EVERYMAN,
I WILL GO WITH THEE,
AND BE THY GUIDE,
IN THY MOST NEED
TO GO BY THY SIDE

RICHARD FORD

THE BASCOMBE NOVELS

THE SPORTSWRITER
INDEPENDENCE DAY
THE LAY OF THE LAND

WITH AN INTRODUCTION
BY THE AUTHOR

EVERYMAN'S LIBRARY
Alfred A. Knopf   New York   London   Toronto

319

THIS IS A BORZOI BOOK
PUBLISHED BY ALFRED A. KNOPF

First included in Everyman's Library, 2009

The Sportswriter Copyright © 1986 by Richard Ford
Independence Day Copyright © 1995 by Richard Ford
The Lay of the Land Copyright © 2006 by Richard Ford
Originally published in the USA by Vintage Books (*The Sportswriter*) and
Alfred A. Knopf (*Independence Day, The Lay of the Land*).
First published in the UK by Bloomsbury Publishing Plc,
and reprinted by arrangement.

Introduction Copyright © 2009 by Richard Ford
Bibliography and Chronology Copyright © 2009 by Everyman's Library
Typography by Peter B. Willberg

Portions of *The Sportswriter* were previously published in *Esquire*; portions
of *Independence Day* were previously published in *Antaeus, Esquire*, and
The New Yorker; portions of *The Lay of the Land* previously appeared in slightly
different form in *The New Yorker*.

Grateful acknowledgment is made to: Famous Music Corporation for
permission to reprint "Isn't It Romantic?" (excerpt) by Lorenz Hart and
Richard Rodgers, copyright © 1932 by Famous Music Corporation, copyright
renewed 1959 by Famous Music Corporation; Doubleday, a division of
Random House, Inc. for "The Waking" (excerpt) from *The Collected Poems of
Theodore Roethke*, copyright © 1953 by Theodore Roethke; Swallow Press/
Ohio University Press, Athens, Ohio (www.ohioswallow.com) for "To What
Strangers, What Welcome" (excerpt) by J. V. Cunningham, from *The Poems of
J. V. Cunningham*, copyright © 1997 by J. V. Cunningham.

All rights reserved. Published in the United States by Alfred A. Knopf,
a division of Random House, Inc., New York, and in Canada by Random
House of Canada Limited, Toronto. Distributed by Random House, Inc.,
New York. Published in the United Kingdom by Everyman's Library,
Northburgh House, 10 Northburgh Street, London EC1V 0AT, and
distributed by Random House (UK) Ltd.

US website: www.randomhouse.com/everymans

ISBN: 978-0-307-26903-4 (US)
978-1-84159-319-7 (UK)

A CIP catalogue reference for this book is available from the British Library

Book design by Barbara de Wilde and Carol Devine Carson

Typeset in the UK by AccComputing, North Barrow, Somerset

Printed and bound in Germany by GGP Media GmbH, Pössneck

C O N T E N T S

INTRODUCTION

Over the last twenty years, goodwilled readers have occasionally asked me if Frank Bascombe, the yearning, sometimes vexatious, narrator of the three novels that make up this sizeable volume – if Frank Bascombe was intended to be an American "everyman?" By this I think these readers mean: is Frank at least partly an *emblem*? Poised there in the final clattering quadrant of the last century, beset with dilemmas and joys, equipped with his suburban New Jersey skill-set and ethical outlook – do Frank's fears, dedications, devilings and amusements stand somewhat for our own?

Naturally, I'm flattered to hear such a question, since it might mean the questioner has read at least one of these books and tried to make use of it. And I can certainly imagine that a millennial standard-bearer might be worth having; a sort of generalizable, meditative, desk-top embodiment of our otherwise unapplauded selves – one who's not so accurately drawn as to cause discomfort, but still recognizable enough to make us feel a bit more visible *to ourselves,* possibly re-certify us as persuasive characters in our own daily dramas.

But the truth is that Frank Bascombe as "everyman" was never my intention. Not only would I have no idea how to go about writing such a full-service literary incarnation, but I'm also sure I'd find the whole business to be not much fun in the doing. And I still want to like what I'm doing.

In nearly forty years of writing stories of varying lengths and shapes and, in the process, making up quite a large number of characters, I've always tried to abide by E. M. Forster's famous dictum from *Aspects of the Novel* that says fictional characters should possess "the incalculability of life." To me, this means that characters in novels (the ones we read *and* the ones we write) should be as variegated and vivid of detail and as hard to predict and make generalizations about as the people we actually meet every day. This incalculability would seem to have the effect of drawing us curiously nearer to characters in order to get a better, more discerning look at them, inasmuch

vii

as characters are usually the principal formal features by which fiction gets its many points across. These vivid, surprising details – themselves well-rendered in language – will be their own source of illuminating pleasure. And the whole complex process will eventuate in our ability to be more interested in the characters, as well as in those real people we meet outside the book's covers. In my view, this is why almost all novels – even the darkest ones – are fundamentally optimistic in nature: because they confirm that complex human life is a fit subject for our interest; and they presume a future where they'll be read, their virtues savored, their lessons put into practice. (I should add, as a counterweight to Forster, that I have also taken to heart Robert Frost's advice meant specifically for writers: that what we do when we write represents the last of our childhood, and we may for that reason practice it somewhat irresponsibly.)

Neither of these two directives seems to mean that human beings are really just muddles and that writing about them can be pretty much a frolicsome crap-shoot. Forster and Frost each took life and writing more seriously than that. But together these prescriptions do suggest to me, anyway, that imaginative writing should admit to the dazzling particularity and indeterminacy of life-as-a-subject, and that to act on this perception of life – by representing it as it is – can actually be pleasurable and produce very interesting results. And it's from this understanding that I founded my conviction that drawing up and reading sociologically, demographically, even anatomically correct embodiments of a larger class of humans – which is how I imagine writing an *everyman* would be – is a writing ambition that falls short of both life and art's most glorious possibilities.

The art critic Robert Hughes once wrote of Cézanne that instead of possessing a theory about painting, Cézanne relied on *sensation*, "the experience," Hughes wrote, "of being up against the world – fugitive, and yet painfully solid, imperious in its thereness and constantly, unrelentingly new." I conceive of writing novels in something of the same way. Regarding my own writing habits, I try to play down the part about the world being painful, unrelenting, and imperious – even though it can be all these things. But I do not play down the raw sensation part. My novelist's version of sensation, of being up against the world, is to keep my nose pressed similarly up to the palpable, mutable, visible, audible, smellable and for the most part disorderly world, flooded as it is with exquisite, intractable, irresistible, details. And where Cézanne had paint as his affectionate medium, I have language, which I either find or invent, in order to mediate and imagine the world for my reader, and in a manner (again, to quote Hughes) that's in accord with experience's "density."

Of course, you can say that I operate with *some* kind of theory. So did Cézanne. His "theory" was that he'd already seen other paintings achieve marvelous effects, and believed that there were such real things as people, who act and look one way and another, and that it mattered to us what they do, so that representing them in a painting was a way of imagining how the world can matter more than we might've expected, and even be beautiful. It's a fairly loose theory. But it's more or less my theory for writing novels. And it has nothing to do – at least that I can see – with writing generalizable, freight-bearing characters who become *everymen*.

To my mind, and faithful to Frost, these three Frank Bascombe novels, along with everything else I've ever written, have been largely born out of fortuity. First, I fortuitously decided I wanted to write a book. I then collected a lot of seemingly random and what seemed like significant things out of the world, things I wanted to make fit into my prospective book – events, memories, snippets of what someone said, places, names of places, ideas – all, again, conveyed in language (sometimes just words I liked and wanted to put into play). After that, I set about trying to intuit that unruly language into a linear shape that was clear enough to make a reader temporarily give up disbelief and suppose that herein lies a provoking world with interesting people in it. And I did this with the certainty that even if I were working straight from life, and was trying to deliver perfect facsimiles of people directly to the page, the truth is that the instant one puts pen to paper, fidelity to fact – or to one's original intention or even sensation itself – almost always goes flying out the window because language is an independent agent different from sensation, and tends to find its own loyalties in whimsy, context, the time of day, the author's mood, sometimes even maybe the old original intention – but many times not. Northrop Frye once wrote that "literature is a disinterested use of words. You need to have nothing riding on the outcome." Another way of saying that is: the blue Bic pen glides along the page and surprising things always spill out of it.

From such a lyrical process I suppose one *could* produce an everyman. But even if you were very skillful, you'd have to be very, *very* lucky. And it was never my intention anyway. Of course, it's always my wish that readers do with my books what Walter Benjamin thought readers should do with stories – and as I mentioned before: make use of them. And one more example of such a use might be to believe that a character is *like* and/or interestingly *unlike* the reader him- or herself, so that the character's fate or behavior serves that reader to renew his sensuous and emotional life and uncover new awareness. To some extent the spectator always makes the picture. And possibly some spectators who see Frank Bascombe simply have use for him as an everyman.

But, vastly more than I want my characters to atomize into some general or even personal applicability, I want them first to be radiant in verbal and intellectual particularity, to *not* be an everyman but to revel in being specifically *this* man, this woman, this son, this daughter with all his or her incalculability intact. And I make characters with this intention because I think we were all made and become interesting and dramatic and true by the very same method – which is to say, again, rather fortuitously.

I realize I may not be telling a prospective reader exactly what she or he wants to know by way of an introduction to this "trilogy," but am only saying what's on my mind as I've begun to think about them all together for the first time – and wanting to free a new reader from some binding and unlikeable expectancies, while admitting him to better ones. These three novels were never really imagined as a trilogy, but only "developed" to that status one book at a time, leaving me pleasantly surprised, and pleasantly bemused, by the result.

INTRODUCTION

I've always imagined the novels I've written to be entirely independent and free-standing enterprises – one book not requiring a previous book to become understandable. And this was true also of these three, although much industry was devoted by me, as I wrote the second two, to "linking" them and creating an illusion of chronological sequence, of a developing (i.e. aging) main character, with a cohort of recurring secondary characters, recurring landscapes, historical event, and more.

I wrote *The Sportswriter* in a period of sustained panic in the middle 1980s – most of the novel written while I was living in New Jersey, Vermont and Montana – and at a time when my writing vocation was threatening to dematerialize in front of me, literally frightening me into a bolder effort than I ever supposed myself capable. *Independence Day* – begun in 1992, in a rented, seaside house in Jamestown, Rhode Island – I first imagined as a novel with no relation to any other book I'd written. It was to be a story about a beleaguered, well-intentioned divorced father who takes his "difficult," estranged teenage son on a trip to the Baseball Hall of Fame in Cooperstown, New York – and in so doing draws himself and his son emotionally closer to each other. All seemed to go well through the planning stages (a year). But over that time I began to notice that all the father's projected calculations about life and events seemed, in my notes, to "sound" like Frank Bascombe's – the character who'd narrated *The Sportswriter*. I made dogged efforts to scuttle all thought of a "linked" book. I was fearful of helplessly writing that first novel over again; fearful of having more ambition than skill or sense; fearful of gloomy failure. And yet these fears finally succumbed to the recognition that to be given a "voice" and with it an already-plausible character who can transact the complex world in reasonably intelligent, truthful, even mirthful ways, was just too much of a gift from the writing gods to decline. And so *Independence Day*, after some considerable pre-writing adjustments to my original plan, came into existence.

The Lay of the Land, last and longest of these novels, represents as much as anything a straight-on and somewhat less fearful acceptance of the forward momentum of the two previous books, and a concession by me that I'd backed myself into a corner and could either accept the "ambition" to write a third book in train with the others, or else be a pathetic coward for not trying. And in that way, over the next four years – from 2002 to 2006 – these *Bascombe Novels* came to their completion.

If it seems that fear played a large part in conceiving these three books, it might just be that fear plays a large part in any work that aspires to the lofty condition of literature. Fear of the unknown. Fear of failure, again. Fear of not, at least, trying to meet the challenge of one's youthful aspirations. Fear, of course, might be the wrong word, or maybe an indelicate word. Another writer might describe the same experience differently – for instance, as the excitation of the protracted creative moment. I've already insisted though that fortuity played a part, and idleness, and lucky availability. So it seems that all kinds of less-than-majestic human impulses have played their part, and that Thoreau might have been right when he said that a writer is a man who, having nothing to do, finds something to do. Surely one of the sublime allures of literature and a reason people want to know more about its origins and to draw near to them, is that part of literature's breathtaking miracle is its sheer unlikeliness in the hands of its makers, the chance that, given all, it just might never have happened.

If any of this seems close to the truth, then consider yourself to have encountered something about human beings, of which writers are a sub-species: that we go on being human even when we want to be better; and also something about the habit of art, that great, intense, optimistic and forward-thinking seduction that seeks magically to change base metal into gold. This alchemy, and our willingness to test it may have something to do with what some people (but not I) romantically call talent. But even if the current efforts here don't turn out to be in every case 24 carat, know at least that I trusted to luck and industry, incalculability and disinterest as well as I possibly could, and that the habit of art is no less a precious habit for having been the guiding spirit of these books that follow.

Richard Ford

SELECT BIBLIOGRAPHY

———

WORKS BY RICHARD FORD

A Piece of My Heart, Harper & Row, New York, 1976.
The Ultimate Good Luck, Houghton Mifflin Co., Boston, MA, 1981.
The Sportswriter, Vintage Contemporaries, New York, 1986.
Rock Springs, Atlantic Monthly Press, New York, 1987.
Wildlife, Atlantic Monthly Press, New York, 1990.
Independence Day, Alfred A. Knopf, New York, 1995.
Women With Men, Alfred A. Knopf, New York, 1997.
A Multitude of Sins, Alfred A. Knopf, New York, 2002.
Vintage Ford, Vintage Contemporaries, New York, 2004.
The Lay of the Land, Alfred A. Knopf, New York, 2006.

C H R O N O L O G Y

———

1936 Outbreak of Spanish Civil War. Hitler and Mussolini form
Rome–Berlin Axis. Edward VIII abdicates; George VI crowned in UK.
Stalin's "Great Purge" of the Communist Party (to 1938).
1938 Germany annexes Austria; Munich crisis.
1940 Fall of France; Battle of Britain.

1941 Japan attacks Pearl Harbor; US enters WW II.

1944 Normandy landings and liberation of Paris.

1945 Unconditional surrender of Germany. Roosevelt dies; Truman becomes
US president. US drops atomic bombs on Hiroshima and Nagasaki. End of
WW II. United Nations founded.

1948 Jewish State of Israel comes into existence. Russian blockade of West
Berlin.

1950 Korean War (to 1953).

DATE	AUTHOR'S LIFE	LITERARY CONTEXT
1952	His father suffers a heart attack. As a result, he begins spending summers in the Marion Hotel (managed by his maternal grandfather) in Little Rock, Arkansas.	1952 Beckett: *Waiting for Godot*. Mary McCarthy: *The Groves of Academe*. Flannery O'Connor: *Wise Blood*. Hemingway: *The Old Man and the Sea*.
1953		1953 Bellow: *The Adventures of Augie March*.
1954		1954 Amis: *Lucky Jim*.
1955		1955 Flannery O'Connor: *A Good Man Is Hard to Find*. Nabokov: *Lolita*. Greene: *The Quiet American*. Baldwin: *Notes of a Native Son* (essays). Miller: *A View from the Bridge*.
1956		1956 Osborne: *Look Back in Anger*. Barth: *The Floating Opera*. Camus: *The Fall*.
1957		1957 Kerouac: *On the Road*. Cheever: *The Wapshot Chronicle*.
1958		1958 Barth: *The End of the Road*.
1959		1959 Burroughs: *Naked Lunch*. Grass: *The Tin Drum*. Bellow: *Henderson the Rain King*.
1960	His father suffers a second and fatal heart attack.	1960 Updike: *Rabbit, Run*. Barth: *The Sot-Weed Factor*.
1961		1961 Percy: *The Moviegoer*. Yates: *Revolutionary Road*. Heller: *Catch-22*.
1962	Graduates from Murrah High School in Jackson, Mississippi. Enrolls at Michigan State University majoring in hotel management but instantly changes major to English.	1962 Nabokov: *Pale Fire*. Solzhenitsyn: *One Day in the Life of Ivan Denisovich*.
1963		1963 Oates: *By the North Gate* (stories).
1964	Enlists in US Marine Corps.	1964 Bellow: *Herzog*. Cheever: *The Wapshot Scandal*.

CHRONOLOGY

1952 Eisenhower elected US president.

1953 Death of Stalin.

1954 Vietnam War (to 1975).

1956 Soviets invade Hungary. Suez crisis.

1957 Civil Rights Commission established in US to safeguard voting rights.

1959 Fidel Castro seizes power in Cuba and forms a socialist government.

1960 Kennedy elected US president.

1961 Anti-Castro force supported by CIA attempts invasion of Cuba at Bay of Pigs. Yuri Gagarin becomes first man in space. Construction of Berlin Wall.
1962 Cuban missile crisis.

1963 Assassination of Kennedy; Johnson becomes US president.

1964 Civil Rights Act prohibits discrimination in the US. Nobel Peace Prize awarded to Martin Luther King.

DATE	AUTHOR'S LIFE	LITERARY CONTEXT
1965	Honorably discharge from US Marine Corps, having contracted hepatitis.	1965 Wolfe: *The Kandy-Kolored Tangerine-Flake Streamline Baby*. Mailer: *An American Dream*.
1966	Receives BA in English from Michigan State University. Teaches junior high school in Flint, Michigan.	1966 Percy: *The Last Gentleman*. Capote: *In Cold Blood*. Barth: *Giles Goat-Boy*.
1967	Attends Washington University Law School in St. Louis, Missouri, for one semester.	1967 Styron: *The Confessions of Nat Turner*. Márquez: *One Hundred Years of Solitude*. Oates: *A Garden of Earthly Delights*.
1968	Marries Kristina Hensley. Moves to New York and briefly works for *American Druggist* as an assistant science editor.	1968 Solzhenitsyn: *Cancer Ward*. Exley: *A Fan's Notes*. Barth: *Lost in the Funhouse* (stories).
1969		1969 Roth: *Portnoy's Complaint*. Oates: *Them*. Cheever: *Bullet Park*.
1970	Receives MFA in Creative Writing from the University of California at Irvine, where he studied with Oakley Hall and E. L. Doctorow. Moves to Chicago, Illinois.	1970 Bellow: *Mr. Sammler's Planet*. Oates: *The Wheel of Love*.
1971	Begins three-year fellowship in University of Michigan Society of Fellows.	1971 Updike: *Rabbit Redux*. Flannery O'Connor: *The Complete Stories*. Percy: *Love in the Ruins*. Oates: *Wonderland*.
1972		1972 Welty: *The Optimist's Daughter*.
1973		1973 Pynchon: *Gravity's Rainbow*. Solzhenitsyn: *The Gulag Archipelago* (to 1975). Stone: *Dog Soldiers*. Oates: *Do With Me What You Will*.
1974		1974 Heller: *Something Happened*. Roth: *My Life as a Man*.
1975	Teaches for a year as assistant professor at the University of Michigan.	1975 Bellow: *Humboldt's Gift*.

CHRONOLOGY

1965 US begins bombing North Vietnam. Malcolm X is assassinated.

1966 Mao launches Cultural Revolution in China. Revolutionary nationalist organization the Black Panther Party is founded in Oakland, California.

1967 Six-Day War between Israel and Arab states. Racial violence breaks out in many US cities; President Johnson appoints a commission to look into causes. 75,000 young people gather at Haight-Ashbury, California for "Summer of Love." Argentinian-born guerrilla Che Guevara is shot dead in Bolivia.

1968 Students protest in US and throughout Europe. Martin Luther King assassinated; violent reactions throughout US. Soviet invasion of Czechoslovakia. Nixon elected US president.

1969 US troops begin to withdraw from Vietnam. US astronaut Neil Armstrong becomes first man on the moon. Woodstock rock festival in New York State attracts 400,000 fans.
1970 Death of de Gaulle in France.

1972 Israeli building at Olympic Village near Munich attacked by Arab guerrillas; eleven Israeli athletes are killed. Strategic Arms Limitation Treaty (SALT I) signed by US and USSR.
1973 US Supreme Court suspends capital punishment (until 1976).

1974 Nixon resigns as the result of Watergate scandal; Ford becomes US president.
1975 Vietnam War ends.

THE BASCOMBE NOVELS

DATE	AUTHOR'S LIFE	LITERARY CONTEXT
1976	First novel, *A Piece of My Heart*, is published. Moves to Princeton, New Jersey.	1976 Carver: *Will You Please Be Quiet, Please?* (stories).
1977	Awarded a Guggenheim Foundation fellowship.	1977 Morrison: *Song of Solomon.* Percy: *Lancelot.* Cheever: *Falconer.*
1978	Teaches at Williams College in Williamston, Massachusetts.	1978 Cheever: *The Stories of John Cheever.*
1979	Awarded a National Endowment for the Arts fellowship. Teaches at Princeton University as George Perkins Fellow in the Humanities.	1979 Mailer: *The Executioner's Story.* Roth: *The Ghost Writer.* Oates: *Unholy Loves.*
1980		1980 Percy: *The Second Coming.* Welty: *The Collected Stories of Eudora Welty.*
1981	*The Ultimate Good Luck* is published. Quits writing fiction and moves to New York to work as a sportswriter for *Inside Sports* magazine, but the publication folds. Mother dies.	1981 Rushdie: *Midnight's Children.* Roth: *Zuckerman Unbound.* Updike: *Rabbit Is Rich.*
1982		1982 Márquez: *Chronicle of a Death Foretold.* Walker: *The Color Purple.* Barth: *Sabbatical: A Romance.*
1983	Stories are published in the following anthologies: *Matters of Life and Death*, ed. Tobias Wolff; *Dirty Realism: Writing from America*, ed. Bill Buford; and *Fifty Great Years of Esquire Fiction*, ed. L. Rust Hills. *American Tropical*, a play, is produced by the Actors Theatre of Louisville.	1983 Updike: *Hugging the Shore* (essays). Carver: *Cathedral* (stories). Welty: *One Writer's Beginnings* (memoir).
1984		1984 McInerney: *Bright Lights, Big City.* Oates: *Last Days* (stories).
1985		1985 Márquez: *Love in the Time of Cholera.* Delillo: *White Noise.* Cormac McCarthy: *Blood Meridian.*

CHRONOLOGY

1976 Death of Mao Tse-Tung in China. Carter elected US president.

1978 Camp David Agreement between Carter, President Sadat of Egypt and Israeli prime minister Begin.

1979 The Shah of Iran is forced into exile, and an Islamic state is established under the Ayatollah Khomeini. Margaret Thatcher elected first female prime minister in UK. Carter and Brezhnev sign SALT II arms limitation treaty. Soviet troops occupy Afghanistan.

1980 Lech Walesa leads strikes in Gdansk, Poland. Iran–Iraq War begins (to 1988). Reagan elected US president.

1981 Attempted assassination of Reagan in Washington. President Sadat killed by Islamic fundamentalists in Egypt.

1982 Argentina occupies Falkland Islands, resulting in war with Britain.

1983 US troops invade Granada after the government is overthrown.

1984 Famine in Ethiopia. Indira Gandhi assassinated in India. Reagan re-elected US president in landslide victory over Democrat Walter Mondale.

1985 Gorbachev becomes General Secretary of Communist Party in USSR; period of reform begins.

DATE	AUTHOR'S LIFE	LITERARY CONTEXT
1986	*The Sportswriter* is published. Short stories win the Best American Short Stories Prize and the Pushcart Prize. *The Sportswriter* is named one of *Time* magazine's five best books of 1986. It is also a finalist for the PEN/Faulkner Award for Fiction. Awarded National Endowment for the Arts fellowship.	1986 DeLillo: *End Zone.* Munro: *The Progress of Love.* Atwood: *The Handmaid's Tale.* Wolff: *The Night in Question: Stories.* Oates: *Raven's Wing* (stories).
1987	Wins the Mississippi Academy of Arts and Letters Award for Literature. *Rock Springs*, a short story collection, is published.	1987 Wolfe: *The Bonfire of the Vanities.* Morrison: *Beloved.* Percy: *The Thanatos Syndrome.*
1988	Wins the New York Public Library's "Literary Lion" Award and the Northwest Booksellers Award for Fiction.	1988 Rushdie: *The Satanic Verses.* Carver: *Where I'm Calling From* (stories).
1989	Wins the American Academy of Arts and Letters Award in Literature. Moves to New Orleans.	1989 DeLillo: *Libra.* Márquez: *The General in His Labyrinth.* Atwood: *Cat's Eye.* Wolff: *This Boy's Life: A Memoir.*
1990	*Wildlife* is published as well as *The Best American Short Stories* (editor).	1990 Pynchon: *Vineland.* Updike: *Rabbit at Rest.*
1991	Wins Echoing Green Foundation Award for Literature. The film *Bright Angel* (based on his screenplay) is released. The play *American Tropical* is published.	1991 Updike: *Odd Jobs* (essays).
1992	Appointed Avery Hopwell Memorial Lecturer at the University of Michigan. Serves as founding director of the William Faulkner Foundation, University of Rennes, Paris, France. *The Granta Book of the American Short Story* (editor) is published.	1992 Cormac McCarthy: *All the Pretty Horses.*
1993	Wins the Lyndhurst Prize as well as the Mississippi Governor's Award for Artistic Achievement. Receives a Fulbright Fellowship (Sweden).	1993 Roth: *Operation Shylock.*

CHRONOLOGY

1986 Nuclear explosion at Chernobyl, USSR. US bombs Libya. Gorbachev–Reagan summit.

1988 George Bush elected US president over Democrat Michael Dukakis. Gorbachev announces significant troop reductions and withdrawal from Afghanistan, signaling an end to the Cold War.

1989 Communism collapses in Eastern Europe. Fall of the Berlin Wall. First democratic elections in USSR. Tiananmen Square massacre in China.

1990 End of Communist monopoly in USSR. Yeltsin elected first leader of Russian Federation. Nelson Mandela released after 27 years' imprisonment. John Major becomes prime minister in UK.

1991 Gulf War. Bush and Gorbachev sign START arms reduction treaty. Central government in USSR suspended. War begins in former Yugoslavia. End of apartheid in South Africa.

1992: Riots in Los Angeles. Clinton elected US president.

1993 Palestinian leader Arafat and Israeli prime minister Rabin sign peace agreement in US. Maastricht Treaty (creating European Union) ratified.

DATE	AUTHOR'S LIFE	LITERARY CONTEXT
1994	Teaches for a year as a lecturer at Harvard University. Awarded an honorary doctorate from the University of Rennes.	1994 Heller: *Closing Time.*
1995	Wins the Rea Award for the Short Story. *Independence Day* is published.	1995 Guterson: *Snow Falling on Cedars.* Rushdie: *The Moor's Last Sigh.*
1996	Wins Pulitzer Prize and PEN/Faulkner Award for *Independence Day.* Awarded the Honorary Doctorate of Humane Letters from Loyola University, New Orleans. Named *Officier, l'Ordre des Arts et des Lettres* by the French government.	1996 Updike: *In the Beauty of the Lilies.*
1997	Serves as a visiting professor at Northwestern University, Evanston, Illinois, until 1999. Receives the Award of Merit in the Novel from the American Academy of Arts and Letters. *Women with Men* (a collection of three novellas) is published.	1997 Roth: *American Pastoral.* McEwan: *Enduring Love.* Bellow: *The Actual.*
1998	Awarded Honorary Doctorate of Humane Letters from the University of Michigan and elected to the American Academy of Arts and Letters. *The Essential Tales of Chekhov* (editor), *Eudora Welty: The Complete Novels, Stories, Essays, and Memoir* (co-editor with Michael Kreyling), and *The Granta Book of the American Long Story* (editor) are published.	1998 Morrison: *Paradise.* DeLillo: *Underworld.* Heller: *Now and Then.* McEwan: *Amsterdam.* Roth: *I Married a Communist.*
1999	*The Best American Sportswriting* (editor) is published.	1999 Sontag: *In America.* Rushdie: *The Ground Beneath Her Feet.*
2000	Moves to East Boothbay, Maine.	2000 Bellow: *Ravelstein.* Roth: *The Human Stain.* Atwood: *The Blind Assassin.*
2001	Receives the PEN/Malamud Award for Excellence in the Short Story.	2001 Franzen: *The Corrections.* Russo: *Empire Falls.*

CHRONOLOGY

THE BASCOMBE NOVELS

DATE	AUTHOR'S LIFE	LITERARY CONTEXT
2002	*A Multitude of Sins* (stories) is published.	
2003		2003 Lowell: *The Collected Poems of Robert Lowell.*
2004	*Vintage Ford* (a collection of previously published short fiction) is published.	2004 Roth: *The Plot Against America.*
2005	*The Lay of the Land* is published and named as *New York Times* Book of the Year.	2005 McCarthy: *No Country for Old Men.*
2006		2006 Updike: *Terrorist.* McCarthy: *The Road.* McInerney: *The Good Life.*
2007	*The New Granta Book of the American Short Story* (editor) is published.	2007 Russo: *Bridge of Sighs.* Roth: *Exit Ghost.*
2008		

CHRONOLOGY

2003 American and British troops invade Iraq. Saddam Hussein captured by US troops.

2004 Terrorist bombings in Madrid. George W. Bush re-elected as US president over Democrat John Kerry. Indian Ocean tsunami.

2005 Blair re-elected prime minister in UK. Terrorist bombings in London. IRA formally orders end to its armed campaign (since 1969). First forced evacuation of settlers under Israel Unilateral Disengagement Plan. Hurricane Katrina causes breaches in levees and widespread flooding of New Orleans.

2006 Stephen Harper becomes first Conservative prime minister in Canada in 13 years. Iran announces that it has joined the "nuclear club."

2007 A suicidal student kills 32 people on the campus of Virginia Tech University. Yeltsin dies. Gordon Brown elected prime minister in UK. President Bush orders gradual reductions in US forces in Iraq while rejecting calls to end the war. Al Gore and UN climate scientists win Nobel Peace Prize. Deadliest year for US troops in Iraq, with at least 853 military deaths.

2008 Senator Barack Obama, a democrat from Illinois, becomes the first African-American to be nominated as his party's candidate for the US presidency.

THE SPORTSWRITER

Kristina

CHAPTER 1

MY NAME is Frank Bascombe. I am a sportswriter.

For the past fourteen years I have lived here at 19 Hoving Road, Haddam, New Jersey, in a large Tudor house bought when a book of short stories I wrote sold to a movie producer for a lot of money, and seemed to set my wife and me and our three children—two of whom were not even born yet—up for a good life.

Just exactly what that good life was—the one I expected—I cannot tell you now exactly, though I wouldn't say it has not come to pass, only that much has come in between. I am no longer married to X, for instance. The child we had when everything was starting has died, though there are two others, as I mentioned, who are alive and wonderful children.

I wrote half of a short novel soon after we moved here from New York and then put it in the drawer, where it has been ever since, and from which I don't expect to retrieve it unless something I cannot now imagine happens.

Twelve years ago, when I was twenty-six, and in the blind way of things then, I was offered a job as a sportswriter by the editor of a glossy New York sports magazine you have all heard of, because of a free-lance assignment I had written in a particular way he liked. And to my surprise and everyone else's I quit writing my novel and accepted.

And since then I have worked at nothing but that job, with the exception of vacations, and one three-month period after my son died when I considered a new life and took a job as an instructor in a small private school in western Massachusetts where I ended up not liking things, and couldn't wait to leave and get back here to New Jersey and writing sports.

My life over these twelve years has not been and isn't now a bad one at all. In most ways it's been great. And although the older I get the more things scare me, and the more apparent it is to me that bad things can and do happen to you, very little really worries me or keeps me up at night. I still believe in the possibilities of passion and romance. And I would not change much, if anything at all. I might not choose to get divorced. And my son, Ralph Bascombe, would not die. But that's about it for these matters.

Why, you might ask, would a man give up a promising literary career—there were some good notices—to become a sports-writer?

It's a good question. For now let me say only this: if sports-writing teaches you anything, and there is much truth to it as well as plenty of lies, it is that for your life to be worth anything you must sooner or later face the possibility of terrible, searing regret. Though you must also manage to avoid it or your life will be ruined.

I believe I have done these two things. Faced down regret. Avoided ruin. And I am still here to tell about it.

I HAVE CLIMBED over the metal fence to the cemetery directly behind my house. It is five o'clock on Good Friday morning, April 20. All other houses in the neighborhood are shadowed, and I am waiting for my ex-wife. Today is my son Ralph's birth-day. He would be thirteen and starting manhood. We have met here these last two years, early, before the day is started, to pay our respects to him. Before that we would simply come over together as man and wife.

A spectral fog is lifting off the cemetery grass, and high up in the low atmosphere I hear the wings of geese pinging. A police car has murmured in through the gate, stopped, cut its lights and placed me under surveillance. I saw a match flare briefly inside the car, saw the policeman's face looking at a clipboard.

At the far end of the "new part" a small deer gazes at me where I wait. Now and then its yellow tapetums blink out of the dark toward the old part, where the trees are larger, and where three signers of the Declaration of Independence are buried in sight of my son's grave.

My next-door neighbors, the Deffeyes, are playing tennis, calling their scores in hushed-polite early-morning voices. "Sorry." "Thanks." "Forty-love." Pock. Pock. Pock. "*Ad* to you, dear." "Yes, thank you." "Yours." Pock, pock. I hear their harsh, thrashing nose breaths, their feet scraping. They are into their eighties and no longer need sleep, and so are up at all hours. They have installed glowless barium-sulphur lights that don't shine in my yard and keep me awake. And we have stayed good neighbors if not close friends. I have nothing much in common with them now, and am invited to few of their or anyone else's cocktail parties. People in town are still friendly in a distant way, and I consider them fine people, conservative, decent.

It is not, I have come to understand, easy to have a divorced man as your neighbor. Chaos lurks in him—the viable social contract called into question by the smoky aspect of sex. Most people feel they have to make a choice and it is always easier to choose the wife, which is what my neighbors and friends have mostly done. And though we chitter-chatter across the driveways and hedges and over the tops of each other's cars in the parking lots of grocery stores, remarking on the condition of each other's soffits and down-drains and the likelihood of early winter, sometimes make tentative plans to get together, I hardly ever see them, and I take it in my stride.

Good Friday today is a special day for me, apart from the other specialness. When I woke in the dark this morning, my heart pounding like a tom-tom, it seemed to me as though a change were on its way, as if this dreaminess tinged with expectation, which I have felt for some time now, were lifting off of me into the cool tenebrous dawn.

Today I'm leaving town for Detroit to begin a profile of a famous ex-football player who lives in the city of Walled Lake, Michigan, and is confined to a wheelchair since a waterskiing accident, but who has become an inspiration to his former teammates by demonstrating courage and determination, going back to college, finishing his degree in communications arts, marrying his black physiotherapist and finally becoming honorary chaplain for his old team. "Make a contribution" will be my angle. It is the kind of story I enjoy and find easy to write.

Anticipation rises higher, however, because I'm taking my new girlfriend Vicki Arcenault with me. She has recently moved up to New Jersey from Dallas, but I am already pretty certain I'm in love with her (I haven't mentioned anything about it for fear of making her wary). Two months ago, when I sliced up my thumb sharpening a lawnmower blade in my garage, it was Nurse

Arcenault who stitched me up in the ER at Doctors Hospital, and things have gone on from there. She did her training at Baylor in Waco, and came up here when her marriage gave out. Her family, in fact, lives down in Barnegat Pines, not far away, in a subdivision close to the ocean, and I am scheduled to be exhibit A at Easter dinner—a vouchsafe to them that she has made a successful transition to the northeast, found a safe and good-hearted man, and left bad times including her dagger-head husband Everett far behind. Her father, Wade, is a toll-taker at Exit 9 on the Turnpike, and I cannot expect he will like the difference in our ages. Vicki is thirty. I am thirty-eight. He himself is only in his fifties. But I am in hopes of winning him over and eager as can be under the circumstances. Vicki is a sweet, saucy little black-hair with a delicate width of cheekbone, a broad Texas accent and a matter-of-factness with her raptures that can make a man like me cry out in the night for longing.

You should never think that leaving a marriage sets you loose for cheery womanizing and some exotic life you'd never quite grasped before. Far from true. No one can do that for long. The Divorced Men's Club I belong to here in town has proven that to me if nothing else—we don't talk much about women when we are together and feel relieved just to be men alone. What leaving a marriage released me—and most of us—to, was celibacy and more fidelity than I had ever endured before, though with no one convenient to be faithful to or celibate for. Just a long empty moment. Though everyone should live alone at some time in a life. Not like when you're a kid, summers, or in a single dorm room in some crappy school. But when you're grown up. *Then* be alone. It can be all right. You can end up more within yourself, as the best athletes are, which is worth it. (A basketball player who goes for his patented outside jumper becomes nothing more than the simple wish personified that the ball go in the hole.) In any case, doing the brave thing isn't easy and isn't supposed to be. I do my work and do it well and remain expectant of the best without knowing in the least what it will be. And the bonus is that a little bundle like Nurse Arcenault seems sent straight from heaven.

For several months now I have not taken a trip, and the magazine has found plenty for me to do in New York. It was stated in court by X's sleaze-ball lawyer, Alan, that my travel was the cause of our trouble, especially after Ralph died. And though that isn't technically true—it was a legal reason X and I invented together —it is true that I have always loved the travel that accompanies my job. Vicki has only seen two landscapes in her entire life: the flat, featureless gloom-prairies around Dallas, and New Jersey— a strange unworldliness these days. But I will soon show her the midwest, where old normalcy floats heavy on the humid air, and where I happen to have gone to college.

It is true that much of my sportswriter's work is exactly what you would think: flying in airplanes, arriving and departing airports, checking into and out of downtown hotels, waiting hours in corridors and locker rooms, renting cars, confronting unfriendly bellmen. Late night drinks in unfamiliar bars, up always before dawn, as I am this morning, trying to get a perspective on things. But there is also an assurance to it that I don't suppose I could live happily without. Very early you come to the realization that nothing will ever take you away from yourself. But in these literal and anonymous cities of the nation, your Milwaukees, your St. Louises, your Seattles, your Detroits, even your New Jerseys, something hopeful and unexpected can take place. A woman I met at the college where I briefly taught, once told me I had too many choices, that I was not driven enough by dire necessity. But that is just an illusion and her mistake. Choices are what we all need. And when I walk out into the bricky warp of these American cities, that is exactly what I feel. Choices aplenty. Things I don't know anything about but might like are here, possibly waiting for me. Even if they aren't. The exhilaration of a new arrival. Good light in a restaurant that especially pleases you. A cab driver with an interesting life history to tell. The casual, lilting voice of a woman you don't know, but that you are allowed to listen to in a bar you've never been in, at a time when you would otherwise have been alone. These things are waiting for you. And what could be better? More mysterious? More worth anticipating? Nothing. Not a thing.

THE BARIUM-SULPHUR lights die out over the Deffeyes' tennis court. Delia Deffeyes' patient and troubleless voice, still hushed, begins assuring her husband Caspar that he played well, while they walk toward their dark house in their pressed whites.

The sky has become a milky eye and though it is spring and nearly Easter, the morning has a strangely winter cast to it, as though a high fog is blotting its morning stars. There is no moon at all.

The policeman has finally seen enough and idles out the cemetery gate onto the silent streets. I hear a paper slap on a sidewalk. Far off, I hear the commuter train up to New York making its belling stop at our station—always a consoling sound.

X's brown Citation stops at the blinking red light at Constitution Street, across from the new library, then inches along the cemetery fence on Plum Road, her lights on high beam. The deer has vanished. I walk over to meet her.

X is an old-fashioned, solidly Michigan girl from Birmingham, whom I met in Ann Arbor. Her father, Henry, was a Soapy Williams best-of-his-generation liberal who still owns a plant that stamps out rubber gaskets for a giant machine that stamps out car fenders, though he is now a Republican and rich as a Pharaoh. Her mother, Irma, lives in Mission Viejo, and the two of them are divorced, though her mother still writes me regularly and believes X and I will eventually reconcile, which seems as possible as anything else.

X could choose to move back to Michigan if she wanted to, buy a condominium or a ranch-style home or move out onto the estate her father owns. We discussed it at the divorce, and I did not object. But she has too much pride and independence to move home now. In addition, she is firmly behind the idea of family and wants Paul and Clarissa to be near me, and I'm happy to think she has made a successful adjustment of her new life. Sometimes we do not really become adults until we suffer a good whacking loss, and our lives in a sense catch up with us and wash over us like a wave and everything goes.

Since our divorce she has bought a house in a less expensive but improving section of Haddam called The Presidents by the locals, and has taken a job as teaching pro at Cranbury Hills C.C. She co-captained the Lady Wolverines in college and has lately begun entering some of the local pro-ams, now that her short game has sharpened up, and even placed high in a couple last summer. I believe all her life she has had a yen to try something like this, and being divorced has given her the chance.

What was our life like? I almost don't remember now. Though

I remember *it*, the space of time it occupied. And I remember it fondly.

I suppose our life was the generic one, as the poet said. X was a housewife and had babies, read books, played golf and had friends, while I wrote about sports and went here and there collecting my stories, coming home to write them up, mooning around the house for days in old clothes, taking the train to New York and back now and then. X seemed to take the best possible attitude to my being a sportswriter. She thought it was fine, or at least she said she did and seemed happy. She thought she had married a young Sherwood Anderson with movie possibilities, but it didn't bother her that it didn't turn out that way, and certainly never bothered me. I was happy as a swallow. We went on vacations with our three children. To Cape Cod (which Ralph called Cape God), to Searsport, Maine, to Yellowstone, to the Civil War battlefields at Antietam and Bull Run. We paid bills, shopped, went to movies, bought cars and cameras and insurance, cooked out, went to cocktail parties, visited schools, and romanced each other in the sweet, cagey way of adults. I looked out my window, stood in my yard sunsets with a sense of solace and achievement, cleaned my rain gutters, eyed my shingles, put up storms, fertilized regularly, computed my equity, spoke to my neighbors in an interested voice—the normal applauseless life of us all.

Though toward the end of our marriage I became lost in some dreaminess. Sometimes I would wake up in the morning and open my eyes to X lying beside me breathing, and not recognize her! Not even know what town I was in, or how old I was, or what life it was, so dense was I in my particular dreaminess. I would lie there and try as best I could to extend not knowing, feel that pleasant soaring-out-of-azimuth-and-attitude sensation I grew to like as long as it would last, while twenty possibilities for who, where, what went by. Until suddenly I would get it right and feel a sense of—what? Loss, I think you would say, though loss of what I don't know. My son had died, but I'm unwilling to say that was the cause, or that anything is ever the sole cause of anything else. I know that you can dream your way through an otherwise fine life, and never wake up, which is what I almost did. I believe I have survived that now and nearly put dreaminess behind me, though there is a resolute sadness between X and me that our marriage is over, a sadness that does not feel sad. It is the way you feel at a high school reunion when you hear an old song you used to like played late at night, only you are all alone.

X APPEARS out of the agate cemetery light, loose-gaited and sleepy, wearing deck shoes, baggy corduroys and an old London Fog I gave her years ago. Her hair has been cut short in a new-style way I like. She is a tall girl, big and brown-haired and pretty, who looks younger than she is, which is only thirty-seven. When we re-met fifteen years ago in New York, at a dreary book signing, she was modeling at a Fifth Avenue clothing store, and sometimes even now she has a tendency to slouch and walk about long-strided in a loose-limbed, toes-out way, though when she takes a square stance up over a golf ball, she can smack it a mile. In some ways she has become as much of a genuine athlete as anyone I know. Needless to say, I have the greatest admiration for her, and love her in every way but the strictest one. Sometimes I see her on the street in town or in her car without expecting to and without her knowing it, and I am struck by wonder: what can she want from life now? How could I have ever loved her and let her go.

"It's chilly, still," she says, in a small, firm voice when she is close enough to be heard, her hands stuffed down deep inside her raincoat. It is a voice I love. In many ways it was her voice I loved first, the sharpened midwestern vowels, the succinct glaciated syntax: Binton Herbor, himburg, Gren Repids. It is a voice that knows the minimum of what will suffice, and banks on it. In general I have always liked hearing women talk more than men.

I wonder, in fact, what my own voice will sound like. Will it be a convincing, truth-telling voice? Or a pseudo-sincere, phony, ex-husband one that will stir up trouble? I have a voice that is really mine, a frank, vaguely rural voice more or less like a used car salesman: a no-frills voice that hopes to uncover simple truth by a straight-on application of the facts. I used to practice it when I was in college. "Well, okay, look at it this way," I'd say right out loud. "All right, all right." "Yeah, but look here." As much as any, this constitutes my sportswriter voice, though I have stopped practicing by now.

X leans herself against the curved marble monument of a man named Craig—at a safe distance from me—and presses her lips inward. Up to this moment I have not noticed the cold. But now that she said it, I feel it in my bones and wish I'd worn a sweater.

These pre-dawn meetings were my idea, and in the abstract they seem like a good way for two people like us to share a remaining intimacy. In practice they are as uncomfortable as a hanging, and it's conceivable we will just forgo it next year, though we felt the same way last year. It is simply that I don't know how to mourn and neither does X. Neither of us has the vocabulary or temperament for it, and so we are more prone to pass the time chatting, which isn't always wise.

"Did Paul mention our rendezvous last night?" I say. Paul, my son, is ten. Last night I had an unexpected meeting with him standing in the dark street in front of his house, when his mother was inside and knew nothing of it, and I was lurking about outside. We had a talk about Ralph, and where he was and about how it might be possible to reach him—all of which caused me to go away feeling better. X and I agree in principle that I shouldn't sneak my visits, but this was not that way.

"He told me Daddy was sitting in the car in the dark watching the house like the police." She stares at me curiously.

"It was just an odd day. It ended up fine, though." It was in fact much more than an odd day.

"You could've come in. You're always welcome."

I smile a winning smile at her. "Another time I will." (Sometimes we do strange things and say they're accidents and coincidences, though I want her to believe it *was* a coincidence.)

"I just wondered if something was wrong," X says.

"No. I love him very much."

"Good," X says and sighs.

I have spoken in a voice that pleases me, a voice that is really mine.

X brings a sandwich bag out of her pocket, removes a hard-boiled egg and begins to peel it into the bag. We actually have little to say. We talk on the phone at least twice a week, mostly about the children, who visit me after school while X is still out on the teaching tee. Occasionally I bump into her in the grocery line, or take a table next to hers at the August Inn, and we will have a brief chairback chat. We have tried to stay a modern,

divided family. Our meeting here is only by way of a memorial
for an old life lost.

Still it is a good time to talk. Last year, for instance, X told me
that if she had her life to live over again she would probably wait
to get married and try to make a go of it on the LPGA tour.
Her father had offered to sponsor her, she said, back in 1966—
something she had never told me before. She did not say if she
would marry me when the time came. But she did say she wished
I had finished my novel, that it would have probably made things
better, which surprised me. (She later took that back.) She also
told me, without being particularly critical, that she considered
me a loner, which surprised me too. She said that it was a mistake
to have made as few superficial friends as I have done in my life,
and to have concentrated only on the few things I have concentrated on—her, for one. My children, for another. Sportswriting
and being an ordinary citizen. This did not leave me well enough
armored for the unexpected, was her opinion. She said this was
because I didn't know my parents very well, had gone to a military school, and grown up in the south, which was full of betray-
ers and secret-keepers and untrustworthy people, which I agree
is true, though I never knew any of them. All that originated,
she said, with the outcome of the Civil War. It was much better
to have grown up, she said, as she did, in a place with no apparent
character, where there is nothing ambiguous around to confuse
you or complicate things, where the only thing anybody ever
thought seriously about was the weather.

"Do you think you laugh enough these days?" She finishes
peeling her egg and puts the sack down deep in her coat pocket.
She knows about Vicki, and I've had one or two other girlfriends
since our divorce that I'm sure the children have told her about.
But I do not think she thinks they have turned my basic situation
around much. And maybe she's right. In any case I am happy to
have this apparently intimate, truth-telling conversation, something I do not have very often, and that a marriage can really be
good for.

"You bet I do," I say. "I think I'm doing all right, if that's what
you mean."

"I suppose it is," X says, looking at her boiled egg as if it posed
a small but intriguing problem. "I'm not really worried about
you." She raises her eyes at me in an appraising way. It's possible

my talk with Paul last night has made her think I've gone off my bearings or started drinking.

"I watch Johnny. He's good for a laugh," I say. "I think he gets funnier as I get older. But thanks for asking." All this makes me feel stupid. I smile at her.

X takes a tiny mouse bite out of her white egg. "I apologize for prying into your life."

"It's fine."

X breathes out audibly and speaks softly. "I woke up this morning in the dark, and I suddenly got this idea in my head about Ralph laughing. It made me cry, in fact. But I thought to myself that you have to strive to live your life to the ultimate. Ralph lived his whole life in nine years, and I remember him laughing. I just wanted to be sure you did. You have a lot longer to live."

"My birthday's in two weeks."

"Do you think you'll get married again?" X says with extreme formality, looking up at me. And for a moment what I smell in the dense morning air is a swimming pool! Somewhere nearby. The cool, aqueous suburban chlorine bouquet that reminds me of the summer coming, and all the other better summers of memory. It is a token of the suburbs I love, that from time to time a swimming pool or a barbecue or a leaf fire you'll never ever see will drift provocatively to your nose.

"I guess I don't know," I say. Though in truth I would love to be able to say *Couldn't happen, not on a bet, not this boy.* Except what I do say is nearer to the truth. And just as quick, the silky-summery smell is gone, and the smell of dirt and stolid monuments has won back its proper place. In the quavery gray dawn a window lights up beyond the fence on the third floor of my house. Bosobolo, my African boarder, is awake. His day is beginning and I see his dark shape pass the window. Across the cemetery in the other direction I see yellow lights in the care-taker's cottage, beside which sits the green John Deere backhoe used for dredging graves. The bells of St. Leo the Great begin to chime a Good Friday prayer call. "Christ Died Today, Christ Died Today" (though I believe it is actually "Stabat Mater Dolorosa").

"I think I'll get married again," X says matter-of-factly. Who to, I wonder?

"Who to?" Not—please—one of the fat-wallet 19th-hole clubsters, the big hale 'n' hearty, green-sports-coat types who're always taking her on weekends to the Trapp Family Lodge and getaways to the Poconos, where they take in new Borscht Belt comedians and make love on waterbeds. I hope against all hope not. I know all about those guys. The children tell me. They all drive Oldsmobiles and wear tasseled shoes. And there is every good reason to go out with them, I grant you. Let them spend their money and enjoy their discretionary time. They're decent fellows, I'm sure. But they are not to be married.

"Oh, a software salesman, maybe," X says. "A realtor. Somebody I can beat at golf and bully." She smiles at me a mouth-down smirky smile of unhappiness, and bunches her shoulders to wag them. But unexpectedly she starts to cry through her smile, nodding toward me as if we both knew about it and should've expected this, and that in a way I am to blame, which in a way I am.

The last time I saw X cry was the night our house was broken into, when, in the search for what might've been stolen, she found some letters I'd been getting from a woman in Blanding, Kansas. I don't know why I kept them. They really didn't mean anything to me. I hadn't seen the woman in months and then only once. But I was in the thickest depths of my dreaminess then, and needed—or thought I did—something to anticipate away from my life, even though I had no plans for ever seeing her and was in fact intending to throw the letters away. The burglars had left Polaroid pictures of the inside of our empty house scattered about for us to find when we got back from seeing *The Thirty-Nine Steps* at the Playhouse, plus the words, "We are the stuffed men," spray-painted onto the dining room wall. Ralph had been dead two years. The children were with their grandfather at the Huron Mountain Club, and I was just back from my teaching position at Berkshire College, and was hanging around the house more or less dumb as a cashew, but otherwise in pretty good spirits. X found the letters in a drawer of my office desk while looking for a sock full of silver dollars my mother had left me, and sat on the floor and read them, then handed them to me when I came in with a list of missing cameras, radios and fishing equipment. She asked if I had anything to say, and when I didn't, she went into the bedroom and began tearing apart her hope chest with a claw hammer and a crowbar. She tore it to bits, then took it to the fireplace and burned it while I stood outside in the yard mooning at Cassiopeia and Gemini and feeling invulnerable because of dreaminess and an odd amusement I felt almost everything in my life could be subject to. It might seem that I was "within myself" then. But in fact I was light years away from everything.

In a little while X came outside, with all the lights in the house left shining and her hope chest going up the chimney in smoke—it was June—and sat in a lawn chair in another part of the dark yard from where I was standing and cried loudly. Lurking behind a large rhododendron in the dark, I spoke some hopeful and unconsoling words to her, but I don't think she heard me. My voice had gotten so soft by then as to be inaudible to anyone but myself. I looked up at the smoke of what I found out was her hope chest, full of all those precious things: menus, ticket stubs, photographs, hotel room receipts, place cards, her wedding veil, and wondered what it was, what in the world it *could've been* drifting off into the clear spiritless New Jersey nighttime. It reminded me of the smoke that announced a new Pope—*a new Pope!*—if that is believable now, under those circumstances. And in four months I was divorced. All this seems odd now, and far away, as if it had happened to someone else and I had only read about it. But that was my life then, and it is my life now, and I am in relatively good spirits about it. If there's another thing that sportswriting teaches you, it is that there are no transcendent themes in life. In all cases things are here and they're over, and that has to be enough. The other view is a lie of literature and the liberal arts, which is why I did not succeed as a teacher, and another reason I put my novel away in the drawer and have not taken it out.

"Yes, of course," X says and sniffs. She has almost stopped crying, though I have not tried to comfort her (a privilege I no longer hold). She raises her eyes up to the milky sky and sniffs again. She is still holding the nibbled egg. "When I cried in the dark, I thought about what a big nice boy Ralph Bascombe should be right now, and that I was thirty-seven no matter what. I wondered about what we should all be doing." She shakes her head and squeezes her arms tight against her stomach in a way I have not seen her do in a long time. "It's not your fault, Frank.

I just thought it would be all right if you saw me cry. That's my idea of grief. Isn't that womanish?"

She is waiting for me to say a word now, to liberate us from that old misery of memory and life. It's pretty obvious she feels something is odd today, some freshening in the air to augur a permanent change in things. And I am her boy, happy to do that very thing—let my optimism win back a day or at least the morning or a moment when it all seems lost to grief. My one redeeming strength of character may be that I am good when the chips are down. With success I am worse.

"Why don't I read a poem," I say, and smile a happy old rejected suitor's smile.

"I guess I was supposed to bring it, wasn't I?" X says, wiping her eyes. "I cried instead of bringing a poem." She has become girlish in her tears.

"Well, that's okay," I say and go down into my pants pockets for the poem I have Xeroxed at the office and brought along in case X forgot. Last year I brought Housman's "To An Athlete Dying Young" and made the mistake of not reading it over beforehand. I had not read it since I was in college, but the title made me remember it as something that would be good to read. Which it wasn't. If anything, it was much too literal and dreamily so about real athletes, a subject I have strong feelings about. Ralph in fact had not been much of an athlete. I barely got past "townsman of a stiller town," before I had to stop and just sit staring at the little headstone of red marble, incised with the little words RALPH BASCOMBE.

"Housman hated women, you know," X had said into the awful silence while I sat. "That's nothing against you. I just remembered it from some class. I think he was an old pederast who would've loved Ralph and hated us. Next year I'll bring a poem if that's okay."

"Fine," I had answered miserably. It was after that that she told me about my writing a novel and being a loner, and having wanted to join the LPGA back in the sixties. I think she felt sorry for me—I'm sure of it, in fact—though I also felt sorry for myself.

"Did you bring another Housman poem?" she says now and smirks at me, then turns and throws her nibbled egg as far as she can off into the gravestones and elms of the old part, where it hits soundlessly. She throws as a catcher would, snapping it by her ear in a gainly way, on a tape-line into the shadows. I admire her positive form. To mourn the loss of one child when you have two others is a hard business. And we are not very practiced, though we treat it as a matter of personal dignity and affection so that Ralph's death and our loss will not get entrapped by time and events and ruin our lives in a secret way. In a sense, we can do no wrong here.

Out on Constitution Street an appliance repair truck has stopped at the light. Easler's Philco Repair, driven by Sid (formerly of Sid's Service, a bankrupt). He has worked on my house many times and is heading toward the village square to hav-a-cup at The Coffee Spot before plunging off into the day's kitchens and basements and sump pumps. The day is starting in earnest. A lone pedestrian—a man—walks along the sidewalk, one of the few Negroes in town, walking toward the station in a light-colored, wash-and-wear suit. The sky is still milky, but possibly it will burn off before I leave for the Motor City with Vicki.

"No Housman today," I say.

"Well," X says and smiles, and seats herself on Craig's stone to listen. "If you say so." Lights are numerous and growing dim with the daylight along the backs of houses on my street. I feel warmer.

It is a "Meditation" by Theodore Roethke, who also attended the University of Michigan, something X will be wise to, and I start it in my best, most plausible voice, as if my dead son could hear it down below:

"I have gone into the waste lonely places behind the eye. . . ."

X has already begun to shake her head before I am to the second line, and I stop and look to her to see where the trouble is.

She puches out her lower lip and sits her stone. "I don't like that poem," she says matter-of-factly.

I knew she would know it and have a strong opinion about it. She is still an opinionated Michigan girl, who thinks about things with certainty and is disappointed when the rest of the world doesn't. Such a big strapping things-in-order girl should be in every man's life. They alone are reason enough for the midwest's existence, since that's where most of them thrive. I feel tension rising off me like a fever now. It is possible that reading a poem over a little boy who never cared about poems is not a good idea.

"I thought you'd know it," I say in a congenial voice.

"I shouldn't really say I don't like it," X says coldly. "I just don't believe it, is all."

It is a poem about letting the everyday make you happy—insects, shadows, the color of a woman's hair—something else I have some strong beliefs about. "When I read it, I always think it's me talking," I say.

"I don't think those things in that poem would make anybody happy. They might not make you miserable. But that's all," X says and slips down off the stone. She smiles at me in a manner I do not like, tight-lipped and disparaging, as if she believes I'm wrong about everything and finds it amusing. "Sometimes I don't think anyone can be happy anymore." She puts her hands in her London Fog. She probably has a lesson at seven, or a follow-through seminar, and her mind is ready to be far, far away.

"I think we're all released to the rest of our lives, is my way of looking at it," I say hopefully. "Isn't that true?"

She stares at our son's grave as if he were listening and would be embarrassed to hear us. "I guess."

"Are you really getting married?" I feel my eyes open wide as if I knew the answer already. We are like brother and sister suddenly, Hansel and Gretel, planning their escape to safety.

"I don't know." She wags her shoulders a little, like a girl again, but in resignation as much as anything else. "People want to marry me. I might've reached an age, though, when I don't need men."

"Maybe you *should* get married. Maybe it would make you happy." I do not believe it for a minute, of course. I'm ready to marry her again myself, get life back on track. I miss the sweet specificity of marriage, its firm ballast and sail. X misses it too, I can tell. It's the thing we both feel the lack of. We are having to make everything up now, since nothing is ours by right.

She shakes her head. "What did you and Pauly talk about last night? I felt like it was all men's secrets and I wasn't in on it. I hated it."

"We talked about Ralph. Paul has a theory we can reach him by sending a carrier pigeon to Cape May. It was a good talk."

X smiles at the idea of Paul, who is as dreamy in his own way as I ever was. I have never thought X much liked that in him, and preferred Ralph's certainty since it was more like hers and, as such, admirable. When he was fiercely sick with Reye's, he sat up in bed in the hospital one day, in a delirium, and said, "Marriage is a damnably serious business, particularly in Boston"— something he'd read in Bartlett's, which he used to leaf through, memorizing and reciting. It took me six weeks to track the remark down to Marquand. And by then he was dead and lying right here. But X liked it, thought it proved his mind was working away well underneath the deep coma. Unfortunately it became a kind of motto for our marriage from then till the end, an unmeant malediction Ralph pronounced on us.

"I like your new hair," I say. The new way was a thatch along the back that is very becoming. We are past the end of things now, but I don't want to leave.

X fingers a strand, pulls it straight away from her head and cuts her eyes over at it. "It's dikey, don't you think?"

"No." And indeed I don't.

"Well. It'd gotten to a funny length. I had to do something. They screamed at home when they saw it." She smiles as if she's realized this moment that children become our parents, and we just become children again. "You don't feel old, do you, Frank?" She turns and stares away across the cemetery. "I don't know why I've got all these shitty questions. I feel old today. I'm sure it's because you're going to be thirty-nine."

The black man has come to the corner of Constitution Street and stands waiting as the traffic light flicks from red to green across from the new library. The appliance truck is gone, and a yellow minibus stops and lets black maids out onto the same corner. They are large women in white, tentish maid-dresses, talking and swinging big banger purses, waiting for their white ladies to come and pick them up. The man and women do not speak. "Oh, isn't that the saddest thing you ever saw," X says, staring at the women. "Something about that breaks my heart. I don't know why."

"I really don't feel a bit old," I say, happy to be able to answer a question honestly, and possibly slip in some good advice on the side. "I have to wash my hair a little more often. And sometimes I wake up and my heart's pounding to beat the band—though Fincher Barksdale says it isn't anything to worry about. I think it's a good sign. I'd say it was some kind of urgency, wouldn't you?"

X stares at the maids who are talking in a group of five, watching up the street where their rides will come from. Since our divorce she has developed the capability of complete distraction. She will be talking to you but be a thousand miles away. "You're very adaptable," she says airily.

"I am. I know you don't have a sleeping porch in your house, but you should try sleeping with all your windows open and your clothes on. When you wake up, you're ready to go. I've been doing it for a while now."

X smiles at me again with a tight-lipped smile of condescension, a smile I don't like. We are not Hansel and Gretel anymore. "Do you still see your palmist, what's-her-name?"

"Mrs. Miller. No, less often." I'm not about to admit I tried to see her last night.

"Do you feel like you're at the point of understanding everything that's happened—to us and our life?"

"Sometimes. Today I feel pretty normal about Ralph. It doesn't seem like it's going to make me crazy again."

"You know," X says, looking away. "Last night I lay in bed and thought bats were flying around my room, and when I closed my eyes I just saw a horizon line a long way off, with everything empty and flat like a long dinner table set for one. Isn't that awful?" She shakes her head. "Maybe I should lead a life more like yours."

A small resentment rises in me, though this is not the place for resentment. X's view of my life is that it is a jollier, more close to the grain business than hers, and certainly more that way than I know it to be. She'd probably like to tell me again that I should've gone ahead and written a novel instead of quitting and being a sportswriter, and that she should've done some things differently herself. But that would not be right, at least about me—there were even plenty of times when she thought so herself. Everything looks old gloomy to her now. One strain in her character that our divorce has touched is that she is possibly less resilient than she has been before in her life, and worry about getting older is proof of it. I'd cheer her up if I could, but that is one of the talents I lost a long time ago.

"I'm sorry again," she says. "I'm just feeling blue today.

There's something about your going away that makes me feel like you're leaving for a new life and I'm not."

"I hope I am," I say, "though I doubt it. I hope you are." Nothing, in fact, would I like better than to have a whole new colorful world open up to me today, though I like things pretty well as they are. I will settle for a nice room at the Pontchartrain, a steak Diane and a salad bar in the rotating rooftop restaurant, seeing the Tigers under the lights. I am not hard to make happy.

"Do you ever wish you were younger?" X says moodily.

"No. I'm fairly happy this way."

"I wish it all the time," she says. "That seems stupid, I know."

I have nothing I can say to this.

"You're an optimist, Frank."

"I hope I am." I smile a good yeoman's smile at her.

"Sure, sure," she says, and turns away from me and begins making her way quickly out through the tombstones, her head up toward the white sky, her hands deep in her pockets like any midwestern girl who's run out of luck for the moment but will soon be back as good as new. I hear the bells of St. Leo the Great chime six o'clock, and for some reason I have a feeling I won't see her for a long time, that something is over and something begun, though I cannot tell you for the life of me what those somethings might be.

CHAPTER 2

ALL WE REALLY want is to get to the point where the past can explain nothing about us and we can get on with life. Whose history can ever reveal very much? In my view Americans put too much emphasis on their pasts as a way of defining themselves, which can be death-dealing. I know I'm always heartsick in novels (sometimes I skip these parts altogether; sometimes I close the book and never pick it up again) when the novelist makes his clanking, obligatory trip into the Davy Jones locker of the past. Most pasts, let's face it, aren't very dramatic subjects, and should be just uninteresting enough to release you the instant you're ready (though it's true that when we get to that moment we are often scared to death, feel naked as snakes and have nothing to say).

My own history I think of as a postcard with changing scenes on one side but no particular or memorable messages on the back. You can get detached from your beginnings, as we all know, and not by any malevolent designs, just by life itself, fate, the tug of the ever-present. The stamp of our parents on us and of the past in general is, to my mind, overworked, since at some point we are whole and by ourselves upon the earth, and there is nothing that can change that for better or worse, and so we might as well think about something more promising.

I was born into an ordinary, modern existence in 1945, an only child to decent parents of no irregular point of view, no particular sense of their *place* in history's continuum, just two people afloat on the world and expectant like most others in time, without a daunting conviction about their own consequence. This seems like a fine lineage to me still.

My parents were rural Iowans who left farms near the town of Keota and moved around a lot as young marrieds, settling finally in Biloxi, Mississippi, where my father had some work that involved plating ships with steel at the Ingalls ship-building company, for the Navy, which he'd served in during the war. The year before that they had been in Cicero, doing what I'm not really sure. The year before that in El Reno, Oklahoma, and before that near Davenport, where my father had something to do with the railroad. I'm frankly hazy about his work, though I have enough memory of him: a tall rangy blade-faced man with pale eyes—like me—but with romantically curly hair. I have tried to place him in a Davenport or a Cicero, where I've gone myself to report sports events. But the effect is strange. He was not a man—at least in my memory—for those places.

I remember my father played golf and sometimes I went with him around the flat course on hot days in the Biloxi summer. He played on the Air Force Base links which were tanned and bleached out and frequented by non-coms. This was so my mother could have a day to herself and go to the movies or get her hair fixed or stay home reading movie magazines and cheap novels. Golf seemed to me then the saddest kind of torture, and even my poor father didn't seem to have much fun at it. He was not really the golf type, but more the type to race cars, and he took it up, I believe, in a mindful way because it meant something to him, some measure of success in the world. I remember standing on a tee with him, both of us wearing shorts, looking down the long palm-lined fairway beyond which you could see a sea wall and the Gulf, and seeing him grimace toward the far-away flag as if it represented a fortress he was reluctantly about to lay seige to, and him saying to me, "Well, Franky, do you think I can hit it that far?" And my saying, "I doubt it." He was sweating and smoking a cigarette in the heat, and I have a very clear memory of him looking at me then as if in wonder. Who was I again? What was it I was planning? He seemed struck by such questions. It was not exactly a heartless look, just a look of profoundest wonder and resign.

My father died when I was fourteen, and after that my mother placed me in what she called "the naval academy," which was in fact a little military school near Gulfport called Gulf Pines (we cadets called it Lonesome Pines) and where I never once minded being. In fact, I liked the military bearing that was required there, and I think there is an upright part of my character which at least respects the appearance of rectitude if not the fact, and which school was responsible for. My situation at Lonesome Pines was somewhat more than average, since most of the cadets had come there from the broken homes of rich people or from abandon-ment, or because they had stolen something or burned something down and their families were able to get them off and sent there instead of reform school. Though the other students never seemed any different from me, just boys full of secrecy and not-knowing and abject longing, who thought of this time as some-thing simply to be gotten through, so that no one made attach-ments. It was as if we all sensed we'd be gone someday soon in a sudden instant—often it happened in the middle of the night—and didn't want to get involved. Or else it was that none of us wanted to know anybody later on who was the way we were now.

What I remember of the place was a hot parade ground surrounded by sparse pine trees, a flag pole with an anchor at its base, a stale shallow lake where I learned to sail, a smelly beach and boat house, hot brown stucco classroom buildings and white barracks houses that reeked with mops. There were some ex-Navy warrant officers who taught there—men unsuited for regular teaching. One Negro even taught there, a man named Bud Simmons who coached baseball. The Commandant was an old captain from World War I, named Admiral Legler.

We took our leaves in bunches, out on Highway 1 in the little Gulf Coast towns we could get to by public bus, in the air-conditioned movie and tamale houses, or hanging out in the vicinity of Keesler Air Force Base, in the hot, sandy parking lots of strip joints, all of us in our brown uniforms trying to get the real servicemen to buy us booze, and wretched because we were too young to go in ourselves and had too little money to be able to do anything but squander it.

I went home on holidays to my mother's bungalow in Biloxi, and occasionally I saw her brother Ted who lived not far away, and who came to see me and took me on trips to Mobile and Pensacola, where we did not do much talking. It may be just the fate of boys whose fathers die young never to be young—officially—ourselves; youth being just a brief dream, a prelude of no particular lasting moment before actual life begins.

My only personal athletic experience came there at Lonesome Pines. I tried to play baseball on the school team, under Bud Simmons, the Negro coach. I was relatively tall for my age—though I'm more normal now—and I had the lanky, long-loose-arm grace of a natural ball player. But I could never do it well.

I could always see myself as though from outside, doing the things I was told to do. And that was enough never to do them well or fully. An inbred irony seemed to haunt me, and served no useful purpose but to make me a musing, wiseacre kid, shifty-eyed and secretive—the kind who belongs in exactly such a place as Lonesome Pines. Bud Simmons did what he could with me, including make me throw with my other arm, which I happily did, though it didn't help at all. He referred to my problem as not being able to "give it up," and I knew exactly what he meant. (Today I am amazed when I find athletes who can be full-fledged people and also "give it up" to their sport. That does not happen often, and it is a dear gift from a complex God.)

I did not see so much of my mother in those years. Nor does this seem exceptional to me. It must've happened to thousands of us B. 1945s, and to children in earlier centuries as well. It seems odder that children see their parents *so much* these days, and come to know them better than they probably ever need to. I saw my mother when she could see me. I stayed in her house when I was back from school and we acted like friends. She loved me as much as she was able to, given her altered situation. She might've liked having a closer life with me. I'm sure I would've liked it. But it's possible she was dreamy herself and in no particular mind to know exactly what to do. I'm sure she never thought my father would die, in the same way I didn't think Ralph would die, except he did. She was only thirty-four, a small dark-eyed woman with skin darker than mine, and who strikes me now as having been shocked by how far she had come from where she was born, and having been more absorbed by that than anything. Her life just distracted her the way another person would, not in a hateful or a selfish way, possibly even the way my father had, but that I knew nothing about. I think she must've been worried about going back to Iowa, and didn't want to.

Eventually she went to work in a large hotel called the Buena Vista in Mississippi City as the night cashier, and while she was there she met a man named Jake Ornstein, a jeweler from Chicago, and after a few months in which he made several trips down, she married him and moved to Skokie, Illinois, where she lived until she got cancer and died.

At almost that same time I won an NROTC scholarship through Lonesome Pines, and by pure chance enrolled at the

University of Michigan. The Navy's idea was to achieve a mix, and nobody got to go where they wanted to go, though I don't even remember where I wanted to go, except it probably wasn't there.

I do remember that there were times when I visited my mother in Skokie, taking the fragrant old New York Central from Ann Arbor and spending the weekend lounging around trying to be comfortable and make conversation in that strangely suburban ranch-style house with plastic slipcovers on the furniture and twenty-five clocks on the walls, in a Jewish neighborhood and in a town where I had no attachments. Jake Ornstein was fifteen years older than my mother and was quite a nice fellow, and I got along well with him and his son Irv—better, in fact, than I ended up getting along with my mother. She mentioned she thought my college was "one of the good schools," but treated me like a nephew she didn't know very well, and who worried her, even though she liked me. (She gave me a smoking jacket and pipe when I left for school—she was already in Skokie by then so that my leaving was from there.) For my part I'm sure I stared a lot and kept a distance. I'm sure we both tried to approach one another on some new level that could've flattered us both when we saw how we'd adjusted. But her life had gotten in front of her somehow, and I became someone out of another time, a fact I don't hold against my mother and haven't felt abandoned or disaffected because of it.

What could *her* life have been like, after all? Good, bad, both by turns? A long pathway through which she hoped to be not too unhappy? She knew. But *only* she knew. And I am not prone to judge a life I don't know much about, in particular since things have turned out all right for me. The best I knew then, and still, is of my own life, which at the time my mother was married to Jake Ornstein, I was on fire to get on with. I know that she and Jake were happy, and that I loved my mother very much in whatever way I was able, knowing so little about her. When she died I was still in school. I went to the funeral, acted as a pall-bearer, sat around Jake's house for a weekend afternoon with the people they both knew, tried to think of what my parents had taught me in their lives (I came up with "a sense of indepen-dence"). And that night I got back on the train and slipped out of that life for good. Jake, afterwards, moved to Phoenix, married again, and died of cancer himself. Irv and I kept in touch for a few years, but have drifted apart.

But does that seem like an odd life? Does it seem strange that I do not have a long and storied family history? Or a list of problems and hatreds to brood about—a bill of particular grievances and nostalgias that pretend to explain or trouble everything? Possibly I was born into a different time. But maybe my way is better all around, and is actually the way with most of us and the rest tell lies.

Still. Do I ever wonder what my family would think of me? Of my profession? As a divorced man, a father, a quester after women? As an adult heading for life and death?

Sometimes. Though it never stays with me long. And, indeed, *when* I think of it, I think this: that they would probably have approved of everything I've done—particularly my decision to quit writing and get on to something they would think of as more practical. They would feel about it the way I do: that things sometimes happen for the best. Thinking that way has given me a chance for an interesting if not particularly simple adulthood.

BY 9:30 I have nearly finished the few odds-and-ends details remaining before picking up Vicki and heading for the airport. Usually this would include a cup of coffee with Bosobolo, my boarder from the seminary in town, a custom I enjoy, but not today. We have had some good give-and-takes on such subjects as whether the bliss of the redeemed is heightened by the sufferings of the damned—something he feels Catholic about, but I don't. He is forty-two and from the country of Gabon, and a stern-faced apologist for limitless faith. I usually argue for works, but without any illusions about where it'll get me.

Why take a boarder? To ward off awful loneliness. Why else? The consolation in the disinterested footfalls of another human in an otherwise empty house, especially a six-foot-five-inch Negro from Africa living in your attic, can be considerable. This morning, though, he is away early on his own business and I see him from the window larruping up Hoving Road like a Bible salesman, heading for school—white shirt, black trousers and truck-tread sandals. He has told me that he is a prince in his tribe—the Nwambes—but I have never known an African who wasn't. Like me, he has a wife and two children. We're both Presbyterians, though I am not a good one.

My other duties require the usual phone calls from my desk: first to the magazine, for business with Rhonda Matuzak, my editor, who has dug into the rumors that all is not roses on the Detroit team, which could be a problem. The general feeling at the editors' meeting is I should do the story and take what I get. Sports thrives on this kind of turmoil and patented misinformation, though I am not much interested in it.

Rhonda is divorced and lives alone with two cats in a large dark-walled, high-ceilinged floor-thru in the West Eighties, and is always trying to get me to meet her at Victor's for dinner, or to haul off to some evening's activity after work. Though except for one painful night after my divorce I've always managed just to have a drink at Grand Central, put her in a cab, then hurry off to Penn Station and home.

Rhonda is a tall raw-boned, ash-blond girl in her late thirties with an old-fashioned, chorus-line figure, but with a face like a racehorse and a loud voice I don't like. (Illusion would be well-nigh impossible even with the lights off.) For a time after my divorce everything began to seem profoundly ironic to me. I found myself thinking of other people's worries as sources of amusement and private derision which I thought about at night to make myself feel better. Rhonda helped me out of all that by continuing to invite me to dinner and leaving notes on my desk which said "all loss is relative, Jack," "nobody ever died of a broken heart," and "only the young die good." On the one night I agreed to have dinner with her—at Mallory's on West 70th Street—we ended up in her apartment sitting in facing Bauhaus chairs, with me unhappily coming down with a case of the dreads so thick they seemed to whistle out the heating ducts and swarm the room like a dark mistral. I needed to take a walk in the street for air, I said, and she was considerate enough to believe I was still having trouble getting adjusted to being single again, and not that I was for some reason scared out of my wits to be alone with her. She walked me downstairs and out into the dark and windy canyons of West End Avenue, where we stood at the curb and talked about her favorite subject, American furniture history, and after a while I thanked her, clambered into a cab like a

refugee and beat it down to 33rd Street and my safe train to New
Jersey.

What I didn't tell Rhonda and what is still true, is that I cannot
stand being alone in New York after dark. Gotham takes on a
flashing nighttime character I just can't bear. The lights of bars
demoralize me, the showy glow of taxi cabs whiz-banging down
Fifth Avenue or careening out of the Park Avenue tunnel make
me somehow heartsick and turmoiled and endangered. I feel
adrift and badly so when the editors and the agents stroll out of
their midtown offices in their silly garb, headed for assignations,
idiot softball games or cocktails on the cuff. I can't bear all the
complications, and long for something that is façades-only and
non-literate—the cozy pseudo-colonial Square here in conventional Haddam; the nicotine clouds of New Jersey as seen from
a high office building like mine at dusk; the poignancy of a night-
time train ride back down the long line home. It was bad enough
that one night to have Rhonda "walk me" down West End three
blocks to a good cross street, but it was worse afterwards to ride
in that bouncing, clanging cab clear to the station and then to
dart—my feet feeling frozen—in and down the escalator from
Seventh before the whole city reached out and clutched me like
the pale hand of a dead limo driver.

"Why stay out there like a hermit, Bascombe?" Rhonda is
louder than usual on the phone this morning. As an equalizer
she refers to men by our last names, as if we were all in the Army.
I could never yearn for anyone who called me Bascombe.

"A lot of people are where they belong, Rhonda. I'm one of
them."

"You're talented, God knows." She taps something hard near
the phone with a pencil eraser. "I've read those short stories, you
know. They're very, very good."

"Thanks for saying so."

"Did you ever think about writing another book?"

"No."

"You should. You should move up here. At least stay in sometime. You'd see."

"What would I see?"

"You'd see it's not so bad."

"I'd rather have something wonderful, not just *not so bad*,
Rhonda. I've pretty much got it right here."

"In New Jersey."

"I like it here."

"New Jersey's the back of an old radio, Frank. You should smell the roses."

"I have roses in my yard. I'll talk to you when I get back, Rhonda."

"Great," Rhonda says loudly and blows smoke into the receiver. "Do you want to make any trades before the deadline?" There is an office baseball league that Rhonda is running and I'm in on it this year. It's a good way to ride out a season.

"No. I'm sitting pat."

"All right. Try to get some insider stuff on the NFL draft. Okay? They're putting together the Pigskin Preview Sunday night. You can call it in."

"Thanks, Rhonda. I'll do my best."

"Frank? What're you searching for?"

"Nothing," I say. I hang up before she has a chance to think of something else.

I MAKE MY other calls snappy—one is to an athletic shoe designer in Denver for a "Sports Chek" round-up box I'm pulling together on foot injuries, and which other people in the office have worked on. He tells me there are twenty-six bones in the foot, and only two people in eight will ever know their correct shoe size. Of those two, one will still suffer permanent foot injury before he or she is sixty-two—due to product defect. Women, I learn, are 38 percent more susceptible than men, although men have a higher percentage of painful injuries due to body weight, stress and other athletic-related activities. Men complain less, however, and consequently amount to a hidden statistic.

Another call is to a Carmelite nun in Fayetteville, West Virginia, who is trying to run in the Boston Marathon. Once a polio victim, she is facing an uphill credentials fight in her quest to compete, and I'm glad to put a plug in for her in our "Achievers" column.

I make a follow-up call to the public relations people at the Detroit Football Club to see if they have someone they'd like to speak on behalf of the organization about Herb Wallagher, the ex-lineman, but no one is around.

Finally a call to Herb himself in Walled Lake, to let him know

I'm on my way. The research department has already done a work-up on Herb, and I have a thick pile of his press clips, photo-graphs, as well as transcribed interviews with his parents in Beaver Falls, his college coach at Allegheny, his surgeon, and the girl who was driving the ski boat when Herb was injured and whose life, I've learned, has been changed forever. On the phone Herb is a friendly, ruminative fellow with a Beaver Falls way of swallowing his consonants—*wunt* for wouldn't, *shunt* for shouldn't. I've got before-and-after pictures of him in his play-ing days and today, and in them he does not look like the same person. Then he looks like a grinning tractor-trailer in a plastic helmet. Now he wears black horn-rims, and having lost weight and hair, looks like an overworked insurance agent. Linemen often tend to be more within themselves than most athletes, par-ticularly once they've left the game, and Herb tells me he has decided to go to law school next fall, and that his wife Clarice has signed on for the whole trip. He tells me he doesn't see why anybody *shunt* get all the education they can get, and that you're never too old to learn, and I agree wholeheartedly, though I detect in Herb's voice a nervy formality I can't quite make out, as if something was bothering him but he didn't want to make a fuss about it now. It could easily be the team troubles I've been hearing about. But more than likely this is just the way with all wheelchair victims: after you lift weights, eat a good breakfast, use the toilet, read the paper and bathe, what's left for the day but news broadcasts, reticence and turning inward? A good sense of decorum can make life bearable when otherwise you might be tempted to blow your brains out.

"Listen, I'll sure be glad to see you, Frank." We have never laid eyes on each other and have talked on the phone only once, but I feel like I know him already.

"It'll be good to see you, Herb."

"You miss a lot of things now, you know," Herb says. "Tele-vision's great. But it's not enough."

"We'll have a good talk, Herb."

"We'll have a time, won't we? I know we will."

"I'll say we will. See you tomorrow."

"You take care, Frank. Safe trip and all that."

"Thanks, Herb."

"Think metric, Frank. Hah." Herb hangs up.

*   *   *

WHATEVER'S LEFT to tell of my past can be dispensed with in a New York minute. At Michigan I studied the liberal arts in the College of Literature, Science and the Arts (along with ROTC). I took all the courses I was supposed to, including Latin, spent some time at the *Daily* writing florid little oversensitive movie reviews, and the rest with my feet up in the Sigma Chi house, where one crisp autumn day in 1965, I met X, who was the term party date of a brother of mine named Laddy Nozar, from Benton Harbor, and who—X—impressed me as ungainly and too earnest and not a girl I would ever care to go out with. She was very athletic-looking, with what seemed like too large breasts, and had a way of standing with her arms crossed and one leg in front of the other and slightly turned out that let you know she was probably sizing you up for fun. She seemed like a rich girl, and I didn't like rich Michigan girls, I didn't think. Consequently I never saw her again until that dismal book signing in New York in 1969, not long before I married her.

Shortly after our first meeting—but not because of it—I quit school and joined the Marines. This was in the middle stages of the war, and it seemed the right thing to do—with my military bearing—and the NROTC didn't mind. In fact, I joined with Laddy Nozar and two other boys, at the old post office on Main Street in Ann Arbor and had to cross an embarrassing protest line to do it. Laddy Nozar went to Vietnam and got killed at Con Thien with the Third Marines. The two others finished their tours and now run an ad agency in Aurora, Illinois. As it happened, I contracted a pancreatic syndrome which the doctors thought was Hodgkin's disease but which turned out to be benign, and after two months in Camp Lejeune I was discharged without killing anyone or being killed, but designated a veteran anyway and given benefits.

This event happened when I was twenty-one years old, and I report it only because it was the first time I remember feeling dreamy in my life, though then what I felt was not so pleasant and I think I would've said I felt sullen more than anything. I used to lie in bed in the Navy hospital in North Carolina and think about nothing but dying, which for a while I felt interested in. I'd think about it the way you'd think of a strategy in a ball game, deciding one way then deciding another, seeing myself dead then alive then dead again, as if considerations and options were involved. Then I'd realize I didn't have any choices and that it wasn't going to be that way, and I felt nostalgic for a while, but then got sullen as hell so that the doctors ended up giving me antidepressants to stop my thinking about it altogether, which I did. (This happens to a lot of people who get sick at a young age, and, in fact, can ruin your life.)

What it did for me, though, was let me go back to college, since I had only missed a semester, and, by 1967, entertain the idea I'd been entertaining since reading the seafaring diaries of Joshua Slocum at Lonesome Pines—to write a novel. Mine was to be about a bemused young southerner who joins the Navy but gets discharged with a mysterious disease, goes to New Orleans and loses himself into a hazy world of sex and drugs and rumored gun-running and a futile attempt to reconcile a vertiginous present with the guilty memories of not dying along-side his Navy comrades, all of which is climaxed in a violent tryst with a Methodist minister's wife who seduces him in an abandoned slave-quarters, though other times too, after which his life is shattered and he disappears permanently into the Texas oil fields. It was all told in a series of flashbacks.

This novel was called *Night Wing*, the title of a sentimental nautical painting that hung above the sweetheart couch in the Sigma Chi chapter room (I used a quotation from Marvell up front). In the middle of my senior year I wrapped it up and sent it off to a publisher in New York who wrote back in six months to say it "showed promise," and could he see "other things." The manuscript got lost in the mail back and I never saw it again, and naturally I hadn't kept a copy. Though I can remember the opening lines as clearly as if I had written them this morning. They described the night the narrator of the story was conceived. "It was 1944, and it was April. Dogwoods bloomed in Memphis. The Japanese had not given in and the war plowed on. His father came home from work tired and had a drink, not thinking of the white-coated men with code names, imagining at that moment an atomic bomb. . . ."

After graduation I bought a car and drove straight out to Man-hattan Beach, California, where I rented a room and for four weeks walked in the sand, stared at the women and the oil der-ricks, but could not see much there that was worth writing about —which I'd decided was what I was going to do. I was getting disability money from the Navy by then, which was supposedly going to pay a tuition, and I managed to have the checks cashed by a woman I met who worked in the bursar's office of Los Angeles City College, and who sent them to me where I went, to the village of San Miguel Tehuantepec in Mexico, to write stories like a real writer.

Inside six months of arriving, all in a rush, I wrote twelve stories—one of which was a reduced form of *Night Wing*. Without sending one to a magazine, I shipped the whole book to the publisher I'd been in touch with the year before, who wrote back inside of four weeks to say that his company might publish the book with a number of changes I was only too happy to make, and sent back immediately. He encouraged me to keep writing, which I did, though without much enthusiasm. I had written all I was going to write, if the truth had been known, and there is nothing wrong with that. If more writers knew that, the world would be saved a lot of bad books, and more people—men and women alike—could go on to happier, more productive lives.

The rest is of even less interest. My book, *Blue Autumn*, was officially accepted while I was on the road driving up from San Miguel Tehuantepec. (They wired me a check for $700.) I stopped off that evening and took in a Little League game under the lights in the town of Grants, New Mexico, and drank a bottle of Cold Duck sitting alone in the stands to toast myself and my fortunes. Almost the next day a movie producer offered to buy the book for a good price, and by the time I got to New York—which my editor suggested was a good place to live—I was rich, at least for those times. It was 1968.

Right away I rented a railroad apartment on Perry Street in Greenwich Village and tried to set up some kind of writer's life, a life I actually liked. My book was published in the spring; I gave readings at some small local colleges, interviews on the radio, went out with a lot of girls, acquired a literary agent I still get Christmas cards from. I had my picture in *Newsweek*, stayed up late almost every night drinking and carousing with the new friends I was making, wrote very little (though I stayed at my desk a lot), met X at the book signing on Spring Street and took an advance from my publisher to write a novel I claimed to have an idea for, but had no interest in at all, nor any idea in the world what I could write about.

In the fall of 1969, X and I began to spend a great deal of time together. I took my first trip to the Huron Mountain Club and to the cushy golf clubs her father had memberships in. I found out she was not ungainly or too earnest at all, but was actually a wonderful, unusual, challenging girl (she was still modeling and making plenty of money). We got married in February of 1970, and I began doing some magazine assignments to deflect the agony of writing my novel, which was entitled *Tangier*, and took place in Tangier—where I had never been, but assumed was like Mexico. The first line of *Tangier* was, "Autumn came later that year to the rif of the Low Atlas, and Carson was having an embarrassing time staying publicly sober." It was about a Marine who had deserted the war and wandered across the edges of continents in search of his sense of history, and was told in the first person and also mostly in flashbacks. It sits in my drawer in a closet under a lot of old life-insurance forms and catalogs to this very moment.

In the spring, my book was still in some book stores because a New York reviewer had said, "Mr. Bascombe is a writer who could turn out to be interesting." The movie producer decided he could "see a movie" in my stories, and paid me the rest of the money he owed me (though one was never made). I began churning out more work on *Tangier*, which everybody including me thought I should write. Ralph began to be on the way. X and I were having a fine time going to ball games at Yankee Stadium, driving to Montauk, taking in movies and plays. And suddenly one morning I woke up, stood at the window from which I could see a slice of the Hudson, and recognized that I had to get out of New York immediately.

When I think about it now, I'm not sure why we didn't just move into a larger apartment. If you were to ask X she would tell you it wasn't her idea. Yet something in me just suddenly longed for it. I felt at the time that going into things with a sense of certainty and confidence was everything. And that morning I woke up with the feeling my passport to New York had been invalidated and I had insurmountable wisdom as to the ways of the world; a feeling that we had to get out of town pronto so that my work could flourish in a place where I knew no one and no one knew me and I could perfect my important writer's anonymity.

Faced with this, X put in a vote for Lime Rock, Connecticut, up the Housatonic, where we had taken drives. But I couldn't have been more fearful of that indecisive Judas country. Its minor mountains and sad Shetland-sweater, Volvo-wagon enclaves spoke to me only of despair and deceit, sarcasm and overweening informalities—no real place for a real writer; only for second-rate editors and agents of textbook writers, was my judgment.

For lack of a better idea I cast my vote for New Jersey: a plain, unprepossessing and unexpectant landscape, I thought, and correctly. And for Haddam with its hilly and shady seminary niceness (I'd seen an ad in the *Times*, making it sound like an undiscovered Woodstock, Vermont), where I could invest my movie money in a sound house (I wasn't wrong), and where there was a mix of people (there was), and where a fellow might sit down with good hope and do a serious piece of work himself (I wasn't right there, but couldn't have known it).

X did not think it was worth a hard stand about Connecticut, and in the fall of 1970 we bought the house I now live alone in. X had quit her job to get ready for Ralph. I moved with renewed enthusiasm up to an "office" on the third floor—the part I now rent to Mr. Bosobolo—and set about trying to invent some more serious writing habits and a good attitude toward my novel, which I'd let drift over the summer. In a few months we fell in with a younger group of people (some of whom were writers and editors), began attending rounds of cocktail parties, took walks along the nearby Delaware, went to literary events in Gotham, attended plays in Bucks County, took drives in the country, stayed home evenings to read, were looked upon as a couple who were a little exceptional (I was just twenty-five), and generally felt fine about our lives and the choices we had made. I gave a talk entitled "The Making of a Writer" at the library and to the Rotarians in a neighboring town; wrote a piece in a local magazine about "Why I Live Where I Live," in which I talked about the need to find a place to work that is in most ways "neutral." I worked on an original screenplay for the producer who'd bought my book, and wrote several large magazine pieces—one about a famous center fielder from the old Sally League, who later became a petroleum baron and spent some time in prison for bank fraud, had several wives, but as a parolee went back to his arid West Texas home of Pumpville and built a therapeutic swimming pool for brain-damaged children and even brought Mexicans up for treatment. A year somehow managed to go by. Then I simply stopped writing.

I didn't exactly know I'd stopped writing. For a good while I'd gone to my office every day at eight, come downstairs at lunch and lounged around the house reading research books about Morocco, "doping out a few structural problems," making graphs and plot-flow outlines and character histories. But the fact was, I was washed up. Sometimes I would go upstairs, sit down, and not have any idea of what I was there for, or what it was I meant to write about, and had simply forgotten everything. My mind would wander to sailing on Lake Superior (something I had never done), and after that I would go back downstairs and take a nap. And as if I needed proof I was washed up, when the managing editor at the magazine I now work for called me and asked if I had any interest in going to work writing sports full-time—his magazine, he said, had a nose for good writing of the type he'd seen in my article about the Texas millionaire-convict-Samaritan—I was more than interested. He said he'd seen something complex yet hard-nosed in that piece of writing, in particular the way I didn't try to make the old center fielder either a villain or a hero to the world, and he had a suspicion I might have just the right temperament and eye for detail to do their kind of work, though he said I might just as well think the entire call was a joke. I took the train up the very next morning and had a long talk with the man who had called me, a fat, blue-eyed Chicagoan named Art Fox, and his young assistants, in the old oak-chaired offices the magazine then occupied on Madison and 45th. Art Fox told me that if you're a man in this country you probably already know enough to be a good sportswriter. More than anything, he said, what you needed was a willingness to watch something very similar over and over again, then be able to write about it in two days' time, plus an appreciation of the fact that you're always writing about people who wanted to be doing what they're doing or they wouldn't be doing it, which was the only urgency sportswriting could summon, but also the key to overcoming the irrelevancy of sports itself. After lunch, he took me out into the big room full of old-fashioned cubicles which still had typewriters and wooden desks, and introduced me around. I shook everyone's hand and heard them out about what was on their minds (no one mentioned anything about my book of stories), and at three o'clock I went home in brimming spirits. That night I took X out to a high-priced dinner with champagne at the Golden Pheasant, hauled her off on a romantic moonlight walk up the towpath in a direction we'd never gone, told her all about what I had in mind, what I thought we could practically hope to get from this kind of commitment (I thought plenty), and she simply said she thought it all sounded just fine. I remember that moment, in fact, as one of the happiest of my life.

The rest is history, as they say, until my son Ralph got Reye's syndrome some years later and died, and I launched off into the dreaminess his death may or may not have even caused but didn't help, and my life with X broke apart after seeing *The Thirty-Nine Steps* one night, causing her to send her hope chest chuffing up the chimney stack.

Though as I began by saying, I'm not sure what any of this proves. We all have histories of one kind or another. Some of us have careers that do fine or that do lousy. Something got us to where we are, and nobody's history could've brought another Tom, Dick or Harry to the same place. And to me that fact limits the final usefulness of these stories. To the extent that it's incompletely understood or undisclosed, or just plain fabricated, I suppose it's true that history can make mystery. And I am always vitally interested in life's mysteries, which are never in too great a supply, and which I should say are something very different from the dreaminess I just mentioned. Dreaminess is, among other things, a state of suspended recognition, and a response to too much useless and complicated factuality. Its symptoms can be a long-term interest in the weather, or a sustained soaring feeling, or a bout of the stares that you sometimes can not even know about except in retrospect, when the time may seem fogged. When you are young and you suffer it, it is not so bad and in some ways it's normal and even pleasurable.

But when you get to my age, dreaminess is *not* so pleasurable, at least as a steady diet, and one should avoid it if you're lucky enough to know it exists, which many people aren't. For a time—this was a period after Ralph died—I had no idea about it myself, and in fact thought I was onto something big—changing my life, moorings loosed, women, travel, marching to a different drummer. Though I was wrong.

Which leaves a question which might in fact be interesting.

Why did I quit writing? Forgetting for the moment that I quit writing to become a sportswriter, which is more like being a businessman, or an old-fashioned traveling salesman with a line of novelty household items, than being a genuine writer, since in so many ways words are just our currency, our medium of exchange with our readers, and there is very little that is ever genuinely creative to it at all—even if you're not much more than a fly-swat reporter, as I'm not. Real writing, after all, is something much more complicated and enigmatic than anything usually having to do with sports, though that's not to say a word against sportswriting, which I'd rather do than anything.

Was it just that things did not come easily enough? Or that I couldn't translate my personal recognitions into the ambiguous stuff of complex literature? Or that I had nothing to write about, no more discoveries up my sleeve or the pizzaz to write the more extensive work?

And my answer is: there are those reasons and at least twenty better ones. (Some people only have one book in them. There are worse things.)

One thing certain is that I had somehow lost my sense of anti-cipation at age twenty-five. Anticipation is the sweet pain to know whatever's next—a must for any real writer. And I had no more interest in what I might write next—the next sentence, the next day—than I cared what a rock weighed on Mars. Nor did I think that writing a novel could make me interested again.

Though I minded like all get out the loss of anticipation. And the glossy sports magazine promised me that there would always be something to look forward to, every two weeks. They'd see to it. And it wouldn't be something too hard to handle in words (my first "beat" was swimming, and some of the older writers put me through a pretty vigorous crash apprenticeship, which always happens). I had no special store of sports knowledge, but that wasn't needed. I was as comfortable as an old towel in a locker room, had plenty of opinions and had always admired athletes anyway. The good-spirited, manly presence of naked whites and Negroes has always made me feel well-located, and I was never out of place asking a few easy-to-answer questions and being somewhat less imposing than everybody around.

Plus, I'd be paid. Well paid—and there'd be travel. I would

regularly see "Frank Bascombe" in print above a piece of work-manlike journalism many people would read and possibly enjoy. Occasionally I'd get to be some fellow's guest on a call-in show (a hook-up in my own living room) and answer questions from fans in St. Louis or Omaha, where one of my articles had stirred up a bees' nest of controversy. "This is Eddie from Laclede, Mr. Bascombe, whaddaya think's wrong with the whole concept of competition on the college level these days? I think it stinks, Mr. Bascombe, if you want to know what I think." "Well, Eddie, that's a pretty good question...." Beyond all that I could look forward to the occasional company of good-natured men who, at least on a superficial level, shared my opinions—something you don't often have in the real writer's business.

What I determined to do was write well everything they told me to write—mixed pairs body-building, sky-diving, the luge, Nebraska 8-man football—I could've written three different stories for every assignment. I thought of things in the middle of the night, jumped out of bed, practically ran down to the study and wrote them. Raw material I had up to then—ruminations, fragments of memory, impulses I might've tried to struggle into a short story suddenly seemed like life I already understood clearly and could write about: fighting the battle with age; dis-covering how to think of the future in realistic terms.

It must happen to thousands of people that a late calling is missed, with everything afterwards done halfway—a sense of accomplishment stillborn. But for me it was the reverse. Without knowing I had a natural calling I had hit on a perfect one: to sit in the empty stands of a Florida ball park and hear the sounds of glove leather and chatter; talk to coaches and equipment man-agers in the gusty autumn winds of Wyoming; stand in the grass of a try-out camp in a mid-size Illinois grain town and watch footballs sail through the air; to bone up on the relevant stats, then go home or back to the office, sit down at my desk and write about it.

What could be better, I thought, and still think? How more easily assuage the life-long ache to anticipate than to write sports—an ache only zen masters and coma victims can live happily without?

I have talked this very subject over with Bert Brisker, who was also once a sportswriter for the magazine, but who has since become a book reviewer for one of the slick weeklies, and he has a remarkably similar set of experiences. Bert is as big as a den bear but gentle as they come now that he's stopped drinking. He is the closest acquaintance I still have in town from the old cocktail-dinner party days, and we are always trying to arrange for me to have dinner at their house, though on the one occasion I did, Bert got jittery as a quail halfway through the evening (this was about at the point it became clear we had nothing to talk about), and ended up downing several vodkas and threatening to throw me through the wall. Consequently we see each other only on the train to Gotham, something that happens once a week. It is, I think, the essence of a modern friendship.

Bert was once a poet and has two or three delicate, spindly-thin books I occasionally see in used bookstore racks. For years, he had a wild-man's reputation for getting drunk at public readings and telling audiences of nuns and clubwomen to go straight to hell, then falling off stages into deep trance-like sleeps and getting into fistfights in the homes of professors who had invited him there and thought he was an artist. Eventually, of course, he ended up in a rehab hospital in Minnesota and, later, running a poetry program in a small New Hampshire college—very like the one I taught at—and eventually getting fired for shacking up with most of his female students, several of whom he moved right into the house with his wife. It is not an unusual story, though that was all years ago. He came to sportswriting precisely as I did, and now lives nearby on a farm in the hills outside of Haddam with his second wife, Penny, and their two daughters, and raises sheepdogs in addition to writing about books. Bert's specialty, when he was a sportswriter, was ice hockey, and I will commend him by saying he was very good at making an uninteresting game played by Canadians seem sometimes more than uninteresting. Many of our writers are former college teachers or once-aspiring writers who simply couldn't take it, or rougher-cut graduates of Ivy League schools who didn't want to be stockbrokers or divorce lawyers. The day of the old bulldog reporter up from the Des Moines *Register* or the Fargo *Dakotan*— your Al Bucks and your Granny Rices—are long gone, though that wasn't as true when I started twelve years ago.

Bert and I have talked about this subject on our train rides through the New Jersey beltland—why he quit writing, why I did. And we've agreed, to an extent, that we both got gloomy in an attempt to be serious, and that we didn't understand the vital necessity of the play of light and dark in literature. I thought my stories were good at the time (even today I think I might like them). They seemed to have a feeling for the human dilemma and they *did* seem hard-nosed and old-eyed about things. It was also true, though, that there were a good many descriptions of the weather and the moon, and that most of them were set in places like remote hunting camps on Canadian Lakes, or in the suburbs, or Arizona or Vermont, places I had never been, and many of them ended with men staring out snowy windows in New England boarding schools or with somebody driving fast down a dark dirt road, or banging his hand into a wall or telling someone else he could never *really* love his wife, and bringing on hard emptinesses. They also seemed to depend on silence a lot. I seemed, I felt later, to have been stuck in bad stereotypes. All my men were too serious, too brooding and humorless, characters at loggerheads with imponderable dilemmas, and much less interesting than my female characters, who were always of secondary importance but free-spirited and sharp-witted.

For Bert, being serious meant he ended up writing poems about stones and savaged birds' nests, and empty houses where imaginary brothers he believed were himself had died grisly ritual deaths, until finally, in fact, he could no longer write a line, and substituted getting drunk as a donkey, shacking up with his students and convincing them how important poetry was by boinking the daylights out of them in its name. He has described this to me as a failure to remain "intellectually pliant."

But we were both stuck like kids who had reached the end of what they know they know. I did not, in fact, know how people felt about *most* things—and didn't know what else to do or where to look. And needless to say that is the very place where the great writers—your Tolstoys and your George Eliots—soar off to become great. But because I didn't soar off to become great—and neither did Bert—I have to conclude we suffered a failure of imagination right there in the most obvious way. We lost our authority, if that is a clear way of putting it.

What I did, as I began writing *Tangier*, which I hoped would have some autobiographical parts set in a military school, was become more and more grave—over my literary voice, my sentences and their construction (they became like some heavy metallic embroidery no one including me would want to read), and my themes, which became darker and darker. My characters generally embodied the attitude that life is always going to be a damn nasty and probably baffling business, but somebody has to go on slogging through it. This, of course, can eventually lead to terrible cynicism, since I knew life wasn't like that at all—but was a lot more interesting—only I couldn't write about it that way. Though before that could happen, I lost heart in stringing such things together, became distracted, and quit. Bert assures me his own lines took on the same glum, damask quality. "Waking each day / at the end / of a long cave / soil is jammed / in my nostrils / I bite through / soil and roots / and bones and / dream of a separate existence" were some he quoted me from memory one day right on the train. He quit writing not long after he wrote them and went chasing after his students for relief.

It is no coincidence that I got married just as my literary career and my talents for it were succumbing to gross seriousness. I was crying out, you might say, for the play of light and dark, and there is no play of light and dark quite like marriage and private life. I was seeing that same long and empty horizon that X says she sees now, the table set for one, and I needed to turn from literature back to life, where I could get somewhere. It is no loss to mankind when one writer decides to call it a day. When a tree falls in the forest, who cares but the monkeys?

CHAPTER 3

BY A QUARTER to ten I have surrendered to the day and am in my Malibu and down Hoving Road, headed for the Great Woods Road and the Pheasant Run & Meadow condos where Vicki lives—really nearer to Hightstown than to Haddam proper.

Something brief should be said, I think, about Haddam, where I've lived these fourteen years and could live forever.

It is not a hard town to understand. Picture in your mind a small Connecticut village, say Redding Ridge or Easton, or one of the nicer fieldstone-wall suburbs back of the Merritt Parkway, and Haddam is like these, more so than a typical town in the Garden State.

Settled in 1795 by a wool merchant from Long Island named Wallace Haddam, the town is a largely wooded community of twelve thousand souls set in the low and rolly hills of the New Jersey central section, east of the Delaware. It is on the train line midway between New York and Philadelphia, and for that reason it's not so easy to say what we're a suburb of—commuters go both ways. Though as a result, a small-town, out-of-the-mainstream feeling exists here, as engrossed as any in New Hampshire, but retaining the best of what New Jersey offers: assurance that mystery is never longed for, nor meaningful mystery shunned. This is the reason a town like New Orleans defeats itself. It longs for a mystery it doesn't have and never will, if it ever did. New Orleans should take my advice and take after Haddam, where it is not at all hard for a literalist to contemplate the world.

It is not a churchy town, though there are enough around because of the tiny Theological Institute that's here (a bequest from Wallace Haddam). They have their own brick and copper Scottish Reform Assembly with a choir and organ that raises the roof three days a week. But it is a village with its business in the world.

There is a small, white-painted, colonial Square in the center of town facing north, but no real main street. Most people who live here work elsewhere, often at one of the corporate think-tanks out in the countryside. Otherwise they are seminarians or rich retirees or faculty of De Tocqueville Academy out Highway 160. There are a few high-priced shops behind mullioned windows—men's stores and franchised women's undergarments salons are in ascendance. Book stores are down. Aggressive, sometimes bad-tempered divorcées (some of them seminarians' ex-wives) own most of the shops, and they have given the Square a fussy, homespun air that reminds you of life pictured in catalogs (a view I rather like). It is not a town that seems very busy.

The Post Office holds high ground, since we're a town of mailers and home shoppers. It's no chore to get a walk-in haircut, or if you're out alone at night—which I often was after my divorce—it isn't hard to get a drink bought for you up at the August Inn by some old plaid-pantser watching the ball game, happy to hear a kind word about Ike instead of heading home to his wife. Sometimes for the price of a few daiquiris and some ardent chitchat, it's even possible to coax a languid insurance broker's secretary to drive with you out to a roadhouse up the Delaware, and to take in the warm evening of springtime. Such nights often don't turn out badly, and in the first few months, I spent several in that way without regrets.

There is a small, monied New England émigré contingent, mostly commuters down to Philadelphia with summer houses on the Cape and on Lake Winnepesaukee. And also a smaller southern crowd—mostly Carolinians attached to the seminary—with their own winter places on Beaufort Island and Monteagle. I never fitted exactly into either bunch (even when X and I first got here), but am part of the other, largest group who're happy to be residents year-round, and who act as if we were onto something fundamental that's not a matter of money, I don't think, but of a certain awareness: living in a place is one thing we all went to college to learn how to do properly, and now that we're adults and the time has arrived, we're holding on.

Republicans run the local show, which is not as bad as it might seem. Either they're tall, white-haired, razor-jawed old galoots from Yale with moist blue eyes and aromatic OSS backgrounds; or else retired chamber of commerce boosters, little guys raised in town, with their own circle of local friends, and a conservator's clear view about property values and private enterprise know-how. A handful of narrow-eyed Italians run the police—descendants of the immigrants who were brought over in the twenties to build the seminary library, and who settled The Presidents, where X lives. Between them, the Republicans and Italians, the rule that *location is everything* gets taken seriously, and things run as quietly as anyone could want—which makes you wonder why that combination doesn't run the country better. (I am lucky to be here with my pre-1975 dollars.)

On the down side, taxes are sky high. The sewage system could use a bond issue, particularly in X's neighborhood. But there are hardly any crimes against persons. There are doctors aplenty and a fair hospital. And because of the southerly winds, the climate's as balmy as Baltimore's.

Editors, publishers, *Time* and *Newsweek* writers, CIA agents, entertainment lawyers, business analysts, plus the presidents of a number of great corporations that mold opinion, all live along these curving roads or out in the country in big secluded houses, and take the train to Gotham or Philadelphia. Even the servant classes, who are mostly Negroes, seem fulfilled in their summery, keyboard-awning side streets down Wallace Hill behind the hospital, where they own their own homes.

All in all it is not an interesting town to live in. But that's the way we like it.

Because of that, the movie theater is never noisy after the previews and the thanks-for-not-smoking notices. The weekly paper has mostly realty ads, and small interest in big news. The seminary and boarding school students are rarely in evidence and seem satisfied to stay put behind their iron gates. Both liquor stores, the Gulf station and the book stores are happy to extend credit. The Coffee Spot, where I sometimes ride up early on Ralph's old Schwinn, opens at five a.m. with free coffee. The three banks don't bounce your checks (an officer calls). Black boys and white boys—Ralph was one—play on the same sports teams, study together nights for the SATs and attend the small brick school. And if you lose your wallet, as I have, on some elm-shaded street of historical reproductions— my Tudor is kitty-cornered from a big Second Empire owned by a former Justice of the New Jersey Supreme Court—you can count on getting a call by dinner just before someone's teenage son brings it over with all the credit cards untouched and no mention of a reward.

You could complain that such a town doesn't fit with the way the world works now. That the real world's a worse and devious and complicated place to lead a life in, and I should get out in it with the Rhonda Matuzaks of life.

Though in the two years since my divorce I've sometimes walked out in these winding, bowery streets after dark on some ruminative errand or other and looked in at these same houses, windows lit with bronzy cheer, dark cars hove to the curbs, the sound of laughing and glasses tinking and spirited chatter floating out, and thought to myself: what good rooms these are. What complete life is here, audible—the justice's is the one I'm thinking of. And though I myself wasn't part of it and wouldn't much like it if I were, I was stirred to think all of us were living steadfast and accountable lives.

Who can say? Perhaps the justice himself might have his own dark hours on the streets. Maybe some poor man's life has hung in the balance down in sad Yardville, and the lights in my house —I usually leave them blazing—have given the Justice solace, moved him to think that we all deserve another chance. I may only be inside working over some batting-average charts, or reading *Ring* or poring through a catalog in the breakfast nook, hopeful of nothing more than a good dream. But it is for just such uses that suburban streets are ideal, and the only way neighbors here can be neighborly.

Certainly it's true that since there is so much in the world now, it's harder to judge what is and isn't essential, all the way down to where you should live. That's another reason I quit real writing and got a real job in the reliable business of sports. I didn't know with certainty what to say about the large world, and didn't care to risk speculating. And I still don't. That we all look at it from someplace, and in some hopeful-useful way, is about all I found I could say—my best, most honest effort. And that isn't enough for literature, though it didn't bother me much. Nowadays, I'm willing to say yes to as much as I can: yes to my town, my neighborhood, my neighbor, yes to his car, her lawn and hedge and rain gutters. Let things be the best they can be. Give us all a good night's sleep until it's over.

*   *   *

HOVING ROAD this morning is as sun-dappled and vernal as any privet lane in England. Across town the bells of St. Leo the Great chime a brisk call to worship, which explains why no Italian gardeners are working on any neighbors' lawns, clearing out under the forsythias and cutting back the fire thorns. Some of the houses have sunny Easter-lily decorations on their doors, whereas some still abide by the old Episcopal practice of Christmas wreaths up till Easter morning. There is a nice ecumenical feel of holiday to every street.

The Square this morning is filled up with Easter buyers, and to avoid tie-ups I take the "back door" down Wallace Hill through the little one-ways behind the hospital Emergency entrance and the train station. And soon I am out onto the Great Woods Road, which leads to U.S. 1 and across the main train line into the suave and caressing literalness of the New Jersey coastal shelf. It is the very route I took yesterday afternoon when I drove to Brielle. And whereas then my spirits were tentative— I still had this morning's duties ahead—today they are rising and soaring.

Six miles out, Route 33 is astream with cars, though a remnant fog from early morning has clung to the roadway as it sways and swerves toward Asbury Park. A light rain draws in a soughing curtain of apple greens from the south and across the accompanying landscape, softening the edges of empty out-of-season vegetable stands, farmettes, putt-putts and cheerless Ditch Witch dealers. Though I am not displeased by New Jersey. Far from it. Vice implies virtue to me, even in landscape, and virtue value. An American would be crazy to reject such a place, since it is the most diverting and readable of landscapes, and the language is always American.

'An Attractive Retirement Waits Just Ahead'

Better to come to earth in New Jersey than not to come at all. Or worse, to come to your senses in some spectral place like Colorado or California, or to remain up in the dubious airs searching for some right place that never existed and never will. Stop searching. Face the earth where you can. Literally speaking, it's all you have to go on. Indeed, in its homeliest precincts and turn-outs, the state feels as unpretentious as Cape Cod once might've, and its bustling suburban-with-good-neighbor-industry mix of life makes it the quintessence of the town-and-country spirit. Illusion will never be your adversary here.

An attractive retirement is Pheasant Run & Meadow. I make the turn up the winding asphalt access that passes beneath a great water tower of sleek space-age blue, then divides toward one end or the other of a wide, unused cornfield. Far ahead—a mile, easy—billowing green basswoods stand poised against a platinum sky and behind them the long, girdered "Y" stanchions of a high-voltage line, orange balls strung to its wires to warn away low-flying planes.

Pheasant Run to the left is a theme-organized housing development where all the streets are culs-de-sac with "Hedgerow Place" and "The Thistles" painted onto fake Andrew Wyeth barnboard signs. All the plantings are young, but fancy cars already sit in the driveways. Vicki and I drove through once like tourists, admiring the farm-shingled and old-brick homesteads with price tags bigger than I paid for my three-story in town fourteen years ago. Vicki's father and stepmother live in the same sort of place down in Barnegat Pines, and I have a feeling she would like nothing better than for herself and some prospective hubby to move right in.

Pheasant Meadow sits at the other lower end of the stubble field—a boxy, unscenic complex of low brown-shake buildings overlooking a shallow man-made mud pond, a yellow bulldozer, and some other apartments already half-built. In the ideal plan of things, these are for the younger people just starting in the world and on the way up—secretaries, car salesmen, nurses, who will someday live to buy the complete houses over in Pheasant Run on resale. Starter people, I call them.

Vicki's aqua Dart sits out front in slot 31, still with black and white Texas plates, and shining with polish. The last hiss of rain squall thrums off north into the Brunswicks as I pull in beside her, and the air is thick with a silvery, chemical smell. But before I can get out, and to my surprise, I see Vicki in the front seat of her car, nearly hidden by its big head rest. I roll down the passenger window and she sits peeking out at me from the driver's seat, her black hair orchestrated Loretta Lynn style, two thick swags taken toward the back of her head and ears, then straight down in sausage curls to her shoulders.

Across in the new units two hardhats sit grinning on un-finished Level Two. It's clear they've been having a good time over something before I got here.

"I figured you probably wouldn't show up," Vicki says out her open window, as tentative as a school girl. "I was sitting up there waiting on the phone to ring for you to give me the bad news, and so I just came down here and listened to some tapes I like to hear when I'm sad." She smiles out at me, a sweet-natured, chancy smile. "You're not going to be hot at me are you?"

"If you don't get over here in about two seconds I am," I say.

"I knew it," she says, running her window up quick and grabbing her bag, bouncing out of her Dart and into my life in a twinkling. "I told myself, I said, self, if you go out there he'll come, and sure enough."

All fears are put instantly to rest, leaving the two hardhats shak-ing their heads. I wouldn't mind, as I back out, blinking my lights and wishing them just half the fun I'm expecting. But they'd probably get the wrong idea. As we back up, though, I give them a grin and we wheel out of Pheasant Meadow down the access road toward Route 33 and the NJTP, Vicki cleaving to me, squeezing my arm and sighing like a new cheerleader.

"Why'd you think I wouldn't show up?" I say, as we weave through rain-drenched Hightstown, and I am thinking how glad I am to own a car with an old-fashioned bench seat.

"Oh it's just old silly-milly. Seemed like too good a thing to happen, I guess." Vicki is wearing black slacks that fit her tight but not too, a white, frilly-dressy blouse-and-scarf combination, a blue Ultrasuede jacket straight from Dallas and shoes with clear plastic heels. These are her dressy travel clothes, along with her nylon Le Sac weekender tossed in the back and her little black clutch where she keeps her diaphragm. She is a girl for every modern occasion, and I find I can be interested in the smallest particulars of her life. She stares out as the upright Federalist buildings of Hightstown slide past. "Plus. I had a patient kick out on me last night just right when I was talking to him, asking him questions about how he felt and everything. I wasn't even s'posed to be workin, but a gal got sick. He was this colored man. And he *was* C-liver terminal, already way into uremia when he admitted, which is not *that* bad cause it usually starts 'em dreamin about their pasts and off their current problem." (A tiny sigh of relief as to her whereabouts last night. I had called and found no one there, and my worst fears were loosed.) "Only you don't really get that used to death, which is why I came down to ER from ONC. We're supposed to be used to it and all, but I'm just not. I'd lot rather see a guy busted up and bleeding than some guy dying inside. I guess that was why I started worrying. I knew you went to the cemetery this morning."

"That all went fine, though," I say, and in most ways it did.

Vicki takes a Merit Light out of her little purse and lights up. She is not the kind of girl who smokes, but likes to smoke when she's nervous. I reach a hand across her plump thighs and pull her closer to me, leg-side to leg-side. She lowers her window a crack and blows smoke that way. "When's your birthday, anyway?"

"Next week."

"Okay, that's what you're supposed to say. Now when is it really?"

"That's the truth. I'm going to be thirty-nine." I snake a glance down to see if there's adverse reaction to this news. We have not discussed my age in the eight weeks I've known her. I assume she thinks I'm younger.

"You are not. Liar."

"I'm afraid it's true," I say, and try to smile.

"Well, maybe I'll make you a present of an eight-track, and tape you all my favorites. How'd you like that?" There is no more reaction to this news about my age. There are women I know who care about men's ages, and women who don't. X didn't, and I have always counted that as a sign of good sense. Though where Vicki is concerned—her possible reasons for not caring are probably related to a bad first marriage and a wish to hook up with someone at least kind—it is another in a burgeoning number of happy surprises. Maybe we'll get married in Detroit, fly back and move out to Pheasant Run, and live happily like the rest of our fellow Americans. What would be wrong with that?

"I'd like that fine," I say.

"You weren't mad at me for bein out in the car like a tart?"

"You're too pretty to be mad at."

"That's about what them dimwits thought, too."

We approach the Turnpike, take our ticket and start north,

above the flat, featureless bedrenched Jersey flatlands—a land-scape perfect for easy golf courses, valve plants and flea markets.

The reason Vicki is worried that I would be mad at not getting to come to her door is because she knows I love the tribal ritual of picking her up for our dates, even if I'm hoping to spend the night. Usually I am formal and bring a gift, something I quit doing long ago when X and I went on outings. Though it's true that X and I lived together, and such things are easy to forget. But with Vicki, I usually bring something down from New York, where she has only been once and claims she can't abide. For her part, she is always *almost* ready and pretends I hurry her, runs to the bedroom with straight pins in her mouth, or holding her hair up in back, needing to stitch a hem or iron a pleat. We are throwbacks in this, straight out of an earlier era, but I like this nervous and over-produced manner of things between us. We seem to know what each other wants without really knowing each other, which was a dilemma between X and me at the end. We didn't seem to be tending the same ways. Though it may simply be that at my age I'm satisfied with less and with things less complicated.

Whatever the reason, I'm always happy when I am invited to spend the night or just an hour waiting in the pristine and nursey neatness of Vicki's little 1-BR condo, on which her dad holds the note, and which the two of them furnished in a one-day whirlwind trip to the Miracle Furniture Mile in Paramus.

Vicki made all her own choices: pastel poof-drapes, sun-burst mirror, bright area rugs with abstract designs, loveseat with a horse-and-buggy print, a maple mini-dining room suite, a China-black enamel coffee table, all brown appliances and a whopper Sony. All Wade Arcenault had to do was write a big check and set his little girl's life back on track after the bad events with husband Everett.

Each time I'm inside, all is precisely as it was the time before, as if riveted in place and clean as newsprint: a fresh *Nurse* maga-zine, a soap opera archive and *TV Guide* shingling the piecrust table. A shiny saxophone on its stand unused since high school band days. The guest bathroom spotless. Dishes washed and put away. Everything reliable as the newly-wed suite in the Holiday Inn.

My own house represents other aims, with its comfortable,

over-stuffed entities, full magazine racks, faded orientals, creaky sills and the general residue of mid-life eclecticism—artifacts of a prior life and goals (many unmet), yet evidence that does not announce a life's real quality any more eloquently than a new Barca Lounger or a Kitchen Magician, no matter what you've heard. In fact, I have become a committed no-muss, no-fuss fellow. And the idea appeals to me of starting life over in such a new and genial place with an instant infusion of colorful, fresh and impersonal furnishings. I might've done the same if it hadn't been for Paul and Clarissa, and if I hadn't believed I wasn't so much starting a new life as raising the ante on an old one. And if I hadn't felt our house was still a sound investment. All of which has worked out well, and most nights I drift off to sleep (wherever I am—a St. Louis, an Atlanta, a Milwaukee or even a Pheasant Meadow) convinced I have come away, as they say, with the best of both worlds—the very thing we all crave.

VICKI HAS dowsed her cigarette and begun pinching at her saus- age curls in the visor mirror. "Doesn't it seem strange to you we'd be takin a trip together?" She squinches up her nose, first at her own face then at mine, as if she didn't expect to hear a word she could believe.

"This is what grownups do—go on trips together, stay in hotels, have wonderful times."

"Rilly?"

"Really."

"Well. I guess." She takes a bobby pin out of her blouse cuff and puts it in her mouth. "It just never seemed like anything I'd be doin. Everett and me went to Galveston sometimes. I been to Mexico, but just to cross over." She removes the pin and buries it deep in her black hair. "What *are* you, anyway, by the way?"

"I'm a sportswriter."

"Yes, I know that. I read things you wrote." (This is news to me! What things?) "I mean, are you Libra or the Twins. You said your birthday wasn't but less than a month from now. I want to figure you out."

"I'm the Taurus."

"What does that one mean?" She watches me keenly now out the side of her eye while she finishes with her hair.

"I'm pretty intelligent. I'm not cynical, but I'm intuitive about people, and that might make me seem cynical." All this comes straight from Mrs. Miller, my palmist. It is part of her service to give information like this if I ask her for it, in addition to speculating on the future. I try to see her at least every two weeks. "I'm also pretty generous."

"I'll admit that, at least you been that with me. I wonder if that stuff'll make your dreams come true. I don't know much about it. I guess I could learn more."

"What dreams of yours have come true?"

She folds her arms under her breasts like a high school girlfriend and stares straight ahead for miles. It is possible to think of her as being sixteen and chaste instead of thirty and divorced; as never having witnessed a single bad or unhappy thing, despite the fact she attends death and mayhem nearly every day. "Well, look," she says, staring up the Turnpike. "Did you know I always wanted to go to Detroit?" She pronounces Detroit so as to rhyme with knee-joint.

"No."

"Well then all right. I did though. I almost fell over when you asked me." She puts her chin down as though deep in serious thought and makes a little clucking sound with her tongue. "If you'd asked me to go to Washington, D.C., or Chicago, Illinois, or Timbuktu, I probably would've said no. But when I was a little girl my Daddy used to always say, 'De-troit makes, the world takes.' And that was just such a puzzle to me I figured I *had* to see it. It seemed so unusual, you know, to me. And romantic. He'd gone up there to work after the Korean War, and when he came back he had a picture postcard of a great big tire stood up on its tread. And that's what I wanted to see, but I never got to. I got married instead on the way to no place special. Then I met you."

She smiles up at me sweetly and puts her hand inside my thigh in a way she hasn't quite done before, and I have to keep from swerving and causing a big pile-up. We are just now passing Exit 9, New Brunswick, and I take a secret look over along the line of glass booths, only two of which are lighted OPEN and have cars pulling through. Indistinct, gray figures lean out and lean back, give directions, make change, point toward surface roads for weary travelers. What could be more fortuitous or enticing than to pass the toll booth where the toll-taker's only daughter is with you and creeping up on your big-boy with tender, skillful fingers?

"Do you like my name?" She keeps her hand close up on my leg, her built-on fingernails doing a little audible skip-dance.

"I think it's great."

"Is that right?" She squinches her nose again. "I never liked it, but thanks. I don't mind Arcenault. I like that. But Vicki sounds like a name you'd see on a bracelet at Walgreen's." She glances at me, then back toward the wide estuary and wetlands of the Raritan, stretching like wheat to the tip of Staten Island and the Amboys. "Looks like someplace the world died out there, doesn't it?"

"I like it out there," I say. "Sometimes you can imagine you're in Egypt. Sometimes you can even see the World Trade Center."

She gives my leg a friendly pinch and turns me loose to sit up straight. "Egypt, huh? You probably *would* like that. You're in from the nut department, too. Tell me what that little boy of yours died of?"

"Reye's."

She shakes her head as though mystified. "Boy-shoot. What'd you do when he died?"

This is a question I'm not interested in exploring, though I know she wouldn't ask if she weren't concerned about me and felt some good could come out of it. She is as much a literalist in these matters as I am, and much more savvy about men than I am about women.

"We were both sitting beside his bed. It was early in the morning. Before light. We may have been asleep, really. But a nurse came in and said, 'I'm sorry, Mr. Bascombe, Ralph has expired.' We both just sat there a few minutes, stunned, though we knew it was going to happen. And then she cried a while and I did, too. And then I went home and cooked up some bacon and toast, and ended up watching television. I had a tape of great NBA championships, and I watched that until it got light."

"Death'll make you nutty, won't it?" Vicki rests her head on the seat back, pulls her feet up, and hugs her shiny black knees. Far ahead I see a plane—a great jet—floating earthward where I know Newark airport to be; it is a promising sign. "You know what *we* did when my Mama died?" She glances up, as if to see if I'm still here.

"No."

"We all went out and ate Polynesian. It wasn't a big surprise or anything, either. She had everything you can have and I was working right in Texas Shriners and knew everything from talking to the doctors, which I don't think is really that good. Everett and Daddy, Cade and me, though, went out to the Garland Mall in the middle of the hot afternoon and ate poo-poo pork. We just wanted to eat. I think you want to eat when someone dies. Then we just went and spent money. I bought a gold add-a-bead necklace I didn't need. Daddy bought a three-piece suit at Dillards' and a new wristwatch. Cade bought something. And Everett bought a new-used red Corvette he probably still owns, I guess. He *did* have it." She extends her lower lip over the other one and focuses down beetle-browed on the visible memory of Everett's Corvette, which stands out now more than death. Her nature is to put her faith in objects more than essences. And in most ways that makes her the perfect companion.

Her story, however, has left me with an unexpected gloominess. Some aspects of hidden-life-revealed have a certain bedrock factuality I don't like. I'd be a braver soldier if the story had someone discovering they had Lou Gehrig's disease or a brain tumor on the eve of his last track meet, and deciding to run anyway. But in this I am unprotected from the emotions—vivid ones—of true death, and I suddenly feel, whipping along the girdered Turnpike, exactly as I did that morning I described: bereaved and in jeopardy of greater bereavement sweeping me up.

Women have always *lightened* my burdens, picked up my faltering spirits and exhilarated me with the old anything-goes feeling, though anything doesn't go, of course, and never did.

Only this time the solace-spirit has been sucked out of the car by a vagrant boxcar wind, leaving my stomach twitching and my mouth grimmed as though the worst were happening. I have slipped for a moment out onto that plane where women can't help in the age-old ways (this, of course, is something X said this morning and I passed off). Not that I've lost the old yen, just that the old yen seems suddenly defeatable by facts, the kind you can't sidestep—the essence of a small empty moment.

Vicki eyes me in little threatening glances, her brows arched. "What's the matter, did a bug bite you?"

If we were as far north as the Vince Lombardi Rest Area, I'd

pull in and spend a half-hour admiring Vince's memorabilia—
the bronze bust, the picture of the Five Blocks of Granite, the
famous gabardine overcoat. We have plenty of time today. But
Vince's Area is all the way past Giant's Stadium, and we are here
down among the flaming refineries, without a haven.

"Would you just give me a big hug," I say. "You're a wonderful girl."

And instantly she throws an armlock around me with a neck-
crunching ferocity. "Oh, oh, oh," she sighs into my ear, and as
easy as that (I was not wrong) rapture rises in me. "Does it make
you happy to have me here?" She is patting my cheek softly and
staring straight at it.

"We're going to have us some fun, you better believe what
I say."

"Oh, boy blue," she murmurs, "boy, boy blue." She kisses my
ear until my legs tingle, and I want to squeeze my eyes shut and
give up control. This is enough to bring us back up to ground
level, and send us to the airport with all my old hopes ascendant.

I am easily rescued, it's true.

AT THIS MOMENT it may be of interest to say a word about
athletes, whom I have always admired without feeling the need
to be one or to take them at all seriously, and yet who seem to
me as literal and within themselves as the ancient Greeks (though
with their enterprises always hopeful).

Athletes, by and large, are people who are happy to let their
actions speak for them, happy to be what they do. As a result,
when you talk to an athlete, as I do all the time in locker rooms,
in hotel coffee shops and hallways, standing beside expensive
automobiles—even if he's paying no attention to you at all,
which is very often the case—-he's never likely to feel the least
bit divided, or alienated, or one ounce of existential dread. He
may be thinking about a case of beer, or a barbecue, or some
man-made lake in Oklahoma he wishes he was waterskiing on,
or some girl or a new Chevy shortbed, or a discothèque he owns
as a tax shelter, or just simply himself. But you can bet he isn't
worried one bit about you and what *you're* thinking. His is a rare
selfishness that means he isn't looking around the sides of his
emotions to wonder about alternatives for what he's saying or

thinking about. In fact, athletes at the height of their powers make literalness into a mystery all its own simply by becoming absorbed in what they're doing.

Years of athletic training teach this; the necessity of relinquishing doubt and ambiguity and self-inquiry in favor of a pleasant, self-championing one-dimensionality which has instant rewards in sports. You can even ruin everything with athletes simply by speaking to them in your own everyday voice, a voice possibly full of contingency and speculation. It will scare them to death by demonstrating that the world—where they often don't do too well and sometimes fall into depressions and financial imbroglios and worse once their careers are over—is complexer than what their training has prepared them for. As a result, they much prefer their own voices and questions or the jabber of their teammates (even if it's in Spanish). And if you are a sportswriter you have to tailor yourself to their voices and answers: "How are you going to beat this team, Stu?" Truth, of course, can still be the result— "We're just going out and play our kind of game, Frank, since that's what's got us this far"—but it will be *their* simpler truth, not your complex one—unless, of course, you agree with them, which I often do. (Athletes, of course, are not *always* the dummies they're sometimes portrayed as being, and will often talk intelligently about whatever interests them until your ears turn to cement.)

An athlete, for example, would never let a story like the one Vicki just told me get to him, even though the same feelings might strike him in the heart. He is trained not to let it bother him too much or, if it bothers him more than he can stand, to go outside and hit five hundred balls off the practice tee or run till he drops, or bash himself head-on into a piece of complicated machinery. I admire that quality more than almost any other I can think of. He knows what makes him happy, what makes him mad, and what to do about each. In this way he is a true adult. (Though for that, it's all but impossible for him to be your friend.)

For the last year I was married to X, I was always able to "see around the sides" of whatever I was feeling. If I was mad or ecstatic, I always realized I could just as easily feel or act another way if I wanted to—somber or resentful, ironic or generous— even though I might've been convinced that the way I was acting probably represented the way I *really* felt even if I hadn't seen the other ways open. This can be an appealing way to live your life, since you can convince yourself you're really just a tolerant generalist and kind toward other views.

I even had, in fact, a number of different voices, a voice that wanted to be persuasive, to promote good effects, to express love and be sincere, and make other people happy—even if what I was saying was a total lie and as distant from the truth as Athens is from Nome. It was a voice that totally lacked commitment, though it may well be this is as close as you can ever come to yourself, your own voice, especially with someone you love: mutual agreement with no significant irony.

This is what people mean when they say that so-and-so is "distanced from his feelings." Only it's my belief that when you reach adulthood that distance has to close until you no longer see those choices, but simply do what you do and feel what you feel—marriage you may have to relinquish, of course. "Seeing around" is exactly what I did in my stories (though I didn't know it), and in the novel I abandoned, and one reason why I had to quit. I could always think of other ways I might be feeling about what I was writing, or other voices I might be speaking in. In fact, I could usually think of quite a number of things I might be doing at any moment! And what real writing requires, of course, is that you merge into the *oneness of the writer's vision*—something I could never quite get the hang of, though I tried like hell and eventually sunk myself. X was always clear as spring water about how she felt and why she did everything. She was completely reliable and resistant to nuance and doubt, which made her a wonderful person for a fellow like me to be married to, though I'm not certain she's so sure about things now.

Though about athletes, I want to say just one more thing: you can learn too much about them, even learn to dislike them, just as you can with anybody. When you look very closely, the more everybody seems just alike—unsurprising and factual. And for that reason I sometimes tell less than I know, and for my money the boys in my racket make a mistake with in-depth interviews.

I'd just as soon pull a good heartstring. Write about the skinny Negro kid from Bradenton, Florida, who can't read, suffered rickets and had scrapes with the law, yet who later accepts a basketball scholarship to a major midwestern university, becomes a star, learns to read and eventually majors in psychology, marries a white girl and later starts a consulting firm in Akron. That is a good story. Maybe the white girl would be of eastern European extraction. Her parents would oppose, but get won over.

If all this makes it seem that being a sportswriter is at best a superficial business, that's because it is. And it is not for that reason a bad profession at all. Nor am I, I will admit, altogether imperfectly suited for it.

AT TERMINAL A we become two veteran travelers. I stand in line at United while Vicki goes to powder her nose and buy flight insurance. As it turns out, she is as much a denizen of airports as I am. When everything turned bad with old dagger-head Everett, she informed me on the escalator, she used to drive out to the new airport in Dallas, watch planes leave, and pretend she was on all of them. "If you stayed in that airport for one year," she said, beaming like a carhop as we headed up the glittering ticket concourse full of passengers and loved ones looking for partners, "you'd see everybody in the world. And you'd sure see Charley Pride a hundred times at least."

Vicki also believes flight insurance to be the world's best bargain, and who am I to say no, though I advise her not to make me her beneficiary.

"Well, I guess *not*," she says, with a vaguely disgusted look. "I always make the R.C. Church my heir in everything."

"That's fine then," I say, though she and I have never discussed religion.

"I just went to Catholics when I married Everett, in case you're wondering," she says, and looks at me oddly. "They do a lot for the hospitals. And the Pope's a good old guy I think. I wadn't but a dirty Methodist before, like everybody else in Texas except the Baptists."

"That's great," I say and give her arm a squeeze.

"Freedom to choose," she says, then skitters away toward the insurance machines.

By wide degrees now I am better. Public places always work

this curative on me, and if anything I suffer the opposite of agoraphobia. I enjoy the freely shared air of the public. It is, in a way, my element. Even the yellow-haired Greyhound terminals and murky subway stations make me feel a well-being, that a place has been provided for me and my fellow man together. When I was married to X, I hated the grinding summer weeks we'd spend first at the Huron Mountain Club, and, later, at Sumac Hills down in Birmingham, where her father was a founding member. I hated that still air of privilege and the hushed, nervous noises of midwestern exclusivity. I thought it was bad for the children and kept stealing off with Ralph to the Detroit Zoo and the Belle Isle Botanical Garden, and once all the way out to the Arboretum in Ann Arbor. X's had been an entire life of privilege—clubs and reserved tables and private boxes at the ball game—though I think all that means nothing if you have a sound enough character to weather it, which she has.

Across from me studying the departures board I spy a face I recognize but hope to get away without acknowledging. It is the long face of Fincher Barksdale. Fincher is holding his white United ticket folder and has a big TWA golf bag over his shoulder. Fincher is my internist, and I have visited him, as I said, to inquire about my pounding heart, and have heard from him that it is likely a matter of my age, and that many men approaching forty suffer from symptoms inexplicable to medical science, and that in a while they just go away by themselves.

Fincher is one of those lanky, hairy-handed, hip-thrown, vaguely womanish southerners who usually become bored lawyers or doctors, and whom I don't like, though X and I were friendly with him and his wife, Dusty, when we first came to Haddam and I had a small celebrity with my picture in *Newsweek*. He is a Vanderbilt grad, and older than I am by at least three years though he looks younger. He took his medicine and a solid internist's residency at Hopkins, and though I do not like him one bit, I am happy to have him be my doctor. I try to look away in a hurry, out the big window toward the spiritless skyline of Newark, but I'm sure Fincher has already seen me and is waiting to be sure I've seen him and absolutely don't want to talk to him before he pipes up.

"Now look out here. Where're we slippin off to, brother

Frank." It is Fincher's booming southern baritone, and without even looking I know he is stifling a white, toothy smile, tongue deep in his cheek, and having a wide look around to see who else might be listening in. He extends me his soft hand without actually noticing me. We are not old fraternity brothers. He was a Phi Delt, though he once suggested we might have a distant aunt in common, some Bascombe connection of his from Memphis. But I squelched it.

"Business, Fincher," I say nonchalantly, shaking his long, bony hand, hoping Vicki doesn't come back anytime soon. Fincher is a veteran lecher and would take pleasure in making me squirm on account of my traveling companion. One of the bad things about public places is that you sometimes see people you would pay money not to see.

Fincher is wearing green jackass pants with little crossed ensigns in red, a blue Augusta National pullover and black-tasseled spectator shoes. He looks like a fool, and is undoubtedly flying off on a golfing package somewhere—Kiawah Island, where he shares a condo, or San Diego, where he goes for doctors' conventions six or eight times a year.

"What about you, Fincher?" I say, without the slightest interest.

"Just a hop down to Memphis, Frank, down to Memphis for the holiday." Fincher rocks back on his heels and jingles change in his pockets. He makes no mention of his wife. "Since we lost Daddy, Frank, I go down more, of course. Mother's doing real fine, I'm happy to say. Her friends have closed ranks around her." Fincher is the kind of southerner who will only address you through a web of deep and antic southernness, and who assumes everybody in earshot knows all about his parents and history and wants to hear an update on them at every opportunity. He looks young, but still manages to act sixty-five.

"Glad to hear it, Fincher." I take a peek down past Delta and Allegheny to see if Vicki's coming this way. If Fincher and the two of us are flying the same flight, I'll change airlines.

"Frank, I've got a little business venture I want to tell you about. I started to get into it in the office the other day, but things went right on and got ahead of me. It's something you absolutely ought to consider. We're past the venture capital stages, but you can still get in on the second floor."

"We're due out of here in a minute, Fincher. Maybe next week."

"Now who're we here with, Frank?" A definite mistake there. I have set Fincher nosing all around again like a bird dog.

"With a friend, Fincher."

"I see. Now this is one minute to tell, Frank. Just while we're standing here. See now, some boys and I are starting up a mink ranch right down in south Memphis, Frank. It's always been my dream, for some damn reason." Fincher smiles at me in stupid self-amazement. He is picturing his stupid farm at this moment, I can tell, his tiny lizard's eyes dull with lusterless blue absorption. They are without question the peepers of a fool.

"It'd get hot for the minks, wouldn't it?"

"Oh well, you *have* to air-condition, Frank. Definitely. No way around that mountain. The start-up's sky high, too." Fincher is nodding like a banker, his blond and grayed head a pleasant puzzle of fresh financial wranglings. He crams both hands in his pockets and gives whatever's down there another stern jingle. Though just for the moment I am struck by Fincher's hair, the thinning top of which sinks into view as he glances ritually at his spectators. His hair is barbered into the dopey-blond Tab Hunter brushcut circa 1959, crisp as a saltine and with just a soupçon of odorless colloid to hold it in place. He is the perfect southerner-in-exile, a slew-footed mainstreet change jingler in awful clothes—a breed known only *outside* the south. At Vandy he was the tallish, bookish Memphian meant for a wider world—brushcut, droopy suntans, white bucks, campaign belt and a baggy long-sleeved Oxford shirt, hands stuffed in his pockets, arrogantly bored yet supremely satisfied and accustomed to the view from his eyrie. (Essentially the very way he is now.) At Hopkins he met and married a girl from Goucher who couldn't stand the South and craved the suburbs as if they were the Athens of Pericles, and Fincher has been free ever since to jingle his change and philander around the links with the other southern renegades of whom, as I've said, there is a handsome cadre. When the awful day of reckoning comes to Fincher, I want to be somewhere far away in a boat, I know that.

"Frank," Fincher says, having gone on talking about mink farms while I rode up over the clouds, "now don't you think it'd be a high-water mark for the New South? You care about all those things, don't you?"

"Not much," I say, and the truth is not at all.

"Well now, Frank, everybody thought old Tom Edison was crazy, didn't they?" Fincher pulls his ticket folder out of his back pocket and whacks it across his palm and smirks.

"I'm pretty sure everybody thought Edison was smart, Fincher."

"Okay. You know what I mean, son."

"It's forward thinking, Fincher, I'll give it that much."

And Fincher suddenly assumes an unexpected dazed look as if that was the signal he has been waiting for. And for a moment we stand in silence among hundreds of milling passengers, just the way we might stand together at the window up in the Petroleum Club in Memphis, brainstorming and conniving over next year's tail-gate party at the Commodore–Ole Miss game. Somehow or other Fincher has managed to set himself at ease, despite my reservations with his mink farm, and I actually admire him for it.

"You know, Frank. I've probably never said this to you." Fincher nods his head like a sage old trial judge. "But I admire the hell out of what you do and how you lead your life. There's a lot of us would like to do that, but lack the nerve and the dedication."

"What I do's pretty easy, Fincher. You'd probably be as good at it as I am. You ought to give it a try." I squeeze my toes inside my shoes.

"Now you'd need to tie me up in chains and beat me with a stick to get me to write, Frank. I get the ants nowadays just writing a scrip." Fincher's mouth mulls down in a mock-grimace. He secretly knows he could do it as well as I can and most likely better, but feels the need to pay me some kind of unfelt compliment. "There's a whole lot of us would like to mouse off with a little nurse, too," Fincher says with a big wink.

I turn and look off down the crowded concourse and see Vicki skittering back with her insurance papers, walking with difficulty on her plastic high heels. She looks like a secretary on an urgent trip to the copy machine, elbows thrown out for balance, her feet seemingly made of wood. Fincher *has* seen her and recognized her from the hospital halls, and I am caught.

Fincher has suddenly adopted the old dirty-leg innuendo he perfected in the Phi Delt house down at Vanderbilt, and means to reduce me to fun or force a briny confidence. A sinister uneasiness surrounds us both. He is more untrustworthy than I thought, and I am as on my guard as any man who has something worth defending—though wretched ever to have let him hold me in a conversation. Fincher is threatening to pull the plug on all anticipation, and I'll be damned if I'll let him do it.

"Why don't you mind your own business, Fincher," I say, and look him dead in the eyes. I could punch him in the nose, bloody up his jackass pants, and send him home to Memphis in stitches.

"Now-now-now." Fincher raises his chin and saunters back a half step onto his heels, glancing up over my shoulder toward Vicki. "We're white men, here, Frank."

"I'm not married anymore," I say fiercely. "Anything I do is all right."

"Yes indeed." Fincher flashes his big-tooth smile, but it is for Vicki, not me. I am defeated and cannot help wondering if Fincher hasn't been on this very track before me.

"Well, look what you see when you aren't properly armed," Vicki says, fastening a good grip on my arm, and giving Fincher a nasty little smile to let me know she's got his number. I love her more than I can say.

Fincher mumbles something like "mighty small world," but he has become half-hearted at best. "I got the in-surance," Vicki says and flutters the papers up to me, ignoring Fincher completely. "You might see a name you know if you look. I changed religions, too." Her sweet face is gone plain with seriousness. It is a face I did not even want to see two moments before, but that I welcome now as a friend of my heart. I unfold the thick onionskin sheaf from Mutual of Omaha, and see Vicki's name here as Victory Wanda Arcenault—and mine partway down as beneficiary. The sum is $150,000.

"What about the Pope?" I say.

"He's still a good ole bird. But I'll never *see* him." She blinks her eyes up at me as if a light had burst into view around my ears. "I'll see *you*, though."

I would like to hug her till she squeaked, but not in Fincher's presence. It would give him something to think about, and

I want to give him nothing. At the moment he is standing with his mouth formed into a small, perfect *o*. "Thanks," I say.

"I liked the idea of you spending all that money and thinking about me. It'd make me happy then wherever I was. You could buy a Corvette—only you'd probably want a Cadillac."

"I just want you," I say. "Anyway we'll be together if it crashes."

She rolls her eyes up at the high crystal-lighted airport ceiling. "That's true, isn't it?" She takes the policy back and kneels down to put it in her Le Sac bag.

"I 'spec I'll just steal on off," Fincher says, eyes flashy-darty since something has taken place here outside his ken. He has bent himself slightly at the waist and is on the verge of embarrassment, an emotion he has not felt, in all likelihood, for twenty years.

The concourse has begun welling up around us with people wearing paper tags on their breasts that say "Get-Away." They appear from nowhere and begin flowing in the direction of gates 36–51. The air suddenly smells sweet and peanutty. A plane has been held up for late-arrivers, and a feeling of relief circles us like a spring breeze.

"It's good to see you, Fincher," I say. Fincher, of course, is no more a lecher than the rest of us, and I am relieved to let him and his grave Ichabod's features slip away.

"Uh-huh, you bet," Vicki says and glances at Fincher with distaste, a look he seems to accept with gratitude.

"I guess they're lettin us on a little early." Fincher flashes a smile.

"You have a good trip," I say.

"Yep, yep," Fincher says and hoists his clubs onto his bony shoulder.

"Don't do it in the lake," Vicki says. But Fincher is already out of her range, and I watch him pick up his step with the other expectants, in from Buffalo, his clubs hitched high up, happy to be in with a new crowd, ready for some good earnest talk and arm-squeezing on their way south.

"You and Fincher have a falling out?" I say this in a chummy voice.

"I 'magine we did." Vicki is kneeling, elbow-deep in her weekender bag, digging for something at the bottom. We are next up to have our tickets validated. "He's some kinda joker.

A real sneak-up-behind-you guy if you know what that means. A bad potato. We all watch out for him."

"Did he sneak up behind you?"

"No sir." She looks up at me in surprise. "Nasty mind. I keep an eye on who's back of me."

"What do you think I think?"

"It's on your face like eggs."

"I'm just jealous," I say. "Can't you tell?"

"I wouldn't know." She finds a tiny perfume phial from her bag, uncaps it and takes it to her neck and arms while she kneels on the airport floor. She smiles up at me in a spicy way I know she knows I like. "You ain't got nothin to worry about, lemme tell you, Mister. You're numero uno and there's no number two."

"Tell me about Fincher, then."

"One-a-these days. You won't be surprised, though, I'll tell you that."

"You'd be surprised what surprises me."

"And what *don't* surprise me. Ever." She stands to take my hand in the ticket line. Her hand's moist, and the air smells of Chanel No. 5.

"You win."

"Right. I'm a winner all the way," she says airily. And if I could make the moment last—lost in the anticipation of a safe trip, a fatal crash, a howling success, a grinding bitter failure—I would, and never leave this airport, never gain on or rejoin myself, and never know what's to come, the way you always have to know, though it's only the same, the same you waiting.

CHAPTER 4

ON THE PLANE we are in the midwest from the first moment we take our seats. The entire tourist cabin of our 727 virtually vibrates with its grave ying-yangy appeal. Hefty stewardesses with smiles that say "Hey, I could love you once we're down and safe" stow away our carry-ons. Vicki folds her weekender strap inside and hands it up. "Gaish, now is that ever neat," says a big blond one named Sue and puts her hands on her hips in horsey admiration. "I wanta show Barb that. We've got the pits with our luggage. Where're you guys headed?" Sue's smile shows a big canine that is vaguely tan-colored, but she is full of welcome and good spirits. Her father was in the Air Force and she has a lot of athletic younger brothers, I would stake my life on it. She's seen plenty.

"De-troit," Vicki announces proudly, taking a secret peek at me.

Sue cocks her blond head to the side with pride. "You gyz'll love Detroit."

"Well, I'm really lookin forward to it," Vicki says with a grin.

"Greet, reelly greet," Sue says and sways off to start the coffee around. All about me, almost immediately, people begin to converse in the soft nasalish voices and mildish sentiments familiar from my college days. Everyone seems to be a native Detroiter heading home for the holidays, and no one coming west just to visit but us. Someone nearby claims to have stayed up and watched an entire telethon and missed two days of work. Someone else headed up to "the thumb" on a fishing trip but had motor trouble and ended up marooned in Bad Axe for a weekend. Someone had started Wayne State and pledged Sigma Nu but by last Christmas was back to work at his dad's sheet metal business. It might be said, of course, that the interiors of all up-to-date conveyances of travel put one in mind of the midwest. The snug-fitted overhead bins, the comfy pastel recliners, disappearing tray-tables and smorgasbord air of anything-you-want-within-sensible-limits. All products of midwestern ingenuity, as surely as a waltz is Viennese.

In a little while Barb and Sue circulate back and conduct a serious Q&A with Vicki about her weekender bag, which neither of them has seen the exact likes of, they say, and Vicki is only too happy to discuss. Barb is a squat little strawberry blondie with too much powder makeup and slightly heavy hands. She is interested in something called "price points" and "mean value mark-up," and whether or not an identical bag couldn't be bought at Hudson's boutique in a mall near her own condo in Royal Oak; it turns out she studied retailing in college. Vicki says hers came from Joske's, but that's all she knows, and the girls talk about Dallas for a while (Barb and Sue have both been based there at different times) and Vicki says she likes a store called Spivey's and a rib place in Cockrell Hill called Atomic Ribs. They all three like each other a lot. Then all at once we're in the air rising out over the cloud-shaded Watchungs and a bright blue-green industrial river, toward Pennsylvania, making for Lake Erie, and the girls slide off to other duties. Vicki picks up the arm rest and shoves close to me on our three-across seats, her shiny, encased thigh as hard as a saucepan, her breath drowsy with excitement. We are well above the morning's storminess now.

"What're you thinking about, old Mr. Man?" She has attached her pair of pink earphones around her neck.

"About what a sweet thigh you've got and how much I'd like to pull it my way."

"Well you surely can. Won't nobody see you but Suzie and little Barbara, and they don't care long as no clothes come off. That wasn't what you were thinking anyway. I know about you, old tricky."

"I was thinking about Candid Camera. The talking mailbox. I think that's about the funniest thing I've ever seen in my life."

"I like 'em, too. Ole Allen Funk. I thought I saw him one day in the hospital. I'd heard he lived someplace around. But then it wasn't. A lot of people look alike now, you know it? But that still isn't it. I'll just let you run on."

"You're a smart girl."

"I got a good memory, which you need to nurse. But I'm not really smart. I wouldn't have married Everett if I had been." She fattens her cheeks and smiles at me. "Are you not gonna tell me what you're sitting there worrying?" She takes a good two-armed hold on my arm and squeezes it. She is a girl who likes squeezing. "Or am I gon have to squeeze you till you talk." She is strong, which I think would also be a requirement for a nurse, though I am sure she doesn't really care what's on my mind.

In truth, of course, I have nothing to answer. Undoubtedly I was thinking something, but most things I find myself thinking seem to fly right out of my mind and I can't remember them at all. It is a trait of character which made being a writer hard and often downright tedious. I either had to sit down and write out whatever I happened to be thinking about at any time of the day or night I happened to think it, or else just forget it all, which is what happened at the end of the time I was working on my novel. Finally I became happy to forget everything and let it all lapse. Real writers have to be more attentive, of course, and attentive was what I wasn't much interested in being.

I do not think, in any event, it's a good idea to want to know what people are thinking (that would disqualify you as a writer right there, since what else is literature but somebody telling us what somebody else is thinking). For my money there are at least a hundred good reasons not to want to know such things. People never tell the truth anyway. And most people's minds, like mine, never contain much worth reporting, in which case they just make something up that's patently ridiculous instead of saying the truth—namely, I was thinking nothing. The other side, of course, is that you will run the risk of being told the *very* truth of what someone is thinking, which can turn out to be something you don't want to hear, or that makes you mad, and ought to be kept private anyway. I remember when I was a boy in Mississippi, maybe fifteen years old—just before I left for Lonesome Pines—a friend of mine got killed in a hunting accident. The very night after, Charlieboy Neblett and I (he was one of my few friends in Biloxi) sat out in Charlieboy's car drinking beer and complaining about our having thought, then forgiving each other for thinking, that we were glad Teddy Twiford got killed. If Teddy's mother had come by just then and asked us what we were thinking, she would've been flab-bergasted to find out what lousy friends of Teddy's we were. Though in fact we weren't lousy friends at all. Things just come into your mind on their own and aren't your fault. So I learned this all those years ago—that you don't need to be held responsible for what you think, and that by and large you don't have any business knowing what other people think. Full disclosure never does anybody any favors, and in any event there are few enough people in the world who are sufficiently within themselves to make such disclosure pretty unreliable right from the start. All added to the fact that this constitutes intrusion where you least need to be intruded upon, and where telling can actually do harm to everyone involved.

I remember, in fact, the Lebanese woman I knew at Berkshire College saying to me, after I told her how much I loved her: "I'll always tell you the truth, unless of course I'm lying to you." Which at first I didn't think was a very good idea; though stewing over it after a while I realized that it was actually a piece of great luck. I was being promised truth *and* mystery—not an easy combination. There would be important things I would and wouldn't know, and I could count on it, could look forward to it, muse on it, worry about it if I was idiot enough, which I wasn't, and all I had to do was agree, and be forever freed.

She was a literary deconstructionist and had a mind trained for that kind of distinction. And she managed to make a policy out of a fact of life: how much of someone you can actually get to know about. Very little. Though I don't think in the three vertiginous months we spent together she ever lied to me. There was never a reason to! I saw to that by never asking a question whose answer wasn't already obvious. X and I might in fact have made a better go of it if she could've tried that strategy out on me by not asking me to explain anything that night I stood out in the rhododendrons marveling at Gemini and Cassiopeia, while her hope chest was fast going up the chimney. She might've understood my predicament for what it was—an expression of love and inevitability, instead of just love's failure. Though I will not complain about it. She is fine now, I think, in most ways. And if she is not as certain about things as she once was, that is not a tragedy, and I think she will be better as time goes on.

By the time the copilot pokes his head through the tourist class curtain and gives us all the high sign, Vicki has drifted off to sleep, her head on a tiny pillow, her mouth slightly ajar. I intended to show her Lake Erie, which we're now passing high above, green and shimmering, with gray Ontario out ahead. She is tired from too much anticipation, and I want her full of energy for our whirlwind trip. She can see the lake on the flight home, and be a slug-a-bed on Sunday night when we return from her parents.

An odd thing happened to me last night, and I would like to say something about it because it touches on the whole business of full disclosure, and because it has stayed on my mind ever since. It is, of course, what I wasn't prepared to tell Vicki.

For the past two years I have been a member of a small group in town which we got together and called—with admirable literalness—the Divorced Men's Club. There are five of us in all, though the constituency has changed once or twice, since one fellow got married again and moved away from Haddam to Phil-adelphia, and another died of cancer. In both instances someone has come along at just the right time to fill in the space, and we have all been happy to have five since that number seems to strike a balance. There have been several times when I have nearly quit the club, if you can call it a club, since I don't think of myself as a classic joiner and don't feel, at least anymore, that I need the club's support. In fact, almost all of it bores the crap out of me, and ever since I began to concentrate on becoming more within myself I've felt like I was over the shoals and headed back to the mainstream of my own lived life. But there have been good reasons to stay. I did not want to be the first to leave as a matter of choice. That seemed niggardly to me—gloating that I had "come through," whereas maybe the others hadn't, even though no one has ever admitted that we do anything to support one another. To start with, none of us is that kind of confessional, soulful type. We are all educated. One fellow is a banker. One works in a local think-tank. One is a seminarian, and the last guy is a stocks analyst. Ours is much more a jocular towel-popping raffish-rogueishness than anything too serious. What we mostly do is head down to the August, puff cigars, talk in booming busi-nessmen's voices and yuk it up once a month. Or else we pile into Carter Knott's old van and head down to a ball game in Philadelphia or go fishing over at the shore, where we get a special party deal at Ben Mouzakis' Paramount Show Boat Dock.

Though there's another reason I don't leave the club. And that is that *none* of the five of us is the type to be in a club for divorced men—none of us in fact even seems to belong in a place like Haddam—given our particular circumstances. And yet we are there each time, as full of dread and timidness as conscripts to a firing squad, doing what we can to be as chatty and polite as Rotarians—ending nights, wherever we are, talking about life and sports and business, hunched over our solemn knees, some holding red-ended cigarettes as the boat heads into the lighted dock, or before last call at the Press Box Bar on Walnut Street, all doing our best for each other and for non-confessional personal expression. Actually we hardly know each other and sometimes can barely keep the ball moving before a drink arrives. Likewise there have been times when I couldn't wait to get away and promised myself never to come back. But given our characters, I believe this is the most in friendship any of us can hope for. (X is dead right about me in this regard.) In any case the suburbs are not a place where friendships flourish. And even though I cannot say we like each other, I definitely can say that we don't *dislike* each other, which may be exactly the quiddity of all friendships that have not begun with fellows you knew before your own life became known to you—which is the case with me, and, I suppose, for the others, though I truly don't know them well enough to say.

We met—the original five—because we'd all signed up for the "Back in Action" courses at Haddam High School, courses designed expressly for people like us, who didn't feel comfortable in service clubs. I was enrolled in "Twentieth-Century American Presidents and Their Foreign Policies." A couple of the other fellows were in "Water-Color Foundations" or "Straight-Talking" and we used to stand round the coffee urn on our breaks keeping our eyes diverted from the poor, sad, skinny divorced women who wanted to go home with us and start crying at 4 a.m. One thing led to another, and by the time our courses were half over we'd started going over to the August, jawing about fishing trips to Alaska and baseball trades, singling out one another's idiosyncrasies, and assigning funny names for each other like "ole Knot-head" for Carter Knott, the banker; "ole Basset Hound" for Frank Bascombe; "ole Jay-Jay" for Jay Pilcher—who, inside of a year, died alone in his house with a brain tumor he never even knew about. Perfect Babbitts, really, all of us, even though to some extent we understood that.

In a way, I suppose you could say all of us were and are lost, and know it, and we simply try to settle into our lost-ness as comfortably and with as much good manners and little curiosity as we can. And perhaps the only reason we have not quit is that we can't think of a compelling reason to. When we do think of a good reason we'll all no doubt quit in an instant. And I may be getting close.

But that is not so much the point as a way of getting around to it.

Yesterday was the day of our spring fishing excursion for flukes and weakfish, out of Brielle. Knot-head Knott made all the arrangements, and while Ben Mouzakis does not give us one of his boats all to ourselves for the money we pay, he usually just books one other party of congenial fellows for the afternoon and takes us out at cost since he knows we'll talk it up in Haddam and come back ourselves next year, and because I honestly think he enjoys our company. We are all good fellows for an afternoon.

I had left Haddam in the glum spirits I've fallen into each year on the day before Ralph's birthday. It had rained early just the way it did today, but by the time I had come round the traffic rotary in Neptune and turned toward the south Shore Points, the rain had swept up into the Amboys leaving me drenched in the supra-real seashore sunshine and traffic hum of Shark River, as indistinguishable from my fellow Jerseyites as a druggist from Sea Girt.

It is of course an anonymity I desire. And New Jersey has plenty to spare. A passing glance down off the bridge-lock at Avon and along the day-trip docks where the plastic pennants flutter and shore breezes dance always assures me that any one of these burly Bermuda-shorts fellows waiting impatiently with their burly wives for the *Sea Fox* to weigh its anchor or the *Jersey Lady* to cast off, could just as well be me, heading out after monkfish off Mantoloking or Deauville. Such random identifications always strike me as good practice. Better to think that you're like your fellow man than to think—like some professors I knew at Berkshire College—that no man could be you or take your place, which is crazy and leads straight to melancholy for a life that never existed, and to ridicule.

Anyone could be anyone else in most ways. Face the facts.

Though possibly because of my skittishness, yesterday the

Bermuda-shorts guys on the docks didn't seem altogether hopeful from my distance. They seemed to be wandering off bandy-legged from their spouses down the dock planks, arms folded, faces querulous in the mealy sunshine, their natural Jersey pessimism working up a fear that the day might go wrong—in fact *couldn't* go right. Someone would charge them too much for an unwanted and insignificant service; the wife would get seasick and force the boat in early; there'd be no fish and the day would end with a sad chowder at a rueful chowder house a stone's throw from home. In other words, all's ahead to be regretted; better to start now. I could've yelled right out to them: Cheer up! Chances are better than you think. Things could pan out. You could have a whale of a time, so climb aboard. Though I didn't have quite the spirits for it.

But as it happened, I would not have been more right. Ben Mouzakis had chartered half the boat to a family of Greeks—the Spanelises—from his own home village near Parga on the Ionian, and the divorced men were all on best behavior, acting like good-will ambassadors on a fortunate posting, assisting the women with their stubby rods, baiting hooks with brown chub and untangling backlashed reels. The Greek men had their own way of fixing on bait so that it was harder to pick clean, and a good deal of time was spent learning this procedure. Ben Mouzakis eventually broke out some retsina, and by six o'clock fishing was over, the few fluke caught off the "secret reef" were packed in ice, the radio was beamed into a Greek station in New Brunswick, and everyone—the divorced men and the Spanelises, two men, three pretty women and two children—were sitting inside the long gallery cabin, elbows on knees, nodding and cupping glasses of wine and talking solemnly with the best good-neighborly tolerance about the value of the drachma, Melina Mercouri and the trip to Yosemite the Spanelises were planning for June if their money held out.

I was contented with the way the day had turned out. Sometimes an awful sense of loss comes over me when I am with these men, as profound as a tropical low. Though it has been worse in the past than yesterday. Something about them—earnest, all good-hearted fellows—seems as dreamy to me as it's possible to be, dreamier than I am by far. And dreamy people often do not mix well, no matter what you might believe.

Dreamy people actually have little to offer one another, tend in fact to neutralize each other's dreaminess into bleary nugatude. Misery does not want company—happiness does. Which is why I have learned to stay clear of other sportswriters when I'm not working—avoid them like piranhas—since sportswriters are often the dreamiest people of all. It is another reason I will not stay in Gotham after dark. More than one drink with the boys from the office at Wally's, a popular Third Avenue watering hole, and the dreads come right down out of the fake tin ceiling and the Tiffany hanging lamps like cyanide. My knee starts to hop under the table, and in three minutes I'm emptied of all conviction and struck dumb as a shoe and want nothing but to sit and stare away at the pictures on the wall, or at how the moldings fit the ceiling or how the mirrors in the back bar reflect a different room from the one I'm in, and fantasize about how much I'm going to enjoy my trip home. A group of sportswriters together can narrow your view far beyond pessimism, since the worst of them tend to be cynics looking only for false drama in the germs of human defeat.

Beyond that, what is it that makes me back off from even the best like-minded small talk when there is no chance of the willies nor the least taint of cynicism, and when in principle at least I like the whole idea of comradeship (otherwise why would I go fishing with the Divorced Men)? Simply, that I hate for things to get finally pinned down, for possibilities to be narrowed by the shabby impingement of facts—even the simple fact of comradeship. I am always hoping for a great surprise to open in what has always been a possible place for it—comradeship among professionals; friendship among peers; passion and romance. Only when the facts are made clear, I can't bear it, and run away as fast as I can—to Vicki, or to sitting up all night in the breakfast nook gazing at catalogs or to writing a good sports story or to some woman in a far-off city whom I know I'll never see again. It's exactly like when you were young and dreaming of your family's vacation; only when the trip was over, you were left faced with the empty husks of your dreams and the fear that that's what life will mostly be—the husks of your dreams lying around you. I suppose I will always fear that whatever *this* is, is *it*.

Even so, I have been happy enough on the Divorced Men's fishing trips. My habit is not to rent a rod and reel but to walk around and exchange a wry word with the men who are fishing like demons, go get their beers, sit in the passengers' cabin and watch television, or go up top and stand beside Ben and watch the sonar on the pilot's deck, where he finds the fish like clouds of white metal on the dark green baize. Ben never remembers my name, though after a while he recognizes me as someone named John, and we have diverse conversations about the economy or Russian fishing vessels or baseball, which Ben is a fanatic for, and which serves as a good man-to-man connection.

On yesterday's excursion I finished the day doing what I like best, standing at the iron rail near the bow of the *Mantoloking Belle* staring off at the jeweled shore lights of New Jersey, brightening as dark fell, and feeling full of wonder and illusion— like a Columbus or a pilgrim seeing the continent of his dreams take shape in the dusk for the first time. My plans for the evening were to be at Vicki's by eight, to surprise her with an intimate German dinner at Truegel's Red Palace on the river at Lambertville—celebrating two months of love—then have her home early. Altogether it was not a bad bunch of prospects.

Down the railing from me, staring as I was into the sequined gloom, was Walter Luckett, pensive as a judge and quite possibly cold in the spring night, from the way he was hunched over his elbows.

Walter is the newest member of the Divorced Men. He took Rocko Ferguson's place when Rocko got remarried and moved down to Philadelphia, and came in as an old acquaintance of Carter Knott's from Harvard Business School. Walter is from Coshocton, Ohio, attended Grinnell, and pronounces Ohio as if it both begins and ends in a U. He is a special-industries analyst for Dexter & Warburton in New York and looks like it, with tortoise-shell glasses and short, slicked hair. Occasionally I spy him on the train platform going to work, but we rarely speak. In fact I know almost nothing else about him. Carter Knott told me Walter's wife, Yolanda, left him and ran off to Bimini with a water ski instructor; that it'd been a big shock, but he seemed to be "handling things better now." That could happen to any of us, of course, and the Divorced Men seemed like just the thing for him.

Occasionally, I've slipped out to the Weirkeeper's Tavern after eleven—I do this sometimes to see the sports final on the big screen—and there was Walter, a little drunk and talkative. Once he yelled out, "Hey Frank! Where're all the women?" after which I couldn't wait to get out.

Another time I was in The Coffee Spot at dinnertime when Walter came in. He sat down in the booth across from me, and we talked about the Jaycees and what a bunch of phonies he thought they all were, and about the quality of silk underwear you can get out of most catalogs. Some, he said, were made in Korea, but the best ones came right from China; it was one of his industries. And then we just sat for a long time—a hundred years, it felt like—while our eyes tried to find a place to rest, until they finally settled on each other. And then we sat and stared at each other for four, maybe five horrible, horrible minutes, then Walter just got up and walked out without ordering anything or saying another word. Since then he has never mentioned that terrible moment, and I have frankly tried to duck him and on two occasions know that he walked in the door at the August, saw me and walked out again—something I respect him for. All together, I think I like Walter Luckett. He does not really belong in a divorced men's club any more than I do, but he is willing to try it on for size, not because he thinks he'll eventually like it, or that this is the thing he's always missed, but because it's in some ways the last thing in the world he can imagine doing, and probably feels he should do it for that reason alone. We should all know what's at the end of our ropes and how it feels to be there.

"Do you happen to know what I like about standing here at the rail and looking out at the coast, Frank?" Walter said softly, after I had declined to speak a word.

"What's that, Walter?" I was surprised he had even noticed me. Walter had caught one weakfish all afternoon, the biggest one caught, and after that he had quit fishing and curled up with a book on one of the bench seats.

"I like seeing things from an angle you don't live them. You know what I mean?"

"Sure," I said.

"I'm out there embedded in life every day. Then I come just a mile offshore, and it's dark, and suddenly it's all different. Better. Right?" Walter looks around at me. He is not a large man, and tonight he is wearing white walking shorts, a baggy blue tennis shirt and deck shoes, which makes him seem even smaller.

"It seems better. Probably that's why we come out here."

"Right," Walter said, and stared for a time out at the darkly dazzling coast, the sound of water slapping the side of the boat. Far up I could see the glow of the Asbury Park ferris wheel, and due north the ice-box glow of Gotham. It was consoling to see those lights and know that lives were there, and mine was here. And for the moment I was glad to have come along, and considered the Divorced Men all pretty darn solid fellows. Most of them, in fact, were inside the main cabin yakking with the Spanelises, having the time of their lives. "It's not the way I always see it though, Frank," Walter said soberly, clasping his hands over the rail and leaning on his forearms.

"How do you usually see it, Walter?"

"Okay. It's funny. When I was a kid in eastern Ohio, our whole family used to take these long trips. Fairly long, anyway. From Coshocton, in the east part of the state, all the way to Timewell, Illinois, which is in the west part of that state. All of it just flatland, you know. One county same with another one. And I used to ride in the car while my sister played hubcaps or lucky-lives-license or whatever, concentrating on remembering certain things—a house or maybe a silo or a swell of land, or just a bunch of pigs, something I'd be able to remember on the way back. So it would be the same to me, all part of the same experience, I guess. Probably everybody does that. I *still* do. Don't you do it?" As Walter looked at me again, his glasses caught a glint of shore light and twinkled at me.

"I guess I'm your opposite here, Walter," I said. "The highway never seems the same coming and going to me. I even think about meeting myself in the cars I pass. I actually forget it all pretty much right away, though I tend to forget a lot of things."

"That's a better way to be," Walter said.

"To me, it makes the world more interesting."

"I guess I'm having to learn that, Frank," Walter said and shook his head.

"Is something bothering you, Walter," I said—and shouldn't have, since I broke the rules of the Divorced Men's Club, which is that we're none of us much interested in that kind of self-expression.

"No," Walter said moodily. "Nothing's bothering me." And he stood for a while staring out at the jet coast of Jersey—the boxy beach house lights linking us to whatever hopeful life was proceeding there. "Let me just ask you something, Frank," Walter said.

"All right."

"Who do you have to confide in?" Walter did not look at me when he said this, though I somehow felt his smooth soft face was both sad and hopeful at the same moment.

"I guess I don't, to tell the truth," I said. "I mean I don't have anyone."

"Did you not even confide in your wife?"

"No," I said. "We talked about things plenty of times. That's for sure. Maybe we don't mean the same thing by confiding. I'm not particularly a private person."

"Good. That's good," Walter said. I could tell he was puzzled but also satisfied by my answer, and what's more I had given him the best answer I could. "Frank, I'll see you later," Walter said unexpectedly and gave me a pat on the arm, and walked off down the deck into the dark where one of the Spanelis men was still fishing, though it was black on the water and the tart spring air was chilling enough that I went inside and watched a couple of innings of a Yankees game on the boat's TV.

Once we got in, though, and all said our goodbyes, and the divorced men had given the few weakfish and fluke they'd caught to the Spanelis kids, I was walking across the gravel lot to my car, ready to head straight for Vicki's and steal her away to Lambert-ville, and here was Walter Luckett scuffing his deck shoes along-side my car and looking, in the dark, strangely like a man who wanted to borrow some money.

"What-say now, Wally," I said cheerfully, and went about put-ting the key in the door lock. I had an hour to get there, and I was for getting going. Vicki goes to bed early even when she doesn't have to work the next day. She is damned serious about her nursing career, and likes being bright and cheerful, since she believes many of her patients have no one who understands their predicament. The result is I don't drop in after eight, no matter what.

"This is a helluva life, isn't it, Frank?" Walter said and leaned against my back fender, arms folded, staring off as if in amuse-ment as the other divorced men and the Spanelises were barging out of the lot up toward Route 35, their lights brightly swaying.

They were honking horns and yelling, and the Spanelis kids were squealing.

"It sure is, Walter." I opened my door and stopped to look at him in the dark. He stuffed his hands in his pockets and bunched his shoulders. He had on a pale sweater draped in the old lank, country club style. "I think it's a pretty good life, though."

"You couldn't really plan it, could you?"

"You certainly couldn't."

"There's so much you can't foresee, yet it's all laid out and clear."

"You look cold, Walter."

"Let me buy you a drink, Frank."

"Can't tonight. Got things to do." I smiled at him conspiratorially.

"Just a bone warmer. We can sneak right over into the Manasquan." Across the lot was the Manasquan Bar, a barny old hip-roofed fisherman's roadhouse with a red BAR sign on top. Ben Mouzakis had invested in it with his wife's brother, Evangelis, as he told me once when we talked about tax shelters up on deck. "What d'ya say?" Walter said and started off. "Let's drink one, Frank."

I did not want to have a nightcap with Walter Luckett. I wanted to go speeding back toward Vicki and drowsy Lambert-ville while the last flickers of sunlight clung in the western sky. The memory of those awful centuries spent in The Coffee Spot rose up in my thoughts suddenly, and I almost jumped in the car and rammed out of the lot like a desperado. But I didn't. I stood and looked at Walter, who by now had walked halfway across the empty lot in his walking shorts and sweater, and had turned toward me and assumed a posture I can only describe as heart-breaking. And I could not say no. Walter and I had something in common—something insignificant, but something that his heartbreaking posture made undeniable. Walter and I were both men, Vicki or no Vicki, Lambertville or no Lambertville.

"Only one," I said into the parking lot darkness. "I've got a date."

"You'll make it," Walter said, lost now in the bleary seaside low-lights of Brielle. "I'll see to that myself."

In the Manasquan Walter ordered a scotch and I ordered a gin, and for a while we sat in complete uncomfortable silence and stared at the old pictures behind the bar that showed record stripers caught off the dock. I thought I could detect Ben Mouzakis in several—a chesty young roughneck of the Fifties, a big immigrant's crazy grin, no shirt, muscles bristling, standing beside some other taller men in khakis and two hundred dead fish strung along a rafter board.

The Manasquan is a dark, pine-board, tar-smelling pile of sticks inside and in truth it is one of my favorite places for small departures. Any other time I wouldn't have minded being there one bit. It has a long teak bar with a quasi-nautical motif, and no one makes the first attempt to be friendly, though drinks are poured honestly and at a reasonable price for a touristy seaside area. Sometimes, arriving too early for our excursion, I have walked over, taken a seat at the bar and bought a good greasy hamburger and felt right at home reading a newspaper or watching TV alongside the few watchcap fishermen who huddle and mutter at the end of the bar, and the woman or two who float around speaking brashly to strangers. It is a place where you'd be happy to consider yourself a regular, though when all is said and done you have nothing at all in common with anyone there except some speechless tenor of spirit only you know a damn thing about.

"Frank, were you ever an athlete?" Walter said forthrightly after our long and studious staring.

"Just an athletic supporter, Walter," I said and gave him a grin to set him at his ease. He obviously had something on his mind; and the sooner he got it out, the sooner I could be blazing a trail west.

Walter smiled back at me ironically, gave his nose a disapproving pinch, pushed up at his glasses. Walter, I realized, was actually a handsome man, and it made me like him. It isn't easy for handsome people to be themselves, or even try to be. And I had a feeling Walter was trying to be himself for the moment, and I liked him for that reason, though I wished he'd get on with it.

"You were out at Michigan, is that right," Walter asked.

"Right."

"That's Ann Arbor, not East Lansing."

"Right."

"I know that's different." Walter nodded thoughtfully and

sniffed again. "You couldn't be an athlete there, I comprehend that. That's like a factory."

"It wasn't that bad."

"I was an athlete out at Grinnell. Anybody could be one. It wasn't a big thing, although I'm sure it's gotten bigger now. I never go back anymore."

"I don't go back to Ann Arbor, either. What'd you do?"

"Wrestled. One forty-five. We wrestled against Carleton and Macalester and those places. I wasn't very good."

"Those are good schools, though."

"They *are* good schools," Walter said. "Though you don't hear much about them. I guess everybody wants to talk about sports, right?" Walter looked at me seriously.

"Sometimes," I said. "But I don't mind it. Other people know a lot more about sports than I do, to tell you the truth. It's a pretty innocent part of people, and talking has the effect of bringing us all together on a good level." I don't know why I started talking to Walter in this Grantland Rice after-dinner speech way, except that he seemed to want that and it was truthfully the only thing I could think of. (It's also true that I believe every word of it, and it's a lot better than talking about some pretentious book that only one person's read.)

Walter moved the ice around in his drink using his finger. "What would you say's the worst part about your job, Frank? I hate traveling myself, and I have to do it. I bet that's it, right?"

"I don't mind it," I said. "There're things about it I'm not sure I could live without anymore. In particular, now that I'm home alone."

"Okay, sure." Walter drank down his scotch in one gulp and signaled for another in one continuous finger-wiggle gesture. "So it's not the travel. Okay, that's good."

"I think the hardest part about my job, Walter, since you asked, is that people expect me to make things better when I come. If I come to interview them or write about them or just call them up on the phone, they want to be enriched. I'm not talking about money. It's just part of the natural illusion of my profession. The fact is, we can sometimes not make things worse, or we can make things worse. But we can't usually make things better for individuals. Sometimes we can for groups. But then not always."

"Interesting." Walter Luckett nodded as though it was anything but interesting. "What do you mean, worse?"

"I mean sometimes things can seem worse just by not being better. I don't know if I ever thought about it before," I said. "But I think it's right."

"People don't have any right to think you can make life better for them," Walter said soberly. "But it's what they want, all right. I agree."

"I don't know about rights," I said. "It'd be nice if we could. I think I once thought I could."

"Not me," Walter said. "One lousy marriage proved that."

"It's a disappointment. I don't mean marriage is a disappointment. Just ending it."

"I guess." Walter looked down at the fishermen at the dim-lit end of the bar, where they were huddling over some playing cards with fat Evangelis. One of the men laughed out loud, then another man put the cards in his coat pocket and smirked, and the talk got quiet. I would've given anything for a peek at those cards and to have had a good laugh with the fishermen instead of being land-locked with Walter. "Your marriage wasn't disappointing to you, then?" Walter said in a way I found vaguely insulting. Walter had just the tips of his slender fingers touching the glass of scotch, and then he looked at me accusingly.

"No. It was really a wonderful marriage. What I remember of it."

"My wife's in Bimini," Walter said. "My ex-wife, I need to say now. She went down there with a man named Eddie Pitcock, a man I've never seen and know nothing about except his name, which I know from a private detective I hired. I could find out a lot more. But who cares? Eddie Pitcock's his name. Isn't that a name for the guy who runs away with your wife?"

"It's just a name, Walter."

Walter pinched his nose again and sniffed.

"Right. You're right about that. That isn't what I want to talk about anyway, Frank."

"Let's talk about sports, then."

Walter stared intently at the fish pictures behind the bar and breathed forcefully through his nose. "I feel pretty self-important hauling you over here like this, Frank. I'm sorry. I'm not usually self-important. I don't want this to be the story of my life."

Walter had completely ignored my offer of a good sports conversation, which seemed to mean something more serious was on
the way, something I was going to be sorry about. "It isn't a very
amusing life. I'm sure of that."

"I understand," I said. "Maybe you just wanted to have a
drink and sit in a bar with someone you knew but didn't have to
confide in. That makes plenty of sense. I've done that."

"Frank, I went in a bar in New York two nights ago, and I
let a man pick me up. Then I went to a hotel with him—the
Americana, as a matter of fact—and slept with him." Walter
stared furiously out into the fishing pictures. He stared so hard
that I knew he would like nothing in the world better than to be
one of those happy, proud khaki-clad fishermen displaying his
fat stripers to the sun on a happy July day, say, in 1956, when we
would have been, Walter and me, eleven years old—assuming we
are the same age. I would've been doubly happy at the moment to
be there myself.

"Is that what you wanted to tell me, Walter?"

"Yes." Walter Luckett said this as if stunned, looking deadly
serious.

"Well," I said. "It doesn't matter to me."

"I know that," Walter said, his chin vaguely moving up and
down in a kind of secret nod to himself. "I knew that ahead of
time. Or I thought I did."

"Well, that's fine, then," I said. "Isn't it?"

"I *feel* pretty bad, Frank," Walter said. "I don't feel dirty or
ashamed. It's not a scandal. I probably ought to feel stupid, but
I don't even feel that way. I just feel bad. It's like it's loosed a bad
feeling in me."

"Do you think you want to do it again, Walter?"

"I doubt it. I hope not, anyway," Walter said. "He was a nice
guy, I'll just say that. He wasn't one of these leather bullies or
what have you. And neither am I. He's got a wife and kids up in
north Jersey. Passaic County. I'll probably never see him again.
And I'll never do that again, I hope. Though I could, I guess.
I certainly don't think anyone would care if I did. You know?"
Walter drank down his scotch and quickly cut his eyes to me.
I wondered if we were talking loud enough for the fishermen
to hear us. They would probably have something to say about
Walter's experience if we wanted to include them.

"Why do you think you told me, Walter?"

"I think I wanted to tell you, Frank, because I knew you wouldn't care. I felt like I knew the kind of guy you are. And if you did care, I could feel better because I'd know I was better than you. I have some real admiration for you, Frank. I got your book out of the library when I joined the group, though I admit I haven't read it. But I felt like you were a guy who didn't hold opinions."

"I've got a lot of opinions," I said. "But I tend to keep them to myself, usually."

"I know that. But not about something like this. Am I right?"

"It doesn't matter to me. If I have an opinion about it, I'll only know about it later."

"I'd be happy if you wouldn't tell me about it then, frankly, if you do. I don't think it would do me any good. I don't really think of this as a confession, Frank, because I don't really want a response from you. And I know you don't like confessions."

"No, I don't," I said. "I think most things are better if you just let them be lonely facts."

"I agree," Walter said confidently.

"You did tell me, though, Walter."

"Frank, I needed a context. I think that's what friends are for." Walter jiggled ice in his glass in a summary fashion, like a conventioneer.

"I don't know," I said.

"Women are better at this kind of thing, I think," Walter said.

"I never thought about it."

"I think women, Frank, sleep together all the time and don't really bother with it. I believe Yolanda did. They understand friendship better in the long run."

"Do you think you and this fellow, whatever his name is, are friends?"

"Probably not, Frank. No. But you and I are. I can say that I don't have a better friend in the world than you are right now."

"Well that's good, Walter. Do you feel better?"

Walter thumped the space between his brown eyes with his middle finger and let go a deep breath. "No. No. No, I don't. I didn't even think I would, to tell you the truth. I don't think I told you to feel better. Like I said, I didn't want anything back. I just didn't want it to be my secret. I don't like secrets."

"So, how do you feel?"

"About what?" Walter stared at me strangely.

"About sleeping with this man. What else have we been talking about?" I darted a look down the long bar. One of the fishermen was sitting staring at us, apart from the others who were watching a TV above the cash register, watching the Yankees game. The fisherman looked drunk, and I suspected he wasn't really listening to what we were saying, though that was no sign he couldn't hear it by accident. "Or about telling me. I don't know," I said almost in a whisper. "Either one."

"Have you ever been poor, Frank?" Walter glanced at the fisherman, then back at me.

"No. Not really."

"Me, too. Or me either. I haven't been. But that's exactly how I feel now. Like I'm impoverished, just suddenly. Not that I want anything. Not that I even can lose anything. I just feel bad, though I'm probably not going to kill myself."

"Do you think that's what being poor's like? Feeling bad?"

"Maybe," Walter said. "It's my version anyway. Maybe you've got a better one."

"No. Not really. That's fine."

"Maybe we all need to be poor, Frank. Just once. Just to earn the right to live."

"Maybe so, Walter. I hope not. I wouldn't like it much."

"But don't you feel sometimes, Frank, like you're living way up on the top of life, and not really living all of it, all the way down deep?"

"No. I never felt that way, Walter. I just always felt like I was living all the life I could."

"Well, then you're lucky," Walter Luckett said bluntly. He tapped his glass on the bar. Evangelis looked around, but Walter waved him off. He let a couple of ice cubes wiggle around in his mouth a moment. "You've got a date, don't you pal?" He tried to smile around the ice cubes and looked stupid.

"I did, anyway."

"Oh, you'll be fine," Walter said. He laid a crisp five-dollar bill out on the bar. He probably had plenty of such bills in his pocket. He adjusted his sweater around his shoulders. "Let's take a walk, Frank."

We walked out of the bar, past the fishermen and Evangelis,

standing under the TV looking up at the color screen and the game. The fishermen who'd been staring at us still sat staring at the space where we'd been. "Come back, fellas," Evangelis said, smiling, though we were already out the door.

Awash down the boat channel and the dark Manasquan River, the night air was fresher than I could've imagined it, a cool, after-rain airishness, an evening to soothe away human troubles. Over the water, halyards were belling on the metal masts in the dark, a lonely elegiac sound. Lighted condos rose above the far river bank.

"Tell me something, would you." Walter took a deep breath and let it out. Two young black men holding their own gear and plastic bait-buckets were loitering on the gangplank of the *Mantoloking Belle*, ready for an all-night adventure. Ben Mouzakis stood in his pilot's house staring down at them from the dark.

"If I can," I said.

Walter seemed to be feeling better in spite of himself. "Why'd you quit writing?"

"Oh that's a long story, Walter." I crammed my hands in my pockets and weaseled away a step or two toward my car.

"I guess so, I guess so. Sure. They're all long stories, aren't they?"

"I'll tell you sometime, since we're friends, Walter. But not right now."

"Frank, I'd like that. I really would. Sit down over a drink and hear it all out. We've all got our stories, don't we?"

"Mine's a pretty simple one."

"Well, good. I like 'em simple."

"Take care, Walter. You'll feel better tomorrow."

"You take care, Frank."

Walter started toward his car at the far end of the gravel lot, though when he was twenty yards from me he started running for some reason, and ran until I couldn't see him anymore, only his white shorts and his thin legs fading in the night.

CENTRAL JERSEY dozed in a sweet spring somnolence. DJ's as far south as Tom's River crooned along the seaboard that it was after eight. Nighttime streets were clearing from Bangor to Cape Canaveral, and I was out of luck with Vicki, though I tried to make good time.

At Freehold I stopped for the hell of it and called her apartment where no one answered; she unplugged the phone after bedtime. I called the nurses' private hospital number—a number I'm not supposed to know, reserved for loved ones in case of emergency; the regular hospital number with the last digit changed to zero. A woman answered in a startled voice and said her records showed Miss Arcenault wasn't scheduled. Was it an emergency? No. Thanks, I said.

For some reason I called my house. The answering machine clicked on with my voice, cheerier than I could bear to hear myself. I beeped for a message and there was X's managerial-professional voice saying she would meet me the next morning. I hung up before she was finished.

Once, when our basset hound, Mr. Toby, was killed by a car that didn't bother to stop—right on Hoving Road—X, in tears, said she wished that time could just be snatched back. Precious seconds and deeds retrieved for a better try at things. And I thought, while I dug the grave behind the forsythias along the cemetery fence, that it was like a woman to grieve over a simple fact in that hopeless-extravagant way. Maturity, as I conceived it, was recognizing what was bad or peculiar in life, admitting it has to stay that way, and going ahead with the best of things. Only that's exactly what I craved now! A precious hour returned to me; a part of Walter's sad disclosures held over till a later date—hardly the best of things.

What's friendship's realest measure?

I'll tell you. The amount of precious time you'll squander on someone else's calamities and fuck-ups.

And as a consequence, zipping along the Jersey darkside past practical Hightstown, feeling ornery as a bunkhouse cook, the baddies suddenly swarmed my car like a charnel mist so dense that not even opening the window would rout them.

Nothing in the world is as hopeful as knowing a woman you like is somewhere thinking about only you. Conversely, there is no badness anywhere as acute as the badness of no woman out in the world thinking about you. Or worse. That one has quit because of some bone-headedness on your part. It is like looking out an airplane window and finding the earth has disappeared. No loneliness can compete with that. And New Jersey, muted and adaptable, is the perfect landscape for that very loneliness, its other pleasures notwithstanding. Michigan comes close, with its long, sad vistas, its desolate sunsets over squatty frame houses, second-growth forests, flat interstates and dog-eared towns like Dowagiac and Munising. But *only* close. New Jersey's is the purest loneliness of all.

By disclosing an intimacy he absolutely didn't have to disclose (he didn't want advice, after all), Walter Luckett was guilty of both spoiling my superb anticipation and illuminating a set of facts-of-life I'd have been happy never to know about.

There are things in this world—plenty of them—we don't need to know the facts about. The noisome fact of two men's snuggle-buggle in some Seventh Avenue drummer's hotel has *no* mystery to it—the way, say, an electric guitar or "the twist" or an old Studebaker have no mystery either. Only facts. Walter and Mr. Whoever could live together twenty years, sell antiques, change to real estate, adopt a Korean child, change their wills, buy a summer house on Vinalhaven, fall out of love a dozen times and back again, go back to women more than once and finally find love together as senior citizens. And still not have it.

By now it seemed more than possible that Vicki had gotten bored and hied off with some oncologist from upstairs, in his dream machine Jag, and at that moment was whirling into the sunset, a thermos of mai tais on the console and Engelbert Humperdinck groaning on the eight-track.

What, then, was left for me to do but make the best of things.

I drove to Route 1, then south to Mrs. Miller's little brick ranchette on a long, grassy lot between an Exxon and a Rusty Jones, where a chiropractor once kept a practice. Several older, low-slung bomber cars were in the driveway, and the lights were lit behind drawn curtains, but her *Reader-Adviser* sign was dark. I was too late here, too, though the curtained lights certainly spoke of some secret, possibly exotic goings on inside; enough to excite my curiosity, and in fact enough to excite the curiosity of anyone driving south through the night toward Philadelphia with only glum prospects to consider.

Mrs. Miller and I have done business two years now, since just before X and I got divorced, and I've become a well-known face to all the aunts and uncles and cousins who lounge around inside in the tiny, overfurnished rooms, talking in secret, low voices and drinking coffee at all hours of the day and night. They were probably, I guessed, doing exactly that and no more now, and in fact if I had walked in I'd have been as welcome as a cousin to have an after-hours consultation, inquire about my prospects for the rest of the week. But I preferred to respect her privacy, since, like a writer, her place of business is also her home.

There is nothing complicated about how I began seeing Mrs. Miller. I was driving down Route 1 heading for the hardware store with Clary and Paul in the back seat—we were intent on buying a bicycle pump—and I simply saw her open-palm *Reader-Adviser* sign and pulled in. Probably I had passed it two hundred times over the years, and never noticed. I don't remember feeling out of sorts, though it's not always possible to remember. But I believe when it comes time to see a reader-adviser you know it, if, that is, you aren't at full-scale war with your best instincts.

For a moment I paused at the end of the driveway. I cut my lights and sat a moment watching the windows, since Mrs. Miller, her house, her business, her relatives, her life, posed altogether a small but genuine source of pleasure and wonder. It was as much for that reason that I went to see her once a week, and so found it satisfying enough last night just to be there.

Mrs. Miller's advice, indeed, is almost always just the standard reader-adviser advice and frequently completely wrong: "I see you are coming into much money soon" (not true). "I see a long life" (not likely, though I wouldn't argue). "You are a good man at heart" (uncertain). And she gives me the same or similar advice almost every week, with provisory adjustments that have to do mostly with the weather: "Things will brighten for you" (on rainy days). "Your future is not completely clear" (on cloudy days). There are even days she doesn't recognize me and gives me a puzzled look when I enter. Though she giggles like a schoolgirl when we're finished and says "See you next time" (never using my name), and occasionally dispenses with giving me one of her cards, which has typed at the bottom, below the raised crystal ball emblem: A PLACE TO BRING YOUR FRIENDS AND FEEL NO EMBARRASSMENT—I AM NOT A GYPSY.

I am certainly not embarrassed to go there, you can bet on that. Since for five dollars she will lead you into a dimly lit back bedroom of her sturdy suburban house, where there is plastic-brocade drapery over the window. (I wondered, first time through, if a little Levantine cousin or sister wouldn't be waiting there. But no.) There the light is greenish-amber, and a tiny radio plays softly sinuous Greek-sounding flute music. There is an actual clouded crystal ball on the card table (she has never used this) and several stacks of oversized tarot cards. Once we're in place she will hold my hand, trace its tender lines, wrinkle her brows as if my palm revealed hard matters, look puzzled or relieved and finally say hopeful, thoughtful things that no other strangers would ever think to say to me.

She is *the stranger who takes your life seriously*, the personage we all go into each day in hopes of meeting, the friend to the great mass of us not at odds with much; not disabled from anything; not "sick" in the strictest sense.

She herself is a handsome, dusky-skinned woman in her thirties or forties, a bit overweight and vaguely condescending, but completely agreeable down deep—so much so that at the end of our conferences she will almost always entertain a question or two as a bonus. I write these questions on scraps of paper during the week, though I almost always lose them and end up asking simple, factual-essential questions like: "Will Paul and Clarissa be safe from harm this week?" (a continued source of concern for anyone, especially me). Her answers, in turn, tend always to the bright side concerning my happiness, though toward the precautionary concerning my children: "No harm will come to them if you are a good father." (I have told her about Ralph long ago.) Once, in a panic for a good question, I asked if the Tigers could possibly finish tied for the American League East, in which case a one-game, winner-take-all tie-breaker with Baltimore would've been the decider. And this made her angry. Betting advice, she said, was more expensive than five dollars, and then charged me ten without giving me an answer.

I have learned over time that when her answers to my questions have been wrong, the best thing to think is that somehow it's my fault things didn't turn out.

But where else can you get, on demand, hopeful, inspiring projections for the real future? Where else, on a windy day in January, can you drive out beset by blue devils and in five minutes be semi-reliably assured by a relative stranger that you are who you think you are, and that things aren't going to turn out so crappy after all?

Would a Doctor Freud be so obliging, I've wondered? Would

he be any more likely to know anything, and tell you? I doubt it. In fact, in the bad days after my divorce I met a girl in St. Louis who had by then—she was in her mid-twenties and a buxom looker—spent thousands of dollars and hours consulting the most highly respected psychiatrist in that shadowy bricktop town, until one day she bounced into the office, full of high spirits. "Oh, Dr. Fasnacht," she proclaimed, "I woke up this morning and realized I'm cured! I'm ready to stop my visits and go out into the world on my own as a full-fledged citizen. You've cured me. You've made me so happy!" To which the old swindler replied: "Why, this is disastrous news. Your wish to end your therapy is the most distressing evidence of your terrible need to continue. You are much more ill than I ever thought. Now lie down."

Mrs. Miller would never give anyone such mopish opinions. Her strategy would be to give a much more promising than usual reading for that day, shake your hand, (possibly) forgo the five dollars as a lucky sign and say with eyebrows raised, "Come back when things puzzle you." Her philosophy is: *A good day's a good day. We get few enough of them in a lifetime. Go and enjoy it.*

And that is only the literal part of Mrs. Miller's—what can I call it best? Her service? Treatment? Poor words for mystery. Since for me, mystery is the crucial part, and in fact the *only* thing I find to have value at this stage in my life—midway around the track.

Mystery is the attractive condition a thing (an object, an action, a person) possesses which you know a little about but don't know about completely. It is the twiney promise of unknown things (effects, interworkings, suspicions) which you must be wise enough to explore not too deeply, for fear you will dead-end in nothing but facts.

A typical mystery would be traveling to Cleveland, a town you have never liked, meeting a beautiful girl, going for a lobster dinner during which you talk about an island off of Maine where you have both been with former lovers and had terrific times, and which talking about now revivifies so much you run upstairs and woggle the bejesus out of each other. Next morning all is well. You fly off to another city, forget about the girl. But you also feel differently about Cleveland for the rest of your life, but can't exactly remember why.

Mrs. Miller, when I come to her for a five-dollar consultation, does not disclose the world to me, nor my future in it. She merely encourages and assures me about it, admits me briefly to the mystery that surrounds her own life, which then sends me home with high hopes, aswarm with curiosities and wonder on the very lowest level: Who is this Mrs. Miller if she is not a Gypsy? A Jew? A Moroccan? Is "Miller" her real name? Who are those other people inside—relatives? Husbands? Are they citizens of this state? What enterprise are they up to? Are guns for sale? Passports? Foreign currency? On a slightly higher level: How do *I* seem? (Who has not wanted to ask his doctor that?) Though I am fierce to find out not one fleck more than is incidental to my visits, since finding out more would only make me the loser, submerge me in dull facts, and require me to seek some other mystery or do without.

As I expected would happen, simply proximity to the glow through her warm curtains—like the antique light of another century—plucked my spirits up like a hitchhiker who catches a ride when all hope was lost. More seemed suddenly possible, and near, whereas before nothing did. Though as I glanced back nostalgically at Mrs. Miller's squared ranchette, I sensed the front door had opened an inch. Someone there was watching me, wondering who I was, what I'd been up to. A love car? The police? A drunk sleeping it off? I was not even sure the door had opened, so that this was as much a riddle to me as I was to whomever I took to be there. A shared riddle, if he/she existed, a perfect give and take in the spirit of a marriage. And I slid off quickly into the south-bound traffic as renewed as a baby born to middle life.

I TOOK THE first jug-handle turn and zipped back up the Great Woods Road through the dark apple orchards, sod farms, beefalo barns, the playing fields of De Tocqueville Academy and the modern world-headquarters lawns, all of which keep Haddam sheltered from the dazzling hubcap emporia, dairy barns and swank Radio Shack hurdy-gurdy down Route 1 toward the sullen city of brotherly love. I was not ready for bed now. Far from it. Factuality and loneliness had been put in their places, and an anticipation awakened. The day, changed to a spring evening, held promise only an adventure would unearth.

I idled down Seminary Street, abstracted and empty in the
lemony vapor of suburban eventide. (It could always be a sad
town.) The two stoplights at either end were flashing yellow, and
on the south side of the square only Officer Carnevale waited in
his murmuring cruiser, lost in police-radio funk, ready to catch
speeders and fleeing ten-speed thieves. Even the seminary was
silent—Gothic solemnity and canary lights from the quarreled
windows aglimmer through the elms and buttonwoods. Ser-
monizing midterms were soon, and everybody'd buckled down.
Only Carnevale's exhaust said a towny soul was breathing inside
a hundred miles, where above the trees the gladlights of New
York City paled the sky.

Nine o'clock on the Thursday before Easter far down the suburban train line. A town, almost any town, would seem to have
secrets all its own. Though if you believed that you'd be wrong.
Haddam in fact is as straightforward and plumb-literal as a fire
hydrant, which more than anything else makes it the pleasant
place it is.

None of us could stand it if every place were a grizzled
Chicago or a bilgy Los Angeles—towns, like Gotham, of genuine woven intricacy. We all need our simple, unambiguous, even
factitious townscapes like mine. Places without challenge or
double-ranked complexity. Give me a little Anyplace, a grinning, toe-tapping Terre Haute or wide-eyed Bismarck, with
stable property values, regular garbage pick-up, good drainage,
ample parking, located not far from a major airport, and I'll beat
the birds up singing every morning.

I slowed to take a peek at the marquee of the First Presbyterian,
at the edge of the seminary grounds. I occasionally pop in on a
given Sunday just to see what they're up to and lift my spirits
with a hymn. X and I attended when we first moved here, but
she eventually lost interest, and I began working Sundays. Years
ago, when I was a senior and in need of an antidote to the puddling, laughless, guilty ironies of midwar Ann Arbor, I began
attending a liberal and nondogmatic Westminster group on
Maynard Street. The preacher, who referred to himself as a
"moderator," was a tall, acned, open-collared scarecrow who
aimed his mumbled sermons toward world starvation, the U N
and S E A T O, and who seemed embarrassed when it came time
to stand up and pray and always kept his darting eyes open.

A skinny little anorexic wife was his assistant—they were both from Muskegon—and our congregation consisted mostly of elderly professors' widows, a few confused and homely coeds and a homosexual or two just coming to grips with things.

I lasted five weeks, then put my Bible away and started staying up Saturday nights at the fraternity and getting good and drunk. Christianity, like everything else in the Ann Arbor of those times, was too factual and problem-solving-oriented. The spirit was made flesh too matter-of-factly. Small-scale rapture and ecstasy (what I'd come for) were out of the question given the mess the world was in. Consequently I loathed going.

But the First Presbyterians of Haddam offer a good, safe-and-sound approach to things. Their ardent hope is to bring you down to earth by causing your spirit to lift—a kind of complex spiritual orienteering. The regulars all have no doubts about what they're there for; they're there to be saved or give a damned good impression of it, and nobody's pulling the wool over anybody else's eyes.

What I could read off the marquee, however, seemed strange business, though it will probably turn out to be as ordinary as toast—a trick to lure the once-a-year guys into thinking church has changed.

"The Race To The Tomb"

The preacher will have some witty, eyebrow-arching joke to start off: "Now this fella, Jesus, he was really some heckuva peculiar kind of guy, wouldn't you say so?" And we all would. Then straight away we'd get to the hard-nosed corroborating of the resurrection and suggesting how such a fate might be ours.

I slipped on by, gave Officer Carnevale the lucky thumbs-up, which he managed moodily to return, then drove straight over to The Presidents—up Tyler, down Pierce and winding a sinewy way to Cleveland Street, before stopping under a giant tupelo across from 116, X's little white clapboard colonial. Her Citation sat in the narrow drive, an unknown blue car parked at the curb.

Quick as a ferret I left my car, crossed the street, crouched and laid my hand on the hood of the unknown blue car—a Thunderbird—then stole back to mine before anyone on Cleveland Street could see. As I had hoped, the Bird was as cold as a murderer's heart, and I was relieved to believe it belonged to a neighbor, or to some relative visiting the Armentis next door.

Though it could've been a suitor I knew nothing about—one of the fat-belly credit card boys from the country club, a thought which changed relief back to doubt.

My plan had been to pay an innocent visit. I hadn't seen Paul and Clarissa in four days, a long interval in the normal course of our lives. The two of them usually waltz by after school, eat a sandwich, sit and chat together, rummage around their former rooms the way they used to, play Yahtzee or Clue, read books, all while I try by fervent misdirection to prove a continuity in their little lives with my presence. Periodically I quit the work I'm doing and clump upstairs to tease and flirt with them, answer their questions, challenge them and try to woo them back to me in some plain and forthright way, a strategy they're wise to but don't mind because they love me, know I love them, and have no choice, really. We are, all four of us in this, a solid and divided family, doing our level bests to see our duty clearly.

Last night I hoped to stay for a drink, see the kids to bed, yak with X for half an hour, then end up, possibly, spending the night on the couch, something I hadn't done in some time (not, in fact, since I met Vicki) but felt a fierce urge to do suddenly.

Still if I'd gone hat-in-hand up to the door, on a mission of somber fatherhood, I couldn't be sure I wouldn't have interrupted an *intime*—the kids away on overnights at the Armentis, the lights turned up to facilitate the best atmosphere of grownup-bittersweet-excitement-since-so-much-has-gone-before, for the benefit of neighbors interested in seeing a proud woman make the best of a fractured life. I would've been thunderstruck to intercept some well-dressed corporate-level type with love in his eyes, athwart the precise couch I hoped to curl up on. X would've been in her rights to say I'd torpedoed her attempts at getting her feet on the ground, and the fellow would've been in his rights to run me out or punch me. And we'd have both ended up having to leave (the two men always have to trudge off into the night alone, though occasionally they become friends if they meet up later in a bar).

My whole scenario, in short, had lost its glow, and I was left in the dark understory, facing the blue intruder car with nothing to do more than breathe the plush air and endorse X's neighborhood. The Presidents, with their precise fifty-foot frontages, their mature mulberries and straight sidewalks, are actually an excellent location for a young, divorced lady with children, steady means and an independent bent, to dig her heels in. Up and down the street are other young free-thinking people on the way someplace in the world, sharp-eyed, idealistic folks who spotted a good investment and acted fast, and now have some value to sit on. The immigrant Italians who built them (some chosen right out of Sears catalogs) now prefer Delray Beach and Fort Myers and citizens' groups more their own age, and have left their neighborhoods to the young, though hardly ever their own young, who prefer the likes of Pheasant Run and Kendall Park. The banks have proved compassionate with mortgage points and variable rates, and as a result the young liberals—most of them prospering stockbrokers, corporate speech writers, and public defenders—have revived a proud, close-knit neighborhood and property-value ethic where everybody looks after everybody else's kids and grinds their own espresso. Bright new façades and paint jobs. New footings dug. A reshingled weather stoop. Smart art-deco numerals and a pane of discreetly stained glass done at home. All of it promisingly modern.

X, I think, is happy here. My children are close to their school, their friends and me. It is not the same as Hoving Road where we all once hung our hats, but things change in ways none of us can expect, no matter how damn much we know or how smart and good-intentioned each of us is or thinks he is. Who'd know that Ralph would die? Who'd know that certainty would grow rare as diamonds? Who'd know our home would be broken into and everything suddenly break apart? Did Walter Luckett know he'd meet Mr. Wrong two nights ago and alter his life again after his wife already had? No, you bet not. None of our lives is really ordinary; nothing humdrum in our delights or our disasters. Everything is as problematic as geometry when it's affairs of the heart in question. A life can simply change the way a day changes—sunny to rain, like the song says. But it can also change again.

The clock at St. Leo the Great sounded ten, and something began happening at 116 Cleveland.

The yellow stoop light flashed on. Someone inside spoke in a tone of patient instruction, and the front door opened. My son, Paul, stepped out.

Paul in tennis shorts, and a Minnesota Twins shirt I brought him from a trip I took. He is ten, small and not overly clever yet, a serious, distractable boy with a good heart, and all the sweet qualities of second sons: patience, curiosity, some useful inventiveness, sentimentality, a building vocabulary, even though he is not much of a reader. I have tried to think that things will turn out well for him, though when we powwow up in his room, a place he keeps furnished with Sierra Club posters of eagles and large Audubon mergansers and grebes, he always seems to display a moody enthrallment, as if there is some sovereign event in his life he senses is important but cannot for some reason remember. Naturally I am very proud of him, and his sister, too. They both carry on like soldiers.

Paul had brought outside with him one of the birds from his dovecote. A mottled rock dove, a handsome winger. He toted it manfully to the curb, using the two-handed professional bird handler's way he's taught himself. I surveilled him like a spy, slumped behind the steering wheel, the shadow of the big tupelo making me not especially noticeable, though Paul was too intent on his own business to see me.

At the curb he took the pigeon in one small hand, slipped the hood and neatly pocketed it. The bird cocked its head peckishly at his new surroundings. The sight, though, of Paul's familiar, serious face calmed it.

Paul studied the pigeon for a time, grappling it once again in both hands, and via the still darkness I could hear his boy's voice talking. He was coaching the bird in some language he had practiced. "Remember this house." "Fly this special route." "Be careful of this hazard or that obstacle." "Think of all we've worked on." "Remember who your friends are"—all of it good advice. When he'd finished, he held the bird to his nose and sniffed behind its beaky head. I saw him close his eyes, and then it was up, pitched, the bird's large bright wings seizing the night instantly, up and gone and out of sight like a thought, its wings white and then quickly small as it cleared the closure of trees—gone.

Paul looked up a moment, watching it. Then, as if he'd forgotten all about any loosed bird, he turned and stared at me across the street, slouched like Officer Carnevale in my cruiser car. He had seen me probably for quite some time, but had gone on with his business like a big boy who knows he's watched and doesn't care for it, but understands those are the rules.

Paul walked across the street in his little boy's ungainly gait but with a gainly smile, a smile he'd give, I know, to a total stranger.

"Hi Dad," he said through the window.

"Hi, Paul."

"So what's up?" He still smiled at me like an innocent boy.

"Just sort of sitting here now."

"Is it all right?"

"It's great. Whose car's that out front there?"

Paul looked back behind him at the Thunderbird. "The Litzes." (Neighbor, lawyer, no problem.) "Are you coming inside?"

"I just wanted to check up on you folks. Just being a patrol car."

"Clary's asleep. Mom's watching news," Paul said, adopting his mother's way of dropping definite articles, a midwest mannerism. *They went to market. She has flu. We bought tickets.*

"Who was that you gave his freedom to?"

"Ole Vassar." Paul looked up the street. Paul names his birds after hillbilly tunesters—Ernest, Chet, Loretta, Bobby, Jerry Lee—and had adopted his father's partiality for *ole* as a term of pure endearment. I could've hauled him through the window and hugged him till we both cried out, so much did I love him at that moment. "I didn't give him his freedom right off, though."

"Ole Vassar has a mission first, then?"

"Yes sir," Paul said and looked down at the pavement. It was clear I was burdening his privacy, of which he has plenty. But I knew he felt he had to talk about Vassar now.

"What's Vassar's mission?" I asked bravely.

"To see Ralph."

"Ralph. What's he going to see Ralph for?"

Paul sighed a small boy's put-on sigh, transformed back from a big boy. "To see if he's all right. And tell him about us."

"You mean it's a report."

"Yeah. I guess." Head still down at the pavement.

"On all of us?"

"Yeah."

"And how did it come out?"

"Good." Paul avoided my eyes in another direction.

"My part okay, too?"

"Your part wasn't too long. But it was good."

"That's all right. Just so I made it in. When's Ole Vassar reporting back?"

"He isn't. I told him he could live in Cape May."

"Why is that?"

"Because Ralph's dead. I think."

I had taken him and his sister to Cape May only last fall, and I was interested now that he supposed the dead lived there. "It's a one-way mission, then."

"Right."

Paul stared fiercely at the door of my car and not at me, and I could sense he was confused by all this talk of dead people. Kids are most at home with sincerity and the living (who could blame them?), unlike adults, who sometimes do not have an unironical bone in their bodies, even for things that are precisely in front of them and can threaten their existence. Paul's and mine, though, has always been a friendship founded on sincerity's rock.

"What do you know tonight to tickle me?" I said. Paul is a secret cataloger of corny jokes and can make anyone laugh out loud, even at a joke they've heard before, though he often chooses to withhold. I myself envy his memory.

For this question, though, he had to consider. He wagged his head backwards in pretend-thought, and stared into the tree boughs as if all the good jokes were up there. (What did I say about things always changing and surprising us? Who would've thought a drive down a dark street could produce a conversation with my own son! One in which I find out he's in contact with his dead brother—a promising psychological indicator, though a bit unnerving—plus get to hear a joke as well.)

"Ummm, all right," Paul said. He was all Johnny now. By the way he stuffed his hands in his pockets and averted his mouth I could tell he thought it was a pretty funny one.

"Ready?" I said. With anyone else this would spoil the joke. But with Paul it is protocol.

"Ready," he said. "Who speaks Irish and lives in your back yard?"

"I don't know." I give in straight away.

"Paddy O'Furniture." Paul could not hold back his laughter a second and neither could I. We both held our sides—he in the street, I in my car. We laughed like monkeys loud and long until tears rose in his eyes and mine, and I knew if we did not rein ourselves in, his mother would be out wondering (silently) about my "judgment." Ethnics, though, are among our favorite joke topics.

"That's a prize-winner," I said, wiping a tear from my eye.

"I have another one, too. A better one," he said, grinning and trying not to grin at the same time.

"I have to drive home now, sonny," I said. "You'll have to remember it for me."

"Aren't you coming inside?" Paul's little eyes met mine. "You can sleep on the couch."

"Not tonight," I said, joy bounding in my heart for this sweet Uncle Milty. I would've accepted his invitation if I could, taken him up and tickled his ribs and put him in his bed. "Rain Czech." (One of our oldest standbys.)

"Can I tell Mom?" He had sprung past the strange confusion of my not coming inside, and on to the next most important issue: disclosure, the reporting of what had happened. In this he is not at all like his father, but he may come to it in time.

"Say I was driving by, and saw you and we stopped and had a conversation like old-timers."

"Even though it isn't true?"

"Even though it isn't true."

Paul looked at me curiously. It was not the lie I had instructed him to tell—which he might or might not tell, depending on his own ethical considerations—but something else that had occurred to him.

"How long do you think it'll take Ole Vassar to find Ralph?" he said very seriously.

"He's probably almost there now."

Paul's face went somber as a churchman's. "I wouldn't like it to take forever," he said. "That'd be too long."

"Goodnight, son," I said, suddenly full of anticipation of quite another kind. I started my motor.

"Goodnight, Dad." He broke a smile for me. "Happy dreams."

"You have happy dreams your own self."

He walked back across Cleveland Street to his mother's house, while I eased away into darkness toward home.

THE AIR IN Detroit Metro is bright crackling factory air. New cars revolve glitteringly down every concourse. Paul Anka sings tonight at Cobo Hall, a flashing billboard tells us. All the hotels are palaces, all the residents our best friends. Even Negroes look different here—healthy, smiling, prosperous, expensive-suited, going places with briefcases.

Our fellow passengers are all meeting people, it turns out, and are not resident Michiganders at all, though they all have come from here originally, and their relatives are their mirror-image: the women ash-blond, hippy, smiling; the men blow-dried and silent-mouthed, secretive, wearing modern versions of old-time car coats and Tyroleans, earnest beefsteak handshakes extended. This is a car coat place, a place of wintry snuggle-up, a place I'm glad to have landed. If you seek a beautiful peninsula, look around you.

Barb and Sue walk us down the concourse. They have bags-on-wheels, snazzy red blazers and shoulder purses, and they are both in jolly moods. They are looking forward to "fun week-ends," they say, and Sue gives Vicki a big lascivious wink. Barb says that Sue is married to a "major hunk" from Lake Orion who owns a bump shop, and that she may quit flying soon to get the oven warmed up. She and Ron, her own husband, she says, "are still 'dining out.' "

"Don't let this old gal fool ya," Sue sings out with a big grin. "She's a party doll. The things I could tell you would fill a book. Some of the trips we go on. Whoa." Sue rolls her eyes and snaps her blond head famously.

"Just don't pay any attention to all that," Barb says. "Just enjoy yourselves, you two, and hev a seef trip home."

"We surely will," Vicki boasts, smiling her newcomer's smile. "And you have a nice night, too, okay?"

"No stopping us," Sue calls back, and off the two go toward

the crew check-in, gabbing like college girls with the handsomest boys on campus waiting at the curb in big convertibles and the housemother already hoodwinked.

"Weren't they just nice?" Vicki says, looking sentimentally detached in the midst of the mile-long Detroit bustle. She has grown momentarily pensive, though I suspect this is also from too much anticipation, and she will be herself in a jiffy. She is a great anticipator, as much as I am and maybe more. "I didn't realize those gals were that nice and all."

"They sure were," I say, thinking of all the cheerleaders Sue and Barb are the spitting image of. Put a bulky letter-sweater on either of them, a flippy pleated skirt and bobby sox, and my heart would swell for them. "They were wonderful."

"How wonderful?" Vicki says, giving me a suspicious frown.

"About one half as wonderful as you." I grab her close to me high up under her tender arm. We are awash in shuffling Detroiters, a rock in a stream.

"Lilacs are pretty, too, but they make an ugly bush," Vicki says, her eyes knowledgeable and small. "You've got the wander-eye, mister. No wonder your wife signed them papers on you."

"That's in the past, though," I say. "I'm all yours, if you want me. We could get married right now."

"I had one forever already that didn't last," Vicki says, meanly. "You're talking like a nut now. I just came here to see the sights, so let's go see 'em." She beetles her brows as if something had briefly confused her, then the shiny smile breaks through once again and she reclaims the moment. I am, of course, talking like a nut, though I'd marry her in a flash, in the airport nondenominational chaplain's office, with a United skycap as my best man, Barb and Sue as cosmetologically perfect bridesmaids. "Let's get the bags, what d'ya say, boy?" she says, perky now, and on the move. "I want to get a look at that big tire 'fore they tear the sucker down." She arches her brows at me and there's a secret fragrant promise embedded, a sex code known only to nurses. How can I say no? "You sure have got a case of the dismal stares, all of a suddenly," she says, ten yards away now. "Let's get going."

Anything can happen in another city. I had forgotten that, though it takes a real country girl to bring it home. Then I'm away, catching up, smiling, trundling on eager feet toward the baggage carrousels.

*   *   *

DETROIT, CITY of lost industrial dreams, floats out around us like a mirage of some sane and glaciated life. Skies are gray as a tarn, the winds up and gusting. Flying papers and cellophane skirmish over the Ford Expressway and whap the sides of our suburban Flxible like flak as we lug our way toward Center City. Flat, dormered houses and new, brick-mansard condos run side by side in the complicated urban-industrial mix. And, as always, there is the expectation of new "weather" around the corner. Batten down the hatches. A useful pessimism abounds here and awaits.

I have read that with enough time American civilization will make the midwest of any place, New York included. And from here that seems not at all bad. Here is a great place to be in love; to get a land-grant education; to own a mortgage; to see a game under the lights as the old dusky daylight falls to blue-black, a backdrop of stars and stony buildings, while friendly Negroes and Polacks roll their pants legs up, sit side by side, feeling the cool Canadian breeze off the lake. So much that is explicable in American life is made in Detroit.

And I could be a perfect native if I wasn't settled in New Jersey. I could move here, join the Michigan alums and buy a new car every year right at the factory door. Nothing would suit me better in middle life than to set up in a little cedar-shake builder's-design in Royal Oak or Dearborn and have a try at another Michigan girl (or possibly even the same one, since we would have all that ready-made to build on). My magazine could install me as the midwest office. It might even spark me to try my hand at something more adventurous—a guiding service to the northern lakes, for example. A change to pleasant surroundings is always a tonic for creativity.

"IT'S JUST like it's still winter here." Vicki's nose is to the bus's tinted window. We have passed the big tire miles back. She peered at it silently as we drifted by, a tourist seeing a lesser pyramid. "Well," she said as a big fenced-in Ford plant, flat and wide as Nebraska, hauled next into view, "I got that all behind me."

"If you don't like the weather, wait ten minutes. That's an expression we used to say in college."

She fattens her cheeks as Walter Reuther Boulevard flashes by, then the Fisher Building and the lumpish Olympia rises in the furred, gray distance. "They say that in Texas all the time. They prob'ly say it everywhere." She looks back at the cityscape. "You know what my daddy says about De-troit?"

"He must not've liked it very much."

"When I told him I was coming out today with you, he just said, 'If De-troit was ever a state, it'd be New Jersey.'" She smiles at me cunningly.

"Detroit doesn't have the diversity, though I really like both places."

"He likes New Jersey, but he didn't like this place." We swerve into the long concrete trench of the Lodge freeway, headed to midtown. "He hasn't ever liked a place much, which I always thought was kind of a shame. This place doesn't look so bad, though. Lots of colored, but that's all right with me. They gotta live, too." She nods seriously to herself, then takes my hand and squeezes it as we enter a vapor-lit freeway tunnel which takes us to the riverfront and the Pontchartrain.

"This was the first city I ever knew. We used to come into town when I was in college and go to burlesque shows and smoke cigars. It seemed like the first American city to me."

"That's the way Dallas is to me. I'm not upset to be gone from it, though. Not a little teensy." She purses her lips hard and turns loose of my hand. "My life's lots better now, I'll tell you that."

"Where *would* you rather be?" I ask as the milky light of Jefferson Avenue dawns into our dark bus and passengers begin to murmur and clutch belongings up and down the aisle. Someone asks the driver about another stop farther along the hotel loop. We are all of us itchy to be there.

Vicki looks at me solemnly, as if the gravity of this city had entered her, making all lightheartedness seem sham. She is a girl who knows how to be serious. I had hoped, of course, she'd say there's no place she'd rather be than with m-e me. But I cannot mold *all* her wishes to my model for them, fulfill her every dream as I do my own. Yet she is as unguarded to this Detroit chill as I am, and secretly it makes me proud of her.

"Didn't you say you went to college around here some-where?" She's thinking of something hard for her to come to, a glimmering of a thought.

"About forty miles away."

"Well, what was that like?"

"It was a nice town with trees all around. A nice park for spring afternoons, decent profs."

"Do you miss it? I bet you do. I bet it was the best time in your life and you wish you had it back. Tell the truth."

"No ma'am," I say. And it's true. "I wouldn't change from right this moment."

"Ahhh," Vicki says skeptically, then turns toward me in her seat, suddenly intense. "Do you swear to it?"

"I swear to it."

She fastens her lips together again and smacks them, her eyes cast to the side for thinking power. "Well, it idn't true with me. This is to answer where would I rather be."

"Oh."

Our Flxible comes hiss to a lumbering stop in front of our hotel. Doors up front fold open. Passengers move into the aisle. Behind Vicki out the tinted glass I see Jefferson Avenue, gray cars moiling by and beyond it Cobo, where Paul Anka is singing tonight. And far away across the river, the skyline of Windsor— glum, low, retrograde, benumbed reflection of the U.S. (The very first thing I did after Ralph was buried was buy a Harley-Davidson motorcycle and take off driving west. I got as far as Buffalo, halfway across the Peace Bridge, then lost my heart and turned back. Something in Canada had taken the breath of spirit out of me, and I promised never to go back, though of course I have.)

"When I think about where would I rather be," Vicki says dreamily, "what I think about is my first day of nursing school out in Waco. All of us were lined up in the girls' dorm lobby, clear from the reception desk out to the Coke machine between the double doors. Fifty girls. And across from where I was stand- ing was this bulletin board behind a little glass window. And I could see myself in it. And written on that bulletin board in white letters on black was 'We're glad you're here' with an exclamation. And I remember thinking to myself, 'You're here to help people and you're the prettiest one, and you're going to have a wonderful life.' I remember that *so* clearly, you know? A very wonderful life." She shakes her head. "I always think of that." We are last to leave the bus now, and other passengers are ready to depart. The driver is folding closed the baggage doors, our two sit on the damp and crowded sidewalk. "I don't mean to be ole gloomy-doomy."

"You're not a bit of gloomy-doomy," I say. "I don't think that for a minute."

"And I don't want you to think I'm not glad to be here with you, because I am. It's the happiest day of my life in a long time, 'cause I just love all of this so much. This big ole town. I just love it so much. I didn't need to answer that right now, that's all. It's one of my failings. I always answer questions I don't need to. I'd do better just going along."

"It's me that shouldn't ask it. But you're going to let me make you happy, aren't you?" I smile hopefully at her. What business do I have wanting to know any of this? I'm my own worst enemy.

"I'm happy. God, I'm *real* happy." And she throws her arms around me and cries a tiny tear on my cheek (a tear, I want to believe, of happiness), just as the driver cranes his neck in and waves us out. "I'd marry you," she whispers. "I didn't mean to make fun of you asking me. I'll marry you any time."

"We'll try to fit it into our agenda, then," I say and touch her moist soft cheek as she smiles through another fugitive tear.

And then we are up and out and down and into the dashing wet wind of Detroit, and the squabbly street where our suitcases sit in a sop of old melted snow like cast-off smudges. A lone policeman stands watching, ready to chart their destination from this moment on. Vicki squeezes my arm, her cheek on my shoulder, as I heft the two cases. Her plaid canvas is airy; mine, full of sportswriter paraphernalia, is a brick.

And I feel exactly what at this debarking moment?

At least a hundred things at once, all competing to take the moment and make it their own, reduce undramatic life to a gritty, knowable kernel.

This, of course, is a minor but pernicious lie of literature, that at times like these, after significant or disappointing divulgences, at arrivals or departures of obvious importance, when touchdowns are scored, knock-outs recorded, loved ones buried, orgasms notched, that at such times we are any of us altogether *in* an emotion, that we are within ourselves and not able to detect other emotions we might also be feeling, or be about to feel, or prefer to feel. If it's literature's job to tell the truth about these moments, it usually fails, in my opinion, and it's the writer's fault for falling into such conventions. (I tried to explain all of this to my students at Berkshire College, using Joyce's epiphanies as a good example of falsehood. But none of them understood the first thing I was talking about, and I began to feel that if they didn't already know most of what I wanted to tell them, they were doomed anyway—a pretty good reason to get out of the teaching business.)

What I feel, in truth, as I swing these two suitcases off the wet concrete and our blue bus sighs and rumbles from the curbside toward its other routed hotels, and bellboys lurk behind thick glass intent on selling us assistance, is, in a word: a *disturbance*. As though I were relinquishing something venerable but in need of relinquishing. I feel a quickening in my pulse. I feel a strong sense of lurking evil (the modern experience of pleasure coupled with the certainty that it will end). I feel a conviction that I have no ethics at all and little consistency. I sense the possibility of terrible regret in the brash air. I feel the need suddenly to confide (though not in Vicki or anyone else I know). I feel as literal as I've ever felt—stranded, uncomplicated as an immigrant. All these I feel at once. And I feel the urge—which I suppress—to cry, the way a man would, for these same reasons, and more.

That is the truth of what I feel and think. To expect anything less or different is idiotic. Bad sportswriters are always wanting to know such things, though they never want to know the truth, never have a place for that in their stories. Athletes probably think and feel the fewest things of anyone at important times—their training sees to that—though even they can be counted on to have more than one thing in their mind at a time.

"I'll carry my own bag," Vicki says, pressed against me like my shadow, sniffing away a final tear of arrival happiness. "It's light as a feather duster."

"You're not going to do anything from now on out but have fun," I say, both bags up and moving. "You just let me see a smile."

And she smiles a smile as big as Texas. "Look, I ain't p.g., you know," she says as the pneumatic hotel doors glide away. "I always carry what's mine."

*   *   *

IT IS FOUR-THIRTY by the time we get to our room, a tidy rectangle of pretentious midwestern pseudo-luxury—a prearranged fruit basket, a bottle of domestic champagne, blue bachelor buttons in a Chinese vase, red-flocked whorehouse wall décor and a big bed. There is an eleventh-story fisheye view upriver toward the gaunt Ren-Cen and gray pseudopodial Belle Isle in the middle distance—the shimmer-lights of suburbs reaching north and west out of sight.

Vicki takes a supervisory look in all spaces—closets, shower, bureau drawers—makes ooo's and oh's over what's here free of charge by way of toiletries and toweling, then establishes herself in an armchair at the window, pops the champagne and begins to take everything in. It is exactly as I'd hoped: pleased to respectful silence by the splendor of things—a vote that I have done things the way they were meant to be.

I take the opportunity for some necessary phoning.

First, a "touch base" call to Herb to firm up tomorrow's plans. He is in laughing good spirits and invites us to have dinner with him and Clarice at a steak place in Novi, but I plead fatigue and prior commitments, and Herb says that's great. He has become decidedly upbeat and shaken his glumness of the morning. (He is on pretty serious mood stabilizers, is my guess. Who wouldn't be?) We hang up, but in two minutes Herb calls back to check whether he's given me right directions for the special shortcut once we leave I-96. Since his injury, he says, he's suffered mild dyslexia and gets numbers turned around half the time with some pretty hilarious results. "I do the same thing, Herb," I say, "only I call it normal." But Herb hangs up without saying anything.

Next I call Henry Dykstra, X's father, out in Birmingham. I have made it my policy to keep in touch with him since the divorce. And though things were strained and extremely formal between us while X's and my affairs were in the lawyers' hands, we have settled back since then into an even better, more frank relationship than we ever had. Henry believes it was Ralph's death pure and simple that caused our marriage to go kaput, and feels a good measure of sympathy for me—something I don't mind having, even if my own beliefs about these matters are a good deal more complex. I have also stayed an intermediary message-carrier between Henry and his wife, Irma, out in

Mission Viejo, since she writes to me regularly, and I have let him know that I can be trusted to keep a confidence and to relay timely information which is often something surprisingly intimate and personal. "The old plow still works," he once asked me to tell her, and I did, though she never answered that I know of. Families are very hard to break apart forever. I know that.

Henry is a robust seventy-one and, like me, has not remarried, though he often makes veiled but conspicuous references to women's names without explanation. My personal belief—seconded by X—is that he's as happy as a ram living on his estate by himself and would've had it that way from the day X was born if he could've negotiated Irma. He is an industrialist of the old school, who worked his way up in the Thirties and has never really understood the concept of an intimate life, which I contend is not his fault, though X thinks otherwise and sometimes claims to dislike him.

"We're going broke, Franky," Henry says, in a bad temper. "The whole damn country has its pants around its ankles to the unions. And we elected the S.O.B.s who're doing it to us. Isn't that something? Republicans? I wouldn't give you a goddamned nickel for the first one they ever made. I stand somewhere to the right of Attila the Hun, I guess is what that means."

"I'm not much up on it, Henry. It sounds tricky to me."

"Tricky! It isn't tricky. If I wanted to steal and lay off everybody at my plant I could live for a hundred years, exactly the way I live now. Never leave the house. Never leave the chair! I came up a Reuther man, you know that, Frank. Life-long. It's these gangsters in Washington. All of them. They're all goddamn criminals, want to run me in the ground. Retire me out of the gasket business. What's going on at home, anyway? You still divorced?"

"Things're great, Henry. Today's Ralph's birthday."

"Is that so?" Henry does not like to talk about this, I know, but for me it is a day of some importance, and I don't mind mentioning it.

"I think he would've made a fine adult, Henry. I'm sure of that."

For a moment then there is stupefied emptiness in our connection while we think over lost chances.

"Why don't you come out here and we'll get drunk," Henry says abruptly. "I'll have Lula fix duck en brochette. I killed the sons-of-bitches myself. We can call up some whores. I've got their private phone numbers right here. Don't think I don't call them, either."

"That'd be great, Henry. But I'm not alone."

"Got a shady lady with you yourself?" Henry guffaws.

"No, a nice girl."

"Where're you staying?"

"Downtown. I have to go back tomorrow. I'm on business today."

"Okay, okay. Tell me why you think our golfing friend left you, Frank? Tell the truth. I can't get it off my mind today, for some damn reason."

"I think she wanted her life put back in her own hands, Henry. There's not much else to it."

"She always thought I ruined her life for men. It's a hell of a thing to hear. I never ruined anybody's life. And neither did you."

"I don't really think she thinks that now."

"She *told* me she did last week! As late as that. I'm glad I'm old. It's enough life. You're here, then you're not."

"I wasn't always such a great guy, Henry. I tried hard but sometimes you can just fool yourself about yourself."

"Forget all that," Henry says. "God forgave Noah. You can forgive yourself. Who's your shady lady?"

"You'd like her. Her name's Vicki." Vicki swings her smiling head around and holds up a glass of champagne to toast me.

"Bring her out here, I'll meet her. What a name. Vicki."

"Another visit, Henry. We're on a short schedule this time." Vicki goes back to watching the night fall.

"I don't blame you," Henry says brashly. "You know, Frank, sometimes the fact of living with somebody makes living with them impossible. Irma and I were just like that. I sent her to California one January, and that was twenty years ago. She's a lot happier. So you stay down there with Vicki whatever."

"It's hard to know another person. I admit that."

"You're better off assuming anybody'll do anything, anytime, than that they won't. That way you're safe. Even my own daughter."

"I wish I could come out there and get drunk with you, Henry, that's the truth. I'm glad we're pals. Irma told me to tell you she'd seen a real good performance of *The Fantasticks* in Mission Viejo. And it made her think of you."

"Irma did?" Henry says. "What's the fantastics?"

"It's a play."

"Well, that's good then, isn't it?"

"Any messages to go back? I'll probably write her next week. She sent me a birthday card. I could add something."

"I never really knew Irma, Frank. Isn't that something?"

"You were pretty busy making a living, though, Henry."

"She could've had boyfriends and I wouldn't have even noticed. I hope she did. *I* certainly did. All I wanted."

"I wouldn't worry about that. Irma's happy. She's seventy years old."

"In July."

"What about a message. Anything you want to say?"

"Tell her I have bladder cancer."

"Is that true?"

"I *will* have, if I don't have something else first. Who cares anyway?"

"I care. You have to think of something else, or I'll think of something for you."

"How's Paul and how's Clarissa?"

"They're fine. We're taking a car trip around Lake Erie this summer. And we'll be stopping to see you. They're already talking about it."

"We'll go up to the U.P."

"There might not be time for that." (I hope not.) "They just want to see you. They love you very much."

"That's great, though I don't know how they could. What do you think about the Maize and Blue, Franky?"

"A powerhouse, is my guess, Henry. All the seniors are back, and the big Swede from Pellston's in there again. I hear pretty awesome stories. It's an impressive show out there." This is the only ritual part of our conversations. I always check with the college football boys, particularly our new managing editor, a little neurasthenic, chain-smoking Bostonian named Eddie Frieder, so I can pass along some insider's information to Henry, who never went to college, but is a fierce Wolverine fan nonetheless. It is the only use he can think to make of my profession, and I'm not at all sure he doesn't concoct an interest just to please me, though I don't much like football per se. (People have some big misunderstandings about sportswriters.) "You're going to see some fancy alignments in the defensive backfield this fall, that's all I'll say, Henry."

"All they need now is to fire that meathead who runs the whole show. He's a loser, if you ask me. I don't care how many games he wins."

"The players all seem to like him, from what I hear."

"What the hell do they know? Look. The means don't always justify the end to me, Frank. That's what's wrong with this country. You ought to write about that. The abasement of life's intrinsic qualities. That's a story."

"You're probably right, Henry."

"I feel hot about this whole issue, Frank. Sports is just a paradigm of life, right? Otherwise who'd care a goddamn thing about it?"

"I know people can see it that way." (I try to avoid that idea, myself.) "But it's pretty reductive. Life doesn't need a metaphor in my opinion."

"Whatever that means. Just get rid of that guy, Frank. He's a Nazi." Henry says this word to rhyme with snazzy in the old-fashioned way. "His popularity's his biggest threat." In fact, the coach in question is quite a good coach and will probably end up in the Hall of Fame in Canton, Ohio. He and Henry are almost exactly alike as human beings.

"I'll pass a word along, Henry. Why don't you write a letter to *The Readers Speak*."

"I don't have time. You do it. I trust you that far."

Light is falling outside the Pontchartrain now. Vicki sits in the shadows, her back to me, hugging her knees and staring out toward the Seagram's sign upriver half a mile, red and gold in the twilight, while little Canuck houses light up like fireflies on a dark and faraway lake beach where I have been. I could want nothing more than to hug her now, feel her strong Texas back, and fall into a nestle we'd break off only when the room service waiter tapped at our door. But I can't be sure she hasn't lulled to sleep in the sheer relief of expectations met—one of life's true blessings. In a hundred ways we could not be more alike, Vicki and I, and I miss her badly, though she is only twelve feet away and I could touch her shoulder in the dark with hardly a move (this is one of the prime evils of being an anticipator).

"Frank, we don't amount to much. I don't know why we go to the trouble of having opinions," Henry says.

"It puts off the empty moment. That's what I think."

"What the hell's that? I don't know what that is."

"Then you must've been pretty skillful all your life, Henry. That's great, though. It's what I strive for."

"How old will you be next birthday? You said you had a birthday." For some reason Henry is gruff about this subject.

"Thirty-nine, next week."

"Thirty-nine's young. Thirty-nine's nothing. You're a remarkable man, Frank."

"I don't think I'm that remarkable, Henry."

"Well no, you're not. But I advise you, though, to think you are. I'd be nowhere if I didn't think I was perfect."

"I'll think of it as a birthday present, Henry. Advice for my later years."

"I'll send you out a leather wallet. Fill it up."

"I've got some ideas that'll do just as good as a fat wallet."

"Is this this Vicki trick you're talking about?"

"Right."

"I agree wholeheartedly. Everybody ought to have a Vicki in his life. Two'd even be better. Just don't marry her, Frank. In my experience these Vickis aren't for marrying. They're sporting only."

"I've got to be going now, Henry." Our conversations often tend this way, toward his being a nice old uncle and then, as if by policy, making me want to tell him to go to hell.

"Okay. You're mad at me now, I know it. But I don't give a goddamn if you are. I know what I think."

"Fill your wallet up with that then, Henry, if you get my meaning."

"I get it. I'm not an idiot like you are."

"I thought you said I was pretty remarkable."

"You are. You're a pretty remarkable moron. And I love you like a son."

"This is the point to hang up now, Henry. Thanks. I'm glad to hear that."

"Marry my daughter again if you want to. You have my permission."

"Good night, Henry. I feel the same way." But like Herb Wallagher, Henry has already hung up on me, and never hears my parting words, which I sing off into the empty phone lines like a wilderness cry.

VICKI HAS indeed gone to sleep in her chair, a cold stream of auto lights below, pouring up Jefferson toward the Grosse Pointes: Park, Farms, Shores, Woods, communities tidy and entrenched in midwestern surety.

I am hungry as an animal now, though when I rouse her with a hand on her soft shoulder, ready for a crab soufflé or a lobsteak, amenable to à la carte up on the revolving roof, she wakes with a different menu in mind—one a fellow would need to be ready for the old folks' home to pass up. (She has drunk all the champagne, and is ready for some fun.)

She reaches and pulls me onto her chair so I'm across her lap and can smell the soft olive scent of her sleepy breath. Beyond the window glass in the starless drifting Detroit night an ore barge with red and green running lights aglow hangs on the current toward Lake Erie and the blast furnaces of Cleveland.

"Oh, you sweet old sweet man," Vicki says to me, and wiggles herself comfortable. She gives me a moist soft kiss on the mouth, and hums down in her chest. "I read someplace that if the Taurus tells you he loves you, you're s'posed to believe it. Is that so?"

"You're a wonderful girl."

"Hmmmm. But . . ." She smiles and hums.

I have a good handful of her excellent breast now, and what a wonderful bunch she is, a treasure trove for a man interested in romance. "Doesn't that make you happy?"

"Oh, that does. You know that. You're the only one for me." She is no part a dreamer, I know it, but a literalist from the word go, happy to let the world please her in the small ways it can (true of fewer and fewer people, women especially). Though it is probably not an easy thing to be here with me, in a strange glassy hotel in a cold and sinister town, strange as man to a mandrill, and to believe you are in love.

"Oh, my my my," she whispers.

"Tell me what'll make you happiest. That's what I'm here for, and that's the truth" (or most of it).

"Well, don't let's sit on this ole chair all night and let that big ole granddaddy bed go to waste. I'm a firecracker just thinking about you. I didn't think you'd *ever* get off that phone."

"I'm off now."

"You better look out then."

And then the cold room folds around us, and we become lost in simple nighttime love gloom, boats rafted together through a blear passage of small perils. A fair, tender Texas girl in a dark séance. Nothing could be better, more cordial than that. Nothing. Take this from a man who knows.

BEFORE MY marriage ended but after Ralph died, in that wandering two-year period when I bought a Harley-Davidson, drove to Buffalo, taught at a college, suffered that dreaminess I have only lately begun to come out from under, and began to lose my close moorings with X without even noticing the slippage, I must've slept with eighteen different women—a number I don't consider high, or especially scandalous or surprising under the circumstances. X, I'm sure, knew it, and in retrospect I can see that she did her best to accommodate it, tried to make me feel not so miserable by not asking questions, not demanding a strict accounting of my days when I would be off working in some sports mecca—a Denver or a St. Louis—expecting, I feel sure, that one day or other I would wake up out of it, as she thought she already had (but probably at this moment would be willing to doubt, wherever she might be—safe I hope).

None of this would've been so terrible, I believe, if I hadn't reached a point with the women I was "seeing," at which I was trying to simulate complete immersion—something anyone who travels for a living knows is a bad idea. But when times got bad, I would, for example, find myself after a game alone in the pressbox of some concrete and steel American sports palace. Often as not there would be a girl reporter finishing up her late running story (my eyes were sharpened for just such stragglers), and we would end up having a few martinis in some atmospheric-panoramic bar, then driving out in my renter to some little suburban foot-lit lanai apartment with rattan carpets, where a daughter waited—a little Mandy or Gretchen—and no hubby, and where before I knew it the baby would be asleep, the music turned low, wine poured, and the reporter and I would be plopped in bed together. And bango! All at once I was longing with all my worth to be a part of that life, longing to enter completely into that little existence of hers as a full (if brief) participant, share her secret illusions, hopes. "I love you," I've heard myself say more than once to a Becky, Sharon, Susie or Marge I hadn't known longer than *four hours and fifteen minutes*! And being absolutely certain I did; and, to prove it, loosing a barrage of pryings, human-interest questions—demands, in other words, to know as many of the whys and whos and whats of her life as I could. All of it the better to get *into* her life, lose that terrible distance that separated us, for a few drifting hours close the door, simulate intimacy, interest, anticipation, then resolve them all in a night's squiggly romance and closure. "Why did you go to Penn State when you could've gone to Bryn Mawr?" *I see.* "What year did your ex-husband actually get out of the service?" *Hmmm.* "Why did your sister get along better with your parents than you did?" *Makes sense.* (As if knowing anything could make any difference.)

This, of course, was the world's worst, most craven cynicism. Not the invigorating little roll in the hay part, which shouldn't bother anyone, but the demand for full-disclosure when I had nothing to disclose in return and could take no responsible interest in anything except the hope (laughable) that we could "stay friends," and how early I could slip out the next morning and be about my business or head for home. It was also the worst kind of sentimentalizing—feeling sorry for someone in her lonely life (which is what I almost always felt, though I wouldn't have admitted it), turning that into pathos, pathos into interest, and finally turning that into sex. It's exactly what the worst sportswriters do when they push their noses into the face of someone who has just had his head beaten in and ask, "What were you thinking of, Mario, between the time your head began to look like a savage tomato and the moment they counted you out?"

What I was doing, though I didn't figure it out until long after I'd spent three months at Berkshire College—living with Selma Jassim, who wasn't interested in disclosure—was trying to be within myself by being as nearly as possible *within* somebody else. It is not a new approach to romance. And it doesn't work. In fact, it leads to a terrible dreaminess and the worst kind of abstraction and unreachableness.

How I expected to be within some little Elaine, Barb, Sue or Sharon I barely knew when I wasn't even doing it with X *in my own life* is a good question. Though the answer is clear. I couldn't.

Bert Brisker would probably say about me, that at that time I wasn't "intellectually pliant" enough, since what I was after was illusion complete and on a short-term, closed-end basis. And what I should've been happy with was the plain, elementary rapture a woman—any woman I happened to like—could confer, no questions asked, after which I could've gone home and let life please me in the ways I'd always let it. Though it's a rare man who can find real wonder in the familiar, once luck's running against him—which it was.

By the time I came back from teaching three months, which was near the end of this two years, I'd actually quit the whole business with women. But X had been home with Paul and Clary, and had not been communicating, and had begun reading *The New Republic*, *The National Review* and *China Today*, something she'd never done before, and seemed remote. I fell immediately into a kind of dreamy monogamy that did nothing but make X feel like a fool—she said so eventually—for putting up with me until her own uncertainty got aroused. I was around the house every day, but not around to do any good for anybody, just reading catalogs, lying charitably to avoid full disclosure, smiling at my children, feeling odd, visiting Mrs. Miller weekly, musing ironically about the number of different answers I could give to almost any question I was asked, watching sports and Johnny on television, wearing putter pants and plaid shirts I'd bought from L.L. Bean, going up to New York once a week and being a moderately good but committed sportswriter—all the while X's face became indistinct, and my voice grew softer and softer until it was barely audible, even to me. Her belief—at least her way of putting things since then—was that I'd grown "untrustworthy," which is not surprising, since I probably was, if what she wanted was to be made happy by my making life as certain as could be, which I could've sooner flown than do then. And when I couldn't do that, she just began to suspect the worst about everything, for which I don't blame her either, though I could tell that wasn't a good idea. I contend that I felt pretty trustworthy then, in spite of everything—if she could've simply trusted just that I loved her, which I did. (Married life requires shared mystery even when all the facts are known.) I'd have come around before too long, I'm sure of that, and I'd have certainly been happy to have things stay the way they were while hoping for improvements. If you lose all hope, you can always find it again.

Only our house got broken into, hateful Polaroids scattered around, the letters from the woman in Kansas found, and X seemed suddenly to think we were too far gone, farther gone than we knew, and life just seemed unascendant and to break between us, not savagely or even tragically, just ineluctably, as the real writers say.

A lot happens to you in your life and comes to bear midway: your parents can die (mine, though, died years before), your marriage can change and even depart, a child can succumb, your profession can start to seem hollow. You can lose all hope. Any one thing would be enough to send you into a spin. And correspondingly it is hard to say what *causes* what, since in one important sense *everything* causes everything else.

So with all this true, how can I say I "love" Vicki Arcenault? How can I trust my instincts all over again?

A good question, but one I haven't avoided asking myself, for fear of causing more chaos in everybody's life.

And the answer like most other reliable answers is in parts.

I have relinquished a great deal. I've stopped worrying about being completely *within* someone else since you can't be anyway—a pleasant unquestioning mystery has been the result. I've also become less sober-sided and "writerly serious," and worry less about the complexities of things, looking at life in more simple and literal ways. I have also stopped looking around what I feel to something else I might be feeling. With all those eighteen women, I was so bound up creating and resolving a complicated illusion of life that I lost track of what I was up to—that I ought to be having a whale of a good time and forget about everything else.

When you are fully in your emotions, when they are simple and appealing enough to be in, and the distance is closed between what you feel and what you might *also* feel, then your instincts can be trusted. It is the difference between a man who quits his job to become a fishing guide on Lake Big Trout, and who one day as he is paddling his canoe into the dock at dusk, stops paddling to admire the sunset and realizes how much he wants to be a fishing guide on Lake Big Trout; and another man who has made the same decision, stopped paddling at the same time, felt how glad he was, but also thought he could probably be a guide on Windigo Lake if he decided to, and might also get a better deal on canoes.

Another way of describing this is that it's the difference between being a literalist and a factualist. A literalist is a man who will enjoy an afternoon watching people while stranded in an airport in Chicago, while a factualist can't stop wondering why his plane was late out of Salt Lake, and gauging whether they'll still serve dinner or just a snack.

And finally, when I say to Vicki Arcenault, "I love you," I'm not saying anything but the obvious. Who cares if I don't love her forever? Or she me? Nothing persists. I love her now, and I'm not deluding myself or her. What else does truth have to hold?

AT TWELVE-FORTY-FIVE I am awake. Vicki sleeps beside me, breathing lightly with a soft clicking in her throat. In the room there is the dense dimensionless feeling of going to sleep in the dark though waking up still in the dark and wondering about the hours till dawn: how many will there be still? Will I suffer some unexpected despair? How am I likely to pass the time? I am usually —as I've said—such a first-rate sleeper that I'm not bothered by these questions. Though I'm certain part of my trouble is the ordinary thrill of being here, with this woman, free to do anything I please—that familiar old *school's out* we all look and hope for. Tonight would be a good time to take a solo walk in the dark city streets, turn my collar up, get some things thought out. But I have nothing to think out.

I turn on the television with the sound off, something I often do when I'm on the road alone, while I browse a player roster or sharpen up some notes. I love the television in other cities, the assurance of looking up from my chair in some strange room to see a familiar newscaster talking in his familiar Nebraska accents, clad in a familiarly unappealing suit before a featureless civic backdrop (I can never remember the actual news); or to see an anonymous but completely engrossing athletic event acted out in a characterless domed arena, under the same lemony light, to the tune of the same faint zizzing, many miles from anywhere my face would be known. These comprise a comfort I would not like to do without.

On television the station reruns a pro basketball game I am only too happy to watch. Detroit plays Seattle. (Reruns, incidentally, are where you learn a game inside and out. They're far superior to the actual game in the actual place it's played, where things are usually pretty boring and you often forget altogether about what you're there for and find yourself getting interested in other things.)

I go get Vicki's Le Sac bag, open it up and take out one of her Merits, and light it. I have not smoked a cigarette in at least twenty years. Not since I was a freshman in college and attended a fraternity smoker where older boys gave me Chesterfields and I stood against a wall, hands in pockets, and tried to look like the boy everyone would want to ask to join: the silent, slender southern boy with eyes older than his years, something already jaded and over-experienced about him. Just the one we need.

While I'm at it, I push down through the bag. Here is a rosary (predictable). The United inflight magazine (swiped). A card of extra pearlescent buttons (useful). Car keys to the Dart on a big brass ring with a V insignia. An open tube of Velamints. Two movie ticket stubs from a theater where Vicki and I saw part of an old Charlton Heston movie (until I fell asleep). The flight-insurance policy. A paperback copy of a novel, *Love's Last Journey*, by someone named Simone La Noire. And a fat, brown leather wallet with a tooled western-motif of a big horse head on shiny grain.

In it—right up front—is a picture of a man I've never seen before, a swank-looking greaseball character, wearing an open-collared white shirt and a white big-knit shepherd's roll cardigan. The fellow has thick, black eyebrows, a complicated but strict system of dark hair waves, narrow eyeslits and a knifey smile set in the pouting, mocking angle of swarthy self-congratulation. Around his pencil-neck is a gold cross on a chain. It is Everett.

The carpet king from the other Big D is a leering, hip-sprung lounge lizard in a fourth-rate Vegas motel; the kind of fellow who wears his cigarettes under his shirt sleeve, possesses long, skinny arms and steely fingers, and as a policy drinks huge amounts of cheap beer at all hours of the day and night. I would recognize him anywhere. Lonesome Pines was full of such types, from the best possible homes, and all capable of the sorriest depravities. I couldn't be more disappointed to find his picture here. Nor more perplexed. It's possible that he is a superior, good-natured yokel and were we ever to meet (which we won't), we'd cement a sensible common ground from which to express earnestly our different opinions about the world. (Sports, in fact, is the perfect *lingua franca* for such crabwise advances between successive boyfriends and husbands who might otherwise fall into vicious fistfights.)

But in truth I couldn't give a damn about Everett's selling points. And I am of a mind to flush his picture down the commode then stand my ground when the first complaint is offered.

I take a deep, annoyed drag on my cigarette and attempt a difficult French Inhale I once saw practiced in college. But the smoke gets started backwards in my throat and not up my nose, and suddenly I'm seized by a terrifying airlessness and have to suppress a horrible gagging. I make a swift stagger into the bathroom and close the door to keep from waking Vicki with a loud grunt-cough that purples my face.

In the bathroom mirror I resemble a wretched sex-offender— cigarette dangling in my fingers, blue-piped pajamas rumpled, my face gaunt from gasping, the stern light pinching my eyes narrow as Everett's. I am not a pretty sight, and I'm not a bit happy to see myself here. I should have gone out in the streets alone and figured out something to figure out. Certain situations dictate to you how they should be used to advantage. And you should always follow the conventional wisdom in those cases— in fact, in all cases. Always go up on deck to watch the sun come up. Always take a late-night swim after your hosts are in bed. Always take a hike in the woods near your friends' cabin and try to find a new route to the waterfall or an old barn to explore. If nothing else you save yourself giving in to a more personal curiosity and the trouble that always seems to cause. I have gone poking around after full disclosure before my disavowal of it is barely out of my mouth—a disappointing testimony to self-delusion, even more disappointing than finding dagger-head

Everett's picture in Vicki's pocketbook where, after all, it had every right to be and I had none.

When I exit the bathroom Vicki is seated at the dressing table, smoking one of her own Merits, elbow on the chair back, the TV off, looking sultry and alien as a dancehall girl. She is wearing a black crepe de Chine "push up" nightgown and matching toeless mules. I don't like the spiky looks of this (though it's conceivable I might've liked it earlier in the evening) since it looks like something Everett would like, might even have bought himself as a final, fragrant memento. I would not stand for it one minute if I was calling the shots, which I'm not.

"I didn't mean to wake you up," I say balefully and slink to the end of the big granddaddy bed, two feet from her sovereign knees, where I take a seat. Evil has begun to lurk the room, ready to grip with its cold literal claws. My heart begins pounding the way it was when I woke up this morning, and I feel as if my voice may become inaudible.

I am caught. Though I would save the moment, save us from anger and regret and even more disclosure, the enemy of intimacy. I wish I could blurt out a new truth; that I suffer from a secret brain tumor and sometimes do inexplicable things I afterwards can't discuss; or that I'm writing a piece on pro basketball and need to see the end of the Seattle game where Seattle throws up a zone and everything comes down to one shot the way it always does. The saved moment is the true art of love.

Staring, though, at Vicki's sculptured, vaguely padded knees, I now am clearly lost and feel the ultimate slipping away again, bereavement threatening like thunder to roll in and take its place.

"So what is it you were lookin for in my bag?" she says. Hers is a frown of focused disdain. I am the least favorite student caught looking for the gradebook in the teacher's desk. She is the friendly substitute there for one day only (though we all wish she were the regular one) but who knows a sneak when she sees him.

"I wasn't looking for anything, really. I wasn't looking." I *was* looking, of course. And this is the wrong lie, though a lie is absolutely what's needed. My first tiny skirmish with the facts goes into the debit column. My voice falls ten full decibels. This has happened before.

"I don't keep secrets," she says now in a flat voice. "I suppose you do though."

"Sometimes I do." I lose nothing admitting that.

"And you lie about things, too."

"Only if it's completely necessary. Otherwise never." (It is better than confiding.)

"And like lovin me, too, I guess?"

A sweet girl's heart only speaks truths. Evil suddenly takes an unexpected rebuke. "You're wrong there," I say, and nothing could be truer.

"Humph," she says. Her brow gathers over small prosecutorial eyes. "And I'm s'pose to believe that now, right? With you rammaging around my things and smokin cigarettes and me dreaming away?"

"You don't have to believe it for it to be true." I put my elbows on my knees, honest-injun style.

"I hate a snake," she says, looking coldly around at the ashtray beside her as if a dead snake were coiled right there. "I just swear I do. I stay way clear of 'em. Cause I seen plenty. Right? They're not hard to recognize, either." She cuts her eyes away at the door to the hall and sniffs a little mirthless laugh. "That was just a lie on me, wadn't it?"

"The only way you'll find that out, I guess, is just to stay put." Out in the chilly streets I hear a police siren wail down the wide, dark avenue and drawl off into the traffic. Some poor soul is having it worse than I am.

"So what about getting married?" she says archly.

"That, too."

She smirks her mouth into a look of disillusionment and shakes her head. She stubs out her cigarette carefully in the ashtray. She has seen this all before. Motel rooms. Two a.m. Strange sights. The sounds of strange cities and sirens. Lying boys out for the fun and a short trip home. Empty moments. The least of us has seen a hundred. It is no wonder mystery and its frail muted beauties have such a son-of-a-bitching hard time of it. They're way out-numbered and ill-equipped in the best of times.

"Well-o-well," she says and shrugs, hands down between her knees in a fated way.

But still, something has been won back, some aspirant tragedy averted. I am not even sure what it is, since evil still floods the room up to the cornices. The Lebanese woman I knew at Berk-shire College would never have let this happen, no matter what

I had done to provoke it, since she was steeled for such things by a life of Muslim disinterest. X wouldn't either, though for other, even better reasons (she expected more). Vicki is hopeful, but not of much, and so is never far from disappointment.

Still, the worst reconciliation with a woman is better than the best one you work out with yourself.

"There's nothing in this bag worth stealin, or even finding out about," Vicki says wearily, everting her lips at her weekender as if it were a wreckage that has washed ashore after years of not being missed. "Money," she says languidly, "I keep hid in a special place. That's one secret I keep. You won't get that."

I want to hug her knees, though this is clearly hands-to-yourself time. The slightest wrong move will see me on the phone locating another room on another floor, possibly in the Sheraton, four cold and lonely blocks away, and no coat to keep out the slick Canadian damp.

Vicki peers over at the glass desktop, at her wallet open alongside her cigarettes. The snapshot of brain-dead Everett leers upwards (it may in fact be hard to tell my somber, earnest face from his).

"I really believe there's only six people in the world," she says in a softened voice, staring down at Everett's mug. "I'd been thinking you might be one. An important one. But I think you had too many girlfriends already. Maybe you're somebody else's one."

"You might be wrong. I could still make the line-up."

She looks at me distrustfully. "Eyes are important to me, okay? They're windows to your soul. And your eyes . . . I used to think I could see your soul back in there. But now. . . ." She shakes her head in doubt.

"What do you see?" I don't want to hear the answer. It is a question I would never even ask Mrs. Miller, and one she'd never take it upon herself to speculate about. We do not, after all, deal in truths, only potentialities. Too much truth can be worse than death, and last longer.

"I don't know," Vicki says, in a thin wispy way, which means I had better not pursue it or she'll decide. "What're you so interested in my stepbrother for?" She looks at me oddly.

"I don't know your stepbrother," I say.

She picks up the wallet and holds the snapshot up so I am

looking directly into the swarthy smart-aleck's face. "Him," she says. "This poor old thing, here."

So much of life can't be foreseen. A hundred private explanations and exculpations come rushing up into my throat, and I have to swallow hard to hold them back. Though, of course, there is nothing to say. Like all needless excuses, the unraveling is not worth the time. However, I feel a swirling dreaminess, an old familiar bemusement, suddenly rise into my appreciation of everything around me. Irony is returned. I have a feeling that if I tried to speak now, my mouth would move, but no sound would occur. And it would scare us both to death. Why, in God's name, isn't it possible to let ignorance stay ignorance?

"That poor boy's already dead and gone to heaven," Vicki says. She turns the picture toward her and looks at it appraisingly. "He got killed at Fort Sill, Oklahoma. A Army truck hit him. He's my Daddy's wife's son. Was. Bernard Twill. Beany Twill." She pops the wallet closed and puts it on the table. "I didn't even really know him. Lynette just gave me his picture for my wallet when he died. I don't know how come I kept it." She looks at me in a sweet way. "I'm not stayin mad. It's just an old purse with nothin in it. Women're strange on their purses."

"I'm going to get back in bed," I say in a voice that is hardly a whisper.

"Long as you're happy, to hell with the rest. That's a good motto, isn't it?"

"Sure. It's great," I say, crawling into the big cold bed. "I'm sorry about all this."

She smiles and sits looking at me as I pull the sheet up around my chin and begin to think that it is not a hard life to imagine, not at all, mine and Vicki Arcenault's. In fact, I would like it as well as it's possible to like any life: a life of small flourishes and clean napkins. A life where sex plays an ever-important nightly role—better than with any of the eighteen or so women I knew before and "loved." A life appreciative of history and its generations. A life of possible fidelity, of going fishing with some best friend, of having a little Sheila or a little Matthew of our own, of buying a fifth-wheel travel trailer—a cruising brute—and from its tiny portholes seeing the country. Paul and Clarissa could come along and join our gang. I could sell my house and move not to Pheasant Run but to an old Quakerstone in Bucks County.

Possibly when our work is done, a tour in the Peace Corps or Vista—of "doing something with our lives." I wouldn't need to sleep in my clothes or wake up on the floor. I could forget about being *in* my emotions and not be bothered by such things.

In short, a natural extension of almost all my current attitudes taken out beyond what I now know.

And what's wrong with that? Isn't it what we all want? To look out toward the horizon and see a bright, softened future awaiting us? An attractive retirement?

Vicki turns on the television and takes up a rapt stare at its flicking luminance. It's ice skating at 2 a.m. (basketball's a memory). Austria, by the looks of it. Cinzano and Rolex decorate the boards. Tai and Randy are skating under steely control. He is Mr. Elegance—flying camels, double Salchows, perfect splits and lofts. She is all in the world a man could want, vulnerable yet fiery, lithe as a swan, in this their once-in-a-lifetime, everything-right for a flawless 10. Together they perform a perfect double axel, two soaring triple toe loops, a spinning Lutz jump, then come to rest with Tai in a death spiral on the white ice, Randy her goodly knight. And the Austrians cannot control it one more second. These two are as good as the Protopopovs, and they're Americans. Who cares if they missed the Olympics? Who cares if rumors are true that they despise each other? Who cares if Tai is not so beautiful up close (who is, *ever*)? She is still exotic as a Berber with regal thighs and thunderous breasts. And what's important is they have given it their everything, as they always do, and every Austrian wishes he could be an American for just one minute and can't resist feeling right with the world.

"Oh, don't you just love them two?" Vicki says, sitting cross-legged on her chair, smoking a cigarette and peering into the brightly lit screen as though staring into a colorful dream-life.

"It's pretty wonderful," I say.

"Sometimes I want to be her *so* much," she says, blowing smoke out the corner of her mouth. "Really. Ole Randy. . . ."

I turn and close my eyes and try to sleep as the applause goes on, and outside in the cold Detroit streets more sirens follow the first one into the night. And for a moment I find it is really quite easy and agreeable not to know what's next, as if the sirens were going out into this night for no one but me.

SNOW. By the time I leave my bed, a blanket of the gently falling white stuff has covered the concrete river banks from Cobo to the Ren-Cen, the river sliding by brackish and coffee-colored under a quilted Michigan sky. So much for a game under the lights. Spring has suddenly disappeared and winter stepped in. I am certain by tomorrow the same weather will have reached New Jersey (we are a day behind the midwest in weather matters), though by then, here will have thawed and grown mild again. If you don't like the weather, wait ten minutes.

Vicki is still deep asleep in her black crepe de Chine, and though I would like to wake her and have a good heart-to-heart, last night feels otherwordly, and optimism about "us two" is what's in need of emphasizing. A talk can always wait till later.

I shower and dress in a hurry, pockets loaded with note pads and a small recorder, and head off to breakfast and my trip to Walled Lake. I leave a note on the bed table saying I'll be back by noon, and she should watch a movie on HBO and have a big breakfast sent up.

The Pontchartrain lobby has a nice languorous-sensuous Saturday feel despite the new snow, which the bellhops all agree is "freakish" and can't last past noon, though a number of guests are lining up to check out for the airport. The black newsstand girl sells me a *Free Press* with a big smile and a yawn. "I'm bout shoulda stayed in bed," she laughs in a put-on accent. On the rack there is an issue of my magazine with a story I wrote about the surge in synchronized swimming in Mexico—all the digging work was done by staff. I'm tempted to make some mention of it just in passing, but I wander off to breakfast instead.

In the La Mediterranée Room I order two poached, dry toast and juice, and ask the waiter to hurry, while I check on the early leaders in the AL East—who's been sent down, who's up for a cup of coffee. The *Free Press* sports section has always been my favorite. Photographs galore. A crisp wide-eyed layout with big, readable coldtype print and a hometown writing style anyone could feel at home with. There is a place for literature, but a bigger one for sentences that are meant to be read, not mused over: "Former Brother Rice standout, Phil Staransky, who picked up a couple timely hits in Wednesday's twi-nighter, on the way to going three-for-four, already has plenty of experts around Michigan and Trumbull betting he'll see more time at third before the club starts its first swing west. Pitching Coach Eddie Gonzalez says there's no doubt the Hamtramck native 'figures in the big club's plans, especially,' Gonzalez notes, 'since the young man left off trying to pull everything and began swinging with his head.'" When I was in college I had a pledge bring it right to my bed every morning, and was even a mail subscriber when we first moved to Haddam. From time to time I think of quitting the magazine and coming back out to do a column. Though I'm sure it's too late for that now. (The local sports boys never take kindly to the national magazine writers because we make more money. And in fact, I've been given haywire information from a few old beat writers, which, if I'd used it, would've made me look stupid in print.)

It has the feeling of an odd morning, despite the friendly anonymity of the hotel. A distinct buzzing has begun in the pit of my stomach, a feeling that is not unpleasant but insistent. Several people I saw in the lobby have reminded me of other people I know, an indicator that something exceptional's afoot. A man in the checkout line reminded me of—of all people—Walter Luckett. Even the black shop girl put me in mind of Peggy Connover, the woman I used to write in Kansas and whose letters caused X to leave me. Peggy, in fact, was Swedish and would laugh to think she looked a bit Negroid. Like all signs, these can be good or bad, and I choose to infer from them that life, anyone's life, is not as disconnected and random as it might feel, and that down deep we're all reaching out for a decent rewarding contact every chance we get.

Last night, after Vicki went to sleep, I experienced the strangest dream, a dream I've never had before and one I would rather not have again. I am not much of a dreamer to begin with, and almost never remember them past the moment just before my eyes open. When I do, I can usually ascribe everything to something I've eaten in the afternoon, or to a book I'd been reading. And for the most part there's never much that's familiar in them anyway.

But in this dream I was confronted by someone I knew—a man —but had forgotten—though not completely, because there were flashes of recollection I couldn't quite organize into a firm picture-memory. This man mentions to me—so obliquely that now I can't even remember what he said—something shameful about me, clearly shameful, and it scares me that he might know more and that I've forgotten it, but shouldn't have. The effect of all this was to shock me roundly, though not to wake me up. When I did wake up at eight, I remembered the entire dream clear as a bell, though I could not fill in names or faces or the shame I might've incurred.

Besides not being a good collector of my dreams, I am not much a believer in them either or their supposed significance. Everyone I've ever talked to about dreams—and Mrs. Miller, I'm happy to say, feels exactly as I do, and will not listen to anyone's dreams—everyone always interprets their dreams to mean something unpleasant, some lurid intention or ungenerous, guilty desire crammed back into the subconscious cave where its only chance is to cause trouble at a later time.

Whereas what *I* am a proponent of is forgetting. Forgetting dreams, grievances, old flaws in character—mine and others'. To me there is no hope unless we can forget what's said and gone before, and forgive it.

Which is exactly why this particular dream is bothersome. It is *about* forgetting, and yet there seems to be a distinct thread of unforgiving in it, which is the source of the shock I felt even deep in sleep, in an old town where I feel as comfortable as a Cossack in Kiev, and where I want nothing more than that the present be happy and for the future—as it always does—to look after itself. I would prefer to think of all signs as good signs, or else to pay no attention to them at all. There are enough bad signs all around (read the *New York Times*) not to pick out any particular one for attention. In the case of my dream, I can't even think of what I ought to be anxious about, since I am eager— even ascendant. And if it is that I'm anxious in the old mossy existential sense, it will have to stay news to me.

It is, of course, an irony of ironies that X should've left me because of Peggy Connover's letters, since Peggy and I had never committed the least indiscretion.

She was a woman I met on a plane from Kansas City to Minneapolis, and whom in the space of an afternoon, a dinner, and an evening, I came to know as much about as you could know in that length of time. She was thirty-two and not at all an appealing woman. She was plump with large, white teeth and a perfectly pie-shaped face. She was leaving her family with four children, back in the town of Blanding, Kansas, where her husband sold insulation, to go live with her sister in northern Minnesota and become a poet. She was a good-natured woman, with a nice dimpled smile, and on the plane she began to tell me about her life—how she had gone to Antioch, studied history, played field hockey, marched in peace marches, written poems. She told me about her parents who were Swedish immigrants—a fact that had always embarrassed her; that she dreamed sometimes of huge trucks going over cliffs and woke up terrified; about writing poems that she showed to her husband, Van, then hearing him laugh at them, though he later told her he was proud of her. She told me she had been a sexpot in college, and had married Van, who was from Miami of Ohio, because she loved him, but that they weren't on the same level educationally, which hadn't mattered then, but did now, which was why she felt she was leaving him.

When we got off the plane she asked me, standing in the concourse, where I was staying, and when I told her the Ramada, she said she could just as easily stay there and that maybe we could have dinner together because she liked talking to me. And since I had nothing else to do, I said okay.

In the next five hours we had a buffet dinner, then after that went down to my room to drink a bottle of German wine she had bought for her sister, and she talked some more, with me just adding a word here and there. She told me about her break with Lutheranism, about her philosophy of child-rearing, about her theories of Abstract Expressionism, the global village, and a Great Books course she'd built up to teach somewhere if the chance ever came along.

At eleven-fifteen, she stopped talking, looked down at her pudgy hands and smiled. "Frank," she said, "I just want to tell you that I've been thinking about sleeping with you this whole time. But I don't really think I should." She shook her head. "I know we're supposed to do what our senses dictate, and I'm very attracted to you, but I just don't think it would be right, do you?"

Her face looked troubled by this, but when she looked at me a big hopeful smile came on her lips. And what I felt for her then was a great and comprehending nostalgia, because for some reason I thought I knew just exactly how she felt, alone and at the world's mercy, the same way I'd felt when I'd been in the Marines, suffering from an unknown disease with no one but unfriendly nurses and doctors to check on me, and I had had to think about dying when I didn't want to. And what it made me feel about Peggy Connover was that I wanted to make love to her—more, in fact, than I'd wanted to do that in a long time. It's possible, let me tell you, to become suddenly attracted to a woman you don't really find attractive; a woman you'd never want to take to dinner, or pick up at a cocktail party, or look twice at in an elevator, only just suddenly it happens, which was the case with Peggy.

Though what I said was, "No, Peggy, I don't think it would be right. I think it'd cause a lot of trouble." I don't know why I said this or said it in this way, since it wasn't what *my* senses were dictating.

Peggy's face lit up with pleasure, and also, I think, surprise. (This is always the most vulnerable time in such encounters. At the very moment you absolve yourself of any intention to do wrong, you often roll right into each other's arms. Though we didn't.) What happened was that Peggy came over to the bed where I was sitting, sat beside me, took my hand and squeezed it, gave me a big damp kiss on the cheek and sat smiling at me as if I were a man like no other. She told me how lucky she felt to meet me and not some "other type," since she was vulnerable that night, she said, and probably "fair game." We talked for a while about how she was probably going to feel in the morning after having drunk all that wine, and that we would probably want a lot of coffee. Then she said that if it was all right she'd like to find something I'd written and read it and write me about it. And I said I'd like that. Then as if by some secret signal she came around the bed, pulled back the covers, climbed in beside me and went immediately to snoring sleep. I slept beside her the rest of the night fully clothed, on top of the covers, and never touched her once. And in the morning I left before she woke up, to go interview a football coach, and never saw her again.

After about a month, a fat letter—the first of several from Peggy Connover—arrived at the house, full of talk about her kids, humorous remarks about her welfare, her weight, her ailments, about Van, whom she'd decided to go back to live with, what plans she was making for their life; but also about stories of mine she'd read in the magazine and had comments on (she liked some but not every one), all of it in the same chatty voice as when we'd talked, closing each time with "Well, Frank, hope to see you again real soon. Love, Peg." All of which I was happy to hear about, and even answer a time or two, since it pleased me that, as we had never been more than friends, we could still be, with everything hunky-dory. And it pleased me that somewhere out in the remote world someone was thinking of me for no bad reason at all, and even wishing me well.

These, of course, were the letters X found in the drawer of my desk when she was looking for the sack of silver dollars she feared might've been stolen. And it was these letters that in some way made our life seem to break apart for her, and made continuing somehow seem impossible (I found it likewise impossible to explain anything then, since much else was wrong already). X believed, I think, when she read Peggy Connover's letters, that if these chatty, normal over-the-fence-sounding sentiments were hidden there in my drawer (they weren't hidden, of course), in all probability more letters full of similar good sense and breezy humor were going out (she was right). And that there was none of that around the house for her. And she began to think, then, that love was simply a transferable commodity for me—which may even be true—and she didn't like that. And what she suddenly concluded was that she didn't want to, or have to, be married to someone like me a second longer—which is exactly how it happened.

OUTSIDE, IT IS no longer snowing, but the streets impress me as too icy to risk a rental car. Our time in town feels already much too short, and in bad weather even the idea of the botanical garden begins to sink into the unlikely zone—though for Vicki, my guess is, it will make no difference.

I'm sorry, however, to miss a renter. There is nothing quite like the first moments inside a big, strapping fleet-clean LTD or Montego—mileage checked, tank full, seat adjusted, the heavy door closed tight, the stirring "new" smell in your nostrils—the confidence that here is a car better even than the one you own (and even better than that, since you have only to ask for another one if this one craps out). To me, there is no feeling of freedom-within-sensible-limits quite like that. New today. New tomorrow. Eternal renewal on a manageable scale.

I walk down to the snowy cab queue at Larned Street, but as I reach the icy corner I am stopped short and for a moment by a sound. On the chill Saturday morning airs, a faint *hsss* murmurs up the city streets from the sewers and alleyways, as if a cold wind was thrashing ditch grass somewhere nearby and, out here near the river, on the edge of things, I was in danger. Of what I have no idea. Though what I know, of course, is that I am running a tricky race now with my spirits, trusting my enthusiasm will out-strip the perils of usual, midwestern literalness which can gang up against you quick and do you in like a doomed prisoner.

My cab driver is a giant Negro named Lorenzo Smallwood, who reminds me of the actor Sydney Greenstreet, and who drives with both arms straight out in front of him. On the dash-board he has an assortment of small framed pictures of babies, two pairs of baby shoes and a mat of white fringe, though he is not much for talking, and we get quickly out into the snowy traffic, weaving around dingy warehouse blocks and old hotels to Grand River, then head for the northwest suburbs. It is faster today, Mr. Smallwood says with humming uninterest, to stay on the "real streets," and avoid "the Lodge," where it's already wall-to-wall assholes heading for their cabins up north.

Strathmore, Brightmoor, Redford, Livonia, another Miracle Mile. We speed through the little connected burgs and townlets beyond the interior city, along white-frame dormered-Cape streets, into solider red-brick Jewish sections until we emerge onto a wide boulevard with shopping malls and thick clusters of traffic lights, the houses newer and settled in squared-off tracts. Outside everyone is "dressed for it," a point of traditional pride among Michiganders. A freak spring snowstorm means nothing.

Everyone still has "snows" on his Plymouth, and a winter face of workmanlike weather how-to. Michigan is a place where every man is handy with a jumper cable, a metal lathe and a snow blower. The mechanical nuts-and-bolts of anything is never a problem here. It's what's reliable and appealing in such an otherwise gray and unprepossessing panorama.

Far out crowded Grand River I am struck by what seems like thousands of restaurants, and by how dedicated the population is to going out to eat. As much as cars, meals are what's on people's minds. Though there is a small and heart-swelling glory to these places—chop houses, hofbraus, rathskellers, rib joints, cafés of all good quality. Part of life's essence is here. And on a brooding spring eve, a fast foray out to any one of them can be just enough to make any out-of-the-way loneliness bearable another night-time through. In most ways, I can promise you, Michigan knows exactly what it's doing. It knows the enemy and the odds.

Mr. Smallwood pulls into a white enamel drive-in called The Squatter, and asks if I want a sinker. I am full to the gills from breakfast, but while he is inside I step out and give a call back to the Pontchartrain. I have briefly won back some enthusiasm for the day—the buzzing in my stomach having subsided—and I want to share it all with Vicki, since there is no telling what new world and circumstances she has waked to, given the night's shenanigans and the strange, whitened landscape confronting her in the daylight.

"I was just layin here watching the television," she says in a bright voice. "Just like you said for me to do in your cute note. I already ordered up a Virgin Mary and a honey pull-apart. There's nothing on TV yet, though. A movie's next, supposedly."

"I'm sorry about last night," I say softly, my voice taking a sudden decibel dive, so that I can barely make it out myself in the traffic noise on Grand River.

"What happened last night, lessee?" I can hear the TV and the sound of ice cubes in her Virgin Mary tinking against the glass. It is a reassuring sound, and I wish I could be there to snuggle up under the warm covers with her and wait for the movie.

"I wasn't at my best, but I'll do better," I say almost soundlessly. I smell warm hash browns, a waffle, an order of French toast humming out of The Squatter's exhaust fan, and I am suddenly starving.

"This hotel's a good place to spend your money," she says, ignoring me completely.

"Well then, go spend some."

"I'm watching something real cerebral right now," she says, distracted. "It's about how the government takes back fifteen tons of old money every week. Mostly just ones. That's the work-horse bill. A hundred-dollar bill lasts for years, though it dudn't in my pocket, I'll tell you that. They *are* trying to figure out how to make shingles out of them. But right now all they can make is note pads."

"Are you having a swell time?"

"So far." She laughs a happy girlish laugh. I see Mr. Small-wood come rolling out the front of The Squatter, a small white paper bag in one huge hand and a sinker half in his mouth. The snow has already begun to melt to slush in the curb gutters.

"I love you, okay," I say, and suddenly feel terribly feeble. My heart pounds down on itself like an anvil, and I have that old ague-sense that my next breath will bring down a curtain of bright red over my eyes, and I will slump to the phone booth glass and cease altogether. "I love you," I hear myself murmur again.

"It's okay with me. But you're a nut, I'll tell you that." She is gay now. "A real Brazil nut. But I like you. Is that all you called up here to say?"

"You just wait'll I get back," I say, "I'll. . . ." But for some reason I do not finish the sentence.

"Do you miss your wife?" she says as gay as can be.

"Are you crazy?" It is clear she has not gotten my point.

"Oh boy. You're some kind of something," she says. I hear silverware clink against plates, the sound of the receiver getting far away from her. "Now you hurry back and let me go and watch this." Clickety-click.

TEN MINUTES later we are into the rolling landscape of snowy farmettes and wide cottage-bound lakes beyond the perimeter of true Detroit suburbia, the white-flight areas stretching clear to Lansing. It is here that Mr. Smallwood suggests we turn off the meter and arrange a flat rate, which, when I agree, starts him whistling and suggesting he could hang around till I'm ready to go back. He has friends, he says, in nearby Wixom, and we agree that I'll be ready to roll by noon. I remember, briefly, a boy I knew in college from Wixom, Eddy Loukinen, and I enjoy a fond wonder as to where Eddy might be—running a car dealership in his hometown, or down in Royal Oak with his own construction firm. Possibly an insulated window frame outlet in the UP—trading cars every year, checking his market shares, quitting smoking, flying to the islands, slipping around on his wife. These were the futures we all had looking at us in 1967. Good choices. We were not all radicals and wild-eyes. And most of my bunch would tell you they're glad to have a good thirty years left to see what surprises life brings. The possibility of a happy ending. It is not unique to me.

It takes two gas station stops to find Herb's. Both owners claim to know him and to work on his cars exclusively. And both give me a suspicious, bill-collector look, as if I might be looking for big Herb to do him harm or steal his fame. And in each instance Mr. Smallwood and I drive off feeling that phone calls are being made, a protective community rising to a misconstrued threat against its fallen hero. All of which makes me realize just how often I am with people I don't know and who don't know me, and who come to know me—Frank Bascombe—only as a sportswriter. It is possibly not the best way to go into the world, as I explained to Walter two nights ago; with no confidants, with no real allies except ex-allies; no lovers except a Vicki Arcenault or her ilk. Though maybe this is the best for me, given my character and past, which at most are inconclusive. I could have things much worse. At least as a stranger to almost everyone and a sportswriter to boot, I have a clean slate almost every day of my life, a chance not to be negative, to give someone unknown a pat on the back, to recognize courage and improvement, to take the battle with cynicism head-on and win.

Out front of Herb's house, I'm greeted from around the side by a loud "Hey now!" before I can even see who's talking. Mr. Smallwood stares out his closed cab window. He has heard of Herb, he's said, though he has the story of Herb's life wrong and thinks Herb is a Negro. In any case he wants to see him before he cuts out for Wixom.

Herb's house is on curvy little Glacier Way, a hundred yards from Walled Lake itself and not far from the amusement park that operates summers only. I came here long ago, when I was in college, to a dense, festering old barrely dancehall called the Walled Lake Casino. It was at the time when line dances were popular in Michigan, and my two friends and I drove over from Ann Arbor with the thought of picking up some women, though of course we knew no one for forty miles and ended up standing against the firred, scarred old walls being wry and sarcastic about everyone and drinking Cokes spiked with whiskey. Since then, Mr. Smallwood has informed me, the Casino has burned down.

Herb's house is like the other houses around it—a little white Cape showing a lot of dormered roof and with a small picture window on one side of the front door. The kind of house a tool-and-dye maker would own—a sober Fifties structure with a small yard, a two-car garage in back and a van in the drive with HERB'S on its blue Michigan plates.

Herb wheels into view from around the corner of the house, making tire tracks in the melting snow. The moment he is visible, Mr. Smallwood puts his cab in gear and goes whooshing off down the street and around the corner, leaving me alone in the front yard with Herb Wallagher, stranded like a prowler.

"I thought you'd be bigger," Herb shouts with a big gap-toothed grin. He shoots a great hand out at me, and when I embrace it he nearly hauls me down to the ground.

"I thought *you'd* be smaller, Herb," I say, though this is a lie. He is much smaller than I thought. His legs have shrunk and his shoulders are bony. Only his head and arms are good-sized, giving him a gaping, storkish appearance behind his thick horn-rims. He has twice cut himself shaving and doctored it with toilet paper, and is wearing a T-shirt that says BIONIC on the front, and a pair of glen-plaid Bermudas below which a brand new pair of red tennis shoes peek out. It is hard to think of Herb as an athlete.

"I like to be outside on a day like this, Frank. It's a wonderful day, isn't it?" Herb looks all around at the sky like a caged man, making his head go loose on its stem.

"It's a great day, Herb." We both, for the moment, affect the corny accents of Kansas hay farmers, though Herb is dead wrong about the weather. It looks like it may snow again and go nasty before the morning is over.

"Every year it got to be spring, ya know, I'd start thinking about motorcycles or some kind of hot car to buy. I had four or five cars and two or three bikes." Herb sits looking away toward a spot above the coping of the house across the street, a house exactly like his except for the pale-blue roof. Beyond it several streets away Walled Lake shines through the yard gaps like metal. I am sorry to hear Herb referring to his life in the past tense. It is not an optimistic sign. "Well, Frank, how do you wanna get this over with," Herb almost shouts at me in his put-on Kansas brogue. He smiles another big fierce smile, then pops both his hands on the black, plastic armrests of his chair as though he'd like nothing better than to spring up and strangle me. "You wanna go in the house or walk to the lake or what? It's your choice."

"Let's try the lake, Herb," I say. "I used to come over here when I was in college. I'd be happy to see it again."

"Clarice!" Herb bellows, frowning up toward the little front door, squirming in his chair and muling it to face the way he wants. He is not interested in my past, though that's no crime since I am not much interested myself. "Clar-eeeece!"

The door opens behind the storm-glass and a slender, pretty black woman with extremely short hair and wearing jeans steps half out onto the step. She gives me a watery half-smile. "Clarice, this is old Frank Bascombe. He's gonna try to make a monkey outa me, but I'm going to kick his keister for him. We're going to the lake. You better bring us a coupla bathing suits, cause we might take a swim." Herb grins back at me in mockery.

"I'm keeping my distance from him, Mrs. Wallagher." I give her a friendly smile to match the frail one she has given me.

"Herb'll talk too much to swim," Clarice says, shaking her head patiently at Herb the perennial bad boy.

"Okay, okay, don't let's get her started," Herb growls, then grins. It is their little burlesque, though it's an odd thing to see in people of two different races, and so young. Herb couldn't be thirty-four yet, though he looks fifty. And Clarice has entered that long, pale, uncertain middle existence in which years behind you is not a faithful measure of life. Possibly she is thirty, but she is Herb's wife, and that fact has made everything else—race, age, hopes—fade. They are like retirees, and neither has gotten what he or she bargained for.

When I look around, Herb has wheeled himself down the walk and is already out in the street. I offer his pretty little wife a little wave which she answers with a wave, and I go off hauling up the rear after Herb.

"Okay now, Frank, what's this bunch of lies supposed be about," Herb says gruffly as we whirl along. There is one more street of lined Capes—some with campers and boat trailers out front—then a wider artery road that leads back to the expressway, and beyond that is the lake, lined with small cottages owned mostly, I'm sure, by people from the city—policemen, successful car salesmen, retired teachers. All are closed and shuttered for the winter. It is not a particularly nice place, a shabby summer community of unattractive bungalows. Not the neighborhood I'd expected for an ex-all-pro.

"I've got my mind on an update on Herb Wallagher, Herb. How he's doing, what're his plans, how life's treating him. Maybe a little inspirational business on the subject of character for people with their own worries. Maybe a touch of optimism in the soup."

"All *right*," Herb says. "Super. Super."

"I know readers would be interested in hearing about your job as spirit coach. Guys you played with taking their cue from you on going the extra half-mile. That kind of thing."

"I'm not going to be doing that anymore, Frank," Herb says grimly, pushing harder on his wheels. "I'm planning to retire."

"Why so, Herb?" (Not the best news for starters.)

"I just wasn't getting the job done down there, Frank. Too much bullshit involved."

An uneasy silence descends as we cross the road to Walled Lake. Most of the snow has melted here and only a gray crust remains on the shoulder where passersby have tossed their refuse. A hundred years ago, this country would've been wooded and the lake splendid and beautiful. A perfect place for a picnic. But now it has all been ruined by houses and cars.

Herb coasts on down the concrete boat ramp in between two boarded-up and fenced-in cottages, and wheels furiously up onto the plank dock. Across Walled Lake is the expressway, and up the lakeside beyond the cottages a roller coaster track curves above the tree line. The Casino must've been nearby, though I see no sign of it.

"It's funny," Herb says, where he can see the lake from an elevation. "When I first saw you, you had a halo around your head. A big gold halo. Do you ever notice that, Frank?" Herb whips his big head around and grins at me, then looks back at the empty lake.

"I never have, Herb." I take a seat on the pipe banister that runs the length of the dock at the end of which two aluminum boats ride in the shallow water.

"No?" Herb says. "Well." He pauses a moment in a reverie. "I'm glad you came, Frank," he says, but does not look at me.

"I'm glad to be here, Herb."

"I get mad sometimes, Frank, you know? God *damn* it. I just get boiling." Herb suddenly whacks both his big open hands on the black armrests, and shakes his head.

"What makes you mad, Herb?" I have not taken a note yet, of course, nor have I touched my recorder, something I will need to do since I have a terrible memory. I am always too involved with things to pay strict attention. Though I feel like the interview has yet to get started. Herb and I are still getting to know each other on a personal level, and I've found you can rush an interview and come away with such a distorted sense of a person that he couldn't recognize himself in print—the first sign of a badly written story.

"Do you have theories about art, Frank?" Herb says, setting his jaw firmly in one fist. "I mean do you, uh, have any fully developed concepts of, say, how what the artist sees relates to what is finally put on the canvas?"

"I guess not," I say. "I like Winslow Homer a lot."

"All right. He's a good one. He's plenty good," Herb says, and smiles a helpless smile up at me.

"He'd paint Walled Lake here, and it'd feel and look pretty much like this, I think."

"Maybe he would." Herb looks away at the lake.

"How long did you play pro ball, Herb?"

"Eleven years," Herb says moodily. "One in Canada. One in Chicago. Then they traded me over here. And I stayed. You know I've been reading Ulysses Grant, Frank." He nods profoundly. "When Grant was dying, you know, he said, 'I think I am a verb instead of a personal pronoun. A verb signifies to be; to do; to suffer. I signify all three.'" Herb takes off his glasses and holds them in his big linesman's fingers, examining their frames. His eyes are red. "That has some truth to it, Frank. But what the hell do you think he meant by that? A verb?" Herb looks up at me with a face full of worry. "I've been worried about that for weeks."

"I couldn't begin to say, Herb. Maybe he was taking stock. Sometimes we think things are more important than they are."

"That doesn't sound good, though, does it?" Herb looks back at his glasses.

"It's hard to say."

"Your halo's gone now, Frank. You know it? You've become like the rest of the people."

"That's okay, isn't it? I don't mind." It's pretty clear to me that Herb suffers from some damned serious mood swings and in all probability has missed out on a stabilizing pill. Possibly this is his gesture of straight-talk and soul-baring, but I don't think it will make for a very good interview. Interviews always go better when athletes feel fairly certain about the world and are ready to comment on it.

"I'll just tell you what I think it means," Herb says, narrowing his weakened eyes. "I think he thought he'd just become an act. You understand that, Frank? And that act was dying."

"I see."

"And that's terrible to see things that way. Not to *be* but just to do."

"Well, that was just how Grant saw things, Herb. He had some other wrong ideas, too. Plenty of them."

"This is goddamn real life here, Frank. Get serious!" Herb's face struggles with the fiercest intensity, then just as promptly goes blank. "I was just reading the other day that Americans always feel like the real life is somewhere else. Down the road, around the bend. But this is it right here." Herb cracks his palms on his armrests again. "You know what I'm getting at Frank?"

"I think so, Herb. I'm trying."

"God damn it!" Herb breathes a savage sigh. "You haven't even taken any notes yet."

"I keep it up here, Herb," I say and give my head a poke.

Herb stares up at me darkly. "You know what it's like to lose the use of your legs, Frank?"

"No I don't, Herb. I guess that's pretty obvious."

"Have you ever had someone close to you die?"

"Yes." I could actually see myself getting angry at Herb before this is over.

"Okay," Herb says. "Your legs go silent, Frank. I can't hear mine anymore." Herb smiles a wild smile at me meant to indicate there might be a hell of a lot more I don't know about the world. People, of course, are always getting you all wrong. Because you come to interview them, they automatically think you're just using them to confirm the store of what's already known in the world. But where I'm concerned, that couldn't be wronger. It's true I have expected a different Herb Wallagher from the Herb Wallagher I've found, a stouter, chin-out, better tempered kind of guy, a guy who'd pick up the back of a compact car to help you out of a jam if he could. And what I found is someone who seems as dreamy as a barn owl. But the lesson is not new to me. You can't go into these things thinking you know what can't be known. That ought to be rule one in every journalism class and textbook; too much of life, even the life you think you should know, the life of athletes, can't be foreseen.

There is major silence now that Herb has told me what it's like not to have his legs to use. It is not an empty moment, not for me anyway, and I am not discouraged. I would still like to think there's the possibility for a story here. Maybe by going off his medicine Herb will finally come back to his senses with some unexpected and interesting ideas to bring up and end up talking a blue streak. That happens every day.

"Do you ever miss playing football, Herb?" I say, and smile hopefully.

"What?" Herb is drawn back from a muse the glassy lake has momentarily fostered. He looks at me as though he had never seen me before. I hear trucks pounding the interstate corridor to Lansing. The wind has wandered back now and a chill picks up off the black water.

"Do you ever miss athletics?"

Herb stares at me reproachfully. "You're an asshole, Frank, you know that?"

"Why do you say that?"

"You don't know me."

"That's what I'm *doing* here, Herb. I'd *like* to get to know you and write a damn good story about you. Paint you as you are. Because I think that's pretty interesting and complex in itself."

"You're just an asshole, Frank, yep, and you're not going to get any inspiration out of me. I dropped all that. I don't have to do for anybody, and that means you. Especially you, you asshole. I don't play ball anymore." Herb plucks a piece of the toilet paper off his cheek and peers at it for blood.

"I'm ready to give up on inspiration, Herb. It was just a place to start."

"Do you want to hear the dream I have over and over?" Herb rolls the paper between his fingers, then pushes himself out toward the end of the dock. I sit on the pipe banister, looking at his back. Herb's bony shoulders are like wings, his neck thin and rucked, his head yellowish and balding. I do not know if he knows where I am or not, or even where *he* is.

"I'd be glad to hear a dream," I say.

Herb stares off toward the lake as if it contained all his hopes gone cold. "I have a dream about these three old women in a stalled car on a dark road. Two of them are taking their grandmother, who's old, really old, back to a nursing home. Just someplace. Say New York state, or Pennsylvania. I come along in my Jeep—I *had* a Jeep once—and I stop and ask if I can help them. And they say yes. No one's come by in a long time. And I can tell they're worried about me. One woman has her money out to pay me before I even start. And they've got this flat tire. I shine my Jeep lights on their car and I can see this worried old grandmother, her face low in the front seat. A chicken-wattle neck. The two other women stand with me while I change the tire. And as I'm doing it I think about killing all three of them. Just strangling them with my hands, then driving off because no one would ever know who did it, since I wasn't a killer or even known to be there. But I look around then, and I see these deer staring at me out of the trees. These yellow eyes. And that's it. I wake up." Herb twists his wheelchair and faces me. "How's that for a dream? Whaddaya think, Frank? You've got a halo again, by the way. It just came back. You look idiotic." Herb suddenly breaks out in laughter, his whole body rumbling and his mouth wide as a canyon. Herb, I see, is as crazy as a betsey bug, and I want nothing in the world more than to get as far away from him as I can. Interview or no interview. Inspiration or no inspiration.

Interviewing a crazy man is a waste of anybody's time who's not crazy himself. And I'm glad, in fact, that Herb is in his chair at the moment since it's possible he would strangle *me* if he could.

"It's probably time we head back, Herb."

He has taken his glasses off and begun wiping them on his BIONIC shirt. But he is really still laughing. "Sure, okay."

"I've got all I need for a good story. And it's getting pretty chilly out here."

"You're full of shit, Frank," Herb says, smiling across the empty boat dock. On the lake a pair of ducks flies low across the surface, fast and slicing. They make an abrupt turn, then skin into the shiny water and become invisible. "Oh Frank, you're really full of shit." Herb shakes his head in complete amazement.

Herb pushes along beside me in his silver chair while we make our way back up Glacier Way in silence. Everything has become confused, though why, exactly, I don't know. It's possible I've had a bad effect on him. Sometimes when people realize sports-writers are just men or women they become resentful. (People often want others to be better than they are themselves.) But under these circumstances it is all but impossible to make a contribution, or to give an honest effort of any kind. It is, in fact, enough to make you want to hit the road for a pharmaceuticals house, of which New Jersey has plenty.

"We didn't talk much about football," Herb says thoughtfully. He is now as sane and reflective as an old sextant.

"I guess it didn't seem it was much on your mind, Herb."

"It really seems insignificant now, Frank. It's really a pretty crummy preparation for life, I've come to believe."

"But I'd still think it had some lessons to teach to the people who played it. Perseverance. Team work. Comradeship. That kind of thing."

"Forget all that crap, Frank. I've got the rest of my life handed to me if I can figure it out. I've got some pretty big plans. Sports is just a memory to me."

"You mean law school and all that."

Herb nods at me like an undertaker. "That's it."

"You've got a lot of courage, Herb. It takes courage to be you, I think."

"Maybe," Herb says, considering that idea. "Sometimes I'm afraid, though, Frank. I'll tell ya. Scared to death." We're just

two guys jawing now. Just the way I'd hoped. Maybe a straightforward old-fashioned interview could still be worked out. I feel
for my tape recorder.

"Sometimes I'm afraid, Herb. It's natural to the breed, I'd say."

"All *right*," Herb says and chuckles, nodding in forced
agreement.

I see Mr. Smallwood's yellow Checker waiting out front of
Herb's house as we round the curve, his visit to Wixom apparently gone awry. It has grown colder since we've been outside,
and the sky has lowered. By nighttime it will be snowing to beat
the band, and Vicki and I will be glad to be far from here. It is a
strange turn of events, not what I would've expected, but I, on
the other hand, am still not surprised.

As we pass by, a man wearing a brown car coat comes out of
his house, holding a can of motor oil. His is a house in the same
architectural order as Herb's, though with a room added on
where the driveway once went into the back. The man stands
beside his car—a new Olds with its hood up—and gives Herb a
wave and a "howzitgoin."

"Primo. Numero uno," Herb calls back with a grin and waves
his arm as if he's waving to a crowd. "This guy's interviewing
me. I'm giving him a helluva time."

"Don't take nobody's crap," the man shouts, and bends his
short trunk under the murky hood of the Olds.

"The neighbors still think I play on the team," Herb says in a
hushed voice, pushing himself up Glacier Way toward his wife
and home.

"How's that?"

"Well, I keep my injury pretty well a secret. Another guy plays
in my place. With my number. I hope you won't write about
that and ruin it."

"No way, Herb. You've got my word on that."

Herb looks up at me as we approach Mr. Smallwood's cab,
and gives me a look full of wonder. "How come you do it, Frank.
Tell the truth."

"How come I do what, Herb?" Though I know what's coming.

For some reason Herb seems to be having a hard time making
his head be still. It's wandering all around. "You couldn't really
like sports, Frank," he says. "You don't look like a guy who likes
sports."

"I like some better than others." It is not that uncommon a question, really.

"But wouldn't you rather talk about something else?" Herb shakes his big head, still wondrous. "What about Winslow Homer?"

"I'd talk to you about him, Herb. Any time. Writing about something is a lot different from doing the thing itself. Does that clear anything up?" For some reason my diaphragm, or its vicinity, feels like it is quaking again.

"Pret-ty interesting, Frank." Herb nods at me with genuine admiration. "I'm not sure it explains a goddamn thing, but it's interesting. I'll give you that."

"It's pretty hard to explain your own life, Herb." I'm sure my quaking is visible, though maybe not to Herb, for whom the whole world might quake all the time. He's still having trouble keeping his head stationary. "I think I've said enough. I'm supposed to be asking you questions."

"I'm a verb, Frank. Verbs don't answer questions."

"Don't think that way, Herb." My diaphragm is crackling. Herb and I have not been together an hour, but there is a strong sense around him that he would like to strangle *someone*, and not be choosy whose neck he got his hands on. When you have spent so much of your life whamming into people and hurting them, it must be hard just to call a halt to it and sit down. It must be hard to do anything else, it seems to me, but keep on whamming. In any case, I'm always most at ease when I know the way out. There is something to be avoided here, and I intend to avoid it. "I'm going to try to write a good story, Herb," I say, inching toward the back of Smallwood's Checker.

Clarice Wallagher has stepped out onto the front stoop and stands watching us. She calls Herb's name and smiles wearily. This must happen to everyone: meetings ending in stunned silences out front; a waiting cab; Herb proclaiming himself a verb. My greatest admiration is hers. I'd hoped to have a word with her on the subject of Herb's heroism-in-life, but that has gone past us. I simply hope there is a consolation for her late on dark nights.

"Herb," Clarice says in a pretty voice that cracks on the cold Michigan wind.

"Okay!" Herb shouts heroically. "Gotta go, Frank, gotta go.

You oughta write my life story. You'd make six figures." We shake hands, and once again Herb tries to jerk me to my knees. There is an odd smell on Herb now, a metallic smell that is the odor of his chair. His cheek is bleeding from where he peeled off the paper. "I wanted you to see some old game films before you left. I could put the kebosh on 'em, Frank. Don't let this chair fool ya."

"We'll do it next time, Herb, that's a promise."

Mr. Smallwood starts his cab with a loud whooshing and drops it into drive so that the body bucks half a foot forward.

"I don't know what happens sometimes, Frank." Herb's sad blue eyes suddenly fill with hot tears, and he shakes his big head to dash them away. It is the sadness of elusive life glimpsed and unfairly lost, and the following, lifelong contest with bitter facts. Pity, in other words, for himself, and as justly earned as a game ball. Only I do not want to feel it and won't. It is too close to regret to play fast and loose with. And the only thing worse than terrible regret is unearned terrible regret. And for that reason I will not bend to it, will, in fact, go on to the bottom with my own ship.

I take four quick steps back. "I'm glad I met you, Herb."

Herb stares at me, his face distorted by unhappiness. "Yeah sure," he says.

And I am into the boxy, musty backseat of Mr. Smallwood's Checker, and we shush off down Glacier Way without even so much as a goodbye to Clarice, leaving Herb sitting in the empty street, in his chair, waving goodbye to our tail lights, his sad face astream with helpless and literal tears.

CHAPTER 7

MR. SMALLWOOD is the best possible confederate for my circumstances.

"You look like you could use a pick-me-up," he says, once we are going, and hands back a bottle half out of its flimsy paper bag. I drink down a good gulp that makes me flubber my lips— it is peppermint and sweet as cough syrup, but I'm happy to have it in me, and take a second big gulp. "You musta had you a *time*," Mr. Smallwood says as we hiss past the remnants of a long, charred building on the landward side of the lakefront road. A dismembered line of cabins stands opposite. The big building was once a Quonset hut with a barn built on behind, though snow is piled on its blackened interior timbers, one of which is a long bar. Grass has grown up. No one, apparently, has thought to find a new use for the land. My past in decomposition and trivial disarray.

"These peoples out here're cra-zy," Mr. Smallwood announces widely, steering chauffeur-style with one huge hand on the plastic steering knob, the other stretched over the seat back. "Sur-burban peoples, I'm tellin you. Houses full of guns, everybody mad all the time. Oughta cool out, if you ask me. I ain't been out here in years, couldn't even figure out which street was which. I used to come out here all the time." We pull up onto the expressway back toward Big D, invisible now in mossy green clouds that tell of snow and possibly a marooning storm. "Look here now." Mr. Smallwood catches my eye in the rearview and leans backwards in his driver's seat for a speculative stretch. "How much money you got?"

"Why?"

"Well, for a hundred dollars I could make a phone call up here at a gas station and the first thing you know, somebody be done made you feel a whole lot better." Mr. Smallwood grins a big happy grin at the back seat, and I think for a moment about a hundred dollar whore, the kindness she might bring, like the pharmacy sending over an expensive prescription to get you through a rough night. A trip to the hot springs. Something wordless to patch the tissue of innocent words that holds life in its most positive attitude. Too much serious talk and self-explanation and you're a goner.

What Herb needs, of course, and can't have, is to strap on a set of pads and beat the daylights out of somebody and quit worrying about theories of art. He is a man without a sport, when a sport is exactly what he needs. With better luck we might've summoned up a vivider memory of his playing days, seen the game films. Herb could get back within himself, shake off alienation and dreary doubt, and play through pain—be the inspiration he was put on earth to be.

I tell Mr. Smallwood no thanks, and he chuckles in a mirthful-derisive way. Then for a while we wind back toward town without speaking, taking the Lodge this time since the snow is off and the traffic gone north, leaving the expressway gray and wintry.

Across from Tiger Stadium, Mr. Smallwood stops at a liquor store owned, he says, by his brother-in-law, a little Fort Knox of steel mesh and heavy bullet-proof glass. Across the avenue the big stadium hulks up white and lifeless. A message on its marquee says simply, "Sorry Folks. Have a Good One."

Mr. Smallwood ambles across and buys another pint bottle of schnapps, which I insist on paying for, and he and I treat ourselves to a warm elevation of spirits on the short trip down to the Pontchartrain. He says he is a Tiger fan and that he believes it's time for a dynasty. He also tells me that his parents moved up from Magnolia, Arkansas, in the Forties, and that for a while he attended Wayne State before he got married and went to work at Dodge Main. He quit that last year, he says, a jump ahead of the lay-offs, and bought his taxi. And he is happy to name his own hours now and to go home every day at noon for lunch with his wife and to rest an hour before getting back onto the street for the afternoon rush. Someday he hopes to retire to Arkansas. He doesn't ask me about myself, either too courteous or too engaged in his own interesting life of work and discretionary time. His is a nice life, a life that would be easy to envy if you didn't have one just as good. I calculate him to be not much older than I am.

At the hotel Mr. Smallwood leans across the seat to where he can see me out on the windy pavement putting money back in my wallet. For an instant I think he means to shake my hand, but that is not on his mind at all. I have already paid him our agreed fare, and the schnapps bottle is on the floor beside his considerable leg. My gift to him.

"There's a good chop house down on Larned," he says in a tour guide's voice and with a grin that makes me wonder if he isn't making fun of me. "Steaks big as this." He holds two big chunky fingers two full inches apart. "You can walk from here. It's safe. I take the wife now and then. You can drink some wine, have a good time." For some reason Mr. Smallwood has started talking like a second generation Swede, and I understand he isn't making fun of me at all, only trying to be a good ambassador for his city, putting on the voice he has learned for it.

"That's great," I say, not quite hearing all this insider's dining advice, turning an ear instead into the windy sibilance of the city air. Snow flakes are falling now.

"Come on back when the weather's nicer," he says. "You'll like it a whole lot better."

"When will that be?" I smile, giving him the old Michigan straight line.

"Ten minutes maybe." He cracks a big wisecracker's grin, the same as his hundred-dollar-whore grin. And with the slap-shut of the yellow door, he shoots off down the street, leaving me at the hissing curbside as solitary as a lonely end.

THOUGH NOT for long.

Back in the room, the TV is on without sound. The drapery is drawn and two trays of dishes are set outside. Vicki lies naked as a jaybird on the rumpled bed, drinking a 7-Up and reading the in-flight magazine. Air in the room is hot and close, changed from the sleep-soft night smell. Only the sad old familiarity from the dreamy days after Ralph died is left: lost in strangerville with a girl I don't know well enough and can't figure how to revive an interest in (or, for her sake, an interest in me that would compensate). It is a tinny, minor-key feeling, a far-flung longing for conviction among the convictionless.

"I'm sure glad to see *you*," she says, giving me a happy smile in the blinky TV light. I stand in the little dark entryway, my two feet heavy as anchors, and I can't help thinking of my life as a scene in some steamy bus station novel. *Big Sledge moved toward the girl cat-quick, trapping her where he'd wanted her, between his cheap drifter's suitcase and the pile of greasy tire chains against the back of the lube bay. Now she would see what's what. They both would.* "How'd everything work out with your old football guy?"

"Dandy." I go to the window, pull back the heavy curtain and look out. Snow is dazzling an inch from my face, falling in burly flakes onto Jefferson Avenue. The river is lost in white, as is Cobo. In the street, flashing yellow beacons signal the first snow-plows. I feel I can hear their skid and clatter, but I'm sure I do not. "I don't like the looks of this weather. We might have to change our plans."

"A-Okay," she says. "I'm just happy to be here today with you. I can go to the aquarium someplace else. They must be alike." She sets her 7-Up on her bare belly and stares at it, thinking.

"I wanted this to be a nice vacation for you, though. I had a lot of plans."

"Well, keep 'em, cause I've had a plenty good time. I ordered beer-batter shrimp up here, which was a meal in itself. I put on my clothes and went downstairs and looked in the shops which're nice, though they're like Dallas's in a lot of similar ways. I think I might've seen Paul Anka, but I'm not sure. He's about half the size I thought he'd be if it was him, and I already knew he was tiny."

I sit in the chair beside the coffee table. Her uncovered beauty is unexpectedly what I need to make the transition back (the familiar can still surprise and should). Hers is an altogether ordinary nakedness, a sleek curve of bust, a plump darkening thigh tapered to a dainty ankle, a willing smile of no particular intention—all in all, a nice bundle for a lonely fellow to call his in a strange city when time's to kill.

On television the face of a pallid newsman is working dramatically without sound. *Believe!* his eyes say. *This stuff is the God's truth. It's what you want.*

"Do you believe women and men can just be friends," Vicki says.

"I guess so," I say, "once the razzle-dazzle's over. I like the razzle-dazzle though."

"Yeah, me too." Her smile broadens and she crosses her arms over her soft breasts. She has, I can tell, been captured by a thought, an event she likes and wants to share. At heart she could not be kinder and could make someone the most reward- ing wife. Only for some reason it does not seem as likely to be me as it once did. She may have caught this very mood in the wind today and be as puzzled by it as I am. Though she is nobody's fool.

"I called Everett on the phone," she says, and looks down at her knees, which are bent upwards. "I used *my* charge number."

"You could've used this one."

"Well. I used mine, anyway."

"How *is* old Everett?" Of course I have never seen ole Everett and can be as chummy as a barber with the far-off idea of him.

"He's okay. He's into Alaska now. He said people need carpets up there. He also said he's shaved his head bald as a cue ball. I told him I was in a big suite, looking out at a renaissance center. I didn't say where."

"What'd he think about that."

" 'As the world turns,' is what he said, which is about standard. He wanted to know would I send him back his stereo I got in the divorce. Everything's sky high up there, I guess, and if you come with all you need, you start ahead."

"Did he want you to go with him?"

"No, he did not. And I wouldn't either. You don't have to marry somebody like Everett but once in a lifetime. Twice'll kill you. He's got some ole gal with him, anyway, I'm sure."

"What did he want, then?"

"I called him, remember." She frowns at me. "He didn't want anything. Haven't you ever got the phonies in your life?"

"Only when I'm lonesome, sweetheart. I didn't think you were lonesome."

"Right," she says and looks at the silent television.

Detroit, I can see now, has not affected her exactly as I had hoped, and she has become wary. Of what? Possibly in the lobby she saw someone who reminded her too much of herself (that can happen to inexperienced travelers). Or worse. That *no* one there reminded her of anyone she ever knew. Both can be threatening to a good frame of mind and usher in a gloomy remoteness. Though calling up an old lover or husband can be the perfect antidote. They always remind you of where you've been and where you think you're going. And if you're lucky, wherever you are at the moment—in the Motor City, in a snow-storm—can seem like *the* right place on the planet. Though I'm not certain Vicki has been so lucky. She may have found an old flame burning and not know what to do about it.

"Do you feel like you wanted to be friends with Everett?" I start with the most innocent of questions and work toward the most sensitive.

"No-ho way." She reaches down and pulls the sheet up over her. She is even warier now. It may be she wants to tell me some-thing and can't quite find the words. But if I'm to be relegated to the trash heap of friendship, I want to do a friend's one duty: let her be herself. Though I'd be happier to snuggle up under the sheets and rassle around till plane time.

"Did you hang up feeling like you wanted to be friends with *me*?" I say, and smile at her.

Vicki turns over on the big bed and faces the other wall, the white sheet clutched up under her chin and the crisp hotel per-cale stretched over her like a winding. I have hit the tender spot. A day and a night with me has made even Everett look good. Something else is needed, and I don't fit the bill even with champers, a demi-suite, bachelor buttons and a view of Canada. Maybe that isn't even surprising when you come down to it, since by scaling down my own pleasures I may have sold short her hopes for herself. I, however, am an expert in taking things like this lying down. For writers—even sportswriters—bad news is always easier than good, since it is, after all, more familiar.

"I don't want to be friends. Not *just*," Vicki says in a tiny, mouse voice from a mound of white covers. "I really thought I was gettin a new start with you."

"Well, what happened to make you think you weren't? Just because you caught me going through your purse?"

"Shoot. That didn't matter," she says, smally. "Live and let die, I say. You can't help yourself. Yesterday wasn't the tiptop day for you in the year."

"Then, what's the matter?" I wonder, in fact, how many times I have said that or something equal to it to a woman passing palely through my life. *What're you thinking? What's made you so quiet? You seem suddenly different. What's the matter?* Love *me* is what this means, of course. Or at least, second best: surrender. Or at the *very* least, take some time regaling me with why you won't, and maybe by the end you will.

Outside a wind makes a sharp oceanic *woo* around the corner of the hotel, then off into the cold, paltry Detroit afternoon. By five it could as easily turn to rain, by six the stars could be out and by nighttime Vicki and I could be strolling down Larned for a steak or a chop. You can never completely count on things out here. Life is counterpoised against a mean wind that could suddenly cease.

"Well," Vicki says, and turns over to face me out of a grotto of pillows and sheets. "When I went downstairs, you know, when you were gone? I just went to be a part of something. I didn't need anything. And I went in the little newsstand down there, and I picked up this paperback. *How To Take On The World*, by Doctor Barton. Because I felt like I was starting over in one way, like I said. You and me. So I stood there at the rack and read one chapter called 'Our New-Agers.' Which was about these people who won't eat potato chips and who join these self-discovery groups, and drink mineral water and have literary discussions every day. People that think it oughta be easy to express their feelings and be how you seem. And I just started cryin, cause I realized that that was you, and I was someplace way off the beam. Back with the potato chips and people who aren't inner-looking. Here we'd come all the way out here, and all I could do was eat shrimp and watch TV and cry. And it wasn't working out. So I thought maybe we could be friends if you wanted to. I called up Everett because I knew I could bring it off with him and quit crying. I knew I was better off than him." A big handsome tear leaves her eye, goes off her nose and vanishes into the pillow. I have managed to make two different people cry inside of two hours. I am doing something wrong. Though what?

Cynicism.

I have become more cynical than old Iago, since there is no cynicism like lifelong self-love and the tunnel vision in which you yourself are all that's visible at the tunnel's end. It's embarrassing. Likewise, there's nothing guaranteed to make people feel more worthless than to think someone is trying to help them—even if you're not. A cynical "New-Ager" is exactly me, a sad introspecter and potato chip avoider with a queasy heart-to-heart mentality—though I would give the crown jewels not to be, or at least not be thought to be.

My only hope now is to deny everything—friendship, disillusionment, embarrassment, the future, the past—and make my stand for the present. If I can hold her close in this cold-hot afternoon, kiss her and hug away her worries with ardor, so that when the sun is down and the wind stops and a spring evening draws us, maybe I will love her after all, and she me, and all this will just have been the result of too little sleep in a strange town, schnapps and Herb.

"I'm not really a New-Ager," I say and take a seat on the bed shoulder, where I can touch her cheek, warm as a baby's. "I'm just an old-fashioned Joe who's been misunderstood. Let's pretend we just got here and it's late at night, and I had you in my old-fashioned arms to love."

"Oh my." She puts a tentative hand on my shoulder and gives it a friendly pat. "I bet you think I got it all wrong." She gives a stout sniff. "That I can't even make myself miserable and do it right."

"You're just no good at messin up." I put a heavy hand on her soft breast. "You just have to let good things be good if they will. Don't worry about more than you have to."

"I shouldn't read, is what it is. It always gets me in trouble." She reaches both hands around my neck and pulls hard, so hard once again a crippling pain goes down my back clear to my buttocks.

"Oh," I say, involuntarily. On TV a skier is just about to push out the timer gate onto a slope longer and higher than any I've ever seen. Snow is falling wherever he is. I wouldn't do what he's doing for a million dollars.

"Oh my," she says, for I have found her in the lemony light. "My, my, my."

"You sweet girl," I say. "Who wouldn't love you?"

Outside in the cold city the wind goes *woo* again and I can, I think, hear the tufted snow dashing against the window, sending shivers through every soul in Detroit who thinks he knows a thing or two and who is willing to bet his life on it. I leave the TV on, since even now, in its prying presence, I still find it consoling.

*　　*　　*

BY FIVE o'clock, we have taken a cab trip up Jefferson to the
Belle Isle Botanical Garden, and are back in the room suffering
a case of the wall-stare willies, something sportswriters know a
lot about. We are like the family of a traveling salesman, come
along for the adventure and diversion, but who find themselves
with too much time to kill while business gets conducted; too
many unfamiliar streets leading too far away; too little going on
in the hotel lobby to make people-watching all that rewarding.

The Botanical Garden turned out to be cold and alien-feeling,
though we trudged down aisles of ferns and succulents and
passion flowers until Vicki announced a headache. The most
interesting rooms all seemed to be closed—in particular a recreation of an eighteenth-century French herb garden, which
we could see through the glass door and that caught both our
fancies. A sign hung in the window saying Detroit was not generous enough in its tax attitudes to support this century properly.
And in less than an hour we were back out in the cold and snow
of afternoon on the windy concrete steps. A muddy playing field
stretched away from us toward the boat basin, with the big river
invisible and low behind a crescent-line of poplar saplings. Public
places can sometimes let you down no matter how promising
they start out.

Delivered back outside our hotel, I offered a short walk
down Larned to "a great little steak house I know about."
Though when we had gone as far as Woodward, everyone we
saw had become black and vaguely menacing, the taxis and
police all unexplainably disappeared, and Vicki clung to me
ashiver from the wintry norther that'd dropped in on us from
bland Canada.

"I'm not really dressed for this, I don't think," she said beneath
my arm, and smiled a daunted smile. "I'd settle for a Tuna Alladin
at the coffee shop, if that's okay with you."

"I guess they've moved the steak place," I said and gazed up
weekend-empty Woodward toward the Grand Circus where,
when I was a college boy, Eddy Loukinen, Golfball Kirkland
and I cruised the burlesque houses and the schooner bars, then
drove the forty miles back to campus full of the mystique of
soldiers on a last leave before shipping out to fates you wouldn't
smile about. It was incongruous to me, in fact, that the year
could've been 1963. Not '73 or '53. Sometimes I can even

forget my own age and the year I'm living in, and think I am twenty, a kid starting new in the world—a greener, confused by life at its beginning.

"Towns aren't even towns anymore," Vicki said, sensing my distraction with this sad evolution, and giving me a hug around my middle. "Dallas wasn't *ever* one, when you get right down to it. It's just a suburb looking for a place to light."

"I remember they had a first class wine list there," I said, still gazing up Woodward toward the phantom steak house, past the old Sheraton and into the abandonment and dazzle of sex clubs and White Castles and *bibliothèques sensuelles* stretching to where snow made a backdrop.

"I can taste the cheddar cheese already," she said in reference to her Tuna Alladin, trying to be upbeat. "I bet they've got just as good a wine for half the price back at the hotel. You're just looking for someplace else to spend your money again." And she was right, and wheeled me around and set us off back to the Pontch, watching our toes on the snowy pavement, taking long, slew-footed strides and laughing like conventioneers turned loose on the old town.

Though by five we are room-bound here, driven in by un-seasonable weather and the forbidding streets of this city. We have tried to make the most of everything that's come our way: a belly-buster lunch in the Frontenac Grill complete with a bottle of Michigan beaujolais. A long nap in a fresh bed, after which I have stood at the window and watched another ore barge down from Lake Superior ply the snowy river, headed, like the one last night, for Cleveland or Ashtabula. It's possible I should put in a call to Herb, or even to Clarice, though I don't know what I'd say and finally lack the courage. I might also call Rhonda Matuzak to report I've found out nothing usable for the Pigskin Preview. People are in the office this weekend, though it's doubt-ful anyone's counting on me. Mine, for the moment, is not the best sportswriter's attitude.

"I'll tell you what let's do," Vicki says suddenly. She is seated at the vanity twisting in some Navajo earrings she has bought with her money at the gift shop. They are tiny as pin-heads, lovely and blue as hyacinths.

"You just name it," I say, looking up from the *Out on the Town*, which I've read cover to cover without finding one local attraction I have the heart for—including Paul Anka, who's already left town. Even a cab ride to Tiger Stadium and a Mexican dinner seem somehow second rate.

"Let's go on out to the airport and stand-by for a flight. Nobody goes any place on Saturday. I remember from when I used to watch planes for fun, they used to let people on with tickets for other days. They're good about that."

"I thought we'd make a festive night of it," I say half-heartedly. "I was planning on Greek Town. There's still plenty to do here."

"Sometimes, you know, you just get the bug to sleep in your own bed, don't you think that's so? We're s'posed to be at Daddy's tomorrow before noon anyway. This'll make it easier."

"Aren't you going to be disappointed to miss souvlaki and baklava?"

"I don't even know where they're located so how could I miss 'em? I bet you have to drive through some snow to get there though."

"I haven't been much of a high-flier this trip. I don't really know what happened."

"Nothing did." Looking in the mirror, Vicki pulls back her dark curls to model the Navajos, pinched in behind her plump cheeks. She turns to the side to see and gives me a reassuring smile via the mirror. "I don't have to ride the merry-go-round to have fun. I take mine from who I'm with, not what I do. I've had the best time I could, just being with you, and you're a clubfoot not to know it."

"What if the airport's closed?"

"Then I'll sit and read stories to you out of movie magazines. There's worse things than spending the night in the airport. Sometimes I'd rather be there than lots of places."

"It wouldn't be that bad, would it?"

"No sir. Put yourself in one of those little TV chairs, eat dinner in a good restaurant. Get your shoes shined. It'd take you all night to hit the high spots."

"I'll call us a bellman," I say, and stand up.

"I don't know why we waited this long." She smiles at me.

"I guess I was waiting for something exciting and unusual to happen. I always hope for that. It's my weakness."

"You have to know, though, when what you're waiting for

says, 'Smile, you're on candid camera.' Then you got to be ready to smile."

And I do smile, at her, as I reach for the phone to ring the bell captain. A small future brightens, and not a bad one, but an ordinary good one. And, as I dial, I feel the sky of this long day lighten about me now for the first time, and the clouds begin at last to ascend.

BY TEN we are in New Jersey as if by miracle of time travel, returned from the flat midwest to the diverse seaboard. Vicki has slept across Lake Erie once again after reading to me several excerpts from *Daytime Confidential*, all of which made me laugh, but which she took more seriously and seemed to want to mull over. I read a good deal of *Love's Last Journey* and found it not bad at all. There was no long flashback prologue to get past, and the writer proved pretty skillful at getting the ball rolling by page two. I woke her only when the pilot banked over what I estimated to be Red Bank, with bright Gotham (the Statue of Liberty tiny but distinct, like a Japanese doll of herself) and all of New Jersey spread out like a glittering diamond apron, the Atlantic and Pennsylvania looming dark as the Arctic.

"What's *that* thing," Vicki asked, staring and pointing below us into the distant carnival of civilized lights.

"That's the Turnpike. You can see where it meets the Garden State at Woodbridge and heads to New York."

"Hey-o," she said.

"I think it's beautiful from up here."

"You prob'ly do," she said. "No telling what you'll think's beautiful next. A junk yard I guess."

"I think you're beautiful."

"More than a junk yard. A junk yard in New Jersey?"

"Almost." I squeezed her strong little arm and held it to me.

"You said the wrong thing now." Her eyes narrowed in mock pique. "I liked you to this point. But I don't see how this can go on."

"You'll break my heart."

"It won't be the first one I broke, will it?"

"What if I'm better?"

" 'Bout too late," she said. "You should of considered all that before you were even born." She shook her head as though she meant every word of it, then settled back and closed her eyes to sleep as our silver ship perfected its descent to earth.

BY ELEVEN-FIFTEEN I have delivered us to Pheasant Meadow. It has become a clear and intensely full-featured night, with the moon waning and tomorrow's weather giving no sign of arriving from Detroit. It's the very kind of night that used to make me disoriented and dizzy—the sort of night I stood out in the yard in, while X was inside burning her hope chest, and charted Cassiopeia and Gemini in the northern sky and felt vulnerable beside the rhododendrons. Since then, to be truthful, I have never felt all that easy with the clear night sky, as if I was seeing it from the top of a high building and afraid to look down. (I tend to prefer broken cirrus or mackerel clouds to a pure, starry vault.)

"Don't bother walkin me," Vicki says, already out the car door and with her head back inside the window. I have stopped behind her Dart. The hard-hat guys from yesterday have finished off a phony mansard across the lot, although none of the finished buildings have roofs like that. Naturally I was hoping for an invitation inside—a nightcap. But I see my hopes on that front are slim. She has become skittish now, as though someone else was waiting upstairs.

"Tomorrow's the day he rolled back the stone and raised up from the dead," she says in all seriousness, staring straight at me as if I was expected to recite a psalm. She has her Le Sac weekender looped over her shoulder and her Navajo earrings on. "I might go to early mass, just for keeping us safe, that and the in-surance. Or I might go to the drive-in Methodists in Hightstown. One's official as the other. I'm thinking twice about lapsin. I'd ask you to come, but I know you wouldn't like it."

"I'd like the music."

"Whatever floats your boat, I guess," she says. We have been together for two days now, shared another geography, slept in one bed, been quiet together and attended each other's pleasures and courtesy like married folk. Only now the end is in sight, and neither of us can find the handle to a proper parting. Flippancy and a vague churlishness is her protocol. Unwitting politeness is mine. It is not a good mix.

"I'm going to see you tomorrow, aren't I?" I am cheerful, bending to see her and seeing beyond her the big blue space-age water tank and beyond that the big Easter moon.

"You better be on time. Daddy's picky 'bout when he eats. And it takes a whole hour to get there."

"I'm looking forward to it a lot." This is not entirely true, but it is my official attitude. This part of tomorrow is actually alive with fearsome ambiguity.

"You hadn't even met him yet. Wait'll you meet my step-mother. She's a breed apart. If you like her you'll like broccoli. But Daddy's somethin. You *better* like him, only he probably won't like you. Or least that's how he'll act. His true thoughts will come to light later. Not that it matters."

"You love me, don't you?" When I lean up to be kissed, she gazes down on me with a pert, appraising face. I cannot help wondering if she's not considering Everett right now and an Alaskan adventure.

"Maybe. What if I do?"

"Then you'll give me a kiss and ask me to spend the night."

"No way on that," she says, and gives her hand a big Dinah Shore kiss and smacks me hard across the cheek with it. "That's what you got comin. Signed, sealed and delivered, ole Mister Smart." And then she is off, skittering toward the darkened apartments, across the skimpy lawn and in the lighted outside door and out of sight. And I am left alone in my Malibu, staring at the glossy moon as if it were all of mystery and anticipation, all the things we are happy to leave and happier yet to see come toward us new again.

CHAPTER 8

A SUSPICIOUS light shines in my living room. A strange car sits at the curb. On the third floor Bosobolo's desk lamp is lit, though it is after midnight. Easter undoubtedly means special preparations for him, possibly a sermon at one of the Institute's satellite churches which he services now and then to fine-tune his evangelizing techniques. He has put up a wreath on the front door, a decision we have discussed earlier that won my approval. All the houses on Hoving Road are silent and dark, odd for a Saturday night, when there is usually entertaining going on and windows brightened. In the clear sky above the buttonwoods and tulip trees, I can see only the lemony glitter of Gotham lighting the heavens fifty miles away, as though a great event was going on there—a state fair, say, or a firestorm. And I am happy to see it, happy to be this far from the action, on the leeward side of what the wider world deems important.

In my house stands Walter Luckett.

More accurately, waiting in the room I now use as a cozy study, an old side porch with French doors, overstuffed summerish furniture, brass lamps with maps for shades (bought from a catalog), bookshelves to the ceiling and a purplish Persian rug that came with the house. It is the room I normally consider *mine*, though I am not hard-nosed about it. But even Bosobolo, who has the run of everything, stays clear without having to be asked. It is the room where I finally gave up work on *Tangier*, where I do most of my sportswriting, where my typewriter sits on my desk. And when X left me, it was in this room that I slept every night until I could face going back upstairs. Most people have such comfortable, significant places if they own a home, and Walter Luckett is standing in the middle of mine with a wry self-derisive smirk that probably caused a certain kind of brainy, pock-marked girl back in Coshocton to think, "Well, now. Here's something new to the planet. . . . More's here than meets the eye," and later to put up with hell and foolishness to be his date.

Though I can't say it makes me glad to see him, since I'm tired, and as recently as twelve hours ago was in faraway Walled Lake, having a conversation with a crazy man out of which I won't get a story to write. What I want to do is put that behind me and hit the hay. Tomorrow like all tomorrows could still be a banner day.

Walter is holding a copy of a canvas luggage catalog, and, upon seeing me, has rolled it into a tight little megaphone. "Frank. Your butler let me in, or I wouldn't be here at this hour. You have my word on that."

"It's okay, Walter. He's not my butler, though, he's my roomer. What's up?"

I set down my one-suiter bought from the very catalog he is now spindling. I like this room very much, its brassy, honeyed glow, paint peeling insignificantly off its moldings, the couches and leather chairs and hatchcover table all arranged in a careless, unpretentious way that is immensely inviting. I would like nothing more than to curl up anywhere here and doze off for seven or eight unmolested hours.

Walter is wearing the same blue tennis shirt and walking shorts he wore in the Manasquan two nights ago, a pair of sockless loafers and a barracuda jacket with a plaid lining (referred to as a *jerk's suit* in my fraternity). In all likelihood it is the same suit-of-casual-clothes Walter has worn since Grinnell days. Only behind his tortoise-shells, his eyes look vanquished, and his slick bond-salesman's hair could stand a washing. Walter looks, in other words, like private death, though I have a feeling he is here to share some of it with me.

"Frank, I haven't slept for three days," Walter blurts and takes two tentative steps forward. "Not since I talked to you over at the shore." He squeezes the Gokey catalog into the tightest tube possible.

"Let's make you a drink, Walter," I say. "And let me have that catalog before you tear it apart."

"No thanks, Frank. I'm not staying."

"How about a beer?"

"No beer." Walter sits down in a big armchair across from my chair, and leans up, forearms to knees: the posture of the confessional, something we Presbyterians know little about.

Walter is sitting under a framed map of Block Island, where X and I once sailed. I gave the map to her as a birthday present, but laid claim to it in the divorce. X complained until I said the map meant something to me, which caused her to relent instantly —and it does. It is a link to palmier times when life was simple and ungrieved. It is a museum piece of a kind, and I'm sorry to see Walter Luckett's beleaguered visage beneath it now.

"Frank, this is a helluva house. I mean, when I thought you had a colored butler with a British accent, it didn't surprise me at all." Walter looks around wide-eyed and approving. "Say about how long you've owned it." Walter smiles a big first-bike kid's grin.

"Fourteen years, Walter." I pour myself a good level of warm gin from a bottle I keep behind the children's *World Books* and drink it down with a gulp.

"Now that's old dollars. Plus location. Plus the interest rates from that era. That adds up. I have clients over here, old man Nat Farquerson for one. I live over in The Presidents now, Coolidge Street. Not a bad part of town, don't you think?"

"My wife lives on Cleveland. My former wife, I guess I should say."

"My wife's in Bimini, of course, with Eddie Pitcock. Of all things."

"I remember you said."

Walter's eyes go slitted, and he frowns up at me as if what I'd just said deserved nothing better than a damn good whipping. A silence envelops the room, and I cannot suppress an impolite yawn.

"Frank, let me get right to this. I'm sorry. Since this Americana business I've just been dead in my tracks. My whole life is just agonizing around this one goddamn event. Christ. I've done so much worse in my life, Frank. Believe me. I once screwed a thirteen-year-old girl when I was twenty and married, and bragged about it to friends. I slept like a baby. Like a baby! And there's worse than that, too. But I can't get this one out of my mind. I'm thirty-six, Frank. And everything seems very bad to me. I've quit *becoming*, is what it feels like. Only I stopped at the wrong time." A smile of wonder passes over Walter's dazed face, and he shakes his head. His is the face of a haunted war veteran with wounds. Only to my thinking it's a private matter, which no one but him should be required to care a wink about. "What're you thinking right now, Frank," Walter asks hopefully.

"I wasn't thinking anything, really." I give my own head a shake to let Walter know I'm an earnest war veteran myself, though in fact I'm lost in a kind of fog about Vicki. Wondering if she's expecting me to call and for us to make up, wondering for some reason if I'll ever see her again.

Walter leans up hard on his knees, looking more grim than earnest. "What did you think when I said what I said two nights ago? When I originally told you? Pretty idiotic, huh?"

"It didn't seem idiotic, Walter. Things happen. That's all I thought."

"I'm not putting babies in freezers, am I, Frank?"

"I didn't think so."

Walter's face sinks solemner still, in the manner of a man considering new frontiers. He would like me to ask him a good telling question, something that will then let him tell me a lot of things I don't want to know. But if I have agreed to listen, I have also agreed not to ask. This is the only badge of true friendship I'm sure of: not to be curious. Whatever Walter is up to may be as novel as teaching chickens to drive cars, but I don't want the whole lowdown. It's too late in the night. I'm ready for bed. And besides, I have no exact experience in these matters. I'm not sure what anyone—including trained experts—ought to say except, "All right now, son, let's get you on over to the state hospital and let those boys give you a shot of something that'll bring you back to the right side of things."

"What do you worry about, Frank, if you don't mind my asking?" Walter is still ghost-solemn.

"Really not that much, Walter. Sometimes at night my heart pounds. But it goes back to normal when I turn the light."

"You're a man with rules, Frank. You don't mind, do you, if I say that? You have ethics about a lot of important things."

"I don't mind, Walter, but I don't think I have any ethics at all, really. I just do as little harm as I can. Anything else seems too hard." I smile at Walter in a bland way.

"Do you think *I've* done harm, Frank? Do you think you're better than I am?"

"I think it doesn't matter, Walter, to tell you the truth. We're all the same."

"That's evading me, Frank, because I admire codes, myself. In everything." Walter sits back, folds his arms, and looks at me appraisingly. It's possible Walter and I will end up in a fistfight before this is over. Though I would run out the door to avoid it. In fact, I feel a nice snugged wooziness rising in me from the gin. And I would be happy to take this right up to bed.

"Good, Walter." I stare fervently at Block Island, trying to find X's and my first landfall from all those years ago. Sandy Point. I scan the bookshelves behind Walter's head as if I expected to see those very words on a friendly spine.

"But let me ask you, Frank, what do you do when something worries you and you can't make it stop. You try and try and it won't." Walter's eyes become exhilarated, as if he'd just willed into being something that was furious and snapping and threatening to swirl him away.

"Well, I take a hot bath sometimes. Or a midnight walk. Or I read a catalog. Get drunk. Sometimes, I guess, I get in bed and think dirty thoughts about women. That always makes me feel better. Or I'll listen to the short-wave. Or watch Johnny Carson. I don't usually get in such a bad state, Walter." I smile to let him know I'm at least half-serious. "Maybe I should more often."

Upstairs, I hear Bosobolo walk down his hall to his bathroom, hear his door close and his toilet flush. It's a nice homey sound—as always—his last office before turning in. A long, satisfying leak. I envy him more than anyone could know.

"You know what I think, Frank?"

"What, Walter."

"You don't seem to be somebody who knows he's going to die, that's what." Walter suddenly ducks his head, like a man someone has menaced and who has barely gotten out of the way.

"I guess you're right." I smile a smile of failed tolerance. Though Walter's words deliver a cold blue impact on me—the first clump of loamy dirt thrumping off the pine box, mourners climbing back into their Buicks, doors slamming in unison. Who the hell wants to think about that now? It's one a.m. on a day of resurrection and renewal the world over. I want to talk about dying now as much as I want to play a tune out my behind.

"Maybe you just need a good laugh, Walter. I try to laugh every day. What did the brassiere say to the hat?"

"I don't know. What *did* it say, Frank?" Walter is not much amused, but then I am not much amused by Walter.

" 'You go on ahead, I'll give these two a lift.' " I stare at him.

He smirks but doesn't laugh. "If you don't think that's hilarious, Walter, you should. It's really funny." In fact I have a hard time suppressing a big guffaw myself, though we're at basement-level seriousness now. No jokes.

"Maybe you think I need a hobby or something. Right?" Walter's still smirking, though not in a friendly way.

"You just need to see things from another angle, Walter. That's all. You aren't giving yourself much of a break." Maybe a hundred dollar whore would be a good new angle. Or an evening course in astronomy. I was thirty-seven before I knew that more than one star could be the North Star; it was a huge surprise and still has the aura of a genuine wonder for me.

"You know what's true, Frank?"

"What, Walter."

"What's true, Frank, is that when we get to be adults we all of a sudden become the thing viewed, not the viewer anymore. Do you know what I mean?"

"I guess so." And I *do* know what he means, and with a marksman's clarity. Divorce has plenty of these little encounter-group lessons to teach. Only I'll be goddamned if I'm going to trade epiphanies with Walter. We don't even go in for that stuff at the Divorced Men's Club. "Walter, I'm pretty beat, I've had a long day."

"And I'll tell you something else, Frank, even though you didn't ask me. I'm not going to be cynical enough to ignore that fact. I'm not going to find a hobby or be a goddamn jokemaster. Cynicism makes you feel smart, I know it, even when you aren't smart."

"Maybe so. I wasn't suggesting you take up fly-tying."

"Frank, I don't know what the hell I've gotten myself into, and there's no use acting like I'm smart. I wouldn't be in this if I was. I just feel on display in this mess, and I'm scared to death." Walter shakes his head in contrite bafflement. "I'm sorry about all this, Frank. I wanted to keep improving myself, by myself."

"It's all right, Walter. I'm not sure, though, if you *can* improve yourself much. Why don't I fix us both a drink." Unexpectedly, though, my heart suddenly goes out to Walter the self-improver, trying to go it alone. Walter is the real New-Ager, and in truth, he and I are not much different. I've made discoveries he'll make when he calms down, though the days when I could stay up all night, riled up about some *point d'honneur* or a new novel or bracing up a boon pal through some rough seas are long gone. I am too old for all that without even being very old. A next day—any new day—means too much to me. I am too much anticipator, my eye on the future of things. The best I can offer is a nightcap, and a room for the night where Walter can sleep with the light on.

"Frank, I'll have a drink. That's white of you. Then I'll get the hell out of here."

"Why don't you just bed down here tonight. You can claim the couch, or there's an extra bed in the kids' room. That'd be fine." I pour us both a glass of gin, and hand one to Walter. I've stashed away some roly-poly Baltimore Colts glasses I bought from a Balfour catalog when I was in college, in the days when Unitas and Raymond Berry were the big stars. And now seems to me the perfect time to crack them out. Sports are always a good distraction from life at its dreariest.

"This is nice of you, Franko," Walter says, looking strangely at the little rearing blue Colt, shiny and decaled into the nubbly glass from years ago. "Great glasses." He smiles up in wonderment. There is a part of me Walter absolutely cannot fathom, though he doesn't really want to fathom it. In fact he is not interested in me at all. He might even sense that I am in no way interested in him, that I'm simply performing a Samaritan's duty I would perform for anyone (preferably a woman) I didn't think was going to kill me. Still, some basic elements of my character keep breaking into his train of thought. Like my Colts glasses. At his house he has leaded Waterfords, crystals etched with salmon, and sterling goblets—unless, of course, Yolanda got it all, which I doubt since Walter is cagier than that.

"Salud," Walter says in a craven way.

"Cheers, Walter."

He puts the glass down immediately and drums his fingers on the chair arm, then stares a hole right into me.

"He's just a guy, Frank." Walter sniffs and gives his head a hard shake. "A monies analyst right on the Street with me. Two kids. Wife named Priscilla up in Newfoundland."

"What the hell are they doing way up there?"

"New Jersey, Frank. Newfoundland, New Jersey. Passaic County." A place where X and I used to drive on Sundays and eat in a turkey-with-all-the-trimmings restaurant. Perfect little bucolic America set in the New Jersey reservoir district, an hour's commute from Gotham. "I don't know what you'd want to say about either of us," Walter says.

"Nothing might be enough."

"He's an okay guy is what I'm saying. Okay?" Walter clasps his hands in his lap and gives me a semi-hurt look. "I went over to his firm to cash some certificates for a customer, and somehow we just started talking. He follows the same no-loads I do. And you know you can just talk. I was late already, and we decided to go down to the Funicular and drink till the traffic cleared. And one conversation just led to another. I mean, we talked about everything from petrochemicals in the liquid container industry to small-college football. He's a Dickinson grad, it turns out. But the first thing I knew, it was nine-thirty and we'd talked for three hours!" Walter rubs his hands over his small handsome face, right up under his glasses and into his eye sockets.

"That doesn't seem strange, Walter. You could've just shaken hands and headed on home. It's what you and I do. It's what most people do." (And ought to do!)

"Frank, I know it." He resettles his tortoise-shells using both sets of fingers. There's nothing for me to say. Walter acts like a man in a trance and waking him, I'm afraid, will only confuse things and make them go on forever. With any luck this will all end soon, and I can hop into bed. "Do you want to hear it, Frank?"

"I don't want to hear anything that'll embarrass me, Walter. Not in *any* way. I don't know you well enough."

"This isn't embarrassing. Not a bit." Walter swivels to the side and reaches for his glass, looking at me hopefully.

"It's right there." I point to the gin.

Walter goes and pours himself a drink, then slumps back in his easy chair and drinks it down. Bolting, we used to call it at Michigan. Walter just *bolted* his drink. It occurs to me, in fact, that I could *be* in Michigan at this very moment, that Vicki and I might've driven out to Ann Arbor and be eating a late supper at the Pretzel Bell. Flank steak and hot mustard with a side of red cabbage. I have made an error in my critical choices. "Do you know who Ida Simms is, Frank?" Walter looks at me judiciously, his lower lip pressed tightly above his upper. He means to imply

an icy logic's being applied—the rest from here on out will deal
only in the bedrock and provable facts. No gushy sentiment for
this boy.

"It sounds familiar, Walter. But I don't know why."

"Her picture was in all the papers last year, Frank. An older
lady with a Nineteen-forties hairdo. It looked like some kind
of advertisement, which in a way it was. The woman who just
disappeared? Got out of a cab at Penn Station, with two little
poodles on a leash, and nobody's seen her since? The family ran
the ads with her picture, asking for calls if anybody knew anything. Somebody dear to them who walked right out of the
world. Boom." Walter shakes his head, both comforted and
astonished by what a strange world it is. "She'd had mental problems, Frank, been in hospitals. All that came out. You'd have to
figure the signs weren't too good for her if you were the family.
The impulse to do away with yourself must get pretty strong in
those circumstances."

Walter looks at me with his blue eyes shining significantly, and
I'm forced to look up squarely at Block Island again. "You never
can tell, Walter. People are gone ten years, then one day they
wake up in St. Petersburg on the Sunshine Skyway, and everything's fine."

"I know it. That's true." Walter stares down at his loafers.
"We talked about the whole business, Frank. Yolanda and I. She
thought the picture was some kind of a fake, a massage parlor or
something phony. But I couldn't. I didn't know anymore than
she did. Except here was a picture of this woman, Frank, looking
like somebody's mother somewhere, yours or mine, her hair all
done up like the Forties, and a scared smile on her face like she
knew she was in trouble, and I just was not ready to think fake.
I told Yolanda she ought to believe it wasn't a fake just because
it might not be. You know what I mean?"

"I guess." I saw the picture, in fact, twenty times at least.
Whoever was running it had had the bright idea of putting it on
the sports page of the *Times*, which I read just before the obits.
I'd wondered myself if Ida Simms wasn't a unisex barber shop
or an erotic catering service, and somebody'd just thought of
using a picture of his mother as an ad. I finally forgot about it
and got interested in the spring trades.

"Now one day," Walter says, "I was looking at the paper, and

I said, 'I really wonder where this poor woman is.' And Yolanda, which was typical of her actually, said, 'There isn't any woman, Walter. It's just a come-on for some damn thing. If you don't believe me, I'll call and you can listen in on the extension.' I said I wouldn't listen in on anything because even if she was right, she ought to be wrong. I wouldn't want somebody giving up on me, would you?"

"What happened next?"

"She called, Frank. And a man answered. Yolanda said, 'Who's this?' And the man I guess said, 'This is Mr. Simms speaking. Do you have any word about my wife?' It was a special line, of course. And Yolanda said, 'No, I don't. But I'd like to know if this is on the level.' And the man said, 'Yes, on the level. My wife's been missing since February and we're crazy out of our minds worrying. We can offer a reward.' Yolanda just said, 'Sorry. I don't know anything.' And she hung up. This was about six weeks before she left with this Pitcock character." Walter's eyes grow narrow as if he can see Pitcock in the cross hairs of a high-powered rifle.

"What does that have to do with anything?"

"It's just cynical, is my point. That's all."

"I think you're way too finicky on this, Walter."

"Maybe so. Though I couldn't get it out of my mind. That poor woman wandering around God knows where—lost, maybe. Crazy. And everybody thinking her picture was an ad for something filthy, just a dirty joke. The helplessness of it got to me."

"Anything's possible, Walter." I can't suppress another yawn.

Walter suddenly presses his hands together between his bald knees, and fixes on me an odd supplicant's look. "I know anything's possible, Frank. But when I mentioned it to Warren, he said he thought it was a tragedy, the whole thing, and a shame nobody had called up with some news to put her family at ease. Even that she was dead would've been a relief."

"I doubt that."

"Okay, that's a point. We all have to die. That's not going to be any goddamn tragedy. The bad thing is a shitty, cynical, insensitive life, somebody like Yolanda calling those poor people up and making their lives miserable for an extra five minutes just because she couldn't stand not to make a joke out of dying. Something that's all around us. . . ."

"Oh, for Christ sake."

"That's okay, Frank. Never mind. I still want to tell you the rest, at least the part that won't embarrass you."

Though how could hearing about Walter's moment of magic do anything but bore me the same as watching an industrial training film, or hearing a lecture on the physics of the three-point stance. What could I hear that I couldn't figure out already if I was interested? The private parts of man are no amusement to me (only the public).

"It was like a friendship, Frank." Walter is suddenly as sorry-eyed as a pallbearer. "If you can believe that." (What is there for me to say?) "I guess I can't really explain my feelings, can I? All I know is what he said. 'Death's no tragedy,' something strange, I don't know. And then I said, 'Let's get out of here.' Just like you would with a woman you thought you were in love with. Neither of us was shocked. We just got up, walked out of the Funicular onto Bowling Green, got in a cab and headed uptown."

"How'd you choose the Americana?" I have absolutely no earthly reason to want to know that, of course. What I'd like to do is grab Walter by his barracuda lapels and throw him out.

"His firm keeps some rooms blocked up there, Frank, for the fellas who work late. I guess that probably seems pretty ironic to you, doesn't it?"

"I don't know, Walter, you have to go somewhere, I guess."

"It sounds silly, even to me. Two Wall Street guys going at it in the Americana. You get caught in your own silliness sometimes, Frank, don't you?" He's aching to tell me the whole miserable business.

"So what's going to happen, Walter. Are you going to see Warren, or whatever his name is again?"

"Frank, who knows. I doubt it. He's pretty happy up in Newfoundland, I guess. Marriage to me is founded on the myth of perpetuity, and I think I'm wedded pretty firmly to the here and now at this point in time." Walter sniffs in a professional way, though I have no idea on earth what he could be talking about. He could as easily be reciting the Gettysburg Address in Swahili. "Warren doesn't feel that way from all I can learn. Which is fine. I don't think I'm made to be one of those guys anyway, Frank. Though I was never closer to anyone in my life. Not Yolanda. Not even my mom and dad, which is pretty scary for a farm kid from Ohio." Walter offers me a big, scared, kid-from-Ohio-grin. "I gave up all that perpetuity business, which after all is just founded on a fear of death. You know that, of course. It's the big business concept all over again. I'm not afraid of dying suddenly, Frank, and leaving everything in a mess. Are you?"

"I'm nervous about it, Walter, I'll admit that."

"Would you do what I did, Frank? Tell the truth."

"I guess I'm still stuck on the perpetuity concept. I'm pretty conventional. I don't mean to disapprove, Walter. Because I don't."

Walter cocks his head when he hears this. He has just heard some unexpected good news, and his blue, sad eyes narrow as if they saw down a long corridor where the light had gone dim as all past time. He holds me in this bespectacled gaze for a long moment, maybe a half-minute. And I know exactly what he is seeing, or trying to see, since from time to time I've assiduously tried to see the same thing—with X before she left me for good.

Himself is what Walter's trying to see! If some old-fashioned, conventional Walter Luckettness is recognizable in conventional and forgiving Frank Bascombeness, maybe things won't be so bad. Walter wants to know if he can save himself from being lost out in the sinister and uncharted waters he's somehow gotten himself into. (For all his recklessness, Walter is basically a sound senator, and not much a seeker of the unknown.)

"Frank," Walter says, cracking a big smile, wriggling back in his chair and giving his head an incongruous shake. (For the moment he has staunched badness.) "Did you ever wish somebody or something could just pick you up and move you way, way far off?"

"Plenty of times. That's why I'm in the business I'm in. I can get on a plane and that happens. That's what I was telling you about traveling the other night."

"Well, that's how I felt when I first came in here tonight, Frank—when your colored boy let me in and I was just wandering around here waiting. I didn't feel like there was any place far away enough, and I was caught in the middle of a helluva big mess, and everything was just making it worse. Do you remember how we used to feel when we were kids? Everything out of bounds, just off the map, and we weren't responsible."

"It was great, Walter, wasn't it." What I'm thinking about is the fraternity, which was great. Splendid. Whiskey, card games, girls.

"Before I got here tonight everything seemed to count against me in some crappy way."

"I'm glad you came, then, Walter."

"I am too. I *do* feel better, thanks to you. Maybe it was us swapping some ideas back and forth. I feel like some new opportunity is just about to present itself. By the way, Frank, do you ever go duck hunting?" Walter smiles a big, generous smile.

"No."

"Well, let's *go* duck hunting, then. I've got all kinds of guns. I was just looking at them yesterday, cleaning them up. You can have one. I'd like you to come back to Coshocton with me, meet my family. Maybe next fall. That Ohio River country is really something. I used to go every single day of the season when I was a kid. You know, as far as Ohio seems, it's not really that far. Just down the Penn Turnpike. I haven't been going back lately, but I'm ready to start. My folks are getting old. What about your folks, Frank, where are they now?"

"They're dead, Walter."

"Ah well, sure. We lose 'em, Frank. What plans have you got?"

"When?"

"This summer, say." Walter is veritably beaming. I wish he would go home.

"I'm going to take my kids up around Lake Erie." What business is it of his what plans I have? Everything, to him, is pertinent now.

"Real good idea."

"I've just about had it, Walter. It's been a long day."

"I was in despair when I came here, Frank. A lot of life seemed behind me. And now it doesn't. What can I do? Do you want to go out and have some eggs? There's a good place on Route 1. What d'ya say to a breakfast?" Walter is on his feet, hands in his pockets, rocking back on his heels.

"I think I'll just hit the hay, Walter. The couch is your kingdom."

Walter reaches down, picks up his Colts glass, admires it, then hands it over to me. "I think I'll get in my car and drive around. That'll settle me down."

"I'll leave the door unlocked."

"Okay," Walter says with a brash laugh. "Frank, let me give you an extra key to *my* place. You can't tell when you're going to want to disappear for a while. My place is yours."

"Aren't you going to be in it, Walter?"

"Sure, but it can't hurt. Just so you'll know you can always drop out of sight when you want to." Walter hands me the key. I have no idea why Walter would think I'd ever need to drop out of sight.

"That's nice of you." I put the key in my pocket and give Walter a good-natured smile meant to make him leave.

"Frank," Walter says. Then without my expecting it or being able to duck or run, Walter grabs my cheek and kisses me! And I am struck dumb. Though not for long. I shove him backwards and in one spasm of wretchedness shout, "Quit it, Walter, I don't want to be kissed!"

Walter blushes red as Christmas and looks dazed. "Sure, sure," he says. I know I have missed Walter's point here, but I have not missed my own point, not on your life. I would kiss a camel rather than have Walter kiss me on the cheek again. He does not get to first base with me, no matter how much he feels at home.

Walter stands blinking behind his tortoise-shells. "We lose control by degrees, don't we, Frank?"

"Go home, Walter." I'm peevish now.

"Maybe I can, Frank. Thanks to you." Walter smiles his somber war-vet's smile and walks out the door.

In a moment I hear his car start. From the window I see the headlights on the street and the car—it is an MG—buzz sadly away. Walter gives me two quick honks and disappears around the curve. I am sure he will call when he gets home; he is that kind of High-school Harry. And as I settle onto the couch as I used to in the old days when X was gone, fully clothed, a Gokey catalog for reading, I unplug my phone—a small, silent concession to the way lived life works. Don't call, my silent message says, I'll be sleeping. Dreaming sweet dreams. Don't call. Friendship is a lie of life. Don't call.

IN THE FIRST six months after Ralph died, while I was in the deepest depths of my worst dreaminess, I began to order as many catalogs into the house as I could. At least forty, I'm sure, came every three months. I would, finally, have to throw a box away to let the others in. X didn't seem to mind and, in fact, eventually became as interested as I was, so that quite a few of the catalogs came targeted for her. During that time—it was summer—we spent at least one evening a week couched in the sun room or sitting in the breakfast nook leafing through the colorful pages, making Magic Marker checks for the things we wanted, dog-earing pages, filling out order blanks with our Bankcard numbers (most of which we never mailed) and jotting down important toll-free numbers for when we might want to call.

I had animal-call catalogs, which brought a recording of a dying baby rabbit. Dog-collar catalogs. Catalogs for canvas luggage that would stand up to Africa. Catalogs for expeditions to foreign lands with single women. Catalogs for all manner of outerwear for every possible occasion, in every climate. I had rare-book catalogs, record catalogs, exotic hand-tool catalogs, lawn-ornament catalogs from Italy, flower-seed catalogs, gun catalogs, sexual-implement catalogs, catalogs for hammocks, weathervanes, barbecue accessories, exotic animals, spurtles, slug catchers. I had all the catalogs you could have, and if I found out about another one I'd write or call up and ask for it.

X and I came to believe, for a time, that satisfying all our purchasing needs from catalogs was the very way of life that suited us and our circumstances; that we were the kind of people for whom catalog-buying was better than going out into the world and wasting time in shopping malls, or going to New York, or even going out into the shady business streets of Haddam to find what we needed. A lot of people we knew in town did the very same thing and believed that was where the best and most unusual merchandise came from. You can see the UPS truck on our street every day still, leaving off hammocks and smokers and God knows what all—packs of barbecue mitts and pirate chest mailboxes and entire gazebos.

For me, though, there was something other than the mere ease of purchase in all this, in the hours spent going through pages seeking the most virtuous screwdriver or the beer bottle cap rehabilitator obtainable nowhere else but from a PO box in Nebraska. It was that the life portrayed in these catalogs seemed irresistible. Something about my frame of mind made me love the abundance of the purely ordinary and pseudo-exotic (which always turns out ordinary if you go the distance and place your order). I loved the idea of merchandise, and I loved those ordinary good American faces pictured there, people wearing their asbestos welding aprons, holding their cane fishing rods, checking their generators with their new screwdriver lights, wearing their saddle oxfords, their same wool nighties, month after month, season after season. In me it fostered an odd assurance that some things outside my life were okay still; that the same men and women standing by the familiar brick fireplaces, or by the same comfortable canopy beds, holding these same shotguns or blow poles or boot warmers or boxes of kindling sticks could see a good day before their eyes right into perpetuity. Things were knowable, safe-and-sound. Everybody with exactly what they need or could get. A perfect illustration of how the literal can become the mildly mysterious.

More than once on a given night when X and I sat with nothing to say to each other (though we weren't angry or disaffected), it proved just the thing to enter that glimpsed but perfectly commonplace life—where all that mattered was that you had that houndstooth sport coat by Halloween or owned the finest doormat money could buy, or that all your friends recognized "Jacques," your Brittany, from a long distance away at night, and could call him by the name stitched on his collar and save him from the log truck bearing down on him just over the rise.

We all take our solace where we can. And *there* seemed like a life—though we couldn't just send to Vermont or Wisconsin or Seattle for it, but a life just the same—that was better than dreaminess and silence in a big old house where unprovoked death had taken its sad toll.

All of which passed in time, as I got more interested in women and X did whatever she did to accommodate her loss. Months later, when I had departed home to teach at Berkshire College, I found myself alone one night in the little dance professor's house the college rented for me at the low end of the campus near the Tuwoosic River, doing what I did in those first couple of weeks to the exclusion of practically everything else—poring over a catalog. (The faculty lounge was full of them, leading me to be sure I was not alone.) In this instance I was going through the supplement of a pricey hunting outfitter based in West Ovid, New Hampshire, at the foot of the White Mountains, barely eighty miles from where I sat at that moment. Up the hillside that night, a group of students was holding a sing-along (I was meant to be in attendance), and a cool, crisp burnt-apple smell swam with the New England air and flooded my open window, making the possibility of going as remote as Neptune. I was deep in size comparisons of Swiss wicker-and-leather picnic baskets, and just flipping back toward clearance items on the black-and-white insert pages, my thoughts on a fumble-free flashlight, ankle warmers for the chilly nights ahead, a predator-pruf feeder, when suddenly what do I see on page 88 but a familiar set of eyes.

After how many years? The narrow, half-squinty, mirthful sparkle I had seen a hundred times over—though on page 88 *only* the eyes were visible behind a black silk balaclava worn by a woman modeling a pair of silk underwear from Formosa.

Off in the darkening surround, the sounds of "Scarborough Fair" drifted into the purple hills, and the smell of elm and apple wood floated lushly through my open window, but I couldn't care less.

I flipped forward and back. And suddenly here was Mindy Levinson on almost every page: with long brown hair and a tentative smile, a Swedish Angora jacket over her shoulder (not looking the least bit Jewish); farther back, standing by a red Vermont barn, wearing a Harris Tweed casual jacket and appearing proud and arrogant; just inside the cover in an Austrian hat, but seeming repentant of some untold misdeed; elsewhere toward the back, ensconced in a comfy New Hampshire kitchen, starting a fire with a brass spark-igniter made in the shape of a duck's head. And later still, coralling a bunch of munchkin kids all wearing rabbit's fur puppet hats.

When she was my first college love interest, Mindy and I used to slip off campus, into her parents' Royal Oak home and boink the daylights out of each other for days on end. It was Mindy who had traveled with me on a tour of Hemingway Country and stayed out on a beach at Walloon Lake while fireflies twinkled. She was the first girl I ever lied to a room clerk because of. Later, of course, she married a slimy land developer named Spencer Karp and settled down in the Detroit suburb of Hazel Park near her parents and had kids before I was even through with school.

But I could not have been more stupefied. Out of a disorderly and not especially welcome present came a friendly, charitable face from the past (not an experience I have that often). Here was Mindy Levinson smiling at me twenty times out of a shiny life I might've had if I'd just gone to law school, gotten bored with corporate practice, dropped it all, moved up to New Hampshire, hung out my shingle, and set up my wife in a town-and-country dress shop all her own—a pretty life, prizable and beckoning, apparently without a crumb of alienation or desperate midnight heart's pounding. A fairy-tale life for real adults.

Where, I wondered, *was* Mindy? Where was Spencer Karp? Why did she not look Jewish now? What about Detroit?

What I did was immediately pick up the phone, dial the twenty-four-hour toll-free number and talk to a sleepy-sounding older woman whom I directed to the catalog page with the kids in the puppet hats and ordered three. As I was reading off my credit card number, I happened to say that the woman in that picture looked strangely familiar, like my sister from whom I was separated by the adoption agency. Did the company use local women for their models? I asked. "Yes," came the stoical reply. Did she know who this particular woman might be? There was then a pause. "I don't know nothin about that kind of thing," the woman said suspiciously. "Is this all you want to buy?" She sighed with exasperation and lack of sleep. I admitted it was but that I had decided not to buy the puppet hats after all, after which the woman cut me off.

I sat for a while and gazed out my screenless window into the yellow-lit dale of Berkshire College, where the maples and oaks were still in summer leaf, listening to "Scarborough Fair" change to "Michael, Row the Boat Ashore," and then to "Try to Remember," trying indeed to remember as much as I could about Mindy and those long-ago days in Ann Arbor, sensing both mystery and coincidence, and considering the small stirring caused by the two brown eyes behind the black balaclava, and the non-Jewish smile in a popcorn sweater.

A certain kind of mystery requires investigation so that a better, more complicated mystery can open up like an exotic flower. Many mysteries are not that easy to wreck and will stand some basic inquiry.

Mine entailed getting up at the crack of dawn the next day and driving the eighty miles over to West Ovid, strolling into the store whose catalog I brought with me, and asking the clerk straight out who this woman in the moleskin ratcatchers was, since she looked like a woman I had gone to college with and who had married my best friend in the service from whom I'd been separated in a Vietnamese POW camp and did not know the fate of to this very moment.

The cash register woman—a dwarfish, ruby-faced little Hampshirewoman—was only too happy to tell me that the woman in question was Mrs. Mindy Strayhorn, wife of Dr. Pete Strayhorn, whose dental office was down in the middle of town, and that all I had to do was go down there, walk in the office and see if he was my long-lost friend. I was not the first person, she said, to recognize old friends in the catalog, but that most people, when they inquired, turned out to be mistaken.

I could not get out the door fast enough. And not to Doc Strayhorn's, needless to say. But to the phone booth in front of the Jeep dealership across the road, where I looked up Strayhorn on Raffles Road and dialed Mindy without catching a breath or blinking an eye.

"Frank Bascombe?" she said, and I would've known her playful voice in a crowded subway car. "My goodness. How in the world did you ever find us here?"

"You're in the catalog," I said.

"Oh, well sure." She laughed in an embarrassed way. "Isn't that funny. I do it for the clothes discount, but Pete thinks it isn't quite nice."

"You really look great."

"Do I?"

"Darn right. You're prettier than ever. A whole lot prettier."

"Well, I had my nose fixed after I married Spencer. He hated my old one. I'm glad you like it."

"Where is Spencer?"

"Oh, Spencer. I divorced him. He was a crumb, you know." (I did know.) "I've lived here ten years now, Frank. I'm married to a nice man who's a dentist. We have children with perfect teeth."

"Great. It sounds like a great life. Plus you do the modeling."

"Isn't that a riot? How are you? What's happened to you in seventeen years? A lot, I'll bet."

"Quite a bit," I said. "I don't want to talk about that, though."

"Okay."

Red and silver streamers were spinning outside down the front of the Jeep dealership's lot. Two long lines of Cherokees and Apaches sat in the brisk New England sunlight. It soon would be winter, and the mountains at this latitude were already red and yellow higher up. In a day I would have to begin teaching students I already knew I wasn't going to like, and everything seemed to be starting on a new and perilous course. I knew, though, I wanted to see Mindy Levinson Karp Strayhorn one last time. Many, many things would've changed, but if she was who she was, I would still be me.

"Mindy?"

"What?"

"I'd sure like to see you." I felt myself grinning persuasively at the phone.

"When did you have in mind, Frank?"

"In ten minutes? I'm down the street right now. I was just passing through town."

"Ten minutes. That'll be great. It's pretty easy to find our house. Let me give you directions."

The rest of it was short but all I'd hoped for (though possibly not what you would think). I drove to her house, a rambling remodeled Moravian farmhouse with a barn, plenty of out-buildings and a pleasant pond that reflected the sky and the geese that swam on it. There was a golden dog and a housekeeper who looked at me suspiciously. Two children who might've been ten and eight, and a taller girl who might've been seventeen stood at the back end of the hall and smiled at me when their mother and I left. Mindy and I took a drive in my car with the top down toward Sunapee Lake and caught up on things. I told her about X and Ralph and my other children and my writing career and sportswriting and my plans to try teaching for a short while, all of which seemed not to interest her much, but in a pleasant way (I didn't expect anything different). She told me about Spencer Karp and about her husband and her children and how much she appreciated "just the general mental attitude" of the people up here in the "north country," and how in her mind the whole nation was changing not so much for the better as for the worse, and nobody could make her go back to Detroit now. At first she was guarded and skittish and talked like a travel agent as we skimmed along the highway, sitting over by the door as if she wasn't sure I wasn't some dark destroyer come to wreck her existence with out-of-date memories. After a while, though, when she saw how tame I really was, how enthusiastic, how all I wanted was to be near her life for a couple of hours, unquestioning and intending only to admire all from a distance and not to try and "go in" or to get her in the sack in some shabby motel on the way to Concord (exactly like I used to), then she liked me all over again and laughed and was happy the rest of the time. In fact, she eventually couldn't help giving me a kiss and a hug every little while, and putting her head on my shoulder once we were far enough from West Ovid that no one she knew would see her. She even told me she didn't intend to tell Pete about my visit, because that would make it all "the more delicious," which made me kiss her again and embarrass her.

And then I simply drove her home. She was wearing a mint-colored cotton dirndl right out of the catalog and which she raised above her excellent knees when she was sitting in the car. And she looked as pretty as her picture, which is how I remember her, and how I think of her each time I see her, season onto season, wearing one set of bright traditional clothes after another, on and on into a perfect future.

And what I felt as I drove back the long, slow road that evening toward the little town where Berkshire College sits, crossed the Connecticut and plowed my way into picture postcard Vermont, was: better. Better in all the possible ways. X and I were finally too modern for this kind of perfect, crystallized life—no matter how ours was turning out at the moment. But I had glimpsed a nearly perfect life of a kind, as literally perfect as the catalog promised it could be. And I had done it in a casual, offhand way, which was why Mindy liked me again and could kiss and hug me shamelessly. I had taken nothing away with me, had ruined nothing (though with another kiss I could've gotten her to that motel in Concord). I had had, in essence, a brief love affair not-quite. And that was quite enough for me, or for any man trying to get on a better, straighter track, trying to see the brighter side of things and put an end to his dreaminess, which I hoped was on the run by then, though I was certainly wrong.

A GRAY, SILVERMANE mist inhabits my room. I lie on the floor of the upstairs sleeping porch, fully clothed, my head cushioned by the boards, which are cold and morning-slicked by mist. In this posture I would often wake up in the months after X left. I would go to sleep reading catalogs, out like a light on the couch as I was last night, or in my bed or in the breakfast nook—but wake up on these same cold deals, still dressed and stiff as a mummy, with no memory of moving. I do not yet know what to make of it. Back then it didn't necessarily seem a bad sign, and it doesn't now. And though a longing permeates the cool morning, it is familiar enough, and I'm happy to lie still and listen to my heart harmlessly thump. It is Easter.

What I hear are typical Sunday sounds. Someone raking spring leaves in a nearby yard, finishing a chore begun months ago; a single horn blat from the first train down—moms and dads early for services at the Institute. A fat paper slaps the pavement. A rustle of voices next door at the Deffeyes' as they putter in the early dark. I hear the squeeze-squeak of Bosobolo in his room, his radio tuned low for all-night gospel. I hear a jogger on my street heading toward town. And far away in the stillness of pre-dawn—as far away, even, as the next sleeping town—I hear bells chiming a companionable Easter call. And I hear also: weeping. The low susurrus of a real grief being grieved somewhere in the cemetery, close by in the dark.

I go stand at the window and peer down into the early dawn, through the leafing copper beech and the tulip tree, but I can see nothing beneath the pale clouds-and-stars sky—only the low profiled shadows of white monuments and trees. No deer look up at me.

I have heard such sounds before. Early is the suburban hour for grieving—midway of a two mile run; a stop-off on the way to work or the 7-11. I have never seen a figure there, yet each one sounds the same, a woman almost always, crying tears of loneliness and remorse. (Actually, I once stood and listened, and after a while someone—a man—began to laugh and talk Chinese.)

I lie back on the bed and listen to the sounds of Easter—the optimist's holiday, the holiday with the suburbs in mind, the day for all those with sunny dispositions and a staunch belief in the middle view, a tiny, tidy holiday to remember sweetly and indistinctly as the very same day through all your life. I cannot remember a rainy Easter, or one when the sun didn't shine its heart out. Death, after all, is a mystery Christians can't get cozy with. It is too severe and unequivocal, a mistake in adding, we think. And we raise a clamor against it, call on the sun to stay cheery, preach the most rousing of sermons. "Well, now, let's us just hunker down to a *real* miracle, while we're putting two and two together." (A knowing, homiletic grin.) "Let's just let plasma physics and bubble chambers and quarks try and explain *this* one." (Grinning, nodding parishioners; sun beaming to beat the band through modern, abstract-ecumenical, permanently sunny window glass. Organ oratorio. Hearts expanding to victory.)

My only wish is that my sweet boy Ralph Bascombe could wake up from *his* sleep-out and come in the house for a good Easter tussle like we used to, then be off to once-a-year services. What a day that would be! What a boy! Many things would be different. Many things would never have changed.

X, I know, is not taking Paul and Clarissa to church, a fact which worries me—not because they will turn out godless (I couldn't care less) but because she is bringing them up to be perfect little factualists and information accumulators with no particular reverence or speculative interest for what's not known. Easter will soon seem like nothing more than a lurid folk custom, one they'll forget before they're past puberty. A myth. Naturally, there was no time for religion in the Dykstra household, where facts and figures reigned, though Irma tells me she has begun "experimenting" with Orange County Holy Rollerism, which makes me worry that the scales might tip for my own two once they get to the end of what can be sensibly, literally disclosed—which is where extremism lurks. You can, after all, know too damn much and end up with a big thumping loss you can't replenish. (Paul's mission for his pigeon three nights ago is an encouraging, countervailing sign.)

They may already know too much about their mother and father—nothing being more factual than divorce, where so much has to be explained and worked through intelligently (though they have tried to stay equable). I've noticed this is often the time when children begin calling their parents by their first names, becoming little ironists after their parents' faults. What could be lonelier for a parent than to be criticized by his child on a first-name basis? What if they were mean children, or by knowing too much, *became* mean? The plain facts of my alone life could make them tear me apart like maenads.

I am of a generation that did not know their parents as just plain folks—as Tom and Agnes. Eddie and Wanda. Ted and Dorie—as democratically undifferentiable from their children as ballots in a box. I never once thought to call my parents by their first names, never thought of their lives—remote as they were— as being like mine, their fears the equal of my fears, their smallest desires mirrors of everyone else's. They were my parents— higher in terms absolute and unknowable. I didn't know how they financed their cars. When they made love or how they liked it. Who they had their insurance with. What their doctor told them privately (though they must've both heard bad news eventually). They simply loved me, and I them. The rest, they didn't feel the need to blab about. That there should always be something important I wouldn't know, but could wonder at, wander near, yet never be certain about was, as far as I'm concerned, their greatest gift and lesson. "You don't need to know that" was something I was told all the time. I have no idea what they had in mind by not telling me. Probably nothing. Possibly they thought I would come to truths (and facts) on my own; or maybe—and this is my real guess—they thought I'd never know and be happier for it, and that not knowing would itself be pretty significant and satisfying.

And how right they were! And how hopeful to think my own surviving children could enjoy some confident mysteries in life, and not fall prey to idiotic factualism or the indignity of endless explanation. I would protect them from it if I could. Divorce and dreary parenting have, of course, made that next to impossible, though day to day I give it my most honest effort.

To get a divorce in a town this size, I should say, is not the least bit pleasant—though it is easy, and in so many ways the town is made for it, appreciates it, and knows how to act by way of supplying "support groups" (a woman's counseling unit called X the day of our settlement and invited her to a brown bag lunch at the library). Still, it is troubling to be a litigant in the building where you have gone to pay parking fines or retrieved stolen bikes, been supposed a solid citizen by stenos and beat cops. It leaves you with a bankrupt feeling, since the law here is not made to notice you or even to be noticed, only to give you respectable, disinterested sway. From what I hear, Las Vegas divorces are much better since no one notices anything.

Ours was the most amicable of partings. We could've stayed married, of course, and waited until things got better, but that was not what happened. Alan, X's little lawyer with fragrant dreams of a rich entertainment practice—XKEs awaiting him on tarmacs, chorus girls with giant tits—huddled up with my big, slope-shouldered, bearded, ex-Peace Corps, ex-alcoholic Middlebury guy and, across a mahogany table in Alan's office, struck a bargain in an hour. In principle I surrendered everything, though X didn't want much. I kept this house in exchange for helping her buy hers with my half of the savings. I laid claim to the Block Island map and three or four other treasures. We agreed on "irreconcilable differences" as the theme for our appearance in court, then all trooped across the street together and sat chatting uncomfortably in the back until our case was called. And in less than another hour we were "done," as they say in Michigan. X flew off with the children to a golf-and-swim holiday on Mackinac Island, to "open some space." I drove home, got drunk as a monkey and cried until dark.

What else could I do? The cleansing ritual of strong fluids and hot, balming tears is all we have native to us. I looked around for some Rupert Brooke poems or a copy of *The Prophet* but couldn't find them. Around eight, I stretched out on the couch, put a taped NBA slam-dunk contest on television, ate a pimento cheese sandwich, began to feel better and went to sleep watching Johnny. And my sleep, I remember, was one of the most sound and dreamless sleeps of my life—till eight-thirty the next day when I woke up hungry as a lion and as trusting to the future as a blind sky-diver.

Was I not alienated? Depressed? Ashamed? In need of violent

cheering up? Schitzy? On the edge? My answer is, not much.
Dreamy as Tarzan, perhaps. Lonely. Though in a way that I got
over after a while. But not chance's victim. I got myself busy
after breakfast, finishing up work on a six-pronged analysis of
major-leaguers' base stealing styles, and before I knew it I was
back in the thick of things. Which is how it's stayed. Bert Brisker
told me that after his divorce he went crazy, broke into his ex-
wife's house while she was gone on vacation, threw bricks
through the TV screen, slept in her bed and emptied cat shit in
all her drawers. But that is not the way I felt. We can make too
much of our misfortunes.

EVER SINCE I was in the Marines (I was only in six months) I've
been an early riser, and have done my best thinking then. I used
to lie nervously in my bunk, wide awake, waiting for the reveille
record, my mind thrumming, mapping out how I could do better
that day, make the Marine Corps take notice and be proud of
me; make myself less a victim of the funks and incongruities
my fellow officer candidates were wrestling with, rise to rank
quickly, and as a result help protect the lives of my men once we
got situated over in Vietnam, where I felt they'd have a lot on
their minds (like getting blown to smithereens). I had the advantage of an education, I thought, and I'd need to be their eyes and
ears over and above the level they themselves could see and hear.
I was an idiot, of course, but we're almost always wrong when
we are young.

What I'd like to do as I lie here, and before the day burgeons
into a glowing Easter, is put together some useful ideas about
Herb, just a detail or two to act as magnets for what else will occur
to me in the next days, which is the way good sportswriting gets
done. You hardly ever just sit down and write it cold, staring at
an empty yellow sheet expecting yourself to summon up every
good idea you'll have ready at the first moment. That can be the
scariest thing in the world. Instead, what you try to do is honor
your random instincts, catch yourself off guard, and write a sentence or an unexpected descriptive line—the way the air smelled
one day, or how the wind lifted and tricked off the lake surface
in a peculiar way that might later make the story inevitable. Once
those notes are on record, you put them away and let them draw

up an agenda of their own that you can discover later when you're sorting through things just before the deadline, and it's time to write.

Herb, though, is no easy nut to crack, since he's obviously as alienated as Camus. It would've helped if I'd filed away one perception or recorded a quote, but I didn't know what to say or think anymore than I know now. The way the air smelled or the wind shifted or what song was playing on the radio as we drove out, don't seem to figure. Simple, declarative sentences just don't exactly flock to big Herb's aid. Everything is minor key, subjunctive and contingent. *Herb Wallagher's got his eye on the future these days* (at least until his mood stabilizer wears through). *Herb Wallagher has seen life from both sides* (and doesn't think much of either one). *It would be easy for Herb Wallagher to take a dim view of life* (if he wasn't already as crazy as a road lizard).

The cheap-drama artists of my profession would, of course, make quick work of Herb. They're specialists at nosing out failure: hinting a fighter's legs as suspect once he's over thirty and finally in his prime; reporting a hitter's wrists are stiff just when he's learned to go the opposite way and can help the team by advancing runners. They see only the germs of defeat in victory, venality in all human endeavor.

Sportswriters are sometimes damned bad men, and create a life of lies and false tragedies. In Herb's case, they'd order up a grainy black-and-white fisheye of Herb in his wheelchair, wearing his BIONIC shirt and running shoes, looking like a caged child molester; take in enough of his crummy neighborhood to get the "flavor"; stand Clarice somewhere in the background looking haggard and lost like somebody's abandoned slave out of the dustbowl, then start things off with: "Quo Vadis Herb Wallagher?" The idea being to make us feel sorry enough for Herb, or some *idea* of Herb, to convince us we're all really like him and tragically involved, when in fact nothing of the kind is true, since Herb isn't even a very likable guy and most of us aren't in wheelchairs. (If I were paying salaries, those guys would be on the street looking for a living where they couldn't do any harm.)

Though what can I write that's better? I'm not certain. Some life does not give in to a sportswriter's point of view. It ought to

be possible to take a rear-guard approach, to look for drama in
the concept of retrenchment, to find the grit of the survivor in
Herb—something several hundred thousand people would be
glad to read with a stiff martini on a Sunday afternoon before
dinner (we all have our optimal readers and times), something
that draws the weave of lived life tighter. It's what's next that
I have to work on. Though in the end, this is all I ask for: to
participate briefly in the lives of others at a low level; to speak in
a plain, truth-telling voice; to not take myself too seriously; and
then to have done with it. Since after all, it is one thing to write
sports, but another thing entirely to live a life.

BY NINE I am up, dressed in my work clothes and out in the side
yard nosing around the flower beds like a porch hound. Following my speculations about Herb, I went back to sleep and woke
up happy and alert—my mind empty, the sun speckling through
the beech leaves and not a hint of ugly Detroit weather on the
horizon. My trip to the Arcenaults, however, is still two hours
off, and as is sometimes the case these days, I do not have quite
enough to do. One of the down-side factors to living alone is
that you sometimes get overly absorbed with how exact segments
of time are consumed, and can begin to feel a pleasure with life
that is hopelessly tinged with longing.

   Beyond my hemlock hedge Delia Deffeyes is out in her yard
in tennis whites, reading the newspaper, something I've seen her
do a hundred times. She and Caspar have had their morning
game, and now he has gone in for a nap. The Deffeyes and I have
a policy which says that simply seeing each other in our yards is
no reason to have a conversation, and normally we pass polite
offhand waves and smiling nods and go about our business.
Though I never mind an impromptu conversation. I am not a
man who hoards his privacy, and if I am out in my yard spreading
Vigaro or inspecting my crocuses, I am per se available for an
encounter. Delia and I do occasionally engage in nuts and bolts
publishing talk with reference to a book she's writing for the
historical society on European traditions in New Jersey architecture. My experience is years old, but I maintain a kind of
plain-talk, common-sense expertise about matters: "Any editor
worth his or her salt ought to appreciate the hell out of the kind

of attention to detail you're willing to give. You can't take that for granted, that's all I know." It *is* all I know, but Delia seems willing to take a word to the wise. She is eighty-two, born to a storied American business family in Morocco during the Protectorate, and has seen a wide world. Caspar has retired out of the diplomatic corps and came to the seminary afterward to teach ethics. Neither of them has too many years left on earth. (It is, in fact, a revelation to live in a town with a seminary, since like Caspar, seminarians are not a bit what you'd think. Most of them are not pious Bible-pounders at all, but sharp-eyed liberal Ivy League types with bony, tanned-leg second wives, and who'll stand with you toe to toe at a cocktail party, drink scotch and talk about their timeshare condos in Telluride.)

Delia spies me down behind the children's jungle gym, fingering a rose bud that's ready to bloom, and wanders over to the hemlock hedge shaking her head, though apparently still reading. It is her signal and the premise of our neighborliness—all our conversations are just extensions of the last one, even though they are often on different subjects and months apart.

"Now here, Frank, look at this." Delia holds up the front page of the *Times* to show me something. Church bells have begun clamoring and gonging across town. On all streets families are off to Sunday school in spanking new Easter get-ups—cars washed and polished to look like new, all arguments suspended. "What do you think about what our government's doing to the poor people in Central America?"

"I haven't kept very close tabs on that, Delia," I say from the roses. "What's going on down there now?" I give her a sunny smile and walk over to the hedge.

Her moist blue eyes are large with effrontery. (Her hair is the precise blue color of her eyes.) "Well, they're mining all the ports down there, in, let's see," she takes a quick peek, "Nicaragua." She crushes the open paper down in front of her and blinks at me. Delia is small and brown and wrinkled as an iguana, but has plenty of strong opinions about world affairs and how they ought to work out. "Caspar's extremely discouraged about it. He thinks it'll be another Vietnam. He's in the house right now calling up all his people in Washington trying to find out what's really going on. He may still have some influence, he thinks, though I don't see how he could."

"I've been out of town a couple of days, Dee." I stand and admire Dee and Caspar's pair of pink pottery flamingos which they bought in Mexico.

"Well, I don't see why we should mine each other's ports, Frank. Do you? Honestly?" She shakes her head in private disappointment with our entire government, as though it had been one of her very favorites but suddenly become incomprehensible. For the moment, though, my mind's as empty as a jug, captured by the belling at the seminary carillon. "Come my soul, thou must be waking; now is breaking o'er the earth another day." I find I cannot bring up the name or the face of the man who is president, and instead I see, unaccountably, the actor Richard Chamberlain, wearing a burnoose and a nicely trimmed Edwardian beard.

"I guess it would depend on what the cause was. But it doesn't sound good to me." I smile across the flat-trimmed hedge. I have to work at being a full adult around Delia, since if I'm not careful our age difference—roughly forty-five years—can have the effect of making me feel like I'm ten.

"We're hypocrites, Frank, if that's our policy. You should bear in mind Disraeli's warning about the conservative governments."

"I don't remember that, I guess."

"That they're organized hypocrisy, and he wasn't wrong about that."

"I remember Thomas Wolfe wrote about making the world safe for hypocrisy. But that's not the same."

"Caspar and I think that the States should build a wall all along the Mexican frontier, as large as the Great Wall, and man it with armed men, and make it clear to those countries that we have problems of our own up here."

"That's a good idea."

"Then we could at least solve our own problem with the black man." I don't exactly know what Delia and Caspar think about Bosobolo, but I do not intend asking. For being anti-colonial, Delia has some pretty strong colonial instincts. "You writers, Frank. Always ready to set sail with any wind that blows."

"The wind can blow you interesting places, Dee." I say this with only mock seriousness, since Delia knows my heart.

"I see your wife at the grocery, and she doesn't seem very happy to me, Frank. And those two sweet babies."

"They're all fine, Dee. Maybe you caught her on a bad day. Her golf game gets her down sometimes. She really didn't get a fair start on a real career. I think she's trying to make up for lost time."

"I do too, Frank." Delia nods, her face like lean old glove leather, then folds her paper in a neat paperboy's fold that's wonderful to see. I'm ready to dawdle away back to the roses and crab apples. Delia and I are sympathetic to each other's private causes, and both realize it, and that is good enough for me. For a moment I spy Frisker, her seal-point, sleuthing around the hibiscus below Caspar's flag pole, staring up at the bird feeder where a junco's perched. Frisker has been known to prowl my roof at night and wake me up, and I've thought about getting a slingshot, but so far haven't. "Man wasn't meant to live alone, Frank," Delia says significantly, eyeing me closely all of a sudden.

"It has its pluses, Delia. I've adjusted pretty well now."

"How long has it been since you read *The Sun Also Rises*, Frank?"

"It's probably been a while now."

"You should reread it," Delia says. "There're important lessons there. That man knew something. Caspar met him in Paris once."

"He was always one of my favorites." Not true, though a lie's what's asked for. It's not surprising that Delia's view of the complex world dates from about 1925. In fact it might have been a better time back then.

"Caspar and I were married in our sixties, you know."

"I didn't realize that."

"Oh, yes. Caspar had a nice fat wife who died. I even met her once. Of course, my own poor husband died years before. Caspar and I went out of wedlock in Fez, in 1942, and kept aware of each other's whereabouts afterwards. When I heard Alma, his fat wife, had died, I called him up. I was with a niece in Maine by then, and in two months Caspar and I were married and living just below Mount Reconnaissance in Guam, which was his last posting. I certainly didn't expect what I got from life, Frank. But I didn't waste time either." She smiles fiercely, as if she can see my future and the certainty that it will not be quite as wonderful.

"It's a beautiful day, isn't it, Dee?"

"It is, yes. It's quite lovely. I believe it's Easter."

"I can't remember a prettier one."

"I can't either, Frank. Why don't you come over this week and have a scotch with Caspar. He'd love for you to come talk men's talk. I think he's pretty upset by all this mining." In the fourteen years I've lived here, I have been in the Deffeyes' house only two times (both times to fix something), and Delia means no harm by one more insincere invitation. We have reached the natural end of our neighborliness, though she's too polite to admit the inevitability of it, a quality I like in her. I gaze up from the yard into the still blue Easter morning and, to my surprise, see a balloon, large upon the currents of a gleaming atmosphere, its mooring lines adangle, a big red moon with a smiling face on its bloated bag. Two tiny stick-figure heads peer down from the basket, point arms at us, pull a chain which produces a far-off gasping.

Where did they leave earth, I wonder? The grounds of a nearby world headquarters? A rich man's mansion on the Delaware? How far can they see on a clear day? Are they safe? Do they *feel* safe?

Delia does not seem to notice, and awaits my answer to her invitation.

"I'll do that, Dee." I smile. "Tell Cap I'll stop by this week. I've got a joke to tell him."

"Any day but Tuesday." She smiles a prissy smile. This is the usual complication. "He misses men, I'm afraid."

Delia strays away now with her paper to her sunny lawn and tennis court, me to my barbecue pit and roses and day, upward-tending in most all ways, one I'll be happy to put into the file of Easters spent richly and forgotten.

Gong, go the bells in town. Gong, gong, gong, gong, gong.

JUST BEFORE ten I put in a call to X, to wish the children happy Easter. It is now a holiday we "trade," and this the first one when I haven't been around. Though no one's home on Cleveland Street. X's answer message says that if I'm interested in golf lessons I should leave my name and number. In the background I hear Clary say "Later, bird brain," and break up laughing. There is an edge in X's voice now, something strange to me, an all-business, money-in-the-bank brassiness that reminds me of

her father. It makes me wonder if my family is off smorging in
Bucks County with one of X's software or realtor friends, some
big hairy-armed guy in a green sports jacket, with everything on
the company cuff.

I decide not to leave a message (though I'd like to).

For some reason I call Walter Luckett's number and let the
phone ring a long time without an answer while I stare out on
the paisley Easter street. Where would I be if I were Walter? In
some bully bar in the West Village? Cruising the elmy streets
of insular Newfoundland in a devil's own fury? Hitting some
backboard balls at the high school before taking in *The Robe* at
Lost Bridge Mall? I'm not even certain I care to know. Some
people were not made to have best friends, and I might be one.
Walter might be another, though for different reasons. Acquaint-
anceship usually suffices for me, which was more or less the one
important lesson learned from my Lebanese girlfriend, Selma
Jassim, at Berkshire College, since if anything, she believed
mutual confidences of almost any kind were just a lot of baloney.

I decided to go teach at Berkshire College—I know now—to
deflect the pain of terrible regret—the same reason I quit writing
my novel, years ago, and began to write sports; the same reason
most of us make our dramatic turns to the right and left about
midway, and the same reason some people drive right off the
course and into the ditch.

One afternoon a year after Ralph died, I was at home on one
of the week-long breaks that occur at the magazine between
large assignments, and when we are supposed to rest up and
re-establish a semblance of regular life. I was sitting in the breakfast nook—it was in May—reading some piled-up copies of *Life*
when the phone rang. The man calling said his name was Arthur
Winston and he was married to Beth Winston, who was the sister
of my former literary agent, Sid Fleisher, whom I had not heard
from since he had written us a condolence card. Arthur Winston
said he was the chairman of the English Department at Berkshire
College in Massachusetts, and he had been talking to Sid in Sid's
house in Katonah, and Sid had mentioned a writer he had once
represented who had written one good book of short stories, but
then quit writing entirely. One thing led to another, Arthur said,
and he had ended up with the book, which he claimed to have
read and admired. He asked if I had been writing any other short

stories since then, and for some reason I gave him an evasive answer which could've made him think I had, and that with a little coaxing I could actually be induced to write plenty more (though none of this was true). He said to me then that he was over a pretty big barrel. The usual writer at Berkshire, an older man whose name I didn't know, had suddenly gone berserk at the end of the spring semester and started vicious fist fights with several people—one of them a woman—and had begun carrying a gun under his coat, so that he had been institutionalized and would not be back in the fall. Arthur Winston said he knew it was a long shot, but that Sid Fleisher had said I was a "pretty interesting" fellow who'd lived a "pretty unusual" life since quitting writing, and he—Arthur—thought maybe a semester of teaching would be just the thing to get my work fired up again, and if I wanted to do it he would consider it a personal favor to him and would see to it I taught anything I pleased. And I simply said "Yes, that's fine," and that I would be there in the fall.

I do not exactly know what got into my thinking. I had never thought about such a thing in my life, and in one way it couldn't have been crazier. The magazine, of course, is always happy to extend leaves for what it considers widening experiences. But when I told X she just stood there in the kitchen and stared out the window at the Deffeyes' tennis court where Paul and Clary were watching Caspar play with one of his octogenarian friends —each old man wearing a crisp white sweater and hitting bright orange balls in high looping volleys—and said "What about us? We can't move to Massachusetts. I don't want to go there."

"That's fine," I said, actually for a moment seeing myself leading a graduation day exercise at some tiny Gothic-looking campus, wearing a floppy cap and crimson gown, carrying a scepter, and being the soul of everyone's admiration. "I'll commute," I said. "The three of you can come up odd weekends. We'll go stay in country inns with cider mills. We'll have a wonderful time. It'll be easy." I was suddenly eager to get up there.

"Have you lost your mind?" X turned and looked at me as if she could in fact see that I'd lost my mind. She smiled at me in an odd way then, and it seemed she knew something bad was happening but was powerless to help. (This was during the worst of the time with the other women, and she had been doing a lot of holding her peace.)

"No. I haven't lost my mind," I said, smiling guiltily. "This is something I've always wanted to do." (Which was a total lie.) "There's no time like the present if you ask me. What do you think?" I went over to give her a pat on the arm, and she just turned and went out into the yard. And that was the last time we ever talked about it. I started making arrangements with the college to provide me a house. I asked for and received my leave from the magazine (a Breadth Fellowship was what they called it). My texts were mailed down midway through the summer, and I did what I felt like was proper preparation. Then at the first of September I packed the Chevy and drove up.

WHAT I FOUND, of course, when I got my feet under me was that I had about as much business teaching in college as a duck has riding a bicycle, since what was true was that in spite of my very best efforts I had *nothing to teach*.

It's rare, when you think about it, that anyone ever would, given that the world is as complicated as a microchip and we all learn it slowly. I knew plenty of things, a whole lifetime's collection. But it was all just about myself, and significant only to me (love is transferable; location isn't actually everything). But I didn't care to reduce any of it to fifty minute intervals, to words and a voice ideal for any eighteen-year-old to understand. That's dangerous as a snake and runs the risk of discouraging and baffling students—whom I didn't even like—though more crucially of reducing *yourself*, your emotions, your own value system —your life—to an interesting syllabus topic. Obviously this has a lot to do with "seeing around," which I was in the grip of then but trying my best to get out of. When you are not seeing around, you're likely to speak in your own voice and tell the truth as you know it and not for public approval. When you *are* seeing around, you're pretty damn willing to say anything—the most sinister lie or the most clownish idiocy known to man—if you think it might make someone happy. Teachers, I should say, are highly susceptible to seeing around, and can practice it to the worst possible consequence.

I could twine off sports anecdotes, Marine Corps stories, college jokes, occasionally vet an easy Williams poem to profit, tell a joke in Latin, wave my arms around like a poet to demonstrate enthusiasm. But that was all just to get through fifty minutes. When it came time to teach, literature seemed wide and undifferentiable—not at all distillable—and I did not know where to start. Mostly I would stand at the tall windows distracted as a camel while one of my students discussed an interesting short story he had found on his own, and I mused out at the dying elms and the green grass and the road to Boston, and wondered what the place might've looked like a hundred years ago, before the new library was put up and the student center, and before they added the biplane sculpture to the lawn to celebrate the age of flight. Before, in other words, it all got ruined by modernity gone haywire.

The fellows in my department, God knows, couldn't have been a better bunch. To their way of thinking, I was a "mature writer" trying to get back on my feet after a "promising start" followed by a fallow period devoted to "pursuing other interests," and they were willing to go to bat for me. To make them all feel better I claimed to be putting together a new collection based on my experiences as a sportswriter, but in truth any thought I had for such an enterprise fled like thunder the minute I set foot on campus. I'd see a copy of my book at a dozen different houses at a dozen different dinner parties (the same library copy that made its way around ahead of me). And though no one ever mentioned it, I was to understand that it had been read closely and remarked on admiringly and in private by people who mattered. One crisp October evening at the house of a Dickens scholar, I inconspicuously removed it off the coffee table, put it in the snappy autumn fire and stood and watched it burn (with the same satisfaction X must've felt when her hope chest billowed up our chimney), then went in to dinner, ate chicken Kiev and had a good time talking in a pseudo-English accent about departmental politics and anti-Semitism in T. S. Eliot. I ended up late that night in a bar across the New York line, with Selma, who had also been a guest, arguing the virtues of the American labor movement and the checkered career of Emil Mazey with a bunch of right-to-work conservatives, and afterward sleeping in a motel.

My colleagues, I should say, were all fiercely interested in sports, especially baseball, and could carry on informative brass-tacks conversations about how statistics lie, hitting zones and

who the great all-time bench managers had been—bull sessions
that could last half an evening. They often knew much more than
I did and wanted to talk for hours about exotic rule applications,
who covers what on a double-steal, and the "personalities" of
ball parks. They would often alter their own English or urban
accents to a vaguely southern, "athletic" accent and then talk
that way for hours, which also happened at Haddam cocktail
parties. I even had some confide wistfully that they wished they'd
done what I did, but had never seen where the "gap" was in a
young life that let you think about such a thing as being a sportswriter. All of them, of course, had gone right out of college,
raced through graduate school, and as far as possible gotten jobs,
tenure, and a life set for them. If they'd had any "gaps," they
didn't acknowledge them, since that might've had something to
do with a failure of some kind—a bad grade, a low board score
or a wishy-washy recommendation by an important professor,
something that had scared the bejesus out of them and that they
wanted to forget all about now.

Still, I could tell it confused them that something had happened to me that hadn't happened to them, and that here I was
in their midst, and not such a bad guy after all, when their lives
seemed both perfect and perfectly ordinary. They would smile
at me and shake their heads, arms folded, pipes clenched tight,
ties adjusted, and for some reason I didn't and still can't understand, listen to me talk! (whereas they wouldn't listen to each
other for a second). I was specimen-proof that life could be
different from theirs and still be life, and they marveled at it.

Writing sports was, I think, inviting to them just the way it's
inviting to me, and also exotic, but because of its literalness it
sometimes embarrassed and scared them and made them laugh
and fold and refold their arms like Zulus.

They all seemed, however, extremely encouraging that I give
another try at real writing. That was something they could
understand a fellow wanting to do and then failing at nobly. They
respected deeply the nobility of small failures since that was what
they suspected of themselves. Though for my lights they thought
too little of themselves, and didn't realize how much all of us are
in the very same boat, and how much it is an imperfect boat.

I do not hold to the old belief that professors like writers
because they can see us fail in a grander and sillier and therefore

more unequivocal way than they have. On the contrary, they like to see someone trying, giving it all up to set a permanent mark. They may also be absolutely expecting to watch you fail, but they aren't really cynical types at all. And since I wasn't trying to set any marks (they simply *thought I* was and had some admiration for me for that reason) I probably got the best the place had to offer.

The only people whom I can say with certainty I didn't get along with were the "junior people," the sad, pencil-mouthed and wretched hopefuls. They hated the sight of me. I was, I think, too much like them—unprotected in the world—yet different in a way they found infuriating, incriminating and irrelevant. Nothing is more inciteful of disdain than somebody doing something other than what you're doing, not doing it badly but not complaining about it (though at the moment I was as much at sea as a man can be). They looked on me with real disgust and usually wouldn't even speak, as if certain human enterprise was synonymous with laughable failure, though at the same time as if something about me seemed familiar and might figure dimly in their futures if things did not work out. The gallows, I imagine, is less scary to the condemned man than to the one not yet sentenced.

I told them without rancor or the first wish to worry them that if they didn't get tenure they might give sportswriting a serious try, as other people in that situation had. Though they never appeared to like that advice. I think they didn't appreciate the concept of interchangeability, and no one ever came by to apply for a job after they were let go.

Finally, though, what I couldn't stand was not what you might think.

I didn't mind the endless rounds of meetings, which I sat through wearing a smile and with nothing whatsoever in my mind. I didn't care a mouse's fart for "learning"—didn't even feel I understood what it meant in their language—since I couldn't begin to make my students see the world I saw. I ended up feeling an aching remorse for the boys, especially the poor athletes, and could only think of the girls in terms of what they looked like in their vivid underwear. But I was impressed with my colleagues' professionalism: that they knew where all "their books" were in the library, knew the new acquisitions by heart, never had to waste time at the card catalog. I enjoyed bumping into them down in the lower level stacks, gossiping and elbowing one another about female faculty, tenure, sharing some joke they'd heard or whatever scandal had turned up in *TLS* that week. What they did, how they conducted life, was every bit as I would've done if I was them—treated the world like an irrelevant rib-tickler, and their own comfortable lives like an elite men's club. I never once felt a sense of superiority, and would be surprised if they did. I didn't object to the fisherman's sweaters, the Wallabies, pipes, dictionary games, charades, the long dinner party palaver about "sibs" and "La Maz" and college boards and experimental treatments for autism, the frank talk about lesbianism and who was right in the Falklands (I liked Argentina). I even got used to the little, smirky, insider mailbox-talk passed between people I had just eaten dinner with the night before, but who, the next morning, would address me only in sly, crypto-ironic references from whatever we'd talked about last night: "... put *this* memo in *The Cantos*, right, Frank? See if Ole Ezra can translate that. Haw!" Live and let live is my motto. I'm at home with most interest groups, even in the speakers' bureau at the magazine, for whom I occasionally journey into the country to talk to citizens about the philosophy of building-from-within, or to deliver canned sports anecdotes.

To the contrary. These eternally youthful, soft-handed, lank-shouldered, blameless fellows—along with a couple of wiry lesbians—were all right with me. They could always give in to their genuine boyishness around me, which was something their wives encouraged. They could quit playing at being serious and surrender to giggly silliness most any time after a few drinks, the same as real folks.

And deep down, I think, they liked me, since that's how I treated them—like decent Joes, even the lesbians, who seemed to appreciate it. They'd have been happy to have me around longer, maybe forever, or else why would they have asked me to "stay on" when they could tell that something was wrong with me, with my life, something that made me melancholy, though all of them were careful enough never to say a word about it.

What I did hate, though, and what finally sent me at a run out of town after dark at the end of term, without saying goodbye or even turning in my grades, was that with the exception of Selma, the place was all anti-mystery types right to the core—-men and women both—all expert in the arts of explaining, explicating and dissecting, and by these means promoting permanence. For me that made for the worst kind of despairs, and finally I couldn't stand their grinning, hopeful teacher faces. Teachers, let me tell you, are born deceivers of the lowest sort, since what they want from life is impossible—time-freed, existential youth forever. It commits them to terrible deceptions and departures from the truth. And literature, being lasting, is their ticket.

Everything about the place was meant to be lasting—life no less than the bricks in the library and books of literature, especially when seen through the keyhole of their incumbent themes: eternal returns, the domination of man by the machine, the continuing saga of choosing middling life over zesty death, on and on to a wormy stupor. Real mystery—the very reason to read (and certainly write) any book—was to them a thing to dismantle, distill and mine out into rubble they could tyrannize into sorry but more permanent explanations; monuments to themselves, in other words. In my view all teachers should be required to stop teaching at age thirty-two and not allowed to resume until they're sixty-five, so that they can *live* their lives, not teach them away—live lives full of ambiguity and transience and regret and wonder, be asked to explain nothing in public until very near the end when they can't do anything else.

Explaining is where we all get into trouble.

What's true, of course, is that they were doing exactly what I was doing—keeping regret at arm's length, which is wise if you understand it exactly. But they had all decided they really didn't have to regret anything ever again! Or be responsible to anything that wasn't absolutely permanent and consoling. A blameless life. Which is not wise at all, since the very best you can do is try and keep the regret you can't avoid from ruining your life until you can get a start on whatever's coming.

Consequently, when these same people are suddenly faced with a real ambiguity or a real regret, say something as simple as telling a sensitive young colleague they probably like and have had dinner with a hundred times, to go and seek employment elsewhere; or as complicated as a full-bore, rollicking infidelity right in their own homes (colleges are lousy with it)—they couldn't be more bungling, less ready, or more willing to fall to pieces because they can't explain it to themselves, or wanting to, won't; or worse yet, willing to deny the whole beeswax.

Some things can't be explained. They just are. And after a while they disappear, usually forever, or become interesting in another way. Literature's consolations are always temporary, while life is quick to begin again. It is better not even to look so hard, to leave off explaining. Nothing makes me more queasy than to spend time with people who don't know that and who can't forget, and for whom such knowledge isn't a cornerstone of life.

Partly as a result, Selma Jassim and I gave ourselves up to the frothiest kind of impermanence—reveled in it, staved off regret and the memory of loss with it. (Muslims, let me tell you, are a race of people who understand impermanence. More so even than sportswriters.)

A person with a cold eye might say what happened between Selma and me—after our romantic dinner in the starchy fire-placed Vermont Yankee Inn the very night I put X and the children on the bus—was simply an example of the usual shabby little intrigues visiting firemen in small New England colleges are expected to get embroiled in, since there's nothing else to do from bleary week to bleary week, and you're not really into the swing of things. And my answer is that in the grip of desperate dreaminess even the most trivial of human connections can bear a witness, and sometimes can actually improve a life that's stranded. (Beyond that, you can never successfully argue the case for your own passions.)

X had come up with the children the second weekend I was there (I'd just seen Mindy Levinson). She brought a pair of brass candlesticks for my little house, neatened the whole place up, sat in one of my classes, went with me to faculty parties two nights in a row and seemed to have a good time. She slept late and took a long autumnish walk with me along the Tuwoosic, during which we talked about a spring driving trip with the children down to the Big Bend Country, something she had been reading about. But as we were driving out to the Bay State Tavern for the three of them to catch the bus home Sunday morning, she looked across the seat at me and said "I really don't have any idea what you're doing up here, Frank. But it really all seems pretty extremely stupid to me, and I want you to resign and come home right now with us. It's not so great being home without you."

I told her, of course, that I couldn't just leave. (Though if I had I might still be married, and I had the feeling she was dead right about my staying; that another failed writer would crawl out of the woodwork and be in my place in less than twenty-four hours, and Arthur Winston would never think of my "interesting" face again.) I felt, however, that something had brought me up there and it may have been ridiculous, but I thought I needed to see what it was—which is what I told X. Plus, I'd given my word. I told her, lamely, that I wanted her to come up every weekend, and she could even take Paul out of school and move all three of them in with me (which was, needless to say, even more ridiculous).

When I said all this, X sat in the car staring out at the waiting bus, then sighed and said sadly "I'm not coming back up here anymore at all, Frank. Something's in the air up here that makes me feel old and completely silly. So you'll just have to go it alone."

And with that she got out with Paul and Clary, and lugged their big bag onto the bus. When they climbed aboard the children both cried (X didn't), and they left me standing alone and dazed, waving at them from the Bay State parking lot.

What Selma and I did after that and for the next thirteen weeks before I went back home to New Jersey and divorce, was simply share a fitful existence. She was an acerbic cold-eyed Arab of dusky beauty, who was thirty-six at the time (exactly my age), but seemed older than I was. She had come to Berkshire College that fall from Paris only to obtain a visa (she said), so she could find a rich American "industrialist," marry him, then settle down in a rich suburb for a happy life. (She knew a pleasant, easy existence staunched almost any kind of unhappiness.)

I never visited home again until the semester was over, and X never wrote me or even called. And what Selma and I did to amuse ourselves was stay inside my little faculty cottage lolling in bed, or else drive in my Malibu wherever we could go in the time we had away from campus, talking for hours about whatever interested us—conversations I actually remember as the most engrossing of my entire life—primarily, of course, because they were stolen. We drove to Boston, up to

Maine, down into Westchester, far up into Vermont, and as far west as Binghamton. We stayed in small motels, ate in roadhouses, stopped for drinks in bars with names like The Mohawk, The Eagle and The Adams—dark, remote, millstone places where the outside world rarely entered, and where we knew no one and were cause for no notice: a tall, long-necked Arab woman in sleek black silks, smoking French cigarettes, and an ordinary-looking Joe in a crew-neck sweater, chinos and a John Deere Tractor cap I'd affected when I got to Berkshire. We were tourists headed to and from nowhere.

We hardly ever talked about literary subjects. She was a critical theorist and as far as I could tell had only the darkest, most ironic contempt for all of literature. (As a joke, she invented a scheme for taking all the "I" pronouns out of one of F. Scott Fitzgerald's novels and gave a seminar on it that all our colleagues said was "ingenious.") What we talked about instead were small-talk things—why a particularly brilliant hillside of sugar maples changed their color at different schedules and what that might suggest of disease; why American highways ran though the places they did; what it was like to drive in London (where I have never been and she had been a student); her first husband, who was British; my only wife; an acting career she'd abandoned; how I felt about compulsory military service at various crucial stages in my life—nothing of great interest, though anything that came along and that we could chatter about without implying a future (we had no delusions about that). Yet it all served to make one day passable before we had to go back to teach, something I came to loathe. I found out a great deal about her in the course of things, though I never asked any of it, and it was always understood that I really knew nothing. There were other people in her life, I knew that, a good many of them, men and women both, people who lived in foreign countries—some possibly even in prison—others who were estranged for reasons that she simply wouldn't go into. For a period of one week I felt extremely strongly about her, entertained all kinds of impractical and romantic notions, things I never went into, and then I abandoned them all. I told her I loved her a hundred times, usually in chuckling, dare-devilish ways we both understood was a lot of hooey, since she laughed at the idea of almost any kind of usual affection and claimed love was an emotion she had no interest in finding out about.

She had only one, I thought, strange attachment, which was the subject of altruism and which she lectured me about at length the first morning we woke up together, when she was standing around naked in my sunny little house smoking cigarettes and staring out the window at the Tuwoosic as if it were the Irrawaddy. She said altruism drove Arabs crazy because it was always "phony" (a word she liked). She grew furious when she talked about it, threw her head from side to side and shouted and laughed, while I simply sat in bed and admired her. It was not religion or economics that fueled the flames of world hatreds, she felt; it was altruism. She told me that first morning, with a grave look, that by the time she was eighteen she'd survived two drug addictions, a "profound" involvement with terrorists in which she hinted she'd killed people; been kidnaped, raped, imprisoned, had flirtations with a number of dark *isms*, all of which had galvanized her intellect and forged unassuageably her belief that she knew why people did things—to suit themselves and no other reason—which was why she preferred to stay as remote as possible. She said she disliked the Christian members of the faculty (not the Jews), and not because of the self-satisfied squalor of their collegiate lives which she made laughing, sneering reference to (though only because they weren't rich), but because the Christians thought they were altruists and pretended to be generous and well-meaning. The only remedy for altruism, she felt, was either to be very poor or enormously rich. And she knew which of those she wanted.

What Selma thought about me I'm not exactly sure. I thought *she* was simply a knock-out, though I'm not certain she didn't think of me as pathetic, despite expressing admiration for me of the kind every American would like to inspire when traveling to far-away, more advanced cultures. I would sometimes get into sudden states of agitation during which I would clam up and get somber as a mental patient or else begin directing vicious remarks toward something I knew nothing about—often, near the end of the term, it was some colleague I'd decided had slighted me, but whom I really had nothing against and usually had never even met. Selma would humor me at that point and say she'd never met anyone like me; that I was the savvy, hard-nosed realist she had heard real Americans were (puny academics fell far below), but that I also had a thoughtful, complicatedly whole-hearted and vulnerable side which made the whole mix of my character intellectually exotic and brilliant. She said it had been a positive step to quit real writing and become a sports-writer, which she knew practically nothing about, but saw just as a way of making a living that wasn't hard. She thought my being at Berkshire College was as ridiculous as X did, and as her own presence there. Though in truth what I really think she thought of me was that we were alike, both of us displaced and distracted out of our brainpans and looking for ways to get along. "You might just as well have been a Muslim," she said more than once and raised her long sharp nose in a way I knew she meant as estimable. "You should've been a sportswriter, too," I said. (I didn't know what I meant by that, though we both laughed about it like apes.)

From a distance it could seem that Selma and I existed on the most dallying edge of cynicism. Though that would be dead wrong, since to be truly cynical (such as when I romanced all those eighteen women in all those major sports venues of this nation) you have to hoodwink yourself about your feelings. And we knew exactly what we were doing and what we were existing on. No phony love, or sentimentality, or bogus interest. No pathos. But only on anticipation, which can be as good as any-thing else, including love. She understood perfectly that when the object of anticipation becomes paramount, trouble begins to lurk like a panther. And since she wanted nothing from me— I was not an industrialist and had many more problems than I needed; and since I wanted nothing from her but to have her in my car or in my bed, laughing and touring the quilted New Eng-land landscape like leaf-peepers, we thrived. (I figured this out later, since we never talked about it.)

What we anticipated no one of course could ever make a whole, free-standing life out of and expect it to last very long. A nighttime drive to get dinner at a state-line roadhouse, in which you cruise through hills and autumn-smelling woods and feel almost too cold before you're home. A phone's sudden ring-ing on an Indian summer night when insects buzz but you have expected it. The sound of a car outside your house and a door swinging closed. The noise of what becomes a familiar deep breathing. The sound of cigarette smoke against a telephone, the tinkle-chink of ice cubes from a caressing silence. The Tuwoosic rilling in your sleep, and the slow positive feeling that all might not be entirely lost—followed by the old standard closure and sighs of intimacy. She gave in to the literal in life but almost nothing else, and for that reason mystery emanated from her like a fire alarm. And there isn't much more to life without much more complication.

There was, I should say, no one thing that happened between us, nothing that either of us said that made a difference to our lives longer than a moment. The particulars would only seem as ordinary as they were. For the two of us, ours was just a version of life briefly perfected (though in a way that showed me something) and that ended.

In any case, what more did I have to look forward to? My semester? My bunch of smiling, explaining colleagues? Life without my first son? My diminishing life at home with X? The gradual numbly-crumbly toward the end stripe? I don't know. I didn't know then. I simply found out that you couldn't know another person's life, and might as well not even try. And when it was all over (we simply went out for a drink at the Bay State and said goodbye as if we'd just met each other), I left campus after dark and headed back to New Jersey without even reporting my grades (I mailed them in), eager but apprehensive as a pilgrim, but without a flicker of loss or remorse. All bets were off from the start and no one had his or her heart broken or suffered regret, or even had their feelings hurt much. And that does not happen often in a complex world, which is worth remembering.

The day of the night of my sudden leaving, I was sitting in my office high in Old Mather Library daydreaming out the window while I should've been reading some final papers and figuring grades, when a knock came at my door. (I'd had my office changed to the remotest place possible so, I told them, I could work on my book, but actually it was so students wouldn't be tempted to drop in, and so Selma and I could have some privacy.)

At the door was the wife of one of the young associate professors, a fellow I'd barely gotten to know and who I suspected didn't much like me from the arrogant way he acted. His wife, though, was named Melody, and she and I had once had a long and friendly conversation at Arthur Winston's first-of-the-year cocktail party (which X had attended) about *The Firebird*, which I had never seen performed and knew nothing about. Afterwards she always acted like she thought I was an interesting new addition to things, and always gave me a nice smile when she saw me. She was a small mouse-haired woman with brown teary-looking eyes and, I thought, a seductive mouth that her husband probably didn't like, but I did.

At my door she seemed nervous and half-embarrassed, and seemed to want to get inside and shut us in. It was December and she was bundled up for the snow, and had on, I remember, a Peruvian cap with ear flaps that came to a peak, and some kind of woolly boots.

When I closed the door she sat down on the student's chair and immediately took out a cigarette and began smoking. I sat down and smiled at her, with my back to the window.

"Frank," she said suddenly, as if the words were simply colliding around inside her head and getting out only by accident, "I know we don't know each other very well. But I've wanted to see you again ever since we had that wonderful talk at Arthur's. That was an important talk for me. I hope you know that."

"I enjoyed it myself, Melody." (Though I didn't remember much more about it than that Melody had said she'd once hoped to be a dancer, but that her father had always been against it, and much of her life after that had been in defiance of her old man and all men. I remember thinking that she possibly thought of me as something other than a man.)

"I'm starting a dance company right in town here," Melody said. "I've gotten local backing. I think Berkshire students will probably be in it, and the school's going to get involved. I'm taking lessons again, driving to Boston twice a week. Seth's taking care of the children. It's pretty hectic these days, but it's made a big difference. None of it will really get off the ground till next fall at the earliest, but it all started the night we talked about *The Firebird*." She smiled at me, full of pride for herself.

"That's great to hear, Melody," I said. "I have a lot of admiration for you. I know Seth's proud of you. He's mentioned it to me." (A total lie.)

"Frank, my life's really changed. With Seth particularly. I haven't moved out on him. And I'm not going to—at least not right away. But I've demanded my freedom. Freedom to do anything I want with whoever I want to do it with."

"That's good," I said. But I didn't know really if it was

that good. I swiveled and looked out the window at the snowy quadrangle below, where some idiot students were building a snow fortress, then looked at the clock on the wall as if I had an appointment. I didn't.

"Frank. I don't know how to say this, but I have to say it this way, because that's the way it is. I want to have an affair. And I'd like to ask you to have it with me." She smiled a cold little smile that didn't make her plummy lips look the least bit kissable. "I know you're involved with Selma. But you can be involved with me, too, can't you?" She unbuttoned her heavy coat and let it slip behind her, and I could see she was wearing a leotard that was purple on one side and white on the other, the Berkshire College colors. "I can be appealing," she said, and pulled down one shoulder of her leotard and exposed there in my office a very handsome breast, and began to take the other shoulder, the purple one, down.

But I said, "Melody, wait a minute. This is pretty unusual."

"Everything I've done has been usual, Frank. I'm ready to get laid a lot now. Why shouldn't I?"

"That's a good idea," I said. "But you just wait right here for me. I want to do one thing. Put your coat back on." I picked up her coat off the floor where she'd dropped it, and put it around her shoulders where she sat now with both of her lovely breasts exposed, and her lips looking as full and beautiful as they probably ever would, and her purple and white leotard down to her waist. And I went out into the hall, closed the door behind me, picked up my coat off the coat rack at the bottom of the stairs and walked out into the quad, heading for my car. The students were putting the finishing touches to their snow fort and were already starting to pelt each other and yell. Classes were over. Exams were still too far away to worry. It is the best time to be on a college campus and to be leaving.

When I was halfway across the quadrangle, whom should I see but Seth Fairbanks, Melody's husband, slogging toward the gym carrying a bag full of books and a squash racquet. He was a slender, wiry man with a thin black mustache who'd gone to NYU, and taught the 18th century but also some modern novels. We had once talked about some of my favorites, and it turned out he hated everything I had ever liked and had airtight arguments for why they were laughable.

"Where to, Professor Bascombe," Seth Fairbanks said, with a derisory smile. "Heading to the library?" This was meant as some sort of joke I didn't understand. But I put a grin on my face, thinking of his wife shivering up in my office at that moment, just beyond a window that was in sight of where we were walking (if she was still there). It was five o'clock, and the day was gray and nearly dark, and we probably couldn't have been seen anyway.

"Going home to grade a set of essays, Seth," I said in a jolly voice. "I've had them writing about Robbe-Grillet." (Another lie. My students had made up their own assignments and also suggested what grade they thought they should get.) "He's a pretty smart cookie."

"I'd like to see how you phrased your questions. Drop it in my box in the morning. I might learn something. I'm teaching *The Voyeur* myself." Seth could barely suppress a laugh.

"You bet," I said. I could see my car, caked with snow, as we walked down the hill toward the lot. The old brown gymnasium was across the road, its lights burning yellow in the dusk. It was about to turn cold, and the winter would be a long one.

"I'm getting ready to teach a course in the uncanny, Frank, just for winter minisemester." I could see Seth's breath in the cold. "There're a lot of books about the weird and unusual that aren't cheap books, but real literature. I've got a little theory about it. Somebody needs to be reading those books."

"I'd like to hear about it," I said.

"I'll put a syllabus in your box. We can have lunch next week."

"That'd be great, Seth."

"It's the best of both worlds up here, Frank. I think you ought to stay on a semester. All this sportswriting can wait. You might decide you liked it up here and want to stay." Seth smiled. I knew he meant nothing of the kind. But I was going to oblige him.

"It's worth thinking about, Seth. I'll do it."

"Right." Seth raised his racquet to gesture goodbye as we reached my car, and he turned toward the gym and down the hill. I stood and looked up at the dark window of my office where Seth's wife had been, but was now in all likelihood gone home. And that seemed like the best idea to me. And I got in my car, started it up, and turned for home myself.

*   *   *

AT TEN-THIRTY I'm cleaned up, shaved and dressed in my Easter best—a two-piece seersucker Palm Beach I've had since college. On my way out the back, I see Bosobolo striding in through the front door. He has let Frisker slip inside and shoot down the hall past me to the kitchen.

I stop in the doorway and for a moment look him up and down in an arch, appraising way. He is a man I admire, a bony African with an austere face, almost certain the kind to have a long aboriginal penis. We believe we have the same off-beat, low-key sense of humor we've always thought as unique, and for that reason are shrewd and respectful toward each other. He likes it that I live alone with no apparent self-pity and that occasionally Vicki spends the night. I respect him for studying Hobbes as an antidote to over-spiritualizing over at the Institute.

He is dressed in his black missionary pants, white short-sleeves and sandals, but with a loudly ugly orange necktie he bought on 42nd Street the day he arrived from Gabon, and that makes him look like an old blues man. Two times lately, from my car window, I've seen him arm-in-arm with a dumpy white seminary girl half his age, the two of them strolling on the edge of the grounds. Obviously steamy romance is brewing up in her little garret or possibly even upstairs here.

What a piece of exoticism it must be! A savage old prince, old enough to be her father, whonking away on her like a frat boy.

Seeing me, Bosobolo stops under the hanging crystal lamp X inherited from her aunt, and peers at me down the hall as if I were far away. He would like, I already know, to get upstairs and turn on Brother Jimmy Waldrup from North Carolina, whom he deeply admires, though he's complained he can't understand how Brother Jimmy keeps so much in his head at once and cries so easily. He has pages of observer notes I've seen in his room. His education here is a complete one.

"How was Sunday school?" I say, unable to suppress a wry grin. Everything between us assumes the air of a complex irony.

"Yes, quite fine," he says, keeping his distance but looking serious and vaguely fussy. "You'd've enjoyed *your*self. I saw the Second Methodist Professional Advanced Men. I explained origins of the resurrection myth." He smiles a haughty smile. "The Neanderthal thought the cave bear was dead, then found out it wasn't." I can, of course, guess exactly what the professional men—group insurance sharpshooters and branch bank veeps—thought about this particular news. I'm certain they're having a few words about it now out at Howard Johnson's.

"Sounds way too anthropomorphic to me, Gus." Gus is what he's called by the Institute professors, who can't pronounce his actual first name which is full of combative consonants, though he actually seems to like being called Gus.

"Our aim is to reconcile," he says and takes a step back. "The deity enters wherever he can. In other words." His black eyes dart up the stairs and back. I would love to grill him about his little seminary squeeze, but he would be indignant. He is married with numerous children, and probably doesn't take his new arrangement jokingly. There is not enough Fincher Barksdale in me.

I shake my head in mock seriousness. "I just don't think you can make sense out of all that. Sorry." We're talking end to end in the hall, a distance in which no one can be too serious.

"Einstein believed in a God," he says quickly. "There is a clear line of logic. You should come to the discussions." He is carrying his big black gospel, though his bony fingers wrap across the front and obscure the title completely.

"I'd be afraid of using up mystery."

"We are not listening to Bach," he says. "Our faith's involved. You'd have nothing to lose." He smiles at me, proud of this reference to Bach, whom he knows I admire, and whom we both know is exhaustible.

"Do you have any doubters down at the Second Methodist?"

"Very many. I only offer what has been always available. Someday they'll all die and find out."

"That's awful strict."

Bosobolo's eyes twinkle with mirth and firmness. He is the authority here. "When I am back home, I will be more compassionate."

He raises his eyebrows and inches toward the stairs. He hasn't mentioned Walter's visit last night. He'd be amused, I'm sure, to know that Walter thought he was the butler. On the morning airishness down the middle of my house I smell his grainy sweat, a smell that goes deep in my nose and delivers a vague stinging warning: this man is no one to trifle with. Religion is not sports to him.

"How about Hobbes," I say, ready to let him go. "Do you discuss him?"

"He was a Christian, too. Temporality interested him." He is telling me in so many words, yes, he's romancing the dumpy little seminary chicken, and no, he won't repudiate it, and I should mind my own business. "You should probably come."

"I've got too much worldly business."

"Well then, today's the day for it," he says. He raises his empty hand in a wave and starts up the stairs two at a time. "God is smiling for you today," he calls from the gloomy upper story.

"Good," I say. "I'm smiling back at him." I go back to the kitchen first to find Frisker, and then to be on my way.

ON THE way through town I cruise up Seminary Street, which dead-ends on the Institute grounds and the small First Presbyterian, its white steeple pointing at the clouds. The Square is church-empty (though plenty of cars are parked). A man in an orange jacket, seated in a wheelchair, peers into the closed ice cream shop, and our one black policeman stands on the curb, heavy with police gear. The De Tocqueville minibus rumbles out ahead of me and disappears down Wallace Road. Both traffic lights click to green in the watery sunlight. It is a perfect time for a robbery.

I turn south toward Barnegat Pines, but after a block I make a sweeping U-turn—what Ralph used to call a "hard left"—and pull back into the empty Disabled slot at the side of the Presbyterians.

Leaving the motor on, I duck in a side door at the back. Ushers are milling, holding sheafs of special deckle-edged vanilla Easter Service bulletins. They are local businessmen, in brown suits and tie clasps, ready to whisper a "gladjerhere" as if they'd known you all your life and had your pew picked out. No seating during prayers, doxologies and Holy Communion. Slip in during hymns, announcements and, of course, collection.

This is my favorite place in church, the very farthest back door. This is where my mother used to stand with me the few times we ever went in Biloxi. I cannot sit still in a pew, and always have to leave early, disturbing people and feeling embarrassed.

The fellow who greets me has on a name tag that says "Al."

Someone has written "Big" before it in a red marker. I recognize him from the hardware store and The Coffee Spot. He is in fact a big man in his fifties, who wears big clothes and smells of Aqua Velva and cigarettes. When I edge in close to his door, which is open revealing rows of praying heads, he eases over by me, puts a giant hand on my shoulder and whispers, "We'll put you right in there in a minute. Plenty of good seats in front." Aqua Velva washes over me. Big Al wears a big purple and gold Masonic knucklebuster, and his hairy hand is as wide as a stirrup. He slips me a bulletin and I hear him breathe down deep in his troubled lungs. The other ushers are all praying, staring ferociously at their toes and the bright red carpet, their eyes resolutely open.

"I'll just stand a minute, if it's all right," I whisper. We are old friends after all, both lifelong Presbyterians.

"Sure-you-bet, Jim. Stay right there." Big Al nods in complete assurance, then eases back with the other ushers and bows his head dramatically. (It is not surprising that he thinks of me as someone else, since nothing here could matter less than my own identity.)

The sanctuary is swimming in permanent, churchy light and jam-packed with heads and flowered hats bowed in beseechment. The minister, who seems a half-mile away, is a hale and serious barrel-chested, rambling-Jack type with a bushy beard and an Episcopal bib—without any doubt a seminary prof. He gives in to the old bafflement in a loud actor's voice, his arms raised so his gown makes great black bat wings over the lilied altar. "And we take, Oh Lord, this day as a great, great gift. A promise that life begins again. Here we are on this earth . . . our day to day comings. . . ." Predictably on and on. I listen wide-eyed, as if hearing a great new secret revealed, a promised message I must deliver to a faraway city. And I feel . . . what, exactly?

A good ecumenist's question, for a well-grounded fellow like me. Though the answer is plain and simple, or I wouldn't be here at all.

I feel just as I wanted to feel, and knew I would when I made that hard left and came barreling back to the parking lot—a sweet and expanding hieratic ardor and free elevation above low spirits, a swoony, hot tingle right down to my toe tips, something akin to what sailors in the brig must feel when the president visits their ship. Suddenly I'm home, without fear, anxiety, or for that matter even any burdensome reverence. I'm not even in jeopardy of being bested at religion here—it's not that kind of place—and can feel damn pleased with both myself and my fellow man. A rare immanence is mine, things falling back and away in the promise that more's around here than meets the eye, even though it is of course a sham and will last only as far as my car. Better this than nothing, though. Or worse. To have hollow sorrow. Or regret. Or to be derailed by the spiky fact of being alone.

Then suddenly: "Rise my soul and stretch thy wings, thy better portion trace; Rise from transitory things toward heaven, thy destined place...." My voice springs forth strong and unequivocal, with Big Al's baritone behind me in the chorus of confident, repentant suburbanites. (I can never think what the words mean or even imply.) The organ rattles the windows, raises the roof, tickles the ribs, sends a stirring through all our bellies—Jim's, the ushers', the preacher's.

And then I'm gone.

A secret high sign to big Al, who understands me and everything perfectly and clasps his big stirrupy hands in front of him in a Masonic one-man handshake. It is time for the "Race to the Tomb," and I am in no need of messages, having taken in all I want and can use, am "saved" in the only way I can be (*pro tempore*), and am ready to march on toward dark temporality, my banners all aflutter.

CHAPTER 10

UNDER THE visor I have a Johnny Horizon Let's-Clean-Up-America map, printed for the Bicentennial, and taped to the dash a page of directions in Vicki's own hand on the "smart way" to get to Barnegat Pines. 206-A to 530-E to 70-S and (swerving briefly north) to an unnumbered county road referred to only as Double Trouble Road, which supposedly delivers you neat as a whistle to where you're going.

Her directions route me past the most ordinary but satisfying New Jersey vistas, those parts that remind you of the other places you've been in your life, but in New Jersey are grouped like squares in a puzzle. It is a good time to put the top down and let in the winds.

Much of what I pass, of course, looks precisely like everyplace else *in* the state, and the dog-leg boundaries make it tricky to keep cardinal points aligned. The effect of driving south and east is to make you feel you're going south and west and that you're lost, or sometimes that you're headed nowhere. Clean industry abounds. Valve plants. A Congoleum factory. U-Haul sheds. A sand and gravel pit close by a glass works. An Airedale kennel. The Quaker Home for Confused Friends. A mall with a nautical theme. Several signs that say HERE! Suddenly it is a high pale sky and a feeling like Florida, but a mile farther on, it is the Mississippi Delta—civilized life flattened below high power lines, the earth laid out in great vegetative tracts where Negroes fish from low bridges, and Mount Holly lumps on the far horizon just before the Delaware. Beyond that lies Maine.

I stop in the town of Pemberton near Fort Dix, and put in another call to X to express Easter greetings. Her recording talks in the same brassy business voice, and this time I leave a number—the Arcenaults'—where she can reach me. I also put in a call to Walter. He is on my mind today, although no one answers at his house.

In Bamber—a town that is no more than a post office and small lake across Route 530—I stop for a drink in a cozy rough-pine roadhouse with yellow lowlights and log tables. Sweet Lou's Sportsman's B'ar, owned—the signs inside all say—by a famous ex-center on the '56 Giants, Sweet Lou Calcagno. Jack Dempsey, Spike Jones, Lou Costello, Ike and a host of others have all been close friends of Sweet Lou's and contributed pictures to the walls, showing themselves embracing a smiling, crewcut bruiser in an open collar shirt who looks like he could eat a football.

Sweet Lou isn't around at the moment, but when I sit down at the bar, a heavy pale-skinned woman in her fifties with beehive hair and elastic slacks comes out from a swinging door to the back and begins to clean an ashtray.

"Where's Lou today," I ask after I've ordered a whiskey. I would, in fact, like to meet him, maybe set up a *Where Are They Now* feature: "Former Giant lugnut Lou Calcagno once had a dream. Not to run a fumble in for a touchdown or to play in a league championship or to enter the Hall of Fame, but to own a little watering trough in his downstate Jersey home of Bamber, a quiet, traditional place where friends and fans could come and reminisce about the old glory days. . . ."

"Lou who?" the woman says, lighting a cigarette and blowing smoke away from me out the corner of her mouth.

I widen my grin. "*Sweet* Lou."

"He's where he is. How long since you been in?"

"A while, I guess it's been."

"I guess too." She narrows her eyes. "Maybe in your other life."

"I used to be a big fan of his," I say, though this isn't true. I'm not even sure I ever heard of him. To be honest, I feel like an idiot.

"He's dead. He's *been* dead maybe, thirty years? That's approximately where he is."

"I'm sorry to know that," I say.

"Right. Lou was a real nunce," the woman says, finishing wiping out the ashtray. "And he was a big nunce. I was married to him." She pours herself a cup of coffee and stares at me. "I don't wanna ruin your dreams. But. You know?"

"What happened?"

"Well," she says, "some gangsters drove over here from Mount Holly and walked him into the parking lot out there like it was friends and shot him twenty or thirty times. That did it."

"What the hell had he done to *them*?"

She shakes her head. "No idea. I was right here where I am behind this bar. They came in, three of them, all little rats. They said they wanted Lou to come out and talk, and when he did, boom. Nobody came back in to explain."

"Did they catch the people?"

"Nope. They did not. Not one was caught. Lou and I were getting divorced anyway. But I was working for him afternoons."

I look around the dark bar where Sweet Lou stares down at me from long ago and life, surrounded by his smiling friends and fans, an athlete who left sports a success to achieve a prosperous life in Bamber, which was no doubt his home, or near it, yet came to a bad end. Not the way these things usually turn out and not exactly what you'd want to read about before dinner behind a chilled martini.

Someone else, I see, is in the bar, an older gray-haired man in an expensive-looking silverish suit sitting talking to a young woman in red slacks. They are in the corner by the window. Above them is a huge somber-looking bear's head.

I cluck my tongue and look at Lou's widow. "It's nice you keep the place this way."

"He had it in his will that all these had to be left up, or I'd have changed it, what, a hundred years ago? It has to stay a B'ar, too, and buy from his distributorship. Otherwise I lose it to his guinea cousins in Teaneck. So I ignore him. I forget whose picture it is, really. He wanted to run everybody's life."

"Do you still own the distributorship?"

"My son by my second marriage. It fell in his lap." She sniffs, smokes, stares out the small front door glass which casts a pale inward light.

"That's not so bad."

"It was the best thing he ever did, I guess. After he was in the ground he did it. Which figures."

"My name's Frank Bascombe, by the way. I'm a sportswriter." I put my dollar on the bar and drink up my whiskey.

"Mrs. Phillips," she says and shakes my hand. "My other husband's dead, too." She stares at me without interest and opens a saltine packet from a basket of them on the bar. "I haven't seen one of you guys in years. They used to come all the time to interview Fatso. From Philly. He kept 'em in stitches. He knew jokes by the hundreds." She drops the little red saltine ribbon into the clean ashtray and breaks the cracker in two.

"I'm sorry I didn't know him." I'm on my feet now, smiling, sympathetic, but ready to go.

"Well, I'm sorry I did. So we're even." Mrs. Phillips stubs out her cigarette before biting the saltine. She looks at it curiously as if considering Lou Calcagno all over again. "No, I take it back," she says. "He wasn't so awful *all* the time." She gives me a sour smile. "Quote me. How's that. Not all the time." She turns and walks stoutly down the bar toward a TV that is dark. The other two patrons are getting up to go, and I am left with my own smile and nothing to say but, "Okay. Thanks. I'll do it."

OUTSIDE IN the white-shell parking lot there is the promise of approaching new weather—Detroit weather—though the sun is shining. A wet wind has arrived over Bamber Lake, unsettling the dust, bending the pines along the row of empty lake cottages, sending the Sportsman's B'ar sign wagging. The older man and the young woman in slacks climb into a red Cadillac and drive away toward the west, where a bank of quilty clouds has lowered the sky. I stand beside my car and think first of Lou Calcagno coming to his sad end where I am parked, and that this is exactly the place for such things, a place that was something once. I think about the balloonists I saw this morning, and if they will get down and moored before the stiff blow comes. I am glad to be away from home today, to be off in the heart of a landscape that is unknown to me, glad to be bumping up against a world that is not mine or of my devising. There are times when life seems not so great but better than anything else, and when you're happy to be alive, though not exactly ecstatic.

I run the top up now against a chill. In a minute's time I'm fast down the road out of scrubby Bamber, headed for my own rendezvous on Double Trouble Road.

VICKI'S DIRECTIONS, it turns out, are perfect. Straight through the seaside townlet of Barnegat Pines, cross a drawbridge spanning a tarnished arm of a metallic-looking bay, loop through some beachy rental bungalows and turn right onto a man-made

peninsula and a pleasant, meandering curbless street of new pastel
split-levels with green lawns, underground utilities and attached
garages. Sherri-Lyn Woods, the area is named, and there are
streets like it along other parallel peninsulas nearby, though there
are no woods in sight. Most of the houses have boat docks out
back with a boat of some kind tied up—a boxy cabin-fisherman
or a sleek-hulled outboard. All in all it is a vaguely nautical-
feeling community, though all the houses down the street look
Californiaish and casual.

The Arcenaults' house at 1411 Arctic Spruce is vaguely similar
to the others, though hanging on its front at the place where the
two levels join behind beige siding there is a near life-size figure
of Jesus-crucified that makes it immediately distinctive. Jesus
in his suburban agony. Bloody eyes. Flimsy body. Feet already
beginning to sag and give up the ghost. A look of redoubtable
woe and calm. He is painted a lighter shade of beige than the
siding and looks distinctly Mediterranean.

The Arcenaults—the swaying plaque out front says—and I
wheel in just ahead of unkind weather and come to rest beside
Vicki's Dart.

"LYNETTE JUST had to have ole Jesus hung out there," Vicki
whispers, when we're only half in the door, where she has met
me looking put out. "I think he's the tackiest thing in the entire
world and *I'm* a Catholic. You're thirty minutes late, anyway."
She is a vision in a pink jersey dress, serious rose-colored heels,
snapping stockings and crimson fingernails, her black hair
uncurled and simplified for home.

Everybody, she says, is scattered through the house on all
levels at once, and I am only able to meet Elvis Presley, a tiny
white poodle wearing a diamond collar, and Lynette, Vicki's
stepmother, who comes to the kitchen door in a chef's apron,
holding a spoon and sings out "Hi, hi." She is a pert and
pretty little second wife with bright red hair and bunchy hips
descending to ankletted ankles. Vicki whispers that she hails
from Lodi, West Virginia, and is a thick-as-rock hillbilly, though
I have the feeling we could be friendly if Vicki'd allow it. She
is cooking meat and the house airs smell warm and thick. "Hope
you like your lamb well, well, *well* done, Franky," Lynette

says, disappearing back into the kitchen. "That's the way Wade Arcenault likes his."

"Great. That's exactly how I like mine," I lie, and am suddenly aware that not only am I late but I haven't brought a gift for anybody, not a flower, a greeting card, or an Easter bonbon. I am certain Vicki has noticed.

"You better put plenty of mint jelly on my plate." Vicki rolls her eyes, then says to my ear, "You don't either like it well done."

Vicki and I sit on a big salmon-colored couch, with our backs to a picture window that faces Arctic Spruce Drive. The drapes are open and an amber storm light colors the room, which has old-master prints on the walls—a Van Gogh, a Constable seascape, and "The Blue Boy." A plush blue carpet (a hunch tells me Everett had a hand here) covers the floor wall to wall. The house has exactly the feel of Vicki's apartment, but its effect on me—in my youthful seersucker—is that I am the teacher who has given Vicki a bad mark at midterm and who has been invited to Sunday dinner to prove the family's solid one before finals. It isn't a bad way to feel, and when dinner is over I'm sure I can leave in a hurry.

The television, a cabinet model the size of a large doghouse, is showing another NBA game without sound. I would be happy to watch it the rest of the afternoon, while Vicki reads *Love's Last Journey,* and forget all about dinner.

"I'm hot, aren't you hot?" Vicki says, and she suddenly jumps up, crosses the room and twists the thermostat drastically. Cooling, forced air hits me almost immediately from a high wall louver. She switches around, showing her nice fanny and gives me a witchy smile. This is a different girl at home, there's no doubting that. "No need us smotherin indoors, is it?"

We sit for a while and silently watch the Knicks beat hell out of the Cavaliers. Cleveland plays its regular leggy, agitating garage-ball game while the Knicks seem club-footed and awkward as giraffes but inexplicably score more points, which makes the Cleveland crowd good and mad. Two giant Negroes start to scuffle after a loose ball, and a vicious fight breaks out almost instantly. Players, black and white, fall all over the floor like trees, and the game quickly becomes a free-for-all the referees can't handle. Police come onto the floor and begin grabbing people, smiles on their big Slovak faces, and things seem likely to get worse. It is a usual Cleveland tactic.

Vicki clicks off the picture with a remote box hidden between the couch cushions, leaving me wide-eyed and silent. She jerks her dress down around her sleek knees and sits up high like a job applicant. I can see the broad, all-business outline of her brassiere (she needs a good-sized one) through the stretchy pink fabric. I would like to snake a hand round to one of those breasts and pull her back for an Easter kiss, which I still have not been given. Meat smell is everywhere.

"Did you read that *Parade* today," she asks, giving her jersey another tug and staring across the room at an electric organ sitting against the wall underneath the flat and florid Van Gogh.

"I guess not," I say, though I can't remember actually what I have been doing. Waiting to be here. My sole occupation for the day.

"Ole Walter Scott's said that a woman washed her hair with a honey shampoo and walked out in the backyard with a wet head and got stung to death by bees." She casts a fishy eye around at me. "Does that sound like the truth?"

"What happened to the woman who washed her hair with beer? Did she end up marrying a Polack?"

She tosses her head around. "You're a regular Red Skeleton, aren't you?"

Out in the kitchen Lynette drops a pan with a loud bangety bang. "Scuze me, kids," she calls out and laughs.

"You drop the set out of your ring?" Vicki says loudly.

"I coulda said something else," Lynette says, "but I won't on Easter."

"Small favors, please," Vicki says.

"I *had* a ring that big once," Lynette's friendly voice says.

"So where'd *he* go?" Vicki says and gives me a hot look. She and Lynette are not the best of friends. I wish, though, that they could pretend to be for the afternoon.

"That poor man died of cancer before you were in the picture," Lynette says light-heartedly.

"Was that about the time you converted over?"

Lynette's beaming face pops around the kitchen door molding, her eyes sharpened. "Shortly after, sweetheart, that's right."

"I guess you needed help and guidance."

"We all do, don't we, Vicki sweet? Even Franky, I bet."

"He's Presbyterian."

"Well-o-well." Lynette is gone from the door back to her stove. "Back in the hills we called them the country club, though I understand they've gotten pious since Vatican II. The Catholics got easier and the others had to get harder."

"I doubt the Catholics got any easier," I say, though for this Vicki fires me a savage look of warning.

Lynette suddenly reappears, nodding seriously at me and pulling a curl of damp orange hair off her temple. She still seems someone a person could like. "We ought none of us to get lax the way this world is headed," she says.

"Lynette works at the Catholic crisis center in Forked River," Vicki says in a tired singsong.

"That's mighty right, sweetheart." Lynette smiles, then is gone again and begins making thick stirring noises in a bowl. Vicki looks as disgusted with everything as it's possible to be.

"What it comes down to is she answers the phone," Vicki whispers, but loud enough. "And they call that a crisis-line." She flounces back on the couch and buries her chin over in her collarbone, staring at the wall. "I guess I've seen a crisis or two. Some guy came in one time down in Dallas with his entire *thing* sticking out of his friend's pocket, and we had to sew that gentleman right back on."

"Alienation didn't work out, you see." Lynette speaks energetically from the kitchen. "That's what we're finding out now from the colleges. A *lot* of people want to get back in the world now, so to speak. And I don't try to force my religion onto them. I'll stay on a line as much as eight straight hours with some individual and he won't be Catholic at all. Course, I have to stay in bed two days after that. We all wear headphones." Lynette walks into the doorway, cradling a big crockery bowl in her arms like a farm wife. Her smile is the most patient one in the world. But she has the look of a woman who wants to start something. "Some crises don't bleed out in the open, Vicky hon."

"Whoop-dee-do," Vicki says and rolls her eyes.

"Now you're a writer, right?" Lynette says.

"Yes, ma'am."

"Well, that's awfully nice too." Lynette gazes down lovingly into her bowl while she thinks this over. "Do you ever sometimes write religious tracts?"

"No ma'am, I never have. I'm a sportswriter."

Vicki signals the TV to start again, and sighs. On the screen a tiny dark-skinned man is diving off a high cliff into a narrow inlet of surging white water. "Acapulco," Vicki mutters.

Lynette is smiling at me now. My answer, whatever it was, has been enough for her, and she just wants to take this chance to look me over.

"Well, Lynette, why don't you stare at Frank an hour or two," Vicki nearly shouts and crosses her arms angrily.

"I just want to see him, hon. I like to have one time to see a whole person clearly. Then I know them. It doesn't hurt a thing. Frank can tell I mean only good, can't you, Frank?"

"Absolutely." I smile.

"I'm glad I ain't livin here," Vicki snaps.

"That's why you have a nice place all your own," Lynette says amiably. "Of course, I've never been invited there." She ambles into the steamy, meaty kitchen, leaving the two of us on the couch alone with the cliff-divers.

"You and me ought to have a talk," Vicki says sternly, her eyes suddenly red and full of tears. The forced air comes on again and drums us both with a cool mechanical influx. Elvis Presley trots to the door and looks at us. "Get outa here, Elvis Presley," Vicki says. Elvis Presley turns around and trots into the dining room.

"What about?" I smile hopefully.

"Just a bunch of things." She wipes her eyes with her finger-tips, which requires her to duck her head.

"About you and me?"

"Yes." She makes her pouty lips go sour. And once again my poor heart drums fast. Who knows why? To save me? I don't have a liar's clue to what needs to be said between us, but her mood is a mood with unhappy finality in it.

Why, though, can't everything—just for today—wait? Wait a beat as the actor says. Just go on without change a bit longer? Why can't every sweet untranscendent thing we know or think we know go on along a little longer without closure having to rear its practical head? Walter *Luckless* Luckett could not have been more right about me. I don't like to think of this or that thing ending, or even changing. Death, the old streamliner, is not my friend, nor will he ever be.

Though I can't put off whatever this is, and maybe I don't even want to. She is a demon after changes today, her whole person exuding transition. Only there's no real need for it, is there? (*Thunk-a, thunk-a thunk*, my heart's pumping.) We haven't even had dinner yet, not tasted the lamb cooked hard as a coaster. I have yet to meet her father and her brother. I had sheltered hope that her dad and I could become bosom buddies even if Vicki and I didn't work things out. He and I could still be friends. If his tire went flat some rainy night in Haddam or Hightstown or anyplace within my area code, he could call me up, I'd drive out to get him, we'd have a drink while the tire was being fixed at Frenchy's and he would go off into the Jersey darkness certain he had a friend worthy of his trust and who looked down life's corridor more or less the way he did. Maybe we could take the brother fishing at Manasquan (no need to bring the women in on it). Vicki could be married to Sweet Lou Calcagno's stepson over in Bamber, have a wonderful life as a beer distributor's wife with all the hullygully of kids. And I could be the trusted family friend with a heart of gold. I'd renounce my failed suitor's glower for the demeanor of a wise old uncle. That would be enough for me, just the natural playing out of the pleasing present.

Vicki stares out the window at the houses along Arctic Spruce, her arm on the couch back. Sometimes it is possible to see in her face the lineaments of the older woman she will be, when her features will take on dimension, weight around the chin, a character more serious than now. She will undoubtedly be stout in later life, which is not always a hopeful sign.

Amber light has turned the lawns as green as England. In driveways all up the curving curbless street sit bright new cars—Chryslers, Olds, Buicks—each one with a hefty, moneyed look. In the middle distance a great white RV sits in a side yard. Smoke curls from almost every white brick chimney, though it is not cold enough by a long shot. Some doors have wreaths up since Christmas. My trailing wind has arrived.

Someone, I see, has set white croquet wickets around the Arcenaults' front lawn. Two striped stakes face each other at less than regulation distance. Games have been planned for the day, and here is how I will paint my trapdoor to escape the incoming empty moment I feel.

"Let's play," I say, giving Vicki's arm an uncle's squeeze. This is not a ruse I'm up to, only a break in the broody unfinished silence we've fallen victims to.

She looks amazed, though she isn't. Her eyes round out like dimes. "In all this wind and the rain comin?"

"It isn't raining yet."

"Man-o-man-o-man," Vicki says, and snaps her fingers in hot succession. "It's your funeral." But she is off the couch quick, and headed for some upstairs storage room for mallets.

On television, CBS is trying to get us settled back into basketball, now that things are under control again. However, each time they show what's happening on the court, a short, bulb-nosed, red-faced man wearing a loud, checked sport coat comes into the picture shouting "Aw, fuck you" soundlessly at someone on the New York team, waving a stubby arm in disgust. This checked coat guy is one of my favorites. Mutt Greene, the Cleve-lands' G.M. I interviewed him once just after I'd restarted life as a sportswriter. He was a coach in Chicago then, but by his own choice has since moved up to the front office in another city, where I'm sure life seems better. He said to me "People surprise you, Frank, with just how fuckin stupid they are." He was smoking a big expensive cigar in a cramped coach's office under the Chicago arena. "I mean, do you *actually* realize how much adult conversation is spent on this fuckin business? Facts treated like they were opinions just for the simple purpose of talking about it longer? Some people might think that's interesting, bub, but I'll tell you. It's romanticizing a goddamn rock by calling it a mountain range to me. People waste a helluva lot of time they could be putting to useful purposes. This is a game. See it and forget about it." Afterwards we got involved in a pretty lively conversation about grass seeds and the piss-poor choices you face when your trouble was a high water table and inadequate drain-age, which was not my problem, but was the case at his home on Hilton Head.

The interview wasn't very productive on the subject of "see-ing the keys" in classic big-man, small-man match-ups, which is what I was after. But I think of it as informative, though I don't agree with everything he said. Still, he was happy to sit down with a young sportswriter and teach a lesson in life. "Keep things in perspective and give an honest effort" is what I took back to the Sheraton Commander that night. And when you've done with that take an interest in a new grass seed or an old Count Basie record you've missed listening to lately, or a catalog or a cocktail waitress, which—the last of these—is precisely what I did and wasn't sorry about it.

On the court now the players are paying everyone murderous looks and pointing long bony fingers as threats. In particular the black players look fierce, and the white boys, pale and thin-armed, seem to want to be peacemakers, though they are actu-ally just trying to stay out of trouble's way. The trainer, a squat, worried-looking man in white pants, is trying to pull Mutt Greene down a runway below the stands. But Mutt is fighting mad. To him, real life's going on here. Nothing's for show. He has lost all perspective and wants to raise a little hell about the Knicks' way of playing. He's come out of the stands to show what he's worth, and I admire him for it. I'm sure he misses the old life.

Suddenly the picture flicks and another cliff-diver stands staring down at his frothy fate. CBS has given up.

Elvis Presley trots into the kitchen door again, jingling his little diamond collar, and sniffs the air. He is uncertain about me, and who could blame him?

Lynette is right behind him, her eyes sparkly and furtive but full of good cheer. "Elvis Presley 'bout runs this whole family." She taps Elvis Presley lightly with her toe. "He's fixed, of course, so you don't have to worry about your leg. He idn't but half a man, but we do love him."

Elvis Presley sits in the doorway and stares at me.

"He's something," I say.

"Doesn't Vicki seem like she's worried to you?" Lynette's voice becomes cautionary. Her bright eyes are speculative and she crosses her arms in absolute slow motion.

"She seems just fine to me."

"Well, I thought maybe since you all went to De-troit, some-thing unhappy'd happened."

So! Everybody including Elvis Presley knows everything, and wants to turn it to their own purposes, no matter how idle. A full-disclosure family. No secrets unless individuals make

decisions for themselves, which runs the risk of general disapproval. Vicki has obviously told an aromatic little-but-not-
enough, and Lynette wants filling in. She is not exactly as I want
her to be, and as of this moment I transfer fully back to Vicki's
alliance.

"Everything's great that I know of." I admit nothing with a
smile.

"Well good-should, then." Lynette nods happily. "We all just
love her and want the best for her. She's the bravest ole thing."

No answer. No "Why is she brave?" or "Tell me what you
make of Everett?" or "In fact, she *is* seeming just the least little
bit peculiar all of a sudden." Nothing from me, except "She's
wonderful," and another grin.

"Yes she is now," Lynette beams, but full of warning. Then
she is gone again, leaving Elvis Presley in the doorway, frozen in
an empty stare.

In the time it takes Vicki to come back with the mallets, her
brother Cade comes pushing through the front door. He has
been out back tying down a tarp on his Boston Whaler, and when
I shake his hand it is rock-fleshed and chilled. Cade is twenty-
five, a boat mechanic in nearby Toms River, and a mauler of a
fellow in a white T-shirt and jeans. He is, Vicki has told me,
on the "wait list" for the State Police Academy and has already
developed a flat-eyed, officer's uninterest for the peculiarities of
his fellow man.

"Down from Haddam, huh?" Cade grunts, once we've let go
of each other's hands and are standing hard-by with nothing to
say. His speech does not betray one trace of Texas, where he
grew up, and instead he has developed now into full-fledged
Jersey young-manhood with an aura of no-place/no-time
surrounding him like poison. He looms beside me like a mast
and stares furiously out the front window. "I useta know a girl
in South Brunswick. Useta take her skatin in a rink on 130. You
might know where that is?" A snicker and a sneer appear on his
lips at once.

"I know exactly," I say and sink my hands deep in my pockets.
Indeed I've watched my own two precious children (and once
my third) skate there for hours on end while I hugged the rail in
estranged admiration.

"There's a Mann's Tri-Plex in there now, I guess," Cade says, looking around the room as if perplexed by getting into this embarrassing conversation in the first place. He'd feel much better if he could put the cuffs on me and push me head-down into the back seat of a cruiser. On the ride downtown we could both relax, be ourselves, and he could share a cruel joke with me and his partner—amigos in our roles, as God intended. As it is I'm from an outside world, the type of helpless citizen who owns the expensive boats he repairs; the know-nothings with no mechanical skills he hates for the way we take care of property he himself can't afford. I am not who normally comes for dinner, and he's having a hard time being human about me.

My advice to him, though unspoken, is that he'd better get used to me and mine, since I am the people he'll be giving tickets to sooner or later, average solid citizens whose ways and mores he'll ridicule at the risk of getting into a peck of trouble. I can, in fact, be of use to him, could be instructive of the outside world if he would let me.

"Uhn, where's Vicki?" Cade looks suddenly caged, glancing around the room as if she might be hiding behind a chair. Simultaneously he opens his thick fist to display a piece of silvery, tooled metal.

"She's gone to get croquet mallets," I say. "What's that?"

Cade stares down at the two-inch piece of tubular metal and purses his lips. "Spacer," he says and then is silent a moment. "Germans make it. It's the best in the world. And it's a real piece of crap's what it is."

"What's it to?" My hands are firm and deep in my pockets. I'm willing to take an interest in "spacer" for the moment.

"Boat," Cade says darkly. "We should be making these things over here. That way they'd last."

"You're right about that," I say. "It's too bad."

"I mean, what're you gonna do if you're out on the ocean and this thing cracks? Like this." One greasy finger fine-points a hairline fissure in the spacer's side, something I'd never have noticed. Cade's dark eyes grow hooded with suppressed annoyance. "You gonna call for a German? Is that it? I'll tell you what you'd do, mister." His eyes find me gazing stupidly at the spacer, which seems obscure and unimportant. "You kiss your ass goodbye if a storm comes up." Cade nods grimly and pops his big hand shut like a clam. All his feelings are pretty closely positioned into this conceit—the strongest chain is no stronger than its weakest link, and he's resolved never to be that link in his personal life, where *he's* in control. This is the central fact of all tragedy, though to me it's not much to get excited about. His is the policeman's outlook, mine the sportswriter's. To me a weak link bears some watching, and you'd better have replacements handy in case it goes. But in the meantime it could be interesting to see how it bears up and tries to do its job under some bad conditions, all the while giving its best in the other areas where it's strong. I've always thought of myself as a type of human weak link, working against odds and fate, and I'm not about to give up on myself. Cade, on the other hand, wants to lock up us offenders and weak links so we'll never again see the light of day and worry anybody. We would have a hard time being good friends, this I can see.

"You been to Atlantic City lately?" Cade says suspiciously.

"Not in a long time." X and I went on our honeymoon there, stayed in the old Hadden Hall, walked on the boardwalk and had the time of our lives. I haven't been back since, except once for a karate match, when I flew in after dark and left two hours later. I doubt Cade is interested in this.

"It's all ruined now," Cade says, shaking his head in dismay. "Hookers and spic teenagers all over. It useta be good. And I'm not even prejudiced."

"I'd heard it's changed."

"Changed?" Cade smirks, the first sign of a real smile I've seen so far. "Nagasaki changed, right?" Cade suddenly flings his head toward the kitchen. "I'm hungry enough eat a lug wrench." And a strangely happy smile breaks over his tragic big bullard's face. "I've got to go wash up or Lynette'll shoot me." He shakes his head, appreciative and grinning.

Suddenly all is good cheer. Whatever troubled him is gone now. Atlantic City. Weak links. Faulty spacers. Spics. Criminals he will someday arrest and later want to joke with on the long ride downtown. All gone. This is a feature of his outlook I have not expected. He can forget and be happy—a real strength. A good meal is waiting somewhere. A TV game. A beer. Clear sailing beyond the squall-line of life. It isn't so bad, when you don't think of it.

*   *   *

IN THE front yard Vicki displays for me the most excellent way to hit a croquet ball, the between-the-straddled-legs address, which lets her give her ball a good straight ride that makes her whoop with pleasure. I am a side-approacher by nature, having played some golf at Lonesome Pines and when I first married X. I also enjoy hitting the stupid striper with one hand, though I give up *touch* every time. Vicki gives me dark and disreputable looks when I hit, then even more aggressively straddles her green ball and hikes her skirt above her knees to get the straightest pendulum swing. She's half around the course before I'm through a wicket, though I'm a tinge dreamy now, my mind not truly on our game.

The Detroit weather has arrived finally, though it is not the same storm. All the anger has gone out of it, and it consents to being just a gusty, plucky breeze with a few sprinklings of icy rain—a mild suburban shower at best, though the light has passed from Sunday amber to late afternoon aquamarine. In fact it's wonderful to be out of doors and away from the house, even though we play under the eyes of crucified Jesus. I have no idea where Vicki's father is. Is this interpretable as a dark sign, a gesture of unwelcome? Should I be asking what I'm doing here? I was, after all, invited, though I feel in an unavoidable way as alone as a nomad.

"You havin fun?" Vicki says. She has managed to nest her green stripe close enough to my yellow ball to give it a good clacking whack under her stockinged foot, scooting it through the grass and into the flowerbed where it is lost among the snapdragons against the house.

"I *was* doing pretty good."

"Gogetchanotherball. Get a red one—they're lucky." She stands like a woodsman, with her mallet on her shoulder. She has but two wickets remaining, and pretends to want me to catch up.

"I resign," I say and smile.

"Say what?"

"That's what you say in chess. I'm not a match for you, not even a patch on your jeans."

"Chest nothin, you're the one wanted to play, and now you're the one quittin. Go on and get a ball."

"No I won't. I'm no good at games, not since I was little."

"People bet on this game in Texas. It's taken very serious."

"That's why I'm no good at it."

I take a seat on the damp porch step beside her red shoes and admire the green-tinted light and the lovely curving street. This snaky peninsula is the work of some enterprising developer who's carted it in with trucks and reclaimed it from a swamp. And it has not been a bad idea. You could just as easily be in Hyannis Port if you closed your eyes, which for a moment I do.

Vicki goes back to hitting her green stripe, but carelessly now, using my method to show she isn't serious. "When I was a lil girl I saw *Alice in Wonderland*, Cade and me. You know?" She looks up to see if I'm listening. "In the part where they played croquet with ostriches' heads, or whatever those pink birds are, I cried bloody murder, 'cause I thought it killed 'em. I hated to see anything get hurt even then. That's why I'm a nurse."

"Flamingos," I say and smile down at her.

"Is that what they were? Well, I know I cried about 'em." Whack-crack. Her green makes a hard driving run toward the striped stake, then twirls by on the left. "There you go, that's your fault. Shoot-a-mile." She stands thrown-hipped in the breeze. I watch her with terrible desire. "You don't play games, but you write about 'em all the time. That's backwards."

"I like it that way."

"How'd you like ole Cade. Idn't he great?"

"He's a good fellow."

"If he'd let me dress him he'd be a whole lot better, I'll tell you that. Cade needs him a little girlfriend. He's got being a policeman on the brain." She comes over and sits on the step below mine, hugs her knees and tucks her skirt up under her. Her hair is sweet-smelling. While she was gone she has put on a good deal of Chanel No. 5.

I wish we could not talk about Cade now, but I have nothing much to substitute for him. Vicki has no interest in the upcoming NFL draft, or the early lead the Tigers have opened up in the East, or who might be ahead in the Knicks game, so I'm content to sit on the porch like a lazy freeholder, breathe in the salt air and look upwards at the daylight moon. In its own way this is quite inspiring.

"So how do you like it out here?" Vicki looks at me up over her shoulder, then back at the house across the street—another split-level, but with an oriental façade, its cornices tweaked, and painted China red.

"It's great."

"You don't fit in at all, you know that."

"I'm here to see you. I'm not trying to fit in."

"I guess," she says, and hugs her knees hard.

"Where's your dad? I sort of have the feeling he's ducking me."

"No way for that, José."

"I could get lost in a hurry, you know, if being here is one bit of trouble."

"Right, you're a heap of trouble. Breakin things and spillin food and roughin up poor ole Cade. Maybe you *had* better leave."

She turns and gives me a different look, a look you'd give a man trying to recite the Lord's Prayer in pig Latin. "Just don't be dumb," she says. "That man dudn't duck nobody. He's in the basement with his hobby. He probably dudn't even know you're here." She glares into the moiling sky. "If anybody's trouble it's ole you-know-who in there. But I can't talk about that. It's his poison, let him drink it."

"Just like you're mine." I scoot down a step so I can hug her shoulders around tight. No one up or down Arctic Spruce could care less, a far different place from prudent Michigan. The feeling out here is we can hug and smooch on the steps till our arms fall off and it'll be just fine with folks.

Her shoulders rise and settle inside my bear's hug. "I'm not so sweet," she says.

"Don't tell me any bad news now."

She furrows her brow. "Well, look."

"It's okay. I give you my word; whatever it is, later's good enough." I breathe in washed sweetness from her warm hair.

"Well, I do have something to tell you."

"I just don't want to spoil this afternoon."

"Maybe it won't."

"Do I really have to hear it?"

"I think you should, yes." She sighs. "You know that clam-handed old sawbones you were talkin to at the airport the other day? The one I came up and killed with a look?"

"I don't want to know about you and Fincher," I say. "It

would count as a terrible part of my day. I command you never to tell me." I stare at the swarming green sky. A small Cessna mutters across our airspace, seeking, I'm sure, a safe landing in Manahawkin or Ship Bottom, ahead of the storm. It does not seem a bit like Easter now, only another day without safeguards. Though the more normal the April day the better for me. Holidays can hold too many disappointments that I then have to accommodate.

"Look. I hadn't been with that ole character."

"Okay. That's good to hear."

"It's *your ex*. She's slippin off with him. The only reason I know is that I've seen her pick him up at the ER entrance three or four times. She's got the light brown Citation, right?"

"What?"

"Well," Vicki says. "If it hadn't been he kissed her, I would've thought it was just innocent. But it idn't innocent. That's why I acted so peculiar at the airport. I figured ya'll was about to fight."

"Maybe it was somebody else," I say. "There's a lot of brown cars. G.M. made millions of them. They're wonderful cars."

"G.M." She shakes her head in a teacherly way. "Not with your wife in 'em, they don't."

And for a sudden moment my mind simply ceases—which isn't even so unusual, and there are times when nothing else will help. Sitting next to Ralph's bed at the instant the nurse came in and said, "I'm sorry, Ralph has expired" (he was actually cold as an oyster when I touched his small clenched fist, and had been dead probably for an hour), at that moment when I knew he was dead, I remember my mind stopping. No other thought occurred to me immediately. No association or memory latched on to the event, or to the next one, for that matter, whatever it might've been. I don't remember. No lines of poetry. No epiphanies. The room became like a picture of a room, though more greenish and murky for that time of the morning, and then it sank away and became tiny—as though I was having a look at it through the wrong end of a telescope. I have since heard this explained as a protective mechanism of the mind, and that I should be grateful for it. Though I'm certain it was brought on as much by fatigue as the shock of grief.

Nothing now grows smaller because of this unexpected news,

though the air around me is tinged a stormy bottle green. The Chinese split-level maintains its ground in full view. Nothing has been thrown for a loop. I simply find myself staring across Arctic Spruce Drive at a chimney painted white, from which a gusty wind is drawing smoke at an angle perfectly perpendicular to the flue. All the draperies are closed. The grass out front is unspeakably green. You could putt on it and expect a good true roll to the cup.

I admit I am surprised; that the picture Vicki would like to paint of X *kissing* Fincher Barksdale in the front seat of her Citation outside the emergency room—when he is just off the cancer ward, smelling of disease and bodies—is as revulsive as any I could think of on my own. That the next scene, the one she hasn't painted yet, of wherever the two of them are slying off to for whatever itchy plans they have, clouds up pretty fast—aided by the revulsion. At the same time it's true I have to fight back a black hole of betrayal—for me and for Fincher's wife, Dusty, which is totally unwarranted since she might not even care and I hardly know her anymore. This in turn makes me feel a sense of Fincher's lizard's depravity, which brings about more disgust.

But a *thought* I do not think. Nor contrive a mean and explicatory synthesis to formulate my position regarding what I've heard.

In other words, I do not exactly respond; except to remember: *people will surprise you.*

"I guess not," I say agreeably, and stare off.

Vicki has twisted around to face me, her face above the split horizon of my two knees. She looks concerned, but willing to swap this look for a happy one. "So what're you thinkin?"

"Nothing." I smile, revulsion faded in me, leaving me only a little weak. I am glad I don't have to stand up. The simple words "You cannot" come to mind, but I don't have a finish for the phrase. "You cannot . . . what?" Dance? Fly? Sing an aria? Control the lives of others? Be happy all the time? "Why is it so important to tell me that just now?" I ask in a sudden but friendly way.

"Well, I just hate secrets. And I had this one with me a while. And if I waited any longer you might get to feeling so good that maybe I couldn't tell you at all or it'd ruin your whole day. I coulda told you in De-troit, but that would've been awful."

She nods at me soberly, chin out, as if she couldn't agree more with what she's just heard herself say. "This way, you got time to get over it."

"I appreciate your thinking about me," I say, though I'm sorry she is such a spendthrift of secrets.

"You're my ole pardner, aren't you?" She gives me a pat on my knees and the grin she's wanted to give me all along. It's nice to see, in spite of everything.

"What am I again?"

"My ole pardner. That's what I use to call Daddy when I was a little bitty thing." She bats her eyes at me.

"I'm more than that, at least I *used* to be. I still want to be, anyway." And I have to staunch a terrible tear that fills my eye like a freshet.

In some of the heart's business there is really no net gain. Let someone who knows tell you.

"Why, you bet," Vicki says. "But cain't we be friends, too? I'm gon always want to be your pardner." She plants a big fishy kiss upon my cold cheek. And up above me the sky swirls and tears apart, and on my face I feel the first serious drop of storm that's all along been waiting for its time.

WADE ARCENAULT is a cheery, round-eyed, crewcut fellow with a plainsman's square face and hearty laugh. I instantly recognize him from Exit 9, where he has taken my money hundreds of times but doesn't recognize me now. He is not a large man, hardly taller than Lynette, though his forearms, exposed and khaki sleeves up for washing at the sink, are ropy and tanned. He gives my hand a good wet shake right where he's washing. With a sly-secret smile he tells me he's been "down in his devil's dungeon" rewiring a Sunbeam fry-pan for Lynette to use to make Dutch Babies—her favorite Easter dessert. The pan sits splendidly fixed now on the counter top.

He is not at all what I expected. I had envisioned a wiry, squint-eyed little pissant—a gun store owner type, with fading flagrant tattoos of women on emaciated biceps, a man with a cruel streak for Negroes. But that is the man of bad stereotype, the kind my writing career foundered over and probably should have. The world is a more engaging and less dramatic place than writers ever give it credit for being. And for a moment Wade and I do nothing more than stand and stare at the fry-pan's drastic utilitarian lines like deaf-mutes, unable to get a better subject out in the open.

"So now how was the trip down, Frank?" Wade says with brusque heartiness. There is a frontier tautness in his character that makes him instantly trustworthy and appealing, a man with his priorities straight and a permanent twinkle in his eye that says he expects someone—me, maybe—to tell him something that will make him extremely happy. Nothing, in fact, would please me more.

"I came down through Pemberton and Bamber, Wade. It's one of my favorite drives. I'd like to take a canoe in the Rancocas one of these days. Parts of Africa must be a lot like that."

"Isn't it something, Frank?" Wade Arcenault's eyes ramble around in their sockets, seeking what, I don't know. Strange to say, Wade has no more of a Texas accent than Cade. "This is our little Garden of Eden down here, and we want to keep it so the outsiders don't ruin it for us, which is why I don't mind driving fifty miles to work. Though I guess I shouldn't be closing the drawbridge." His clear eyes sparkle with admission. "We're all from someplace else these days, Frank. People who were born right here don't even recognize it anymore. I've talked to them."

"But I bet they like it. This peninsula is a good idea."

"There's just the *ti*-niest little erosion problem out back," Wade says, finishing drying his hands with a dish towel. "But we've got our builder, this smart young Rutger's grad, Pete Calcagno." (A name I know!) "He's done his share with his backhoe and sandbags, and he'll get her licked, is what I think." Wade beams at me. "Most people want to do right, is my concept."

"I agree." And I most surely do! It is certainly true of me, and unquestionably true of Wade Arcenault. He, after all, bought his divorced daughter a house full of new furniture, and stood by and let her pick out every stick, then stepped up and wrote a whopper check so she could get a good start in a new northern environment. A lot of people would like to do that, but not many would follow through all the way.

Wade's blue eyes cut mischievously toward the basement door. Something I've done or said seems to have made him take to me, at least in a preliminary way. "Lynette," he says loudly, putting his eyes on the ceiling. "Have I got time to take this boy down to my devil's dungeon?" He gives me a wide wink and looks upwards again. (Maybe we'll be able to get a fishing trip planned, no matter how things go with Vicki.)

"I doubt if Grant's army could be expected to stop you, could it?" Lynette smiles in at us through the serving bay to the dining room, shakes her pretty red head, and waves us on.

In through the living room door I spy Vicki and Cade sitting on the salmon couch having what looks like an intimate talk. Cade's wardrobe and stultifying social life are no doubt under reappraisal.

Wade goes tromping off down the dark basement steps with me right behind. And immediately the heavy kitchen air is exchanged for the cool, chemically pungent odors indigenous to suburban basements where the owner is nobody's fool and has his termite contract up-to-date. I am one of their number.

"All right now, stay there, Frank," Wade says, lost in darkness ahead of me, his steps crossing concrete. Behind me Lynette's plump arm closes the kitchen door.

"Hold your horses, now." Wherever he is, Wade is enthusiastic.

I hold on to a wood 2 × 6 banister, not certain of even one more step. Something, I sense, is large and in front of me.

Wade is fiddling with metal objects, possibly the shade of a utility lamp, a fuse-box door, possibly a box of keys. "Ahh, the Christ," he mutters.

Suddenly a light flutters on, not a utility lamp but a shimmering white fluorescence in the raftered ceiling. What I see first in the light is not, I think, what I'm supposed to see. I see a big picture of the world photographed from outer space, fastened to the cinderblock wall above Wade's workbench. In it, all of space is blue and empty, and North America clear as in a dream, from miles away, in perfect outline white against a dark surrounding sea.

"What d'you think, Frank?" Wade says with pride.

My eyes try to find him, but instead find, directly in front of me where I could touch it, a big black car—so close I can't make out what it is, though it certainly is a car, with plenty of chrome and a glassy black finish. CHRYSLER is lettered above big wide louvered grillwork.

"By God, Wade," I say and find him down the long-fendered side, his hand on the tip of a high rear fin above the red taillight. He's grinning like a TV salesman who this time has put together something really special, something the little woman will *have* to like, something anyone in his nut would be proud to own as an investment, since its value can only increase.

It is a big box-safe of a car with fat whitewalls, ballistic bumpers, and an air of postwar styling-with-substance that makes my Malibu only a sad reminder.

"They don't make these anymore, Frank." Wade pauses to let these words hold sway. "I restored it myself. Cade helped me some, but he got bored soon as the motor work was over. Bought this off a soapstone Greek in Little Egg, and you should've seen it. Brown. Full of holes. Chrome half gone. Just a Swiss cheese, is what it was." Wade looks at the finish as if it might have murmured. It's chilly in the basement, and the Chrysler seems as cold and hard as a black diamond. "The roll-pleat inside still needs work," Wade admits.

"How'd you get it in here?"

Wade grins. He's been waiting for this one. "One Bilco door, back around there where you can't see it. The tow truck just slid it down. Cade and I had a ramp rigged out of channel irons. I had to relearn welding. You know anything about arc welding, Frank?"

"Not a damn thing," I say. "I should, though." I look at the photo of the earth again. It is a good thing to have, I think, for maintaining a sense of perspective, though in its homely sur-roundings the globe seems as exotic as a tapestry.

"Not necessary," Wade says soberly. "The principles are all pretty straightforward. Resistance is the whole thing. You'd pick it up in a minute." Wade smiles at the thought that I might some-day own a marketable skill.

"What're you going to do with it, Wade?" I say, a question that just came to me.

"I haven't thought about that," Wade says.

"Do you ever drive it?"

"Oh, I do. Yes. I start it up and drive it a foot one way and a foot or two back. There isn't much room down here." He stuffs his hands in his pockets and leans sideways on the fender, looking up and around at the low rafters into the dark cinderblock crawl space. Above us I hear muffled voices, the sound of footsteps squeezing from kitchen to dining room. I hear Cade's clomping off in another direction, no doubt upstairs to change clothes. I hear Elvis Presley's paws tick the kitchen floor. Then nothing. Wade and I are silent in the presence of his Chrysler and each other.

This situation could, of course, result in disaster, as many such situations do. A fear of what he may innocently ask me now, or a greater fear that I may have nothing special to say in answer and be left standing here as mute as a rocker panel—these make me wish I were back upstairs seeing the Knicks whip tar out of the Cavaliers, cheek-by-jowl with my old friend Cade. Sports is a first-rate safety valve when you and your whole value system are brought under friendly but unexpected scrutiny.

"Just what kind of fellow are you?" would be a perfectly natural curiosity. "What are your intentions regarding my daughter?" ("I'm not at all sure" would not be much of an answer.) "Who in the world do you think you are?" (I'd be stumped.) Suddenly I feel cold, though Wade doesn't seem to have any tricks up his sleeve. He is someone with codes I respect and that I would like to like me. All the best signs, in other words, are not so different from all the worst. Wade puts his fingertips to the porcelain-black fender and stares at them. I'm sure if I were closer every feature of me would be spelled out clear as a mirror.

"Frank," Wade says, "do you like fish?" He looks up at me almost imploringly.

"You bet I do."

"You do, huh?"

"I sure do."

Wade peers down at the shiny black surface again. "I was just thinking maybe you and me could go eat at the Red Lobster some night, get away from these women. Really have us a talk. You ever been there?"

"I sure have. Plenty of times." In fact, when X and I were first divorced, I went practically no place else. All the waitresses got to know me, knew I liked the broiled bluefish not overcooked and went out of their way to cheer me up, which is exactly what they're paid to do but usually don't.

"I go just for the haddock," Wade says. "It's a meal in itself. I call it the poor man's lobster."

"We ought to go. It'd be great." I slip my cold hands in my jacket pockets. All in all I would still jump at the chance to get back upstairs.

"Frank, where're your parents?" Wade looks gravely at me.

"They're both dead, Wade," I say. "A long time now."

"Mine, too." He nods. "Both of 'em gone. We all come from nowhere in the end, right?"

"I guess I don't really mind that part," I say.

"Right, right, right, right." Wade has crossed his arms and backed up against the Chrysler fender. He gives me a right-angles glance, then stares off into the crawl space again. "What brought you to New Jersey? You're a writer, is that right?"

"It's a pretty long story, Wade. I was married before. I've got two kids up in Haddam. It would take some time to explain all that." I smile in a way I hope will head him off, though I know Wade probably doesn't give a damn about it. He's just trying to be friendly.

"Frank, I like women. How about you?" Wade swivels his crewcut head toward me and grins, a straightforward grin of amusement, founded on the old anticipation of pleasure, the source of eighty percent of all happiness. It is the same to him as liking haddock, though more interesting because it might turn out to be a little dirty.

"I guess I do too, Wade." And I smile broadly back.

Wade raises his chin in an "I-knew-it" way, and puts his tongue against his cheek. "I've never wanted a night out with the boys in my life, Frank. What fun that is, I don't know."

"Not much," I say. And I think of my doleful nights in the "Back in Action" course, and with the Divorced Men, floating higgledy-piggledy on the chilly waters off Mantoloking like an army planning its renewed attack upon the beaches of lived life. I silently pledge never again to be in their number. I am finished with that and them. Life's ashore, after all (though God love them).

"Now don't get me wrong, Frank," Wade says warily, still staring off, as if I was standing somewhere else. "I'm not into your and Vicki's business. You two'll just have to fight that out."

"It gets complicated."

"You bet it does. It's hard to know what to want at your age. How old are you, anyway, Frank?"

"Thirty-eight," I say. "How old are you?"

"Fifty-six. I was forty-nine when my wife died of cancer."

"That's young, Wade."

"We were living in Irving, Texas, then. I was a petroleum engineer for Beutler Oil, worked a mile from a house I owned outright. I had a daughter married. I took my son to Cowboys' games. We lived what we thought was a good life. And then, bang, we suffered a heckuva terrible loss. Just overnight, it seemed like. Vicki and Cade just were wrecked by it. So you bet I know what complicated is." He nods toward his own private miseries.

"I know it was a hard time," I say.

"Divorce must be something like that, Frank. Lynette's divorced from a pretty decent guy, you know. Her second husband—her first died, too—I've met him. He's a decent guy, though we're not friends. But they couldn't make it together. It's no reflection. She's had a son killed in Oklahoma, herself."

Vicki has apparently mentioned Ralph, which is all right with me. He is, after all, part of my permanent public record. His lost life serves to further explain and punctuate mine. Wade, I'm happy to say, is doing his best here to "take me on as an individual," to speak in his own voice, and let me speak in mine, to be as within himself as it's possible to be with someone he doesn't know and could just as easily hate on sight. He could be giving me the third-degree down here, and I'd like to let him know I appreciate it that he isn't—though I'm not sure how to. By being direct and unambiguous and nothing like what I expected, he has left me nothing to say.

"Wade, what part of Texas did you grow up in?" I say, and grin hopefully.

"I'm from northeast Nebraska, Frank. Oakland, Nebraska." He scratches the back of his hand, perhaps thinking of wheat fields. "I went to *school* in Texas, now. Started in 1953 at A&M. Already married. Vicki was on the way, I think. It took me forever to graduate, and I worked in the oil fields all that time. But what I was saying about women, though, was that when my first wife, Esther, died, I was afraid I wouldn't be interested in women anymore. You know? You can just lose interest in women, Frank. I don't mean in a lead-in-your-pencil sense. But up here." Wade looks at me and points a finger right at the middle of his forehead. "You lose touch with *you*," he says.

"With your own needs. And I did that. Vicki can tell you about it, 'cause she took care of me." Wade rolls his eyes in a way that is ridiculously outside his character, though I've seen Vicki do it plenty of times, and it is entirely possible that he learned it from her. It is a woman's gesture and makes Wade seem womanly, as if life had taught him some harder lessons than he was man enough to suffer. "I did some crazy, crazy things along in there, Frank," Wade says and smiles in a self-forgiving way (he is no New-Ager, I can tell you that). "I kidnaped a baby out of a shopping mall. Now is that crazy?" Wade looks at me in amazement. "A little colored baby girl. I can't even tell you why now. At the time I would've said it was reaching out for commitment, I guess. Crying in the wilderness. I'd have been doing my crying on death row if they'd caught me, I can tell you that. And I damn well would've deserved it." Wade nods solemnly into the shadows as if all his darkest motives were imprisoned there now and could not reach him anymore.

"That's a helluva thing to do, Wade. What'd you do about it?"

"It was one *hell* of a pickle, Frank. Fortunately I returned that little baby to its stroller. But I'd already had it in the car with me. God knows what I would've done with it. That's when you hit the twilight zone."

"Maybe you didn't want to do it. That you didn't follow up on that is a pretty good argument, if you ask me."

"I know that theory all right, Frank. But I'll tell you what happened. I bumped into this Aggie classmate, Buck Larsen. It was at a reunion in College Station. We hadn't seen each other in probably twenty-six years. And it so happens he was with the Turnpike Authority. And we just started jabbering like you do. I told him that Esther had died, on and on, kids, women, tears, and that I had to get out of Dallas. I didn't even know it myself, you understand? You know how that is. You're the writer."

"Pretty well, I guess." (At least he and Buck didn't go to a motel.)

"It's pretty hard to tell where your intentions lie exactly, isn't it?" Wade offers me a pitiful smile.

"It's a lot easier in books. I know that."

"Damn right it is. We read some books at A&M. Not *that* many, I guess." Now we can both grin together. "Where'd you attend, Frank?"

"Michigan."

"East Lansing, right?"

"Ann Arbor."

"Well. You read more books there than I did at College Station, I know that."

"Just looking at everything around here now, it looks like you made the right choices, Wade."

"Frank, I guess so." With his toe Wade pokes at a scuff of dry concrete on the floor. He pressures it until it's clear it won't budge, then he shakes his head. "Your life can change a hundred ways, I'll tell you that."

"I know it, Wade."

"I took a job with the Turnpike Authority. I left Cade with Esther's folks in Irving and came up and lived a bachelor's life for a year. As far away from my other life as I could get. I went from being an engineer in Texas to being a toll-taker in New Jersey in a week's time. With help of course. It was a step down. With a big cut in pay. But I didn't care because I was a total wreck, Frank. You don't think you're a total wreck, but you are, and I had to start over again, get taken up by a new place, as crazy a place as this is, it didn't matter. I'm a problem-solver by nature, Frank. Engineers always are. And this was my problem. If you ask me, Americans are too sensitive to moving down in rank. It isn't so bad."

"It doesn't sound easy though. It makes my problems seem pretty small in comparison."

"I can't tell you if it was easy or not." His forehead ravels as if he wished he could, would like to be able to talk about that too, only it is lost to him now—a mercy. "You know, son. There's a fellow works for us up at Exit 9. I won't say his name. Except in 1959, he was living out west near Yellowstone. Had a wife and three children, a house and a mortgage. A job, a life. One night he'd been to a bar and was on his way home. And just after he left, a whole side of a mountain collapsed down on the bar. He stopped in the middle of the highway, he told me, and he could see back in the moonlight to where a lot of lights had been that were all gone because this huge landslide had taken place. Killed everybody but him. And do you know what he did?" Wade raises his eyebrows and squints, both at the same time.

"I've got a pretty good idea." (Who in a modern world wouldn't?)

"Well, and you'd be right. He got in his car and drove east. He said he felt like somebody'd just said, 'Here, Nick, here's your whole life being handed to you again. See if you can't do better this time.' And he's reported dead right now out in Idaho or Wyoming, or one of those states. Insurance paid. Who knows where his family is? His kids? And he works right beside me on the Turnpike, happy as a man can be. I'd never tell it, of course. And I'm a lot luckier than he is. We both just had new lives served to us, and a conviction to do something with them." Wade looks at me seriously, rubs his palms delicately on the chrome door handle beside him. He wants me to know that he's discovered something important late in life, something worth knowing when very few people ever discover anything by just living. He'd like to pass some wisdom along from the for-what-it's-worth department, though I can't help wondering what his friend's wife would think if she ever came through Exit 9 at just the right moment. It could happen. "Do you want to get married again, Frank?"

"I don't know."

"That's a good answer," Wade says. "I didn't think I did. Living alone didn't seem so bad after being married for twenty-nine years. What do you think?"

"It has its pluses, Wade. Did you meet Lynette up here?"

"I met her at a rock concert, and don't ask me what I was doing there because I couldn't tell you. This was in Atlantic City, three years ago. I'm not a joiner, and if you're not a joiner you can end up in some pretty strange places proving to yourself how independent you are."

"I usually end up staying home reading. Though I get in my car sometimes and drive all day, too. It sounds like what you're talking about."

"That's not so good, doesn't sound to me like."

"It isn't always, no."

"Well, anyway. Here was ole Lynette. She's about your age, Frank. Been widowed, divorced, and came to this concert with a Spanish guy who was about twenty-five. And he had just up and disappeared on her. I won't tell you all the gory details. But we ended up out at the Howard Johnson's on the freeway drinking coffee and talking the truth to each other till four in the morning. It turns out we both had a yearning to do something useful and positive with what time we had left to us, and neither one of us was much of a perfectionist, by which I mean we both knew we weren't exactly perfect for each other." Wade folds his arms and looks stern.

"How long before you got married, Wade? Not that long, I'll bet." I direct a sly grin at Wade because a big sly grin needs to come on his face at the thought of that starry night on the smoggy Atlantic City Expressway, and I'm glad to help him out. It must've seemed to them that they had beached together on a blasted, deserted shingle, and were damned lucky to be there. It is not a bad story, and worth a hundred grins.

"Not *that* long, Frank," Wade says proudly, cracking the very grin needed to get into the spirit of that old charmed time again. "Her divorce was settled, and we didn't see any use waiting. She's a Catholic, after all. A divorce was bad enough. And she didn't want us to be living together, which would've been fine with me. Only in a month I was married, and had this house! Boy!" Wade smiles and shakes his head at the remarkable singularity of unplanned life.

"You struck it rich, I'd say."

"Well, Lynette and I are opposites of a sort. She's pretty definite about things. And I'm a lot less definite, nowadays anyway. She takes being a Catholic pretty seriously—more so since her son got killed. And I kinda let her have her way there. I joined just for her sake, but we don't hold mass here, Frank. I'd say we were just alike in the one thing that counts—we're not rich people, and I'm not sure we really love each other or need to, but we want to be a good force in a small world and give a good accounting in the time that's left." Wade looks at me on the steps as if I were going to judge him, and he was hoping I'd come down and give him a big crack on the shoulders like a linebacker. I'm sure he has told me all this—a subject we might've gotten into in greater depth at the Red Lobster, and where I might've done more of the talking—because he wants to give me a fair sense of what the family is here, just in case I was weighing joining up. And it's true that the Arcenaults are a world apart from what I expected. Only better. Wade couldn't recommend himself or his tidy life to me in sweeter, more agreeable terms. What better prospects than to hitch up here. Forge a commitment in Sherri-Lyn Woods (odd weekends and holidays). I might eventually make friends with Cade, write him a subtle letter of recommendation to a good junior college; get him interested in marketing techniques instead of police work and guns. I might buy my own Whaler and dock it behind the house. It could be a damn good ordinary life, that's for sure.

Though for some reason I am nervous and embarrassed. My hands are still cold and stiff, and I stuff them inside my pants pockets and stare at Wade blank as a tomb door. That I withhold at just this moment is a major failing in my character.

"Frank," Wade says, sharp-eyed and studious now. "I want to hear from you on this. Do you think it's too little to do with your life? Just collect tolls, raise a family, work on an old car like this, go out on the ocean with your son and fish for fluke? Maybe love your wife?"

I cannot answer fast enough, all reluctance aside. "No," I almost shout. "Not a bit. I think it's goddamn great, Wade, and you're a damn lucky son of a bitch to get it." (I'm shocked to hear myself call Wade a son of a bitch.)

"There's more romance, I'd guess, in what you do, though, Frank. I don't see a lot of the world where I stand, though I've already seen plenty of it."

"Our lives are probably a lot more alike than you'd think, Wade. If you don't mind my saying so, yours might even be better."

"There are a lot of things went into an old car like this, if you get my meaning." Wade smiles proudly now, happy for my vote of approval. "Little touches I can't put into words. I'll come down here at four in the morning sometimes and tinker till daylight. And I have it to look forward to when I drive home. And I'll tell you this, son. Any day I come up upstairs, I'm happy as a lark, and my devils are in their dungeon."

"That's great, Wade."

"And it's every bit of it completely knowable, son. Wires and bolts. I could show you everything, though I can't tell you. You could sure do it yourself." He looks at me and shakes his head in amazement. Wade is not a full-disclosure kind of man, no matter how it might seem. And in this case, I know exactly what he's discovered, know the worth and pleasure it can be to anyone. Though for some strange reason, as I look down at Wade looking up at me, what I think of is Wade alone, walking down a long empty hospital corridor, holding a single suitcase, stopping at a numberless door and peeking in on a neat, empty room where the bed is turned down and harsh sunlight comes through a window, and things inside are clean as they can be. *Tests* are what he's here for. Many, many of them. And once he's walked in the room he will never be the same. This is the beginning of the end, and frankly it scares me witless and gives me a terrible shudder. I would like to hug him now, tell him to stay out of hospitals, meet the reaper at home. But I can't. He would get the wrong idea and everything between us would be ruined just when it's started so well.

Above us, in the fitful activity of the house, someone has begun to play the bass intro to "What'd I Say" on the electric organ, the four low minor-note sex-and-anticipation vamp before ole Ray starts his moan. The hum sinks through the rafters and fills the basement with an unavoidable new atmosphere. Despair.

Wade glances at the ceiling, happy as a man could have any right to be. It is as if he knew this very thing would happen and hears it as a signal that his house is in superb working order and ready for him to find his place in it once again. He is a man completely without a subtext, a literalist of the first order.

"I feel, Frank, like I've seen your face before. It's familiar to me. Isn't that strange?"

"You must see a lot of faces, Wade, wouldn't you guess?"

"Everybody in New Jersey's at least once." Wade flashes the patented toll-taker's grin. "But I don't remember many. Yours is just a face I remember. I thought it the moment I saw you."

I can't bear to tell Wade that he has taken my $1.05 four hundred times, smiled and told me to have myself "a super day," as I whirled off into the rough scrimmage of Route 1-South. That would be too ordinary an answer for his special kind of question, and for this charged moment. Wade is after mystery here, and I am not about to deny him. It would be as if Mr. Smallwood from Detroit had turned out to be a former grease jockey at Frenchy Montreux's Gulf, who had changed my oil and given me lubes, only I hadn't noticed, but suddenly did and pointed it out: mystery, first winded, then ruined by fact. I would rather stay on the side of good omens, be part of the inexplicable, an unexpected bellwether for whatever is ahead. Discretion, oddly enough, is the best response for a man of stalled responses.

Behind me the kitchen door opens, and I turn to see Lynette's cute cheerleader's face peering down at both of us, looking amused—a palpable relief, though I read in her look that this whole man-talk-below-decks business has been scheduled in advance and that she's been minding the kitchen clock for a pre-arranged moment to call us topside. I'm the lucky subject (but not the victim) of other people's scheming, and that is never bad. It is, in fact, a cozy feeling, even if it can be put to no good use.

The brooding, churchy Ray Charles chords come down louder now. This is Vicki's work. "You men can talk old cars all day if you want to, but there's folks ready to sit down." Lynette's eyes twinkle with impatient good humor. She can tell everything's A-Okay down here. And she's right. If we are not great friends, we soon will be.

"How 'bout let's eat a piece of dead sheep, Frank?" Wade laughs, giving his belly a rub. "Agnus dei," he chortles up toward Lynette.

"That is *not* what it is," Lynette says, and rolls her eyes in the (I see now) Arcenault manner. "What'll he say next, Frank? Agnus Dei is what *you* are, Wade, not what we're eatin. Heavens."

"I'm sure too tough to chew, Frank, I'll tell you that right now. Haw." And up out of the shadowy basement we come—all hands on deck—into the warm and sunlit kitchen, the whole Arcenault crew arrived and ready for ritual Sunday grub.

DINNER IS a more ceremonial business than I would've guessed. Lynette has transformed her dining room into a hot little jewel box, crystal-candle chandelier, best silver and linens laid. The instant we're seated she has us all join hands around the obloid so that I end up uneasily grabbing both Wade's and Cade's (no resistance from Cade) while Vicki holds Wade's and Lynette's. And I can't help thinking—eyes stitched shut, peering soundlessly down into the familiar death-ball of liquid crimson flame behind which waits an infinity of black soul's abyss from which nothing but Wade and Cade's cumbersome hands can keep me from tumbling—what strange, good luck to be reckoned among these people like a relative welcome from Peoria. Though I can't keep from wondering where my own children are at this moment, and where X is—my hope being that they are not sharing a fatherless, prix fixe Easter brunch at some deserted seaside Ramada in Asbury Park with Barksdale, back on the sneak from Memphis, taking my place. That news I could've passed a happy day without, though we can never stop what comes to us by right. I am overdue, in fact, for a comeuppance, and lucky not to be spending the day cruising some mall for an Easter takeout— the way poor Walter Luckett no doubt is, lost in the savage wilderness of civil life.

Lynette's blessing is amiably brief and upbeat-ecumenical in its particulars—I assume for my benefit—taking into account the day and the troubled world we live in but leaving out Vatican II and any saintly references unquestionably on her mind—where they count—and winding up with a mention of her son, Beany, in a soldier's grave at Fort Dix but present in everyone's mind, including mine. (Molten flames, in fact, give way at the end to reveal Beany's knifey mug leering at me out from oblivion's sanctum.)

Wade and Cade have both put on garish flower ties and sports jackets, and look like vaudevillians. Vicki gives double cross-eyes at me when I smile at her and attempt to act comfortable among the family. Talk is of the weather as we dig into the lamb, then a brief pass into state politics; then Cade's chances of an early call-up at the police academy and speculation about whether uniforms will be assigned the first morning, or if more tests will need to be passed, which Cade seems to view as a grim possibility. He leads a discussion on the effect of driving fifty-five, noting that it's all right for everybody else but not him. Then Lynette's work on the Catholic crisis-line, then Vicki's work at the hospital, which everyone agrees is both as difficult and rewarding a service to mankind as can be—more, by implication, than Lynette's. No one mentions our weekend in the faraway Motor City, though I have the feeling Lynette is trying to find a place for the word Detroit in practically every sentence, to let us all know she wasn't born yesterday and isn't making a stink since Vicki, like all other divorced gals, can take care of her own beeswax.

Cade cracks a baiting smile and asks me who I like in the AL East, to which I answer Boston (my least favorite team). I, of course, am behind Detroit all the way, and know in fact that certain crucial trades and a new pitching coach will make them virtually unstoppable come September.

"Boston. Hnuhn." Cade leers into his plate. "Never see it."

"Wait and see," I say with absolute assuredness. "There're a hundred and sixty-two games. They could make one smart trade by the deadline and pretty much have it their way."

"It'd have to be for Ty Cobb." Cade guffaws and eyes his father slavishly, his mouth full of a dinner roll.

I laugh the loudest while Vicki crosses her eyes again, since she knows I've led Cade to the joke like a trained donkey.

Lynette smiles attentively and maneuvers her lamb hunk, English peas and mint jelly all nearer one another on her plate. She is an understanding listener, but she is a straightforward questioner too, someone who wouldn't let you off easy if you called up the crisis-line with a silly crisis. It seems she has me fixed in her mind. "Now were you in the service, Frank?" she says pleasantly.

"The Marines, but I got sick and was discharged."

Lynette's face portrays real concern. "What happened?"

"I had a blood syndrome that made a doctor think I was dying of cancer. I wasn't, but nobody figured it out for a while."

"You were lucky, then, weren't you?" Lynette is thinking of poor dead Beany again, cold in the Catholic section of the Fort Dix cemetery. Life is never fair.

"I was headed over in six more months, so I guess so. Yes ma'am."

"You don't have to ma'am me, Frank," Lynette says and bats her eyes all around. She smiles dreamily down the table at Wade, who smiles back at her in his best old southern gent manner. "My former husband was in Vietnam in the Coast Guard," Lynette says. "Not many knew the Guard was even there. But I have letters postmarked the Mekong Delta and Saigon."

"Where've you got 'em hid?" Vicki smirks at everyone.

"Past is past, sweetheart. I threw them out when I met that man right there." Lynette nods and smiles at Wade. "We don't need to pretend, do we. Everybody's been married here except Cade."

Cade blinks his dark eyes like a puzzled bull.

"Those guys saw some real tough action," Wade says. "Stan told me, Lynette's ex-husband, that he probably killed two hundred people he never saw, just riding along shooting the jungle day after day, night after night." Wade shakes his head.

"That's really something," I say.

"Right," Cade grunts sarcastically.

"Are you sorry not to have seen real action," Lynette says, turning to me.

"He sees enough," Vicki says and smirks again. "That's my department."

Lynette smiles dimly at her. "Be nice, sweetheart. Try to be, anyway."

"I'm perfect," Vicki says. "Don't I *look* perfect?"

"I'd have some more of that lamb," I say. "Cade, can I pass some your way?" Cade gives me a devious look as I catch a slab of gray lamb and pass him the platter. For some reason, my mind cannot come up with a good sports topic, though it's trying like a computer. All I can think is facts. Batting averages. Dates. Seating capacities. Third-down ratios of last year's Super Bowl opponents (though I can't remember which teams actually played). Sometimes sports are no help.

"Frank, I'd be interested to hear you out on this one," Wade says, swallowing a big wedge of lamb. "Just in your journalist's opinion, are we, would you say, in a prewar or a postwar situation in this country right now?" Wade shakes his head in earnest dismay. "I guess I get sour about things sometimes. I wish I didn't."

"I haven't paid much attention to politics the last few years, to tell the truth, Wade. My opinion never seemed worth much."

"I hope there's a world war before I'm too old to be in it. That's all I know," Cade says.

"That's what Beany thought, Cade." Lynette frowns at Cade.

"Well," he says to his plate after a moment's numbed silence.

"Now seriously, Frank," Wade says. "How can you stay isolated from events on a grand scale, is my question." Wade isn't badgering me. It is just the earnest way of his mind.

"I write sports, Wade. If I can write a piece for the magazine on, say, what's happening to the team concept here in America, and do a good job there, I feel pretty good about things. Pretty patriotic, like I'm not isolating myself."

"That makes sense." Wade nods at me thoughtfully. He is leaning on his elbows, over his plate, hands clasped. "I can buy that."

"What *has* happened to the team concept," Lynette asks, and looks at everyone by turns. "I'm not sure I know even what that is."

"That's pretty complicated," Wade says, "wouldn't you say so, Frank?"

"If you talk to athletes and coaches the way I do, that's all you hear, from the pros especially. Baseball, football. The line is, everybody has a role to play, and if anybody isn't willing to play his role, then he doesn't fit into the team's plans."

"It sounds all right to me, Frank," Lynette says.

"It's all a crocka shit's what it is." Cade scowls miserably at his own two hands, which are on the table. "They're just all assholes. They wouldn't know a team if it bit 'em on the ass. They're all prima donnas. Half of 'em are queers, too."

"That's certainly intelligent, Cade," Vicki says. "Thanks very much for your brilliant comment. Why don't you tell us some more of your philosophies."

"That wasn't too nice, Cade," Lynette says. "Frank had the floor then."

"Ppptttt," Cade gives a Bronx cheer and rolls his eyes.

"Is that some new language you learned working on boats?" Vicki says.

"Okay, seriously, Frank." Wade is still leaning up on his elbows like a jurist. He's hit a subject with some meat on its bones, and he's ready to saw right in. "I think Lynette's got a pretty valid point in what she says here." (Forgetting for the moment Cade's opinion.) "I mean, what's the matter with following your assignment on the team? When I was working oil rigs, that's exactly how we did it. And I'll tell you, too, it worked."

"Well, maybe it's too small a point. Only the way these guys use team concept is too much like a machine to me, Wade. Too much like one of those oil wells. It leaves out the player's part—to play or not play; to play well or not so well. To give his all. What all these guys mean by team concept is just cogs in the machine. It forgets a guy has to decide to do it again every day, and that men don't work like machines. I don't think that's a crazy point, Wade. It's just the nineteenth-century idea—dynamos and all that baloney—and I don't much like it."

"But in the end, the result's the same, isn't it?" Wade says seriously. "Our team wins." He blinks hard at me.

"If everybody decides that's what they want, it is. If they can perform well enough and long enough. It's just the *if* I'm concerned about, Wade. I worry about the *decide* part, too, I guess. We take too much for granted. What if I just don't want to win that bad, or can't?"

"Then you shouldn't be on the team." Wade seems utterly puzzled (and I can't blame him). "Maybe we agree and I don't know it, Frank?"

"It's all niggers with big salaries shootin dope, if you ask me," Cade says. "I think if everybody carried a gun, everything'd work a lot better."

"Oh, Christ." Vicki throws down her napkin and stares away into the living room.

"Who's he?" Cade gapes.

"You can just be excused, Cade Arcenault," Lynette says crisply, with utter certainty. "You can leave and live with the other cavemen. Tell Cade, Wade. He can leave the table."

"Cade." Wade beams an unmistakable look of unmentionable violence Cade's way. "Put the lock on that, mister." But Cade cannot stop smirking and lurks back in his chair like a criminal, folding his big arms and balling his fists in hatred. Wade balls his own fists and butts them together softly in front of him, while his eyes return to a point two inches out onto the white field of linen tablecloth. He is cogitating about teams still, about what makes one and what doesn't. I could jawbone about this till it's time to start home again, though I admit the whole subject has begun to make me vaguely uneasy.

"What you're telling me then, Frank, and I may have this all bum-fuzzled up. But it seems to me you're saying this idea—" Wade arches his eyebrows and smiles up at me in a beatific way "—leaves out our human element. Am I right?"

"That says it well, Wade." I nod in complete agreement. Wade has got this in terms he likes now (and a pretty versatile sports cliché at that). And I am pleased as a good son to go along with him. "A team is really intriguing to me, Wade. It's an event, not a thing. It's time but not a watch. You can't reduce it to mechanics and roles."

Wade nods, holding his chin between his thumbs and index fingers. "All right, all right, I guess I understand."

"The way the guys are talking about it now, Wade, leaves out the whole idea of the hero, something I'm personally not willing to give up on yet. Ty Cobb wouldn't have been a role-player." I give Cade a hopeful look, but his eyes are drowsy and suffused with loathing. My knee begins to twitch under the table.

"I'm not either," Lynette says, her eyes alarmed.

"It also leaves out why the greatest players, Ty Cobb or Babe Ruth, sometimes don't perform as greatly as they should. And why the best teams lose, and teams that shouldn't win, do. That's team play of another kind, I think, Wade. It's not role-playing and machines like a lot of these guys'll tell you."

"I think I understand, Wade," Lynette says, nodding. "He's saying athletes and all these sports people are just not too smart."

"I guess it's giving a good accounting, sweetheart, is what it comes down to," Wade says somberly. "Sometimes it'll be enough. Sometimes it isn't going to be." He purses his lips and stares at my idea like a crystal vase suspended in his mind's rare ether.

I stare at my own plateful of second helping I haven't touched and won't, the pallid lamb congealed and hard as a wood chip, and the untouched peas and broccoli flower alongside it cold as Christmas. "When I can make that point in one of our 'Our Editors Think' columns, Wade, that half a million people'll read, then I figure I've addressed the big picture. What you said: events on a grand scale. I don't know what else I really can do after that."

"That's everything in life right there, is my belief," Lynette says, though she's thinking of another subject, and her bright green eyes scout the table for anyone who hasn't finished his or hers yet.

In the kitchen an electric coffeemaker clicks, then spurts, then sighs like an iron lung, and I get an unexpected whiff of Cade who smells of lube jobs and postadolescent fury. He cannot help himself here. His short life—Dallas to Barnegat Pines —has not been especially wonderful up to now, and he knows it. Though to my small regret, there's nothing on God's green earth I can do to make it better for him. My future letter-of-recommendation and fishing excursions with just the three men cut no ice with him. Perhaps one day he will stop me for speeding, and we can have the talk we can't have now, see eye-to-eye on crucial issues—patriotism and the final rankings in the American League East, subjects that would bring us to blows in a second this afternoon. Life will work out better for Cade once he buttons on a uniform and gets comfortable in his black-and-white machine. He is an enforcer, natural born, and it's possible he has a good heart. If there are better things in the world to be, there are worse, too. Far worse.

Vicki is staring down at her full plate, but glances up once out the tops of her eyes and gives me a disheartened sour-mouth of disgust. There is trouble, as I've suspected, on the horizon. I have talked too much to suit her and, worse, said the wrong things. And worse yet, jabbered on like a drunk old uncle in a voice she's never heard, a secular Norman Vincent Pealeish tone I use for the speaker's bureau and that even makes me squeamish sometimes when I hear it on tape. This may have amounted to a betrayal, a devalued intimacy, an illusion torn, causing doubt to bloom into dislike. Our own talk is always of the jokey-quippy-irony style and lets us leap happily over "certain things" to other "certain things"—cozy intimacy, sex and rapture, ours in a heartbeat. But now I may have stepped out of what she thinks she knows and feels safe about, and become some Gildersleeve she doesn't know, yet instinctively distrusts. There is no betrayal like voice betrayal, I can tell you that. Women hate it. Sometimes X would hear me say something—something as innocent as saying "Wis-sconsin" when I usually said "Wisconsin"—and turn hawk-eyed with suspicion, wander around the house for twenty minutes in a brown brood. "Something you said didn't sound like you," she'd say after a while. "I can't remember what it was, but it wasn't the way you talk." I, of course, would be stumped for what to answer, other than to say that if I said it, it must be me.

Though I should know it's a bad idea to accompany anyone but yourself home for the holidays. Holidays with strangers never turn out right, except in remote train stations, Vermont ski lodges or the Bahamas.

"Who'll have coffee?" Lynette says brightly. "I've got decaf." She is clearing dishes smartly.

"Knicks," Cade mutters, pounding to his feet and slumping off.

"Nix to you too, Cade," Lynette says, pushing through the kitchen door, arms laden. She turns to frown, then cuts her eyes at Wade who is sitting with a pleasant, distracted look on his square face, palms flat on the tablecloth thinking about team concept and the grand scale of things. She widely mouths words to the effect of getting a point across to this Cade Arcenault outfit, or there'll be hell to pay, then vanishes out the door, letting back in a new scent of strong coffee.

Wade is galvanized, and gives Vicki and me a put-on smile, rising from the head of the table, looking small and uncomfortable in the loose-fitting sports jacket and ugly tie—unquestionably a joke present from the family or the men at the toll plaza. He has worn it as a token of good spirits, but they have temporarily abandoned him. "I guess I've got a couple things to do," he says miserably.

"Don't you rough up on that boy now," Vicki threatens in a whisper. Her eyes are savage slits. "Life ain't peaches-and-milk for him either."

Wade looks at me and smiles helplessly, and once again I imagine him peeping into an empty hospital room from which he'll never return.

"Cade's fine, sister," he says with a smile, then wanders off to find Cade, already deep in some squarish room of his down a hallway on another level.

"It'll be all right," I say, soft and sober-voiced now, meant to start me back on the road to intimacy. "There's just too many new people in Cade's life. I wouldn't be any good at it either." I smile and nod in one fell motion.

Vicki raises an eyebrow—I am a strange man with inexpert opinions concerning her family life, something she needs like a new navel. She turns a dinner spoon over and over in her fingers like a rosary. The boat collar of her pink jersey has slid a fraction off-center exposing a patch of starkly white brassiere strap. It is inspiring, and I wish this were the important business we were up to instead of old dismal-serious—though I have only myself to blame. *Sic transit gloria mundi.* When is that ever not true?

"Your father's a great guy," I say, my voice becoming softer with each word. I should be silent, portray a different fellow entirely, affect some hidden antagonism of my own to balance hers. Only I'm simply not able to. "He reminds me of a great athlete. I'm sure he'll never have a nervous breakdown."

Lynette clatters dessert plates and coffee cups in the kitchen. She's listening to us, and Vicki knows it. Anything said now will be for a wider consumption.

"Daddy and Cade oughta be living here by theirselves," Vicki says scornfully. "He oughtn't to be hooked up with this ole gal. They oughta be both big bachelors havin the time of their lives."

"He seems pretty happy to me."

"Don't start on me 'bout my own daddy, if you please. I know *you* well enough, don't I? I ought to know *him!*" Her eyes grow sparkly with dislike. "What's all that guff you were spewin about. Patriotism. Team con-cept. You sounded like a preacher. I just about mortified."

"They're things I believe in. More people could stand to think that way, if you ask me."

"Well, you oughta believe them to yourself quietly then. I can't take this."

At this moment, Elvis Presley comes to the living room door and stares up at me. He's heard something he doesn't like and intends to find out if I'm responsible. "I don't even like men," Vicki says, staring belligerently at her spoon. "Ya'll don't make yourselves happy ten minutes at a time. You and Everett both. Y'act like tormented dogs. Plus, you bring it all on yourselves."

"I think it's you that's unhappy."

"Yeah? But it's really you, though, idn't it? You hate everything."

"I'm pretty happy." I put on a big smile, though it's true I am heartsick. "You make me happy. I know that. You can count on that."

"Oh boy. Here we go. I shouldn't of told you about your ex and whatever his name is. You been Serious Sam ever since."

"I'm not Serious Sam. I don't even care about that."

"Shoot. You should've seen your face when I told you."

"Look at it now, though." My grin is ear-to-ear, though it is impossible to argue in behalf of your own good spirits without defeating them completely and getting mad as hell. Elvis Presley has seen enough and goes back behind the couch. "Why don't we just get married?" I say. "Isn't that a good idea?"

"Because I don't love you enough, that's why." She looks

away. More dishes clatter in the kitchen. Cups settle noisily into saucers. Far away, in a room I know nothing of, a phone rings softly.

"Now that's the phone," I hear Lynette say to no one in particular, and the ringing stops.

"Yes you do," I say brightly. "That's just a bunch of hooey. I'll get right down on my knees right now." I get onto my knees and walk on them all the way around the table to where she sits, thighs crossed regally and entombed in taut panty hose. "A man's on his knees to plead and beg with you to marry him. He'd be faithful, and take out the garbage and do dishes and cook, or at least pay someone to do it. How can you say no?"

"It ain't gon be hard," she says giggling, embarrassed at me for yet another reason.

"Frank?"

My name. Unexpected. Called from somewhere in the unexplored cave of the house. Wade's voice. Probably he and Cade want me up there to watch the end of the Knicks game—once again everything decided in the last twenty seconds. But wild horses couldn't pull me away from here. This is serious.

"Ho, Wade," I call out, still on my knees in my pleader's pose in front of his regal daughter. One more bout of ardent pleading-tickling and we'll both be laughing, and she'll be mine. And why shouldn't she? My *always* needn't be forever. I'm ready for the plunge, nervy as a cliff-diver. Though if down the line things go rotten we can both climb the cliffs again. Life is long.

"Phone's for you," Wade calls. "You can take it up here in Lynette's and my room." Wade sounds sobered and bedeviled, a pitiable presence from the top of the stairs. A door clicks softly shut.

"Who's that?" Vicki says scratchily, tugging on her pink skirt as if we'd been caught in heavy petting. Her brassiere strap is now exposed completely.

"I don't know." Though I have a terrible bone-aching crisis fear that I have forgotten something important and am about to stare disaster in the face. A special assignment I was supposed to write but have somehow completely neglected, everyone up in New York rushing round in emergency moods trying to find me. Or possibly an Easter date I made months ago and have overlooked, though there's no one I know well enough to ask me.

I cannot guess who it is. I plant a quick kiss of promised return on Vicki's stockinged knee, get to my feet and head off to investigate. "Don't move," I say. The kitchen door is just opening as I leave.

Above floors, a dark and short carpeted hall leads to a bathroom at the end where a light is on. Two doors are shut on one side, but on the other, one stands open, a bluish light shining through. Ahead of me I hear a thermostat click and the sound of whooshing air.

I step into Wade and Lynette's nuptial sanctum where the blue light radiates from a bed lamp. The bed is also blue, a skirted-and-flounced four-poster canopy, king-sized and wide as a peaceful lake. Nothing is an inch out of place. Rugs raked. Vanity sparkling. No underwear or socks piled on the blue Ultrasuede loveseat beside the window overlooking the windy boat channel. The door to the bathroom is discreetly closed. A smell of face powder lingers. The room is perfect as a place where strangers can accept personal phone calls.

The phone is on the bed table, its conscientious little night light glowing dimly.

"Hello," I say, with no idea what I will hear, and sink expectant into the soft flounced silence.

"Frank?" X's voice, solemn, reliable, sociable. I am instantly exhilarated to hear her. But there is an undertone I do not comprehend. Something beyond speech, which is why she is the only one who can call me.

I feel a freeze going right to the bottom of my feet. "What's the matter?"

"It's all right," she says. "Everyone's all right. Everyone's fine here. Well, everyone's not, actually. Someone named, let's see, Walter Luckett is dead, apparently. I guess I don't know him. He sounds familiar, but I don't know why. Who is he?"

"What do you mean, he's dead?" Consolation spurts right back up through me. "I was with him last night. At home. He isn't dead."

She sighs into the receiver, and a dumb silence opens on the line. I hear Wade Arcenault's voice, soft and evocative, speaking to his son across the hall behind a closed door. A television mumbles in the background, a low crowd noise and a ref's distant whistle. "Now in the best of all possible worlds. . . ." Wade can be heard to say.

"Well," X says quietly, "the police called here about thirty minutes ago. They think he's dead. There's a letter. He left it for you."

"What do you mean?" I say, and am bewildered. "You sound like he killed himself."

"He shot himself, the policeman said, with a duck gun."

"Oh no."

"His wife's out of town, evidently."

"She's in Bimini with Eddie Pitcock."

"Hmm," X says. "Well."

"Well what?"

"Nothing. I'm sorry to call you. I just listened to your message."

"Where're the children?"

"They're here. They're worried, but it isn't your fault. Clary answered the phone when the police called. Are you with what's-her-face?" (A first-rate Michigan expression of practiced indifference.)

"Vicki." Vicki Whatsherface.

"Just wondering."

"Walter came to the house last night and stayed late."

"Well," X says, "I'm sorry. Was he a friend of yours, then?"

"I guess so." Somebody in Cade's room claps his hands loudly three times in succession, then whistles.

"Are you all right, Frank?"

"I'm shocked." In fact, I can feel my fingertips turning cold. I lie down backwards on the silky bedspread.

"The police want you to call them."

"Where was he?"

"Two blocks from here. At 118 Coolidge. I may have even heard the shot. It isn't that far."

I stare up through the open canopy into an absolutely blue ceiling. "What am I supposed to do? Did you already say that?"

"Call a Sergeant Benivalle. Are you all right? Would you like me to come meet you someplace?"

Cade lets out a loud, raucous laugh across the hall.

"Isn't that the goddamn truth!" Wade says in high spirits. "It is the god-*damndest* thing, I swear."

"I'd like you to meet me someplace," I say in a whisper. "I'll have to call you, though."

"Where in the world are you?" (This, in her old scolding lover's style of talk: "Where *will* you turn up next?" "Where in the *world* have you been?")

"Barnegat Pines," I say softly.

"Wherever that is."

"Can I call you?"

"You can come over here if you want to. Of course."

"I'll call soon as I know what to do." I have no idea why I should be whispering.

"Call the police, all right?"

"All right."

"I know it's not a happy call."

"It's hard to think about right now. Poor Walter." In the pale blue ceiling I wish I could see something I recognized. Almost anything would do.

"Call me when you get here, Frank."

Though of course there is nothing to see above me. "I will," I say. X hangs up without saying anything, as if "Frank" were the same as saying "Goodbye. I love you."

I call information for the Haddam police and dial it immediately. As I wait I try to remember if I've ever laid eyes on Sergeant Benivalle, though there's no doubt I have. I've seen the whole guinea lot of them at Village Hall. In the normal carryings-on of life they are unavoidable and familiar as luggage.

"Mr. Bascombe," a voice says carefully. "Is that right?"

"Yes."

I recognize him straight off—a big chesty, small-eyed detective with terrible acne scars and a flat-top. He is a man with soft thick hands he used, in fact, to take my fingerprints when our house was broken into. I remember their softness from years ago. He is a good guy by my memory, though I know he'd never remember me.

And in fact Sergeant Benivalle might as well be talking to a recording. Death and survivorship have become the equivalents of pianos to a house-mover—big items, but a day's work that will end.

He explains in a voice void of interest that he would like me to offer positive identification of "the deceased." No one nearby will, and I reluctantly agree to. Yolanda is unreachable in Bimini, though he seems not to be bothered by it. He says he will have to give me a Thermofax of Walter's letter, since he needs it to keep "for evidence." Since Walter left another note for the police, there is no suspicion of foul play. Walter killed himself, he says, by blowing his brains out with a duck gun, and the time of death was about one p.m. (I was playing croquet on the lawn.) He bolted the shotgun, Sergeant Benivalle says, to the top of the television set and rigged a remote control to release the trigger. The TV was on when people arrived—the Knicks and Cavaliers from Richfield.

"Now, Mr. Bascombe," the Sergeant says, using his private, off-duty voice. I hear him riffling through papers, blowing smoke into the receiver. He is sitting, I know, at a metal desk, his mind wandering past other crimes, other events of more concern. It is Easter there, too, after all. "Can I ask you something personal?"

"What?"

"Well." Papers riffle, a metal drawer closes. "Were you and this Mr. Luckett, uh, sorta into it?"

"Do you mean did we have an argument, no."

"I don't, uhm, mean an argument. I mean, were you romantically linked. It would help to know that."

"Why would it help you to know that?"

Sergeant Benivalle sighs, his chair squeaks. He blows smoke into the receiver again. "Just to account for the, uh, event in question here. No big deal. You of course don't have to answer."

"No," I say. "We were just friends. We belonged to a divorced men's club together. This seems like an intrusion to me."

"I'm sort of in the intrusion business down here, Mr. Bascombe." Drawers open and close.

"All right. I just don't exactly see why that has to be an issue."

"It's okay, thanks," Sergeant Benivalle says wearily (I'm not sure what he means by this either). "If I'm not here, ask for the copy with the watch officer. Tell 'em who you are so you can, ah, identify the deceased. All right?" His voice has suddenly brightened for no reason.

"I'll do that," I say irritably.

"Thanks," Sergeant Benivalle says. "Have a good day."

I hang up the phone.

*   *   *

THOUGH IT is *not* a good day, nor is it going to be. Easter has turned to rain and bickering and death. There's no saving it now.

"Whaaaat?" Vicki shouts, all shock and surprise at the death of someone she has never met, her face creased into a look of pain and uninterested disbelief.

"Why, oouu noouu," Lynette exclaims, making the sign of the cross twice and in a devil's own hurry, without leaving the kitchen door. "Poor man. Poor man."

I've told them only that a friend of mine is dead and I have to go back right away. Dutch Babies and piping hot coffee sit all around, though Wade and Cade are still upstairs ironing things out.

"Well course you do," Lynette says sympathetically. "You better go on right now."

"Dyouwanme to go with you?" For some reason Vicki grins at this idea.

Why do I have the feeling she and Lynette have struck some sympathetic pact while I was on the phone? An understanding that puts a ceiling and a floor to old grievances and excludes me—the family closing ranks suddenly and officially, leaving me in the cold. This is the grim side of the non-nuclear family—its capacity to pile disaster on disaster. (Son of a bitch!) After I leave they'll stoke the fire, haul out the sheet music and sing favorite oldies—together alone. I am called away at the very worst time, before they realize how much they all really like me and want someone just like me around forever. Preemptive, ill-meant death has intruded. Its gluey odors are spread over me. I can smell them myself.

"No," I say. "There wouldn't be anything for you to do anyway. You go on and stay here."

"Well it's the God's truth, idn't it?" Vicki gets up and comes to stand beside me in the dining room archway, looping her arm encouragingly through mine. "I'll walk with you out, though."

"Lynette...." I start to say, but Lynette is already waving a spoon at me from the end of the table.

"Now don't say a word, Franky Bascombe. Just go see 'bout your friend who needs you."

"Tell Wade and Cade I'm sorry." I want more than anything not to leave, to be around another hour to sing "Edelweiss" and doze off in my chair while Vicki files her nails and daydreams.

"About what? What is it's going on?" Wade has heard commotion and come right down to see what all the trouble is about. He's at the top of the stairs, half a level above us, leaning over as if he were about to fly.

"Let me explain it all to you later, Dad," Lynette says, and raises her fingers to her lips.

"You two haven't had a fuss, have you?" Wade's look is pure bafflement. "I hope nobody's mad. Why are you leaving, Frank?"

"His best friend's dead, that's all," Vicki says. "That's what the phone call was about." It's clear she wants me out of here and in a hurry, and intends to be on the phone to the daggerhead in Texas before my key is in the ignition.

Though what have I done that's so wrong? Can a longed-for life sink below the waves because a tone in my voice wasn't exactly appreciated? Can affections be frail as that? Mine are heartier.

"Wade, I'm just as sorry as hell about this." I reach up the short carpeted stairway to shake his hard hand. Bafflement has not altogether left him nor me.

"Me too, son. I hope you'll come on back here. We're not going anyplace."

"He'll come back," Lynette chirps. "Vicki'll see to that." (Vicki is silent on this subject.)

"Tell Cade goodbye," I say.

"Will do." Wade comes down and squares me up with a small earnest hand on my shoulder—half a manly hug. "Come back and we'll go out fishing." Wade makes a squeaky, embarrassed laugh, and in fact looks slightly dizzy.

"I'll do it, Wade." And God knows I would. Though that will never happen in a hundred moons, and I will never see his face again outside a toll plaza. We will never stalk, hungry as bears, into a Red Lobster, never be friends in the ways I had hoped— ways to last a lifetime.

I wave them all goodbye.

ON THE front lawn everything including our empty croquet wickets is lost and gray and gone straight to hell. I stand in the fluttering wind and sight down the unpeopled curve of Arctic Spruce to the point where it sweeps from sight, all its plantings fresh and immature, its houses split-level and perfectly isosceles. Wade Arcenault is a lucky man to live here, and I am, at heart, cast down to loss in its presence.

Vicki knows I'm stalling and tampers with the door latch of my Malibu until, as if by magic, it swings open.

She is bemused, in no mind for words. I, of course, would talk till midnight if I thought it could improve my chances.

"Why don't we just go get a motel room right now?" I paint a grin on my face. "You haven't been to Cape May. We could have a big time."

"What about your ole dead guy? Herb?" Vicki sets her chin up haughtily. "What about him?"

"Walter." She's made me feel slightly embarrassed. "He's not going anywhere. But I'm still alive. Frank's still among the living."

"I'd be ashamed," Vicki says, shoving the door wide open between us. The wind now has a wintry grit in it. The front has passed quickly and left us in a gray spring chill. In half a minute, she is going. This is the last chance to love her.

"Well, I'm not," I say loudly into the wind. "I didn't kill *my* self. I want you to go off and let me love you. And tomorrow we'll get married."

"Not hardly." She looks glumly at the dry black weather stripping on my poor car's poor window frame. She picks off a piece with a crimson fingernail.

"Why not?" I say. "*I* want to. This time yesterday we were in bed like newlyweds. I was one of the only six people in the world then. What the hell happened? Did you just go crazy? Twenty minutes ago you were happy as a monkey."

"No way *I* went crazy, José," she says coarsely.

"My name's not José, goddamn it." I cast a wintry eye at Lynette's spurious beigey Jesus nailed to the siding. He makes life a perfect misery for as many as he can, then never takes the heat. He should try resurrection in today's complex world. He'd fall right off His cross on His ass. He couldn't sell newspapers.

"We don't have none of the same interests, doesn't look like," Vicki says nearly inaudibly, fumbling a finger at her blue Navajo earring. "I just figured that out sitting at the table."

"But *I'm* interested in *you!*" I shout. "Isn't that enough?" The wind is kicking up. From around the house Wade's Boston

Whaler blunks against the dock. My own words are broken and carried off like chaff.

"Not to be married, it isn't," she says, her jaw set in certainty. "Just foolin like what we been doin is one thing. But that won't get you all the way to death."

"What will? Just tell me and I'll do it. I want to go all the way to death with you." Words, my best refuge and oldest allies, are suddenly acting to no avail, and I am helpless. In the wind, in fact, words hardly seem to clear my mouth. It is like a dream in which my friends turn against me and then disappear—a poor man's Caesar dream, a nightmare in itself. "Look here. I'll get interested in nursing. I'll read some books and we can talk about nursing all the goddamn time."

Vicki tries to smile but looks dumbfounded. "I don't know what to say, really."

"Say yes! Or at least something intelligent. I might just kidnap you."

"Right you won't." She curls her lip and narrows her eyes, a look I've never seen and that scares me. She is without fear if fearlessness is what's asked for. But just so long as she is fearlessly mine.

"I'm not going to be fooled with," I say, and move toward her.

"I just don't love you enough to marry you." She throws down her hands in exasperation. "I don't love you in the right way. So just go on. You're liable to say anything, and I don't like that." Her hair has become whipped and tangled.

"There isn't any right way," I say. "There's just love and not love. You're crazy."

"You'll see," she says.

"Get in this car." I pull back the door. (She has decided not to love me because I might change her, but she couldn't be more wrong. It is I who'll happily bend.) "You just think you want some little life like Lynette's to complain about, but I'm going to give you the best of all worlds. You don't know how happy you're going to be." I give her a big signpost grin and step forward to put my arms around her, but she busts me full in the mouth with a mean little itchy fist that catches me midstride and sends me to the turf. I manage to grab onto the car door to ease my fall, but the punch is a looping girl's left hook straight from the shoulder, and I actually walked directly into it, eyes wide open.

"I'll 'bout knock you silly," she says furiously, both fists balled like little grapeshoots, thumbs inward. "Last guy took holt of me went to eye surgery."

And I can't help smiling. It is the end to all things, of course. But a proper end. I taste thick, squeamish blood in my mouth. (My hope is that no one inside has seen this and feels the need to help me.) When I look up, she has backed off a half step, and to the right of dolorous Jesus I see Cade's big head peering down at me, impassive as Buddha. Though in all ways Cade does not matter in this, and I don't mind his seeing me in defeat. It is an experience he already knows, and would sympathize with if he could.

"Get on up and go see your dead guy," Vicki says in a quavery, cautionary voice.

"Okay." I'm still smiling my dopey Joe Palooka smile. Possibly there are even stars and whirligigs shooting above my head. I might not be in complete control, but I'm certain I can drive.

"You awright, aren't you?" She will not come a step closer, but squints an assessing eye at me long-distance. I'm sure I am pale as potatoes, though I'm not ashamed to be decked by a strong girl who can turn grown men over in their beds and get them in and out of distant bathrooms single-handed. In fact, it confirms everything I have always believed of her. There may be hope yet for us. This may be the very love she's been seeking but hasn't trusted, and needed only to whop me good to make us both realize it.

"Why don't you call me tomorrow?" I say, sprawled on my elbows, my head starting to ache, though I'm still smiling a good loser's smile.

"I doubt that." She crosses her arms like Maggie in the funnies. Who is a better Jiggs than I am? Who is worse at learning from his experience?

"You better go inside," I say. "It's an indignity for you to see me get on my feet."

"I didn't mean to hit you," she says in a bossy way.

"Like hell. You'd've knocked me out if you knew how to make a fist. You make a girl's fist."

"I don't hit too many."

"Go on," I say.

"You sure you're awright?"

"Would you call me tomorrow?"

"Maybe, maybe not." I can actually hear her stockings scrape as she turns and starts back across the lawn in the wind, her arms swinging, each foot planted toe-down to keep from sinking in the sod. She does not look back—as she shouldn't—and quickly disappears into the house. Cade has likewise left the window. And for a time then I sit where I've fallen beside my car and stare up at the rending clouds, trying to make the world around me stop its terrifying spin. Everything has seemed beckoning and ahead, though I am unsure now if life has not suddenly passed me like a big rumbling semi and left me flattened here by the road.

WINDS BUFFET me on my way home and impede my progress. It has, in fact, been a terrible weekend weatherwise, though who could've predicted it on Friday morning at my son's grave.

My choice of routes home is not a wise one—the Parkway—where there is no consoling landscape, only pines and sad sedgy hummocks and distant power right-of-ways trailing skyward toward Lakehurst and soulful Fort Dix. An occasional Pontiac dealer's sign or a tennis bubble peeps above the conifers, but these are far too meager and abstracted. I'm on the old knife-edge of dread, without constructive distance from what's to come, and I see only the long, empty horizon that X told me about but that I was too idiotic to fear.

All the traffic is coming up from Atlantic City and the beaches in a hurry, and at Route 98 I consult the map and turn out hoping to square off to Route 9 and then, by driving the farmy section lines toward Freehold, get home. The foul weather has moved on past, and on the radio unexpected stations turn up with unexpected news—what's for lunch tomorrow at the Senior Citizens' Center in South Amboy (city chicken and Texas Toast); the weather in Kalispell and Coeur d'Alene (much summerier than here). On the feminist station from New Brunswick, a woman with a sexy voice reads dirty passages from *Tropic of Cancer*—Van Norden's soliloquy on love, where he compares orgasm to holy communion, then prays for a woman who's better than he is. "Find me a cunt like that, will you?" Van Norden pleads. "If you could do that I'd give you my job." Afterwards the female DJ gives poor Miller a good whipping for his attitudes, followed immediately by a "get acquainted" offer for a sex club not far from my office. I stay tuned until winds carry the words away and I'm left with the pleasant if brief idea of a hundred dollar whore waiting for me somewhere if I only had the gumption to find her and didn't have other duties. Unhappy ones. The worst kind.

Suddenly, in two dreadful minutes, I make an inventory of *everything* that could possibly turn out better in the next twenty-four to thirty-six hours, and come up with nothing except a wavering mirage memory of Selma Jassim from years ago and our late-night hours, half-asleep and half-drunk and in a high state of excitement, with her moaning in unintelligible Arabic and me in animal anticipation (all this when I should've been reading student essays). Of course I can't remember one thing we could've said, or how we kept each other interested very long with the little we had to offer from the fringes of our upturned lives. Though anything is possible, any amount of rapturous transport, when you're lonely enough and at the nubbins end of your rope. Mutinous freedom awaits there for those who can bear it.

What I actually remember are long sinuous sighs in the night and the intermittent tinkle of ice cubes from glasses, her cigarette smoke in the dark of the dance-lady's house and the still October air turned electric with longing. And then, the next day, the long fog of having been up and awake all night, and a sense of accomplishment for having gotten through the night at all.

I don't regret a moment of it, the way you wouldn't regret wolfing down the last crumbly morsel of, say, the blackberry cobbler you had when you were snowbound in December on a rural highway in Wyoming and no one knew you were there, and the sun setting on you for the last time. Regret is not part of that, I'll tell you (even though knowing her absolutely lengthened the distance between X and me at the time, and made me dreamy and untalkative at the wrong crucial moment).

But I am no martyr to a past. And halfway through the town of Adelphia, New Jersey, on Business 524, I pull into an empty Acme lot and put in a call to Providence, where I think she might be. A voice could help. Better than four hundred-dollar prostitutes and a free trip to Coeur d'Alene.

In the phone booth I lean heavily on the cool plexiglas, staring at a wire shopping cart stranded in the empty parking lot, while the operator in faraway 401 runs through her listings. At a distance across the blacktop, a burger joint is open on Easter. Ground Zero Burg—a relic of the old low-slung Forties places with sliding screens, windows all around and striped awnings. A lone black car sits nosed under the awning, a carhop leaned in talking to the driver. The sky is white and skating toward the ocean at top speed. Things can happen to you. I know that. Evil lurks most everywhere, and death is too severe for most ordinary remedies. I have dealt with them before.

A ring and then an answer straightaway.

"Halloo."

"Selma?" An inexplicable name, I know, but it's pronounced differently in Arabic.

"Yes?"

"Hi Selma, it's Frank. Frank Bascombe."

Silence. Puzzlement. "Oh. Yes. Of course. And how are you?" Cigarette smoke in the receiver. Nothing surprising here.

"Fine. I'm fine." I couldn't be worse, though I won't admit it. And what next? I have nothing else to say. What do we expect other people can do for us? One of my problems is that I am *not* a problem-solver. I rely on others, even though I like to think I don't.

"So. How long has it been?" It's damn good of her to try and make conversation with me, since I seem incapable of it.

"Three years, Selma. Seems like a long time."

"Ah, yes. And you still write . . . what was it you wrote that I thought so amusing?"

"Sports."

"Sports. Yes indeed. I remember now." She laughs. "Not novels."

"No."

"Good. It made you so happy."

I watch the stoplight on Route 524 as it changes from yellow to red, and try to picture the room where she is sitting. A Queen Anne-style house, white or blue, on College Hill. Angell Street or Brown Street. The view from the window: a nice prospect of elms and streets running down to the old factory piles with the big bay far in the hazy afterground. If only I could be there instead of a parking lot in Adelphia. I would be miles happier. New prospects. Real possibilities rising like new mountains. I could be convinced in no time flat that things weren't so bad. "Frank?" Selma says into the musing silence at my end. I am putting a sail in on the bay, calculating winds and seas. Populating a different world.

"What."

"Are you sure you're feeling well? You sound quite strange.

I'm always very happy to hear from you. But you don't sound particularly as if you're all right. Exactly where are you now?"

"In New Jersey. In a phone booth in a town called Adelphia. I'm not as good as I could be. But that's all right. I just wanted to hear your voice and think about you."

"Well, that's very nice. Why don't you tell me what's wrong." The familiar tinkle of a single ice cube (some things remain the same). I wonder if she is wearing her Al Fatah burnoose right now, which drove our Jewish colleagues crazy. (In private, of course, they loved it.)

"What are you doing right now," I say, staring across the Acme lot. The name "Shelby" has been scratched on the glass in front of my eyes. A cool urine scent hangs around me. At Ground Zero Burg the carhop suddenly stands back from the lone car, hands on her hips in what looks like disgust. Trouble may be brewing there. They don't know how good they have it.

"Oh. Well. I'm reading today," Selma says and sighs. "What else do I do?"

"Tell me what. I haven't read a book in I don't know when. I wish I had. The last one I read wasn't very good."

"Robert Frost. I'm meant to teach him in a week's time."

"That sounds great. I like Frost."

"Great? I don't know about that." Tinkle, tinkle.

"It sounds great to me. I'll tell you that. You're going to take all the I's out of it, aren't you?"

"Yes, of course." A laugh. "What silliness that was. He's a bore, though, really. Just a mean child who wrote. Occasionally he's amusing, I suppose. He's short, leastways. I've read Jane Austen now."

"She's great, too."

Angry blue-white smoke spews suddenly from underneath the tires of the black car, though there's no sound. The carhop turns and steps languidly up onto the curb, unimpressed. The car bolts back, halts, then squeals forward directly at her, but she doesn't even bother to move as the bumper bulls her way, stopping short and diving. She raises her arm and gives the driver the finger, and the car spurts back again with more white smoke, all the way into the Acme lot, and makes a one-eighty right out of TV. Whoever's driving knows his business. Adelphia may be where race drivers live, for all I know.

"So, well. Are you married now, Frank?"

"No. Are you? Have you found an industrialist yet?"

"No." Silence, followed by a cruel laugh. "People ask me to marry them . . . quite a number, in fact. But. They're all idiots and very poor."

"What about me?" I take another mental glimpse out her window into the atmospheric Narragansett town and bay. Plenty of sails. It's all wonderful.

"What about you?" She laughs again and sips her drink. "Are you rich?"

"I'm still interested."

"*Are* you?"

"You're damn right I am."

"Well, that's good." She is amused—why shouldn't she be? General amusement was always her position vis-à-vis the western world. There is no harm meant, really. Frost and I are just a couple of cutups. I don't even mind admitting I feel a tiny bit better. And what has it cost anyone? Two minutes of palaver charged to my home phone.

For some reason the car in the Acme lot has stopped. It is a long Trans-Am, one of the sharky-looking GMs with a wind fin like a road racer. A small head rides low behind the wheel. Suddenly more white smoke blurts from underneath the raised tires, though the car doesn't exactly move but seems to want to move—the driver is standing on the brake, is my guess. Then the car positively leaps forward ahead of all its tire-smoke and fishtails across the Acme lot (I'm sure the driver is having a devil of a time holding it straight), barely misses one of the light stanchions, achieves traction, flashes by a second stanchion, and whonks right into the empty grocery cart, sending it flying, end-over-end, casters rocketing, plastic handles splintered, red "Property of Acme" sign sailing up into the white sky, and the bulk of the basket atumble-and-whirligig right at the phone booth where I'm talking to Selma in Rhode Island, the Ocean State.

The shattered cart hits—BANG—into the phone booth, busts out a low pane of plexiglas and rocks the whole frame. "Christ," I shout.

"What was that," Selma says from Providence. "What's happened, Frank? Has something gone wrong?"

"No it's fine."

"It sounded like an explosion in a war."

Dust has been shaken all over me, and the Trans-Am has stopped just beyond where it hit the shopping cart, its motor throbbing, *ga-lug, ga-lug*.

"A kid hit a shopping cart in his car and it flew over here and crashed into this phone booth. A pane of glass came out and broke. It's strange." The glass pane is now leaned against my knee.

"Well. I suppose I don't understand."

"It's hard to understand, really."

The driver's door on the Trans-Am opens and a Negro boy in sunglasses gets out and stares at me, his head barely clearing the top of the window. He seems to be considering the distance between us. I don't know if he's thinking of going ahead and ramming the phone booth or not.

"Wait a minute." I step out to where he can see me. I wave and he waves back, and then he gets back in his car and slowly backs up twenty yards—for no reason at all, since he's in the middle of an empty lot—and drives slowly around toward the exit by Ground Zero. As he turns out into the street, he honks at the carhop, and once again she gives him the finger. She, of course, is white.

"What's actually happening," Selma asks. "Is someone hurting you?"

"No. They missed me." With my foot I shove the corner of the shopping cart back out the broken window. A breeze flows in at knee level. Across the lot the carhop is talking to someone about what's just happened. This would make a good Candid Camera segment, though it isn't clear who the joke would be on. "I'm sorry to call you up and then have all this go crash." The cart falls free out the window.

"It doesn't matter," Selma says, and laughs.

"It must seem like I live a life of chaos and confusion," I say, thinking about Walter's face for the first time all afternoon. I see it alive, then stone dead, and I can't help thinking he has made a terrible mistake, something I might've warned him about, except I didn't think of it in time.

"Well, yes. I suppose it does seem that way." Selma sounds amused again. "But it doesn't matter, either. It doesn't seem to bother you."

"Listen. How about if I took the train up to see you tonight? Or I could drive. How about it?"

"No. That wouldn't work out too well."

"Okay." I am feeling light-headed now. "How about later in the week? I'm not very busy these days."

"Maybe so. Yes." (Scant enthusiasm for this plan, though who would want me as an after-midnight guest?) "It might not be that good an idea to come, really." Her voice implies several things, a plethora of better choices.

"Okay," I say, and find it possible to cheer up a little. "I'm glad to get to talk to you."

"Yes, it's very very nice. It's always *very* nice to hear from you."

What I'd like to say is: *Go to hell, there aren't that many better choices in the world than me. Look around. Do yourself a favor.* But what kind of man would say that? "I should probably go. I have to drive home."

"Yes. All right," Selma says. "You should be careful."

"Go to hell," I say.

"Yes, goodbye," Selma says—Queen Anne house, bright prospects, tidy faculty life, sailboats, leafy streets all spinning around every which way, and all suddenly gone.

I step out of the shambles into the breezy parking lot, my heart thumping like an outboard. A few slow cars cruise Route 524, though the town, here on its outer edge, lies sunk in the secular aimlessness of Sunday that Easter only worsens for the lonely of the world. And for some reason I feel stupid. The colored boy in the Trans-Am slides by, looks at me and registers no recognition, then heads on out to the nappy countryside, running the yellow light toward Point Pleasant and the beaches, more white girls on his mind. His dashboard, I can see, is covered with white fur.

How exactly did I get to here, is what I would like to know, since my usual need, when I find myself in unaccustomed environs, is to add things up, consider what forces have led me here, and to wonder if this course is typical of what I would call my life, or if it is only extraordinary and nothing to worry about.

Quo vadis, in other words. No easy question. And at the moment I have no answers.

"Ahnnn, you aren't dead, are ya?" A voice speaks to me.

I turn and am facing a thin, sallow-faced girl with vaguely spavinous hips. Her sleeveless T-shirt has a rock group's name, THE BLOOD COUNTS, stenciled on its flat front, her pink jeans pronounce all out of happy proportion the bone-spread of her hips. She is the carhop from Ground Zero Burg, the girl who gives men the finger. She has come to get a first-hand look at me.

"I don't think so," I say.

"You oughta call the cops on that little boogie," she says in a nasty voice meant to portray hatred, but failing. "I seen what he didja. I use to live with his brother, Floyd Emerson. He isn't that way."

"Maybe he didn't mean to do it."

"Uh-huh," she says, blinking over at the shattered telephone booth and the crumpled cart, then back at me. "You don't already look too sharp. Your knee's bleedin. I think you banged your mouth. I'd call the cops."

"I hurt my mouth before," I say, looking at my knee, where the seersucker has been razored and blood has soaked through the blue stripes. "I didn't think I got hurt."

"You better siddown before you fall down then," she says. "You look like you're gonna die."

I squint at the orange awnings of the Ground Zero, fluttering like pennants in the breeze, and feel weak. The girl, the broken phone booth, the bent shopping cart suddenly seem a far distance from where I am. Inexplicably far. A gull shouts in the high white sky, and I have to stand against my car fender for balance. "I don't see why that should be true," I say with a smile, though I'm not quite sure I know what I mean. And for a little while then, I do not remember anything.

THE GIRL has gone and come back. She stands by the door of my car, holding out a tall brown and white Humdinger cup. I am in the driver's seat, but with my feet sticking out on the pavement like a dazed accident victim.

I try to smile. She's smoking a cigarette, the hard pack stuck in her jeans pocket so the outline shows. A thick diesely smell is in the air. "What's that," I ask.

"A float. Wayne made it for you. Drink it."

"Okay." I take the foamy cup and drink. The root beer is

sweet and creamy and hurts my teeth with goodness. "Wonderful," I say, and reach in my pocket for money.

"Naa, ya can't, it's free," she says, and looks away. "Where're you going?"

I drink some more of my float. "Haddam."

"Where's that at?"

"West of here, over by the river."

"Ahnnnn, the river," she says and glances skeptically out at the wide street. She is maybe sixteen, but you can't really tell. I would hate to have Clary looking like her, though now that is pretty much out of my hands. I wouldn't mind, however, if Clary were as kind as she seems to be.

"What's your name?"

"Debra. Spanelis. Your knee's quit." She looks at my torn knee with revulsion. "A good cleaner'd fix that."

"Thanks. Spanelis is a Greek name, isn't it?"

"Yeah. So how'd you know?" She looks away and draws on her cigarette.

"I met some Greek people the other night on a boat. They were named Spanelis. They were wonderful people."

"It's, like, a common, a real common Greek name." She depresses the door lock button then pulls it back up, taking a flickering look at me as if I were the rarest of exotic bird. "I tried to get you a band-aid, but Wayne doesn't keep 'em anymore." I say nothing as she stares at me. "So, like. Whaddaya do?" She has adopted a new sleepy way of talking, as if nothing could bore her more than I do. Again I hear a gull cry. My lip, where Vicki socked me, throbs like a goddamn boil.

"I'm a sportswriter."

"Uh-huh." She parks one hip against the door molding and leans into it. "Whaddaya write about?"

"Well. I write about football and baseball, and players." I take a sip of my sweet, cold float. I actually feel better. Who would've thought a root-beer float could restore both faith and health, or that I would find it in as half-caste a town as this, a place wizened to a few car lots, an adult book store, a shut-down drive-in movie up the road—remnants of a boom that never boomed. From this emerges a Samaritan. A Debra.

"So," she says, scanning the highway again, her little gray eyes squinting as if she expects to see someone she doesn't know drive by. "Do you have a favorite team and all?" She smirks as if the whole idea embarrassed her.

"I like the Detroit Tigers for baseball. Some sports I don't like at all."

"Like what?"

"Hockey."

"Right. Forget it. They had a fight and a game broke out."

"That's my feeling."

"So, were you, like, a pretty great jock sometime when you were young?"

"I liked baseball then, too, except I couldn't hit or run."

"Uh-huh. Same here." She takes a preposterous puff on her cigarette and exhales all the smoke out her mouth and into the shopping center air. "So. How'd you get interested in it? Did you read about it someplace?"

"I went to college. Then when I got older, I failed at everything else, and that's all I could do."

Debra looks down at me, worry hooding her eyes. Her idea of a big success has a different story line, one that doesn't confess any start-up problems. I can teach her a damned useful lesson in life about that. "That doesn't sound so great," she says.

"It is pretty great, though. Successful life doesn't always follow a straight course to the top. Sometimes things don't work out and you have to change the way you look at things. But you don't want to stop and get discouraged when the chips are all down. That'd be the worst time. If I'd stopped when things went the wrong way, I'd be a goner."

Debra sighs. Her eyes fall from my face to my torn and bloody knee, to my scuffed wingtips and back up to the damp, soft Humdinger I'm holding in both hands. I'm not what she had in mind for a great success, but I hope she won't ignore what I've said. A little of the real truth can make a big impression.

"Have you got any plans," I ask.

Debra takes a cigarette drag that requires her to lift her chin in the air. "Whadda ya mean?"

"College. Not that that's necessary. It's just an idea of what to do next."

"I'd like to go out and work in Yellowstone Park," she says. "I heard about that." She looks down at her BLOOD COUNTS T-shirt.

But I'm immediately enthusiastic. "That's a great idea. I wanted to do that myself once." In fact, I actually considered it while I was poring over life choices after my divorce. A blue plastic name tag that said: FRANK: NEW JERSEY seemed good at the time. I thought I could manage the gift shop in the Old Faithful Inn. "About how old are you, Debra?"

"Eighteen." She stares studiously at the barrel of her cigarette as if she'd noticed some defect in it. "Like in July."

"Well, that's the perfect age for Yellowstone. You're probably graduating this spring, right?"

"I quit." She drops the cigarette on the blacktop and mashes out the hot end with her sneaker.

"Well, that probably doesn't even matter to the people out there. They're interested in everybody."

"Yeah. . . ."

"Listen, I think it's a good idea. It'll sure widen some horizons for you." I'd be happy to write a recommendation for her on magazine letterhead: *Debra Spanelis is not at all the kind of girl you meet every day.* They would take her in a heartbeat.

"I've got a baby," Debra says and sighs. "I doubt if the Yellowstone people would let him come." She looks at me, flat-eyed, her mouth hard and womanish, then glances away at the Ground Zero, carless, awning flaps aflutter.

She has lost all interest in me, and I can't blame her. I might as well have been speaking French from the planet Pluto. I am not an answer man of any kind.

"I guess not," I say dimly.

Debra's eyes come back round to me, and she is unexpectedly loose-limbed. My Humdinger is soft and waxy, and there's no longer much for us to say. Some meetings don't lead anyone anywhere better—an unassailable fact of life. Some small empty moments cannot be avoided, no matter how hard good will and expectations for the best try to make it so.

"So how do you feel now?" Like a lawyer, she touches her chin with her index finger.

"Better. A lot better. This made a lot of difference." I smile hopefully at my Humdinger.

"It used to be medicine, I guess." She throws her hip to one side and holds onto the window glass with her fingertips. "Do you think it's bad if I don't have any of my plans set yet?" She squints at me, trying to guess my real answer in case I decide to lie.

"Not one bit," I say. "You'll have plans. And they won't be long in coming, either. You'll see." I blink at her uncertainly. "Your life'll change fifty ways before you're twenty-five."

"Cause I'm gettin older, okay? I don't wanna piss away my whole life." She drums her fingernails on the window glass, then leaves off. I can't help thinking of Herb Wallagher's dream of death and hatred. Everybody has the most perfect right to be happy, but sometimes there's nothing you can do to help yourself.

"You won't," I say. "It's all ahead of you." I give her a big encouraging grin, though I don't think it can do the trick for either of us.

"Yeah, okay." She smiles for the first time, a shy-girl's smile of politeness and misgiving. "I gotta go." She glances over at the Ground Zero, where a yellow Corvette has slid in under the awning, its red blinker blinking.

"Can I give you a ride?"

"Naa, I can walk."

"Thanks a million." She looks at the phone booth where the shopping cart is resting against the frame, and the receiver has fallen off its hook. It's a bleak-looking place. I would hate to make a phone call from it now.

"Did you ever like write about skiing?" she says, and shakes her head at me as if she knows my answer before I say it. The breeze blows up dust and sprinkles our faces with it.

"No. I don't even know how to ski."

"Me neither," she says and smiles again, then sighs. "So. Okay. Have a nice day. What's your name, what'd you say it was?" She is already leaving.

"Frank." For some reason I do not say my last name.

"Frank," she says.

As I watch her walk out into the lot toward the Ground Zero, her hands fishing in her pocket for a new cigarette, shoulders hunched against a cold breeze that isn't blowing, her hopes for a nice day, I could guess, are as good as mine, both of us out in the wind, expectant, available for an improvement. And my hopes are that a little luck will come both our ways. Life is not always ascendant.

CHAPTER 12

IT IS THE bottom of the day, the deep well of shadows and springy half-light when late afternoon becomes early evening and we all want to sit down in a leather chair by an open window, have a drink near someone we love or like, read the sports and possibly doze for a while, then wake before the day is gone all the way, walk our cool yards and hear the birds chirp in the trees their sweet eventide songs. It is for such dewy interludes that our suburbs were built. And entered cautiously, they can serve us well no matter what our stations in life, no matter we have the aforementioned liberty or don't. At times I can long so for that simple measure of day and place—when, say, I'm alone in misty Spokane or chilly Boston—that an unreasonable tear nearly comes to my eye. It is a pastoral kind of longing, of course, but we can all have it.

Things seem to move faster now.

I buzz through Freehold, turn east at the trotter track, then wrangle toward Route 1, past Pheasant Run & Meadow. A Good Life Is Affordable Here, reads the other side of the sign.

On the Trenton station the announcer has a sports quiz going to which I do not know one answer, though I take educated guesses. Whose record did Babe Ruth break when he hit sixty in 1927? Harry Heilmann is my guess, though the answer was, "His own." Who was the MVP in the Junior Circuit in '50? George Kell, the Newport Flash, is my choice. Phil Rizutto, the Glendale Spaghetti, is the answer. In most ways I am content not to know such information, and to think of sportswriting not as a real profession but more as an agreeable frame of mind, a *way* of going about things rather than things you exactly do or know. A reasonable guess is a source of pleasure, since it makes me feel like one of the crowd rather than a human FORTRAN spitting out stats and reducing sports to unsavory accountancy. When sports stops being a matter for speculation, even idle, aimless, misinformed speculation, something's gone haywire—no matter what Mutt Greene thinks—and it'll be time to get out of the business and for the cliometricians and computer whizzes from Price Waterhouse to take over the show.

At the intersection of Routes 1 and 533, I head south toward Mrs. Miller's. I would like the consultation I missed on Thursday, possibly even a full reading. If, for instance, Mrs. Miller were to tell me I was risking a severe emotional breakdown if I identified Walter in the morgue and would possibly never see my children as long as I lived, I'd start thinking about Alaska king crab and a night of HBO in a Philadelphia-area Travel-Lodge, and a new look at things in the morning. Why sneer in the face of unhappy prophecy?

Unfortunately, however, Mrs. Miller's little brick-and-asphalt ranchette looks locked up tighter than Dick's hatband. No dusty Buicks sit in the drive. No sign of the usual snarling Doberman in the fenced-in back. The Millers (what could their name really be?) are gone for the holiday, and I have now missed consultations two times running—not a good sign in itself.

I pull into the drive and sit as I did three nights ago, staring at an opening in the heavy drawdrapes as if I could will someone to be there. I give my horn an "accidental" toot. I'd be happy to see the opening widen, a door inched back behind the dusty metal screen, as it did the last time. A nice niece would do. I'd pay ten bucks to make small talk with a dark-skinned female in-law. She wouldn't need divining powers. I'd still come away better.

But that is not to be. Cars beat the highway behind me, and no niece comes to signal. No door cracks. The future, at least my part in it, remains unassured, and I will need to take extra care of myself. I pull back out onto Route 1 toward home, just missing a big honking tractor-trailer headed south, and my jaw still throbbing from Vicki's knuckle sandwich, now two hours old.

I TAKE THE front way into Haddam, curling up King George Road and Bank Street, along the north lawns of the Institute and through the Square. Though once in the village limits I am at a loss for what to do first, and am struck by an unfriendliness of the town, the smallish way it offers no clue for how to go about things—no priority established, no monumental structures to determine a true middle, no Main Street to organize things. And I see again it can be a sad town, a silent, nothing-happening, keep-to-yourself Sunday town—the library closed and green-shaded. Frenchy's abandoned. The Coffee Spot empty (Sunday *Times* scattered from the breakfast crowd). The Institute lies remote and tree-shadowed, a remaining family from the morning services, standing on the Square with their son. It is unexpectedly a foreign place, as strange as Moline or Oslo, its usual informal welcomeness reefed in as if some terror was about, a crusty death's smell, a different bouquet from the swimming pool odor I trust.

I park in my drive and go in to put on new clothes. Hoving Road is somnolent, as blue-shaded and leaden as a Bonnard. The Deffeyes' sprinkler hisses, and up a few houses the Justice has set a badminton net onto his long lawn. An old Ford Woody sits in his drive. Somewhere near abouts I hear the sounds of light chatter-talk and glasses clinking in our cozy local backyard fashion—an Easter Egg hunt finished, the children asleep, the sound of a single swimmer diving in. But this is the day's extent. A private stay-home with the family till past dark. Wreaths are off all doors. The world once more a place we know well.

Inside, my house has a strange public smell to it, a smell I would like on any other day but that today seems unwholesome. Upstairs, I put Merthiolate and a big band-aid on my knee, and change to chinos and a faded red madras shirt I bought at Brooks Brothers the year my book was published. A casual look can sometimes keep you remote from events.

I haven't thought much about Walter. Occasionally his face has plunged into my thinking, an expectant sad-eyed face, the sober, impractical fellow I stood railside with on the *Mantoloking Belle* speculating about the lives ashore we were both embedded in, how we tended to see the world from two pretty distinct angles, but that on balance it didn't matter much.

Which was all *I* needed! I didn't need to know about Yolanda and Eddie Pitcock. Certainly not about his monkeyshines at the Americana. We didn't need to become *established*. That is not my long suit.

No one answers when I call up to Bosobolo. He and his Miss Right, D.D., are no doubt being entertained "in the home" by some old chicken-necked Christology professor, and at this very moment he is probably backed into a bookshelved corner, clutching his ebony elbow and a glass of chablis, while Dr. So-and-so prattles about the hermeneutics of getting the goods on that old radical Paul the Apostle. Bosobolo, I'm sure, has other goods on his mind but is learning to be a first-class American. Though he could have it worse. He could still be running around in the jungle, dressed in a palm tutu. Or he could be me, morgue-bound and fighting a willowy despair.

My plan, which I've come to momentarily, is to call X, go do what I have to at the police, possibly see X—at her house (a remote chance to see my children)—then do *what* I haven't a clue. The plan doesn't reach far, though the literal possibilities might be just a source of worry.

A silent red "3" blinks on the answering machine, when I go to call X. "1" is in all likelihood Vicki wondering if I made it home safely and wanting to set up a powwow somewhere in the public domain where we can end love like grownups—less stridency and fewer lefts to the chin—a final half-turn of the old gem.

And she is right, of course, and smart to be. We don't really share enough of the "big" interests. I am merely mad for her. And at best she is unclear about me, which leaves us where in six months' time? I would never be enough for a Texas girl, anyway. Fascination has its virtuous limits. She needs attention to more than I could give mine to: to Walter Scott's column, to being a New-Ager, to setting up a love nest, to a hundred things I really don't care that much about but that grip her imagination. Consequently I'll cut loose without complaining (though I'd be willing to spend one more happy night in Pheasant Meadow and then call it quits).

I punch the message button.

> *Beep.* Frank, it's Carter Knott. I'm sneaking off to the Vet tomorrow for the Cardinals game. I guess I can't get enough of you guys. I'm calling Walter too. It's Sunday morning. Call me at home. *Click.*

Beep. Hey you ole rascal-thing.
I thought you were comin at
eleven-thirty. We're all mad
at you down here so you better
not show your face. You know
who this is, dontcha? *Click.*

Beep. Frank, this is Walter
Luckett, Jr., speaking. It's twelve
o'clock sharp here, Frank. I
was just throwing away some
old *Newsweeks*, and I found
this photograph of that DC-10
that went down a year or so
ago out in Chicago. O'Hare.
You might remember that.
Frank, you can see all those
people's heads in the windows
looking out. It's really
something. And I just can't
help wondering what they
must've been thinking about,
since they *are* riding a bomb.
A big, silver bomb. That's
about all I had in mind now.
Uhhmm. So long. *Click.*

Is this what he'd have told me if I'd been here to answer? What
an Easter greeting! A chummy slice o' life to pass along while
you're rigging your own blast-off into the next world. A *while
you were out* from the grave! What else can happen?

I still cannot think a long thought about Walter. Though
what I do think about is poor Ralph Bascombe, in *his* last hours
on earth, only four blocks from here in Doctors Hospital and a
lifetime away now. In his last days Ralph changed. Even in his
features, he looked to me like a bird, a strangely straining gooney
bird, and not like a nine-year-old boy sick to death and weary of
unfinished life. Once he barked out loud at me like a dog, sharp
and distinct, then he flopped up and down in his bed and
laughed. Then his eyes shot open and burned at me, as if he knew
me better than I knew myself and could see all my faults. I was

in my chair beside his bed, holding his water cup and his terrible bendable straw. X was at the window, musing out at a sunny parking lot (and probably the cemetery). Ralph said loudly at me, "Oh, you son of a bitch, what are you doing holding that stupid glass? I could kill you for that." And then he fell asleep again. And X and I just stared at each other and laughed. It's true, we laughed and laughed until we cried with laughter. Not with fear or pain. What else was there to do, we must've said silently, and agreed that a good laugh was all right this time. No one would mind. It was at no one's expense, and no one but the two of us would hear it—not even Ralph. It may seem callous, but we had that between ourselves, and who's to be the judge when intimacy's at work? It was one of our last moments of unalloyed tenderness in the world.

Though I suppose that in this memory of bereavement there is some for poor Walter, as wrongly and surely dead as my son, and just as absurd. I have tried not to be part of it. But why shouldn't I? We all deserve mankind's pity, his grief. And maybe never more than when we go outside its usual reaches and can't get back.

No one answers at X's house. She may be taking the children to a friend's. Are we going to have to have another heart-to-heart, I wonder. Am I going to be the recipient of other unhappy news? Is Fincher Barksdale leaving Dusty and getting X knee-deep in mink-ranching in Memphis? On what thin strand does all equilibrium dangle?

I leave a message saying I'll be by soon, then I'm off to the police, to have a look at Walter, though I have hope that a responsible citizen—possibly one of the Divorced Men with a police scanner—will already have come forward and performed this service for me.

The police station occupies part of the new brick-and-glass car-dealerish Village Hall where I rode out the heart-sore days of my divorce. The Hall is located near some of our nicer, more established residences, and it is closed now except for the brightly lighted cubicles in the back where the police hang out. From the outside where you drive around the circular entry, the last drowsy hours of Easter have softened its staunch Republican look. But it remains a house of hazards to me, a place where I'm uneasy each time I set my foot indoors.

Sergeant Benivalle, it turns out, is still on duty when I give my name to the watch officer, a young Italian-looking brushcut fellow wearing an enormous pistol and a gold name plate that says, PATRIARCA. He is in wry spirits, I can tell, and smiles a secret smile that implies some pretty good off-color jokes have been going the rounds all day, and were we a jot better friends he'd let me in on the whole hilarious business. My own smile, though, is not in tune for jokes, and after writing down my name he wanders off to find the sergeant.

I sit down on the public bench beside a big framed town map, breathing in the floor-mop smell of waiting rooms, leaning on my knees and peering out the glass doors through the lobby and across the lawn of elms and ginkgoes and spring maples. Outside is all almond light now, and in an hour a dreamy celestial darkness will return and one more day find its end. And what a day! Not a typical one at all. And yet it ends as softly, in as velvet a hush and airish a calm as any. Death is not a compatible presence here-abouts, and everything is in connivance—forces municipal and private—to say it isn't so; it's only a misreading, a wrong rumor to be forgotten. No harm done. This is not the place to die and be noticed, though it isn't a bad place to live, all things considered.

Two cyclists glide across my view. A man ahead, a woman behind; a child in a child's secure-seat strapped snug to Papa. All three are white-helmeted. Red pennants wag on spars in the dusk. All three are on their way home from an informal prayer get-together somewhere down some street, at some Danish-modern Unitarian hug-a-friend church where cider's on tap and *damn* and *hell* are permissible—life on the continual upswing week after week. (It is the effect of a seminary in your town.) Now they're headed homeward, fresh and nuclear, their frail magneto lights whispering a gangway to old darkness. Here come the Jamiesons. Mark, Pat and baby Jeff. Here comes life. All clear. Nothing can stop us now.

But they are wrong, wrong these Jamiesons. I should tell them. Life-forever is a lie of the suburbs—its worst lie—and a fact worth knowing before you get caught in its fragrant silly dream. Just ask Walter Luckett. He'd tell you, if he could.

Sergeant Benivalle appears through a back office door, and he's exactly the fellow I expected, the chesty, flat-top, sad-eyed man with bad acne scars and mitts the size of work gloves. His mother must not have been a spaghetti-bender, since his eyes are pale and his square head stolid and Nordic. (His stomach, though, is firmly Italian and envelops his belt buckle, squeezing the little silver snub-nose strapped above his wallet.) He is not a man to shake hands, but looks at the red EXIT sign above our heads when we meet. "We can just sit here, Mr. Bascombe," he says. His voice is hoarse, wearier than earlier in the day.

We sit on the shiny bench while he fingers through a manila file. Officer Patriarca takes his seat behind the watch desk window, props up his feet and begins glancing through a *Road & Track* with a black drag-strip hero-turned-TV-personality smiling on the front.

Sergeant Benivalle sighs deeply and shuffles sheets of paper. Silent as a prisoner, I await him.

"Ahhh. Okay now. We've been in touch with family . . . a sister . . . in . . . Ohio, I guess. So . . ." He lifts a stapled page briefly to reveal a bright photograph of a man's feet clad in a pair of rope sandals, toes pointed upward. Absolutely these are Walter's feet, which I hope will be identification enough. *Bascombe identifies deceased from picture of feet.* "So that," Sergeant Benivalle says slowly, "should eliminate your need to identify the, uh, deceased."

"I didn't really feel that need, anyway," I say.

Sergeant Benivalle glances at me dismissively. "We have fingerprints coming, of course. But it's just easier to get a positive this way."

"I understand."

"Now," he says, flipping more pages. It's surprising how much paper work has already been compiled. (Was Walter in some other kind of trouble?) "Now," he says again and looks at me. "You're the sportswriter, aren't you?"

"Right." I smile weakly.

Sergeant Benivalle glances back into his papers. "Who's taking the AL East this year?"

"Detroit. They're pretty good."

He sighs. "Yep. Prolly so. I wish I had time to see a game. But I'm busy." He protrudes his bottom lip, looking down. "I play a little golf, once in a blue moon."

"My wife's the teaching pro over at Cranbury Hills," I say, though I add quickly, "my ex-wife, I mean."

"That right?" Benivalle says, forgetting golf entirely. "I've got grass asthma," he says, and since I can add nothing to that, I say nothing. "Do you," he pauses, "have any idea why this Mr., uh, Luckett would take his own life, Mr. Bascombe, just off the top of your head?"

"No. I guess he gave up hope. That's all."

"Um-huh, um-huh." Sergeant Benivalle reads down his folder. Inside, a form has been typed: HOMICIDE REPORT. "That usually happens at Christmas a lot more. Not that many people do it on Easter."

"I never thought much about it."

Sergeant Benivalle wheezes when he breathes, a small peeping noise down inside his chest. He fingers toward the back of the file. "I could never write," he says thoughtfully. "I wouldn't know what to say. That must be hard."

"It's really not too hard."

"Um-huh. Well. I've got this, uh, copy of this letter for you." He slides a slick Thermofax sheet out the back of his sheaf, holding it out daintily by a corner. "We keep the original, which you can claim in three months if the estate agrees to release it to you." He looks at me.

"Okay." I take the page by another of its greasy corners. It is badly copied in gray with a nasty embalming-fluid odor all over it. I see the script is a neat, very small longhand, with a signature near the bottom.

"Be careful with that stuff, it gets in your clothes. Cops smell like it all the time, it's how you know we're in the neighborhood." He closes his folder, reaches in his pocket and takes out a pack of Kools.

"I'll read it later," I say and fold the letter in thirds, then sit holding it, waiting for whatever is supposed to happen next to happen. We are both of us immobilized by how simple all this has been.

Sergeant Benivalle lights his cigarette and inserts the burnt match into the book behind the others. The two of us sit then and stare at the yellow street map of the town we live in—each probably looking at the street where his own house sits. They couldn't be far apart. Prolly he lives in The Presidents.

"Where'd you say this guy's wife was again?" Benivalle says, breathing smoke hugely into his lungs. Though he looks at least fifty, he is no older than I am. His life cannot have been an easy one so far.

"She went to Bimini with another man."

He blows smoke, then sniffs loudly two times. "That's the shits." He braces against the curved back of the bench, clenching his cigarette in his teeth, thinking about Bimini. "There's gotta be better things to do about it than kill yourself, though. It isn't that bad. Wouldn't you think?" He turns his big head and fixes me with eyes blue as fjords. He hasn't liked this business with Walter one bit better than I have, and he'd like somebody to say a word to help him out of worrying about it.

"I sure would think so," I say and nod.

"Boy-o-boy. Mmmmph. What a mess." He extends both his legs and crosses them at the ankles. It is his way of inviting conversation between menfolk, though I'm stumped for what to say. It's possible he would understand if I said nothing.

"Do you think it would be all right if I went over to Walter's house?" I actually surprise myself by saying this.

Sergeant Benivalle looks at me strangely. "What do you want to do that for?"

"Just to have a look. I wouldn't stay long. It's just probably the only way I'm going to get grips on this whole business. He gave me a key."

Sergeant Benivalle grunts, thinking about this request. He smokes his cigarette and stares at the smoke he exhales. "Sure," he says almost indifferently. "Just don't take anything out. The family has claims on everything. Okay?"

"I won't." Everyone trusts everyone here. And why not? No one's ever up to anything that could cause harm to anyone but themselves. "Are you married, Sergeant," I ask.

"Divorced." He throws a narrow, flinty look my way, his eyes piggy with suspicion. "Why?"

"Well. Some of us, we're all of us divorced men—there's a lot of us in town these days—we get together now and then. It's nothing serious. We just gang up for a beer at the August once a month. Go to a ball game or two. We went fishing last week, in fact. I thought if you'd like to, I'd give you a call. It's a pretty good group. Everything's informal."

Sergeant Benivalle holds his Kool between his big thumb and his crooked forefinger, like a movie Frenchman, and flicks off an ash toward the polished floor. "Busy," he says and sniffs. "Police work. . . ." He starts to say more, then stops. "I forget what I was going to say." He stares at the marble floor.

I have embarrassed him without meaning to, and I'd just as soon leave now. It's possible Sergeant Benivalle is nothing but Cade Arcenault years later, and I should leave him to his police work. Though it never hurts to show someone that their own monumental concerns and peculiar problems are really just like everybody else's. We all have our own police work to do.

"I'll still call you, okay?" I grin like a salesman.

"I doubt I'll make it," he says, suddenly distracted.

"Well. We're pretty flexible. I don't come myself, sometimes. But I like the idea of going."

"Yeah," Sergeant Benivalle says, and once again fattens his heavy lower lip.

"I guess I'll take off," I say.

He blinks at me as if waked up from a dream. "How come you have a key to that place?" He cannot not be a policeman, a fact I find satisfying. He is hard to imagine as anything else.

"Walter just gave it to me. I don't know why. I don't know if he had many friends."

"People don't usually give their keys to people." He shakes his head and clicks back in his mouth.

"People do weird things, I guess."

"All the time," he says and sniffs again. "Here," he says. He reaches in his pocket behind his pack of Kools and pulls out a little blue plastic card case. "Keep this if you go over there." He hands me a printed card with his name and title and the Haddam town seal printed on it. "Gene Benivalle. Sergeant of Detectives." His no doubt unlisted home number is printed at the bottom. I could call him about the Divorced Men's Club at this very number, as I'm sure he knows.

"Okay." I stand up.

"Just don't take anything, right?" he says hoarsely, sitting on the bench with his sheaf of papers in front of his stomach. "That'd be wrong."

I stuff his card in my shirt pocket. "Maybe we'll see you some night."

"Nah," he says, pushing his foot down hard on his cigarette and blowing smoke across his big knees.

"I'll probably call you anyway."

"Whatever," he says, wearily. "I'm always here."

"So long," I say.

But he doesn't like goodbyes. He's not the type any more than he's the handshake type. I leave him where he sits, under the red EXIT sign in the lobby, staring out the glass door at me as I go.

X'S CAR sits alongside mine in the deepening dusk in front of Village Hall. She herself sits on the front fender carrying on a coaxing conversation with our two children, who are performing cartwheels on the public lawn and giggling. Paul is unwilling to fling his legs high enough in the air to achieve perfect balance, but Clarissa is expert from hours of practice, and even in her gingham granny dress, which I gave her, she can "walk the clouds," her cotton panties astonishing in the failed daylight. On the front bumper of X's car is a sticker that says "I'd Rather Be Golfing."

"I bought these two some ice cream, and this is the result," X says, when I sit up on the warm fender beside her. She has not looked at me, merely taken my existence for granted from the evidence of my car. "It seems to have brought out the kid in them."

"Dad," Paul shouts from the grass. "Clary's going in the circus."

"*Please* scratch glass," Clary says and immediately gets onto her hands again. They aren't surprised to see me, though I notice they've passed a secret look between themselves. Their usual days are alive with secrets, and toward me they feel both secret humor and secret sympathy. They'd be happy for us to start a rough-house on the lawn the way we do at home, but now we can't. Paul probably has a new joke by now, better than the one from Thursday night.

"She's pretty good, isn't she?" I call out.

"I meant it as a compliment, all right?" Paul stands, hands on his hips in a girlish way. He and I suffer misunderstanding poorly. Clary lets herself fall on her bottom and laughs. She looks like her grandfather and has his almost silvery hair.

"I think it's odd that a town like this could have a morgue, don't you?" X says, musing. She's wearing a bright green-and-red sailcloth wraparound and a mint-colored knitted Brooks' shirt like the ones I wear, and looks coolly clubby. She smoothes the material over her knees and lets her heels kick against the tire wall. She is in a generous mood.

"I never thought about it," I say, watching my children with admiration. "But I guess it's surprising."

"One of Paul's friends is a pathologist's son, and he says there's a very modern facility in the basement in there." She gazes at the brick-and-glass façade with placid interest. "No coroner, though. He drives down from New Brunswick on a circuit of some kind." For the first time she looks at me eye to eye. "How are *you*?"

I am happy to hear this confiding voice again. "I'm all right. This day'll be over with."

"Sorry I had to call you at wherever that was."

"It's fine. Walter died. We can't help that."

"Did you have to *view* him?"

"No. His relatives are coming from Ohio."

"Suicide is very Ohio, you know."

"I guess." Hers, as always, is a perfect Michigan attitude. No one there has any patience for Ohio.

"What about his wife?"

"They're divorced."

"Well. You poor old guy," she says and pats me on my knee and gives me a quick and unexpected smile. "Want me to buy you a drink? The August is open. I'll run these two Indians home." She glances into the near dark, where our children are sitting in a private powwow on the grass. They are each other's confidants in all crucial matters.

"I'm okay. Are you going to marry Fincher?"

She glances at me impassively then looks away. "I certainly am not. He's married unless something's changed in three days."

"Vicki says you two are the hot topic in the Emergency Room."

"Vicki-schmicky," she says and sighs audibly through her nostrils. "Surely she's mistaken. Surely you can't be interested."

"He's an asshole and a change-jingler, that's all. He's down in Memphis starting an air-conditioned mink ranch at this very moment. That's the kind of guy he is."

"I'm aware."

"It's true."

"True?" X looks at me heartlessly. I am the asshole here, of course, but I don't care. Something seems at stake. The stability and sanctity of my divorce.

"I thought you were interested in software salesmen."

"I'll marry *and fuck*," she whispers terribly, "whoever I choose."

"Sorry," I say, but I'm not. Out on Seminary Street I see the lights go on weakly, blink once, then stay on.

"Men *always* think other men are assholes," X says, coldly. "It's surprising how often they're right."

"Does Fincher think I'm an asshole?"

"He's intimidated by you. And anyway, he isn't so bad. He's pretty certain about some things in his life. He just doesn't show it."

"How about Dusty?"

"Frank, I will take your children to Michigan and you'll never see them again, except for two weeks every summer in the Huron Mountain Club with my father to chaperone. This if you don't lay off me at this moment. How would you like that?" She isn't serious about this, and it's possible, I think now, that Vicki has made this whole business up for reasons of her own, though I would rather believe it was a mistake. X sighs again wearily. "I gave Fincher putting lessons, because he's playing in a college reunion tournament in Memphis. He was embarrassed about it, so we went over to Bucks County to Idlegreen and putted for a few days. He needed to improve his confidence."

"Did you put some iron in his putter?" I would like to ask about the putative kiss, but the moment's passed.

It is full dark now, and we are silent and alone in it. Cars murmur along Cromwell Lane, their headlights sweeping in the direction of the Institute, where an "Easter sing" is no doubt on for tonight. St. Leo the Great chimes out a last chance, admonitory call. Three uniformed policemen stroll outside laughing, heading off for a supper at home. I recognize officers Carnevale and Patriarca, whom I imagine, for some reason, to be distant cousins. They walk in lock step toward their personal cars and pay no attention to us. It is a dreamy, average, vertiginous evening in the suburbs—not too much on excitement, only the lives of isolated individuals in the harmonious secrecy of a somber age.

I can't deny I'm relieved about Fincher Barksdale, though—

a misunderstanding, that is what I'm ready to believe. "Your father sent a message," I say.

"Oh?" Her face grows instantly skeptical.

"He told me to tell your mother he has bladder cancer."

"She told him the same thing once when I was a little girl, and he forgot to ask her about it the next day and went away on business. Only now it's different. It's a way to make them feel passionate. She'll think that's hilarious."

"He said I could marry you again if I wanted to."

X sniffs, then looks into her hands as if one might contain something she's forgotten. "He can't stop giving me away."

"He's a nice guy, isn't he?"

"No, he's not." She casts a secret glance at me. "I'm sorry about your friend. Was he a nice, good friend?" The footlights that illumine the shrubbery around Village Hall all go on at once. A Negro janitor steps to the glass door and peers out between his palms, then wanders back with a long dust mop in tow. It is cool now out of doors. A car horn blows briefly. The policemen's taillights disappear down the dark streets.

"No. I didn't know him very well."

"What could've happened?" I hear my children giggle in the damp grass, sweet music of not-to-worry-in-this-world.

"He quit being interested in what's next, I guess. I don't know. I tend not to be much of an alarmist."

"You don't worry that it was your fault, do you?"

"I hadn't thought about that. I don't see how."

"You have awfully odd relationships. I don't know how you stand it."

"I don't have any relationships at all."

"I know that. But it's the way you like it."

Clarissa calls out from the darkness haltingly, wanting to know the exact time. It is 7:36. She is beginning to feel a strangeness out of doors, as though she might suddenly be cut loose and abandoned. "It's early," Paul whispers.

"I'm going over to Walter's house tonight. Would you like to come with me?"

X turns to me with a look of outlandish surprise. "What on earth? Did he have something of yours?"

"No. I just want to go by there. He gave me a key, and I want to use it. The police don't mind if I don't take anything."

"It's ghoulish."

I sit in silence, then, and listen for meaningful sounds in the darkness—a train whistle far out on the main line, a long-haul trucker drumming up Route 1 from as far away as Arkansas, a small plane humming through the angelic night sky—anything to console us two in these last thin moments. Genuinely good conversations with your ex-wife are limited by the widening territories of intimacy from which you're restricted. It is finally okay, I guess. "That's fine," I say.

"But you're probably going anyway, aren't you?" X looks at me, then stares out at the lighted foyer of Village Hall, through which is the tax assessor's glassed-in office. We can both see the janitor with his dust mop moving in slow motion.

"I guess so," I say. "It's really all right."

"Why?" She looks at me with narrow eyes, her look of skepticism at earthly uncertainties, entities she has never much liked.

"I don't need to say. Men feel things women don't. You don't have to disapprove of it."

"You do such odd things." She smiles sympathetically, though magisterially also. "You're so vague sometimes. Are you *really* all right? You looked pale when I could see you."

"I'm not completely all right. But I will be." I could tell her about Vicki knocking my block off, and being hit by a shopping cart. But what the hell good would it do? It would be in the way of full disclosure, and neither of us wants that again, now or ever. We have probably been here too long.

"We just see each other about deaths now," X says, somberly. "Isn't that sad?"

"Most divorced people don't see each other at all. Walter's wife went to Bimini, and he never saw her again. So I think we do pretty well. We have wonderful children. We don't live very far apart."

"Do you love me," X says.

"Yes."

"I was wondering about it. I haven't asked you in a long time."

"I'm always glad to tell you, though."

"I haven't really heard it in a long time, except from the children. I'm sure you've heard it several times."

"No." (Though it would be a lie to say I haven't heard it at all.)

"Sometimes I think about you being involved with all

different kinds of people I don't know anything about, and it seems so odd. I don't like the feeling."

"I'm involved with fewer people all the time."

"Does that make you lonely?"

"No. Not a bit."

The fender of her Citation has grown cold in the darkness. Our two children—weary at last of each other's secrets—have climbed to their feet and are standing out in the dark like shy ghosts of themselves, wanting to be pleased and made over. It is like old times in a way. They stand not far from us and stare, wondering what's going on, saying nothing, exactly like their very ghosts might.

"Do you really want me to go over there with you?" X says, blinking but ready to give in.

"You don't have to."

"Yes. Well," she says and sniffs a little chuckle laugh. "I can drop these two at the Armentis' for half a hour. They like it over there, anyway. I don't know what might happen to you alone."

"I'll pay if it costs anything."

X shakes her head and slides off the fender. "You'll pay, huh?" The moon has appeared suddenly over the stalky elms—a bright, wide and ethereal world above us, illuminating trees and patches of empty street and the older white residences beyond. She glances at me in amusement. "Who did you think was going to pay?" She laughs.

"I just wanted to be a good sport."

"What do you really care most about in the world? That's the question of the hour, I think."

"You. That's all."

X laughs again and opens the door wide. "You're a sport, all right. You're the original sport."

I smile at her in the public darkness. My children pile past me inside. The car door closes. And once again we are off.

WALTER'S PLACE at 118 Coolidge is a two-story cinderblock apartment row between two nicer older colonials whose young-couple-owners have sunk reasonable money into them, and are home tonight. I've never noticed the place, though there is a streetlight out front and it is only two streets over from X's house, and a block exactly like hers in every way but for this very building. The windowless front has been decorated with aluminum strips made like Venetian blinds, with "The Catalina" painted in script across it and backed by a wan light. Exterior lights along the side-facing doors burn visibly to the street. It is a place for abject senior seminarians, confirmed bachelors and divorcées—people in transition—and it is not, I think, such a bad place. I wouldn't have minded it in Ann Arbor in the middle Sixties, say, or even today if I was fresh out of law school, trying to get my legs under me before starting life in earnest and annexing a little wife. Though it is not a place I'd be happy to end up, or even pass through as a way-station toward somewhere else in adult life. The Catalina would be too unpromising for those conditions. And it would certainly not be a place I'd choose to die. Seeing it makes me wonder exactly what kind of lovers' nest Yolanda and Eddie Pitcock share in Bimini. I'm sure it's nothing like this. I'm sure a blue ocean is nearby, and cooling breezes rattling banana palms, and wind chimes punctuating languorous afternoons. Better on all accounts.

X parks behind Walter's MG, and we walk up the concrete to the mailboxes where a single buggy globe shines dimly. Walter's business card has been pruned to fit the space marked 6-D, and we start down the lower row of doors where I hear the mutter of televisions.

"It's *dank* here," X says. "I've never been anyplace I could actually say was dank. Have you?"

"Locker rooms," I say, "in some of the older stadiums."

"I suppose that shouldn't surprise me, should it?"

"I doubt if Walter liked it much either."

"Well, he's fixed that."

6-D's outside light is off, and a bright orange sticker masks the door saying POLICE INVESTIGATION. AUTHORIZED ENTRY ONLY. I turn the key and open the door into darkness.

A small green light and the tiny numerals 7:53 shine from the black. I own the very same clock at home.

"This *is* very, *very* unpleasant," X says. "I think this man would hate my coming in here."

"You can go back," I say.

A smell is in the room and seems not to belong there, a medical smell from a doctor's office closed for vacation.

"Can't we turn on a light?"

Though for a moment I can't find a wall switch, and when I do it is out of service. "This doesn't work."

"Well, for God's sake find a lamp. I don't like his clock."

I bump across the dark floor, the furniture around me thick as elephants. I brush what feels like a leather couch, scrape a leg on an end table, pat across the back of a chair, then somewhere in the middle of the room touch the neck of a hanging lamp and pull the chain.

X appears alone in the doorway, her face fixed in a frown. "Well, for God's sake," she says again.

"I just want to see it," I say, standing in the middle of Walter's living room, seeing spots.

The hanging lamp casts dishy yellow light everywhere, though it is, in truth, a perfectly nice room. There are varnished paneled walls and a doorway leading to a dark bedroom. A pullman kitchen is behind a counter-thru, everything there put away and straight. There is plenty of big comfortable, new-looking furniture—a red leather couch across from a big RCA 24 with bolt holes on top where Walter has attached his duck gun. A set of barbells leans in a corner, several tables hold lamps with interesting oriental shades. A small mahogany secretary sits against a wall with blank paper and pencils laid out neatly as though Walter had intended to do some serious writing.

On the wall outside the bedroom door is a gallery of framed photographs I am eager to see. Pictured is the '66 Grinnell wrestling team in black and white with Walter, a rangy 145-er, kneeling in an old wire-window gym, arms folded thick, sober as an Indian. Under that is a pretty blond girl with a slightly heavy upper lip and wide-spaced eyes—no doubt Yolanda—taken in a row boat with the wind blowing. Here is the Delta Chi fraternity on risers; here is a picture of two stern-looking senior citizens, a man in a stiff wool suit, a woman in a flowered dress—Ma and Pa Luckett in Coshocton, without doubt. Here is Walter in a full-traction leg-cast on a hospital bed beside a pretty nurse, both giving a big thumbs-up; and Walter in a convict's suit and cap beside Yolanda in a dancehall getup, each sneering. Walter has framed his Harvard Business School acceptance letter, and to the side there is a picture of a younger Walter seated at a desk with a stack of businessy-looking papers, smoking a Meerschaum pipe.

At the bottom, and to my surprise, is a photo of the Divorced Men's Club ganged around our big circular table in the August. It is during one of our Thursday night sessions. I'm holding a huge beer mug and wearing an idiot grin, listening animatedly to something Knot-head Knott is spieling about and am undoubtedly bored blind. Knot-head is holding back a big guffaw, but I have no recollection of what we might've been talking about. I do not even remember the time's happening, and seeing it makes me feel it all must've been in Walter's imagination.

I poke my head back into the bedroom and snap on the ceiling light. Here it is sparer than out front, but still satisfactory in its own way. An aquarium sits on the dresser, its lurid light exposing floating, tiny black mollies. Walter's bed has a geometric-design cover with three oversized pillows, and on the night table there is a copy of my book, *Blue Autumn*, with my author's picture face-up, and myself looking remarkably lean and ironic. I am drinking a beer, elbowed-in to an open air bar in San Miguel Tehuantepec. I have a crewcut and am smoking a cigarette, and couldn't look more ridiculous. "Mr. Bascombe," my biography says, "is a young American living in Mexico. He was born at the end of World War II, served in the Marines, and has attended the University of Michigan." I pick it up and see it is the Haddam Public Library copy, with the plastic cover taken off. (Walter has boosted it! He told me in the Manasquan that he had a library copy, but I didn't believe him.) He has jotted small pluses and zeros by certain titles on the contents page. I'd like to see more about that, possibly take the book with me, though I know there's an inventory inside Sergeant Benivalle's folder. I set the book back, take a quick look around—shoes, shoetrees, a skinny closet of suits and shirts, a silent butler, a computer terminal on the floor in the corner, an air-conditioner built through from the outside, a Grinnell pennant—the unextraordinary remains of a life at loose ends.

X is seated on the edge of the leather couch, her wrists on her knees, looking at a red ceramic lobster peeking out over the rim of a large green "dip bowl" on the coffee table. "You know?" She stares closely at the lobster's eyes. Her voice makes a hollow, echoey sound.

"What?"

"It reminds me of a frat house in here, a Phi Delt's room I used to go into. Ron something. Ron Kirk. It was fixed up exactly this way, like a dentist's office somebody'd lived in. Just horrible boy's stuff. I bet there's a set of *Playboy*s in here somewhere. I looked around for it a little." She shakes her head in wonder. On the floor in front of the coffee table is more orange tape the police have laid around the chair Walter was sitting in, a chair that is missing. Two large dark brown stains have dried on one of the hooked rugs, and these have been covered with clear plastic, then taped. An area on the wall has also been covered and sealed. X has made no reference to either of them. "You're just so strange, Frank, my God. I don't see how any of you get along alone." She blinks up at me, smiling, curious at who would kill himself, wishing for a common-sensical explanation for such a strange event. "You know?"

"I was just wondering how Walter rigged up the switch. He was probably an expert."

"Do you think you understand all this?"

"I think so."

"Then tell me, would you?"

"Walter gave himself up to the here and now, but got stranded. Then I think he got excited, and all he knew how to do was sentimentalize his life, which made him regret everything. If he'd made it past today he'd have been fine, I think." I pick up an Americana matchbook off the kitchen counter, and read the address and phone number to myself. Below it is a copy of *Bimini Today* with a photograph on the cover of a long silver beach. I put the matchbook down.

"Do you think you were supposed to help him?" X says, still smiling. "He seems so conventional. Just seeing in here."

"He should've helped himself" is my answer, and in fact it is what I believe. "You can't be too conventional. That's what'll save you." And for a moment a sudden unwanted grief sweeps up in me; a grief, I suppose, for possibilities misconstrued, for consolation not taken (which is what grief is all about). I share, I know, and only for a moment, the grief poor Walter must've felt alone here but shouldn't have. This is not a perfectly good room. There's little here for small mystery and hope and anticipation to flicker on—yet there's nothing so corrupting or so lonely here as to be unworkable. I could hang in here until I got myself headed right, though I'd see that I did it in a hurry.

"You look like your best friend died, sweetheart," X says.

I smile at her and she stands up in the shadowy, death-smelling room, taller than I usually think of her, her shadow rising to the nubbly ceiling.

"Let's leave," she says and smiles back in a friendly way.

I think a moment about the drinking glasses Walter probably owned, that I'm sure I was right about them, though I won't bother looking. "You know," I say, "I suddenly had this feeling we should make love. Let's close the door there and get in bed."

X stares at me in sudden and fierce disbelief. (I can see she is horrified by this idea, and I wish I could take the words back right away, since it was a preposterous thing to say, and I didn't mean a word of it.) "That's something we don't do anymore. Don't you remember?" X says, bitterly. "That's what divorce means. You're really a terrible man."

"I'm sorry," I say. Sergeant Benivalle would understand this and have a strategy for getting it straightened out. It has not been the best day of either of our lives, after all.

"I remember why I divorced you now." X turns away, reaching the door in three unexpectedly long steps. "You've really *become* awful. You weren't always awful. But now you are. I don't like you very much at all."

"I guess I am," I say and try to smile. "But you don't have to be afraid."

"I'm not afraid," she says, and laughs a hard little laugh, turning through the doorway just as a small man in a white shirt arrives into it. It stops her cold to see him.

The man's eyes look wide behind thick glasses, and he blocks X's way without intending to. He leans around her to look at me. "Are you the sister and brother?" he says.

I lean exactly as he does, trying to see him and look pleasant. "No," I say. "I'm a friend of Walter's." This is the only explanation I have, and I can see from his expression that it isn't enough. He is a youngish Frank Sinatra type with pale, knobby cheeks and curly hair (possibly he's not as young as he looks, since he has a dry librarian's air about him). He suspects something's up, though, and means to get to the bottom of it pronto using this very air. His presence makes me realize how little I have to do with anything here, and that X was right. It's just lucky we were not getting into bed.

"You don't belong here," the young man says. He is for some

reason flustered and trying to decide whether to get damn good and mad about everything. Conceivably I could show him Sergeant Benivalle's card.

"Are you the manager?"

"Yes. What are you stealing? You can't take anything."

"We're not taking anything."

"Excuse me," X says, and shoulders past the man into the dark. She has nothing more to say to me. I listen to her footsteps down the sidewalk and feel awful.

The man blinks at me in the living room's light. "What the hell *are* you doing here? I'm going to call the police about it. We'll get—"

"They know about it already," I say wearily. Here without a doubt is where I should present Sergeant Benivalle's card, but I do not have the heart.

"What do you want here?" the man says painfully, stranded in the doorway.

"I don't know. I forgot."

"Are you some kind of newspaperman?"

"No. I was just Walter's friend."

"No one's allowed in here but the family. So just get out."

"Are you a friend of Walter's, too?"

He blinks several times at this particular question. "I was," the man says. "I certainly was."

"Then why didn't you go down and identify him?"

"Just get out," the man says, and looks dazed.

"Okay." I start to turn off the light, and remember my book in the dark bedroom. I would like to take it with me to return to the library. "I'm sorry," I say.

"I'll turn that off," the man says abruptly. "You just leave."

"Thanks." I walk past the man, brushing his sleeve, then out where the air awaits me, sweet and thick and running full of fears.

x sits in her Citation beneath the streetlight, motor idling, the dashboard lights green in her face. She has waited here for me.

I lean in the passenger window, where the air is warm and smells like X's perfume. "I don't see why we had to go in there," she says stonily.

"I'm sorry about it. It's my fault. I didn't mean that in there."

"You are *such* a cliché. God." X shakes her head, though she is still angry.

This is perfectly true, of course. It is also true that I have tried for a kind of sneaky full disclosure, been caught at it, and am about to be left empty-handed.

"I don't really see why I have to distinguish myself, though I'm a grown man. I don't have to impress anybody now."

"You just embarrass me. But that's right." She nods, staring unhappily straight into the night. "I was going to ask you to come home with me. Isn't that funny? I left the kids at the Armentis'."

"I'd go. That's a great idea."

"Well, no." X reaches round and buckles her seat belt over her wonderfully skirted thighs, sets both hands on the steering wheel. "That little man in there just seemed so strange to me. Was he a friend of your friend's?"

"I don't know. He never mentioned him." She is probably worrying that Walter and I were "romantically linked."

"Maybe your friend was just meant to kill himself." She smiles at me with too much irony, too much, anyway, for people who have known each other as long as we have, and slept together, had children, loved each other and been divorced. Irony ought to be outlawed from this kind of situation. It is a pain in the ass and doesn't help anybody. Hers, regrettably, is a typical midwestern response to the complicated human dilemma.

"Walter didn't understand his own resources. He didn't have to do this. It seems to me you could stand to be more adaptable yourself. We could just go home right now. No one's there."

"I don't think so." She smiles still.

"I still want to," I say. I grin through the window. I smell the exhaust flooding underneath me, feel the car shuddering behind its safe headlights. The change scoop between the bucket seats, I see, is filled with orange golf tees.

"You're not a real bad man. I'm sorry. I don't think divorce has worked wonders for you." She puts the car into gear so that it lurches, yet doesn't quite leave. "It was just a bad idea I had."

"Your loved ones are the ones you're supposed to trust," I say. "Who's after that?"

She smiles at me a sad, lonely smile out of the instrument panel twilight. "I don't know." I can see her eyes dancing in tears.

"I don't know either. It's getting to be a problem."

X lets off on her brake and I step back in the grass. Her Citation hesitates, then hisses off from me up Coolidge and into the night. And I am left alone in the cool silence of dead Walter's yard and MG, an unknown apartment house behind me, a neighborhood where I am not known, a man with no place to go in particular—out, for the moment, of any good ideas, at the sad end of a sad day that in a better world would never have occurred at all.

WHERE, IN FACT, do you go if you're me?

Where do sportswriters go when the day is, in every way, done, and the possibilities so limited that neither good nor bad seems a threat? (I'd be happy to go to sleep, but that doesn't seem available.)

It is not, though, a genuine empty moment, and as such, war needn't be waged against it. It need not even be avoided or faced up to with particular daring. It is not the prologue to terrible regret. An empty moment requires both real expectation and its eventual defeat by the forces of fate. And I have no such hopes to dash. For the moment, I'm beyond all hopes, much as I was on the night X burned her hope chest while I watched the stars.

Walter would say that I have become neither the seer nor the thing seen—as invisible as Claude Rains in the movie, though I have no enemies to get back at, no debts to pay off. Invisibility, in truth, is not so bad. We should all try to know it better, use it to our advantage the way Claude Rains didn't, since at one time or other—like it or not—we all become invisible, loosed from body and duty, left to drift on the night breeze, to do as we will, to cast about for what we would like to be when we next occur. That, let me promise you, is not an empty moment. And further yet from real regret. (Maybe Walter *was* interested in me, but who knows? Or cares?) Just to slide away like a whisper down the wind is no small freedom, and if we're lucky enough to win such a setting-free, even if it's bad events that cause it, we should use it, for it is the only naturally occurring consolation that comes to us, sole and sovereign, without props or the forbearance of others—among whom I mean to include God himself, who does not let us stay invisible long, since that is a state he reserves for himself.

God does not help those who are invisible too.

*   *   *

I DRIVE, an invisible man, through the slumberous, hilled, post-Easter streets of Haddam. And as I have already sensed, it is not a good place for death. Death's a preposterous intruder. A breach. A building that won't fit with the others. An enigma as complete as Sanskrit. Full-blown cities are much better at putting up with it. So much else finds a place there, a death as small as Walter's would fit in cozy, receive its full sympathies and be forgotten.

Haddam is, however, a first-class place for invisibility—it is practically made for it. I cruise down Hoving Road past my own dark house set back in its beeches. Bosobolo has not returned (still away in the bramble bush with plain Jane). I could talk to him about invisibility, though it's possible a true African would know less than one of our local Negroes, and I would end up explaining a lot to start with, though eventually he would catch on—committed as he is to the unseen.

I cruise through the dark cemetery where my son is put to rest, and where the invisible virtually screams at you, cries out for quiet, quiet and more quiet. I could go sit on Craig's stone and be silent and invisible with Ralph in our old musing way. But I would soon be up against my own heavy factuality, and consolation would come to a standstill.

I drive by X's house, where there is bright light from every window, and a feeling of bustle and things-on-tap behind closed doors, as if everyone were leaving. There's nothing for me here. My only hope would be to make trouble, extenuate circumstances for everybody, do some shouting and break a lamp. And I—it should come as no surprise—lack the heart for that too. It's nine p.m., and I know where my children are.

Where is there to go that's fun, I wonder?

I drive past the August, where a red glow warms the side bar window, and where I'm sure a life-long resident or a divorced man sits wanting company—a commodity I'm low on.

Down Cromwell Lane at Village Hall a light still burns in the glass lobby—in the tax office the janitor stands at the front door staring out, his mop at order arms. Somewhere far off a train whistles, then a siren sings through the heavy elms of the Institute grounds. I catch the wink of lights, hear the soft spring monotone of all hometown suburbs. Someone might say there's nothing quite so lonely as a suburban street at night when you are all alone. But he would be dead wrong. For my money, there're a lot of things worse. A seat on the New York Stock Exchange, for instance. A silent death at sea with no one to notice your going under. Herb Wallagher's life. These would be worse. In fact, I could make a list as long as your arm.

I drive down the cobblestone hill to the depot, where, if I'm right, a train will soon be arriving. It is not bad to sit in some placeless dark and watch commuters step off into splashy car lights, striding toward the promise of bounteous hugs, cool wall-papered rooms, drinks mixed, ice in the bucket, a newspaper, a long undisturbed evening of national news and sleep. I began coming here soon after my divorce to watch people I knew come home from Gotham, watch them be met, hugged, kissed, patted, assisted with luggage, then driven away in cars. And you might believe I was envious, or heartsick, or angling some way to feel wronged. But I found it one of the most hopeful and worthwhile things, and after a time, when the train had gone and the station was empty again and the taxis had drifted back up to the center of town, I went home to bed almost always in rising spirits. To take pleasure in the consolations of others, even the small ones, is possible. And more than that: it sometimes becomes damned necessary when enough of the chips are down. It takes a depth of character as noble and enduring as willingness to come off the bench to play a great game knowing full well that you'll never be a regular; or as one who chooses not to hop into bed with your best friend's beautiful wife. Walter Luckett could be alive today if he'd known that.

But I am right.

Out of the burly-bushy steel darkness down the line comes the clatter of the night's last arrival from Philadelphia, on its way back to New York. Trainmen lean out the silver vestibules, eye-ing the passing station, taking notice of the two waiting cars with workmanlike uninterest. Theirs is another life I wouldn't like, though I'm ready to believe it has moments of real satisfaction. I'm sure I would pay undue attention to my passengers, would stand around hearing what they had on their minds, learning where they were off to, conversing with them on train travel in general, picking up a phone number here and there, and never get my tickets clipped on time and end up being let go—no better at that than I'd be at arc welding.

The local squeezes to a halt beside the station. The trainmen are down on the concrete, swinging their tiny flashes like police even before the last cars are bucked stopped. The lone taxi switches on its orange dome light and the two waiter cars rev engines in unison.

Within the yellow-lit coaches, pale dreamy faces stare out into the Easter night. *Where are we now*, they seem to ask. *Who lives here? Is this a safe place? Or what?* Their features are glassy and smooth with drowse.

I stroll to the platform and up under the awning, hands in pockets, stepping lively on my toes as if I'm expecting—a loved one, a girlfriend, a best friend from college long out of touch. The two trainmen give me the mackerel eye and begin some exclusive talk they've been putting off. But I don't feel the least excluded, since I enjoy this closeness to trains and the great moment they exude, their implacable hissing noise and purpose. I read somewhere it is psychologically beneficial to stand near things greater and more powerful than you yourself, so as to dwarf yourself (and your piddlyass bothers) by comparison. To do so, the writer said, released the spirit from its everyday moorings, and accounted for why Montanans and Sherpas, who live near daunting mountains, aren't much at complaining or nettlesome introspection. He was writing about better "uses" to be made of skyscrapers, and if you ask me the guy was right on the money. All alone now beside the humming train cars, I actually do feel my moorings slacken, and I will say it again, perhaps for the last time: there is mystery everywhere, even in a vulgar, urine-scented, suburban depot such as this. You have only to let yourself in for it. You can never know what's coming next. Always there is the chance it will be—miraculous to say—something you want.

Off the train steps a buxom young nun, in the blackest, most orthodox habit, carrying a slick attaché case and a storky umbrella. She is bright-eyed, round-faced, smiling, and passes a teasing "thanks, goodbye" to the trainmen, who touch their hats and smile, but also give her a swarthy look the instant her back is turned. She is met by no one, and trudges past me cheerfully, heading, I'm sure, up to the seminary on some ecclesiastical business with the Presbyterians. As she passes me by I give her a smile, for she will encounter no dangers on our streets, I can assure her. No would-be rapists or scroungy types.

Though she seems like someone to look danger in the eye and call its bluff.

Next, two business types with loose ties, single-suiters and expensive briefcases—lawyers, without doubt, up from Philadelphia or the nation's capital, come to do business with one or another of the world headquarters that dot the local landscape. Both are Jews, and both look dog-tired, ready for a martini, a bath, a set of clean sheets and a made-for-TV movie. They crawl into the taxi. I hear one say "The August," and in no time they go murmuring up the hill, the taxi's taillights red as smudged roses.

Two blond women scurry out, give each other big phony hugs, then jump in the two waiting cars—each driven by a man—and disappear. For an instant, I thought one of them was familiar, someone I might've met at a cocktail party in the old days. A spiky married Laura or Suzannah with boyish hips, red silk pants and leathery skin: someone of my own rough age, whom I more than likely bored the nose off of but was too bored back by to stop. Possibly a friend of X's, who knows the truth about me. One blonde indeed did give me a lashing, feral half-glance before stepping into her waiting Grand Prix and delivering Mr. Inside a big well-rehearsed kiss, but she seemed not to recognize me. A big problem of being divorced in a town this size is that all the women immediately become your wife's friends whether they know her or not. And that's not just paranoia. Being a man gets harder all the time.

The trainmen part company and sidle back toward their vestibules. The wig-wag headlight careers over the open rails. The inside passengers have all gone back to sleep. It is time, almost, to turn to home. And do what?

Out of the far silver car comes a last departer. A small fawn-haired woman of the frail but vaguely pretty category, not of this town. That much is clear the moment her shoes—the kind with heels lower than the toes—touch ground. She is wearing a tent dress, though she is wire-thin, with a pleasant, scrubbed look on her wren's features, and a self-orienting way of looking round about, which makes her turn her nose up testingly to the air. In one hand she is carrying some kind of deep Brazilian wicker basket as luggage, on top of which she's strapped a bulky knitted sweater. And in the other there's a fat copy of what I can make out as *The Life of Teddy Roosevelt*, with plenty of paper bookmarks sprouting from the pages.

She sniffs the air as if she's just detrained in the Punjab, and turning her head with a scent, moves to say a word to the older of the two trainmen, who points her in the direction the nun has taken, up the hill into town and directly by me, leaned against a girder beside the phalanx of newspaper boxes, growing sleepy in the springtime evening.

The word "taxi" is spoken, and both of them look toward the empty parking spaces and shake heads. My Malibu sits alone across the street, angled into the murky Rose of Sharon hedge behind the regional playhouse—a dark and barely detectable blob. I see the two of them look toward me again, and I sense a connection being made. "Maybe that gentleman right there will give you a lift into town," one of them is saying. "This is a town of gentle folk. Not one in ten thousand will murder you."

I am unexpectedly visible!

The woman turns with her orienteering wren's look. She and I are the same vintage. We have learned to trust strange people in the Sixties, and it hasn't yet dawned on us that it might've been a mistake (though one clue should've been our own perfidies).

Hands thrust in back pockets, though, I am ready to be used; to lend a hand, prove myself guileless as old Huck. There might, in fact, be a late-night cocktail invitation in the works as a "thankee," an *intime* in the dark taproom of the August, alongside the bushed lawyers. After that, who knows? More? Less?

Deep in my pocket my fingers touch an inconclusive paper. Walter's poor letter, folded in thirds and tucked behind my wallet, forgotten to this moment. And a sudden cheerless warmth rises out under my chin and stings my ears and scalp.

This is Walter's sister, this woman! Wicker basket. Healthy shoes. Roosevelt bio. She has already arrived for her doleful duties, and with enough dry, grief-dispelling practicality to send a drowning man clambering for the bottom. She is some miserable Montessori teacher from Coshocton. A woman with a reading list and an agenda, friends in the Peace Corps, an NPR program log deep in her Brazil bag. A tidy, chestless Pat or Fran from Oberlin or Reed, with high board scores. My heart pounds a tomtom for the now disappeared blondie, whirling away in her Grand Prix to some out-of-the-way Italian snuggery with the nerve to stay open Easters. I ache to be along. Dinner could be on me. Drinks. The tip. Don't leave me to sensible grief and a night of plain-talk. (Of course I'm not sure it's her, but neither am I sure it isn't.) This woman has the look to me of trouble's sister, and I'd rather put my trust in my heart and my money where my mouth isn't.

"Excuse me, please," scratchy Fran/Pat says in her bony, businesslike voice as she comes toward me. She has an iron handshake, I'm sure, and knows death to be just one of life's slow curves you have to stand in on, brother or no brother. I would hate to see what else she has in that basket. "I wonder if you'd mind terribly. . . ." She speaks in a phony boarding school accent, nose up, seeing me—if at all—out the bottom third of her eyes.

The train discharges a loud hiss. A bell rings a last shrilling peel. "Boooard," the trainman shouts from his dark vestibule. The train lurches, and in that sudden instant I am aboard, hurt knee and all, unexpectedly a passenger, and away. "I'm sorry," I say, as my face slides past, "I've got to catch a train."

The woman stands blinking as I recede, her mouth open for the next words I will not have to hear, words for which even a roll in the hay would not be antidote.

She grows small—gnawingly small and dim—in the powdery depot light, poised in a moment when certainty became confusion; confused among other things, that people do things so differently out here, that people are more abrupt, less willing to commit themselves, less schooled in old-fashioned manners; confused why the least of God's children would do anyone a bad turn by not helping. Maybe Pat/Fran is right. It *is* confusing, though sometimes—let me say—it's better not to take a chance. You can take too many chances and end up with nothing but regret to keep you company through a night that simply—for the life of you—won't end.

CHAPTER 13

CLATTER-DE-CLACK, we swagger and sway up through the bleak-lit corridor of evening Jersey. Mine is one of the old coaches with woven brown plastic seats and bilgy window glass. A cooked metal odor fills the aisles and clings to the luggage racks, as the old lights flicker and dim. It is another side to the public accommodation coin.

Still, it's not bad to be moving. With the traveling seat turned toward me, it's easy to make myself comfortable, feet up, and watch float past the sidereal townlets of Edison, Metuchen, Metropark, Rahway, and Elizabeth.

Of course, I have no earthly idea where I'm bound or what to do once I get there. Fast getaways from sinister forces are sometimes essential, though what follows can mean puzzlement. I haven't ridden the night train *to* New York, I'm sure, since X and I rode up to see *Porgy and Bess* one winter night when it snowed. How long ago—five years? Eight? The specific past has a way of blending, an occurrence I don't particularly mind. And tonight the prospect of detraining in Gotham seems less spooky than usual. It seems a more local-feeling place with a sweet air of the illicit, like a woman you barely know and barely want, but who lets you anyway. Things change. We have that to look forward to. In fact, climbing down tonight onto the streets of any of these little crypto-homey Jersey burgs could heave me into a panic worse than New York ever has.

Only a few solitary passengers share my coach. Most are sleeping, and I don't recognize any as faces I saw from the platform. I wouldn't even mind seeing someone I knew. Bert Brisker would be a welcome companion, full of some long, newsy ramble about the book he's reviewing or some interview he's conducted with a famous author. I'd be interested to hear his opinion about the future of the modern novel. (I miss this clubby in-crowd talk, the chance to make good on the conviction that your formal education hasn't left you completely shipwrecked.)

Usually Bert is deep in his own work, and I'm in mine. And once
we leave the platform, where we chuckle and grouse in special
code talk, we rarely utter another word. But I'd be glad now for
some friendly jawboning. I haven't done enough of that; it is a
bad part of being in the company of athletes and people I don't
know well and will never know, people who have damned little
of general interest to talk about. To be a sportswriter, sad to say
it, is to live your life mostly with your thoughts, and only the
edge of others'. That's exactly why Bert got out of the business,
and why he's at home tonight with Penny and his girls and his
sheepdogs, watching Shakespeare on HBO, or dozing off with
a good book. And why I'm alone on an empty, bad-smelling
milk train, headed into a dark kingdom I have always feared.

The young mackerel-eye trainman sways into my car and gives
me a look of distrust as he processes my ticket money and dedi-
cates a stub on my seatback. He does not like it that I have to buy
my passage en route, or that I wouldn't give a lift to Walter's
sister back up the line, or that I'm wearing a madras shirt and
seem happy and so much his opposite when the rest of the world
known to him—in his sheeny black conductor's suit—is strictly
where it belongs. He is not yet thirty, by my guess, and I give
him a good customer's no-sweat smile to let him know it's really
all right. I'm no threat to any of his beliefs. In fact, I probably
share most of them. I can tell, though, by his fisheye that he
doesn't like the night and what it holds—inconstant, marauding,
sinister, peaceless thing to be steered clear of here inside the
thrumming tube of his professional obligation. And since I've
come out of it, unexpectedly, I am suspect too. Quick as he can,
he pockets his punch, scans the other passengers' stubs down the
aisle and abandons me for the bar car, where I see him begin
talking to the Negro waiter.

When I paid for my ticket, I've once again fingered Walter's
letter, and under the circumstances there's nothing to do but read
it, which I do, starting in Rahway, with the aid of the pained
little overhead light.

> Dear Franko,
>   I woke up today with the clearest idea of what I need to
> do. I'm absolutely certain about it. Write a novel! I don't
> know what the hell it will be for or who'll read it or any of

that, but I've got the writer's itch now and whoever wants to read it can or they can forget about it. I've gotten beyond everything, and that feels good!

What I wrote was: "Eddie Grimes waked up on Easter morning and heard the train whistle far away in a forgotten suburban station. His very first thought of the day was, 'You lose control by degrees.'" That seemed like a hell of a good first line. Eddie Grimes is me. It's a novel about me, with my own ideas and personal concepts and beliefs built into it. It's hard to think of your own life's themes. You'd think anyone could do it. But I'm finding it very, very hard. Pretty close to impossible. I can think of yours a lot better, Frank. I'm conservative, passionate, inventive, and fair—as an investment banker, which works great! But it's hard to get that down and translated into the novel form, I see. I've gotten side-tracked in this.

Maybe a good way to start a novel is with a suicide note. That'd be a built-in narrative hook. I know it's been done before. But what hasn't? It was new to me, right? I'm not worried about that.

I've gone away and come back. The suicide note idea doesn't really lead anywhere interesting novel-wise, Frank. I'm not sure which fickle master I'm trying to serve here (ha-ha). I apologize for the message about the airplane, by the way. I was just trying to manipulate my feelings, get the right mood going for writing. I hope you're not pissed off. I admire you all the more now for the work you've done. I still consider you my best friend, even though we don't really know each other that well.

I tried to call Yolanda earlier. No answer, then busy. Then no answer. I also got things straightened out with Warren. That was a fine thing I did there. I admit I should've just been friends with him. But I didn't. So what, right? Sue me. Take care of yourself, Frank.

I would like this to be an interesting letter anyway if it can't be a best-selling novel. I feel I know exactly what I'm doing now. This is not phony baloney. You're supposed to be crazy when you kill yourself? Well forget that. You'll never be saner. That's for sure.

Frank, here's the kicker now, alright? I have a daughter! And I know all about what you're thinking. But, I do. She's nineteen. One of those ill-begotten teenage liaisons back in Ohio early in the summer, sophomore year, when I was nineteen myself! Her name is Susan—Suzie Smith. She lives in Sarasota, Fla, with her mother, Janet, who lives with some sailor or highway patrolman. I don't know which. I send them checks still. I'd like to go down there and shed some light on all this for her. And me, too. I've never actually seen her. There was a lot of trouble at the time. Of course it wouldn't happen today. But I feel very close to her. And you're the only person who'll be able to make sense out of this, Franko. I hope you don't mind my asking you to go down there and have a talk with her. Thanks in advance. You needed the vacation, right?

I really haven't felt this clear-headed about things since I was out at Grinnell and had to make the decison to move up to 152, and give up at 145 where I was successful, because there was someone there all of a sudden who was better—a freshman, no less. I had to give up or make a big decision. I finally won matches at the higher weight, but I was never as good. I never was prideful again either. I'm not prideful now, but I think I have a right to be.

All best,

Wally

All *best*? Talk about losing your authority! All best, then go boom-blow-your-brains-out? How do we get bound up with people we don't even know, is my question for the answer man. I'd give anything in the world at this moment never to have known Walter Luckett, Jr., or that he could be alive so I could drop him like a hot potato, and he could have no one to address his dumb-ass letter to and have to figure out the big questions all by himself. Maybe he could've finished his novel then. In a way, if it weren't for me being his friend, he'd be alive.

Whose life ever has permanent mystery built into it anyway? An astronaut? The heavyweight champ? A Ubangi tribesman? Even old Bosobolo has to pursue an advanced degree, and then it's not a sure thing, which accounts for his love interest on the side. If Walter were here I'd shake the bejesus out of him.

He could've found Mrs. Miller (if he knew about her); or read catalogs into the night; or turned on Johnny; or called up a hundred dollar whore for a house call. He could've hunted up a reason to keep breathing. What else is the ordinary world good for except to supply reasons not to check out early?

Walter's circumstances would be a good argument for a trip to Bimini to settle his debts, or a camping trip to Yellowstone in a land yacht. Only now I don't even have *those* luxuries. What I have is awful, mealy factual death, which once you start to think of it, won't go away and inhabits your life like a dead skunk under the porch.

And a daughter? No way. I have my own daughter. One day soon enough she'll want to hear some explaining, too. And that, frankly, is all I care about; the answers I come up with then. What happened to Walter on this earth is Walter's own lookout. I'm sorry as hell, but he had his chance like the rest of us.

SUDDENLY WE are through the rank, larky meadowlands and entered in the long tunnel to Gotham, where the lights go out and you can't see beyond your reflected self in gritty window glass, and I have the sudden feeling of falling out of space and into a perilous dream—a dream, in fact, I used to suffer after my divorce (though I am sure it's primed this time by Walter) in which I am in bed with someone I don't know and cannot—must not—touch (a woman, thank God), but whom I must lie beside for hours and hours on end in a state of fear and excitation and scalding guilt. It is a terrible dream, but it wouldn't surprise me if all men didn't have it at one time or other. Or many times. And in truth, after I had had it for six months I got used to it and could go back to sleep within five minutes. Though if I wasn't already on the floor, I was at least on the edge of the bed when I woke up, cramped and achy as though clinging at the edge of a lifeboat on a vast and moody sea. Like all things bad and good, we get used to them, and they pass us by with age.

In ten minutes we have docked in the vault of Penn Station, and I am up and out of its hot tunnel, across the bright upper lobby, my dream faded in the crowd of derelicts and Easter returnees, then out onto breezy Seventh Avenue and the wide prospects of Gotham on a warm Easter night. It is now ten-fifteen. I have no idea what I'm supposed to do.

Though I am not sorry to be here. The usual demoralizing fire-storm of speeding cabs, banging lights and owl-voiced urban-ness has yet to send me careening into the toe-squeezing funk of complication and obscurity, in which everything becomes too important and too dangerous to be tolerable. Here, out on Seventh and 34th, I feel an unaccustomed lankness, a post-coital midwestern caress to things—the always dusky air still high and hollowish, streets alive with the girdering wheels of hungry traffic that pours past me and quickly vanishes.

And I sense, standing in the exit crowds from a Shaggy Chrys-anthemum show at the Garden, gazing across at the marquee and night lights of the old Statler Hotel, that a person could have a few laughs here, might even find the exhilaration of a woman tolerable excitement, given the right quarters and timing. A person might even have his actions speak (if briefly) for them-selves—something that never seemed possible here before—and actually put up with the old ethicless illicit for a while before escape became essential. This must be how all suburbanites feel when the suburbs suddenly go queer and queasy on them; that things cannot continue to fall away forever, and it's high time for a new, quick age to dawn. It's embarrassing to be so unworldly and timid at my age.

But still. What am I to do in this fragile truce? If I'm not simply ready to sprint back downstairs, buy my return and sleep all the way home, what am I *supposed* to do?

My answer, even with the city tamed and seemingly willing to meet my needs halfway, just proves my lack of expertise with the complicated life of real city-dwellers. I jump in the first cruis-ing cab and beat it uptown to 56th and Park, where I practice my sportswriter's trade. There's nothing I'd rather do than try out some fresh strategies on Herb and turn that emblem of desolation into something better, even if it means putting a wrench to a fact or two.

THE TWENTY-SECOND floor is abuzz with fluorescent light down the rows of cubicles. When I leave the elevator, I hear loud, contentious voices wrangling in the back offices. "Aw-right ... Aw-*right!*" Then: "Naaa-na,na,na,na. He's glue. Pure donkey." Then: "*I don't* believe this. This guy'll be alive in your nightmares, believe me. Be-*leeve* me!" It's the Pigskin Preview. The NFL draft is in ten days, and they are in extraordinary session.

I head toward my own cubicle, but stop and stick my head in the crowded conference room. Inside, sits a long Formica table littered with yellow hamburger bags and ashtrays and paper coffee cups, thick green ring-bound notebooks, a green computer screen showing a list of names drawn up. A white grease-pencil board is leaned against the wall. The entire football staff with a few of the younger boys on the low end of the masthead are staring in eagle-eyed attention through a layer of smoke at a big video machine showing a football play on a wide imitation-grass field. This is the skull session where our experts decide the first forty college players to be picked by the pros and in what order. After the World Series Roundup it is the most important issue of the year. As a young staffer, I sat in on these very sessions, chewed a cold cigar, shouted my favorites the way these boys are going at it (there's one female at the back I'm vaguely familiar with) and it became a damned valuable experience. Younger writers, researchers and interns out of Yale and Bowdoin get to see how these old heads do their stuff, how things really go on. The older writers would normally just settle this kind of thing over drinks at a sushi place around the corner. But for the Preview—and to their credit—they bring all the machinery out in the open and run the show as though it were really democratic. Later they'll all wind up strolling into the early morning streets, feeling good about themselves and football and the world in general, laughing and swearing, and having a round or two at some spudbuster bar over on Third Avenue. Sometimes they'll all stay out till dawn, and by nine can be seen around the coffee machine, or floating back to their desks with bushed-but-satisfied looks, ready to put the whole business into print.

Plenty of times I've seen writers, famous novelists and essayists, even poets, with names you'd recognize and whose work I admire, drift through these offices on one high-priced assignment or other. I have seen the anxious, weaselly lonely looks in their eyes, seen them sit at the desk we give them in a far cubicle, put their feet up and start at once to talk in loud, jokey, bluff, inviting voices, trying like everything to feel like members of the staff, holding court, acting like good guys, ready to give advice or offer opinions on anything anybody wants to know. In other words, having the time of their lives.

And who could blame them? Writers—all writers—need to belong. Only for real writers, unfortunately, their club is a club with just one member.

The Pigskin Preview boys are at odds over the talents of a big Polack from Iowa State who has speed and heart, versus a venomous-looking black cornerback from a small Baptist college, in Georgia, who's tiger quick and blessed with natural talent. Big cigars wag from clenched fingers. Piles of print-out rap sheets are scattered around. All eyes are on the screen as the black boy— referred to as Tyrone the Murderer—in a blue and orange #19 delivers a blow to a spindly white wide-out that would put most people right onto a respirator. Both players, however, bounce up like toys and Tyrone pats the white boy on the butt as they trot back to their huddles.

"Son of a bitch, The Murderer was on *that* play," a junior man from someplace like Williams shouts. "The bastard started late, missed his key, and still delivered like a fucking freight train." Eddie Frieder, the managing editor, teeth clenching a cigarette, and wearing a Red Sox cap, raises his brows and nods, then goes back to making computations. He's in charge here, but you'd never know. Agreement ripples among the other younger men, though it's clear there's still division. Two men express uneasiness with The Murderer's friendly pat on the backside. They suspect the pros might translate it into an impure competitive instinct, while others think it's a mark of good character on The Murderer's part. "This guy's no higher than eight in round two," they seem to agree.

"What do you think, Frank?" Eddie looks up at the door where I'm half-hidden, wanting not to be singled out.

All eyes see me—a smiling, slender, slightly flushed man in a madras shirt and chinos. A couple of young guys put down pencils and stare. I'm not a pigskin prognosticator; Eddie, in fact, knows I don't even like football, though I'll probably end up rewriting a lot of what gets done here and putting together a

sidebar about The Murderer's life-long fear of inheriting his
dad's fatal alcoholism (that can take a notch out of one's competitive instinct).

"I hear good things about this Hawaiian kid, from Arkansas
A&M," I say. "He runs a four-five and likes contact."

"Gone already!" four people shout at once. Heads shake.
Eyes blink. Everyone returns to his rap sheet. Someone rerolls
The Murderer's murderous tackle, and people scribble, which
reminds me again that I have found out nothing in Detroit for
use here. "Denver's got him on a player-to-be-named with
Miami. He can't miss," Eddie Frieder says officially, then looks
at his notes.

"Here's our next millionaire, Mike," someone cracks.

"You're the experts," I say. "I just got in from Altoona."
I wave to Eddie, then slip away down the row of cubicles to
my own.

MY DESK. My typewriter. My video console. My rolodex. My
extra shirt hung on the modular wall. My phone with three lines.
My tight window-view into the city's darkness. My pictures:
Paul and Clary under an umbrella and smiling during a Mets'
rain delay. X and Clary wearing Six Flags T-shirts, taken on our
front steps six months before our divorce (X looks happy, progressive in spirit). Ralph on a birthday pony in our backyard
my own.

MY DESK. My typewriter. My video console. My rolodex. My
second, glasses cleaned, hair combed—beatific. In the first he is
simply an athlete.

My plan of attack is to write on a legal pad the very first
things that come into my head—sentences, phrases, a concept,
a balancing word or detail. When I was writing seriously I used
to sit for hours over a sentence—usually one I hadn't written
yet, and usually without the first idea of what I was trying to
say. (That should've been a clue to me.) But the moment I started
writing sports, I found out it really didn't matter that much
what the sentence looked like, or even if it made sense, since
somebody else—Rhonda Matuzak, for instance—was going to

have it the way she liked it before it went into print. I got into the habit of putting down whatever occurred to me, and before long the truth of most things turned out to be waiting just over the edge of worried thought, and eventually I could write with practically no editing at all. If I ever write another short story I'm going to use the same technique; the way I would if I were writing about an American hockey player who becomes a skid-row drunk, rehabilitates himself at AA, scores forty goals and wins the Stanley Cup as the captain and conscience of the Quebec Nordiques.

In the case of Herb Wallagher I write: *Possibilities Limited.*

I think for a moment, then, about the first trip I ever made to New York. It was 1967. The fall. Mindy Levinson and I drove all night from Ann Arbor in one of my fraternity brothers' cars so I could attend a law school interview at NYU. (There was a brief period when I got out of the Marines, when I wanted more than anything to be a lawyer and work for the FBI.) Mindy and I stayed—as man and wife—in the old Albert Pick on Lexington Avenue, rode the IRT to Greenwich Village, bought a brass wedding ring to make things look legal and spent the rest of our time in bed woogling around in each other's businesses and watching sports on TV. Early the very next morning I took a taxi to Washington Square and attended my interview. I sat and talked amiably with a studious-looking fellow I'm now sure was only a senior work-study student, but who impressed me as a young and eccentric Constitutional genius. I didn't know the answers to any of the questions he asked me, nor, in fact, had I ever even thought of anything like the questions he had in mind. Later that day Mindy and I checked out of the hotel, drove across the George Washington Bridge, down the Turnpike and back to Ann Arbor, with me feeling I'd done a better than fair job answering the questions that *should've* been important but weren't even asked, and that I would end up editing the law review.

Naturally I wasn't even admitted to NYU, nor to any other of the law schools I applied to. And today I can't walk through Washington Square without thinking of that time with minor regret and longing. What might've happened, is what I usually think. How would life be different? And my feeling is, given the swarming, unforeseeable nature of the world, things could've turned out exactly as they have, give or take a couple of small matters: Divorce. Children. Changes in careers. Life in a town like Haddam. In this there is something consoling, though I don't mind saying there is also something eerie.

I go back again to Herb and write: *Herb Wallagher doesn't play ball anymore.*

I think, then, of the people I might possibly call at this hour. 10:45 p.m. I could call Providence again. Possibly X, though activities at her house made me think she is already on her way to the Poconos or elsewhere. I could call Mindy Levinson in New Hampshire. I could call Vicki at her parents'. I could call my mother-in-law in Mission Viejo, where it's only a quarter till eight, with the sun barely behind Catalina on an Easter ocean. I could call Clarice Wallagher, since it's possible she's up late most nights, wondering what's happened to her life. All of these people would talk to me, I know for a fact. But I am almost certain none of them would particularly want to.

I return to Herb once more; *The way Herb Wallagher sees it, real life's staring at you everyday. It's not something you need to go looking for.*

"Hi," a voice with an almost nautical lilt to it says behind me.

I swivel around, and framed there in the aluminum rectangle is a face to save a drowning man. A big self-assured smile. A swag of honey hair with two plaited strips pulled back on each side in a complex private-school style. Skin the clarity of a tulip. Long fingers. Pale blond skim of hair on her arm, which at the moment she is rubbing lightly with her palm. Khaki culottes. A white cotton blouse concealing a pair of considerable grapefruits.

"Hi." I smile back.

She rests a hip against the door frame. Below the culottes' hems her legs are taut and shiny as a cavalry saddle. I don't exactly know where to look, though the big smile says: *Look square at what you like, Jack. That's what God made it for.* "You're Frank Bascombe, aren't you?" She's still smiling as if she knows something. A secret.

"Yes. I am." My face grows pleasantly warm.

Eyes twinkle and brows arch. A look of admiration with nothing shady necessarily implied—a punctilio taught in the best New England boarding schools and mastered in adulthood— the simple but provoking wish to make oneself completely understood. "I'm sorry to butt in. I've just wanted to meet you ever since I've been here."

"Do you work here," I ask disingenuously, since I know with absolute certainty that she works here. I saw her down a corridor a month ago—not to mention ten minutes ago at the Pigskin Preview—and have looked up her employment files to see if she had the right background for some research. She is an intern down from Dartmouth, a Melissa or a Kate. Though at the moment I can't remember, since her kind of beauty is usually zealously overseen by some thick-necked Dartmouth Dan, with whom she is sharing an efficiency on the Upper East Side, taking their "term off" together to decide if a marriage is the wise decision at this point in time. I remember, however, her family is from Milton, Mass., her father a small-scale politician with a name I vaguely recognize as lustrous in Harvard athletics (he is a chum of some higher-up at the magazine). I can even picture him—small, chunky, shoulder-swinging, a scrappy in-fighter who got in Harvard on grades then lettered in two sports though no one in his family had ever made it out of the potato patch. A fellow I would usually like. And here is his sunny-faced daughter down to season her résumé with interesting extras for med school, or for when she enters local politics in Vermont/New Hampshire midway through her divorce from Dartmouth Dan. None of it is a bad idea.

But the sight of her in my doorway, healthy as a kayaker, Boston brogue, "experienced" already in ways you can only dream about, is a sight for mean eyes. Maybe Dartmouth Dan is off crewing dad's 12-metre, or still up in Hanover cramming for the business boards. Maybe he doesn't even find this big suavely beautiful girl "interesting" anymore (a decision he'll regret), or finds her wrong for his career (which demands someone shorter or a little less bossy), or needing better family ties or French. These mistakes still happen. If they didn't, how could any of us face a new day?

"I was just sitting in on the football meeting," Melissa/Kate says. She leans back to glance down the corridor. Voices trail away toward elevators. Forecasting work is over. Her hair is cut bluntly toward her sweet little helical ears so she can flick it as she just did. "My name's Catherine Flaherty," she says. "I'm interning here this spring. From Dartmouth. I don't want to intrude. You're probably real busy." A shy, secretive smile and another hair flick.

"I wasn't having much luck staying busy, to tell you the truth." I push back in my swivel chair and lace my hands behind my skull. "I don't mind a little company."

Another smile, the slightest bit permissive. *There's something kinda neat about you*, it says, *but don't get me wrong*. I give her my own firm, promise-not-to grin.

"I really just wanted to tell you I've read your stories in the magazine and really admire them a lot."

"That's kind of you, thanks." I nod as harmless as old Uncle Gus. "I try to take the job here pretty seriously."

"I'm *not* being kind." Her eyes flash. She is a woman who can be both chatty and challenging. I'm sure she can turn on the irony, too, when the situation asks for it.

"No. I don't believe you'd be kind for a minute. It's just nice of you to say so, even if you're not being nice." I rest my jaw, right where Vicki has slugged it, in the soft palm of my hand.

"Fair 'nuff." Her smile says I'm a pretty good guy after all. All is computed in smiles.

"How's the old Pigskin going?" I say, with forced jauntiness.

"Well, it's pretty exciting, I guess," she says. "They finally just throw out their graphs and ratings and play their hunches. Then the yelling really starts. I liked it."

"Well, we do try to factor in all the intangibles," I say. "When I started here, I had a heck of a time figuring out why anybody was right, ever, or even how they knew anything." I nod, pleased at what is, of course, a major truth of a lived life, though there's no reason to think that this Catherine Flaherty hasn't known it longer than I have. She is all of twenty, but has the sharp-eyed look of knowing more than I do about the very things I care most about—which is the fruit of a privileged life. "You thinking of taking a crack at this when school's over?" I say, hoping to hear *Yep, you bet I am*. But she looks instantly pensive, as though she doesn't want to disappoint me.

"Well, I took the Med-Cats already, and I spent all this time applying. I oughta hear any day now. But I wanted to try this, too. I always thought it'd be neat." She starts another wide smile, but her eyes suddenly go serious as if I might take offense at the least glimmer of what's fun. What she really wants is a piece of good strong advice, a vote in one direction or the other. "My brother played hockey at Bowdoin," she says for no reason I can think of.

"Well," I say happily and without one grain of sincerity, "you can't go wrong with the medical profession." I swivel back in mock spiritedness and tap my fingertips on the armrest. "Medicine's a pretty damn good choice. You participate in people's lives in a pretty useful way, which is important to me. Though my belief is you can do that as a sportswriter—pretty well, in fact." My hurt knee gives off a bony throb, a throb almost surely engineered by my heart.

"What made you want to be a sportswriter?" Catherine Flaherty says. She's not a girl to fritter. Her father has taught her a thing or two.

"Well. Somebody asked me at a time when I really didn't have a single better idea, to tell you the truth. I'd just run out of goals. I was trying to write a novel at the time, and that wasn't going like I wanted it to. I was happy to drop that and come on board. And I haven't regretted it a minute."

"Did you ever finish your novel?"

"Nope. I guess I could if I wanted to. The trouble seemed to me that unless I was Cheever or O'Hara, nobody was going to read what I wrote, even if I finished it, which I couldn't guarantee. This way, though, I have a lot of readers and can still turn my attention to things that matter to me. This is, after I'd earned some respect."

"Well, everything you write seems to have a purpose to show something important. I'm not sure I could do that. I may be too cynical," Catherine says.

"If you're worried about it, you probably aren't. That's what I've found. I worry about it all the time myself. A lot of guys in this business never think about it. And some of those are the mathematical guys. But my thinking is, you can learn how not to be cynical—if you're interested enough. Somebody could teach you what the warning signs are. I could probably teach you myself in no time." Knee throbbing, heart a-pounding: Let me be your teacher.

"What's a typical warning sign?" She grins and flicks her honey hair in a this-oughta-be-good way.

"Well, *not* worrying about it is one. And you already do that.

Another is catching yourself feeling sorry for somebody you're writing about, since the next person you're liable to feel sorry for is you, and then you're in real trouble. If I ever find myself feeling like somebody's life's a tragedy, I'm pretty sure I'm making a big mistake, and I start over right away. And I don't really think I've ever felt stumped or alienated doing things that way. Real writers feel alienated all the time. I've read where they've admitted it."

"Do you think doctors feel alienated?" Catherine looks worried (as well she might). I can't help thinking about Fincher and the dismal, jackass life he must lead. Though it could be worse.

"I don't see how they can avoid some of it, really" is my answer. "They see an awful lot of misery and meanness. You could give medical school an honest try, and then if that doesn't work out you can be pretty sure of a job writing sports. You could probably come right back here, in fact."

She gives me her best eye-twinkling smile, long Beantown teeth catching the light like opals. We're all alone here now. Empty cubicles stretch in empty rows all the way to the empty reception area and the empty elevator banks—a perfect place for love to blossom. We've got things in hand and plenty to share—her admiration for me, my advice about her future, my admiration for her, her respect for my opinion (which may rival even her old man). Forget that I'm twice her age, possibly older. Too much gets made of age in this country. Europeans smirk behind our backs, while looking forward to what good might be between now and death. Catherine Flaherty and I are just two people here, with plenty in common, plenty on our minds and a yen for a real give-and-take.

"You're really *great*," she volunteers. "You're just a real optimist. Like my father. All my worries just seem like little tiny things that'll work out." Her smile says she means every word of it, and I can't wait to start passing more wisdom her way.

"I like to think of myself as pretty much a literalist," I say. "Whatever happens to us is going to be literal when it happens. I just try to arrange things the best way I know how according to my abilities." I glance around behind at my desk as if I'd just remembered and wanted to refer to something important—a phantom copy of *Leaves of Grass* or a thumbed-up Ayn Rand hardback. But there's only my empty yellow legal pad with false starts jotted down like an old grocery list. "Unless you're a real Calvinist, of course, the possibilities really aren't limited one bit," I say, pursing my lips.

"My family's Presbyterian," Catherine Flaherty says, and perfectly mimics my own tight-lipped expression. (I'd have given racetrack odds she was on the Pope's team.)

"That's my bunch, too. But I've let my lines go a little slack. I think that's probably okay, though. My hands are pretty full these days."

"I've got a lot to learn, too. I guess."

And for a long moment sober silence reigns while the lights hum softly above us.

"What've they got you doing around here to soak up experience," I ask expansively. Whatever idea is dawning on me is still below the horizon, and I don't intend to seem calculating, which would send her out of here in a hurry. (I realize at this moment how much I would hate to meet her father, though I assume he's a great guy.)

"Well, I've just done some telephone interviewing, and that's sort of interesting. The retired crew coach at Princeton was a Russian defector in the fifties and smuggled out information about H-bombs during athletic meets. That was all hushed up, I guess, and the government had his job at Princeton all ready for him."

"Sounds good," I say. And it does. A low-grade intrigue, something to get your teeth in.

"But I have a hard time asking good questions." She wrinkles her brow to show genuine concern with her craft. "Mine are too complicated, and no one says much."

"That isn't surprising," I say. "You just have to keep questions simple and remember to ask the same ones over and over again, sometimes in different words. Most athletes are really dying to tell you the whole truth. You just need to get out of their way. That's exactly why a lot of sportswriters get cynical as hell. Their role's a lot smaller than they thought, and that turns them sour. All they've done, though, is learn how to be good at their business."

Catherine Flaherty leans against the aluminum door jamb, eyes gleaming, mouth uncertain, and says exactly nothing at this important moment, merely nods her pretty head. Yes. Yes.

It's all up to me.

The clear moon on this night has posted a smooth silver hump above my dark horizon, and I have only to stand up, put my hands firmly on my chest like St. Stephen and suggest we stroll out into the cool air of Park Avenue, maybe veer over to Second for a sandwich and a beer at someplace I will have to know about (but don't yet), then let the dreamy night take care of itself and us from there on. A couple. Regulation city-dwellers, arm-in-arm under that dog moon, familiars strolling the easy streets, old hands at the new business of romance.

I take a peek at the clock above Eddie Frieder's cubicle, see through his office window, in fact, and out through the bright night at the building across the street. The windows there are yellow with old-fashioned light. A heavy man in a vest stands looking down toward the avenue. Toward what? What is on his mind, I cannot help wondering. A set of alternatives that don't appeal to him? A dilemma that could consume his night in calculating? A future blacker than the night itself? Behind him, someone I cannot see speaks to him or calls his name, and he turns away, raises his hands in a gesture of acceptance and steps from view.

By Eddie Frieder's clock it is the eleventh hour exactly. Easter night. The office is silent and still, but for a far-away computer's hum and for the clock itself, which snakes to its next minute station. There is a sweet smell on the odorless air—the smell of Catherine Flaherty, a smell of full closets, of secret private-school shenanigans, of dark (but not too dark) rendezvous. And for a moment I am stopped from speech and motion, and imagine precisely how she will take on the duty of loving me. It is, of course, a way I know already, cannot help but know, all things considered (that's one subject that does not surprise you once you're an adult). It will be the most semi-serious of ways. Not the way she would love Dartmouth Dan, nor the way she will love the lucky man she is likely to marry—some wide-eyed Columbia grad with a family law practice all in place. But something in the middle of those, a way that means to say: This is pretty serious, though only for experience sake; I'd be the most surprised little girl in Boston if this turns out to be important at all; it'll be interesting, you bet, and I'll look back on it someday and feel sure I did the right thing and all, but not be sure exactly why I think so; full steam ahead.

And what's my attitude? At some point nothing else really matters *but* your attitude—your hopes, your risks, your sacrifices, your potential islands of regret and reward—as you enter what is no more than rote experience upon the earth.

Mine, I'm happy to say, is the best possible.

"Well, hey," I say in a stirring voice, hands upon my breast. "What say we get out of here and take a walk? I haven't eaten since lunch, and I could pretty much eat a lug wrench right now. I'll buy you a sandwich."

Catherine Flaherty bites a piece of her lip as she smiles a smile even bigger than mine and colors flower in her tulip cheeks. This is a pretty good idea, she means to say, full of sentiment. (Though she is already nodding a business woman's agreement before she speaks.) "Sounds really *great*." She flips her hair in a definitive way. "I guess I'm pretty hungry too. Just let me get my coat, and we'll go for it."

"It's a deal," I say.

I hear her feet slip-skip down the carpeted corridor, hear the door to the ladies' sigh open, sigh back, bump shut (always the practical girl). And there is no nicer time on earth than now—everything in the offing, nothing gone wrong, all potential—the very polar opposite of how I felt driving home the other night, when everything was on the skids and nothing within a thousand kilometers worth anticipating. This is really all life is worth, when you come down to it.

The light across the street is off now. Though as I stand watching (my bum knee good as new), waiting for this irresistible, sentimental girl's return, I can't be certain that the man I saw there—the heavy man in his vest and tie, surprised by the sudden sound of a voice and his own name, a sound he didn't expect—I can't be certain he's not there still, looking out over the night streets of a friendly town, alone. And I step closer to the glass and try to find him through the dark, stare hard, hoping for even an illusion of a face, of someone there watching me here. Far below I can sense the sound of cars and life in motion. Behind me I hear the door sigh closed again and footsteps coming. And I sense that it's not possible to see there anymore, though my guess is no one's watching me. No one's noticed me standing here at all.

THE END

LIFE WILL ALWAYS be without a natural, convincing closure. Except one.

Walter was buried in Coshocton, Ohio, on the very day I sounded the horns of my thirty-ninth birthday. I didn't go to his funeral, though I almost did. (Carter Knott went.) In spite of everything, I could not feel that I had a place there. For a day or two he was kept over in Mangum & Gayden's on Winthrop Street, where Ralph was four years ago, and then was driven back to the midwest by long-haul truck. It turns out it wasn't his sister I saw on the train platform in Haddam that night, but some other woman. Walter's sister, Joyce Ellen, is a heavy-set, bespectacled, YWCA-type who has never married and wears mannish suits and ties, is as nice a person as you will ever meet, and has never read Teddy Roosevelt's *Life*. She and I had a long, friendly visit at a coffee shop in New York, where we talked about the letter Walter had left and about Walter in general. Joyce said he was a kind of enigma to her and her entire family, and that he hadn't been in close touch with them for some time. Only in the last week of his life, she said, Walter had called up several times to talk about hunting and the possibility of moving back there and setting up a business and even about me, whom he described as his best friend. Joyce said she thought there was something very strange about her brother, and she wasn't all that surprised when the call came in. "You can feel these things coming," she said (though I do not agree). She said she hoped Yolanda wouldn't come to the funeral, and I have a suspicion she got her wish.

Walter's death, I suppose you could say, has had the effect on me that death means to have; of reminding me of my responsibility to a somewhat larger world. Though it came at a time when I didn't much want to think about that, and I still don't find it easy to accommodate and am not completely sure what I can do differently. Walter's story about a daughter born out of wedlock and grown up now in Florida was, it turns out, not true, but simply a gentle joke. He knew, I think, that I would never run the risk of letting him down, and he was right. I flew to Sarasota, did a good bit of sleuthing, including some calls about birth records in Coshocton. I called Joyce Ellen, even hired a detective who cost me a good bit of money but turned up nothing and no one. And I've decided that the whole goose chase was just his one last attempt at withholding full disclosure. A novelistic red herring. And I admire Walter for it, since for me such a gesture has the feel of secrecies, a quality Walter's own life lacked, though he tried for it. I think that Walter might've even figured out something important before he turned the television on for the last time, though I wouldn't want to try to speak for him. But you can easily believe that some private questions get answered—just in the nature of things—as you anticipate the hammer falling.

Coming to Florida has had a good effect on me, and I have stayed on these few months—it is now September—though I don't think I will stay forever. Coming to the bottom of the country provokes a nice sensation, a tropical certainty that something will happen to you here. The whole place seems alive with modest hopes. People in Florida, I've discovered, are here to get away from things, to seek no end of life, and there is a crispness and a rightness to most everyone I meet that I find likable. No one is trying to rook anybody else, as my mother used to say, and contrary to all reports. Many people are here from Michigan, the blue plates on their cars and pickups much in evidence. It is not like New Jersey, but it is not bad.

The time since last April has gone by fast, in an almost technicolor-telescopic way—much faster than I'm used to having it go—which may be Florida's great virtue, instead of the warm weather: time goes by fast in a perfectly timeless way. Not a bit like Gotham, where you seem to feel every second you are alive, but somehow miss everything else.

With my bank savings, I have leased a sporty, sea-green Datsun on a closed-end basis and left my car and my house in Bosobolo's care. This has allowed him—as he explained in a letter—to bring his wife over from Gabon and to live a real married life in America. I don't know the fate of the dumpy white girl. Possibly he has put her aside, though possibly not. And neither do I know what my neighbors think of this new arrangement—seeing

Bosobolo out in the yard, surveying the spirea and the hemlocks, stretching his long arms and yawning like a lord.

I have a furnished adults-only condo out on a pleasant enough beachy place called Longboat Key, and have taken a leave of indefinite absence from the magazine. And for these few months I've lived a life of agreeable miscellany. At night someone will often put on some Big Band or reggae records, and men and women will gather around the pool and mix up some drinks and dance and chitter-chat. There are, naturally, plenty of girls in bathing suits and sundresses, and once in a while one of them consents to spend a night with me, then drifts away the next day back to whatever interested her before: a job, another man, travel. A few agreeable homosexuals live here, as well as an abundance of retired Navy men—midwestern guys in most cases, some of them my age—with a lot of time and energy on their hands and not enough to do. The Navy men have stories about Vietnam and Korea that all together would make a good book. And one or two have asked me about writing their life stories once they learned I write for a living. Though when all that begins to bore me, or when I don't feel up to it, I take a walk out to the water which is just beyond the retaining wall and hike a while in the late daylight, when the sky is truly high and white, and watch the horizon go dark toward Cuba, and the last tourist plane of the day angle up toward who knows where. I like the flat plexus of the Gulf, and the sensation that there is a vast, troubling landscape underwater all lost, with only the definite land remaining, a sad and flat and melancholy prairie that can be lonely but in an appealing way. I've even driven up to the Sunshine Skyway, where I have thought of Ida Simms, and of the night Walter and I talked about her and of how much she meant to him. I have wondered if she ever woke up there or in the Seychelles or some such place and went home to her family. Probably not.

I realize I have told all this because unbeknownst to me, on that Thursday those months ago, I awoke with a feeling, a stirring, that any number of things were going to change and be settled and come to an end soon, and I might have something to tell that would be important and even interesting. And now I am at the point of not knowing the outcome of things once again, a frame of mind that pleases me. I sense that I have faced up to a great empty moment in life but without suffering the usual terrible regret—which is, after all, the way I began to describe this.

Some days I drive over in my Datsun and roam around the Grapefruit League parks, where not a lot is going on now. The Tigers have clinched at least a magic number, and seem to me unstoppable. Around the player complex there is a strange, anxious merriment. A few prospects are beginning in the fall instructional leagues, Latin boys plus a few older players on their way down the ladder, some of whom I even know from years ago. Hanging around on their own, they're hoping to motivate some kid to hit or shake a bad attitude and to impress someone as being a good coach or a scout, maybe with a farm club out in Iowa, and in that way live a life of their choosing. It is a poignant life here, and play is haphazard at best, listless in its pleasures, and everyone waits for victory. A good human-interest article could be worked up from this small world. An old catcher actually came up to me and confessed he had diabetes and was going blind, and thought it might make a good story for younger readers. But I'll never write it, just as I never properly wrote about Herb Wallagher and had to accept defeat there. Some life is only life, and unconjugatable, just as to some questions there are no answers. Just nothing to say. I have passed the catcher's story and my thoughts on to Catherine Flaherty, in the event her current plans do not work out.

Things occur to me differently now, just as they might to a character at the end of a good short story. I have different words for what I see and anticipate, even different sorts of thoughts and reactions; more mature ones, ones that seem to really count. If I could write a short story, I would. But I don't believe I could, and do not plan to try, which doesn't worry me. It seems enough to go out to the park like a good Michigander, get the sun on my face while somewhere nearby I hear the hiss and pop of ball on glove leather. That may be a sportwriter's dreamlife. Sometimes I even feel like the man Wade told me about whose life disappeared in the landslide.

Though it's not true that my old life has been swept away entirely. Since coming here the surprise is that I have had the chance to touch base with honest-to-goodness relatives, some cousins of my father's who wrote me in Gotham through Irv Ornstein (my mother's stepson) to say that a Great-Uncle Eulice had died in California, and that they would like to see me if I was ever in Florida. Of course, I didn't know them and doubt I had ever heard their names. But I'm glad that I have now, as they are genuine salt of the earth, and I am better that they wrote, and that I have taken the time to get to know them.

Buster Bascombe is a retired railroad brakeman with a serious heart problem that could take him any hour of the day or night. And Empress, his wife, is a pixyish little right-winger who reads books like *Masters of Deceit* and believes we need to re-establish the gold standard, quit paying our taxes, abandon Yalta and the UN, and who smokes Camels a mile a minute and sells a little real estate on the side (though she is not as bad as those people often seem). Both of them are ex-alcoholics, and still manage to believe in most of the principles I do. Their house is a big yellow stucco bungalow outside Nokomis, on the Tamiami Trail, and I've driven down at least four times and had steak dinners with them and their grown children—Eddie, Claire Boothe, and (to my surprise) Ralph.

These Florida Bascombes are, to my mind, a grand family of a modern sort who trust that the world has some important things still in it, and who believe life has given them more than they ever expected or deserved of it, not excepting that young Eddie at the present time is out of work. I'm proud to be the novelty member of their family.

Buster is a big humid-eyed, pale-skinned jolly man who sees a palmist about his heart trouble and enjoys taking strangers like me into his confidence. "Your daddy was a clever man, now don't you think he wasn't," he has told me on his screened back porch after dinner, in the sweet aroma of grapefruit groves and azaleas. I hardly remember my father, and so it is all news to me, news even that *anyone* knew him. "He had a way of seeing the future like no one else," Buster says and grins. He'd never met my mother. And my admission that I hardly remember anyone from back then doesn't faze him. It is merely a regrettable mistake of fate he is willing to try to correct for me, even though I have no interesting confidences to return. And truthfully, when I drive back up Highway 24 just as the light is falling beyond my condo, behind its wide avenue of date palms and lampposts, I am usually (if only momentarily) glad to have a past, even an imputed and remote one. There is something to that. It is not a burden, though I've always thought of it as one. I cannot say that we all need a past in full literary fashion, or that one is much useful in the end. But a small one doesn't hurt, especially if you're already in a life of your own choosing. "You choose your friends," Empress said to me when I first arrived, "but where your family is concerned you don't choose."

FINALLY, WHAT is left to say? It is not a very complicated business, I don't think.

My heart still beats, though not, in truth, exactly as it did before.

My voice is as strong and plausible as I can ever remember it, and has not gone soft on me since that Easter day in Barnegat Pines.

I have stayed in close touch with Catherine Flaherty, and after the two days we spent together in her untidy little flat on East 5th Street, we saw a good deal of one another until I picked up and came down here. She is a wonderful, curious-minded, tendentious girl, ironic in the precise ways I half-suspected, and serious things continue to be mentioned between us. She has started med school at Dartmouth, and plans to fly here for Thanksgiving if I'm still here, though there's no reason to think I will be. It turns out there is no Dartmouth Dan, which should be a lesson to all of us: the best girls oftentimes go unchosen, probably precisely because they are the best. It is enough for me to realize this, and for us to act like two college kids, talking on the phone until late at night, planning holiday visits, secretly hoping never to see each other again. I doubt ours is a true romance. I am too old for her; she is too smart for me. (I would never have the nerve to meet her father, whose name is "Punch" Flaherty, and who is planning a run for Congress.) Though as a postscript, I'll admit I have been wrong altogether about her attitudes toward love and lovemaking, and have also been pleased to find out she is a modern enough girl not to think that I can make things better for her one way or another, even though I wish I could.

From Vicki Arcenault I have not heard so much as a word, and I wouldn't be surprised to learn that she has moved to Alaska and reconciled with her first husband and new love, skin-head

Everett, and that they have become New-Agers together, sitting in hot tubs discussing their goals and diets, taking on a cold world with *Consumer Reports*, assured of who they are and what they want. The world will be hers, not mine. I could've postponed her development, but only for a while, and we'd surely have ended in bitter divorce. My guess is, and it's not a happy one, that she will one day discover she doesn't like men and never did (just as she said), her father included, and will carry a banner in public with those very words written on it. That is the way with things: expectations reversed in matters of the heart; love, a victim of chance and fate; the thing we say we'll never do is the very thing, after all, we want to do most.

I believe now she told me a lie about Fincher Barksdale and my former wife, though it was finally not a hurtful lie. Maybe she's embarrassed about it all. But she had purposes of her own to serve, and if I was not going to confide in her (and I wasn't) there was no reason for her to confide in me. I wasn't harmed more than a sore jaw can harm you, and I hold no bad feelings. Sailor-Vee, as she herself often said.

I have finally resigned from the Divorced Men's Club. Though after Walter's death it really seemed to me there was not much enthusiasm left. It did not seem to serve its purpose very well, and the other men, I think, will eventually just go back to being friends in the old-fashioned ways.

Regarding my children, they are planning a visit, though they have planned to come all summer long, and it could be their mother suspects I'm leading an unsavory bachelor's life here and will not send them. Somehow something always seems to come up. They were disappointed not to take our trip around Lake Erie, but there will be other times while they are still young.

X's mother, Irma, has moved back to Michigan with Henry. Together again after twenty years. They are afraid, I'm sure, of dying alone. Unlike me, they can feel time flying. In her last letter Irma said, "I read in the *Free Press*, Franky, *many* prominent people—except for one woman broadcaster—read the sports sometime early each day. I think that's encouraging. Don't you?" (I do.) "I think you should pay closer attention."

Regarding X herself, I can only say, who knows? She does not think I'm a terrible man, which is more than most marriages have to go on into the future. She has lately begun competing on the mideast club pro tour, challenging other groups of women in Pennsylvania and Delaware. She told me on the phone that lately she's played the best golf of her life, putts with supreme confidence, and has a deft command over her long irons—skills she isn't even sure she would have if she'd played competitively all these years. She also said there are parts of her life she would take back, though she wasn't specific about which ones. I am afraid she has become more introspective now, which is not always a hopeful sign. She talked about moving, but did not say where. She said she would not get married. She said she might take flying lessons. Nothing would surprise me. Just before she hung up the last time she asked me why I hadn't consoled her on the night our house was broken into, those years ago, and I told her that it all seemed at once so idiotic and yet so inexplicable that I simply had not known what I could say, but that I was sorry, and that it was a failure on my part. (I didn't have a heart to say I'd spoken, but she hadn't heard me.)

As I've said, life has only one certain closure. It is possible to love someone, and no one else, and still not live with that one person or even see her. Anything or anyone who says different is a liar or a sentimentalist or worse. It is possible to be married, to divorce, then to come back together with a whole new set of understandings that you'd never have liked or even understood before in your earlier life, but that to your surprise now seems absolutely perfect. The only truth that can never be a lie, let me tell you, is life itself—the thing that happens.

Will I ever live in Haddam, New Jersey, again? I haven't the slightest idea.

Will I be a sportswriter again and do those things I did and loved doing when I did them? Ditto.

I read in the *St. Petersburg Times* a week ago that a boy had died in De Tocqueville Academy, the son of a famous astronaut, which is why it made the news, though he died quietly. Of course it made me think of Ralph, my son, who did not die quietly at all, but howling mad, with a voice all his own, full of crazy curses and outrage and even jokes. And I realized that my own mourning for him is finally over—even as the astronaut's is just beginning. Grief, real grief, is relatively short, though mourning can be long.

I walked out of the condos onto the flat lithesome beach this morning, and took a walk in my swimming trunks and no shirt on. And I thought that one natural effect of life is to cover you in a thin layer of . . . what? A film? A residue or skin of all the things you've done and been and said and erred at? I'm not sure. But you *are* under it, and for a long time, and only rarely do you know it, except that for some unexpected reason or opportunity you come out—for an hour or even for a moment—and you suddenly feel pretty good. And in that magical instant you realize how long it's been since you felt just that way. Have you been ill, you ask. Is life itself an illness or a syndrome? Who knows? We've all felt that way, I'm confident, since there's no way that I could feel what hundreds of millions of other citizens haven't.

Only suddenly, then, you are out of it—that film, that skin of life—as when you were a kid. And you think: this must've been the way it was *once in my life*, though you didn't know it then, and don't really even remember it—a feeling of wind on your cheeks and your arms, of being released, let loose, of being the light-floater. And since that is not how it has been for a long time, you want, this time, to make it last, this glistening one moment, this cool air, this new living, so that you can preserve a feeling of it, inasmuch as when it comes again it may just be too late. You may just be too old. And in truth, of course, this may be the last time that you will ever feel this way again.

INDEPENDENCE DAY

Kristina

IN HADDAM, summer floats over tree-softened streets like a sweet lotion balm from a careless, languorous god, and the world falls in tune with its own mysterious anthems. Shaded lawns lie still and damp in the early a.m. Outside, on peaceful-morning Cleveland Street, I hear the footfalls of a lone jogger, tramping past and down the hill toward Taft Lane and across to the Choir College, there to run in the damp grass. In the Negro trace, men sit on stoops, pants legs rolled above their sock tops, sipping coffee in the growing, easeful heat. The marriage enrichment class (4 to 6) has let out at the high school, its members sleepy-eyed and dazed, bound for bed again. While on the green grid-iron pallet our varsity band begins its two-a-day drills, revving up for the 4th: "Boom-Haddam, boom-Haddam, boom-boom-ba-boom. Haddam-Haddam, up'n-at-'em! Boom-boom-ba-boom!"

Elsewhere up the seaboard the sky, I know, reads hazy. The heat closes in, a metal smell clocks through the nostrils. Already the first clouds of a summer T-storm lurk on the mountain horizons, and it's hotter where *they* live than where we live. Far out on the main line the breeze is right to hear the Amtrak, "The Merchants' special," hurtle past for Philly. And along on the same breeze, a sea-salt smell floats in from miles and miles away, mingling with shadowy rhododendron aromas and the last of the summer's staunch azaleas.

Though back on my street, the first shaded block of Cleveland, sweet silence reigns. A block away, someone patiently bounces a driveway ball: squeak ... then breathing ... then a laugh, a cough ... "All *riiight*, that's the *waaay*." None of it too loud. In front of the Zumbros', two doors down, the streets crew is finishing a quiet smoke before cranking their machines and unsettling the dust again. We're repaving this summer, putting in a new "line," resodding the neutral ground, setting new curbs, using our proud new tax dollars—the workers all Cape

Verdeans and wily Hondurans from poorer towns north of here. Sergeantsville and Little York. They sit and stare silently beside their yellow front-loaders, ground flatteners and backhoes, their sleek private cars—Camaros and Chevy low-riders—parked around the corner, away from the dust and where it will be shady later on.

And suddenly the carillon at St. Leo the Great begins: gong, gong, gong, gong, gong, gong, then a sweet, bright admonitory matinal air by old Wesley himself: "Wake the day, ye who would be saved, wake the day, let your souls be laved."

THOUGH ALL is not exactly kosher here, in spite of a good beginning. (When is anything *exactly* kosher?)

I myself, Frank Bascombe, was mugged on Coolidge Street, one street over, late in April, spiritedly legging it home from a closing at our realty office just at dusk, a sense of achievement lightening my step, still hoping to catch the evening news, a bottle of Roederer—a gift from a grateful seller I'd made a bundle for—under my arm. Three young boys, one of whom I thought I'd seen before—an Asian—yet couldn't later name, came careering ziggy-zaggy down the sidewalk on minibikes, conked me in the head with a giant Pepsi bottle, and rode off howling. Nothing was stolen or broken, though I was knocked silly on the ground, and sat in the grass for ten minutes, unnoticed in a whirling daze.

Later, in early May, the Zumbros' house and one other were burgled twice in the same week (they missed some things the first time and came back to get them).

And then, to all our bewilderment, Clair Devane, our one black agent, a woman I was briefly but intensely "linked with" two years ago, was murdered in May inside a condo she was showing out the Great Woods Road, near Hightstown: roped and tied, raped and stabbed. No good clues left—just a pink while-you-were-out slip lying in the parquet entry, the message in her own looping hand: "Luther family. Just started looking. Mid-90's. 3 p.m. Get key. Dinner with Eddie." Eddie was her fiancé.

Plus, falling property values now ride through the trees like an odorless, colorless mist settling through the still air where all breathe it in, all sense it, though our new amenities—the new police cruisers, the new crosswalks, the trimmed tree branches, the buried electric, the refurbished band shell, the plans for the 4th of July parade—do what they civically can to ease our minds off worrying, convince us our worries aren't worries, or at least not ours alone but everyone's—no one's—and that staying the course, holding the line, riding the cyclical nature of things are what this country's all about, and thinking otherwise is to drive optimism into retreat, to be paranoid and in need of expensive "treatment" out-of-state.

And practically speaking, while bearing in mind that one event rarely causes another in a simple way, it must mean *something* to a town, to the local *esprit*, for its values on the open market to fall. (Why else would real estate prices be an index to the national well-being?) If, for instance, some otherwise healthy charcoal briquette firm's stock took a nosedive, the *company* would react ASAP. Its "people" would stay at their desks an extra hour past dark (unless they were fired outright); men would go home more dog-tired than usual, carrying no flowers, would stand longer in the violet evening hours staring up at the tree limbs in need of trimming, would talk less kindly to their kids, would opt for an extra Pimm's before dinner alone with the wife, then wake oddly at four with nothing much, but nothing good, in mind. Just restless.

And so it is in Haddam, where all around, our summer swoon notwithstanding, there's a new sense of a wild world being just beyond our perimeter, an untallied apprehension among our residents, one I believe they'll never get used to, one they'll die before accommodating.

A sad fact, of course, about adult life is that you see the very things you'll never adapt to coming toward you on the horizon. You see them as the problems they are, you worry like hell about them, you make provisions, take precautions, fashion adjustments; you tell yourself you'll have to change your way of doing things. Only you don't. You can't. Somehow it's already too late. And maybe it's even worse than that: maybe the thing you see coming from far away is not the real thing, the thing that scares you, but its aftermath. And what you've feared will happen has already taken place. This is similar in spirit to the realization that all the great new advances of medical science will have no benefit for us at all, though we cheer them on, hope a vaccine might be ready in time, think things could still get better. Only it's too late there too. And in that very way our life gets over before we know it. We miss it. And like the poet said: "The ways we miss our lives are life."

THIS MORNING I am up early, in my upstairs office under the eaves, going over a listing logged in as an "Exclusive" just at closing last night, and for which I may already have willing buyers later today. Listings frequently appear in this unexpected, providential way: An owner belts back a few Manhattans, takes an afternoon trip around the yard to police up bits of paper blown from the neighbors' garbage, rakes the last of the winter's damp, fecund leaves from under the forsythia beneath which lies buried his old Dalmatian, Pepper, makes a close inspection of the hemlocks he and his wife planted as a hedge when they were young marrieds long ago, takes a nostalgic walk back through rooms he's painted, baths grouted far past midnight, along the way has two more stiff ones followed hard by a sudden great welling and suppressed heart's cry for a long-lost life we must all (if we care to go on living) let go of . . . And boom: in two minutes more he's on the phone, interrupting some realtor from a quiet dinner at home, and in ten more minutes the whole deed's done. It's progress of a sort. (By lucky coincidence, my clients the Joe Markhams will have driven down from Vermont this very night, and conceivably I could complete the circuit—listing to sale— in a single day's time. The record, not mine, is four minutes.)

My other duty this early morning involves writing the editorial for our firm's monthly "Buyer vs. Seller" guide (sent free to every breathing freeholder on the Haddam tax rolls). This month I'm fine-tuning my thoughts on the likely real estate fallout from the approaching Democratic Convention, when the uninspirational Governor Dukakis, spirit-genius of the sinister Massachusetts Miracle, will grab the prize, then roll on to victory in November—my personal hope, but a prospect that paralyzes most Haddam property owners with fear, since they're almost all Republicans, love Reagan like Catholics love the Pope, yet also feel dumbfounded and double-crossed by the clownish spectacle of Vice President Bush as their new leader. My arguing tack departs from Emerson's famous line in *Self-Reliance*, "To be great is to be misunderstood," which I've rigged into a thesis that claims Governor Dukakis has in mind more "pure pocketbook issues" than most voters think; that economic insecurity is a plus for the Democrats; and that interest rates, on the skids all year, will hit 11 percent by New Year's no matter if William Jennings Bryan is elected President and the silver standard reinstituted. (These sentiments also scare Republicans to death.) "So what the hell," is the essence of my clincher, "things could get worse in a hurry. Now's the time to test the realty waters. Sell! (or Buy)."

IN THESE summery days my own life, at least frontally, is simplicity's model. I live happily if slightly bemusedly in a forty-four-year-old bachelor's way in my former wife's house at 116 Cleveland, in the "Presidents Streets" section of Haddam, New Jersey, where I'm employed as a Realtor Associate by the Lauren-Schwindell firm on Seminary Street. I should say, perhaps, the house formerly owned by formerly my wife, Ann Dykstra, now Mrs. Charley O'Dell of 86 Swallow Lane, Deep River, CT. Both my children live there too, though I'm not certain how happy they are or even should be.

The configuration of life events that led me to this profession and to this very house could, I suppose, seem unusual if your model for human continuance is some *Middletown* white paper from early in the century and geared to Indiana, or an "ideal American family life" profile as promoted by some right-wing think-tank—several of whose directors live here in Haddam—but that are just propaganda for a mode of life no one could live without access to the very impulse-suppressing, nostalgia-provoking drugs they don't want you to have (though I'm sure *they* have them by the tractor-trailer loads). But to anyone reasonable, my life will seem more or less normal-under-the-microscope, full of contingencies and incongruities none of us escapes and which do little harm in an existence that otherwise goes unnoticed.

This morning, however, I'm setting off on a weekend trip with my only son, which promises, unlike most of my seekings, to be starred by weighty life events. There is, in fact, an odd feeling of *lasts* to this excursion, as if some signal period in life—mine *and* his—is coming, if not to a full close, then at least toward some tightening, transforming twist in the kaleidoscope, a change I'd be foolish to take lightly and don't. (The impulse to read *Self-Reliance* is significant here, as is the holiday itself—my favorite secular one for being public and for its implicit goal of leaving us only as it found us: free.) All of this comes—in surfeit—near the anniversary of my divorce, a time when I routinely feel broody and insubstantial, and spend days puzzling over that summer seven years ago, when life swerved badly and I, somehow at a loss, failed to right its course.

Yet prior to all that I'm off this afternoon, south to South Mantoloking, on the Jersey Shore, for my usual Friday evening rendezvous with my lady friend (there aren't any politer or better words, finally), blond, tall and leggy Sally Caldwell. Though even here trouble may be brewing.

For ten months now, Sally and I have carried on what's seemed to me a perfect "your place and mine" romance, affording each other generous portions of companionship, confidence (on an as-needed basis), within-reason reliability and plenty of spicy, untranscendent transport—all with ample "space" allotted and the complete presumption of laissez-faire (which I don't have much use for), while remaining fully respectful of the high-priced lessons and vividly cataloged mistakes of adulthood.

Not love, it's true. Not exactly. But closer to love than the puny goods most married folks dole out.

And yet in the last weeks, for reasons I can't explain, what I can only call a strange *awkwardness* has been aroused in each of us, extending all the way to our usually stirring lovemaking and even to the frequency of our visits; as if the hold we keep on the other's attentions and affections is changing and loosening, and it's now our business to form a new grip, for a longer, more serious attachment—only neither of us has yet proved quite able, and we are perplexed by the failure.

Last night, sometime after midnight, when I'd already slept for an hour, waked up twice twisting my pillow and fretting about Paul's and my journey, downed a glass of milk, watched the Weather Channel, then settled back to read a chapter of *The Declaration of Independence*—Carl Becker's classic, which, along with *Self-Reliance*, I plan to use as key "texts" for communicating with my troubled son and thereby transmitting to him important info—Sally called. (These volumes by the way

aren't a bit grinding, stuffy or boring, the way they seemed in
school, but are brimming with useful, insightful lessons applicable directly or metaphorically to the ropy dilemmas of life.)

"Hi, hi. What's new?" she said, a tone of uneasy restraint in
her usually silky voice, as if midnight calls were not our regular
practice, which they aren't.

"I was just reading Carl Becker, who's terrific," I said, though
on alert. "He thought that the whole Declaration of Independence was an attempt to prove rebellion was the wrong word for
what the founding fathers were up to. It was a war over a word
choice. That's pretty amazing."

She sighed. "What was the right word?"

"Oh. Common sense. Nature. Progress. God's will. Karma.
Nirvana. It pretty much all meant the same thing to Jefferson and
Adams and those guys. They were smarter than we are."

"I thought it was more important than that," she said. Then
she said, "Life seems congested to me. Just suddenly tonight.
Does it to you?" I was aware coded messages were being sent,
but I had no idea how to translate them. Possibly, I thought,
this was an opening gambit to an announcement that she never
wanted to see me again—which has happened. ("Congested"
being used in its secondary meaning as: "unbearable.") "Something's crying out to be noticed, I just don't know what it is,"
she said. "But it must have to do with you and I. Don't you
agree?"

"Well. Maybe," I said. "I don't know." I was propped up by
my bed lamp, under my favorite framed map of Block Island,
the musty old annotated Becker on my chest, the window fan
(I've opted for no air-conditioning) drawing cool, sweet suburban midnight onto my bedcovers. Nothing I could think of
was missing right then, besides sleep.

"I just feel things are congested and I'm missing something,"
Sally said again. "Are you sure you don't feel that way?"

"You have to miss some things to have others." This was an
idiotic answer. I felt I might possibly be asleep but tomorrow
still have a hard time convincing myself this conversation hadn't
happened—which is also not that infrequent with me.

"I had a dream tonight," Sally said. "We were in your house
in Haddam, and you kept neatening everything up. I was your
wife somehow, but I felt terrible anxiety. There was blue water

in our toilet bowl, and at some point you and I shook hands, standing on your front steps—just like you'd sold me your own house. And then I saw you shooting away out across the middle of a big cornfield with your arms stretched out like Christ or something, just like back in Illinois." Where she's from, the stolid, Christian corn belt. "It was peaceful in a way. But the whole effect was that everything was very, very busy and hectic and no one could get anything done right. And I felt this anxiety right in my dream. Then I woke up and I wanted to call you."

"I'm glad you did," I said. "It doesn't sound like anything that bad, though. You weren't being chased by wild animals who looked like me, or getting pushed out of airplanes."

"No," she said, and seemed to consider those fates. Far away in the night I could hear a train. "Except I felt so anxious. It was very vivid. I don't usually have vivid dreams."

"I try to forget my dreams."

"I know. You're very proud of it."

"No I'm not. But they don't ever seem mysterious enough. I'd remember them if they seemed very interesting. Tonight I dreamed I was reading, and I *was* reading."

"You don't seem too engaged. Maybe now isn't a good time to talk seriously." She sounded embarrassed, as if I was making fun of her, which I wasn't.

"I'm glad to hear your voice, though," I said, thinking she was right. It was the middle of the night. Little good begins then.

"I'm sorry I got you up."

"You didn't get me up." At this point, though, and unbeknownst to her, I turned out my light and lay breathing, listening to the train in the cool dark. "You just want something you're not getting, is my guess. It's not unusual." In Sally's case, it could be any one of a number of things.

"Don't you ever feel that way?"

"No. I feel like I have a lot as it is. I have you."

"That's very nice," she said, not so warmly.

"It *is* nice."

"I guess I'll be seeing you tomorrow, won't I?"

"You bet. I'll be there with bells on."

"Great," she said. "Sleep tight. Don't dream."

"I will. I won't." And I put the phone down.

It would be untruthful to pretend that what Sally was wrestling with last night was some want or absence I didn't feel myself. And perhaps I'm simply a poor bet for her or anybody, since I so like the tintinnabulation of early romance yet lack the urge to do more than ignore it when that sweet sonority threatens to develop into something else. A successful practice of my middle life, a time I think of as the Existence Period, has been to ignore much of what I don't like or that seems worrisome and embroiling, and then usually see it go away. But I'm as aware of "things" as Sally is, and imagine this may be the first signal (or possibly it's the thirty-seventh) that we might soon no longer "see" each other. And I feel regret, would like to find a way of reviving things. Only, as per my practice, I'm willing to let matters go as they go and see what happens. Perhaps they'll even get better. It's as possible as not.

THE MATTER of greater magnitude and utmost importance, though, involves my son, Paul Bascombe, who is fifteen. Two and a half months ago, just after tax time and six weeks before his school year ended in Deep River, he was arrested for shoplifting three boxes of 4X condoms ("Magnums") from a display-dispenser in the Finast down in Essex. His acts were surveilled by an "eye in the sky" camera hidden above the male hygiene products. And when a tiny though uniformed Vietnamese security person (a female) approached him just beyond the checkout, where as a diversionary tactic he'd bought a bottle of Grecian Formula, he bolted but was wrestled to the ground, whereupon he screamed that the woman was "a goddamned spick asshole," kicked her in the thigh, hit her in the mouth (conceivably by accident) and pulled out a fair amount of hair before she could apply a police stranglehold and with the help of a pharmacist and another customer get the cuffs on him. (His mother had him out in an hour.)

The security guard naturally enough has pressed criminal charges of assault and battery, as well as for the violation of some of her civil rights, and there have even been "hate crime" and "making an example" rumblings out of the Essex juvenile authorities. (I consider this only as election-year bluster plus community rivalry.)

Meanwhile, Paul has been through myriad pretrial interviews, plus hours of tangled psychological evaluations of his personality, attitudes and mental state—two of which sessions I attended, found unremarkable but fair, though I have not yet seen the results. For these proceedings he has had not a lawyer but an "ombudsman," who's a social worker trained in legal matters, and who his mother has talked to but I haven't. His first actual court date is to be this Tuesday morning, the day after the 4th of July.

Paul for his part has admitted everything yet has told me he feels not very guilty, that the woman rushed him from behind and scared the shit out of him so that he thought he might be being murdered and needed to defend himself; that he shouldn't have said what he said, that it was a mistake, but he's promised he has nothing against any other races or genders and in fact feels "betrayed" himself—by what, he hasn't said. He's claimed to have had no specific use in mind for the condoms (a relief if true) and probably would've used them only in a practical joke against Charley O'Dell, his mother's husband, whom he, along with his father, dislikes.

For a brief time I thought of taking a leave from the realty office, sub-letting a condo somewhere down the road from Deep River and keeping in touch with Paul on a daily basis. But his mother disapproved. She didn't want me around, and said so. She also believed that unless things got worse, life should remain as "normal" as possible until his hearing. She and I have continued to talk it over every bit—Haddam to Deep River—and she is of the belief that all this will pass, that he is simply going through a phase and doesn't, in fact, have a syndrome or a mania, as someone might think. (It is her Michigan stoicism that allows her to equate endurance with progress.) But as a result, I've seen less of him than I'd like in the last two months, though I have now proposed bringing him down to Haddam to live with me in the fall, which Ann has so far been leery of.

She has, however—because she isn't crazy—hauled him to New Haven to be "privately evaluated" by a fancy shrink, an experience Paul claims he enjoyed and lied through like a pirate. Ann even went so far as to send him for twelve days in mid-May to an expensive health camp in the Berkshires, Camp Wanapi (called "Camp Unhappy" by the inmates), where he was judged to be "too inactive" and therefore encouraged to wear mime makeup and spend part of every day sitting in an invisible chair with an invisible pane of glass in front of him, smiling and looking surprised and grimacing at passersby. (This was, of course, also videotaped.) The camp counselors, who were all secretly "milieu therapists" in mufti—loose white tee-shirts, baggy khaki shorts, muscle-bound calves, dog whistles, lanyards, clipboards, preternaturally geared up for unstructured heart-to-hearts— expressed the opinion that Paul was intellectually beyond his years (language and reasoning skills off the Stanford charts) but was emotionally underdeveloped (closer to age twelve), which in their view posed "a problem." So that even though he acts and talks like a shrewd sophomore in the honors program at Beloit, full of sly jokes and double entendres (he has also recently shot up to 5'8", with a new layer of quaky pudge all over), his feelings still get hurt in the manner of a child who knows much less about the world than a Girl Scout.

Since Camp Unhappy, he has also begun exhibiting an unusual number of unusual symptoms: he has complained about an inability to yawn and sneeze properly; he has remarked about a mysterious "tingling" at the end of his penis; he has complained about not liking how his teeth "line up." And he has from time to time made unexpected barking noises—leering like a Cheshire, afterwards—and for several days made soft but audible *eeeck-eeecking* sounds by drawing breath back down his throat with his mouth closed, usually with a look of dismay on his face. His mother has tried to talk to him about this, has re-consulted the shrink (who's advised many more sessions), and has even gotten Charley to "step in." Paul at first claimed he couldn't imagine what anybody was talking about, that all seemed normal to him, then later he said that making noises satisfied a legitimate inner urge and didn't bother others, and that they should get over their problems with it, and him.

In these charged months I have tried, in essence, to increase my own ombudsman's involvement, conducting early-morning phone conversations with him (one of which I'm awaiting hopefully this morning) and taking him and now and then his sister, Clarissa, on fishing trips to the Red Man Club, an exclusive anglers' hideaway I joined for this very purpose. I have also taken him once to Atlantic City on a boys-only junket to see Mel Tormé at TropWorld, and twice to Sally's seashore house, there to be idle-hours bums, swimming in the ocean when syringes and solid human waste weren't competing for room, walking the beach and talking over affairs of the world and himself in a nondirected way until way after dark.

In these talks, Paul has revealed much: most notably, that he's waging a complex but losing struggle to forget certain things. He remembers, for instance, a dog we had years ago when we were all a nuclear family together in Haddam, a sweet, wiggly, old basset hound named Mr. Toby, who none of us could love enough and all doted on like candy, but who got flattened late one summer afternoon right in front of our house during a family cookout. Poor Mr. Toby actually clambered up off the Hoving Road pavement and in a dying dash galumphed straight to Paul and leaped into his arms before shuddering, wailing once and croaking. Paul has told me in these last weeks that even then (at only age six) he was afraid the incident would stay in his mind, possibly even for the rest of his life, and ruin it. For weeks and weeks, he said, he lay awake in his room thinking about Mr. Toby and worrying about the fact that he was thinking about it. Though eventually the memory had gone away, until just after the Finast rubber incident, when it came back, and now he thinks about Mr. Toby "a lot" (possibly constantly), thinks that Mr. Toby should be alive still and we should have him—and by extension, of course, that his poor brother, Ralph, who died of Reye's, should also be alive (as he surely should) and we should all still be we. There are even ways, he's said, in which all this is not that unpleasant to think about, since he remembers much of that early time, before bad things happened, as having been "fun." And in that sense, his is a rare species of nostalgia.

He has also told me that as of recently he has begun to picture the thinking process, and that his seems to be made of "concentric rings," bright like hula hoops, one of which is memory, and that he tries but can't make them all "fit down flush on top of each other" in the congruent way he thinks they should—except sometimes just before the precise moment of sleep, when he can briefly forget about everything and feel happy. He has likewise told me about what he refers to as "thinking he's thinking," by which he tries to maintain continuous monitorship of all his thoughts as a way of "understanding" himself and being under control and therefore making life better (though by doing so, of course, he threatens to drive himself nuts). In a way his "problem" is simple: he has become compelled to figure out life and how to live it far too early, long before he's seen a sufficient number of unfixable crises cruise past him like damaged boats and realized that fixing one in six is a damn good average and the rest you have to let go—a useful coping skill of the Existence Period.

All this is not a good recipe, I know. In fact, it's a bad recipe: a formula for a life stifled by ironies and disappointments, as one little outer character tries to make friends with or exert control over another, submerged, one, but can't. (He could end up as an academic, or a U.N. translator.) Plus, he's left-handed and so is already threatened by earlier-than-usual loss of life, by greater chances of being blinded by flying objects, scalded by pans of hot grease, bitten by rabid dogs, hit by cars piloted by other left-handers, of deciding to live in the Third World, of not getting the ball over the plate consistently and of being divorced like his Dad and Mom.

My fatherly job, needless to say, is not at all easy at this enforced distance of miles: to coax by some middleman's charm his two foreign selves, his present and his childish past, into a better, more robust and outward-tending relationship—like separate, angry nations seeking one government—and to sponsor self-tolerance as a theme for the future. This, of course, is what any father should do in any life, and I have tried, despite the impediments of divorce and time and not always knowing my adversary. Only it seems plain to me now, and as Ann believes, I have not been completely successful.

But bright and early tomorrow I am picking him up all the way in Connecticut and staging for both our benefits a split-the-breeze father-and-son driving campaign in which we will visit as many sports halls of fame as humanly possible in one forty-eight-hour period (this being only two), winding up in storied Cooperstown, where we'll stay in the venerable Deerslayer Inn, fish on scenic Lake Otsego, shoot off safe and ethical fireworks, eat like castaways, and somehow along the way I'll work (I hope) the miracle only a father can work. Which is to say: if your son begins suddenly to fall at a headlong rate, you must through the agency of love and greater age throw him a line and haul him back. (All this somehow before delivering him to his mother in

NYC and getting myself back here to Haddam, where I myself, for reasons of familiarity, am best off on the 4th of July.)

And yet, and yet. Even a good idea can be misguided if embarked on in ignorance. And who could help wondering: is my surviving son already out of reach and crazy as a betsy bug, or headed fast in that dire direction? Are his problems the product of haywire neurotransmitters, only solvable by preemptive chemicals? (This was the New Haven guy's, Dr. Stopler's, initial view.) Will he turn gradually into a sly recluse with a bad complexion, rotten teeth, bitten nails, yellow eyes, who abandons school early, hits the road, falls in with the wrong bunch, tries drugs, and finally becomes convinced *trouble* is his only dependable friend, until one sunny Saturday it, too, betrays him in some unthought-of and unbearable way, after which he stops off at a suburban gun store, then spirits on to some quilty mayhem in a public place? (This I frankly don't expect, since he has yet to exhibit any of the "big three" of childhood homicidal dementia: attraction to fire, the need to torture helpless animals, or bedwetting; and because he is in fact quite softhearted and mirthful, and always has been.) Or, and in the best-case scenario, is he— as happens to us all and as his mother hopes—merely going through a phase, so that in eight weeks he'll be trying out for lonely end on the Deep River JV?

God only knows, right? *Really* knows?

For me, alone without him most of the time, truly the worst part is that I believe he should now be at an age when he cannot imagine one bad thing happening to him, ever. And yet he can. And sometimes at the Shore or standing streamside at the Red Man Club as the sun dies and leaves the water black and bottomless, I have looked into his sweet, pale, impermanent boy's face and known that he squints out at a future he's unsure of, from a vantage point he already knows he doesn't like, but toward which he soldiers on because he thinks he should and because even though in his heart of hearts he knows we're not alike, he wishes we were and for that likeness to give him assurance.

Naturally enough, I can explain almost nothing to him. Fatherhood by itself doesn't provide wisdom worth imparting. Though in preparation for our trip, I've sent him copies of *Self-Reliance* and the Declaration, and suggested he take a browse. These are not your ordinary fatherly offerings, I admit; yet

I believe his instincts are sound and he will help himself if he can, and that independence is, in fact, what he lacks—independence from whatever holds him captive: memory, history, bad events he struggles with, can't control, but feels he should.

A parent's view of what's wrong or right with his kid is probably less accurate than even the next-door neighbor's, who sees the child's life perfectly through a gap in the curtain. I, of course, would like to tell him how to live life and do better in a hundred engaging ways, just as I tell myself: that nothing ever neatly "fits," that mistakes must be made, bad things forgotten. But in our short exposures I seem only able to talk glancingly, skittishly before shying away, cautious not to be wrong, not to quiz or fight him, not to be his therapist but his Dad. So that in all likelihood I will never provide good cure for his disease, will never even imagine correctly what his disease is, but will only suffer it with him for a time and then depart.

The worst of being a parent is my fate, then: being an adult. Not owning the right language; not dreading the same dreads and contingencies and missed chances; the fate of knowing much yet having to stand like a lamppost with its lamp lit, hoping my child will see the glow and venture closer for the illumination and warmth it mutely offers.

OUTSIDE IN the still, quiet morning, I hear a car door close, then the muffled voice (softened to the early hour) of Skip McPherson, my neighbor across the street. He is returning from his summer hockey league in East Brunswick (ice time available only before daylight). Many mornings I've seen him and his bachelor CPA chums lounging on his front steps drinking a quiet beer, still in their pads and jerseys, their skates and sticks piled on the sidewalk. Skip's team has adopted the ruddy Indian-warrior insignia and hard-check skating style of the '70 Chicago Blackhawks (Skip hails from Aurora), and Skip himself has taken the number 21 in honor of his hero, Stan Mikita. Sometimes when I'm up early and out picking up the Trenton *Times*, we'll talk sports curb to curb. He frequently has a butterfly bandage over his eye, or a gummy fat lip, or a complicated knee brace that stiffens his leg, but he's always high-spirited and acts as if I'm the best neighbor in the world, though he has little notion of me

other than that I'm a realtor—some older guy. He is typical of
the young professionals who bought into the Presidents Streets
in the middle Eighties and paid a big price, and who are sticking
it out now, gradually fixing up their houses, sitting on their
equity and waiting for the market to fire up.

In my "Buyer vs. Seller" editorial I've noted that even though
most people won't be happy with *whoever* wins the election, 54
percent of them still expect to be better off this time next year.
(I've omitted the companion statistic, cribbed from the *New York
Times*, that only 24 percent feel the *country* will be better off.
Why these numbers shouldn't be the same, is anybody's guess.)

And then suddenly, it is seven-thirty. My phone comes alive.
It is my son.

"Hi," Paul says lamely.

"Hi, son," I say, the model of upbeat father-at-a-remove.
Music is playing somewhere, and I think for a moment it's
outside my window—the streets crew, possibly, or Skip—then
I recognize the heavy, fuzzed-out *thunga-thyunga-thunga-thyunga*
and realize Paul has his headphones on and is listening to Mam-
moth Deth or some such group he likes while he's also listening
to me. "What's going on up there, son? Everything okay?"

"Yeah." *Thunga-thyunga.* "Everything's okay."

"Are we all set? Canton, Ohio, tomorrow, the Cowgirl Hall
of Fame by Sunday?" We have compiled a list of all the halls of
fame there are, including the Anthracite Hall of Fame in Scranton, the Clown Hall of Fame in Delavan, Wisconsin, the Cotton
Hall of Fame in Greenwood, Mississippi, and the Cowgirl in
Beaton, Texas. We've vowed to visit them all in two days, though
of course we can't and will have to satisfy ourselves with basketball, in Springfield (it's close to his house), and Cooperstown—
which I'm counting on to be the *ur*-father–son meeting ground,
offering the assurances of a spiritually neutral spectator sport
made seemingly meaningful by its context in idealized male
history. (I have never been there, but the brochures suggest I'm
right.)

"Yeah. We're all set." *Thunga-thyunga-thunga-thyunga.* Paul has
turned it up.

"Are you still pretty keen to be going?" Two days are paltry,
we both recognize but pretend we don't.

"Yeah," Paul says noncommittally.

"Are you still in bed, son?"

"Yeah. I am. Still in bed." This doesn't seem like a great sign, though of course it's only seven-thirty.

There is really nothing for us to talk about every morning. In any normal life, we would pass each other going this way and that, to and fro, exchange pleasantries or casual bits of wry or impertinent information, feel varyingly in touch with each other or out in harmless ways. But under the terms of our un-normal life we have to make extra efforts, even if they're wastes of time.

"Did you have any good dreams last night?" I sit forward in my chair, stare straight into the cool mulberry leaves out my window. This way it is possible to concentrate totally. Paul sometimes has wacky dreams, though it may be he invents them to have something to tell.

"Yeah, I did." He sounds distracted, but then the *thunga-thyunga-thunga-thyunga* goes very low. (Last night was apparently a good one for dreaming.)

"Want to tell me about it?"

"I was a baby, right?"

"Right."

He is tampering with something metallic. I hear a metal *snap!* "But I was a really ugly baby? *Really* ugly. And my parents were not you or Mom, but they kept leaving me at home and going off to parties. Veddy, veddy posh parties."

"Where was this?"

"Here. I don't know. Somewhere."

"In Deep Water?" Deep Water is his wisenheimer's name for Deep River, calculated precisely to make Charley O'Dell feel as unappreciated as possible. He conceivably has less use for Charley than even I do.

"Yep. Deep Water. And that's the *way* it is." He adopts his perfect-pitch Walter Cronkite voice. A headshrinker, I'm confident, would read signs of dread and fear in Paul's dream and be right. Fear of abandonment. Of castration. Of death—all solid fears, the same ones I entertain. He at least seems willing to make a joke out of it.

"Anything else going on?"

"Mom and Charley had a big fight last night."

"Sorry to hear that. About what?"

"Stuff, I guess. I don't know." I hear the weatherman on *Good*

Morning America giving us the good news for the weekend. Paul has activated his TV now and doesn't want to talk more about his mother's marital dustup; he simply wants to announce it so he can refer to it usefully on our trip. For a while I've sensed (with an acuity unique to ex-husbands) that something wasn't right with Ann. Early menopause, early nostalgia all her own, late-breaking regret. All are possible. Or maybe Charley has a honey, some little busty button-nosed waitress from the boatyard diner in Old Saybrook. Their union, though, has lasted four years, which seems long enough under the circumstances—since its chief frailty is that Charley's nobody anyone in her right mind should ever marry in the first place.

"So look. Your ole Dad's got to go sell a house this morning. Slam home my pitch. Reel in the big fish."

"D. O. Volente," Paul says.

"You got it. The Volente family from Upper High Point, North Carolina." He has decided, from his one year of Latin, that D. O. Volente is the patron saint of realtors and must be courted like a good Samaritan—shown every house, given the best deals, accorded every courtesy, made to pay no vigorish—or bad things will happen. Since the rubber incident our life has largely been conducted as a reticule of jokes, quips, double entendres, horse laughs, whose excuse for being, of course, is love. "Be a pal to your mother today, okay, pal?" I say.

"I'm her pal. She's just a bitch."

"No she's not. Her life's harder than yours, believe it or not. She has to deal with you. How's your sister?"

"Great." His sister Clary is twelve and as sage as Paul is callow. "Tell her I'll see her tomorrow, okay?"

The volume suddenly zooms up on the TV, another man's voice blabbing at a high-decibel level about Mike Tyson making 22 mil for beating Michael Spinks in ninety-one seconds. "I'd let him sock *me* in the kisser for half that much," the man says. "Did you hear that?" Paul says. "He'd let him 'sock him in the kisser.'" He loves this kind of tricky punning talk, thinks it's hilarious.

"Yeah. But you be ready to go when I get there tomorrow, okay? We have to hit the ground running if we expect to get to Beaton, Texas."

"He was Beaton to the punch, then socked in the kisser. Are

you gonna get married again?" He says this shyly. Why, I don't know.

"No, never. I love you, okay? Did you look at the Declaration of Independence and those brochures? I expect you to have your ducks in a row."

"No," he says. "But I've got one, okay?" This refers to a real joke.

"Tell me. I'll use it on my clients."

"A horse comes into a bar and orders a beer," Paul says, deadpan. "What does the bartender say?"

"I give up."

" 'Gee, why the long face?' "

Silence on his end of the line, a silence that says we each know what the other is thinking and are splitting our sides in silent laughter—the best, giddiest laughter of all. My right eyelid gives a predictable flicker. Now would be a perfect moment—with silent laughter as sad counterpoint—to think a melancholy thought, ponder a lost something or other, conduct a quick review of life's misread menu of what's important and what's not. But what I feel instead is acceptance hedging on satisfaction and a faint promise for the day just beginning. There is no such thing as a false sense of well-being.

"Great," I say. "That's great. But what's a horse doing in a bar?"

"I don't know," Paul says. "Maybe dancing."

"Having a drink," I say. "Somebody led him to it."

Outside, on the warming lawns of Cleveland Street, Skip McPherson shouts, "He shoots, he *scooooores!*" Restrained laughter floats up, a beer can goes *kee-runch*, another manly voice says, "Old slapshot, ooold slapshot, yesssireeobert." Down the block I hear a diesel growl to life like a lion waking. The streets crew is up and going.

"I'll catch you tomorrow, son," I say. "Okay?"

"Yeah," Paul says, "catch you tomorrow. Okay." And then we hang up.

CHAPTER 2

ON SEMINARY STREET at 8:15, Independence Day is the mounting spirit of the weekend, and all outward signs of life mean to rise with it. The 4th is still three days off, but traffic is jamming into Frenchy's Gulf and through the parking lot at Pelcher's Market, citizens shouting out greetings from the dry cleaners and Town Liquors, as the morning heat is drumming up. Plenty of our residents are already taking off for Blue Hill and Little Compton; or, like my neighbors the Zumbros, with time on their hands, to dude ranches in Montana or expensive trout water in Idaho. Everyone's mind-set reads the same: avoid the rush, get a jump, hit the road, put pedal to the metal. Exit is the seaboard's #1 priority.

My first order of business is to make an early stop at one of two rental houses I own, with a mind to collecting the rent, then do a quick sweep through the realty office to drop off my editorial, pick up the key for the house I'm showing in Penns Neck and have a last-minute map-out session with the Lewis twins, Everick and Wardell, the agency's "utility men," regarding our planned participation in Monday's holiday events. As it happens, our part simply amounts to handing out free hot dogs and root beer from a portable "dogs-on-wheels" stand I myself own and am lending to the cause (all proceeds to Clair Devane's two orphaned children).

Up Seminary, which since the boom has become a kind of Miracle Mile "main street" none of us ever wished for, all merchants are staging sidewalk "firecracker sales," setting out derelict merchandise they haven't moved since Christmas and draping sun racks with patriotic bunting and gimmicky signs that say wasting hard-earned money is the American way. Virtual Profusion has laid in extra bunches of low-quality daisies and red bachelor buttons to draw the bushed businessman or seminarian hiking home in a funk but determined to seem festive ("Say it with cheap flowers"). Brad Hulbert, our gay shoe-store owner, has stacked boxes of one-size-only oddities along his front window and stationed his tanned and bored little catamite, Todd, on a stool behind an open-air cash register. And the bookstore has hauled out its overstocks—piles of cheap dictionaries, atlases and unsellable '88 calendars, plus last season's computer games, all of it heaped high on a banquet table to be eyed and picked over by larcenous teens like my son.

For the first time, though, since I moved here in 1970, two businesses on Seminary have left their stores standing empty, their management clearing out under cover of darkness, owing people money and merchandise. One has since resurfaced in the Nutley Mall, the other hasn't been heard from. Indeed, many of the high-dollar franchises—places that never staged a sale— have now gone through takeovers and Chapter 11 reorganizations and given way to second-echelon high-dollar places where sales are a way of life. This spring, Pelcher's postponed a grand reopening of its specialty meat-and-cheese boutique; a Japanese car dealership suddenly went belly-up and now sits empty on Route 27. And on the weekend streets there's even a different crowd of visitors. In the early Eighties, when the Haddam population ballooned from twelve to twenty thousand, and I was still writing for a flashy sports magazine, our typical weekenders were suave New Yorkers—rich SoHo residents in bizarre get-ups and well-heeled East Siders come down to "the country" for the day, having heard it was a quaint little village here, one worth seeing, still unspoiled, approximately the way Greenwich or New Canaan used to be fifty years ago, which was at least partly true, then.

Now those same people are either staying at home in their cement-and-burglar-barred pillboxes and getting into urban pioneering or whatever their checkbooks allow; or else they've sold out and gone back to KC or decided to make a new start in the Twin Cities or Portland, where life's slower (and cheaper). Though plenty, I'm sure, are lonely and bored silly wherever they are and are wishing someone would try to rob them.

But in Haddam, their place has been taken by, of all things, more Jerseyites, down from Baleville and Totowa or up the dog-leg from Vineland and Millville—day-trippers driving 206 "just to remember where it goes" and who stop in here (unhappily rechristened "Haddam the Pleasant" by the village council) for a snack and a look-around. These people—I've watched them through the office window when I've been "on point" on the weekend—all seem to be a less purposeful lot of humans. They have more kids that're noisier, drive rattier cars with exterior parts missing and don't mind parking in handicap spaces or across a driveway or beside a fire hydrant as though they didn't have fire hydrants where they come from. They keep the yogurt franchise jumping and bang down truckloads of chocolate-chip cookies, but few of them ever sit down at The Two Lawyers for an actual lunch, fewer still spend a night in the August Inn, and none get interested in houses—though sometimes they'll waste half your day larky-farking around looking at places they'll forget the instant they're back in their Firebirds and Montegos, beetle-browing it down to Manahawkin. (Shax Murphy, who took over the agency when old man Otto Schwindell passed on, tried instituting a credit check before allowing a house to be shown over 400K. But the rest of us did some lobbying after a rock star got turned away, then spent two million at Century 21.)

I turn off Seminary out of the holiday traffic, coast down Constitution Street behind downtown, past the library, across Plum Road at the blinker, and cruise along outside the metal-picket fence behind which my son Ralph Bascombe lies buried, out as far as Haddam Medical Center, where I make a left at Erato, then over to Clio, where my two rental houses sit in their quiet neighborhood.

It might seem unusual that a man my age and nature (unadventuresome) would get involved in potentially venal landlording, chockablock as it is with shady, unreliable tenants, vicious damage-deposit squabbles, dishonest repair persons, bad checks, hectoring late-night phone calls over roof leaks, sewage backups, sidewalk repairs, barking dogs, crummy water heaters, falling plaster and noisy parties requiring the police being called, often eventuating in lengthy lawsuits. The quick and simple answer is that I decided none of these potential nightmares would be my story, which is how it's mostly happened. The two houses I own, side by side, are on a quiet, well-treed street in the established black neighborhood known as Wallace Hill, snugged in between our small CBD and the richer white demesnes on the west side, more or less behind the hospital. Reliable, relatively prosperous middle-aged and older Negro families have lived here for decades in small, close-set homes they keep in much better than average condition and whose values (with a few eyesore exceptions) have gone steadily up—if not keeping exact pace with the white sections, at least approximating them but also not suffering price slippage related to recent sags in white-collar employment. It's America like it used to be, only blacker.

Most of the residents on these streets are blue-collar professionals—plumbers or small-engine mechanics or lawn-care partners who work out of garage setups that come right off their taxes. There are a couple of elderly Pullman porters and several working moms who're teachers, plus plenty of retirees whose mortgages are paid off and who are perfectly happy to be going nowhere. Lately a few black dentists and internists and three trial lawyer couples have decided to move back to a neighborhood similar to where they grew up, or at least where they might've grown up if their families hadn't been trial lawyers and dentists themselves, and they hadn't gone to Andover and Brown. Eventually, of course, as in-town property becomes more valuable (they aren't making any more of it), all the families here will realize big profits and move away to Arizona or down South, where their ancestors were once property themselves, and the whole area will be gentrified by incoming whites and rich blacks, after which my small investment, with its few-but-bearable headaches, will turn into a gold mine. (This demographic shifting is, in fact, slower-moving in the stable black neighborhoods, since there aren't that many places for a well-heeled black American to go that's better than where he or she already is.)

Though that isn't the whole picture.

Since my divorce and, more pointedly, after my former life came to a sudden end and I suffered what must've been a kind of survivable "psychic detachment" and took off in a fugue for Florida and afterward to as far away as France, I had been uneasily aware that I had never done very much in my life that was honestly good except for myself and my loved ones (and not all of them would agree even with that). Writing sports, as anyone can tell you who's ever done it or read it, is at best offering a harmless way to burn up a few unpromising brain cells while someone eats breakfast cereal, waits nervously in the doctor's office for CAT-scan results or mulls away dreamy, solitary minutes in the can. And as far as my own hometown was concerned, apart from transporting the occasional half-flattened squirrel to the vet, or calling the fire department once when my elderly neighbors the Deffeyes let their gas barbecue set their back porch on fire and threatened the neighborhood, or some other act of tepid suburban heroism, I'd probably contributed as little to the commonweal as it was possible for a busy man to contribute without being plain evil. This, though I'd lived in Haddam fifteen years, ridden the prosperity curve right through the roof, enjoyed its civic amenities, sent my kids to its schools, made frequent and regular use of the streets, curb cuts, sewers, water mains, police and fire, plus various other departments dedicated to my well-being. Almost two years ago, however, while driving home in a weary semi-daze after a long, unproductive morning of house showings, I took a wrong turn and ended up behind Haddam Medical Center on little Clio Street, where most of our town's Negro citizens were sitting out on their porches in the late August heat, fanning themselves and chatting porch to porch, pitchers of iced tea and jars of water at their feet and little oscillating fans connected with cords through the windows to keep the air moving. As I drove past they all looked out at me serenely (or so I judged). One elderly woman waved. A group of boys stood on the street corner wearing baggy athletic shorts, holding basketballs, smoking cigarettes and talking, their arms draped around each other's shoulders. None of them seemed to notice me, or do anything menacing. So that for some reason I felt compelled to make the block and do the whole tour over, which I did—complete with the old woman waving as if she'd never laid eyes on me or my car in her life, much less two minutes before.

And what I thought, when I'd driven around a third time, was that I'd passed down this street and the four or five others like it in the darktown section of Haddam at least *five hundred* times in the decade and a half I'd lived here, and didn't know a single soul; I had been invited into no one's home, had paid no social calls, never sold a house here, had probably never even walked down a single sidewalk (though I had no fear about doing it day or night). And yet I considered this to be a bedrock, first-rate neighborhood and these souls its just and sovereign protectors.

On my fourth trip around the block, naturally no one waved

at me (two people in fact came to the top of their porch steps and frowned, and the boys with the basketballs glowered with their hands on their hips). However, I had seen two identical next-door houses—single-story, American-vernacular frame structures in slightly run-down condition, with keyboard awnings, brick-veneer half-fronts, raised, roofed porches and a fenced alley in between, both with a Trenton realty company's FOR SALE sign out front. I discreetly jotted down the phone number, then went straight to the office and put in a call to investigate price and the possibility of buying both places. I hadn't been in the realty business long and was happy to think about diversifying my assets and stashing money away where it'd be hard to get at. And I thought that if I could buy both houses at a bargain, I could then rent them to whoever wanted to live there—black retirees on fixed incomes, or not-entirely-healthy elderlies still able to look after their affairs and not be a burden on their kids, or young-marrieds in need of a sensibly priced but sturdy leg up in life—people I could assure a comfortable existence in the face of housing costs going sky-high and until such time as they could move into a perpetual-care facility or buy a starter home of their own. All of which would bestow on me the satisfaction of reinvesting in my community, providing affordable housing options, maintaining a neighborhood integrity I admired, while covering my financial backside and establishing a greater sense of connectedness, something I'd lacked since before Ann moved to Deep River two years before.

I would, I felt, be the perfect modern landlord: a man of superior sympathies and sound investments, with something to donate from years of accumulated life led thoughtfully if not always at complete peace. Everybody on the street would be happy to see my car come cruising by, because they'd know I was probably stopping in to install a new faucet kit in the kitchen, or to service the washer-dryer, or was just paying a visit to see if everybody was feeling good about things, which they always, I felt sure, would be. (Most people with an urge to diversify, I knew, would've checked with their accountant, bought beachfront condos on Marco Island, limited their loss exposure, set aside one unit for themselves, one for their grandchildren, put the others with a management company, then cleared the whole business out of their mind April to April.)

What I thought I had to offer was a deep appreciation for the sense of belonging and permanence the citizens of these streets might totally lack in Haddam (through no fault of their own), yet might long for the way the rest of us long for paradise. When Ann and I—expecting the arrival of our son, Ralph—first came to Haddam from New York and moved into our Tudor-style house on Hoving Road, we landed with the uneasy immigrant sense that everybody but the two of us had been here since before Columbus and they all damn well wanted us to feel that way; that there was some secret insider knowledge we didn't have simply because we'd shown up when we did—too late—yet unfortunately it was knowledge we could also never acquire, for more or less the same reasons. (This is total baloney, of course. Most people are late arrivals wherever they live, as selling real estate makes clear in fifteen minutes, though for Ann and me the uneasy feeling lasted a decade.)

But the residents of Haddam's black neighborhood, I concluded, had possibly never felt at home where they were either, even though they and their relatives might've been here a hundred years and had never done anything but make us white late-arrivers feel welcome at their own expense. And so what I thought I could do was at least help make two families feel at home and let the rest of the neighbors observe it.

Therefore, with a relatively small down, I quickly snapped up the two houses on Clio Street, presented myself at the front door of each as the new owner and gave my pledge to the two startled families inside that I intended to keep the houses as rental properties, all reliances and responsibilities to be meticulously honored, and that they could feel confident about staying put as long as they wanted.

The first family, the Harrises, immediately asked me in for coffee and carrot cake, and we got started on a good relationship that has lasted to the present—though they've since retired and moved in with their children in Cape Canaveral.

The other family, however, the McLeods, were unfortunately miles different. They are a mixed-race family—man and wife with two small children. Larry McLeod is a middle-aged former black militant who's married to a younger white woman and works in the mobile-home construction industry in nearby Englishtown. The day I came to his door he opened it wearing a tight red tee-shirt that had *Keep on shooting 'til the last mother-fucker be dead* stenciled across the front. A big automatic pistol was lying just inside the door on a table, and not surprisingly it was the second thing my eyes lit on. Larry has long arms and bulging, venous biceps, as if he might've been an athlete once (a kick boxer, I decided), and acted surly as hell, wanting to know why I was bothering him during the part of the day when he was usually asleep, and even going so far as to tell me he didn't believe I owned the house and was just there to hassle him. Inside on the couch I could see his skinny little white wife, Betty, watching TV with their kids—all three of them looking wan and drugged in the watery light. There was also an odd, bestilled odor inside the house, something I could almost identify but not quite, though it was like the air in a closet full of shoes that has been shut up for years.

Larry kept on seeming mad as a bulldog and glaring at me through the latched screen. I told him exactly what I'd told the elderly Harrises—all responsibilities and reliances meticulously honored, etc., etc., though I specifically mentioned to him the requirement of keeping up the rent, which I spontaneously decided to drop by ten dollars. I added that I wanted the neighborhood to stay intact, with housing available and affordable for the people who lived there, and while I intended to make needed capital improvements to both houses he should feel confident these would not be reflected in rent increases. I explained that with this plan I could realistically foresee a net gain just by keeping the property in excellent condition, deducting expenses from my taxes, keeping my tenants happy and possibly selling out when I was ready to retire—though I allowed that seemed a long way off.

I smiled at Larry through the metal screen. "Uh-huh," was the total of what he had to say, though he glanced over his shoulder once as if he was about to instruct his wife to come interpret something I'd said. Then he returned his gaze to me and looked down at the pistol on the table. "That's registered," he said. "Check it out." The pistol was big and black, looked well oiled and completely bursting with bullets—able to do an innocent world irretrievable damage. I wondered what he needed it for.

"That's good," I said cheerfully. "I'm sure we'll be seeing each other."

"Is that it?" Larry said.

"That's about it."

"All right then," he said, and closed the door in my face.

SINCE THIS first meeting nearly two years ago, Larry McLeod and I have not much enriched or broadened each other's world-views. After a few months of sending his rent check by mail he simply stopped, so that I now have to go by the house every first of the month and ask for it. If he's there, Larry always acts menacing and routinely asks me when I plan to get something fixed—though I've kept everything in both houses in good condition the entire time and have never let longer than a day go by to have a drain unplugged or a ball float replaced. On the other hand, if Betty McLeod happens to answer the door she simply stares out at me as if she's never seen me before and has in any case stopped communicating with words. She almost never has the rent check herself, so when I see her pale, scraggly-haired little pointy-nosed face appear like a specter behind the screen, I know I'm out of luck. Sometimes neither of us even speaks. I just stand on the porch trying to look pleasant, while she peers silently out as if she were staring not at me but at the street beyond. Finally she just shakes her head, begins pushing the door closed, and I understand I am not getting paid that day.

This morning when I park at 44 Clio it is eight-thirty and already a third way up the day's heat ladder and as still and sticky as a summer morning in New Orleans. Parked cars line both sides, and a few birds are chirping in the sycamores planted in the neutral ground decades ago. Two elderly women stand farther down the sidewalk chatting at the corner of Erato, leaning on brooms. A radio plays somewhere behind a window screen—an old Bobby Bland tune I knew all the words to when I was in college but now can't even remember the title of. A somber mix of vernal lethargy and minor domestic tension fills the air like a funeral dirge.

The Harrises' house sits still empty, our agency's green-and-gray FOR RENT sign in the yard, the new white metal siding and new three-way windows with plastic screens glistening dully in the sunlight. The aluminum flashing I installed below the chimney and above the eaves makes the house look spanking new, which in most ways it is, since I also installed soffit vents, roll-in insulation in the attic (upping the R factor to 23), refooted half the foundation and still mean to put up crime bars as soon as I find a tenant. The Harrises have been gone now for half a year, and I frankly don't understand my failure to attract a tenant, since rentals are tight as a drumhead and I have priced it fairly at $575, utilities included. A young black mortuarial student from Trenton came close, but his wife felt the commute was too long. Then two sexy black legal secretaries came frisking through, though for some reason felt the neighborhood wasn't safe enough. I of course had a long explanation ready for why it was probably the safest neighborhood in town: our one black policeman lives within shouting distance, the hospital is only three blocks away, people on the block get to know one another and pay attention as a matter of course; and how in the one break-in in anybody's memory, citizen-neighbors charged out of their houses and brought the crook to ground before he got to the corner. (That the crook turned out to be the son of the black policeman, I didn't mention.) But it was no use.

For reasons of my restricted access, the McLeods' house isn't yet as spiffy as the former Harrises'. The seedy brick veneer's still in place, and a couple of porch boards will soon begin "weathering" if nothing's done. Though hiking up the front steps I can hear the new window unit humming on the side (Larry demanded it, though I got it *used* out of one of our management properties), and I'm sure someone's home.

I give the doorbell one short ring, then stand back and put a businesslike but altogether friendly smile on my face. Anyone inside knows who's out here, as do all the neighbors. I glance around and down the hot, shaded street. The two women are still talking beside their brooms, the radio is still playing blues in some hot indoors. "Honey Bee," I remember, is the Bobby Bland song, but can't yet think of the words. I notice the grass in both yards is long and yellowed in spots, and the spirea Sylvania Harris planted and kept watered to a fare-thee-well are scrawny and dry and brown and probably rotten at the roots. I lean around and take a quick look down the fenced side yard between houses. Pink and blue hydrangeas are barely blooming along the foundation walls where they conceal the gas and water meters, and both areas seem deserted and unused, inviting to a burglar.

I ring the bell again, suddenly conscious that no one's answering and that I'll have to come back after the weekend, when the rent will be more in arrears and possibly in jeopardy of being forgotten. Ever since I became the owner here, I've wondered if I shouldn't just move out of my house on Cleveland—put it up for sale—and transfer into my rental unit as a cost-cutting, future-securing measure, and as a way of putting my money where my mouth is in the human-relations arena. Eventually the McLeods would take off out of pure dislike for me, and I could then locate new tenants to be my neighbors (possibly a Hmong family to spice the mix). Though under current market stresses my house on Cleveland could conceivably sit empty for months, after which I could get lowballed and sustain a major whomping—even acting as my own agent and carrying the paper. Whereas, on the other hand, finding a quality, short-term renter for a larger house like mine, even in Haddam, is a tricky proposition and rarely works out happily.

I ring the doorbell one more time, stand back to the top of the steps, listen for sounds within—footfalls, a back door closing, a muffled voice, the sound of kids' bare feet running. But nothing. This has happened before. Someone's, of course, inside, but no one's answering, and short of using my landlord's key or calling the police and saying I'm "worried" about the inhabitants, I have nothing to do but fold my tents and come again, possibly later in the day.

BACK UP on busy Seminary Street, I park in front of the Lauren-Schwindell building and make a fast turn through the office, where the usual holiday realty-office languor hangs over the still-empty desks, blank Real-trom consoles and copy machines. Almost everyone, including the younger agents, has stood steadfastly in bed an extra hour, pretending the holiday exodus means no one's doing any real business and that anybody who needs to can just jolly well call them at home. Only Everick and Wardell are glimpsable, passing in and out of the back storage room, the outside door to the parking lot left standing open. They're returning FOR SALE signs retrieved from the ditches and woodlots where our local teenagers toss them once they're tired of having them on their walls at home or when their mothers won't stand for it any longer. (We offer a no-questions-asked, three-dollar "capture fee" for every one brought in, and Everick and Wardell—grave-faced, gangly, beanpole bachelor twins in their late fifties, who are lifelong Haddamites and oddly enough Trenton State graduates—have made a science out of knowing exactly where to search.) The Lewises, who I usually find impossible to tell apart, live around the corner from my two rentals in a duplex left them by their parents, and in fact are tight-fisted, no-nonsense landlords in their own right, owning a block of senior-citizen units in Neshanic, from which they enjoy a nice profit. Yet they still work part-time for the agency and regularly do minor upkeep chores for me on Clio Street, duties they perform with a severe, distinctly put-upon efficiency that might make someone out of the know conclude they resented me. Though that is not at all the case, since they have both told me on more than one occasion that by being born in Mississippi, even with all the heavy baggage that brings along, I naturally possess a truer instinct for members of their race than any white northerner could ever approximate. This is, of course, not one bit true, though theirs is an old-style racial stationlessness that forever causes baseless "verities" to persist on with the implacable force of truth.

Our receptionist, Miss Vonda Lusk, has I see exited the ladies room and parked herself halfway down the row of empty desks, with a smoke and a Coke, and is sitting, one leg crossed and swinging, happily answering the phones and leafing through *Time* magazine till we shut down in earnest at noon. She is a big, tall, bulgy-busted, wry-humored blonde who wears a ton of makeup, bright-colored, ludicrously skimpy cocktail dresses to work, and lives in nearby Grovers Mills where she was head majorette back in 1980. She was also best friends with Clair Devane, our murdered agent, and regularly wants to discuss "the case" with me because she seems to know Clair and I once had a discreet special something of our own. "I think they're not pushing this thing hard enough," is her persistent view of the police attitude. "If she'd been a local white girl you'd have seen a big difference. You'd have FBI here out your butt." Three white men, in fact, were taken into custody for a day, though they were let go, and in the weeks since then it's true that no apparent progress has been made, though Clair's boyfriend is a well-connected black bond lawyer in a good firm in town, and the realty board along with his partners have established a $5,000 reward. Yet it's also true that the FBI made inquiries before deciding Clair's death was not a federal crime but a simple murder.

In the office we've at least officially left her desk unoccupied until the murderer is found (though in fact business hasn't been good enough to hire somebody in her place). And Vonda for her part has kept a piece of black ribbon taped across Clair's chair and a single rose in a murky bud vase on the empty wood-grain top. We are all warned against forgetting.

This morning, though, Vonda has global matters more in mind. She is a current-events buff, reads all the magazines in the office and has her *Time* folded over on her amply exposed thigh. "Look here, Frank, are you a single-warhead guy or a ten-warhead guy?" She sings this out when she sees me and flashes me her big okay-what's-up-with-you smile. She's wearing an outlandish red, white and blue off-the-shoulder taffeta getup that wouldn't let her pick a dime up off a countertop and stay decent. There is nothing between us but banter.

"I'm still a single-warhead guy," I say, heading for the front now with three listing sheets, Everick and Wardell having taken one look at me and ducked out the back (not unusual), so that I've deposited in their message box some already prepared instructions for where and when to park the dogs-on-wheels stand beside the Haddam Green once they've trailered it Monday from Franks, the root beer stand I own west of town on Route 31. This is the way they prefer to conduct all affairs—indirectly and at a distance. "I think there're too many warheads around these days," I say, heading toward the door.

"Well then, you're in deep doo-doo on your vision thing, according to *Time*." She's twirling a strand of golden hair around her little finger. She's a yellow-dog Democrat and knows I'm one too, and thinks—unless I miss my guess—that we could have some fun together.

"We'll have to talk about it," I say.

"That's quite all right," she says archly. "I'm sure you're busy. Did you know Dukakis speaks fluent Spanish?" This is not for me but for whoever might be listening, as if the empty office were jammed with interested people. Only I'm out *la puerta* seeming not to hear and as quick as possible back to the cool serenity of my Crown Victoria.

BY NINE I'm on my way out King George Road toward the Sleepy Hollow Motel on Route 1, to pick up Joe and Phyllis Markham and (it's my hope) sell them our new listing by noon.

Haddam out this woodsy way doesn't seem like a town in the throes of a price decline. An old and wealthy settlement, founded in 1795 by disgruntled Quaker merchants who split off from their more liberal Long Island neighbors, traveled south and set up things the right way, Haddam looks prosperous and confidently single-minded about its civic expectations. The housing stock boasts plenty of big 19th-century Second Empires and bracketed villas (now owned by high-priced lawyers and software CEOs) with cupolas and belvederes and oriels punctuating the basic architectural *lingua*, which is Greek with Federalist details, and post-Revolutionary stone houses fitted with fanlights, columned entries and Roman-y flutings. These houses were all big-ticket items the day the last door got hung in 1830, and hardly any turn up on the market except in vindictive divorces in which a spouse wants a big FOR SALE sign stuck out front of a former love nest to get the goat of the party of the second part. Even the few "village-in" Georgian row houses have in the last five years become prestige addresses and are all owned by rich widows, privacy-hungry gay husbands and surgeons from Philadelphia who keep them as country places they can hie off to with their nurse-anesthetists during the color season.

Though looks, of course, can be deceiving and usually are. Asking prices have yet to reflect it, but banks have slowly begun rationing money and coming back to us realtors with "problems" about appraisals. Many sellers who'd nailed down early-retirement plans at Lake of the Ozarks or for a "more intimate" place in Snowmass, now that the kids are finished at UVA, are taking a wait-and-see attitude and deciding Haddam's a lot better place to live than they'd imagined when they thought their houses were worth a fortune. (I didn't get into the residential housing business at exactly the optimum moment; in fact, I got in at almost the worst possible moment—a year before the big gut-check of last October.)

Yet like most people I remain optimistic, and feel the boom paid off no matter what things feel like at the moment. The Boro of Haddam was able to annex the Township of Haddam, which deepened our tax base and gave us a chance to lift our building moratorium and reinvest in infrastructure (the excavation in front of my house is a good illustration). And because of the influx of stockbrokers and rich entertainment lawyers early in the decade, several village landmarks were spared, as well as some late-Victorian residences that were falling in because their owners had grown old, moved to Sun City or died. At the same time, in the moderate-to-low range, where I've shown house after house to the Markhams, prices have gone on rising slowly, as they have since the beginning of the century; so that most of our median-incomers, including our African Haddamites, can still sell out once they're ready to quit paying high taxes, take a fistful of dollars along with a sense of accomplishment, and move back to Des Moines or Port-au-Prince, buy a house and live off their savings. Prosperity is not always bad news.

At the end of King George Road, where sod farms open out wide like a green hayfield in Kansas, I make the turn onto once-countrified Quakertown Road, then a hard left back onto Route 1, then through the jug handle at Grangers Mill Road, which lets me work back to the Sleepy Hollow and avoid a half hour of pre-4th get-away traffic. Off on the right, Quakertown Mall sits desolated on its wide plain of parking lot, now mostly empty, a smattering of cars at either end, where the anchors—a Sears and a Goldbloom's—are still hanging on, the original developers now doing business out of a federal lockup in Minnesota. Even the Cinema XII on the backside is down to one feature, showing on only two screens. The marquee says: *B. Streisand: A Star Is Bored* ∗∗ *Return engagement* ∗∗ *Congradulations Bertie and Stash*.

My clients the Markhams, whom I'm meeting at nine-fifteen, are from tiny Island Pond, Vermont, in the far northeast corner, and their dilemma is now the dilemma of many Americans. Sometime in the indistinct Sixties, each with a then-spouse, they departed unpromising flatlander lives (Joe was a trig teacher in Aliquippa, Phyllis a plump, copper-haired, slightly bulgy-eyed housewife from the D.C. area) and trailered up to Vermont in search of a sunnier, less predictable *Weltansicht*. Time and fate soon took their unsurprising courses: spouses wandered off with other people's spouses; their kids got busily into drugs, got pregnant, got married, then disappeared to California or Canada or Tibet or Wiesbaden, West Germany. Joe and Phyllis each floated around uneasily for two or three years in intersecting circles of neighborhood friends and off-again, on-again *Weltansichts*, taking classes, starting new degrees, trying new mates and eventually giving in to what had been available and obvious all along: true and eyes-open love for each other. Almost immediately, Joe Markham—who's a stout, aggressive little bullet-eyed, short-armed, hairy-backed Bob Hoskins type of about my age, who played nose guard for the Aliquippa Fighting Quips and who's not obviously "creative"—started having good luck with the pots and sand-cast sculptures in abstract forms he'd been making, projects he'd only fiddled around with before and that his first wife, Melody, had made vicious fun of before moving back to Beaver Falls, leaving him alone with his regular job for the Department of Social Services. Phyllis meanwhile began realizing she, in fact, had an untapped genius for designing slick, lush-looking pamphlets on fancy paper she could actually make herself (she designed Joe's first big mailing). And before they knew it they were shipping Joe's art and Phyllis's sumptuous descriptive booklets all over hell. Joe's pots began showing up in big department stores in Colorado and California and as expensive specialty items in ritzy mail order catalogs, and to both their amazement were winning prizes at prestigious crafts fairs the two of them didn't even have time to attend, they were so busy.

Pretty soon they'd built themselves a big new house with cantilevered cathedral ceilings and a hand-laid hearth and chimney, using stones off the place, the whole thing hidden at the end of a private wooded road behind an old apple orchard. They started teaching free studio classes to small groups of motivated students at Lyndon State as a way of giving something back to the community that had nurtured them through assorted rough periods, and eventually they had another child, Sonja, named for one of Joe's Croatian relatives.

Both of them, of course, realized they'd been lucky as snake charmers, given the mistakes they'd made and all that had gone kaflooey in their lives. Though neither did they view "the

Vermont life" as necessarily the ultimate destination. Each of them had pretty harsh opinions about professional dropouts and trust-fund hippies who were nothing more than nonproducers in a society in need of new ideas. "I didn't want to wake up one morning," Joe said to me the first day they came in the office, looking like bedraggled, wide-eyed missionaries, "and be a fifty-five-year-old asshole with a bandanna and a goddamn earring and nothing to talk about but how Vermont's all fucked up since a lot of people just like me showed up to ruin it."

Sonja needed to go to a better school, they decided, so she could eventually get into an even better school. Their previous batch of kids had all trooped off in serapes and Sorels and down jackets to the local schools, and that hadn't worked out very well. Joe's oldest boy, Seamus, had already done time for armed robbery, toured three detoxes and was learning-disabled; a girl, Dot, got married to a Hell's Commando at sixteen and hadn't been heard from in a long time. Another boy, Federico, Phyllis's son, was making the Army a career. And so, based on these sobering but instructive experiences, they understandably wanted something more promising for little Sonja.

They therefore made a study of where schools were best and the lifestyle pretty congenial, and where they could have some access to NYC markets for Joe's work, and Haddam came at the top in every category. Joe blanketed the area with letters and résumés and found a job working on the production end for a new textbook publisher, Leverage Books in Hightstown, a job that took advantage of his math and computer background. Phyllis found out there were several paper groups in town, and that they could go on making pots and sculptures in a studio Joe would build or renovate or rent, and could keep sending his work out with Phyllis's imaginative brochures, yet embark on a whole new adventure where schools were good, streets safe and everything basked in a sunny drug-free zone.

Their first visit was in March—which they correctly felt was when "everything" came on the market. They wanted to take their time, survey the whole spectrum, work out a carefully reasoned decision, make an offer on a house by May first and be out watering the lawn by the 4th. They realized, of course, as Phyllis Markham told me, that they'd probably need to "scale back" some. The world had changed in many ways while they were plopped down in Vermont. Money wasn't worth as much, and you needed more of it. Though all told they felt they'd had a good life in Vermont, saved some money over the past few years and wouldn't have done anything—divorce, wandering alone at loose ends, kid troubles—one bit differently.

They decided to sell their own new hand-built house at the first opportunity, and found a young movie producer willing to take it on a ten-year balloon with a small down. They wanted, Joe told me, to create a situation with no fallback. They put their furniture in some friends' dry barn, took over some other friends' cabin while they were away on vacation, and set off for Haddam in their old Saab one Sunday night, ready to present themselves as home buyers at somebody's desk on Monday morning.

Only they were in for the shock of their lives!

What the Markhams were in the market for—as I told them—was absolutely clear and they were dead right to want it: a modest three-bedroom with charm and maybe a few nice touches, though in keeping with the scaled-back, education-first ethic they'd opted for. A house with hardwood floors, crown moldings, a small carved mantel, plain banisters, mullioned windows, perhaps a window seat. A Cape or a converted saltbox set back on a small chunk of land bordering some curmudgeonly old farmer's cornfield or else a little pond or stream. Pre-war, or just after. Slightly out of the way. A lawn with maybe a healthy maple tree, some mature plantings, an attached garage possibly needing improvement. Assumable note or owner-finance, something they could live with. Nothing ostentatious: a sensible home for the recast nuclear family commencing life's third quartile with a kid on board. Something in the 148K area, up to three thousand square feet, close to a middle school, with a walk to the grocery.

THE ONLY problem was, and is, that houses like that, the ones the Markhams still google-dream about as they plow down the Taconic, mooning out at the little woods-ensconced rooftops and country lanes floating past, with mossy, overgrown stone walls winding back to mysterious-wondrous home possibilities in Columbia County—those houses are history. Ancient history. And those prices quit floating around at about the time Joe was saying good-bye to Melody and turning his attentions to plump, round-breasted and winsome Phyllis. Say 1976. Try four-fifty today if you can find it.

And I *maybe* could come close if the buyer weren't in a big hurry and didn't faint when the bank appraisal came in at thirty-under-asking, and the owner wanted 25 percent as earnest money and hadn't yet heard of a concept called owner finance.

The houses I *could* show them all fell significantly below their dream. The current median Haddam-area house goes for 149K, which buys you a builder-design colonial in an almost completed development in not-all-that-nearby Mallards Landing: 1,900 sq ft, including garage, three-bedroom, two-bath, expandable, no fplc, basement or carpets, sited on a 50-by-200-foot lot "clustered" to preserve the theme of open space and in full view of a fiberglass-bottom "pond." All of which cast them into a deep gloom pit and, after three weeks of looking, made them not even willing to haul out of the car and walk through most of the houses where I'd made appointments.

Other than that, I showed them an assortment of older village-in houses inside their price window—mostly small, dark two-bedrooms with vaguely Greek façades, originally built for the servants of the rich before the turn of the century and owned now either by descendants of immigrant Sicilians who came to New Jersey to be stone-masons on the chapel at the Theological Institute, or else by service-industry employees, shopkeepers or Negroes. For the most part those houses are unkempt, shrunken versions of grander homes across town—I know because Ann and I rented one when we moved in eighteen years ago—only the rooms are square with few windows, low-ceilinged and connected in incongruous ways so that inside you feel as closed in and on edge as you would in a cheap chiropractor's office. Kitchens are all on the back, rarely is there more than one bath (unless the place has been fixed up, in which case the price is double); most of the houses have wet basements, old termite damage, unsolvable structural enigmas, cast-iron piping with suspicions of lead, subcode wiring and postage-stamp yards. And for this you pay full price just to get anybody to break wind in your direction. Sellers are always the last line of defense against reality and the first to feel their soleness threatened by mysterious market corrections. (Buyers are the second.)

On two occasions I actually ended up showing houses to *Sonja* (who's my daughter's age!) in hopes she'd see something she liked (a primly painted "pink room" that could be hers, a particularly nifty place to snug a VCR, some kitchen built-ins she thought were neat), then go traipsing back down the walk burbling that this was the place she'd dreamed of all her little life and her Mom and Dad simply had to see it.

Only that never happened. On both of these charades, as Sonja went clattering around the empty rooms, wondering, I'm sure, how a twelve-year-old is supposed to buy a house, I peeked through the curtains and saw Joe and Phyllis waging a corrosive argument inside my car—something that'd been brewing all day—both of them facing forward, he in the front, she in the back, snarling but not actually looking at each other. Once or twice Joe'd whip his head around, focus-in his dark little eyes as intent as an ape, growl something withering, and Phyllis would cross her plump arms and stare out hatefully at the house and shake her head without bothering to answer. Pretty soon we were out and headed to our next venue.

Unhappily, the Markhams, out of ignorance and pigheadedness, have failed to intuit the one gnostic truth of real estate (a truth impossible to reveal without seeming dishonest and cynical): that people never find or buy the house they say they want. A market economy, so I've learned, is not even remotely premised on anybody getting what he wants. The premise is that you're presented with what you might've thought you didn't want, but what's available, whereupon you give in and start finding ways to feel good about it and yourself. And not that there's anything wrong with that scheme. Why should you only get what you think you want, or be limited by what you can simply plan on? Life's never like that, and if you're smart you'll decide it's better the way it is.

My own approach in all these matters and specifically so far as the Markhams are concerned has been to make perfectly clear who pays my salary (the seller) and that my job is to familiarize them with our area, let them decide if they want to settle here, and then use my accumulated goodwill to sell them, in fact, a house. I've also impressed on them that I go about selling houses the way I'd want one sold to me: by not being a realty wind sock; by not advertising views I don't mostly believe in; by not showing clients a house they've already said they won't like by pretending the subject never came up; by not saying a house is "interesting" or "has potential" if I think it's a dump; and finally by not trying to make people believe in *me* (not that I'm untrustworthy—I simply don't invite trust) but by asking them to believe in whatever they hold dearest—themselves, money, God, permanence, progress, or just a house they see and like and decide to live in—and to act accordingly.

All told today, the Markhams have looked at forty-five houses—dragging more and more grimly down from and back to Vermont—though many of these listings were seen only from the window of my car as we rolled slowly along the curbside. "I wouldn't live in that particular shithole," Joe would say, fuming out at a house where I'd made an appointment. "Don't waste your time here, Frank," Phyllis would offer, and away we'd go. Or Phyllis would observe from the back seat: "Joe can't stand stucco construction. He doesn't want to be the one to say so, so I'll just make it easier. He grew up in a stucco house in Aliquippa. Also, we'd rather not share a driveway."

And these weren't bad houses. There wasn't a certifiable "fixer-upper," "handyman special," or a "just needs love" in the lot (Haddam doesn't have these anyway). I haven't shown them one yet that the three of them couldn't have made a damn good fresh start in with a little elbow grease, a limited renovation budget and some spatial imagination.

Since March, though, the Markhams have yet to make a purchase, tender an offer, write an earnest-money check or even see a house twice, and consequently have become despondent as we've entered the dog days of midsummer. In my own life during this period, I've made eight satisfactory home sales, shown a hundred other houses to thirty different people, gone to the Shore or off with my kids any number of weekends, watched (from my bed) the Final 4, opening day at Wrigley, the French Open and three rounds of Wimbledon; and on the more somber side, I've watched the presidential campaigns grind on in disheartening fashion, observed my forty-fourth birthday, and sensed my son gradually become a source of worry and pain to himself and me. There have also been, in this time frame, two fiery jetliner crashes far from our shores; Iraq has poisoned many Kurdish villagers, President Reagan has visited Russia; there's been a coup in Haiti, drought has crippled the country's mid-section and the Lakers have won the NBA crown. Life, as noted, has gone on.

Meanwhile, the Markhams have begun "eating into their down" from the movie producer now living in their dream house and, Joe believes, producing porn movies using local teens. Like-wise Joe's severance pay at Vermont Social Services has come and gone, and he's nearing the end of his piled-up vacation money. Phyllis, to her dismay, has begun suffering painful and possibly ominous female problems that have required midweek trips to Burlington for testing, plus two biopsies and a discussion of surgery. Their Saab has started overheating and sputtering on the daily commutes Phyllis makes to Sonja's dance class in Crafts-bury. And as if that weren't enough, their friends are now home from their geological vacation to the Great Slave Lake, so that Joe and Phyllis are having to give thought to moving into the original and long-abandoned "home place" on their own former property and possibly applying for welfare.

Beyond all that, the Markhams have had to face the degree of unknown involved in buying a house—unknown likely to affect their whole life, even if they were rich movie stars or the key-boardist for the Rolling Stones. Buying a house will, after all, partly determine what they'll be worrying about but don't yet know, what consoling window views they'll be taking (or not), where they'll have bitter arguments and make love, where and under what conditions they'll feel trapped by life or safe from the storm, where those spirited parts of themselves they'll eventually leave behind (however over-prized) will be entombed, where they might die or get sick and wish they were dead, where they'll return after funerals or after they're divorced, like I did.

After which all these unknown facts of life to come have then to be figured into what they still don't know about a house itself, right along with the potentially grievous certainty that they *will* know a *great* deal the instant they sign the papers, walk in, close the door and it's theirs; and then later will know even a great deal more that's possibly not good, though they want none of it to turn out badly for them or anyone they love. Sometimes I don't understand why anybody buys a house, or for that matter does anything with a tangible downside.

As part of my service to the Markhams, I've tried to come up with some stop-gap accommodations. Addressing that feeling of not knowing *is*, after all, my job, and I'm aware what fears come quaking and quivering into most clients' hearts after a lengthy, unsatisfactory realty experience: Is this guy a crook? Will he lie to me and steal my money? Is this street being rezoned C-1 and he's in on the ground floor of a new chain of hospices or drug rehab centers? I know also that the single biggest cause of client "jumps" (other than realtor rudeness or blatant stupidity) is the embittering suspicion that the agent isn't paying any attention to your wishes. "He's just showing us what he hasn't already been able to unload and trying to make us like it"; or "She's never shown us anything like what we said we were interested in"; or "He's just pissing away our time driving us around town and letting us buy him lunch."

In early May I came up with a furnished condominium in a remodeled Victorian mansion on Burr Street, behind the Haddam Playhouse, complete with utilities and covered off-street parking. It was steep at $1,500, but it was close to schools and Phyllis could've managed without a second car if they'd stayed put till Joe started work. Joe, though, swore he'd lived in his last "shitty cold-water flat" in 1964, when he was a sophomore at Duquesne, and didn't intend to start Sonja off in some oppressive new school environment with a bunch of rich, neurotic suburban kids while the three of them lived like transient apartment rats. She'd never outlive it. He'd rather, he said, forget the whole shittaree. A week later I turned up a perfectly workable brick-and-shingle bungalow on a narrow street behind Pelcher's—a bolt-hole, to be sure, but a place they could get into with some lease-to-buy furniture and a few odds and ends of their own, exactly the way Ann and I and everybody else used to live when we were first married and thought everything was great and getting greater. Joe, however, refused to even drive by.

Since early June, Joe has grown increasingly sullen and mean-spirited, as though he's begun to see the world in a whole new way he doesn't like and is working up some severe defense mechanisms. Phyllis has called me twice late at night, once when she'd been crying, and hinted Joe was not an easy man to live with. She said he'd begun disappearing for parts of the day and had started throwing pots at night over in a woman artist friend's studio, drinking a lot of beer and coming home after midnight.

Among her other worries, Phyllis is convinced he might just forget the whole damn thing—the move, Sonja's schooling, Leverage Books, even their marriage—and sink back into an aimless nonconformist's life he lived before they got together and charted a new path to the waterfall. It was possible, she said, that Joe couldn't stand the consequences of real intimacy, which to her meant sharing your troubles as well as your achievements with the person you loved, and it seemed also possible that the act of trying to buy a house had opened the door on some dark corridors in herself that she was fearful of going down, though she thankfully seemed unready to discuss which these might be.

In so many sad words, the Markhams are faced with a potentially calamitous careen down a slippery socio-emotio-economic slope, something they could never have imagined six months ago. Plus, I know they have begun to brood about all the other big missteps they've taken in the past, the high cost of these, and how they don't want to make any more like that. As regret goes, theirs, of course, is not unusual in kind. Though finally the worst thing about regret is that it makes you duck the chance of suffering new regret just as you get a glimmer that nothing's worth doing unless it has the potential to fuck up your whole life.

A TANGY metallic fruitiness filters through the Jersey ozone—the scent of overheated motors and truck brakes on Route 1—reaching clear back to the rolly back road where I am now passing by an opulent new pharmaceutical world headquarters abutting a healthy wheat field managed by the soil-research people up at Rutgers. Just beyond this is Mallards Landing (two ducks coasting-in on a colonial-looking sign made to resemble wood), its houses-to-be as yet only studded in on skimpy slabs, their bald, red-dirt yards awaiting sod. Orange and green pennants fly along the roadside: "Models Open." "Pleasure You Can Afford!" "New Jersey's Best-Kept Secret." But there are still long ragged heaps of bulldozed timber and stumps piled up and smoldering two hundred yards to one side, more or less where the community center will be. And a quarter mile back and beyond the far wall of third-growth hardwoods where no animal is native, a big oil-storage depot lumps up and into what's becoming thickened and stormy air, the beacons on its two great canisters blinking a red and silver *steer clear, steer clear* to the circling gulls and the jumbo jets on Newark approach.

When I make the final right into the Sleepy Hollow, two cars are nosed into the potholed lot, though only one has the tiresome green Vermont plate—a rusted-out, lighter-green Nova, borrowed from the Markhams' Slave Lake friends, and with a muddy bumper sticker that says ANESTHETISTS ARE NOMADS. A cagier realtor would've already phoned up with some manufactured "good news" about an unexpected price reduction in a previously out-of-reach house, and left this message at the desk last night as a form of torture and enticement. But the truth is I've become a little sick of the Markhams—given our long campaign—and have fallen into a not especially hospitable mood, so that I simply stop midway in the lot, hoping some emanations of my arrival will penetrate the flimsy motel walls and expel them both out the door in grateful, apologetic humors, fully ready to slam down their earnest money the instant they set eyes on this house in Penns Neck that, of course, I have yet to tell them about.

A thin curtain does indeed part in the little square window of room #7. Joe Markham's round, rueful face—which looks changed (though I can't say how)—floats in a small sea of blackness. The face turns, its lips move. I make a little wave, then the curtain closes, followed in five seconds by the banged-up pink door opening, and Phyllis Markham, in the uncomfortable gait of a woman not accustomed to getting fat, strides out into the midmorning heat. Phyllis, I see from the driver's seat, has somehow amplified her red hair's coppery color to make it both brighter and darker, and has also bobbed it dramatically into a puffy, mushroomy bowl favored by sexless older moms in better-than-average suburbs, and which in Phyllis's case exposes her tiny ears and makes her neck look shorter. She's dressed in baggy khaki culottes, sandals and a thick damask Mexican pullover to hide her extra girth. Like me, she is in her forties, though unclear where, and she carries herself as if there were a new burden of true woe on the earth and only she knows about it.

"All set?" I say, my window down now, cracking a smile into the new pre-storm breeze. I think about Paul's horse joke and consider telling it, as I said I would.

"He says he's not going," Phyllis says, her bottom lip slightly enlarged and dark, making me wonder if Joe has given her a stiff smack this morning. Though Phyllis's lips are her best feature and it's more likely Joe has gifted himself with a manly morning's woogling to take his mind off his realty woes.

I'm still smiling. "What's the problem?" I say. Paper trash and parking lot grit are kicking around on the hot breeze now, and when I peek in the rearview there's a dark-purple thunderhead closing fast from the west, toiling the skies and torquing up winds, making ready to dump a big bucket of rain on us. Not a good augury for a home sale.

"We had an argument on the way down." Phyllis lowers her eyes, then casts an unhappy look back at the pink door, as if she expects Joe to come bursting through it in camo gear, screaming expletives and commands and locking and loading an M-16. She takes a self-protective look at the teeming sky. "I wonder if you'd mind just talking to him." She says this in a clipped, back-of-the-mouth voice, then elevates her small nose and stiffens her lips as two tears teeter inside her eyelids. (I've forgotten how much Joe's gooby western PA accent has rubbed off on her.)

Most Americans will eventually transact at least some portion of their important lives in the presence of realtors or as a result of something a realtor has done or said. And yet my view is, people should get their domestic rhubarbs, verbal fisticuffs and emotional jugular-snatching completely out of the way *before* they show up for a house tour. I'm more or less at ease with steely silences, bitter cryptic asides, eyes rolled to heaven and dagger stares passed between prospective home buyers, signaling but not actually putting on display more dramatic after-midnight wrist-twistings, shoutings and real rock-'em, sock-'em discord. But the client's code of conduct ought to say: Suppress all important horseshit by appointment time so I can get on with my job of lifting sagging spirits, opening fresh, unexpected choices, and offering much-needed assistance toward life's betterment. (I haven't said so, but the Markhams are on the brink of being written off, and I in fact feel a strong temptation just to run up my window, hit reverse, shoot back into the traffic and head for the Shore.)

But instead I simply say, "What would you like me to say?"

"Just tell him there's a great house," she says in a tiny, defeated voice.

"Where's Sonja?" I'm wondering if she's inside, alone with her dad.

"We had to leave her home." Phyllis shakes her head sadly. "She was showing signs of stress. She's lost weight, and she wet the bed night before last. This has been pretty tough for all of us, I guess." (She has yet to torch any animals, apparently.)

I reluctantly push open my door. Occupying the lot beside the Sleepy Hollow, inside a little fenced and razor-wire enclosure, is a shabby hubcap emporium, its shiny silvery wares nailed and hung up everywhere, all of it clanking and stuttering and shimmering in the breeze. Two old white men stand inside the compound in front of a little clatter-board shack that's completely armored with shiny hubcaps. One of them is laughing about something, his arms crossed over his big belly, swaying side to side. The other seems not to hear, just stares at Phyllis and me as if some different kind of transaction were going on.

"That's exactly what I was going to tell him anyway," I say, and try to smile again. Phyllis and Joe are obviously nearing a realty meltdown, and the threat is they may just dribble off elsewhere, feeling the need for an unattainable fresh start, and end up buying the first shitty split-level they see with another agent.

Phyllis says nothing, as if she hasn't heard me, and just looks morose and steps out of the way, hugging her arms as I head for the pink door, feeling oddly jaunty with the breeze at my back.

I half tap, half push on the door, which is ajar. It's dark and warm inside and smells like roach dope and Phyllis's coconut shampoo. "Howzit goin' in here?" I say into the gloom, my voice, if not full of confidence, at least half full of false confidence. The door to a lighted bathroom is open; a suitcase and some strewn clothes are on top of an unmade bed. I have the feeling Joe might be on the crapper and I may have to conduct a serious conversation about housing possibilities with him there.

Though I make him out then. He's sitting in a big plastic-covered recliner chair back in a shadowed corner between the bed and the curtained window where I saw his face before. He's wearing—I can make out—turquoise flip-flops, tight silver Mylar-looking stretch shorts and some sort of singlet muscle shirt. His short, meaty arms are on the recliner's arms, his feet on the elevated footrest and his head firmly back on the cushion, so that he looks like an astronaut waiting for the first big G thrust to drive him into oblivion.

"*Sooou*," Joe says meanly in his Aliquippa accent. "You got a house you want to sell me? Some dump?"

"Well, I do think I've got something you ought to see, Joe, I really do." I am just addressing the room, not specifically Joe. I would sell a house to anyone who happened to be here.

"Like what?" Joe is unmoving in his spaceship chair.

"Well. Like pre-war," I say, trying to bring back to memory what Joe wants in a house. "A yard on the side and in back and in front too. Mature plantings. Inside, I think you'll like it." I've never been inside, of course. My info comes from the rap sheet. Though I may have driven past with an agents' cavalcade, in which case you can pretty well guess about the inside.

"It's just your shitty job to say that, Bascombe." Joe has never called me "Bascombe" before, and I don't like it. Joe, I notice, has the beginnings of an aggressive little goatee encircling his small red mouth, which makes it seem both smaller and redder, as though it served some different function. Joe's muscle shirt, I also see, has *Potters Do It With Their Fingers* stenciled on the front. It's clear he and Phyllis are suffering some pronounced personality and appearance alterations—not that unusual in advanced stages of house hunting.

I'm self-conscious peeking in the dark doorway with the warm, blustery storm breeze whipping at my backside. I wish Joe would just get the hell on with what we're all here for.

"D'you know what *I* want?" Joe's begun to fiddle for something on the table beside him—a package of generic cigarettes. As far as I know, Joe hasn't been a smoker until this morning. He lights up now though, using a cheap little plastic lighter, and blows a huge cloud of smoke into the dark. I'm certain Joe considers himself a ladies' man in this outfit.

"I thought you came down here to buy a house," I say.

"What I want is for reality to set in," Joe says in a smug voice, setting his lighter down. "I've been kidding myself about all this bullshit down here. The whole goddamn mess. I feel like my whole goddamn life has been in behalf of bullshit. I figured it out this morning while I was taking a dump. You don't get it, do you?"

"What's that?" Holding this conversation with Joe is like consulting a cut-rate oracle (something I in fact once did).

"You think your life's leading someplace, Bascombe. You *do* think that way. But I saw myself this morning. I closed the door to the head and there I was in the mirror, looking straight at myself in my most human moment in this bottom-feeder motel I wouldn't have taken a whore to when I was in college, just about to go look at some house I would never have wanted to live in in a hundred years. Plus, I'm taking a fucked-up job just to be able to afford it. That's something, isn't it? There's a sweet scenario."

"You haven't seen the house yet." I glance back and see that Phyllis has climbed into the back seat of my car before the rain starts but is staring at me through the windshield. She's worried Joe's scotching their last chance at a good house, which he may be.

Big, noisy splats of warm rain all at once begin thumping the car roof. The wind gusts up dirty. It is truly a bad day for a show-ing, since ordinary people don't buy houses in a rainstorm.

Joe takes a big, theatrical drag on his generic and funnels smoke expertly out his nostrils. "Is it a Haddam address?" he asks (ever a prime consideration).

I'm briefly bemused by Joe's belief that I'm a man who believes life's leading someplace. I *have* thought that way other times in life, but one of the fundamental easements of the Exis-tence Period is not letting whether it is or whether it isn't worry you—as loony as that might be. "No," I say, recollecting myself. "It's not. It's in Penns Neck."

"I see." Joe's stupid half-bearded red mouth rises and lowers in the dark. "Penns Neck. I live in Penns Neck, New Jersey. What does that mean?"

"I don't know," I say. "Nothing, I guess, if you don't want it to." (Or better yet if the bank doesn't want you to, or if you've got a mean Chapter 7 lurking in your portfolio, or a felony con-viction, or too many late payments on your Trinitron, or happen to enjoy the services of a heart valve. In that case it's back to Vermont.) "I've shown you a lot of houses, Joe," I say, "and you haven't liked any of them. But I don't think you'd say I tried to force you into any of them."

"You don't offer advice, is that it?" Joe is still cemented to his lounge chair, where he obviously feels in a powerful command modality.

"Well. Shop around for a mortgage," I say. "Get a foundation inspection. Don't budget more than you can pay. Buy low, sell high. The rest isn't really my business."

"Right," Joe says, and smirks. "I know who pays your salary."

"You can always offer six percent less than asking. That's up to you. I'll still get paid, though."

Joe takes another drastic slag-down on his weed. "You know, I like to have a view of things from above," he says, absolutely mysteriously.

"Great," I say. Behind me, air is changing rapidly with the rain, cooling my back and neck as the front passes by. A sweet rain aroma envelops me. Thunder is rumbling over Route 1.

"You remember what I said when you first came in here?"

"You said something about reality setting in. That's all I remember." I'm staring at him impatiently through the murk, in his flip-flops and Mylar shorts. Not your customary house-hunting attire. I take a surreptitious look at my watch. Nine-thirty.

"I've completely quit becoming," Joe says, and actually smiles. "I'm not out on the margins where new discoveries take place anymore."

"I think that's probably too severe, Joe. You're not doing plasma research, you're just trying to buy a house. You know, it's my experience that it's when you don't think you're making progress that you're probably making plenty." This is a faith I in fact hold—the Existence Period notwithstanding—and one I plan to pass on to my son if I can ever get where he is, which at the moment seems out of the question.

"When I got divorced, Frank, and started trying to make pots up in East Burke, Vermont"—Joe crosses his short legs and cozies down authoritatively in his lounger—"I didn't have the foggiest idea about what I was doing. Okay? I was out of control, actually. But things just worked out. Same when Phyllis and I got together—just slammed into each other one day. But I'm not out of control anymore."

"Maybe you are more than you think, Joe."

"Nope. I'm *in* control way too much. That's the problem."

"I think you're confusing things you're already sure about, Joe. All this has been pretty stressful on you."

"But I'm on the verge of something here, I think. That's the important part."

"Of what?" I say. "I think you're going to find this Houlihan house pretty interesting." Houlihan is the owner of the Penns Neck property.

"I don't mean *that*." He pops both his chunky little fists on the plastic armrests. Joe may be verging on a major disorientation here—a legitimate rent in the cloth. This actually appears in textbooks: Client abruptly begins to see the world in some entirely new way he feels certain, had he only seen it earlier, would've directed him down a path of vastly greater happiness—only (and this, of course, is the insane part) he inexplicably senses that way's still open to him; that the past, just this once, doesn't operate the way it usually operates. Which is to say, irrevocably. Oddly enough, only home buyers in the low to middle range have these delusions, and for the most part all they bring about is trouble.

Joe suddenly bucks up out of his chair and goes slappety-slap through the dark little room, taking big puffs on his cigarette, looking into the bathroom, then crossing and peeping out between the curtains to where Phyllis waits in my car. He then turns like an undersized gorilla in a cage and stalks past the TV to the bathroom door, his back to me, and stares out the frosted, louvered window that reveals the dingy motel rear alley, where there's a blue garbage lugger, full to brimming with white PVC piping, which I sense Joe finds significant. Our talk now has the flavor of a hostage situation.

"What do you think you mean, Joe?" I say, because I detect that what he's looking for, like anybody on the skewers of dilemma, is *sanction*: agreement from beyond himself. A nice house he could both afford and fall in love with the instant he sees it could be a perfect sanction, a sign some community recognizes him in the only way communities ever recognize anything: financially (tactfully expressed as a matter of compatibility).

"What I mean, Bascombe," Joe says, leaning against the door-jamb and staring pseudo-casually through the bathroom at the blue load lugger (the mirror where he's caught himself on the can must be just behind the door), "is that the reason we haven't bought a house in four months is that I don't *want* to goddamned buy one. And the reason for that is I don't want to get trapped in some shitty life I'll never get out of except by dying." Joe swivels toward me—a small, round man with hirsute butcher's arms and a little sorcerer's beard, who's come to the sudden precipice of what's left of life a little quicker than he knows how to cope with. It's not what I was hoping for, but anyone could appreciate his predicament.

"It *is* a big decision, Joe," I say, wanting to sound sympathetic. "If you buy a house, you own it. That's for sure."

"So are you giving up on me? Is that it?" Joe says this with a mean sneer, as if he's observed now what a shabby piece of realty dreck I am, only interested in the ones that sell themselves. He is probably indulging in the idyll of what it'd be like to be a realtor himself, and what superior genius strategies he'd choose to get his point across to a crafty, interesting, hard-nut-to-crack guy like Joe Markham. This is another well-documented sign, but a good one: when your client begins to see things as a realtor, half the battle's won.

My wish of course is that after today Joe will spend a sizable portion if not every minute of his twilight years in Penns Neck, NJ, and it's even possible he believes it'll happen, himself. My job, therefore, is to keep him on the rails—to supply sanction *pro tempore*, until I get him into a buy-sell agreement and cinch the rest of his life around him like a saddle on a bucking horse. Only it's not that simple, since Joe at the moment is feeling isolated and scared through no fault of anyone but him. So that what I'm counting on is the phenomenon by which most people will feel they're not being strong-armed if they're simply allowed to advocate (as stupidly as they please) the position opposite the one they're really taking. This is just another way we create the fiction that we're in control of anything.

"I'm not giving up on you, Joe," I say, feeling a less pleasant dampness on my back now and inching forward into the room. Traffic noise is being softened by the rain. "I just go about selling houses the way I'd want one sold to me. And if I bust my ass showing you property, setting up appointments, checking out this and that till I'm purple in the face, then you suddenly back out, I'll be ready to say you made the right decision if I believe it."

"Do you believe it this time?" Joe is still sneering, but not quite as much. He senses we're getting to the brassier tacks now, where I take off my realtor's hat and let him know what's right and what's wrong in the larger sphere, which he can then ignore.

"I sense your reluctance pretty plainly, Joe."

"Right," Joe says adamantly. "If you feel like you're tossing your life in the ter-let, why go through with it, right?"

"You'll have plenty more opportunities before you're finished."

"Yup," Joe says. I hazard another look toward Phyllis, whose mushroom head is in motionless silhouette inside my car. The glass has already fogged up from her heavy body exhalations. "These things aren't easy," he says, and tosses his stubby cigarette directly into the toilet he was no doubt referring to.

"If we're not going to do this, we better get Phyllis out of the car before she suffocates in there," I say. "I've got some other things to do today. I'm going away with my son for the holiday."

"I didn't know you had a son," Joe says. He, of course, has never asked me one question about me in four months, which is fine, since it's not his business.

"And a daughter. They live in Connecticut with their mother." I smile a friendly, not-your-business smile.

"Oh yeah."

"Let me get Phyllis," I say. "She'll need a little talking to by you, I think."

"Okay, but let me just ask one thing." Joe crosses his short arms and leans against the doorjamb, feigning even greater casualness. (Now that he's off the hook, he has the luxury of getting back on it of his own free and misunderstood will.)

"Shoot."

"What do you think's going to happen to the realty market?"

"Short term? Long term?" I'm acting ready to go.

"Let's say short."

"Short? More of the same's my guess. Prices are soft. Lenders are pretty retrenched. I expect it to last the summer, then rates'll probably bump up around ten-nine or so after Labor Day. Course, if one high-priced house sells way under market, the whole structure'll adjust overnight and we'll all have a field day. It's pretty much a matter of perception out there."

Joe stares at me, trying to act as though he's mulling this over and fitting his own vital data into some new mosaic. Though if he's smart he's also thinking about the cannibalistic financial forces gnashing and churning the world he's claiming he's about to march back into—instead of buying a house, fixing his costs onto a thirty-year note and situating his small brood behind its solid wall. "I see," he says sagely, nodding his fuzzy little chin. "And what about the long term?"

I take another stagy peek at Phyllis, though I can't see her now. Possibly she's started hitchhiking down Route 1 to Baltimore.

"The long term's less good. For you, that is. Prices'll jump after the first of the year. That's for sure. Rates'll spurt up. Property really doesn't go down in the Haddam area as a whole. All boats pretty much rise on a rising whatever." I smile at him blandly. In realty, all boats most certainly *do* rise on a rising whatever. But it's still being right that makes you rich.

Joe, I'm sure, has been brooding all over again this morning about his whopper miscues—miscues about marriage, divorce, remarriage, letting Dot marry a Hell's Commando, whether he should've quit teaching trig in Aliquippa, whether he should've joined the Marines and right now be getting out with a fat pension and qualifying for a VA loan. All this is a natural part of the aging process, in which you find yourself with less to do and more opportunities to eat your guts out regretting everything you *have* done. But Joe doesn't want to make another whopper, since one more big one might just send him to the bottom.

Except he doesn't know bread from butter beans about which is the fatal miscue and which is the smartest idea he ever had.

"Frank, I've just been standing here thinking," he says, and peers back out the dirty bathroom louvers as if he'd heard someone call his name. Joe may at this moment be close to deciding what he actually thinks. "Maybe I need a new way to look at things."

"Maybe you ought to try looking at things across a flat plain, Joe," I say. "I've always thought that looking at things from above, like you said, forced you to see all things as the same height and made decisions a lot harder. Some things are just bigger than others. Or smaller. And I think another thing too."

"What's that?" Joe's brows give the appearance of knitting together. He is vigorously trying to fit my "viewpoint" metaphor into his own current predicament of homelessness.

"It really won't hurt you to take a quick run over to this Penns

Neck house. You're already down here. Phyllis is in the car, scared to death you're not going to look at it."

"Frank, what do you think about me?" Joe says. At some point of dislocatedness, this is what all clients start longing to know. Though it's almost always insincere and finally meaningless, since once their business is over they go right back to thinking you're either a crook or a moron. Realty is not a friendly business. It only seems to be.

"Joe, I may just queer my whole deal here," I say, "but what I think is you've done your best to find a house, you've stuck to your principles, you've put up with anxiety as long as you know how. You've acted responsibly, in other words. And if this Penns Neck house is anywhere close to what you like, I think you ought to take the plunge. Quit hanging onto the side of the pool."

"Yeah, but you're paid to think that, though," Joe says, sulky again in the bathroom door. "Right?"

But I'm ready for him. "Right. And if I can get you to spend a hundred and fifty on this house, then I can quit working and move to Kitzbühel, and you can thank me by sending me a bottle of good gin at Christmas because you're not freezing your nuts off in a barn while Sonja gets further behind in school and Phyllis files fucking divorce papers on you because you can't make up your mind."

"Point taken," Joe says, moodily.

"I really don't want to go into it any further," I say. There's no place further to go, of course, realty being not a very complex matter. "I'm going to take Phyllis on up to Penns Neck, Joe. And if she likes it we'll come get you and you can make up your mind. If she doesn't I'll bring her back anyway. It's a win–win proposition. In the meantime you can stay here and look at things from above."

Joe stares at me guiltily. "Okay, I'll just come along." He virtually blurts this out, having apparently blundered into the sanction he was looking for: the win–win, the sanction not to be an idiot. "I've come all this fucking way."

With my damp right arm I give a quick thumbs-up wave out to Phyllis, who I hope is still in the car.

Joe begins picking up change off the dresser top, stuffing a fat wallet into the tight waistband of his shorts. "I should let you and Phyllis figure this whole goddamn thing out and follow along like a goddamn pooch."

"You're still looking at things from above." I smile at Joe across the dark room.

"You just see everything from the fucking middle, that's all," Joe says, scratching his bristly, balding head and looking around the room as though he'd forgotten something. I have no idea what he means by this and am fairly sure he couldn't explain it either. "If I died right now, you'd go on about your business."

"What else should I do?" I say. "I'd be sorry I hadn't sold you a house, though. I promise you that. Because you at least could've died at home instead of in the Sleepy Hollow."

"Tell it to my widow out there," Joe Markham says, and stalks by me and out the door, leaving me to pull it shut and to get out to my car before I'm soaked to my toes. All this for the sake of what? A sale.

CHAPTER 3

IN MY AIR-CONDITIONED Crown Vic heading up Route 1 both Markhams sit, Joe in front, Phyllis in back, staring out at the rainy morning bustle and rush as though they were in a funeral cortege for a relative neither of them liked. Any rainy summer morning, of course, has the seeds of gloomy alienation sown in. But a rainy summer morning far from home—when your personal clouds don't move but hang—can easily produce the feeling of the world as seen from the grave. This I know.

My own view is that the realty dreads (which is what the Markhams have, pure and simple) originate not in actual house buying, which could just as easily be one of life's most hopeful optional experiences; or even in the fear of losing money, which is not unique to realty; but in the cold, unwelcome, built-in-America realization that we're just like the other schmo, wishing his wishes, lusting his stunted lusts, quaking over his idiot frights and fantasies, all of us popped out from the same unchinkable mold. And as we come nearer the moment of closing—when the deal's sealed and written down in a book in the courthouse—what we sense is that we're being tucked even deeper, more anonymously, into the weave of culture, and it's even less likely we'll make it to Kitzbühel. What we all want, of course, is all our best options left open as long as possible; we want not to have taken any obvious turns, but also not to have misread the correct turn the way some other boy-o would. As a unique strain of anxiety, it makes for a vicious three-way split that drives us all crazy as lab rats.

If I, for instance, were to ask the Markhams, staring stonily now at rain-drenched exurbia, cartage trucks and Mercedes wagons sluicing by, spewing water right into their mute faces—ask them if they were self-conscious about leaving homespun Vermont and copping an easier, more conventional life of curbs, reliable fire protection, garbage pickup three days a week, they'd be irate. *Jesus, no*, they'd shout. *We simply discovered we had some pretty damn unique needs that could only be met by some suburban virtues we'd never even heard about before.* (Good schools, malls, curbs, adequate fire protection, etc.) I'm sure, in fact, the Markhams feel like pioneers, reclaiming the suburbs from people (like me) who've taken them for granted for years and given them their bad name. Though I'd be surprised if the distaste they feel about being in the wagon with everybody else isn't teamed with the usual pioneer conservatism about not venturing *too* far—in this case toward a glut of too many cinemas, too-safe streets, too much garbage pickup, too-clean water—the suburban experiential ante raised to dizzier and dizzier heights.

My job—and I often succeed—is to draw them back toward a chummier feeling, make them less anxious both about the unknown *and* the obvious: the ways they're like their neighbors (all insignificant) and the happy but crucial ways they're not. When I fail at this task, when I sell a house but leave the buyers with an intact pioneer anxiety, it usually means they'll be out and on the road again in 3.86 years instead of settling in and letting time slip past the way people (that is, the rest of us) do who have nothing that pressing on their minds.

I TURN OFF Route 1 onto NJ 571 at Penns Neck and hand Phyllis and Joe two fresh listing sheets so they can begin placing the Houlihan house into a neighborhood context. Neither of them has had much to say on the drive up—I assume they're letting their early-morning emotional bruises heal in silence. Phyllis has posed one question about "the radon problem," which she said was more serious than a lot of their Vermont neighbors would ever admit. Her blue, exophthalmic eyes grew hooded, as if radon was only one item in a Pandora's box of North-country menace and grimness she'd grown prematurely old worrying about. Among them: asbestos in the school heating system, heavy metals in the well water, B. coli bacteria, wood smoke, hydrocarbons, rabid foxes, squirrels, voles, plus cluster flies, black ice, frozen mud—the wilderness experience up the yin-yang.

I, however, assured her radon wasn't a big problem in central New Jersey, owing to our sandy-loamy soil, and most people I knew had had their houses "crawled" and sealed around 1981, when the last scare swept through.

Joe has had even less to say. As we neared the 571 turnoff he peered back once through his side mirror at the streaming road-way behind and asked in a mumbling voice where Penns Neck *was*. "It's in the Haddam area," I said, "but across Route 1 nearer the train line, which is a plus."

He was silent for a while, then said, "I don't want to live in an area."

"You don't what?" Phyllis said. She was leafing through the green-jacketed *Self-Reliance* I have brought along for Paul (my old, worn, individually bound copy from college).

"The Boston area, the tristate area, the New York area. Nobody ever said the Vermont area, or the Aliquippa area," Joe said. "They just said the places."

"Some people said the Vermont area," Phyllis answered, flip-ping pages smartly.

"The D.C. area," Joe said as a reproach. Phyllis said nothing. "Chicagoland," Joe continued. "The Metro area. The Dallas area."

"I guess you have to chalk it up to perception again," I said, passing the little metal Penns Neck sign, which looked like a license plate, nearly hidden by some clumpy yew trees. "We're in Penns Neck now," I said, though no one answered.

Penns Neck is not in fact much of a town, much less an area: a few tidy, middle-rank residential streets situated on either side of busy 571, which connects the serenely tree-studded and affluent groves of nearby Haddam with the gradually sloping, light-industrial, overpopulous coastal plain where housing is abundant and affordable but the Markhams aren't interested. In decades past, Penns Neck would've boasted a spruced-up, Dutchy-Quakery village character, islanded by fertile cornfields, well-tended stone walls, maple and hickory farmsteads teem-ing with wildlife. Only now it's become just one more aging bedroom community for other larger, newer bedroom com-munities, in spite of the fact that its housing stock has withstood modernity's rush, leaving it with an earnest old-style-suburban appeal. There is, however, no intact town center left, only a couple of at-home antique shops, a lawn-mower repair and a gas station—deli hard by the state road. The town office (I've checked into this) has actually been moved to the next town down Route 1 and into a mini-mall. At the Haddam Realty Board I've heard the sentiment bruited that the state should unincorporate Penns Neck and drop it onto the county tax rolls, which would sweeten the rates. In the past three years I've sold two houses here, though both families have since departed for better jobs in upstate New York.

But in truth I'm showing the Markhams a Penns Neck house not because I think it'll be the house they've waited for me to show them all along, but because what's here is what they can afford and because I think they may be dejected enough to buy it.

Once we turn left off 571 onto narrow Friendship Lane, pass a series of intersecting residential streets to the north, ending up at Charity Street, the beating-whomping hum of Route 1 traffic fades out of earshot and the silken, seamless ambience of quiet houses all in neat, close rows amid tall trees, nice-ish shrubberies and edged lawns with morning sprinklers hissing, plus no overnight parking—all this begins to fill the space that worry likes to occupy.

The Houlihan house, at 212 Charity, is forthright and not even so little, a remodeled gable-roofed American farmhouse set back on a shaded and shrubbed double lot among some old hardwoods and younger pines, farther from the street than any of its neighbors, and also elevated enough in its siting to suggest it once meant more than it means now. It has, in fact, the nicer, larger, slightly out-of-place look of having been the "original farmhouse" when all this was nothing but cow pastures and farmland, and pheasants and unrabid foxes coursed the turnip rows and real estate meant zip. It also has a new bright-green shingled roof, a solid-looking brick front stoop, and white wooden siding a generation older but of more or less the same material as the other houses on the street, which are smaller one-story, design-book ranches with attached pole garages and little concrete walks straight to the curb, where mailboxes are posted house after house after house.

But here—and to my complete surprise, since I see I've, in fact, never seen it before—here might be the house the Markhams have been hoping for; the fabled long-shot house, the one I'd never shown them, the little Cape set too far back, with too many trees, the old caretaker's cottage from the once-grand manor now gone, a place requiring "imagination," a place no other clients could quite "visualize," a house with "a story" or "a ghost," but which might have a *je-ne-sais-quoi* attraction for a couple as amusingly offbeat as the Markhams. (Again, such houses do exist. They've usually just been retrofitted into single-practice laser-gynecological clinics run by doctors with Costa Rican M.D.'s and are most often found along older, major thoroughfares and not in actual neighborhoods in towns like Penns Neck.)

Our "Lauren-Schwindell Exclusive" sign is staked out front on the sloping lawn with *Julie Loukinen*, the listing agent's name, dangling from the bottom. The grass has been newly trimmed, shrubbery pruned, the driveway swept clear to the back. There are lights inside, glowing humidly in the post-storm gloom. A car, an older Merc, sits in the driveway, and the door behind the front screen is standing open (aka no central air). This could be Julie's car, though we haven't planned to show the house as a team, so that it probably belongs to owner Houlihan, who (I've arranged this with Julie) is right now supposed to be eating a late breakfast at Denny's courtesy of me.

The Markhams sit silent, noses first in their listing sheets then to the windows. This has often been the point when Joe announces he's seen quite enough.

"Is that it?" Phyllis says.

"It's our sign," I say, turning in the driveway and pulling up halfway. Rain has stopped now. Beyond the old Merc, at the end of the drive behind the house, a detached wooden garage is visible, plus an enticing angle-slice of green from the shaded back yard. No crime bars are on any windows or doors.

"What's the heating?" Joe—veteran Vermonter—says, squinting out the windshield, his listing sheet in his lap.

"Circulating hot water, electric baseboards in the den," I say verbatim from the same sheet.

"How old?"

"Nineteen twenty-four. Not in the floodplain, and the side lot's buildable if you ever want to sell or add on."

Joe casts a dark frown of ecological betrayal at me, as if the very idea of parceling off vacant lots was a crime of rain-forest-type gravity which no one should even be allowed to conceptualize. (He himself would more than conceptualize it if he ever needed the money, or were getting divorced. I of course conceptualize it all the time.)

"It has a nice front yard," I say. "Shade's your hidden asset."

"What kind of trees?" Joe says, scowling and concentrating on the side yard.

"Let's see," I say, leaning and looking out past his thick, hair-matte chest. "One's a copper beech. That one's a split-leaf maple, I'd say. One's a sugar maple—which you should like. There's a red oak. And one may be a ginkgo. It's a good mix soilwise."

"Ginkgoes stink," Joe says, fixed in his seat, as is Phyllis, neither one offering to get out. "What's it border on the back side?"

"We'll need to look at that," I say, though of course I know.

"Is that the owner?" Phyllis says, looking out.

A figure has come to the door and is rubbernecking from behind the shadowy screen: a man—not large—in a shirt and tie with no jacket. I'm not sure he even sees us.

"We'll just have to find that out," I say, hoping not, but easing the car a notch farther up the drive before shutting it off and immediately opening my door to the summer heat.

ONCE OUT, Phyllis steams right up the walk, moving with the same wobble-gaited unwieldiness as before, toes slightly out, arms working, intent on loving as much as possible before Joe can weigh in with the bad news.

Joe, though, in his silver shorts, flip-flops and pathetic muscle shirt, hangs back with me, then stops stock-still on the walk to survey the lawn, the street and the neighboring houses, which are Fifties constructions and cheaper, but with fewer maintenance worries and more modest, less burdensome lawns. The Houlihans' is in fact the nicest house on the street, which can become a scratchy price issue with an experienced buyer but probably will not be today.

I have grabbed my clipboard and put on my red nylon windbreaker from the back seat. The jacket has the Lauren-Schwindell *Societas Progressioni Commissa* crest on the breast and a big white stenciled REALTOR across the back, like an FBI agent's. I'm wearing it today in spite of the heat and humidity to get a point across to the Markhams: I'm not their friend; it's business, not a hobby; there's something at issue. Time's a-wastin'.

"It ain't Vermont, is it?" Joe muses as we stand side by side in the last drippy moments of the morning's wet weather. This is exactly what he's said at similar moments outside any number of other houses in the last four months, though he probably doesn't remember. And what he means is: *Well, fuck this. If you can't show me Vermont, then why the hell are you showing me a goddamned thing?* After which, often before Phyllis has even made it to the front door, we've turned around and left. This is why Phyllis caught fire to get inside. I, however, am frankly glad just to get Joe out of the car and this far, no matter what his objections might later be.

"It's New Jersey, Joe," I say as always. "And it's pretty nice, too. You got tired of Vermont."

Which has usually prompted Joe to say ruefully, "Yeah, and what a stupid fuck I am." Only this time he says "Yeah" and looks at me soulfully, his little flat brown irises gone flatter, as if some essential lambency has droozled out and he has faced certain facts.

"That's not a net loss," I say, zipping my jacket halfway up and feeling my toes, damp from standing in the rain back at the Sleepy Hollow. "You don't have to buy this house." Which is a hell of a thing for a realtor to say, instead of: "You goddamn *do* have to buy it. It's God's patent will that you buy it. He'll be furious at you if you don't. Your wife'll leave you and take your daughter to Garden Grove and enroll her in an Assembly of God school, and you'll never see her again if you don't buy this son of a bitch by lunchtime." Yet what I go on airily to say is: "You can always head back to Island Pond tonight and be there in time to watch the crows come home to roost."

Joe is not susceptible to other people's witticisms and looks up at me strangely (I'm a few inches taller than he is, though he's a little bullock). He clearly starts to say one thing in one tone of voice (sarcastic, without doubt), then just lets it go and stares out at the unpretentious row of hip-roofed, frame-with-brick-façade houses (some *with* crime bars), all built when he was a teenager, and where now, across Charity Street at 213, a young, shockingly red-haired woman—brighter red even than Phyllis's—is pushing a big black-plastic garbage-can-on-wheels to the curb for the last pickup before the 4th.

The woman is obviously a young mom, in blue jeans cut off midthigh, sockless tennies and a blue work shirt sloppily but calculatedly cinched in a Marilyn Monroe knot just below her breasts. When she squares her plastic can up beside her mailbox, she looks at us and waves a cheery, careless wave that means she knows who we are—new-neighbor candidates, more lively maybe than the current owner.

I wave back, but Joe doesn't. Possibly he is thinking about seeing things across a flat plain.

"I was just thinking as we were driving over here . . . ," he says, watching young Marilyn flounce back up the driveway and disappear into an empty carport. A door closes, a screen slams. ". . . that wherever you took us today was going to be where I was going to live for the rest of my life." (I was right.) "A decision almost entirely in other people's hands. And that in fact my judgment's no good anymore." (Joe hasn't tumbled to my telling him he didn't have to buy this place.) "I don't know what the hell's the right thing anymore. All I do is hold out as long as I can in hopes the really fucked-up choices will start to *look* fucked up, and I'll be saved at least that much. You know what I mean?"

"I guess so." I can hear Phyllis yakking inside, introducing herself to whoever was at the front door—not, I still hope, Houlihan himself. I would like to get inside, but I can't leave Joe here under the dripping oaks in a brown study whose net yield might be double-decker despair and a botched chance at an offer.

Across in 213, the redhead we've watched suddenly whips open the draw drapes in a far-end bedroom window. I see only her head, but she is watching us brazenly. Joe is still lost in his bad-judgment funk.

"The other day Phyl and Sonja were off in Craftsbury," he says, somberly, "and I got on the phone and called a woman I used to know. Just called her up. Out in Boise. I had a little— really a not so little—thing with her after my first marriage went south. Just before that happened, actually. She's a potter too. Makes finished-looking stuff she sells to Nordstrom's. And after we'd talked a while, just past events and whatnot, she said she had to get off the phone and wanted to know my number. But when I told her she laughed. She said, 'God, Joe, there were a whole lot of pay-phone numbers for you in my book, but none of the *M*'s are you now.'" Joe stuffs his little hands up under his damp armpits and ponders this, staring in the direction of 213.

"She didn't mean anything by that," I say, still wanting to get a move on. Phyllis has not gone much farther than inside the door yet. I can hear her sing-songy voice exclaiming that everything in sight's the nicest she ever saw. "You probably ended it on a good note way back then, didn't you? Otherwise you wouldn't have called her."

"Oh, absolutely." Joe's little goatee works first this way and then that, as if he is double-checking his memory on all counts. "No blood let. Ever. But I really thought she'd call me later to say we needed to get together—which I was willing to do, to be honest. This house-buying business pushes you to extremes." Willing-wife-deceiver Joe looks at me importantly.

"Right," I say.

"But she never called. At least I never knew if she did." He nods, still staring across at 213, which is painted a not very bright green on the wood above the brick and has a faded red front door no one ever uses. The bedroom curtain zips closed. Joe hasn't been paying attention there. Some somnolent quality in the moment or the place or the misty rain or the distant rumble of Route 1 has rendered him unexpectedly capable of thinking a whole thought through.

"I don't think it's that meaningful, though, Joe," I say.

"And I don't even care a goddamned thing about this woman," he says. "If she'd called me and said she was flying out to Burlington and wanted to meet me in a Holiday Inn and fuck me to death, I'd have most likely begged off." Joe is not aware he has contradicted himself inside of a minute.

"Maybe she just figured that out and decided to let it go herself. Saved you the trouble."

"But I'm just struck about my judgment," Joe says sadly. "I was sure she'd call. That's all. It was something *she* did, not something I did, or was even right about. Everything happened without me. Just like what's going on here."

"Maybe you'll like this house," I say lamely. The big front picture-window curtain at 213 now goes slashing back, and young red-haired Marilyn is standing in the middle, fixing us with what seems to me from here to be an accusing frown, as if whatever she took us for was making her mad enough to flash us the evil eye.

"You must've had this happen." Joe looks toward me but not at me, in fact, looks right straight back over my left shoulder, which is his usual and most comfortable mode of address. "We're the same age. You've been divorced. Had lots of women."

"We need to go on inside, Joe," I say. Though I am sympathetic. Not trusting your judgment—and, worse, *knowing* you shouldn't trust it for some damn substantial reasons—can be one of the major causes and also one of the least tolerable ongoing features of the Existence Period, one you have to fine-tune out by the use of caution. "But let me just try to say this to you." I cross my hands in front of my fly, holding my clipboard down there like an insurance adjuster. "When I got divorced, I was sure things had all happened *to* me and that I hadn't really acted and was probably a coward and at least an asshole. Who knows if I was right? But I made one promise to myself, and that was that I'd never complain about my life, and just go on and try to do my best, mistakes and all, since there's only so much anybody can do to make things come out right, judgment or no judgment. And I've kept my promise. And I don't think you're the kind of guy to fashion a life by avoiding mistakes. You make choices and live with them, even if you don't feel like you've chosen a damn thing." Joe may think, and I hope he does, that I've paid him a compliment of the rarest kind for being untranslatable.

His little bristle-mouth again makes a characteristic O, which he is totally oblivious to, his eyes going narrow as razor cuts. "Sounds like you're telling me to shut up."

"I just want us to have a look at this house so you and Phyllis can think about what you want to do. And I don't want you to worry about making a mistake before you even have a chance to make one."

Joe shakes his head, sneers, then sighs—a habit I intensely dislike, and for that reason I hope he buys the Houlihan house and discovers an eyelash too late that it's sitting over a sinkhole. "My profs at Duquesne always said I overintellectualized too much." He sneers again.

"That's what I was trying to suggest," I say, just as the flame-haired woman in 213 whisks across the picture-window space, north to south, totally in the buff, a big protuberant pair of white breasts leading the way, her arms out Isadora Duncan style, her good, muscular legs leaping and striding like a painting on an antique urn. "Wow, look at that," I say. Joe, though, has shaken his head again over what a brainy guy he is, chuckled and ambled on off, and is already mounting the steps of what might be his last home on earth. Though what he's just missed is a neighbor's neighborly way of letting the prospective buyer know what he's getting into out here, and frankly it's a sight that causes my estimation of Penns Neck to go up and off the charts. It has mystery and the unexpected as its hidden assets—much better than shade —and Joe, had he seen it, might also have seen where his own interests lay and known exactly what to do.

STEPPING INSIDE the little arched front foyer, I can hear Phyllis far in the back already having an important-sounding conversation about gypsy moths, and about what her recent experience has been in Vermont. She is having this, I feel sure, with Ted Houlihan, who shouldn't be here haunting his own house, badgering the shit out of my clients, satisfying himself they're the kind of "solid" (meaning white) folks he'll be comfortable passing his precious fee simple on to.

All the table lamps have been turned on. The floors are shiny, ashtrays cleaned, radiator tops dusted, floor moldings scrubbed, doorknobs polished. A welcome waxy smell deodorizes all— a sound selling strategy for creating the illusion that nobody actually lives here.

Joe, without even offering to greet the owner, goes right into his inspection modality, which he conducts with a brusque and speechless air of military thoroughness. In his smushed-pecker shorts, he takes a quick turn through the living room, which contains mint-condition Fifties couches, sturdy upholstered wing chairs, polished end tables, a sky-blue area rug and some elderly, store-bought prints of bird dogs, parrots in trees and lovers by a peaceful sylvan lake. He leans into the dining room, scans its heavy, polished eight-piece mahogany table-and-chairs ensemble. His beady eyes survey the crown moldings, the chair rails, the swinging kitchen door. He twists the rheostat, brightening then dimming the pink salad-bowl globe, then turns and heads back through the living room and down the central hall, where lights are also on and there's a security panel with a keypad of oversized cartoon numbers, friendly to older users. With me right behind, Joe strides slappety-slap into each bedroom, takes an unimpressed look around, slides open then closed a closet door, mentally adds up the number of grounded wall sockets, steps to the window, takes in the view, gives each window a little lift to determine if it's hung correctly or painted shut, then makes for the bathrooms.

In the pink-tiled master bath, he goes for the sink, twists on both taps full blast and waits, assessing the flow, how long the hot takes, how efficiently the drain drains. He flushes the toilet and stares at the bowl to time the "retrieval." In the "little" bath he raises the thin, new-style venetian blinds and stares out again at the park-like yard, as though contemplating the peaceful vista he would have *après le bain* or during another prolonged nature call. (Once a client, an eminent German economist from one of the local think-tanks, actually dropped trou and plopped down for a real test.)

During all such inspections, over nearly four months, and with me in attendance, Joe has stopped looking the instant he recorded three major demerits: too few sockets, more than two squishy floorboards, any unrepaired ceiling water stain, any kind of crack or odd wall angle indicating settling or "pulling away." Customarily he has also spoken very little, making only infrequent, undesignated hums. In one split-level in Pennington, he wondered out loud about the possibility of undetected root damage from an older linden tree planted close to the foundation; another time, in Haddam, he mumbled the words "lead-based paint" as he strode through a daylight basement, checking for seepage. In each case no response was asked from me, since he'd already found plenty not to like, starting with the price, which he later said, in both instances, indicated the owners needed to have their heads uncorked from their asses.

When Joe makes his plunge into the basement (where I'm happy not to go), flipping the light switch on at the top and then off again at the bottom, I take my opportunity to wander back where Phyllis stands with, indeed, Ted Houlihan at the glass door to the back yard. Here, an afterthought rumpus room *cum* live-in kitchen gives pleasingly onto a neat brick patio surrounded by luau torches, viewable through a big picture window (a neighborhood staple) that also exhibits some seepage discoloration around its frame—a defect Joe won't miss if he gets this far.

Ted Houlihan is a recently widowed engineer, not long retired from the R&D division of a nearby kitchen appliance firm. He is a sharp-eyed little white-haired seventy-plus-year-old, in faded chinos, penny loafers, an old short-sleeved, nicely frayed blue oxford shirt and a blue-and-red rep tie, and looks like the happiest man in Penns Neck. (He looks, in fact, eerily like the old honey-voiced chorister Fred Waring, who was a favorite of mine in the Fifties but in private was a martinet and a bully despite having an old softy's reputation.)

Ted gives me a big sincere back-over-his-shoulder smile when I arrive in my REALTOR windbreaker. It is our first meeting, and he would make me happy if he'd take this opportunity to head for Denny's. Noisy *boom, boom, boom* racketing has begun below-floors, as if Joe were breaking through the foundation with a sledgehammer.

"I was just about to explain to Mrs. Markham, Mr. Bascombe," Ted Houlihan says as we shake hands—his is small and tough as a walnut, mine pulpy and for some reason damp. "I've been diagnosed with testicular cancer here just last month, and I've got a son out in Tucson who's a surgeon, and he's going to do the operation himself. I'd sort of been mulling over selling for months, but just decided yesterday enough was enough." (Which it certainly is.)

Phyllis (and who wouldn't?) has reacted to this cancer news with a look of pale distress. No doubt it puts her in mind of her own problems—which is reason # fourteen to keep owners miles away from clients: they inevitably heave murky, irresolvable personal issues into the sales arena, often making my job all but impossible.

Though unless I'm way off, Phyllis is already well dazzled and charmed by everything. The back yard is a grassy little mini-Watteau, with carpets of deep-green pachysandra ringing the large trees. Rhodies, wistarias and peonies are set out all over everywhere. A good-size Japanese rock garden containing a little toy maple has been artfully situated under a big dripping oak that looks thoroughly robust and in no danger of falling over into the house. Plus, against the side of the garage is an actual pergola, clustered all over with dense, ropy grapevines and honeysuckle, with a little rustic English-looking iron settee placed underneath like a wedding bower—just the setting for renewing your sacred oaths on a clear late-summer's evening, followed by some ardent alfresco lovemaking.

"I was just saying to Mr. Houlihan what a lovely yard it is," Phyllis says, recovering herself and smiling a little dazedly at the thought of the man in front of her having his nuts snipped by his own son. Joe has stopped banging on whatever he was banging on downstairs, though I hear other metal-to-metal scraping and prying coming up through the floorboards.

"I've got a bunch of old pictures someplace of the house and the yard back in 1955 when we bought it. My wife thought it was the prettiest place she'd ever seen *then*. There was a farmer's field and a big stone silo out back and a cow lot and a milk parlor." Ted points a leathery finger toward the back property line, where there's a thick tropical-bamboo stand backed by a high plank fence painted the exact same shade of unnoticeably dark green. The fence continues in both directions behind the next-door neighbors' houses until it goes out of sight.

"What's back there, now?" Phyllis says. She has the look of "this is the one, this is the place" written all over her flushed, puffy face. Joe is currently clumping up the basement steps, his excavations and explorings now complete. I picture him as a miner in a metal-cage elevator rising miles and miles out of the deep Pennsylvania earth, his face caked, his eye sockets white, a bunged-up lunch pail under his ham-hock arm and a dim beacon light on his helmet. I am betting the next thing Ted Houlihan says isn't going to faze Phyllis Markham one iota.

"Oh, the state put its little facility back there," Ted Houlihan says genially. "Though they're pretty good neighbors."

"What kind of facility?" Phyllis says, smiling.

"Mmm. It's a little minimum security unit," Ted says. "It's just one of these country clubs. Nothing serious."

"For what?" Phyllis says, still happy. "What kind of security?"

"For you and me, I guess," Ted says, and looks over at me. "Isn't that right, Mr. Bascombe?"

"It's the State of New Jersey's minimum security facility," I say chummily. "It's where they put the mayor of Burlington, and bankers, and ordinary people like Ted and me. And Joe." I smile a little co-conspirator's smile.

"*It's* back there?" Phyllis says. Her eyes find Joe, who has emerged from down under—no coal-dust tan or headlamp or lunch-box, just his flip-flops, jersey shirt and shorts with his wallet stuck in his belt—come in to be cordial. He's seen some things he likes and is thinking about possibilities. "Did you hear what Frank said?" Her full and curvaceous mouth shows a slight sign of stiffening concern. For some reason she puts her palm flat on top of her bobbed red hair and blinks, as though she were holding something down inside her skull.

"I missed it," Joe says, rubbing his hands together. There is in fact a black dust smudge on his naked shoulder, where he's been rooting around. He looks happily at the three of us—his first on-record pleased expression in weeks. He again makes no effort to introduce himself to Ted.

"There's a prison behind that fence." Phyllis points out the picture window, across the little spruced-up lawn.

"Is that right?" Joe says, still smiling. He sort of ducks so he can see out the window. "What's that mean?" He has yet to notice the seepage.

"There's criminals in cells behind the back yard," Phyllis says. She looks at Ted Houlihan and tries to seem agreeable, as if this were just an irksome little sticking point to be worked out as a contingency in a contract ("Owner agrees to remove state prison on or before date of closing"). "Isn't that right," she asks, her blue eyes larger and intenser than usual.

"Not really cells, per se," Ted says, thoroughly relaxed. "It's more like a campus atmosphere—tennis courts, swimming pools, college classes. You can attend classes there yourself. A good many of the residents go home on weekends. I really wouldn't call it a prison."

"That's interesting," Joe Markham says, nodding out at the bamboo curtain and the green plank wall behind it. "You can't really see it, can you?"

"Did you know about this?" Phyllis says to me, still agreeable.

"Absolutely," I say, sorry to be involved. "It's on the listing sheet." I scan down my page. "Adjoins state land on north property line."

"I thought that meant something else," Phyllis says.

"I've actually never even been over there," Ted Houlihan says, Mr. Upbeat. "They have their own fence behind ours, which you can't see. And you never hear a sound. Bells or sirens or anything. They do have nice chimes on Christmas Day. I know the gal across the street works there. It's the biggest employer in Penns Neck."

"I just think it might be a problem for Sonja," Phyllis says quietly to everyone.

"I don't think there's a threat to anything or anyone," I say, thinking about Marilyn Monroe across the way, strapping on her hogleg and heading off to work every morning. What must the prisoners think? "I mean, Machine Gun Kelly's not in there. It's probably just people we all voted for and will again." I smile around, thinking this might be a correct time for Ted to walk us through his own security setup.

"We've come up quite a bit in value since they built it," Ted says. "The rest of the area—including Haddam, I should say—has lost some ground. I feel like I'm probably really leaving at the wrong time." He gives all three of us a sad-but-foxy Fred Waring grin.

"You're sure leaving a goddamned good house, I'll just tell you that," Joe says self-importantly. "I had a look at the floor joists and the sills. They don't cut 'em that wide anymore, except in Vermont." He gives Phyllis a narrow-eyed, approving frown meant to announce he's found a house he likes even if Alcatraz is next door. Joe has turned a corner now—a mysterious transit no man can chart for another. "The pipes and the wiring are all copper. The sockets are all three-prongs. You don't see that in an older home." Joe stares at Ted Houlihan almost irritably. I'm sure he would like to dope out the entire house plan in detail.

"My wife liked everything up to code," Ted says, a little sheepish.

"Where's she now?" Joe has the listing sheet out and is giving it a good perusing.

"She's dead," Ted says, and lets his gaze for an instant slip out to his bosky lawn to glide among the white peonies and yew shrubs, up under the pergola and through the wistarias. A little glistening and chartless passage has been glimpsed open and he's wandered in, and there is a golden cornfield beyond, and he and the missus are in their wondrous primes. (It is not foreign ground to me, this passage, though under my strict rules of existence it opens but rarely.)

Joe is running his stubby finger and snapping eyes over some listing sheet fine points, undoubtedly pertaining to "extras" and "rm sz," and "schls." Noting the "sq ftge" for his new work space. He is house-buying Joe now, death on the scent of a good deal.

"Joe, you asked Mr. Houlihan about his wife, and she's dead," Phyllis says.

"Hm?" Joe says.

"She's lying right there in the kitchen floor, bleeding out her ears, in fact." I'd like to say this in old reverie-lost Ted's defense, but I don't.

"Oh yeah, I know, I'm sorry to know that," Joe says. He holds the listing sheet down and frowns at Phyllis and me and lastly at Ted Houlihan, as if we'd all been shouting at him "She's dead, she's dead, you asshole, she's dead," while he's been sound asleep. "I am, I really am," he says. "When did this happen?" Joe gives me a look of incredulity.

"Two years ago," Ted says, back from the past and regarding Joe kindly. His is an honest face of life's sad dwindling. Joe shakes his head as if there were things in life you just couldn't explain.

"Let's see the rest of the house," Phyllis says, weary with let-down. "I'd still like to see it."

"You bet," I say.

"I am *very* interested in the house," Joe says to no one. "It's got a lot of features I like. I really do."

"I'll stay with Mr. Markham here," Ted Houlihan says, still unintroduced. "Let's go out and have a look at the garage." He opens the glass door to the sweet, past-besotted yard, while Phyllis and I head moodily back into the house for what, I'm afraid, will now be only a hollow formality.

PHYLLIS, AS expected, takes only polite interest, barely poking her head into the staid little bedrooms and baths, taking pleasant but brief notice of the plastic-decor laundry hampers and pink cotton bath mats, emitting an occasional "I see" or "That's nice" toward a tub-and-shower that looks brand-new. Once she murmurs, "I haven't seen that in years," toward a phone nook built into the end of the hall.

"It's been taken care of," she says, standing in the front foyer but stealing a look through to the back to where Joe is now out by the bamboo wall, short arms crossed, listing sheet in hand, jawing with Ted in a pool of midmorning sunlight. She would like to leave. "I liked it so much at first," she says, turning to gaze out the front, where sexy Marilyn-the-prison-guard's garbage can waits at the curb.

"My advice is just to think about it," I say, sounding insipid even to myself. My job, though, is to place a light finger on the scale of judgment when I sense the moment requires, when a potential buyer has a gold-plated chance to make herself happy by becoming an owner. "What I wonder about, Phyllis, when I sell a house is whether a client's getting his or her money's worth." I say this as I feel it—truly. "You might think I'd wonder about whether he or she gets their dream house, or if they get the house they originally wanted. Getting your money's worth, though, getting value, is frankly more important—particularly in the current economy. When the correction comes, value will be what things stand on. And in this house"—I cast a theatrical look around and up at the ceiling as if that was where value generally staked its pennant—"in this house I think you've got the value." And I do. (My windbreaker is beginning to stoke up inside, but I don't want to take it off just yet.)

"I don't want to live next door to a prison," Phyllis says almost pleadingly, and walks to the screen and looks out, her pudgy hands stuffed in her culotte pockets. (It may be she is attempting one simulated act of ownership—the innocent pause of an everyday to stare out a front door—trying to feel where the "catch" comes and *if* it comes, the needling thought that somewhere nearby's a TV-room full of carefree tax cheats, randy priests and scheming pension-fund CEOs who are her leering neighbors, and whether that's as intolerable as she's thought.)

Phyllis shakes her head, as if an unsavory taste had just been located. "I always felt I was a liberal. But I guess I'm not," she says. "I think there ought to be these types of institutions for certain types of criminals, but I shouldn't have to live next to one and raise my daughter there."

"We're all a little less flexible as we get older," I say. I should tell her about Clair Devane being murdered in a condo, and me being bopped to the pavement by larking Orientals. A convenient good-neighbor prison wouldn't be all that bad.

I hear Joe and Ted laugh like Rotarians out back, Joe going "Ho-ho-ho." A greasy, gassy fragrance has wafted out from the

kitchen, supplanting the clean, furniture-wax smell. (I'm surprised Joe could've missed it.) Ted and his wife may have mooned
around here half gassed and happy as goats for decades, never
knowing quite why.

"What do you do about your testicles? Is that bad?" Phyllis
says, still solemn.

"I'm not much of an expert," I say. I need to haul Phyllis back
from life's darker corridor, where she seems to be venturing, and
push us on to the more positive aspects of close-by prison living.

"I was just thinking about getting old." Phyllis gives her little
mushroom top a one-finger scratching. "And how fucked up
it is." She, for this moment, is seeing all God's children as a
dying breed (possibly the gas leak is responsible), killed off not
by disease but by MRIs, biopsies, sonograms and cold, blunt
instruments unsoothingly entered into our most unwelcoming
recesses. "I guess I have to have a hysterectomy," she says,
facing the front yard but speaking serenely. "I haven't even told
Joe yet."

"I'm sorry to hear that," I say, unclear whether that's the
correct and wished-for sympathy.

"Yeah. So. Ho-hum," she says sadly, her wide backside to me.
She may be dousing tears. But I'm frozen in my saddle. A less
advertised part of the realtor's job is overcoming natural client
morbidity—the quickening, queasy realization that by buying
a house you're taking over someone else's decays and lurking
problems, troubles you'll be responsible for till doomsday and
that do nothing more than replace troubles of your own, old ones
you've finally gotten used to. There are tricks of the trade to deal
with this sort of recoil: stressing value (I just did it); stressing
workmanship (Joe did that); stressing an older home's longevity,
its being finished with settling pains, blah, blah, blah (Ted did
exactly that); stressing general economic insecurity (I did that in
my editorial this morning and will see that Phyllis gets a copy by
sundown).

Only for Phyllis's particular distress and dismay I have no antidote, except to wish for a kinder world. It hardly counts.

"The whole country seems in a mess to me, Frank. We really
can't afford to live in Vermont, if you want to know the truth.
But now we can't live down here either. And with my health
concerns, we need to put down some roots." Phyllis sniffs, as if

the tears she's been fighting have retreated. "I'm riding a hormonal roller coaster today. I'm sorry. I just see everything black."

"I don't think things are that bad, Phyllis. I think, for instance, this is a good house with good value, just the way I've said, and you and Joe would be happy here, and so would Sonja, and you'd never worry about your neighbors at all. No one knows his neighbors in the suburbs anyway. It's not like Vermont." I peek down at my listing sheet to see if there's anything new and diverting I can stress: "fplc," "gar/cpt," "lndry," priced right at 155K. Solid value considerations but nothing to bring the hormonal roller coaster into the station.

I gaze in puzzlement at her ill-defined posterior and have a sudden, fleeting curiosity about, of all things, her and Joe's sex life. Would it be jolly and jokey? Prayerful and restrained? Rowdy, growling and obstreperous? Phyllis has an indefinite milky allure that is not always obvious—encased and bundled as she is, and slightly bulge-eyed in her fitless, matron-designer clothes—some yielding, unmaternal *abundance* that could certainly get a rise out of some lonely PTA dad in corduroys and a flannel shirt, encountered by surprise in the chilly intimacy of the grade-school parking lot after parents' night.

The truth is, however, we know little and can find out precious little more about others, even though we stand in their presence, hear their complaints, ride the roller coaster with them, sell them houses, consider the happiness of their children—only in a flash or a gasp or the slam of a car door to see them disappear and be gone forever. Perfect strangers.

And yet, it is one of the themes of the Existence Period that interest can mingle successfully with uninterest in this way, intimacy with transience, caring with the obdurate uncaring. Until very recently (I'm not sure when it stopped) I believed this was the *only* way of the world; maturity's balance. Only more things seem to need sorting out now: either in favor of complete uninterest (ending things with Sally might be an example) or else going whole hog (not ending things with Sally might be another example).

"You know, Frank . . ." Her misty moment past, Phyllis has walked by me into the Houlihans' living room, stepped to the front window beside a little leafed butler's table and, just like the redhead across the street, pulled open the drapes, letting in a

warm, midmorning light, which defeats the room's funeral stillness by causing its fussy couches and feminine mint dishes, its
antimacassars and polished knickknacks (all of which Ted has left
sentimentally in place), to seem to shine from within. "I was just
standing there thinking that maybe no one gets the house they
want." Phyllis glances around the room in an interested, friendly
way, as if she liked the new light but thought the furniture needed
rearranging.

"Well, if I can find it for them they do. And if they can afford
it. You *are* best off coming as close as you can and trying to bring
life to a place, not just depending on the place to supply it for
you." I give her my own version of a willing smile. This is a
positive sign, though of course we're not really addressing each
other now; we're merely setting forth our points of view, and
everything depends on whose act is better. It is a form of
strategizing pseudo-communication I've gotten used to in the
realty business. (Real talk—the kind you have with a loved one
such as your former wife back when you were her husband—
real talk is out of the question.)

"Do you have a prison behind your house?" Phyllis says
bluntly. She gazes at her toes, which are pinched into her sandals,
their nails painted scarlet. They seem to imply something to her.

"No, but I *do* live in my ex-wife's former house," I say, "and
I live alone, and my son's an epileptic who has to wear a football
helmet all day, and I've decided to live in her house just to give
him a little semblance of continuity when he comes to visit, since
his life expectancy's not so great. So I've made *some* adjustments
to necessity." I blink at her. This is about her, not about me.

Phyllis was not expecting this, and looks stunned, suddenly
acknowledging how much everything up to now has been usual
salesmanship, usual aggravating clienthood; but that now everything is suddenly *down to it*: her and Joe's *actual situation* being
attended to diligently by a man with even bigger woes than they
have, who sleeps less well, visits more physicians, has more
worrisome phone calls, during which he spends more anxious
time on hold while gloomy charts are being read, and whose life
generally matters more than theirs by his being closer to the grave
(not necessarily his own).

"Frank, I don't mean to compare wounds with bruises,"
Phyllis says abjectly. "I'm sorry. I'm just feeling a lot of pressure

along with everything else." She gives me a sad Stan Laurel smile and lowers her chin just like old Stan. Her face, I see, is a malleable and sweet putty face, perfect for alternative children's theater in the Northeast Kingdom. But no less right for Penns Neck, where a thespian group she might head up could do *Peter Pan* or *The Fantasticks* (minus the "Rape" song) for the lonely, sticky-fingered ex-comptrollers and malpractitioners across the fence, leaving them with at least a temporary feeling that life isn't all that ruined, that there's still hope on the outside, that there are a lot of possibilities left—even if there aren't.

I hear Ted and Joe scraping their damp dogs on the back steps, then stamping the welcome mat and Joe saying, "Now that'd be a *real* reality check, I'll tell you," while gentle, clever Ted says, "I've just decided for the time I have left, Joe, to let go all the nonessentials."

"I envy that, don't think I don't," Joe says. "Boy-oh-boy, I could get rid of some of those, all right."

Phyllis and I both hear this. Each of us knows that one of us is the first nonessential Joe would like to put behind him.

"Phyllis, I figure we've all got scars and bruises," I say, "but I just don't want them to cause you to miss a damn good deal on a wonderful house when it's in your grasp here."

"Is there anything else we can see today?" Phyllis says dispiritedly.

I sway back slightly on my heels, arms enfolding my clipboard. "I could show you a new development." I'm thinking of Mallards Landing, of course, where slash is smoldering and maybe two units are finished and the Markhams will go out of their gourds the minute they lay eyes on the flapping pennants. "The young developer's a heck of a good guy. They're all in your range. But you indicated you didn't want to consider new homes."

"No," Phyllis says darkly. "You know, Frank, Joe's a manic-depressive."

"No, I didn't know that." I hug my clipboard tighter. (I'm beginning to cook like a cabbage in my windbreaker.) I mean, though, to hold my ground. Manic-depressives, convicted felons, men and women with garish tattoos over every inch of their skin: all are entitled to a hook to hang their hats on if they've got the scratch. This claim for Joe's looniness is probably a complete lie, a ploy to let me know she's a worthy opponent in the realty struggle (for some reason her female troubles still seem legit). "Phyllis, you and Joe need to do some serious thinking about this house." I stare profoundly into her obstinate blue eyes, which I realize for the first time must have contacts, since no blue nearly similar to that occurs in nature.

She is framed by the window, her small hands clasped in front like a schoolmarm lording a trick question over a schoolboy dunce. "Do you feel sometimes"—the light glowing around Phyllis seems to have brought her in contact with the forces of saintliness—"that no one's looking out for you anymore?" She smiles faintly. The creases at the corners of her mouth make weals in her cheeks.

"Every day." I try to beam back a martyrish look.

"I had that feeling when I got married the first time. When I was twenty and a sophomore at Towson. And I had it this morning again at the motel—the first time in years." She rolls her eyes in a zany way.

Joe and Ted are making a noisy second trek over the floor plan now. Ted's unscrolling some old blueprints he's kept squirreled away. They will soon barge into Phyllis's and my little séance.

"I think that feeling's natural, Phyllis, and I think you and Joe take care of each other just fine." I peek to see if the orienteers are here yet. I hear them tromping over the defunct floor furnace, talking importantly about the attic.

Phyllis shakes her head and smiles a beatified smile. "The trick's changing the water to wine, isn't it?"

I have no idea what this might mean, though I give her a lawyerly-brotherly look that says this competition's over. I could even give her a pat on her plump shoulder, except she'd get wary. "Phyllis, look," I say. "People think there're just two ways for things to go. A worked-out way and a not-worked-out way. But I think most things start one way, then we steer them where we want them to go. And no matter how you feel at the time you buy a house—even if you don't buy this one or don't buy one from me at all—you're going to have to—"

And then our séance *is* over. Ted and Joe come trooping back down the hall from where they've decided not to take a cob-webby tour up the "disappearing" stairway to eyeball some metal rafter gussets Ted installed when Hurricane Lulu passed by in

'58, blowing hay straw through tree trunks, moving yachts miles inland and leveling grander houses than Ted's. It's too hot upstairs.

"God's in the details," one of the new best friends observes. But adds, "Or is it the devil?"

Phyllis looks peacefully at the entry, into which the two of them go first one way and then the other before locating us in the l/r. Ted, coming into view with his blueprints, looks to my estimation satisfied with everything. Joe, in his immature goatee, his vulgar shorts and *Potters Do It With Their Fingers* shirt, seems on the verge of some form of hysteria.

"I've seen enough," Joe shouts like a railroad conductor, taking a quick estimation of the living room as if he'd never seen it in his life. He jams his thick knuckles together in satisfaction. "I can make up my mind on what I've seen."

"Okay," I say. "We'll take a drive, then." (Code for: We'll go to breakfast and write up a full-price offer and be back in an hour.) I give Ted Houlihan an assuring nod. Unexpectedly he's proved a key player in an ad hoc divide-and-conquer scheme. His memories, his poor dead wife, his faulty *cojones*, his Milquetoast Fred Waring soft-shoe worldview and casual attire, are first-rate selling tools. He could be a realtor.

"This place won't stay on the market long," Joe shouts to anyone in the neighborhood who's interested. He swivels around and starts for the front door in some kind of beehive panic.

"Well, we'll see," Ted Houlihan says, and gives me and Phyllis a doubtful smile, scrolling his blueprints tighter. "I know that place across the fence disturbs you, Mrs. Markham. But I've always felt it made the whole neighborhood safer and more cohesive. It's not much different from having AT&T or RCA, if you get what I mean."

"I understand," Phyllis says, unmoved.

Joe is already through the front door, down the steps and out onto the lawn, scoping out the roofline, the fascial boards, the soffits, his hair-framed mouth gaped open as he searches for sags in the ridgeboard or ice damage under the eaves. Possibly it is manic-depression medicine that causes his lips to be so red. Joe, I think, needs a bit of tending to.

I find a *Frank Bascombe, Realtor Associate* card in my windbreaker pocket and slip it onto the umbrella stand outside the living-room door, where I've spent the last ten minutes keeping Phyllis in the corral.

"We'll be in touch," I say to Ted. (More code. Less specific.)

"Yes, indeed," Ted says, smiling warmly.

And then out Phyllis goes, hips swaying, sandals clicking, shaking Ted's little hand on the fly and saying something about its being a lovely house and a pity he has to sell it, but heading right out to where Joe's trying to get a clear bead on things through whatever fog it's his bewildered lot to see through.

"They'll never buy it," Ted says gamely as I head toward the door. His is not disappointment but possibly misplaced satisfaction at having foreign elements turned away, permitting a brief retreat into the comfortable bittersweet domesticity that's still his. Joe out the door would be a relief for anyone.

"I can't tell, Ted," I say. "You don't know what other people will do. If I did, I'd be in another line of work."

"It'd be nice to think that the place was valuable to others. I'd feel good about that. There's not a lot of corroboration there for us anymore."

"Not what we'd like. But that's my part in this." Phyllis and Joe are standing beside my car, looking at the house as though it were an ocean liner just casting off for open seas. "Just don't underestimate your own house, Ted," I say, and once again grab his little hard-biscuit hand and give it an affirming shake. I take a last whiff of gas leak. (I'll hear Joe out on this subject inside of five minutes.) "Don't be surprised if I come back with an offer this morning. They won't see a house as good as yours, and I mean to make that clear as Christmas."

"A guy once climbed over the fence while I was out back sacking leaves," Ted says. "Susan and I took him inside, gave him some coffee and an egg salad sandwich. Turned out he was an alderman from West Orange. He'd just gotten in over his head. But he ended up helping me bag leaves for an hour, then going back over. We got a Christmas card from him for a while."

"He's probably back in politics," I say, happy Ted has spared Phyllis this anecdote.

"Probably."

"We'll be in touch."

"I'll be right here," Ted says. He closes the front door behind me.

*   *   *

INSIDE THE CAR, the Markhams seem to want to get rid of me as fast as possible, and, more important, neither one makes a peep about an offer.

As we're pulling out the drive we all notice another realtor's car slowing to a stop, a young couple front and back—the woman videotaping the Houlihan place through the passenger window. The driver's-side sign on the big shiny Buick door says BUY AND LARGE REALTY—*Freehold, NJ.*

"This place'll be history by sundown," Joe says flatly, seated beside me, his get-up-and-go oddly got-up-and-gone. No mention of any gas odor. Phyllis has had no real chance to browbeat him, but a look can raze cities.

"Could be," I say, staring knives at the BUY AND LARGE Buick. Ted Houlihan may have already reneged on our *exclusive*, and I'm tempted to step out and explain some things to everybody involved. Though the sight of competing buyers could put a special, urgent onus to act on Phyllis and Joe, who watch these new people in disapproving silence as I drive us back down Charity Street.

On the way to Route 1, Phyllis—who has now put on dark glasses and looks like a diva—suddenly insists I drive them "around" so she can see the prison. Consequently, I negotiate us back through the less nice, bordering neighborhoods, curve in behind a new Sheraton and a big Episcopal church with a wide, empty parking lot, then merge out onto Route 1 north of Penns Neck, where, a half mile down the road in what looks like a mowed hayfield, there sits, three hundred yards back, a complex of low, indistinct flat-green buildings fenced all around and refenced closer in, which altogether constitutes the offending "big house." We can see basketball backboards, a baseball diamond, several fenced and lighted tennis courts, a high-dive platform over what might very well be an Olympic-size pool, some paved and winding "reflection paths" leading out into open stretches of field where pairs of men—some apparently elderly and limping—are strolling and chatting and wearing street clothes instead of prison monkey garb. There's also, apparently for atmosphere, a large flock of Canada geese milling and nosing around a flat, ovoid pond.

I, naturally, have passed this place incalculable times but have paid it only the briefest attention (which is what the prison planners expected, the whole shebang as unremarkable as a golf course). Though looked at now, a grassy, summery compound with substantial trees ranked beyond its boundaries, where an inmate can do any damn thing he wants but leave—read a book, watch color TV, think about the future—and where one's debts to society can be unobtrusively retired in a year or two, it seems like a place anyone might be glad to pause just to get things sorted out and cut through the crap.

"It looks like some goddamn junior college," Joe Markham says, still talking in the higher decibels but seeming calmer now. We're stopped on the opposite shoulder, with traffic booming past, and are rubbernecking the fence and the official silver-and-black sign that reads: N.J. MEN'S FACILITY—A MINIMUM SECURITY ENVIRONMENT, behind which New Jersey, American and Penal System flags all rustle on separate poles in the faint, damp breezes. There's no guardhouse here, no razor wire, no electric fences, no watchtowers with burp guns, stun grenades, searchlights, no leg-chewing canines—just a discreet automatic gate with a discreet speaker box and a small security camera on a post. No biggie.

"It doesn't look that bad, does it?" I say.

"Where's our house from here?" Joe says, still loudly, leaning to see across me.

We study the row of big trees which is Penns Neck, the Houlihan house on Charity Street invisible within.

"You can't see it," Phyllis says, "but it's back there."

"Out of sight, out of mind," Joe says. He flashes a look back at Phyllis in her shades. A giant dump truck blows past, rocking the car on its chassis. "They have a gap in the fence where you can trade recipes." He snorts.

"A cake with a file in it," Phyllis says, her face unresigned. I try to catch her eye in the rearview, but can't. "I don't see it."

"I goddamned see it," Joe growls.

We sit staring for thirty more seconds, and then it's off we go.

AS A NEGATIVE inducement and a double cincher, I drive us out past Mallards Landing, where everything is as it was two hours ago, only wetter. A few workmen are moving inside the half-studded homes. A crew of black men is loading wads of damp sod off a flatbed and stacking them in front of the MODEL that's supposedly OPEN but isn't and in fact looks like a movie façade where a fictionalized American family would someday pay the fictionalized mortgage. It puts me and, I'm sure, the Markhams in mind of the prison we just left.

"Like I was saying to Phyllis," I say to Joe, "these are in your price window, but they're not what you described."

"I'd rather have AIDS than live in that junk," Joe snarls, and doesn't look at Phyllis, who sits in the back, peering out toward the strobing oil-storage depot and the bulldozed piles of now unsmoldering trees. *Why have I come here?* she is almost certainly thinking. *How long a ride back is it by Vermont Transit?* She could be down at the Lyndonville Farmers' Co-op at this very moment, a clean red kerchief on her head, she and Sonja blithely but responsibly shopping for the holiday—surprise fruits for the "big fruit bowl" she'll take to the Independence Day bash. Chinese kites would be tethered above the veggie stalls. Someone would be playing a dulcimer and singing quirky mountain tunes full up with sexual double meanings. Labs and goldens by the dozens would be scratching and lounging around, wearing colorful bandanna collars of their own. Where has that all disappeared to, she is wondering. What have I done?

Suddenly *crash-boom!* Somewhere miles aloft in the peaceful atmosphere, invisible to all, a war jet breaks the barrier of harmonious sound and dream, reverbs rumbling toward mountaintops and down the coastal slope. Phyllis jumps. "Oh fuck," she says. "What was that?"

"I broke wind. Sorry," Joe says, smirking at me, and then we say no more.

AT THE Sleepy Hollow, the Markhams, who have ridden the rest of the way in total motionless silence, seem now reluctant to depart my car. The scabby motel lot is empty except for their ancient borrowed Nova with its mismatched tires and moronic anesthetists' sticker caked with Green Mountain road dirt. A small, pinkly dressed maid wearing her dark hair in a bun is flickering in and out the doorway to #7, loading a night's soiled linen and towels into a cloth hamper and carting in stacks of fresh.

The Markhams would both rather be dead than anywhere that's available to them, and for a heady, unwise moment I consider letting them follow me home, setting them up for a weekend of house discussion on Cleveland Street—a safe, depression-free base from which they could walk to a movie, eat a decent bluefish or manicotti dinner at the August Inn, window-shop down Seminary Street till Phyllis can't stand not to live here, or at least nearby.

Though that is simply not in the cards, and my heart strikes two and a half sharp, admonitory beats at the very thought. Not only do I not like the idea of them rummaging around in my life's accoutrements (which they would absolutely do, then lie about it), but since we're not talking offer, I want them left as solitary as Siberia so they can get their options straight. They could always, of course, move themselves up to the new Sheraton or the Cabot Lodge and pay the freight. Though in its own way each of these is as dismal as the Sleepy Hollow. In my former sportswriter's life I often sought shelter and even exotic romance in such spiritless hideaways, and often, briefly, found it. But no more. No way.

Joe has gone all the way through his list of questions left unanswered on the listing sheet, which he has spindled, then folded, his former lion's certainty now beginning to wane. "Any chance of a lease option back there at Houlihan's?" he says, as we all three just sit.

"No."

"Any chance Houlihan might come off a buck fifty-five?"

"Make an offer."

"When can Houlihan vacate?"

"Minimum time. He has cancer."

"Would you negotiate the commission down to four percent?"

(This comes as no surprise.) "No."

"What's the bank renting money for these days?"

(Again.) "Ten-four on a thirty-year fixed, plus a point, plus an application fee."

We skirl down through everything Joe can dredge up. I have turned the a/c vent into my face until I almost decide again to let them move into my house. Except, forty-five showings is the statistical point of no return, and the Markhams have today gone to forty-six. Clients, after this point, frequently don't buy a house but shove off to other locales, or else do something nutty like take a freighter to Bahrain or climb the Matterhorn. Plus, I might have a hard time getting them to leave. (In truth, I'm ready to cut the Markhams loose, let them set off toward a fresh start in the Amboys.)

Though of course they might just as well say, "Okay. Let's just get the sonofabitch bought and quit niggly-pigglying around. We're in for the full boat. Let's get an offer sheet filled out." I've got a boxful in my trunk. "Here's five grand. We're moving into the Sheraton Tara. You get your sorry ass back over to Houli-han's, tell him to get his bags packed for Tucson or go fuck him-self, because one fifty's all we're offering because that's all we've got. Take an hour to decide."

People do that. Houses get sold on the spot; checks get writ-ten, escrow accounts opened, moving companies called from windy pay phones outside HoJo's. It makes my job one hell of a lot easier. Though when it happens that way it's usually rich Texans or maxillary surgeons or political operatives fired for financial misdealings and looking for a place to hide out until they can be players again. Rarely does it happen with potters and their pudgy paper-making wives who wander back to civiliza-tion from piddly-ass Vermont with emaciated wallets and not a clue about what makes the world go around but plenty of opinions about how it ought to.

Joe sits in the front seat grinding his molars, breathing audibly and staring out at the foreign national swamping out their soiled room with a mop and a bottle of Pine-Sol. Phyllis, in her Marginalia shades, sits thinking—what? It's anybody's guess. There's no question left to ask, no worry to express, no resolve or ultimatum worth enunciating. They've reached the point where nothing's left to do but act. Or not.

But by God, Joe doesn't like it even in spite of loving the house, and sits inventorying his brain for something more to say, some barrier to erect. Likely it will have to do with "seeing from above" again, or wanting to make some great discovery.

"Maybe we *should* think about renting," Phyllis says vacantly. I have her in my mirror, keeping to herself like a bereaved widow. She has been staring at the hubcap bazaar next door, where no one's visible in the rain-soaked yard, though the

hubcaps sparkle and clank in the breeze. She may be seeing something as a metaphor for something else.

Unexpectedly, though, she sits forward and lays a consolidating
mitt on Joe's bare, hairy shoulder, which causes him to jump like
he'd been stabbed. Though he quickly detects this as a gesture of
solidarity and tenderness, and lumpily reaches round and grubs
her hand with his. All patrols and units are now being called in.
A unified response is imminent. It is the bedrock gesture of
marriage, something I have somehow missed out on, and rue.

"Most of your better rentals turn up when the Institute term
ends and people leave. That was last month," I say. "You didn't
like anything then."

"Is there anything we might get into temporarily?" Joe says,
limply holding Phyllis's plump fingers as though she were laid
out beside him in a hospital bed.

"I've got a place *I* own," I say. "It might not be what you
want."

"What's wrong with it?" Joe and Phyllis say in suspicious
unison.

"Nothing's wrong with it," I say. "It happens to be in a black
neighborhood."

"Oh Je-sus. Here we go," Joe says, as if this was a long-
foreseeable and finally sprung trap. "That's all I need. Spooks.
Thanks for nothin'." He shakes his head in disgust.

"That's not how we look at things in Haddam, Joe," I say
coolly. "That's not how I practice realty."

"Well, good for you," he says, seething but still holding
Phyllis's hand, probably tighter than she likes. "You don't live
there," he fumes. "And you don't have kids."

"I do have kids," I say. "And I'd happily live there with them
if I didn't already live someplace else." I give Joe a hard, iron-
browed frown meant to say that beyond what he already doesn't
know about, the world he left behind in nineteen seventy-
whatever is an empty crater, and he'll get no sympathy here if it
turns out he doesn't like the present.

"What you got, some shotgun shacks you collect rent on every
Saturday morning?" Joe says this in a mealy, nasty way. "My old
man ran that scam in Aliquippa. He ran it with Chinamen. He
carried a pistol in his belt where they could see it. I used to sit in
the car."

"I don't have a pistol," I say. "I'm just doing you a favor by mentioning it."

"Thanks. Forget about it."

"We could go look at it," Phyllis says, squeezing Joe's hairy knuckles, which he's balled up now into a menacing little fist.

"In a million years, maybe. But only maybe." Joe yanks up the door latch, letting hot Route 1 whoosh in.

"The Houlihan house is worth thinking about," I say to the car seat Joe is vacating, giving a sidelong look to Phyllis in the back.

"You realty guys," Joe says from outside, where I can just see his ball-packer shorts. "You're always nosing after the fucking sale." He then just stalks off in the direction of the cleaning woman, who's standing beside her laundry hamper and his very room, looking at Joe as if he were a strange sight (which he is).

"Joe's not a good compromiser," Phyllis says lamely. "He may be having dosage problems too."

"He's free to do whatever he wants, as far as I'm concerned."

"I know," Phyllis says. "You're very patient with us. I'm sorry we're so much trouble." She pats me on *my* shoulder, just the way she did asshole Joe. A victory pat. I don't much appreciate it.

"It's my job," I say.

"We'll be in touch with you, Frank," Phyllis says, struggling to exit her door to the hot morning heading toward eleven.

"That's just great, Phyllis," I say. "Call me at the office and leave a message. I'll be in Connecticut with my son. I don't get to spend that much time with him. We can do pretty much everything on the phone if there's anything to talk about."

"We're trying, Frank," Phyllis says, blinking pathetically at the idea of my son who's an epileptic, but not wanting to mention it. "We're really trying here."

"I can tell," I lie, and turn and give her a contrite smile, which for some reason drives her right out of the doorway and across the hot little crumbling motel lot in search of her unlikely husband.

I NOW FIND myself in a whir to get back into town, and so split the breeze over the steamy pavement up Route 1, retaking King George Road for the directest route to Seminary Street. I have more of the day returned to me than I'd expected, and I mean to put it to use by making a second stop by the McLeods', before driving out to Franks on Route 31, then heading straight down to South Mantoloking for some earlier than usual quality time with Sally, plus dinner.

I'd hoped, of course, to be back in the office, running the numbers on an offer or already delivering same to Ted Houlihan, hustling to get various balls rolling—calling a contractor for a structural inspection, getting the earnest money deposited, vetting the termite contract, dialing up Fox McKinney at Garden State Savings for a fast track through to the mortgage board. There's absolutely nothing an owner likes better than a quick, firm reply to his sell decision. Philosophically, as Ted said, it indicates the world is more or less the way we best feature it. (Most of what we unhappily hear back from the world being: "Boy, we're back-ordered on that one, it'll take six weeks"; or, "I thought they quit making those gizmos in '58"; or, "You'll have to have that part milled special, and the only guy who does it is on a walking trip through Swaziland. Take a vacation, we'll call you.") And yet if an agent can pry loose a well-conceived offer on an entirely new listing, the likelihood of clear sailing all the way to closing is geometrically increased by the simple weight of seller satisfaction, confidence, a feeling of corroboration and a sense of immanent meaning. *Real* closure in other words.

Consequently, it's a good strategy to set the Markhams adrift as I just did, let them wheeze around in their clunker Nova, brooding about all the houses in all the neighborhoods they've sneered at, then crawl back for a nap in the Sleepy Hollow—one in which they doze off in daylight but awake startled, disoriented and demoralized after dark, lying side by side, staring at the greasy motel walls, listening to the traffic drum past, everyone but them bound for cozy seaside holiday arrangements where youthful, happy, perfect-toothed loved ones wave greetings from lighted porches and doorways, holding big pitchers of cold gin. (I myself hope shortly to be arriving for just such a welcome—to be a cheerful, eagerly awaited addition to the general store of holiday fun, having a million laughs, feeling the world's woe rise off me someplace where the Markhams can't reach me. Possibly bright and early tomorrow there'll either be a frantic call from Joe wanting to slam a bid in by noon, or else no call—confoundment having taken over and driven them back to Vermont and public assistance—in which case I'll be rid of them. Win–win again.)

It's perfectly evident that the Markhams haven't looked in life's mirror in a while—forget about Joe's surprise look this morning. Vermont's spiritual mandate, after all, is that you don't look at your*self*, but spend years gazing at everything *else* as penetratingly as possible in the conviction that everything out there more or less stands for you, and everything's pretty damn great because you are. (Emerson has some different opinions about this.) Only, with home buying as your goal, there's no real getting around a certain self-viewing.

Right about now, unless I miss my guess, Joe and Phyllis are lying just as I pictured them, stiff as planks, side by side, fully clothed on their narrow bed, staring up into the dim, flyspeck ceiling with all the lights off, realizing as silent as corpses that they can't *help* seeing themselves. They are the lonely, haunted people soon to be seen standing in a driveway or sitting on a couch or a cramped patio chair (wherever they land next), peering disconcertedly into a TV camera while being interviewed by the six o'clock news not merely as average Americans but as people caught in the real estate crunch, indistinct members of an indistinct class they don't want to be members of—the frustrated, the ones on the bubble, the ones who suffer, those forced to live anonymous and glum on short cul-de-sac streets named after the builder's daughter or her grade-school friends.

And the only thing that'll save them is to figure out a way to think about themselves and most everything else *differently*; formulate fresh understandings based on the faith that for new fires to kindle, old ones have to be dashed; and based less on isolating, boneheaded obstinance and more, for instance, on the wish to make each other happy without neutralizing the private self—which was why they showed up in New Jersey in the first place instead of staying in the mountains and becoming smug casualties of their own idiotic miscues.

With the Markhams, of course, it's hard to believe they'll work it out. A year from now Joe would be the first person to kick back at a summer solstice party in some neighbor's new-mown hay meadow, sipping homemade lager and grazing a hand-fired plate full of vegetarian lasagna—naked kids a-frolic in the twilight, the smell of compost, the sound of a brook and a gas generator in the background—and hold forth on the subject of change and how anybody's a coward who can't do it: a philosophy naturally honed on his and Phyllis's own life experiences (which include divorce, inadequate parenting practices, adultery, self-importance, and spatial dislocation).

Though it's change that's driving him crackers *now*. The Markhams say they won't compromise on their ideal. But they aren't compromising! They can't afford their ideal. And not buying what you can't afford's not a compromise; it's reality speaking English. To get anywhere you have to learn to speak the same language back.

And yet they may find hidden strengths: their fumbling, lurching Sistine Chapel touch across the car seat was a promising signal, but it's one they'll need to elaborate over the weekend, when they're on their own. And inasmuch as I'm not in possession of their check, on their own's where they'll be—sweating it but also, I hope, commencing the process of self-seeing as a sacred initiation to a fuller later life.

IT MIGHT be of some interest to say how I came to be a Residential Specialist, distant as it is from my prior vocations of failed short-story writer and sports journalist. A good *liver* would be a man or woman who'd distilled all of life that's important down to a few inter-related principles and events, which are easy to explain in fifteen minutes and don't require a lot of perplexed pauses and apologies for this or that being hard to understand exactly if you weren't there. (Finally, almost nobody else *is* ever able to "be there," and in many cases it's too bad *you* have to be.) And it is in this streamlined, distilled sense that it's possible to say my former wife's getting remarried and moving to Connecticut is what brought me to where I am.

Five years ago, at the end of a bad season that my friend Dr. Catherine Flaherty described as "maybe a kind of major crisis," or "the end of something stressful followed by the beginning of something indistinct," I one day simply quit my job at a large sports magazine in New York and moved myself to Florida, and then in the following year to France, where I had never been but decided I needed to go.

In the ensuing winter, the previously mentioned Dr. Flaherty, then age twenty-three and not yet a doctor, interrupted her medical studies at Dartmouth and flew to Paris to spend "a season" with me—entirely against her father's best judgment (who could blame him?) and without the slightest expectance that the world held out any future for her and me together or that the future even needed to be taken into account. The two of us struck off on a driving tour in a rented Peugeot to wherever seemed interesting on the European map, with me paying the freight from the proceeds of my magazine-stock buyout and Catherine doing all the complicated map reading, food ordering, direction seeking, bathroom locating, phone calling, and bellman paying. She had, naturally, been to Europe at least twenty times before she was out of Choate and could in all instances remember and easily lead us straight to a "neat little hilltop restaurant" above the Dordogne, or "an interesting place for very late lunch" near the Palacio in Madrid, or find the route to a house that was once Strindberg's wife's home outside Stockholm. The whole trip had for her the virtue of an aimless, nostalgic return to past triumphs in the company of a non-traditional "other," just before life—serious adult life—began in earnest and fun was forgotten forever; while for me it was more of an anxious dash across a foreign but thrilling *exterior* landscape, commenced in hopes of arriving at a temporary refuge where I'd feel rewarded, revived, less anxious, possibly even happy and at peace.

It's not necessary to say much of what we did. (Such pseudo-romantic excursions must all be more or less alike and closed-ended.) We eventually "settled" in the town of Saint-Valéry-sur-Somme, in Channel-side Picardy. There we passed the better part of two months together, spent a great deal of my money, rode bicycles, read plenty of books, visited battlefields and cathedrals, tried sculling on the canals, walked pensively along the grassy verge of the old estuarial river, watching French fishermen catch perch, walked pensively around the bay to the alabaster village of Le Crotoy, then walked back, made much love. I also practiced my college French, chatted up the English tourists, stared at sailboats, flew kites, ate many gritty *moules meunières*, listened to much "traditional" jazz, slept when I wanted to and even when I didn't, woke at midnight and stared at the sky as though I needed to get a clearer view of something but wasn't sure what it was. I did all this until I felt perfectly okay, not in love with Catherine Flaherty but not unhappy, although also futureless, disused and bored—the way, I imagine, extended time in Europe makes any American who cares to stay an American feel (possibly similar to how a larcenous small-town road commissioner feels during the latter part of his stay in the Penns Neck minimum security facility).

Though what I in time began to sense in France was actually a kind of disguised urgency (disguised, as urgency often is, as unurgency), a feeling completely different from the old clicking, whirly, suspenseful perturbations I'd felt in my last days as a sportswriter: of being divorced, full of regret, and needing to pursue women just to keep myself pacified, amused and slightly dreamy. This new variety was more a deep-beating urgency having to do with me and me only, not me *and* somebody. It was, I now believe, the profound low thrum of my middle life seeking to be seized rather than painlessly avoided. (There's nothing like spending eight weeks alone with a woman two decades your junior to make you wise to the fact that you'll someday disappear, make you bored daffy by the concept of youth, and dismally aware how impossible it is ever to be "with" another human being.)

One evening then, over a plate of *ficelle picarde* and one more glass of tolerable Pouilly-Fumé, it occurred to me that being there with winsome, honey-haired, sweetly ironic Catherine was indeed a kind of dream and a dream I'd wanted to have, only it was now a dream that was holding me back—from what, I wasn't sure, but I needed to find out. Needless to say, she had to have been bored silly by me but had gone on acting, in a vaguely amused way, as if I was a "pretty funny ole guy" with pretty interesting, eccentric habits, not one bit to be taken lightly "as a man," and that being in Saint-Valéry with me had made all the difference in getting her young life started in the most properly seasoned way, and she would remember it all forever. She didn't, however, mind if I left or if she stayed, or if we both left or stayed. She already had plans to leave, which she hadn't thought to tell me about yet; and in any case, when I was seventy and in adult Pampers, she'd have been fiftyish, in a surly mood from all she'd missed and in no rush to humor me—which by then would be all I'd want. So that there was no thought of a long haul for the two of us.

But in just that short an order and on that very evening, and without a harsh word, we kissed and broke camp—she back to Dartmouth, and me back to . . .

Haddam. Where I landed not only with a new feeling of great purpose and a fury to suddenly *do* something serious for my own good and possibly even others', but also with the feeling of renewal I'd gone far to look for and that immediately translated into a homey connectedness to Haddam itself, which felt at that celestial moment like my spiritual residence more than any place I'd ever been, inasmuch as it *was* the place I instinctively and in a heat came charging back to. (Of course, having come first to life in a true *place*, and one as monotonously, lankly *itself* as the

Mississippi Gulf Coast, I couldn't be truly surprised that a simple *setting* such as Haddam—willing to be so little itself—would seem, on second look, a great relief and damned easy to cozy up to.)

Before, when I was in town writing sports, as a married, then later, divorced man, I'd always fancied myself a spectral presence, like a ship cruising foggy banks, hoping to hang near and in hearing distance of the beach but without ever bashing into it. Now, though, by reason of Haddam's or any suburb's capacity to accommodate any but the rankest outsider (a special lenience which can make us miss even the most impersonal housing tract or condo development), I felt *towny*: a guy who shares a scuzzy joke with the Neapolitan produce man, who knows exactly the haircut he'll get at Barber's barbershop but goes there anyway, who's voted for more than three mayors and can remember how things used to be before something else happened and as a result feels right at home. These feelings of course ride the froth of one's sense of hope and personal likelihood.

Every age of life has its own little pennant to fly. And mine upon returning to Haddam was decidedly two-sided. On one side was a feeling of bright synchronicity in which everything I thought about—regaining a close touch with my two children after having flown the coop for a while, getting my feet wet in some new life's enterprise, possibly waging a campaign to reclaim lost ground with Ann—all these hopeful activities seemed to be, as though guided by a lightless beam, what my whole life was all about. I was in a charmed state in which nothing was alien and nothing could resist me if I turned my mind to it. (Psychiatrists like the one my son visits warn us about such feelings, flagging us all away from the poison of euphoria and hauling us back to flat earth, where they want us to be.)

The other feeling, the one that balanced the first, was a sensation that everything I then contemplated was limited or at least underwritten by the "plain fact of my existence": that I was after all only a human being, as untranscendent as a tree trunk, and that everything I might do had to be calculated against the weight of the practical and according to the standard considerations of: Would it work? and, What good would it do for me or anybody?

I now think of this balancing of urgent forces as having begun the Existence Period, the high-wire act of normalcy, the part that comes *after* the big struggle which led to the big blow-up, the time in life when whatever was going to affect us "later" actually affects us, a period when we go along more or less self-directed and happy, though we might not choose to mention or even remember it later were we to tell the story of our lives, so steeped is such a time in the small dramas and minor adjustments of spending quality time simply with ourselves.

Certain crucial jettisonings, though, seemed necessary for this passage to be a success—just as Ted Houlihan mentioned to Joe Markham an hour ago but which probably didn't register. Most people, once they reach a certain age, troop through their days struggling like hell with the concept of completeness, keeping up with all the things that were ever part of them, as a way of maintaining the illusion that they bring themselves fully to life. These things usually amount to being able to remember the birthday of the first person they "surrendered" to, or the first calypso record they ever bought, or the poignant line in *Our Town* that seemed to sum life up back in 1960.

Most of these you just have to give up on, along with the whole idea of completeness, since after a while you get so fouled up with all you did and surrendered to and failed at and fought and didn't like, that you can't make any progress. Another way of saying this is that when you're young your opponent is the future; but when you're not young, your opponent's the past and everything you've done in it and the problem of getting away from it. (My son Paul may be an exception.)

My own feelings were that since I'd jettisoned employment, marriage, nostalgia and swampy regret, I was now rightfully a man a-quiver with possibility and purpose—similar to a way you might feel just prior to taking up the sport of, say, glacier skiing; and not for sharpening your acuities or tempting grisly death, but simply to celebrate the hum of the human spirit. (I could not, of course, have told you what my purpose actually was, which probably meant my purpose was just to have a purpose. Though I'm certain I was afraid that if I didn't use my life, even in a ridiculous way, I'd lose it—what people used to say about your dick when I was a kid.)

My qualifications for a new undertaking were, first, that I was not one bit preoccupied with how things *used to be*. You're usually wrong about how things used to be anyway, except that you used to be happier—only you may not have known it at the time, or might've been unable to seize it, so stuck were you in life's gooeyness; or, as is often the case, you might never have been quite as happy as you like to believe you were.

The second of my qualifications was that intimacy had begun to matter less to me. (It had been losing ground since my marriage came to a halt and other attractions failed.) And by intimacy I mean the real kind, the kind you have with only one person (or maybe two or three) in a lifetime; not the kind where you're willing to talk to someone you're close to about laxative choices or your dental problems; or, if it's a woman, about her menstrual cycle, or your aching prostate. These are private, not intimate. But I mean the real stuff—*silent intimacies*—when spoken words, divulgences, promises, oaths are almost insignificant: the intimacy of the fervently understood and sympathized with, having nothing to do with being a "straight shooter" or a truth teller, or with being able to be "open" with strangers (these don't mean anything anyway). To *none* of these, though, was I in debt, and in fact I felt I could head right into my new frame of reference—whatever was beginning—pretty well prepared and buttoned up.

Third, but not last, I wasn't actually worried that I was a coward. (This seemed important and still does.) Years earlier, in my sportswriting days, Ann and I were once walking out of a Knicks–Bullets night game at the Garden, when some loony up ahead began brandishing a pistol and threatening to open up on everybody all around. Word went back like a windstorm over wheat stalks. "Gun! He's got a GUN! Watch it!" I quickly pulled Ann inside a men's room door, hoping to get some concrete between the gun muzzle and us. Though in twenty seconds the gunman was tackled and kicked to sawdust by a squad of New York's quick-witted finest, and thank God no one was hurt.

But Ann said to me when we were in the car, waiting in a drizzle to enter the bleak tunnel back to New Jersey, "Did you realize you jumped *behind* me when that guy had his gun?" She smiled at me in a tired but sympathetic way.

"That's not what I did!" I said. "I jumped in the rest room and pulled you in with me."

"You did that too. But you also grabbed me by my shoulders and got behind me. Not that I blame you. It happened in a hurry." She drew a wavy vertical line in the window fog and put a dot at the bottom.

"It did happen in a hurry. But you're wrong about *what* happened," I said, flustered because in fact it *had* all happened fast, I'd acted solely on instinct and couldn't remember much.

"Well, if that's what happened," she said confidently, "then tell me if the man—if it was a man—was colored or white." Ann has never gotten over her old man's Michigan racial epithets.

"I don't know," I said as we made the curve down into the lurid world of the tunnel. "It was too crowded. He was too far up ahead. We couldn't see him."

"*I* could," she said, sitting straighter and flattening her skirt across her knees. "He wasn't actually that far. He might've shot one of us. He was a small brown-colored man, and he had a small black revolver. If we passed him on the street I'd recognize him again. Not that it matters. You were trying to do the right thing. I'm happy I was no less than the second person you thought to protect when you thought you were in danger." She smiled at me again and patted my leg infuriatingly, and we were all the way to Exit 9 before I could think of anything to say.

But for years it bothered me (who wouldn't be bothered?). My belief had always been with the ancient Greeks, that the most important events in life are physical events. And it bothered me that in (I now realize) the last opportunity I might've had to throw myself in front of my dearest loved one, it appeared I'd pushed my dearest loved one in front of myself as cravenly as a slinking cur (appearances are just as bad when cowardliness is at issue).

And yet I found that when Ann and I divorced because she couldn't put up with me and my various aberrations of grief and longing owing to the death of our first son, and just flew the coop (a physical act if there ever was one), I quit worrying about cowardice almost immediately and decided she'd been wrong. Though even if she'd been right, I felt it was braver to live with the specific knowledge of cowardice and look for improvements than never to know anything about myself on that front; and better, too, to go on believing, as we all do in our daydreams, that when the robber jumps out of the alley brandishing the skinning knife or the large-caliber pistol, terrorizing you and your wife and plenty of innocent bystanders (old people in wheelchairs, your high-school math teacher, Miss Hawthorne, who was patient when you couldn't get the swing of plane geometry and thus changed your life forever), that there'll be time for you (me) to act heroically ("I just don't think you've got nuts big enough to use that thing, mister, so you might as well hand it over and get out of here"). Better to wish the best for yourself; better also (and this isn't easy) that others wish it too.

IT WOULD be of no great interest to hear me expound on all I tried and started out to do during this time—1984, the Orwellian year, when Reagan was reelected to the term soon to end, the one he has more or less napped through when he wasn't starting wars or lying about it and getting the country into plenty of trouble.

For the first few months, I spent three mornings a week reading to the blind down at WHAD-FM (98.6). Michener novels and *Doctor Zhivago* were the blind people's favorites, and it is still something I occasionally stop off and do when I have time, and take real satisfaction in. I also looked briefly into the possibility of becoming a court reporter (my mother had always thought that would be a wonderful job because it served a useful purpose and you'd always be in demand). Later, and for one entire week, I attended classes in heavy-equipment operation, which I enjoyed but didn't finish (I was determined to aim at less predictable choices for a man with my background). I likewise tried getting a contract to write an "as told to" book but couldn't get my former literary agency interested since I had no particular subject in mind and they by then were only interested in young writers with surefire projects. And for three weeks I actually worked as an inspector for a company that certified as "excellent" crummy motels and restaurants across the Middle West, though that didn't work because of all the lonely time spent in the car.

At this same time, I also got busy shoring up my responsibilities with my two children (then ages eleven and eight), who were living with their mother on Cleveland Street and growing up between our two households in ordinary divorced-family style, which they seemed reconciled to, if not completely happy about.

I joined the high-priced Red Man Club during this period, with a mind to teaching the two of them respect for nature's bounty; and I was also planning a nostalgic update trip to Mississippi, for my old military school's class reunion, as well as a trip to the Catskills for a murder-mystery weekend, a hike up the Appalachian Trail and a guided float down the Wading River. (I was, as I said, fully conscious that taking an extended flier to Florida, then France, had not been scrupulous fathering practice and I needed to do better; though I felt it was arguable that if one of my parents had done the same thing I'd have understood, as long as they said they loved me and hadn't both vamoosed at once.)

All told, I felt I was positioning myself well for whatever good might come along and was even giving tentative thought to approaching Ann for an older-but-wiser reconsideration of the marriage option, when one evening in early June Ann herself called up and announced that she and Charley O'Dell were getting married, she was selling her house, quitting her job, putting the children in new schools, moving kit and caboodle, lock, stock and barrel, the whole nine yards up to Deep River and not coming back. She hoped I wouldn't be upset.

And I simply didn't know what in the hell to say or think, much less feel, and for several seconds I just stood holding the receiver to my ear as if the line had gone dead, or as if some lethal current had connected through my ear to my brain and struck me cold as a haddock.

Anybody, of course, could've seen it coming. I'd met Charley O'Dell, age fifty-seven (tall, prematurely white-haired, rich, big-boned, big-schnozzed, big-jawed, literal-as-a-dictionary architect), on various occasions having to do with the delivery and pickup of my children, and had at that time officially declared him a "no-threat." O'Dell is commandant of his own pretentious one-man design firm, housed in a converted seamen's chapel built on stilts (!) at the marsh edge in Deep River, and of course pilots his own 25-foot Alerion, built with his own callused hands and fitted with sails sewn at night while listening to Vivaldi, yakkedy, yakkedy, yak. We once stood one spring night, on the little front stoop of Ann's house—now mine—and yammered for thirty minutes with not one grain of sincerity or goodwill about diplomatic strategies for corraling the Scandinavians into the EEC, something I knew not a fig about and cared less. "Now if you ask me, Frank, the Danes are the key to the whole square-headed pack out there"—one tanned, naked knobby knee hiked up on Ann's stoop railing, one bespoke deck shoe dangling half off his long big toe, chin balanced pseudo-judiciously on big fist. Charley's usual attire when he isn't wearing a bow tie and a blazer is a big white tee-shirt and khaki canvas walking shorts, something they must hand out at graduation at Yale. I, that night, stared him straight in the eyes as if I were paying rapt attention, though in fact I was sucking one of my molars where I'd discovered a randy taste in an area I couldn't floss, and was also thinking that if I could hypnotize him and will him into disappearing I could have some time alone with my ex-wife.

Ann, however (suspiciously), wouldn't give in on the several evenings she and I paused together by my car in the silent dark of divorced former mates who still love each other, wouldn't crack smirky jokes at Charley's expense, the way she always had about all her other suitors—jokes about their taste in suits or their dreary jobs, their breath, the reported savage personalities of their ex-wives. Mum was always the word where Charley was concerned. (I guessed wrongly it was respect for his age.) But I should've paid closer attention and torpedoed him the way any man would who's in charge of his senses.

As a result, though, when Ann gave me the bad news on the phone that June evening just at cocktail hour—the sun having cleared the yardarm in butler's pantries all over Haddam, and trays of ice were being cracked into crystal buckets, leaded tumblers and slender Swedish pitchers, the vermouth hauled out wryly, the smell of juniper flaring the nostrils of many a bushed but deserving ex-hubby—I was kicked square in the head.

And my first on-record thought was of course that I had been bitterly, scaldingly betrayed just at a critical point—the point at which I'd gotten things almost "turned around" for the long canter back to the barn—the commencing point of life's gentle amelioration, all sins forgiven, all lesions healed.

"Married?" I, in essence, shouted, my heart making one palpable, possibly audible clunk at the bottom of its cavity. "Married to who?"

"To Charley O'Dell," Ann said, unduly calm in the face of calamitous news.

"You're marrying the bricklayer!" I said. "Why?"

"I guess because I want somebody to make love to me more than three times after which I never see them again." She said this calmly too. "You just go to France and I don't hear from you for months"—which wasn't true—"I actually think the children need a better life than that. And also because I don't want to die in Haddam, and because I'd like to see the Connecticut in the morning mist and go sailing in a skiff. I guess, in more traditional terms, I'm in love with him. What'd you think?"

"Those seem like good reasons," I said, light-headed.

"I'm happy you approve."

"I don't approve," I said, breathless, as if I'd come straight inside from a long run. "You're moving the kids away too?"

"It's not in our decree that I can't," she said.

"What do *they* think?" I felt my heart thunk-a-thunk again at the thought of the children. This, of course, was a serious issue, and one that becomes urgent decades beyond divorce itself: the issue of what the children think of their father if their mother remarries. (He almost never fares well. There are books about this, and they aren't funny: the father is seen either as a stooge wearing goat horns or a brute betrayer who forced Mom into marrying a hairy outsider who invariably treats the kids with irony, ill-disguised contempt and annoyance. Either way, insult is glommed onto injury.)

"They think it's wonderful," Ann said. "Or they should. I think they expect me to be happy."

"Sure, why not?" I said numbly.

"Right. Why not."

And then there was a long, cold silence, which we both knew to be the silence of the millennium, the silence of divorce, of being fatigued by love parceled out and withheld in the unfair ways it had been, by love lost when something should've made it not be lost but didn't, the silence of death—long before death might even be winked at.

"That's all I really have to say now," she said. A heavy curtain had parted briefly, then closed again.

I was *in fact* standing in the butler's pantry at 19 Hoving Road, staring out the little round nautically paned fo'c'sle window into my side yard, where the big copper beech cast ominous puddles of purple, pre-dark shadow over the green grasses and shrubs of late-spring evening.

"When's all this happening?" I said almost apologetically. I put my hand to my cheek, and my cheek was cold.

"In two months."

"What about the club?" Ann had stayed on as a part-time teaching pro at Cranbury Hills and had once briefly been an aspirant to the state ladies' pro-am. She'd actually met Charley there, on the cadge with his reciprocating membership from the Old Lyme Country Club. She had told me (I thought) all about him: a sort of nice older man she felt comfortable with.

"I've taught enough women to play golf now," she said briskly, then paused. "I put my house on the market this morning with Lauren-Schwindell."

"Maybe I'll buy it," I said rashly.

"That'd certainly be novel."

I had no idea why I'd say anything so preposterous, except to have something bold to say instead of breaking into hysterical laughter or howls of grief. But then I said, "Maybe I'll sell this place and move into your house."

And as quick as the words left my mouth I had the dead-eyed conviction that I was going to do exactly that, and in a hurry— perhaps so she could never get rid of me. (That may be what marriage means in laymen's terms: a relation you have with the one person in the world you can't get rid of except by dying.)

"I think I'll leave the real estate ventures to you," Ann said, ready to get off the phone.

"Is Charley there?" It seemed conceivable I might just storm over right then and bust him up, bloody his tee-shirt, put some extra years on him.

"No, he's not, and don't come over here, please. I'm crying now, and you don't get to see that." I hadn't *heard* her crying and concluded she was lying to make me feel like a louse, which was how I felt even though I hadn't done anything lousy. *She* was getting married. I was the one getting left behind like a cripple.

"Don't worry," I said, "I don't want to spoil any of the fun."

And then suddenly, the receiver pressed to my ear, another even more inert silence filled the optic lines connecting us. And I had the sharpest pain that Ann *was* going to die, not in Haddam and not immediately, not even soon, but not so long from then either—at the end of a period of time that, because she was abandoning me for the arms of another, would pass almost imperceptibly, her life's extinguishment paying out beyond my knowing via a series of small, exquisite doctors' appointments, anxieties, dismays, unhappy lab reports, gloomy X rays, tiny struggles, tiny victories, reprieves, then failures (life's inventory of morose happenstance), at the sudden, misty conclusion of which a call would come or a voice mail or a fax or a mailgram, saying: "Ann Dykstra died Tuesday morning. Services yesterday. Thought you'd want to know. Condolences. C. O'Dell." After which my own life would be ruined and over with, big time! (It's a matter of my age that all new events threaten to ruin my precious remaining years. Nothing like this feeling happens when you're thirty-two.)

And of course it was just cheap sentimentalism—the kind the gods frown down on from Olympus and send avengers to punish the small-time con men of emotion for practicing. Only sometimes you can't feel anything about a subject without hypothesizing its extinction. And that *is* how I felt: full of sadness that Ann was going away to start the part of her life that would end in her death; at which time I'd be elsewhere, piddling around at nothing very important, the way I had since coming back from Europe or—depending on your point of view—the way I had for twenty years. I'd be unthought of or worse, thought of only as "a man Ann was once married to. . . . I'm not sure where he is now. He was strange."

Yet I felt, if I was to have a part, any part in it at all, it would have to be spoken right then—on the phone, streets away but different neighborhoods (the geography of divorce), me alone in my house, feeling, as recently as ten minutes prior, hopeful about my unruined prospects but suddenly feeling as divorced as a man can be.

"Don't marry him, sweetheart! Marry me! Again! Let's sell both our shitty houses and move to Quoddy Head, where I'll buy a small newspaper from the proceeds. You can learn to sail your skiff off Grand Manan, and the kids can learn to set type by hand, be wary little seafarers, grow adept with lobster pots, trade in their Jersey accents, go to Bowdoin and Bates." These are words I *didn't* say into the dense millennial silence available to me. They would've been laughed at, since I'd had years to say them before then and hadn't—which Dr. Stopler of New Haven will tell you means I didn't really want to.

"I think I understand all this," I said instead, in a convinced voice, as I poured myself a convincing amount of gin, bypassing the vermouth. "And I love you, by the way."

"Please," Ann said. "Just please. You love me? What difference does that make? I'm finished with what I had to tell you, anyway." She was and is the kind of bedrock literalist who takes no interest in the far-fetched (the things I sometimes feel I'm *only* interested in), which is I'm sure why she married Charley.

"To say that some important truths are founded on flimsy evidence really isn't saying much." I voiced this view meekly.

"That's your philosophy, Frank, not mine. I've heard it for years. It only matters to you how long some improbable thing holds up, right?"

I took my first sip of just-cold-enough gin. I could feel the slow exhilaration of a long, honing talk coming. There aren't very many better feelings. "For some people the improbable can last long enough to become true," I said.

"And for other people it can't. And if you were about to ask me to marry you instead of Charley, don't. I won't. I don't want to."

"I was just trying to speak to an ephemeral truth at a moment of transition and trudge on beyond it."

"Trudge on, then," Ann said. "I've got to cook dinner for the children. I do want to admit this, though: I thought that it'd be you who'd get married again after we got divorced. To some bimbo. I admit I was wrong."

"Maybe you don't know me very well."

"I'm sorry."

"Thanks for calling me," I said. "Congratulations."

"Sure. It was nothing." Then she said good-bye and hung up.

BUT . . . NOTHING? It was nothing?

It was something!

I bolted my gin in one shuddering, breathless gulp, to wash down frothing bitterness. Nothing? It was epochal. And I didn't care if it was blue-blood Charley from Deep River, pencil-neck, breast-pocket-penholder Waldo from Bell Labs or tattooed Lonnie down at the car wash: I'd have felt the same. Like shit!

Up to that moment, Ann and I had had a nice, cozy-efficient system worked out, one by which we lived separate lives in separate houses in one small, tidy, peril-free town. We had flings, woes, despairs, joys, a whole gearbox full of life's meshings and unmeshings, on and on, but fundamentally we were the same two people who'd gotten married and divorced, only set in different equipoise: same planets, different orbits, same solar system. But in a pinch, a real pinch, say a head-on car crash requiring extended life support or a prolonged bout of chemo, no one but the other would've been in attendance, buttonholing the doctors, chatting up the nurses, judiciously closing and open- ing heavy curtains, monitoring the game shows through the long, silent afternoons, shooing away prying neighbors and long- ignored relatives, former boyfriends, girlfriends, old nemeses come to make up—shepherding them all back down the long hallways, speaking in confidential whispers, saying "She had a good night," or "He's resting now." All this while the patient dozed, and the necessary machines clicked and whirred and sighed. And all just so we could be alone. Which is to say we had standing in the other's dire moments, even if not in the happy ones.

Eventually, after a long recovery during which one or the other would have had to relearn some basic human life functions up to now taken for granted (walking, breathing, pissing), certain key conversations would've taken place, certain dour admissions been offered if not already offered in moments of extremis, and important truths reconciled so that a new and (this time) binding union could be forged.

Or maybe not. Maybe we would simply have parted again, though with new strengths and insights and respects achieved through the fragile life experiences of the other.

But all of that was gone like a fart in a skillet. And jeez Louise! If I'd thought back in '81 that Ann would get remarried, I'd have fought it like a Viking instead of giving in to divorce like a queasy, uninspired saint. And I'd have fought it for a damn good reason: because no matter where she held the mortgage papers, she completely supposed my existence. My life was (and to some vague extent still is) played out on a stage in which she's con- tinually in the audience (whether she's paying attention or not). All my decent, reasonable, patient, loving components were developed in the experimental theater of our old life together, and I realized that by moving house up to Deep River she was striking most of the components, dismembering the entire illusion, intending to hook up with another, leaving me with only faint, worn-out costumes to play myself with.

Naturally enough, I fell into a deep, sulfurous, unsynchronous gloom, stayed at home, called no one for days, drank a lot more gin, reconsidered heavy-equipment-operator's class and becoming an unwieldy embarrassment to people who knew me, and overall felt myself becoming significantly less substantial.

I spoke once or twice to my children, who seemed to calculate their mother's marriage to Charley O'Dell with the alacrity with which a small investor notices a gain in a stock he feels certain he'll eventually lose money on. Though he'd later change his mind, Paul uncomfortably declared Charley to be an "okay" guy and admitted having gone to a Giants game with him in November (something I hadn't heard about because I was in Florida and contemplating going to France). Clarissa seemed more interested in the wedding itself than in the conception of remarriage, which didn't seem to worry her much. She was concerned with what she was going to wear, where everyone would stay (the Griswold Inn in Essex) and if I could be invited ("No"), plus whether she could be a bridesmaid if I got married in the future (which she said she hoped I would). All three of us talked about all these matters for a while via extension phones. I tried to calm fears, sweeten prospects and simplify growing confusions about my own and their possible unhappiness, until there was nothing left to say, after which we parted company, never to speak under those exact circumstances or in those same innocent voices again. Gone. Poof.

THE WEDDING itself was an intimate though elegant "on the grounds" affair at Charley's house—"The Knoll" (pretentious hand-hewn post-and-beam Nantucket cottage adaptation: giant windows, wood from Norway and Mongolia, everything built-in flush, rabbeted, solar panels, heated floors, Finnish sauna, on and on and on). Ann's mother flew in from Mission Viejo, Charley's aged parents somehow motored down from Blue Hill or Northeast Harbor or some such magnate's enclave, with the happy couple flying off to the Huron Mountain Club, where Ann's father had left her his membership.

But no sooner had Ann solemnized her retreaded vows than I plunged forward with my own plans (founded on my previously explained sense of practicality, since high-spirited synchronicity hadn't fared well) to purchase her house on Cleveland Street for four ninety-five, and to get rid of my big old soffit-sagging half-timber on Hoving Road, where I'd lived nearly every minute of my life in Haddam and where I mistakenly thought I could live forever, but which now seemed to be one more commitment holding me back. Houses can have this almost authorial power over us, seeming to ruin or make perfect our lives just by persisting in one place longer than we can. (In either case it's a power worth defeating.)

Ann's house was a crisp, well-kept freestanding Greek Revival town house of a style and 1920s vintage typical of the succinct, nice-but-not-finicky central Jersey architectural temper—a place she'd bought on the cheap (with my help) after our divorce and done some modernizing work on ("opening out" the back, adding skylights and crown moldings, repointing some basement piers, finishing off the third floor to be Paul's lair, then giving the clapboards a new white paint job and new green shutters).

In truth, the house was a natural for me, since I'd already spent a three-years collection of sleepless nights there when a child was sick or when, in the early days of our sad divorced limbo, I'd sometimes gotten the jimjams so bad Ann would take pity on me and let me slip in and sleep on the couch.

It felt like home, in other words; and if not my home, at least my kids' home, *someone's* home. Whereas since Ann's announcement, my old place had begun to feel barny and murky, murmurous and queer, and myself strangely outdistanced as its owner—in the yard cranking away on the Lawn-Boy, or standing in my driveway, hands on hips, supervising from below the patching of a new squirrel hole under the chimney flashing. I was no longer, I felt, preserving anything *for* anything, even for myself, but was just going through the motions, joining life's rough timbers end to end.

Consequently, I got promptly over to Lauren-Schwindell and threw my hat in both rings at once: hers to buy, mine to sell. My thinking was, if lightning struck and Charley and his new bride came unglued during week one, Ann and I could forge our new beginning in her house (then later move to Maine more or less as newlyweds).

So, before the O'Dells returned home (no annulment was pending), I'd entered a full-price cash offer on 116 Cleveland and, through a savvy intercession by old man Otto Schwindell himself, reached an extremely advantageous deal with the Theological Institute to take over my house for the purpose of converting it into the Ecumenical Center where guests like Bishop Tutu, the Dalai Lama and the head of the Icelandic Federation of Churches could hold high-level confabs about the fate of the world's soul, and still find accommodations homey enough to slip down after midnight for a snack.

The Institute's Board of Overseers was, in fact, highly sensitive to my tax situation, since my house appraised out at an eye-popping million two, near the peak of the boom. Their lawyers were able to set up a healthy annuity which earns interest for me and later passes on to Paul and Clarissa, and by whose terms I in essence donated my house as an outright gift, claimed a whopper deduction and afterward received a generous "consultant's" fee in what I think of as temporal affairs. (This tax loophole has since been closed, but too late, since what's done's done.)

One bright and green August day, I simply walked out the door and down the steps of my house, leaving all my furniture except for books and nostalgic attachments (my map of Block Island, a hatch-cover table, a leather chair I liked, my marriage bed), drove over to Ann's house on Cleveland, with all her old-new furniture sitting exactly where she'd left it, and took up residence. I was allowed to keep my old phone number.

And truth to tell I hardly noticed the difference, so often had I lain awake nights in my old place or roamed the rooms and halls of hers when all were sleeping—searching, I suppose, for where I fit in, or where I'd gone wrong, or how I could breathe air into my ghostly self and become a recognizable if changed-for-the-better figure in their sweet lives or my own. One house is as good as another for this kind of private enterprise. And the poet was right again: "Let the wingèd Fancy roam, / Pleasure never is at home."

*   *   *

GETTING GOING in the realty business followed as a natural off-spring of selling my house and buying Ann's. Once all was settled and I was "at home" on Cleveland Street, I started thinking again about new enterprises, about diversification and stashing my new money someplace smart. A ministorage in New Sharon, a train-station lobster house rehab, a chain of low-maintenance self-serv car washes—all rose as possibles. Though none did I immediately bite for, since I still somehow felt frozen in place, unable or unwilling or just uninspired to move into action. Without Ann and my kids nearby, I, in fact, felt as lonely and inessential and exposed as a lighthouse keeper in broad daylight.

Unmarried men in their forties, if we don't subside entirely into the landscape, often lose important credibility and can even attract unwholesome attention in a small, conservative community. And in Haddam, in my new circumstances, I felt I was perhaps becoming the personage I least wanted to be and, in the years since my divorce, had feared being: the suspicious bachelor, the man whose life has no mystery, the graying, slightly jowly, slightly too tanned and trim middle-ager, driving around town in a cheesy '58 Chevy ragtop polished to a squeak, always alone on balmy summer nights, wearing a faded yellow polo shirt and green suntans, elbow over the window top, listening to progressive jazz, while smiling and pretending to have everything under control, when in fact there was nothing *to* control.

One morning in November, though, Rolly Mounger, one of the broker-agents at Lauren-Schwindell, and the one who had walked me through my buyout with the Institute and who is a big ex-Fairleigh Dickinson nose-tackle out of Plano, Texas, called up to advise me about some tax forms I needed to get hold of after New Year's and to fill me in on some "investment entities" dealing with government refinance grants for a bankrupt apartment complex in Kendall Park that he was putting together with "other principals"—just in case I wanted a first crack (I didn't). He said, however, as if in passing, that he himself was just before pulling up stakes and heading to Seattle to get involved with some lucrative commercial concepts he didn't want to get particular about; and would I like to come over and talk to some people about coming on there as a residential specialist. My name, he said, had come up "seriously" any number of times from several different sources (why, and who,

I couldn't guess and never found out and I'm sure now it was a total lie). It was generally thought, he said, I had strong natural credentials "per se" for their line of work: which was to say I was looking to get into a new situation; I wasn't hurting for dough (a big plus in any line of work); I knew the area, was single and had a pleasant personality. Plus, I was mature—meaning over forty—and I didn't seem to have a lot of attachments in the community, a factor that made selling houses one hell of a lot easier.

What did I think?

Training, paperwork and "all that good boool dukie," Rolly said, could be plowed under right on the job while I went nights to a three-month course up at the Weiboldt Realty Training Institute in New Brunswick, after which I could take the state boards and start printing money like the rest of them.

And the truth was, having parted with or been departed from by most everything, until I was left almost devoid of all expectation, I thought it was a reasonable idea. In those last three months I'd begun to feel that living through the consequences of my various rash acts and bad decisions had had its downsides as well as its purported rewards, and if it was possible to be at a complete loss without being miserable about it, that's what I was. I'd started going fishing alone at the Red Man Club three afternoons a week, sometimes staying overnight in the little beaverboard cabin meant for keeping elderly members out of the rain, taking a book up with me but ultimately just lying there in the dark listening to big fish kerplunking and mosquitoes bopping the screen, while not very far away the bangety-bang of I-80 soothed the night and, out east, Gotham shone like a temple set to fire by infidels. I still registered a faint tingle of the synchronicity I'd felt when I got back from France. I was still dead set on taking the kids to Mississippi and the Pine Barrens once they were settled, and had even joined AAA and gotten color-coded maps with sidebars to various attractions down side roads (Cooperstown and the Hall of Fame was in fact one of them).

But tiny things—things I'd never even noticed when Ann lived in Haddam and we shared responsibilities and I held down my sportswriting job—had begun to get the better of me. Some little worry, some little anything, would settle into my thinking—for instance, how was I going to get my car serviced on Tuesday but also get to the airport to sign for a Greek rug I'd ordered from Thessaloníki and had been waiting on for months and was sure some thieving airport worker would steal if I wasn't there to lay hands on it the instant it came down the conveyer? Should I rent a car? Should I send someone? Who? And would that person even be willing to go if I could think of who he or she was, or would that person think I was an idiot? Should I call the broker in Greece and tell him to delay the shipping? Should I call the freight company and say I'd be a day late getting up there and would they please see to it the rug was kept in a safe place until my car was ready? I'd wake up right in the Red Man Club cabin, my heart booming, or in my own new house, brooding about such things, sweating, clenching my fists, scheming how to get this plus a hundred *other* simple, ordinary things done, as if everything were a crisis as big as my health. Later I'd start to think about how stupid it was to carry such things around all day. I'd decide then to trust fate, go up and get it when I could or maybe never, or to forget the fucking rug and just go fishing. Though then I'd start to fear I was letting everything go, that my life was spinning crazy-out-of-azimuth, proportion and common sense flying out the window like pie plates. Then I'd realize that years later I'd look back on this period as a "bad time," when I was "w*aaaay* out there at the edge," my everyday conduct as erratic and zany as a roomful of chimps, only I was the last to notice (again, one's neighbors would be the first: "He really sort of stayed to himself a lot, though he seemed like a pretty nice guy. I wouldn't have expected anything like *this*!").

Now, of course, in 1988, driving into sunny Haddam with better hopes for the day squirreling around my belly, I know the source of that devilment. I'd paid handsome dues to the brotherhood of consolidated mistake-makers, and having survived as well as I had, I wanted my goddamned benefits: I wanted *everything* to go my way and to be happy *all the time*, and I was wild it wouldn't work out like that. I wanted the Greek rug delivery not to interfere with getting my windshield washer pump replaced. I wanted the fact that I had left France and Catherine Flaherty and come home in the best spirit of enterprise and good works to still somehow reward me in big numbers. I wanted the fact that my wife had managed to divorce me *again* and *worse*, and even divorce my kids from me, to become a fact of life I got smoothly used to and made the most of. I wanted a lot of things, in other words (these are just samples). And I'm not in fact sure all this didn't constitute another "kind of major crisis," though it may also be how you feel when you survive one.

But what I wanted more than anything was to quit being deviled so I could have a chance for the rest, and it occurred to me once I'd listened to Rolly Mounger's idea that I might try out a new thought (since I wasn't making any other headway): I might just take seriously his list of my "qualifications" and let them lead me toward the unexpected—instead of going on worrying about how happy I was all the time—after which worries and contingencies might glide away like leaves on a slack tide, and I might find myself, if not in the warp of many highly dramatic events, reckless furies and rocketing joie de vivre, still as close to day-to-day happy as I could be. This code of conduct, of course, is the most self-preserving and salubrious tenet of the Existence Period and makes real estate its ideal occupation.

I told Rolly Mounger I'd give his suggestion some serious thought, even though I said the idea pretty much came out of left field. He said there was no hurry to make a decision about becoming a realtor, that down at their office everyone had gotten there by different routes and timetables, and there were no two alike. He himself, he said, had been a supermarket developer and before that a policy strategist for a Libertarian state senate candidate. One person had a Ph.D. in American literature; another had left a seat on the Exchange; a third was a dentist! They all worked as independents but acted in concert whenever possible, which gave everybody a damn good feeling. Everybody had made a "ton of money" in the last few years and expected to make a ton more before the big correction came ("the whole industry" knew it was coming). From his point of view, which he admitted favored the commercial side, all you needed to do to wake up rich was "get with your money people, put some key factors and some financing on the table," locate some un-improved parcels your group can handle the debt service and taxes on for twelve to eighteen months, then once the time's up sell out the whole trunkload to some Johnny-come-lately Arabs or Japs and start cashing in your chips. "Let your money people run the risk gauntlet," Rolly said. "You just sit tight in the middle seat and take your commissions." (You could always, of course, "participate" yourself, and he admitted he had. But the exposure could be substantial.)

To figure all this out took me no time at all. If everybody came at it from all angles, I thought maybe I could find one of my own to work—relying on the concept that you don't sell a house to someone, you sell a life (this had so far been my experience). In this way I could still pursue my original plan to do for others while looking after Number One, which seemed a good aspiration as I entered a part of life when I'd decided to expect less, hope for modest improvements and be willing to split the difference.

I went down to the office in three days and got introduced around to everybody—a crew of souls who seemed like people you wouldn't mind working out of the same office with. A short, bunchy-necked, thick-waisted dyke in a business suit and wing tips, named Peg, with Buick-bumper breasts, braces on her teeth and hair bleached silver (she was the Ph.D.). There was a tall, salt-and-pepper, blue-blazer Harvard grad in his late fifties—this was Shax Murphy, who's since bought the agency and who'd retired out of some brokerage firm and still owned a house in Vinalhaven. He had his long, gray-flanneled legs stretched out in the aisle between desks, one big shiny cordovan oxford on top of the other, his face red as a western sunset from years of gentlemanly drinking, and I took to him instantly because when I shook his hand he had just put down a dog-eared copy of *Paterson*, which made me think he probably had life in pretty much the right perspective. "You just need to remember the three most important words in the 'relaty budnus,' Frank, and you'll do fine in this shop," he said, jiggering his heavy brows up and down mock seriously. 'Locution, locution, locution.'" He sniffed loudly through his big ruby nose, rolled his eyes and went right back to reading.

Everyone else in the office at that time—two or three young realtor associates and the dentist—has left since the '86 slide began to seem like a long fall-off. All of them were people without solid stakes in town or capital to back them up, and they quickly scattered back out of sight—to vet school at Michigan State, back home to New Hampshire, one in the Navy, and of course Clair Devane, who came later and met an unhappy end.

Old man Schwindell accorded me only the briefest, most

cursory of interviews. He was an old, palely grim, wispy-haired, flaking-skinned little tyrant in an out-of-season seersucker suit and whom I'd seen in town for years, knew nothing about and viewed as a curio—though it was he who'd done the behind-the-scenes knitting of my deal with the Institute. He was also the "dean" of New Jersey realtors and had thirty plaques on his office wall saying as much, along with framed photos of himself with movie stars and generals and prizefighters he'd sold homes to. No longer officially active, he held forth in the back office, hunched behind a cluttered old glass-topped desk with his coat always on, smoking Pall Malls.

"Do you believe in progress, Bascombe?" Old man Schwindell squinted his almost hueless blue eyes up at me. He had a big mustache yellowed by eight million Pall Malls, and his grizzled hair was thick on the sides and growing out his ears but was thin on top and falling out in clusters. He suddenly groped behind himself without looking, clutched at the clear plastic hose attached to a big oxygen cylinder on wheels, yanked it and strapped a little elastic band around his head so that a tiny clear nozzle fit up into his nose and fed him air. "You know that's our motto," he gasped, routing his eyes down to monkey with his lifeline.

"That's what Rolly's told me," I said. Rolly had never mentioned word one about progress, had talked only about risk gauntlets, capital gains taxes and exposure, all of which he was dead against.

"I'm not going to ask you about it now. Don't worry," old man Schwindell said, not entirely satisfied with his flow, straining around to twist a green knob on the cylinder and succeeding only in getting half a good breath. "When you've been around here and know something," he said with difficulty, "I'll ask you to tell me *your* definition of progress. And if you give me the wrong answer, I'll get rid of you on the spot." He swiveled back around and gave me a mean little ocher-toothed leer, his air apparatus getting in the way of his mouth, though his breathing was going much more smoothly, so that he might've felt like he wasn't about to die that very minute. "How's that? Is that fair?"

"I think that's fair," I said. "I'll try to give you a good answer."

"Don't give me a good answer. Give me the right answer!"

he shouted. "Nobody should graduate the sixth grade without an idea of what progress is all about. Don't you think so?"

"I agree completely," I said, and I did, though mine had been suffering some setbacks.

"Then you're good enough to start. You don't have to be any good anyway. Realty sells itself in this town. Or it used to." He started fiddling more furiously with his breathing tubes, trying to get the holes to line up better with his old hairy nostrils. And my interview was over, though I stood there for almost another minute before I recognized he wasn't going to say anything else, so that I just eventually let myself out.

And for all practical purposes I was on my sweet way after that. Rolly Mounger took me to lunch at The Two Lawyers. I'd have a "break-in period," he told me, of about three months, when I'd be on salary (no insurance or benefits). Everybody would chip in and rotate me around the office, see to it I learned the MLS hardware and the office lingo. I'd go on *"beaucoup"* house show-ings and closings and inspections and realty caravans, "just to get to know whatever," all this while I was going to class at my own expense—"three hundred bucks *más o menos.*" At the end of the course I'd take the state exam at the La Quinta in Trenton, then "jump right in on the commission side and start root-hoggin'."

"I wish I could tell you there was one goddamn hard thing about any of this, Frank," Rolly said in amazement. "But"—and he shook his jowly, buzz-cut head—"if it was *so* goddamned hard why would I be doing it? Hard work's what the other asshole does." And with that he cut a big bracking fart right into his Naugahyde chair and looked all around at the other lunchers, grinning like a farm boy. "You know, your soul's not supposed to be in this," he said. "This is realty. *Reality's* something else—that's when you're born and you die. This is the in-between stuff here."

"I get it," I said, though I thought my personal take on the job probably wouldn't be just like Rolly's.

And that was that. In six months old man Schwindell gorked off in the front seat of his Sedan de Ville, stopped at the light at the corner of Venetian Way and Lipizzaner Road, a man-and-wife ophthalmologist team in the car, on their way to the preclosing walk-through at the retired New Jersey Supreme Court Justice's house, down the street from my former home

on Hoving (the deal naturally fell through). By then Rolly
Mounger was steaming along selling time-shares to Seattleites,
most of the young people in our office had taken off for better
pickings in distant area codes, and I'd passed the board and was
out hawking listings.

Though based on strict cash flow and forgetting about taxes,
it was already true by then that a person could rent for half the
cost of buying, and a lot of our clients were beginning to wise
up. In addition—as I have ever so patiently told the Markhams,
fidgeting now out in the Sleepy Hollow—housing costs were
rising faster than incomes, at about 4.9 percent. Plus, plenty of
other signs were bad. Employment was down. Expansion was
way out of balance. Building permits were taking a nosedive. It
was "what the monkey does on the other side of the stick," Shax
Murphy said. And those who had no choice or, like me, had
choices but no wish to pursue them, all dug in for the long night
that becomes winter.

But truth to say, I was as happy as I expected to be. I enjoyed
being on the periphery of the business community and having
the chance to stay up with trends—trends I didn't even know
existed back when I was writing sports. I liked the feeling of
earning a living by the sweat of my brow, even if I didn't need
the money, still don't work that hard and don't always earn a
great deal. And I managed to achieve an even fuller appreciation
of the Existence Period; began to see it as a good, permanent
and adaptable strategy for meeting life's contingencies other than
head-on.

For a brief time I took some small interest in forecast colloquia,
attended the VA and FHA update meetings and a few taking-
control-of-the-market seminars. I attended the state Realty
Roundtable, sat in on the Fair Housing Panel down in Trenton.
I delivered Christmas packages to the elderly, helped coach the
T-ball team, even dressed up like a clown and rode from Haddam
to New Brunswick in a circus wagon to try to spruce up the
public perception of realtors as being, if not a bunch of crooks,
at least a bunch of phonies and losers.

But eventually I let most of it slide. A couple of young hotshot
associates have come in since I signed on, and they're fired up to
put on clown suits to prove a point. Whereas I don't feel like I'm
trying to prove a point anymore.

And yet I still like the sunny, paisley-through-the-maples exhilaration of exiting my car and escorting motivated clients up some new and strange walkway and right on into whatever's waiting—an unoccupied house on a summer-warm morning when it's chillier indoors than out, even if the house isn't much to brag about, or even if I've shown it twenty-nine times and the bank's got it on the foreclosure rolls. I enjoy going into other people's rooms and nosing around at their things, while hoping to hear a groan of pleasure, an "Ahhh, now *this*, this is more like it," or a whispered approval between a man and wife over some waterfowl design worked into the fireplace paneling, then surprisingly repeated in the bathroom tiles; or share the satisfaction over some small grace note—a downstairs-upstairs light switch that'll save a man possible injury when he's stumbling up to bed half sloshed, having gone to sleep on the couch watching the Knicks long after his wife has turned in because she can't stand basketball.

Beyond all that, since two years ago I've bought no new houses on Clio Street or elsewhere. I ride herd on my small hot dog empire. I write my editorials and have as always few friends outside of work. I take part in the annual Parade of Homes, standing in the entryway of our fanciest listings with a big smile on my chops. I play an occasional game of volleyball behind St. Leo's with the co-ed teams from other businesses. And I go fishing as much as I can at the Red Man Club, where I sometimes take Sally Caldwell in violation of Rule 1 but never see other members, and where I've learned over time to catch a fish, to marvel a moment at its opaline beauties and then to put it back. And of course I act as parent and guardian to my two children, though they are far away now and getting farther.

I try, in other words, to keep something finite and acceptably doable on my mind and not disappear. Though it's true that sometimes in the glide, when worries and contingencies are floating off, I sense I myself am afloat and cannot always feel the sides of where I am, nor know what to expect. So that to the musical question "What's it all about, Alfie?" I'm not sure I'd know the answer. Although to the old taunt that says, "Get a life," I can say, "I already have an existence, thanks."

And this may perfectly well constitute progress the way old man Schwindell had it in mind. His wouldn't have been some philosopher's enigma about human improvement over the passage of time used frugally, or an economist's theorem about profit and loss, or the greater good for the greater number. He wanted, I believe, to hear something from me to convince him I was simply *alive*, and that by doing whatever I was doing—selling houses—I was extending life and my own interest in it, strengthening my tolerance for it and the tolerance of innocent, unnamed others. That was undoubtedly what made him "dean" and kept him going. He wanted me to feel a little every day—and a little would've been enough—like I felt the day after I speared a liner bare-handed in the right-field stands at Veterans Stadium, hot off the bat of some black avenger from Chicago, with my son and daughter present and awed to silence with admiration and astoundment for their Dad (everyone around me stood up and applauded as my hand began to swell up like a tomato). How I felt at that moment was that life would never get better than that—though later what I thought, upon calmer reflection, was that it had merely been just a damn good thing to happen, and my life wasn't a zero. I'm certain old Otto would've been satisfied if I'd come in and said something along those lines: "Well, Mr. Schwindell, I don't know very much about progress, and truthfully, since I became a realtor my life hasn't been totally transformed; but I don't feel like I'm in jeopardy of disappearing into thin air, and that's about all I have to say." He would, I'm certain, have sent me back to the field with a clap on the back and a hearty go-get-'em.

And this in fact may be how the Existence Period helps create or at least partly stimulates the condition of honest independence: inasmuch as when you're in it you're visible as you are, though not necessarily very noticeable to yourself or others, and yet you maintain reason enough and courage in a time of waning urgency to go toward where your interests lie as though it mattered that you get there.

THE RAIN that dumped buckets on Route 1 and Penns Neck has missed Wallace Hill, so that all the hot, neat houses are shut up tight as nickels with their window units humming, the pavement already giving off wavy lines no one's willing to tread through at eleven-thirty. Later, when I'm long gone to South Mantoloking and shade inches beyond the eaves and sycamores, all the front porches will be full, laughter and greetings crisscrossing the way as on my first drive-by. Though now everyone who's not at work or in summer school or in jail is sitting in the TV darkness watching game shows and waiting for lunch.

The McLeods' house looks as it did at 8:30, though someone in the last three hours has removed my FOR RENT sign from in front of the Harrises', and I pull to a halt there, careful not to stop in front of the McLeods' and alert them. I climb out into the clammy heat, ditch my windbreaker and hike up onto the dry lawn and take a look around. I check down both sides of the house, behind the hydrangeas and the rose of Sharon bush and up on the tiny porch as if the sign stealers had just uprooted the thing and tossed it, which according to Everick and Wardell is what usually happens. Only it's not here now.

I step back out to my car, open the trunk for another sign from the several (FOR SALE, OPEN HOUSE, REDUCED, CONTRACT PENDING) that're stacked there with my box of offer sheets, along with my suitbag and fishing rods, three Frisbees, two ball mitts, baseballs and the fireworks I've ordered special from relatives in Florida—all important paraphernalia for my trip with Paul.

I bring the new FOR RENT up onto the lawn, find the two holes the previous sign occupied, waggle the stiff metal legs in until they stop, and with my toe mash some grassy ground around so that everything looks as it did. Then I close up the trunk, wipe the sweat off my arms and brow, using my handkerchief, and walk straight to the McLeods' front door, where, though I mean to ring the bell, I like a criminal step to the side and peer through the front window into the living room, where it's murky as twilight. I can make out both McLeod kids huddled on a couch, eyes glued like zombies to the TV (little Winnie is clutching a stuffed bunny in her tiny hands). Neither one of them seems to see me, though suddenly the older one, Nelson, jerks his curly head around and stares at the window as if it were just another TV screen, and I was in the picture.

I wave a little friendly wave and grin. I would like to get this over with and get going to Franks and on to Sally's.

Nelson continues staring at me out of the dark room's dreamy light as though he expects me to disappear in a few more seconds. He and his sister are watching Wimbledon, and I suddenly realize that I have no business whatsoever gawking in the window and am actually running a serious risk hothead Larry will blow my head off.

Little Nelson gazes at me until I wave again, step away from the window, move back to the door and ring the bell. Like a shot, his bare feet hit the floor and pound out of the room, heading I hope to get his lazy parents up out of bed. An interior door slams, and far, far away I hear a voice below the a/c hum, a voice I can't make out, saying what, I'm not sure, though it's certainly about me. I look out at the street of white, green, blue and pink frame houses with green and red roofs and neat little cemetery-plot yards—some with overgrown tomato plants along the foundation walls, others with sweet-pea vines running up side lattices and porch poles. It could be a neighborhood in the Mississippi Delta, though the local cars at the curb are all snazzy van conversions and late-model Fords and Chevys (Negroes are among the most loyal advocates of "Buy American").

A large elderly black woman, pushing an aluminum walker over which a yellow tea towel is draped, stumps out the screen door of the house directly across the street. When she sees me on the McLeods' porch she stops and stares. This is Myrlene Beavers, who waved at me hospitably the first two times I cruised the block, back in 1986, when I was deciding to buy into her neighborhood. Her husband, Tom, has died within the year, and Myrlene—the Harrises tell me by letter—has gone into a decline.

"Who you lookin' fo'?" Myrlene shouts out at me across the street.

"I'm just looking for Larry, Myrlene," I shout back and wave amiably. She and Mr. Beavers were both diabetics, and Myrlene is losing the rest of her sight to milky cataracts. "It's me, Myrlene," I call out. "It's Frank Bascombe."

"Sho' better not be," Myrlene says, her steely hair all tufted out in crazy stalks. "I'm tellin' you right now." She's wearing a bright-orange Hawaiian-print muumuu, and her ankles are swollen and bound up in bandages. I am aware she may fall slap over dead if she gets excited.

"It's all right, Myrlene," I call out. "I'm just visiting Larry. Don't worry. Everything's all right."

"I'm callin' the po-lice," Mrs. Beavers says, and goes stumping around so she can get back through her front door, the walker scraping the porch boards ahead of her.

"No, don't call the police," I shout. I should jog across and let her see it's me, that I'm not a burglar or a process server, only a rent collector—more or less the way Joe Markham said. Myrlene and I had several cordial conversations when the Harrises were still here—she from her porch, me going to and from my car. But something has happened now.

Though just as I'm about to hustle across and stop her from calling the cops, more bare feet come thundering toward the door, which suddenly quakes with locks and bolts being keyed and thrown, then opens to reveal Nelson in the crack, sandy-curly headed and light tan skin, a little mulatto Jackie Cooper. His face is below the nail latch on the screen, and staring down on him I feel like a giant. He says nothing, just peers up at me with his small, brown, skeptical eyes. He is six, bare-chested and wearing only a pair of purple-and-gold Lakers shorts. A draft of air-conditioned air slips past my face, which again is sweating. "Advantage, Miss Navratilova," an English woman's bland voice says, after which spectators applaud. (It's a replay from yesterday.)

"Nelson, how you doin'?" I say enthusiastically. We have never spoken, and Nelson just stares up at me and blinks as if I were speaking Swahili. "Your folks home today?"

He takes a look over his shoulder, then back at me. "Nelson, why don't you tell your folks Mr. Bascombe's at the front door, okay? Tell 'em I'm just here for the rent, not to murder anybody." This may be the wrong brand of humor for Nelson.

I would like not to peek in farther. It's, after all, my house, and I have a right to see in under extraordinary circumstances. But Nelson and Winnie may be home by themselves, and I wouldn't want to be inside alone with them. I have the sensation from behind me of Myrlene Beavers yelling inside her house: an unidentified white man is trying to break into Larry McLeod's private home in broad daylight. "Nelson," I say, sweating through my shirt and feeling unexpectedly trapped, "why don't you let me lean inside and call your Dad? Okay?" I offer him a big persuasive nod, then pull back the screen door, which surprisingly isn't latched, and push my face into the cool, swimming air. "Larry," I say fairly loudly into the dark room. "I'm just here for the rent." Winnie, clutching her stuffed rabbit, seems asleep. The TV's showing the deep greens of the All England Club.

Nelson looks straight up at me still (I'm leaning directly over him), then turns and goes and reseats himself on the couch by his sister, whose eyes open slowly, then close.

"Larry!" I call in again. "Are you in here?" Larry's big pistol is absent from the table, which may mean, of course, he has it in his possession.

I hear what sounds like a drawer opening and shutting in a back room; then a door slams. What would a panel of eight blacks and four whites—a jury of my peers—say if because of wishing to collect my rent I turned out to be a pre-holiday homicide statistic? I'm sure I'd be found at fault.

I step back from the door and turn a wary look over at the Beavers' house. Myrlene's orange muumuu is swimming like a mirage behind the screen, where she's watching me.

"It's all right, Myrlene," I say at nothing, which causes the muumuu specter to recede into the shadows.

"What's the matter?"

I turn quickly, and Betty McLeod is behind the screen, which she is this instant latching. She looks out at me with an unwelcoming frown. She's wearing a quilted pink housecoat and holding its scalloped collar closed with her skinny papery fingers.

"Nothing's the *matter*," I say, shaking my head in a way that probably makes me look deranged. "I think Mrs. Beavers just called the cops on me. I'm just trying to collect the rent." I'd like to look amused about it, but I'm not.

"Larry isn't here. He'll be home tonight, so you'll have to come back." Betty says this as though I'd been yelling in her face.

"Okay," I say, and smile mirthlessly. "Just tell him I came by like every other month. And the rent's due."

"He'll pay you," she says in a sour voice.

"That's great, then." Far back in the house, I hear a toilet flushing, water slackly then more vigorously touring the new pipes I had installed less than a year ago and paid a pretty penny for. Larry has no doubt just waked up, had his long morning piss and is holing up in the bathroom until I'm dispensed with.

Betty McLeod blinks at me defiantly as we both listen to the water trickle. She is a sallow, pointy-faced little Grinnell grad, off the farm near Minnetonka, who married Larry while she was

doing a social work M.A. at Columbia and he was working himself through trade school at some uptown community
college. He'd been a Green Beret and was searching for a way
out of the city hell (all this I learned from the Harrises). Betty's
Zion Lutheran parents naturally had a conniption when she and
Larry came home their first Christmas with baby Nelson in a
bassinet, though they've reportedly recovered. But since moving
to Haddam, the McLeods have lived an increasingly reclusive
life, with Betty staying inside all the time, Larry going off to his
night job at the mobile-home factory and the kids being their
only outward signs. It's not so different from many people's lives.

In truth I don't much like Betty McLeod, despite wanting to
rent the house to her and Larry because I think they're probably
courageous. To my notice she's always worn a perpetually disappointed look that says she regrets all her major life choices yet
feels absolutely certain she made the right moral decision in
every instance, and is better than you because of it. It's the typical
three-way liberal paradox: anxiety mingled with pride and self-
loathing. The McLeods are also, I'm afraid, the kind of family
who could someday go paranoid and barricade themselves in
their (my) house, issue confused manifestos, fire shots at the
police and eventually torch everything, killing all within. (This,
of course, is no reason to evict them.)

"Well," I say, moving back to the top step as if to leave, "I
hope everything's A-okay around the house." Betty looks at me
reproachfully. Though just then her eyes leave mine, move to
the side, and I turn around to see one of our new black-and-
white police cruisers stopping behind my car. Two uniformed
officers are inside. One—the passenger—is talking into a two-
way radio.

"He's still over there!" Myrlene Beavers bawls from inside her
house, totally lost from sight. "That white man! Go on and git
him. He's breakin' in."

The policeman who was talking on the radio says something
to his partner-driver that makes them both laugh, then he gets
out without his hat on and begins to stroll up the walk.

The cop, of course, is an officer I've known since I arrived in
Haddam—Sergeant Balducci, who is only answering disturbance calls today because of the holiday. He is from a large local
family of Sicilian policemen, and he and I have often passed

words on street corners or chatted reticently over coffee at the
Coffee Spot, though we've actually never "met." I have tried to
talk him out of a half-dozen parking tickets (all unsuccessfully),
and he once assisted me when I'd locked my keys in my car
outside Town Liquors. He has also cited me for three moving
violations, come into my house to investigate a burglary years
ago when I was married, once stopped me for questioning and
patted me down not long after my divorce, when I was given to
long midnight rambles on my neighborhood streets, during
which I often admonished myself in a loud, desperate voice. In
all these dealings he has stayed as abstracted as a tax collector,
though always officially polite. (Frankly, I've always thought of
him as an asshole.)

Sergeant Balducci approaches almost to the bottom of the
porch steps without having looked at either Betty McLeod or
me. He hitches up on the heavyweight black belt containing all
his police gear—Mace canister, radio, cuffs, a ring of keys, black-
jack, his big service automatic. He is wearing his iron-creased
blue and black HPD uniform with its various quasi-military
markings, stripes and insignia, and either he has gained weight
around his thick midsection or he's wearing a flak vest under
his shirt.

He looks up at me as if he'd never laid eyes on me before. He
is five-ten with a heavy-browed, large-pored face as vacant as the
moon, his hair cut in a regimental flattop.

"We got a problem out here, folks?" Sergeant Balducci says,
setting one polished police boot on the bottom step.

"Nothing's wrong," I say, and for some reason am breathless,
as if more's wrong here than could ever meet the eye. I mean, of
course, to look guilt-free. "Mrs. Beavers just got the wrong idea
in her head." I know she's watching everything like an eagle, her
mind apparently departed for elsewhere.

"Is that right?" Sergeant Balducci says and looks at Betty
McLeod.

"Nothing's wrong," she says inertly, behind her screen.

"We have a reported break-in in progress at this address."
Sergeant Balducci's voice is his official voice. "Do you live here,
ma'am?" He says this to Betty.

Betty nods but adds nothing helpful.

"And did anybody break into your house or attempt to?"

"Not that I know of," she says.

"What's *your* business here?" Officer Balducci says to me, gazing around at the yard to see if he can notice anything out of the everyday—a broken pane of glass, a bloody ball-peen hammer, a gun with a silencer.

"I'm the owner," I say. "I was just stopping by on some business." I don't want to say I'm here hawking the rent, as if collecting rent were a crime.

"You're the owner of *this* house?" Officer Balducci's still glancing casually around but finally settles his gaze back on me.

"Yes, and that one too." I motion toward the Harrises' empty ex-home.

"What's your name again?" he says, producing a little yellow spiral notebook and a ballpoint from his back pocket.

"Bascombe," I say. "Frank Bascombe."

"Frank . . . ," he says as he writes, "Bascombe. Owner."

"Right," I say.

"I think I've seen you before, haven't I?" He looks slowly down, then up at me.

"Yes," I say, and immediately picture myself in a lineup with a lot of unshaven sex-crime suspects, being given the once-over by Betty McLeod behind a two-way mirror. He has known a great deal about my life, once, but has simply let it recede.

"Did I arrest you one time for D and D?"

"I don't know what D and D is, but you didn't arrest me for it. You gave me a ticket twice"—three times, actually—"for turning right on red on Hoving Road after not making a full stop. Once when I didn't do it and once when I did."

"That's a pretty good average." Sergeant Balducci smiles, mocking me as he's writing in his notebook. He asks Betty McLeod her name, too, and enters that in his little book.

Myrlene Beavers comes scraping out onto her porch, a yellow cordless phone to her ear. A few neighbors have appeared on their porches to see what's what. One of them also has a cordless. She and Myrlene are doubtless connected up.

"Well," Sergeant Balducci says, dotting a few i's and shoving his notebook back in his pocket. He is still smiling mockingly. "We'll check this out."

"Fine," I say, "but I didn't try to break into this house." And I'm breathless again. "That old lady's nuts across the street."

I glare over at the traitorous Myrlene, gabbling away like a goose to her neighbor two houses down.

"People all watch out for each other in this neighborhood, Mr. Bascombe," Sergeant Balducci says, and looks up at me pseudo-seriously, then looks at Betty McLeod. "They have to. If you have any more trouble, Mrs. McLeod, just give us a call."

"All right," is all Betty McLeod says.

"She didn't have any trouble *this* time!" I say, and give Betty a betrayed look.

Sergeant Balducci takes a semi-interested glance up at me from the concrete walk of my house. "I could give you some time to cool off," he says in an uninflected way.

"I *am* cooled off," I say angrily. "I'm not mad at anything."

"That's good," he says. "I wouldn't want you to get your bowels in an uproar."

On the tip of my tongue are these words: "Gee thanks. And how would you like to bite my ass?" Only the look of his short, stout arms stuffed like fat salamis into his short blue shirtsleeves makes me suspect Sergeant Balducci is probably a specialist in broken collarbones and deadly chokeholds of the type practiced on my son. And I literally bite the tip of my tongue and look bleakly across Clio Street at Myrlene Beavers, blabbing on her cheap Christmas phone and watching me—or some blurry image of a white devil she's identified me to be—as if she expected me to suddenly catch flame and explode in a sulfurous flash. It's too bad her husband's gone, is what I know. The good Mr. Beavers would've made this all square.

Sergeant Balducci begins ambling back toward his cruiser Plymouth, his waist radio making fuzzy, meaningless crackles. When he opens the door, he leans in and says something to his partner and they both laugh as the Sarge squeezes in and notes something on a clipboard stuck to the dash. I hear the word "owner," and another laugh. Then the door shuts and they ease away, their big duals murmuring importantly.

Betty McLeod has not moved behind her screen, her two little mulatto kids now peeping around each side of her housecoat. Her face reveals no sympathy, no puzzlement, no bitterness, not even a memory of these.

"I'll just come back when Larry's home," I say hopelessly.

"All right then."

I fasten a firm, accusing look on her. "Who else is here?" I say. "I heard the toilet running."

"My sister," Betty says. "Is that any of your business?"

I look hard at her, trying to read truth in her beaky little features. A sibling from Red Wing? A willowy, big-handed Sigrid, taking a holiday from her own Nordic woes to commiserate with her ethical sis. Conceivable, but not likely. "No," I say, and shake my head.

And then Betty McLeod, on no particular cue, simply shuts her front door, leaving me on the porch empty-handed with the equatorial sun beating on my head. Inside, she goes through the relocking-the-locks ritual, and for a long moment I stand listening and feeling forlorn; then I just start off toward my car with nothing left of good to do. I will now be after the 4th getting my rent, if I get it then.

Myrlene Beavers is still on the porch of her tiny white abode with sweet peas twirling up the posts, her hair frazzled and damp, her big fingers clenching the rubber walker like handholds on a roller coaster. Other neighbors have now gone back inside.

"Hey!" she calls out at me. "Did they catch that guy?" Her little yellow phone is hooked to her walker with a plastic coathanger rig-up. No doubt her kids have bought it so they can all keep in touch. "They was tryin' to break in over at Larry's. You musta scared him off."

"They caught him," I say. "He's not a threat anymore."

"That's good!" she says, a big falsey-toothy smile opening onto her face. "You do a wonderful job for us. We're all grateful to you."

"We just do our best," I say.

"Did you never know my husband?"

I put my hands on my doorframe and look consolingly at poor fast-departing Myrlene, soon to join her beloved in the other place. "I sure did," I say.

"Now he was a wonderful man," Mrs. Beavers says, taking the words from my very thought. She shakes her head at his lost visage.

"We all miss him," I say.

"I guess we do," she says, and starts her halting, painful way back inside her house. "I guess we sho 'nuf do."

CHAPTER 5

I DRIVE WINDINGLY out Montmorency Road into Haddam horse country—our little Lexington—where fences are long, white and orthogonal, pastures wide and sloping, and roads (Rickett's Creek Close, Drumming Log Way, Peacock Glen) slip across shaded, rocky rills via wooden bridges and through the quaking aspens back to rich men's domiciles snugged deep in summer foliage. Here, the Fish & Game quietly releases hatchery trout each spring so well-furnished sportsmen/home owners with gear from Hardy's can hike down and wet a line; and here, wedges of old-growth hardwoods still loom, trees that saw Revolutionary armies rumble past, heard the bugles, shouts and defiance cries of earlier Americans in their freedom swivet, and beneath which now tawny-haired heiresses in jodhpurs stroll to the paddock with a mind for a noon ride alone. Occasionally I've shown houses out this way, though their owners, fat and bedizened as pharaohs, and who should be giddy with the world's gifts, always seem the least pleasant people in the world and the most likely to treat you like part-time yard help when you show up to "present their marvelous home." Mostly, Shax Murphy handles these properties for our office, since by nature he possesses the right brand of inbred cynicism to find it all hilarious, and likes nothing more than peeling the skin off rich clients a centimeter at a time. I, on the other hand, cleave to the homier market, whose homespun spirit I prize.

I think now, with regard to the disagreeable McLeods, that my mistake has been pretty plain: I should've hauled them over for a cookout the minute I closed on their house, gotten them into some lawn chairs on the deck, slammed a double margarita in both of them, served up a rack of ranch-style ribs, corn on the cob, tomato and onion salad and a key lime pie, and all after would've been jake. Later, when matters took a sour turn (as always happens between landlord and tenant, unless the tenants are inclined toward gratitude, or the landlord's a fool), we'd have had some instant history for ballast against suspicion and ill will, which are now unhappily the status quo. Why I didn't I don't know, except that it's not my nature.

I LITERALLY BASHED right into Franks one summer night a year ago, driving home tired and foggy-eyed from the Red Man Club, where I'd fished till ten. In its then incarnation as Bemish's Birch Beer Depot, it rose appealingly up out of the night as I rounded a curve on Route 31, my eyes smarting and heavy, my mouth dry as burlap, the perfect precondition for a root beer.

Everybody over forty (unless they were born in the Bronx) has pristine and uncomplicated memories of such places: low, orange-painted wooden bunker boxes with sliding-screen customers' windows, strings of yellow bulbs outside, whitewashed tree trunks and trash barrels, white car tires designating proper parking etiquette, plenty of instructional signs on the trees and big frozen mugs of too-cold root beer you could enjoy on picnic tables by a brook or else drink off metal trays with your squeeze in the dark, radio-lit sanctity of your '57 Ford.

As soon as I saw this one I angled straight toward the lot, though at the precise moment I turned I apparently dozed off and drove right across the white-tire barrier, over a petunia bed, and gave one of the green picnic tables a board-cracking whack, which brought the owner, Karl Bemish, booming out the side door in his paper cap and his apron, wanting to know what in the hell I featured myself doing, and pretty sure I was drunk and in need of being arrested.

None of it came to anything unhappy (far from it). I was naturally enough awakened by the crash, climbed out apologizing at a high rate of speed, offered to take a breathalyzer, peeled off three hundred bucks to cover all damages and explained I'd been fishing, not closing down some gin mill in Frenchtown, and had veered into the lot because I thought the place was so goddamned irresistible out here by the brook with strings of bulbs and white trees, and in fact still wanted a root beer if he could see his way clear to selling me one.

Karl let himself be talked out of being mad by stuffing my wad of money in his apron pocket and relying on good character to concede that sometimes innocent things happen and sometimes (if rarely) the stated cause of an event is the real cause.

With my root beer in hand, I took a table that wasn't cracked and sat smilingly beside babbling Trendle Brook, my thoughts on my father stopping with me in just such places in the long-ago Fifties, in the far-away South, when as a Navy purchasing officer he had taken me on trips so my mother could recover from the chaos of being home alone with me night and day.

After a while Karl Bemish came out, having switched off all but one string of bulbs. He was carrying another root beer for me and a real suds for himself, and sat down across the table, happy to have a late-night chit-chat with a stranger who in spite of some initial suspiciousness seemed to be a good person to end the day with by virtue of being the only one around.

Karl, of course, did all the talking. (There were apparently insufficient opportunities to talk to his customers through the sliding window.) He was a widower, he said, and had been employed in the ergonomics field up in Tarrytown for almost thirty years. His wife, Millie, had died three years before, and he'd just decided to take his retirement, cash in his company stock and go looking for something imaginative to do (this sounded familiar). He knew plenty about ergonomics, a science I'd never even heard of, but nothing about retail trade or the food service industry or dealing with the public. And he admitted he'd bought the birch beer stand totally on a whim, after seeing it advertised in an entrepreneurs magazine. Where he had grown up, in the little upstate Polish community of Pulaski, New York, there'd been a place just like his right by a little stream that ran into Lake Ontario, and it of course was the "real meeting place" for all the kids and the grown-ups too. He'd met his wife there and even remembered working in the place and wearing a brown cotton smock with his name stitched in darker brown script on the front and a brown paper cap, though he admitted he could never find any actual evidence he'd worked there and had probably just dreamed it up as a way better to furnish his past. He remembered that place and time, though, as the best of his life, and his own birch beer stand served, he felt, to commemorate it.

"Of course, things haven't worked out exactly perfect here now," Karl said, taking his white paper cap off and setting it on the sticky planks of the picnic table, revealing his smooth, lacquered-looking dome, shiny under the string of lights strung back to the Depot. He was sixty-five and a big sausage-handed, small-eared guy who looked more like he might've loaded bricks for a living.

"It sure seems awful good to me," I said, taking an admiring look around. Everything was newly painted, washed, picked up, as GI'd as a hospital grounds. "I'd think you pretty much had a gold mine out here." I nodded approvingly, full to the gills with rich and creamy root beer.

"Super my first year and a half. I did super," Karl Bemish said. "The previous guy had let the place run down. And I put some money in it and fixed everything up. People in the little communities out here said it was great to see an old place restored and wanted to see it catch on again, and people like you stopped by late. It became a meeting place again, or started to. And I guess I got overexcited, 'cause I added a machine to make these slush puppies. I had some cash flow. Then I bought a yogurt machine. Then I bought a trailer kitchen to cater parties with. Then I got this idea from the entrepreneurs magazine to buy an old railroad dining car to fix up as a restaurant and put it beside here; maybe have a waiter out there, a limited menu, rig it up with chrome fixtures, original tables, bud vases, carpets. For special occasions." Karl looked over his shoulder in the direction of the brook and frowned. "It's all back there. I bought the goddamn thing from a place in Lackawanna and had it trucked down here in two pieces and set up right on a length of track. That's about when I ran out of money." Karl shook his head and brushed at a mosquito camped out on his pate.

"That's a shame," I said, peering into the dark and making out a blacker-than-normal hulk sitting still and ominous in the night. The original bad idea.

"I had big plans going," Karl Bemish said, and smiled across the table in a defeated way meant to suggest again that innocent things happen but that big ideas are inherently big mistakes.

"But you're still doing fine," I said. "You can just hold off on expansion till you renew your capital base." These were expressions I'd only recently learned in the realty business and hardly knew the meaning of.

"I'm carrying pretty stiff debt," Karl said dolefully, as if that were equivalent to toting around a hunk of lead in his heart.

With his flat pink thumbnail he stabbed at a hardened root beer droplet bonded to the tabletop. "I'm about, oh, six months from two tits up out here." He sniffed and dug away at the scab of sweetness, baked on by a long summer of shitty luck.

"Can't you recapitalize?" I said. "Sell off the dining car, maybe take out an equity loan?" More realty lingo.

"Don't got the equity," Karl said. "And no one wants a god-damned dining car in central Jersey."

I was ready to drag myself home by then, have a real drink and pile into bed. But I said, "So what do you think you're going to do?"

"I need an investor to come in and clear my debt, then maybe trust me not to run us into the ground again. You know anybody like that? 'Cause I'm going to lose this pop stand before I have a chance to prove I'm not a complete asshole. It'll be too bad." Karl was not making an attempt at a joke, as my son would've.

I looked around behind Karl Bemish, at his little orange birch beer outlet—neat, hand-lettered signs all over the trees: "Walk dogs here ONLY!" "PLEASE don't litter." "Our customers are our BEST FRIENDS." "THANKS, come again." "BIRCH BEER is GOOD for YOU." It was a sweet little operation, with, I imagine, plenty of local goodwill and a favorable suburban-semi-rural location—a few old farms nearby, with small but prospering vegetable patches, the odd nursery *cum* cider mill, some decades-old hippie pottery operations and one or two mediocre, mostly treeless golf courses. New housing soon would be sprouting up in the open pastures. Traffic flow was good at the intersection of 518 and 31, where there was already a two-way stop and as growth continued there would have to be a light, since 31, if no longer the main road, was at least the scenic *former* main road from the north-western counties down to the state house in Trenton. All of which spelled money.

It might really be, I thought, that all Karl Bemish needed was a little debt relief, a partner to consult with and oversee capital decisions while he ran the day-to-day. And for some reason (partly, I'm sure, because I shared a slice of nostalgic past with old Karl) I just couldn't say no.

I said to him right out under the gum trees, with mosquitoes thickening around our two heads, that I myself might be interested in some sort of partnership possibility. He seemed not the least bit surprised at this and immediately started spieling about several great ideas he had, all of which I thought would never work and told him so as a way of letting him know (and myself too) that I could be firm on some things. We talked for another hour, till nearly one, then I gave him my card, told him to call me at the office the next day and said if I didn't wake up feeling like I needed to have my brain replaced, maybe we could sit down again, go over his books and records, lay out his debts versus his assets, income and cash flow and if there weren't any tax problems or black holes (like boozing or a gambling problem), maybe I'd buy in for a piece of his birch beer action.

All of which seemed to please the daylights out of Karl, from the evidence of how many times he nodded his head solemnly and said, "Yep, sure, okee, yep, sure, okee. Right, right, right."

But who wouldn't be happy! A man comes crashing out of the night into your place of business, apparently drunk and wrecking the shit out of your picnic table and petunia beds. Yet before the dust even settles, you and he are making plans to be partners and to haul you out of a mud hole you'd gotten yourself in by a combination of dumb optimism, ineptitude and greed. Who wouldn't think the horn of plenty had been laid, big end forward, right outside his door?

And in fact inside of a month everything was pretty much in place, as the high rollers say. I bought into Karl's operation at the agreed-to amount of 35 thousand, which in essence zero-balanced his creditor debt, and also—because Karl was completely broke—took a controlling interest.

I immediately got busy selling off the slush puppy and yogurt machines to a restaurant wholesaler over in Allentown. I got in touch with the company up in Lackawanna that sold Karl the dining car, "The Pride of Buffalo," and they agreed to return a fifth of what they could get from reselling it, plus they'd haul it away. I sold off the copy and fax machines Karl had bought expecting eventually to further diversify by offering his roadway clients a wider variety of services than just birch beer. I eliminated several novelty food items Karl had also bought equipment for but never got operational because of space and money problems—a machine for making pronto pups; another, almost identical machine for (and only for) making New Orleans–style beignets. Karl had catalogs for daiquiri makers (in case he got a liquor license), a six-burner crepe stove and a lot of other crap no one in central New Jersey had ever heard of. It occurred to me during this time that after his wife's death Karl may have suffered a nervous breakdown or possibly a series of small strokes that left his decision-making faculty slightly bent.

Yet pretty soon, by application of nothing but common sense, I had things under control and was able to split the proceeds of the equipment sales with Karl and to put back half of mine into working capital (I decided, on a lark, to keep the kitchen-on-wheels). I also filled Karl in on some of my own newly minted, commonsense-rooted business acumen, all of which I'd picked up around the realty office. The biggest mistake, I told him, was an impulse to replicate a good thing so as to try to make it twice as good (this almost never works). And the second was that people failed not simply because they were greedy but because they got bored with regular life and with what they were doing— even things they liked—and farted away their hard-won gains just trying to stay amused. My view was, keep your costs down, make it simple, don't permit yourself the luxury of boredom, build up a clientele, then later sell to some doofus who can go broke making your idea "better." (None of this had I ever done, of course: all I'd done was buy two rental houses and sell my own house to buy my ex-wife's—hardly qualifying me for the trading pit.) I expounded these maxims to Karl while two enormous black men from Allentown Restaurant Outfitters were fork-lifting his slush puppy and yogurt machines out the back door onto a rental truck. It was, I thought, a vivid object lesson.

The last alterations I made in our business strategies were, first, to change the name of the place from Bemish's Birch Beer Depot (too big a mouthful) to Franks, no apostrophe (I liked the pun plus the straightforward appeal). And on top of that I declared that only two things would a human being buy when he pulled off the road at our sign: a frosty mug of root beer and a hell of a good Polish wurst-dog of the sort everyone always dreams about and wishes they could find while driving through some semi-scenic backwater with a hunger on. Karl Bemish, a saved man now in his white, monogrammed tunic, paper cap and shiny dome, was of course promptly established as owner-operator, yukking it up with his old customers, making crude, half-assed jokes about the "bun man" and generally feeling like he'd gotten his life back on track since the much-too-early death of his precious wife. And for me, for whom it was all pretty simple and amusing, our transaction was more or less what I'd been searching for when I came back from France but didn't find: a chance to help another, do a good deed well and diversify in a way that would pay dividends (as it's begun to) without driving myself crazy. We should all be so lucky.

I EMERGE OUT of the woodsy Haddam back roads to the intersection with 31, over which a state utility crew with a cherry picker is just suspending the prophesied new stoplight, the crew members standing around in white hard hats and work clothes, watching the procedure as if it were an act of legerdemain. A temporary sign says "Your highway taxes at work—SLOW." A few cars are pulling cautiously around, then heading off south toward Trenton.

Franks, with its new brown and orange mug-with-frothy-bubbles sign, sits kitty-cornered from the yellow highway truck. A lone customer car sits off to one side on the newly re-asphalted lot, its driver cool behind tinted windows. Karl's old red VW Beetle is parked by the back door, the red OPEN card in the window. And as I park I admit I unreservedly admire all, including the silver kitchen-on-wheels converted now into a dogs-on-wheels, glistening in the corner of the lot, all polished up by Everick and Wardell and ready to be hauled into Haddam early Monday. Some quality of its single-use efficiency, its compactness and portability, make it seem like the best purchase I've ever made, including even my house, though of course I have scarcely any use for it and should probably sell it before it depreciates out of existence.

Karl and I have forged an unwritten agreement that at least once a week I drive out and troop the colors, a practice I enjoy and especially today after my disconcerting wire-crossings with the Markhams and Betty McLeod—neither one typical of my days, which are almost always pleasant. Karl, during our first year together, which included the market sinkhole last fall (we coasted through unfazed), has begun treating me like a spirited but slightly too headstrong young maverick boss and has re-invented himself as an eccentric but faithful lifelong employee whose job it is to snipe at me in a salty, Walter Brennanish way, thereby keeping me on a true compass course. (He is much happier being an employee than running the show, which I'm sure comes from years in the ergonomics industry; though I have never thought of myself as anyone's boss, since at times I feel I'm hardly my own.)

When I step inside the "Employees only" side door, Karl is behind the sliding window, reading the Trenton *Times*, perched on two stacked red plastic milk cartons from the days when he made malts. It is hot as a broiler back here, and Karl has a little rubber-bladed Hammacher Schlemmer fan trained on his face. As usual, everything is spotless, since Karl has dark worries of getting what he calls a "C card" from the county health officer and so spends hours every night scouring and polishing, mopping and rinsing, until you could sit right down on the concrete and eat a four-course meal and never give one thought to salmonella.

"I'll tell you, I'm getting goddamn anxious about my economic future now, aren't you?" he says in a loud, scoffing voice. Karl has on his plastic reading specs and hasn't otherwise remarked my arrival. He's dressed in his summer issue: short-sleeved white tunic, laundry-supplied black-and-white checkered knee shorts that let his thick, mealy, sausage-veined calves "breathe," short black nylon socks and black crepe-soled brogans. An ancient transistor, tuned to the all-polka station in Wilkes-Barre, is playing "There Is No Beer in Heaven" at a low volume.

"I'm just interested in the Democrats to see how they'll fuck up next," I say, as though we'd been talking for hours, walking back to open the rear door onto the brookside picnic area to get some breeze going. (Karl is a lifelong Democrat who began voting Republican in the last decade but still thinks of himself as a nonconforming Jacksonian. To me, these are the true turncoats, though Karl in most ways is not a bad citizen.)

Since I have no special mission here today, I begin counting packages of hot dog buns, cans of condiments (spice relish, mustard, mayo, ketchup, diced onions), checking the meat delivery and the extra kegs of root beer I've ordered for the "Firecracker Weenie Firecracker" concession.

"Looks like housing starts fell *way* off last month again, twelve point two from May. The dumb fucks. It's gotta mean trouble to the realty business, right?" Karl gives the *Times* a good snapping as though to get the words lined up straighter. It pleases him for us to talk in this quasi-familial way (he is finally an old nostalgian where I'm concerned), as if we had come a long ways together and learned the same hard human lessons of decency and need. He peers at me over the newspaper, removes his half glasses, then stands and looks out the window as the car that's been parked by the picnic tables idles out onto Route 31 and slowly starts north toward Ringoes. The backup bell on the highway department truck starts dinging away and a heavy, black man's voice sings out, "Come-awn-back, nah, come-awn-back."

"Units sold is down five from a year ago, though," I say, while I estimate packages of Polish weenies in the cold box, frigid air hitting my face like a bright light. "Maybe it means people are going to buy houses already built. That's my guess." In fact that *is* what'll happen, and the sorry-ass Markhams better be getting in touch with me and their brains *toute de suite.*

"Dukakis takes credit for the big Massachusetts Miracle, it's only right he takes it for the big Taxachusetts Fuck-up. I'm glad I live in *Joisey* now." Karl says this listlessly, still mooning out the window at the newly lined lot.

"Well." I turn back toward him, ready to quote him my "Buyer vs. Seller" column eye-to-eye, but I confront his big checkered behind and two pale, meaty legs underneath. The rest of him is geezering around, watching the workers and their cherry picker and the new stoplight going up.

"And hot dogs," Karl observes, having heard me say something I haven't said, his voice faint for most of it being directed into the hot day, and making it easier for me to hear the polka music, which is pleasing. I am as ever always pleased to be here. "I don't think anybody gives a shit about this election anyway," Karl says, still facing out. "It's just like the fuckin' all-star game. Big buildup, then nothin'." Karl makes a juicy fart noise with his mouth for proper emphasis. "We're all distanced from government. It don't mean anything in our lives. We're in limbo." He is undoubtedly quoting some right-wing columnist he read exactly two minutes ago in the Trenton *Times.* Karl couldn't care less about government or limbo.

I, however, have nothing more I can do now, and my gaze wanders through the side door, back out to the lot, where the portable silver dog stand sits in the sun on its shiny new tires, its collapsible green-and-white awning furled above its delivery window, the whole outfit chained to a fifty-gallon oil drum filled with concrete that is itself bolted to a slab set in the ground (Karl's idea for discouraging thievery). Seeing outside from this angle, though, and particularly viewing the feasible but also in most ways sweetly ridiculous hot dog trailer, makes me feel suddenly, unexpectedly distanced from all except what's here, as though Karl and I were all each other had in the world. (Which of course isn't true: Karl has nieces in Green Bay; I have two children in Connecticut, an ex-wife, and a girlfriend I'm right now keen to see.) Why this feeling, why now, why here, I couldn't tell you.

"You know, I was just reading in the paper yesterday . . ." Karl pulls his bulk off the counter and swivels around toward me. He reaches down and switches off the polka festival. ". . . that there's a decline in songbirds now that's directly credited to the suburbs."

"I didn't know that." I stare at his smooth, pink features.

"It's true. Predatory animals that thrive in disturbed areas eat the songbird eggs and young. Vireos. Flycatchers. Warblers. Thrushes. They're all taking a real beating."

"That's too bad," I say, not knowing what else to offer. Karl is a facts man. His idea of a worthwhile give-and-take is to confront you with something you've never dreamed of, an obscure koan of history, a rash of irrefutable statistics such as that New Jersey has the highest effective property-tax rate in the nation, or that one of every three Latin Americans lives in Los Angeles, something that explains nothing but makes any except the most banal response inescapable, and then to look at you for a reply—which can only ever amount to: "Well, what d'you know," or "Well, I'll be goddamned." Actual, speculative, unprogrammed dialogue between human beings is unappetizing to him, his ergonomic training notwithstanding. I am, I realize, ready to leave now.

"Listen," Karl says, forgetting the dark fate of vireos, "I think we might be being cased out here."

"What do you mean?" A trickle of oily, hot-doggy sweat leaves my hairline and heads underground into my left ear before I can finger it stopped.

"Well, last night, see, just at eleven"—Karl has both hands on the counter edge behind him, as if he were about to propel him-self upward—"I was scrubbin' up. And these two Mexicans drove in. Real slow. Then they drove off down Thirty-one, and in about ten minutes here they come back. Just pulled through slow again, and then left again."

"How do you know they were Mexicans?" I feel myself squinting at him.

"They *were* Mexicans. They were Mexican-*looking*," Karl says, exasperated. "Two small guys with black hair and GI haircuts, driving a blue Monza, lowered, with tinted windows and those red and green salsa lights going around the license tag? Those weren't Mexicans? Okay. Hondurans then. But that doesn't really make a lot of difference, does it?"

"Did you know them?" I give a worried look out the open customer window, as though the suspicious foreigners were there now.

"No. But they came back about an hour ago and bought birch beers. Pennsylvania plates. CEY 146. I wrote it all down."

"Did you let the sheriff know?"

"They said there's still no law yet against driving through a drive-in. If there were, we wouldn't be in business."

"Well." Again I don't know what else to say. In most ways it is a statement like the one about songbird decline. Though I'm not happy to hear about suspicious lurkers in lowered Monzas. It's news no small businessman wants to hear. "Did you ask the sheriff to check by special?" A little more oily sweat slides down my cheek.

"I'm not supposed to worry, just pay attention." Karl picks up his rubber-bladed fan and holds it so it blows warm air at my face. "I just hope if the little cocksuckers decide to rob us, they don't kill me. Or half kill me."

"Just fork over all the money," I say seriously. "We can replace that. No heroics." I wish Karl would put the fan away.

"I want a chance to protect myself," he says, and makes his own quick assessment outside, via the customer window. I'd never considered protecting myself until I got bonked in the head by the Asian kid with the big Pepsi bottle. Though what I thought of doing then was concealing a handgun, lying in wait at the same place the next evening and blasting all three of them—which was not a workable idea.

Behind Karl I see the gang of state stoplight installers swagger-ing in a scattered group across the highway and on into our parking lot, still wearing their hard hats and thick insulated gloves. A couple are animatedly dusting off their thick pants, a couple are laughing. Half are black and half white, though they're taking their break together as if they are best of friends. "I'll have the big weenie," I hear one say from a distance, making the others laugh some more. " 'She said *hungrily*,' " someone else says. And they all laugh again (too boisterous to be sincere).

I, though, want to get out of here, get back in my car, jack the a/c to the max and lickety-split head to the Shore before I get corralled into building Polish dogs and serving up root beer and watching out for stickup artists. I occasionally hold down the fort when Karl takes off for some medical checkup or to have his choppers adjusted, but I don't like it and feel like an asshole every time. Karl, however, loves nothing better than the idea of "the boss" donning a paper cap.

He has already started lining up cold mugs out of the freezer box. "How's old Paul?" he says, forgetting about the Mexicans. "You oughta bring him out here and leave him with me a couple of days. I'll shape him up." Karl knows all about Paul's brush with the law over filched condoms, and his view is that all fifteen-year-olds need shaping up. I'm sure Paul would pay big money to spend two free-wheeling days out here with Karl, cracking jokes and double entendres, garbaging down limitless root beers and Polish dogs and generally driving Karl nuts.

But not a chance. The vision of Karl's little second-floor bach-elor apartment over in Lambertville, with all his old furniture from his prior Tarrytown life, his pictures of his dead wife, his closets full of elderly "man's" things, odorous old toiletries on dressertop doilies, the green rubber drain rack, all the strange smells of lonely habits—I'd be grateful if Paul lived an entire life without having to experience that firsthand. And for fear of a hundred things: that a set of "mature" snapshots might just get left on a table, or a "funny magazine" turn up among the *Time*s and *Argosy*s under the TV stand, possibly an odd pair of "novelty undershorts" Karl might wear only at home and decide my son would think was "a gas." Such notions come to solitary older men, happen without plan, and then boom—piggy's in the soup before you know it! So that with all due respect to Karl, whom

I'm happy to be in the hot dog business with and who has never given a hint something might be fishy about himself, a parent has to be vigilant (though it's unarguable I have not been as vigilant as I should've been).

All the state workers are standing outside now, staring at the closed sliding window as if they expected it to speak to them. There are seven or so, and they're digging into their pockets for lunch money. "So how's it going out there? You guys ready for a dog?" Karl shouts through the little window, as much to me as the state guys, as though we both know what we know—that this place is a friggin' gold mine.

"I think I'll sneak on out," I say.

"Yeah, okay," Karl says brightly, but now busily.

"Got a hamburg?" someone outside says to the screen.

"No burgs, just dogs," Karl answers, and viciously slides back the screen. "Just dogs and birch beer, boys," he says, turning cheery, leaning into the window, his big damp haunch hoisted once again into the air.

"I'll see you, Karl," I say. "Everick and Wardell will be here early Monday."

"Right. You bet," Karl shouts. He has no idea what I've said. He has entered his medium—dogs 'n' sweet suds—and his happy abstraction from life is my welcome cue to leave.

I MAKE A southerly diversion below Haddam now, take streaming 295 up from Philadelphia, bypass Trenton and skirt the campus of De Tocqueville Academy, where Paul could attend when and if he comes to live with me and had the least interest, even though I would personally prefer the public schools. Then I head off onto the spanky new I-195 spur for more or less a bullet shot across the wide, subsident residential plain (Imlaystown, Jackson Mills, Squankum—all viewed from freeway level), toward the Shore.

I have not gone far before I pass above Pheasant Meadow, sprawled along the "old" Great Woods Road directly in the corridor of great silver high-voltage towers made in the shape of tuning forks. An older dilapidated sign just off the freeway announces: AN ATTRACTIVE RETIREMENT WAITS JUST AHEAD.

Pheasant Meadow, not old but already gone visibly to seed, is the condo community where our black agent, Clair Devane, met her grim, still unsolved and inexplicable death. And in fact, as I watch it drift by below me, its low, boxy, brown-shake buildings set in what was once a farmer's field, now abutting a strip of pastel medical arts plazas and a half-built Chi-Chi's, it seems so plainly the native architecture of lost promise and early death (though it's possible I'm being too harsh, since not even so long ago, I—arch-ordinary American—was a suitor to love there myself, wooing, in its tiny paper-walled, nubbly-ceilinged rooms, its dimly lit entryways and parking desert, a fine Texas girl who liked me some but finally had more sense than I did).

Clair was a fresh young realty associate from Talladega, Alabama, who'd gone to Spelman, married a hotshot computer whiz from Morehouse working his way up through an aggressive new software company in Upper Darby, and who for a sweet moment thought her life had locked into a true course. Except before she knew it she'd ended up with no husband, two kids to raise and no work experience except once having been an R A in her dormitory and, later, having kept the books for Zeta Phi Beta imaginatively enough that at year's end a big surplus was available to stage a carnival for underprivileged Atlanta kids and also to have a mixer with the Omegas at Georgia Tech.

On a fall Sunday in 1985, during an afternoon drive "in the country," which included a mosey through Haddam, she and her husband, Vernell, fell into a ferocious, screaming fight right in the middle of after-church traffic on Seminary Street. Vernell had just announced in the car that he had somehow fallen into true love with a female colleague at Datanomics and was the very next morning (!) moving out to L.A. to "be with her" while she started a new company of her own, designing educational packages targeted for the D I Y home-repair industry. He allowed to Clair that he might drift back in a few months, depending on how things went and on how much he missed her and the kids, though he couldn't be sure.

Clair, however, just opened the car door, stepped out right at the stoplight at Seminary and Bank, across from the First Presbyterian (where I occasionally "worship") and simply started walking, looking in store windows as she went and smilingly whispering, "Die, Vernell, die right now," to all the white, contrite Presbyterians whose eyes she met. (She told me this story at an Appleby's out on Route 1, when we were at the height of our ardent but short-lived amours.)

Later that afternoon she checked into the August Inn and called her sister-in-law in Philadelphia, revealing Vernell's treachery and telling her to go get the kids at the baby-sitter's and put them on the first flight to Birmingham, where her mother would be waiting to take them back to Talladega.

And the next morning—Monday—Clair simply hit the bricks, looking for work. She told me she felt that even though she didn't see many people who looked like her, Haddam seemed as good a town as any and a damn sight better than the City of Brotherly Love, where life had come unstitched, and that the measure of any human being worthy of the world's trust and esteem was her ability to make something good out of something shitty by reading the signs right: the signs being that some strong force had crossed Vernell off the list and at the same time put her down in Haddam across from a church. This she considered to be the hand of God.

In no time she found a job as a receptionist in our office (this was less than a year after I came on board). In a few weeks she'd started the agent's course I took up at the Weiboldt school. And in two months she had her kids back, had bought a used Honda Civic and was set up in an apartment in Ewingville with a manageable rent, a pleasant, tree-lined drive to Haddam and a new and unexpected sense of possibility wrought from disaster. If she wasn't a hundred percent free and clear, she was at least free and making ends meet, and before long she started seeing me on the Q.T., and when that didn't seem to work she got together with a nice, somewhat older Negro attorney from a good local firm, whose wife had died and whose bad-tempered kids were all grown and gone.

It is a good story: human enterprise and good character triumphing over adversity and bad character, and everybody in our office coming to love her like their sister (though she never really sold much to the moneyed white clientele Haddam attracts like sheep, but came to specialize in rentals and condo turn-arounds, which are not much of our market).

And yet completely mysteriously, in a routine showing of one of her condos right out here below me in Pheasant Meadow, a condo she'd shown ten times before and to which she arrived early to turn on lights, flush the toilets and open the windows—all normal chores—she was confronted by what the state police believe were at least three men. (As I said before, indications were that they were white, though I couldn't say what those indications were.) For two days, Everick and Wardell were extensively questioned, due to their access to keys, but they were completely exonerated. The unknown men, though, bound Clair hand and foot, gagged her with clear plastic tape, then raped and murdered her, slashing her throat with a packing knife.

Drugs were at first thought to be a motive, not that she was in any way implicated. It was speculated the unnamed men could've been repackaging bricks of cocaine, and Clair just walked unluckily in. The police know that empty condos in remote or declining locations, developments where good times have come and gone or never even came, often serve as havens for illicit transactions of all kinds—drug deals, the delivery of kidnaped Brazilian babies to rich childless Americans, the storage of various contrabands including dead bodies and auto parts, cigarettes and animals—anything that might profit from the broad-daylight anonymity condos are designed to provide. Our receptionist, Vonda, has a private-public theory that the owners, some young Bengali businessmen from New York, are at the bottom of everything and have a secret interest in pushing condo prices down for tax reasons (several agencies, including ours, have stopped showing property there). But there's no proof nor any reason to imagine anyone would *need* to kill as sweet a soul as Clair was for their purposes to win out. Only they did.

Immediately after Clair's murder, the women in our office, along with most of the other female realtors in town, formed mutual-protection groups. Some have begun to carry guns and Mace canisters and Tasers to work and right on out to houses they are showing. Women realtors now go around only in twos. Several have enrolled in martial arts classes, and "grieving and coping" sessions are still going on in different offices after business hours. (We men were encouraged to come, but I felt I already knew plenty about grieving and enough about coping.) There is even a clearinghouse number whereby any female agent can ask for and be given a male escort to any showing she feels uneasy about; and twice I've gone out just to be there when the clients show up, in case there was any funny business (there hasn't been any). None of these precautions, needless to say, can be discussed with the clients, who would hot-foot it out of town at the first sniff of danger. In both instances I was simply introduced as Ms. So-and-so's "associate," no explanations given; and when the coast proved clear, I inconspicuously departed.

Since May, all the realtors in Haddam have contributed to the Clair Devane Fund for her kids' education ($3,000 has so far been raised, enough for two full days at Harvard). Yet in spite of all the gloominess and hollow feeling, and the practical realization that "this kind of thing *can* happen here, and did," that no one is very far from a crime statistic, and the general recognition of how much we take our safety for granted—in spite of all that, no one talks about Clair much now, other than Vonda, whose cause she somehow is. Clair's kids have moved out with Vernell in Canoga Park, her fiancé, Eddie, is in quiet mourning (though he has already been seen lunching with one of the legal secretaries who considered renting my house). Even I have made my peace, having said my explicit adieus long before, when she was alive. Eventually her desk will be manned by someone else and business will go on—sad to say, but true—which is the way people want it. And in that regard, as well as respecting the most private of evidence, it can sometime already seem as though Clair Devane had not fully existed in anyone's life but her very own.

NOWADAYS I END up driving over once a week to pass a jolly-intimate evening with Sally Caldwell. We often attend a movie, later slip out to some little end-of-a-pier place for an amberjack steak, a pitcher of martinis, sometimes a stroll along a beach or out some jetty, following which events take care of themselves. Though often as not I end up driving home in the moonlight alone, my heart pulsing regularly, my windows wide open, a man in charge of his own tent stakes and personal equipment, my head full of vivid but fast-disappearing memories and no anxious expectancies for a late-night phone call (like this morning's) full of longing and confusion, or demands that I spell out my intentions and come back immediately, or bitter accusations that I have not been forthright in every conceivable way. (I may not have, of course; forthright being a greater challenge than would seem, though my intentions are always good if few.) Our relationship, in fact, hasn't seemed to need more attention to theme or direction but has proceeded or at least persisted on autopilot, like a small plane flying out over a peaceful ocean with no one exactly in command.

Not of course that this is *best*—life's paradigm mapped out to perfection. It's simply what is: *fine* in the eternity of the here and now.

Best would be ... well, *good* for a time was Cathy Flaherty in a wintry, many-windowed flat overlooking the estuary in Saint-Valéry (walks along the cold Picardy coast, fishermen fishing, foggy views across foggy bays, etc., etc.). *Good* was the early days (even the middle to late days) of my unrequited love for Nurse Vicki Arcenault of Pheasant Meadow and Barnegat Pines (now a Catholic mother of two in Reno, where she heads the trauma unit at Reno St. Veronica's). *Good* was even much of my sports-writing work (for a time, at least), my days back then happily dedicated to giving voice to the inarticulate and inane in order that an abstracted-but-still-yearning readership be painlessly diverted.

All that was *good*, sometimes even mysterious, sometimes so outwardly complicated as to *seem* interesting and even transporting, which is what most life gets by on and what we'll take as scrip against what's eternally due us.

But *best*? There's no use going through that card sort. Best's a concept without reference once you're married and have loused that up; maybe even once you've had your first banana split at age five and find, upon finishing it off, that you could handle another one. Forget best, in other words. Best's gone.

MY LADY FRIEND Sally Caldwell is the widow of a boy I attended Gulf Pines Military Academy with, Wally "Weasel" Caldwell of Lake Forest, Illinois; and for that reason Sally and I sometimes act as if we have a long, bittersweet history together of love lost and fate reconciled—which we don't. Sally, who's forty-two, merely saw my snapshot, address and a short personal reminiscence of Wally in the *Pine Boughs* alumni book printed for our 20th Gulf Pines reunion, which I didn't attend. At the time she didn't know me from Bela Lugosi's ghost. Only in trying to dream up a good reminiscence and skimming through my old yearbook for somebody I could attribute something amusing to,

I chose Wally and sent in a mirthful but affectionate account that made fleeting reference to his having once drunkenly washed his socks in a urinal (a complete fabrication; I, in fact, chose him because I discovered from another school publication that he was deceased). But it was my "reminiscence" that Sally happened to see. I barely, in fact, had any memory of Wally, except that he was a fat, bespectacled boy with blackheads who was always trying to smoke Chesterfields using a cigarette holder—a character who, in spite of a certain likeness, turned out not to be Wally Caldwell at all but somebody else, whose name I never could remember. I have since explained my whole gambit to Sally, and we have had a good laugh about it.

I learned later from Sally that Wally had gone to Vietnam about the time I enlisted in the Marines, had come damn close to getting blown to bits in some ridiculous Navy mishap which left him intermittently distracted, though he came home to Chicago (Sally and two kids waiting devotedly), unpacked his bags, talked about studying biology, but after two weeks simply disappeared. Completely. Gone. The End. A nice boy who would've made a better than average horticulturist, became forever a mystery.

Sally, however, unlike the calculating Ann Dykstra, never remarried. Finally, for IRS reasons, she was forced to obtain a divorce by having Wally declared a croaker. But she went right on and raised her kids as a single mom in the Chicago suburb of Hoffman Estates, earned her B.A. in marketing administration from Loyola while holding down a full-time job in the adventure-travel industry. Wally's well-heeled Lake Forest parents provided her with make-ends-meet money and moral support, having realized she was not the cause of their son's going loony and that some human conditions are beyond love's reach.

Years went by.

But as quick as the kids were old enough to be safely dumped out of the nest, Sally put into motion her plan for setting sail with whatever fresh wind was blowing. And in 1983, on a rental-car trip to Atlantic City, she happened to turn off the Garden State in search of a clean rest room, stumbled all at once upon the Shore, South Mantoloking and the big old Queen-Anne-style double-gallery beach house facing the sea, a place she could afford with her parents' and in-laws' help, and where her kids would be happy coming home to with their friends and spouses, while she got her feet wet in some new business enterprise. (As it happened, as marketing director and later owner of an agency that finds tickets to Broadway shows for people in the later stages of terminal illness but who somehow think that seeing a revival of *Oliver* or the original London cast of *Hair* will make life—discolored by impending death—seem brighter. Curtain Call is her company's name.)

I luckily enough got into the picture when Sally read my bio and reminiscence about ersatz Wally in the *Pine Boughs*, saw I was a realtor in central New Jersey and tracked me down, thinking I might help her find bigger space for her business.

I came over one Saturday morning almost a year ago, and got a look at her—angularly pretty, frosted-blond, blue-eyed, tall in the extreme, with long, flashing model's legs (one an inch shorter than the other from a freak tennis accident, but not an issue) and the occasional habit of looking at you out the corner of her eyes as though most of what you were talking about was mighty damn silly. I took her to lunch at Johnny Matassa's in Point Pleasant, a lunch that lasted well past dark and moved over subjects far afield of office space—Vietnam, the coming election prospects for the Democrats, the sad state of American theater and elder care, and how lucky we were to have kids who weren't drug addicts, young litigators-to-be or maladjusted sociopaths (my luck there may be waning). And from there the rest was old hat: the inevitable usual, with a weather eye out for health concerns.

AT LOWER SQUANKUM I turn off then slide over to NJ 34, which becomes NJ 35, the beach highway, and head into the steamy swarm of 4th of July early-bird traffic, those who so love misery and wall-to-wall car companionship that they're willing to rise before dawn and drive ten hours from Ohio. (Many of these Buckeye Staters, I notice, are Bush supporters, which makes the holiday spirit seem meanly expropriated.)

Along the beach drag through Bay Head and West Manto-loking, patriotic pennants and American flags are snapping along the curbside, and down the short streets past the seawall I can see sails tilting and springing at close quarters on a hazy blue-steel sea. Though there's no actual feel of shimmery patriot fervor, just the everyday summery wrangle of loud Harleys, mopeds, topless Jeeps with jutting surfboards, squeezed in too close to Lincolns and Prowlers with stickers saying TRY BURNING THIS ONE! Here the baked sidewalks are cluttered with itchy, skinny bikini'd teens waiting on line for saltwater taffy and snow cones, while out on the beach the wooden lifeguard stands are occupied by brawny hunks and hunkettes, their arms folded, staring thoughtlessly at the waves. Parking lots are all full; motels, efficiencies and trailer hookups on the landward side have been booked for months, their renter-occupants basking in lawn chairs brought from home, or stretched out reading on skimpy porches bordered by holly shrubs. Others simply stand on old, Thirties shuffle-board pavements, sticks in hand, wondering: Wasn't this once—summer—a time of inner joy?

Though off to the right the view inland opens behind the town toward the broad reach of cloudy, brackish estuarial veldt, wintry and sprouted with low-tide pussy willows, rose hips and rotting boat husks stuck in the muck; and, overseeing all, farther and across, a great water tower, pink as a primrose, beyond which regimented housing takes up again. Silver Bay this is, its sky fletched with darkened gulls gliding to sea behind the morning's storm. I pass a lone and leathered biker, standing on the shoulder beside his broken-down chopper just watching, taking it all in across the panoramic estuary, trying, I suppose, to imagine how to get from here to there, where help might be.

And I am then into South Mantoloking and am almost "home."

I stop along the beach road at a store where LIQUOR is sold, buy two bottles of Round Hill Fumé Blanc '83, eat a candy bar (my last bite was at six), then walk out onto the windy, salty sidewalk to call for messages, unwilling not to know if the Markhams have resurfaced.

Message one of five, in fact, is Joe Markham, at noon in the full dudgeon of his helpless state. "Yeah. Bascombe? Joe Markham speaking. Gimme a call. Area code 609 259-6834. That's it." Clunk. Words like bullets. Perhaps he can wait a bit.

Message two. A cold call. "Right. Mr. Bascombe? My name is Fred Koeppel. Maybe Mr. Blankenship mentioned my name." (Mr. Who?) "I'm considering putting my house on the market up in Griggstown. I'm sure it'll go pretty quick. It's a sellers' market, so I'm told. Anyway, I'd like to discuss it with you. Maybe let you list it if we can work a fair commission. It'll sell itself, is my view. It'll just be paperwork for you. My number is . . ." A commission, fair or unfair, is 6 percent. Click.

Message three. "Joe Markham." (Basically the same news.) "Yeah. Bascombe. Gimme a call. Area code 609 259-6834." Clunk. "Oh yeah, it's one or whatever on Friday."

Message four. Phyllis Markham. "Hi, Frank. Try to get in touch with us." Bright as a sprite. "We have some questions. Okay? Sorry to bother you." Clunk.

Message five. A voice I don't recognize though briefly imagine to be Larry McLeod: "Look, chump! Ah-mo-ha-tuh-fuck-you-up, unu-stan-where-ahm-cummin-frum? Cause"—more distinct now, as if somebody else was talking—"I'm like sicka *yo* shit. Got it, chump? Fuckah?" Clunk. We get used to these in the realty biz. The police philosophy is, if they're calling, they're harmless. Larry, however, wouldn't leave such a message no matter how hot under the collar he'd gotten at my thinking I deserve to be paid money for letting him live in my house. Some part of him, I believe, is too dignified.

I'm relieved there's no call from Ann or Paul, or worse. When Paul was hauled away to juvenile detention by the Essex P.D. and Ann had to go get him out, it was Charley O'Dell who called to say, "Look, Frank, this'll all parse out right. Just hold steady. We'll be in touch." Parse out. Hold steady. *WE?* I haven't wanted to hear such niceness again, but been touchy I might have to. Charley, though (obviously at Ann's request), has since then been mum about Paul's problems, leaving them for his real parents to hassle over and try to fix.

Charley, of course, owns his own probs: a big, dirty-blond, overweight, bad-tempered, pimply-faced daughter named Ivy (who Paul refers to as IV), a student in an experimental writing program in NYC, who's currently living with her professor, aged sixty-six (older even than Charley), while writing a novel surgerying her parents' breakup when she was thirteen, a book that (according to Paul, who's had parts read to him) boasts as its first lines: "An orgasm, Lulu believed, was like God—something she'd heard was good but didn't really believe in. Though her father had very different ideas." In another life I might be sympathetic to Charley, but not in this one.

*　　*　　*

SALLY'S RAMBLING dark-green beach house at the end of narrow Asbury Street is, when I hike up the old concrete seawall steps alongside and attain the beach-level promenade, locked, and she surprisingly gone, though all the side-opening windows upstairs and down are thrown out to catch a breeze. I am still early.

I, for a while, have had my own set of keys, though for a moment I simply stand on the shaded porch (plastic wine sack in hand) and gaze at the quiet, underused stretch of beach, the silent, absolute Atlantic and the gray-blue sky against which more near-in sailboats and Windsurfers joust in the summer haze. Farther out, a dark freighter inches north on the horizon. It is not so far from here that in my distant, postdivorce days I set sail for many a night's charter cruise with the Divorced Men's Club, all of us drinking grappa and angling for weakfish off Manasquan, a solemn, hopeful, joyless crew, mostly scattered now, most remarried, two dead, a couple still in town. Back in '83 we'd come over as a group, using the occasion of a midnight fishing excursion to put an even firmer lock on our complaints and sorrows—important training for the Existence Period, and good practice if your resolve is never to complain about life.

On the beach, beyond the sandy concrete walk, moms under beach umbrellas lie fast asleep on their heavy sides, arms flung over sleeping babies. Secretaries with a half day off to start the long weekend are lying on their bellies, shoulder to shoulder, chatting, winking and smoking cigarettes in their two-pieces. Tiny, stick-figure boys stand bare-chested at the margins of the small surf, shading their eyes as dogs trot by, tanned joggers jog and elderlies in pastel garb stroll behind them in the fractured light. Here is human hum in the barely moving air and surf-sigh, the low scrim of radio notes and water subsiding over words spoken in whispers. Something in it moves me as though to a tear (but not quite); some sensation that I have been here, or nearby, been at dire pains here time-ago and am here now again, sharing the air just as then. Only nothing signifies, nothing gives a nod. The sea closes up, and so does the land.

I am not sure what chokes me up: either the place's familiarity or its rigid reluctance to act familiar. It is another useful theme and exercise of the Existence Period, and a patent lesson of the realty profession, to cease sanctifying places—houses, beaches, hometowns, a street corner where you once kissed a girl, a parade ground where you marched in line, a courthouse where you secured a divorce on a cloudy day in July but where there is now no sign of you, no mention in the air's breath that you were there or that you were ever, importantly you, or that you even *were.* We may feel they *ought* to, *should* confer something—sanction, again—because of events that transpired there once; light a warming fire to animate us when we're well nigh inanimate and sunk. But they don't. Places never cooperate by revering you back when you need it. In fact, they almost always let you down, as the Markhams found out in Vermont and now New Jersey. Best just to swallow back your tear, get accustomed to the minor sentimentals and shove off to whatever's next, not whatever was. Place means nothing.

DOWN THE wide, cool center hall I head to the shadowy, high, tin-ceilinged kitchen that smells of garlic, fruit and refrigerator freon, where I unload my wine into the big Sub-Zero. A "Curtain Call" note is stuck on the door: "FB. Go jump in the ocean. See you at 6. Have fun. S." No words about where she might be, or why it's necessary to use both the "F" and the "B." Perhaps another "F" lurks in the wings.

Sally's house, as I make my way up toward a nap, always reminds me of my own former family pile on Hoving Road— too many big wainscoted downstairs rooms with bulky oak paneling, pocket doors and thick chair rails, too much heavy plaster and a God's own excess of storage and closet space. Plus murky, mildewy back stairways, floors worn smooth and creaky with use, dented crown moldings, medallions, escutcheons, defunct gas wall fixtures from a bygone era, leaded glass, carved newel posts and the odd nipple button for a bell only servants (like canines) could hear—a house to raise a family in a bygone fashion or retire to if you've got the scratch to keep it up.

But for me, Sally's is a place of peculiar unease on account of its capacity to create a damned unrealistic, even scary, illusion of the future—which is one more reason I couldn't stand my own, could barely even sleep in it when I got back from France, in spite of high hopes. Suddenly I couldn't bear its woozy, fusty, weighted clubbiness, its heavy false promise that since the appearance of things can stay the same, life'll take care of itself too. (I knew better.) This is why I couldn't wait to get my hands on Ann's, with its re-habbed everything—clean sheetrock, new, sealed skylights made in Minnesota, polyurethaned floors, thermopanes, level-headed aluminum siding—nothing consecrated by or for all time, only certified as a building serviceable enough to live in for an uncertain while. Sally, though, who's already as cut off from her past as an amnesia victim, doesn't see things this way. She is calmer, smarter than I am, less a creature of extremes. Her house, to her, is just a nice old house she sleeps in, a comfortably convincing stage set for a life played out in the foreground, which is a quality she's perfected and that I find admirable, since it so matches what I would have be my own.

Up the heavy oak stairs, I make straight for the brown-curtained and breezy bedroom on the front of the house. It has become a point of policy with Sally—whether she's here or in New York with a vanload of Lou Gehrig's sufferers seeing *Carnival*—that I have my own space when I show up. (So far there's been no quibbling about where I sleep once the sun goes down—her room on the back). But this small, eave-shaded, semi-garret overlooking the beach and the end of Asbury Street has been designated mine, though it would otherwise be a spare: brown gingham wallpaper, an antique ceiling fan, a few tasteful but manly grouse-hunting prints, an oak dresser, a double bed with brass rainbow headboard, an armoire converted to a TV closet, a mahogany clotheshorse, all serviced by its own demure small forest-green and oak bathroom—a layout perfect for someone (a man) you don't know too well but sort of like.

I draw the curtains, strip down and crawl between the cool blue-paisley sheets, my feet still clammy from being rained on. Only when I reach to turn off the bedside lamp, I notice on the table a book that was not here last week, a red hand-me-down paperback of *Democracy in America*, a book I defy anyone to read who is not on some form of life support; and beside it, conspicuously, is a set of gold cuff links engraved with the anchor, ball and chain of the USMC, my old service branch (though I didn't last long). I pluck up one cuff link—it has a nice jeweler's heft in my palm. I try, leaning on my bare elbow, to remember through the haze of time if these are Marine issue, or just some trinket an old leatherneck had "crafted" to memorialize a burnished valiance far from home.

Except I don't want to wonder over the origin of cuff links, or whose starchy cuffs they might link; or if they were left for my private perusal, or pertain to Sally calling up last night to complain about life's congestions. If I were married to Sally Caldwell, I would wonder about that. But I'm not. If "my room" on Fridays and Saturdays becomes Colonel Rex "Knuckles" Trueblood's on Tuesdays and Wednesdays, I only hope that we never cross paths. This is a matter to be filed under "laissez-faire" in our arrangement. Divorce, if it works, should rid you of these destination-less stresses, or at least that's the way I feel now that welcome sleep approaches.

I thumb quickly back through the old, soft-sided de Tocqueville, Vol. II, check its yellowed title page for ownership, note any underlinings, margin notes (nothing), then remember my experiment from college: supine, holding the book up at a proper viewing distance, I open it at random and begin to read, testing how many seconds will pass before my eyes close, the book sinks and I fall off the cushiony cliff to dreamland.

I commence: "How Democratic Institutions and Manners Tend to Raise Rents and Shorten the Terms of Leases." Too boring even to sleep through. Outside I hear girls giggling on the beach, hear the tame surf as a soft, sleep-bringing ocean breeze raises and floats the window curtain.

I thumb back farther and start again: "What Causes Almost All Americans to Follow Industrial Callings." Nothing.

Again: "Why So Many Ambitious Men and So Little Lofty Ambitions Are to Be Found in the United States." Possibly I can get my teeth into this at least for eight seconds: "The first thing that strikes a traveler to the United States is the innumerable multitudes of those who seek to emerge from their original condition; and the second is the rarity of lofty ambition to be observed in the midst of universally ambitious stir of society. No Americans are devoid of a yearning desire to rise but hardly any appear to entertain hopes of great magnitude or to pursue lofty aims. . . ."

I set the book back on the table beside the Marine cuff links and lie now more awake than asleep, listening to the children's voices and, farther away, nearer the continent's sandy crust, a woman's voice saying, "I'm not hard to understand. Why are you so goddamn difficult?" Followed by a man's evener voice, as if embarrassed: "I'm *not*," he says, "I'm not. I'm really, really not." They talk more, but their sounds fade in the light airishness of Jersey seaside.

Then, suddenly, peering up at the brassy fan listlessly turning, I for some reason wince—*whing-crack!*—as though a rock or a scary shadow or a sharp projectile had flashed close and just missed maiming me, making my whole head whip to the right, setting my heart to pounding thunk-a, thunk-a, thunk-a, thunk-a, exactly the way it did the summer evening Ann announced she was marrying Frank Lloyd O'Dell and moving to Deep River and stealing my kids.

But why now?

There are winces, of course, and there are other winces. There is the "love wince," the shudder—often with accompanying animal groan—of hot-rivet sex imagined, followed frequently by a sense of loss thick enough to upholster a sofa. There is the "grief wince," the one you experience in bed at 5 a.m., when the phone rings and some stranger tells you your mother or your first son has "regretfully" expired; this is normally attended by a chest-emptying sorrow which is almost like relief but not quite. There is the "wince of fury," when your neighbor's Irish setter, Prince Sterling, has been barking at squirrels' shadows for months, night after night, keeping you awake and in an agitation verging on dementia, though unexpectedly you confront the neighbor at the end of his driveway at dusk, only to be told you're blowing the whole dog-barking thing way out of proportion, that you're too tightly wrapped and need to smell the roses. This wince is often followed by a shot to the chops and can also be called "the Billy Budd."

What I have just suffered, though, is none of these and has left me light-headed and tingling, as if an electrical charge had been administered via terminals strapped to my neck. Black spots wander my vision, my ears feel as though glass tumblers were pressed over them.

But then, just as quickly, I can hear the beach voices again, the slap of a book being closed, a feathery laugh, somebody's sandy sandals being slapped together, a palm being smacked on someone's tender red back and the searing "owwwweeee," while the tide fondly chides the ever-retreating shingle.

What I feel rising in me now (a consequence of my "big-time

wince") is a strange curiosity as to what exactly in the hell I'm doing here; and its stern companion sensation that I really ought to be somewhere else. Though where? Where I'm wanted more than just expected? Where I fit in better? Where I'm more purely ecstatic and not just glad? At least someplace where meeting the terms, conditions and limitations set on life are not so front and center. Where the rules are not the game.

Time was when a moment like this one—stretched out in a cool, inviting house not my own, drifting toward a nap, but also thrillingly awaiting the arrival of a sweet, wonderful and sympathetic visitor, eager to provide what I need because she needs it too—time was when this state was the best damned feeling on God's earth, in fact was the very feeling the word "life" was coined for, plus all the more intoxicating and delectable because I recognized it even as it was happening, and knew with certainty no one else did or could, so that I could have it all, all, all to myself, the way I had nothing else.

Here, now, all the props are in place, light and windage set; Sally is doubtless on her way at this instant, eager (or at least willing) to run up, jump in bed, find once more the key to my heart and give it a good cranking-up turn, thereby routing last night's entire squadron of worries.

Only the old giddyup (mine) is vanished, and I'm not lying here a-buzz and a-thrill but listening haphazard to voices on the beach—the way I used to feel, would like to feel, gone. Left is only some ether of its presence and a hungrified wonder about where it might be and will it ever come back. Nullity, in other words. Who the hell wouldn't wince?

Possibly this is one more version of "disappearing into your life," the way career telephone company bigwigs, overdutiful parents and owners of wholesale lumber companies are said to do and never know it. You simply reach a point at which everything looks the same but nothing matters much. There's no evidence you're dead, but you act that way.

But to dispel this wan, cavern-of-winds feeling, I try fervently now to picture the first girl I ever "went" with, willing like a high-schooler to project lurid mind-pictures and arouse myself into taking matters in hand, after which sleep's a cinch. Except my film's a blank; I can't seem to remember my first sexual conduction, though experts swear it's the one act you *never* forget, long after you've forgotten how to ride a bicycle. It's there on your mind when you're parked on a porch in your diaper at the old folks' home, lost in a row of other dozing seniors, hoping to get a little color in your cheeks before lunch is served.

My hunch, though, is that it was a little pasty brunette named Brenda Patterson, whom a military-school classmate and I convinced to go "golfing" with us on the hot Bermuda-grass links at Keesler AFB, in Mississippi, then half-pleaded, half-teased and almost certainly browbeat into taking her pants down in a stinking little plywood men's room beside the 9th green, this in exchange for our—me and my pal "Angle" Carlisle—grim-facedly returning the favor (we were fourteen; the rest is hazy).

Otherwise it was years later in Ann Arbor, when, nuzzling under some cedar shrubs in the Arboretum, below the New York Central trestle, I made an effort in full watery daylight to convince a girl named Mindy Levinson to let me do it just with our pants half down, our young tender flesh all over stickers and twigs. I remember she said yes, though, as uninspired as it now seems, I'm not even certain if I went through with it.

Abruptly now my mind goes electric with sentences, words, strings of unrelateds running on in semi-syntactical disarray. I sometimes can go to sleep this way, in a swoony process of returning sense to nonsense (the pressure to make sense is for me always an onerous, sometimes sleepless one). In my brain I hear: *Try burning life's congested Buckeye State biker . . . There is a natural order of things in the cocktail dress . . . I'm fluent in the hysterectomy warhead (don't I?) . . . Give them the Locution, come awn back, nah, come awn, the long term's less good for you . . . The devil's in the details, or is it God . . .*

Not this time, apparently. (What kinship these bits enjoy is a brainteaser for Dr. Stopler, not me.)

Sometimes, though not *that* often, I wish I were still a writer, since so much goes through anybody's mind and right out the window, whereas, for a writer—even a shitty writer—so much less is lost. If you get divorced from your wife, for instance, and later think back to a time, say, twelve years before, when you almost broke up the first time but didn't because you decided you loved each other too much or were too smart, or because you both had gumption and a shred of good character, then later after everything *was* finished, you decided you actually *should've* gotten divorced long before because you think now you missed something wonderful and irreplaceable and as a result are filled with whistling longing you can't seem to shake—*if you were a writer*, even a half-baked short-story writer, you'd have someplace to put that fact buildup so you wouldn't have to think about it all the time. You'd just write it all down, put quotes around the most gruesome and rueful lines, stick them in somebody's mouth who doesn't exist (or better, a thinly disguised enemy of yours), turn it into pathos and get it all off your ledger for the enjoyment of others.

Not that you ever truly *lose* anything, of course—as Paul is finding out with pain and difficulty—no matter how careless you are or how skilled at forgetting, or even if you're a writer as good as Saul Bellow. Though you do have to teach yourself not to cart it all around inside until you rot or explode. (The Existence Period, let me say, is made special for this sort of adjusting.)

For example. I never worry about whether or not my parents felt rewarded because they only had me or if they might've wanted another child (a memory-based anxiety that could drive the right person nuts). And it's simply because I once wrote a story about a small, loving family living on the Mississippi Gulf Coast who have one child but sort of want another one, ya-ta-ya-ta-ya-ta—ending with the mother taking a solitary boat ride on a hot windy day (very much like this one) out to Horn Island, where she walks on the sand barefoot, picks up a few old beer cans and stares back at the mainland until she realizes, due to something being said by a nun to some nearby crippled children, that wishing for things that can't be is—you guessed it—like being on an island with strangers and picking up old beer cans, when what she needs to do is get back to the boat (which is just whistling) and return to her son and husband, who are that day on a bass-fishing trip but will soon be back, wanting supper, and who that very morning have told her how much they both love her, but which has succeeded only in making her sad and lonely as a hermit and in need of a boat ride. . . .

This story, of course, is in a book of stories I wrote, under the title, "Waiting Offshore." Though since I stopped writing stories eighteen years ago I've had to find other ways to cope with unpleasant and worrisome thoughts. (Ignoring them is one way.)

When Ann and I were first married and living in NYC, in 1969, and I was scribbling away like a demon, hanging around my agent's office on 35th Street and showing Ann my precious pages every night, she used to stand at the window pouting because she could never find, she felt, much direct evidence of herself in my work—no cameos, no tall, slouchingly athletic golfer types of strong, resolute Dutch extraction, saying calamitously witty or incisive things to take the starch out of lesser women or men, who, naturally, would all be sluts or bores. What I used to tell her was—and God smite me if I'm lying almost twenty years later—that if I could encapsulate her in words, it would mean I'd rendered her less complex than she was and would therefore signify I was already living at a distance from her, which would eventuate in my setting her aside like a memory or a worry (which happened anyway, but not for that reason and not with complete success).

Indeed, I often tried telling her that her contribution was not to be a character but to make my little efforts at creation *urgent* by being so wonderful that I loved her; stories being after all just words giving varied form to larger, compelling but otherwise speechless mysteries such as love and passion. In that way, I explained, she was my muse; muses being not comely, playful feminine elves who sit on your shoulder suggesting better word choices and tittering when you get one right, but powerful life-and-death forces that threaten to suck you right out the bottom of your boat unless you can heave enough crates and boxes—words, in a writer's case—into the breach. (I have not found a replacement for this force as yet, which may explain how I've been feeling lately and especially here today.)

Ann, of course, in her overly factual, Michigan-Dutch way, didn't like the part that seemed to be my secret, and always assumed I was simply bullshitting her. If we were to have a heart-to-heart at this very minute, she would finally get around to asking me why I never wrote about her. And my answer would be that it was because I didn't want to use her up, bind her in words, set her aside, consign her to a "place" where she would be known, but always as less than she was. (She still wouldn't believe me.)

I try running all this end to end as I watch the ceiling fan baffle light around my room's shadowy atmosphere: *Ann wishes for . . .*

Horn Island . . . God smite my Round Hill elves . . . try burning this one . . .

Someplace far, far away I seem to hear footsteps, then the softened sound of a wine cork being squeezed, then popped, a spoon set down gently on a metal stovetop, a hushed radio playing the theme music of the news broadcast I regularly tune to, a phone ringing and being answered in a grateful voice, followed by condoning laughter—a sweet and precious domestic sonority I so rarely feel these days that I would lie here and listen till way past dark if I only, only could.

I LUMBER DOWN the stairs, my teeth brushed, my face washed, though groggy and misaligned in time. My teeth in fact don't feel they're in the right occlusion either, as if I'd gnashed them in some dream (no doubt a dismal "night guard" is in my future).

It is twilight. I've slept for hours without believing I slept at all, and feel no longer fuguish but exhausted, as though I'd dreamed of running a race, my legs heavy and achy clear up to my groin.

When I come around the newel post I can see, out the open front doorway, a few darkened figures on the beach and, farther out, the lights of a familiar oil platform that can't be seen in the hazy daytime, its tiny white lights cutting the dark eastern sky like diamonds. I wonder where the freighter is, the one I saw before—no doubt well into harbor.

A lone, dim candle burns in the kitchen, though the little security panel—just as in Ted Houlihan's house—blinks a green all-clear from down the hall. Sally usually maintains lights-off till there's none left abroad, then sets scented candles through the house and goes barefoot. It is a habit I've almost learned to respect, along with her cagey sidelong looks that let you know she's got your number.

No one is in the kitchen, where the beige candle flickers on the counter for my sake. A shadowy spray of purple irises and white wistaria have been arranged in a ceramic vase to dress up the table. A green crockery bowl of cooling bow ties sits beside a loaf of French bread, my bottle of Round Hill in its little chilling sleeve. Two forks, two knives, two spoons, two plates, two napkins.

I pour a glass and head for the porch.

"I don't think I hear you with your bells on," Sally says, while I'm still trooping down the hall. Outside, to my surprise it is almost full dark, the beach apparently empty, as if the last two minutes had occupied a full hour. "I'm just taking in the glory of the day's end," she continues, "though I came up an hour ago and watched you sleep." She smiles around at me from the porch shadows and extends her hand back, which I touch, though I stay by the door, overtaken for a moment by the waves breaking white-crested out of the night. Part of our "understanding" is not to be falsely effusive, as though unmeant effusiveness was what got our whole generation in trouble somewhere back up the line. I wonder forlornly if she will take up where she left off last night, with me flying across cornfields looking like Christ almighty, and her odd feelings of things being congested—both of which are encrypted complaints about me that I understand but don't know how to answer. I have yet to speak. "I'm sorry I woke you up last night. I just felt so odd," she says. She's seated in a big wood rocker, in a long white caftan slit up both sides to let her hike her long legs and bare feet up. Her yellow hair is pulled back and held with a silver barrette, her skin brown from beach life, her teeth luminous. A damp perfume of sweet bath oil floats away on the porch air.

"I hope I wasn't snoring," I say.

"Nope. Nope. You're a wife's dream. You never snore. I hope you saw I put de Tocqueville out for you since you're taking a trip and also reading history in the middle of the night. I always liked him."

"Me too," I lie.

She gives me the look then. Her features are narrow, her nose is sharp, her chin angular and freckled—a sleek package. She is wearing thin silver earrings and heavy turquoise bracelets. "You *did* say something about Ann—speaking of wives, or former wives." This is the reason for the look, not my lying about de Tocqueville.

"I only remember dreaming about somebody not getting his insurance premiums paid on time, and then about if it was better to be killed or tortured and then killed."

"I know what I'd choose." She takes a sip of wine, holding the round glass in both palms and focusing into the dark that has taken over the beach. New York's damp glow brightens the lusterless sky. Out on the main drag cars are racing; tires squeal, one siren goes *woop*.

Whenever Sally turns ruminant, I assume she's brooding over Wally, her long-lost, now roaming the ozone, somewhere amongst these frigid stars, "dead" to the world but (more than likely) not to her. Her situation is much like mine—divorced in a generic sense—with all of divorce's shaky unfinality, which, when all else fails, your mind chews on like a piece of sour meat you just won't swallow.

I sometimes imagine that one night right at dusk she'll be here on her porch, wondering away as now, and up'll stride ole Wal, a big grin on his kisser, more slew-footed than she remembered, softer around center field, wide-eyed and more pudding-faced, but altogether himself, having suddenly, in the midst of a thriving florist's career in Bellingham or his textile manufacturer's life in downstate Pekin, just waked up in a movie, say, or on a ferry, or midway of the Sunshine Bridge, and immediately begun the journey back to where he'd veered off on that long-ago morning in Hoffman Estates. (I'd rather not be present for this reunion.) In my story they embrace, cry, eat dinner in the kitchen, drink too much vino, find it easier to talk than either of them would've thought, later head back to the porch, sit in the dark, hold hands (optional), start to get cozy, consider a trek up the flight of stairs to the bedroom, where another candle's lit—thinking as they consider this what a strange but not altogether supportable thrill it would be. Then they just snap out of it, laugh a little, grow embarrassed at the mutually unacknowledged prospect, then grow less chummy, in fact cold and impatient, until it's clear there's not enough language to fill the space of years and absence, plus Wally (aka Bert, Ned, whatever) is needed back in Pekin or the Pacific Northwest by his new/old wife and semi-grown kids. So that shortly past midnight off he goes, down the walkway to oblivion with all the other court-appointed but not-quite dead (not that much different from what Sally and I do together, though I always show up again).

Anything more, of course, would be too complex and rueful: the whole bunch of them ending up on TV, dressed in suits, sitting painfully on couches—the kids, the wives, the boyfriend, a family priest, the psychiatrist, all there to explain what they're feeling to bleachers full of cakey fat women eager to stand up and say they themselves "would prolly have to feel a lot of jealousy, you know?" if they were in either wife's place, and really "no one could be sure if Wally was telling the truth about where . . ." True, true, true. And who cares?

Somewhere on the water a boat neither of us can see suddenly becomes a launch pad for a bright, fusey, sparkly projectile that arcs into the inky air and explodes into luminous pink and green effusions that brighten the whole sky like creation's dawn, then pops and fizzles as other, minor detonations go off, before the whole gizmo weakens and dies out of view like an evanescing spirit of nighttime.

Invisible on the beach, people say *Ooooo* and *Aaahhh* in unison and applaud each pop. Their presence is a surprise. We wait for the next boomp, whoosh and burst, but none occurs. "Oh," I hear someone say in a falling voice. "Shit." "But one was nice," someone says. "One ain't enough a-nuthin," is the answer.

"That was my first official 'firework' of the holiday," Sally says cheerfully. "That's always very exciting." Where she's looking the sky is smoky and bluish against the black. We are, the two of us, suspended here as though waiting on some other ignition.

"My mother used to buy little ones in Mississippi," I offer, "and let them pop off in her fingers. 'Teensies,' she called them." I'm still leaned amiably on the doorframe, glass dangling in my hand, like a movie star in a celebrity still. Two sips on a mostly empty stomach, and I'm mildly tipsy.

Sally looks at me doubtfully. "Was she very frustrated with life, your Mom?"

"Not that I know of."

"Well. Somebody might say she was trying to wake herself up."

"Maybe," I say, made uncomfortable by thinking of my guileless parents in some revisionist's way, a way that were I only briefly to pursue it would no doubt explain my whole life to now. Better to write a story about it.

"When *I* was a little girl in Illinois, *my* parents always managed to have a big fight on New Year's Eve," Sally says. "There'd always be yelling and things being thrown and cars starting late at night. They drank too much, of course. But my sisters and I would get terribly excited because of the fireworks display at

Pine Lake. And we'd always want to bundle up and drive out and watch from the car, except the car was always gone, and so we'd have to stand in the front yard in the snow or wind and see whatever we could, which wasn't much. I'm sure we made up most of what we said we saw. So fireworks always make me feel like a girl, which is probably pretty silly. They *should* make me feel cheated, but they don't. Did you sell a house to your Vermont people, by the way?"

"I've got them simmering." (I hope.)

"You're very skillful at your profession, aren't you? You sell houses when no one else sells them." She rocks forward then back, using just her shoulders, the big rocker grinding the porch boards.

"It's not a very hard job. It's just driving around in the car with strangers, then later talking to them on the phone."

"That's what my job's like," Sally says happily, still rocking. Sally's job is more admirable but fuller of sorrows. I wouldn't get within a hundred miles of it. Though suddenly and badly now I want to kiss her, touch her shoulder or her waist or somewhere, have a good whiff of her sweet, oiled skin on this warm evening. I therefore make my way clump-a-clump across the noisy boards, lean awkwardly down like an oversize doctor seeking a heartbeat with his naked ear, and give her cheek and also her neck a smooch I'd be happy to have lead to almost anything.

"Hey, hey, stop that," she says only half-jokingly, as I breathe in the exotics of her neck, feel the dampness of her scapula. Along her cheek just below her ear is the faintest skim of blond down, a delicate, perhaps sensitive feature I've always found inflaming but have never been sure how I should attend to. My smooch, though, gives rise to little more than one well-meant, not overly tight wrist squeeze and a willing tilt of head in my general direction, following which I stand up with my empty glass, peer across the beach at nothing, then clump back to take my listening post holding up the doorframe, half aware of some infraction but uncertain what it is. Possibly even more restrictions are in effect.

What I'd like is not to make rigorous, manly, night-ending love now or in two minutes, but to have *already* done so; to have it on my record as a deed performed and well, and to have a lank, friendly, guard-down love's afterease be ours; me to be the goodly swain who somehow rescues an evening from the shallows of nullity—what I suffered before my nap and which it's been my magician's trick to save us from over these months, by arriving always brimming with good ideas (much as I try to do with Paul or anybody), setting in motion day trips to the *Intrepid* Sea-Air-Space Museum, a canoe ride on the Batsto, a weekend junket to the Gettysburg battlefield, capped off by a balloon trip Sally was game for but not me. Not to mention a three-day Vermont color tour last fall that didn't work out, since we spent most of two days stuck in a cavalcade of slow-moving leaf-peepers in tour buses and Winnebagos, plus the prices were jacked up, the beds too small and the food terrible. (We ended up driving back one night early, feeling old and tired—Sally slept most of the way—and in no mood even to suffer a drink together when I let her off at the foot of Asbury Street.)

"I made bow ties," Sally says very assuredly, after the long silence occasioned by my unwanted kiss, during which we both realized we are not about to head upstairs for any fun. "That's your favorite, correct? *Farfalline?*"

"It's sure the food I most like to *see*," I say.

She smiles around again, stretches her long legs out until her ankles make smart little pops. "I'm coming apart at my seams, so it seems," she says. In fact, she's an aggressive tennis player who hates to lose and, in spite of her one leg being docked, can scissor the daylights out of a grown man.

"Are you over there thinking about Wally?" I say, for no good reason except I thought it.

"Wally Caldwell?" She says this as if the name were new to her.

"It was just something I thought. From my distance here."

"The name alone survives," she says. "Too long ago." I don't believe her, but it doesn't matter. "I had to give up on that name. He left *me, and* his children. So." She shakes her thick blond hair as if the specter of Weasel Wally were right out in the dark, seeking admission to our conversation, and she'd rejected him. "What I *was* thinking about—because when I drove all the way to New York today to pick up some tickets, I was also thinking it then—was you, and about you being here when I came home, and what we'd do, and just what a sweet man you always are."

This is not a good harbinger, mark my words.

"I *want* to be a sweet man," I say, hoping this will have the effect of stopping whatever she is about to say next. Only in rock-solid marriages can you hope to hear that you're a sweet man without a "but" following along afterward like a displeasing goat. In many ways a rock-solid marriage has a lot to say for itself. "But what?"

"But nothing. That's all." Sally hugs her knees, her long bare feet side by side on the front edge of her rocker seat, her long body swaying forward and back. "Does there have to be a 'but'?"

"Maybe that's what *I* am." I should make a goat noise.

"A butt? Well. I was just driving along thinking I liked you. That's all. I can try to be harder to get along with."

"I'm pretty happy with you," I say. An odd little smirky smile etches along my silly mouth and hardens back up into my cheeks without my willing it.

Sally turns all the way sideways and peers up at me in the gloom of the porch. A straight address. "Well, good."

I say nothing, just smirk.

"Why are you smiling like that?" she says. "You look strange."

"I don't really know," I say, and poke my finger in my cheek and push, which makes the sturdy little smile retreat back into my regular citizen's mien.

Sally squints at me as if she's able to visualize something hidden in my face, something she's never seen but wants to verify because she always suspected it was there.

"I always think about the Fourth of July as if I needed to have something accomplished by now, or decided," she says. "Maybe that was one of my problems last night. It's from going to school in the summers for so long. The fall just seems too late. I don't even know late for what."

I, though, am thinking about a more successful color tour. Michigan: Petoskey, Harbor Springs, Charlevoix. A weekend on Mackinaw Island, riding a tandem. (All things, of course, I did with Ann. Nothing's new.)

Sally raises both her arms above her head, joins hands and does a slinky yoga stretch, getting the kinks out of everything and causing her bracelets to slide up her arm in a jangly little cascade. This pace of things, this occasional lapse into silence, this un-urgency or ruminance, is near the heart of some matter with us now. I wish it would vamoose. "I'm boring you," she says, arms aloft, luminous. She's nobody's pushover and a wonderful sight to see. A smart man should find a way to love her.

"You're not boring me," I say, feeling for some reason elated. (Possibly the leading edge of a cool front has passed, and everybody on the seaboard just felt better all at once.) "I don't mind it that you like me. I think it's great." Possibly I should kiss her again. A real one.

"You see other women, don't you?" she says, and begins to shuffle her feet into a pair of flat gold sandals.

"Not really."

"What's 'not really'?" She picks her wine glass up off the floor. A mosquito is buzzing my ear. I'm more than ready to head inside and forget this topic.

"I don't. That's all. I guess if somebody came along who I wanted to see"—"see": a word I hate; I'm happier with "boff" or "boink," "roger" or "diddle"—"then I feel like that'd be okay. With me, I mean."

"Right," Sally says curtly.

Whatever spirit has moved her to put her sandals on has passed now. I hear her take a deep breath, wait, then let it slowly out. She is holding her glass by its smooth round base.

"I think you see other men," I say hopefully. Cuff links come to mind.

"Of course." She nods, staring over the porch banister toward small yellow dots embedded in darkness at an incomprehensible distance. I think again of us Divorced Men, huddled for safety's sake on our bestilled vessel, staring longingly at the mysterious land (possibly at this very house), imagining lives, parties, cool restaurants, late-night carryings-on we ached to be in on. Any one of us would've swum ashore against the flood to do what I'm doing. "I have this odd feeling about seeing other men," Sally says meticulously. "That I *do* it but I'm not planning anything." To my huge surprise, though I'm not certain, I think she scoops a tear from the corner of her eye and massages it dry between her fingers. This is why we are staying on the porch. I of course didn't know she was *actually* "seeing" other men.

"What would you like to be waiting on?" I say, too earnestly.

"Oh, I don't know." She sniffs to signify I needn't worry about further tears. "Waiting's just a bad habit. I've done it before. Nothing, I guess." She runs her fingers back through her thick hair, gives her head a tiny clearing shake. I'd like to ask about the anchor, ball and chain, but this is not the moment, since all I'd do is find out. "Do you think *you're* waiting for something to happen?" She looks up at me again, skeptically. Whatever my answer, she's expecting it to be annoying or deceitful or possibly stupid.

"No," I say, an attempt at frankness—something I probably can't bring off right now. "I don't know what it'd be for either."

"So," Sally says. "Where's the good part in anything if you don't think something good's coming, or you're going to get a prize at the end? What's the good mystery?"

"The good mystery's how long anything can go on the way it is. That's enough for me." The Existence Period par excellence. Sally and Ann are united in their distaste for this view.

"My oh my oh *my*!" She leans her head back and stares up at the starless ceiling and laughs an odd high-pitched girlish *ha-ha-ha*. "I underestimated you. That's good. I . . . never mind. You're right. You're completely right."

"I'd be happy to be wrong," I say, and look, I'm sure, goofy.

"Fine," Sally says, looking at me as if I were the rarest of rare species. "Waiting to be proved wrong, though—that's not exactly taking the bull by the horns, is it, Franky?"

"I never really understood why anybody'd take a bull by its horns in the first place," I say. "That's the dangerous end." I don't much like being called "Franky," as though I were six and of indeterminate gender.

"Well, look." She is now sarcastic. "This is just an experiment. It's not personal." Her eyes flash, even in the dark, catching light from somewhere, maybe the house next door, where lamps have been switched on, making it look cozy and inviting indoors. I wouldn't mind being over there. "What does it mean to you to tell somebody you love them? Or her?"

"I don't really have anybody to say that to." This is not a comforting question.

"But if you did? Someday you might." This inquiry suggests I have become an engaging but totally out-of-the-question visitor from another ethical system.

"I'd be careful about it."

"You're always careful." Sally knows plenty about my life—

that I am sometimes finicky but in fact often not careful. More of irony.

"I'd be *more* careful," I say.

"What would you mean if you said it, though?" She may in fact believe my answer will someday mean something important to her, explain why certain paths were taken, others abandoned: "It was a time in my life I was lucky enough to survive"; or "This'll explain why I got out of New Jersey and went to work with the natives in Pago Pago."

"Well," I say, since she deserves an honest answer, "it's provisional. I guess I'd mean I see enough in someone I liked that I'd want to make up a whole person out of that part, and want to keep that person around."

"What does that have to do with being in love?" She is intent, almost prayerful, staring at me in what I believe may be a hopeful manner.

"Well, we'd have to agree that that was what love was, or is. Maybe that's too severe." (Though I don't really think so.)

"It *is* severe," she says. A fishing boat sounds a horn out in the ocean dark.

"I didn't want to exaggerate," I say. "When I got divorced I promised I'd never complain about how things turned out. And not exaggerating is a way of making sure I don't have anything to complain about." This is what I tried explaining to smushed-dick Joe this morning. With no success. (Though what can it mean for one's desideratum to come up twice in one day?)

"You can probably be talked out of your severe view of love, though, can't you? Maybe that's what you meant by being happy to be wrong." Sally stands as she says this, once again raises her arms, wine glass in hand, and twists herself side to side. The fact that one leg is shorter than the other is not apparent. She is five feet ten. Almost my height.

"I haven't thought so."

"It really wouldn't be easy, I guess, would it? It'd take something unusual." She is watching the beach where someone has just started an illegal campfire, which makes the night for this moment seem sweet and cheerful. But from sudden, sheer discomfort, and also affection and admiration for her scrupulousness, I'm compelled to grab my arms around her from behind and give her a hug and a smoochy schnuzzle that works out better than the last one. She is no longer humid underneath her caftan, where she seems to my notice to be wearing no clothes, and is sweeter than sweet. Though her arms stay limp at her side. No reciprocation. "At least you don't need to worry how to trust all over again. All that awful shit, the stuff my dying people never talk about. They don't have time."

"Trust's for the birds," I say, my arms still around her. I live for just these moments, the froth of a moment's pseudo-intimacy and pleasure just when you don't expect it. It is wonderful. Though I don't believe we have accomplished much, and I'm sorry.

"Well," Sally says, regaining her footing and pushing my cloying arms off in a testy way without turning around, making for the door, her limp now detectable. "Trust's for the birds. Isn't it just. That's the way it has to be, though."

"I'm pretty hungry," I say.

She walks off the porch, lets the screen slap shut. "Come in then and eat your bow ties. You have miles to go before you sleep."

Though as the sound of her bare feet recedes down the hall, I am alone in the warm sea smells mixed with the driftwood smoke, a barbecue smell that's perfect for the holiday. Someone next door turns on a radio, loud at first, then softer. *E-Z Listn'n* from New Brunswick. Liza is singing, and I myself drift like smoke for a minute in the music: "Isn't it romantic? Music in the night . . . Moving shadows write the oldest magic . . . I hear the breezes playing . . . You were meant for love . . . Isn't it romantic?"

AT DINNER, eaten at the round oak table under bright ceiling light, seated either side of the vase sprouting purple irises and white wistaria and a wicker cornucopia spilling summery legumes, our talk is eclectic, upbeat, a little dizzying. It is, I understand, a prelude to departure, with all memory of languor and serious discussion of love's particulars off-limits now, vanished like smoke in the sea breeze. (The police have since arrived, and the firemakers hauled off to jail the instant they complained about the beach being owned by God.)

In the candlelight Sally is spirited, her blue eyes moist and

shining, her splendid angular face tanned and softened. We fork
up bow ties and yak about movies we haven't seen but would
like to (Me—*Moonstruck*, *Wall Street*; she—*Empire of the Sun*,
possibly *The Dead*); we talk about possible panic in the soybean
market now that rain has ended the drought in the parched
Middle West; we discuss "drouth" and "drought"; I tell her
about the Markhams and the McLeods and my problems there,
which leads somehow to a discussion of a Negro columnist who
shot a trespasser in his yard, which prompts Sally to admit she
sometimes carries a handgun in her purse, right in South
Mantoloking, though she believes it will probably be the instrument that kills her. For a brief time I talk about Paul, noting that
he is not much attracted to fire, doesn't torture animals, isn't a
bed-wetter that I know of, and that my hopes are he will live
with me in the fall.

Then (from some strange compulsion) I charge into realty.
I report there were 2,036 shopping centers built in the U.S. two
years ago, but now the numbers are "way off," with many big
projects stalled. I affirm that I don't see the election mattering a
hill of beans to the realty market, which provokes Sally to
remember what rates were back in the bicentennial year (8.75
percent), when, I recall to her, I was thirty-one and living on
Hoving Road. While she mixes Jersey blueberries in kirsch for
spooning over sponge cake, I try to steer us clear of the too-
recent past, talk on about Grandfather Bascombe losing the
family farm in Iowa over a gambling debt and coming in late at
night, eating a bowl of berries of some kind in the kitchen, then
stepping out onto the front porch and shooting himself.

I have noticed, however, throughout dinner that Sally and
I have continued to make long and often unyielding eye contact.
Once, while making coffee using the filter-and-plunger system,
she's stolen a glimpse at me as if to acknowledge we've gotten to
know each other a lot better now, have ventured closer, but that
I've been acting strange or crazy and might just leap up and start
reciting Shakespeare in pig Latin or whistling "Yankee Doodle"
through my butt.

Toward ten, though, we have kicked back in our captain's
chairs, a new candle lit, having finished coffee and gone back to
the Round Hill. Sally has bunched her dense hair back, and we
are launched into a discussion of our individual self-perceptions

(mine basically as a comic character; Sally's a "facilitator," though from time to time, she says, "as a dark and pretty ruthless obstructor"—which I've never noticed). She sees me, she says, in an odd priestly mode, which is in fact the worst thing I can imagine, since priests are the least self-aware, most unenlightened, irresolute, isolated and frustrated people on the earth (politicians are second). I decide to ignore this, or at least to treat it as disguised goodwill and to mean I, too, am a kind of facilitator, which I would be if I could. I tell her I see her as a great beauty with a sound head on her shoulders, who I find compelling and unsusceptible to being made up in the way I explained earlier, which is true (I'm still shaken by being perceived as a priest). We venture on toward the issue of strong feelings, how they're maybe more important than love. I explain (why, I'm not sure, when it's not particularly true) that I'm having a helluva good time these days, refer to the Existence Period, which I have mentioned before, in other contexts. I fully admit that this part of my life may someday be—except for her—hard to remember with precision, and that sometimes I feel beyond affection's grasp but that's just being human and no cause for worry. I also tell her I could acceptably end my life as the "dean" of New Jersey realtors, a crusty old bird who's forgotten more than the younger men could ever know. (Otto Schwindell without the Pall Malls or the hair growing out my ears.) She says quite confidently, all the while smiling at me, that she hopes I can get around to doing something memorable, and for a moment I think again about bringing up the Marine cuff links and their general relation to things memorable, and possibly dropping in Ann's name—not wanting to seem unable to or as if Ann's very existence were a reproach to Sally, which it isn't. I decide not to do either of these.

Gradually, then, there comes into Sally's voice a tone of greater gravity, some chin-down throatiness I've heard before and on just such well-wrought evenings as this, yellow light twiny and flickering, the summer heat gone off, an occasional bug bouncing off the front screen; a tone that all by itself says, "Let's us give a thought to something a little more direct to make us both feel good, seal the evening with an act of simple charity and desire." My own voice, I'm sure, has the same oaken burr.

Only there's the old nerviness in my lower belly (and in hers too, it's my guess), an agitation connected to a thought that won't go away and that each of us is waiting for the other to admit—something important that leaves sweetly sighing desire back in the dust. Which is: that we've both by our own private means decided not to see each other anymore. (Though "decided" is not the word. Accepted, conceded, demurred— these are more in the ballpark.) There's plenty of everything between us, enough for a lifetime's consolation, with extras. But that's somehow not sufficient, and once that is understood, nothing much is left to say (is there?). In both the long run and the short, nothing between us seems to matter enough. These facts we both acknowledge with the aforementioned throaty tones and with these words that Sally actually speaks: "It's time for you to hit the road, Bub." She beams at me through the candle flicker as though she were somehow proud of us, or for us. (For what?) She's long since taken off her turquoise bracelets and stacked them on the table, moving them here and there as we've talked, like a player at a Ouija board. When I stand up she begins putting them on again. "I hope it all goes super with Paul," she says smilingly.

The hall clock chimes 10:30. I look around as though a closer timepiece might be handy, but I've known almost the exact minute for an hour.

"Yep," I say, "me too," and stretch my own arms upward and yawn.

She's standing now beside the table, fingers just touching the grain, smiling still, like my most steadfast admirer. "Do you want me to make more coffee?"

"I drive better asleep," I say, and produce a witless grin.

Then off I go, rumbling right down the hall past the winking green security panel—which might as well have changed to red.

Sally follows at a distance of ten feet and not fast, her limp pronounced for her being barefooted. She's allowing me to let myself out.

"So, okay." I turn around. She's still smiling, no less than eight feet back. But I am not smiling. In the time taken to walk to the screen door I've become willing to be asked to stay, to get up early, have some coffee and beat it to Connecticut after a night of adieus and possible reconsiderations. I close my eyes and fake a little weaving stagger meant to indicate *Boy, I'm sleepier than I thought and conceivably even a danger to myself and others.* But I've waited too long expecting something to happen *to* me; and if I were to ask, I'm confident she'd simply phone up the Cabot Lodge in Neptune and check me in. I can't even have my old room back. My visit has become like a house showing in which I leave nothing but my card in the foyer.

"I'm real glad you came," Sally says. I'm afraid she might even "put 'er there" and with it push me out the door I came through months ago in all innocence. Worse treatment than Wally.

But she doesn't. She walks up, grasps my short shirtsleeves above my elbows—we are at eye level—and plants one on me hard but not mean, and says in a little breath that wouldn't extinguish a candle, "Bye-bye."

"Bye-bye," I say, trying to mimic her seductive whisper and translate it possibly into hello. My heart races.

But I'm history. Out the door and down the steps. Along the sandy concrete beach walk in the fading barbecue aroma, down sandy steps to Asbury Street at the lighted other end of which Ocean Avenue streams with cruising lovers on parade. I crawl into my Crown Vic; though as I start up I crane around and survey the shadowy cars behind me on both sides, hoping to spy the other guy, whoever he is, if he is, someone on the lurk in summer khakis, waiting for me to clear out so he can march back along my tracks and into my vested place in Sally's house and heart.

But there's no one spying that I can see. A cat runs from one line of parked cars to the one I'm in. A porch light blinks down Asbury Street. Lights are on in most all the houses, TVs warmly humming. There's nothing, nothing to be suspicious of, nothing to think about, nothing to hold me here another second. I turn the wheel, back out, look up briefly at my empty window, then motor on.

CHAPTER 6

UP THE INK-DARK seaboard, into the stillborn, ocean-rich night, my windows open wide for wakefulness: the Garden State, Red Bank, Matawan, Cheesequake, the steep bridge ascent over the Raritan and, beyond, the sallow grid-lights of Woodbridge.

There's, of course, a ton of traffic. Certain Americans will only take their summer jaunts after dark, when "it's easier on the engine," "there're fewer cops," "the gas stations lower the rates." The interchange at Exit 11 is aswarm with red taillights: U-Hauls, trailers, step vans, station wagons, tow dollies, land yachts, all cramming through, their drivers restless for someplace that can't wait till morning: a new home in Barrington, a holiday rental on Lake Memphrémagog, an awkward reunion at a more successful brother's chalet at Mount Whiteface—everyone with kids on board and screaming, a Port-a-Crib lashed to the top carry, desert bag harnessed to the front bumper, the whole, damn family belted in so tight that an easy breath can't be drawn.

And, too, it's that time of the month—when leases expire, contracts are up, payments come due. Car windows in the Turn-pike line reveal drawn faces behind steering wheels, frowns of concern over whether a certain check's cleared or if someone left behind is calling the law to report furniture removed, locks jimmied, garages entered without permission—a license number noted as a car disappears down a quiet suburban street. Holidays are not always festive events.

Cops, needless to say, are out in force. Up ahead of me on the Turnpike, blue lights flash far and near as I clear the toll plaza and start toward Carteret and the flaming refinery fields and cooling vats of Elizabeth. I have had, I realize, one glass of Round Hill too many and am now squinting into the shimmer lights and MERGE LEFT arrows, where road repavers are working late under banks of da-brite spots—our highway taxes at work here too.

It would've been smart, of course, just to pack Sally in with me, lock the house, activate the alarm, inaugurate a new stratagem for the rescue of collapsing love, since I'm at this moment positive that no matter what decision was entered an hour ago, it'll never happen that way. Beyond an indistinct but critical point in life (near my own age, to be sure), most of your latter-day resolves fall apart and you end up either doing whatever's damn well easiest or else whatever you feel strongest about. (These two in fact can get mixed up and cause plenty of mischief.) At the same time it also gets harder and harder to believe you can control anything via principle or discipline, though we all talk as if we can, and actually try like hell. I feel certain, batting past Newark airport, that Sally would've dropped everything and come with me if I'd as much as asked. (How this would go over with Ann would be another bridge to cross.) Paul, I'm sure, would've thought it was fine. He and Sally could've become secret pals in league against me, and who knows what might've been in store for the three of us. For starters, I wouldn't be alone in this traffic-gunk metallurgic air shaft, bound for an empty set of sheets in who knows what motel in who knows what state.

An important truth about my day-to-day affairs is that I maintain a good share of flexibility, such that my personal time and whereabouts are often not of the essence. When poor sweet Clair Devane met her three o'clock at Pheasant Meadow and got pulled into a buzz saw of bad luck, a whole network of alarms and anguish cries bespeaking love, honor, dependency immediately sounded—north to south, coast to coast. Her very *moment* as a lost human entity was at once seismically registered on all she'd touched. But on any day *I* can rise and go about all my normal duties in a normal way; or I could drive down to Trenton, pull off a convenience-store stickup or a contract hit, then fly off to Caribou, Alberta, walk off naked into the muskeg and no one would notice much of anything out of the ordinary about my life, or even register I was gone. It could take days, possibly weeks, for serious personal dust to be raised. (It's not exactly as if I didn't exist, but that I don't exist *as much.*) So, if I didn't appear tomorrow to get my son, or if I showed up with Sally as a provocative late sign-up to my team, if I showed up with the fat lady from the circus or a box of spitting cobras, as little as possible would be made of it by all concerned, partly in order that everybody retain as much of their own personal freedom and flexibility as possible, and partly because I just wouldn't be noticed that much *per se*. (This reflects my own wishes, of course—the unhurried nature of my single life in the grip of the Existence Period—though it may also imply that laissez-faire is not precisely the same as independence.)

Where Sally's concerned, however, I take responsibility for how things went tonight. Since, in spite of other successful adjustments, I have yet to learn to *want* properly. When I've been with Sally for longer than a day—plowing over the Green Mountains, or snug-a-bug in a big matrimonial suite at the Gettysburg Battlefield Colonial Inn, or just sitting staring at oil rigs and trawler lights riding the Atlantic, as we were tonight, what I always think is, Why don't I love you?—which instantly makes me feel sorry for her and, after that, for myself, which can lead to bitterness and sarcasm or just evenings like tonight, when bruised feelings lurk below surface niceties (though still well above *deep* feelings).

But what bothers me about Sally—unlike Ann, who still superintends everything about me just by being alive and sharing ineluctable history—is that Sally superintends nothing, presupposes nothing and in essence promises to do nothing remotely like that (except *like* me, as she admitted she does). And whereas in marriage there's the gnashing, cold but also cozy fear that after a while there'll be no *me* left, only *me chemically amalgamated with another*, the proposition with Sally is that there's *just* me. Forever. I alone would go on being responsible for everything that had me in it; no cushiony "chemistry" or heady synchronicity to fall back on, no *other*, only me and my acts, her and hers, somehow together—which of course is much more fearsome.

This is the very source of the joint feeling we both had sitting on the dark porch: that we weren't waiting for anything to happen or change. What might've seemed like hollow, ritual acts or ritual feelings between us were, in fact, neither hollow nor ritual, but real acts and honest feelings—not nullity, not at all. That was the way we actually felt tonight at the actual time we felt it: simply present, alone and together. There was nothing really wrong with it. If you wanted to you might call our "relationship" the Existence Period shared.

Obviously what I need to do is simply "cut through," make

clear and understood what it is I do like about Sally (which is damn plenty), give in to whatever's worth wanting, accept what's offered, change the loaded question from "Why don't I love you?" to the better, more answerable "How can I love you?" Though if I'm successful it would probably mean resuming life at about the point, give or take, where a good marriage would've brought me, had I been able to last at it long enough.

PAST EXIT 16W and across the Hackensack River from Giants Stadium, I curve off into the Vince Lombardi Rest Area to gas up, take a leak, clear my head with coffee and check for messages.

The "Vince" is a little red-brick Colonial Williamsburg-looking pavilion, whose parking lot this midnight is hopping with cars, tour buses, motor homes, pickups—all my adversaries from the Turnpike—their passengers and drivers trooping dazedly inside through a scattering of sea gulls and under the woozy orange lights, toting diaper bags, thermoses and in-car trash receptacles, their minds fixed on sacks of Roy Rogers burgers, Giants novelty items, joke condoms, with a quick exit peep at the Vince memorabilia collection from the great man's glory days on the "Seven Blocks of Granite," later as win-or-die Packer headman and later still as elder statesman of the resurgent Skins (when pride still mattered). Vince, of course, was born in Brooklyn, but began his coaching career at nearby Englewood's St. Cecilia's, which is why he has his own rest area. (Sportswriting leaves you with such memories as these.)

As there's a lull at the pumps, I gas up first, then park on the back forty, among the long-haul trucks and idling buses, and hike across the lot and into the lobby, where it's as chaotic as a department store at Christmas yet also, strangely, half asleep (like an old-time Vegas casino at 4 a.m.), with its dark video arcade bing-jinging, long lines at the Roy's and Nathan's Famous and families walking around semi-catatonically eating, or else sitting arguing at plastic tables full of paper trash. Nothing suggests the 4th of July.

I make my visit to the cavernous men's room, where the urinals flush the instant you're done and on the walls, appropriately enough, there're no pictures of Vince. I pass through the "Express Coffee Only" line at Roy's, then carry my paper cup over to the phone bank, which as usual is being held hostage by twenty truckers in plaid shirts with big chained-on wallets, all leaning into the little metal phone cubbies, fingers sealing their ears, maundering to someone time zones away.

I wait till one of them hauls up on his jeans and saunters off like a man who's just committed a secret sex act, then I set up shop and call for my messages, which I haven't heard since three—nearly nine hours and counting. (My receiver holds onto the gritty warmth of the trucker's grip as well as the lime-cologne odor from the rest room dispensers, a smell many women must find it possible to get used to.)

Message one (of ten!) is from Karl Bemish: "Frank, yeah. So's you know. The little Frito Banditos just cruised through. CEY 146. Note that down in case they kill me. Another Mexican's in the back seat this time through. I phoned the sheriff. Nothing to worry about." Clunk.

Message two is another call from Joe Markham: "Look, Bascombe. Goddamn it. 259-6834. Call me. 609 area code. We'll be here tonight." Clunk.

Message three is a hang-up—undoubtedly Joe, going ballistic and becoming speechless.

Message four, though, is from Paul, in a mood of fierce hilarity. "Boss? Hello dere, boss?" His less than perfect Rochester voice. Someone else's squeaky laughter is in the background. "If you needs to get laid, crawl up a chicken's ass and *wait!*" Louder hilarity, possibly Paul's girlfriend, the troubling Stephanie Deridder, though also possibly Clarissa Bascombe, his accomplice. "Okay, okay now. Wait." He's starting a new routine. This is not very good news. "You insect, you parasite, you worm! It's Dr. Rection here. Dr. Hugh G. Rection, calling with your test results. It doesn't look good for you, Frank. Oncology recapitulates ontogeny." He couldn't know what this means. "Bark, bark, bark, bark, bark." This, of course, is very bad, though they're both laughing like monkeys. Change clicks in a pay phone slot. "Next stop the Black Forest. I'll have the torte, pleeeezzz. Bark, bark, bark, bark, bark. Make that two, t-o-o, doc-tah." I hear the sound of the receiver being dropped, I hear them walking away giggling. I wait and wait and wait for them to come back (as though they were really there and I could speak to Paul, as though it wasn't all recorded hours ago). But they don't, and the tape stops. A bad call, about which I feel at a complete loss.

Message five is from Ann (strained, businesslike, a tone for the plumber who fixed her pipes wrong). "Frank, call me, please. All right? Use my private number: 203 526-1689. It's important. Thanks." Click.

Message six, Ann again: "Frank. Call me please? Anytime tonight, wherever you are—526-1689." Click.

Message seven, another hang-up.

Message eight, Joe Markham: "We're on our way to Vermont. So fuck you, asshole. You prick! You try to do—" Clunk! Good riddance.

Message nine, Joe again (what a surprise): "We're on our way to Vermont right now. So stick this message up your ass." Clunk.

Message ten, Sally: "Hi." A long, thought-organizing pause, then a sigh. "I should've been better tonight. I just . . . I don't know what." Pause. Sigh. "But—I'm sorry. I wish you were still here, even if you don't. Wish, wish, wish. Let's . . . umm . . . Sure. Just call me when you get home. Maybe I'll come for a visit. Bye-bye." Clunk.

Except for the last, an unusually unsettling collection of messages for 11:50 p.m.

I dial Ann and she answers immediately.

"What's going on?" I say, more anxious than I care to sound.

"I'm sorry," she says in an unsorry-sounding voice. "It's gotten a little out of hand here today. Paul flipped out, and I thought maybe you could get up here early and take him off, but it's okay now. Where are you?"

"At the Vince Lombardi."

"The fence what?"

"It's on the Turnpike." She has in fact used the facilities here. Years ago, of course. "I can make it in two hours," I say. "What happened?"

"Oh. He and Charley got into a fracas in the boathouse, about the right way and the wrong way to varnish Charley's dinghy. He hit Charley in the jaw with an oarlock. I think maybe he didn't mean to, but it knocked him down. Almost knocked him out."

"Is he all right?"

"He's all right. No bones broken."

"I mean is *Paul* all right?"

A pause for adjustment. "Yes," she says. "He is. He disappeared for a while, but he came home about nine—which breaks his court curfew. Has he called you?"

"He left me a message." No need for details: barking, hysterical laughter. (To be great is to be misunderstood.)

"Was he crazy?"

"He just seemed excited. I guessed he was with Stephanie." Ann and I are of one mind about Stephanie, which is that *their* chemistry is wrong. In our view, for Stephanie's parents to send her to a military school for girls—possibly in Tennessee—would be good.

"He's very upset. I don't really know why." Ann takes a sip of something that has ice cubes in it. She has changed her drinking habits since moving to Connecticut, from bourbon (when she was married to me) to vodka gimlets, over whose proper preparation Charley O'Dell apparently exercises total mastery. Ann in general is much harder to read these days, which I assume is the point of divorce. Though on the subject of *why now* for Paul, my belief is that on any given day there're truckloads of good excuses for "flipping out." Paul, in particular, could find plenty. It's surprising we all don't do it more.

"How's Clary?"

"Okay. They've gone to sleep in his room now. She says she wants to look out for him."

"Girls mature faster than boys, I guess. How's Charley? Did he get his dinghy waxed right?"

"He has a big lump. Look, I'm sorry. It's all right now. Where is it you're taking him again?"

"To the basketball and baseball halls of fame." This suddenly sounds overpoweringly stupid. "Do you want me to call him?" My son with his own line, a proper Connecticut teen.

"Just come get him like you planned." She's ill at ease now, itchy to get off.

"How are you?" Comes to my mind that I haven't seen her in weeks. Not so long, but long. Though for some reason it makes me mad.

"All right. Fine," she says wearily, avoiding the personal pronoun.

"Are you spending enough time in skiffs? Getting to see the morning mist?"

"What're you indicating with that tone?"

"I don't know." I actually don't know. "It just makes me feel better."

Phone silence descends. Video arcade and Roy Rogers clatter rises and encapsulates me. Another plaid-shirted, blue-jeaned wavy-haired, big-wallet trucker is now waiting midway of the lobby, glomming a sheaf of businessy-looking papers, staring hatchets at me as if I were on his private line.

"Tell me something that's the truth," I say to Ann. I have no idea why, but my voice to me sounds intimate and means to ask intimacy in return.

I, however, know the look on Ann's face now. She has closed her eyes, then opened them so as to be looking in an entirely different direction. She has elevated her chin to stare next at the lacquered ceiling of whatever exquisite, architecturally *sui generis* room she's occupying. Her lips are pursed in an unyielding little line. I'm actually happy not to see this, since it would shut me up like a truant. "I don't really care what you mean by that," she says in an icy voice. "This isn't a friendly conversation. It's just necessary."

"I just wished you had something important to tell me, or something interesting or wholehearted. That's all. Nothing personal." I'm fishing for a sign of the argument, the one Paul said she'd had with Charley. Nothing more innocent.

Ann says nothing. So I say meagerly, "I'll tell *you* something interesting."

"Not wholehearted?" she says crossly.

"Well ..." I, of course, have opened my mouth without knowing what words to bring forth, what beliefs to proclaim or validate, what human condition to hold under my tiny microscope. It's frightening. And yet it's what everybody does— learning how you stand by hearing yourself talk. (Locution, locution, locution.)

What I *almost* say is: "I'm getting married." Though I somehow stop myself after "I'm," which sounds enough like "Um." Except it *is* what I want to say, since it announces something important to *do*, and the only reason I don't say it (other than that it's not true) is that I'd end up responsible for the story and later have to invent a series of fictitious "subsequent" events and shocking turns of fate to get me off the hook. Plus I'd risk being found out and looking pathetic to my children, who already have reservations about me.

The hillbilly trucker is still glaring at me. He is a tall, hip-sprung guy with depressed cheekbones and beady sunken eyes. Probably he is another lime-cologne devotee. His watchband, I notice, is formed by linked, gold-plated pull-tabs, and he in fact points to the watch face and mouths the words *I'm late.* I, though, simply mouth some nonsense words back, then turn into the stale little semi-cubicle separating me from the other humans.

"Are you still there?" Ann says irritably.

"Umm. Yeah," my heart whomping once, unexpectedly. I am staring at my undrunk coffee. "I was thinking," I say, still slightly confused (perhaps I'm still buzzed), "that when you get divorced you think everything changes and you shed a lot of stuff. But I don't think you shed a goddamn thing; you just take more on, like cargo. That's how you find out the limits of your character and the difference between *can't* and *won't*. You might find out you're a little cynical too."

"I have to tell you I don't have any idea what you're talking about. Are you drunk?"

"I might be. But what I said is still true." My right eye flutters, along with my heartbeat going bim-bam. I have scared myself.

"Well, who knows," she says.

"Do you feel like a person who was ever married before?" I wedge my shoulder farther up into my little metal phone coffin for whatever quiet there is.

"I don't *feel* like I was married," Ann says, even more irritable. "I was. A long time ago. To you."

"Seven years ago on the eighteenth," I say, though all at once there's the ice-water-down-the-back recognition that *I* am actually *talking* to Ann. Right now. Rather than doing what I do most all the time—*not* talking to her, or hearing recorded messages of her voice, yet having her on my mind. I'm tempted to tell her how peculiar this feels, as a way of trying to woo her back to me. Though after that, what? Then, loud enough to make me jump out of my shoes, *Boom-boom-boom-ding-ding-ding! Crrraaaaaash!* Somebody in the hellhole video chamber across the concourse has hit some kind of lurid jackpot. Other players—spectral, drugged-looking teens—drift nearer for a gander. "I'm beginning not to feel like I used to feel." I say this under the noise.

"And how is that?" Ann says. "You mean you can't feel what it's like to feel married?"

"Right. Something like that."

"It's because you're *not* married. You should *get* married. We'd all feel better."

"It's pretty nice being married to ole Charley, is it?" I'm glad I didn't blub out I was getting married. I'd have missed this.

"Yes, it is. And he's not old. And it's not any of your business. So don't ask me about it, and please don't think because I won't answer you that *that* means anything." Silence again. I hear her glass tinkle and get set firmly down on some solid surface. "My life's private," she says after swallowing, "and it's not that I can't discuss it; I *won't* discuss it. There's no subject to discuss. It's just words. You may be the most cynical man in the world."

"I hope I'm not," I say, with what feels like an idiotic smile emerging unbidden onto my features.

"You should go back to writing stories, Frank. You quit too soon." I hear a drawer open and close wherever she is, my mind ablaze with possibility. "You could have everybody saying what you wanted them to, then, and everything would work out perfectly—for you anyway. Except it wouldn't really be happening, which you also like."

"Do you think that's what I want?" Something like this very thought, of course, is what put me to sleep at Sally's today.

"You just want everything to seem perfect and everybody to seem pleased. And you're willing to let *seem* equal *be*. It makes pleasing anybody be an act of cowardice. None of this is new news. I don't know why I'm bothering."

"I asked you to." This is a sneak frontal assault on the Existence Period.

"You said to tell you something that was the truth. This is simply obvious."

"Or reliable. I'd settle for that too."

"I want to go to sleep. Please? Okay? I've had a trying day. I don't want to argue with you."

"We're not arguing." I hear the drawer open and close again. Back in the gift-shop complex, a man shouts, "I brake for beer," and laughs like hell.

"Everything's in quotes with you, Frank. Nothing's really solid. Every time I talk to you I feel like everything's being written by you. Even my lines. That's awful. Isn't it? Or sad?"

"Not if you liked them."

"Oh, well . . . ," Ann says, as if a bright light had flashed somewhere outside a window in an otherwise limitless dark, and she had been moved by its extraordinary brilliance and for a moment become transported. "I guess so," she says, seemingly amazed. "I've just gotten very sleepy. I have to go. You wore me out." These are the most intimate words she's addressed to me in years! (I have no idea what might've inspired them.) Though sadder than what she thinks is sad is the fact that hearing them leaves me nothing to say, no lines I even can write for her. Moving closer, even slightly, even for a heartbeat, is just another form of storytelling.

"I'll be there in the morning," I say brightly.

"Fine, fine," Ann says. "That'll be fine, sweetheart." (A slip of the tongue.) "Paul'll be glad to see you." She hangs up before I can even say good-bye.

A NUMBER of travelers have now cycled out of the Vince heading back to the night, awake enough for another hour of driving before sleep or the police catch up. The trucker who's been fish-eyeing me is now talking to another of his ilk, also wearing a plaid shirt (in green; shirts only available in truck stops). The second guy is gigantic with a huge Milwaukee goiter, red suspenders, a piggy crew cut and an oversize silver-and-gold rodeo-champeen belt buckle to keep his jeans cinched up over his, I'm sure, minuscule private parts. They're both shaking their heads disgustedly at me. Clearly their business is more important than mine—a 900 number for finding out which of their favorite hookers are working the BP lot on Route 17 north of Suffern. I'm sure they're Republicans; I probably seem like the most obvious caller to intimidate.

I decide, though, in a moment of discomposure over Ann, to call the Markhams, since my bet is Joe's all talk about clearing out, and he and Phyllis are right now sitting up stolidly watching HBO, the very thing they lack but yearn for in Island Pond.

The switchboard rings for a long time before it's answered by a woman who was asleep one moment before and who says Sleepy Hollow so it sounds like "slippery olive."

"Those left, I think," she says in an achy, light-in-your-eyes voice. "I saw 'em packin' their vehicle around nine, I guess. But lemme ring it."

And in an instant, Joe is on the line.

"Hi, Joe, it's Frank Bascombe," I say, arch-cheerful. "Sorry to fall out of touch. I've had some family problems I couldn't get out of." (My son poleaxed his mother's hubby with an oarlock, then started barking like a Pomeranian, which has caused us all to drop back a couple of squares.)

"Who do you think *this* is?" Joe says, obviously gloating to Phyllis, who's no doubt parked beside him in a swampy TV glow, bingeing on Pringles. I hear a bell ding on Joe's end and someone jabbering in Spanish. They're apparently watching boxing from Mexico, which has probably put Joe in a fighting mood. "I thought I told you we were gettin' out of here."

"I hoped I'd catch you before you got away, just see if there're any questions. Maybe you'd made a decision. I'll call back in the morning if that's better." I ignore the fact that Joe has called me an asshole and a prick on my machine.

"We already got another realtor," Joe says contemptuously.

"Well, I've shown you what there is out there that *I* know about. But the Houlihan house is worth a serious thought. We'll see some movement there pretty quick if the other agencies are on the case. It may be a good time to make an offer if you thought you wanted to."

"You're talking to yourself," Joe sneers. I hear a bottle clink the rim of a glass, then another glass. "Go, go, go," I hear him say in a brash voice—obviously to Phyllis.

"Let me talk to him," she says.

"You're not going to talk to him. What else do you want to tell me?" Joe says, so I can hear the receiver scrape his dopey goatee. "We're watching the fights. It's the last round. Then we're leaving." Joe's forgotten already about the supposed other realtor.

"I'm just checking in. Your message sounded a little agitated."

"That was three hundred and fifty years ago. We're seeing a new person tomorrow. We would've made an offer six hours ago. Now we won't."

"Maybe seeing someone else is a good strategy at this point in time," I say—I hope—infuriatingly.

"Good. I'm glad you're glad."

"If there's anything I can do for you and Phyllis, you know my number."

"I know it. Zero. Zero, zero, zero, zero, zero, zero."

"In 609. Be sure to tell Phyllis I said good-bye."

"Bascombe sends you warm greetings, dear," Joe says snidely.

"Lemme talk," I hear her say.

"A two letter word ending in O." Joe stretches *o* out to a long diphthongal *uhhoouu*, just the way the bozos do in the Beaver Valley.

"You don't have to be such a turd," she says. "He's doing the best he can."

"You mean he's a shithead?" Joe says, partly covering the mouthpiece so I can hear what he's called me but still pretend not to, and he can say what he pleases but pretend not to have said it. After a certain point, which may be a point I've already passed, I don't give a rusty fuck anymore.

Though their situation is pretty much what I imagined this morning: that they'd enter a terrible trial-by-fire period having to do with their sense of themselves, a period which they'd exit disoriented. Afterward they'd wander in a fog until they reached a point of deciding something, which is when I'd wanted to talk to them. As it is, I've called while they're still disoriented and merely *seem* decisive. If I'd waited until tomorrow, they'd both be in straitjackets and ready to roll; inasmuch as what's true for them is true for any of us (and a sign of maturer years): you can rave, break furniture, get drunk, crack up your Nova and beat your knuckles bloody on the glass bricks of the exterior wall of whatever dismal room you're temporarily housed in, but in the end you won't have changed the basic situation and you'll still have to make the decision you didn't want to make before, and probably you'll make it in the very way you'd resented and that brought on all the raving and psychic fireworks.

Choices are limited, in other words. Though the Markhams have spent too long in addlebrained Vermont—picking berries, spying on deer and making homespun clothes using time-honored methods—to know it. In a sense, I provide a service somewhat wider in scope than at first it might seem—a free reality check.

"Frank?" Phyllis is now on the line. Bumping and scraping of motel furniture starts in the background, as if Joe were loading it all in the car.

"Still here," I say, though I'm thinking I'll give Sally a call. Conceivably I can fly her up to Bradley in the morning, where Paul and I could nab her on the way to the Basketball Hall of Fame, then proceed to Cooperstown in a new-dimensional family modality: divorced father, plus son living in another state and undergoing mental sturm und drang, plus father's widowed girlfriend, for whom he feels considerable affection and ambiguity, and whom he may marry or else never see again. Paul would view it as right for our times.

"I guess Joe and I have sort of pulled together on this whole thing now," Phyllis says. Phyllis sounds to me like she's having to exert physical force to talk, as if she's being stuffed in a closet or having to squeeze between big rocks. I imagine her in a pink granny gown, her arms plump above the elbows, possibly wearing socks due to unaccustomed air-conditioning.

"That's just great." *Bing, bing, bingety-bing.* Kids are racking up big numbers on the Samurai Showdown across in the arcade. The Vince operates more like a small-town mall than a part-time sports shrine.

"I'm sorry it's turned out this way after all the work you put in," she says, somehow and with effort freeing herself from whatever's restraining her. Possibly she and Joe are arm-wrestling.

"We'll fight on another day," I say cheerfully. I'm sure she means to tell me her and Joe's complex reasoning for changing boats midstream. Though I'm only willing to hear her spiel it out because telling it will make her feel desperate the instant she's finished. For donkeyish clients like the Markhams, the worst option is having to act on your own advice; whereas letting a paid professional like me tell you what to do is much easier, safer and more comforting, since the advice will always be to follow convention. "Just so you feel like you've made the right decision," I say. I'm still thinking vividly about Sally flying up to meet me: a clear mental picture of her getting in a small plane, in high spirits, carrying an overnight bag.

"Frank, Joe said he could see himself standing in the driveway being interviewed by a local TV reporter," Phyllis says sheep-ishly, "and he didn't want to be that person, not in the Houlihan house." I must've already talked to Joe about my theory of seeing yourself and learning to like it, since he's now claimed it as his own patented wisdom. Joe has apparently left the room.

"What was he being interviewed about?" I say.

"That didn't matter, Frank. It was the whole situation."

Outside the glass doors in the orange-lit parking lot, a big gold-and-green cruiser bus pulls past the entrance, *Eureka* writ-ten on its side in lavish, curving scripted letters. I've seen these buses while driving to Sally's via the Garden State. They're usually crammed with schnockered Canucks headed for Atlantic City to gamble at Trump Castle. They motor straight through, arrive at 1 a.m., gamble forty-eight hours without cease (eats and drinks on the cuff), then hustle back on board and sleep the whole way back to Trois-Rivières, arriving in time for half a day's work on Monday. Someone's idea of fun. I'd like to get on my way before a crew of them comes storming in.

Phyllis, though, has won a round, somehow letting Joe convince himself he's the bad-tempered, tight-fisted old non-compromiser who put the ki-bosh on the Houlihan house. "We also feel, Frank," Phyllis drones, "and I feel this as strongly as Joe, that we don't want to be bossed around by a false economy."

"Which economy is that?" I say.

"The housing one. If we don't get in now, it could be better later."

"Well, that's true. You never get in the river the same place twice," I say dully. "I'm curious, though, if you know where you're going to live by the time school starts."

"Uh-huh," Phyllis says competently. "We think if worse comes to worst, Joe can rent a bachelor place near his work and I can stay on temporarily in Island Pond. Sonja can go right on with her friends in school. We plan to talk to the other relator about that." Phyllis actually says "relator," something I've never heard her say, indicating to me she's reverting to a previous per-sonality matrix—more desperate, but more calculating (also not unusual).

"Well, that's all pretty sound reasoning," I say.

"Do you think that, really?" Phyllis says, undisguised fear suddenly working through her voice like a pitchfork. "Joe says he didn't have a feeling anything significant ever happened in any of the places you showed us. But I wasn't sure."

"I wonder what he had in mind there?" I say. Possibly a celebrity murder? Or the discovery of a new solar system from an attic-window telescope?

"Well, he thinks if we're leaving Vermont we should be moving into a sphere of more important events that would bring us both up in some way. The places you showed us he didn't think did that. Your houses might be better for someone else, maybe."

"They aren't my houses, Phyllis. They belong to other people. I just sell them. Plenty of people do okay in them."

"I'm sure," Phyllis says glumly. "But you know what I mean."

"Not really," I say. Joe's theory of significant events suggests to me he's lost his new finger-hold on sanction. Though I'm not interested. If Joe rents a little *dépendance* in Manalapan, and Phyllis finds "meaningful" work substituting in the Island Pond alternative crafts school, gets into a new "paper group" with a cadre of acid-tongued but spiritually supportive women friends, while Sonja makes the pep squad at Lyndon Academy, marriage Markham-style will be a dead letter by Turkey Day. Which is the real issue here, of course (a profounder text runs beneath all realty decisions): Is being together worth the unbelievable horseshit required to satisfy the other's needs? Or would it just be more fun to go it alone? "Looking at houses is a pretty good test of what you're all about, Phyllis," I say (the very last thing she wants to hear).

"I would've looked at your colored house, Frank—I mean your rental. But Joe just didn't feel right about it."

"Phyllis, I'm at a pay phone on the Turnpike, so I better be going before a truck runs over me. But our rental market's pretty tight, I think you'll find." I spy a phalanx of chortling Canadians, most of them in Bermudas, rumbling across the lot, all primed to hit the can, down a gut-bomb, have a sniff at the Vince trophy case, then grab one last en-route catnap before nonstop gaming commences.

"Frank, I don't know what to say." I hear something made of glass being knocked over and broken into a lot of pieces. "Oh, shit," Phyllis says. "This isn't, by the way, a realtor in Haddam. She's more in the East Brunswick area." A portion of central New Jersey resembling the sere suburban scrub fields of

Youngstown. It's also where Skip McPherson rents ice time before daylight.

"Well, that'll have a whole new feel for you guys" (the Youngstown feel).

"It's sort of starting over, though, isn't it?" Phyllis says, giving in to bewilderment.

"Well, maybe Joe'll picture himself better up there. And there really isn't any starting over involved, Phyllis. It's all part of your ongoing search."

"What do you think's going to happen to us, Frank?"

The Canadians are now bustling into the lobby, elbowing each other and yucking it up like hockey fans—men and women alike. They are big, healthy, happy, well-adjusted white people who aren't about to miss any meals or get dressed up for no good reason. They break off into pairs and threes, guys and gals, and go yodeling off through the metal double doors to the rest rooms. (The best all-around Americans, in my view, are Canadians. I, in fact, should think of moving there, since it has all the good qualities of the states and almost none of the bad, plus cradle-to-grave health care and a fraction of the murders we generate. An attractive retirement waits just beyond the forty-ninth parallel.)

"Did you hear me, Frank?"

"I hear you, Phyllis. Loud and clear." The last of the laughing Canadian women, purses in hand, disappear into the women's, where they immediately start unloading on the men and gassing about how "lucky" they were to hook up with a bunch of cabbage-heads like these guys. "You and Joe are just over-wrought about happiness, Phyllis. You should just buy the first house you halfway like from your new realtor and start making yourselves happy. It's not all that tricky."

"I'm just in a black mood because of my operation, I guess," Phyllis says. "I know we're pretty lucky. Some young people can't even afford a home now."

"Some older people too." I wonder if Phyllis visualizes herself and Joe as among the nation's young. "I gotta get a move on here," I say.

"How's your son? Didn't you tell me he had Hotchkin's or brain damage or something?"

"He's making a comeback, Phyllis." Until this afternoon. "He's quite a boy. Thanks for asking."

"Joe needs a lot of maintenance right now too," Phyllis says, to keep me on the phone. (Some woman in the rest room lets out an Indian whoop that sets the rest of them howling. I hear a stall door bang shut. "Yew-guyz . . . Jeeeeez-us," one of the men answers from next door.) "We've seen some changes in our relationship, Frank. It's not easy to let someone into your inner circle if you're both second-timers."

"It's not easy for first-timers either," I say impatiently. Phyllis seems to be angling for something. Though what? I once had a client—the wife of a church history professor and a mother of three, one of whom was autistic and got left in the car in a restraining harness—who asked me if I had any interest in getting naked with her on the polished floor of a ranch-style home in Belle Mead, a house her husband liked but she wanted a second look at because she felt the floor plan lacked "flow." An instance of pure transference. Though no one in the realty business isn't clued in to the sexual dimension: hours spent alone in close quarters (front seats of cars, provocatively empty houses); the not-quite-false aura of vulnerability and surrenderment; the possibility of a future in the same grid pattern, of unexpected, tingly sightings at the end of the lettuce rack, squirmy, almost-missed eye contact across a hot summer parking lot or through a plate-glass window with a spouse present. There have been instances in these three years and a half when I haven't been a model citizen. Except you can lose your license for that kind of stunt and become a bad joke in the community, neither of which I care to risk as much as I might once have.

Still, for some reason, I find myself imagining fleshy Phyllis not in a pink petunia print but a skimpy slip over her bare underneath, holding a tumbler of warm Scotch while she talks, and peeking out the blinds at the grainy-lit Sleepy Hollow parking lot as the innkeeper's eighteen-year-old half-Polynesian son, Mombo, shirtless and muscles bulging, hauls a garbage bag around to the dumpster outside their bathroom in which sluggo Joe is grouchily tending to more of nature's unthrilling needs behind closed doors. This is the second time today I've thought of Phyllis "in this way," her health situation notwithstanding. My question, however, is: why?

"So you live alone?" Phyllis says.

"What's that?"

"Because Joe had at one time thought you might be gay, that's all."

"Nope. A frayed knot, as my son says." Though I'm baffled. In two hours I have been suspected of being a priest, a shithead and now, a homo. I'm apparently not getting my message across. I hear another round-bell go *ding*, as Joe turns up the TV from Mexico.

"Well," Phyllis says, whispering, "I just wished for a second I was going wherever you were going, Frank. That might be nice."

"You wouldn't have a good time with me, Phyllis. I can promise that."

"Oh. It's just crazy. Crazy, crazy talk." Too bad she can't get on the bus with the Canadians. "You're a good listener, Frank. I'm sure it's a plus in your profession."

"Sometimes. But not always."

"You're just modest."

"Good luck to you two," I say.

"Well, we'll see you, Frank. You be good. Thanks."

Clunk.

THE TRUCKERS who've been glowering at me have wandered off. And both sets of Canadians now emerge from their comfort stations, hands damp, noses blown, faces splashed, hair wet-combed, shirttails for the moment tucked, yaw-hawing about whatever nasty secrets were shared around inside. They march off into Roy's, their skinny, uniformed bus driver standing just outside the glass doors, having a smoke and some P & Q in the hot night. He cuts his eyes my way, sees me down the phone bank watching him, shakes his head as if we both knew all about it, tosses his smoke and walks out of view.

Without as much as one guarded thought left from dinner, I punch in Sally's number, feeling that I've made a bad decision where she's concerned, should've stayed and wooed my way out of the woods like a man who knows how to get messages across. (This of course may turn out to be a worse decision—tired, half drunk, fretful, not in control of my speech. Though sometimes it's better to make a bad decision than no decision at all.)

But Sally, from her message, must be in a similar frame of

mind, and what I'd like to do is turn around and beat it back to her house, scramble into bed with her and have us go slap to sleep like old marrieds, then tomorrow haul her along, and begin instilling proper wanting practices into my life, and fun to boot, and quit being the man holding out. Forty psychics able to find Jimmy Hoffa in a landfill, or to tell you what street your missing twin Norbert's living on in Great Falls, couldn't tell me what's a "better deal" than Sally Caldwell. (Of course, one of the Existence Period's bedrock paradoxes is that just when you think you're emerging, you may actually be wading further in.)

"Uffda, ya goddamn knucklehead," one of the Canadians yorks out as I listen intently to Sally's phone ring and ring and ring.

Though I'm quick to the next decision: leave a message saying I *would*'ve zoomed back but didn't know where she was, yet I stand prepared to charter a Piper Comanche, zoom her up to Springfield, where Paul and I'll pick her up in time for lunch. Zoom, zoom.

But instead of her sweet voice and diversionary, security-conscious message—"Hi! We're not here, but your call is important to us"—I get rings and more rings. I actually picture the phone vibrating all to hell on its table beside her big teester bed, which in my tableau is lovingly turned down but empty. I pound in the number again and try to visualize Sally dashing out of the shower or just coming in from a pensive midnight walk on Mantoloking beach, taking the front steps two at a time, forgetting her limp, hoping it's me. And it is. Only, ring, ring, ring, ring.

An overcooked, nearly nauseating hot dog smell floats across the lobby from Nathan's. "And your mind's a sewer too," one of the Canuck women sounds off at one of the men standing in line.

"So and what's yers, eh? An operating room? I'm not married t'ya, okay?"

"Yet," another man guffaws.

Defeated, I'm nonetheless ready to go, and take off striding right out through the lobby. Gaunt boys from Moonachie and Nutley are straying in toward the Mortal Kombat and Drug War machines, angling for the big kills. New weary-eyed travelers wander through the front doors, seeking relief of some stripe, ignoring the Vince trophy case—too much on a late night. I should, right here and now, buy something to bring Clarissa, but there's nothing for sale but football crap and postcards showing the NJ Tpk in all four seasonal moods (I'll have to find something tomorrow), and I pass out of the air-conditioning right by the Eureka driver, leaning one leg up on his idling juggernaut, surrounded now by white gulls standing motionless in the dark.

UP AGAIN onto the streaming, light-choked Turnpike, my dashboard digital indicating 12:40. It's tomorrow already, July 2, and my personal aspirations are now trained on sleep, since the rest of tomorrow will be a testing day if everything goes in all details perfectly, which it won't; so that, I'm determined—late departure and all—to put my woolly head down *someplace* in the Constitution State, as a small token of progress and encouragement to my journey.

But the Turnpike thwarts me. Along with construction slowdowns, entrance ramps merging, MEN WORKING, left-lane breakdowns and a hot mechanical foreboding that the entire seaboard might simply explode, there's now even more furious, grinding-mad-in-the-dark traffic and general vehicular desperation, as if to be caught in New Jersey after tonight will mean sure death.

At Exit 18 E & W, where the Turnpike ends, cars are stacked before, beyond, around and out of sight toward the George Washington Bridge. Automated signs over the lanes counsel way-worn travelers to EXPECT LONG DELAYS, TAKE ALTERNATE ROUTE. More responsible advice would be: LOOK AT YOUR HOLE CARD. HEAD FOR HOME. I envision miles and miles of backup on the Cross Bronx (myself dangled squeamishly above the teeming hellish urban no-man's-land below), followed by multiple-injury accidents on the Hutch, more long toll-booth tie-ups on the thruway, a blear monotony of NO VACANCYs clear to Old Saybrook and beyond, culminating in me sleeping on the back seat in some mosquito-plagued rest area and (worst case) being trussed and maimed, robbed and murdered, by anguished teens—who might right now be following me from the Vince—my body left for crows' food, silent on a peak in Darien.

So, as ill advised, I take an alternate route.

Though there is no truly alternate route, only *another* route, a longer, barely chartable, indefensible fool's route of sailing west to get east: up to 80, where untold cars are all flooding eastward, then west to Hackensack, up 17 past Paramus, onto the Garden State north (again!), though eerily enough there's little traffic; through River Edge and Oradell and Westwood, and two tolls to the New York line, then east to Nyack and the Tappan Zee, down over Tarrytown (once home to Karl Bemish) to where the East opens up just as the North must have once for old Henry Hudson himself.

What on a good summer night should take thirty minutes— the G.W. to Greenwich and straight into a pricey little inn with a moon-shot water view—takes me an hour and fifteen, and I am *still* south of Katonah, my eyes jinking and smarting, phantoms leaping from ditches and barrow pits, the threat of spontaneous dozing forcing me to grip the wheel like a Le Mans driver having a heart attack. Several times I consider just giving in, pulling off, falling over sideways from fatigue, surrendering to whatever the night stalkers lurking on the outskirts of Pleasantville and Valhalla have dreamed up for me—my car down on its rims, my trunk jimmied, luggage and realty signs strewn around, my wallet lifted by shadowy figures in Air Jordans.

But I'm too close. And instead of staying on big, safe, reliable 287 up to big, safe, reliable 684 and pushing the extra twenty miles to Danbury (a virtual Motel City, with maybe an all-night liquor outlet), I turn north on the Sawmill (its homespun name alone makes me sleepy) and head toward Katonah, checking my AAA atlas for the quickest route into CT.

Then, almost unnoticeable, a tiny wooden sign—CONNECTI-CUT—with a small hand-painted arrow seeming to point right out of the 1930s. And I make for it, down NY 35, my headlights vacuuming its narrow, winding, stone-walled, woods-to-the-verge alleyways toward Ridgefield, which I calculate (distances that look long on the map are actually short) to be twelve miles. And in ten minutes flat I'm there, the sleeping village rising into pretty, bucolic view, meaning that I've somehow crossed the state line without knowing it.

Ridgefield, as I drive cautiously up and through, my eyes peeled for cops and motels, is a hamlet that even in the pallor of its barium-sulfur streetlights would remind anyone but a lifelong

Ridgefielder of Haddam, New Jersey—only richer. A narrow, English high street emerges from the woodsy south end, leads through a hickory-shaded, lush-lawned, deep-pocketed mansion district of mixed architectural character, each mansion with big-time security in place, winds through a quaint, shingled, basically Tudor CBD of attached shops (rich realtors, a classic-car showroom, a Japanese deli, a fly-tiers shop, a wine & liquor, a Food For Thought Books). A walled war-memorial green lies just at village center, flanked by big Protestant churches and two more mansions converted to lawyers' offices. The Lions meet Wednesday, the Kiwanis Thursday. Other, shorter streets bend away to delve and meander through more modest but still richly tree-lined neighborhoods, with lanes named Baldy, Pudding, Toddy Hill, Scarlet Oak and Jasper. Plainly, anyone living below the Cross Bronx would move here if he or she could pay the freight.

But if you're driving through at 2:19, "town" slips by before you know it, and you're too quick through it and out onto Route 7, having passed no place to stop and ask or caught no glimpse of a friendly motel sign—only a pair of darkened inns (Le Chateau and Le Perigord), where a fellow could tuck into a lobster thermidor across from his secretary, or a veal scarpatti and a baked Alaska with his son from some nearby prep school. But don't expect a room. Ridgefield's a town that invites no one to linger, where the services contemplate residents only, but which makes it in my book a piss-poor place to live.

Exhausted and disappointed, I make a reluctant left at the light onto 7, resigned to sag into Danbury, fifteen miles farther on and by now full to the brim with darkened cars nosed into darkened motel lots. I have done this all wrong. A forceful stand at Sally's or at the very least tarrying in Tarrytown would've saved me.

Yet ahead in the gloom where 7 crosses the Ridgefield line and disappears back into the hinterland of scrub-brush Connecticut, I see the quavery red neon glimmer I've given up hoping for. MOTEL. And under it, in smaller, fuzzier letters, the life-restoring VACANCY. I aim at it like a missile.

But when I wheel into the little half-moon lot (it's the Sea Breeze, though no sea's near enough to offer breezes), there's a commotion in progress. Motel guests are out of their rooms in bathrobes, slippers and tee-shirts. The state police are abundantly present—more blue flashers turning—while a big white-and-orange ambulance van, its strobes popping and its back door open, appears ready to receive a passenger. The whole lot has the backlit, half-speed unreality of a movie set (not what I'd hoped for) and I'm tempted just to drive on, though again that would mean conking out on the car seat and hoping no one kills me.

All the police activity is going on at one end of the lot, in front of the last unit in line; so I park near the other end, beyond the office, where lights are on and a customer counter is visible through the window. If I can be assigned a room away from the action, I may still get one-third night's measure of sleep.

Inside the office the air-conditioning's cranked up high, and a powerful cooking smell from a rear apartment beyond a red drapery makes the air dense and stinging. The clerk is a slender, dull-looking subcontinental whose eyes flicker up at me from a desk behind the counter. He's talking on the phone at a blazing speed and in a language I recognize as not my own. Without pausing, he fingers a little registration card off a stack he has, slides it up onto the glass countertop, where a pen's attached to a little chain. Several hand-lettered and unequivocal instructions have been pressed under the glass, relating to one's use of one's room: no pets, no calls charged, no cooking, no hourly rates, no extra guests, no operation of a business (none of these is currently in my plans).

The clerk, who has on a regulation dirty-collared, short-sleeved white shirt and black slacks, goes right on talking, even becoming at one point agitated and loudly vociferous while I finish filling out the guest card and slide it across with my Visa. At this instant he simply puts the receiver down, clears his throat, stands and starts scribbling on the card with his own ballpoint. My needs are apparently enough like other guests' that we can skip pleasantries.

"So what's happened down at the other end?" I say, hoping I'll hear everything's all over and wasn't any great shakes to begin with. Possibly an on-site demo of police practices for the benefit of the Ridgefield town fathers.

"Don't worry," the clerk says in a fussy voice guaranteed to make anyone worry. "Everything is fine now."

He whips my Visa through the credit-check box, glances at

me, doesn't smile, just takes a weary breath and waits for the green numbers to certify I'm a fair risk for $52.80.

"What happened, though?" I feign absolute no-worry.

He sighs. "It's just best to stay away." He's used to answering questions only about room rates and checkout times. He has a long, slender neck that would look much better on a woman, and wisps of little mannish mustache hairs that shadow the corners of his mouth. He does not inspire wide trust.

"Just curious," I say. "I wasn't planning on wandering down there." I look back through the window, where the police and ambulance lights are still buffeting the dark. Several gawker cars have stopped on Route 7, their drivers' faces lit by the flashes. Two Connecticut state troopers in wide Stetsons are conferring beside their cruiser, arms folded, their stiff, tight-fitting uniforms making them seem brawny and stern though unquestionably even-handed.

"Some people maybe got robbed down there," the clerk says, pushing a Visa receipt out for my Frank Bascombe. At this moment a short, round-waisted thick-haired woman in a red-and-black sari and a badgered expression appears at the doorway drapery. She buzzes something to the clerk, then vanishes. For some reason I sense she's been talking via extension to whomever he was talking to, and he's now required again—possibly to catch hell from relatives in Karachi about whatever's happening outside.

"How'd it happen?" I say, putting my name on the dotted line.

"We don't know." He shakes his head, comparing signatures, then pulling the delicate leaves off the receipt, having never even acknowledged the woman who came and left. She, I'm sure, is the person responsible for the venomous cooking smell. "They check in. In a little while some big agitation in there. I don't see what happened."

"Anybody get hurt?" I stare at my Visa receipt in his hand, wishing I hadn't signed it.

"Maybe. I don't know." He hands me my card, receipt and a key. "Get the key deposit when you check out. Ten o'clock is the time."

"Swell," I say, and smile hopelessly, thinking of heading to Danbury.

"It's on the other end, okay?" he says, pointing toward the

hoped-for wing, smiling perfunctorily and showing his straight little teeth. He has to be freezing in his short sleeves, though right away he returns to the phone and begins muttering in his tangly tongue, his voice going to a hush in case I might know a word or two of Urdu and spill some important beans.

Back out on the lot, night air feels even more electrified and stoked. Other motel guests have started to drift back, but police radios are crackling, the bugged-up red MOTEL sign hums and an even denser feeling of subsonic noises vibrates off the cruisers and the ambulance and the cars stopped along the highway. Somewhere close by a skunk has been aroused, its hot scent swarming out of the trees beyond the lights. I think of Paul, not so far from here now, and will him to be in bed asleep, as I should be.

The last door in the line of motel doors has been opened now, and harsh lights are on inside, with shadows passing quickly. Several policemen, local Joes, are standing around a two-tone blue Chevy Suburban parked directly in front of the room, all its five doors open, its interior lights on. A Boston Whaler is in tow behind the Suburban and is filled with recreation gear—a bicycle, water skis, some strapped-together lawn furniture, scuba tanks and a wooden doghouse. The local cops are shining flashlights around inside. A big leering Bugs has been stuck to a back side window with suction cups.

"Y'ain't safe no mo' nowhere," a man's thick voice says, and actually makes me jump. I look around fast and find an immense, heavy-breathing Negro standing behind me wearing a green Mayflower moving van uniform. He's holding a black attaché case under his arm, and above his breast pocket, under a red *Mayflower*, the word *Tanks* is stitched within a yellow oval. He's watching what I'm watching.

We're right behind my parked Crown Victoria, and the instant I see him I also notice his Mayflower van parked across Route 7 in the turnout for a seasonal produce stand, closed at this hour.

"What's going on down there?" I say.

"Kids broke on into some people's room owns that Suburban, and robbed 'em. Then they killed the guy. They got 'em both over there"—he points—"in that po-lice car. Somebody oughta just go over there and pop 'em both in the melon and be done with it." Mr. Tanks (first name, last, nickname?) breathes in again momentously. He has a lineman's wide smudge-pot face, a huge big-nostril nose and all but invisible deep-set eyes. His uniform includes ludicrous green walking shorts that barely manage around his butt and thighs, and black nylon knee socks that show off his beefsteak calves. He is a head shorter than me, but it's no chore to feature him bear-hugging an armoire or a new Amana down several flights of stairs.

The two troopers, I determine, are standing guard at their car, which is stopped in the precise middle of the lot with its head-lights still on. Through the back window I can make out in the darkness first one white face and then a second one—boys' faces, tilted forward to indicate both are handcuffed. Neither is talking, and both seem to be watching the troopers. The boy I can see more clearly seems to smile in reply to Mr. Tanks's having pointed him out.

The sight of the two faces, though, causes me a sudden jittery interior flutter like a fan blade spinning in my belly. I wonder if I'm about to wince again, but I don't. "How do they know they did it?"

" 'Cause they run, that's why," Mr. Tanks says, confidently. "I was out on number seven. And the police car come around me going a hundred. And two miles on down, here they all were. Two of 'em spread out on the hood. Hadn't been five minutes. Trooper tol' me about it." Mr. Tanks breathes another threaten-ing breath. His thick truckdriver's smell is a nice leathery fragrance mingled with what must be the scent of moving pads. "Bridgeport," he murmurs, making *port* sound like *pote*. "Killin' to be killin'."

"Where are the other people from?" I say.

"I guess Utah." He is silent a moment. Then he says, "Pullin' that little boat."

Just then two male ambulance attendants in red shirts appear in the motel door, horsing a collapsible metal stretcher out into the night. A long black plastic bag that looks like it should hold a set of golf clubs is strapped on top and lumpy from the body inside. A moment later a small, thick-necked, tough-looking white man in a white short-sleeved shirt and tie, and wearing a pistol, and a badge on a string around his neck, escorts a blond woman in a thin blue flowered dress out the door, holding her upper arm as though she were under arrest. They walk quickly toward the state troopers' car, where one of the troopers opens the back door and starts to pull out the boy who's smiled before. But the detective speaks something out in front of him, and the trooper simply stands aside and lets the boy stay put, while the other trooper produces a flashlight.

The detective directs the blond woman to the open car door. She seems very light on her feet. The trooper shines his flash straight into the face of the boy closest. His skin is ghostly and looks damp even from here, his hair buzzed almost bare on the sides but left long in the back. He gazes up into the light as if he's willing to expose everything there is to know about him.

The woman only briefly looks at him, then turns her head away. The boy says something—I see his lips move—and the woman says something to the detective. Then they both turn and walk briskly back toward the room. The troopers quickly close the car door, then climb in the front seat, both sides. Their siren makes a loud *wheep-whoop*, their blue flasher flashes once, and their car—a Crown Vic just like mine—idles forward a few yards before it makes an engine roar, skitters its wheels and shoots out onto 7, where it disappears to the north, its siren coming on again but far out of sight.

"Where *you* tryin' to get?" Mr. Tanks says gruffly. He is now carefully unfolding two sticks of Spearmint, which he inserts into his large mouth both at once. He goes on clutching his attaché case.

"Deep River," I say, nearly silenced by what I've just witnessed. "I'm picking up my son." The jittery flutter has stopped in my stomach.

The watchers out on Route 7 are starting to creep away. The ambulance, now closed, its interior lights out, backs cautiously away from the motel door, then eases off in the direction the troopers have gone—to Danbury is my guess—its silver and red lights turning but with no siren.

"*Then* where you two goin'?" He is crushing his gum wrapper and chewing vigorously. He wears a great chunky diamond-and-gold-crusted ring on his right ring finger, something a large person might design for himself or possibly get by winning the Super Bowl.

"We're going to the Baseball Hall of Fame." I look around at him amiably. "Did you ever go there?"

"Uh-uh," he says, and shakes his head, his mouth emitting a loud Spearminty sweetness. Mr. Tanks's hair is short and dense and black, but doesn't grow on all parts of his head. Islands of his glistening black scalp appear here and there, making him look older than I'm sure he is. We're probably the same age. "What line of work you do?"

The VACANCY sign goes silently off, then the MOTEL sign itself, leaving only a humming red NO illuminated. The clerk lowers the blinds inside the office, switches them closed, and the office lights go almost immediately out.

We aren't socializing here, I realize, only bearing brief dual witness to the perilous character of life and our uncertain presences in it. Otherwise there's no reason for us to stand here together.

"Real estate," I say, "down in Haddam, New Jersey. About two and a half hours from here."

"That's a rich man's town," Mr. Tanks says, still chewing rapidly.

"*Some* rich people live there," I say. "But some folks just sell real estate. Where do you live?"

"Divorced," Mr. Tanks says. "I 'bout live in that rig." He swivels his big midnight face in the direction of his truck.

There in the shadows Mr. Tanks's enormous trailer displays a jaunty good ship *Mayflower* in green, abreast a jaunty sea of yellow. It's the most nearly patriotic sight I've seen in the Ridgefield area. I think of Mr. Tanks snugged up in his high-tech sleep cocoon, decked out (for some reason) in red silk pj's, earphones plugged into an Al Hibbler CD, perusing a *Playboy* or a *Smithsonian* and munching a gourmet sandwich purchased somewhere back down the line and heated up in his mini-micro. It's as good as what I do. Possibly the Markhams should consider long-haul trucking instead of the suburbs. "That must not be so bad," I say.

"It gets old. Cramped gets old," he says. Mr. Tanks must weigh 290. "I *own* a home out in Alhambra."

"Does your wife live there, then?"

"Uh-uh," Mr. Tanks grunts. "My furniture stays out there. I pay it a visit once in a while when I miss it."

Down at the lighted room where a murder has taken place, the local cops shut the Suburban's doors and wander inside, talking quietly, their local-cop hats pushed back on their heads. Mr.

Tanks and I are the last observers left. I'm sure it's close to three. I yearn for bed and sleep, though I don't want to leave Mr. Tanks alone.

"Lemme just ask you a question." Mr. Tanks is holding his attaché still under his giant arm and gravely chewing his Spearmint. "Since you're into real estate now" (as if I'd only been in it a couple of weeks). He doesn't look at me. It may embarrass him to address me in terms of my profession. "I'm thinking about selling my home." He stares straight away into the dark.

"The one in Alhambra?"

"Uh-huh." He breathes again noisily through his big nostrils.

"California's holding onto its value is all I hear, if that's what you want to know."

"I bought in seventy-six." Another big sigh.

"Then you're in great shape," I say, though why I'd say that I don't know, since I've never been in Alhambra, don't know the tax base, the racial makeup, the comp situation or the market status. I'll probably visit *the* Alhambra before I visit Mr. Tanks's Alhambra.

"What I'm wonderin' is," Mr. Tanks says and wipes his big hand over his face, "if I oughtn't not to move out here."

"To Ridgefield?" Not an obvious match.

"It don't matter where."

"Do you have any friends and family out here?"

"Naw."

"Is the Mayflower home office out here someplace?"

He shakes his head. "They don't matter where you live. You just drivin' for them."

I look at Mr. Tanks curiously. "Do you like it out here?" Meaning the seaboard, the Del-Mar-Va to Eastport, from the Water Gap to Block Island.

"It's pretty good," he says. His cavey eyes narrow and flicker at me, as if he'd caught a whiff suggesting I might be amused by him.

But I'm not! I understand (I think) perfectly well what he's getting at. If he'd answered in the usual way—that his Aunt Pansy lived in Brockton, or his brother Sherman in Trenton, or if he was positioning himself for a managerial charge inside corporate Mayflower, home offices, say, in Frederick, MD, or Ayer, Mass., and needed to move nearer—that would make sound sense.

Though it would be a whole lot less interesting on the human side. But if I'm right, his question is of a much more omenish and divining nature, having to do with the character of eventuality (not rust-belt economics or the downturn in per-square-foot residential in the Hartford-Waterbury metroplex).

Instead, his is the sort of colloquy most of us engage in alone with only our silent selves, and that with the right answers can give rise to rich feelings of synchronicity of the kind I came back from France full of four years ago: when everything is glitteringly about *you*, and everything you do seems led by a warm, invisible astral beam issuing from a point too far away in space to posit but that's leading you to the place—if you can just follow and stay lined up—you *know* you want to be. Christians have their grimmer version of this beam; Jainists do too. Probably so do ice dancers, bucking-bronco riders and grief counselors. Mr. Tanks is one of the multitude seeking, with hope, to emerge from a condition he's grown weary of in pursuit of something better, and wants to know what he should do—a profound inquiry.

I'd of course love to help with this alignment of small stars, and without making him worry I'm a loony or a realty shark or a homosexual with polyracial endomorphic appetites. In the most magnanimous sense, such assistance is the heart of the realty profession.

I fold my arms and let myself sway sideways so my thigh pushes against the back bumper of my Crown Victoria. I wait a few seconds, then say, "I think I know exactly what you're getting at."

"What about?" Mr. Tanks says suspiciously.

"About wondering where you ought to go," I say in as unaggressive, unsharky, unhomophilic a way as possible.

"Yeah, but that don't really matter," Mr. Tanks says, instantly shying off the subject now that he's raised it. "But okay," he says, still showing interest. "I'd like to set down someplace else, you know? Like a neighborhood."

"Would you live there?" I say in a helpful, professional voice. "Or would it just be someplace for your furniture to live?"

"I'd live there," Mr. Tanks says, and nods, looking up at the sky as though wishing to envision a future. "If I liked it, I wouldn't necessarily even mind being in someplace I've lived before. You understand what I mean?"

"Pretty much," I say, meaning "perfectly."

"The East Coast just seems sorta homey to me." Mr. Tanks suddenly looks around at his truck as if he's heard a sound and expects to see someone scaling the side, ready to break in and steal his TV. Though there's no one.

"Where'd you grow up?" I say.

He continues staring at his truck and away from me. "Michigan. Old man was a chiropractor in the U.P. Wasn't too many Negroes doing that work."

"I bet not. Do you like it up there?"

"Oh yeah. I love it."

There's no use blabbing that I'm an old Wolverine or that we probably have experiences in common. Divorce, for starters. My memories, in any case, would probably conflict with his.

"Then why don't you go back and buy a house? Or build one? That seems like a no-brainer to me."

Mr. Tanks turns and gives me a wary look, as if I might've been referring to *his* brain. "My ex-wife stays up there now. That don't work."

"Do you have any children?"

"Uh-uh. That's why I ain't been to the Hall of Fame." His big eyebrows lower. (What business is it of mine if he has children?)

"Well. I'll just say this." I would still like to encourage Mr. Tanks with some useful facts offered as data for his search for what to do next. I in fact feel some anxiety that he doesn't know how specifically I appreciate how he feels and that I've felt the same way myself. No disappointment is quite like the failure to share a crucial understanding. "I just *want* to say this," I begin again, correcting myself. "I'm selling houses these days. And I live in a pretty nice town down there. And we're about to see a rise in prices, and I believe interest rates'll head up by the end of the year and maybe even before."

"That's too rich down there. I been down there. I moved some basketball player's mother into some big house. Then moved her out again a year later."

"You're right, it's not cheap. But let me just say that most experts believe a purchase price two and a half times your annual pre-tax income is a realistic debt load. And I've got houses right now, in the Boro of Haddam"—all shown to the Markhams, all promptly trashed—"at two-fifty, and I'll have more as time goes on. And I feel like in the long run, whether it's Dukakis or Bush or Jackson"—fat chance—"prices are going to stay up in New Jersey."

"Uh-huh," Mr. Tanks says, making me feel exactly like a realty shark (which is possibly what you are if you're a realtor at all).

Only my view is, if I sell you a house in a town where life's tolerable, then I've done you a big favor. And if I try and don't succeed, then you've got a view you like better (assuming you can afford it). Plus, I don't cotton to the idea of raising the draw-bridge, which Mr. Tanks probably has experience with. I mean to guarantee the same rights and freedoms for all. And if that means merchandising New Jersey dirt like dog-nuts so we all get our one sweet piece, then so be it. We'll all be dead in forty years anyway.

I won't (or can't), in other words, be easily shamed. And Mr. Tanks would make a good addition and be as welcome on Cleve-land Street as his pocketbook could make him (he'd, of course, have to stash his truck someplace else). And I'm not doing any-body a favor if I don't try to get him interested.

"So what's the worst part about being a realtor?" He's staring around somewhere else again—above the Sea Breeze roofline, where the humpy moon has floated higher and wears a fuzzy halo. Mr. Tanks is now signaling me that he's not ready to buy a house in New Jersey, which is fine. He may conduct conversa-tions like this with everyone—his "thing" being to ramble on dolefully about wishing he could *be* someplace better—and I've spoiled the fun by trying to figure out where and how. He may feel fine dedicating his life to moving other people hither and yon.

"My name's Frank Bascombe, by the way." A gesture of hello and good-bye, poking my hand toward Mr. Tanks's strenuous green belly. He administers a halfhearted little jiggling of just my fingers. Mr. Tanks might look like a guard for old Vince back in the Bart Starr-Fuzzy Thurston gravy days, but he shakes hands like a debutante.

"Tanks," is all he grunts.

"Well, really, I don't know if it has a worst part," I say, address-ing the realtor question and feeling a sudden, brain-flattening fatigue and the painful need for sleep. I pause for a breath. "When *I* don't like it so much, I try not to notice it and stay home reading a book. But I guess if it has to have a bad side, it's having clients think I want to sell them a house they don't like, or that I don't care if they like it or not. Which is never true." I pull my hand over my face and push my eyelids up to keep them open.

"You don't like being misinterpreted, is that it?" Mr. Tanks looks amused. He makes an odd gurgly chuckle deep in his throat, which makes me self-conscious.

"I guess so. Or not."

"I figured you guys was all crooks," Mr. Tanks says as though talking about something else *to* someone else. "Like a used-car guy, only 'cept with houses. Or burial insurance. Something like that."

"Some people feel that way, I guess." I'm thinking that we're at this moment two feet away from my trunkful of realty signs, blank offer sheets, earnest money receipts, listing forms, prospect memos, PRICE REDUCED and SORRY, YOU MISSED IT stickers. Burglar's tools, to Mr. Tanks. "Really, a main concern *is* avoiding misrepresentation. I wouldn't want to do anything to you that I wouldn't want done to me—at least as far as realty goes." This did not come out sounding right (due to exhaustion).

"Hunh," is all Mr. Tanks offers. Our time for bearing witness to life's strangeness is nearly over.

Suddenly, at the end of the row of motel units, out the door of the lighted room we've been waiting a vigil over, come two uniformed local police, followed by the tough-nut detective, followed by a uniformed policewoman, holding the arm of the young blue-dressed wife who's in turn holding the small hand of a tiny blond girl, who looks apprehensively all around in the dark and back behind her into the room she's left, though suddenly, by dint of memory, she turns and looks up at ole Bugs, stuck to the window of the Suburban, leering his nutty brains out. She's wearing neat little yellow shorts and tennies with white socks, and a hot-pink pullover that has a red heart on the front like a target. She is slightly knock-kneed. When she gazes around again and sees no one she recognizes, she fastens her eyes on Mr. Tanks as she's led across the lot to an unmarked vehicle that will take her and her mother elsewhere, to some other Connecticut town, where a terrible-awful thing *hasn't* happened. There, to sleep.

They have left their room standing open, the Whaler jammed with stealable gear somebody should see about locking up or storing. (This I would've waked up and worried about in the middle of the night back in 1984, even if it were my loved one who was killed.)

Though just as the young woman ducks into the dark car, she looks back at her room and at the Suburban and the Sea Breeze and then to the left at Mr. Tanks and me, her companions of a sort, watching her with distant compassion as she encounters grief and confusion and loss all alone and all at once. Her face comes up, light catches it so that I see the look of startlement on her fresh young features. It is her first scent, the first light-glimmer, that she's no longer connected in the old manner of two hours ago but into some new network now, where caution is both substance and connector. (It is not so different from the look on the boy's face who killed her husband.) I, of course, could connect with her—give a word or a look. But it would be only momentary, whereas caution is what she needs now, and what's dawning. To learn a lesson of caution at a young age is not the worst thing.

Her face disappears into the squad car. The door closes hard, and in half of one minute they are all gone—the local boys in their Fairfield Sheriff's cruiser, murmuring ahead, gumball flashing; the unmarked car with the policewoman driving—off in the direction opposite, where the ambulance has gone. Again, when they are all out of sight into the scrub-timber distance, a siren rises. They will not be back tonight.

"I bet they got their insurance paid up," Mr. Tanks says. "Mormons. You know *they're* paid up. Them people don't let nothin' slide." He consults his wristwatch, sunk into his great arm. Time of day means nothing to him. I don't know how he knows they were Mormons. "You know how to keep a Mormon from stealin' your sandwich when you go fishin', don't you?"

"How?" It is an odd moment for a quip.

"Take another Mormon witchyou." Mr. Tanks makes his deep-chested *hunh* noise again. This is his way of resolving the unresolvable.

I, though, have had it in mind—since his position on realtors is that we're first cousins to odometer-spinning car dealers and burial plot scammers—to ask about his views on moving-van drivers. We hear plenty of adverse opinions of *them* in my business, where they're generally considered the loose cannons of the removal industry. But I'm certain he wouldn't have an opinion. I'd be surprised if Mr. Tanks practiced many analytical views of himself. He is no doubt happiest concentrating on whatever's beyond his windshield. In this way he's like a Vermonter.

In the thick trees behind the Sea Breeze I hear a dog barking, perhaps at the skunk, and somewhere else, faintly, a phone ringing. Mr. Tanks and I have not shared much, in spite of my wishing we could. We are, I'm afraid, not naturals for each other.

"I guess I'll hit the hay," I say as if the idea has just come to me. I offer Mr. Tanks a hopeful smile, which awards no closure, only its surface appeal.

"Talk about misinterpreted and not being misinterpreted." Mr. Tanks still has in mind our conversation from before (a surprise).

"Right," I say, not knowing what's right.

"Maybe I'm gon' come down there to New Jersey and buy a big house from you," he announces imperially. I'm beginning to inch away toward my room.

"I wish you'd do that. That'd be great."

"You got some expensive neighborhoods where they'll let me park my truck?"

"That might take some time to find," I say. "But we could work up something." A ministorage up in Kendall Park, for instance.

"We could work on that, huh?" Mr. Tanks yawns a cavernous yawn and closes his eyes as he rolls his big furry head back in the moonlight.

"Absolutely. Where do you park in Alhambra?"

He turns, to notice I'm farther away now. "You got any niggers down there in your part of New Jersey?"

"Plenty of 'em," I say.

Mr. Tanks looks at me steadily, and of course, even as sleepy as I am, I'm awfully sorry to have said that, yet have no way to yank the words back. I just stop, one foot up on the Sea Breeze walkway, and look helpless to the world and fate.

"'Cause I wouldn't care to be the only pea in the pod down there, you understand?" Mr. Tanks seems earnestly if briefly to be considering a move, committing to a life in New Jersey, miles and miles from lonely Alhambra and lightless, glacial Michigan.

"I bet you'd be happy there," I say meekly.

"Maybe I'll have to call you up," Mr. Tanks says. He, too, is walking away, striding off almost jauntily, his short beer-keg legs prized apart in his green spectator shorts but close together at the knees as if a rolling gait did not come easy for him, his big arms in motion despite his attaché case being mashed under one of them.

"That'd be great." I need to give him my card so he can call me if he rumbles in late, finds no place to park and no one to be helpful. But he is already keying his way in. His room is three away from the murder scene. A light burns inside. And before I can call out and mention my card or say "Good night," or say anything more, he has stepped inside his door and quickly closed it.

IN MY Sea Breeze double, I run the a/c up to medium, get the lights off and myself into bed as fast as possible, praying for quick sleep, which seemed so overpowering ten minutes or an hour ago. The thought nags me that I should call Sally (who cares if it's three-thirty? I have an important offer to make). But the phone here circuits through the Pakistani switchboard, and everyone there's long asleep.

And then—and not for the first time today but for the first time since my talk with Ann on the Turnpike—I think a worrisome, urgent-feeling thought for Paul, under siege at this minute by phantom and real-life woes, and a court date as his official rite of passage into life beyond parent and child. I could want for better. Though I could also want him to stop braining people with oarlocks and blithely stealing condoms and struggling with security guards, to stop grieving for dogs a decade dead, and barking the case for their return. Dr. Stopler says (arrogantly) he could be grieving the loss of whoever we hoped he would be. But I don't know who that boy is or was (unless of course it's his dead brother—which it isn't). My wish has consistently been to strengthen the constitution of whoever he is whenever I meet him—though that is not always the same boy, and because I'm only a part-timer, possibly I have been insufficient at my job too.

So that clearly I must do better, must adopt the view that my son needs what only I can supply (even if it's not true) and then try for all I'm worth to imagine just what that something might be.

And then a scant sleep comes, which is more sleep versus unsleep than true rest, but in which for reasons of proximity to death, I dream, half muse of Clair and our sweet-as-tea-cakes winter's romance, commencing four months after she joined our office and ending three months down the road, when she met the older, dignified Negro lawyer who was perfect for her and made my small excitations excess baggage.

Clair was a perfect little dreamboat, with wide liquid-brown eyes, short muscular legs that widened slightly but didn't soften in the high-ups, extra-white teeth with red-lipstick lips that made her smile as much as she could (even when she wasn't happy) and a flipped, meringuey hair configuration she and her roomies at Spelman had borrowed from the Miss Black America pageant that stayed resilient through nights of ardent lovemaking. She had a high, confident, thick-tongued, singsongy Alabama voice, with the hint of a lisp, and wore tight wool skirts, iron-leg panty hose and pastel cashmere sweaters that showed off her wondrous ebony skin so that every time I saw an extra inch of it I squirmed and itched to get her alone. (She in many ways dressed and conducted herself exactly like the local white girls I knew in Biloxi when I was at Gulf Pines back in 1960, and for that sweet reason seemed to me quite old-fashioned and familiar.)

For reasons of her country-style, strict Christian family up-bringing, Clair was unswerving in her demand to keep our little attachment just between us two, whereas I lacked a restraining self-consciousness of any kind and especially about being a forty-two-year-old divorced white man smitten to jibbers over a twenty-five-year-old black woman with kids (it's arguable I might've avoided the whole thing for sound professional and crabby small-town reasons, only of course I didn't). To me it was all as natural as grass sprouting, and I floated along on its harmless effusions, enjoying it and myself the way you'd enjoy a high-school reunion where you meet a girl nobody ever thought was beautiful way-back-when, but who now looks like the prettiest girl you ever dreamed of, except you're still the only one who thinks so and therefore get her all to yourself.

To Clair, though, the two of us together bore a "tinge" (her

Alabama word meaning bad shadow), which naturally made *us* all the more giddy and distracting to me, but to her made *us* seem exactly wrong and doomed, and an item she absolutely didn't want her ex-husband, Vernell, or her mother, in Talladega, ever getting wind of. So that for our most intimate moments we ended up skulking around on the sly: her blue Civic slipping into my Cleveland Street garage under cover of night, and she slipping in the back door; or worse yet, rendezvousing for dinner plus surreptitious hand-holding and smooching in angst-thick public places such as the HoJo's in Hightstown, the Red Lobster in Trenton or the Embers in Yardley, spiritless venues where Clair felt completely invisible and comfortable and where she drank Fuzzy Navels till she was giggly, then slipped out to the car and made out with me in the dark till our lips were numb and our bodies limp.

Though we also spent plenty of ordinary, cloudy-wintry Sundays with her kids, hauling up and down both sides of the Delaware, treading the towpath, viewing the pleasing but un-spectacular river sights like any modern couple whose life of ups and downs had rendered them thus 'n' so, but whose remarkable equanimity in the face of uphill social odds made everyone who saw or sat across from us in Applebee's in New Hope or stood in line behind us at yogurt shops feel good about themselves and all of life in general. I often remarked that she and I were impersonating the very complexly ethical, culturally diverse family unit that millions of liberal white Americans were burn-ing to validate, and that the whole arrangement felt pretty good to me in addition to being hilarious. She, however, didn't like this attitude since it made her feel—in her sweet Talladega lisp—"*thstood*-out." And for that reason (and not that it's a small one) we probably missed a longer run at bliss.

Race, of course, was not our official fatal defect. Instead, Clair insisted my helpless age was the issue that kept us from a real future that I from time to time couldn't keep from wanting in the worst way. We therefore settled ourselves into a little on-going pocket drama in which I created the role of avuncular but charmingly randy white professor who'd sacrificed a successful but hopelessly stodgy prior life to "work" for his remaining productive years in a (one-student) private college, where Clair was the beautiful, intelligent, voluble, slightly naive but feisty, yet basically kindhearted valedictorian, who realized we two shared lofty but hopeless ideals, and who in the service of simple human charity was willing to woogle around with me in private, hypertensive but futureless (due to our years) lovemaking, and to moon at my aging mug over fish-stick dinners and doughy pancakes in soulless franchise eateries while pretending to everybody she knew that such a thing was absolutely out of the question. (No one was fooled a minute, of course, as Shax Murphy informed me—with a discomforting wink—the day after Clair's memorial service.)

Clair's feeling was ironclad, simple and candidly set out: we were laughably all wrong for each other and wouldn't last the season; though our wrongness served a good purpose in getting her through a bad patch when her finances were rocky, her emotions in a tangle and she didn't know anyone in Haddam and was too proud to head back to Alabama. (Dr. Stopler would probably say she wanted to cauterize something in herself and used me as the white-hot tool.) Whereas for me, fantasies of permanence aside as she demanded, Clair made bachelor life interesting, entertaining and enticingly exotic in a hundred thrilling ways, aroused my keen admiration, and kept me in good spirits, while I acclimated myself to the realty business and my kids being gone.

"Now, when I was back in college, see," Clair once said to me in her high, sweetly monotonous, lispy voice (we were butt naked, lounging in the evening-lit upstairs front bedroom of my former wife's former house), "we all used to *laaaaugh* and laugh about hookin' up with some rich ole white guy. Like some fat bank president or big politician. That was our cruel joke, you know? Like, 'Now, when you marry that ole white fool,' this or that thing was going to happen to you. He was s'posed to try to give you a new car or some trip to Europe, and then you were gonna trick him. You know how girls are."

"Sort of," I said, thinking of course that I had a daughter but didn't know how girls were, except that mine would probably one day be just like Clair: sweet, certain of everything, basically untrusting for sound reasons. "What was so wrong about us ole white guys?"

"Oh well, *you* know," Clair said, raising onto her sharp little elbow and looking at me as if I'd just shown up on the surface of the earth and needed harsh instruction. "Y'all are all boring.

White men *are* boring. You're just not as bad as the rest of them. Yet."

"You get more interesting the longer you stay alive, is my view," I said, wanting to put a good word in for my race and age. "Maybe that's why you'll learn to like me more, not less, and won't be able to live without me."

"Uh-huh, you got that wrong," she said, thinking, I'm sure, about her own life, which to date hadn't been that peachy but, I'd have argued, was looking up. It was true, though, she had very little facility for actually thinking about me and never in the time we knew each other asked me five questions about my children or my life before I met her. (Though I never minded, since I was sure some little personal exegesis would only have proved what she already expected.)

"If we didn't get more interesting," I said, happy to belabor a moot point, "all the other crap we put up with in life might drive us right out of it."

"Us Baptists don't believe that, now," she said, flinging her arm across my chest and jamming her hard chin into my bare ribs. "What's his name—Aristotle—Aristotle canceled his class today. He got sick of hearing his own voice and couldn't make it."

"I don't have anything to teach you," I said, thrilled as usual.

"That's *not* wrong," Clair said. "I'm not going to keep you that long anyway. You'll start to get boring on me, start repeating yourself. I'll be right out of here."

Which was not very different from what happened.

One March morning I showed up at the office early (my usual) to type an offer sheet for a presentation later that day. Clair had nearly finished her classes to get her realtor's certification and was at her desk, studying. She was never at ease addressing private-life matters in the office setting, yet as soon as I sat down she got up, wearing a little peach-colored skirt-and-sweater combo and red high heels, came right over to my desk by the front window, took a seat and said very matter-of-factly that she had met a man that week, bond lawyer McSweeny, whom she'd decided to start "dating," and therefore had decided to stop "dating" me.

I remember being perfectly dazed: first, by her altogether firing-squad certainty; and then by how damned unhappy the whole prospect made me. I smiled, though, and nodded as if I'd

been thinking along those lines myself (I definitely hadn't) and
told her that in my view she was probably doing the right thing,
then went on smiling more disingenuously, until my cheeks
ached.

She said she'd finally talked to her mother about me, and her
mother had immediately told her, in what Clair said were actually "crude" terms, to get as far away from me as possible (I'm
sure it wasn't my age), even if it meant spending her nights home
alone or moving away from Haddam or finding another job in
another city—which I said was too strong a medicine. I would
just obligingly step aside, hope she was happy and feel lucky to
have had the time with her I'd had, though I told her I didn't
think we'd done anything but what men and women had done
to and for each other through the ages. My saying this clearly
made her aggravated. (She was not well practiced at being argued
with, either.) So that I just finally shut up about it and grinned at
her again like a half-wit, as a way of saying (I guessed) good-bye.

Why I didn't protest, I'm not exactly sure, since I was stung,
and surprisingly near to the heart, and spent days afterward
tinkering with convoluted futuristic scenarios in which life
would've been goddamned tough but that sheer off-the-map
novelty and unlikelihood might've proved the final missing
ingredients to true and abiding love—in which case she'd sacrificed to convention a type of mountaintop victory reserved for
only the brave and enlightened few. It's, however, undoubtedly
true that my idyll with permanence was entirely founded on
Clair's being a total impossibility, which means she was finally
never more than a featured player in some Existence Period
melodrama of my own devising (nothing to be proud of, but not
radically different from my cameo in her short life).

After our abrupt sayonara she returned to her desk, resumed
studying her realty books—and with this new state of affairs in
effect, we stayed on at our desks for another whole hour and a
half, doing work! Our colleagues arrived and departed. We both
entered into amused, even jocular, conversations with several
different individuals. I once asked her about the disposition of a
bank foreclosure, and she answered me as equably and cheerfully as you would expect in any well-run office bent on profit.
Neither one of us said anything else of moment, and I eventually
finished my offer sheet, made a couple of cold client calls, did

part of a crossword, wrote a letter, put on my coat and wandered around in it for a few minutes, wisecracking with Shax Murphy, and finally just wandered out and down to the Coffee Spot, after which I did not come back—all the while (I suppose) Clair stayed at her desk, concentrating like a cleric. And basically that was that.

In short order she and lawyer McSweeny became a nice, viable, single-race item in town. (Though she began treating me, in my view, with unneeded correctness in the office, which became, of course, the only place I ever saw her.) Everybody agreed the two of them were lucky to find each other when attractive members of their race were scarce as diamonds. Predictable difficulties came up to prevent their speedy marriage: Ed's grasping grown kids caused a ruckus about Clair's age and financial situation (Ed, naturally, is *my* age, and loaded). Clair's ex-husband, Vernell, declared Chapter 11 in Canoga Park and tried to reopen their divorce decree. Clair's grandmother died in Mobile, her mother broke her hip, her younger brother got put in jail—the usual wearisome inventory of life's encroachments. In the long run it all would've worked out, with Clair and Ed married to the tune of a clearly worded prenuptial agreement. Clair would've moved into Ed's big late Victorian out on Cromwell Lane, would've had a flower garden and a nicer car than a Honda Civic. Her two kids would've grown to like going to school with white children and in time forgotten there was a difference. She would've gone on selling condos and gotten better at it. Ed's grown children would've finally accepted her for the truehearted, straight-talking, slightly overcertain girl she was, and not as just some hick gold-panner they needed to sic their own lawyers on. She and Ed, in time, would have enjoyed a somewhat isolated suburban existence, with a few but not many people regularly over for dinner, and even fewer close friends— a life spent with each other in a way most people would pay money to know how to pull off but can't because their days are too full of rich opportunity they just can't say no to.

Except that one spring afternoon Clair happened out to Pheasant Meadow and in an entirely professional way got trapped in a bad situation and ended up as dead as the Mormon traveler in the body bag down in room 15.

And as I lie in bed here, still alive myself, the Fedders blowing brisk, chemically cooled breezes across my sheets, I try to find solace against the way this memory and the night's events make me feel, which is: bracketed, limbo'd, unable to budge, as illustrated amply by Mr. Tanks and me standing side by side in the murderous night, unable to strike a spark, utter a convincingly encouraging word to the other, be of assistance, shout halloo, dip a wing; unable at the sad passage of another human to the barren beyond to share a hope for the future. Whereas, had we but been able, our spirits might've lightened.

Death, veteran of death that I am, seems so near now, so plentiful, so oh-so-drastic and significant, that it scares me witless. Though in a few hours I'll embark with my son upon the other tack, the hopeful, life-affirming, anti-nullity one, armed only with words and myself to build a case, and nothing half as dramatic and persuasive as a black body bag, or lost memories of lost love.

Suddenly my heart again goes bangety-bang, bangety-bangety-bang, as if I myself were about to exit life in a hurry. And if I could, I would spring up, switch on the light, dial someone and shout right down into the hard little receiver, "It's okay. I got away. It was goddamned close, I'll tell ya. It didn't get me, though. I smelled its breath, saw its red eyes in the dark, shining. A clammy hand touched mine. But I made it. I survived. Wait for me. Wait for me. Not that much is left to do." Only there's no one. No one here or anywhere near to say any of this to. And I'm sorry, sorry, sorry, sorry, sorry.

CHAPTER 7

EIGHT A.M. Things speed up.

On my way out of the Sea Breeze I remember to hike across, scale the green side of Mr. Tanks's Peterbilt and squeeze a business card under his king-size windshield wiper, with a personal note on the back saying: "Mr. T. Good meeting you. Call up any time. FB." I include my home phone. (The art of the sale first demands imagining the sale.) Strangely enough, when I take a quick curious peek inside the driver's capsule, on the passenger's seat I see a clutter of *Reader's Digest* condenseds and on top of it an enormous yellow cat wearing a gold collar and staring up at me as if I were an illusion. (Pets are not welcome in the Sea Breeze, and Mr. Tanks is no doubt a consummate player-by-the-rules.) I notice also, as I climb down the cab's outer shell, and just in front of the door, a name, painted in ornate red script and set in quotes: "*Cyril.*" Mr. Tanks is a man deserving of study.

Back in the lot to leave my key (forgoing my deposit), I see that the Suburban with its Boston Whaler rig is gone now, and yellow "crime scene" tape is stretched across the closed door to #15. And I realize then that I've dreamed about it all: of a sealed room, of a car being towed off in the dark by small, muscular, sweaty white men in sleeveless shirts, shouting, "Come on back, come on back," followed by the sound of scary chains and winches and big motors revving, then someone shouting, "Okay, okay, okay."

AT 8:45 I STOP bleary-eyed for coffee at the Friendly's in Hawleyville. After consulting my atlas, I decide on the Yankee Expressway to Waterbury and over to Meriden, a jog across and down to Middletown—where adjunct Charley "teaches" Wesleyan coeds to distinguish which column is Ionic and which Doric—then CT 9 straight into Deep River; this instead of drag-assing all the way down to Norwalk and 95 as I meant to do last night, driving east along the Sound with, I'm certain, four trillion other Americans craving a safe and sane holiday, yet doing everything they can to prevent me from having one.

In Friendly's I browse through the Norwalk *Hour* for any mention of last night's tragedy, although I'm sure it happened too late. I learn here, however, that Axis Sally has died in Ohio, aged eighty-seven and an honors graduate of Ohio Wesleyan; Martina has out-dueled Chris in three sets; hydrologists in Illinois have decided to draw down Lake Michigan to channel water into the more important and drought-starved Mississippi; and Vice President Bush has declared prosperity to be at "a record high" (though as if to call him a liar there are sidebar reports of declines in prices, mutual funds and CDs, declines in factory orders and aircraft demands—all "pocketbook" issues Dullard Dukakis needs to shanghai or lose his ass in a bucket).

After paying, I make my strategic calls squeezed between the double doors of Friendly's "lobby": one to my answering machine, disclosing nothing—a relief; another to Sally, intending to offer a private charter to anyplace I can meet her—no answer, not even a recording, causing my gut to wrench like someone had tightened a rope around it and jerked downward.

Apprehensively then I call Karl Bemish, first at the root beer palace, where there's no reason for him to be yet, then at his bachelor digs in Lambertville, where he answers on the second ring.

"Everything's jake here, Frank," he shouts, to my inquiry about the felonious Mexicans. "Aw yeah, I should've called you back last night. I called the sheriff instead. I expected some action, really. But. False alarm. They never showed up again, the little fucks."

"I don't want you being in danger down there, Karl." Customers stream in and out beside me, opening the door, jostling me, letting in hot air.

"I've got my alley sweeper, you know," Karl says.

"You've got your what? What's that?"

"A sawed-off twelve-gauge pump," Karl says supremely, and grunts an evil laugh. "A serious piece of machinery."

This is the first I've heard of an alley sweeper, and I don't like it. In fact, it scares me silly. "I don't think it's a good idea to have an alley sweeper at the root beer stand, Karl." Karl doesn't like me to call it root beer, or a "stand," but that's how I think of it. What else is it? An office?

"Well, it beats lying facedown behind the birch beer cooler drinking your brains out of your paper hat. Or maybe I'm wrong about that," Karl says coolly.

"Jesus Christ, Karl."

"Just don't worry. I don't even bring it out till after ten."

"Do the police know about it?"

"Hell, they *told* me where to buy it. Up in Scotch Plains." Karl shouts this too. "I shouldn't have blabbed it to you. You're such a goddamn nervous nelly."

"It makes me goddamn nervous," I say, and it does. "I can't use you dead. I'd have to serve the root beer myself, plus our insurance won't pay off if you're killed with an unlicensed gun in there. I'd probably get sued."

"You just go on and have a holiday with your kid. I'll hold down Fort Apache. I've got some other things to do this morning. I'm not alone here."

There's no more getting through to Karl now. My window's just been shut. "Leave me a message if anything's strange, would you do that?" I say this in an unlikely-to-be-acknowledged voice.

"I plan to be out of touch *all* morning," Karl says, and makes a dumb hardee-har-har laugh, then hangs up.

I immediately dial Sally again, in case she's been out picking up croissants and the *Daily Argonaut*. But nothing.

My last call is to Ted Houlihan—for an update, but also to grill him on the status of our office "exclusive." Making client calls is actually one of the most satisfying parts of my work. Rolly Mounger was right on the money when he said real estate has almost nothing to do with the state of one's soul; consequently a necessary business call is tantamount to an enjoyable game of Ping-Pong. "It's Frank Bascombe, Ted. How's everything going down there?"

"Everything's just fine, Frank." Ted sounds frailer than yesterday, but as happy as he claims. A slow gas leak may create an unbeatable euphoria.

"Just wanted to tell you my clients are taking a day to think about it, Ted. They were impressed with the house. But they've looked at a lot of houses, and they need to push themselves beyond a threshold now. I do think the last house I showed them, though, is the one they ought to buy, and that was yours."

"Super," Ted says. "Just super."

"Anybody else been through to look?" The crucial question.

"Oh, a few yesterday. Some people right after your folks." Followed by not unexpected but still aggravating bad news.

"Ted, I have to remind you that we've got an office exclusive on your house. That's what the Markhams are acting in reliance of. They're under the impression they've got a little time to think without any outside pressure. We got all that stapled down ahead of time."

"Well, I don't know, Frank," Ted says dimly. Conceivably, of course, Julie Loukinen has played down the exclusivity clause for fear Ted would balk, and just put it on the sign anyway. It's also likely Ted's known far and wide as a perpetual "potential," and Buy and Large or whoever else is involved is simply horning in on the chance of splitting a commission; this versus our suing the shit out of them and queering the whole deal—a strategy tantamount to walking in the winning run, something you never want to do. A third possibility is that Ted's as crooked as a cork-screw and wouldn't tell the truth to God in his heaven. The supposedly bum testicle story could be part of the act. (Nothing should surprise anybody anymore.)

"Look, Ted," I say. "Just step out and take a look at that green-and-gray sign and see if it doesn't say 'exclusive.' I'm not going to make a big deal out of it right now, because I'm up in Connecticut. But I'm going to get it straight on Tuesday."

"How is it up there?" Ted says, daffy as a duck.

"It's hot."

"Are you up at Mount Tom?"

"No. I'm in Hawleyville. But if you'd just be considerate enough, Ted, not to show the house to anyone else, maybe we can avoid a big lawsuit. My clients deserve a chance to make an offer." Not that they haven't had ample chance, or that they aren't right now cruising the deserted, lusterless streets of East Brunswick, hoping to find something much better.

"I wouldn't mind that," Ted says, energetic now.

"Great, then," I say. "I'll get back to you in a hurry."

"The people after you yesterday said they'd be coming in with an offer this morning."

"If they do, Ted," and I say this threateningly, "remember my clients have first refusal. It's in writing." Or it should be. Of course this is standard realty baloney, routinely purveyed by both sides: the "bright 'n' early in the morning" offer. In general, people (buyers, usually) who trot out this "promise" are either making themselves feel substantial and will have forgotten it entirely by five o'clock, or else they're deluding themselves by supposing the mere prospect of a fat offer makes everybody feel better. Naturally, only generous offers you can pinch between your thumb and index finger make everybody *actually* feel better. And until one of those comes into view, there's nothing to get excited about (though a rising tide of seller's angst never hurt anybody).

"Frank, do you know what's a very strange thing I've learned," Ted says in a seeming state of goofy wonderment.

"What's that?" Through the window I'm watching a van full of retarded kids off-load in the Friendly's lot—teenage tongue-thrusters, frail cross-eyed girls, chubby Down's survivors of unspecified gender—eight or so, bumbling out onto the hot tarmac in elastic-band shorts of various hues, sneakers and dark blue tee-shirts that have YALE printed on the front. Their counselors, two strapping college girls in matching brown shorts and white pullovers, who look like they go to Oberlin and play water polo, get the van locked up while the kids stand staring in all different directions.

"I've learned that I really enjoy showing people my house," Ted rambles on. "Everyone who's seen it seemed to like it a lot and they all think Susan and I did all right here. That's a good feeling to have. I expected to hate it and feel a lot of grief at having my life invaded. You know what I mean?"

"Yeah," I say. My interest in Ted is dwindling fast since I realize there's a decent chance he's a real estate scammer. "It just means you're ready to move on, Ted. You're ready for Albuquerque and all that sunshine." (And to have your nuts preserved in amber.)

"My son's a surgeon in Tucson, Frank. I'm going out for surgery in September."

"I remember." (I got the city wrong.) The gaggle of afflicted teens and their two big, tan-legged, water-polo-type minders are making for the door now, some of the kids in full charge, and all but a couple wearing plastic crash helmets strapped under their chins like linebackers. "Ted, I just wanted to touch base here, see how your day went yesterday. And I needed to remind you about the 'exclusive.' That's a serious agreement, Ted."

"Okay then," Ted says buoyantly. "Thanks for telling me." I imagine him, white-haired, soft hands, diminutively handsome in his dimpled Fred Waring way, framed in his back window, marveling out at the bamboo wall that has long shielded him from his peaceable prison. It leaves me with a dull feeling that I've gone about this wrong. I should've stayed close to the Markhams, but my instincts said otherwise. "Frank, I'm thinking that if I get this cancer thing behind me I might just give realty a try. I think I might have a gift for it. What do you think?"

"Sure. But it doesn't take a gift, Ted. It's like being a writer. A man with nothing to do finds something to do. I've got to hit the road now. I've got to pick up my son."

"Good for you," Ted says. "Go right on. We'll talk another time."

"You bet," I say darkly, and then that's over.

The kids are clustered at the glass doors now, their counselors wading through them, laughing. One Down's boy is giving the door handle a vicious jerking and making a fierce face at the pane, in which he can no doubt see his reflection. The rest of them are still looking around and up and down and back.

When the first counselor drags the door open with the Down's kid still attached to it, he glares at her and makes a loud, fully uninhibited roar as the door lets hot air right into my face. Then the whole bunch comes scuttling in and past, heading for the second door.

"Oops," the first tall girl says to me with a wondrously bountiful grin. "We're sorry, we're a little clumsy." She moves on by in the current of little feebs in their Eli shirts. Her own shirt has a bright-red shield on its breast that says *Challenges, Inc.* and below that, *Wendy*. I give her a smile of encouragement as she gets shoved past.

Suddenly the little Down's kid whirls left, still attached to the door, and roars again, conceivably at me, his dark teeth clenched and worn to nubs, one little doughboy arm raised, fist balled. I am poised by the phone, smiling down at him, my hopes for the day attempting to scale the ladder of possibility.

"That means he likes you," says the second counselor—
Megan—inching past at the back of the pack. She's putting me
on, of course. What the roar means is: "Stay away from these
two honeys or I'll eat your face." (People in many ways are the
same.)

"He seems to know me," I say to golden-armed Megan.

"Oh, he knows you." Her face is freckled with sunshine, her
eyes as plain brown as Cathy Flaherty's were dazzling. "They
look alike to us, but they can pick you and me out a mile away.
They have a sixth sense." She smiles without a whit of self-
consciousness, a smile to inspire minutes but possibly not hours
of longing. The inner door to Friendly's hisses open, then slowly
shuts behind her. I head at that moment out into the sunny
morning to begin my last leg to Deep River.

BY 9:50, feeling late, late, late, I'm larruping down-hill-and-up
toward Middletown, Waterbury and Meriden, being already lost
in the morning's silvery haze. CT 147 is as verdant, curvy and
pleasant as a hedgerow lane in Ireland minus the hedgerows. Tiny
pocket reservoirs, cozy roadside state parks, pint-size ski "mountains" perfect for high-school teams, and sturdy frame homes
edging the road with satellite dishes out back, show up around
every curve. Many houses, I notice, are for sale, and quite a few
display yellow plastic ribbons on their tree trunks. I can't now
remember what Americans are being held prisoner or where and
by whom, though it's easy to conceive *somewhere, somebody* must
be. Otherwise the ribbons are wishful thinking, a yearning
for another Grenada-type tidy-little-war which worked out so
happily for all concerned. Patriotic feelings are much more
warming when focused on something finite, and there's nothing
like focusing on kicking somebody's ass or depriving them of
their freedom to make you feel free as a bird yourself.

My thoughts, though, unwillingly run again to the pathetic
Markhams, no doubt at this very minute touring some grisly cul-
de-sac, accompanied by a nasal-voiced, thick-thighed residential
specialist demoralizing the shit out of them with chatter. An
indecent, unprofessional part of me hopes that by day's end, faced
with calling me and crawling back to 212 Charity with a full-
price offer, they jump for the last house of the day, some

standing-empty, dormered Cape whose prior owners gave it to the bank when they transferred-out to Moose Jaw back in '84, some dire shell on a slab, with negative R factors, potential for radon, a seeping septic, in need of emergency gutter work before the leaves fly.

Why, in an otherwise pleasant and profitable summer season, the Markhams would so shadow my mind isn't clear, unless it's that after much finagling, obstruction and idiot discouragement at every level, I have now fashioned the Easter egg, filled it with the right sweet stuff, made the hole and put their eye right to it; and yet I'm afraid they'll never see inside, after which their lives will be worse—my belief being that once you're offered something good, you ought to be smart enough to take it.

Years back, I remember, in the month before Ann and I moved to Haddam, new, happy suburban ethers full in our noses, we got it in mind to buy a practical-sturdy Volvo. We drove out in my mother's old Chrysler Newport to the dealership in Hastings-on-Hudson, kibitzed around the showroom for a hour and a half—chin-rubbing, ear-scratching potential young buyers—fingering the mirror surfaces of some olive-drab five-door job, slipping into and out of its sensible seats, sniffing its chilly perfume, checking out the glove box capacity, the unusual spare tire mounts and jack assembly, finally pretending even to drive it—Ann side by side with me in the driver's seat, both of us staring ahead through the dealership window at a make-believe road to the future as new Volvo owners.

Until, at the end, we simply decided we wouldn't. Who knows why? We were young, spiritedly inventing life by the minute, rejecting this, saying yea to that, completely by whim. And a Volvo, a machine I might even still own and use to transport potting soil or groceries or firewood or keep as a fish car to haul myself to the Red Man Club—a Volvo just didn't suit us. Afterward we drove back into the city toward whatever did suit us, our real future: marriage, parenthood, sportswriting, golf, glee, gloom, death, gyrating unhappiness unable to find a center point, and later, divorce, separation and the long middle passage to now.

Though when I'm in just the right deprived-feeling, past-entangled mood and happen to see one, some brawny-sleek, murmuring black or silver up-to-date-version Volvo, with its enviable safety record, its engine primed to drop out on impact, its boastable storage spaces and one-piece construction, I'm often struck with a heart's pang of *What if?* What if our life had gone in that direction . . . some direction a *car* could've led us and now be emblem for? Different house, different town, different sum total of kids, on and on. Would it all be better? Such things happen, and for as little cause. And it can be paralyzing to think an insignificant decision, a switch thrown this way, not that, could make many things turn out better, even be saved. (My greatest human flaw and strength, not surprisingly, is that I can always imagine anything—a marriage, a conversation, a government—as being different from how it is, a trait that might make one a top-notch trial lawyer or novelist or realtor, but that also seems to produce a somewhat less than reliable and morally feasible human being.)

It's best at this moment not to think much along these lines. Though this I'm sure is another reason why the Markhams come to mind on a weekend when my own life seems at a turning or at least a curving point. Likely as not, Joe and Phyllis know how these things work as well as I do and are scared shitless. Yet, while it's bad to make a wrong move, as maybe I did with the Volvo, it's worse to regret in advance and call it prudence, which I sense is what they're doing roving around East Brunswick. Disaster is no less likely. Better—much, much better—to follow ole Davy Crockett's motto, amended for use by adults: Be sure you're not completely wrong, then go ahead.

BY TEN-THIRTY I'm past bland, collegiate Middletown and up onto Route 9, taking in the semi-panoramic view of the Connecticut (vacationers assiduously canoeing, jet skiing, windsurfing, sailing, paraskiing or skydiving right into the drink), and then straight downstream the short distance to Deep River.

My chief hope of a secondary nature here is not to lay eyes on Charley, for reasons I perhaps have brought to light already. With luck he'll be nursing his lumpy jaw out of sight, or else waxing his dinghy or sighting a plumb line or doodling in his sketchbook— whatever rich dilettante architects do when they're not competing in marathon gin rummy matches or tying their bow ties blindfolded.

Ann understands I don't precisely loathe Charley, only that I believe that whenever she tells him she loves him there's an asterisk after "love" (like Roger Maris's home run title), referencing prior, superior attainment in that area, as though I'm certain she'll one day pitch it all and begin life's last long pavane with me and me alone (though neither of us seems to want that).

In nearly all my preceding visits, I've ended up feeling I'd snuck onto the property by way of a scaled fence and left (for wherever I'm taking my children—the mollusk exhibit at Woods Hole, a Mets game, a blustery ferry ride to Block Island for a little stolen quality time) as though I was one step ahead of the law. Ann says I fabricate these feelings. But so what? I still have them.

Charley, unlike me, who thinks everything's mutable, is the sort of man who puts his trust in "character," who muses when alone about "standards" and *bona fides*, "parsing" and "winnowing out men from boys," but who (it's my private bet) stands at the foggy mirror in the locker room at the Old Lyme CC thinking about his dick, wishing he had a bigger one, considering if a rectangular glass doesn't distort proportions, deciding eventually that everybody's looks smaller when viewed by its hypercritical owner and that, in absolute terms, his is bigger than it looks because he's tall. Which he is.

One evening, standing together out below the knoll where his house sits, our shoes nuzzling the pea-gravel path that leads down to his boathouse, beyond which is a dense, pinkly-rose-infested estuarial pond protected from the Connecticut by a boundary of tupelo gums, Charley said to me, "Now, you know, Frank, Shakespeare must've been a pretty damn smart cookie." In his big bony hand he was cradling one of his drop-dead vodka gimlets in a thick, hand-blown Mexican tumbler. (He hadn't offered me one, since I wasn't staying.) "I took a look at everything he wrote this year, okay? And I think history's writers just haven't moved the bar up much since sixteen-whatever. He saw human weakness better than anybody ever did, and sympathetically at that." He blinked at me and rolled his tongue around behind his lips. "Isn't that what makes a writer great? Sympathy for human weakness?"

"I don't know. I never thought a thing about it," I said bleakly but churlishly. I already knew Charley thought it was "odd" that a man who once wrote respectable short stories would "end up" selling real estate. He also had views about my living in Ann's old house, though I never asked what they were (I'm sure they're prejudicial).

"All right, but how *do* you see it?" Charley sniffed through his big Episcopalian nose, furrowing his silver eyebrows as if he were smelling a complex bouquet in the evening's mist that was available only to him (and possibly his friends). He was clad in his usual sockless deck shoes, khaki shorts and a tee-shirt, but with a thick blue zippered sweater I'd seen thirty years ago in a J. Press catalog and wondered who in the hell would buy. He is of course as fit as a greyhound and maintains some past master's squash ranking for oldsters.

"I don't really think literature has anything to do with moving the bar up," I said distastefully (I was right). "It has to do with being good in an absolute sense, not better." I now wish I could've punctuated this with a shout of hysterical laughter.

"Okay. That's hopeful." Charley pulled on his long earlobe and looked down, nodding as though he were visualizing the words I'd said. His thick white hair glowed with whatever light was left in the twilight. "That's really a pretty hopeful view," he said solemnly.

"I'm a hopeful man," I said, and promptly felt as hopeless as an exile.

"Fair enough then," he said. "Do you suppose in a hopeful way you and I are ever going to be friends?" He half raised his head and looked at me through his metal-rim glasses. "Friend" I knew to be, in Charley's view, the loftiest of lofty human conditions men of character could aspire to, like Nirvana for Buddhist monks. I never wanted to have friends less in my life.

"No," I said bluntly.

"Why's that, do you think?"

"Because all we have in common is my ex-wife. And eventually you'll feel it's okay to discuss her with me, and that would piss me off."

Charley held onto his earlobe, his gimlet in his other hand. "Might be." He nodded speculatively. "You're always coming across something in someone you love that you can't fathom, aren't you? So then you have to ask somebody. I guess you'd be an obvious choice. Ann's not that simple, as I'm sure you know."

He was doing it already. "I don't know," I said. "No."

"You maybe oughta have another go at it, like I did. Maybe you'd get it right this time." Charley rounded his eyes at me and nodded again.

"Why don't you have a go at a flying fuck at whatever's in range," I said moronically, and glared at him, feeling fairly willing to throw a punch irrespective of his age and excellent physical condition (hoping my children wouldn't see it). I felt a chill rise then like a column of refrigerated air right off the pond, making my arm hairs prickle. It was late May. Little house lights had printed up across the silver plane of the Connecticut. I could hear a boat's bell clanging. At that moment I felt not truly angry enough to cold-cock Charley, but sad, lonesome, lost, unhappy and useless alongside a man I wasn't even interested in enough to hate the way a man with character would.

"You know," Charley said, zipping his sweater up to his glunky Adam's apple and tugging his sleeves as if he'd felt the chill himself. "There's something about you I don't trust, Frank. Maybe architects and realtors don't have that much in common, though you'd think we would." He eyed me just in case I might be about to produce guttural sounds and spring at his throat.

"That's fine," I said. "I wouldn't trust me either if I were you."

Charley gently tossed his glass, ice and all, off onto the lawn. He said, "Frank, you can play sharp and play flat but still be in tune, you know." He seemed disappointed, almost perplexed. Then he just strolled off down the gravel path toward his boathouse. "You won't win 'em all," I heard him say to himself, theatrically from out of the dark. I let him walk all the way down, pull aside the sliding door, enter and close it behind him (I'm sure he had nothing to do there). After that I walked back around his house, got in my car and waited for my children, who were soon to be there with me and be happy.

DEEP RIVER, as I drive hurriedly through, is the epitome of dozing, summery, southern New England ambivalence. A little green-shuttered, swept-sidewalk burg where just-us-regular-folks live in stolid acceptance of watered-down Congregationalist and Roman Catholic moderation; whereas down by the river there's the usual enclave of self-contented, pseudo-reclusive richies who've erected humongous houses on bracken and basswood chases bordering the water, their backs resolutely turned to how the other half lives. Endowed law profs from New Haven, moneyed shysters from Hartford and Springfield, moneyed pensioners from Gotham, all cruise sunnily in to shop at Greta's Green Grocer, The Flower Basket, Edible Kingdom Meats and Liquid Time Liquors (less often to visit Body Artistry Tattoo, Adult Newz-and-Video or the Friendly Loaner pawn), then cruise sunnily back out, their Rovers heaped with good dog food, pancetta, mesquite, chard, fresh tulips and gin—all primed for evening cocktails, lamb shanks on the grill, an hour of happy schmoozing, then off to bed in the cool, fog-enticed river breeze. It is not such a great place to think of your children living (or your ex-wife).

Nothing extravagant seems planned here for Monday. Droopy bunting decorates a few lampposts. A high-school "Freedom Car Wash" is in semi-full swing out on the fire station driveway, a rake-and-hoe promotion in front of the True Value. Several businesses, in fact, have put up red-and-white maple-leaf flags beside Old Glory, signaling some ancient Canuck connection—a group of hapless white settlers no doubt mercifully if unaccountably spared by a company of Montcalm's regulars back in '57, leaving a residuum of "Canadian Currency OK" sentiment in all hearts. Even Donna's Kut'n Kurl boasts a window sign reading "Time for a trim, eh?" But that's it—as if Deep River were simply saying, "Given our long establishment (1635), the spirit of true and complex independence is observed and breathed here every day. Silently. So don't expect much."

I turn toward the river and head down woodsy Selden Neck Lane, which T's into even woodsier, laurel-choked Brainard Settlement House Way, which curves, narrows and switches back onto American holly and hickory-thick Swallow Lane, the road where Ann's, Charley's and my two children's mailbox resides unnoticeably on a thin cedar post, its dark-green letters indicating THE KNOLL. Beside it a rough gravel car path disappears into anonymous trees, so that an atmosphere of exclusive, possibly less than welcoming habitation greets whoever wanders past: people live here, but you don't know them.

My brain, in the time it's taken me to clear town and wind

down into these sylvan purlieus of the rich, has begun to exhibit an unpleasant tightness behind my temples. My neck's stiff, and there's a feeling of tissue expansion in my upper thorax, as if I ought to burp, gag or possibly just split open for relief's sake. I have, of course, slept little and badly. I drank too much at Sally's last night; I've driven too far, devoted too much precious worry time to the Markhams, the McLeods, Ted Houlihan and Karl Bemish, and too little to thinking about my son.

Though of course the most sharp-stick truth is that I'm about to pay my former wife a visit in her subsequent and better life; am about to see my orphaned kids gamboling on the wide lawns of their tonier existence; I may even, in spite of all, have to make humiliating, grinding conversation with Charley O'Dell, whom I'd just as soon tie up on a beach and leave for the crabs. Who wouldn't have a "swelling" in his brain and generalized thoracic edema? I'm surprised it isn't a helluva lot worse.

A small plastic sign I haven't noticed before has been attached to the bottom edge of the mailbox, a little burgundy-colored plaque with green lettering like the box itself, which says: HERE IS A BIRD SANCTUARY. RESPECT IT. PROTECT OUR FUTURE. Karl would be pleased to know vireos are still safe here in Connecticut.

Only directly below the box, on the duffy, weedy ground, lies a bird—a grackle or a big cowbird, its eyes glued shut with death, its stiff feathers swarmed by ants. I peer down on it from behind my window and puzzle: Birds die, we all know that. Birds have coronaries, brain tumors, anemia, suffer bad luck and life's battering, then croak like the rest of us—even in a sanctuary, where nobody has it in for them and everybody dotes on everything they do.

But here? Under their very own sign? Here is odd. And I am, in my brain-tightened unease, suddenly, instantly certain my son's to blame (call it a father's instinct). Plus, animal torture is one of the bad childhood warning signs: meaning he's begun the guerrilla war of spirit-attrition against his foster home, against Charley, against cool lawns, morning mists, matched goldens, sabots, clay courts and solar panels, against all that's happened outside his control. (I don't completely blame him.)

Not that I approve of dispatching blameless tweeties and leaving them by the mailbox as portents of bad things on the wing. I don't approve. It scares me silly. But as little as I hope to be involved in domestic life here, I also believe an ounce of intervention might deter a pound of cure. So, putting my car in park, I shove open my door and climb out into the heat, my brain still expanding, stoop stiffly down, lift the little dull-feathered, ant-swarmed carcass by its wingtip, take a quick look behind me at Swallow Lane curving out of sight, then quick-flip it like a cow chip off into the bushes, where it falls soundlessly, saving my son (I hope) one peck of trouble in a life that may already stretch out long and full of troubles.

Out of ancient habit I quickly raise my fingers for a sniff-check in case I need to go someplace—back up to the Chevron on Route 9—to wash the death smell off. But just as I do, a small dark-blue car (I believe it is a Yugo) with silver lettering and a silver police-shield door decal inscribed with AGAZZIZ SECURITY pulls in to block me where I'm standing beside my car. (Where has *this* come from?)

A slender, blond man in a blue uniform gets quickly out, as though I might just take off running into the trees, but then remains behind his door looking at me with an odd, unhumorous smile—a smile any American would recognize as signifying wariness, arrogance, authority and a conviction that outsiders cause trouble. Possibly he thinks I'm filching mail—ten reggae CD offers, or some prime steaks from Idaho, special for high rollers only.

I lower my fingers—unhappily they *do* smell of feral death—my skull tightened back down into my neck sinews. "Hi," I say, extra cheerful.

"Hi!" the young man says and nods in some unclear sort of agreement. "Whatcha up to?"

I beam probity at him. "I was just going into the O'Dells' here. I've been driving a ways, so I decided to stretch my legs."

"Great," he says, beaming cold indifference back. He is razorish-looking and, although thin, undoubtedly schooled in lethal martial-arts wherewithal. I can't see a firearm, but he's wearing a miniature microphone that allows him to talk to some-one in another location by speaking straight into his own shoul-der. "You friends of the O'Dells, are ya?" he says cheerfully.

"Yep. Sure am."

"I'm sorry, but what was it you threw over in the trees?"

"A bird. That was a bird. A dead one."

"Okay," the officer says, peering over in that direction as if he could see a dead bird, which he can't. "Where'd *it* come from?"

"It got caught behind the outside mirror of my car. I didn't notice it till I opened the door. It was a grackle."

"I see. What was it?" (Perhaps he thinks my story will change under interrogation.)

"Grackle," I say, as if the word itself might induce a humorous response, but I'm wrong.

"You know, this is a wildlife sanctuary back here. There isn't any hunting."

"I didn't hunt for it. I was just disposing of it before I drove in with it on my car mirror. I thought that'd be better. It'll be okay over there." I look where I'm referring.

"Where you driving from?" His young weak eyes twitch toward my blue-and-cream Jersey plates, then quickly back up at me so that if I claim I've just driven in from Oracle, Arizona, or International Falls, he'll know to call for backup.

"I'm from down in Haddam, New Jersey." I adopt a voice that says I'd be glad to help you in any way I can and would write a letter of commendation to your superiors complimenting you on your demeanor the moment I'm back at my desk.

"And what's your name, sir?"

"Bascombe." And I haven't done a goddamn thing, I say silently, but toss one dead bird in the bushes to save everybody trouble (though of course I've lied about it). "Frank Bascombe." Cool air surrounds me from my open car door.

"Okay, Mr. Bascombe. If I could just look at your driver's license, I'll get out of your way here." The young rent-a-cop seems pleased, as if these words are the standard words and he positively loves saying them.

"Sure thing," I say, and in a flash have my wallet out and license forked from its little slot below my realtor certification, my Red Man Club membership, my Maize and Blue Club alumni card.

"If you'd bring it over here and put it on the hood of my car," he says, giving his shoulder mike an adjustment, "I'll have a look at it while you stand back, then I'll put it back and you can pick it up. Is that all right?"

"It's just great. It seems a little elaborate. I could just hand it to you."

I start in the direction of his Yugo, which has a springy little two-way antenna stuck onto its dumpy top. But he nervously says, "Don't approach me, Mr. Bascombe. If you don't want to show your license"—he's eyeing his shoulder mike again—"I can get a Connecticut state trooper out here, and you can explain your case to him." The blond boy's amiable veneer has, in a heartbeat, disappeared to reveal sinister, police-protocol hardass, bent on construing obvious innocence as obvious guilt. I'm sure his real self is right now trying to figure out how Bascombe is spelled, since it's obviously a Jewish name, remembering that New Jersey's chock-full of Jews and spicks and darkies and towelheads and commies, all needing to be rounded up and reminded of a few things. I see his hands drifting somewhere below window level and around toward his backside, where he probably has his heat. (I have not provoked this. I merely am handing over my license.)

"I don't really have a case," I say, renewing my smile and stepping over to his Yugo and laying my license above the headlight. "I'm happy just to play by the rules." I take a few steps back.

The young man waits till I'm ten steps away, then comes round his door and snakes up my license. I can see his idiotic gold nameplate above his blue shirt pocket. *Erik*. Besides his shirt and blue trousers, he's wearing thick crepe-soled auxiliary-police footwear and a dopey little red ascot. I can also see that he's older than he looks, which is twenty-two. Probably he's thirty-five, has multiple applications in with all the local PDs and been turned down due to "irregularities" in his Rorschachs, even though from a distance he looks like the boy any parent would love and spare no expense in sending off to Dartmouth.

Erik steps around behind his open car door and gives my license thorough study, which includes looking up at me for a mug-shot match. I see now he has an almost colorless Hitler Youth mustache on his pale lip, and something tattooed on the back of his hand—a skull, maybe, or a snake coiled around a skull (no doubt a Body Artistry creation). He is also, I can just make out, wearing a tiny gold earring bead in his right lobe. An amusing little combo for Deep River.

He turns my license over, apparently to see if I'm an organ

donor (I'm not), then he walks it back around, lays it on the Yugo's hood and returns to his protective door. I still can't tell if he's packin'.

"There you go," he says, with a remnant of his former warmth. I don't know what he's learned, since it wouldn't say on my license if I was a serial killer. "We just have a lot of strangers drive in here, Mr. Bascombe. People who live in here really don't like being harassed. Which is why we have a job, I guess." He grins amiably. We're friends now.

"I hate it myself," I say, coming over and snugging my license back in my billfold. I wonder if Erik got a whiff of the dead-bird stink.

"You'd probably be surprised the number of wackos come off that I-Ninety-five and end up back in here, roaming around."

"I believe it," I say. "A hundred percent." And then for some reason I am enervated, as if I'd been to jail for days and had just this very moment stepped out into harsh daylight.

"Particularly on your holidays," says Erik the sociologist. "And especially *this* holiday. This one brings out the psychos from *all* over. New York, New Jersey, Pennsylvania." He shakes his head. Those are the states where most lunatics live if you're him. "You old friends with Mr. O'Dell?" He smiles, protected by his door. "I like him a lot."

"No," I say, stepping back to my car, which has cold air still pouring out, making me feel even more enervated.

"You're just business acquaintances, I guess," he says. "You an architect?"

"No," I say. "My ex-wife's married to Mr. O'Dell, and I'm picking up my son to take him on a trip. Does that seem like a good idea?" I can easily imagine wanting to harm Erik.

"Wow, that sounds pretty serious." He leers from behind his open blue door. He's, of course, got me figured now: I'm a defeated, pathetic figure engaged in a demeaning and hopeless mission—not nearly as interesting as a wacko. Though even my kind can cause trouble, can have a trunkful of phosphorous grenades and plastique and be bent on neighborhood mayhem.

"It's not that serious," I say, pausing, looking at him. "It's something I enjoy."

"Is Paul *your* son?" Erik says. He brings his forefinger up to his earring, a small gesture of dominion.

"Yep. You know Paul?"

"Oh yeah," Erik says, smirking. "We're all acquainted with Paul."

"All who? What does that mean?" I feel my brows thicken.

"We've all had contact with Paul." Erik starts lowering himself back into his stupid Yugo.

"I'm sure he hasn't caused you any trouble," I say, thinking that he probably has, and will again. Erik is the kind of monkey Paul would consider a barrel of laughs.

Erik is speaking from the driver's seat now; I can't make his words out. No doubt he's saying something smart-assed he doesn't intend me to hear. Or else he's radioing messages via his shoulder. He drops the Yugo in reverse, scoots back out the drive and wheels around.

I consider saying something vicious, running over and screaming in his window. But I can't afford to get arrested in my ex-wife's driveway. So I only wave, and he waves back. I think he says, "Have a good day," in his policey, insincere way, before heading slowly up Swallow Lane out of my sight.

MY DAUGHTER, Clarissa, is the first living soul I spy as I drive tired-eyed into compound O'Dell. She is far below the big house, on the ample lawn slope above the pond, committedly whacking a yellow tetherball all by her lonesome, oblivious as a sparrow to me here in my car, surveilling her from afar.

I pull up to the back of the house (the front faces the lawn, the air, the water, the sunrise and, for what I know, the path to all knowledge) and climb wearily out into the hot, chirpy morning, reconciled to finding Paul by myself.

Charley's house is, of course, a glorious erection, chalky-blue-shingled and white-trimmed, with a complex gabled roof, tall paneless windows and a big sashaying porch around three sides that gives onto the lawn down some white steps to the very spot where Charley and I discussed Shakespeare and came to the conclusion we neither one trusted the other.

I wedge in sideways through the row of purple-blooming hydrangeas (contrast my poor dried-up remnants on Clio Street), stagger only slightly, but walk on out onto the hot shadowless grass, feeling light-legged and dazed, my eyelids flickering, my eyes darting side to side to see who might see me first (such entrances are never dignified). I have, to my eternal infamy, forgotten to buy a gift this morning, a love and peace offering to appease Clarissa for not taking her along with her brother. What I'd give for a colorful Vince Lombardi sweatband or a Seven Blocks of Granite book of inspirational halftime quotes. It would be our joke. I am lost here.

Clarissa ceases larking with the tetherball when she sees me and stands eyes-shaded, averting her face and waving, though she can't tell it's me she sees—possibly hopes it is and not a plainclothes policeman come to ask questions about her brother.

I wave back, realizing for some reason known only to God that I have begun to *limp*, as though a war had intervened since I last saw my loved ones and I had returned a changed and beaten veteran. Though Clarissa will not notice. Even as rarely as she sees me—once a month nowadays—I am a timeless fixture, and nothing would seem unusual; an eye patch, a prosthetic arm, allnew teeth: none would rate a mention.

"Hi-dee, hi-dee, hi-dee," she sings out when it's clearly me she's waving welcome to. She wears strong contacts and can't see distances well, but doesn't care. She darts and springs barefoot toward me across the dry grass, ready to deliver a big power hug around my aching neck—which every time hurts like a hammerlock and makes me groan.

"I came as soon as I heard the news," I say. (In our makeshift, make-believe life I always arrive just in time to face some dire emergency—Clarissa and I being the responsible adults, Paul and their mother the temperamental kids in need of rescue.) I am still limping, though my heart's going strong with simple pleasure, all tightness in my brain miraculously dispatched.

"Paul's in the house with Mom, getting ready and probably having an argument."

Clarissa, in brilliant red shorts over her blue Speedo suit, jumps up and gives me her hammer hug, and I swing her like a tetherball before letting her sink weak-kneed into the grass. She has a wonderful smell—dampness and girlish perfume applied hours before, now faded. Beyond us is the boathouse crime scene, the pond again dense with pink fleabane and wild callas and, farther on, the row of dense motionless tupelos and the invisible river, above which a squad of pelicans executes a slow and graceful upward soar.

"Where's the man of the house?" I let myself down heavily beside her, my back against the tetherball pole. Clarissa's legs are thin and tanned and golden-sheeny-haired, her bare feet milky and without a blemish. She arranges herself belly-down, chin-propped, her eyes clear behind her contacts and fastened on me, her face a prettier version of my own: small nose, blue eyes, cheekbones more obvious than her mother's, whose broad, Dutch forehead and coarse hair match Paul's looks almost completely.

"He's work-ing now in his studi-o-o." She looks at me knowingly and without much irony. It's life to her, all of this—few tragedies, few great singing victories, everything pretty much good or okay. We are well paired in our family unit.

Charley's studio is half visible beyond a row of deep-green hardwoods that boundaries the lawn and stops at the pond's edge. I see a glint off its tin roof, its row of cypress stilts holding up a catwalk (a project Charley and his roommate doped out as a joke freshman year, back in '44, but that Charley "always wanted to build").

"So how's the weather?" I say, relieved to know where he is.

"Oh, it's fine," Clarissa says noncommittally. A skim of sweat is on her temples from belting the tetherball. My back's already sweaty through my shirt.

"And how's your brother?"

"Weird. But okay." Maintaining her belly-down, she rotates her head around on its slender stem, some routine from dance class or gymnastics, though an unmistakable signal: she is Paul's *buen amiga*; the two of them are closer than the two of us; this all could've been different with better parents, but isn't; do not fail to notice it.

"Is your mom okay too?"

Clarissa stops rotating her head and wrinkles her nose as though I'd announced an unsavory subject, then rolls over on her back and stares skyward. "She's much worse," she says, and looks unconvincingly worried.

"Worse than what?"

"Than you!" She rounds her eyes upward in mock surprise. "She and Charley had a howler this week. And they had one last week too. And one the week before." "Howlers" mean big disputes, not embarrassing verbal miscues. "Hmmmm, hmm, hmm," she says, meaning most of what she knows is being retained silently. I of course can't quiz her on this subject—a cardinal rule once divorce has become the governing institution—though I wish I knew more.

I pluck up a blade of grass, press it between my two thumbs like a woodwind reed and blow, making a sputtery, squawky but still fairly successful soprano sax note, a skill from eons back.

"Can you play 'Gypsy Road' or 'Born in the U.S.A.'?" She sits up.

"That's my whole repertoire on grass," I say, putting my two hands down on both her kneecaps, which are cold and bony and soft all at once. Conceivably she can smell dead grackle. "Your ole Dad loves you," I say. "I'm sorry I have to kidnap Paul and not all two of you. I'd rather travel as a trio."

"He's much needier now," Clarissa says, and drags a blade of grass all her own across the backs of both my hands where they rest on her perfect kneecaps. "I'm way ahead of him emotionally. I'll have my period pretty soon." She looks up at me profoundly, fattens the corners of her mouth and slowly lets her eyes cross and keeps them that way.

"Well, that's good to know," I say, my heart going ker-whonk, my eyes suddenly hot and unhappily moist—not with unhappy tears, but with unhappy sweat that has busted out on my forehead. "And how old *are* you?" I say, ker-whonk. "Thirty-seven or thirty-eight?"

"Thirty-twelve," she says, and lightly pokes my knuckles with the grass blade.

"Okay, that's old enough. You don't need to be any older. You're perfect."

"Charley knows Bush," she says with a sour face. "Did you hear that?" Her blue eyes elevate gravely to mine. This is bottom-line business to her. All that Charley might conceivably have been forgiven is reassigned to him with this choice bit of news. My daughter, like her old man, is a Democrat of the New Deal bent and considers most Republicans and particularly V. P. Bush barely mentionable dickheads.

"I guess I knew that without knowing it." I scour my two fingers on the turf to clean off the death smell.

"He's for the party of money, tradition and influence," she says, way too big for her britches, since Charley's tradition and influence are paying her bills, keeping her in tetherballs, tutus and violin lessons. She is for the party of no tradition, no influence, no nothing, also like her father.

"He has his rights," I say, and add a lackluster "I mean that." I can't help conjuring what Charley's cheek looks like where Paul has whopped him.

Clarissa stares at her blade of grass, wondering, I'm sure, why she has to accord Charley any rights. "Sweetheart," I say solemnly, "is there anything you can tell me about ole Paul? I don't want you to tell me a deep dark secret, just maybe a shallow light one. It would be as-you-know-held-in-strictest-confidence." I say this last to make it halfway a joke and let her feel comradely about providing me some lowdown.

She stares at the thick grass carpet in silence, then angles her head over and squints up at the house with the flowering bushes and the white porch and stairs. Atop the highmost roof pinnacle, in the midst of all the springing angles and gable ends, is an American flag (a small one) on a staff, rustling in an unfelt breeze.

"Are you sad?" she says. In her sun-blond hair I see a tiny red ribbon tied in a bow, something I hadn't noticed but instantly revere her for, since along with her question it makes her seem a person of complex privacies.

"No, I'm not sad, except that you can't go with Paul and me to Cooperstown. And I forgot to bring you anything. That's pretty sad."

"Do you have a car phone?" She raises her eyes accusingly.

"No."

"Do you have a beeper?"

"No, afraid not." I smile at her knowingly.

"How do you keep up with your calls then?" She squints again, making her look a hundred.

"I guess I don't get that many calls. Sometimes there's a message from you on my answering box, though not that often."

"I know."

"You didn't answer me about Paul, sweetheart. All I really want to do is be a good pappy if I can."

"His problems are all stress-related," she says officially. She plucks up another blade of quite green and dry grass and slips it into the cuff of my chinos where I'm cross-legged beside her.

"What stress is he suffering from?"

"I don't know."

"Is that your best diagnosis?"

"Yes."

"How 'bout you? Do you have any stress-related problems?"

"No." She shakes her head, makes a pruny pucker with her lips. "Mine'll come out later, if I have any."

"Who told you so?"

"TV." She looks at me earnestly as though to say that TV has its good points too.

Somewhere high in the firmament I hear a hawk cry out, or possibly an osprey, though when I look up I can't see it.

"What can I do about Paul's stress-related problems?" I say, and, God be gracious, I wish she'd pipe up with a nice answer. I'd put it in place before the sun sets. Somewhere, then, another noise—not a hawk but a thumping, a door slamming or a window being shut, a drawer being closed. When I look up, Ann is standing at the porch rail, watching down on us across the lawn. I sense she's just arrived but would like my chat with Clarissa to come to a close and for me to get on with my business. I make a friendly ex-husband-who-wishes-no-trouble wave, a gesture that makes me feel not so good. "I believe that's your mom," I say.

Clarissa looks up at the porch. "Yeah hi," she says.

"We better dust off our britches here." She will, I see, out of ancient, honorable loyalty, offer no help with her brother. She fears, I suppose, divulging compromising secrets while claiming only to love him. Children are wise to adult ways now, thanks to us.

"Paul might be happier if you could maybe live in Deep River. Or maybe Old Saybrook," she says as if these words require immense discipline, nodding her head slightly with each one. (Parents can break up, fall out of love, get searingly divorced, marry others, move miles away; but as far as kids are concerned, most of it's tolerable if one parent will just tag along behind the other like a slave.)

There was, of course, in the savage period after Ann moved away in '84, a dolorous time when I haunted these very hills and streamsides like a shamus; cruised its middle-school parking lots, its street corners and back alleys, cased its arcades and skating rinks, its Finasts and Burger Kings, merely to be in visual contact with where my children *might* spend the days and afternoons they could've been spending with me. I even went so far as to price a condo in Essex, a sterile little listening post from which I could keep "in touch," keep love alive.

Only it would've made me even more morose, as morose as a hundred lost hounds, to wake up alone in a condo! In Essex! Awaiting my appointed pickup hour with the kids, expecting to take them back where? To my condo? And afterward, glowering back down 95 for a befuddled workweek till Friday, when the lunacy commenced again? There are parents who don't blink an eye at that kind of bashing around, who'd ruin their own lives and everybody's within ten miles if they can prove—long after all the horses are out of the barn—that they've always been good and faithful providers.

But I simply am not one of these; and I have been willing to see my kids less often, for the three of us to shuttlecock up and back, so that I can keep alive in Haddam a life they can fit into, even if precariously, when they will, and meanwhile maintain my sanity, instead of forcing myself into places where I don't belong and making everybody hate me. It's not the best solution, since I miss them achingly. But it's better to be a less than perfect dad than a perfect goofball.

And in any case, with the condo option, they would still grow up and leave in a heartbeat; Ann and Charley would get divorced. And I'd be stuck (worst case) with a devalued condo I couldn't give away. Eventually, I'd sell Cleveland Street as a downsizing measure, perhaps move up here to keep my mortgage company, and grimly pass my last years alone in Essex watching TV in a pair of old corduroys, a cardigan and Hush Puppies, while helping out evenings in some small bookshop, where I'd occasionally see Charley dodder in, place an order and never recognize me.

Such things happen! We realtors are often the very ones called in for damage control. Though thankfully my frenzy subsided and I stayed put where I was and more or less knew my place. Haddam, New Jersey.

"Sweetheart," I say tenderly to my daughter, "if I lived up here, your mother wouldn't like it at all, and you and Paul wouldn't come stay in your own rooms and see your old friends-in-need. Sometimes you can change things and just make them worse."

"I know," she says bluntly. I'm sure Ann hasn't discussed with her Paul's coming to live with me, and I have no idea what her opinion will be. Perhaps she'll welcome it, loyalty aside. I might, if I were her.

She reaches fingers into her yellow hair, her mouth going into a scowl of application. She pulls the little red bow out along the fine blond strands until she frees it still tied, and hands it to me rather matter-of-factly. "Here's *my* latest present," she says. "You can be my bow."

"That's another kind of bow," I say, taking the little frill in my hand and squeezing it. "They're spelled different."

"Yeah, I know. It's okay, though, this time."

"Thanks." Once again, sadly, I have nothing to trade as an act of devotion.

And then she is up and on her bare feet, spanking the seat of her red shorts and shaking out her hair, looking down like a small lioness with a tangled mane. I am less quick but am up too, using the tetherball pole. I look toward the house, where no one's standing on the porch now. A smile is for some reason on my lips, my hand on my daughter's bony bare shoulder, her red bow, my badge of courage, clutched in my other hand, as we start—the two of us—together up the wide hill.

"DID YOU ever take trips in Mississippi with your father?" Ann asks without genuine interest. We are seated opposite each other on the big porch. The Connecticut River, visible now above the serrated treetops, is a-glitter with dainty sailboats sporting rust-colored sails, their masts steadfast as the wind transports them up the current toward Hartford. All boats of a certain class rising on a rising tide.

"Sure, you bet. Sometimes we went over to Florida. Once we went to Norfolk and visited the Great Dismal Swamp on the way back." She used to know this but has now forgotten.

"Was it dismal?"

"Absolutely." I smile at her in a collegial way, since that is what we are.

"And so did you two always get along great?" She looks away across the lawn below us.

"We got along pretty great. My mother wasn't around to complicate things, so we were on our best behavior. Three was more complicated."

"Women just enjoy disrupting men's lives," she says.

We are fixed firmly in two oversize green wicker chairs furnished with oversize flowery cushions of some lush and complex lily-pad pattern. Ann has brought out an ole-timey amber-glass pitcher of iced tea, which Clarissa has fixed and drawn a fat happy face on. The tea and glasses and little pewter ice bucket are situated on a low table at knee level, as we, the two of us, wait for Paul, who was up late and slow now to rustle his bones. (I notice no warm-hearted carryover from our sentimental sign-off at the Vince last night.)

Ann runs a comb-of-fingers back through her thick, athletically shortened hair, which she's highlighted so sudden blond strands shine from within and look pretty. She's wearing white golfing shorts and an expensive-looking sleeveless top of some earthy taupe color that fits loose and shows her breasts off semi-mysteriously, and tan, sockless tassel shoes that cause her tanned legs to look even longer and stauncher, stirring in me a low-boil sexual whir that makes me gladder to be alive than I ever expected to feel today. I've noticed in the last year a subtle widening of Ann's wonderful derriere and a faint thickening and loosening of the flesh above her knees and upper arms. To my view, a certain tense girlishness, always present (and which I never really liked), has begun subsiding and been replaced by a softer, womanly but in every way more substantial and appealing adultness I admire immensely. (I might mention this if I had time to make clear I liked it; though I see she is wearing Charley's pretentiously plain gold band today, and the whole idea seems ridiculous.)

She has not asked me to come inside to wait, though I'd already decided to stay clear of the glassed-in, malaise-filled "family room," which I can just see into through the long mirror-tinted windows beside me. Charley has of course installed a big antique telescope there, complete with all the necessary brass knobs and fittings, engraved logarithmic calibrations and moon phases, and with which I'm sure he can bring in the Tower of London if he takes a notion. I can also make out the ghostly-white beast of a grand piano and beside it a beaux arts music stand, where Ann and Clarissa almost certainly play Mendelssohn duets for Charley's delectation on many a cold winter's eve. It is a tiresome recognition.

Truth is, the one time I ever waited inside (picking up the kids for a day trip to the fish elevator at South Hadley), I ended up waiting alone for nearly an hour, leafing through the coffee-table library (*Classic Holes of Golf, Erotic Cemetery Art, Sailing*), eventually working my way down to a hot-pink flyer from a women's clinic in New London, offering an enhance-your-sexual-performance workshop, which made me instantly panicky. Prudenter now just to stay on the porch and risk feeling like a grinning high-school kid forced to make deadpan parental chitchat while I await my date.

Ann has already explained to me how yesterday was much worse than I knew, worse than she explained last night when she said I thought "be" and "seem" were the same concept (which may have been true once but isn't now). Not only, it seems, did Paul wound poor Charley with an oarlock from his own damned dinghy, but he also informed his mother in the very living room I won't enter and in front of damaged-goods Charley himself that she "needed" to get rid of "asshole Chuck." After that, he marched out, got in his mother's Mercedes wagon and hit off on a brief tear, barrel-assing unlicensed out the driveway at a high speed, missing the very first curve on Swallow Lane and side-swiping a two-hundred-year-old mountain ash on the neighbor's property (a lawyer, of course). In the process he banged his head into the steering wheel, popped the air bag and cut his ear, so that he had to take a stitch at the Old Saybrook walk-in clinic. Erik, the man from Agazziz, arrived moments after the crash—similar to how he apprehended me—and escorted him home. No police were called. Later he disappeared again, on foot, and came home long past dark (Ann heard him bark once in his room).

She of course called Dr. Stopler, who calmly informed her that medical science knew mighty damn little about how the old mind works in relation to the old brain—whether they're one and the same pancake, two parts of one pancake, or just altogether different pancakes that somehow work in unison (like an automobile clutch). However, distressed family relations were pretty clear bugaboo factors leading to childhood mental illness, and from what he already knew, Paul did have some qualifying preconditions: dead brother, divorced parents, absent father, two major household moves before puberty (plus Charley O'Dell for a stepdad).

He did allow, though, that when he'd conducted his evaluative "chat" with Paul back in May, prior to his Camp Wanapi visit, Paul had failed entirely to exhibit low self-esteem, suicide idea-tion, neurological dysfunction; he was not particularly "opposi-tional" (then), hadn't suffered an IQ nosedive and didn't display any conduct disorders—which meant he didn't set a fire or murder any birds. In fact, the doctor said, he'd demonstrated a "real capacity for compassion and a canny ability to put himself in another's shoes." Though circumstances could always change overnight; and Paul could easily be suffering any and every one of the aforementioned maladies at this very minute, and might've abandoned all compassion.

"I'm really just pissed off at him now," Ann says. She is stand-ing, looking out over the porch rail where I first saw her today, staring across the apron of shining river toward the few small white house façades catching the sun from deep in the encroach-ment of solid greens. Once again I steal an approving look at her new substantial-without-sacrificing-sexual-specificity woman-liness. Her lips, I notice, seem fuller now, as if she might've had them "enhanced." (Such surgeries can sweep through the more well-to-do communities like new kitchen appliances.) She rubs the back of one muscular calf with the top of her other shoe and sighs. "You may not know how exactly lucky you've had it," she says, after a period of silent staring.

I mean to say nothing. A careful review of how lucky I am could too easily involve more airing of my "be/seem" misdeeds and tie into the possibility that I'm a coward or a liar or worse. I scratch my nose and can *still* smell grackle on my fingers.

She looks around at where I sit still not very comfortably silent on my lily pad.

"Would you agree to seeing Dr. Stopler?"

"As a patient?" I blink.

"As a co-parent," she says. "*And* as a patient."

"I'm really not based in New Haven," I say. "And I never much liked shrinks. They just try to make you act like every-body else."

"You don't have that to worry about." She regards me in an impatient older-sister way. "I just thought if you and I, or maybe you and I and Paul, went down, we might iron some things out. That's all."

"We can invite Charley, if you want to. He's probably got some ironing out that needs doing. He's a co-parent too, right?"

"He'll go. If I ask him."

I look around at the mirror window behind which sits the spectral white piano and a lot of ultra-modern, rectilinear blond-wood furniture arranged meticulously between long, sherbet-colored walls so as to maximize the experience of an interesting inner space while remaining unimaginably comfy. Reflected, I see the azure sky, part of the lawn, an inch of the boathouse roof and a line of far treetops. It is a vacant vista, the acme of opulent American dreariness Ann has for some reason married into. I feel like getting up and walking out onto the lawn—waiting for my son in the grass. I don't care to see Dr. Stopler and have my weaknesses vetted. My weaknesses, after all, have taken me this far.

Behind the glass, though, and unexpectedly, the insubstantial figure of my daughter becomes visible crossing left to right, intending where, I don't know. As she passes she gazes out at us—her parents, bickering—and, blithely assuming I can't see her, flips one or both of us the bird in a spiraling, heightening, conjuring motion like an ornate salaam, then disappears through a door to another segment of the house.

"I'll think about Dr. Stopler," I say. "I'm still not sure what a milieu therapist is, though."

The corners of Ann's mouth thicken with disapproval—of me. "Maybe you could think of your children as a form of self-discovery. Maybe you'd see your interest in it then and do something a little more wholeheartedly yourself." Ann's view is that I'm a half-hearted parent; my view is that I do the best I know how.

"Maybe," I say, though the thought of dread-filled weekly drives to dread-filled New Haven for expensive fifty-five dread-filled minutes of *mea culpa! mea culpa!* gushered into the weary, dread-resistant map of some Austrian headshrinker is enough to set anybody's escape mechanisms working overtime.

The fact is, of course, Ann maintains a very unclear picture of me and my current life's outlines. She has never appreciated the realty business or why I enjoy it—doesn't think it actually involves *doing* anything. She knows nothing of my private life beyond what the kids snitch about in offhand ways, doesn't know what trips I take, what books I read. I've over time become fuzzier and fuzzier, which given her old Michigan factualism makes her inclined to disapprove of almost anything I might do except possibly joining the Red Cross and dedicating my life to feeding starving people on faraway shores (not a bad second choice, but even that might not save me from pathos). In all important ways I'm no better in her mind than I was when our divorce was made final—whereas, of course, she has made great strides.

Only I don't actually mind it, since not having a clear picture makes her long for one and in so doing indirectly long for me (or that's my position). Absence, in this scheme, both creates and fills a much-needed void.

But it's not all positive: when you're divorced you're always wondering (I am anyway, sometimes to the point of granite pre-occupation) what your ex-spouse is thinking about you, how she's viewing your decisions (assuming she thinks you make any), whether she's envious or approving or condescending or sneeringly reproachful, or just indifferent. Your life, because of this, can become goddamned awful and decline into being a "function" of your view of *her* view—like watching the salesman in the clothing store mirror to see if he's admiring you in the loud plaid suit you haven't quite decided to buy, but will if he seems to approve. Therefore, what I'd prefer Ann's view to be is: of a man who's made a spirited recovery from a lost and unhappy union, and gone on to discover wholesome choices and pretty solutions to life's thorny dilemmas. Failing that, I'd be happy to keep her in the dark.

Though in the end the real trick to divorce remains, given this refractory increase in perspectives, not viewing *yourself* ironically and losing heart. You have, on the one hand, such an obsessively detailed and minute view of yourself from your prior existence, and on the other hand, an equally specific view of yourself *later on*, that it becomes almost impossible not to see yourself as a puny human oxymoron, and damn near impossible sometimes to recognize who your self is at all. Only you must. Writers in fact survive this condition better than almost anyone, since they understand that almost everything—e-v-e-r-y-t-h-i-n-g—is not really made up of "views" but words, which, should you not like them, you can change. (This actually isn't very different from what Ann told me last night on the phone in the Vince Lombardi.)

Ann has assumed a seat on the porch railing, one strong, winsome brown knee up, the other swinging. She is half facing me and half observing the red-sailed regatta, most of whose hulls have moved behind the treeline. "I'm sorry," she says moodily. "Tell me where you two're going, again? You told me last night. I forgot."

"We're heading up to Springfield this morning." I say this cheerfully, happy to change the subject away from me. "We're having a 'sports lunch' at the Basketball Hall of Fame. Then we're driving over to Cooperstown by tonight." No use mentioning a possible late crew addition of Sally Caldwell. "We're touring the Baseball Hall of Fame tomorrow morning, and I'll have him in the city at the stroke of six." I smile a reliable, You're in good hands with Allstate smile.

"He's not really a big baseball fan, is he?" She says this almost plaintively.

"He knows more than you think he knows. Plus, going's the ur-father–son experience." I erase my smile to let her know I'm only half bluffing.

"So have you thought up some important fatherly things to say to solve his problems?" She squints at me and tugs at her earlobe exactly the way Charley does.

I, however, intend not to give away what I'll say to Paul on our trip, since it's too easy to break one's fragile skein of worthwhile purpose by jousting with casual third-party skepticism. Ann is not in a good frame of mind to validate fragile worthwhile purposes, especially mine.

"My view is sort of a facilitator's view," I say, hopefully. "I just think he's got some problems figuring out a good conception of himself"—to put it mildly—"and I want to offer a better one so he doesn't get too attached to the one he's hanging onto now, which doesn't seem too successful. A defective attitude can get to be your friend if you don't look out. It's sort of a problem in risk management. He has to risk trying to improve by giving up what's maybe comfortable but not working. It's not easy."

I would smile again, but my mouth has gone dry as cardboard saying this much and trying to seem what I am—sincere. I drink down a gulp of ice tea, which is sweet the way a child would like it and has lemon and mint and cinnamon and God knows what else in it, and tastes terrible. Clarissa's finger-drawn happy face has droozled down and become a scowling jack-o'-lantern in the heat.

"Do you think you're a good person to instruct him about risk management?" Ann suddenly looks toward the river as if she'd heard an unfamiliar sound out in the summer atmosphere. A fishy breeze has in fact risen offshore and moved upriver, carrying all manner of sounds and smells she might not expect.

"I'm not that bad at it," I say.

"No." She is still looking off. "Not at risk management. I guess not."

I hear a noise myself, unfamiliar and nearby, and stand up to the porch rail and peer over the lawn, hoping I'll see Paul coming up the hill. But to the left, at the edge of the hardwoods, I can see, instead, all of Charley's studio. As advertised, it is a proper old New England seaman's chapel raised ten cockamamie feet above the pond surface on cypress pilings and connected to land by a catwalk. The church paint has been blasted off, leaving the lapped boards exposed. Windows are big, tall, clear lancets. The tin roof simmers in the sun of nearly noon.

And then Charley himself makes an appearance on the little back deck (happily in miniature), fresh from this morning's sore-jawed brainstorms, cooking up super plans for some rich neuro-surgeon's ski palace in Big Sky, or a snorkeling hideaway in Cabo Cartouche—Berlioz still booming in his oversized ears. Bare-chested, tanned and silver-topped, in his usual khaki shorts, he is transporting from inside what looks like a plate of something, which he places on a low table beside a single wooden chair. I wish I could crank his big telescope down and survey the oar-lock damage. That would interest me. (It's never easy to see why your ex-wife marries the man she marries if it isn't you again.)

I would like, however, to talk about Paul now: about the possibility of his coming down to Haddam to live, so as to stop limiting my fathering to weekends and holidays. I haven't entirely thought through all the changes to my own private dockets that his arrival will necessitate, the new noises and new smells in my air, new concerns for time, privacy, modesty; possibly a new appreciation for my own *moment* and freedoms; my *role*: a man retuned to the traditional, riding herd on a son full time, duties dads are made for and that I have missed but crave. (I could also bear to hear about the howlers Ann and Charley have been conducting, though that isn't my business and could easily turn out to be nothing: mischief Clarissa and Paul dreamed up to confuse everyone's agenda.)

But I'm thwarted by what to say, and frankly inhibited by Ann. (Perhaps this is another goal of divorce—to reinstitute the inhibitions you dispensed with when things were peachy.) It's tempting just to push off toward less controversial topics, like I did last night: my headaches with the Markhams and McLeods, rising interest rates, the election, Mr. Tanks—my most unforgettable character—with his truck, his gold-collared kitty and his *Reader's Digest* condenseds, a personal docket that makes my own Existence Period look like ten years of sunshine.

But Ann suddenly says, apropos of nothing but also, of course, of everything, "It's not really easy being an ex-spouse, is it? There isn't much use for us in the grand plan. We don't help anything go forward. We just float around unattached, even if we're not unattached." She rubs her nose with the back of her hand and snuffs. It's as if she's seen us outside our real bodies, like ghosts above the river, and is wishing we'd go away.

"There's always one thing we can do." She makes a point of rarely using my name unless she's angry, so that most of the time I just seem to overhear her and offer a surprise reply.

"And what's that?" She looks at me disapprovingly, her dark brows clouded, her leg twitching in a barely detectable, spasmic way.

"Get married to each other again," I say, "just to state the obvious." (Though not necessarily the inevitable.) "Last year I sold houses to three couples"—two, actually—"each of whom was at one time married, and who got divorced and married, then divorced, then married their original true love again. If you can say it you can do it, I guess."

"We can put that on your tombstone," Ann says with patent distaste. "It's the story of your life. You don't know what you're going to say next, so you don't know what's a good idea. But if it wasn't a good idea to be married to you seven years ago, why would it be a better idea now? *You're* not any better." (This is unproved.) "It's conceivable you're worse."

"You're happily married anyway," I say, pleased with myself, though wondering who the "special someone" will be who'll make decisions about my tombstone. Best if it could be me.

Ann scrutinizes Charley treading long-strided, barefooted, bare-chested back inside his studio, no doubt to see if his miso is ready and to dig the soy sauce and shallots out of the Swedish mini-fridge. Charley, I notice, walks in a decidedly head-forward, hump-shouldered, craning way that makes him look surprisingly old—he's only sixty-one—but which makes *me* experience a sudden, unexpected and absolutely unwanted and impolitic sympathy for him. A good head shot with an oarlock is more telling on a man his age.

"You like thinking I ought to be sorry I married Charley. But I'm not sorry. Not at all," Ann says, her tan shoe giving another nervous little twitch. "He's a much better person than you are"—grossly unproved—"not that you have any reason to believe that, since you don't know him. He even has a good opinion of you. He tries to be a pal to these children. He thinks we've done a better than average job with them." (No mention of his daughter the novelist.) "He's nice to me. He tells the truth. He's faithful." My ass as a bet on that, though I could be wrong. Some men are. Plus, I'd like to hear an example of some sovereign truth Charley professes—no doubt some self-congratulating GOP Euclideanism: A penny saved is a penny earned; buy low, sell high; old Shakespeare sure knew his potatoes. My unmerited sympathy for him goes flapping away.

"I guess I didn't realize he held me in high esteem," I say (and I'm sure he doesn't). "Maybe we should be best friends. He asked me about that once. I was forced to decline."

Ann just shakes her head, rejecting me the way a great actor rejects a heckler in the audience—utterly and without really noticing.

"Frank, you know when we were all living down in Haddam five years ago, in that sick little arrangement you thrived on, and you were fucking that little Texas bimbo and having the time of your life, I actually put an ad in the *Pennysaver*, advertising myself as a woman who seeks male companionship. I actually risked boredom and rape just to keep things the way you liked them."

This is not the first time I've heard about the *Pennysaver* etc. And Vicki Arcenault was far from a bimbo. "We could've gotten remarried again anytime," I say. "And I wasn't having the time of my life. You divorced *me*, if you can remember precisely. We could've moved back in together. All kinds of things could've happened instead of what did." Possibly I'm about to hear that the most difficult milieu adjustment of my adult life didn't really have to be made (if only I'd been clairvoyant). It's the worst news anyone could hear, and for a nickel I'd pop Ann right in the chops.

"I didn't want to marry you." She keeps shaking her head, though less forcefully. "I just should've left, that's all. Do you even think you know why you and I got unmarried?" She takes a brief, angling look at me—uncomfortably like Sally's look. I'd rather not be delving into the past now, but into the future or at least the present, where I'm most at home. It's all my fault, though, for rashly bringing up the queasy matter of—or at least the word—marriage.

"I'm on record," I say, to answer her fair and square, "as believing our son died and you and I tried to cope with it but couldn't. Then I left home for a time and had some girlfriends, and you filed for divorce because you wanted me gone." I look at her haltingly, as if in describing that time in our life I'd as much as stated a Goya could've easily been painted by a grandmother in Des Moines. "Maybe I'm wrong."

Ann is nodding as if she's trying to get my view straight in her head. "I divorced you," she says slowly and meticulously, "because I didn't like you. And I didn't like you because I didn't trust you. Do you think you ever told me the truth once, the whole truth?" She taps her fingers on her bare thigh, not looking my way. (This is the perpetual theme of her life: the search for truth, and truth's defeat by the forces of contingency, most frequently represented by yours truly.)

"Tell the truth about what?" I say.

"Anything," she says, gone rigid.

"I told you I loved you. That was true. I told you I didn't want to get divorced. That was true too. What else was there?"

"There were important things that weren't being admitted by you. There's no use going into it now." She nods some more as if to ratify this. Though there is in her voice unexpected sadness and even a tremor of remorse, which makes my heart swell and my air passage stiffen, so that for one long festering moment I'm unable to speak. (I've been badly slipped up on here: she is distraught and dejected, and I cannot answer.)

"For a time," she continues, very, very softly and carefully, having slightly recovered herself, "for a long time, really, I knew we weren't all the way *to* the truth with each other. But that was okay, because we were trying to get there together. But suddenly I just felt hopeless, and I saw that truth didn't really exist to you. Though you got it from me the whole time."

Ann was forever suspecting other people were happier than she was, that other husbands loved their wives more, achieved greater intimacy, on and on. It is probably not unusual in modern life, though untrue of ours. But this is the final, belated, judgment on our ancient history: why love failed, why life broke into this many pieces and made this pattern, who at long last is to blame. Me. (Why now, I don't know. I still, in fact, don't know with any clarity what she's talking about.) And yet I so suddenly want to put my hand on her knee in hopes of consoling her that I do—I put my hand on her knee in hopes of consoling her. God knows how I can.

"Can't you tell me something specific?" I say gently. "Women? Or something I thought? Or something you thought I thought? Just some way you felt about me?"

"It wasn't something specific," she says painstakingly. Then stops. "Let's just talk about buying and selling houses now. Okay? You're very good at that." She turns an unpleasant and estimating eye on me. She doesn't bother to remove my warm and clammy hand from her smooth knee. "I wanted somebody with a true heart, that's all. That wasn't you."

"Goddamn it, I have a true heart," I say. Shocked. "And I *am* better. You can *get* better. You wouldn't know anyway."

"I came to realize," she says, uninterested in me, "that you were never entirely there. And this was long before Ralph died, but also after."

"But I loved you," I say, suddenly just angry as hell. "I wanted to go on being your husband. What else from the land of truth did you want? I didn't have anything else to tell you. *That* was the truth. There's plenty about anybody you can't know and are better off not to, for Christ sake. Not that I even know what they are. There's plenty about you, stuff that doesn't even matter. Plus, where the hell was I if I wasn't there?"

"I don't know. Where you still are. Down in Haddam. I just wanted things to be clear and certain."

"I do have a true heart," I shout, and I'm tempted again to give her a whack, though only on the knee. "You're one of those people who think God's *only* in the details, but then if they aren't the precise right details, life's all fucked up. You invent things that don't exist, then you worry about being denied whatever they are. And then you miss the things that *do* exist. Maybe it's you, you know? Maybe some truths don't even have words, or maybe the truth was what you wanted least, or maybe you're a woman of damn little faith. Or low self-esteem, or something."

I take my hand off her knee, unwilling now to be her consoler.

"We don't really need to go into this."

"You started it! You started it last night, about being and seeming, as if you were the world's expert on being. You just wanted something else, that's all. Something beyond what there is." She's right, of course, that we shouldn't go on with this, since this is an argument any two humans can have, could have, have had, no doubt are having at this moment all over the country to properly inaugurate the holiday. It really has nothing to do with the two of us. In a sense, we don't even exist, taken together.

I look around at the long porch, the great blue house on its big lawn, the shimmering windows behind which my two children are imprisoned, possibly lost to me. Charley has not come out onto his little porch again. What I'd thought he was doing—eating his ethical lunch in the ethical sunshine while we two battered at each other far above and out of earshot—is probably all wrong. I know nothing about him and should be kinder.

Ann just shakes her head again, without words accompanying. She eases herself down off the porch rail, lifts her chin, runs one finger from her temple back through her hair, and takes a quick look at the mirror window as if she saw someone coming—which she does: our son, Paul. Finally.

"I'm sorry," I say. "I'm sorry I drove you crazy when we were married. If I'd known I was going to, I wouldn't ever have married you. You're probably right, I rely on how I make things seem. It's my problem."

"I thought you thought how I thought," she says softly. "Maybe that's mine."

"I tried. I should've. I loved you very much all the time."

"Some things just can't be fixed later, can they?" she says.

"No, not later," I say. "Not later they can't."

And that is essentially and finally that.

"WHY THE long face?" Paul says to his mother and also to me. He has arrived, smirking, onto the porch looking far too much like the murder boy from Ridgefield last midnight, as committed to bad luck as a death row convict. And to my surprise he's even pudgier and somehow taller, with thick, adult eyebrows even more like his mom's, but with a bad, pasty complexion—nothing like he looked as recently as a month ago, and not enough anymore (or ever) like the small, gullible boy who kept pigeons at his home in Haddam. (How do these things change so fast?) His hair has been cut in some new, dopey, skint-sided, buzzed-up way, so that his busted ear is evident in its bloody little bandage. Plus, his gait is a new big-shoe, pigeon-toed, heel-scrape, shoulder-slump sidle by which he seems to give human shape to the abstract concept of condescending disapproval for everything in sight (the effects of stress, no doubt). He simply stands before us now—his parents—doing nothing. "I thought of a good homonym while I was getting dressed," he says slyly to either or both of us. " 'Meatier' and 'meteor.' Only they mean the same thing." He smirks, wishing to do nothing out here more than present himself in a way we won't like, someone who's lost IQ points or might be considering it.

"We were just discussing you," I say. I'd meant to mention something about Dr. Rection, to speak to him via private code, but I don't. I am in fact sorry to see him.

His mother, however, steps right up to him—essentially ignoring him and me—grips his chin with her strong golfer's thumb and index finger, and turns his head to examine his split ear. (He is nearly her height.) Paul is carrying a black gym bag with *Paramount Pictures—Reach Your Peak* stenciled on its side in white (Stephanie's stepfather is a studio exec, so I'm told) and is wearing big black-and-red clunker Reeboks with silver lightning bolts on the sides, long and baggy black shorts, and a long midnight-blue tee-shirt that has *Happiness Is Being Single* printed on the front below a painting of a bright-red Corvette. He is a boy you can read, though he also is someone you'd be sorry to encounter on a city street. Or in your home.

Ann asks him in a private voice if he has what he needs (he has), if he has money (he does), if he knows where to meet in Penn Station (yes), if he feels all right (no answer). He cuts his knifey eyes at me and screws up one side of his mouth as if we're somehow in league against her. (We aren't.)

Then Ann abruptly says, "So okay, you don't look great, but go wait in the car, please. I want to have a word with your father."

Paul wrinkles his mouth into a mirthless little all-knowing look of scorn having to do with the very notion of his mother talking to his father. He has become a smirker by nature. But how? When?

"What happened to your ear, by the way?" I say, knowing what happened.

"I punished it," he says. "It heard a bunch of things I didn't like." He says this in a mechanistic monotone. I give him a little push in the direction he's come from, back through the house and out toward the car. And so he goes.

"I'D APPRECIATE it if you'd try to be careful with him," Ann says. "I want him back in good shape for his court appearance Tuesday." She has sought to lead me the way Paul has gone, "back through," but I'm having no part of her sinister house beautiful, with its poisonous élan, spiffy lines and bloodless color scheme. I lead us (I'm still inexplicably limping) down the steps to the lawn and around via the safer grass and through the shrubberies to the pea-gravel driveway, just the way a yardman would. "I think he's injury prone," she says quietly, following me. "I had a dream about him having an accident."

I step through the green-leafed, thick-smelling hydrangeas, blooming a vivid purple. "My dreams are always like the six o'clock news," I say. "Everything happening to other people." The sexual whir I experienced on seeing Ann is now long gone.

"That's fine about your dreams," she says, hands in pockets. "This one happened to be mine."

I don't wish to think about terrible injury. "He's gotten

fat," I say. "Is he on mood stabilizers or neuroblockers or something?"

Paul and Clarissa are already conferring by my car. She is smaller and holding his left wrist in both her hands and trying to raise it to the top of her head in some kind of sisterly trick he's not cooperating with. "Come *on!*" I hear her say. "You putz."

Ann says, "He's not on anything. He's just growing up." Across the gravel lot is a robust five-bay garage that matches the house in every loving detail, including the miniature copper weather vane milled into the shape of a squash racket. Two bay doors are open, and two Mercedeses with Constitution State plates are nosed into the shadows. I wonder where Paul's station wagon is. "Dr. Stopler said he displays qualities of an only child, which is too bad in a way."

"I was an only child. I liked it."

"He's just *not* one. Dr. Stopler also said"—she's ignoring me, and why shouldn't she?—"not to talk to him too much about current events. They cause anxiety."

"I guess they do," I say. I am ready to say something caustic about childhood to seal my proprietorship of this day—revive Wittgenstein about living in the present meaning to live forever, blah, blah, blah. But I simply call a halt. No good's to come. All boats fall on a bitter tide—children know it better than anyone. "Do you think you know what's making him worse, just all of a sudden?"

She shakes her head, grips her right wrist with her left hand, and twists the two together, then gives me a small bleak smile. "You and me, I guess. What else?"

"I guess I was wanting a more complicated answer."

"Well, good for you." She rubs her other wrist the same way. "I'm sure you'll think of one."

"Maybe I'll have put on my tombstone 'He expected a more complicated answer.'"

"Let's quit talking about this, okay? We'll be at the Yale Club just for tonight if you need to call." She looks at me in a nose-wrinkled way and slouches a shoulder. She has not meant to be so harsh.

Ann, in amongst the hydrangeas, and for the first time today looks purely beautiful—pretty enough for me to exhale, my mind to open outward, and for me to gaze at her in a way I once gazed at her all the time, every single day of our old life together in Haddam. Now would be the perfect moment for a future-refashioning kiss, or for her to tell me she's dying of leukemia, or me to tell her I am. But that doesn't happen. She is smiling her stalwart's smile now, one that's long since disappointed and can face most anything if need be—lies, lies and more lies.

"You two have a good time," she says. "And please be careful with him."

"He's my son," I say idiotically.

"Oh, I know that. He's just like you." And then she turns and walks back toward the yard, continuing on, I suspect, out of sight and down to the water to have her lunch with her husband.

CHAPTER 8

CLARISSA BASCOMBE has snugged something tiny and secret into Paul's hand as we were leaving. And on our way up to Hartford, on our way up to Springfield, on our way to the Basketball Hall of Fame, he has held it without acknowledgment while I've yodeled away spiritedly about what I've thought will break our ice, get our ball rolling, fan our coals—start, via the right foot, what now feels like our last and most important journey together as father and son (though it probably isn't).

Once we swerve off busy CT 9 onto busier, car-clogged I-91, go past the grimy jai alai palace and a new casino run by Indians, I set off on my first "interesting topic": just how hard it is right here, ten miles south of Hartford, on July 2, 1988, when everything seems of a piece, to credit that on July 2, 1776, all the colonies on the seaboard distrusted the bejesus out of each other, were acting like separate, fierce warrior nations scared to death of falling property values and what religion their neighbors were practicing (like now), and yet still knew they needed to be happier and safer and went about doing their best to figure out how. (If this seems completely nutty, it's not, under the syllabus topic of "Reconciling Past and Present: From Fragmentation to Unity and Independence." It's totally relevant—in my view— to Paul's difficulty in integrating his fractured past with his hectic present so that the two connect up in a commonsense way and make him free and independent rather than staying disconnected and distracted and driving him bat-shit crazy. History's lessons are subtle lessons, inviting us to remember and forget selectively, and therefore are much better than psychiatry's, where you're forced to remember everything.)

"John Adams," I say, "said getting the colonies all to agree to be independent together was like trying to get thirteen clocks to strike at the same second."

"Who's John Adams?" Paul says, bored—his pale, bare, beginning-to-be-hairy legs crossed in a concertedly unmanly manner, one Reebok with its Day-Glo-yellow lacing hiked up threateningly near the gearshift lever.

"John Adams was the first Vice President," I say. "He was the first person to say it was a stupid job. In public, that is. That was in 1797. Did you bring your copy of the Declaration of Independence?"

"Nuhhhn." This may mean either.

He is staring out at the reemerged Connecticut, where a sleek powerboat is pulling a tiny female water-skier, billowing the river's shiny skin. In a bright-yellow life vest, the girl heels *waaaaay* back against her towrope, carving a high, translucent spume out of the crusty wake.

"Why are you driving so eff-ing slow?" he says to be droll. Then, in a mocking old-granny's voice, "Everybody passes me, but I get there just as fast as the rest of 'em."

I, of course, intend to drive as fast as I want and no faster, but take an appraising look at him, my first since we shoved off from Deep River. His ear that wasn't bammed by the Mercedes's steering wheel has some gray fuzzy litter in it. Paul also doesn't much smell good, smells in fact like unbathed, sleep-in-your-clothes mustiness. He also doesn't seem to have brushed his teeth in a while. Possibly he is reverting to nature. "The original framers, you know," I say hopefully, but instantly getting the Constitution's authors muddled up with the signers of the Declaration (my persistent miscue, though Paul would never know), "they wanted to be free to make new mistakes, not just keep making the same old ones over and over as separate colonies and without showing much progress. That's why they decided to band together and be independent and were willing to sacrifice some controls they'd always had in hopes of getting something better—in their case, better trade with the outside world."

Paul looks at me contemptuously, as if I were an old radio tuned to a droning station that's almost amusing. "Framers? Do you mean farmers?"

"Some of them *were* farmers," I say. There's no use trying to haul this business back. I'm not facilitating good contact yet. "But people who won't quit making the same mistakes over and over are what we call conservatives. And the conservatives were all against independence, including Benjamin Franklin's son, who eventually got deported to Connecticut, just like you."

"So are conservatives farmers?" he says, feigning puzzlement but ridiculing me.

"A lot of them are," I say, "though they shouldn't be. What'd your sister give you?" I'm watching his closed left fist. We are quickly coming up into the Hartford traffic bottleneck. Elaborate road construction is on the right, between the interstate and the river—a soaring new off-ramp, a new parallel lane, arrows flashing, yellow behemoths full of Connecticut earth rumbling along beside us, white men in plastic hats and white shirts standing out in the snappy hot breeze, staring at thick scrolls of plans.

Paul looks at his fist as if he has no idea of what it contains, then slowly opens it, revealing a small yellow bow, the twin of the red one Clarissa gave me. "She gave you one," he mutters. "A red one. She said you said you wanted to be her bow, but it was spelled another way." I'm shocked at what a shady, behind-the-scenes conniver my daughter is. Paul holds the two loose ends of his yellow bow and pulls them tight so the two loops daintily involute and make a knot. Then he puts the whole in his mouth and swallows it. "Umm," he says, and smiles at me evilly. "Good ribbance." (He's constructed this event, including the change in his sister's story, just for a punch line.)

"I guess I'll save mine till later."

"She gave me another one for later." He gives me his slant-eyed look. He is far ahead of me and will, I know, be a struggle.

"So okay, what's the problem with you and Charley?" I am maneuvering us past the Hartford downtown, the little gold-domed capital nearly lost in among big insurance high-rises. "Can't you two be civilized?"

"I can. He's an asshole." Paul is watching out his side as a squad of befezzed Shriners on Harleys comes alongside us. The Shriners are big, overstuffed, fat-cheeked guys dressed in gold-and-green silk harem guard getups with goggles and gloves and motorcycle boots. On their giant red Electra Glides they're as imposing as real harem guards, and of course are riding in safety-first staggered formation, their motor noise even through the closed window loud and oppressive.

"Does braining him with an oarlock seem like a good solution to his being an asshole?" This will be my lone, unfelt concession to Charley's welfare.

The lead Shriner has spied Paul and given him a grinning,

gloved thumbs-up. He and his crew are all big, jolly cream puffs, no doubt on their way to perform figure eights and seamless circles within circles for happy, grateful, shopping-center crowds, then hurry off to lead a parade down some town's Main Street.

"It's just *a* solution," Paul says, returning the lead harem guard's thumbs-up, putting his forehead to the window and grinning back sarcastically. "I like these guys. Charley should be one. What do you call them?"

"Shriners," I say, returning a thumbs-up from my side.

"What do they do?"

"It's not that easy to explain," I say, keeping us in our lane.

"I like their suits." He makes a muffled and unexpected little bark, a clipped Three Stooges, testy-terrier bark. He doesn't seem to want me to hear it but can't resist doing it again. One of the Shriners seems to catch on and makes what looks like a barking gesture of his own, then gives another thumbs-up.

"Are you barking again, son?" I sneak a look at him and swerve slightly to the right. An accident here would mean complete defeat.

"I guess so."

"Why is that? Do you think you're barking for Mr. Toby or something?"

"I *need* to do it." He's told me several times that in his view people now say "need" when they mean "want," which he thinks is hilarious. The Shriners drift back in the slow lane, probably nervous after I swerved at them. "It makes me feel better. I don't have to do it."

And frankly there's nothing I feel I can say if greeting the world with an occasional bark instead of the normal "Howzit goin'" or a thumbs-up makes him feel better. What's to get excited about? It might prove a hindrance under SAT testing conditions, or be a problem if he *only* barked and never spoke for the rest of his life. But I don't see it as that serious. No doubt, like all else, it will pass. I should probably try it. It might make *me* feel better.

"So are we going to the Basketball Hall of Fame or not?" he says, as though we'd been arguing about it. His mind is now who knows where? Possibly thinking he's thinking about Mr. Toby and thinking he wishes he weren't.

"We definitely are," I say. "It's coming up pretty quick. Are you stoked for it?"

"Yeah," he says. "Because I have to take a leak when we get there." And that's all he says for miles.

IN A HASTY thirty minutes we slide off 91 into Springfield and go touring round through the old mill town, following the disappearing brown-and-white BB. HALL OF FAME signs until we're all the way north of downtown and pulled to a halt across from a dense brick housing project on a wide and windy trash-strewn boulevard by the on-ramp to the interstate we were just on. Lost.

Here is a marooned Burger King, attended around the outside by many young black men, and beside it, beyond the parking lot, a billboard showing Governor Dukakis smiling his insincere smile and surrounded by euphoric, well-fed, healthy-looking but poor children of every race and creed and color. No garbage has been picked up here for several days, and a conspicuous number of vehicles are abandoned or pillaged along the streetside. A hall of fame, any hall of fame within twenty miles of this spot, seems not worth the risk of being shot. In fact, I'm willing to just forget the whole thing and head for the Mass Pike, turn west and strike off for Cooperstown (170 miles), which would have us rolling into the Deerslayer Inn, where I've booked us a twin, just in time for cocktail hour.

And yet to bag it would be to translate mere lost directions into defeat (a poor lesson on a voyage meant to instruct). Plus *not* going, now that we're at street level, would be tantamount to temperamental; and in my worst 3 a.m. computations of self and character, temperamental's the thing I'm not, the thing that even a so-so father mustn't be.

Paul, who is ever suspicious of my resolve, has said nothing, just stared at Governor Dukakis through the windshield as if he were the most normal thing in the world.

I therefore execute a fast U-turn back toward town, cruise right into a BP delimart, ask directions out the window from a Negro customer just leaving, who courteously routes us back onto the interstate south. And in five minutes we're on the highway then off again, but this time at a perfectly well marked BBHOF exit, at the end of which we wind around booming freeway pilings and run smack into the Hall of Fame parking lot, where many cars are parked and where a neat little grass lawn with wood benches and saplings for picnickers and reflective roundball enthusiasts borders the Connecticut, sliding by, glistening, just beyond.

When I shut the motor off, Paul and I simply sit and stare through the saplings at the old factory husks on the far side of the river as if we expected some great sign to suddenly flash up, shouting "No! Here! It's over here now! You're in the wrong place! You missed us! You've done it wrong again!"

I should, of course, seize this inert moment of arrival to introduce old Emerson, the optimistic fatalist, to the trip's agenda, haul *Self-Reliance* out of the back seat, where Phyllis had it last. In particular I might try out the astute "Discontent is the want of self-reliance; it is infirmity of will." Or else something on the order of accepting the place providence has found for you, the society of your contemporaries, the connection of events. Each seems to me immensely serviceable if, however, they aren't contradictory.

Paul twists around and frowns back at the metal-and-glass Hall of Fame edifice, which looks less like a time-honored place of legend and enshrinement than a high-tech dental clinic, with its mulberry-colored, fake concrete-slab façade being just the ticket for putting edgy patients at their ease when they arrive for the first-time-ever cleaning and prophylaxis: "Here no one will harm, overcharge or give you bad news." Above these doors, though, are cloth banners in several bright colors, spelling out BASKETBALL: AMERICA'S GAME.

As he looks back, I notice Paul has a thick, ugly, inflamed and unhealthy-looking seed wart on the side of his right hand below his little finger. I also note, to my dismay, what may be a blue tattoo on the inside of his right wrist, something that looks like what a prisoner might do and Paul may have done himself. It spells a word I can't make out, though I don't like it and decide immediately that if his mother can't pay attention to his personal self, I'll have to.

"So what's inside?" he says.

"All kinds of good stuff," I say, postponing Emerson and trying to ignore the tattoo while mounting some roundball enthusiasm, since I want to get out of the car, possibly grab a sandwich inside and make a last-ditch phone plea to S. Mantoloking. "They've got films and uniform displays and photographs and chances to shoot baskets. I sent you the brochures." I'm not making it sound spectacular enough. Driving off might still be easier.

Paul gives me a self-satisfied look, as if a picture of himself shooting a basket were a source of amusement. For half a dollar I'd give *him* a flat-hand pop in the mouth too, for having a god-damned tattoo. Though that would violate, within our first hour together, my personal commitment to quality time.

"You can stand beside a big cutout of Wilt the Stilt and see how you match up sizewise," I say. Our air-conditioning is beginning to dissipate at idle.

"Who's Milt the Stilt?"

This I know he knows. He was a Sixers fan at the time he moved away. We went to games. He saw pictures. A basket in fact is bracketed at this moment to my garage on Cleveland Street. He is now, though, onto complexer games.

"He was a famous proctologist," I say. "Anyway, let's pick up a burger. I told your mother I'd buy you a sports lunch. Maybe they'll have a slam-dunk burger."

His eyes narrow at me across the seat. His tongue flicks nervously into each corner of his mouth. He likes this. His eyelashes, I notice for the first time (also like his mother's), have become ridiculously long. I can't keep up with him. "Are you hungry enough to eat the asshole out of a dead skunk?" he says, and blinks at me brazenly.

"Yeah, I'm pretty hungry." I pop open my door and let stiff dieselly breeze, freeway slam and the gamy river scent all flood inside in one hot, lethal breath. I am also tired of him already.

"Well, you're pretty hungry, then," he says. He has no good follow-up, so that all he can say is: "Do you think I have symptoms that need treatment?"

"No, I don't think you have any symptoms, son," I say down into the car. "I think you have a personality, which may be worse in your case." I should ask him about the dead bird but can't bring myself to.

"A-balone," Paul says. I stand and gaze over the hot roof of my car, over the Connecticut, over the green west of Massachusetts, where soon we'll be driving. I feel for some reason lonely as a shipwreck. "How do you say 'I'm hungry' in Italian?" he says.

"Ciao," I say. This is our oldest-timiest, most reliable, jokey way of conducting father–son business. Only today, due to technical difficulties beyond all control, it doesn't seem exactly to work. And our words get carried off in the breeze, with no one to care if we speak the intricate language of love or don't. Being a parent can be the worst of discontents.

"Ciao," Paul says. He has not heard me. "Ciao. How soon they forget." He is climbing out now, ready for our trip inside.

ONCE IN, Paul and I wander like lost souls who have paid five bucks to enter purgatory. (I have finally quit limping.)

Strategically placed, widely modern staircases with purple velvet crowd-control cords move us and others, herd-like, all the way up to Level 3, where the theme is basketball-history-in-a-nutshell. The air, here, is hypercleaned and frigid as Nome (to discourage lingering), everyone whispers like funeral-parlor guests, and lights are low to show off various long corridors of spotlit mummy-case artifacts preserved behind glass only a multiple-warhead missile could penetrate. Here is a thumbnail bio of inventor Naismith (who turns out to have been a Canadian!), alongside a replica of the old Doc's original scrawled-on-an-envelope basketball master plan: "To devise a game to be played in a gymnasium." (Success was certainly his.) Farther on is a black-and-white picture display featuring Forrest "Phogg" Allen, beloved old Jayhawks chalkboard wizard from the Twenties, and next to that, a replica of the "original" peach basket, along with a tribute to YMCAs everywhere. On all the walls there are grainy, treasured period photos of "the game" being played in shadowy wire-window gyms by skinny unathletic white boys, plus two hundred old uniform jerseys hung from the dark rafters like ghosts in a spook house.

A few listless families enter a dark little Action Theatre, which Paul avoids by hitting the can, though I watch from the doorway as the history of the game unfolds before our preprandial eyes, while the action sounds of the game are piped in.

In eight minutes we progress briskly down to Level 2, where there's more of the same, though it's more up-to-date and recognizable, at least to me. Paul expresses a passing spectator's interest in Bob Lanier's size 22 shoe, a red-and-yellow plastic cross-section model of an as-yet-unmangled human knee, and a film viewable in another little planetarium-like theater, dramatizing how preternaturally large basketball players are and what they can all "do with the ball," in contrast to how minuscule and talentless the rest of us have to suffer through life being. In this way it is a true shrine—devoted to making ordinary people feel like insignificant outsiders, which Paul seems not to mind. (The Vince was in fact more welcoming.)

"We played at camp," he says flatly as we pause outside the amphitheater, both of us looking in as huge, muscular, uniformed black men ram ball after ball through hoop after hoop on a mesmerizing four-sided screen, to the crowd's rapt amazement and smattered applause.

"And so were you a major force," I ask. "Or an intimidator, possibly a franchise or an impact player?" I'm happy to have unfreighted exchange on any subject, though I stare at his shorts, tee-shirt and skinhead and don't like any of it. He seems to me to be in disguise.

"Not really," he says, absolutely earnest. "I can't jump. Or run. Or shoot, and I'm a lefty. And I don't give a shit. So I'm not really cut out for it."

"Lanier was a lefty," I say. "So was Russell." He may not know who they are, even though he'd recognize their shoes. The audience in the jam-o-rama amphitheater makes a low "Ooooo" of utter reverence. Other men with their boys stand beside us, looking in, uninterested in sitting down.

"We weren't really playing to win anyway," Paul says.

"What were you playing for? Fun?"

"Thur-uh-py," he says to make a joke of it, though he seems unironic. "Some of the kids would always forget what month it was, and some of them talked too loud or had seizures, which was bad. And if we played basketball, even stupid basketball, they all got better for a while. We had 'share your thoughts' after every game, and everybody had a lot better thoughts. For a while at least. Not me. Chuck played basketball at Yale." Paul's hands are in his shorts pockets as he stares at the ceiling, which is industrial modern and shadowy, with metal girders, trusses, rafters, sprinkling-system pipes, all painted black. Basketball, I think, is American's postindustrial national pastime.

"Was he any good?" I may as well ask.

"I don't know," he says, digging a finger into his mossy ear and creasing the corner of his mouth like a country hick. A second loud "Ooooo" comes from inside. Someone, a woman, shouts out, "Yes! I swear to God. Look at that!" I don't know what she saw.

"You know the one thing you can do that's truly unique to you and that society can't affect in any way?" he says. "We learned this in camp."

"I guess not." People out here with us are starting to stray away.

"Sneeze. If you sneeze in some stupid-fuck way, or in a loud way that pisses people off in movies, they just have to go along with it. Nobody can say, 'Sneeze a different way, asshole.'"

"Who told you that?"

"I don't remember."

"Does that seem unusual?"

"Yes." Gradually he lets his eyes come down from the ceiling but not to me. His finger quits excavating his ear. He is now uncomfortable for being unironic and a kid.

"Don't you know that's the way everything is when you get to be old? Everybody lets you do anything you want to. If they don't like it, they just don't show up anymore."

"Sounds great," Paul says, and actually smiles, as if such a world where people left you alone was an exhibit he'd like to see.

"Maybe it is," I say, "maybe it isn't."

"What's the most misunderstood automotive accessory?" He's ready to derail serious talk, alert to the dangers inherent in my earnest voice.

"I don't know. An air filter," I say, as the dunk-o-rama film gets over in the auditorium. I have seen no big cutout of Milt the Stilt, as was promised.

"That's pretty close." Paul nods very seriously. "It's a snow tire. You don't appreciate it until you need it, but then it's usually too late."

"Why does that make it misunderstood? Why not just under-appreciated?"

"They're the same," he says, and starts walking away.

"I see. Maybe you're right." And we both walk off then toward the stairs.

* * *

ON LEVEL 1, there's a busy gift boutique, a small room dedicated to sports media (zero fascination for me), an authentic locker room exhibit, a vending machine oasis, plus some gimmicky, hands-on exhibits Paul takes mild interest in. I decide to make my call to Sally before we hit the road. Though I have yet to see a legitimate snack bar, so that Paul wanders off in his new heavy-gaited, pigeon-toed, arm-swinging way I hate, to the vending-machine canteen with money I've supplied (since his is evidently for some other uses—a possible kidnap emergency) and my order to bring back "something good."

The phone area is a nice, secluded, low-lit little alcove beside the bathrooms, with thick, noise-muffling wall-to-wall covering everything, and the latest black phone technology—credit card slits, green computer screens and buttons to amplify sound in case you can't believe what you're hearing. It is an ideal place for a crank or ransom call.

Sally, when I punch in her 609 number, answers thrillingly on the first jingle.

"So where in the world are *you*?" she says, her voice tingly and happy but also a voice that's taking a reading. "I left you a long and poignant message last night. I may have been drunk."

"And I tried to call you right back all this morning, to see if you'd fly up here in a chartered Cessna and come to Coopers-town with us. Paul thinks it'd be great. We'd have some fun."

"Well. My goodness. I don't know," Sally says, acting happily confused. "Where are you right now?"

"Right now I'm in the Basketball Hall of Fame. I mean we're visiting it—we're not enshrined here. Not yet anyway." I feel the most buoyant good spirit expand in my chest. All is not pissed away.

"But isn't that in Ohio?"

"No, it's in Springfield, Mass, where the first peach basket was nailed to the first barn door and the rest is history. Football's in Ohio. We don't have time for that."

"Where *are* you going, again?"

She is enjoying all this, possibly relieved, acting breathless and appealed to. Plans might still spring to life. "Cooperstown, New York. One hundred seventy miles away," I say enthusiastically. A woman several nooks down leans back and glowers at me as if I were making a call that amplified my voice in her receiver.

Possibly she feels at risk being near a person in legitimately high spirits. "So whaddaya say?" I say. "Fly up to Albany right now, and we'll pick you up." I *am* talking too loud and need to put a lid on it before a Hall of Fame SWAT team is summoned. "I'm serious," I say, more modulated, but more serious too.

"Well, you're very sweet to ask."

"I *am* very sweet. That's right. But I'm not letting you off the hook." I say this a bit too loud again. "I just woke up this morning and realized I was crazy as hell last night and that I'm crazy about you. And I don't want to wait till Monday or whenever the hell." For a nickel I'd muster Paul right back to the car and beat it back down to South Mantoloking along with all the other beach yahoos. Though I'd be a bad man for doing so. Being willing to invite Sally in on our sacred hombre-to-hombre is already bad enough—though like anybody else, Paul'd have more fun being along on something technically illicit. The world, as I told him, lets you do what you want if you can live with the consequences. We're all free agents.

"Could I ask you something?" she says, two jots too serious.

"I don't know," I say. "It may be too serious. I'm not a serious man. And it can't be about you not coming up here."

"Would you tell me what you find so enthralling now that you didn't notice last night?" Sally says this in a self-mocking, good-natured way. But important info is being sought. Who could blame her?

"Well," I say, my mind suddenly whirring. A man exits the bathroom, so that I get a stern whiff of urinal soap. "You're a grown-up, and you're exactly the way you seem, at least as far as I can tell. Everybody's not like that." Including me. "And you're loyal and you have a quality of straight-talking impartiality"—this sounds wrong—"that isn't inconsistent with passion, which I *really* like. I guess I just have a feeling some things have to be investigated further between you and me or we'll both be sorry. Or *I* will anyway. Plus, you're just about the prettiest woman I know."

"I'm just about *not* the prettiest woman you know," Sally says. "I'm pretty in a usual way. And I'm forty-two. And I'm too tall." She sighs as though being tall made her tired.

"Look, just get on a plane and come up here, and we'll talk all about how pretty you are or aren't while the moon sets on

romantic Lake Otsego and we enjoy a complimentary cocktail."
While Paul goes who knows where? "I just feel a tidal attraction
to you, and all boats rise on a rising tide."

"Your boat seems to rise most when I'm not around," Sally
says with distinctly diminished good nature. (It's possible I'm not
providing convincing answers again.) The woman in the far
phone nook snaps closed an immense black patent-leather purse
and goes striding quickly out. "Do you remember saying you
wanted to be the 'dean' of New Jersey realtors last night? Do you
even remember that? You talked all about soybeans and drought
and shopping centers. We drank a lot. But you were in a state of
some kind. You also said you were beyond affection. Maybe
you're still in some state." (I should probably toss off a couple of
barks to prove I'm nuts.) "Did you visit your wife?"

This is not the wisest tack for her to take, and I should actually
warn her off. But I simply stare at my little black phone screen,
where it states in cool green letters: *Do you wish to make another
call?*

"Right. I did," I say.

"And how was that—was that nice?"

"Not particularly."

"Do you think you like her better when she's not around?"

"She's not 'not around,' " I say. "We're divorced. She's remarried to a sea captain. It's like Wally. She's *officially* dead, only
we still talk." I'm suddenly as deflated by a thought of Ann as
I was happy to be thinking of Sally, and what I'm tempted to say
is, "But the real surprise is she's leaving ole Cap'n Chuck, and
we're getting married again and moving to New Mexico to start
up an FM station for the blind. That's really the reason I'm
calling—not to invite you to come up here, just to give you my
good news. Aren't you happy for me?" There's an unwieldy
silence on the line, after which I say: "I really just called up to
say I had a good time last night."

"I wish you'd stayed. That's what my message said, if you
haven't heard it yet." Now she is mum. Our little contretemps
and my little rising tide have gone off together in a stout, chilly
breeze. Good spirits are notoriously more fragile than bad.

A tall, big-chested man in a pale-blue jumpsuit comes strolling down the phone alcove, holding a little girl by the hand.
They stop along the opposite phone bank, where the man begins

to make a call, reading off a paper scrap as the little girl, in a frilly pink skirt and a white cowboy shirt, watches him. She looks at me across the shadowy way—a look, like mine, of needing sleep.

"Are you still there?" Sally says, possibly apologetic.

"I was watching a guy make a phone call. I guess he reminds me of Wally, though he shouldn't, since I don't think I ever saw Wally."

Another mum pause. "You really have very few sharp angles, you know, Frank. You're too smooth from one thing to the next. I can't keep up with you very well."

"That's what my wife thinks too. Maybe you two should discuss it. I think I'm just more at ease in the mainstream. It's my version of sublime."

"And you're also very cautious, you know," Sally says. "And you're noncommittal. You know that, don't you? I'm sure that's what you meant last night about being beyond affection. You're smooth and you're cautious and you're noncommittal. That's not a very easy combination for me." (Or a good one, I'm sure.)

"My judgments aren't very sound," I say, "so I just try not to cause too much trouble." Joe Markham said something like this yesterday. Maybe I'm being transformed into Joe. "But when I feel something strong, I guess I jump in. That's how I feel right now." (Or did.)

"Or you seem to anyway," Sally says. "Are you and Paul having lots of fun?" A shift back in the direction of rising spirits, speaking of smooth.

"Yeah. Loads and loads. You would too." I get a faint but putrid sniff of the dead grackle still on my receiver hand. Apparently it's to be on my skin forever and ever. I intend to ignore this last remark about *seeming* to jump in.

"I'm sorry you don't think your judgment's very sound," Sally says, falsely perky. "That doesn't bode very well for how you say you feel about me either, does it?"

"Whose cuff links were those on the bed table?" This, of course, is rash and against all good judgment. But I'm indignant, even though I have no good right to be.

"They were Wally's," Sally says, perky but not falsely. "Did you think they belonged to somebody else? I just got them out to send to his mother."

"Wally was in the Navy, I thought. He almost got blown up in a boat. Isn't that right?"

"He did. But he was in the Marines. Not that it matters. You just made up the Navy for him. It's all right."

"Okay. Yeah, I was callin' about this house you got for rent on Friar Tuck Drive," I hear the big man say across the alcove. His little girl is staring up at her dad/unc/abductor as if he'd told her he needed some moral support and she should focus all her thoughts his way. "What's the rent on that one?" he says. He is a southwesterner, possibly a twangy Texan. Though he isn't wearing dusty old Noconas but a pair of white Keds no-lace low-tops of the male-nurse/minimum-security-prisoner variety. These are Texans without a ranch. My guess is he's busted out of the oil patch, a new-age Joad moving his precious little brood up to the rust belt to set life spinning in a new orbit. It occurs to me the McLeods may likewise be in hot financial water and be in need of a break but are too stubborn to say so. That would change my attitude about the rent, though not totally.

"Frank, did you hear what I said, or have you just drifted off into space?"

"I was watching the same guy trying to rent a house. I wish I had something I could show him in Springfield. Of course, I don't live here."

"Okay-yay," Sally says, ready for our conversation to float off too. I have registered whose cuff links they were, though they aren't any of my business. The Navy–Marine mixup I can't explain. "Is it pretty up there?" she asks brightly.

"Yeah, it's beautiful. But really," I say, suddenly picturing Sally's face, a winning face, worth wanting to kiss. "Don't you want to come up here? I'm popping for everything. Your money's no good. All you can eat. Double stamps. Carte blanche."

"Why don't you just call me some other time, okay? I'll be home tonight. You're very distracted. You're probably tired."

"Are you sure? I'd really like to see you." I should mention that I'm not beyond affection, because I'm not.

"I'm sure," she says. "And I'm just going to say good-bye now."

"Okay," I say. "Okay."

"Good-bye now," she says, and we hang up.

The little cowgirl across the alcove gives me a fretful look.

Possibly I was talking too loud again. Her big Texan daddy swivels half around to look at me. He has a big tough-jawed face, unruly dark hair and enormous pipe-fitter's mitts. "No," he says decisively into the phone. "No, that ain't gonna work, that's way outa line. Forget that." He hangs up, crumpling his little scratch of paper, which he drops on the carpet.

He fishes in his breast pocket, pulls out a pack of Kools, takes one out with his mouth, still holding little Suzie's hand, lights up one-handed with a thick, mean-looking Zippo. He blows a big, frustrated, lung-shuddering drag right at the international NO SMOKING insignia attached to the carpeted ceiling, and I immediately expect to be drenched in cold chemicals, for alarms to trigger, security people to skid around the corner on the dead run. But nothing happens. He gives me an antagonistic look where I'm lost in front of my phone screen. "You got a problem?" he says, fishing back in his cigarette pocket for something he doesn't find.

"No," I say, grinning. "I just have a daughter about your daughter's age"—a total fabrication, followed hard by another one—"and she just reminded me of her."

The man looks down at the child, who must be eight and who looks up at him smiling, charmed by being noticed but unsure exactly how to be charmed. "You want me to sell this one to you?" he says, at which moment the little girl throws her head back and lets her whole self go limp so she's hanging off his big mitt, smiling and shaking her pretty head.

"Nope, nope, nope, nope, nope," she says.

"They're too expensive for me," he says in his Texas accent. He raises his child off the ground, limp as a carcass, and gives her a dainty little swing out.

"You cain't sell me," she says in a throaty, bossy voice. "I'm not for sale."

"You're for sale big time, that's whut," he says. I smile at his joke—a helpless fatherish way of expressing love to a stranger in a time of hardship. I should appreciate it. "You don't have a house to rent, do you?"

"Sorry," I say. "I'm not from Springfield. I'm just here for a visit. My son's running around in here someplace."

"You know how long it takes to get up here from Oklahoma?" he says, his cigarette in one side of his big mouth.

"It's probably not that quick."

"Two days, two nights straight. And we been in the KOA for three damn days. I got a highway job starts up in a week, and I can't find anything. I'm gonna have to send this orphan back."

"Not me," the little girl says in her bossy voice and lets her knees give way, hanging on. "I'm not an orphan."

"You!" the big guy says to his daughter and frowns, though not angrily. "You're my whole damn problem. If I didn't have you with me, *somebody* would've been considerate of me by now." He gives me a big leer and a roll of the eyes. "Stand up on your feet, Kristy."

"You're a redneck," his daughter says, and laughs.

"I might be, and I might be worse than that," he says more seriously. "You think your daughter's like this outfit?" He's already starting to walk away, holding his daughter's tiny hand in his great one.

"They're both pretty sweet when they want to be, I bet," I say, watching his child's quick knock-kneed steps and thinking of Clarissa giving Ann and me, or possibly just me, the finger. "The holiday'll probably change everything." Though I don't know how. "I'll bet you find someplace to stay today."

"It's that or drastic measures," he says, walking away toward the lobby.

"What's that mean?" his daughter says, hanging onto his hand. "What's drastic measures?"

"Being your ole man, for starters," he says, as they go out of sight. Then he adds, "But it might mean a whole lot of things too."

PAUL, WHEN I walk out to find him, is not waiting with an arm-load of vending-machine provisions but has taken up an observer position alongside "The Shoot-Out" exhibit, which dominates one whole wall-side of Level 1 and where a lot of visitors have already become noisy participators.

"The Shoot-Out" is nothing more than a big humming people-mover conveyor belt, just like in an airport, but built right alongside and at the same level as a spotlit arena area, full of basketball backboards, hoops and posts, at varying heights and distances from the belt—ten feet, five yards, two feet, ten yards. Along beside the moving handrail and between the little arena and the people-mover itself, a trough of basketballs is continuously being replenished through a suction tube under the floor, exactly in the manner of a bowling alley rack. A human being getting on the moving floor (as many already are) and traveling at approximately one half of one mile an hour, can simply pick up ball after ball and shoot basket after basket— jump shots, hooks, two-hand sets, over the back, one's whole repertoire—until he reaches the other end, where he steps off. (Such a screwy but ingenious machine has undoubtedly been invented by someone with a dual major in Crowd Control and Automated Playground Management from Southern Cal, and anybody in his right mind would've fought to get ground-floor money in on it. In fact, if the Hall of Fame management didn't insist that you first mull past murky old Phogg Allen pictures and replicas of Bob Lanier's dogs, everyone would spend his whole visit right down here where the real action is, and the rest of the building could go back to being a dentist's office.)

A pocket-size grandstand has been built just on the other side of the conveyor, and plenty of spectators are up there now, noisily ya-hooing and razzing their kids, brothers, nephews, stepsons who're taking the ride and trying to shoot the eyes out of all the baskets.

Paul, who's on the sidelines by the entrance gate, where there's a line of kids waiting to get on, seems on the alert, as though he were running the whole contraption. He is, however, watching a scrappy, thick-thighed white kid in a New York Knicks uniform, who's hustling around among the backboards, kicking trapped balls toward the suction tube gutter, tipping stuck balls out of the nets, snapping vicious passes back at kids on the conveyor and occasionally taking a graceless little short-armed hook shot, which always goes in, no matter what basket he shoots at. No doubt he's the manager's son.

"Did you try out your patented two-hand set yet?" I say, coming up right behind Paul and over the noise. I instantly smell his sour sweat smell when I put my hand on his shoulder. There's also, I can see, a thick scabby jag in his scalp, where whoever authored his skint haircut made a mistake. (Where are such things done?)

"That'd be good, wouldn't it," he says coldly, going on watching the white kid. "That nitwit thinks because he works here his game's gonna improve. Except the floor's tilted and the baskets aren't regulation. So he's actually fucked." This seems to make him satisfied. He has purchased no food that I can see.

"You better give it a try," I say over the basketball clatter and the thrum the giant machine's making. I feel exactly like a dad among other real dads, encouraging my son to do what he doesn't want to do because he's afraid he'll be bad at it.

"D'you always dribble before you shoot?" someone in the bleachers shouts out at the moving conveyor. A short bald man who's about to try a precarious hook shot yells back without even looking: "Why don't you try eating me," then wings a shot that misses everything and causes other people in the bleachers to laugh.

"You do it." Paul snorts a disparaging little snuffle. "I saw some Nets scouts in the crowd." The Nets are his favorite team to belittle, because they're no good and from New Jersey.

"Okay, but then *you* have to do it." I cuff his shoulder in an unnatural comradely way, catching another unappetizing look at his offended ear.

"I don't *have* to do anything," he says without looking at me, just watching the bright, indoor air a-throng with orange balls.

"Okay, you just watch me, then," I say lamely.

I step around him and into line and am quickly right up to the little gate behind a small black kid. I take a look back at Paul, who's watching me, leaning an elbow on the plywood fence that separates the arena from the waiting line, his face completely unawed, as if he expects to see me do something stupid beyond all previous efforts.

"Check out how my balls rotate," I call back at him, hoping it'll embarrass him, but he doesn't seem to hear me.

And then I'm up on the rumbling belt, moving right to left as the rack of balls and the little forest of stage-lit baskets, backboards and poles begins quickly gliding past in the opposite way. I'm instantly nervous about falling down, and don't make a move toward a ball. The black kid in front of me has on a huge purple-and-gold team jacket that says *Mr. New Hampshire Basketball* on the back in sparkling gold letters, and he seems able to handle at least three balls at any one time, virtually spewing shots at every goal, every height, every distance, and with each shot emitting a short, breathy *whoof* like a boxer throwing a punch. And of course everything goes spinning in: a bank, a set, a one-hander, a fall-away, a short-arm hook like the ball boy's—everything but an alley-oop and a lean-in power jam.

I lay hands on my first ball halfway through the ride, still not confident about my balance, my heart suddenly starting to beat fast because other shooters are behind me. I frown out toward the clutter of red metal posts and orange baskets, set my feet as well as I can, cock the ball behind my ear and heave up a high arching shot that misses the basket I expected to hit, strikes a lower one, bounces out and nearly drops in the very lowest goal, which I hadn't actually seen.

I quick grab another ball as Mr. New Hampshire Basketball is putting up shot after shot, making his stagy little *whoof* noise and hitting nothing but net. I take similar aim at a medium-height basket at a medium distance, hoist my shot off one-handed, though well gyroed by a good rotation I learned from watching TV, and come pretty damn close to making it, though one of Mr. Basketball's shots hisses through just ahead and knocks mine down off into the gutter. (I also lose my balance and have to grab the plastic escalator handrail to keep from falling over sideways and causing a pileup.) Mr. B. flashes me a suspicious look over his gigantic purple roll collar, as if I'd been trying to mess with his head. I smile at him and mutter, "Lucky."

"You're supposed to dribble *before* you shoot, you cluck," the same idiot yorks out again amid a lot of other shouting and metallic hum and machinery smell. I turn around and take a squinty look at the crowd, which is essentially invisible because of the bright lights on the baskets. I don't really give a shit who yelled at me, though I'm sure it's not someone whose son is in the audience, smirking.

I complete one more wayward shot before I'm to the end—a lumpy, again off-balance one-hander that clears everything and drops behind the baskets and the wooden barrier, where basketballs aren't supposed to go. "Good arch!" the little wiseacre gymrat kid cracks as he climbs back to retrieve my ball. "Wanna play horse for a million bucks?"

"Maybe I'll have to start trying, then," I say, my heart pounding as I step off the belt onto terra firma, all the excitement over now.

Mr. New Hampshire Basketball is already walking away

toward the sports-media gallery with his father, a tall black man in a green silk Celtics jacket and matching green leisure pants, his long arm over the boy's scrawny shoulders, no doubt laying out a superior strategy for rubbing off the screen, picking up the dribble, taking the J while drawing the foul—all just words to me, a former sportswriter, with no practical application on earth.

Paul is staring at me down the length of the conveyor. Conceivably he's been barking his approval while I've been shooting but doesn't want it known now. I have in fact enjoyed the whole thing thoroughly.

"Take your best shot!" I shout through the loud crowd noise. The ball boy, off to one side now, is chatting up his chunky, pony-tailed blond sweetheart, laying his two meaty hands on her two firm shoulders and goo-gooing in her eyes like Clark Gable. For some reason, having I'm sure to do with queuing theory, no one is on the conveyor at the moment. "Come on," I shout at Paul with false rancor. "You can't do any worse than I did!" Only a few spectators remain in the darkened grandstand. Others are heading off to other exhibits. It is the perfect time for Paul. "Come on, Stretch," I say—something I vaguely remember from a sports movie.

Paul's lips move—words I just as well can't hear. A jocose "Up your ass" or a lusty "Why don't you eat shit"—his favorite swear words from another, antique vintage (mine). He looks behind him, where there's now mostly empty lobby, then just ambles slowly up to the entrance in his clumsy, toes-in gait, pauses to look down toward me again with what appears to be disgust, stares for a moment at the spotlit baskets and stanchions, and then simply steps on, completely alone.

The conveyor moves him seemingly much more slowly than I myself was moved, and certainly leisurely enough to get off six or seven good shots and even to dribble before he shoots. The ball boy takes a casually demeaning look to where Paul is moving along in his garbage-pail shoes and sinister haircut, hands fixed oddly on his hips. He cracks a nasty grin, says something to his girlfriend so she'll look, which she does, though in a kinder, more indulgent older-girl's way at the goony boy who can't help being goony but has a big heart and racks up top math scores (which he doesn't).

When he comes to the end—having faced the baskets the

whole way, never once looking at me, just staring into the little arena like a mesmerist, never taking a shot or even touching a ball, only gliding—he just wobbles off on the carpet and walks over and stands by me, where I've been watching like any other dad.

"High fives," a straggler shouts in a ridiculing voice from the grandstand.

"Next time think about trying a shot," I say, ignoring the shout, since I'm happy with his efforts.

"Are we coming back here anytime soon?" He looks at me, his small gray eyes showing concern.

"No," I say. "You can come back with *your* son." Another batch of adults is invading the bleachers, with more sons and daughters plus a few dads beginning to line up at the gate, checking out how the whole gizmo works, calculating the fun they're about to have.

"I liked that," Paul says, looking at the stage-lit posts and baskets. I hear the surprising voice of some boy he once was (seemingly only a month ago, now disappeared). "I'm thinking I'm thinking all the time, you know? Except when I was on that thing I quit. It was nice."

"Maybe you should do it again," I say, "before it gets crowded." Unhappily, there's no way for him to stay on The Shoot-Out for the rest of his days.

"No, that's okay." He's watching new kids glide away from the gate, new balls arching into the vivid air, the first inevitable misses. "I don't usually like things like that. This was an exception. I don't usually like things I'm supposed to like." He stares at the other kids empathetically. This cannot be a simple truth to admit to your father—that you don't like the things you're supposed to like. It is adult wisdom, though most grown men would fail of it.

"Your ole man isn't very good at it either. If it makes you feel any better. He'd like to be. Maybe you can tell me what you liked about it that made you quit thinking you're thinking."

"You're not that old." Paul looks at me peevishly.

"Forty-four."

"Umm," he says—a thought possibly too fretsome to speak. "You could still improve."

"I don't know," I say. "Your mother doesn't think so." This doesn't qualify as a current event.

"Do you know the best airline?"

"No, let's hear it."

"Northwest," Paul says seriously. "Because it flies to the Twin Cities of Minneapolis and Saint Paul." And suddenly he's trying to suppress a big guffaw. For some reason this is funny.

"Maybe I'll take you out there sometime on a camping trip." I watch basketballs fill the interior air like bubbles.

"Do they have a hall of fame in Minnesota?"

"Probably not."

"Okay, good," he says. "We can go anytime, then."

ON OUR way out we make a fast foray through the gift boutique. Paul, at my instruction, picks out tiny gold basketball earrings for his sister and a plastic basketball paperweight for his mother— gifts he feels uncertain they'll like, though I tell him they will. We discuss a rabbit's foot with a basketball attached as an olive branch gesture for Charley, but Paul goes balky after staring at it a minute. "He has everything he wants," he says grudgingly, without adding "including your wife and your kids." So that after buying two tee-shirts for ourselves, we pass back out into the parking lot with Charley ungifted, which suits both of us perfectly.

On the asphalt it is full, hot Massachusetts afternoon. New cars have arrived. The river has gone ranker and more hazy. We've spent forty-five minutes in this hall of fame, which pleases me since we got our fill, exchanged words of hope, encountered specific subjects of immediate interest and concern (Paul thinking he's thinking) and seem to have emerged a unit. A better start than I expected.

The big, jumpsuited Oklahoman is sprawled out with his tiny daughter under one of the linden saplings by the river's retaining wall. They are enjoying their lunch from tinfoil packets spread on the ground, and drinking out of an Igloo cooler, using paper cups. He has his Keds and socks off and his pants rolled up like a farmer. Little Kristy is as pristine as an Easter present and talking to him in a confidential, animated way, wiggling one of his toes with her two hands while he stares at the sky. I'm tempted to wander over and offer a word of parting, talk to them twice because I've talked to them once, act as a better welcome committee for the Northeast Corridor, dream up some insider dope "I just thought about" and am glad to find him still here to share—something in the realty line. As always, I'm moved by the displacement woes of other Americans.

Only there's nothing I know that he doesn't (such is the nature of realty lore), and I decide against it and just stand at my car door and watch them respectfully—their backs to me, their modest picnic offering this big, panoramic, foreign-seeming river as comfort and company, all their hopes focused on a new settlement. Some people do nicely on their own and by the truest reckoning set themselves down where they'll be happiest.

"Care to guess how hungry I am?" Paul says over the hot car roof, waiting for me to unlock his side. He is squinting in the sun, looking unsavory as a little perpetrator.

"Let's see," I say. "You were supposed to get us something from the fucking vending machines." I say "fucking" just to amuse him. The freeway pounds along behind us—cars, vans, U-Hauls, buses—America on a move-in Saturday afternoon.

"I guess I just fucked up," he says to challenge me back. "But I could eat the asshole out of a dead Whopper." An insolent leer further disfigures his pudgy kid's features.

"Soup'd be better on an empty brain," I say, and pop his door lock.

"Okay, doc-taaah! Doc-tah, doc-tah, doc-tah," he says, snapping open his door and ducking in. I hear him bark in the car. "Bark, bark, bark, bark." I don't know what this is to signify: happiness (like a real dog)? Happiness's defeat at the hands of uncertainty? Fear and hope, I seem to remember from someplace, are alike underneath.

From the linden tree shade, Kristy hears something in the afternoon breeze—a dog barking somewhere, my son in our car. She turns and looks toward me, puzzled. I wave at her, a fugitive wave her bumpkin father doesn't see. Then I duck my own head into the hot-as-an-oven car with my son and we are on our way to Cooperstown.

AT ONE O'CLOCK, we pull in for a pit stop, and I send Paul for a sack of Whalers and Diet Pepsi while I wash dead grackle off my hand in the men's. And then we're off spinning again down the pike, past the Appalachian Trail and through the lowly Berkshires, where not long ago Paul was a camper at Camp Unhappy, though he makes no mention of it now, so screwed down is he into his own woolly concerns—thinking he's thinking, silently barking, his penis possibly tingling.

After a half hour of breathing Paul's sour-meat odor, I make a suggestion that he take off his *Happiness Is Being Single* shirt and put on his new one for a change of scenery and as an emblematic suiting-up for the trip. And to my surprise he agrees, skinning the old fouled one off right in the seat, unabashedly exposing his untanned, unhairy and surprisingly jiggly torso. (Possibly he'll be a big fatty, unlike Ann or me; though it doesn't make any difference if he will simply live past fifteen.)

The new shirt is Xtra large, long and white, with nothing but a big super-real orange basketball on its front and the words *The Rock* underneath in red block letters. It smells new and starched and chemically clean and, I'm hoping, will mask Paul's unwashed, gunky aroma until we check into the Deerslayer Inn, he can take a forced bath and I can throw his old one away on the sly.

For a while after our Whalers, Paul again grows moodily silent, then heavy-eyed, then slips off to a snooze while green boiler-plate Massachusetts countryside scrolls past on both sides. I turn on the radio for a holiday weather and traffic check and conceivably to learn the facts of last night's murder, which, for all the time and driving that's elapsed, occurred only eighty miles south, still well within the central New England area, the small radar sweep of grief, loss, outrage. But nothing comes in on AM or FM, only the ordinary news of holiday fatality: six for Connecticut, six for Mass., two for Vermont, ten for NY; plus five drownings, three boating *per se*, two falls from high places, one choking, one "fireworks related." No knifings. Evidently last night's death was not charged to the holiday.

I "seek" around then, happy to have Paul out of action and for my mind to find its own comfort level: a medical call-in from Pittsfield offers "painless erection help"; a Christian money-matters holiday radiothon from Schaghticoke is interpreting the Creator's views on Chapter 13 filings (He thinks some are okay). Another station profiles lifers in Attica selling Girl Scout cookies "in the population." "We *do* think we shouldn't be totally prevented from adding to the larger good"—laughter from other cons—"but we don't go around knocking on each other's cells wearing little green outfits either." Though a falsetto voice adds, "Not this afternoon anyway."

I turn it off as we get into the static zone at the New York border. And with my son beside me, his scissored and gouged head against his cool window glass, his mind in some swarming, memory-plagued darkness which causes his fingers to dance and his cheek to twitch like a puppy's in a dream of escape, my own mind bends with unexpected admiration toward meisterbuilder O'Dell's big blue house on the knoll; and to what a great, if impersonal, true-to-your-dreams *home* it is—a place any modern family of whatever configuration or marital riggery ought to feel lamebrained not to make a reasonably good go of life in. A type of "go" I could never quite catch the trick of, even in the most halcyon days, when we all were a tidy family in our own sub-stantial house in Haddam. I somehow could never create a sufficiently thick warp and woof, never manufacture enough domestic assumables that we could get on to assuming them. I was always gone too much with my sportswriting work; never felt owning was enough different from renting (except that you couldn't leave). In my mind a sense of contingency and the pos-sibility of imminent change in status underlay everything, though we stayed for more than a decade, and I stayed longer. It always seemed to me enough just to know that someone loved you and would go on loving you forever (as I tried to convince Ann again today, and she rejected again), and that the *mise-en-scène* for love was only that and not a character in the play itself.

Charley of course is of the decidedly *other* view, the one that believes a good structure implies a good structure (which is why he's so handy with plain truth: he has the mind of a true Republican). It was fine with him, as I happen to know via discreet inquiries, that his old man owned a seat on the commodities exchange, kept an unadvertised pied-à-terre on Park Avenue, supported an entire Corsican second family in Forest Hills, was barely a gray eminence whom young Charles hardly ever saw and referred to only as "Father" when he hap-pened to catch a glimpse (never Dad or Herb or Walt or Phil). All was jake as long as there was a venerable old slate-roofed, many-chimneyed, thickly pillared, leaded-glass-windowed, deep-hedged, fieldstone Georgian *residence* reliably there in Old

Greenwich, reeking of fog and privet and boat varnish, brass polish, damp tennies and extra trunks you could borrow in the poolhouse. This, in Charley's view, constitutes life and no doubt truth: strict physical moorings. A roof over your head to prove you have a head. Why else be an architect?

And for some reason now, tooling along westward with my son in tow—and not because either of us gives a particular shit about baseball, but because we simply have no properer place to go for our semi-sacred purposes—I feel Charley might just not be wrong in his rich-boy's manorial worldview. It might *be* better if things were more anchored. (Vice President Bush, the Connecticut Texan, would certainly agree.)

Though there's something in me that's possibly a little off and which I'm sure would make finding firm anchorage a problem. I'm not, for instance, as optimistic as one ought to be (relations with Sally Caldwell are a good example); or else I'm much too optimistic (Sally qualifies again). I don't come back from bad events as readily as one should (or as I used to); or else the reverse—I'm too adept at forgetting and don't remember enough of what it is I'm supposed to resume (the Markhams serve here). And for all my insistent prating that they—the Markhams—haul themselves into clearer view, I've never seen myself all that exactly, or as sharing the frame with those others I might share it with—causing me often to be far too tolerant to those who don't deserve it; or, where I myself am concerned, too little sympathetic when I should be more. These uncertainties contribute, I'm sure, to my being a classic (and possibly chickenshit) liberal, and may even help to drive my surviving son nutty and set him barking and baying at the moon.

Though specifically where he is concerned, I dearly wish I could speak from some more established *place*—the way Charley would were he the father of the first part—rather than from this constellation of stars among which I smoothly orbit, traffic and glide. Indeed, if I could see myself as occupying a fixed point rather than being in a process (the quiddity of the Existence Period), things might grow better for us both—myself and barking son. And in this Ann may simply be right when she says children are a signature mark of self-discovery and that what's wrong with Paul is nothing but what's wrong with us. Though how to change it?

*   *   *

SPIRITING ON across the Hudson and past Albany—the "Capital Region"—I am on the lookout now for I-88, the blue Catskills rising abruptly into view to the south, hazy and softly solid, with smoky mares' tails running across the range. Following his nap Paul has fished into his Paramount bag and produced a Walkman and a copy of *The New Yorker*. He's inquired moodily about the availability of tapes, and I've offered my "collection" from the glove compartment: Crosby, Stills and Nash from 1970, which is broken; Laurence Olivier reading Rilke, also broken; *Ol' Blue Eyes Does the Standards*, Parts I and II, which I bought one lonely night from an 800 number in Montana; two sales motivation speeches all agents were given in March and that I have yet to listen to; plus a tape of myself reading *Doctor Zhivago* (to the blind), given as a Christmas gift by the station manager who thought I'd done a bang-up job and ought to get some pleasure from my efforts. I've never put it on either, since I'm not that much for tapes. I still prefer books.

Paul tries the *Doctor Zhivago*, tunes it in on his Walkman for approximately two minutes, then begins looking at me with an expression of phony, wide-eyed astoundment and eventually says, his earphones still on, "This is very revealing: 'Ruffina Onissimovna was a woman of advanced views, entirely unprejudiced and well disposed toward everything that she called positive and vital.' " He smiles a narrow, belittling smile, though I say nothing, since for some reason it embarrasses me. He clicks in the Sinatra then, and I can hear Frank's tiny buzzy-bee voice deep inside his ear jacks. Paul picks up his *New Yorker* and begins reading in stony silence.

But almost the instant we're south of Albany and out of sight of its unlovely civic skyscrapers, all vistas turn wondrous and swoopingly dramatic and as literary and history-soaked as anything in England or France. A sign by a turnout announces we have now entered the CENTRAL LEATHERSTOCKING AREA, and just beyond, as if on cue, the great corrugated glacial trough widens out for miles to the southwest as the highway climbs, and the butt ends of the Catskills cast swart afternoon shadows onto lower hills dotted by pocket quarries, tiny hamlets and pristine farmsteads with wind machines whirring to undetectable winds. Everything out ahead suddenly says, "A helluva massive continent lies this way, pal, so you better be mindful." (It's the perfect landscape for a not very good novel, and I'm sorry I didn't bring my four-in-one Cooper to read aloud after dinner and once we're staked out on the porch. It would beat being taunted about *Doctor Zhivago*.)

In my official view, absolutely nothing should be missed from here on, geography offering a natural corroboration to Emerson's view that power resides in moments of transition, in "shooting the gulf, in darting to an aim." Paul could do himself a heap of good to set aside his *New Yorker* and try contemplating his own status in these useful terms: transition, jettisoning the past. "Life only avails, not having lived." I should've bought a tape of it and not a book.

But he's locked down in a bit-lip sound cocoon of "Two sweethearts in the summer wind," and reading "Talk of the Town" with his lips moving, and couldn't give a sweet rat's fart about what interesting movie's playing outside his window. Traveling *is* finally a fool's paradise.

I make a brief scenic turnout below Cobleskill to stretch my back (my coccyx has now begun aching). Leaving Paul in the seat, I climb out into the little breezy lot and walk to the sandstone parapet beyond which the luminous Pleistocene valley leaps out stark and vast and green and brown-peaked with the animal grandeur of an inland empire any bona fide pioneer would've quaked before trying to tame. I actually climb onto the wall and take several deep clean breaths, do several strenuous jumping jacks and squat thrusts, touch my toes, pop my fingers, rotate my neck as the sweet odors float in on the watery air. Beyond me hawks soar, martins dip, a tiny airplane buzzes, a distant hang glider like a dragonfly wheels and sways in the rising molecules. A door in a far-off, invisible house slams audibly shut, a car horn blows, a dog barks. And visible on the hillside opposite, where the sun paints a yellow square upon the western gradient, a tractor, tiny but detectably red, halts its progress in an emerald field; a tiny, hatted figure climbs down, pauses, then starts on foot back up the hill he's tractored down. He moves for a long, slow ways above and away from his machine, turns and goes a distance along a curved rim top, then resolutely, undramatically goes over, disappears at his own pace to whatever world's beyond. It is a fine moment to savor, even alone, though I wish my son could break loose and share it.

You can lead a horse to water, but you can't make him sing opera.

I stand and stare a while at nothing in particular, my exercise ended, my back loosened, my son entombed in the car reading a magazine. The yellow square begins gradually to fade on the opposite hillside, then moves mysteriously left, darkens the green hayfield instead of lighting it, and I decide—satisfied and palpably enlivened—to pack it in.

Somebody has left a plastic bag of Styrofoam "popcorn" half out of the trash can—the pale-green kernels that Christmas wreaths or your repaired Orvis reel comes boxed in. A new warm afternoon breeze is shifting wispy kernels here and there around the lot. I stop before climbing in to jam the bag down farther and to police up what bits I can with two hands.

Paul looks up from his *New Yorker* and stares at me where I'm tidying up the asphalt around the car. I merely look back at him from my side of the window, my hands full of clingy green stuff. He fingers his cut ear under his Walkman, blinks, then slowly makes his fingers into a pistol, points it at his temple, produces a silent little "boom" sound with his lips, throws his head back in terrible mock death, then goes back to reading. It's scary. Anyone would think so. Especially a father. But it's also funny as hell. He is not so bad a boy.

SHORT-TERM destinations are by far the best.

Paul and I skirt the outskirts of Oneonta a little past five, turn north on Route 28 along the newly rose Susquehanna, and in truth are almost there. (Geography, while instructive, is also the Northeast's soundest selling point and best-kept secret, since in three hours you can stand on the lapping shores of Long Island Sound, staring like Jay Gatz at a beacon light that lures you to, or away from, your fate; yet in three hours you can be heading for cocktails damn near where old Natty drew first blood—the two locales as unalike as Seattle is to Waco.)

Route 28 takes a pretty hickory-and-maple-shaded course straight upriver through tiny postcard villages, past farms, woodlots and single-family roadside split-levels and ranches. Here is a cut-ur-own Xmas tree lot, a pick-ur-own raspberry patch and apple orchard, a second-echelon B&B tucked into a hillside sugarbush; an attack-dog academy, an ugly clear-cut bordered by a low-yield hay meadow with Guernsey cows grazing to the edge of a gravel pit.

Here you'd expect to find no planning boards, PUDs, finicky building codes, septic standards, sidewalk ordinances or ridgetop laws; just an as yet unspoilt place to site your summer cabin or mobile home where and exactly how you want it, right down the road from a good Guinea restaurant, with its own marinara and Genesee on tap, and where a 10 a.m. night owl's mass is still celebrated Sundays at St. Joe's in Milford. It's the perfect mix, in other words, of small-scale Vermont atmospherics with unpretentious, upstate hardscrabble, all an afternoon's drive from the G.W. Bridge. (Dark rumors may now and then surface that it's also a prime location for big-city muscle to off-load their mistakes, but no place is without a downside.)

Meanwhile, my spirits have taken a strong upward turn and I'd now like to try hauling Paul into a planned off-the-cuff give-and-take squarely on the notion of Independence Day itself, and to point out that the holiday isn't just a moth-bit old relic-joke with men dressed up like Uncle Sam and harem guards on hogs doing circles within circles in shopping-mall lots; but in fact it's an observance of human possibility, which applies a canny pressure on each of us to contemplate what we're dependent on (barking in honor of dead basset hounds, thinking we're thinking, penis tingling, etc.) and after that to consider in what ways we're independent or might be; and finally how we might decide—for the general good—not to worry about it much at all.

This may be the only way an as-needed parent can in good faith make contact with his son's life problems; which is to say sidereally, by raising a canopy of useful postulates above him like stars and hoping he'll connect them up to his own sightings and views like an astronomer. Anything more purely parental—wading in and doing some stern stable-cleaning about stealing rubbers, wrecking cars, kicking security personnel, braining stepfathers (who might even deserve it), torturing innocent birds, eventually hauling up his court appearance and how that might correlate inversely with coming to Haddam to live with me and after that with his chances of ever getting into Williams on a "need scholarship"—simply wouldn't work. In the dizzyingly brief time we have together, he would only retreat into raucous barking, furtive smiles and sullener silences, ending up with me in a fury and in all likelihood ferrying him back to Deep River, feeling myself to be (and being) a ruinous failure. I don't, after all, know what's wrong with him, am not even certain anything is, or that *wrong* isn't just a metaphor for something else, which may itself already be a metaphor. Though probably what's amiss, if anything, is not much different from what's indistinctly amiss with all of us at one time or another—we're not happy, we don't know why, and we drive ourselves loony trying to get better.

Paul has stashed his Walkman back in his bag and set his *New Yorker* on the dash, where it reflects distractingly in the windshield, but he has also grabbed up the slender green-jacketed Emerson off the back seat, where it's been on top of my red REALTOR windbreaker, and begun giving it a look. This is better than I could've planned, though it's clear he hasn't cracked the copy I mailed him.

"Do you think you'd rather have a child with Down's syndrome or a child with just regular mental illness?" he says, leafing casually backward through *Self-Reliance* as if it were *Time*.

"I'm pretty pleased with how you and Clarissa turned out. So I guess I'd rather have neither one." A mental mug shot of the little feral Mongoloid back in Friendly's hours ago opens a cruel vein of awareness that Paul may think he's that or heading that way.

"Choose," Paul says, still leafing. "Then give me your reasons."

On the right, outside pretty little Federalist Milford, we cruise by the Corvette Hall of Fame, a shrine Paul, if he saw it, would vigorously insist on touring since, for reasons of Charley's Old Greenwich tastes, he's claimed the Corvette as his favorite car. (He likes them, he says, because they'll melt.) Only he doesn't see it because he's looking through Emerson! (Plus, I'm now headed for the barn and a tall, stiff drink and an evening in a big wicker rocker made by native artisans working with local materials.)

"Ordinary mental illness, then," I say. "You can sometimes cure that. Down's syndrome you're pretty much stuck with."

Paul's eyes, his mother's slate-gray ones, flicker at me astutely, acknowledging something—I'm not certain what. "Sometimes," he says in a dark voice.

"Do you still want to be a mime?" We have passed out along the little Susquehanna again—more postcard corn patches, blue and white silos, more snowmobile repairs.

"I didn't *want* to be a mime. That was a joke at camp. I *want* to be a cartoonist. I just can't draw." He scratches his scalp with the warty side of his hand and sniffs, then makes a seemingly involuntary little *eeeck* noise back in his throat, grimaces, then stations both hands in front of his face, palms out, doing the man-in-the-glass-box and, looking over at me, still grimacing, silently mouthing "Help me, help me." He then quits and immediately begins flipping Emerson pages backward again. "What's this supposed to be about?" He stares down at the page he happens to have opened. "Is it a novel?"

"It's a terrific book," I say, uncertain how to promote it. "It's got—"

"You've got a lot of things underlined in it," Paul says. "You must've had it in college." (A rare reference to my having had a life prior to his. For a boy in the clench of the past, he has little interest in life before his own. My or his mother's family history, for instance, lack novelty. Not that I entirely blame him.)

"You're welcome to read it."

"Wel-come, welcome," he says to mock me. "And that's the *way* it is, Frank," he says, reverting to his Cronkite voice again, staring down at *Self-Reliance* on his lap as though it interested him.

Then almost surprisingly we are on the south fringes of Cooperstown, coming in past a fenced sale lot packed with used speedboats, another lot with "bigfoot" trucks, a prim white Methodist church with a VACATION BIBLE SCHOOL sign, right in line with a smattering of neat, overpriced, Forties-vintage mom and pop motels with their lots already full of luggage-crammed sedans and station wagons. At the actual village limits sign, a big new billboard demands the passerby "Vote Yes!" However, I see no signs for the Deerslayer or the Hall of Fame, which simply means to me that Cooperstown doesn't put its trust in celebrity or glamour but prefers standing on its own civic feet.

" 'The great man,' " Paul reads in a pseudo-reverent Charlton Heston voice, " 'is he who in the midst of the crowd keeps with perfect sweetness the independence of solitude.' Blah, blah, blah, blah-blah, blah, blah. Glub, glub, glub. 'The objection to conforming to usages that have become dead to you is that it scatters your force. It loses your time and blurs the impression of your character.' Quack, quack, quack, quack. I am the great man, the grape man, the grapefruit, I am the fish stick—"

"To be great is usually to be misunderstood," I say, watching traffic and looking for signs. "That's a good line for you to remember. There're some other good ones."

"I've got enough things I remember already," he says. "I'm drowning. Glub, glub, glub." He raises his hands and makes swimming-drowning motions, then makes a quick, confidential *eeeck* like an old gate needing oiling, then grimaces again.

"Reading it's good enough, then. There's not going to be a test."

"Test. Tests make me really mad," Paul says, and suddenly with his dirty fingers rips out the page he's just read from.

"Don't do that!" I make a grab for it, crunching the green cover so that I dent its shiny paper. "You have to be a complete nitwit asshole to do that!" I stuff the book between my legs, though Paul still has the torn page and is folding it carefully into quarters. This qualifies as oppositional.

"I'll keep it instead of remembering it." He maintains his poise, while mine's all lost. He sticks the folded page into his shorts pocket and looks out his window the other way. I am glaring at him. "I just took a page from your book." He says this in his Heston voice. "Do you by the way see yourself as a complete failure?"

"At what?" I say bitterly. "And get this fucking *New Yorker* off the dashboard." I grab it and wing it in the back. We're now encountering increased vehicular traffic, entering shady little bendy-narrow village streets. Two paperboys sit side by side on a street corner, folding from stacks of afternoon papers. Outside, the air—which of course I can't feel—looks cool and moist and inviting, though I'm sure it's hot.

"At anything." He makes his little *eeeck* sound far down his throat, as if I'm not supposed to hear it.

My chest feels emptied with outrage and regret (over a page in a book?), but I answer because I'm asked. "My marriage to your mother and your upbringing. These haven't been the major accomplishments in my current term. Everything else is absolutely great, though." I am gaunt with how little I want to be in the car alone with my son, only barely arrived upon the storied streets of our destination. My jaw has gone steely, my back aches again and the interior feels thick and airless, as if I'm being gassed by fearsome dread. I wish to a lonely, faraway and inattentive god that Sally Caldwell were in this car with us; or better yet, that Sally was here and Paul was back in Deep River, torturing birds, inflicting injuries and dispensing his smoky dread within the population there. (The Existence Period was patented to ward off such unwelcome feelings. Only it isn't working.)

"Do you remember how old Mr. Toby would be if he hadn't gotten run over?"

I'm just about to ask him if he's been snuffing grackles for fun. "Thirteen, why?" My eyes are fast seeking any DEERSLAYER INN sign.

"That's something I can't quit thinking about," he says for possibly the thirtieth time, as we come to the center-of-town intersection, where some kids dressed exactly like Paul are slouching delinquently on the corner curb, playing idiotic Hacky Sack right in among the passersby. Town seems to be a little brick and white-shuttered village, shaded by big scarlet oaks and hickories, all as charming and snappily tended to as a well-kept cemetery.

"Why do you think you think about that?" I say irritably.

"I don't know. It seems like it ruined everything that was fixed back then."

"It didn't. Nothing's fixed anyway. Why don't you try writing some of it down." For some reason I feel aggravated by the story of my mother and the nun on Horn Island and wanting (God knows why) more children.

"You mean like a journal?" He eyes me dubiously.

"Right. Like that."

"We did that at camp. Then we used our journals to wipe our asses and threw them in bonfires. That was the best use for them."

Around and down the cross street I now unexpectedly see the Baseball Hall of Fame, a pale-red-brick Greek Revival, post-office-looking building, and I make a quick, hazardous right off what was Chestnut and onto what is Main, postponing my drink for a drive-by and a closer look.

Full of baseball vacationers, Main Street has the soullessly equable, bustly air of a better-than-average small-college town the week the kids come back for fall. Shops on both sides are selling showcases full of baseball *everything*: uniforms, cards, posters, bumper stickers, no doubt hubcaps and condoms; and these share the street with just ordinary villagey business entities—a drugstore, a dad 'n' lad, two flower shops, a tavern, a German bakery and several realty offices, their mullioned windows crammed with snapshots of A-frames and "view properties" on Lake So-and-so.

Unlike stolid Deep River and stiff-necked Ridgefield, Cooperstown has more than ample 4th of July street regalia strung up on the lampposts and crossing wires, stoplights and even parking meters, as if to say there's a right way to do things and this is it. Posters on every corner promise a "Big Celebrity Parade" with "country music stars" on Monday, and all visitors strolling the sidewalks seem glad to be here. It seems in fact and on first blush like an ideal place to live, worship, thrive, raise a family, grow old, get sick and die. And yet: Some suspicion lurks—in the crowds themselves, in the too-frequent street-corner baskets of redder-than-red geraniums and the too-visible French *poubelle* trash containers, in the telltale sight of a red double-decker City of Westminster bus and there being no *mention* of the Hall of Fame *anywhere*—that the town is just a replica (of a legitimate place), a period backdrop to the Hall of Fame or to something even less specific, with nothing authentic (crime, despair, litter, the rapture) really going on no matter what civic illusion the city fathers maintain. (In this way, of course, it's no less than what I imagined, and still a potentially perfect setting in which to woo one's son away from his problems and bestow good counsel—if, that is, one's son weren't an asshole.)

We cruise slowly by the unimpressive little brick-arched entry-way to the Hall, with its even more post-office-ish, Old-Glory-on-a-pole look and a single flourishing sugar maple out front. Several noisy citizens seem to be parading in a little circle on the sidewalk, doing their best, it looks like, to get in the way of paying customers who have walked over from nearby inns or hotels or RV parks and want to get inside for a quick evening tour. These circlers all have placards and signs and sandwich boards and, when I let Paul's window down to hear, are chanting what sounds like "shooter, shooter, shooter." (It's hard to know what could be worth picketing in a place like this.)

"So who're those morons?" Paul says, and makes a quick *eeeck* followed by a look of dismay.

"I got here when you did," I say.

"Hooter, hooter, hooter, hooter," he says in a gruff, giant's voice. "Neuter, neuter, neuter, neuter."

"That's the Baseball Hall of Fame right there, though." I'm disappointed, to be honest, but with no right to be. "You've seen it now, so we can go home if you want to."

"Hooter, hooter, hooter," Paul says. "Eeeck, eeeck."

"Do you want to just get it over with? I'll get you back to New York early tonight. You can stay at the Yale Club."

"I'd rather stay up here a whole lot longer," Paul says, still watching out his window.

"Okay," I say, deciding he means he'd rather not go to New York. Though the air of anger flushes right out of me then, and I see my job as father once again to be a permanent, lifelong undertaking.

"What actually supposedly happened here? I forgot." He is musing out at the milling sidewalk traffic.

"Baseball was supposedly dreamed up here in 1839, by Abner Doubleday, though nobody really believes that." All info courtesy of brochures. "It's just a myth to allow customers to focus their interests and get the most out of the game. It's like the Declaration of Independence being signed on the Fourth of July, when it was actually signed some other time." This, of course, is straight from avuncular old Becker and probably a waste of time now. Though I mean to persist. "It's a shorthand to keep you from getting all bound up in unimportant details and missing some deeper point. I don't remember what the point is with baseball, though." A second wave of deep fatigue suddenly descends. It's tempting to pull over and go to sleep on the seat and see who's here when I wake up.

"So this is all just bullshit," Paul says, watching out.

"Not exactly. A lot of things we think are true aren't, just like a lot of things that are, you don't have to give a shit about. You have to make your own assessments. Life's full of little potted lessons like that."

"Why, thank you, then. Thank you, thank you, thank you,

thank you." He looks at me with amusement, but he is scornful. I could easily pass out.

Though I'm still not to be turned aside, under the syllabus topic of separating the wheat from the chaff, or possibly it's the woods from the trees. "You shouldn't get trapped by situations that don't make you happy," I say. "I'm not always very good at it. I fuck up a lot. But I try."

"I'm trying," he says—to my great and heart-wrenching surprise—moved by something. A platitude. The strength of a simple platitude. What else do I offer? "I don't really know what I'm supposed to do."

"Well, if you're trying, that's all you can do."

"Eeeck," he says quietly. "Hooter."

"Hooter. Right," I say, and we motor on.

I drive us farther down Main into the tree-thick neighborhood of expensive and familiar Federalist and well-preserved Greek Revivals—all in primo condition and shaded by two-hundred-year-old beeches and red oaks—which in Haddam would cost a million eight and never come on the market (friends sell to friends to keep us realtors out of it). A couple here, though, have signs on their lawns, one with a JUST REDUCED sticker. Another paperboy is here, walking his route, swinging his swag sack full of afternoon dailies. An older man, in bright-red jackass pants and a yellow shirt, is standing in a yard behind a picket fence, holding an icy drink and raising his free hand for the boy to throw him a paper, which he does, and which the man snags. The boy turns toward us idling past, waves a furtive little wave at Paul, mistaking him for someone he knows, then quickly douses it and looks off. Paul, though, waves back! As though he thought, like a good dreamer, that if we all still lived in Haddam and life was revised back to what it should be, this boy would be him.

"Do you like my clothes?" he says, closing his window with the button.

"Not much," I say, steering the curve around onto another shaded street, where there's a blue HOSPITAL sign, and women in nurses' garb and men in doctors' smocks with dangling stethoscopes are walking down the sidewalk, headed for home. "Do you like mine?"

Paul looks me over seriously—chinos, Weejuns, yellow socks,

Black Watch plaid short-sleeve from Mountain Eyrie Outfitters in Leech Lake, Minnesota, clothes I've worn as long as he's known me, the same as I wore the day I stepped off the New York Central in Ann Arbor in 1963 and am at home in still. Generic clothing.

"No," Paul says.

"But see," I say, the crunched *Self-Reliance* still under my thigh, "in my line of work I'm supposed to dress in a way that makes clients feel sorry for me, or better yet superior to me. I think I accomplish that pretty well." Paul looks over at me again with a distasteful look that might be ready to slide into sarcasm, only he doesn't know if I'm making fun of him. He says nothing. Though what I've just told him, of course, is merely true.

I steer us back now through a nice but less nice neighborhood of red- and green-shuttered houses on narrower streets, thinking by this route to wind back to 28 and find the Deerslayer. Plenty's for sale here too. Cooperstown, it seems, is up for grabs.

"What's your new tattoo say?"

Paul instantly holds his right wrist up for me to see, and what I make out upside down is the word "insect," stained in dull-blue Bic-pen-looking ink right into his tender flesh. "Did you think that up by yourself," I say, "or did someone help you?"

Paul sniffs. "In the next century we're all going to be enslaved by the insects that survive this century's pesticides. With this I acknowledge being in a band of maladapted creatures whose time is coming to a close. I hope the new leaders will treat me as a friend." He again sniffs, then worries his nose with his dirty fingers.

"Is that a lyric from some rock song?" I'm getting us back into the traffic flow, heading toward the center of town again. We have made a circle.

"It's just common knowledge," Paul says, rubbing his knee with his wart.

Almost immediately I see a sign I missed when Paul and I were arguing: a tall, rail-thin, buckskin-and-high-moccasined pioneer man in profile, holding a flintlock rifle, standing on a lakeshore with triangular pine trees in the background. DEERSLAYER INN STRAIGHT AHEAD. A blessed promise.

"Don't you have a better view of human progress than that?" I push right out across Main among the late-Saturday traffic and trolley vans shunting tourists hither and yon. Lake Otsego is unexpectedly straight out ahead—lush, Norwegian-looking headlands miles away on its far shore, lumping north into the hazy Adirondacks.

"Too many things are bothering me all the time. It gets to be old."

"You know," I say, ignoring him, "those guys who founded this whole place thought if they didn't shake loose of old dependencies they'd be vulnerable to the world's innate wildness—"

"By place do you mean Cooperstown?"

"No. I don't. I meant something else."

"So who was Cooperstown named after?" he says, facing toward the sparkling lake as if it were space he was considering flying off into.

"James Fenimore Cooper," I say. "He was a famous American novelist who wrote books about Indians playing baseball." Paul flashes me a look of halfway pleasant uncertainty. He knows I'm tired of him and may be making fun of him again. Though I can also see in his features—as I have other times, and as the dappled light passes over them—the adult face he'll most likely end up with: large, grave, ironic, possibly gullible, possibly gentle, but not likely so happy. Not my face, but a way mine could've been with fewer coping skills. "Do you think *you're* a failure?" I say, slowing across from the Deerslayer, ready to turn up the drive through two rows of tall spruces beyond which is the longed-for inn, its Victorian porches shaded deep in the late day, the big chairs I've daydreamed about occupied by a few contented travelers, but with room for more.

"At what?" Paul says. "I haven't had enough time to fail yet. I'm still learning how." I wait for traffic to clear. Lake Otsego is beside us now, flat and breezeless through an afternoon haze.

"I mean at being a kid. An ass-o-lescent. Whatever it is you think you are now." My blinker is blinking, my palms gripping the wheel.

"Sure, Frank," Paul says arrogantly, possibly not even knowing what he's agreeing to.

"Well, you're not," I say. "So you're just going to have to figure out something else to think about yourself, because you're not. I love you. And don't call me Frank, goddamn it. I don't want my son to call me Frank. It makes me feel like your fucking stepfather. Why don't you tell me a joke. I could use a joke. You're good at that."

And then a sudden stellar quiet settles on us two, waiting to turn, as if a rough barrier had been reached, tried, failed at but then briskly gotten over before we knew it or how. I for some reason sense that Paul might cry, or at least nearly cry—an event I haven't witnessed in a long time and that he has officially ceased yet might try again just this once for old times' sake.

But in fact it's my own eyes that go hot and steamy, though I couldn't tell you why (other than my age).

"Can you hold your breath for fifty-five seconds straight?" Paul says as I swing up across the highway.

"I don't know. Maybe."

"Do it," Paul says, looking straight at me, deadpan. "Just stop the car." He is opaque and gloating with something hilarious.

And so, in the shady drive to the Deerslayer, I do. I hit the brakes. "All right, I'm holding it," I say. "This better be really funny. I'm ready for a drink."

He clamps his mouth shut and closes his eyes, and I close mine, and we wait together in the a/c wind and engine murmur and thermostat click while I count, one-one-thousand, two-one-thousand, three-one-thousand . . .

When I closed my eyes the dashboard digital read 5:14, and when I open them it reads 5:15. Paul has his open, though he seems to be counting silently like a zealot speaking some private beseechments to God.

"Okay. Fifty-five. What's the punch line? I'm in a hurry." My foot is easing off the brake. " 'I didn't know shit could hold its breath so long?' Is it that good?"

"Fifty-five is how long the first jolt lasts in the electric chair. I read that in a magazine. Did you think it seemed like a long time or a short time?" He blinks at me, curious.

"It seemed pretty long to me," I say unhappily. "And that wasn't very funny."

"Me too," he says, fingering his bunged-up ear rim and inspecting his finger for blood. "It's supposed to knock you out, though."

"That'd be a lot better," I say. Parents, of course, think about dying day and night—especially when they see their children one weekend a month. It's not so surprising their children would follow suit.

"You just lose everything when you lose your sense of humor," Paul says in a mock-official voice.

And I'm back in gear then, tires skidding on pine needles and up into the cool and (I hope) blissful removes of the Deerslayer. A bell is gonging. I see an old belfry stand in the side yard being clappered by a smiling young woman in a white tunic and chef's hat, waving to us as we arrive, just like in some travelogue of happy summer days in Cooperstown. I wheel in feeling as if we were late and everybody had been distracted by our absence, only now we've arrived and everything can start.

CHAPTER 9

THE DEERSLAYER is as perfect as I'd hoped—a wide, rambling, spavined late Victorian with yellow scalloped mansards, spindle-lathed porch railings, creaky stairs leading to long, shadowy, disinfectant-smelling hallways, little twin pig-iron bedsteads, a table fan, and a bath at the end of the hall.

Downstairs there's a long, slumberous living room with ancient-smelling slipcovered couches, a scabbed-up old Kimball spinet, a "take one, leave one" library, with dinner served in the shadowy dining room between 5:30 and 7:00 ("No late diners please!"). There is, however and unfortunately, no bar, no complimentary cocktails, no canapés, no TV. (I have embellished it some, but who could blame me?) And yet it still seems to me a perfect place where a man can sleep with a teenage boy in his room and arouse no suspicions.

Drinkless, then, I stretch out on the too-soft mattress while Paul goes "exploring." I relax my jaw sinews, twist my back a little, unlimber my toes in the table-fan breeze and wait to let sleep steal upon me like a bushman out of the twilight. To this end I again braid together new nonsense components, which seep into my mind like anesthesia. *We better dust off our Sally Caldwell . . . I'm sorry I drove your erection you putz . . . Phogg Allen, the long face . . . eat your face . . . You musta been a beautiful Doctor Zhivago, you stranger in the Susquehanna . . .* And I'm gone off into tunneling darkness before I can even welcome it.

And then, sooner than I wanted, I'm emerged—lushly, my head spinning in darkness, alone, my son nowhere near me.

For a time I lie still, as a cool lake breeze circulates thickly around the spruce and elms and into the room through the soft fan whir. Somewhere nearby a bug zapper toasts one after another of the big north-woods Sabre-jet mosquitoes, and above me on the ceiling a smoke detector beams its little red-eye signal out of the dark.

Floors below I hear fork and plate noises, chairs scraping,

muffled laughter followed by footfalls trudging up the stairs past my door, the sound of a door closing and soon a toilet-flush—water skittering, splashing through pipes. Then the door reopens and more heavy footfalls fade into night.

Through a wall I hear someone sawin' 'em off just the way I must've been—stertorous, diligent, thorough-sounding breaths. Someone's playing "Inchworm" on the spinet. I hear a car door open in the gravel lot below my window—the muffled *ping, ping, ping* of the interior "door open" bell—then a man and a woman talking in low voices, affectionately. "It's dirt cheap here, really," the male says in a whisper, as if others needed to be kept in the dark.

"Yeah, but then what?" the female says, and giggles. "What would we do?"

"What d'ya do anywhere?" he says. "Go fishing, play golf, eat dinner, fuck your wife. Just like home."

"I choose window number four," she says. "There's not enough of *that* back home." She giggles again. Then thump, the trunk is slammed; chirp, a car alarm activated; crunch, their feet cross the gravel headed toward the lake. They are talking houses. I know. Tomorrow they'll do some window-browsing, check with an agent, look through some listing books, see one house, maybe two, to get a feel, discuss a feasible "down," then wander dreamily off down Main Street and never think one thought of it again. Not that it's always that way. Some guys write out whopper checks, ship their furnishings, establish whole new lives in two weeks—and *then* think better of it all, after which they list the house again with the same realtor, take a beating on the carrying charges, shell out a penalty for early pay-off, and in this way, in the process of mistake and correction, the economy remains vibrant. In that sense real estate is not about finding your dream house but getting rid of it.

I give a wistful thought to Paul and wonder where he could be in a strange but peril-free town after dark. Possibly he and the Hacky Sack gang from Main and Chestnut have forged lifelong bonds and removed to a dingy diner for cottage fries, waffles and burgers at his expense. He may, after all, lack precise peer grouping in Deep River—where everyone's at least old enough to be an adult. In Haddam he'll do better.

"Jeepers," I hear someone—a woman's nasally voice say,

mounting the creaky stairs to floor three. "I told Mark"—
Merk—"why can't she just move to the Cities, where we can
keep an eye on her, then Dad won't have to drive so far for his
dialysis? He's completely helpless without her."

"So then what'd Mark say to that?" another woman's equally
nasally voice says without true interest—heavy treading down
the hall away from my door.

"Oh, you know Mark. He's such a clod." A key in a lock, a
door opening back. "He didn't say too much." Slam.

SINCE I HAVE napped in my clothes (an irresistible luxury),
I change only my shirt, slip on shoes, stretch my spine backward
and forward, tramp woozily down to the communal bathroom
for a visit and a face washing, then amble downstairs to have a
look at things, locate Paul and get a tip on dinner; I've by now
missed the inn's: spaghetti, salad, garlic bread, tapioca, all highly
praised on the "Weekly Score Card" left on my dressertop
("Mmmmmm," one penciled-in comment by a previous guest).

In the long, brown-carpeted parlor all the old parchment
lamps are burning cheerily and several guests are engrossed in
gin games or Clue or reading newspapers or books out of the
library, but saying little. A too-strong cinnamon candle is somewhere smoldering, and above the cold fireplace hangs a shadowy
six-foot-tall portrait of a man in full leather gear with a silly,
compromised expression on his U-shaped face. This is the Deerslayer himself. A big, elderly, long-eared, ham-handed Swede-
looking guy is yakking away to a Japanese man in confidential
tones about "invasive surgeries" and the extremes he'd be willing
to suffer to avoid them. And across the room a horsey, middle-
aged southern-sounding woman in a red-and-white polka-dot
dress is seated at the piano, talking too loudly to another woman,
in a foam neck brace. The polka-dot woman's eyes roam the long
room, wanting to know who might be listening and being wildly
entertained by what she's yammering about, which is whether
you can ever trust a handsome man married to a not-so-pretty
woman. "Clampin' a big padlock on my china cabinet'd be my
first official move," she says in a loud voice. She spies me in the
doorway contentedly watching the tableau of easygoing inn life
(exactly how any prospective proprietor would fantasize it: every

room filled, everybody's credit card slip salted away in the safe, no refunds offered, everybody in bed by ten). Her eyes snap at me. She offers me a long-toothed, savage stare and waves my way as if she knew me from Bogalusa or Minter City—maybe she simply recognizes a fellow southerner (something in the submissive, shruggy set of my shoulders). "Hey, you! All right! Come on down here, I see you," she shouts toward the door, rings flashing, bracelets banging, dentures a-twinkle. I wave good-naturedly, but fearing I'll end up piano-side having my brains turned to suet, I step discreetly back and out of the doorway, then hustle down the front under-the-stairs hallway to make some calls.

I would certainly like to call Sally and *should* call for messages. The Markhams could've come back from around the bend, and there might be an all-clear from Karl. These subjects have blessedly slipped my mind for several hours, but I haven't noticed much relief in the bargain.

Someone (no doubt the old southern number) has begun playing "Lullaby of Birdland" at a slow, lugubrious pace, so that the whole atmosphere on floor one suddenly feels calculated to drive everyone to bed.

I wait for messages, staring at a diagram illustrating the five steps that will save someone from choking, and fingering a stack of pink tickets from a dinner theater in Susquehanna, PA. *Annie Get Your Gun* is playing this very night, and the stack of playbills on the telephone table rings with the critics' kudos: "Everybody's first rate"—Binghamton *Press & Sun Bulletin*; "Move over 'Cats' "—Scranton *Times*; "This baby's got legs under her"—Cooperstown *Republican*. I can't help conjuring up Sally's review: "My team of death's-door opening-nighters simply couldn't get enough of it. We laughed, we cried, we damn near died"—*Curtain Call Newsletter*.

Beeeeep. "Hello, Mr. Bascombe, this is Fred Koeppel calling again from Griggstown. I know it's a holiday weekend, but I'd like to get a little action going on my house right away. Maybe show it on Monday if we can get the commission worked out. . . ." Click. Ditto.

Beeeeep. "Hello, Frank, it's Phyllis." Pause while she clears her throat, as though she's been asleep. "East Brunswick was a *total* nightmare. Total. Why'n't you tell us, for God's sake? Joe got depressed after one house. I think he may be headed for a big cave-in. So anyway, we've reconsidered about the Hanrahan place, which I'm ready to change my mind about it, I guess. Nothing's forever. If we don't like it we can just sell it. Joe liked it anyway. I'll get over worrying about the prison. I'm at a phone booth here." A deepening change comes into her voice (signifying what?). "Joe's asleep. Actually I'm having a drink at the bar at the Raritan Ramada. Quite a day. *Quite* a day." Another long pause, representing possible stocktaking within the Markham ménage. "I wish I could talk to you. But. I hope you get this message tonight and call us up in the morning so we can get our offer over to old man Hanrahan. I'm sorry about Joe being such a butt. He's not easy, I realize that." A third pause, during which I hear her say, "Yeah, sure," to someone. Then: "Call us at the Ramada. 201-452-6022. I'm probably going to be up late. We couldn't stand that other place anymore. I hope you and your son are getting to share a lot." Click.

Except for the boozy longing (which I ignore), there's no shocker here. East Brunswick's well known for dreary, down-market, cookie-cutter uniformity. It is not a viable alternative even to Penns Neck, though I'm surprised the Markhams came around so soon. It's too bad they couldn't have taken the evening, shot up to Susquehanna for *Annie* and chicken piccante. They'd have laughed, they'd have cried, and Phyllis could've found ways to start getting over worrying about the prison in her back yard. Of course, it won't surprise me if "old man Hanrahan's" house is realty history by now. Good things don't hang around while half-wits split hair follicles, even in this economy.

I instantly put in a call to Penns Neck, to get Ted on the alert for an early-morning offer. (I'll get Julie Loukinen to deliver it.) But the phone rings and rings and rings and rings. I repunch it, taking care to mentally picture each digit, then let it ring possibly thirty times while I stare down the front hall past the old grandfather clock and the portrait of General Doubleday and through the open screen door into the night and farther through trees to the diamond-twinkle lights of another, grander inn across on the lakeshore, a place I didn't see this afternoon. All the ranked windows there are warmly lit, car headlights coming and going like some swank casino in a far-off seaside country. Out on the Deerslayer's porch the high backs of the big Adirondack rockers are swaying as my fellow guests snooze away their spaghetti dinners, murmur and chuckle about the day—something bust-a-gut hilarious somebody's son has piped up with in front of the Heinie Manusch bust, something else about the pros and cons of opening a copy shop in a town this size, something further about Governor Dukakis, whom someone, probably a fellow Democrat, laughingly refers to as "that Beantown Jerkimo."

But nothing in Penns Neck. Ted may have slipped off to an Independence Day open house across the fence.

I try Sally's number, since she said to call and since I intend to renew our amorous connections the instant I let Paul off in Gotham, a time that now feels many miles and hours from now but isn't. (With one's children everything happens in a flash; there's never a now, only a then, after which you're left wondering what took place and trying to imagine if it can take place again so's you'll notice.)

"Hello-o," Sally says in a happy, airy voice, as if she'd just been in the yard, pinning up clothes on a sunny line.

"Hi," I say, relieved and cheered for an answer somewhere. "It's me again."

"Me again? Well. Good. How are you, Me? Still pretty distracted? It's a wonderful night at the beach. I wish you could distract yourself down to here. I'm on the porch, I can hear music, I ate radicchio and mushrooms tonight, and I've had some nice Duck's Wing fumé blanc. I hope you two're having as splendid a time wherever you are. Where are you?"

"In Cooperstown. And we are. It's great. You should be here." I picture one long, shiny leg, a shoe (gold, in my mind) dangling out over her porch banister into darkness, a big sparkling glass in her lounging hand (a banner night for women tipplers). "Have you got any company?" Apprehension's knife enters my voice; even I hear it.

"Nope. No company. No suitors scaling the walls tonight."

"That's good."

"I guess," she says, clearing her throat just the way Phyllis did. "You're extremely sweet to call me. I'm sorry I asked you about your old wife today. That was indiscreet and insensitive of me. I'll never do it again."

"I still want you to come up here." This is not literally true, though it's not far from true. (I'm certain she won't come anyway.)

"Well," Sally says, as though she were smiling into the dark, her voice going briefly weak, then coming back strong. "I'm thinking very seriously about you, Frank. Even though you were very rude or at least odd on the phone today. Maybe you couldn't help it."

"Maybe not," I say. "But that's great. I've been thinking seriously about you."

"Have you?"

"You bet. I thought last night you and I came to a crossroads, and we went in the wrong direction." Something in the South Mantoloking background makes me think I hear surf sighing and piling onto the beach, a blissful, longed-for sound here in the steamy Deerslayer hallway—though conceivably it's only weak batteries in Sally's cordless phone. "I think we need to do some things a lot differently," I say.

Sally has a sip of her fumé blanc right by the receiver. "I thought over what you said about loving someone. And I thought you were very honest. But it seemed very cold too. You don't think you're cold, do you?"

"No one ever told me I was. I've been told about plenty of other faults." (Some quite recently.) Whoever's playing "Lullaby of Birdland" in the living room stops and switches straight into "The Happy Wanderer" at an allegretto clip, the heavy bass notes flat and metallic. Someone claps along for two bars, then quits. A man out on the porch laughs and says, "I think I'm a happy wanderer myself."

"So I've just had this odd feeling all afternoon," Sally says. "About what you said and what I said to you, about being non-committal and smooth. That *is* how you are. But then if I have strong feelings about you, shouldn't I just follow them? If I have a chance? I believe I could figure things out better when I was younger. I certainly always thought I could alter the course of things if I wanted to. Didn't you say you had a tidal something or other about me? Tides were in it."

"I said I had a tidal attraction to you. And I do." Possibly we can move beyond smooth and noncommittal here. Someone—a woman—starts loudly singing "Balls-de-reee, balls-de-rah" in a quavery voice and laughing. Possibly it's the loudmouth in polka dots who gave me the barbarous eyeball.

"What does that mean, tidal attraction?" Sally says.

"It's hard to put into words. It's just strong and persistent, though. I'm sure of that. I think it's harder to say what you like than what you don't."

"Well," Sally says almost sadly. "Last night I thought I was in a tide pulling me toward you. Only that isn't what happened. So I'm not very sure. That's what I've been thinking about."

"It's not bad if it's pulling you toward me, is it?"

"I don't think so. But I got nervous about it, and I'm not used to being nervous. It's not my nature. I got in the car and drove all the way to Lakewood and saw *The Dead*. Then I had my radicchio and mushrooms by myself at Johnny Matassa's, where you and I had our first encounter."

"Did you feel better?" I say, fingering up two *Annie* ducats, wondering if a character in *The Dead* reminded her of me.

"Not completely. No. I still couldn't understand if the unchangeable course was toward you or away from you. It's a dilemma."

"I love you," I say, totally startling myself. A tide of another nature has just swirled me into very deep, possibly dark water. These words are not untrue, or don't feel untrue, but I didn't need to say them at this very moment (though only an asshole would take them back).

"I'm sorry," Sally says, reasonably enough. "What is it? What?"

"You heard me." The living room pianist is playing "The Happy Wanderer" much louder now—just banging away. The Japanese man who's been hearing all about invasive surgeries walks out of the living room smiling, but immediately stops smiling when he hits the hall. He sees me and shakes his head as if he were responsible for the music but now it won't stop. He heads up the front stairs. Paul and I will be happy to be on floor 3.

"What's that mean, Frank?"

"I just realized I wanted to say it to you. And so I said it. I don't know everything it means"—to put it mildly—"but I know it doesn't mean nothing."

"But didn't you tell me you'd have to make somebody up to love them? And didn't you say this was a time in your life you probably wouldn't even remember later?"

"Maybe that time's over, or it's changing." I feel jittery and squeamish saying so. "But I wouldn't make you up anyway. It isn't even possible. I told you that this afternoon." I'm wondering, though, what if I'd said "don't" in front of the verb? Then what? Could that be the way life progresses at my age? A-stumble *into* darkness and *out* of the light? You discover you love someone by trying it without "don't" in front of the verb? Nothing vectored by your *self* or by what *is*? If so, it's not good.

There's a pause on the line, during which Sally is, understandably, thinking. I'm mightily interested in asking if she might love me, since she'd mean something different by it, which would be good. We could sort out the differences. But I don't ask.

"The Happy Wanderer" comes to a crashing end, followed by complete, relieved silence in the living room. I hear the Japanese man's feet treading the squeaky hall above me, then a door click closed. I hear pots being banged and scrubbed beyond the wall in the kitchen. Out on the dark porch the big rockers are rocking still, their occupants no doubt staring moodily across at the nicer inn that's too ritzy for them and probably not worth the money.

"It's very odd," Sally says, clearing her throat again as though changing the subject away from love, which is okay with me. "After I talked to you today from wherever you were, and before I went to see *The Dead*, I walked up the beach a while—you'd asked me about Wally's cuff links, and I just got this idea in my head. And when I came home I called his mother out in Lake Forest, and I demanded to know where he is. It just occurred to me for some reason that she'd always known and wouldn't tell me. That was the big secret, in spite of everything. And I've never even been a person who thought there *was* a big secret." (Unlike, say, Ann.)

"What did she tell you?" This would be an interesting new wrinkle in the tapestry. *Wally: The Sequel.*

"She didn't know where he was. She actually started crying on the phone, the poor old thing. It was terrible. *I* was terrible. I said I was sorry, but I'm sure she doesn't forgive me. I certainly wouldn't forgive me. I told you I can be ruthless sometimes."

"Did you feel better?"

"No. I just have to forget it, that's all. You can still see your ex-wife even if you don't want to. I don't know which is better."

"That's why people carve hearts on trees, I guess," I say, and feel idiotic for saying it, but for a moment also desolate, as if some chance has been once again missed by me. Ann seems all the more insubstantial and distant for being substantial and not even very distant.

"I sound very un-smart to myself," Sally says, ignoring my remark about trees. She takes a drink of wine, bumping the phone with the glass rim. "Maybe I'm undergoing the early signs of something. Self-pitying failure to make a significant contribution in the world."

"That's not true a bit," I say. "You help dying people and make them happier. You make a hell of a contribution. A lot more than I make."

"Women don't usually have midlife crises, do they?" she says. "Though maybe women who're alone do."

"Do you love me?" I say rashly.

"Would you even like that?"

"Sure. I'd think it was great."

"Don't you think I'm too mild? I think I'm very mild."

"No! I don't think you're mild. I think you're wonderful." The receiver for some reason is tightly pinned to my ear.

"I think I'm mild."

"Maybe you feel mild about me." I hope not, and my eyes fall again upon the little stack of pink dinner-theater tickets. They are, I see, for July 2, 1987—exactly a year ago. "If it's free, how good could it be?"—F. Bascombe.

"I *would* like to know something." She could very well want to know plenty.

"I'll tell you anything. No holding back. The whole truth."

"Tell me why you're attracted to women your own age?" This harks back to a conversation we had on our gloom-infested fall excursion to Vermont to peep at leaves, eat overcooked crown roasts and wait in stationary lines of bus traffic, later to retreat homeward in a debrided, funky silence. On the way up and in soaring early spirits, I explained, off the cuff and unsolicited, that younger women (who I'd had in mind I can't remember, but somebody in her middle twenties and not very smart) always wanted to cheer me up and sympathize with me, except that finally bored the socks off me, since I didn't want to be sympathized with and was cheerful enough on my own. We were whizzing up the Taconic, and I went on to say it seemed like a textbook definition of adulthood that you gave up trying to be a cheerleader for the person you loved and just took him or her on as he or she was—assuming you liked him (or her). Sally made no reply at the time, as though she thought I was just making something up for her benefit and wasn't interested. (In fact, I might already have been coaching myself against making *people* up for the purpose of loving them.)

"Well," I say, aware I could blow the whole deal with an inept turn of phrase, "younger women always want everything to be a success and have love depend on it. But some things can't be a success and you love somebody anyway."

Silence again intervenes. Again I think I hear surf languidly sudsing against the sandy shingle.

Sally says, "I don't think that's exactly what you said last fall."

"But it's pretty close," I say, "and it's what I meant and what I mean now. And what do you care? You're my age, or almost. And I don't love anybody else." (Except my ex-wife, which is a non-issue.)

"I guess I'm concerned that you're making me up different from how I am. Maybe you think there's only one person in the world for anybody, and so you keep making her up. Not that I mind being improved on, but you have to stick to my particular facts."

"I have to forget about making people up," I say guiltily, sorry I ever gave utterance to the idea. "And I don't think there's just one person for anybody. At least I hope to hell not, since I haven't done so well yet."

"We have some more fireworks out on the water here," Sally says dreamily. "That's very nice. Maybe I'm just feeling susceptible tonight. I felt good when you called."

"I *still* feel good," I say, and suddenly the bony, horse-face woman who's been banging the piano to death strides out into the foyer and looks down the hall straight at me, where I'm leaning on the wall above the phone table. She's in step with the plump woman in the neck brace, whom she's no doubt been making sing "Balls-de-reee, balls-de-rah." She issues me another savage-eyebrowed look, as if I was where she knew I'd be and up to my pants pockets in the deceit of some angelic and unsuspecting wifey. "Look. I'm in a public phone here. But I feel a lot better. I just want to see you tomorrow if I can't see you in ten minutes."

"Where?" Sally says smally, still susceptible.

"Anywhere. Name it. I'll come down there in a Cessna." The two women stay standing in the lighted foyer, unabashedly ogling me and listening in.

"Are you still taking Paul to the train in New York?"

"By six o'clock," I say, wondering where Paul could be at this minute.

"Well, I could take a train up there and meet you. I'd like that. I'd like to spend the Fourth of July with you."

"You know, it's my favorite holiday of a non-religious nature." I am enthused to hear her even warily agreeable, though she can seem more agreeable than she is. (I have to tabulate all the declarations and forswearings I've committed to in the last ten minutes.) "You didn't answer my question, though."

"Oh." She sniffs once. "You're not really very easy to fix on. And I don't think I'd be a good long-term lover or a wife for somebody like that. I had a husband who was hard to fix on."

"That's all right," I say. Though surely I'm not as elusive as Wally! The Wally who's been gone for damn near twenty years!

"Is that all right? For me to be a not very good lover or wife?" She pauses to think about this novel idea. "Don't you care, or are you just not putting any pressure on me to do anything?"

"I care," I say. "But I'd actually just be happy to hear any good words."

"Everything isn't just about how you say it," Sally says, very formally. "And I wouldn't know what to say anyway. I don't think we mean the same things when we say the same things." (As predicted.)

"That's fine too. As long as you're not sure you *don't* love me. I read a poem someplace that said perfect love was not knowing you weren't in love. Maybe that's what this is."

"Oh my," she says, and sounds sorrowful. "That's too complicated, Frank, and it's not very different from how it was last night. It's not very encouraging to me."

"It's different because I get to see you tomorrow. Meet me at seven at Rocky and Carlo's on Thirty-third and Seventh. We'll start new from there."

"Well," she says. "Are we making a business deal to be in love? Is that what's happening?"

"No, it's not. But it's a good deal, though. Everything's up front for a change." She laughs. And then I try to laugh but can't and have to fake laughing.

"Okay, okay," she says, in a not very hopeful voice. "I'll see you tomorrow."

"You better believe it," I say in a better one. And we hang up. Though the instant she's off I depress the plunger and shout into the empty line, "And so you're nothing but a fucking ass-hole, are you? Well, I'll have you killed before Labor Day, and that's God's promise." I snap a vicious look around at the two women, framed by the screen door, peering at me. "I'll see you in hell," I say into the dead line, and slam the phone down as the women turn and head hastily upstairs to their beds.

I TAKE A quick peek out onto the porch to see if Paul's there. He's not—only one of the gin players is left, asleep but managing to rock his rocker anyway. I make an investigative turn through the smelly dining room, where the light's still on and the big boarding-house lazy Susan table is cleared and shining dully from being wiped with a greasy rag. Through the two-way kitchen door open at the back I see the young woman who was clanging the dinner bell, wearing a chef's hat and waving when Paul and I arrived. She's seated at a long metal table in the brackish light, smoking a cigarette and flipping through a magazine, her hand around a can of Genny, her chef's hat in front of her. Clearly she's immersed in her own well-earned and private quality time. But nothing would make me happier than a warmed-up plate of dinner spaghetti with a couple of cold-as-they-may-be slabs of garlic bread and maybe a brew of my own. I'd eat right here, standing up, or sneak a plate to my room by the back stairs so no other guests would have to know about it. ("The next thing, everybody'll want to eat late, and we'll be serving dinner from now to Christmas. It's hard to know where to draw the line in these things"—which of course is true.)

"Hi," I say in through the kitchen door, one room into the next, sounding meeker than I want to sound.

The young woman—who's still wearing a chef's boxy-looking white tunic, institutional baggy pants and a red neckerchief—turns and gives me a skeptical, unwelcoming look. A round tin ashtray sits on the table in front of her, beside a package of

Winstons. She looks back and flicks her smoke on the ashtray's rim.

"What can I do you for?" she says without looking up at me. I take a couple of minuscule steps nearer the doorframe. In fact, I hate to be the one asking for special treatment, who wants his dinner late, his laundry returned without his ticket, who can't find his stub for his prints, has to have his tires rotated *this* afternoon because he needs to drive to Buffalo in the morning and the left front seems to be wearing a little unevenly. I prefer my regular place in line. Only tonight, after 10 p.m., worn uneven myself from a long, befuddling day with my son, I'm willing to bend the rules like anyone else.

"I thought I might get a good tip on dinner somewhere," I say, with a you-know-what-I-really-mean look. My tired eyes dart around to what I can see of the kitchen: a giant cold box, a black eight-burner Vulcan, a bulky silver pot-washer, its door open, four big tub-sinks, dry as a desert, all utensils—pots, pans, skillets, whisks, spatulas—dangling like weaponry from a rack on the rear wall. Nowhere do I see a still-warm pot of spaghetti with a metal spoon handle poked up over the top. Nothing's doing here food-wise.

"I guess the Tunnicliff's kitchen shuts off at nine." The lady chef glances at her wristwatch and shakes her head without looking up. "You just missed that by an hour. I'm sorry to break the news."

She is a harder-boiled piece of business than I guessed. Frizzy blond hair, pallid indoor skin, blotchy where I can't now see, thick little wrists and neck, and wandering breasts not well captained inside her chef's getup. She is twenty-nine, no doubt, with a kid at home she's slow getting back to, and in all likelihood rides a big Harley to work. (Almost certainly she's the innkeeper's squeeze.) Though whatever her arrangements, they haven't left her easy to win over.

"Got any better ideas?" My stomach produces an audible querking noise as if on cue.

She takes a drag on her Winston and turns her head slightly to the side and blows smoke the other way. I can see the magazine she's reading is *Achieve Super Marital Sex* (something you might get mail order). I can also see she's not wearing a wedding ring, though that's not my business. "If you want to drive down to

Oneonta, there's a Chinese stays open till midnight. Their egg drop's almost edible." She yawns and stifles it halfway.

"That's a pretty fur piece," I say, grinning witlessly. I sniff a gamy pilot light/old stale food smell reminiscent of Ted Houlihan's house. I of course hate egg drop soup, know no one who actually likes it, and hold my ground.

"Twenty-five air miles." She flips the pages of her magazine to one that has pictures I'm not close enough to see.

"Nothing else open in town, then, huh?" I am less convincing, I can tell.

"Bars. This is just a little hick burg. It pretends different. But what else is new." She flips another page nonchalantly, then leans forward to get a better look at something—possibly a defter "mounting strategy" or some fancy new penetration protocol, a tricky Swedish "apparatus" for manipulating previously undiscovered parts and zones, ingenuity for making life better than ever. (My own parts, I realize dimly, have not been manipulated in a coon's age, except in the age-old way; I wonder bleakly if Paul might not be somewhere in the menaceless warp of Cooperstown, having his own parts ardently worked over while I'm here begging a little supper.)

"Look," I say, "you think there's any chance I could get a little leftover spaghetti? I'm as hungry as a bear, and I'd be glad to eat it cold. Or I'd eat something else that was handy. Maybe some tapioca or a sandwich." I edge in the door to make my presence more a feature in the room.

She shakes her frizzy head and thumps her Genny, still intent on her sex magazine. "Jeremy hangs a big lock on the fridge so nobody can come down for Dagwoods, which used to happen, especially with the Japanese. They're apparently always starving. But I'm not trusted with the combination, 'cause I'd just stand back and let you have it all."

I look to the dimly shining Traulsen cold box, and indeed there's a hasp and bail soldered right onto it, and a big impregnable-looking lock—something it'd be a lot of trouble to jimmy off.

I'm close enough, though, to see the diagram that's captured the chef's special attention: a full page of four-panel drawings showing a man and woman, both naked, and painted using translucent, unprurient pastels, in front of a completely nonsexual pea-green background of hazy bedroom details (all emblematic of marriage). Fido-style is the theme here. In panel #1 they're both on their knees; in #2 "he's" standing and "she's" half draped off a bed, fully "offered"; in #3 they're both standing, and I can't see #4, though I'd like to.

"You finding some new recipes in there?" I leer down at her.

Her head twists around and up, and she gives me a brazen, pouty-mouth look that says: Mind your own business or I'll mind it for you. It makes me immediately like her, even if she won't unlock the fridge and build me up a Dagwood. This, I think, is the end of dinner, though my bet is she's got the combination committed to memory.

"I thought you wanted a sandwich," she says, looking back, amused at the canine escapades of two idealized pastel versions of married people who look like us. "Whatta you think she's saying?" She points her short finger, which has some flour dried on its fingernail, at #1, in which the female is looking back around at the already hooked-up male, as if she's just had a good new idea. " 'Knock, knock, Who's there?' " the chef says. " 'Did you hear the garage door?' or 'Do you mind if I balance my checkbook?' " She tours her tongue roguishly around in her cheek and looks mock-disgusted, as if this were all just shameless.

"Maybe they're talking about a sandwich," I say, experiencing a gradual resituating of my own little-thought-of below-decks apparatus.

"Maybe they are," she says, leaning back again while she smokes. "Maybe she's sayin', 'Now, did you remember to buy Bibb lettuce, or did you get that old iceberg again?' "

"What's your name?" I say. (My talk with Sally has been more serious and relieving than actual fun.)

"C-h-a-r, Char," she says. She has a pop of her Genny and swallows it down. "Which is short for Charlane, not Charlotte and not Charmayne. My older sisters are blessed with those."

"Your pop must've been named Charles."

"You know him?" she says. "Great big loud guy with a tiny little brain?"

"I don't think so." I'm waiting for her to flip another page, interested to see what else our panelists come up with.

"Funny," she says, putting her Winston between her teeth so the smoke makes her squint, and pushing the bulky chef's sleeves above her fragile elbows. She is more delicate on second notice. Her outfit is what makes her look chunky and tough. The "chef look" is not a good look for her.

"How'd you get to be a chef?" I say, happier, even just for a moment, to be here in the lighted kitchen with a woman rather than scrounging a burger in the dark or struggling to make contact with my son.

"Oh, well, first I attended Harvard and got a Ph.D.—let's see—in, ah, can opening. Then I did my postdoctoral work in eggs and toast buttering. That must've been at MIT."

"I bet it's harder than English."

"You *would* think so." She lays the page over to reveal more pastel panels, this time spotlighting fellatio, with some vivid but tasteful close-ups showing everything you'd ever want to know from a picture. The female panelist, I notice, now has her hair tied back in an accommodating ponytail. "My, my," Char says.

"You a subscriber?" I say archly. My stomach makes another deep, organic-sounding grumble-gurgle.

"I just read what the guests leave after meals. That's all." Char pauses longer at the fellatio panels. "This was left under one of the chairs. I'll be interested by who asks about it tomorrow. My guess I'll get to keep it."

I picture ole horseface stealing down after lights-out to give the room a tumble.

"Listen," I say, with the sudden realization (again) that I can do anything I want (except get a plate of spaghetti). "Would you like to strike out to one of those bars and let me buy you another beer while I have a gin and maybe a sandwich? My name's Frank Bascombe, by the way." I give her a smile, wondering if we should shake hands.

"And by the way?" Char says, mocking me. She snaps the magazine shut back-to-front, and on the back is a full-page color ad for a thick, pink, anatomically audacious but rather fuzzily photographed dildo that some comical prior reader has drawn a red Happy Face on the business end of. "Well, hel-lo," Char says, peering down at the pink appendage grinning back off the tabletop. "Aren't *we* happy?" The dildo is referred to in the ad as "Mr. Standard Pleasure Unit," though I'm dubious about what it has to do with the standard marriage realities. Under standard circumstances, "Mr. Pleasure" would be a hard act to follow.

"He" in fact doesn't have a particularly good effect on my own enthusiasm and leaves me oddly glum.

"Maybe I'll let you walk me over to the Tunnicliff," Char says, sliding the magazine out across the slick tabletop, rejecting Mr. Pleasure Unit as pie in the sky. She pushes back in her metal chair and turns her attention finally to me. "That's halfway home. And we'll say good night at that point."

"Great. That's great," I say. "That'll be a good end to the night for me."

She stays seated, however, squeezes her eyes shut, then pops them open as if she's just emerged from a trance, then woggles her head around to loosen everything up at the end of a long day's hard chefing. "What line of work you in, Frank?" She's not quite ready to get up, possibly deciding she needs more background on me.

"Residential realty."

"Where at?" She fingers her Winston hard pack as though she's thinking about something else.

"Down in Haddam, in New Jersey. About four hours from here."

"Never hoid of it," she says.

"It's a pretty well-kept secret."

"You in the Millionth Dollar Club? I'd be impressed if you were." She raises her eyebrows.

"Me too," I say. (In Haddam, of course, the Millionth Dollar Club had better be joined by Valentine's Day, or you're out of business by Easter.)

"I prefer to rent," Char says, staring inertly at the distant *Achieve Super Marital Sex* where she's shoved it away, with Mr. Standard Pleasure Unit's happy face turned up. "Actually I want to get into a condo, but a car costs what a house *used* to cost. And I'm still paying off my car." (Not a Harley.)

"You can rent these days," I say cheerfully, "for about half the cost of buying and save money to boot." (There's in fact no use telling her that at her age—twenty-eight or thirty-three—she's looking at a life of more of the same unless she robs a bank or marries a banker.)

"Well," Char says, suddenly motivated by something—an idea, a memory, a determination not to bellyache to a stranger. "I guess I just need to find a rich husband." She raps both sets of knuckles hard on the tabletop, grasps her pack of smokes and stands up (she is not very tall). "Let me get out of my Pillsbury doughgirl outfit." She's walking slowly away toward a little door off the kitchen, which when she opens it and snaps on the light within reveals a tiny, fluorescent-lit bathroom. "I'll meet you out on the piazza later," she says.

"I'll be there," I say at the door as it closes and goes locked.

I WANDER BACK out into the foyer to wait in the cool breeze through the screen. The old bucket-eared Swede is now hunched over the tiny phone where I'd been, his big, rough finger jammed in his other cavernous ear for better hearing. "Well, what makes you a saint, ya satchel-ass sonofabitch?" I hear him say. "For starters, tell me that. I'd like to get that straight tonight."

I look out through the screen, where all the chairs are now empty—everyone safe in bed, plans in motion for an all-out Sunday morning assault on the Hall of Fame.

From the darkness of new-mown grass I hear the distant yet close harmonies of a barbershop quartet, singing what sounds very much like "*Michelle, ma belle, sont des mots qui vont très bien ensemble, très bien ensemble.*" And back among the spruces and elm trunks I see a couple materializing in light-colored summery clothes, arms around, walking in step, returning (I'm certain) from a wonderful five-course dinner in some oak-paneled lake-side *auberge* now closed and locked up tight as Dick's hatband. They're laughing, which makes me realize that it is a good time of night to feel good, to be where you've been headed all day, blissful hours with a significant other still in front of you, half surprised that the day's gone this well, inasmuch as the 4th is the summer's pivotal day, when thoughts turn easily to fall and rapid change and shorter days and feelings of impendment that won't give way till spring. These two are ahead of the game.

They come into view now, in the inn's reflected window glow: he wearing white bucks, seersucker pants, a yellow jacket slung over his shoulder foreign-correspondent style; she in a flimsy pastel-green skirt and a pink Peter Pan blouse. By their flat Ohio vowels I recognize them as the couple from the parking lot back when I lay dozing and their interests lay in property values. Now they have other interests to pursue above floors.

"I ate way too much," he says. "I shouldn't have ordered that Cajun linguine. I'll never get to sleep."

"That's no excuse," she says. "You can sleep when you get home. I've got plans for you."

"You're the expert," he says, not at all eager enough by my standards.

"You're damn right I am," she says, then laughs. "Hah."

I want to be well out of their way when they come through—the lacquer of sex being suddenly too thick around me in the night air—want not to be standing behind the screen with a knowing, Now-you-two-have-a-real-good-sleep smirk on my mug. So, as their shoes hit the steps, I slip back into the living room to wait for my "date."

Two red-shaded lamps have been left on in the long, warm, overfurnished, cinnamon-scented parlor. The Ohioans troop by without seeing me, their voices falling, becoming more intimate as they reach the first landing and then the hallway above. They are full silent as their key enters the lock.

I cruise around the old wainscoted parlor lined with oak bookshelves, a full complement of cast-off butler and drumhead tables, slipcovered couches, wobbly hassocks, nautical-looking brass lamps—all scavenged at antique fairs and roadside flea markets in the Cortland-Binghamton-Oneonta triangle. The scented candle has been extinguished, and bulky shadows encompass the wall art, which includes, in addition to Natty Bumppo himself, a framed, yellowed topo from the Twenties, showing "Lake Otsego and Environs," several portraits of bewhiskered "founders"—doubtless all shopkeepers dressed up to look like presidential candidates—and a sampler hung over the main door, with good advice for the spiritual wanderer: "*Confidences are easy to give, but hard to get back.*"

I mouse over the various tabletops, fingering the reading matter—stacks of old MLS booklets for guests whose vacation idea is to consider putting down roots in an alien locale (the Ohioans, for example). The price of the fancy Federalist pile Paul and I passed this afternoon is eye-poppingly low by Haddam standards at 530K (something has to be wrong with it). Plenty of old *People*s and *American Heritage*s and *National Geographic*s are stacked up on the long library table by the back window. I browse down the shelf containing stiff bound editions of *New York*

History, the Otsego *Times*, *The Encyclopedia of Collectibles*, *American Cage Bird* magazine, *Mechanix Illustrated*, Hersey's *Hiroshima* in three different editions, two whole yards of matched Fenimore Coopers, a *Golden Treasure of Quotable Poetry*, two volumes of *Rails of the World*, surprisingly enough another *Classic Holes of Golf*, a stack of recent Hartford *Courants*—as if somebody had moved here from Hartford and wanted to stay in touch. And to my wonderment and out of all account, among the loose and uncategorized books, here is a single copy of my own now-old book of short stories, *Blue Autumn*, in its original dust jacket, on the front of which is a faded artist's depiction of a 1968-version sensitive-young-man, with a brush cut, an open-collared white shirt, jeans, and an uncertain half smile, standing emblematically alone in the dirt parking lot of a country gas station with an anonymous green pickup (possibly his) visible over his shoulder. Much is implied.

I flinch as always when I see it, since in a panicky time-crunch the artist elected to paint *my* face from my author's photo right onto the cover of my book, so that I see my young self now, made to look perplexed, forever staring out alone from the front of my very first (and only) literary effort.

And yet I cart the book over to one of the red-shaded lamps, full of unexpected thrill. The boxful that I own, shipped to Haddam when the book was remaindered, was left in the attic on Hoving Road, untouched since its arrival and of no more interest to me than a box of clothes that no longer fit.

But *this* book, this *specimen*, sparks interest—since it is after all still "out there," in circulation, still official if somewhat compromised, still striving to the purposes I meant it to: staging raids on the inarticulate, being an ax for the frozen sea within us, providing the satisfactions of belief in the general mess of imprecision. (Nothing's wrong with high-flown purposes, then or now.)

A cake of fine house dust covers the top, so it's clear none of tonight's Clue players has had it down for pre-bedtime sampling. The old binding makes a dry-leaves crackle as I open it back. Pages at the front, I see, are yellow and water-stained, whereas those in the middle are milky, smooth and untouched. I take a look at the aforementioned author photo, a black-and-white taken by my then-girlfriend, Dale McIver: again a young man, though this time with a completely unwarranted confidence etched in his skinny mouth, ludicrously holding a beer and smoking a cigarette (!), an empty sun-lit (possibly Mexican) bar-room and tables behind, staring fixedly at the camera as though he meant to say: "Yep, you just about have to live out here on the wild margins to get this puppy done the way God intended. And *you* probably couldn't hack it, if you want to know the gospel." And I, of course, *couldn't* hack it; chose, in fact, a much easier puppy on a much less wild margin.

Though I'm not displeased to view myself thus—fore and aft, as it were, on my own book, two sides of the issue; not queasy in the hollow of my empty stomach where most of life-that-might've-been finally comes to rest. I carried that sandpaper regret around in me for a time back in 1970, then simply omitted it the way I'd have Paul omit the nightmares and dreads of his child's life stolen away by bad luck and unconscionable adults. Forget, forget, forget.

Nor is this the first time I've happened onto my book *blind*: church book sales, sidewalk tables in Gotham, yard sales in unlikely midwestern cities, one rain-soaked night on top of a trash can behind the Haddam Public Library, where I was groping around in the dark to find the after-hours drop-off. And once, to my dismay, in a friend's house shortly after he'd blown his brains out, though I never thought my book played a part. Once published, a book never strays so far from its author.

But without thinking a thought about its absolute worth, I intend to put my book in Char's hands the moment she arrives and to speak the words I can't now wait to speak: "Who do you think wrote *this*, that I found right here on the shelf below Natty Bumppo's portrait and hard by the J. F. Coopers?" (My two like-nesses will be my proof.) And not that it'll have any important favorable effect on her. But for *me*, finding it still in "use" is high on the manifest of writerly thrills longed for—along with seeing someone you don't know hungrily reading your book on an overland bus in Turkey; or noticing your book on the shelf behind the moderator on *Meet the Press* next to *The Wealth of Nations* and *Giants in the Earth*; or seeing your book on a list of overlooked American masterpieces compiled by former insiders in the Kennedy administration. (None of these has been my good luck yet.)

I blow the dust off and run my finger over the page ends to uncover the original red stain, then flip to the front and survey the contents page, twelve little titles, each as serious as a eulogy: "Words to Die By," "The Camel's Nose," "Epitaph," "Night Wing," "Waiting Offshore," all the way down to the title story —considered my "chance" at something to expand into a novel and thereby break me into the big time.

The book doesn't in fact seem ever to have been opened (only rained on). I turn past the dedication—"To My Parents" (who else?)—back to the title page, ready to greet crisp "Frank Bas-combe," "*Blue Autumn*" and "1969," set out in sturdy, easy-on-the-eyeball Ehrhardt, and to feel the old synchronicity extend to me in the here and now. Except what my eye finds, scrawled over the title page in blue, and in a hand I don't know, is: "For Esther, remembering that really *bleu* autumn with you. Love ya, Dwayne. Spring, 1970," every bit of which has been x-ed through with a smeary lipstick and below it written: "Dwayne. Rhymes with pain. Rhymes with fuck. Rhymes with the biggest mistake of my life. With contempt for you and your cheap tricks. Esther. Winter, 1972." A big red smooch has been plastered on the page below Esther's signature, and this connected by an arrow to the words "My Ass," also in lipstick. This is a good deal different—by virtue of being a great deal less—than what I'd expected.

But what I feel, dizzily, is not wry, bittersweet, ain't-life-strange amusement at poor Dwayne and Esther's hot flame gone smoking under the waves, but a totally unexpected, sickening void opening right in my stomach—right where I said it wouldn't two minutes ago.

Ann, and the end of Ann and me and everything associated with us, comes fuming up in my nostrils suddenly like a thick poison and in a way it never has even in my darkest seven-year despairings, or in the grim aftermath of my periodic revivals of hope. And instead of bellowing like a gored Cyclops, what I instinctively do is whap my book shut and sling it side-arm whirligig across the room, where it smacks the brown wall, knocks loose a crust of Florida-shaped plaster and hits the floor in the crumbles and dust. (Many fates befall books other than being read and treasured.)

The chasm (and what else is it?) between our long-ago time

and this very moment suddenly makes yawningly clear that all is now done and done for; as though she was never *that* she, me never *that* me, as though the two of us had never embarked on a life that would lead to this queer librarial moment (though we did). And rather than being against all odds, it's in precise accordance with the odds: that life would lead to here or someplace just as lonely and spiritless, no less likely than for Dwayne and fiery, heartbroke Esther, our doubles in love. Gone in a hiss and fizzle. (Though if it weren't that tears had just sprung stinging to my eyes, I'd accept my loss with dignity. Since after all I'm the man who counsels abandonment of those precious things you remember but can no longer make hopeful use of.)

I drag my wrist across my cheeks and dab my eyes with my shirtfront. Someone, I sense, is coming from somewhere in the house, and I hustle over, snake up my book, refit its cover, flatten the pages I've busted and carry it back to its coffin slot, where it can sleep for twenty more years—this just as Char appears at the front door, looks out, then sees me standing here like a teary immigrant and saunters in smelling of cigarettes and appley sweetness applied just on the off chance I might be the guy to buy her that condo.

And Char is not the Char of ten minutes ago. She's dressed now in some shrunk-tight jeans with red cowboy boots, a concha belt, a sleeveless black tank top that reveals strong, round, bare athletic shoulders and the breasts I've already envisioned (now in *much* plainer view). She has done "something" to her eyes, and also to her hair, which has made it frizzier. There's rose color in her cheeks, and what seems like glistening lubricant on her lips, so that she's recognizable from when she was a chef, but only just. Though to me she's not nearly as comely as in her boxy whites, when less of her was in view.

But neither am I in the same "place" emotion-wise as ten minutes ago, nor am I exactly used to women with their tits on such nautical display. And I'm now no longer looking forward to being hauled through the door of the Tunnicliff—a place I can all too perfectly picture—and filling the slot as one of "Char's guys from the inn" while the locals grab off their nightly geeze at those hogans, while writing me off as the doofus I am.

"All right, Mr. Pleasure Unit, you ready to roll? Or are you still reading the instructions?" Char's new eyelashes bat closed and open, her small hazel eyes roguishly fixing me. "What's wrong with your eyes? You been in here crying? Is that what I'm getting into?"

"I looked at a book and got dust in my eyes," I say ludicrously.

"I didn't know anybody ever *read* those books. I thought they were just to make the room look cozy." She surveys the shelves, unimpressed. "Jeremy buys 'em by the metric ton from some recycler up in Albany." She sniffs, detecting some of the cinnamon redolence. "Pew. P-U," she says. "Smells like an old folks' home at Christmas in here. I'm in need of a Black Velvet." She fires me off a challenging smile. A smile with a future.

"Great!" I say, thinking I'd feel better if I could just take a walk by myself down to the soggy lakeshore and hear the tinkly, liquid sounds of faceless, nameless others enjoying themselves gaily in long, red-walled rooms lit by crystal chandeliers. Not much to ask.

But I can't back out on something as unfreighted as a simple walk and a drink, especially since it's me did the asking. Canceling will make me out to be a weepy, cringing nutcase who can't go a step without scuttling back three for fear and shame.

"Maybe I'll just have to break down and cook you a fried-egg sandwich à la Charlane. Since you're so starved." She's moving toward the front screen, her hard butt encased in denim like a rodeo wrangler's, her thighs chunky and taut.

"I should try to find my son eventually, I guess," I mutter not quite loud enough to be heard, following onto the porch, where little town lights twinkle in through the trees.

"Say what?" Char gives me a head-cocked look. We're in the solid porch darkness here now.

"My son Paul's here with me," I say. "We're going to the Hall of Fame in the morning."

"Did you leave Mom at home this time?" She rolls her tongue around inside her cheek again. She has heard a warning signal.

"In a sense I did. I'm not married to her anymore."

"So who *are* you married to?"

"Nobody."

"And where's your son gone?" She glances out around at the dark lawn, as if he's there. She runs a finger under her tank top strap, attempting to seem noncommittal. I sniff apple perfume again. That would have to go.

"I don't know where he is," I say, trying to sound both at ease and concerned. "He sort of took off when we got here. I had a nap."

"When was this?"

"I guess five-thirty or a quarter to six. I'm sure he'll be coming back pretty soon." I've lost all heart for everything now—a walk, the Tunnicliff, a drink, *oeufs à la Charlane*. Though my failure is a part of human mystery I understand, even have sympathy for. "I should maybe stick around here. So he can find me." I smile cravenly at her in the darkness.

Out on the highway a dark car rumbles past, its windows open or its top down, loud rock music blaring and thumping through the silent trees. I can make out one scalding phrase only: "Get wet, go deep, take it all." Paul could be there, in the act of disappearing forever, to be seen by me only on milk cartons or grocery store bulletin boards: "Paul Bascombe, 2–8–73, last seen near Baseball Hall of Fame, 7–2–88." It is not a relaxing thought.

"Well, whatever stokes your flame the hottest, I guess," Charlane says, already I hope thinking of something else. "I gotta take off, though." She's leaving down the steps right away, concluding I'm more trouble than I'm worth, though also probably embarrassed for me.

"Do you have any children?" I say just to say something.

"Oh yeah," she says, and half turns back.

"Where's he right now?" I say. "Or she. Or they?"

"*He's* at wilderness survival."

I hear a faint cry then, a woman's high-pitched voice, brief and ululating, from somewhere above. Char looks up and around, a little smile crossing her lips. "Somebody's enjoying her fireworks early."

"What's your son learning to survive?" I say, trying not to think about the Ohioans right above us. Char and I are descending back through the stages of familiarity and in a minute will once again be unknown to each other.

She sighs. "He's with his dad, who lives out in Montana in a tent or a cave someplace. I don't know. I guess they're surviving each other."

"I'm sure you're a great mom," I say, apropos of nothing.

"Eastern religion," she says in a wise-cracky voice. "Motherhood's as close as I come to it." She raises her small nose toward the warm, spruce-scented air and sniffs. "I smelled a lilac just then, but it's too late for lilacs. Musta been somebody's perfume." She squints down hard at me as though I've suddenly moved far, far away and am moving farther (which I am). It's a friendly squint, full of sympathy, and makes me want to come down off the porch and give her a bustly hug, but which would only confuse matters. "I assume you'll find your son," she says. "Or he'll find you. Whatever."

"We will," I say, holding my ground. "Thanks."

"Yep," Char says, and then, as though she's embarrassed by something else, adds, "They don't usually stay gone long. Not long enough, really." Then she hikes off into the trees alone, gone out of sight well before I can manage an audible good-bye.

"*TRÈS AMUSANT*," a voice familiar to me speaks out of the summer's wicking darkness. "*Très, très amusant.* Your most important sexual organ is between your ears. Eeeck, eeeck, eeeck. So use it."

Down the porch, in the last rocking chair in line, Paul is slouched barely visible behind his drawn-up knees, his *The Rock* shirt giving out the only light hereabouts. He's been overhearing my cumbersome parting, no doubt wondering if I'll get around to finding our dinner.

"Howz ur health?" I say, walking down the line of rockers, laying a palm on the smooth spindled back of his and giving it a small, fatherly push.

"Fine 'n' yours?"

"Is that Dr. Rection's anatomy advice?" I am, God knows, full of airy relief he's not departed for Chicago or the Bay Area in the blaring-music car, or not off getting his ashes perilously hauled, or, worse, stretched out in the Cooperstown ER with a wound drip-drip-dripping on the tiles, waiting for some old turkey-neck GP, woozy from the Tunnicliff, to shake his head clear. (If I intend to have him home with me, I'll need to be more vigilant.)

"Was that my new mom?"

"Almost. Did you eat anything?"

"I got a mocktail, some mock turtle soup and a piece of mock apple pie. Don't mock me, please." These are all holdovers from childhood. If I could see his face, it would be worked into a look of secret satisfaction. He seems, however, completely calm. I might be making progress with him and not realizing it (every parent's dearest hope).

"Do you want to call your mother and say you got here safely?"

"Ix-nay." He's tossing a little Hacky Sack up and down in the dark, barely making movement but suggesting he's less calm than seems. I have an aversion to Hacky Sacks. My view is that its skills are perfect only for the sort of brain-dead delinquents who whonked me in the head on my way home from work this spring and sent me sprawling. I understand from it, though, that Paul may have made a connection with the towny kids on the corner.

"Where'd you get that thing?"

"I purchased it." He still hasn't looked around. "At the local Finast." I would still like to ask him if he killed the helpless, driveway grackle, only it now seems too unwieldy a subject. It also seems preposterous to think he could be guilty. "I've got a new question to ask you." He says this in a more assertive voice. Conceivably he's spent the last four hours in a badly lit diner studying Emerson, fingering his Hacky Sack and mulling issues such as whether nature really suffers nothing to remain in her kingdom that can't help itself; or whether every true man is a cause, a country and an age. Good issues for anyone to mull.

"Okay," I say just as assertively, not wanting to seem as eager and encouraged as I am. From across the lawn the tart odor not of lilac but of a car's exhaust reaches my nostrils. I hear an owl, invisible on a nearby spruce bough. *Who-who, who-who, who-who.*

"Okay, do you remember when I was pretty little," Paul says very seriously, "and I used to invent friends? I had some talks with them, and they said things to me, and I'd get pretty involved doing it?" He stares fiercely forward.

"I remember it. Are you doing it again?" This is not about Emerson.

He looks around at me now, as if he wants to see my face. "No. But did it make you feel weird when I did that? Like make you mad or sick and want to puke?"

"I don't think so. Why?" I'm able to make out his eyes. I'm certain he thinks I'm lying.

"You're lying, but it's okay."

"I felt odd about it," I say. "Not any of those other things, though." I am not willing to be called a liar and have no defense in the truth.

"Why were you?" He doesn't seem angry.

"I don't know. I never thought about it."

"Then think. I *need* to know. It's like one of my rings." He shifts back around and trains his gaze across toward the windows of the fancier inn across the road, where fewer warm and yellow room lights are on now. He wants my voice in his ears perfectly distilled. The waning moon has laid a silken, sparkling path dead across the lake, and above its luminance is arrayed a feast of summer stars. He makes, and I vaguely hear it, another tiny *eeeck*, a self-assuring sound, a little rallying *eeeck*.

"It made me feel a little weird," I say uncomfortably. "I thought you were getting preoccupied with something that maybe was hurtful in the long run." (Innocence, what else? Though that word seems not exactly right either.) "I wanted you not to get tricked. I guess maybe it wasn't very generous of me. I'm sorry. Maybe I'm wrong too. I could've just been jealous. I am sorry."

I hear him breathe, air hitting his bare knees where he has them hugged up to his chest. I feel a small loosening of relief, mixed of course with shame for ever making him feel his pre-occupations mattered less than mine. Who'd have thought we'd talk about this?

"It's all right," he says, as if he knew a great, great deal about me.

"Why'd this come to mind?" I say, a warm hand still on his rocking chair, his back still turned to me.

"I just remember it. I liked doing it, and I thought you thought it was bad. Don't you really think something's wrong with me?" he says—unbeknownst to him, fully within his own command now, an adult for just this moment.

"I don't think so. Not especially."

"On a scale of one to five, with five being hopeless?"

"Oh," I say. "One, probably. Or one and a half. It's better than me. Not as good as your sister."

"Do you think I'm shallow?"

"What do you do that's shallow?" I wonder where he's been to come back with these questions.

"Make noises sometimes. Other things."

"They aren't very important."

"Do you remember how old Mr. Toby would be now? I'm sorry to ask that."

"Thirteen," I say bravely. "You did ask me about that today already."

"He could still be alive, though." He rocks forward, then back, then forward. Maybe life will seem better when Mr. Toby reaches the end of his optimum life span. I hold his chair steady. "I'm thinking I'm thinking again," he says as if to himself. "Things don't fit down together right for very long."

"Are you worried about your court hearing?" I pinch his chairback hard between my fingers and hold it nearly still.

"Not especially," he says, copying me. "Were you supposed to give me some big advice about it?"

"Just don't try to be the critic of your age, that's all. Don't be a wise-ankle. Let your best qualities come through naturally. You'll be fine." I touch his clean cotton shoulder, ashamed again, this time for waiting till now to touch him lovingly.

"Are you coming up with me?"

"No. Your mother's going."

"I think Mom's got a boyfriend."

"That's not interesting to me."

"Well, it should be." He says this completely without commitment.

"You don't know. Why do you think you remember everything and think you're thinking?"

"I don't know." He stares out at headlights that are curving along the road in front of our inn. "That stuff just comes back around all the time."

"Do the things seem important to you?"

"Importanter than what?"

"I don't really know. Importanter than something else you might do." The debating club, getting your Junior Life Saver's certificate, anything in the here and now.

"I don't want to have it forever. That'd be completely fucked up." His teeth click down once and grind together hard. "Like today for a while, back at the basketball thing, it went away for a while. Then I got it back."

We pause in silence again. The first adult conversation a man can have with his son is one in which he acknowledges he doesn't know what's good for his own child and has only an out-of-date idea of what's bad. I don't know what to say.

Through the trees now there comes into view a medium-size brown-and-white dog, a springer, loping toward us, a yellow Frisbee in his mouth, his collar jingling, his breath exaggerated and audible. Somewhere out behind him, a man's hearty voice, someone out for a walk in the parky darkness. "Keester! Here, Keester," the voice says. "Come on now, Keester. Fetch it! Keester—here, Keester." Keester, on a mission of his own, stops, looks at us in the porch shadows, sniffs us, his Frisbee clenched tight, while his master strolls on, calling.

"Come on now, Keester," Paul says. "Eeeck, eeeck."

"It's Keester, the wonder dog," I say. Keester seems happy to be just that.

"I was bewildered when I saw I'd turned into a dog—"

"Named Keester," I say. Keester stares up at us now, uncertain why we strangers would know his name. "I guess my thinking is," I say, "you're trying to keep too much under control, son, and it's holding you back. Maybe you're trying to stay in touch with something you liked, but you have to keep going. Even if it's scary and you screw up."

"Uh-huh." He leans his head back toward me and looks up. "How can I not be a critic of my age? Is that something you think's pretty great?"

"It doesn't have to be great," I say. "But for instance, if you go in a restaurant and the floor's marble and the walls are oak, you wouldn't wonder if it's all fake. You'd sit down and order tournedos and be happy. And if you don't like it, or you think it's a mistake to eat there, you just don't come back. Does that make any sense?"

"No." He shakes his head confidently. "I probably wouldn't stop thinking about it. Sometimes it's not that bad to think about it. Keester," he says in a sharp command voice to poor old baffled Keester. "Think! Think, boy! Remember your name."

"It *will* make sense," I say. "You don't have to fight to get everything right, that's all. Sometimes you can relax." I notice two more yellow window squares go dark in the big inn across the way. *Who-who*, goes the owl. *Who-who. Who-who.* He's got Keester in his sights, standing stupidly with his yellow Frisbee, waiting for us to get interested in throwing it, as we always do.

"If you're a tightrope walker in the circus, what's your best trick?" Paul looks up at me, smiling cruelly.

"I don't know. Doing it blindfolded. Doing it naked."

"Falling," Paul says authoritatively.

"That's not a trick," I say. "It's a fuck-up."

"Yeah, but he can't stand the straight and narrow another minute, because it's so boring. And nobody ever knows if he falls or jumps. It's great."

"Who told you about that?" Keester, finally disappointed by us, turns and trots off through the trees, becoming a paler and paler hole in the dark, then is gone.

"Clarissa. She's worse than I am. She just doesn't show it. She doesn't act out anything, because she's sneaky."

"Who says?" I am absolutely certain this isn't true, certain she's just as she seems, flipping the bird behind her parents' backs like any normal girl.

"Dr. Lew D. Zyres sez," Paul says, and suddenly bounds up, with me still clinging to his chairback. "My session's over tonight, Doctah." He starts off toward the front screen, his big shoes noisily clunkety-clunking on the porch boards. He is again trailing a sour smell. Possibly it is the smell of stress-related problems. "We need some fireworks," he says.

"I've got bottle rockets and sparklers in the car. And this wasn't a session. We don't have sessions. This was you and your father having a serious talk."

"People are always shocked at me when I say"—the screen swings open and Paul tromps in out of sight—"ciao."

"I love you," I say to my son, slipping away, but who should hear these words again if only to be able to recall much later on: "Somebody said that to me, and nothing since then has really seemed quite as bad as it might have."

"YOU KNOW, Jerry, the truth is I just began to realize I didn't care what happened to me, you know? Worry and worry about making your life come out right, you know? Regret everything you say or do, everything seems to sabotage you, then you try to quit sabotaging yourself. But then *that's* a mistake. Finally you just have to figure a lot's out of your control, right?"

"Right! Thanks! Bob from Sarnia! Next caller. You're on *Blues Talk*. You're on the air, Oshawa!"

"Hi, Jerry, it's Stan. . . ."

Out my window a tall, blond, bronze-skinned, no-shirt, chisel-chest hombre of about my own age is working a big chamois cloth over a red vintage Mustang with what looks to be red-and-white Wisconsin plates. For some reason he's wearing green lederhosen, and it is his loud and blarey radio that has shaken me awake. Crackling morning light and leafy shadow spread across the gravel and the lawns of neighborhood houses behind the inn. It's Sunday. The lederhosen guy's here for the "Classic Car Parade," which rolls tomorrow, and doesn't want the dust and grime to get ahead of him. His pretty plump-as-a-knödel wife is perched on the fender of *my* car, sunning her short brown legs and smiling. They've hung their bright red floor mats off my bumper to dry.

Another American—Joe Markham, for instance—might snarl out at them: "Getyerfuckinmatsoffyaasshole." But that would spoil a morning, wake the world too early (including my son). Bob from Sarnia has already put it well enough.

By eight I've shaved and showered, using the clammy, tiny-windowed, beaverboard cubicle, already hot and malodorous from the previous user (I spied the woman with the neck brace slipping in, slipping out).

Paul is twisted into his covers when I rouse him with our oldest reveille: "Time's a wastin' . . . miles to go . . . I'm hungry as a bear . . . hop in the shower." We've checked out when we checked in and now have only to eat and beat it.

Then I'm down the stairs, hearing church bells already, as well as the muffled sumptuary noises of belly-buster breakfasts being eaten in the dining room by a group of total strangers who have only the Baseball Hall of Fame in common.

I'm eager to call Ted Houlihan (I forgot to try again last night), and get him ready for a miracle: the Markhams have crumbled; my strategy's borne fruit; his balls are as good as gone. Though the choking-man diagram, here again above the phone as I listen to ring after ring, reminds me unerringly of what realty's all about: we—the Markhams, the bad apples at Buy and Large, Ted, me, the bank, the building inspectors—we're all hankering to get our hands around somebody's neck and strangle the shit out of him for some little half-chewed piece of indigestible gristle we identify as our "nut," the nitty gritty, the carrot that makes the goat trot. Better, of course, to take a higher road, operate on the principle of service and see if things don't turn out better. . . .

"Hello?"

"Hey, good news, Ted!" I shout straight into the receiver. The breakfast club in the next room falls hushed at my voice—as if I'd gone hysterical.

"Good news here too," Ted says.

"Let's hear yours first." I am instantly wary.

"I sold the house," Ted says. "Some new outfit down in New Egypt. Bohemia, or something, Realty. They got it off the MLS. The woman brought a Korean family over last night around eight. And I had an offer in hand by ten." When I was gabbing with Paul about whether or not he's truly hopeless. "I called you around nine and left a message. But I really couldn't say no. They put the money in their trust account night deposit."

"How much?" I say grimly. I experience a small, tight chill and my stomach goes corked.

"What's that?"

"How much did the Koreans pay?"

"Full boat!" Ted says exuberantly. "Sure. One fifty-five. I jewed the girl a point too. She hadn't done anything to earn it. You'd done more by a long shot. Your office gets half, of course."

"My clients just don't have anyplace to live now, Ted." My voice has lowered to a razor-thin whisper. I would be happy to choke Ted with my hands. "We had an exclusive listing with you, we talked about that yesterday, and at the least you were going to get in touch with me so I could put a competitive offer in, which is what I've got authorized." Or nearly. "One fifty-five. Full boat, you said."

"Well." Ted pauses in a funk. "I guess if you want to come back at one-sixty, I could tell the Koreans I forgot. Your office would have to work it out with Bohemia. Evelyn something's the girl's name. She's a little go-getter."

"What I think is, Ted, we're going to have to probably sue you for breach of contract." I say this calmly, but I'm not calm. "Have to tie your house up for a couple of years while the market drops, and let you convalesce at home." All baloney, of course. We've never sued the first client. It's business suicide. Instead, you simply bag your 3 percent, of which I get half, exactly $2,325, maybe make a worthless complaint to the state realty board, and forget about it.

"Well, you have to do what you have to do, I guess," Ted says. I'm sure he's standing once again at the rumpus room window in a sleeveless sweater and chinos, mooning out at his pergola, his luau torches and the bamboo curtain he's just breached in a big way. I wonder if the Koreans even bothered to walk out back last night. Although a big lighted prison might've made them feel safer. They aren't fools.

"Ted, I don't know what to say." The noisy eaters in the next room have started back tink-tink-tinking their flatware, mouths full of pancakes, blabbing about how the berm-improvements work between here and Rochester'll "impact" on driving times to the Falls. Suddenly my chill is over and I'm hot as a sauna bath.

"You might just feel happy for me, Frank, instead of suing me. I'll probably be dead in a year. So it's good I sold my house. I can go live with my son now."

"I really just wanted to sell it for you, Ted." I am made light-headed at the unexpected arousal of death. "I've *got* it sold, in fact," I say faintly.

"You'll find them another house, Frank. I didn't think they much liked it here."

I push my fingertips hard onto the stack of year-old *Annie Get Your Gun* tickets. Someone, I see, has slid the copy of *Achieve Super Marital Sex* underneath the stack, with old Mr. Pleasure Unit's happy face peeking upward. "They liked it a lot," I say, thinking about Betty Hutton in a cowboy hat. "They were cautious, but they're sure now. I hope your Koreans are that reliable."

"Twenty thousand clams. No contingencies," Ted says. "And they know there's other parties interested, so they'll follow up. These people don't throw money away, Frank. They own a sod farm down around Fort Dix, and they want to move up in the world." He would like to burble on about his good fortune now that he's started, but doesn't out of politeness to me.

"I'm just really disappointed, Ted. That's all I can say." Though I'm inventorying my mind for an acceptable fallback, sweat beginning to prickle out of my forehead. I'm to blame for this, for getting diverted from standard practices (though I don't know that I have any practice I could class as standard).

"Who you voting for this fall?" Ted says. "You guys all pull for business, I guess, don't you?" I'm wondering if some computer wizard at Bohemia has hacked into our office circuitry. Or possibly Julie Loukinen, who's new, is double-dipping on our potentials list. I try to remember if I've ever seen her with a scruffy Eastern European-looking boyfriend. Though most likely Ted just listed his house as "exclusive" with everybody who came to the door. (And who can be surprised in a free country? It's laissez-faire: serve your granny to the neighbors for brunch.) "You know neither Dukakis or Bush wants to put out a budget. They don't want to deliver any unhappy news in case it might offend somebody. I'd much rather they told me they were about to fuck me so I wouldn't tense up." Randy new lingo for Ted, the successful house seller. "You want me to take that sign down, by the way?"

"We'll send somebody out," I say glumly.

Then suddenly my line to Penns Neck goes loud with fierce papery static so that I can barely hear Ted jibbering on, half gassed, about fin de siècle qualms and something or other, I don't know what.

"I can't hear you now, Ted," I say into the old gunk-smelling receiver, frowning at the stick-figure man signaling me he's choking, his own hands at his throat, a look of rounded dismay on his balloon face. Then the static stops and I can hear Ted starting in about Bush and Dukakis not being able to tell a good joke if their asses depended on it. I hear him laugh at the whole idea. "So long, Ted," I say, sure he can't hear me.

"I read where Bush accepted Christ as his personal savior. Now there's a joke . . . ," Ted's saying extra loud.

I set the receiver gently in its cradle, understanding this bit of life—his and mine—is now over with. I'm almost grateful.

MY SWORN duty is of course to call the Markhams in a timely manner and break the news, which I try to do, though they're not in their room at the Raritan Ramada. (No doubt they're going through the brunch buffet a second time, cocky for making the right decision—too late.) No one comes on the line after twenty-five rings. I call back to leave a message, but a recording puts me on hold, then leaves me out in murky "hold" purgatory, where an FM station is playing "Jungle Flute." I count to sixty, my hands getting clammy, then decide to call back later since nothing's at stake anymore.

There are other calls I should make. A hectoring, early-bird "business" call to the McLeods, with an innuendo of unspecified pending actions regarding matters of rent irrespective of personal financial pinches; a call to Julie Loukinen just to let her know "somebody" has let Ted swim through the net. A call to Sally to reaffirm all feelings and say whatever comes into my head, no matter how puzzling. None of these, though, do I feel quite up to. Each seems too complicated on a hot morning, none likely to be rewarding.

But just as I turn to go shake Paul loose from his dreams again, I feel a sudden, flushed, almost breathless urge to call Cathy Flaherty in Gotham. Plenty of times I've considered just how welcome (and gratifying) it would be were she just to appear on my doorstep with a bottle of Dom Perignon, demanding an instant barometer reading on me, take my temperature, get the lowdown on how I've *really* been since we last made contact, having naturally enough thought about me no fewer than a million times, with multiple what-ifs embedded everywhere, finally deciding to hunt me down via the Michigan Alumni Association and show up unannounced but "hopefully" not unwelcome. (In my first-draft of the script, we only talk.)

As I was thinking in my room at Sally's two days ago, few things are as pleasing as being asked to do basically nothing but having all good things come to you as if by right. It's exactly what poor Joe Markham wanted to happen with his Boise "friend," except she was too smart for him.

As it happens, I still have Cathy's number committed to memory from the last time I heard her voice, after Ann announced four years ago that she and Charley were tying the knot and taking the kids, and I was tossed for several loop-the-loops, landing me in the realty business. (Back then I only heard Cathy's recorded message and couldn't think of one of my own to leave other than to shout "Help, help, help, help!" and hang up, which I decided against.)

But almost before I know it, I've dialed the old number in old 212—a place once guaranteed to work a strange, funkish, double-whammy of low self-regard on me when I worked there as a sportswriter and life was coming unglued the first time. (Now it seems no stranger than Cleveland; such are the freeing, desanctifying fringe benefits of selling real estate.)

More avid cafeteria-eating noises, commingled with mirthless laughter, rise and ebb from next door. I wait for the 212 circuits to lock in on a ring and an answer to occur to someone—honey-haired, honey-skinned Cathy, I'm happily hoping, by now a bona fide M.D., doing her something-or-other, highly competitive specialty whatchamacallit up at Einstein or Cornell, and conceivably willing (it's also my hope) to take me on for a few moments' out-of-context, ad hominem–pro bono phone "treatment." (I'm actually counting on reverse spin here, by which the sound of Cathy's voice will at once make me feel smart—as can happen—but also feel that I'd better get cracking or face being plowed under by advancing generations with ice water in their veins.)

Ring-ring-ring-a-jing. Ring-ring-ring. Then click. Then a brusque mechanical whir, then another click. It's not promising. Then, finally, a voice—male, young, smug, as yet undisappointed, an insufferable smart aleck for whom outgoing messages are nothing but chances to gloatingly entertain himself, while demonstrating what an asshole he is to us blameless callers-in. "Hi. This is Cathy and Steve's answering mechanism. We're not home now. Really. I promise. We're not lounging in bed making faces and laughing. Cathy's probably at the hospital, saving lives or something like that. I'm probably down at Burnham and Culhane, slicing out a bigger piece of the pie for myself. So just be patient and leave us a message, and when time permits one of us will call you back. Probably it'll be Cathy, since answering machines really kind of bug me. See ya. Bye. Of course wait for the beep."

Beeeeeeeeeeeeeeeeeeeeep, click, then the yawning, paralyzing opportunity to leave the most appropriate of messages. "Hi, Cathy?" I say, exhilarated. "It's Frank." (Less exhilarated.) "Um. Bascombe. Nothing special, really. I'm, uh, it's the Fourth of July, or right about then. I'm just up here in Cooperstown, just happened to think about you." At 8 a.m. "I'm glad to know you're at the hospital. That's a good sign. I'm pretty fine. Up here with my son, Paul, who you don't know." A long pause while the tape's running. "Well, that's about it. By the way, you can tell Steve for me that he can kiss my ass, and I'd be happy to beat the shit out of him any day he can find the time. Bye." Click. I stand a moment, the receiver in my sweaty hand, assessing what I've just done in terms of how it has left me feeling, and also in terms of its character as a small but rash act, possibly foolish and demeaning. And the answer is: better. Much better. Unaccountably. Some idiotic things are well worth doing.

I hike back upstairs to pack, roll Paul out and get the day whacking, since at least for my main purpose (the Markhams aside) it still has some rudiments of promise based on last night's edgy rapprochement and in any case will end soon enough far from here, with Sally at Rocky and Carlo's.

Paul meets me at the head of the stairs, hauling along his Paramount bag and wearing his Walkman ear calipers on his neck. He's groggy and wet-haired, but he's put on fresh baggy maroon shorts, fresh Day-Glo-orange socks and a big new black tee-shirt that for reasons I know nothing of says *Clergy* in white on the front (possibly a rock group). When he sees me coming up he offers me his fat-cheeked, impassive expression, as if knowing about me was one thing but seeing me quite another. "I'm surprised to see a fart-smeller like you up here," he says, then makes a little throaty *oink* and passes on down the stairs.

In five minutes, though, after making a check for telltale wetness in Paul's sheets (nothing), I'm back downstairs with my suit bag and my Olympus, ready for breakfast, except the big dining room is still packed with poky breakfasters and Paul is standing at the doorway, staring in with amused disdain. Charlane, in a tight tee-shirt and the same faded jeans from last night, is serving more plates of flapjacks and bacon and bowls of steaming instant scrambled. She looks at me but seems not to recognize me. So that I quickly decide there's no use waiting (and being ministered to spitefully by Charlane) when we can just as well stash our gear in the car, hike to Main and scare up breakfast for ourselves before the Hall of Fame opens at nine. In other words, let the old Deerslayer sink into history.

Though it hasn't been that bad a place, lack of an honor bar notwithstanding. Inside its walls, I may have ended the seemingly unendable with Ann, dodged a ricochet with Charlane and, possibly, set things on the rails with Sally Caldwell. Plus, Paul and I have skirmished nearer each other's trust, and I have been able at least to speak a few of the way-pointing words I'd prepared for that purpose. All noteworthy accomplishments. With only slightly better luck, the Deerslayer could've become a hallowed and even sacred place where, say, early next century, Paul could come back alone or with a wife or girlfriend or his own troublesome brood, and tell them this was a place he "used to come with his late dad," where life-altering wisdom that made all the difference in later life was passed along—though he might not be able to say with complete certainty what the wisdom was.

Several munching breakfasters (I see no one I recognize) have raised wintry eyes up from their plates to where Paul and I are standing at the dining room door, briefly transfixed by deep currents of good coffee, smoked sausage, hash browns, sticky buns, pancake syrup, scrapple and powdered eggs. Their guarded eyes say, "Hey, we won't be hurried." "We've paid for this." "We're entitled to our own pace." "It's our vacation." "Waitch-yerturn." "Isn't that the joker who was shouting on the phone?" "What about this 'Clergy' shirt?" "Something's fishy here."

Paul, though, his Paramount bag slung to his pudgy shoulder, suddenly sets both his hands palms out against the invisible wall and begins sliding them place to place, here and there, up, down, side to side, a look of empty-mouthed horror contorting his sweet boy's face, and whispering "Help me, help me. I don't want to die."

"So I don't think there's room at the inn for us, son," I say.

"Please don't let me die," Paul continues softly, so only I can hear. "Just don't drop the tablet in the acid. Please, warden." He *is* a sweet, tricky boy and after my heart—my ally just when (or almost when) I feel most in need.

He turns his dying-man's face of hollow-yap horror up to me, his hands now to his cheeks in silent, stricken astonishment. No one in the room has the will to look at him now, their noses back in their vittles like jailbirds. He makes two plainly audible *eeeck*s that seem to come out of the bottom of a shallow well. "Alias Sibelius," he says.

"What's that mean?" I hike my suit bag up, ready to roll.

"It's a good punch line. I can't think of the joke, though. Mom puts arsenic in my food since she got a boyfriend. So my IQ's dropping."

"I'll try to talk to her," I say, and then we are off, no one noticing as we step together out into the morning's hot brilliance, bound for the Hall of Fame.

CHURCH BELLS now clang and clatter all over town, rounding 'em up for morning worship. Well-dressed, pale-faced family groups of three, four and even six march two abreast down every village sidewalk, veering this way toward the Second Methodist, that way toward the Congregationalists, across to Christ Church Episcopal and the First Prez. Others, less well turned out—men in clean but unpressed work khakis and polo shirts, women in red wraparounds, no stockings and a scarf—exit cars to dash into Our Lady of the Lake for a brief and breathless brush with grace before heading off to a waitress job, a tee time or an assignation in some other village.

Paul and I, on the other hand, fit in well with the pilgrim feel of things temporal—nonworshipful, nonpious, camera-toting dads and sons, dads and daughters, in summery togs, winding our certain but vaguely embarrassed way toward the Hall of Fame (as if there were something shameful about going). Cars are moving by us, the Gay Nineties trolleys toting "senior groups" to the town's other attractions—the Fenimore House and the Farmers' Museum, where there are displays and demos of things as they used to be when the world was better. Plus, all the shops are open, ice cream's for sale, music's in the air, the lake's full of water, nothing a visitor could want wouldn't be taken into at least partial account by somebody.

We have parked our gear in the car behind the inn and hiked by dead reckoning down to the marina and into a booth in a little aqua-blue eatery with oversize windows called The Water's Edge, built right out over the water like Charley's studio, only on creosote pilings. Inside, though, it's so rigidly cold that the cheese fries and Denver omelet aromas seem as dank as the inside of an old ice chest, making me feel, in spite of scenic lake views, that we would've been smarter to wait for a place where we'd already paid.

Paul, on our walk over through the short, lakeside back streets lined with homey blue-collar abodes, has raised himself to the best good humor of the trip, and once we're in our red booth has commenced a wide-ranging discourse of what it'd be like to live in Cooperstown.

Working over his Deluxe Belgian, piled with canned whipped cream and gelid strawberries, he declares that if we were to move here he would definitely invest in a "big paper route" (in Deep River, he says, this is an industry bossed over by "Italian greasers" who kick ass on whitebread kids who try to horn in). He likewise says, all sarcasm gone, gray eyes sparkling while he eats, that he'd feel obligated to visit the Hall of Fame once a week until he had it memorized—"Why else live here?"—and that he would eat here at The Water's Edge "religiously every Sunday morning," just like now, would find out all about the Cardiff Giant (another local attraction) and the Farmers' Museum, possibly even work there as a guide, and would probably go out for baseball and football. He also surprisingly informs me, while I'm plowing through my own fast-congealing "Home Run Plate" and occasionally gazing out at a flock of mallards mooching popcorn from boat dock tourists, that he's decided to read all of Emerson when he gets home, since he'll probably be on probation and have more time for reading. He muddles his liquefying whipped cream around over his waffle cleats, getting it conscientiously into all sectors while explaining to me, head down, his Walkman still on his neck, that as a "borderline dyslexic" (this is news to me) he notices more than most people in his age bracket, since he doesn't "process" things as fast and ends up having more opportunity to consider (or get completely derailed by) "certain subjects," which is why he reads the labor-intensive *New Yorker*— "klepto'd out of Chuck's crapper"—and why in fact he's come to believe I need to ditch the realty business—"not interesting enough"—and move away from New Jersey—ditto—possibly to "a place sort of like this one," and maybe get into a business like furniture stripping or bartending, something hands-on and low-stress, and "maybe get back to writing stories." (He has always respected the fact that I was briefly a writer and keeps a signed copy of *Blue Autumn* in his room.)

My heart, needless to say, leaps to him. Beneath the turmoiled surfaces he means everyone everywhere all the best, security guards included. Cooperstown, even before he's stepped through the doors of its magical Hall of Fame, has won a magical victory over him by inducing a stress-free idyll of small-pond-big-fish ordinariness he would dearly love to be his. (Seemingly all his bad-fitting rings have spun down into happy congruence.) Though I can't help wondering if this brief flight of empire-sketching might not be the happiest moment of his life, and in a twinkling he may look back on it with no clarity, no grasp of the details. It may in fact turn out to cause him even greater anxiety and wider warping since he'll never summon up such an idyll again in just this way and yet will never completely forget it or stop wondering about where it's gone. This is the cautionary view I took when he was small and talked to people who weren't there, a view I might've thought would protect him. I should've known, however, as I know now and as it ever is with kids and even those who're older: nothing stays as it is for long and, once again, there's no such thing as a false sense of well-being.

I should raise my Olympus now and snap his picture in this official happy moment. Only I can't risk breaking his spell, since soon enough he'll look again on life and conclude like the rest of us that he used to be happier but can't remember exactly how.

"But look," I say, staying in the spell with him, my hands cold, gazing at the top of his gouged head while he studies his waffle, his mind springing and lurching, his jaw muscles dedicatedly seeking the best alignment for his molars. (I love his fair, delicate scalp.) "I like real estate a lot. It's both forward-thinking and conservative. It was always an ideal of mine to combine those two."

He does not look up. The old skinny-armed fry cook, wearing a stained tee-shirt and a dirty sailor's topper, leers at us from behind the row of empty counter stools and salt-and-pepper caddies. He senses we're locking horns—over a divorce, a change in private schools, a bad report card, a drug bust, whatever visiting dads and sons usually bicker over within his earshot (usually *not* a father's midlife career choices). I flash him a threatening look that makes him shake his head, hang a damp cigarette from his snaggly mouth and reconsider his grill.

Only three other diners are here with us—a man and woman who aren't talking, merely sitting by a window staring at the lake over coffee, and an older, bald man in green pants and green nylon shirt playing an illegal poker machine in the dark and farthest corner, once in a while scoring a noisy win.

"You know the tightrope walker act? About falling off and having that be your great trick?" Paul is ignoring what I've declared about the delicate balance between progressivism and conservatism, with the fulcrum being the realty business. "That was just a joke." He looks up at me, narrows his eyes over his three-quarters scarfed waffle and blinks his long lashes. He is a smarter boy than any.

"I guess I knew that," I lie, clamping eye contact back on him. "But I took you seriously, though. I was just pretty sure you knew that making wild changes didn't have much to do with real self-determination, which is what I want you to have, and which is really pretty much a natural sort of thing. It's not that complicated." I smile at him goonily.

"I've decided where I want to go to college." He inserts one finger in the slick residue of maple syrup, which he's moated all around his waffle, drawing a circle, then licking the sweet off with a pop.

"I'm all leers," I say, which makes him give me an arch look; one more of our jokes from the trunk of lost childhood, *Take it for granite. A new leash on life. Put your monkey where your mouse is.* He, like me, is drawn to the fissures between the literal and the imagined.

"There's this place in California, okay? You go to college and work on a ranch and get to brand cows and learn to rope horses."

"Sounds good," I say, nodding, wanting to keep our spirit level high.

"Yep, it is," he says, a young Gary Cooper.

"You think you can study astrophysics on a cayuse?"

"What's a cayuse?" He's forgotten about being a cartoonist.

"Aren't we going fishing?" he says, and quickly moves his gaze outward to where the big lake extends from the boat slips toward folded indistinct mountain headlands. On the dock's edge a girl is seated wearing a black bathing suit and an orange float vest, a pair of short water skis fastened to her feet. A sleek speedboat with her friends inside, two boys and a girl, rocks at idle fifty feet out, its motor gurgling. All in the boat are watching her on the dock. Suddenly the girl flags her hand up and wide. One boy turns and guns the boat, which even through our window glass gurgles loudly, then roars, seems for an instant to hesitate, then surges, almost leaps to life, its nose up, its rear sunk in foam, catching the thick rope-slack and yanking the girl off the dock and onto her skis, lariating her forward over the water's mirror top away from us, until she is—faster than would seem possible— small upon the lake, a colorless dot against the green hills. "That'd be the butt, Bob," Paul says, watching fiercely. He has seen this, almost exactly, on the Connecticut yesterday, but offers no sign of remembering.

"I guess we're not going fishing," I admit reluctantly. "I don't think we've got time now. I had a big imagination. I just thought we had forever. We may have to miss Canton, Ohio, and Beaton, Texas, too." It doesn't matter to him, I think, though I wonder bleakly if one day he'll be my guardian and do a better job. I also wonder just as bleakly if Ann actually has a boyfriend, and if so where she meets him, and what she wears and if she lies to truth-teller Charley the way I used to lie to her (my guess is she does).

"How many times do you think you'll get married?" Paul says, still watching the faraway skier, not wanting to trade eyes with me on this subject—one he does care about. He looks quickly around behind the grill at the big wall-size color photo of a hamburger on a clean white plate, with a bowl of strangely red soup and a fountain Coke, all coated with grease enough to hold a fly captive till Judgment Day. He has asked me this question as recently as two days ago, I think.

"Oh, I don't know," I say. "Eight, nine times before I'm good 'n' done, I guess." I shut my eyes, then slowly open them so he is in dead center. "What the hell do you care? Have you got some old bag in the stripping business you want me to meet down in Oneonta?" He, of course, knows Sally from our visits to the Shore but has remained significantly silent about her, as he should.

"It doesn't matter," he says almost inaudibly, my fear—the ordinary and abiding parent's fear that he'll miss his childhood—clearly unfounded, given the look on his face. Though Ann's fear, of harm and of his frailty, rises to my mind's view like a warning—a boating mishap, a collision at a bad intersection, a kid's punch-out whereby his tender forehead kisses a curb. Letting him sly away into the dark unguarded last night would definitely be frowned on by the experts, might possibly even be seen as abusive.

He is pick-picking at the duct tape that holds together The Water's Edge's ancient plastic booths. "I wish we could stay here another day," he says.

"Well, we'll have to come back." I'm out with my camera then in half a second. "Lemme make yer pitcher to prove you really came." Paul quickly looks behind him as if to find out who'll mind having his picture taken. The coffee drinkers have slipped away and wandered off down the dock. The poker player has his back humped over his machine. The cook is occupied whipping up a breakfast of his own. Paul looks back at me across the little table, his eyes troubled by a wish for something more, for more to get in the picture—me, possibly. But that's not possible. He is all there is.

"Tell me another good joke," I say in behind my Olympus, through which his girlish boy's face is small but fully captured.

"Have you got the hamburger in the picture?" he says, and looks stern.

"Yeah," I say, "the hamburger's in." And it is.

"That's what I was worried about," he says, then brightly, wonderfully smiles at me.

And that is the picture I will keep of him forever.

UP THE WELCOMINGLY warm morning hill we trudge, side by each, bound finally for the Hall of Fame. It's 9:30, and time is in fact a-wastin'. Though when we round the corner onto sunny Main, a half block from the Hall—red brick, with Greek pediments and dubious trefoils on the gable ends, an architectural rattlebag resembling the building-fund dream of some over-zealous flock of Wesleyans—something again is amiss. Out front, on the sidewalk, another or possibly the same cadre of men and women, boys and girls, is marching a circle, hoisting placards, sporting sandwich boards and chanting what from here—the red-white-and-blue-buntinged corner by Schneider's German Bakery—sounds again like "shooter, shooter, shooter." Though there seem to be more marchers now, plus an encircling group of spectators—fathers and sons, larger families, assorted oldsters, alongside normal every-Sunday parishioners just sprung by Father Damien down at Our Lady—all crowding and observing the marchers and spilling back into the street, slowing traffic and jamming the building entry, the exact coordinates Paul and I are vectored for.

"What's this happy horseshit again?" he says, scowling at the crowd and its nucleus of noisy protesters, which suddenly blossoms into two circles rotating in opposite directions, so that ingress to the Hall is essentially stoppered.

"I guess something *is* worth protesting at the Hall of Fame," I say, admiring the protesters, their (from here) illegible signs jutting in the air and their chants becoming louder as stronger-voiced marchers rotate our way. To me it all has a nice collegial feel of my Ann Arbor days (though I was never involved back then, being a scared-stiff, Dudley Doright frat-rat possessor of a highly revocable NROTC scholarship). Yet it feels laudable today that a spirit of manageable unrest and disagreement can be alive still on the fruited plain, even if it's not associated with anything important.

Paul, however, doesn't know what to say in the face of other people's dissension, accustomed only to his own. "So okay, what're we supposed to do—wait?" he says, and crosses his arms like an old scold. Potential new Hall visitors are drifting past us but stopping soon to take in the spectacle. Some Cooperstown police are standing across Main Street, two bulky men and two small, blue-shirted, terrier women, thumbs in their belts, amused by the whole event, now and then pointing toward something or someone they think is especially comical.

"Protests never last very long, in my experience," I say.

Paul says nothing, only scowls and raises his hand to his teeth and gives his wart a delicate but incisive bite. All this is making him uneasy; his good-kid spirit has gone with the dew. "Can't we just go in around 'em?" he says, tasting his own flesh and blood.

No one, I notice, is getting through or even trying. Most of the spectators, in fact, are looking entertained and talking at the protesters, or taking their pictures. It's nothing too serious. "The idea is for us to be inconvenienced a while, then they'll let us go on in. They have some point they want to make."

"I think the cops oughta arrest 'em," Paul says. He makes one emphatic little *eeeck* midway down his throat and grimaces. (Clearly he has spent more time with Charley than is healthy, since his human-rights attitude favors bulldozer privilege: faced with a blind beggar suffering an epileptic seizure in the revolving door of the University Club, you damn well find a way to bowl through for your court time in the sixty-and-over double-elimination consolation round.) I could easily pose a canny analogy to our nation's early days, in which legitimate grievances were ignored and a crisis followed, but it would fall on uncaring ears. However, I mean to respect the protesters' line even without knowing what it's about. There's time enough for the little we hope to do.

"Let's take a walk," I say, and set my hand on my son's shoulder like a regular ole dad and guide us both out into crowded Main toward the Cooperstown Fire and Rescue station, where glistening yellow vehicles sit out in the driveway on Sunday display, uniformed firefighters and paramedics lounging around the bay doors watching *Breakfast at Wimbledon*. More church cars and several packed Gay Nineties trolleys are stacking up noisily, a few drivers willing to lean on their horns and poke heads irritably out windows to find out what's what. Paul, I can see, is plainly troubled by this delay and mix-up, and I'd like to get us out of the action and avoid another run-in of our own. So I proceed us up the sidewalk against the pedestrian traffic, past more storefronts with sports paraphernalia and trading cards, two open-early taprooms showing nonstop World Series games from the Forties, a movie theater and the tweedy realty office I saw yesterday from the car, with snazzy color snapshots in the window. Where we're headed, I don't know. But unexpectedly as we walk across an open side alley, there, straight left and down the narrow passageway, which widens out at the other sunny end, sits Doubleday Field, hallowed and deep green and decidedly vest pocket in the midmorning light—a most perfect place to see and play a ball game (and distract your bad-tempered son). From somewhere nearby and right on cue, a tootling steam organ begins to play "Take Me Out to the Ball Game," as if our aimless activities were being watched.

"What's that for, Little League?" Paul says, still disapproving and unavailable, done in by his simple failure to gain the Hall of Fame on the first try, though in no time we'll be inside, soaking up the full wonderment: cruising its exhibits, roaming its pavilions, ogling Lou Gehrig's vanity license plate, the Say-Hey Kid's actual glove, Ted Williams's illustrated strike zone and the United Emirates baseball stamp display, while chuckling at Bud and Lou doing "Who's on First" (again)—just the way we did it back in Springfield, only much, much better.

"It's Doubleday Field," I say, warmly admiring it. "Those brochures I sent you explained the whole deal. It's where the Hall of Fame game's played when the new inductees are enshrined in August." I try to think of who'll be ushered in next month, but can't think of any baseball name but Babe Ruth. "It holds ten thousand people, was built in 1939 by the WPA when the country was on its knees and the government was helping to find jobs, which would be nice if it'd do today."

Paul, however, is staring at three public batting cages that are just outside the grandstand wall and from which we both can hear a sharp Coke-bottle *poink* of aluminum meeting horsehide. A small black kid employing a Joe Morgan elbow-trigger stance is at the plate and making repeated, withering contact in what is probably the "fast" cage. It occurs to me, as I'm sure it occurs to Paul, that it is Mr. New Hampshire Basketball again, lording it over everybody in yet another sport, in another town, and that he and his dad are on the same well-intentioned father–son circuit as we two and are having much more fun. Here, though, he's Mr. New Hampshire *Baseball*.

Though of course it's not. This kid has buddies, white and black, hanging on the cage rungs outside, jeering and insulting in a comradely way, encouraging him to miss so they can jump in and take their big-time cuts. One of these is a skinny, bad-posture Hacky Sack punk from yesterday—one of the lowlifes I imagined Paul bonding with last night over cheese fries and burgers. They seem much older than Paul now, and I'm certain he wouldn't know how to address them (unless they communicated by barking).

We walk a ways down the widening alley to the point behind the old brick buildings on Main, where it turns into the Double-day Field parking lot and where several men—men my age—dressed in new-looking big-league uniforms are departing cars with their gloves and bats, hurrying on noisy cleats toward the open grandstand tunnel, as though they were showing up late for a twin bill. Two teams' uniforms are in evidence: the flashy yellow and unappetizing green of the Oakland A's, and the more conservative red, white and blue of the Atlantas. I look for a number or a face I recognize from my years in the press box—somebody who'd be flattered to be remembered—but no one looks familiar.

In fact, two "A's" who pass right by us—R. *Begtzos* and *J. Bergman* stitched to their backs—have sizable Milwaukee goiters and seam-splitting butts, which argue against their having played anytime in recent memory.

"I'm clueless," Paul says. His own outfit is no more appetizing than Bergman's and Begtzos's.

"It's an important part of the whole Cooperstown experience to take a look inside here." I begin moving us toward the tunnel behind the "players." "It's supposed to be good luck." (This I've made up on the spot. But his euphoria has now burned off like ether, and I'm back to conflict-containment drills and getting through our last hours as friendly enemies.)

"I've got a train to catch," he says, following along.

"You'll make it," I say, less friendly myself. "I've got plans of my own."

When we walk through to the end of the tunnel we could easily stroll straight out onto the field where the players are, or else turn and climb steep old concrete steps into the grandstand. Paul shies off from the field as though warned against it and takes the steps. But to me it's irresistible to walk a few yards into the open air, cross the gravel warning track and simply stand on the grass where two teams, ersatz Braves and ersatz A's, are playing catch and limbering stiff, achy joints. Gloves are popping, bats cracking, voices sailing off into the bright air, shouting, "I could catch it if I could see it," or "My leg won't bend that way any-more," or "Watch it, watch it, watch it."

Un-uniformed, I venture far enough that I can see up to the blue sky from within my shadow and all the way out to the right-field fence, where the numbers spell "312," and bleacher seats and treetops and neighborhood rooflines are beyond, and above that a shining MOBIL sign revolves like a radar dish. Heavy, capless men in uniforms sit in the grass below the fence palings, or lie back staring up, taking in moments of deliverance, carefree and obscure. I have no idea what's up here, only that I would love to be them for a moment, complete with a suit and no son.

Paul sits alone on an old grandstand bench, affecting timeless boredom, his Walkman earphones clutching his neck, his chin on a pipe railing. Little is afoot here, the place being mostly empty. A few kids his age are far up in the drafty back rows, cackling and cracking wise. A scattering of chatty wives are below in the reserved seats—women in pantsuits and breezy sundresses, sitting in pairs and threes, viewing the field and players, laughing occasionally, extolling a good catch or merely occupying themselves with the neutral subjects they each are at ease with. And happily—happy as linnets in a warm and gentle wind, with nothing better to do than twitter.

"What'd the bartender say to the mule when he ordered a beer?" I say, coming down the row of seats. I feel I have to break new ground again.

He turns his eyes to me disparagingly without moving his chin off the pipe rail. This won't be funny, his look indicates. His "insect" tattoo is visible. An insult. "Clueless," he says again to be rude.

" 'I'm sorry, sir, what seems to be bothering you?' " I sit beside him, wanted or unwanted, and muse off down the first-base line in silence. A tiny, antique man in a bright white shirt, shoes and trousers is pushing a chalk wheel down the base path. He stops midway and looks where he's been in estimation of his trueness, then resumes toward the sack. I raise my camera and take his picture, then squeeze one off at the field and the players seemingly readying themselves to play, and finally one of the sky with the flag raised but motionless above the "390" sign in center.

"What good is it to come to some beautiful place?" Paul says broodily, his chin still resting on the green pipe, his heavy, downy-haired legs splayed so as to reveal a scar on his knee, a long and pink and still scabby thing of unknown origin.

"The basic idea, I guess, is you'll remember it later and be a lot happier." I could add, "So if you've got some useless or bad memories this'd be a great place to start off-loading them." But what I mean is obvious.

Paul gives me the old dead-eye and shuffles his Reeboks. The hatless ballplayers who have been running sprints and stretching in the outfield are walking in together now, some with their caps on backward, some with arms on each other's shoulders, a couple actually walking backward and clowning it up. "Come ahnnn, Joe Louis!" one of the wives shouts, getting her sports and heroes confused. The other wives all laugh. "Don't yell like that at Fred," one says, "you'll scare him to death."

"I'm sick of not liking stuff," Paul says, seeming not to care. "I'm ready for a big change."

News not unwelcome, since a move to Haddam may be on his horizon. "You're just getting started," I say. "You'll find a lot of things to like."

"That's not what Dr. Stopler says." He stares out at the wide, mostly vacant ballyard.

"Well, fuck Dr. Stopler, then. He's an asshole."

"You don't even know him."

I fleetingly consider telling Paul I'm moving to New Mexico and opening an FM station for the blind. Or that I'm getting married. Or that I have cancer.

"I know him well enough," I say. "Shrinks are all alike." Then I sit silent, resentful of Dr. Stopler for being an authority on all of life—mine included.

"What is it I'm supposed to do again if I'm not supposed to be a critic of my age?" He's been studying this subject since last night. The thought of a whole new leash on life might in fact have inspired his short-lived euphorics.

"Well," I say, watching the players coalesce into two rival but friendly "teams," as a hugely fat man with a tripod and box camera emerges slowly out of the runway, his one leg stiff. The cameraman appraises the sun, then starts to set up in accordance. "I'd like you to come live with me a while, maybe learn to play the trumpet, later go to Bowdoin and study marine biology; and not be so sly and inward while you're there. I'd like you to stay a little gullible and not worry too much about standardized tests. Eventually I'd like you to get married and be as monogamous as possible. Maybe buy a house near the water in Washington State, so I could come visit. I'll be more specific when I have time to direct your every waking movement."

"What's monogamous?"

"It's something like the old math. It's a cumbersome theory nobody practices anymore but that still works."

"Do you think I was ever abused?"

"Nothing I was personally involved in. Maybe you can remember a few minor cruelties. Your memory's pretty good." I stare at him, unwilling to be amused, since his mother and I love him more than he (of all people) will ever know. "Do you want to file a complaint? Maybe talk to your ombudsman about it on Tuesday?"

"No, I guess not."

"You know, you shouldn't think you're not supposed to be happy, Paul. You understand that? You shouldn't get used to not being happy just because you can't make everything fit down right. Everything doesn't fit down right. You have to let some things go, finally." Now would be the moment to bring to light what a quirky old duck Jefferson was—the practical idealist *qua* grammarian—his whole life spent gadgeting out the mysteries of the status quo in quest of a firmer foothold on the future. Or possibly I could borrow a baseball metaphor having to do with some things that happen inside the white lines and those that happen out.

Only I am suddenly stopped cold. Not what I'd planned.

The A's and Braves have formed two team-photo groups down the third-base line, taller men behind, shorter men kneeling (Messrs. Begtzos and Bergman are shorter). The kneeling men have their gloves and a fan of wooden bats arranged prettily on the grassy foreground. A low, portable signboard has been wheeled out and placed in front of them. O'MALLEY'S FAN-TASY BASEBALL CAMP, it says in red block letters, and below it, in temporary lettering: "Braves vs. '67 Red Sox—July 3, 1988." The sign makes all the Braves laugh. None of the Red Sox seem to be present.

Pictures are quickly snapped. The man who has chalked the base paths supervises wheeling the sign over to the canary-suited A's, where he jiggers the letters to read O'MALLEY'S FAN-TASY BASEBALL CAMP: "Athletics vs. '67 Red Sox—July 3, 1988."

All clap when the pictures are done, and players begin straying toward the dugout and down the baselines, or just wandering out onto the infield in their too-tight uniforms, looking as if something wonderfully memorable had just happened but they'd missed it or it wasn't enough, this even though the *big game* with the BoSox, the whole megillah, what it's all about, is still to come. "You look great, Nigel," a husky-voiced wife shouts out from the stands in a yawky Aussie accent. Nigel, who's a big, long-armed and bearded "Brave," with a thick middle and turned-in toes that make him seem shy, pauses on the dugout steps and lifts his blue Atlanta cap like ole Hank on his glory day. "You look damn good," she shouts out. "Damn good on you." Nigel smiles introspectively, nods his head, then ducks into the shadows along the bench with his mates. I should've taken his picture.

For, how else to seize such an instant? How to shout out into the empty air just the right words, and on cue? Frame a moment to last a lifetime?

A dead spot now seems to be where these two days have delivered us—not even inside the Hall of Fame yet, but to an unspectacular moment in a not exactly bona fide ballpark, where two spiritually wrong-footed "clubs" make ready to play a real team whose glories are all behind them, and where by some system of inner weights and measures I have just run out of important words, but before I've said enough, before I've achieved a desired effect, before the momentum of a shared physical act—strolling the hallowed halls, viewing the gloves, license plates, strike zones—can take us up and carry us to a good end. Before I've made of this day a memory worth preserving.

I'd have done better to have us wait with the crowd until the doors were cleared, instead of seeking one more chance at quality time and risking this flat-footed feeling of nothing doing, with our last point of significant agreement being that I had probably not abused my son. (My trust has always been that words can make most things better and there's nothing that can't be improved on. But words *are* required.)

"People my age are on a six-month cycle," Paul says in a reflective adult voice. The "A's" and the "Braves" mill the sidelines, wanting something to happen, something they've paid good money for. I still wouldn't mind joining them. "Probably the way I am now will be different by Christmas. Adults don't have that problem."

"We have other problems," I say.

"Like what?" He looks around at me.

"Our cycles last a lot longer."

"Right," he says. "Then you croak."

I almost say, "Or worse." Which would send his mind off inventorying Mr. Toby, his dead brother, the electric chair, being fed arsenic, the gas chamber—on the hunt for something new and terrible in the world to be obsessed by and later make jokes about. And so I say nothing. My face, I suspect, bears promise of some drollery about death and its too, too little sting. But as I said, I've said all I know.

I hear the steam organ begin tootling away on "Way down upon the Swanee River." Our little ballpark has a lazy, melancholy carnival fruitiness afloat within it now. Paul looks at me shrewdly when I don't answer as expected, the corners of his mouth flickering as if he knows a secret, though I know he doesn't.

"Why don't we head back now?" I say, leaving death unchallenged.

"What are those guys doing down there?" he says, looking quickly to the level playing field, as if he'd just now seen it.

"They're having a great time," I say. "Doesn't it look like fun?"

"It looks like they're not doing anything."

"That's how adults have fun. They're really having the time of their lives. It's just so easy they don't even have to try."

And then we go. Paul first, down the aisle behind the wives, then struggling over the stumpy steps to the runway; and I, having a last fond look at the peaceful field, the men at loose ends but still two teams with games on tap.

We walk through the tunnel's shadows and out into the sunny parking lot, where the steam-organ music seems farther away. Up on Main Street cars are moving. I'm certain the Hall of Fame is open, its morning crises resolved.

The batting cage boys have now shoved off, their metal bats leaned outside the fence, all three cages empty and inviting.

"I believe we have to take a few chops, whatta you think?" I say to Paul. I am not at full strength but am ready, suddenly, for *something*.

Paul estimates the cages from a distance, his clumsy feet turned out now, as slew-footed as the least athletic of boys, heavy and uninspirable.

"Come on," I say, "you can coach." Possibly he makes a tiny double *eeeck* or a fugitive bark; I'm not certain. Though he comes.

Like a militant camp counselor, I lead us straight across to the fenced cages, which are fitted out with fifty-cent coin boxes and draped inside with green netting to keep careening balls from maiming people and injuring the pitching machines, which are themselves big, dark-green, boxy, industrial-looking contraptions that work by feeding balls from a plastic hopper through a chain-drive circuitry that ends with two rubber car tires spinning in opposite tangency at a high rate of speed and from between which each "pitch" is actually *expelled*. Signs posted all around remind you to wear a helmet, protective glasses and gloves, to keep the gates closed, to enter the cage alone, to keep small children, pets, bottles, anything breakable including wheelchair occupants out—and if none of these warnings is convincing, all risk is yours anyway (as if anybody thought different).

The three metal bats leaning on the fence are identically too short, too light, their taped grips much too thin. I tell Paul to stand clear while I "test" one bat, holding it up in front of me like a knight's sword, sighting down its blue aluminum shaft (as I used to do long ago when I played in military school) and for some reason waggling it. I turn sideways of Paul—my camera still on my shoulder—cock the bat behind my ear in a natural-feeling Stan Musial knees-in stance and peer straight at him as though he were Jim Lonborg, the old BoSox righty, ready to rare, kick and fire.

"This is how Stan the Man used to stand in there," I say over my left elbow, my eyes hooded. I trigger a wicked swing, which feels clumsy and ridiculous. Some necessary leverage between my wrists and shoulders feels sprung now, so that my swing could only possibly contact the ball with a slapping motion that wouldn't drive a fruit fly out of the phone booth but would absolutely make me look like a girl.

"Is that how Stan the Man swung?" Paul says.

"Yeah, and it went a fuckin' mile," I say. I hear shouts, a chorus of "I got it, I got it," from inside Doubleday Field. I look around and above the grandstand where we were five minutes ago; white balls arch through the sky, two and three at once, all to be caught but invisible to us here.

Each cage has a title to colorfully reflect the speed of its pitches: "Dyno-Express" (75 mph). "The Minors" (65 mph). "Hot Stove League" (55 mph). I have no reservations about trying my skills in the "Dyno-Express" and so give Paul my camera and two quarters, leaving the batting helmets on their fence hook. I step right inside, close the gate, walk to the batter's box and look out toward the mean green machine as I seek out solid footing a bat's length from the outside corner of the regulation rubber plate that's planted between two scruffy rectangular AstroTurf pads put there to make things look authentic. I once again assume my Musial stance, make a slow, measuring pass of the bat barrel through my putative strike zone, square my knuckles on the handle, rotate the trademark back and line my deck-shoe toes with the center-field flag (though of course there is no flag, only the pitching machine itself and the protective netting, behind which is a sign that says "Home Run?"). I take and release a breath, once more deliberately extend the bat over the plate, then slowly bring it back.

"What time is it?" Paul says.

"Ten. There's no clock in baseball." I glimpse him over my shoulder through the diamond fence wires. He is looking up at the sky and back at the grandstand entrance, where a few fantasy players and their young-looking wives are strolling happy-go-lucky into the sunshine, gloved hands draped over soft shoulders, ball caps turned sideways, everyone ready for a beer, a bratwurst and a few yucks before the big game with Boston.

"Weren't we supposed to do something else?" he says, and looks at me. "Something about a hall of fame?"

"You'll get there," I say. "Trust me."

I again have to establish my stance and settle on a proper balance and repose. But once I'm fixed I say loudly to Paul, "Slap the money in the box," and he does, after which and for a long moment there is calm as the machine radiates a kind of patient human immanence, though this is broken after several seconds by a deep mechanical humming during which a heretofore unnoticed red bulb begins to brighten on top, after which the plastic hopper full of balls begins to vibrate. The machine gives no other sign it means business, but I stare riveted at the black confluence of rubber tires, which have not moved.

"Those greaseballs fucked it up," Paul says behind me. "You wasted your money."

"I don't think so," I say, keeping my balance and stance, my calm intact, bat back, eyes to the machine. My palms and fingers squeeze the bat tape, my shoulders stiffen, though I feel my wrists begin to bend back in a way Stan would deplore but that feels necessary for the raised bat barrel to descend quickly enough to the plane of the ball for me to avoid the girlish *slap* motion I don't want to be "my swing." I hear someone shout out, "Look at that asshole," and can't resist a quick look to see who's being referred to but see no one, then quickly return my gaze to the machine and the two tires, where there's still nothing happening to indicate a "pitch." Until I slightly relax my shoulders to avoid "binding," and it's then the machine makes a more portentous, metallic whirring noise. The black tires start to spin at an instantly great rate. A single ball teeters in full view down a previously unremarked metal channel, then goes "underground" into a smaller slot, after which it or one just like it is viciously spit from between the spinning rubber rings and crosses the plate at a speed so fast and at a distance so easily reachable that I don't even swing, merely let the ball whang the fence behind me and bound back through my legs and out toward an unobserved concrete bunker in front of me whose duty is to route balls back to the hopper. (The basketball version was much jazzier.)

Paul is silent. I do not even turn his way, refixing instead like a sniper on what is my opponent, the slit between the spinning tires. Another interior whirring sound becomes audible. I watch as another ball wobbles down the metal track, disappears and then is shot through space, hissing across the plate directly under my fists and again whanging the fence behind me, untouched and unswung at.

Paul again says nothing. Not "Strike two" or "It sounded high" or "Just try and make contact, Dad." No chuckle or raspberry or fart noise. Not even a bark of encouragement. Only adjudicating silence.

"How many do I get?" I say, merely to hear a sound.

"I just got here," he says.

Though just as I'm picturing the numeral five as the likeliest number, another orange-stitched ball comes rocketing across the plate and rattles the screen, suggesting the machine has possibly quick-pitched me.

Sweat has now appeared upward of my hairline. For ball number four, I extend the stubby bat barrel like a gate barrier straight out into my strike zone and hold it there stiff until the machine generates another pitch, which hits the bat and ricochets off the metal sweet spot with a *dink-poink*, and fouls off against one of the warning signs, finally bouncing back and actually striking me on the heel.

"Bunt," Paul says.

"Fuck you, bunt. Bunt when it's your turn. I'm up here to hit." I'm not looking at him.

"You should be wearing your windbreaker," he says. "You're a wind breaker."

I frown out into the now sinister black crease, twist my fists into the tape, straighten my wrists into a properer Stan-like trigger cock, shift my balance to the ball of my right foot, and ready my left to rise and stride toward contact. The machine whirs, the red light glows, the ball teeters down its metal chase, drops from view, then spanks out from between the rings fast and in full view, at which instant I lunge, flail the blue barrel down into the ordained space, hear my wrists "snap," actually *see* my arms extend, my elbows nearly meet, feel my weight shift as my breath gushes—all just as my eyes squeeze tightly shut. Only this time the ball (unseen, of course) squalls off the bat straight up into the netting, pinballs off two rankled fence surfaces, then falls back to the asphalt in front of me and drains off toward the bunker, leaving me with a ferocious handful of bees I'm determined not to acknowledge.

"Strike five, you're history," Paul says, and I glare back at him as he snaps my picture with my camera, disdainful concentration on his plummy lips. (I can't help seeing what I'll look like: bat slumped to the side, my cheeks sprouting sweat, my hair awry, face distressed by a frown of failure endured in a dopey cause.) "The Sultan of Squat," Paul says, snapping another picture.

"Since you're the expert, you need to try it," I say. Bees are burning my hands.

"Right." Paul shakes his head as though I'd spoken the most preposterous of words. We are completely alone here, though more ersatz players and their real-life wives and kids are strolling carefree and happy across the hot parking lot, their voices crooning praise and good motives. Balls still rise above and arc down upon Doubleday Field. This is the small, consoling music of baseball. For a man to entice his son into a few swings would not be mistreatment.

"What's the matter?" I say, letting myself out of the cage. "If you miss it you can say you meant to miss it. Didn't you say that was the best trick?" (He has already denied this, of course, but for some reason I don't mean to let him.) "Don't you eat stress for lunch?"

Paul holds my camera at belly level below "Clergy" and takes another picture, with an evil smile.

"You're the daredevil tightrope walker, aren't you?" I say, leaning the bat back against the fence, the big green machine now silent behind me. A warm breeze kicks up a skiff of parking lot grit and sweeps it by my sweaty arms. "I think you're walking way too narrow a line here, you need to find a new trick. You have to swing if you're going to hit." I'm wiping sweat off my forearms.

"Like you said." His smile becomes a smirk of dislike. He is still snapping my camera at me, one picture after the next—the same picture.

"What was that? I don't remember."

"Fuck you."

"Oh. Fuck me. Sorry, I did forget that." I come toward him suddenly, pity and murder and love each crying for a time at bat. It is not so rare a fatherly lineup. Children, who sometimes may be angels of self-discovery, are other times the worst people in the world.

When I get in reach of him, I don't know why but I grapple him behind his head, my fingers achy from squeezing my bat, my shoulders weightless as if my arms were nothing. "I just thought," I say, strenuously holding him, "you and me could experience a common humiliation and go off with our arms draped over our shoulders and I'd buy you a beer. We could bond."

"Fuck you! I can't drink. I'm fifteen," Paul says savagely into my chest, where I'm still clutching him.

"Oh, of course, I forgot that too. I'd probably be abusing

you." I pull him in even more harshly, finding his rough buzzed hairline, his Walkman earphones and his neck tendons, forcing his face into my shirtfront so his nose pokes my breastbone and his warty fingers and even my camera push and dig my ribs in rejection. I don't entirely know what I'm doing, or what I want him to do: change, promise, concede, guarantee me something important will be better or pan out, all expressed in language for which there are no words. "And why are you such a little prick?" I say with difficulty. I may be hurting him, but it's a father's right not to be pushed, so that I squeeze him even harder, intent on keeping him till he gives up the demon, renounces all, collapses into hot tears only I can minister to. Dad. His.

But that is not what happens. The two of us begin awkwardly scuffling on the pavement beside the batting cages, and almost immediately, I realize, to attract the interest of tourists and churchgoers out for a Sunday stroll, plus lovers of baseball on their way, as we should be, to the famous shrine—except that we're struggling here. I can almost hear them murmur, "Well, hey now, what's all this about? This can't be good and whole-some. We need to call somebody. Better call. Go ahead and call. The cops. 911. What's the goddamned country coming to?" Though of course they don't speak. They only stop and gaze. Abuse can be mesmerizing.

I loose my grip on my son's neck and let him break away, his fleshy face gray with anger and disgust and shame. My grip has ridden into his cut ear and got it bleeding again, its little bandage rucked off. When I see it, I look in my hand and there is beet-red blood down my middle finger and smeared in my palm.

Paul gapes at me, his left hand—the other's still holding my camera, with which he has gored me in the ribs—gone fiercely into the pocket of his baggy maroon shorts as if he is trying to look casual about being furious. His eyes grow narrow and shiny, though his pupils widen with me in their sight.

"All in fun. No big deal," I say. I flash him a lame, hopeless grin. "High fives." One hand is up for a slap, the other, bloody, one finding my own pocket. Sunglassed tourists continue observing us from forty yards out in the parking lot.

"Gimme the cocksucking bat," Paul seethes and, ignoring my high fives, goes tromping past me, grabbing the blue bat off the fence, kicking the gate open and entering the cage like a man come to a task he's put off for a lifetime. (His Walkman earphones are still on his neck, my camera now lumped in his shorts pocket.)

Inside the "Dyno-Express" cage he stalks to the plate, the bat slung back over his shoulder, and peers down as if into a puddle of water. He suddenly turns back to me with a face of bright hatred, then looks at his toes again as though aligning them with something, the bat still sagging in spite of one attempt to keep it up. He is not a hitter to inspire fear. "Put in the fucking money, Frank," he shouts.

"Bat left, son," I say. "You're a southpaw, remember? And back off a little bit so you can get a swing at it."

Paul gives me a second look, this time with an expression of darkest betrayal, almost a smile. "Just put the money in," he says. And I do. I drop two quarters in the hollow black box.

This time the green machine comes alive much more readily, as if I had previously wakened it, its red top light beaming dully in the sun. The whirring commences and again the whole assembly shudders, the plastic hopper vibrates and the rubber tires start instantly spinning at a high speed. The first white pill exits its bin, tumbles down the metal chute, disappears then at once reappears, blistering across the plate and smacking the screen precisely where I'm standing so that I inch back, thoughtful of my fingers, though they're stuffed in my pockets.

Paul, of course, does not swing. He merely stands staring at the machine, his back to me, his bat still slung behind his head, heavy as a hoe. He is batting right-handed.

"Step back a bit, son," I say again as the machine goes into its girdering second windup, humming and shuddering, and emits another blue darter just past Paul's belly, again thrashing the fence I'm now well back of. (He has, I believe, actually inched in closer.) "Get your bat up to the hitting position," I say. We have performed hitting rituals since he was five, in our yard, on playgrounds, at the Revolutionary War battlefield, in parks, on Cleveland Street (though not recently).

"How fast is it coming?" He says this not to me but to anyone, the machine, the fates that might assist him.

"Seventy-five," I say. "Ryne Duren threw a hundred. Spahn threw ninety. You can get a swing. Don't close your eyes" (like I did). I hear the steam organ playing: "No use in sit-ting a-lone on the shelf, life is a hol-i-day."

The machine goes again into its Rube Goldberg conniption. Paul leans over the plate this time, his bat *still* on his shoulder, gazing, I assume, at the crease where the ball will originate. Though just as it does, he sways an inch back and lets it thunder past and whop the screen again. "Too close, Paul," I say. "That's too close, son. You're gonna brain yourself."

"It's not that fast," he says, and makes a little *eeeck* and a grimace. The machine circuits then into its next-to-last motion. Paul, his bat on his shoulder, watches a moment, and then, to my surprise, takes a short ungainly step forward onto the plate and turns his face to the machine, which, having no brain, or heart, or forbearance, or fear, no experience but throwing, squeezes another ball through its dark warp, out through the sprightly air, and hits my son full in the face and knocks him flat down on his back with a terrible, loud *thwock*. After which everything changes.

In time that does not register as time but as humming motor noise solid in my ear, I am past the metal gate onto the turf and beside him; it is as if I had begun before he was hit. Dropped to my knees, I grab his shoulder, which is squeezed tight, his elbows into his sides, both his hands at his face—covering his eyes, his nose, his cheek, his jaw, his chin—underneath all of which there is a long and almost continuous *wheeee* sound, a sound *he* makes bunched on the plate, a hard, knees-contracted bundle of fright and lightning pain centered where I can't see, though I want to, my hands busy but helpless and my heart sounding in my ears like a cannon, my scalp prickly, damp, airy with fear.

"Let's see it, Paul"—my voice a half octave too high, trying to say it calmly. "Are you all right?" I am hit by ball number five, a sharp blow like a punch off the back of my neck and scalp, skipping smartly on into the netting.

"Wheeee, wheeee, wheeee."

"Let's see, Paul," I say, the air between him and me oddly red-tinted. "Are you all right? Let's see, Paul, are you all right?"

"Wheeee, wheeee, wheeeeee."

People. I hear their footsteps on the concrete. "Just call right now," someone says. "I could hear it halfway to Albany." "Oh boy." "Ohhh boy." The cage door clanks. Shoes. Breathing. Trouser cuffs. Someone's hands. An oiled-leather ball-glove smell. Chanel No. 5.

"Ohhhh!" Paul says in a profound exhalation conceding hurt, and writhes sideways, his elbows still pinned to his sides, his face still covered by his hands, his ear still bleeding from my having grabbed him too hard.

"Paul," I say, all the air still reddish, "let me see, son," my voice giving way slightly, and I am tapping his shoulder with my fingers as if I could wake him up and something else could happen, something not nearly as bad.

"Frank, there's an ambulance coming," someone says from among the legs, hands, breaths all around me, someone who knows me as Frank (other than my son). A man. I hear other footsteps and look up and around, frightened. Braves and A's are outside the fence, gawking in, their wives beside them, their faces dark, troubled. "Wasn't he wearing his helmet?" I hear one inquiry. "No, he wasn't," I say out loud to anyone. "He wasn't wearing anything."

"Wheeee, wheeee," Paul cries out again, his face covered with his hands, his brown head of hair resting squarely on the filthy white plate. These are cries I don't know, cries he has never cried in my hearing.

"Paul," I say. "Paul. Just be still, son." Nothing feels like it's happening to bring help. Though not very far away I hear two sharp *bwoop-bwoop*s, then a heavy engine roar, then *bwoop-bwoop-bwoop*. Someone says, "Okay, great." I'm aware of more feet scuffling. I have my hands pressed tight into Paul's shoulder—his back is to me—feeling how hard his body has become, how unambiguously concentrated on injury it is. Someone says, "Frank, let's let these people try to help. They'll help him. Let them get where you are."

This. This is the worst thing ever.

I stand dizzily and step backward among many others. Someone has my upper arm in his big hand, assisting me gently back, while a stumpy white woman in a white shirt, tight blue shorts, with a huge butt, and then a thinner man in the same clothes but with a stethoscope on his neck, slip past and get onto their hands and knees on the AstroTurf and begin to practice on my son procedures I can't see but that make Paul scream out "Nooooo!" and then "Wheeee" again. I push forward and find myself saying to the people who are here now all around, "Let me talk to him, let me talk to him. It'll be all right," as if he could be persuaded out of being hurt.

But whoever it is here who knows me—a large man—says, "Just stay here a second, Frank, stay still. They'll help. It'll be better if you just stand back and let them."

And so I do. I stand in the crowd as my son is avidly worked on and helped, my heart battering its walls, right to the top of my belly, my fingers cold and sweating. The man who has called me Frank holds onto my arm even yet, says nothing, though I suddenly turn to him and look at his long, smooth-jawed Jewish face, large black eyes with specs and a slick tanned cranium, and say as if I had a right to know, "Who are you?" (Though the words do not actually sound.)

"I'm Irv, Frank. Irv Ornstein. Jake's son." He smiles apologetically and squeezes my arm more tightly.

Whatever has turned the air red now ceases. Here is a name —Irv—and a face (changed) from far away and past. Skokie, 1964. Irv—the good son of my mother's good husband #2, my stepbrother—gone after my mother's death, with his father in tow, to Phoenix.

I do not know what to say to Irv, and simply stare back at him like a specter.

"This is not the best time to meet, I know," Irv says to my voiceless face. "We just saw you on the street this morning, over by the fire station, and I said to Erma: 'I know that guy.' This must be your son who got hurt." Irv is actually whispering and casts a fretful eye now at the medics kneeling over Paul, who screams "Noooo!" again from beneath their efforts.

"That's my son," I say, and move toward his cry, but Irv reins me in once more.

"Just give 'em a couple minutes more, Frank. They know what they're doin'." I look to my other side, and here is a dishy, tiny, wheat-haired woman in her thirties, wearing a tight yellow-and-peach plastic-looking single-piece outfit that resembles a space suit. She has a grip on my other elbow as if she knows me as well as Irv does and the two of them have agreed to prop me up. Possibly she's a weight lifter or an aerobics instructor.

"I'm Erma," she says, and blinks at me like a hatcheck girl. "I'm Irv's friend. I'm sure he's going to be fine. He's just scared, poor thing." She too looks down at the two medics huddled over my son, and her face goes doubtful and her lower lip discreetly extends sympathy. Hers is the Chanel I whiffed.

"It's the left eye," I hear one of the medics say. Then Paul says, "Ohhhh!"

Then I hear someone behind me say, "Oh, ugh." Some of the Braves and A's are already starting to back away. I hear a woman say, "They said it's his eye," and someone else say, "Probably wasn't wearing protective eye covering." Then someone says, "It says 'Clergy.' Maybe he's a minister."

"Where are you now, Frank?" Irv says, still whispering confidentially. His hand seems to encircle my upper arm, his hold on me firm. He is a big, tanned, hairy-looking engineer type, wearing blue designer sweatpants with red piping and a gold cardigan with no shirt under. He is much bigger than I remember him when we were college age, me at Michigan, he at Purdue.

"What?" I hear my own voice sounding calmer than I feel. "New Jersey. Haddam, New Jersey."

"Whaddaya do down there?" Irv whispers.

"Real estate," I say, then look at him again suddenly, at his broad forehead and full, liver-lipped but sympathetic mouth. I remember him absolutely and at the same time have no idea who in the hell he is. I look at his hairy-fingered hand on my arm and see that it has a diamond pinkie ring on its appointed finger.

"We were just coming over to speak to you when your boy got hit," Irv says, giving Erma an approving nod.

"That's good," I say, staring down at the wide, maxi-brassiered back of the fireplug female medic, as if this part of her would be the first to indicate something significant. She struggles to her feet at this very moment and turns to search among us and the two or three others who are still gathered around.

"Anybody responsible for this young man?" she says in a wiry, south Boston *nyak* accent, and extracts a large black walkie-talkie out of her belt holster.

"I'm his father," I say, breathless, and pull away from Irv. She holds her walkie-talkie up toward me as if she expects me to want to speak into it, her finger on the red Talk button.

"Yeah, well," she says in her tough-broad voice. She is a woman of forty, though perhaps younger. Her belt has a blizzard of medical supplies and heavy gear fastened on. "Okay, here's the thing," she says, gone totally businesslike. "We need to get him down to Oneonta pretty fast."

"What's wrong with him?" I say this too loudly, terrified she's about to say his brain has been rendered useless.

"Well, what—did he like get hit with a baseball?" She clicks her walkie-talkie trigger, making it produce a scratchy static sound.

"Yes," I say. "He forgot his helmet."

"Well, he got hit in the eye. Okay? And I can't really tell you if he's got much vision in it, because it's swollen already and got blood all in it, and he won't open it. But he needs to see somebody pretty quick. We take eye injuries down to Oneonta. They've got the staff."

"I'll drive him." My heart makes a bump-a-bump. Cooperstown: not a *real* town for *real* injuries.

"I'd have to get you to sign a form if you take him now," she says. "We can get him down in twenty minutes—it'd take you longer—and we can get him stabilized and monitored." I see her name on her silver nameplate: *Oustalette* (something I need to remember).

"Okay, great. Then I'll just ride with you." I lean to the side to see Paul, but can see only his bare legs and his lightning-bolt shoes and orange socks and the hem of his maroon shorts behind the other paramedic, who's still kneeling beside him.

"Our insurance won't permit that," she says, even more all-business. "You'll have to travel by separate vehicle." She clicks her red Talk button again. She is itchy to go.

"Great. I'll drive." I smile awfully.

"Frank, lemme drive you down," Irv Ornstein says from the side and with full authority, gripping my arm again as if I were about to escape.

"Okay," Ms. Oustalette says, and instantly begins talking tough into her big Motorola without even turning away. "Cooperstown Sixteen? Transporting one white male juvenile ADO to A. O. Fox. Ophthalmic. BP...." There is a moment when I can hear the motor idling on her ambulance, hear two bats pop in quick succession from over the fence in the ballpark. Then all at once five immense jet planes come cracking in over us, low and ridiculously close together, their wings steady as knife blades, their *smack-shwoosh* eruption following a heart's beat behind. All present look up, shocked. All the planes are deep blue against the morning blue sky. (Would anyone believe it was still morning?) Ms. Oustalette doesn't even look up as she awaits her confirmation.

"Blue Angels," Irv says into my deafened ear. "Pretty close. They've got a show here tomorrow."

I step away from Irv's grip, my ears hollowed, and move toward Paul, where the other medic has just left and he is on his back alone, pale as an egg, his hands covering his eyes, his soft stomach, bare beneath his *Clergy* shirt, rising and settling heavily with his breath. He is making a low, throaty grunt of deep pain.

"Paul?" I say, the Blue Angels roaring off in the distance over the lake.

"Uhn," is all he says.

"That was just the Blue Angels that flew over. This is gonna be okay."

"Uhn," he says again, not moving his hands, his lips parted and dry, his ear not bleeding now, his "insect" tattoo the thing I can see best—his concession to the next century's mysteries. Paul smells like sweat, and he is sweating freely and is cold, as I am.

"It's Dad," I say.

"Uhn-nuh."

I reach into his shorts pocket and delicately slide my camera out. I consider removing his Walkman phones but don't. He makes no motion, though his shoes waggle one way and the other on the phony turf. I put my fingers on the blond-fleeced tan line of his thigh. "Don't be afraid of anything," I say.

"I'm fine now," Paul says woozily from under his covering hands, but distinctly. "I'm really fine." He takes a deep breath through his nose and holds it a long, painful moment, then slowly lets it go. I can't see his smacked eye and don't want to, though I would if he asked. Dreamily he says, "Don't give Mom and Clary those presents, okay? They're too shitty." He is too calm.

"Okay," I say. "So. We're going to the hospital in Oneonta. And I'm going down there, too. In another car." No one, I assume, has told him he's going to Oneonta.

"Yep," he says. He removes a hand from one damp gray eye, the one not injured, and looks at me, his other eye still guarded from light and my view. "You have to tell Mom about this?" His one eye blinks at me.

"It's okay," I say, feeling lifted off the ground. "I'll just make a joke out of it."

"Okay." His eye closes. "We're not going to the Hall of Fame now," he says indistinctly.

"You never can tell," I say. "Life's long."

"Oh. Okay." Behind me I hear creaky-squeaky sounds of a stretcher and Irv's deepened official voice saying, "Give 'em some room, give 'em some room, Frank. Let 'em do their job now."

"You just hang on there," I say. But Paul says nothing.

I stand up and am moved back, my Olympus in hand. Paul goes out of sight again as Ms. Oustalette begins to slide a litter board under him. I hear her say "All right?" Irv again is pulling me back. I hear Paul say "Paul Bascombe" to someone's question, then "No" to the subject of allergies, medications and other diseases. Then he is somehow up onto the collapsible stretcher and Irv is still hauling me farther out of the way, clear to the side of the batting cage we are still in. There are but a few people now. A "Brave" and his wife look in at me warily from outside the cage. I don't blame them.

Someone says, "Okay? Let us out."

And then Paul is on his way out, under a blanket, one hand still covering his damaged eye like a war casualty, through the cage door and across the asphalt to the blinking, clicking yellow Life Line ambulance—a Dodge Ram Wagon with antennas, flashers, lights rotating all over.

I watch with Irv as the stretcher is loaded, the doors go closed, both attendants walk around and enter in no great rush. Two more loud *bwoop-bwoop*s sound as their stand-clear, then the engine makes a deep reverberant rumble, lurches into gear, more lights go sharply on, the whole immense machine inches forward, stops, wheels turn, then it is going again, gathering itself, and is quickly gone in the direction of Main without benefit of siren.

CHAPTER 11

IRV-THE-SOLICITOUS is concerned with how to keep my mind off my woes and so drives us back down Route 28 as slowly as a funeral cortege, trusting to cruise control in his blue renter Seville and talking about whatever would take his mind off *his* woes and turn anyone like him toward the bright side. He is wearing big rattan sandals which, with his swarthy balding head and gold cardigan over his hairy chest make him look like nothing as much as a Mafia capo out for a drive. Though in truth he's in the simulator business out in the Valley of the Sun, his particular mission being to design flight simulators where the pilots for all the big airlines learn their business, a skill he acquired along with aeronautical engineering at Cal Tech (though I'm sure I remember him being a Boilermaker).

Irv, however, doesn't want to get into "six-degree freedom, or any of that," which he lets me know to be the high and guiding principle of the simulator racket (roll, pitch, yaw, up, side, backward). "It has to do with what your middle ear's telling you, and it's all pretty routine." He's interested instead in him and me "getting back on track after lo these blows," which involves telling me unexpectedly what a wonderful woman my mother was and what a "real character" his dad was, too, and how lucky they were to find each other in their waning years, and how his dad had confided to him that my mother always wished she could be closer to me after she remarried, but Irv figured she understood pretty well that I could take care of myself and that I was over in Ann Arbor preparing for a damn good career in whatever walk of life I selected (she might be surprised today), and how he'd tried several times over the years to contact me but had never "gotten through."

It occurs to me as we're cruising airily along by the factory sweater outlets and undercoating garages on Route 28, and farther yet past the sugar houses and corn patches and pristine hardwood hillsides rememberable from our trip up yesterday, that Erma, Irv's lady friend, has somehow disappeared and hasn't even been mentioned. And indeed she is a palpable loss, since I'm sure Irv would drive faster if she were in the back seat, and they would talk to each other and defer to my particular woes in silence.

Irv, though, starts spieling about Chicago, which he pronounces *Shu-caw-guh*, telling me he's giving some thought to moving back there, possibly to Lake Forest (near Wally Caldwell's relations), since the aircraft industry's about to take it right in the center hole, in his view. He, along with every other licensed and still-breathing engineer in the world, is a Reagan man, and he's right now expecting to "go with" Bush, yet feels Americans don't like indecisiveness, and Bush doesn't seem much good on that front, only to his mind he's better than any of the "mental dwarfs" my party's currently sponsoring. He hasn't, however, totally ruled out the protest vote or an independent candidate, since the Republicans have sold out the everyday wage earner the way the Nazis sold out "their friends the Czechs." (He does not strike me as a likely Jackson supporter.)

I basically stay silent, thinking sorrowfully of my son and of this day, both of which seem bitter and bottomless losses with absolutely no hope of recovery. There is no *seeming* now. All is *is*. In a better world, Paul would've snagged a line drive barehanded off the bat of one of the ersatz A's, gone trooping off to the Hall of Fame with a proud, satisfyingly swollen mitt, had a satisfactory but not overly good time nosing around through Babe Ruth's locker, taking in the Johnny Bench "out at second" video and hearing the canned crowd noises from the Thirties. Later we could've walked out into the shimmery sunshine of Sunday, caught-ball in hand, gone for a Gay Nineties malt, found some aspirin, had our caricatures drawn together wearing vintage baseball suits, had some well-earned laughs, played Frisbee, set off my bottle rockets along a deserted inlet of the lake and ended the day early, lying in the grass under a surviving elm, with me explaining the ultimate value of good manners and that a commonsense commitment to progress (while only a Christian fiction) can still be a good, pragmatic overlay onto a life that could get dicey and long. Later on, motoring south, I'd have turned off on a back road and let him practice driving, after which we'd forge a plan, once his legal problems are settled, for his coming down to Haddam for school in the fall. A day, in other words, when the past got pushed further away and neutralized, when a promising course was charted for a future based on the postulate that independence and isolation were not the same, when all concentric rings would've snapped down and into place, and a true youthful (barkless, *eeeck*less) synchronicity might've flourished as only in youth it can.

But instead: Remorse. Pain. Reproach. Blindness (or, at the very least, corrective lenses). Gloom. Tedium (involving lengthy, lonely drives up to New Haven and the final failure of progress to mean more than avoidance and denial)—nothing we couldn't have accomplished by staying home or revisiting the fish elevator. (He'll never come to live with me now, I'm sure of it.)

Irv, grown mute out of respect or boredom, crests the last hill above I-88, and through the tinted windshield I can see a long, river-sinuous cornfield opening down the narrow valley of the Susquehanna just where the two roadways meet. There a pheasant bursts out of the high green stalks, flashes just above the tassel tops, sets its wings at a fence row and sails halfway across the four-lane and settles into the median-strip grass.

Who or what scared it, I wonder? Is it safe there in the middle? Can it possibly survive?

"You know, Frank, you can get hooked up to too commanding a metaphor in my business," Irv says, finally sick of being silent and just starting in on whatever he happens to be thinking about as we turn west toward the bricky old town of Oneonta. It is the habit of a man too much alone. I know its symptoms. "Nothing else seems as interesting as simulation when you're in it. Everything seems simulatable. Except," he adds, and looks at me for serious emphasis, "the people who do it best are the people who leave their work at the office. Maybe they're not always the geniuses, but they see simulation as one thing and life as another. It's just a tool, really." Irv gives his own tool a little two-finger nudge inside his sweatpants for comfort's sake. "You get in trouble when you confuse the two."

"I understand, Irv," I say. Irv, who has traveled to Cooperstown for one of O'Malley's Fan-tasy games tomorrow (with the '59 White Sox), is, in fact, a good and sweet man. I wish I knew him better.

"You married, Frank?"

"Not these days," I say, feeling my arms and shoulder joints already stiffening and getting sore, as if *I'd* been in an accident or had aged twenty years in an hour. I'm also grinding my teeth and will, I'm sure, lose more precious angstroms of enamel by morning. I point out to Irv the important blue sign with a white "H," and we begin following its direction down into town, where church is in session everywhere and few cars are on the move.

"Erma's trying out as my third wife," Irv says soberly, seeming to reflect conscientiously on the whole concept of wives (though not on Erma's whereabouts). "You see a big ugly guy like me, Frank, with a pretty gal like Erma, you know everything's just luck. Totally luck. That and being a good listener." He slightly pooches out his thick smooth lips like Mussolini, giving the impression he'd be willing to start listening now if there was anything worth listening to. "Did you guys get a chance to get into the Hall of Fame?"

"We were about to, Irv." I'm watching for another "H" sign but not seeing one, and am nervous we've passed it and will end up at the other end of town and back out on the interstate headed the wrong way, just like in Springfield. Precious time lost.

"You really oughta get back there when this is over. It's a treat. It's an education in itself, really, more than you can take in in a day. Those guys, those early guys, they played because they wanted to. Because they *could*. It wasn't a career for them. It was just a game. Now"—Irv looks disapproving—"it's a business." His voice trails off. I know he's heard himself doing his level best for his long-lost not-quite brother, whom he may remember now in finer detail and have figured out he never liked much and would be happy never to see again, though he still can simulate good cheer and be of service in the way he would to a crippled hitchhiker in a snowstorm, even if the hitchhiker was a convicted felon. "Incidents we can't control make us what we are—eh, Frank?" Irv says, changing subjects as he suddenly takes a sweeping left straight into an unnoticed but landscaped driveway that leads back to a crisp new three-story glass-and-brick hospital building with blinking antennae and microwave dishes on top. The A. O. Fox Hospital. Irv has been paying careful attention; I have been lost in a funk.

"Right, Irv," I say, not catching it all. "At least you can see it that way."

"I'm sure Jack's fine," Irv says, guiding us one-handed through a circular, shrub-lined drive, following the red EMERGENCY signs and stripes. The yellow Cooperstown Life Line ambulance is just swaying back out the drive, its flashers off, its cargo hold dark, as though something deathly has occurred. Ms. Oustalette is at the wheel and talking animatedly while smoking a cigarette, her nameless male partner barely visible in the shadowy passenger's seat.

"Home sweet hospital," Irv says, as he pulls alongside a bank of sliding glass doors designated simply as "Emergency." "Just hop on in, Franky," he says and smiles as I'm already leaving. "I'll park this beast and find you inside."

"Okay." Irv is radiating limitless sympathy, which has nothing to do with liking me. "Thanks, Irv," I say, leaning a moment back down into the door, where it's cool, and out of the hot, gunmetal sunlight.

"Simulate calm," Irv says, hiking one big blue-clad knee up on the leather seat. A tiny bell starts gonging inside.

"He'll probably have to wear glasses, that's all," I say. I shake my head at these wishful words.

"Wait and see. Maybe he's in there right now laughing his ass off."

"That'd be nice," I say, thinking how nice it *would* be and how, if so, it would also be the first time in a long time.

BUT THAT is not the case at all.

Inside at the long apple-green admissions desk I am told by the receptionist that Paul has "gone right in"—which means he is out of my reach behind some thick, shiny metal doors—and that an ophthalmologist has been "called in specially" to have a look at him. If I would take a seat "over there," the doctor will be out pretty soon to talk to me.

My heart has begun whompeting again at the antiseptic hospital colors, frigid surfaces and the strict, odorless, traffic-flow yin-yang of everything within sight and hearing. (All here is new, chrome-looking and hard plastic and, I'm sure, owes its existence to a big bond issue.) And *everything's* lugubriously, despairingly *for* something; nothing's just for itself or, better, for nothing. A basket of red geraniums would be yanked, a copy of *American Cage Bird* magazine tossed like an apple core. A realty guide, a stack of *Annie Get Your Gun* tickets—neither would last five minutes before somebody had it in the trash. People who end up here, these walls say, take no comfort from grace notes.

I sit nervously midway down a row of connected cherry-red high-impact plastic chairs and peer up at a control-less TV, bracketed high and out of reach and where Reverend Jackson in an opened-collared brown safari shirt is being interviewed by a panel of white men in business suits, who're beaming prudish self-confidence at him, as if they found him amusing; though the Reverend is exhibiting his own brand of self-satisfied smugness plus utter disdain, all of it particularly noticeable because the sound's off. (For a time this winter I considered him "my candidate," though I finally decided he couldn't win and would ruin the country if he did, and in either case would eventually tell me everything bad was my fault.) His goose is cooked anyway, and he's only on TV today to be humored.

The glass doors to the outside sigh open, and Irv strolls casually through in his blue sweats and sandals and yellow cardigan. He looks around without seeing me, then turns and walks back out onto the hot sidewalk as the doors shut, as if he'd come in the wrong hospital. A ticker running under Reverend Jackson's shiny brown mug reveals that the Mets defeated Houston, Graf defeated Navratilova, Becker defeated Lendl but is losing to Edberg, and while we're at it that Iraq has poisoned hundreds of Iranians with gas.

Suddenly both metal ER doors swing back, and a small young lemon-haired woman with a scrubbed Scandinavian face and wearing a doctor's smock comes striding out holding a clipboard. Her eyes fall directly on my worried face, alone here in the red relatives' alcove. She walks to the admissions desk, where a nurse points me out, and as I stand already smiling and overgrateful, she heads over with a look—I have to say—that is not a happy look. I would hate for it to be the look that spoke volumes about me, though of course in every way it does.

"Are you Paul's father?" she starts even before she gets to me, flipping pages on her silver clipboard. She's wearing pink tennis shoes that go *squee-kee-gee* on the new tiles, and her smock is open down the front to reveal a crisp tennis dress and short legs as brown and muscled out and thick as an athlete's. She seems totally without makeup or scent, her teeth as white as brand-new.

"Bascombe," I say softly, still grateful. "Frank Bascombe. My son's Paul Bascombe." (A good attitude can oft-times, Gypsies believe, deflect bad news.)

"I'm Dr. Tisaris." She consults her chart again, then fixes me with perfectly flat blue eyes. "Paul's had a very, *very* bad whack to the eye, I'm afraid, Mr. Bascombe. He's suffered what we call a dilation to the upper left arc of his left retina. What this essentially means is—" She blinks at me. "Was he hit with a baseball?" This she simply can't believe; no eye protection, no helmet, no nothing.

"A baseball," I say, possibly inaudibly, my good attitude and Gypsy hope gone, gone. "At Doubleday Field."

"Okay. Well," she says, "what this means is the ball hit him slightly left of center. It's what we call a macula-off injury, which means it drove the left front part of his eye back into the retina and basically flattened it. It was a very, very hard blow."

"It was the Express cage," I say, squinting at Dr. Tisaris. She is pretty, svelte (if short) but sinewy, a little athletic Greek, though she's wearing a wedding ring, so conceivably it's her husband the gastroenterologist who's the Greek and she's as Swedish or Dutch as she looks. Anyone but a fool, however, would feel complete confidence in her, even in tennis clothes.

"At the moment," she says, "he has okay vision in the eye, but he's having bright light flashes, which are typical of a serious dilation. You should probably have a second doctor take a look at him, but my suggestion is we repair it as soon as possible. Before the day's out would be best."

"Dilation. What's a dilation?" I am instantly as cold as mackerel flesh. The nurses at the admissions desk are all three looking at me oddly, and either I've just fainted or am about to faint or have fainted ten minutes ago and am recovering on my feet. Dr. Tisaris, however, model of rigorous antifainting decorum, doesn't seem to notice. So that I simply do not faint but grip my ten toes into the soles of my shoes and hang onto the floor as it dips and sways, all in response to one word. I hear Dr. Tisaris say "detachment" and feel certain she's explaining her medical-ethical perspective toward serious injury and advising me to act in a similar manner. What I hear myself saying is, "I see," then I bite the inside of my cheek until I taste dull, warm blood, then hear myself say, "I have to consult his mother first."

"Is she here?" Clipboard down, a look of unbelief on Dr. Tisaris's face, as if there is no mother.

"She's at the Yale Club."

Dr. Tisaris blinks. There is no Yale Club in Oneonta, I think. "Can you reach her?"

"Yes. I think so," I say, still staggered.

"We should try to get on with this." Her smile is indeed a detached, sober, professional one containing many, many strands of important consideration, none specific to me. I tell her I'd be grateful for the chance to see my son first. But what she says is, "Why don't you make your call, and we'll put a bandage on his eye so he won't scare you to death."

I look down for some reason at her curving, taut thighs beneath her smock and do not speak a word, just stand gripping the floor, tasting my blood, thinking in amazement of my son scaring me to death. She glances down at her two legs, looks up at my face without curiosity, then simply turns and walks away toward the admissions desk, leaving me alone to find a telephone.

AT THE YALE CLUB on Vanderbilt Avenue, Mr. or Mrs. O'Dell is not in. It is noon on a bright Sunday before the 4th of July, and no one, of course, *should* be in. Everyone *should* be just strolling out of Marble Collegiate, beaming magisterially, or happily queuing for the Met or the Modern, or "shooting across to the Carlyle" for a Mozart brunch or up to some special friend's special duplex "in the tower," where there's a hedged veranda with ficuses and azaleas and hibiscus and a magical view of the river.

An extra check, though, uncovers Mrs. O'Dell has left behind a "just-in-case" number, which I punch in inside my scrubbed, green-and-salmon hospital phone nook—just as stout-fellow Irv wanders in again, scans the area, sees me waving, gives a thumbs-up, then turns, hands in his blue sweatpants' pockets and surveys the wide world he's just come from through the glass doors. He is an indispensable man. It's a shame he's not married.

"Windbigler residence," a child's musical voice says. I hear my own daughter, bursting with giggles, in the background.

"Hi," I say, unswervingly upbeat. "Is Mrs. O'Dell there?"

"Yes. She is." A pause for whispering. "Can I say who's calling, plee-yuzzz?"

"Say it's Mr. Bascombe." I am cast low by the insubstantial sound of my name. More concentrated whispers, then a spew of laughter, following which Clarissa comes on the line.

"Hel-*lo*," she says in her version of her mother's lowered serious voice. "This is Ms. Dykstra speaking. Can I be of any use to you, sir?" (She means, of course, Can I be of any service.)

"Yes," I say, my heart opening a little to let a stalk of light enter. "I'd like to order one of the twelve-year-old girls and maybe a pizza."

"What color would you like?" Clarissa says gravely, though she's bored with me already.

"White with a yellow top. Not too big."

"Well, we only have one left. And she's getting bigger, so you'd better place your order. What kind of pizza would you like?"

"Lemme speak to your mom—okay, sweetheart? It's sort of important."

"Paul's barking again, I bet." Clarissa makes a little schnauzer bark of her own, which drives her friend into muffled laughter. (They are, I'm certain, locked away in some wondrous, sound-proof kids' wing, with every amusement, diversion, educational device, aid and software package known to mankind at their fingertips, all of it guaranteed to keep them out of the adults' hair for years.) Her friend makes a couple of little barks too, just for the hell of it. I should probably try one. I might feel better.

"That's not very funny," I say. "Get your mom for me, okay? I need to talk to her."

The receiver goes *blunk* onto some hard surface. "That's what he does," I hear Clarissa say unkindly about her wounded brother. She barks twice more, then a door opens and steps depart. Across the waiting room, Dr. Tisaris emerges again through the emergency room door. She has her smock buttoned now and baggy green surgical trousers down to her feet, which are sheathed in green booties. She is ready to operate. Though she heads over to the admissions desk to impart something to the nurses that makes them all crack up laughing just like my daughter and her friend. A black nurse sings out, "*Giiirl*, I'm tellin' you, I'm tellin' *you* now," then catches herself being noisy, sees me and covers her mouth, turning around the other way to hide more laughter.

"Hello?" Ann says brightly. She has no idea who's calling. Clarissa has kept it as her surprise secret.

"Hi. It's me."

"Are you here *already*?" Her voice says she's happy it's me, has just left a table full of the world's most interesting people, only to find even better pickings here. Maybe I could cab over and join in. (A conspicuous sea change from yesterday—based almost certainly on the welcome discovery that something has finally ended between us.)

"I'm in Oneonta," I say bluntly.

"What's the matter?" she says, as if Oneonta were a city well known for cultivating trouble.

"Paul's had an accident," I say as quickly as I can, so as to get on to the other part. "Not a life-threatening accident"—pause—"but something we need to confer about right away."

"What happened to him?" Alarm fills her voice.

"He got hit in the eye. By a baseball. In a batting cage."

"Is he blind?" More alarm, mixed with conceivable horror.

"No, he's not blind. But it's serious enough. The doctors feel like they need to get him into surgery pretty quick." (I added the plural on my own.)

"Surgery? Where?"

"Here in Oneonta."

"Where *is* it? I thought you were in Cooper's Park."

This, for some reason God knows but I don't, makes me angry. "That's down the road," I say. "Oneonta's a whole other city."

"What do we have to decide?" Cold, stiffening panic now; and not about the part she can't control—the unexplained wounding of her surviving son—but about the part she realizes, in this instant, she *is* accountable for and must decide about and damn well better decide right, because I am not responsible.

"What's wrong with him?" I hear Clarissa spout out officiously, as if she were accountable for something too. "Did he get his eye blown out with fireworks?"

Her mother says, "Shush. No, he did not."

"We have to decide if we want to let them do surgery up here," I say, peevishly. "They think the sooner the better."

"It's his eye?" She is voicing this as she's understanding it. "And they want to operate on it up there?" I know her thick, dark eyebrows are meshed and she's tugging the back of her hair, picking up one strand at a time, tugging and tugging and tugging until she feels a perfect pin-stick of pain. She has done this only in recent years. Never when I lived with her.

"I'm getting another opinion," I say. Though of course I haven't yet. But I will. I gaze at the TV above the waiting-area chairs. Reverend Jackson has vanished. The words "Credit No Good?" are on the screen against a bright blue background. Irv, when I look around, is still inside the sliding doors, Dr. Tisaris gone from the admissions desk. I'll need to find her pronto.

"Can it wait two hours?" Ann says.

"They said today. I don't know." My anger, just as suddenly, has gone.

"I'm going to come up there," she says.

"It takes four hours." Three, actually. "It won't help." I begin thinking of the clogged FDR, holiday inbounds. Major backups on the Triborough. A traffic nightmare. All things I was thinking about on Friday, though now it's Sunday.

"I can get a helicopter from the East River terminal. Charley flies down all the time. I should be there. Just tell me where."

"Oneonta," I say, feeling strangely hollowed at the prospect of Ann.

"I'm going to get on the phone right now on the way and call Henry Burris. He's at Yale–New Haven. They're in the country this weekend. He'll explain all the options, tell me exactly what's wrong with him."

"Detachment," I say. "They say he has a dilated retina. There's no need to come right this second."

"Is he *in* the hospital?" I have the feeling Ann is writing everything down now: *Henry Burris. Oneonta. Detachment, retina, batting cage? Paul, Frank.*

"Of course he's in the hospital," I say. "Where do you think he is?"

"What's the exact name of the hospital, Frank?" She's as deliberate as a scrub nurse; and I a merely dutiful next of kin.

"A. O. Fox. It's probably the only hospital in town."

"Is there an airport there?" Clearly she has written down *airport*.

"I don't know. There should be, if there isn't." Then a silence opens, during which she may in fact have stopped writing.

"Frank, are you all right? You sound not very good."

"I'm not very good. I didn't have my eye knocked out, though."

"He didn't have his eye knocked out really, did he?" Ann says this in a pleading voice of motherhood that can't be escaped.

From the door Irv turns toward me with a worried look, as if he's overheard me say something bitter or argumentative. The black admissions nurse is looking at me too, over the top of her computer terminal.

"No," I say, "he didn't. But he got it knocked. It's not very good."

"Don't let them do anything to him. Please? Until I get there? Can you?" She says this now in a sweet way that is tuned to the helplessness we share and that I would improve if I could but can't. "Will you promise me that?" She has not yet mentioned her dream of injury. She has done me that kindness.

"Absolutely. I'll tell the doctor right now."

"Thank you so much," Ann says. "I'll be there in two hours or less. Just hold on."

"I will. I'll be right here. And so will Paul."

"It won't be very long," Ann says half brightly. "All right?"

"All right."

"Okay then. Okay." And that is all.

FOR TWO HOURS that turn into three hours that turn into four, I walk round and round the little color-keyed lobby, while everything is on hold. (Under better circumstances this would be a natural time to make client calls and take my mind off worrying, but it's not possible now.) Irv, who's decided to toss in the afternoon "drinks party" with the '59 Sox and keep me company, heads out at two and forages a couple of fat bags of Satellite burgers, which we eat mechanically in the plastic chairs while above us on TV the Mets play the Astros in audio-less nontime. Now is not an action period for the ER. Later, when the light fails and too much beer's been guzzled on the lake, an extra base attempted with bone-breaking results, or when somebody who knows all about Roman candles doesn't quite know enough—*then* resources here will be put to the test. As it is, one possibly self-inflicted minor knife wound, an obese woman with unexplained chest pains, one shirtless, shaken-up victim of a one-car rollover come through, but not all at once, and without fanfare (the last chauffeured in by the Cooperstown crew, who frown at me on their way back out). Everyone is eventually set free under his or her own power, all emerging stone-faced and chastened by the sorry outcome of their day. The nurses behind the admissions desk, though, stay in jokey spirits right through. "Now you wait'll tomorrow 'bout this time," one of them says with a look of amazement. "This place'll be jumpin' like Grand Central Station at rush hour. The Fourth's a *biiig* day for hurtin' yourself."

At three, a fat young crew-cut priest passes by, stops and comes back to where Irv and I are watching silent TV, asks in a confessional whisper if everything's under control, and if not, is there anything he can do for us (it's not; there isn't), then heads smilingly off for the ICU wing.

Dr. Tisaris cruises through a time or two, seemingly without enough to do. Once she stops to tell me a "retina man" from Binghamton who did his work at "Mass Eye" has examined Paul (I never saw him arrive) and confirmed a retinal rupture, and "if it'd be okay we'd like to prep him for when your wife gets here, after which we can shoot him in. Dr. Rotollo"—the Binghamton hired gun—"will do the surgery."

Once again I ask if I can see Paul (I haven't since the ambulance left Cooperstown), and Dr. Tisaris looks inconvenienced but says yes, though she needs to keep him still to "minimalize" bleeding, and maybe I might just peek in unbeknownst, since he's had a sedative.

Leaving Irv, I follow her, *squee-kee-gee, squee-kee-gee*, through the double doors into a brightly lit, mint-colored bullpen room smelling of rubbing alcohol, where there are examining bays around on all four walls, each hung with a green hospital curtain. Two special rooms are marked "Surgical" and have heavy, push-in doors with curved handles, and Paul is housed in one of these. When Dr. Tisaris cautiously shoves back the noiseless door, I see my son then, on his back on a bed-on-wheels equipped with metal sidebars, looking very bulky with both his eyes bandaged over like a mummy, but still in his black *Clergy* shirt and maroon shorts and orange socks, minus only his shoes, which sit side by side against the wall. His arms are folded on his chest in an impatient, judicial way, his legs out straight and stiff. A beam of intense light is trained down on his bandaged face, and he's wearing his earphones plugged into a yellow Walkman I've never seen before, and which is resting on his chest. He seems to me in no particular pain and to all appearances except the bandages seems unbothered by the world (or else he's dead, since I can't detect rise or fall in his chest, no tremor in his fingers, no musical toe twitch to whatever he's tuned in to). His ear, I see, has a new bandage.

I would of course dearly love to bound across and kiss him. Or if that couldn't be, at least to do my waiting in here, unacknowledged amongst the instrument trays, oxygen tubes, defibrillator kits, needle dumps and rubber glove dispensers: sit a vigil on a padded stool, be a presence for my son, "useful" at least in principle, since my time for being a real contributor seems nearly over now, in the way that serious, unraveling injury can deflect the course of life and send it careering an all new way, leaving the old, uninjured self and its fussy familiars far back on the road.

But neither of these can happen, and time goes by as I stand with Dr. Tisaris simply watching Paul. A minute. Three. Finally I see a hopeful sigh of breath beneath his shirt and suddenly feel my ears being filled by hissing, so much that if someone spoke to me, said "Frank" again, out loud from behind, I might not hear, would only hear hiss, like air escaping or snow sliding off a roof or wind blowing through a piney bough—a hiss of acceptance.

Paul, then, for no obvious reason, turns his head straight toward us, as if he's heard something (my hiss?) and knows someone is watching, can imagine me or someone through a red-black curtain of molten dark. Out loud, in his boy's voice, he says, "Okay, who's here?" He fiddles sightlessly with his Walkman to kill the volume. He may of course have said it any number of times when no one was present.

"It's Dr. Tisaris, Paul," she says, utterly calm. "Don't be frightened."

All hissing ceases.

"Who's frightened?" he says, staring into his bandages.

"Are you still having flashes of light or vivid colors?"

"Yeah," he says. "A little. Where's my Dad?"

"He's waiting for you." She lays a cool finger upon my wrist. I am not to speak. I am the virus of too much trouble already. "He's waiting for your Mom to get here, so we can fix your eye up." Her starchy smock shifts against the doorframe. I catch a first faint scent of exotica from underneath its folds.

"Tell my Dad he tries to control too much. He worries too much too," Paul says. With his warty, tattooed hand he gropes down at his pleasure unit and gives it a delving scratch just like Irv, as though all lights were out and no one could see anyone. Then he sighs: great wisdom conferring great patience.

"I'll see he gets that message," Dr. Tisaris says in an echoless, professional's voice.

And it is *this* voice that makes me wince, a not-small, mouth-skewing wince up from my knees, sudden and forceful enough that I have to clear my throat, turn my head away and gulp. Here is the voice of the *outer* world become primary: "I'll see he gets that message; I'm sorry, that job's filled; we'd like to ask you some questions; I'm sorry, I can't talk to you now." And so on, and so on, and so on all the way to: "I'm sorry to tell you your father, your mother, your sister, your son, your wife, your dog, your-*anybody*-you-might-ever-know-and-love-and-want-to-survive has left, disappeared, been called away, injured, maimed, expired." While mine—the silenced voice of worry, love, patience, impatience, comradeship, thoughtlessness, understanding and genial acquiescence—is the small voice of the old small life losing ground. The Hall of Fame—impersonal but shareable—was meant as the staging ground for a new life's safe beginning (and nearly, nearly was) but instead has had itself preempted by a regional hospital full of prognoses, voices without echoes, cheery disinterest, cold hard facts impossible to soften. (Why is it we're never quite prepared, as I'm not now, for our plans to work out wrong?)

"Do you have any kids?" Paul asks sagely to his tanned doctor in a voice as echoless as hers.

"Nope," she says, smiling jauntily. "Not yet."

I should stay now, hear his views on child rearing, a subject he has unique experience with. Only my feet won't hear of it and are inching back, shifting direction, then shoving off, getting out of range fast across the bullpen, headed for the doors, much as when I heard him years ago conferring ardently with his made-up "friends" at home and couldn't bear it either, was made too weak and sick at heart by his inspired and almost perfect sufficiency.

"If you have any," I hear him say, "don't ever—" Then that's it, and I am quickly out through the metal doors and back into the cool watery room for relatives, friends, well-wishers, where I now belong.

BY FOUR Ann has not arrived, and Irv and I elect a walk out of the hospital, across the lawn and onto the summery afternoon streets of Oneonta, a town I never once for all my travels imagined myself in; never dreamed I'd be a worried father-in-waiting in, though that has been my MO for moons and moons.

Irv has blossomed into even wider good spirits, the net effect of awaiting dire events that aren't truly dire for him, that will make him sorry if things go bad but never truly bereaved. (Much like your Aunt Beulah's second husband, Bernie from Bismarck, who takes it on himself to tell jokes at your grandfather's funeral and in doing so makes everyone feel a lot better.)

We troop purposefully out across the tonsured Bermuda grass and onto the warm sidewalk where hilly Main drops quickly toward town and is now much busier than when church was going. Here great shagbark hickories and American chestnuts, descendants of our central hardwood forest primeval, have bulged their roots through the aged, crumbly concrete and made strolling a challenge. Ranked along the descending street are old sagging frame residences built on the high ground above retaining walls, going gray and punky from the years and soon to be settling (if work's not done and done soon) into perfect value-lessness. Some are deserted, some have American flags flying, a couple show familiar yellow ribbons, while others show signs that say FOR RENT. FOR SALE. FREE IF YOU MOVE IT. In my trade these are "carpenter's specials," "starter homes for newlys," "not for everyone" homes, "mystery abounds" homes, "make offer" homes—the downward-tending lingo of loss.

Irv, being Irv, means to take up an issue, and in this case the issue is "continuity," which is what his life at least seems to him to be "all about" these days—recognizing, he willingly admits, that his concern may be "tied to" his Jewishness and to the need to strive, to the pressure of history and to a certain significant portion of his life spent on a kibbutz after his first marriage went down the tubes and wrecked continuity big-time, and where he harrowed the dry and unforgiving Bible land, read the Torah, served six nerve-racking months in the Israeli army and eventually married another kibbutznik (from Shaker Heights), a marriage that also didn't last long and ended in scalding, vituperative, religiously dispiriting divorce.

"I learned a lot in the kibbutz, Frank," Irv says, his rattan sandals slapping the split pavement as we head down Main at a good clip. We seem by no particular design to be aiming toward a red Dairy Queen sign below on the Oneonta strip-commercial, a neighborhood where the houses stop and possibly it's unsafe for strangers (a neighborhood in transition).

"Everybody I know who went over there says it was pretty interesting, even if they didn't like it much," I say. I actually know no one but Irv who ever admitted to living on a kibbutz, and all I *do* know I read in the Trenton *Times*. Irv, though, is not a bad advertisement for the life, since he's decent and thoughtful and not at all a pain in the ass. (I've now recalled Irv's boyhood persona: the exuberant, accommodating, gullible-but-complex "big" boy who needed to shave way too early in life.)

"You know, Frank, Judaism doesn't have to be practiced just in the synagogue," Irv says solemnly. "Growing up in Skokie, I didn't always have that impression. Not that my family was ever devout in any way." *Slap-slap, slip-slap, slip-slop.* Local toughs with local sweethearts notched under their bulging biceps are cruising East Main in hot-looking Trans Ams and dark, channeled S-10s. (No Monzas.) Irv and I stand out here like two Latvian rustics in native attire, which isn't that uncomfortable since it's our own country. (A common language alone *should* assure us entry-level acceptance anywhere within a two-thousand-mile radius of Kansas City, though pushing your luck could mean trouble, just like on a kibbutz, and we are now and then glared at.)

"You have any kids, Irv?" I say, not at ease—continuity aside—with religious talk today, happier to be led elsewhere.

"No kids," Irv says. "Didn't want kids, which is what shot my deal with the second wife. She remarried right away and had a bunch. I don't even have any contact with her, which is too bad. They shunned me. You wouldn't think that would happen." Irv seems amazed but sorrowfully willing to accept life's mysteries.

"Self-sufficient thinking's always in short supply in those kinds of places, I guess. Just like with the Baptists and the Presbyterians."

"I guess Sartre said freedom isn't worth a nickel unless you can act on it."

"That sounds like Sartre," I say, thinking all over again what I've always thought about hippie communes, Brook Farms, kibbutzes, goofball utopian ideals of every stripe: let one real independent emerge, and everybody turns into Hitler. And if a good egg like Irv can't make it work for him, the rest of us may as well stay where we are. I don't know what this has to do with continuity, though I'm sure I should.

We pass along by an old building with a dirty junk-store window display piled and jumbled with dented teakettles, wooden hotel coat hangers, busted waffle irons, bits of saddlery, snow tires, empty picture frames, books, lamp shades, plus a whole lot more crap heaped back on a shadowy concrete floor—stuff the last owner couldn't give away when he went bust and just left. In the glass, though, I unexpectedly and unhappily see myself, in brighter colors than the junk but still dim and, to my surprise, a good half a head shorter than Irv and walking along in a semi-*stooped* posture, as if grasping forces were tightening strings and sinews in my gut, causing me to bunch up, humping my shoulders in a way I sure as hell never imagined myself and, now that I see, am shocked by! Irv, of course, is oblivious to his reflection. But I sternly brace back my shoulders and stiffen up like a clothes dummy, take a deep chest breath, give myself a good erective stretching and work my head around like a light-house (not very different from what I did standing on the wall overlooking the Central Leatherstocking Region yesterday, but now with more cause). Irv meanwhile goes back to elaborating on his continuity concerns as we reach the bottom of the hill, passing a low-rent, two-desk real estate office, City of Hills Realty, whose name I don't recognize from the signs I saw farther back.

"Anyway," Irv says, tramping right along, not noticing my furious stretching, opening a button on his gold cardigan to cool off in the warm afternoon. "Do you have a lot of friends?"

"Not too many," I say, my neck worked back, my shoulders squared.

"Same here. Simulators only socialize as a group, but I'd rather take off for a long walk in the desert alone, or maybe go camping."

"I've become an amateur trout fisherman." I walk a little faster now. Moving my shoulders and neck have also awakened an achiness where I was whacked by the baseball.

"See? There you are," meaning what I'm not sure. "How 'bout a girlfriend? You fixed up there?"

"Well," I say, and think an awkward thought about Sally for the first time in too long. I should definitely call South Manto-loking before she gets on the train. Recalculate our plans; aim for tomorrow. "I'm pretty set there, Irv."

"How 'bout marriage plans?"

I smile at Irv, a man with two wives down and one on deck, a man who hasn't seen me in twenty-five years yet who's trying hard to console me against bad events by the honest application of his simple self to mine. Much of human goodness is badly undersold, take it from me. "I'm a bachelor these days, Irv."

Irv nods, satisfied that we're in the same semi-seaworthy boat. "I didn't really explain what I meant about continuity," he says. "It's just my Jewish thing. With other people it's probably different."

"I guess so." I'm picturing the ten separate digits of Sally's phone number, counting the possible rings and her sweet voice in answer.

"I'd think in the realty business you'd get a pretty good exposure to everybody's wish for it. I mean in the community sense."

"What's that?"

"Just continuity," Irv says, smiling, sensing some resistance and maybe considering just letting the subject go (I would). We're across the street from the DQ now, having homed in here through some mutual understanding we haven't needed to voice.

"I don't really think communities are continuous, Irv," I say. "I think of them—and I've got a lot of proof—as isolated, contingent groups trying to improve on an illusion of permanence, which they fully accept as an illusion. If that makes any sense. Buying power is the instrumentality. But continuity, if I understand it at all, doesn't really have much to do with it. Maybe realty's not that commanding a metaphor."

"I guess that makes sense," Irv says, pretty certainly not buying a word of it, though he ought to be satisfied since my definition of community fits right into a general notion of simulation as well as his personal bad experience on the kibbutz. ("Community" is actually one of those words I loathe, since all its hands-on implications are dubious.)

I am braced up straighter now, almost as erect and tall as Irv, though he's meatier from all his months with a Galil strapped to his back while hoeing the dry ground and keeping an eagle eye out for murderous, uncommunity-oriented Arabs.

"Does that seem like enough, though, Frank? The *illusion* of permanence?" Irv says this committedly. It is a subject he no doubt wrangles over with everybody, and may be his *true interest*, one that makes his happy life a sort of formal investigation of firmer stuff beyond the limits of simulation; rather than like mine, a journey toward someplace yet to be determined but that I have good hope for.

"Enough for what?"

We've crossed to the DQ, which true to the old town is an "oldie" itself, in lackluster disrepair since Oneonta has yet to blossom into a destination resort. It's nowhere as nice as Franks, though there are enough similarities to make me feel at home standing in front of it.

"It's still all tied up in my mind with continuity," Irv says, arms folded, reading the hand-lettered menu board from where we're stopped at the back of a short queue of native Oneontans. I scan down for a "dipped" cone, my all-time fave, and feel for just this fleeting moment incongruously happy. "I was remembering while I was waiting for you at the hospital"—Irv allows a look of good-willed perplexity to pass over his big Levantine mouth—"that you and I were around Jake's house together while our parents were married. I was right there when your mother died. We knew each other pretty well. And now twenty-five years of absence go by and we bump into each other up here in the middle of the north woods. And I realized—I realized it pacing around up there worried about Jack and his eye—that you're my only link to that time. I'm not gonna get all worked up over it, but you're as close to family as anyone there is for me. And we don't even know each other." Irv, even as he's making his ice cream choice, and without actually looking at me, lays his big, fleshy, hairy, pinkie-ringed hand heavily onto my shoulder and shakes his head in wonderment. "I don't know, Frank." He looks at me furtively, then stares hard at the big menu. "Life's screwy."

"It is, Irv," I say. "It's screwy as a monkey." I put my smaller hand on Irv's shoulder. And though we don't splutter forward and glom onto each other at the end of the DQ line, we do exchange a number of restrained but unambiguous shoulder pats and glance squeamishly into each other's faces in ways that on any other day but this odd one would set me off up the hill at a dead run.

"We've probably got a lot of things to talk about," Irv says prophetically, keeping his heavy hand where it is, so that I feel forced to keep mine where *it* is, in a sort of unwieldy, arms-length non-embrace. Several Oneontans waiting in front of us have already cast threatening now-just-don't-get-me-involved-in-this frowns our way, as though dangerously unsuppressed effusions were about to splash on everybody like battery acid, with violence a likely outcome. But this is as far as it's going; I could easily tell them as much.

"We might, Irv," I say, not knowing what those things could be.

A shadowy someone inside the Dairy Queen slides back the rickety glass on the SORRY CLOSED window and says from inside, "I can help you down here, folks." The Oneontans all give us a hesitant look as if Irv and I might suddenly rush the other window, though we don't. They turn back toward their own original window, consider it skeptically, then as a group all shift over to number two, giving Irv and me a straight shot to the front.

ON OUR WAY back up the hill we walk side by side, as solemn as two missionaries, I with my fast-dissolving "dip," Irv with a pink "strawberry boat" that snugs perfectly into the palm of one big hand. He seems to be elated but containing his feelings of transcendence owing to the sober protocol of Paul's (Jack's) injury.

He explains to me, though, that lately he's been going through an "odd passage" in life, one he associates with getting to be forty-five (instead of being Jewish). He complains of feeling detached from his own personal history, which has eventuated in a fear (kept within boundaries by his demanding simulator work) that he is diminishing; and if not in an actual physical sense, then definitely in a spiritual one. "It's hard to explain in literal terms and make it seem really serious or clear," he assures me.

I look upward when he says this, my sticky napkin squeezed into a tight dry ball in my palm, my jaw beginning to ratchet tight again after our respite. High above us, sea gulls circle dizzyingly and in great numbers on the clear afternoon air waves, framed by the old green hardwood crowns up the hillside, high enough to seem to make no sound. Why gulls, I wonder, so far from a sea?

Fear of diminishment of course is a concept I know plenty about under the title "fear of disappearance," and would be happy to know not much more. Though in Irv's case it has occasioned what he calls the "catch of dread," a guilty, hopeless, even deathly feeling he experiences just at the moment when anyone else in his right mind might expect to feel exultation—upon seeing sea gulls in dizzying great numbers on a matte of blue sky; or upon stealing an unexpected glimpse down a sun-shot river valley (as I did just yesterday) to a shimmering glacial lake of primordial beauty; on seeing unreserved love in your girlfriend's eyes and knowing she wants to dedicate her life only to your happiness and that you should let her; or just smelling a sudden, heady perfume on a timeworn city sidewalk as you turn a crumbling corner and spy a bed of purple loosestrife and Shasta daisies in full bloom in a public park you had no reason to expect was there. "Little things *and* large," Irv says, referring to whatever has made him feel first wonderful, then terrible, then lessened, then potentially canceled altogether. "It's crazy, but I feel like some bad feeling is sort of eating away at me on the edges." He jabs with his plastic spoon at the bottom of his corrugated pink boat and furrows his big-lug brows.

To tell the truth, I'm surprised to hear this kind of dour talk out of Irv. I'd have guessed his Jewishness plus native optimism would've sheltered him—though of course I'm wrong. Native optimism is that humor most vulnerable to sneak attacks. About Jewishness I don't know.

"My view of marriage"—Irv has earlier admitted a strange unwillingness to tie the knot and make little hard-body Erma Mrs. Ornstein #3—"is that I'm still ready to go whole hog and lose myself in it, but really since about '86 or so I've had this feeling, and this goes along with the dread, of just losing myself period, and in Erma's case of maybe losing myself into the wrong person and being eternally sorry." Irv looks over at me to see, I assume, if I've changed in appearance, having now heard his bitter admissions. "And I do love her, too," he adds as a capper.

We are nearly back to the hospital lawn. The old, settling houses up above the sidewalk behind aged hickories and oaks seem less decrepit now for having been viewed twice in different moods and lights. (A cornerstone principle for your hard-to-sell listing: make 'em see it twice. Things can look better.) I turn and gaze back down the hill and over town. Oneonta seems like a sweet and homey place—admittedly not a place I'd want to sell real estate, but still a fine place to live once your family has gone off and left you to your own devices for combating loneliness. The gulls I've seen have suddenly vanished, and the afternoon air above the treetops is now swept through by evening swifts, taking insects and filling the sky like motes. (I should call the Markhams, as well as Sally, but these needs recede, each as they are counted.)

"Any of that stick to your wall?" Irv says earnestly, knowing he's blathered on like a mental patient and I've said zilch, except it's allowable now since we're brothers.

"All of it does, Irv." I smile, hands down deep in my pockets, letting the warm breeze lave me before I turn back toward the hospital. Naturally, I've felt what Irv is feeling five hundred times over and have no single solution to offer, only the general remedies of persistence, jettisoning, common sense, resilience, good cheer—all tenets of the Existence Period—leaving out the physical isolation and emotional disengagement parts, which cause trouble equal to or greater than the problems they ostensibly solve.

Someone from a passing pickup, a tee-shirted white kid with a mean red mouth and a plump, sneering girlie with her hands parked behind her head, shouts out his window something that sounds like *honi soit qui mal y pense* but isn't, then floors it, laughing. I wave at him good-naturedly, though Irv is captained by his probs.

"I guess I'm sort of surprised to hear you say all that, Irv," I resume, to try and be a help. "But I think a small act of heroism might be to go ahead and try saying yes to Erma. Even if you get whacked. You'll get over it, just like you got over the kibbutz." (I'm a big talker when it's somebody else getting whacked.) "How long ago were you over there, by the way?"

"Fifteen years ago. It left a major impression. But that's interesting for the future," Irv says, nodding, and meaning again that it's *not* interesting at all but the goddamn craziest thing he's ever heard of, though he'll pretend it isn't because he feels sorry for me. (I'd have thought the kibbutz experience was last September, not 1973!) Irv sniffs the air, as if seeking a fragrance he recognizes. "Now's maybe not the time to take that kind of chance, Frank. I'm thinking about the continuity I was boring you with, about getting a clearer sense of where I've come from before I try to find out where I'm going. Just take the pressure off the moment, if you see my point." He looks at me, nodding judiciously.

"How're you going to do that? Get some genealogical charts made up?"

"Well, for instance, today—this afternoon—this has meant something to me along those lines."

"Me too." Though again I'm not completely sure what. Possibly it's something on the order of what Sally said about not ever getting to see Wally and having to get used to it, only in reverse: I *am* getting to see Irv, and I like it, but it doesn't have a profound effect.

"But that's a good sign, isn't it? Someplace in the Torah it says something about beginning to understand long before you know you understand."

"I think that's in *Miracle on 34th Street*," I say, and smile again at Irv, who is kind but goofy from too much simulation and continuity. "I'm pretty sure it says it in *The Prophet* too."

"Never read it," he says gravely. "But let me just show you something, Frank. This'll surprise you." Irv goes groping in his sweatpants' back pocket and comes out with a tiny wafer wallet that probably cost five hundred dollars. Concentrating down-ward, he thumbs through his credit cards and papers, then fingers out something that appears softened by time. "Take a look at that," he says, handing it forward. "I've carried that for years. Five years now. Tell me why."

I turn the card and hold it so the daylight's behind me. (Irv has gone to the trouble of laminating it as a seal of its impor-tance.) And it's not a card at all but a photograph, black and white, encased in layers and re-layers of plastic and for that reason is fogged and dim as memory. Here are four humans in a stately family pose, two parents, two adolescent boys, standing out on some front porch steps, squinting-smiling apprehensively at the camera and into a long-ago patch of light that brightens their faces. Who are these? Where are they? When? Though in a moment I see it's Irv's once-nuclear family in the greenage days in Skokie, when times were sweet and nothing needed simulating.

"Pretty great, Irv." I look up at him, then admire the photo again for politeness' sake and hand it back, ready to re-commence my own parenting tasks, put the pressure back on the moment.

Not far off I hear the wet *thwop-thwop-thwop* and realize the hospital has a helipad for such emergencies as Paul's, and that this is Ann arriving.

"It's us, Frank," Irv says, and looks at me amazed. "It's you and Jake and your mom and me, in Skokie, in 1963. You can see how pretty your mom is, though she looks thin already. We're all there on the porch. Do you even remember it?" Irv stares at me, damp-lipped and happy behind his glasses, holding his precious artifact out for me to see once more.

"I guess I don't." I look again reluctantly at this little pinch-hole window to my long-gone past, feel a quickening torque of heart pain—unexceptional, nothing like Irv's catch of dread—and once again proffer it back. I'm a man who wouldn't recog-nize his own mother. Possibly I should be in politics.

"Me either really." Irv looks appreciatively down at himself for the eight jillionth time, trying to leech some wafting syn-chronicity out of his image, then shakes his head and re-snugs it among his other wallet votives and crams it all back into his pocket, where it belongs.

I survey the sky again for a sight of the chopper but see nothing, not even the swifts.

"I mean, no great big deal, of course." Irv is squaring up his expectations to my rather insufficient response.

"Irv, I better get inside now. I'm pretty sure I hear my wife's helicopter arriving." (Is this a sentence one *usually* says? Or is it me? Or the day?)

"Hey, don't be crazy." Irv's heavy hand is again right up on my shoulder like a gangplank. (My heart has in fact gone rapid with its own *thwopetty-thwop*.) "I wanted to show you what I meant about continuity. It's nothing dangerous. We don't have to cut our arms and mingle blood or anything."

"I might not agree with you about everything, Irv, but I—" and then for an instant I lose my breath entirely and almost gasp, which makes me panic that I'm choking and need a quick Heimlich (if Irv knows how and would oblige). I've done wrong by taking this Dairy Queen walk and letting myself be hoodwinked just like Paul, by cozy, small-town plenitude, lured to think I can float free again against all evidence of real gravity. "But I want you to know," I say just before a second, less terrifying gullet stop, "that I respect how you see the world, and I think you're a great guy." (When in doubt fall back on the old Sigma Chi formula: Ornstein = Great Guy. Let's pledge him, even if he is a Hebe.)

"I don't think I've miscalculated you, Frank," Irv says. He is the stalwart project leader over in the yaw-pitch-and-roll lab now: always flying level even if the rest of us aren't. Though I've been him (more than once) and won't be caught again. Irv is entering his own Existence Period, complete with all the good and not-so-good trimmings, just as it seems I'm exiting it in a pitch-and-tumble mode. We have passed in daylight; we have interfaced, given each other good and earnest feedback. But ours is not life coterminous, though I like him fine.

I start off then toward the hospital doors, my heart popping, my jaw going stiff as an andiron, leaving Irv with my best words for our future as friends. "We'll try to go fishing sometime." I look around for emphasis. He is poised, one long, sandaled foot on the edge of the grass, one off, his bright cardigan catching the sunlight. He is, I know, silently wishing us both clear sailing toward the next horizon.

CHAPTER 12

ANN IS STANDING in the emergency room lobby all alone, in her buttoned-up tan trench coat, bare-legged, wearing worn white running shoes. She looks as if her mind is full of worries, none of which can be solved by seeing me.

"I've been standing here watching you through those doors as you crossed the lawn. And it wasn't until you got to the door that I realized it was you." She smiles at me in a daunted way, takes her hands out of her trench coat pockets, holds my arm and gives me a small kiss, which makes me feel a small bit better (though not actually good). We are less joined than ever now, so much that a kiss can't matter. "I brought Henry Burris with me. That's why I'm so late," she says, immediately all business. "He's already looked at Paul and his chart, and he thinks we ought to fly him down to Yale right away."

I simply stare at her in confoundment. I have indeed missed everything important: her arrival, a new examination, a revised prognosis. "How?" I say, looking hopelessly around the apple-green-and-salmon waiting room walls, as if to say, Well, you can see what *I* bring to the table: Oneonta. It may be a funny name, it may not even be the best, but by God, it's reliable and it's where we are.

"We've already got another helicopter coming that can transport him. It's maybe already here." She looks at me sympathetically.

Behind the admissions desk there is a new crew: two tiny, neat-as-pins Korean girls in high Catholic-nursing-school caps, working over charts like actuaries, plus a listless young blond (a local), engrossed by her computer monitor. None of these knows of my case. It would encourage me to have Irv waltz in, take a seat in the back row and be my ally.

"What does Dr. Tisaris say?" I'm wondering where she is, wishing she would get in on this powwow. Though possibly Ann has already dismissed her and Dr. Rotollo both, put her own surgical team in place while I was out having my "dip." I'll need to apologize to her for a lack of faith.

"She's fine about releasing him," Ann says, "especially to Yale. We just sign a form. I've already signed one. She's very professional. She knows Henry from her residency" (natch). Ann is nodding. Suddenly, though, she peers directly up at my eyes, her gray, flecked irises gone perfectly round and large, shining with straight-ahead imploring. She is not wearing her wedding ring (possibly for the wit's-end, nerves-stripped-bare look). "Frank, I'd just like to do this, okay? So we can get him down to New Haven in fifty minutes? Everything's all set there. It's a half hour to get him prepped and an hour or so in surgery. Henry'll supervise it. Then the best that can happen will." She blinks at me dark-eyed, not wanting to say more, having played the big card first—though she can't help herself. "Or he can be operated on in Oneonta by Dr. Tisaris or whoever, and she may be fine."

"I understand," I say. "What's the risk to him of flying?"

"Smaller than the risk, in Henry's opinion, of doing retinal surgery here." Her features soften and relax. "Henry's done two thousand of these."

"That oughta be enough," I say. "Is he a classmate of Charley's?"

"No. He's older," she says curtly and then is silent. Possibly Henry's our mystery mister; they almost always fill innocent roles as cover. Older, in this case; experienced in treating the ravaged victims of human suffering (such as Ann); uncannily bears Ann's father's name as a karmic asset. Plus, once he saves Paul's vision (days of soulful waiting for the bandages to be removed and sight to re-dawn), it'll be a snap to lay it all out to Charley, who'll wryly, maybe even gratefully, stand aside, outmaneuvered round the final buoy. Charley's a sport, if nothing else. I am much less of one.

"Do you want to know what happened?" I say.

"He got hit with a batting cage, you said." Ann produces a business-size envelope from her trench coat pocket and moves back a step toward the admissions desk, indicating I should come with her. It is another release form. I am releasing my son into the world. Too early.

"He got hit with a baseball, *in* a batting cage," I say.

Ann says nothing, just looks at me as if I'm being overly fastidious about these large-scale events. "Wasn't he wearing a helmet of some kind?" she says, inching back, drawing me on.

"No. He got mad at me and just ran in the cage, and stood there for a couple of pitches, then he just let one hit him in the face. I put the money in for him." I feel my eyes, for the third time in less than twenty-four hours, cloud with hot tears I don't want to be there.

"Oh," Ann says, her envelope in her left hand. One of the Oriental micro-nurses looks up at me in a nose-high, nearsighted way, then goes back to charting. Tears mean nothing in the emergency room.

"I don't think he *wanted* to put his eye out," I say, my eyes brimming. "But he may have wanted to get whacked. To see what it felt like. Haven't you ever felt that way?"

"No," Ann says, and shakes her head, staring at me.

"Well, I have, and I wasn't crazy." I say this much too loudly. "When Ralph died. And after you and I got divorced. I'd have been happy to take a hard one in the eye. It would've been easier than what I *was* doing. I just don't want you to think he's nuts. He's not."

"It was probably just an accident," she says imploringly. "It isn't your fault." Though she is meticulous, her own eyes go shiny against all effort and instinct. I am not supposed to see her cry, remember? It violates the divorce's creed.

"It *is* my fault. Sure it is," I say, terribly. "You even dreamed about it. He should've been wearing protective eye covering and a suit of armor and a crash helmet. You weren't there."

"Don't feel that way," Ann says and actually smiles, though bleakly. I shake my head and wipe my left eye, where there seem to be too many tears. Her seeing me cry is *not* an issue in my code of conduct. There is no issue between us. Which is the issue.

Ann takes a deep unassured breath, then shakes her head as a signal of what I'm not supposed to do now: make things worse. Her left, ringless hand rises as if by itself and places the envelope on the green plastic admissions counter. "I don't think he's crazy. He just may need some assistance right now. He was probably trying to make you notice him."

"We all need assistance. I was just trying to make him *do* something." I am suddenly angry with her for knowing but knowing wrongly what everybody's supposed to do and how and why. "And I *will* feel this way. When your dog gets run over, it's your fault. When your kid gets his eye busted, that's your fault. I was supposed to help manage his risks."

"Okay." She lowers her head, then steps to me and takes one sleeve again as she did when she gave me one small kiss and talked me into agreeing for my son to fly to Yale. She lets her face go sideways against my chest, her body relaxed as a way for me to know she's trying—trying to slip back between the walls of years and words and events, and listen to my heartbeat as a surety that we are both now alive, if we're nothing else, together. "Don't just be mad," she says in a whisper. "Don't be so mad at me."

"I'm not mad at you." I am whispering too, into her dark hair. "I'm just so something else. I don't think I know the word. There's not a word for it, maybe."

"That's what you like, though. Isn't it?" She's holding my arm now, though not too tight, as the nurses behind us politely turn their faces.

"Sometimes," I say. "Sometimes it is. Just not now. I'd like to have a word now. I'm in between words, I guess."

"That's okay." I feel her body grow taut and begin to pull away. She would have a word for it. It's her precise way of truth. "Sign this paper now, won't you? So we can get things going? Get him all fixed up?"

"Sure," I say, letting go. "I'll be glad to."

And of course, finally, I am.

HENRY BURRIS is a dapper, white-thatched, small-handed, ruddy-cheeked little medico in white duck pants, more expensive deck shoes than mine and a pink knit shirt straight—in all probability—from Thomas Pink. He is sixty, has the palest, clearest limestone-blue eyes and when he talks does so in a close, confidential South Carolina low-country drawl, while keeping a light grip on my wrist as he tells me everything's going to be all right with my son. (Zero chance, I now believe, that he and Ann are playing sexual shenanigans, owing chiefly to his height, but also because Henry is famously attached to a highly prized, implausibly leggy and also rich wife named Jonnee Lee Burris, heiress to a gypsum fortune.) Ann has in fact told me, while we waited together like old friends in an airport, that the Burrises are the touchstones for everyone's glowingest marital aspirations there in otherwise divorce-happy Deep River; and likewise in New Haven, where Henry runs Yale-Bunker Eye Clinic, having given up Nobel Prize-caliber research in favor of selfless humanitarian service and family time—not an obvious candidate for a roll in the hay, though who's ever not a candidate?

"Now, Frank, lemme tell ya, I once had to perform a procedure just like the one I'm going to do on young Paul when I was down at Duke twelve years ago. Visiting Professor of Ophthalmology." Henry has already drawn me an impressive freehand picture of Paul's eye but is spindling it now like an unwanted grocery store circular while he's talking (secretly condescending, of course, since I'm his friend's second wife's first husband and probably a goofball with no Yale connections). "It was on a big fat black lady who'd somehow been hit in the eye by some damn kids throwing horse apples right out in her yard. Black kids too, now, not a racial matter."

We are on the back lawn of the hospital, out beside the blue-and-white square landing pad, where a large red Sikorsky from Connecticut Air Ambulance is resting on its sleds, its rotor gliding leisurely around. From out here, a modest hilltop and perfect setting for a picnic, I can see the shaded Catskills, their hazy runnels plowing south to blue sky and, in the intermediate distance below, a fenced cube of public tennis courts, all in use, beyond which I-88 leads to Binghamton and back up to Albany. I can hear no traffic noise, so that the effect on me is actually pleasant.

"And so this black lady said to me, just as we were about to shoot her up with anesthetic, 'Doctah Burris, if today was a fish, I'd sho th'ow it back.' And she grinned the biggest old snaggle-tooth grin, and off she went to sleep." Henry rounds his eyes out wide and tries to suppress a whooping laugh with a phony mouth-shut grimace—his usual bedside performance.

"What happened to her?" Gently I free my wrist and let it dangle, my eyes drawn helplessly back to the copter thirty yards away, where Paul Bascombe is right now being professionally on-loaded by two attendants, in advance of waving good-bye.

"Oh, golly, I'm tellin' you," Henry Burris says, whispering

and raising his voice both at once. "We fixed her *right* up like we're going to do Paul today. She can see as clear as you can, or at least she could then. I'm sure she's dead now. She was eighty-one."

I have complete faith in Henry Burris, due to our talk. He in fact reminds me of a younger, vigorous, more intelligent and no doubt less slippery Ted Houlihan. I have no reluctance about letting him darn away on my son's retina, no sense of this being a terrible blunder or that regret will rise in me like molten metal and harden forever. It is the right thing to do in all ways and, for that reason, rare. "Discretion," Henry Burris has said to me, "is our best route here, since what we worry about in these things are the problems we *can't* see." (Much like a house purchase.) "We've got some doctors who've seen it all down at Yale." (Which I'll bet is true; possibly I should ask what causes wincing.)

My problem is only that I don't know where to attach my own eyes to Henry, can't *sense* him, and not even that I can't tell you what makes him tick. Eyes make him tick: how you fix 'em, what's wrong with 'em, what's good about 'em, how they make us see and sometimes fail to (similar to Dr. Stopler's contrast between the mind and the brain). But what I can't tell, not that it even matters except for my comfort, is what and where his mystery is, the part you'd discover if you knew him for years, learned to respect him professionally, wanted to discover even more and so decided to take a dude-ranch vacation with him up to the Wind Rivers, or went on a twosome freighter trip around the world or a canoe exploration to the uncharted headwaters of the Watanuki. What are his uncertainties, the quality of his peace made with contingency, his worries about the inevitability of joy or tragedy out in the unknown where we all plow the seas: his rationale, based on experience, for the *advisability* of discretion? I know it about Irv, by God, and you could know mine in 8.2 seconds. But in Henry, where a clue would speak volumes and satisfy much, no clue's in sight.

It's possible, of course, that he lacks a specific rationale; that for him it's just eyes, eyes and more eyes, and secondarily a commanding wife with a statuesque bank account, all topped off by his own damn positive attitude. Discretion, in other words, is a standard, not optional, feature. His is the same glacially suitable, semi-affable medical emanation I sensed around Dr. Tisaris, though there was in Dr. T. that whiff of something *else* under her doctor smock. However (and I'm quitting thinking about it now), this is undoubtedly the very emanation you want in a healthcare provider, particularly when your son's in need of serious fixing and you're sure never to see the guy again.

Ann is waiting a few yards away beneath the helipad's red wind sock, talking overattentively to Irv, who's still in his sandals and gold Mafia sweater and is all curled up in his own folded arms and a slightly feminine hip-in, knees-out posture, as if he feels in need of protection from the likes of Ann. They have discovered some mutual cronies from the "Thumb," who went to the same glockenspiel camp in northern Michigan in the Fifties and frolicked like monkeys on the dunes before they were bulldozed to make a park, on and on. For Irv, today is a banner day for continuities, and he seems as engrossed as an Old Testament scholar, although conscious that Ann's and my continuity is kaput and he should therefore hold some measure back (his snapshot, for instance).

Ann has continued to pass a weather eye my way as I've stood with Henry, occasionally signaling me with a faint and faintly puzzled smile, once even a little one-finger wave, as if she suspected me of plotting a last-second dash in under the rotors to save my son from being saved by her and others, and hoped a twinkle in her eye would be enough to head me off. Though I'm not so stubborn and am a man of my word, if allowed to be. She may only want a small gesture of faith. But I feel a change is now in motion, a facing of fact long overdue, so that my good act toward her will be my faithful forbearance.

I have, of course, had a last chance to reenter Paul's brightly lit hospital room and say my good-byes. He lay, as before, seemingly painless and in resolute spirits, his eyes still patched and taped, his feet spraddled over the end of his gurney—a boy grown too big for his furnishings.

"Maybe when I get out of the hospital and if I'm not on probation, I'll come down and stay with you a while," he said, blindly facing the light and as if this were an all-new subject he'd dreamed up in his sedative daze, though it made me light-headed, my arms featherish and tingling, since chances seemed iffy.

"I'm looking forward to it if your mom thinks it's a good

idea," I said. "I'm just sorry we didn't have a very good time today. We didn't get into the Hall of Fame, like you said."

"I'm not hall of fame material. It's the story of my life." He smirked like a forty-year-old. "Is there a Real Estate Hall of Fame?"

"Probably," I said, my hands on the bars of his bed.

"Where would it be? In Buttzville, New Jersey?"

"Or maybe Chagrin Falls. Or Cape Flattery, B.C. Maybe Sinking Springs, PA. One of those."

"Do you think they'd let me in school in Haddam in a pirate's patch?"

"If they'll let you in with what you've got on today, I guess so."

"Do you think they'll remember me?" He exhaled with the tedium of injury, his mind flickering with vivid pictures of school commencing in an old/new town.

"I think you cut a pretty wide swath down there, if I remember it right." I looked studiously down at his nose, wrinkled by the bandage, as if he could know I was concentrating on him.

"I was never really appreciated down there." And then he said, "Did you know more women attempt suicide than men? But men succeed more?" A smirk fattened his cheeks under his bandage.

"It's good to be worse at some things, I guess. You didn't try to kill yourself, did you, son?" I stared even harder at him, feeling my posture suddenly sink with the awful weight of fearsome apprehension.

"I didn't think I was tall enough to get hit. I screwed up. I got taller."

"You're just too big for your britches," I said, hoping he wouldn't lie—to me anyway. "I'm sorry I made you stand up there. That was a big mistake. I wish I'd gotten hit instead."

"You didn't make me." He squinted at the light he couldn't see but could feel. "HBP. Runners advance." He touched his bandaged ear with his warty finger. "Ouch," he said.

I put my hand on his shoulder and pressed down again, as I did in the batting cage, my fingers still bearing a scuff of his blood from my rough-up of this very ear. "It's just my hand," I said.

"What would John Adams say about getting beaned?"

"Who's John Adams?" I said. He smiled a sweet self-satisfied smile at nothing. "I don't know, son. What?"

"I was trying to make up a good one. I thought maybe not seeing would help."

"Are you thinking you're thinking now?"

"No, I'm just thinking."

"Maybe he'd say—"

"Maybe he'd say," Paul interrupted, fully involved, " 'You can lead a horse to water, but you can't make him blank.' John Adams would say that."

"What?" I said, wanting to please him. "Swim? Water-ski? Windsurf? Alias Sibelius?"

"Dance," Paul said authoritatively. "Horses can't dance. When John Adams got beaned, he said, 'You can lead a horse to water, but you can't make him dance.' He'll only dance if he feels like it." I expected an *eeeck* or a bark. Something. But there was nothing.

"I love you, son, okay?" I said, suddenly wanting to clear out and in a hurry. Enough was enough.

"Yep, me too," he said.

"Don't worry, I'll see you soon."

"Ciao."

And I had the feeling he was far out ahead of me then and in many things. Any time spent with your child is partly a damn sad time, the sadness of life a-going, bright, vivid, each time a last. A loss. A glimpse into what could've been. It can be corrupting.

I leaned and kissed his shoulder through his shirt. And it was, luckily, then that the nurses came to make him ready to fly far, far away.

ROTORS, ROTORS, ROTORS, turning now in the warm afternoon. Strange faces appear in the open copter door. Henry Burris shakes my hand in his small trained one, ducks and goes stooping across the blue concrete to clamber in. *Thwop-thwop, thwop-thwop, thwop-thwop.* I give a thought to where Dr. Tisaris might be now—possibly playing mixed doubles on one of the cubed courts below. Well out of it.

Ann, bare-legged in her buttoned-up trench coat, shakes hands like a man with Irv. I see her lips moving and his seeming to mouth it all back verbatim: "Hope, hope, hope, hope, hope." She turns then and walks straight across the grass to where I stand, slightly stooped, thinking about Henry Burris's hands, small enough to get inside a head and fix things. He's got a head for eyes and the hands to match.

"Okay?" Ann says brightly, indestructible. I no longer fear or suppose she could die before I die. I am not indestructible; do not even wish to be. "Where will you be tonight so I can call you?" she says over the *thwop-thwop-thwop*.

"Driving home." I smile. (Her old home.)

"I'll leave a number on your box. What time will you get there?"

"It's just three hours. He and I talked about his coming down with me this fall. He wants to."

"Well," Ann says less loudly, tightening her lips.

"I do great with him almost all the time," I say in the hot, racketing air. "That's a good average for a father."

"We're interested in *him* doing well," she says, then seems sorry. Though I am delivered to silence and perhaps a small catch of dread, a fear of disappearance all over again, a mind's snapshot of my son standing with me on the small lawn of my house, doing nothing, just standing—canceled.

"He'd do great," I say, meaning: I hope he'd do great. My right eye flickers with fatigue and, God knows, everything else.

"Do you really *want* to?" Her eyes squint in the rotor wash, as if I might be telling the biggest of all whoppers. "Don't you think it'd cramp your style?"

"I don't really have a style," I say. "I could borrow his. I'll drive him up to New Haven every week and wear a straitjacket if that's what you want. It'll be fun. I know he needs some help right now." These words are not planned, possibly hysterical, unconvincing. I should probably mention the Markhams' faith in the Haddam school system.

"Do you even like him?" Ann looks skeptical, her hair flattened by the swirling wind.

"I think so," I say. "He's mine. I lost almost everybody else."

"Well," she says and closes her eyes, then opens them, still looking at me. "We'll just have to see when this is over. Your daughter thinks you're great, by the way. You haven't lost everybody."

"That's enough to say." I smile again. "Do you know if he's dyslexic?"

"No." She looks out at the big rumbling copter, whose winds are beating us. She wants to be there, not here. "I don't think he is. Why? Who said he was?"

"No reason, really. Just checking. You should get going."

"Okay." She quickly, harshly grabs me behind my head, her fingers taking my scalp where I'm tender and pulling my face to her mouth, and gives me a harder kiss on my cheek, a kiss in the manner of Sally's kiss two nights ago, but in this instance a kiss to silence all.

Then off she goes toward an air ambulance. Henry Burris is waiting to gangway her in. I, of course, can't see Paul on his strapped-in litter, and he can't see me. I wave as the door slides slap-shut and the rotors rev. A helmeted pilot glances back to see who's in and who's not. I wave at no one. The red ground lights around the concrete square suddenly snap on. A swirl and then a pounding of hot air. Mown grass blasts my legs and into my face and hair. Fine sand dervishes around me. The wind sock flaps valiantly. And then their craft is aloft, its tail rising, miraculously orbiting, its motor gathering itself, and like a spaceship it moves off and begins swiftly to grow smaller, a little, and then more, then smaller and smaller yet, until the blue horizon and the southern mountains enclose it in lusterless, blameless light. And everything, *every thing* I have done today is over with.

STREETS AWAY, in the summoning, glimmery early-morning heat, a car alarm breaks into life, shattering all silences. *Bwoop-bwip! Bwoop-bwip! Bwoop-bwip!* On the front steps of 46 Clio Street, reading my paper, I gaze up into the azure heavens through sycamore boughs, take a breath, blink and wait for peace.

I am here before nine, again in my red REALTOR jacket and my own *The Rock* shirt, awaiting the Markhams, currently on their way down from New Brunswick. Though unlike most of my previous intercourse with them, this time there is not a long story. Possibly there is even a hopeful one.

At the end of yesterday's bewildering if not completely demoralizing events, Irv was good enough to chauffeur me back up to Cooperstown—a drive during which he talked a mile a minute and in an almost desperate way about needing to get out of the simulator business, except that in his current view and based on careful analysis, the rah-rah, back-slap, yahoo days in his industry were all done, so that a policy favoring a career move seemed foolhardy, whereas holding his cards seemed wise. Continuity—an earnest new commanding metaphor—was applicable to all and was taking up the slack for synchronicity (which never carries you far enough).

When we arrived long into the shaded dewy hours of early evening, the Deerslayer lot was jammed full of new vacationer cars and my Ford had been towed away, since inasmuch as I was no longer a paying guest my license number was no longer on file. Irv and I and the resurrected Erma then sat in the office at the Mobil station behind Doubleday Field and waited until the tow-truck driver arrived with keys to the razor-wire impound-ment, during which time I decided to make my necessary calls before paying my sixty dollars, saying good-bye and turning homeward alone.

My second call and inexcusably late was to Rocky and Carlo's, to leave a message with Nick the bartender. Sally would receive this when she got in from South Mantoloking, and among its profuse apologies were instructions to go straight to the Algonquin (my first call), where I'd reserved a big suite for her, there to check in and order room service. Later that night, from the village of Long Eddy, New York, halfway down the Delaware, we spoke and I told her all about the day's lamentable happenings and some odd feeling of peculiar and not easily explainable hope I'd already started to revive by then, after which we were able to impress each other with our seriousness and the possibilities for commitment in ways we admitted were "dangerous" and "anxious-making" and that we had never quite advanced to in the solitary months of only "seeing" each other. (Who knows why we hadn't, except there's nothing like tragedy or at least a grave injury or major inconvenience to cut through red tape and bullshit and reveal anyone's best nature.)

Joe and Phyllis Markham, when I reached them, were as meek as mice on hearing they'd missed their chance on the Houlihan house, that I was now fresh out of good ideas and a long way from home, that my already afflicted son had been poleaxed playing baseball and was at that moment in ominous surgery at Yale– New Haven and would probably lose his vision. In my voice, I know, were the somber tonalities and slow, end-stop rhythms of resignation, of having run the course, made the valiant try in more ways than ten, endured imprecation, come back from the trash heap with no hard feelings, and yet in a moment or two I would say good-bye forever. ("Realty death" is the industry buzzword.)

"Frank, look," Joe said, annoyingly tapping a pencil lead on the receiver from within his medium-priced double at the Raritan Ramada and seeming as clearheaded, plainspoken and ready to own up to reality as a Lutheran preacher at the funeral of his impoverished aunt. "Is there any way Phyl and I could get a peek at that colored rental property you mentioned? I know I got away from myself a little on Friday when I flared up that way. And I probably owe you an apology." (For calling me an asshole, a prick, a shithead? Why not, I thought, though that was as close as we got.) "There's one colored family in Island Pond who's been there since the Underground Railroad. Everybody treats 'em like regular citizens. Sonja goes to school right beside one of them every day."

"Tell him we want to look at it tomorrow," I heard Phyllis say. Changes had occurred aloft, I realized, a storm pushed on out to sea. In the realty business, change is good; from 100 percent *for* to 150 percent *against*, or vice versa, are everyday occurrences and signs of promising instability. My job is to make all that seem normal (and, if possible, make every nutty change in a client's mind seem smarter than anything I myself could've advised).

"Joe, I'll be home tonight around eleven, God willing." I leaned wearily against the window glass at the Mobil, the *da-ding, da-ding, da-ding* of the customer bell going constantly. (There was no use picking up the racial cudgels to try explaining to Joe that it was not "a colored house" but *my* house.) "So if I don't call you, I'll meet you on the porch at forty-six Clio Street at nine a.m. tomorrow."

"Four-six Clio, check," Joe said militarily.

"When can we move in?" Phyllis said from the background.

"Tomorrow morning if you want to. It's ready to go. It just needs airing out."

"It's ready to go," Joe said brusquely.

"Oh, thank God," I heard Phyllis say.

"I guess you heard that," Joe said, brimming with relief and craven satisfaction.

"I'll see you there, Joe." And in that way the deal was sealed.

THE CAR ALARM goes just as suddenly silent, and quiet morning reconvenes. (These almost never herald an actual robbery.) Down the block some kids are hovering around what looks like a red coffee can they've set in the middle of the street. No doubt they're following through on plans for an early-morning detonation to alert the neighbors that it's a holiday. Fireworks, of course, are unthinkably illegal in Haddam, and once the explosion blows, it's automatic that a cruiser will idle through the neighborhood, an HPD officer inquiring if we've heard or seen people shooting or carrying guns. I've noticed Myrlene Beavers twice behind her screen, her walker glinting out of the murk. She seems not to notice me today but to concentrate her vigilance on the boys, one of whom—his little face shiny and black—is sporting a bright Uncle Sam costume and will no doubt be marching in the parade later on (assuming he's not in jail). There is yet no sign of the Markhams, or for that matter the McLeods, whom I also have business with.

Since arriving at eight, I've mowed the small front yard with the (supplied) hand mower, watered the parched grass and sprayed the metal siding using my hose from home. I've cut back the dead hydrangea branches and the spirea and the roses, hauled the refuse to the back alley and opened windows and doors front and back to get air flowing inside the house. I've swept the porch, the front walk, run the tap in all the sinks, flushed the commode, used my broom to jab any cobwebs out from the ceiling corners and finished up by taking down the FOR RENT sign and stowing it in my trunk just to minimize the Markhams' feelings of displacement.

As always, I've noticed an awkward, flat-footed sensation involved with showing my own rental house (though I've done it several times since the Harrises left). The rooms seem somehow too large (or small), too drab and unhopeful, already used up and going nowhere, as though the only thing to truly revive the place would be for me to move in myself and turn it homey with my own possessions and positive attitudes. It's possible, of course, that this reaction is only compensatory for some wrong *take* a potential renter might fall victim to, since my underlying feeling is that I like the house exactly the way I liked it the day I bought it almost two years ago, and the McLeods' house the same. (I've seen a curtain twitch there now, but no face shows behind it—someone observing me, someone who doesn't enjoy paying his or her rent.) I admire its clean, tidy, unassuming adequacy, its sturdy rightness, finished off by the soffit vents, the new wrought-iron banister on the stoop, even the flashing to prevent ice dams and water "creep" during January thaws. It would be my dream house if I were a renter: tight, shipshape, cozy. A no-brainer.

In the Trenton *Times* I find holiday news, most of it not good. A man in Providence has sneaked a peek down a fireworks cannon at the most imperfect of moments and lost his life. Two people in far distant parts of the country have been shot with crossbows (both times at picnics). There's a "rash" of arsons, though fewer boating mishaps than might seem likely. I've even found a squib for the murder I stumbled upon three nights back: the vacationers *were* from Utah; they *were* bound for the Cape; the husband *was* stabbed; the alleged assailants *were* fifteen—the age of my son—and from Bridgeport. No names are given, so that all seems insulated from me now, only the relatives left to bear the brunt.

On the briefer, lighter side, the Beach Boys are at Bally's grandstand for one show only, flag-pole sales have once again skyrocketed, harness racing is celebrating its birthday (150) and a kidney transplant team (five men and a black Lab) is at this hour swimming the Channel—their foreseeable impediments: oil slicks, jellyfish and the twenty-one miles themselves (though not their kidneys).

Though the most interesting news is of two natures. One pertains to the demonstration at the Baseball Hall of Fame yesterday, the one that diverted Paul and me off our course and onward to what fate held in store. The demonstrators who blocked the Hall's doors for an important hour were, it turns out, rising in support of a lovable Yankee shortstop from the Forties, who deserved (they felt) a place, a plaque and a bust inside but who in the view of the sportswriter pundits was never good enough and had come by his obscurity honestly. (I side with the protesters on the principle of *Who cares anyway?*)

Yet of even more exotic interest is the "Haddam story," the discovery by our streets crew of a whole human skeleton unearthed, so the *Times* says, Friday morning at nine (on Cleveland Street, the 100 block) by a backhoe operator trenching our new sewer line under the provisos of our "well-being" bond. Details are sketchy due to the backhoe operator's poor command of English, but there's speculation by the town historian that the remains could be "very old, indeed, by Haddam standards," though another rumor has it that the bones are a "female Negro servant" who disappeared a hundred years ago when the Presidents Streets were a dairy farm. Still another theorizes an Italian construction worker was "buried alive" in the Twenties when the town was replatted. Local residents have already half-seriously named the bones "Homo haddamus pithecarius," and an archaeological team from Fairleigh Dickinson is planning to have a look. Meanwhile, the remains are in the morgue. More later, we think, and hope.

*   *   *

WHEN I ARRIVED last night at eleven, having beaten it home in four hours to an odd day-within-night indigo luminance down the quiet streets of town (many house lights were still lit), a message was waiting from Ann, declaring that Paul had come through his surgery "okay" and there was reason for hope, though he would probably develop glaucoma by fifty and need glasses much sooner. He was "resting comfortably" in any event, and I could call her anytime at a 203 number, a Scottish Inn in Hamden (the closer-in New Haven places already filled again with holiday voyagers).

"It was funny, almost," Ann said drowsily, I supposed from bed. "When he came out of it he just jabbered on and on about the Baseball Hall of Fame. All about the exhibits he'd seen and the ... I guess they're statues. Right? He thought he'd had a splendid time. I asked him how you'd liked it, and he said you hadn't been able to go. He said you'd had a date with somebody. So ... some things are funny."

A languor in Ann's voice made me think of the last year of our marriage, eight years ago nearly, when we made love half waking in the middle of the night (and only then), half aware, half believing the other might be someone else, performing love's acts in a half-ritual, half-blind, purely corporal way that never went on long and didn't qualify as much or dignify passion, so vaguely willed and distant from true intimacy was it, so inhibited by longing and dread. (This was not so long after Ralph's death.)

But where had passion gone? I wondered it all the time. And why, when we needed it so? The morning after such a night's squandering, I'd wake and feel I'd done good for humanity but not much for anyone I knew. Ann would act as if she'd had a dream she only remotely remembered as pleasant. And then it was over for a long time, until our needs would once more rise (sometimes weeks and weeks later) and, aided by sleep, our ancient fears suppressed, we would meet again. Desire, turned to habit, allowed to go sadly astray by fools. (We could do better now, or so I decided last night, since we understand each other better, having nothing to offer or take away and therefore nothing worth holding back or protecting. It is a kind of progress.)

"Has he done any sort of barking?" I asked.

"No," Ann said, "not that I've heard him. Maybe he'll quit that now."

"How's Clarissa?" Emptying my pockets, I'd found the tiny red bow she'd presented me out of her hair, companion to the one Paul had eaten. No doubt, I thought, it's she who'll decide what goes on my tombstone. And she will be exacting.

"Oh, she's fine. She stayed down to see *Cats* and the Italian fireworks over the river. She's interested in taking care of her brother, in addition to being slightly glad it happened."

"That's a dim view." (Although it was probably not a far-fetched one.)

"I feel just a little dim." She sighed, and I could tell, as used to be true, she was in no rush to get off now, could've talked to me for hours, asked and answered many questions (such as why I never wrote about her), laughed, gotten angry, come back from anger, sighed, gotten nowhere, gone to sleep on the phone with me at the other end, and in that way soothed the rub of events. It would've been a perfect time to ask her why she hadn't worn her wedding ring in Oneonta, whether she had a boyfriend, if she and Charley were on the fritz. Plus other queries: Did she really believe I never told the truth and that Charley's dull truths were better? Did she think I was a coward? Didn't she know why I never wrote about her? More, even. Only I found that these questions had no weight now, and that we were, by some dark and final magic, no longer in the other's audience. It was odd. "Did you get anything interesting accomplished in two days? I hope so."

"We didn't get around to any current events," I said to amuse her. "I heard most of his views. We talked over some other important things. It might be better. *He* might be better. I don't know. His accident cut everything short." With my tongue I touched the sore, bitten inside of my mouth. I did not mean to talk specifics with her.

"You two are so much alike, it makes me sad," she said sadly. "I can actually see it in his eyes, and they're *my* eyes. I think I understand you both too well." She breathed in, then out. "What are you doing for the holiday?"

"A date." I said this too forcefully.

"A date. That's a good idea." She paused. "I've become very impersonal now. I felt it when I saw you this afternoon. You seemed very personal, even when I didn't recognize you. I actually envied you. Part of me cares about things, but part doesn't really seem to."

"It's just a phase," I said. "It's just today."

"Do you really think I'm a person of little faith? You accused me of that when you got mad at me. I wanted you to know that it worried me."

"No," I said. "You're not. I was just disappointed in myself. I don't think you are." (Though it's possible she is.)

"I don't want to be," Ann said in a mournful voice. "I certainly wouldn't like it if life was just made up of the specific grievances we could answer all strung together and that was it. I decided that's what you meant about me—that I was a problem solver. That I just liked specific answers to specific questions."

"Liked them instead of what?" I said. Though I guessed I knew.

"Oh. I don't know, Frank. Instead of being interested in important things that're hard to recognize? Like when we were kids. Just life. I'm very tired of some problems."

"It's human nature not to get to the bottom of things."

"And that doesn't ever get uninteresting to you, does it?" I thought she might be smiling, but not necessarily happily.

"Sometimes," I said. "More recently it has."

"A big forest of fallen trees," she said in a dreamy way. "That doesn't seem so bad today."

"Don't you think I could bring him down here in September?" I knew this was not the best time to ask. I had asked seven hours before. But when was the best time? I didn't want to wait.

"Oh," she said, staring I was sure out a frosted air-conditioned window at the small lights of Hamden and the Wilbur Cross, a-stream with cars bound for less adventuresome distances, the holiday almost over before the day even arrived. I would miss it with my son. "We'll have to talk to him. I'll talk to Charley. We'll have to see what his ombudsman says. In principle it might be all right. Isn't that okay to say now?"

"In principle it's fine. I just think I could be some use to him now. You know? More than his ombudsman."

"Ummm," she said. And I couldn't think of anything else to say, staring at the mulberry leafage, my reflection cast back: a man alone at a desk by a telephone, a table lamp, the rest dark. The complex odors of backyard cooking over with hours before still floated out of the evening. "He'll want to know when you're coming to visit him." She said this without inflection.

"I'll drive up Friday. Tell him I'll visit him wherever he's in custody." Then I almost said, "He bought you and Clarissa some presents." But true to my word, I forbore.

And then she was silent, taking time to assess. "Doing anything wholeheartedly is rare. That's probably why you said that. I was shitty the other night, I'm sorry."

"That's okay," I said brightly. "It's harder, that's for sure."

"You know, when I saw you today I felt very good about you. That was the first time in a long time. It seemed very strange. Did you notice it?"

I couldn't answer that, so I just said, "That's not bad, though, is it?" my voice still bright. "That's an advance."

"You always seem like you want something from me," she said. "But I think maybe you just want to make me feel better when you're around. Is that right?"

"I *do* want you to feel better," I said. "That's right." It is part of the Existence Period—and I think now not a good part—to seem to want something but then not to.

Ann paused again. "Do you remember I said it's not easy being an ex-spouse?"

"Yes," I said.

"Well, it's not easy not being one, either."

"No," I said, "it's not," and then I said nothing.

"So. Call up tomorrow," she said cheerfully—disappointed, I knew, by some more complicated, possibly sad, even interesting truth she had heard herself speak and been surprised by but that I hadn't risen to. "Call the hospital. He'll need to talk to his Dad. Maybe he'll tell you about the Hall of Fame."

"Okay," I said softly.

"Bye-bye."

"Bye-bye," I said, and we hung up.

BLAM!

I watch the red coffee can spin high as the rooftops, become a small, whirly shadow on the sky, then lazily sink back toward the hot pavement.

All the kids hightail it down the street, their feet slapping, including Uncle Sam, holding for some reason the top of his head, where he has no tall hat.

"You gon git yo eye put out!" someone shouts.

"Wooo, wooo, wooo, got *damn*!" is what they say in answer. Across Clio Street a young black woman in astonishing yellow short shorts and a yellow buxom halter top leans out over her porch rail, watching the boys as they scatter. The can hits the pavement in front of her house, torn and jagged, bounces and goes still. "Ah-mo beat ya'll butts!" she shouts out as Uncle Sam rounds the corner onto Erato on one hopping, skidding foot, still holding his bare head, and then is gone. "Ah-mo call the cops 'n' *they* gon beat ya'll butts too!" she says. The boys are laughing in the distance. There is, I see, a FOR SALE sign in front of her house, conspicuous in the little privet-hedged and grassy postage-stamp yard. It is new, not ours.

With her hands on the banister, the woman turns her gaze my way, where I'm seated on my porch steps with my paper, gazing back in a neighborly way. She is barefooted and no doubt has just been waked up. " 'Cause ah-mo be *glaaad* to git outa *this* place, y'unnerstan?" she says to the street, to me, to whoever might have a door open or a window ajar and be listening. " 'Cause it's *noisy* up here, ya'll. Ah'm tellin ya'll. Ya'll be nois*eee!*"

I smile at her. She looks at me in my red jacket, then throws her head back and laughs as if I was the silliest person she ever saw. She puts her hand up like a church witness, lowers her head, then wanders back inside.

Crows fly over—two, six, twelve—in ragged, dipping lines, squawking as though to say, "Today is not a holiday for crows. Crows work." I hear the Haddam H.S. band, as I did Friday morning, early again on its practice grounds, rich, full-brass crescendos streets away, a last fine-tuning before the parade. "Com-onna-my-house-my-house-a-com-on" seems to be their rouser. The crows squawk, then dive crazily through the morning's hot air. The neighborhood seems unburdened, peopled, serene.

And then I see the Markhams' beater Nova appear at the top of the street, a half hour late. It slows as though its occupants were consulting a map, then begins again bumpily down my way, approaches the house with my car in front, veers, someone waves from inside, and then, at last, they have come to rest.

*   *   *

"OH, WE GOT into such a bind, Frank," Phyllis says, not quite able to portray for me what she and Joe have been forced through. Her blue eyes seem bluer than ever, as if she has changed to vivider contacts. "We felt like we were strapped to a runaway train. She just wouldn't quit showing us houses." *She*, of course, refers to the horror-show realty associate from East Brunswick. Phyllis looks at me in dejected wonderment for the way some people will act.

We're on the stoop of 46 Clio, paused as though to defeat a final reluctance before commencing our ritual walk-thru. I've already pointed out some improvements—a foundation vent, new flashing—noted the convenience of in-town shopping, hospital, train and schools. (No mention has been made by them of other races in close proximity.)

"I guess she was going to make us buy a house if it killed her," Phyllis says, bringing the Other Realtor story to a close. "Joe sure wanted to murder her. I just wanted to call *you*."

It is of course foregone that they will rent the house and move in as early as within the hour. Though in the spirit of lagniappe I am acting as if all is not yet quite settled. Another realtor might adopt a supercilious spirit toward the Markhams for being hopeless donkeys who wouldn't know a good deal if it grabbed them by the nuts. But to me it's ennobling to help others face their hard choices, pilot them toward a reconciliation with life (it's useful in piloting toward one's own). In this case, I'm helping them believe renting is what they should do (being wise and cautious), by promoting the fantasy that each is acting in his own best interest by attempting to make the other happy.

"Now, I can tell this is a completely stable neighborhood," Joe says with more of an off-duty military style now. (He means, though, no Negroes in evidence, which he takes to be a blessing.) He's remained on the bottom step, small hands inserted in his pockets. He's dressed entirely in Sears khaki and looks like a lumberyard foreman, his nutty goatee gone, his pecker shorts, flip-flops and generic smokes all gone, his little cheeky face as peaceable and wide-eyed as a baby's, his lips pale with medicated normalcy. (The "big cave-in" has apparently been averted.) He is, I'm sure, contemplating the front bumper of my Crown Vic, where sometime in the last three days Paul—or someone like Paul—has affixed a LICK BUSH sticker which, also in the spirit of lagniappe, I'm leaving on.

Joe senses, I'm sure, his gaze carrying across the newly mown lawn and down Clio Street, that this neighborhood is a close replica writ small of the nicer parts of Haddam he was offered and mulishly turned down, and of nicer parts he wasn't offered and couldn't afford. Only he seems happy now, which is my wish for him: to put an end to his unhappy season of wandering, set aside his ideas of the economy's false bottom or whether a significant event ever occurred in this house, to be a chooser instead of a bad-tempered beggar, to view life across a flatter plain (as he may be doing) and come down off the realty frontier.

Though specifically my wish is that the Markhams would move into 46 Clio, ostensibly as a defensive holding action, but gradually get to know their neighbors, talk yard-to-yard, make friends, see the wisdom of bargaining for a break in the rent in exchange for minor upkeep responsibilities, join the PTA, give pottery and papermaking demonstrations at the block association mixers, become active in the ACLU or the Urban League, begin to calculate their enhanced positive cash flow against the dour financial imperatives of ownership in fashioning an improved quality of life, and eventually stay ten years—after which they can move to Siesta Key and buy a condo (if condos still exist in 1998), using the money they've saved by renting. In other words, do in New Jersey exactly what they did in Vermont—arrive and depart—only with happier results. (Conservative, long-term renters are, of course, any landlord's dream.)

"I think we're damn lucky not to have got sucked into that Hanrahan house." Joe looks at me with a bully's self-assurance, as if he's just figured this out by staring down the street—though of course he's only angling for approval (which I'm happy to supply).

"I don't think you ever saw yourself in that house, Joe. I don't really think you liked it." He's still staring off from the bottom step, waiting, I take it, for nothing.

"I didn't like having a prison in my back yard," Phyllis says, fingering the doorbell, which chimes a distant, lonesome two tones back in the empty rooms. She is dressed in her own standard roomy, hip-concealing pleated khakis and sleeveless white ruffle-front blouse that makes her appear swollen. In spite of trying to act plucky, she looks hollow-cheeked and spent, her face too flushed, her fingernails worked down, her eyes moist as if she might start crying for no reason—though her red mushroom cut is as ever neat, clean and fluffy. (Possibly she's experiencing recurrent health woes, though it's more likely her last few days on earth have simply been as rigorous as mine.)

And yet despite these diminishments, I sense an earnest, almost equable acceptance is descending on both the Markhams: certain fires gone out; other, smaller ones being ignited. So that it's conceivable they're on the threshold of unexpected bliss, know it instinctually like a lucky charm but can't quite get it straight, so long has their luck been shitty.

"My view's simple," Joe says, apropos of the lost Hanrahan option. "If somebody buys a house you think you want before you can get it, they just wanted it more than you did. It's no tragedy." He shakes his head at the sound wisdom of this, though once again it's verbatim "realtor's wisdom" I provided long months ago but actually don't mind hearing now.

"You're right there, Joe," I say. "You're really right. Let's take a look inside, whaddaya say?"

A WALK-THRU of an empty house you expect to rent (and not buy and live in till you croak) is not so much a careful inspection as a half-assed once-over in which you hope to find as little as possible to drive you crazy.

The Harrises' house, in spite of opened doors, raised windows and every single tap run for at least a minute, has clung to its unwelcoming older-citizen odor of sink traps and mouse bait, and generally stayed dank and chilly throughout. As a consequence, Phyllis lingers noncommittally near the windows, while Joe heads right off for the bathroom and a quick closet count. She touches the nubbly plaster walls and looks out through the blue blinds, first at the close-by McLeods', then down at the narrow side yard, then into the back, where the garage sits locked up in the morning sunshine, surrounded by a bed of day lilies weeks past bloom. (I've left the push mower against the garage wall where they can notice it.) She tries one sink faucet, opens one cabinet and the refrigerator (which I have somehow failed to inspect but am relieved to find doesn't stink), then walks to the back door, leans and looks out its window, as if in her mind right outside should be a verdant mountain pinnacle in full view, where she could hike today and take a drink from a cold spring, then lie faceup in gentians and columbines as pillowy clouds scud past, causing no car alarms to go off. She has wanted to come here, and now here she is, though it requires a specific moment of wistful renunciation, during which she may once again be seeing *backward* to today from an uncertain future, a time when Joe is "gone," the older kids are even more scattered and alienated, Sonja is with her own second husband and his kids in Tucumcari, and all she can do is wonder how things took the peculiar course they did. Such a view would make anyone but a Taoist Sage a little abstracted.

She turns to me and smiles actually wistfully. I am in the arched doorway connecting the small dining room with the small, neat kitchen, my hands in my red windbreaker pockets. I regard her companionably while fingering the house keys. I am where a loved one would wait below a mistletoe sprig at Christmas, though my reverie of a physical Phyllis has become another holiday statistic.

"We *did* think about just staying permanently in a motel," she says almost as a warning. "Joe considered becoming an independent contractor at the book company. The money's so much better that way, but you pay for your own benefits, which is a big consideration for me now. We met another young couple there who were doing it, but they didn't have a child, and it's hard to go off to school from a Ramada. The clean sheets and cable are attractive to Joe. He even called some nine hundred number at two o'clock this morning about moving to Florida. We were just beyond making sense."

Joe is in the bathroom, studiously testing the sink and both faucets, checking out the medicine cabinet. He does not know how to rent a house and can only think in terms of permanence.

"I expect you all to keep right on looking," I say. "I expect to sell you a house." I smile at her, as I have in other houses, in direr straits than now, which in fact are not so dire but pretty damn good at $575.

"We were burning our candle at both ends, I guess," she says, standing in the middle of the empty red-tiled kitchen. It is not the right trope, but I understand. "We need to burn one end at a time for a while."

"Your candle lasts longer that way," I say idiotically. There isn't much that really needs saying in any case. They're renting, not buying, and she is simply not used to it either. All is fine.

"Bip, bip, bip, bip, bip, bip, bip," Joe can be heard saying back in the bedroom, seizing his chance to check the filters on the window unit.

"How's your son?" Phyllis looks at me oddly, as if it has occurred to her at this very second that I'm not at his bedside but am here showing a short-term rental on the 4th of July with my child on the critical list. A sense of shared parental responsibility but also personal accusation clouds her eyes.

"He came through the surgery real well, thanks." I fidget the keys in my pocket to make a distracting sound. "He'll have to wear glasses. But he's moving down here with me in September." Perhaps in a year, as a trusted older boy, he can even escort Sonja on a date to a mall.

"Well, he's lucky," Phyllis says, swaying a little, her hands judgmentally down in her own generous pockets. "Fireworks are dangerous no matter whose hands they're in. They're banned in Vermont." She now wants me out of her house. In the span of sixty seconds she's assumed responsibility for things here.

"I'm sure he's learned his lesson," I say, and then we stand saying nothing, listening to Joe's footsteps in the other rooms, the sound of closet doors being cracked open and reopened to check for settling, light switches clicked up and down, walls thumped for studs—all activities accompanied by the occasional "Bip, bip, bip" or an "Okay, yep, I get it," now and then an "Uh-oh," though most often "Hmm-hmmm." All, of course, is in perfect, turn-key condition; the house was gone over by Everick and Wardell after the Harrises left, and I have checked it myself (though not lately).

"No basement, huh?" Joe says, appearing suddenly in the hall doorway, from which he takes a quick look around the ceiling and back out toward the open front door. The house is warming now, its floors shiny with outside light, its dank odors shifting away through the open windows. "I'll have to improvise a kiln somewhere else, I guess." (No mention of Phyllis's papermaking needs.)

"They just didn't build 'em in this neighborhood." I nod, touch my sore, bitten cheek with my tonguetip, feel relieved Joe isn't planning to fire pots on site.

"You can bet it's a groundwater consideration," Joe says in a spurious engineer's voice, going to the window and looking out as Phyllis did, straight into the side of the McLeods' house, where my hope is he doesn't come eye-to-eye with a shirtless Larry McLeod aiming his 9-mm. across the side yard. "Anything really bad ever happen in this house, Frank?" He scratches the back of his bristly neck and peers down at something outside that has caught his eye—a cat, possibly.

"Nothing I know about. I guess all houses have pasts. The ones I've lived in all sure did. Somebody's bound to have died in some room here sometime. I just don't know who." I say this to annoy him, knowing he's out of options, and because I know his question is a two-bit subterfuge for broaching the race issue. He doesn't want credit for broaching it, but he'd be happy if I would.

"Just wondering," Joe says. "We built our own house in Vermont, is all. Nothing bad ever happened there." He continues staring down, inventorying other gambits. "I guess this is a drug-free zone." Phyllis looks over at him as if she'd just realized she hated him.

"S'far's I know," I say. "It's a changing universe, of course."

"Right. No shit." Joe shakes his head in the fresh window light.

"Frank can't be held responsible for the neighbors," Phyllis says crabbily (though it's not completely true). She has been standing under the arch with me, looking at the empty walls and floors, possibly envisioning her lost life as a child. Only her mind's made up.

"Who lives next door?" Joe says.

"On the other side, an elderly couple named Broadnax. Rufus was a Pullman porter on the New York Central. You won't see them much, but I'm sure you'll like them. Over on the other side is a younger couple" (of miscreants). "She's from Minnesota. He's a Viet vet. They're interesting folks. I own that house too."

"You own 'em both?" Joe turns and gives me a crafty, squint-eyed look, as if I'd just grown vastly in his estimation and was probably crooked.

"Just these two," I say.

"So you're holdin' onto 'em till they're worth a fortune?" He smirks. For the moment he has begun speaking in a Texas accent.

"They're already worth a fortune. I'm just waiting till they're worth two fortunes."

Joe adopts an even more ludicrous, self-satisfied expression of appreciation. He's always had my number but now sees we are much more of a pair and a lot sharper cookies than he ever thought (even if we are crooked), since socking away for the future's exactly what he believes in doing—and might be doing if he hadn't plunged off on a two-decade *Wanderjahr* to the land of mud season, black ice, disappointing perk tests and feast-or-famine resales, only to reenter the real world with just the vaguest memory of which coin a quarter was and which was a dime.

"It's all still a matter of perception, idn't it?" Joe says enigmatically.

"It seems to be, *these* days," I say, thinking perhaps he's talking about real estate. I more noisily jingle the keys to signal my readiness to get a move on—though I have little to do until noon.

"Okay, well, I'm pretty satisfied here," Joe says decisively, Texas accent gone, nodding his head vigorously. Through the window he's been looking out, and across the side yard, I see little Winnie McLeod's sleepy face behind the thin curtain, frowning at us. "Whaddaya think, baby doll?"

"I can make it nicer," Phyllis says, her voice moving around the empty room like a trapped spirit. (I've never imagined Phyllis as "baby doll" but am willing to.)

"Maybe Frank'll sell it to us when we come into our inheritance." Joe gives me a little tongue-out, sly-boots wink.

"Two inheritances," I say and wink back. "This baby'll cost ya."

"Yeah, okay. Two, then," Joe says. "When we make two fortunes we can own a five-and-a-half-room house in the darky section of Haddam, New Jersey. That's a deal, isn't it? That's a success story you can brag to your grandkids about." Joe rolls his eyes humorously to the ceiling and gives his shiny forehead a thump with his middle finger. "How 'bout the election? How d'ya choose?"

"I'm joined at the hip with the tax-and-spenders, I guess." Joe wouldn't be asking if he weren't at this very moment vacating long-held principles of cultural liberalism in favor of something leaner and meaner and more suitable to his new gestalt. He expects me to sanction this too.

"You mean joined at the wallet," Joe says dopily. "But hell, yes. Me too." This to my absolute surprise. "Just don't ask me. My old man"—the Chinese-slum king of Aliquippa—"had a wide streak of social conscience. He was a Socialist. But what the fuck. Maybe living here'll pound some sense in my head. Now Phyllis, here, she's the mahout, she rides the elephant." Phyllis starts for the door, tired and unamused by politics. Joe fastens on me a gaping, blunt-toothed, baby-faced smile of philosophical comradeship. These things, of course, are never as you expect. Anytime you find you're right, you should be wrong.

IT IS GOOD to stand out on the hot sidewalk with the two of them under the spreading sycamore, and encouraging to see how quickly and tidily permanence asserts its illusion and begins to confer a bounty.

In fifteen minutes the Markhams have become longtime residents, and I their unwieldy, unwished-for guest. An invitation to come back, have lemonade, sit out back on nylon lawn chairs is definitely not forthcoming. They both squint from the pavement to the sun and the untroubled beryl sky as though they judge a good soaking rain—and not my paltry, unremarked watering—to be the only thing that'll do their yard any good.

We have painlessly agreed on a month-to-month, with three months in advance as a security blanket for me—though I've consented to remit a month if they find a house worth buying in the first thirty days (fat chance). I've passed along our agency's "What's The Diff?" booklet, spelling out in layman's terms the pros and cons of renting vs. buying: "Never pay over 20 percent of gross income on housing," although "You always sleep better in a place you own" (debatable). There's nothing, however, about needing to "see" yourself, or securing sanction or the likelihood of significant events ever having occurred in your chosen abode. Those issues are best dealt with by a shrink, not a realtor. Finally we've agreed to sign the papers tomorrow in my office, and I've told them to feel free to haul in their sleeping bags and camp out in their "own house" tonight. Who could say nay?

"Sonja's going to find it real eye-opening here," Phyllis the

Republican says with confidence. "It's what we came down here for, but maybe we didn't know it."

"Reality check," Joe says stonily. They're both referring to the race issue, albeit deviously, while holding each other's hand.

We are beside my car, which gleams blue and hot in the ten o'clock sun. I have the Harrises' accumulated junk mail and the Trenton *Times* tucked under my arm, and have handed over their keys.

I know that filtering up like rare and rich incense in both the Markhams' nostrils is the up-to-now endangered prospect of life's happy continuance—a different notion entirely from Irv Ornstein's indecisive, religio-ethnic-historical one, though he might claim they're the same. An abrupter feeling is the Markhams', though, tantamount to the end of a prison sentence imposed for crimes they've been helpless to avoid: the ordinary misdemeanors and misprisions of life, of which we're all innocent and guilty. Alive but unrecognized in their pleased but dizzied heads is at least now the *possibility* of calling on Myrlene Beavers with a hot huckleberry pie or a blemished-second "gift" pot from Joe's new kiln; or of finding common ground regarding in-law problems with Negro neighbors more their age; of letting little dark-skinned kids sleep over; of nurturing what they both always knew they owned in their hearts but never exactly found an occasion to act on in the monochrome Green Mountains: that magical sixth-sense understanding of the other races, which always made the Markhams see themselves as out-of-the-ordinary white folks.

A police cruiser, our lone Negro officer at the wheel, finally passes slowly by, on the lookout for the Clio Street bombers. He waves perfunctorily and continues on. He is now their neighbor.

"Look, when we get all our shit moved in, we'll get you over here for a meal," Joe says, turning loose Phyllis's hand and trussing a short proprietary arm even more closely about her rounded shoulders. It is obvious she's informed him of her newest medical sorrows, which may be why he came around to renting, which may be why she told him. Another reality check.

"That's a meal I'm happy to wait for," I say, wiping a driblet of sweat off my neck, feeling the touchy spot where I was struck by a baseball in a far-off city. I have expected Joe to bring up the lease-purchase concept at least once, but he hasn't. Possibly he still harbors subconscious suspicions I'm a homosexual, which makes him standoffish.

I take a guarded look up at the old brick-veneer façade and curtained windows at #44, where there is no movement though I know surveillance is ongoing, and where I feel for an uneasy moment certain my $450 is being held hostage to the McLeods' ingrown convictions regarding privacy and soleness, having nothing to do with financial distress, lost jobs or embarrassment (which I would know how to cope with). I am, in fact, less concerned for my money than with the prospect of my own life's happy continuance with this problem unresolved. And yet I'm capable of making more of anything than I should, and I might just as well take a more complex approach to the unknown—such as *never* asking them for another goddamned nickel and seeing what effect that produces over time. Today, after all, is not only the fourth, but the Fourth. And as with the stolid, unpromising, unlikable Markhams, real independence must sometimes be shoved down your throat.

On a street we cannot see, a car alarm (possibly the same one as before) sets off loudly, and at hectic intervals, *bwoop-bwip, bwoop-bwip*, just as the bells at St. Leo's begin tolling ten. It makes for a minor cacophony: thirteen clocks striking at the same second. Joe and Phyllis smile and shake their heads, look around at the heavens as if they were breaking open and this was the only signal they would hear. Though they have decided to try being happy, are in a firm acceptance mode and would agree at this moment to like anything. It must be said, at last, that I admire them.

I take a parting glimpse at Myrlene Beavers's, where the silver bars of her walker are visible behind the screen. She is watching too, phone in her quavering grip, alert to fresh outrage. "Who are *these* people? What do they hope to achieve? If only Tom were alive to take care of it."

I'm shaking Joe Markham's hand almost without knowing it. It is good to leave now, as I have done the best I can by everyone. What more can you do for wayward strangers than to shelter them?

*   *   *

I TAKE A morning's ride up into town now, bent on nothing special—a drive-by of my hot-dog stand on the Green, a pass of the parade's staging grounds for a sniff of the holiday aromas, a cruise (like a tourist's) down my own street to inspect the site of Homo haddamus pithecarius, whose appearance, irrespective of provenance—M or F, human or ape, freedman or slave—I have a certain natural interest in. Who of us, after all, would be buried minus the hope of being returned someday to the air and light, to the curious, the tentative and even affectionate regard of our fellow uprights? None of us, I grant you, would mind a second appraisal with the benefit of some time having passed.

I in fact enjoy such a yearly drive through town, end to end, without my usual purposes to spur me (a property-line check, a roof and foundation write-up, an eleventh-hour visit before a closing), just a drive to take a *look* but not to touch or feel or be involved. Such a tour embodies its own quiet participation, since there is sovereign civic good in being a bystander, a watcher, one of those whom civic substance and display are meant to serve— the public.

Seminary Street has a measly, uncrowded, preparade staticness to it all around. The town's new bunting is swagged on our three stoplights, the sidewalk flags not flying but lank. Citizens on the sidewalks all seem at yawing loose ends, their faces wide and uncommunicative as they stop to watch the parade crew blocking the curbs with sawhorses for the bands and floats that will follow, as if (they seem to say) this *should* be a usual Monday, one *should* be getting other things done and started. Skinny neighborhood boys I don't recognize slalom the hot middle stripes on skateboards, their arms floating out for balance, while at the Virtual Profusion and the former Benetton and Laura Ashley (now in new personas as Foot Locker and The Gap) clerks are shoving sale tables back to their storefronts, preparing to wait in the cool indoors for crowds that may finally come.

It is an odd holiday, to be sure—one a man or woman could easily grow abstracted about, its practical importance to the task of holding back wild and dark misrule never altogether clear or provable; as though independence were *only* private and too crucial to celebrate with others; as though we should all just get on with *being* independent, given that it is after all the normal, commonsensical human condition, to be taken for granted unless opposed or thwarted, in which case unreserved, even absurd measures should be taken to restore or reimagine it (as I've tried to do with my son but that he has accomplished alone). Best maybe just to pass the day as the original signers did and as I prefer to do, in a country-like setting near to home, alone with your thoughts, your fears, your hopes, your "moments of reason" for what new world lies fearsomely ahead.

I cruise now out toward the big unfinished Shop Rite at the eastern verge of town, where Haddam borders on woodsy Haddam Township, past the Shalom Temple, the defunct Jap car dealer and the Magyar Bank, up old Route 27 toward New Brunswick. The Shop Rite was scheduled to be up and going by New Year's, but its satellite businesses (a TCBY, a Color Tile and a Pet Depot) began dragging their feet after the stock market dip and the resultant "chill" in the local climate, so that all work is at present on hold. I, in fact, wouldn't be sad or consider myself an antidevelopment traitor to see the whole shebang fold its tents and leave the business to our merchants in town; turn the land into a people's park or a public vegetable garden; make friends in a new way. (Such things, of course, never happen.)

Out on the wide parking lot, fairly baking in the heat, waits most of our parade, its constituents wandering about in unparade-like disorder: a colonial fife-and-drum band from De Tocqueville Academy; a regiment of coonskin-cap regulars in buckskins, accompanied by several burly men in Mother Hubbards and combat boots (dressed to show independence can be won at the cost of looking ridiculous). Here is a brigade of beefy, wired-up wheelchair vets in American-flag shirts, doing weaves and wheelies while passing basketballs (others simply sit smoking and talking in the sunshine). Waiting, too, is another Mustang regatta, a female clown troupe, some local car dealers in good-guy cowboy hats, ready to chauffeur our elected officials (not yet arrived) in the backs of new convertibles, while a passel of political ingenues are all set to ride behind on a flatbed truck, wearing oversize baby diapers and convict clothes. A swank silver bus parked all by itself under the shadeless Shop Rite sign contains the Fruehlingheisen Banjo and Saxophone Band from Dover, Delaware, most of whose members have postponed coming out. And last but not least, two Chevy bigfoots, one red, one blue, sit mid-lot, ready to rumble down Seminary at parade's end, their tiny cabs like teacups above their giant cleated wheels. (Later on there're plans for them to crush some Japanese cars out at the Revolutionary War Battlefield.) All that's lacking, in my view, are harem guards, who would make Paul Bascombe happy.

From where I stop out on the shoulder for a look, nothing yet seems inspired or up to parade pitch. Several tissue-paper floats are not yet manned or hitched up. The centerpiece Haddam High band has not appeared. And marshals in hot swallowtail coats and tricorne hats are hiking around with walkie-talkies and clipboards, conferring with parade captains and gazing at their watches. All in fact seems timeless and desultory, most of the participants standing alone in the sun in their costumes, looking off much as the fantasy ballplayers did in Cooperstown yesterday, and much, I'm sure, for the same reasons: they're bored, or else full of longing for something they can't quite name.

I decide to make a fast swerve through the lot entrance, avoid the whole parade assemblage and continue back out onto 27 toward town, satisfied that I've glimpsed behind the parade's façade and not been the least disappointed. Even the smallest public rigmarole is a pain in the ass, its true importance measurable not in the final effect but by how willing we are to leave our usual selves behind and by how much colossal bullshit and anarchy we're willing to put up with in a worthwhile cause. I always like it better when clowns seem to try to be happy.

Unexpectedly, though, just as I make my turn around and through the Shop Rite entrance, bent on escape, a man—one of the swallowtail marshals in a hat, red sash and high-buttoned shoes, who's been consulting a clipboard while talking to one of the young men wearing diapers—starts hurriedly toward my moving car. He waves his clipboard as if he knows me and has an aim, means to share a holiday greeting or message, perhaps even get me in on the fun as someone's substitute. (He may have noticed my LICK BUSH sticker and thinks I'm in the mood for high jinks.) Only I'm in another mood, perfectly good but one I'm happy to keep to myself, and so continue swerving without acknowledging him, right back onto 27. There's no telling, after all, who he might be: someone with a lengthy realty complaint, or possibly Mr. Fred Koeppel of Griggstown, who "needs" to discuss a negotiated commission on his house, which'll sell itself

anyway (so let it). Or possibly (and this happens with too great a
frequency) he's somebody from my former married days who
happened to be in the Yale Club just yesterday morning and saw
Ann and wants to report she looks "great," "super," "dynamite"—one of those. But I'm not interested. Independence Day,
at least for the daylight hours, confers upon us the opportunity
to act as independently as we know how. And my determination,
this day, is to stay free of suspicious greetings.

I drive back in on sunny and fast-emptying Seminary, where
the actual civic razzmatazz still seems a good hour off—past the
closed PO, the closed Frenchy's Gulf, the nearly empty August
Inn, the Coffee Spot, around the Square, past the Press Box Bar,
the closed Lauren-Schwindell office, Garden State S&L, the
somnolent Institute itself and the always officially open but actually profoundly closed First Presbyterian, where the WELCOME
sign out front says, *Happy Birthday, America!* ＊ *5K Race* ＊ *HE Can
Help You At The Finish Line!*

Though farther on and across from Village Hall on Haddam
Green there is action, with plenty of citizens already arrived in
musing good spirits. A red-and-white-striped carnival marquee
has been put up in the open middle sward, with our newly refurbished Victorian bandstand shining whitely in the elms and
beeches and crawling with kids. Many Haddamites are simply
out here strolling around as they might on some lane in County
Antrim, though wearing frilly pastel dresses, seersuckers, white
bucks, boaters and pink parasols, and looking—many of them—
like self-conscious extras in a Fifties movie about the South. Out-
of-place country-yokel music is blaring from a little glass-sided
trailer owned by the station where I read *Doctor Zhivago* to the
blind, and the police and fire departments have their free exhibits
of flameproof suits, bomb-defusing shields and sniper rifles set
up side by side under the big tent. The CYO has just begun its
continuous volleyball game, the hospital its free blood pressure
testing, the Lions and AA their joint free-coffee canteen, while
the Young Democrats and Young Republicans are in the process
of hosing down a mudhole for their annual tug-of-war. Otherwise, various village businesses, with their employees turned out
in white aprons and red bow ties, have joined forces behind long
slug-bucket grills to hawk meatless leanburgers, while some
costumed Pennsylvania Dutch dancers perform folk didoes on a

portable dance floor to music only they can hear. Later on, a dog show is planned.

Off to the left, across from the lawn of Village Hall, where seven years ago I achieved the profound and unwelcome independence of divorce, my silver "Firecracker Weenie Firecracker" cart sits in the warm witch hazel shade, attracting a small, dedicated crowd including Uncle Sam and two other Clio Street bombers, a few of my neighbors, plus Ed McSweeny in a business suit and a briefcase and Shax Murphy wearing a pair of pink go-to-hell pants, a bright-green blazer and running shoes— and looking, despite his Harvard background, like nothing so much as a realtor. Wardell and Everick's gleaming onyx faces are visible back inside the trailer under the awning. Dressed in silly waiters' tunics and paper caps, they are dispensing free Polish dogs and waxed-paper root beer mugs and occasionally rattling the "Clair Devane Fund" canisters Vonda has made up in our office. I have tried now on three occasions to sound out the two of them about Clair, whom they adored and treated like a rambunctious niece. But they have avoided me each time. And I've realized, as a consequence, that what I probably wanted was not to hear words about Clair at all but to hear something life-affirming and flattering about *myself*, and they are merely wise to me and have chosen not to let me get started. (Though it's also possible that they've been stung to silence now by the two days when they were held by the police, treated harshly and then released without comment or ceremony—deemed, after all and as they are, entirely innocent.)

And yet, all is as I've expected and modestly planned it: no great shakes, but no small shakes either—a fine achievement for a day such as this, following a day such as that.

I pull unnoticed to the curb on the east edge of the Green, just at Cromwell Lane, let down my window to the music and crowd hum and heat, and simply sit and watch: millers and strollers, oldsters and lovers, singles and families with kids, everyone out for a morning's smiley look-see, then an amble up Seminary for the parade, before hearkening to the day's remains with a practical eye. There is the easeful feeling that the 4th is a day one can leave to chance; though as the hours slide toward dark it will still seem best to find oneself at home. Possibly it's too close to Flag Day, which itself is too close to Memorial Day, which is already too damn close to Father's Day. Too much even well-motivated celebration can pose problems.

I of course think of Paul, cased in gauze and bandages in not-so-far-away Connecticut, who would find something funny to say at the day's innocent expense: "You know you're an American when you . . ." (get socked in the eye). "They laughed at me in America when I . . ." (barked like a Pomeranian). "Americans never, or almost never . . ." (see their fathers every day).

Surprisingly, I have not thought of him at length since early dawn, when I woke up in a gray light and cold from a dream in which, on a lawn like the Deerslayer's, he was dragged to earth by a dog that looked like old Keester and torn bloody, while I stood on the porch nuzzling and whispering with an indistinct woman wearing a bikini and a chef's hat, whom I couldn't break away from to offer help. It is a dream with no mystery—like most dreams—and merely punctuates our puny efforts to gain dominion over our unbrave natures in behalf of advancing toward what we deem to be right. (The complex dilemma of independence is not so simple a matter, which is why we fight to be known by how hard we try rather than by how completely we succeed.)

Though where Paul is concerned I've only just begun trying. And while I don't subscribe to the "crash-bam" theory of human improvement, which says you must knock good sense into your head and bad sense out, yesterday may have cleared our air and accounts and opened, along with wounds, an unexpected window for hope to go free. A *last* in some ways, but a first in others. "The soul becomes," as the great man said, by which he meant, I think, slowly.

LAST NIGHT, when I stopped in the moon-shot river village of Long Eddy, New York, a TOWN MEETING TONITE sign had been posted in both directions. "Reagan Cabinet Minister to Explain Things and Answer Questions" was their important agenda, there on the banks of the Delaware, where just below town single fishermen in ghostly silhouette stood in the darkly glittering stream, their rods and lines flicking and arcing through the hot swarms of insects.

At a pay phone on a closed-up filling station wall, I made a brief reconnaissance call down to Karl Bemish, to learn if the menacing "Mexicans" had had their fates sealed at the business end of Karl's alley sweeper. (Not, I prayed.)

"Oh well, jeez, hell no, Franky. Those guys," Karl said merrily from his cockpit behind the pop-stand window. It was nine. "The cops got them three skunks. They went to knock over a Hillcrest Farms over in New Hope. But the guy runnin' it was a cop himself. And he came out the front blazin' with an AK-47. Shot out the glass, all the tires, penetrated the engine block, cracked the frame, shot all three of 'em in the course. None of them died, though, which is sort of a shame. Did it standing right on the sidewalk. I guess you need to be a cop to run a small business these days."

"Boy," I said, "boy-oh-boy." Across silent, deserted Highway 97, all the windows in the belfried town hall were blazing and plenty of cars and pickups sat parked out front. I wondered who the "Reagan Minister" might've been—possibly someone on his way to prison and a Christian conversion.

"I bet you're having a bang-up time, aren't you, with your kid?" Mugs were clanking in the background. I could hear muffled, satisfied voices of late-night customers as Karl opened and shut the window slide and the cash register dinged. Good emanations, all.

"We had some problems," I said, feeling numbed by the day's menu of sad events, plus the driving, plus my skull and all my bones beginning to ache.

"Ahh, you prolly got your expectations jacked up too high," Karl said, preoccupied yet annoying. "It's like armies moving on their bellies. It's slow going."

"I never thought that's what that meant," I said, good emanations rising away into the mosquitoey darkness.

"D'you think he trusts you?" Clink, clink, clink. "Thanks, guy."

"Yeah. I think he does."

"Well, but you can't tell when you're getting anyplace with kids. You just have to hope they don't grow up like these little Mexican twerps, pulling stickups and getting shot. I take myself out to dinner and drink a toast to good luck every third Sunday in June."

"Why didn't you have any kids, Karl?" A lone citizen of Long

Eddy, a small man in a pale shirt, stepped out the front door to the top of the town hall steps, lit a cigarette and stood drinking in the smoke and considering the evening's sweet benefactions. He was, I supposed, a disgruntled refugee from the cabinet minister's explanations—possibly a moderate—and I felt envy for whatever he might've had on his mind just at that instant, the mere nothing-much of it: the satisfactions of optional community involvement, a point of honest disagreement with a trusted public servant, a short beer later with friends, a short drive home, a quiet after-hours entry to his own bed, followed by the slow caressing carriage to sleep at the hands of a willing other. Could he know, I wondered, how lucky he was? There was hardly a doubt he did.

"Oh, Millie and I tried our best," Karl said drolly. "Or I *guess* we did. Maybe we didn't do it right. Let's see now, first you put it in, then . . ." Karl was obviously in a mood to celebrate not being robbed and murdered. I held the receiver out in the dark so I wouldn't have to hear his rube's routine, and in that splitting instant I missed New Jersey and my life in it with a grinding, exile's poignancy.

"I'm just glad you're all right down there, Karl," I broke back in, without having listened.

"We're pretty damn busy down here," he brayed back. "Fifty paid customers since eleven a.m."

"And no robberies."

"What's that?"

"No robberies," I said more loudly.

"No. Right. We're actually geniuses, Frank. Geniuses on a small scale. We're what this country's all about." Clink, clink, clink, mugs colliding. "Thanks, pal."

"Maybe," I said, watching the pale-shirted man flick away his smoke, spit on the porch steps, run both hands back through his hair and reenter the tall door, revealing a coldly brilliant yellow light within.

"You can't tell me ole Bonzo's uncle's *that* fulla shit," Karl said vehemently, referring to our President of the moment, whose cabinet minister was only yards away from me. "Because if he's that fulla shit, *I'm* fulla shit. And I'm not fulla shit. That's what I know. I'm *not* fulla shit. Not everybody can say that." I wondered what our customers could be thinking, hearing Karl bellowing away behind his little sliding screen about not being fulla shit.

"I don't like him," I said, though it made me feel debilitated to say so.

"Yeah, yeah, yeah. You believe God resides in all of us, nobility of man, help the poor, give it all away. Yakkedy, yakkedy, yak. I believe God resides in heaven, and I'm down here selling birch beer on my own."

"I *don't* believe in God, Karl. I believe it takes all kinds."

"No it don't," he said. Karl might've been drunk or having another small stroke. "What I think is, Frank, you *seem* one way and *are* another, if you want to know the gospel truth, speaking of God. You're a conservative in a fuckin' liberal's zoot suit."

"I'm a liberal in a liberal's zoot suit," I said. Or, I thought, but certainly didn't admit to Karl, a liberal in a conservative's zoot suit. In *three* days I'd been called a burglar, a priest, a homosexual, a nervous nelly, and now a conservative, none of which was true. (It was not an ordinary weekend.) "I do like to help the poor and displaced, Karl. I sure as hell in fact dragged you to the surface when you were tits-up."

"That was just for sport," he said. "And that's why you have so much effing trouble with your son. Your message is all mixed up. You're lucky he'll have anything to do with you at all."

"Why don't you bite my ass, Karl?" I shouted, standing in the dark, wondering if there wasn't some simple, legal way to put Karl out on the street, where he'd have more time to practice psychology. (Spiteful thoughts are not unique to conservatives.)

"I'm too busy to gas with you now," Karl said. I heard the cash register ding again. "Thanks a million. Hey, pardon me, ladies, you want your change, don't you? Two cents is two cents. Next. Come on, don't be shy, sweetheart." I waited for Karl to blast back something else infuriating, something more about my message being mixed. But he simply put the phone down without hanging it up, as if he meant to return, so that for a minute I could hear him going about his business serving customers. But in a while I put my receiver back on the hook and just stared out at the sparkling, alluring river beyond me in the dark, letting my breathing come back to normal.

*   *   *

MY CALL TO the Algonquin and Sally had a completely different, unexpected and altogether positive result, which, when I got home and found out Paul had weathered his surgery as well as could be hoped, allowed me to crawl in bed with all the windows open and the fan on (no more thought of reading Carl Becker or *drifting* to sleep) and to swoon off into profound unconscious while the cicadas sang their songs in the silent trees.

Sally, to my surprise, was as sympathetic as a blood relative to my long story about Paul's getting beaned, our never making it into the Hall of Fame, my having to stay in Oneonta, then heading home late rather than pounding down to NYC to share the night with her, and instead dispatching her to the nicest place I could think of (albeit for another night alone). Sally said she thought she could hear something new in my voice, and for the first time: something "more human" and even "powerful" and "angular," whereas, she reminded me, I had seemed until this weekend "pretty buttoned up and well insulated," "priestly" (this again), often downright "ornery and exclusive," though "down deep" she'd always thought I was a good guy and actually not cold but pretty sympathetic. (I had thought most of these last things about myself for years.) This time, though, she said, she thought she heard worry and some fear in my voice (buzzy timbres familiar, no doubt, from her dying clients' critiques of *Les Misérables* or *M. Butterfly* on their chatty return trips to the Shore, but apparently not incompatible with "powerful" or "angular"). She could tell I'd been "vitally moved" by something "deep and complicated," which my son's injury may have been "only the tip of the iceberg for." It may, she said, have everything to do with my gradual emergence from the Existence Period, which she actually said was a "simulated way to live your life," a sort of "mechanical isolation that couldn't go on forever"; I was probably already off and running into "some other epoch," maybe some more "permanent period" she was glad to see because it boded well for me as a person, even if the two of us didn't end up together (which it seemed might be the case, since she didn't really know what I meant by love and probably wouldn't trust it).

I, of course, was simply relieved she wasn't sitting back with her long legs parked on a silken footrest, ordering tins of Beluga caviar and thousand-dollar bottles of champagne and calling up everybody she knew from Beardsville to Phnom Penh and regaling them at length about what a poor shiftless specimen I was—really just pathetic when you got right down to it—and actually comical (something I'd already admitted to), given my idiotic and juvenile attempts to make good. Just such narrowly missed human connections as this can in fact be fatal, no matter who's at fault, and often result in unrecoverable free fall and a too-hasty conclusion that "the whole goddamn thing's not worth bothering with or it wouldn't be so goddamn confusing all the goddamn time," after which one party (or both) just wanders off and never thinks to look toward the other again. Such is the iffiness of romance.

Sally, however, seemed willing to take a longer look, a deeper breath, blink hard and follow her gut instincts about me, which meant looking for good sides (making me up with the brighter facets out). All of which was damn lucky for me since, standing there by the dark gas station in Long Eddy, I could sense like a faint, sweet perfume in the night the *possibility* of better yet to come, only I had no list of particulars to feel better about, and not much light on my horizon except a keyhole hope to try to *make* it brighter.

And indeed, before I finally climbed back in my car and headed off into the lush night toward Jersey, she began talking at first about whether or not it would ever be possible for *her* to get married after all these years, and then about what kind of permanent epoch might be dawning in *her* life. (Such thoughts are apparently infectious.) She went on to tell me—in much more dramatic tones than Joe Markham had on Friday morning—that she'd had dark moments of doubting her own judgment about many things, and that she worried about not knowing the difference between risking something (which she considered morally necessary) and throwing caution to the winds (which she considered stupid and, I supposed, had to do with me). In several electrifying leaps and connections that made good sense to her, she said she wasn't a woman who thought other adults needed mothering, and if that's what I wanted I should definitely look elsewhere; she said that making her up (which she referred to then as "reassembling") just to make love appealing was actually intolerable, no matter what she'd said yesterday, and that I couldn't just keep switching words around indefinitely to suit myself but needed instead to accept the unmanageable in others; and finally that while she might understand me pretty well and even like me a lot, there was no reason to think that necessarily meant anything about true affection, which she again reminded me I'd said I was beyond anyway. (These accounted, I'm sure, for the feelings of congestion she experienced early Friday morning and that prompted her call to me while I was in bed snuffling over my Becker and the difference between making history and writing it.)

I told her, raptly watching while the last of the night's anglers waded back across the ever darker but still brilliant surface of the Delaware, that I once again had no expectations for re-assembling her, or for mothering either, though from time to time I might need a facilitator (it didn't seem necessary to give in on everything), and that I'd thought in these last days about several aspects of an enduring relationship with her, that it didn't seem at all like a business deal, and that I liked the idea plenty, in fact felt a kind of whirring elevation about her and the whole prospect—which I did. Plus, I had a strong urge to make her happy, which didn't seem in the least way smooth (or cowardly, as Ann had said), and wished in fact she'd take the train to Haddam the next day, by which time the Markhams and the parade would be in the record books and we could resume our speculations into the evening, lie out in the grass on the Great Lawn of the Institute (where I still had privileges as temporal consultant without portfolio) and watch Christian fireworks, after which we might ignite some sparks of our own (a borrowed idea, but still a good one).

"That all sounds nice," Sally said from her suite on West Forty-fourth. "It seems reckless, though. Doesn't it to you? After the other night, when it seemed all so over with?" Her voice suddenly sounded mournful and skeptical at once, which wasn't the tone I'd exactly hoped for.

"Not to me it doesn't," I said out of the dark. "To me it seems great. Even if it *is* reckless it seems great." (Supposedly *I* was the one tarred with the "caution" brush.)

"Something about all those things I said to you about myself and about you, and now taking the train down and lying in the grass watching fireworks. It's suddenly made me feel like I don't know what I'm getting into, like I'm out of place."

"Look," I said, "if Wally shows up, I'll do the honorable thing, assuming I know what it is or who he is."

"Well, that's sweet," she said. "You're sweet. I know you'd try to do that. I'm not going to think about Wally showing up anymore, though."

"That's a good idea," I said. "That's what I'm doing too. So don't worry about feeling out of place. That's what I'm here for."

"That's an encouraging start," she said. "It *is*. It's always encouraging to know what you're here for."

And in that way last night it all began to seem promising and doable, if lacking in long-term specifics. I finished our talk by telling her not that I loved her but that I wasn't beyond affection, which she said she was glad to hear. Then I beat it back down the road toward Haddam as fast as humanly possible.

OUT IN THE unshaded center of the Haddam green, I notice all citizens beginning to look up. Young moms with prams and jogger pairs in Lycra tights, cadres of long-haired boys with skateboards on shoulders, men in bright braces wiping sweat off their brows, all gaze into heaven's vault beyond linden, witch hazel and beech limbs. The Dutch dancers stop their bustle and hurry off the floor, the police and firemen step out of their tent to the grass, seeking to see. Everick and Wardell, Uncle Sam and I (fellow townsman, alone in my car with the sunroof back), each raise eyes to the firmament, while the honky-country music comes to a stop, just as if there were one special moment of portent in this day, to be overseen by some infallible Mr. Big with a knack for coincidence and surprises. Not so far away, still on their practice field, I hear the Haddam band lock down on one sustained note in perfect major-key unison. Then the crowd—as random minglers, they have not precisely *been* a crowd—makes a hushed, suspiring "Ohh" like an assent to a single telepathic message. And suddenly down out of the sky come four men *en parachute!* smoke canisters bracketed to their feet—one red, one white, one blue, one (oddly) bright yellow like a caution to the other three. They for a moment make me dizzy.

The helmeted parachutists, wearing stars 'n' stripes, jumpsuits and cumbersome packs binding their torsos and backsides, all come careening to earth within five seconds, landing semi-gracefully with a hop-skip-jump close by the Dutch dance floor. Each man—and I only guess they're men, though reason would have it they're not *just* men; conceivably they're also kidney-transplant survivors, AIDS patients, unwed mothers, exgamblers or the children of any of these—each *apparent* man promptly flourishes a rakish hand like a circus performer, does a partly-smoke-obscured but still stylish star turn to the crowd and, after a smattering of stunned and I can only say is sincere and relieved applause, begins strenuously reefing in his silks and lines, and sets about getting the hell on to the next jump, in Wickatunk—all this before my momentary dizziness has really begun to clear. (Possibly I'm more drained than I thought.)

Though it is wonderful: a bright and chancy spectacle of short duration enhancing the day's modest storage of fun. More of this would be better all around, even at the risk of someone's chute not opening.

The crowd begins straying apart again, becoming single but gratified minglers. The dancers—skirts bunched in front like frontier women—return to their dance floor, and someone reignites the hillbilly music, with a strutting fiddle and steel guitar out ahead and a throaty female singing, "If you loved me half as much as I loved you."

I climb out of my car onto the grass and stare at the sky to glimpse the plane the jumpers have leaped free of, some little muttering dot on the infinite. As always, this is what interests me: the jump, of course, but the hazardous place jumped *from* even more; the old safety, the ordinary and predictable, which makes a swan dive into invisible empty air seem perfect, lovely, the one thing that'll do. *This* provokes butterflies, ignites danger.

Needless to say, I would never consider it, even if I packed my own gear with a sapper's precision, made friends I could die with, serviced the plane with my own lubricants, turned the prop, piloted the crate to the very spot in space, and even uttered the words they all must utter at least silently as they go—right? "Life's too short" (or long). "I have nothing to lose but my fears" (wrong). "What's anything worth if you won't risk pissing it away?" (Taken together, I'm sure it's what "Geronimo" means in Apache.) I, though, would always find a reason not to risk it; since for me, the wire, the plane, the platform, the bridge, the trestle, the window ledge—these would preoccupy me, flatter my nerve with their own prosy hazards, greater even than the risk of brilliantly daring death. I'm no hero, as my wife suggested years ago.

Nothing's up there to see anyway, no low-flying Cessna or Beech Bonanza recircling the drop site. Only, miles and miles high, the silver-glinting needle's-eye flash of a big Boeing or Lockheed inches its way out to sea and beyond, a sight that on most days would make me long to be anywhere but where I am, but that on this day, with near disaster so close behind me, leaves me happy to be here. In Haddam.

And so I continue my bystander's cruise around town for the purpose of my own and civic betterment.

A loop through the Gothic, bowery, boxwood-hedged Institute grounds and out the "backs" and around and down onto the Presidents Streets—oak-dappled Coolidge, where I was bopped on the head, wider and less gentrified Jefferson, and on to Cleveland, where the search is under way for signs of history and continuance in the dirt in front of my house and the Zumbros'. Though no one's digging this morning. A yellow "crime scene" tape has been stretched around two mulberries and the backhoe, and serves to define the orange-clay hole where evidence has been uncovered. I look down and in from my car window, for some reason not wanting to get out but willing to see something, anything, conclusive—my own dwelling being just to starboard. Yet only a cat stands in the open trench, the McPhersons' big black tom, Gordy, covering up his private business with patience. Time, forward and back, seems suddenly not of the essence on my street, and I ease away having found out nothing, but not at all dissatisfied.

I take a sinuous drive across Taft Lane and up through the Choir College grounds, where it's tranquil and deserted, the flat brick buildings shut tight and echoless for the summer—only the tennis courts in use by citizens in no humor for a parade.

A slow turn then past the high school, where the sixty-member Hornet band is wandering off the practice field, sweltering red tunics slung over their sweaty shoulders, trombones and trumpets in hand, the brawnier instruments—bass drums, sousaphones, cymbals, a bracketed Chinese gong and a portable piano—already strapped atop their waiting school bus, ready for the short trip to the Shop Rite.

On down Pleasant Valley Road along the west boundary fence of the cemetery, wherein tiny American flags bristle from many graves and my first son, Ralph Bascombe, lies near three of the "original signers," but where I will not rest, since early this very morning, in a mood of transition and progress and to take command of final things, I decided (in bed with the atlas) on a burial plot as far from here as is not totally ridiculous. Cut Off, Louisiana, is my first choice; Esperance, New York, was too close. Someplace, though, where there's a peaceful view, little traffic noise, minimum earthly history and where anyone who comes to visit will do so just because he or she means to (nothing on the way to Six Flags or Glacier) and, once arrived, will feel I had my head on straight as to location. Otherwise, to be buried "at home," behind my own old house and forever beside my forever young and lost son, would paralyze me good and proper and possibly keep me from maximizing my remaining years. The thought would never leave me as I went about my daily rounds of house selling: "Someday, someday, someday, I'll be right out there. . . ." It would be worse than having tenure at Princeton.

The strongest feeling I have now when I pass along these streets and lanes and drives and ways and places for my usual reasons—to snapshot a listing, dig up a comp for a market analysis, accompany an appraiser to his tasks—is that holding the line on the life we promised ourselves in the Sixties is getting hard as hell. We want to *feel* our community as a fixed, continuous entity, the way Irv said, as being anchored into the rock of permanence; but we know it's not, that in fact beneath the surface (or rankly all over the surface) it's anything but. We and it are anchored only to contingency like a bottle on a wave, seeking a quiet eddy. The very effort of maintenance can pull you under.

On the brighter side, and in the way that good news can seem like bad, being a realtor, while occasionally rendering you a Pollyanna, also makes you come to grips with contingency and even sell it as a source of strength and father to true self-sufficience, by insisting that you not give up the faith that people have to be housed and will be. In this way, realty is the "True American profession coping hands-on with the fundamental spatial experience of life: more people, less space, fewer choices." (This, of course, was in a book I read.)

*   *   *

TWO, MAKE that *two*, full-size moving vans are parked promi-
nently in front of two houses, side by side, on Loud Road
this late holiday morning, just around the corner from my old
once-happily married house on Hoving. One, a bullish green-
and-white Bekins, is open at all ports; the other, a jauntier
blue-and-white Atlas, is unloading off the back. (Regrettably
there's no green-and-yellow Mayflower.) Signs in front of each
house have identical YOU MISSED IT! stickers plastered over
FOR SALE. Neither is our listing, though neither are they
Bohemia or Buy and Large or some New Egypt outfit, but the
reputable local Century 21 and a new Coldwell Banker just
opened last fall.

Clearly it is a good day for a fresh start, coming or going. My
new tenants must feel this spirit in the air. All neighborhood
lawns mowed, edged and rolled, many façades newly painted,
trimmed and bulwarked since spring, foundations repointed,
trees and plantings green and in full fig. All prices slightly
softened. Indeed, if I didn't rue the sight of them and didn't mind
risking a facedown with Larry McLeod, I'd drive down Clio
Street, see how things have progressed since ten and wish the
Markhams well all over again.

Instead I make my old, familiar turn down fragrant, bonneted
Hoving Road, a turn I virtually never make these days but
should, since my memories have almost all boiled down to good
ones or at least to tolerable, instructive ones, and I have nothing
to fear. Appearances here have remained much the same through
the decade, since it is in essence a rich street of hedges and deep,
shadowed lawns, gazebos in the rear, well-out-of-sight pools and
tennis courts, slate roofs, flagstone verandas, seasonal gardens
somehow always in bloom—country estates, really, shrunk to
town size but retaining the spirit of abundance. Farther up at #4,
the Chief Justice of the NJ Supreme Court has died, though
his widow stays actively on. The Deffeyes, our aged next-door
neighbors from day one, have had their ashes mingled (though
on two foreign shores). The daughter of a famous Soviet dissi-
dent poet, who arrived before I left, seeking only privacy and
pleasant, unthreatening surroundings, but who found instead
diffidence, condescension and cold shoulders, has now departed
for home, where she is rumored to be in an institution. Ditto a
rock star who bought in at #2, visited once, wasn't welcomed,

didn't spend the night—then went back permanently to L.A.
Both listings were ours.

The Institute has done its very best to keep alive a homey,
lived-in feel at my former home, now officially the Chaim Yankowicz Ecumenical Center, and straight ahead amid my old and
amiable beeches, red oaks, Japanese maples and pachysandra. Yet
as I pull to a halt across the street for a long-overdue reconnoitering, I cannot help but register its more plainly institutional
vibes—the original half-timbers replaced and painted a more
burnished mahogany, new security windows and exterior low
lights on the neater, better-kept lawn; the driveway resurfaced,
leveled and converted to semicircular; a metal fire escape on the
east side, where the garage was but isn't now. I've heard from
people in my office that there's also a new "simplified" floor plan,
a digital sprinkler-and-alarm matrix and glowing red EXIT loz-
enges above every exterior door—all to insure the comfort and
security of foreign religious dignitaries who show up, I'm sure,
with nothing more weighty in mind than a little suburban R&R,
some off-the-record chitchat, and a chance to watch cable.

For a while after I sold out, a group of my former neighbors
laid siege to the planning board with complaints and petitions
about increased traffic flow, spot zoning, "strangers on the
block" and weakened price structures should the Institute put its
plans in gear. An injunction was even briefly obtained and two
"old families" who'd been here forty years moved out (to Palm
Beach in both cases, both selling to the Institute for choker
prices). Eventually the furor burned down to embers. The Institute agreed to remove its barely noticeable sign from the head of
the driveway and install some expensive landscaping (two adult
ginkgoes trucked in and added to one property line; my old tulip
tree sacrificed). As a final settlement, the Board of Overseers
bought the house of the lawyer who filed the injunction. After
which everyone got happy, except for a few founder types who
hold it against me and bluster at cocktail parties that they knew
I couldn't afford to live here and didn't belong way back in '70,
and why didn't I just go back to where I came from—though
they're not sure where that is.

And yet and yet, do I sense, as I sit here, a melancholy? The
same scent of loss I sniffed three nights ago at Sally's and almost
shed a tear over, because I'd once merely been *near* there in a

prior epoch of life and was in the neighborhood again, feeling unsanctioned by the place? And so shouldn't I feel it even more *here*, because my stay was longer, because I loved here, buried a son nearby, lost a fine, permanent life here, lived on alone until I couldn't stand it another minute and now find it changed into the Chaim Yankowicz Center, as indifferent to me as a gumdrop? Indeed, it's worth asking again: is there any cause to think a place—any place—within its plaster and joists, its trees and plantings, in its putative essence *ever* shelters some spirit ghost of us as proof of its significance and ours?

No! Not one bit! Only other humans do that, and then only under special circumstances, which is a lesson of the Existence Period worth holding onto. We just have to be smart enough to quit asking places for what they can't provide, and begin to invent other options—the way Joe Markham has, at least temporarily, and my son, Paul, may be doing now—as gestures of our God-required but not God-assured independence.

The truth is—and this may be my faith in progress talking—my old Hoving Road house looks more like a funeral home now than it looks like my house or a house where any past of mine took place. And this odd feeling I have is of having passed on (not in the bad way) to a recognition that ghosts ascribed to places where you once were only confuse matters with their intractable lack of corroborating substance. I frankly think that if I sat here in my car five more minutes, staring out at my old house like a visitant to an oracle's flame, I'd find that what felt like melancholy was just a prelude to bursting out laughing and needlessly freezing a sweet small piece of my heart I'd be better off to keep than lose.

"NOW LOOK HERE, would you buy a used house from this man?" I hear a sly voice speak, and bolt around startled out of my wits to find the flat, grinning moon face of Carter Knott outside my window. Carter's head is cocked to the side, his feet apart, arms crossed like an old judge. He's in damp purple swimming trunks, wet parchment sandals and a short purple terry-cloth cabana jacket that exposes his slightly rounded belly, all of which means he's gotten out of his pool down at #22 and snuck this far just to scare the piss out of me.

I would in fact be embarrassed as hell if anybody else had caught me twaddling away out here like a nutcase. But Carter is arguably my best friend in town, which means he and I "go back" (to my solitary, somber year in the Divorced Men's Club in '83) and also that we regularly bump into each other in the lobby at United Jersey and discuss bidnus, and that we're willing to stand in most any weather outside Cox's News, arms folded around our newspapers, yakking committedly about the chances of the Giants or the Eagles, the Mets or the Phils, whatever exchange won't take longer than ninety seconds, after which we might not see each other for six months, by which time a new sports season and a new set of issues will have taken up. Carter, I'm positive, couldn't tell me where I was born, or when, or what my father's job was, or what college I attended (he would probably guess Auburn), though I know he attended Penn and studied, of all things, classics. He knew Ann when she still lived in Haddam, but he may not know we had a son who died, or why I moved from my old house across the street, or what I do in my spare time. It is our unspoken rule never to exchange dinner invitations or to meet for drinks or lunch, since neither of us would have the least interest in what the other was up to and would both get bored and depressed and end up ruining our relationship. And yet in the way known best to suburbanites, he is my *compañero*.

After the Divorced Men disbanded (I left for France, one member committed suicide, others just drifted off), Carter put together a good post-divorce rebound and was living a free-wheeling bachelor's life in a big custom-built home with vaulted ceilings, fieldstone fireplaces, stained-glass windows and bidets, out in some newly rich man's subdivision beyond Pennington. Somewhere about 1985, Garden State Savings (which he was president of) decided to turn a corner and get into more aggressive instruments, which Carter couldn't see the wisdom in. So that the other stockholders bought him out for a big hunk of change, after which he went happily home to Pennington, got to tinkering with some concepts for converting invisible-pet-fence technology into sophisticated home-security applications. And the next thing he knew, he was running another company, had fifteen employees, four million new dollars in the bank, had been in operation two and a half years and was being wholly bought out by a Dutch company interested in only one tiny microchip adaptation Carter'd been wily enough to apply for a patent on. Carter once again was only too happy to cash out, after which he took in another eight million and bought an outlandish, all-white, ultra-modern, Gothic Revival neighborhood nightmare at #22, married the former wife of one of the aggressive new S&L directors and essentially retired to supervise his portfolio. (Needless to say, his is not the only story in Haddam with these as major plot elements.)

"I figured I'd caught you out here pullin' on old rudy in your red jacket and gettin' teary about your old house," Carter says, hooding his lower lip to look scandalized. He is small and tanned and slender, with short black hair that lies stiffly over on both sides of a wide, straight, scalp-revealing part. He is the standard for what used to be known as the Boston Look, though Carter actually hails from tiny Gouldtown in the New Jersey breadbasket and, though he doesn't look it, is as honest and unpretentious as a feed-store owner.

"I was just doping out a market analysis, Carter," I lie, "getting set to take in the parade. So I'm happy to have you startle the crap out of me." It's evident I have no such appraisal paperwork on the seat, only the Harrises' junk mail and some leftovers from my trip with Paul, most of which are in the back: the basketball paperweight and earring gifts, the crumpled copy of *Self-Reliance*, his Walkman, my Olympus, his copy of *The New Yorker*, his odorous *Happiness Is Being Single* tee-shirt and his Paramount bag containing a copy of the Declaration of Independence and some brochures from the Baseball Hall of Fame. (Carter, though, isn't close enough to see and wouldn't care anyway.)

"Frank, I'm gonna bet you didn't know John Adams and Thomas Jefferson died on the very same day." Carter mimps his regular closed-mouth smile and spreads his tanned legs farther apart, as if this was leading up to a randy joke.

"I didn't," I say, though of course I do, since it came up in the reading for my just completed trip and now seems ludicrous. I'm thinking that Carter looks ludicrous himself in his purple ensemble, standing actually out *in* Hoving Road while he quizzes me about history. "But let me try a guess," I say. "How 'bout July 4th, 1826, fifty years exactly after the signing of the Declaration, and didn't Jefferson say as his last words, 'Is it the Fourth?' "

"Okay, okay. I didn't realize you were a history professor. And Adams said, 'Jefferson still lives.'" Carter smiles self-mockingly. He loves this kind of stagy palaver and kept us all in stitches in the Divorced Men. "My kids let me in on it." He flashes his big straight teeth, which makes me remember how much I like him and the nights with our bereft compatriots, hunched around late tables at the August Inn or the Press Box Bar or out fishing the ocean after midnight, when life was all fucked up and, as such, much simpler than now, and as a group we learned to like it.

"Mine too," I lie (again).

"Both your rascals in fine fettle up in New London or wherever it is?"

"Deep River." Carter is more in the know than I'd have guessed, though a retailing of yesterday's events would cloud his sunny day. (I wonder, though, how he knows.)

I look up Hoving Road as a black Mercedes limo appears and turns right into the semicircular driveway of my old house and passes impressively around to the front door, where I have stood six thousand times contemplating the moon and mare's tails in a winter's sky and letting my spirits rise (sometimes with difficulty, sometimes not) to heaven. A surprising pang circuits through me at this very mind's image, and I'm suddenly afraid I may yield to what I said I wouldn't yield to over a simple domicile—sadness, displacement, lack of sanction. (Though by using Carter's presence I can fight it back.)

"Frank, d'you ever bump into ole Ann?" Carter says soberly for my sake, sticking his two hands up his opposite cabana coat sleeves and giving his forearms a good rough scratching. Carter's calves are as hairless as a turnip, and above his left knee is a deep and slick-pink dent I've of course seen before, where a big gout of tissue and muscle were once scooped violently out. Carter, despite his Boston banker's look and his screwy cabana suit, was once a Ranger in Vietnam, and is in fact a valorous war hero and to me all the more admirable for not being self-conscious about it.

"Not much, Carter," I say to the Ann question and blink my reluctance up at him. The sun is just behind his head.

"You know, I thought I saw her at the Yale–Penn game last fall. She was with a big crowd of people. How long you two been kaput now?"

"Seven years, almost."

"Well, there's your biblical allotment." Carter nods, still scratching his arm like a chimp.

"You catchin' any fish, Carter?" I say. It is Carter who has sponsored me for the Red Man Club, but now never goes himself since his own kids live in California with their mom and tend to meet him in Big Sky or Paris. To my knowledge I'm the only member who regularly plies the Red Man's unruffled waters, and soon expect to do more of it with my son, if I'm lucky enough.

Carter shakes his head. "Frank, I never go," he says regretfully. "It's a scandal. I need to."

"Well, gimme a call." I'm ready to leave, am already thinking about Sally, who's coming at six. Carter's and my ninety seconds are up.

Where the Mercedes has drawn to a halt in front of my former front door, a small, liveried driver in a black cap has jumped out and begun hauling bulky suitcases from the trunk. Then out from the back seat emerges a stupendously tall and thin black African man in a bright jungle-green dashiki and matching cap. He is long and long-headed, splendid enough to be a prince, a virtual Milt the Stilt when he reaches his full elevation. He looks out at the quiet, hedge-bound neighborhood, sees Carter and me scoping him out, and waves a great, slow-moving, pink-palmed hand toward us, letting it wag side to side like a practiced blessing. Carter and I rapidly—me in my car, him out—raise ours and wave back and smile and nod as if we wished we could speak his lingo so he could know the good things we're thinking about him but unfortunately we can't, whereupon the limo driver leads the great man straight into my house.

Carter says nothing, steps back and looks both ways down the curving street. He was not part of the injunction junta but came along afterward and thinks, I'm sure, that the Ecumenical Center is a good neighbor, which is what I always felt would be the case. It's not true that you can get used to anything, but you can get used to much more than you think and even learn to like it.

Carter, it's my guess, is now inventorying his day's thoughts, jokes, headlines, sports scores, trying to determine if there's anything he can say to interest me that won't take over thirty more seconds yet still provide him an exit line so he can go plop back in his pool. I, of course, am doing the same. Save when tragedies strike, there's little that really needs to be said to most people you know.

"So any news about your little agent's murder?" Carter says in a businesslike voice, choosing a proper tragedy and replanting his paper-clad feet even farther apart on the smooth pavement and assuming an expression of dogged, hard-mouthed, law 'n' order intolerance for all unwanted abridgments of personal freedoms.

"We're offering a reward, but not that I know of," I say, hard-mouthed myself, thinking once again of Clair's bright face and her sharp-eyed, self-certain sweetness, which cut me no slack yet brought me to ecstasy, if but briefly. "It's like she got struck by lightning," I say, and realize I'm describing only her disappearance from my life, not her departure from this earth.

Carter shakes his head and makes of his lips a pocket of compressed air, which causes him to look deformed before he lets it all out with a *ptttt* noise. "They oughta just start stringin' those kinda guys up by their dicks and lettin' 'em hang."

"I think so too," I say. And I do.

Because there is truly nothing more to say after this, Carter may be about to ask me my view of the election and its possible radiant lines into the realty business and by that route snake around to politics. He considers himself a "Strong Defense— Goldwater Republican" and likes treading a line of jokey, condescending disparagement toward me. (It is his one unlikable quality, one I've found typical of the suddenly wealthy. Naturally he was a Democrat in college.) But politics is a bad topic for Independence Day.

"I heard you reading *Caravans* on the radio last week," Carter says, nodding. "I really enjoyed that a lot. I just wanted you to know." Though his thinking is suddenly commandeered by a whole new thought. "Okay, now look," he says, his eyes turned intent. "You're our words guy, Frank. I'd think a lot of things these days might make you want to go back to writing stories." Having said this, he looks down, cinches his purple belt tight around his belly and peers at his small feet in their paper sleeves as if something about them has changed.

"Why do you think that, Carter? Does now seem like a dramatic time to be alive? I'm pretty happy with it, but it hasn't to me. I'd find it encouraging if you thought so." The limo is now swinging around to leave, its heavy pipes murmuring against the driveway surface. I'm frankly flattered Carter knows anything about my prior writing life.

My fingers, delving half-consciously between my seat and the passenger's, come up with the tiny red bow Clarissa gave me. Along with Carter's personal crediting of my long-ago and momentary life as a writer, finding this makes me feel measurably better, since my spirits had drooped over thoughts of Clair.

"It just seems to me like a lot more things need explaining these days, Frank." Carter is still peering at his toes. "When you and I were in college, ideas dominated the world—even if most of them were stupid. Now I can't even think of a single new big idea, can you?" He looks up, then down at Clarissa's red bow, which I'm holding in my palm, and wrinkles his nose as though I were presenting him with a riddle. Carter, I sense, has been sitting too long on the sidelines counting his money, so that the world seems both simple and simply screwed up. He may, I'm afraid, be on the brink of voicing some horseshit, right-wing dictum about freedom, banning the income tax, and government interventionism in a free-market economy—"ideas" to feed his need for some certitude and wholeheartedness between now and cocktail hour. He of course is not interested in my former writing career.

But if Carter were to ask me—as a man once did on a plane to Dallas back when I was a sportswriter—what I thought he ought to do with his life now that he'd come into a bank vault full of loot, I'd tell him what I told that man: dedicate your life to public service; do a tour with VISTA or the Red Cross, or hand-deliver essential services to the sick and elderly in West Virginia or Detroit (the man on the Dallas flight wasn't interested in this advice and said he thought he might just "travel" instead). Carter indeed would probably like to be put in touch with Irv Ornstein, once he's retired from his fantasy baseball career. Irv, panting to get free of the simulator business, could tempt Carter with the big new commanding metaphor of *continuity*, and the two of them could start cooking up some sort of self-help scheme to franchise on television and make another fortune.

Or I could suggest he come down just the way I did and have a talk with our crew at L&S, since we have yet to replace Clair but soon must. Stepping into her shoes could satisfy his unsatisfied needs by championing the "idea" of doing something for others. He's at least as qualified as I was, and in some of the same ways— except that he's married.

Or possibly *he* should take up words, pen some stories of his own to fling out into the void. But as for me on that score—I've been there. The air's too thin. Thanks, but no thanks.

I muse up at Carter's small, delicate features, which seem added on to a flat map. I mean to look as though I can't imagine a single idea, good or bad, but know there to be plenty floating around loose. (My most obvious idea would be misconstrued, turned into a debate I don't care to have, ending us up in the politics of stalemate.)

"Most important ideas still probably start with physical acts, Carter," I say (his friend). "You're an old classicist. Maybe what you need to do is get off your butt and stir up some dust."

Carter stares at me a long moment and says nothing, but is clearly thinking. Finally he says, "You know, I *am* still in the Active Reserves. If Bush could get a little conflict fired up when he gets in, I could be called up for serious midlife ass kicking."

"There's an idea, I guess." My daughter's red bow is attached to my little finger like a reminder, and what I'm reminded of is my LICK BUSH sticker, which I'm sorry Carter hasn't seen. Though this is enough, and I ease my car down into gear. The limo's taillights brighten at Venetian Way, swing left and glide from sight. "You might arrange to get yourself killed doing that."

"I-BOG is what we used to say in my platoon: In a blaze of glory." Carter mugs a little and rolls his eyes. He's no fool. His fighting days are long over, and I'm sure he's glad of it. "You relatively happy with your current life's travails, ole Franko? Still planning on staying in town?" He does not exactly mean "travails" but something more innocent, and smiles at me with purest, conversation-ending sincerity built upon the rock of lived life.

"Yep," I say, with goodwill in all ways equal to his. "You already know I believe home's where you pay the mortgage, Carter."

"I'd think real estate might get a little tiresome. About as ridiculous as most jobs."

"So far, not. So far it's fine. You oughta try it, since you're retired."

"I'm not *that* retired." He winks at me for reasons that aren't clear.

"I'm headed for the parade, ole Knott-head. You endure a fine Independence Day."

Carter snaps up a crisp, absurd little army salute in his colorful poolside attire. "Ten-four. Go forth and do well, Cap'n Bascombe. Bring back glory and victory or at least tales of glory and victory. Jefferson still lives."

"I'll do my best," I say, slightly embarrassed. "I'll do my best." And I motor off into my day, smiling.

AND THAT IS simply that. The whole nine yards, that which *it* was all about for a time, ending well, followed by a short drive to a parade.

There is, naturally, much that's left unanswered, much that's left till later, much that's best forgotten. Paul Bascombe, I still believe, will come to live with me for some part of his crucial years. It may not be a month from now or six. A year could go by, and there would still be time enough to participate in his new self-discovery.

It is also possible that I will soon be married, following years supposing I never could again, and so would no longer view myself as the suspicious bachelor, as I admit I sometimes still do. The Permanent Period, this would be, that long, stretching-out time when my dreams would have mystery like any ordinary person's; when whatever I do or say, who I marry, how my kids turn out, becomes what the world—if it makes note at all—knows of me, how I'm seen, understood, even how I think of myself before whatever there is that's wild and unassuagable rises and cheerlessly hauls me off to oblivion.

Up Constitution Street, from my car seat, I now can see the marchers passing beyond crowded spectators' heads, hear the booms of the big drums, the cymbals, see the girls in red and white skirtlets high-prancing, batons spinning, a red banner held aloft ahead of flashing trumpets borrowing the sun's spangly light. It is not a bad day to be on earth.

I park behind our office and beside the Press Box Bar, lock up and then stand out in the noon heat below a whitening sky and begin my satisfied amble up to the crowd. "Ba-boom, ba-boom, ba-boom, ba-boom! Hail to the victors valiant, hail to the conquering heroes . . ." Ours is a familiar fight song, and everyone up ahead of me applauds.

Late last night when I was dead asleep and the worst of my day's events were put to rest after a long trial-by-error followed by the reemergence of some small hope (which is merely human), my phone rang. And when I said hello from the darkness, there was a moment I took to be dead silence on the line, though gradually I heard a breath, then the sound of a receiver touching what must've been a face. There was a sigh, and the sound of someone going, "Ssss, tsss. Uh-huh, uh-huh," followed by an even deeper and less certain "Ummm."

And I suddenly said, because someone was there I felt I knew, "I'm glad you called." I pressed the receiver to my ear and opened my eyes in the dark. "I just got here," I said. "Now's not a bad time at all. This is a full-time job. Let me hear your thinking. I'll try to add a part to the puzzle. It can be simpler than you think."

Whoever was there—and of course I don't know who, really—breathed again two times, three. Then the breath grew thin and brief. I heard another sound, "Uh-huh." Then our connection was gone, and even before I'd put down the phone I'd returned to the deepest sleep imaginable.

And I am in the crowd just as the drums are passing—always the last in line—their *boom-boom-boom*ing in my ears and all around. I see the sun above the street, breathe in the day's rich, warm smell. Someone calls out, "Clear a path, make room, make room, please!" The trumpets go again. My heartbeat quickens. I feel the push, pull, the weave and sway of others.

THE LAY OF THE LAND

Kristina

LAST WEEK, I read in the *Asbury Press* a story that has come to sting me like a nettle. In one sense, it was the usual kind of news item we read every a.m., feel a deep, if not a wide, needle of shock, then horror about, stare off to the heavens for a long moment, until the eye shifts back to different matters—celebrity birthdays, sports briefs, obits, new realty offerings—which tug us on to other concerns, and by mid-morning we've forgotten.

But, under the stunted headline TEX NURSING DEATHS, the story detailed an otherwise-normal day in the nursing department at San Ysidro State Teachers College (Paloma Playa campus) in south Texas. A disgruntled nursing student (these people are always men) entered a building through the front door, proceeded to the classroom where he was supposed to be in attendance and where a test he was supposed to be taking was in progress—rows of student heads all bent to their business. The teacher, Professor Sandra McCurdy, was staring out the window, thinking about who knows what—a pedicure, a fishing trip she would be taking with her husband of twenty-one years, her health. The course, as flat-footed, unsubtle fate would have it, was called "Dying and Death: Ethics, Aesthetics, Proleptics"—something nurses need to know about.

Don-Houston Clevinger, the disgruntled student—a Navy vet and father of two—had already done poorly on the midterm and was probably headed for a bad grade and a ticket home to McAllen. This Clevinger entered the quiet, reverent classroom of test takers, walked among the desks and toward the front to where Ms. McCurdy stood, arms folded, musing out the window, possibly smiling. And he said to her, raising a Glock 9-mm to within six inches of the space just above the mid-point between her eyes, he said, "Are you ready to meet your Maker?" To which Ms. McCurdy, who was forty-six and a better than average teacher and canasta player, and who'd been a flight nurse in Desert Storm, replied, blinking her periwinkle eyes in curiosity only twice, "Yes. Yes, I think I am." Whereupon this Clevinger shot her, turned around slowly to address the astonished nurses-to-be and shot himself in approximately the same place.

I was sitting down when I began to read this—in my glassed-in living room overlooking the grassy dune, the beach and the Atlantic's somnolent shingle. I was actually feeling pretty good about things. It was seven o'clock on a Thursday morning, the week before Thanksgiving. I had a "happy client" closing at ten at the realty office here in Sea-Clift, after which the seller and I were going for a celebratory lunch at Bump's Eat-It-Raw. My recent health concerns—sixty radioactive iodine seeds encased in titanium BBs and smart-bombed into my prostate at the Mayo Clinic—all seemed to be going well (systems up and running, locked and loaded). My Thanksgiving plans for a semi-family at-home occasion hadn't yet started to make me fitful (stress is bad for the iodine seeds' half-life). And I hadn't heard from my wife in six months, which, under the circumstances of her new life and my old one, seemed unsurprising if not ideal. In other words, all the ways that life feels like life at age fifty-five were strewn around me like poppies.

My daughter, Clarissa Bascombe, was still asleep, the house quiet, empty but for the usual coffee aromas and the agreeable weft of dampness. But when I read Ms. McCurdy's reply to her assassin's question (I'm sure he had never contemplated an answer himself), I just stood right up out of my chair, my heart suddenly whonking, my hands, fingers, cold and atingle, my scalp tightened down against my cranium the way it does when a train goes by too close. And I said out loud, with no one to hear me, I said, "Holy shit! How in the world did she ever know that?"

All up and down this middle section of seaboard (the *Press* is the Jersey Shore's paper of record), there must've been hundreds of similar rumblings and inaudible alarms ringing household to household upon Ms. McCurdy's last words being taken in—like distant explosions, registering as wonder and then anxiety in the sensitive. Elephants feel the fatal footfalls of poachers a hundred miles off. Cats exit the room in a hurry when oysters are opened. On and on, and *on* and on. The unseen exists and has properties.

Would I ever say that? was, of course, what my question meant in realspeak, and the question everybody from Highlands to Little Egg would've been darkly pondering. It's not a question, let's face it, that suburban life regularly poses to us. Suburban life, in fact, pretty much does the opposite.

And yet, it might.

Faced with Mr. Clevinger's question and a little pushed for time, I'm sure I would've begun soundlessly inventorying all the things I hadn't done yet—fucked a movie star, adopted Vietnamese orphan twins and sent them to Williams, hiked the Appalachian Trail, brought help to a benighted, drought-ravaged African nation, learned German, been appointed ambassador to a country nobody else wanted but I did. Voted Republican. I would've thought about whether my organ-donor card was signed, whether my list of pallbearers was updated, whether my obituary had the important new details added—whether, in other words, I'd gotten my message out properly. So in all likelihood, what I would've said to Mr. Clevinger as the autumn breezes twirled in through the windows off bright Paloma Playa and the nursing girls held their sweet bubble-gum breaths waiting to hear, would've been: "You know, not really. I guess not. Not quite yet." Whereupon he would've shot me anyway, though conceivably not himself.

When I'd thought only this far through the sad and dreary conundrum, I realized I no longer had my usual interest in the routines of my morning—fifty sit-ups, forty push-ups, some neck stretches, a bowl of cereal and fruit, a manumitting interlude in the men's room—and that what this story of Ms. McCurdy's unhappy end had caused in me was a need for a harsh, invigorating, mind-clearing plunge in the briny. It was the sixteenth of November, a precise week before Thanksgiving, and the Atlantic was as nickel-polished, clean-surfaced and stilly cold as old Neptune's heart. (When you first buy by the ocean, you're positive you'll take a morning dip every single day, and that life will be commensurately happier, last longer, you'll be jollier—the old pump getting a fresh prime at about the hour many are noticing the first symptoms of their myocardial infarct. Only you don't.)

Yet we can all be moved, if we're lucky. And I was—by Ms. McCurdy. So that some contact with the sudden and the actual seemed demanded. And not, as I found my bathing suit in the drawer, got in it and headed barefoot out the side door and down the sandy steps into the brisk beach airishness—not that I was really frightened by the little saga. Death and its low-lying ambuscade don't scare me much. Not anymore. This summer, in clean-lawned, regulation-size, by-the-numbers Rochester, Minnesota, I got over Big-D death in a swift, once-and-for-all and official way. Gave up on the Forever Concept. As things now stand, I won't outlive my mortgage, my twenty-five-year roof, possibly not even my car. My mother's so-so genes—breast-cancer genes giving percolating rise to prostate-cancer genes, giving rise to it's anybody's guess what next—had finally gained a lap on me. Thus the refugees' sad plight in Gaza, the float on the Euro, the hole in the polar ice cap, the big one rumbling in on the Bay Area like a fleet of Harleys, the presence of heavy metals in mothers' milk—all that *seemed* dire, it's true, but was frankly tolerable from my end of the telescope.

It was simply that, moved as I was, and with the coming week full of surprises and the usual holiday morbidities, I wanted reminding in the most sensate of ways that I was alive. In the waning weeks of this millennial year, in which I promised myself as a New Year's/New Century's resolution to simplify some things (but haven't quite yet), I needed to get right, to get to where Ms. McCurdy was at her ending song, or at least close enough to it that if I was faced with something like the question she was faced with, I would give something like the answer she gave.

So, in my bare feet, with a cold breeze pricking my exposed back, chest, legs, I tender-footed it up and across the gritty berm, through the beach grass and off onto the surprisingly cold sand. A white lifeguard stand stood nobly but vacated on the beach. The tide was out, revealing a glistening, black, damp and sloping sand plain. Someone had broken off for firewood the beach sign, so that only OWN RISK was left in red block letters on its standard. Sea-Clift, midline-Jersey Shore, midline-November, can be the best of locales and days. Any one of the 2,300 of us who live here year-round will tell you. The feeling of people nearby enjoying life, whiling it away, out for a ramble, taking it in, is every-where about. Only the people themselves are gone. Gone back to Williamsport and Sparta and Demopolis. Only the solitary-seeming winter residents, the slow joggers, the single-dog walkers, the skinny men with metal detectors—their wives in the van waiting, reading John Grisham—these are who's here. And not even them at 7:00 a.m.

Up the beach and down was mostly empty. A container ship many miles offshore inched along the horizon's flat line. A rain squall that would never reach land hung against the lightening eastern sky. I took a sampling glance back at my house—all mirrored windows, little belvederes, copper copings, a weather vane on the top-most gable. I didn't want Clarissa to get up from her bed, have a stretch and a scratch, cast a welcoming eye toward the sea and suddenly believe that her dad was taking the deep-six plunge alone. Happily, though, I saw no one watching me—only the first sun warming the windows and turning them crimson and hot gold.

Of course, you'd know what I wondered. Who wouldn't? You can't go for a November morning's rejuvenating, self-actualizing dip, craving a taste of the irrefutable, the un-nuanced, of nature's necessity, and not be curious to know if you're on a secret mission. Secret from yourself. Can you? Certainly *some*, I thought, as the languid and surprisingly frigid Atlantic inched up my thighs, the sand creamy and flat under my toes, my dangle parts beginning to retract in alarm, surely *some* slip peacefully over the transom of pleasure craft (as the poet supposedly did), or swim out far too far of an evening, until the land falls dreamily away. But they probably don't say, "Ooops, uh-oh, damn, look-it here. I'm in a real mess now, am I truly not?" Frankly, I'd like to know what the hell they do say while they wait in death's anteroom, the lights of the departing boat growing dim, the water colder, choppier than anticipated. Maybe they *are* a little surprised by themselves, by how *final* events can suddenly seem. Though by then, there's not a whole hell of a lot they can do with the info.

But they're not surprised *qua* surprised. And as I waded up to my waist and began vigorously shivering, a taste of salt on my lips, I recognized I was *not* here, just off the continent's edge, to stage a hasty leave of it. No sir. I was here for the simple reason that I knew I would never have answered Don-Houston Clevin-ger's fatal question the way Sandra McCurdy did, because there was still something I needed to know and didn't, something which the shock of the ocean's burly heft and draw made me feel was still there to be found out and that could make me happy. Academics will say that answering *yes* to death's dire question is the same as answering *no*, and that all things that seem distinct are really identical—that only our need separates the wheat from the chaff. Though it's, of course, their living death that makes them think that way.

But, feeling the ocean climb and lick my chest and my breath go short and shallow—my two arms beginning to resist the float away to nowhere—I knew that death was different, and that I needed to say *no* to it now. And with this certainty, and the shore behind me, the sun bringing glories to the world's slow wakening, I took my plunge and swam a ways to feel my life, before turning back to land and whatever lay waiting for me there.

PART 1

TOMS RIVER, across the Barnegat Bay, teems out ahead of me in the blustery winds and under the high autumnal sun of an American Thanksgiving Tuesday. From the bridge over from Sea-Clift, sunlight diamonds the water below the girdering grid. The white-capped bay surface reveals, at a distance, only a single wet-suited jet-skier plowing and bucking along, clinging to his devil machine as it plunges, wave into steely wave. "Wet and chilly, bad for the willy," we sang in Sigma Chi, "Dry and warm, big as a baby's arm." I take a backward look to see if the NEW JERSEY'S BEST KEPT SECRET sign has survived the tourist season—now over. Each summer, the barrier island on which Sea-Clift sits at almost the southern tip hosts six thousand visitors per linear mile, many geared up for sun 'n fun vandalism and pranksterish grand theft. The sign, which our Realty Round-table paid for when I was chairman, has regularly ended up over the main entrance of the Rutgers University library, up in New Brunswick. Today, I'm happy to see it's where it belongs.

New rows of three-story white-and-pink condos line the mainland shore north and south. Farther up toward Silver Bay and the state wetlands, where bald eagles perch, the low pale-green cinder-block human-cell laboratory owned by a supermarket chain sits alongside a white condom factory owned by Saudis. At this distance, each looks as benign as Sears. Each, in fact, is a good-neighbor clean-industry-partner whose employees and executives send their kids to the local schools and houses of wor-ship, while management puts a stern financial foot down on drugs and pedophiles. Their campuses are well landscaped and policed. Both stabilize the tax base and provide locals a few good yuks.

From the bridge span I can make out the Toms River yacht basin, a forest of empty masts wagging in the breezes, and to the north, a smooth green water tower risen behind the husk of an old nuclear plant currently for sale and scheduled for shutdown in 2002. This is our westward land view across from the Boro of Sea-Clift, and frankly it is a positivist's version of what landscape-seascape has mostly become in a multi-use society.

This morning, I'm driving from Sea-Clift, where I've lived the last eight years, across the sixty-five-mile inland passage over to Haddam, New Jersey, where I once lived for twenty, for a day of diverse duties—some sobering, some fearsome, one purely hopeful. At 12:30, I'm paying a funeral-home visitation to my friend Ernie McAuliffe, who died on Saturday. Later, at four, my former wife, Ann Dykstra, has asked to "meet" me at the school where she works, the prospect of which has ignited piano-wire anxiety as to the possible subjects—my health, her health, our two grown and worrisome children, the surprise announcement of a new cavalier in her life (an event ex-wives feel the need to share). I also mean to make a quick stop by my dentist's for an on-the-fly adjustment to my night guard (which I've brought). And I have a Sponsor appointment at two—which is the hopeful part.

Sponsors is a network of mostly central New Jersey citizens—men and women—whose goal is nothing more than to help people (female Sponsors claim to come at everything from a more humanistic/nurturing angle, but I haven't noticed that in my own life). The idea of Sponsoring is that many people with problems need nothing more than a little sound advice from time to time. These are not problems you'd visit a shrink for, or take drugs to cure, or that require a program Blue Cross would co-pay, but just something you can't quite figure out by yourself, and that won't exactly go away, but that if you could just have a common-sense conversation about, you'd feel a helluva lot better. A good example would be that you own a sailboat but aren't sure how to sail it very well. And after a while you realize you're reluctant even to get in the damn thing for fear of sailing it into some rocks, endangering your life, losing your investment and embittering yourself with embarrassment. Meantime it's sitting in gaspingly expensive dry dock at Brad's Marina in Shark River, suffering subtle structural damage from being out of the water too long, and you're becoming the butt of whispered dumb-ass-novice cracks and slurs by the boatyard staff. You end up never driving down there even when you want to, and instead find yourself trying to avoid ever thinking about your sailboat, like a murder you committed decades ago and have escaped prosecution for by moving to another state and adopting a new identity, but that makes you feel ghastly every morning at four o'clock when you wake up covered with sweat.

Sponsor conversations address just such problems, often focusing on the debilitating effects of ill-advised impulse purchases or bad decisions regarding property or personal services. As a realtor, I know a lot about these things. Another example would be how do you approach your Dutch housekeeper, Bettina, who's stopped cleaning altogether and begun sitting in the kitchen all day drinking coffee, smoking, watching TV and talking on the telephone long-distance, but you can't figure out how to get her on track, or worst case, send her packing. Sponsor advice would be what a friend would say: Get rid of the boat, or else take some private lessons at the yacht club next spring; probably nothing's all that wrong with it for the time being—these things are built to last. Or I'll write out a brief speech for the Sponsoree to deliver to Bettina or leave in the kitchen, which, along with a healthy check, will send her on her way without fuss. She's probably illegal and unhappy herself.

Anybody with a feet-on-the-ground idea of what makes sense in the world can offer advice like this. Yet it's surprising the number of people who have no friends they can ask sound advice from, and no capacity to trust themselves. Things go on driving them crazy even though the solution's usually as easy as tightening a lug nut.

The Sponsor theory is: We offer other humans the chance to be human; to seek and also to find. No donations (or questions) asked.

A DRIVE ACROSS the coastal incline back to Haddam is not at all unusual for me. Despite my last near decade spent happily on the Shore, despite a new wife, new house, a new professional address—Realty-Wise Associates—despite a wholly reframed life, I've kept my Haddam affiliations alive and relatively thriving. A town you used to live in signifies something—possibly interesting—about you: what you were once. And what you *were* always has its private allures and comforts. I still, for instance, keep my Haddam Realty license current and do some referrals and appraisals for United Jersey, where I know most of the officers. For a time, I owned (and expensively maintained) two rental houses, though I sold them in the late-Nineties gentrification boom. And for several years, I sat on the Governor's Board of the Theological Institute—that is, until fanatical Fresh Light Koreans bought the whole damn school, changed the name to the Fresh Light Seminary (salvation through studied acts of discipline) and I was invited to retire. I've also kept my human infrastructure (medical-dental) centered in Haddam, where professional standards are indexed to the tax base. And quite frankly, I often just find solace along the leaf-shaded streets, making note of this change or that improvement, what's been turned into condos, what's on the market at what astronomical price, where historical streets have been revectored, buildings torn down, dressed up, revisaged, as well as silently viewing (mostly from my car window) the familiar pale faces of neighbors I've known since the Seventies, grown softened now and re-charactered by time's passage.

Of course, at some unpredictable but certain moment, I can also experience a heavy curtain-closing sensation all around me; the air grows thin and dense at once, the ground hardens under my feet, the streets yawn wide, the houses all seem too new, and I get the williwaws. At which instant I turn tail, switch on my warning blinkers and beat it back to Sea-Clift, the ocean, the continent's end and my chosen new life—happy not to think about Haddam for another six months.

What is home then, you might wonder? The place you first see daylight, or the place you choose for yourself? Or is it the someplace you just can't keep from going back to, though the air there's grown less breathable, the future's over, where they really don't want you back, and where you once left on a breeze without a rearward glance? Home? Home's a musable concept if you're born to one place, as I was (the syrup-aired southern coast), educated to another (the glaciated mid-continent), come full stop in a third—then spend years finding suitable "homes" for others. Home may only be where you've memorized the grid pattern, where you can pay with a check, where someone you've already met takes your blood pressure, palpates your liver, slips a digit here and there, measures the angstroms gone off your molars bit by bit—in other words, where your primary care-givers await, their pale gloves already pulled on and snugged.

*   *   *

MY OTHER duty for the morning is to act as ad hoc business adviser and confidant to my realty associate Mike Mahoney, about whom some personal data is noteworthy.

Mike hails from faraway Gyangze, Tibet (the real Tibet, not the one in Ohio), and is a five-foot-three-inch, forty-three-year-old realty dynamo with the standard Tibetan's flat, bony-cheeked, beamy Chinaman's face, gun-slit eyes, abbreviated arm length and, in his case, skint black hair through which his beige scalp glistens. "Mike Mahoney" was the "American" name hung on him by coworkers at his first U.S. job at an industrial-linen company in Carteret—his native name, Lobsang Dhargey, being thought by them to be too much of a word sandwich. I've told him that one or the other—Mike Lobsang or Mike Dhargey—could be an interesting fillip for business. But Mike's view is that after fifteen years in this country he's adjusted to Mike Mahoney and likes being "Irish." He has, in fact, become a full-blooded, naturalized American—at the courthouse in Newark with four hundred others. Yet, it's easy to picture him in a magenta robe and sandals, sporting a yellow horn hat and blowing a ceremonial trumpet off the craggy side of Mount Qomolangma—which is often how I think of him, though he never did it. You'd be right to say I never in a hundred years expected to have a Tibetan as my realty associate, and that New Jersey homebuyers might turn skittish at the idea. But at least about the second of these, what might be true is not. In the year and a half he's worked for me, since walking through my Realty-Wise door and asking for a job, Mike has turned out to be a virtual lion of revenue generation and business savvy: unceasingly farming listings, showing properties, exhibiting cold-call tenacity while proving artful at coaxing balky offers, wheedling acceptances, schmoozing with buyers, keeping negotiating parties in the dark, fast-tracking loan applications and getting money into our bank account where it belongs.

Which isn't to say he's a usual person to sell real estate along-side of, even though he's not so different from the real estate seller I've become over the years and for some of the same reasons—neither of us minds being around strangers dawn to dusk, and nothing else seems very suitable. Still, I'm aware some of my competitors smirk behind both our backs when they see Mike out planting Realty-Wise signs in front yards. And though occasionally potential buyers may experience a perplexed moment when a voice inside them shouts, "Wait. I'm being shown a beach bungalow by a fucking Tibetan!"—most clients come around soon enough to think of Mike as someone special who's theirs, and get over his unexpected Asian-ness as I have, to the point they can treat him like any other biped.

Looked at from a satellite circling the earth, Mike is not very different from most real estate agents, who often turn out to be exotics in their own right: ex-Concorde pilots, ex-NFL linebackers, ex-Jack Kerouac scholars, ex-wives whose husbands ran off with Vietnamese au pairs, then wish to God they could come back, but aren't allowed to. The real estate seller's role is, after all, never one you fully *occupy*, no matter how long you do it. You somehow always think of yourself as "really" something else. Mike started his strange life's odyssey in the mid-Eighties as a telemarketer for a U.S. company in Calcutta, where he learned to talk American by taking orders for digital thermocators and moleskin pants from housewives in Pompton Plaines and Bridgeton. And yet with his short gesturing arms, smiley demeanor and aggressively cheerful outlook, he can seem and act just like a bespectacled little Adam's-appled math professor at Iowa State. And indeed, in his duties as a residential specialist, he's comprehended his role as being a "metaphor" for the assimilating, stateless immigrant who'll always be what he is (particularly if he's from Tibet) yet who develops into a useful, purposeful citizen who helps strangers like himself find safe haven under a roof (he told me he's read around in Camus).

Over the last year and a half, Mike has embraced his new calling with gusto by turning himself into a strangely sharp dresser, by fine-tuning a flat, accentless news-anchor delivery (his voice sometimes seems to come from offstage and not out of him), by sending his two kids to a pricey private school in Rumson, by mortgaging himself to the gizzard, by separating from his nice Tibetan wife, driving a fancy silver Infiniti, never speaking Tibetan (easy enough) and by frequenting—and probably supporting—a girlfriend he hasn't told me about. All of which is fine. My only real complaint with him is that he's a Republican. (Officially, he's a registered Libertarian—fiscal conservative, social moderate, which makes you nothing at all.) But he voted for numskull Bush and, like many prosperous newcomers, stakes his pennant on the plutocrat's principle that what's good for him is probably good for all others—which as a world-view and in spite of his infectious enthusiasm, seems to rob him of a measure of inner animation, a human deficit I usually associate with citizens of the Bay Area, but that he would say is because he's a Buddhist.

But as for my role as his business adviser, Mike's name has gotten around some in our mid-Shore real estate circles—it's no longer possible for any single human act to stay long out of the public notice—and as of last week he was contacted by a subdivision developer up in Montmorency County, close to Haddam, with a proposition to enter a partnership. The developer has obtained a purchase option on 150 acres currently planted in Jersey yellow corn, but that lies slap in the middle of the New Jersey wealth belt (bordering the Delaware, bordering Haddam, two hours to Gotham, one from Philly). Houses there—giant mansionettes meant to look like Versailles—go for prices in the troposphere, even with current market wobbles, and anybody with a backhoe, a cell phone and who isn't already doing hard time can get rich without even getting up in the morning.

What Mike brings to the table is that he's a Tibetan *and* an American and therefore qualifies as a bona fide and highly prized minority. Any housing outfit that makes him its president automatically qualifies for big federal subsidy dollars, after which he and his partner can become jillionaires just by filling out a few government documents and letting a bunch of Mexicans do the work.

I've explained to him that in any regular business situation, a typical American entrepreneurial type *might* let him act as substitute towel boy at his racket club—but probably not. Mike, however, believes the business climate's not typical now. Many arrivees to central Jersey, he's told me, are monied subcontinentals with luxury fever—gastroenterologists, hospital administrators and hedge-fund managers—who're sick of their kids not getting into Dalton and Spence and are ready to buy the first day they drive down. The thinking is that these beige-skinned purchasers will look favorably on a development fronted by a well-dressed little guy who sorta looks like them. He and I have also discussed the fact that house sales are already leveling and could pancake by New Year's. Corporate debt's too high. Mortgage rates are at 8.25 but a year ago were at six. The NASDAQ's spongy. The election's going in the toilet (though he doesn't think so). Plus, it's the Millennium, and nobody knows what's happening next, only that something will. I've told him now might be a better time to spend his ethnic capital on a touchless car wash on Route 35, or possibly a U-Store-It or a Kinko's. These businesses are cash cows if you keep an eye on your employees and don't invest much of your own dough. Mike, of course, reads his tea leaves differently.

THIS MORNING, Mike has offered to drive and at this moment has his hands cautiously at ten and two, his eyes hawking the Toms River traffic. He's told me he never got enough driving time in Tibet—for obvious reasons—so he enjoys piloting my big Suburban. It may make him feel more American, since many vehicles in the thick holiday traffic on Route 37 are also Sub-urbans—only most are newer.

Since we rolled out of Sea-Clift and over the bridge toward the Garden State Parkway, he has spoken little. I've noticed in the office that he's recently exhibited broody, deep-ponder states during which he bites his lower lip, sighs and runs his hand back across his bristly skull, frowning apparently at nothing. These gestures, I assume, are standard ones having to do with being an immigrant or being a Buddhist, or with his new business prospects, or with everything at once. I've paid them little attention and am happy to be silently chauffeured today and to take in the scenery while shifting serious thoughts to the outer reaches of my brain—a trick I've gotten good at since Sally's departure last June, and since finding out during the Olympics in August that I'd become host to a slow-growing tumor in my prostate gland. (It *is* a gland, by the way, unlike your dick, which is often said to be, but isn't.)

Route 37, the Toms River Miracle Mile, is already jammed at 9:30 with shopper vehicles moving into and out of every con-ceivable second-tier factory outlet lot, franchise and big-box store, until we're mostly stalled in intersection tie-ups under screaming signage and horn cacophony. Black Friday, the day after Thanksgiving, when merchants hope to inch into the black, is traditionally the retail year's hallowed day, with squadrons of housewives in housecoats and grannies on walkers shouldering past security personnel at Macy's and Bradlees to get their hands on discounted electric carving knives and water-filled ortho- pedic pillows for that special arthritic with the chronically sore C6 and C7. Only this year—due to the mists of economic unease —merchants and their allies, the customers, have designated "gigantic" Black Tuesday and Black Wednesday Sales Days and are flying the banner of EVERYTHING MUST GO!—in case, I guess, the whole country's gone by Friday.

Cars are everywhere, heading in every direction. A giant yellow-and-red MasterCard dirigible floats above the buzzing landscape like a deity. Movie complexes are already opened with queues forming for *Gladiator* and *The Little Vampire*. Crowds press into Target and International Furniture Liquidator ("If we don't have it, you don't want it"). Christmas music's blaring, though it's not clear from where, and the traffic's barely inching. Firemen in asbestos suits and Pilgrim hats are out collecting money in buckets at the mall entrances and stoplights. Ragged groups of people who don't look like Americans skitter across the wide avenue in groups, as though escaping something, while solitary men in gleaming pickups sit smoking, watching, waiting to have their vehicles detailed at the Pow-R-Brush. At the big Hooper Avenue intersection, a TV crew has set up a command post, with a hard-body, shiny-legged Latina, her stiff little butt turned to the gridlock, shouting out to the 6:00 p.m. viewers up the seaboard what all the fuss is about down here.

Yet frankly it all thrills me and sets my stomach tingling. Unbridled commerce isn't generally pretty, but it's always forward-thinking. And since nowadays with my life out of sync and most things in the culture not affecting me much—politics, news, sports, everything but the weather—it feels good that at least commerce keeps me interested like a scientist. Commerce, after all, is basic to my belief system, even though it's true, as modern merchandising theory teaches, that when we shop, we no longer really shop *for* anything. If you're really looking for that liquid stain remover you once saw in your uncle Beckmer's basement that could take the spots off a hyena, or you're seeking a turned brass drawer pull you only need *one of* to finish refurbish- ing the armoire you inherited from Aunt Grony, you'll never find either one. No one who works anyplace knows anything, and everyone's happy to lie to you. "They don't make those anymore." "Those've been back-ordered two years." "That ballpoint company went out of business, moved to Myanmar and now makes sump pumps . . . All we have are these." You have to take what they've got even if you don't want it or never heard of it. It's hard to call this brand of zero-sum merchandising true commerce. But in its apparent aimlessness, it's not so different from the real estate business, where often at the end of the day, someone goes away happy.

We've now made it as far as the Toms River western outskirts. Motels are all full here. Used-car lots are Givin' 'em Away. A bonsai nursery has already moved its tortured little shrubs to the back, and employees are stacking in Christmas trees and wreaths. Flapping flags in many parking lots stand at half-staff—for what reason, I don't know. Other signs shout Y2K MEMORABILIA SCULPTURE! INVEST IN REAL ESTATE NOT STOCKS! TIGHT BUTTS MAKE ME NUTS! WELCOME SUICIDE SURVIVORS. Yellow traffic cones and a giant blinking yellow arrow are making us merge right into one lane, alongside a deep gash in the freshly opened asphalt, beside which large hard-hatted white men stand staring at other men already down in the hole—putting our tax dollars to work.

"I really don't understand that," Mike says, his chin up alertly, the seat run way forward so his toes can reach the pedals and his hands control the wheel. He eyes me as he navigates through the holiday tumult.

I, of course, know what's bothering him. He's seen the WELCOME SUICIDE SURVIVORS sign on the Quality Court marquee. My having cancer makes him possibly worry about me in this regard, which then makes him fret about his own future. When I was at Mayo last August, I left him in charge of Realty-Wise, and he carried on without a hitch. But on his desk last week I saw a *New York Times* article he'd downloaded, explaining how half of all bankruptcies are health-related and that from a purely financial perspective, doing away with oneself's probably a good investment. I've explained to him that one in ten Americans is a cancer survivor, and that my prospects are good (possibly true). But I'm fairly sure that my health is on his mind and has probably brought about today's sudden test-the-waters probing into suburban land-development. Plus, in exactly a week from today I'm flying to Rochester for my first post-procedure follow-up at Mayo, and he may sense I'm feeling anxious—I may be—and is merely feeling the same himself.

Buddhists are naturally unbending on the subject of suicide. They're against it. And even though he's a free-market, de-regulating, *Wall Street Journal*-reading flat-taxer, Mike has also remained a devotee of His Holiness the Dalai Lama. His screen saver at the office actually shows a beaming color photograph of himself beside the diminutive reincarnate, taken at the Meadow-lands last year. He's also displayed three red-white-and-blue prayer flags on the wall behind his desk, with a small painting of the thousand-armed Chenrezig and beside these a signed glossy of Ronald Reagan—all for our clients to puzzle over as they write out their earnest money checks. In the DL's view, utilizing a correct, peaceful-compassionate frame of mind will dissolve all impediments, so that karmically speaking we get exactly what we should get because we're all fathers of ourselves and the world's the result of our doing, etc., etc., etc. Killing yourself, in other words, shouldn't be necessary—about which I'm in complete agreement. Apparently, the smiling-though-exiled precious protector and the great communicating Gipper line up well on this, as on many issues. (I knew nothing about Tibet *or* Buddhists and have had to read up on it at night.)

It's also true that Mike knows something about my Sponsor-ing work, which has made him decide I'm spiritual, which I'm not, and prompted him to address all sorts of provocative moral questions to me and then purposefully fail to understand my answers, thereby proving his superiority—which makes him happy. One of his recent discussion topics has been the Colum-bine massacre, which he believes was caused by falsely pursuing lives of luxury, instead of by the obstinance of pure evil—my view. In the otherwise-pointless Elián González controversy, he sided with the American relatives in a show of immigrant solidarity, while I went with the Cuban Cubans, which just seemed to make sense.

Mike's moral principles, it should be said, have had to learn to operate in happy tandem with the self-interested consumer-mercantile ones of the real estate business. Working for me he gets one-third of 6 percent on all home sales he makes himself

(I take two-thirds because I pay the bills), a bonus on all big-ticket sales *I* make, plus 20 percent on the first month of all summer rentals, which is nothing to bark at. There's another bonus at Christmas if I feel generous. And against that, I pay no benefits, no retirement, no mileage, no nothing—a good arrangement for me. But it's also an arrangement that allows him to live good and buy swanky sporting-business attire from a Filipino small-man shop in Edison. Today he's shown up for his meeting in fawn-colored flared trousers that look like they're made of rubber and cover up his growing little belly, a sleeveless cashmere sweater in a pink ice-cream hue, mirror-glass Brancusi tassel-loafers, yellow silk socks, tinted aviators, and a mustard-colored camel hair blazer currently in the backseat—none of which really makes sense on a Tibetan, but that he thinks makes him credible as an agent. I don't mention it.

And yet there's much about America that baffles him still, in spite of fifteen years' residence and patient study. As a Buddhist, he fails to understand the place of religion in our political doings. He has never been to California or even to Chicago or Ohio, and so lacks the natives' intrinsic appreciation of history as a function of landmass. And even though he's a real estate sales-man, he doesn't finally see why Americans move so much, and isn't interested in my answer: because they can. However, during the time he's been here, he's taken a new name, bought a house, cast three presidential ballots and made some money. He's also memorized the complete *New Jersey Historical Atlas* and can tell you where the spring-loaded window and the paper clip were invented—Millrun and Englewood; where the first manure spreader was field-trialed—in Moretown; and which American city was the first nuclear-free zone—Hoboken. Such readout, he believes, makes him persuasive to home buyers. And in this, he's like many of our citizens, including the ones who go back to the Pilgrims: He's armed himself with just enough information, even if it's wrong, to make him believe that what he wants he deserves, that bafflement is a form of curiosity and that these two together form an inner strength that should let him pick all the low-hanging fruit. And who's to say he's wrong? He may already be as assimilated as he'll ever need to be.

*   *   *

MORE INTERESTING landscape for the citizen scientist now passes my window. A Benjamin Moore paint "test farm," with holiday browsers strolling the grassy aisles, pointing to this or that pastel or maroon tile as if they were for sale. More significant signage: SUCCESS IS ADDICTIVE (a bank); HEALTHY MATE DATING SERVICE; DOLLAR UNIVERSITY INSTITUTE FOR HIGHER EARNING. Then the cement-bunker Ocean County Library, where holiday offerings are advertised out front—a poetry reading on Wednesday, a CPR workshop on Thanksgiving Day, two Philadelphia Phillies players driving over Saturday for an inspirational seminar about infidelity, "the Achilles' heel of big-league sports."

"I just don't understand it," Mike says again, because I haven't answered him the first time he said it. His pointed chin is still elevated, as if he's seeing out the bottom of his expensive yellow glasses. He looks at me, inclining his head toward his shoulder. He's wearing a silver imitation Rolex as thick as a car bumper and looks—behind the wheel—like a pint-sized mafioso on his way to a golf outing. He is a strange vision to be seen from other Suburbans.

"You don't understand 'Tight butts make me nuts'?" I say. "That's pretty basic."

"I don't understand suicide survivors." He keeps careful eyes on the Parkway entrance, a hundred yards ahead of us.

"It just wouldn't work as well if it said 'Welcome Suicide Failures,'" I say. The names Charles Boyer, Socrates, Meriwether Lewis and Virginia Woolf tour my mind. Exemplary suicide success stories.

"Natural death is very dignified," he says. This is the kind of "spiritual" conversation he likes, in which he can further prove his superiority over me. "Avoiding death invites suffering and fear. We shouldn't mock."

"They're not avoiding it and they're not mocking it," I say. "They like getting together in a multipurpose room and having some snacks. Haven't you ever thought about suicide? I thought about it last week."

"Would you attend a suicide survivors meeting?" Mike roams his tongue around the interior of his plump cheek.

"I might if I had time on my hands. I could make up a good story. That's all they want. It's like AA. It's all a process."

Mike's bespectacled face assumes a brows-down ancient look. He doesn't officially approve of self-determination, which he considers to be non-virtuous action and basically pointless. He believes, for instance, that Sally's sudden leaving last June put me in a state of vulnerable anxiety, which resulted from the specific, non-virtuous activity of divisive speech, which was why I got cancer and have titanium BBs percolating inside my prostate, a body part I'm not sure he even believes in. He believes I should meditate myself free of the stressful idea of love-based attachments—which wouldn't be that hard.

A state police blue flasher's now in sight where the on-ramp angles up to enter the Parkway. Cars are backed up all the way down to 37. An ambulance is somewhere behind us, *whoop-whooping*, but we can't pull over due to the road construction. A police copter hovers above the southbound lanes toward Atlantic City. Traffic's halted there in both lanes. Some of the ramp cars are trying to turn around and are getting stuck. People are honking. Smoke rises from somewhere beyond.

"Did you seriously think about suicide?" Mike says.

"You never know if you're serious. You just find out. I've survived to be in Toms River this morning."

A wide, swaying orange-and-white Ocean County EMS meat wagon, bristling with silver strobes, shushes past us on the shoulder, rollicking and roaring. Lights are on inside the swaying box, figures moving about behind the windows, making ready for something.

"Don't go up there," I say, meaning the Parkway. "Take the surface road."

"Shit!" Mike says, and cranes around at the traffic behind us so he's not forced up onto the ramp. "A pain in the ass." Buddhists have no swear words, though cursing in English pleases him because it's meaningless and funny and not non-virtuous. He looks at me in the sly, secret way by which we've come to communicate. He has no real interest in suicide. A significant portion of the essential Mike may now have gone beyond the selfless Buddhist to be the solid New Jersey citizen-realtor. "In your lifetime, you'll spend six and a half years in your car," he says, merging us into the left lane that goes under the Parkway overpass. All the traffic's going there now. "Half the U.S. population lives within fifty miles of the ocean."

"Most of them are right here with us today, I'd say."

"It's good for business," he says. And that is nothing but the truth.

SURFACE ROADS are never a pain in the ass, no matter where we roam. And I'm always interested in what's new, what's abandoned, what's in the offing, what will never be.

Route 37 (after we make a wrong turn onto 530, then correct to 539 and head straight as a bullet up to Cream Ridge) offers rare sights to the conscientious observer. The previous two drought years have rendered the sand-scrubby New Jersey pine flats we're passing a harsh blow, having already been deserted by the subdivision builders in search of better pickings. Vestigial one-strip strip commercials go by now and then, usually with only one store running. Travelers have dumped piles of 24-pack Bud empties in many of the turn-outs, as well as porcelain sinks, washer-dryers, microwaves, serious amounts of crumpled Kleenexes and a clutter of defunct car batteries. Several red-stenciled posters are nailed to roadside oaks, announcing long-forgotten paint-ball battles in the pines. (We're near the perimeter of Fort Dix.) At the turn-off for Collier's Mills Wildlife Management Area, a billboard proclaims a WILD WEST CITY—MASTODON EXHIBIT AND WATER SLIDE. A few cars, dust-caked green Plymouths and a rusted-out Chevy Nova with white shoe-polish 4-$ales on their windshields, sit on the dry shoulder at the woods' edge. One lonely-guy sex shop lurks back in the trees with a blinking red-and-yellow roof sign, awaiting whoever's out here to abandon his pet but finds himself in the mood for some nasty. The White Citizen's Action Alliance has "adopted" the highway. The only car we pass is an Army Humvee driven by a soldier in a helmet and a camo suit.

And though all seems forsaken, back in the pines are occasional tracts of weathered pastel ranch-looking homes on curved streets with fireplugs, curbs and power poles in place. Most of these residences have windows and front doors ply-boarded and spray-painted KEEP OUT, their siding gone gray as a battleship, foundations sunk in grass that's died. It's not clear if these were once lived in or were abandoned brand-new. Although on one of the winding streets that opens onto the highway, Paramour Drive, I make out as we flash by, two boys—twelve-year-olds—side-by-side together on the empty asphalt. One sits on a dirt bike, one's on foot. They're talking while a mopish fluffy dog sits and watches them. The pink house they're in front of has a fallen-in wheelchair ramp to the front door. All its windows are out. No cars are in evidence, no garbage cans, no recycle tubs, no amenities.

In sum, this part of Route 37's the right place to go through a gross of rubbers, shoot .22s, drink two hundred beers, drive fast, toss out an old engine or a load of snow tires or a body. Or, of course, to become a suicide statistic—which I don't mention to Mike, who's sitting forward, paying zero attention to the landscape. It might as well be time travel to him, though he clicks on the radio once for the ten o'clock news. He's, I know, worried that Gore might push through in the Florida Supreme Court, but there's no rumor of that, so that he goes back to silently dry-running his meeting in Montmorency County, and fidgeting over trading in his minority innocence for the chance to wade into the heavy chips—something any natural-born American wouldn't think twice about.

THE MORNING'S plan is that once we make contact with Mike's land developer—at the proposed cornfield site—I'm to take an expert read on the character. Then he and Mike will hie off for a shirtsleeve, elbows-on-the-table, brass-tacks business lunch and afternoon plat-map confab, where Mike'll hear the pitch, look him in the eye and attempt his own cosmic assessment. He and I'll then hook up at 6:45 at the August Inn in Haddam and drive back to Sea-Clift, during which time I'll offer my "gut," take the gloves off, connect some dots, do the math and everything'll come clear. Mike believes I have a "knack for people," a matter in dispute among the actual people who've loved me. Our scheme, of course, is the sort of simple one that makes perfect sense to everybody, and then goes bust no matter how good everyone's intentions were. For that reason, I'm going in with earnest good feeling but little or no expectation of success.

I'VE SAID nothing so far about my own Thanksgiving plans, now just two days away and counting, and that involve my two children. My reticence in this matter may owe to the fact that I've organized events to be purposefully unspectacular—consistent with my unspectacular physical state—and to accommodate as much as possible everyone's personal agendas, biological clocks, comfort zones and need for wiggle room, while offering a pleasantly neutral setting (my house in Sea-Clift) for nonconfrontational familial good cheer. My thought is that by my plan's being unambitious, the holiday won't deteriorate into apprehension, dismay and rage, rocketing people out the doors and back to the Turnpike long before sundown. Thanksgiving *ought* to be the versatile, easy-to-like holiday, suitable to the secular and religious, adaptable to weddings, christenings, funerals, first-date anniversaries, early-season ski trips and new romantic interludes. It often just doesn't work out that way.

As everyone knows, the Thanksgiving "concept" was originally strong-armed onto poor war-worn President Lincoln by an early-prototype forceful-woman editor of a nineteenth-century equivalent of the *Ladies' Home Journal*, with a view to upping subscriptions. And while you can argue that the holiday commemorates ancient rites of fecundity and the Great-Mother-Who-Is-in-the-Earth, it's in fact always honored storewide clearances and stacking 'em deep 'n selling 'em cheap—unless you're a Wampanoag Indian, in which case it celebrates deceit, genocide and man's indifference to who owns what.

Thanksgiving also, of course, signals the beginning of the gloomy Christmas season, vale of aching hearts and unreal hopes, when more suicide successes, abandonments, spousal thumpings, car thefts, firearm discharges and emergency surgeries take place per twenty-four-hour period than any other time of year except the day after the Super Bowl. Days grow ephemeral. No one's adjusted to the light's absence. Many souls buy a ticket to anyplace far off just to be in motion. Worry and unwelcome self-awareness thicken the air. Though strangely enough, it's also a great time to sell houses. The need to make amends for marital bad behavior, or to keep a wary eye on the tax calendar or to deliver on the long-postponed family ski outing to Mount Pisgah—all make people itchy to buy. There's no longer a real off-season for house sales. Houses sell whether you want them to or not.

In my current state of mind, I'd, in fact, be just as happy to lose Christmas and its weak sister New Year's, and ring out the old year quietly with a cocktail by the Sony. One of divorce's undervalued dividends, I should say, is that all the usual dismal holiday festivities can now be avoided, since no one who didn't have to would ever think about seeing the people they used to say they wanted to see but almost certainly never did.

And yet, Thanksgiving won't be ignored. Americans are hard-wired for something to be thankful for. Our national spirit thrives on invented gratitude. Even if Aunt Bella's flat-lined and in custodial care down in Ruckusville, Alabama, we still "need" her to have some white meat and gravy and be thankful, thankful, thankful. After all, *we* are—if only because we're not in her bed-room slippers.

And it *is* churlish not to let the spirit swell—if it can—since little enough's at stake. Contrive, invent, engage—take the chance to be cheerful. Though in the process, one needs to skirt the spiritual dark alleys and emotional cul-de-sacs, subdue all temper flarings and sob sessions with loved ones. Get plenty of sleep. Keep the TV on (the Lions and Pats are playing at noon). Take B vitamins and multiple walks on the beach. Make no decisions more serious than lunch. Get as much sun as possible. In other words, treat Thanksgiving like jet lag.

Once I'd moved from Haddam, married Sally Caldwell and set up life on a steadier footing in Sea-Clift (where, of course, there is no actual clift), the two of us would spend our Thanks-givings together in a cabin in New Hampshire, near where the first Thanksgiving occurred. Sally's former in-laws—parents of her former (AWOL) husband, Wally, and salt-of-the-earth Chicago-North-Shore old New Dealers—owned a summer cottage on Lake Laconic, facing the mountains. Fireplaces were all the heat there was. These were the last bearable days before the pipes were drained, phones turned off, windows shuttered and china locked in the attic. The Caldwells—Warner and Con-stance, then in their seventies—thought of Sally as a beloved but star-crossed family member, and for that reason anything they could do for her couldn't be enough, even with me in attend-ance, as the ambiguous new presence.

Sally and I would drive up from New Jersey on Wednesday night, sleep like corpses, stay in bed under a big tick comforter until we were brave enough to face the morning chill, then scramble around for sweaters, wool pants and boots, making coffee, eating bagels we'd brought from home, reading old *Holidays* and *Psychology Today*s before embarking on a moderately strenuous hike to the French-Canadian massacre site halfway up Mount Deception, after which we took a nap till cocktail hour.

We watched moose in the shallows, eagles in the tree tops, made comical efforts to fish for trout, watched the outfitter's seaplane slide onto the lake, considered getting the outboard going for a trip out to the island where a famous painter had lived. Once, I actually took a dip, but never again. At night we listened to the CBC on the big Stromberg-Carlson. I read. Sally read. The house had plenty of books by Nelson DeMille and Frederick Forsyth. We made love. We drank gin drinks. We found pizzas in the basement freezer. The one rustic restaurant that stayed open offered a Thanksgiving spread on Thursday *and* Friday—for hunters. We each felt this vacation strategy was the best solution, with so many worse solutions available. In other words, we loved it. By Saturday noon, we were bored as hammers (who wouldn't be in New Hampshire?) and antsy to get back to New Jersey. Happy to arrive; happy to leave—the traveler's mantra.

This past Labor Day, when I was far from chipper from my Mayo siege, it occurred to me that the smart plan for the millennial Thanksgiving, with the Caldwells' cottage no longer mine, was to lead a family party back to Lake Laconic, be tourists, take over a B&B, go on walks, wade in cold shallows, paddle canoes, skip rocks, watch for eagles and drink wine (not gin) in the late-autumn splendor. A low-impact holiday for a low moment in life, with my family convened around me.

Except, my son Paul Bascombe, now twenty-seven and leading a fully-embedded, mainstreamed life in Kansas City, where he writes laughable captions for the great megalithic Hallmark greeting-card entity ("an American icon"), said he wouldn't come if he had to drive all the way to "piss-boot New Hampshire." He had to be at work on Monday, and in any case wanted to see his mother, my former wife, now living in Haddam.

My daughter, Clarissa, twenty-five, agreed a soft-landing Lake Laconic holiday might be "restorative" for me and help me get over "a pretty intense summer." She and her girlfriend, the

heart-stoppingly beautiful Cookie Lippincott, her former Harvard roommate, took charge when I flew back from Mayo in a
diaper and in no mood for laughs. (Lesbians make great nurses,
just like you'd think they would: serious but mirthful, generous
but consistent, competent but understanding—even if yours
happens to be your daughter.) During my early recovery days,
I took her and Cookie to the Red Man Club, my sportsman's
hideout on the Pequest, where we shot clay pigeons, played gin
rummy, fished for browns till midnight and slept out on the long
screen porch on fragrant canvas army cots. We took day trips to
the Vet for the last days of the Phillies' season. We visited Atlantic
City and lost our shirts. We hiked Ramapo Mountain—the easy
part. We went on self-guided tours to every passive park, vernal
pond and bird refuge in the guidebook. We read novels together
and talked about them over meals. We managed to assemble a
family unit—not your ordinary one, but what is?—one that got
me back on my feet and pissing straight, took my mind off things
and made me realize I didn't need to worry much about my
daughter (which doesn't go for my son).

But then in the midst of all, Clarissa decided she should take
a sudden, divergent "new" path, and parted with Cookie to "try
men" again before it was too late—whatever that might mean.
Though what it meant at the moment was that with her brother
not attending, my New Hampshire Thanksgiving idyll fell
through in an afternoon, with my house in Sea-Clift elected by
default.

For this Thursday, then, I've ordered a "Big Bird et Tout à
Fait" Thanksgiving package from Eat No Evil Organic in
Mantoloking, where they promise everything's "so yummy you
won't know it's not poisoning you." It comes with bone china,
English cutlery, leaded crystal, Irish napkins as big as Rhode
Island, a case of Sonoma red, all finished with "not-to-die-for
carob pumpkin pie"—no sugar, no flour, lard or anything good.
Two thousand dollars cheap.

I've devised a modest guest list: Clarissa, with possibly a new
boyfriend; Paul with his significant other, driving in from K.C.;
a refound friend from years gone by, widower Wade Arcenault,
who's eighty-something and a strange father-in-law figure to me
(being father to an old flame). I've also invited two of my men
friends from Haddam, Larry Hopper and Hugh Wekkum, good

fellows of my own vintage, former charter members of the Divorced Men's Club and comrades from the bad old days, when we were all freshly singled and at wits' end to know how to tie our shoes. Unlike me—and maybe wiser—neither Hugh nor Larry has married again. At some point they both realized they never would—just couldn't find the low-gear pulling power to mount another love affair, couldn't even imagine kissing women. "I felt like a homeless man groping at a sandwich," Larry has confided with dismay. So with no patience or interest in the old dating metronome, he and Hugh figured out they were seeing more of each other than they were of anybody else. And after Hugh had a by-pass, Larry moved him into his big white Stedman House with attached slave quarters on South Comstock. They've ended up playing golf every day, and Hugh hasn't had any more heart flare-ups. There's no hanky-panky, they assure me, since both are on blood thinners and couldn't hanky the first panky even if the spirit was in them.

I've also thought about inviting my former wife, Ann Dykstra, now a well-provided widow living, as mentioned (of all places), in Haddam, having purchased back her own former house from me at 116 Cleveland (no commission), a house she'd lived in previously, then abandoned and sold to *me* when she married her second husband, Charley O'Dell, and moved to Connecticut, following which I lived there for seven years, then moved to the Shore for my own second try at happiness. Aldous Huxley said—after reading Einstein—that the world is not only stranger than we know but a lot stranger than we *can* know. I don't know if Huxley was divorced, but I'm betting he had to be.

Since Sally's departure in June, and my life-modifying trip to Mayo in August, I've spoken with Ann a few times. Nothing more than business. She conducted the house re-resale using the same vicious little lawyer she'd used to divorce me back in '83, and didn't come to the closing, to which I'd grinningly brought a bouquet of nasturtiums to commemorate (in a good way) life's imperial strangeness. But then, one warm evening in September, just as I'd constructed a forbidden martini and was sitting down in the sunroom to watch the campaign coverage on CNN, Ann called up and just said, "So, how are you?" It was as if she was holding a policy on my life and was checking on her investment. We've always kept our contacts restricted to kid subjects. She didn't understand what Paul was doing in K.C., and wouldn't discuss the concept that her daughter was a lesbian (which I assume she blames me for). Once before, she'd inquired about my health, I lied, and then we didn't know what else to say. And to her more recent question about how I was, I lied again that I was "fine." Then she told me about her mother's Christmas letter describing trouble with her dental implants, and about her once giving holy hell to Ann's since-deceased father, for failing to leave Detroit with her in '72 (when she divorced him) and come enjoy the sunsets in Mission Viejo.

We hung up when that was over.

But. But. Something had been opened. A thought.

Since September, we've had coffee once at the Alchemist & Barrister, exchanged calls about the children's trajectories and plights, gone over house eccentricities only I, as former owner, would know about—furnace warranty, water-pressure worries, inaccurate wiring diagrams. We have not gone into my medical situation, though obviously she's wise to plenty. I don't know if she thinks I'm impotent or have continence issues (not that I know of, and no). But she's exhibited a form of interest. In her husband Charley's last grueling days on earth—he had colon cancer but had forgotten about it because he also had Alzheimer's—I agreed to sit with him and did, since none of his Yale friends were brave enough to. (Life never throws you the straight fastball.) And since then, two years ago, some sort of low ceiling of masking clouds that had for years hung over me where Ann was concerned has slowly opened, and it's almost as if she can now see me as a human being.

Not that either of us wants a "relationship." What's between us is almost entirely clerical-informative in nature and lacking the grit of possibility. Yet there are simply no further grievances needing to be grieved, no final words needing to be spoken, then spoken again. We are what we are—divorced, widowed, abandoned, parents of two adults and one dead son, with just so much of life left to live. It is another facet in the shining gem of the Permanent Period of life that we try to *be* what we *are* in the present—good or not so good—this, so that accepting final credit for ourselves won't be such a shock later on. The world *is* strange, as old Huxley noticed. Though in my view, my and Ann's conduct is also what you might reasonably hope of two people who've known each other over thirty years, never gotten completely outside the other's orbit and now find the other still around and able to make sense.

But the final word: Ann would say no to my invitation if I extended it. She's recently gone to work—just to keep busy—as an admissions high-up at De Tocqueville Academy, where I'm meeting her today, and where she has, Clarissa says, made some new friends among the gentle, introverted, over-diploma'd folk there. She's also, Clarissa reports, been appointed coach of the De Tocqueville Lady Linksters (she captained at Michigan in '69), and, I'm sure, feels life has taken a good turn. None of this, of course, specifically explains why she wants to see me.

POLITICAL PLACARDS sprout along Route 206 when we detour around Haddam toward the north. Local contests—assessor, sheriff, tax collector—were settled weeks back, though a feeling of unfinality hangs in the suburban air. Here, now it's fat yellow Colonial two-of-a-kinds and austere gray saltboxes with the odd redwood deck house peeping through leafless poplars, ash and bushy mountain laurels. Some recidivist Bush sentiment is alive on a few lawns, but mostly it's solid-for-Gore in this moderate, woodsy, newer section of the township (when Ann and I were young newcomers down from Gotham in 1970, it was woods, not woodsy). The placards all insist that we the voters who voted (I went for Gore) really meant it this time and still mean it and won't stand for foolishness. Though of course we will. And indeed, cruising past the uncrowded, familiar roads late in my favorite season, these bosky, privileged precincts feel punky and lank, swooning and ready for a doze. As we used to say, yukking it up in the USMC about recruits who weren't going to make it, "You'll have to wake him up just to kill him." In these parts, it's a good time for an insurrection.

No real commerce flourishes on this stretch of 206. Haddam, in fact, doesn't thrive on regular commerce. Decades of Republican councilmen, building moratoriums, millage turn-downs, adverse zoning reviews, traffic studies, greenbelt referendums and just plain shit-in-your-hat high-handedness have been disincentives for anything more on this end of town than a Forestview Methodist, the odd grandfathered dentist's plaza, a marooned Foremost Farms and one mediocre Italian restaurant the former Boro president's father owns. Housing is Haddam's commerce. Whereas the real business—Kia dealerships, muffler shops, twenty-screen movie palaces, Mr. Goodwrench and the Pep Boys—all that happy horseshit's flourishing across County Line Road, where Haddamites jam in on Saturday mornings before scurrying back home, where it's quiet.

I never minded any of that when I sold houses here. I voted for every moratorium, against every millage to extend services to the boondocks, supported every not-in-my-neighborhood ordinance. In-fill and gentrification are what keep prices fat and are what's kept Haddam a nice place to live. If it becomes the New Jersey chapter of Colonial Williamsburg, with surrounding farmlands morphed into tract-house prairies, carpet outlets and bonsai nurseries, then I can take (and did take) the short view, since the long view was forgone and since that's how people wanted it.

What exactly happened to the short view and that drove me to the Shore like a man in the Kalahari who sees a vision of palm trees and sniffs water in the quavery distance—that's another story.

SINCE WE'VE crossed into Haddam Township, Mike's fallen to sighing again, raking his hand back through his buzzed-off hair, squinting and looking fretful behind his glasses as we head out toward the Montmorency County line. His driving has devolved into fits and spurts in the lighter township traffic. Two times we've been honked at and once given the finger by a pretty black woman in a Jaguar, so that his piloting's begun to get on my nerves.

I again know what he's on about. Mike's belief, and I subscribe to it myself, is that at the exact moment any decision *seems* to be being made, it's usually long after the real decision was actually made—like light we see emitted from stars. Which means we usually make up our minds about important things far too soon and usually with poor information. But we then convince ourselves we *haven't* done that because (a) we know it's boneheaded, and no one wants to be accused of boneheaded-ness; (b) we've ignored our vital needs and don't like to think about them;

(c) deciding but believing we haven't decided gives us a secret from ourselves that's too delicious not to keep. In other words, it makes us happy to bullshit ourselves.

What Mike does to avoid this bad practice—and I know he's fretful about his up-coming meeting—is empty his mind of impure motives so he can communicate with his instincts. He often performs this head-rubbing, frowning ritual right in the realty office before presenting an offer or heading off to a closing. He does this because he knows he frequently holds the power to tip a sale one way or the other and wants things to work out right. I'm sure if you're a Buddhist, you do this all the time about everything. And I'm also sure it doesn't do any good. They teach this brand of soggy crappolio in the "realty psychology" courses that Mike took to get his license. I just came along years too early—back when you only sold houses because you wanted to and it was easy and you liked money.

The other scruple I'm sure is thrumming in Mike's brain is that during his fifteen years in our country he's swung rung to rung up the success ladder, departing one cramped circumstance for a slightly less cramped next one. He arrived from India to his Newark host family, segued on to Carteret and the industrial-linen industry, then to a less nice section of South Amboy, where he worked for an Indian apartment finder. From there to Neptune, Neptune to Lavallette—both times as a realty associate. And from there to me—an impressive climb most Americans would think was great and that would get them started filling up their garages with Harleys and flame-sided Camaros and snow machines and straw deer targets, their front yards sprouting Bush-Cheney placards, their bumpers plastered with stickers that say: I TAKE MY ORDERS FROM THE BIG GUY UPSTAIRS.

But to Mike, the assumption that Lavallette, New Jersey, ought to seem like Nirvana to a smiling little brown man born in a wattle hut in the Himalayas is both true and not true. Deep in his hectic night's sleep, with his estranged wife in her estranged home in the Amboys, his teenagers up late noodling on their laptops with SAT reviews, his Infiniti safely "clubbed" in the driveway, Mike (I would bet) wonders if this is really *it* for him. Or, might there not be just a smidgen more to be clutched at? Real estate, the profession of possibility, can keep such dreams fervid and winy for decades.

Haddam, therefore, makes him as nervous as a debutante. It makes plenty of people feel that way. All that serenely settled, arborial, inward-gazing good life, never confiding about what it knows (property values), so near and yet so far off. All that pretty possibility set apart from the regular social frown and growl. Haddam's rare rich scent is sweetly breathable to him—as we drive past out here on 206—there behind its revetment of Revolutionary oaks and survivor elms, from its lanes and cul-de-sacs, its wood ricks, its leaf rakage, its musing, insider mutter-mutter conversations passed across hedges between like-minded neighbors who barely know one another and wouldn't otherwise speak. Haddam rises in Mike's mind, a citadel he could inhabit and defend.

It's just not likely to happen. Which is fine as long as he doesn't venture too close—which he's almost done—so that his immi-grant life flashes up in grainy black and white and not quite good enough. This, of course, happens to all of us; it's just easier to accept when the whole country's already your own.

"You know, when Ann and I moved to Haddam thirty years ago, none of this was out here," I say to be encouraging as we pass a woodlot soon to be engulfed beside Montmorency Mall. COMMERCIAL SPACE FOR SALE is advertised. "Not even a deer-crossing sign." I smile at him, but he frowns out ahead, his seat pressed close-up to the wheel, his mind in another place, across a gulf from me. "If you lived here then, you wouldn't be home now."

"Ummm," Mike grunts. "I can see that, yes." My attempt doesn't work, and we are for a time sunk in reverential silence.

A MILE INTO Montmorency County, 206 drops into a pleasant jungly sweet-gum and red-clay creek bottom no one's quite figured how to bulldoze yet, and the old road briefly takes on a memorial, country-highway feel. Though we quickly rise again into the village of Belle Fleur, old-style Jersey, with a tall white Presbyterian steeple beside a sovereign little fenced cemetery, and just beyond that, a Seventies-vintage strip development, with two pizza shops, a laundrette, a closed Squire Tux and an H&R Block—and across on the facing side of the road two deserted, dusty-screened redbrick Depression houses (homes to humans

once) from when 206 was a scenic rural pike as innocent and pristine as any back road in Kentucky. Another double-size wooden
sign with big red lettering spells an end to the houses: OWNER
WILL SELL, REMOVE OR TRADE. It's a perfect site for a Jiffy Lube.

Mike takes a left past the church and commences west. And
right away the atmosphere changes, and for the better. Somewhere out ahead of us lies the Delaware, and all can feel the relief.
Though Mike's now consulting his watch and a scribbled-on
pink Post-it while the road (Mullica Road) leaves the strip development for the peaceable town 'n country housing pattern New
Jersey is famous for: deep two-acre lots with curbless frontage,
on which are sited large but not ominous builder-design Capes,
prairie contemporaries and Dutch-door ranches, with now and
then an original eighteenth-century stone farmhouse spruced up
with copper gutters and an attached greenhouse to look new.
Yews, bantam cedars and mountain laurels that were scrubby in
the Seventies are still young-appearing. The earth is flat out here,
poorly drained and clayey. Plus, it's dry as Khartoum. Still, a few
maples and red oaks have matured, and paint jobs look fresh.
Kids' plastic gym sets and chain-link dog runs clutter many back
lawns. Subarus and Horizons stand in new asphalt side drives (the
garages jammed with out-of-date junk). Everything's exactly as
they pictured it when it was all a dream.

Passing on the left now, opposite the houses, lies a perfect,
well-tended cut cornfield extending prettily down to Mullica
Creek, remnant of uses that predate memory but a plus to home
buyers prizing atmosphere. Though you can be sure its pristine
prettiness is giving current owners across the road restless nights
for fear some enterpriser (such as the one driving my car) will
one day happen along, stop for a look-see, make a cell-phone
call and in six months throw up a hundred minimansions that'll
kick shit out of everybody's tax bills, fill the roads, jam the
schools with new students who score eight million on their math
and verbal, who steal the old residents' kids' places at Brown,
and whose families won't speak to anybody because for religious
reasons they don't have to. Town 'n country takes a hike.

Every morning, these original settlers who bought in at 85K—
on what was Mullica Farm Road—frown down at their mutual-
fund numbers, retotal their taxes against retirement investitures
and wonder if now might be the time to roll over their 401s,

move to the Lehigh Valley and try consulting before beating it to Phoenix at age sixty-two. Median house prices out here are at 450K, the fastest market in the land—last year. Only, that's not holding. One or two neighbors already have BY OWNER signs up, which is worrisome. Though to me it's all as natural as pond succession, and no one should regret it. I like the view of landscape in use.

Small, dark-skinned yard personnel with backpack blower units that make them look like spacemen are busy in many yards here, whooshing oceans of late-autumn leaves and heaping them in piles beside great black plastic bags, before hauling them away in their beater trucks. The cold sky has gone cerulean and untroubled (weather being what passes for drama in the suburbs). I don't miss Haddam, but I miss this—the triggering sense of emanation that a drive in what was once the country ratchets up in me. And today especially, since I'm not risking or pitching anything, am off duty and only along for moral support.

"Is Michigan in Lansing or Ann Arbor?" Mike says, blinking expectantly, hands again in the prescribed steering positions. We are nearing our rendezvous and he's on the alert.

He knows I bleed Michigan blue but doesn't really know what that means. "Why?"

"I guess there're some pretty interesting things going on at Michigan State right now." He is speaking officially. Practicing at being authentic.

"Did they discover a featherless turkey in time for Thanksgiving?" I say. "That's what they're good at over there."

A man stands alone on the wide grassy lawn of a bright yellow bay-windowed Dutch contemporary where Halloween pumpkins still line the front walk. He's barefoot, wearing a white tae kwon do suit and is performing stylized Oriental exercises—one leg rising like a mantis while his arms work in an overhand swimming motion. Possibly it's a form of pre-Thanksgiving stress maintenance he's read about in an airline magazine. But something about my Suburban, its rumbling, radiant alien-ness, has made him stop, put palm to brow to shade the sun and follow us as we go past.

"In my new-product seminar last week"—Mike nods as if he's quoting Heraclitus (I, of course, pay for this)—"I saw some interesting figures about the lag between the top of the housing market and the first downturn in askings." His narrow eyes are fixed stonily ahead. I used to eat that kind of computer spurtage for breakfast, and made a bundle doing it. But since I arrived at the Shore, I'm happy to list 'em 'n twist 'em. When man stops wanting ocean-front, it'll be because they've paved the ocean. "I guess they've got a pretty good real estate institute over there," Mike blathers on about Moo-U. "Using some pretty sophisticated costing models. We might plug into their newsletter." Mike can occasionally drone like a grad student, relying on the ritual-reflexive "I guess" to get his most significant points set in concrete. ("I guess Maine's pretty far from San Diego." "I guess a hurricane really whips the wind up." "I guess it gets dark around here once the sun sets.")

"Did you read any reports from Kalamazoo College?"

Mike frowns over at me. He doesn't know what Kalamazoo means, or why it would be side-splittingly hilarious. His round, bespectacled, over-serious face forms a suspicious tight-lipped question mark. Sense of humor can become excess baggage for immigrants, and in any case, Mike's not always great company for extended periods.

Ahead on the left rises an ancient white concrete silo standing in the cornfield, backed by third-growth hardwood through which midday light is flashing. A weathered roadside vegetable stand, years abandoned, sits at the road shoulder, and alongside it a pale blue Cadillac Coupe de Ville. When Ann and I arrived to Haddam blows ago, it was our standard Saturday outing to drive these very county roads, taking in the then-untouched countryside up to Hunterdon County and the river towns, stopping at a country store where they cooked a ham and eggs breakfast in the back, buying a set of andirons or a wicker chair, then pulling over for squash and turnips and slab-sided tomatoes in a place just like this, taking it all home in brown paper sacks. It was long before this became a wealth belt.

I'm thinking this old roadside stall may actually have been one of our regulars. MacDonald's Farm or some such place. Though it wasn't run by a real farmer, but a computer whiz from Bell Labs, who'd taken an early buyout to spend his happy days yakking with customers about the weather and the difference between rutabagas and turnips.

This dilapidated vegetable stand is also clearly our rendezvous

point. Mike, pink Post-it in his fist, swerves us inexpertly straight
across the oncoming lane and rumbles into the little dirt turnout. The Caddy's driver-door immediately swings open, and
a large man begins climbing out. He is a square-jawed, thick-
armed, tanned and taut Mediterranean, wearing clean and
pressed khakis, a white oxford shirt (sleeves rolled Paul Bunyan-
style), sturdy work boots and a braided belt with a silver tape
measure cube riding his hip like a snub-nose. He looks like he
just stepped out of the Sears catalog and is already smiling like
the best, most handsome guy in the world to go into the sprawl
business with. His Caddy has a volunteer fire department tag on
its bumper.

My gut, however, instantly says this is a man to be cautious
of—the too neatly rolled sleeves are the giveaway—a man who
is more or less, but decidedly not, what he seems. My gut also
tells me Mike will fall in love with him in two seconds due to his
large, upright, manly American-ness. If I don't watch out, the
deal'll be done.

"What's this guy's name again?" I've heard it but don't
remember. We're climbing out. The big Caddy guy's already
standing out in the dusty breeze, laving his big hands as if he'd
just washed them in the car. Outside here, the wind's colder than
at the Shore. The barometer's falling. Clouds are fattening to the
west. I have on only my tan barracuda jacket, which isn't warm
enough. Money says this guy's Italian, though he's all spruced
up and could be Greek, which wouldn't be better.

"Tom Benivalle." Mike frowns, grabbing his blazer from the
backseat.

I rest my case.

"Mr. Mahoney?" the big guy announces in a loud voice.
"Tom Benivalle, gladda meetcha." Gruff, let's-cut-the-bullshit
Texas Hill Country drawl resonates in his voice. He's seemingly
not disturbed that a tiny forty-three-year-old Tibetan dressed
like a Mafia golfer and with an Irish name might be his new
partner.

Though it's all an act. Benivalle is a storied central New Jersey
name with much colorful Haddam history in tow. A certain Eug-
ene (Gino) Benivalle, doubtless an uncle, was for a time Haddam
police chief before opting for early retirement to Siesta Key, just
ahead of a trip to Trenton on a statutory rape charge brought by

his fourteen-year-old niece. Tommy, clean-cut, helmet-haired, big schnoz, tiny-dark-eyed good groomer, looks like nothing as much as a cop, up to and including a gold-stud earring. This could be a sting operation. But to catch who?

Mike thrusts himself forward, his face flushed, and gives Benivalle a squinch-eyed, teeth-bared, apologetic grin, along with a double-hander handshake I've counseled him against, since Jerseyites typically grow wary at free-floating goodwill, especially from foreigners who might be Japanese. Though Mike isn't having it. He reluctantly introduces me as his "friend" while buttoning his blazer buttons. We've agreed to keep my part in this hazy, though I already sense he wishes I'd leave. Tom Benivalle enfolds my hand in his big hairy-backed one. His palm's as soft as a puppy's belly, and he transmits an amiable sweet minty smell I recognize as spearmint. He's applied something lacquerish to his forehead-bordering hair that makes it practically sparkle. The prospect that Benivalle might represent shadowy upstate connections isn't unthinkable. But face-to-face with him, my guess is not. My guess is Montclair State, marketing B.A., a tour with Uncle Sam, then home to work for the old man in the wholesale nursery bidnus in West Amwell. Married, then kids, then out on his own, tearing up turf and looking around for new business opportunities. He's probably forty, drives his Caddy to mass, drinks a little Amarone and a little schnapps, plays racquetball, pumps minor iron, puts out the odd chimney fire and voted for Bush but wouldn't actually hurt a centipede. Which is no reason to go into business with him.

Benivalle turns from our handshake and strides off as a gust of November breeze raises grit off Mullica Road and peppers my neck. He's cutting to the chase, heading to the edge of the cornfield to showcase the acreage, demonstrate he's done his homework, before sketching out the business plan. Put the small talk on hold. It's how I'd do it.

Mike and I follow like goslings—Mike flashing me a deviled look meant to stifle early judgment. He's *already* in love with the guy and doesn't want the deal queered. I round my eyes at him in phony surprise, which devils him more.

"Okay. Now our parcel runs straight south to Mullica Creek," Benivalle's saying in a deeper but less LBJish voice, raising a long arm and pointing out toward the silo and the pretty band of trees that follows the water's course (when there's water there). "Which *is* in the floodplain." He glances at me, heavy brows gathering over his black eyes. He knows I know he knows I know. Still, full disclosure, numbers crunched, regulations read and digested: My presence has been registered. It's possible we've met somewhere. Benivalle bites his bottom lip with his top teeth—familiar to me as the stagecraft of our current President. Sharp wind is gusting but fails to disturb a follicle of Benivalle's dense black do. "So," he goes on, "we establish our south lot lines a hundred feet back from the mean high-water mark—the previous hundred-year flood. The creek runs chiefly west to east. So we have about a hundred twenty-five available acres if we clear the woods and grade it off."

Mike is smiling wondrously.

"How many units do you get on a hundred and twenty-five?" I say this because Mike isn't going to.

Benivalle nods. Great question. "Average six thousand with a footprint of about sixty-two per." This means a living room the size of a Fifties tract home. Benivalle tucks his big thumb in under his braided belt, rears back delicately on his boot heels and continues staring toward Mullica Creek as if only in that way can he say what needs saying next. "The state's got its setback laws—you prob'ly know all that—for homes this size. You got some wiggle room on your street widths, but there's not that much you can fudge. So. I'm expecting a density of forty on three-acre lots, leaving some double lots for presale or all-cash offers. Maybe if you got a friend who's interested in building a ten-thousand-footer." A smile at the prospect of such a Taj Mahal. He is now addressing me more than Mike, whom he seems to want to treat benevolently, instead of as just some little foreign team-mascot type who can probably do a good somersault.

"How much do they cost?" Mike finally says.

"High-end, a buck-twenty per," Benivalle answers quick. He, I see, has old, smoothed-over acne craters in both cheeks. It gives him a Neville Brand stolidness, suggesting old humiliations suffered. It also gives him a Neville Brand aura of untrustworthiness that's oddly touching but isn't helped by the earring. No doubt Mrs. B. talks about his face to her girlfriends. He also has extremely regular, straight white teeth, which make him look dull.

"That's seven hundred twenty thousand," I say.

"A-bout." Benivalle laps his bottom lip over his top one and nods. "We don't see much high-end fluctuation out here, Mr. Baxter." Why not Mr. Bastard? "They see it, they buy it, or else they don't. They've all got the dough. Down in Haddam last year, they got a double-digit spike in million-dollar deals. Our problem's the same as theirs."

"What's that?"

Benivalle unaccountably smiles at the luck of it. "Inventory. Used to be it was location in this business, Frank. If I can call you that."

"You bet." I make my cheeks smile.

"Now go over to Hunterdon County and Warren, it's way different. Prices rose twenty-three, twenty-four percent here this year. Median price is four-fifty." Benivalle brusquely scratches his rucked neck like Neville Brand would, and in a way that makes him look older.

"You don't own the land, do you?" Mike suddenly says, forgetting that he's supposed to help buy it. He's been in a swoon since his two-hander was reciprocated. The thought that this out-of-date farmland, this comely but useless woods, this silted, dry creek could be transformed into a flat-as-a-griddle housing tract, on which behemoth-size dwellings in promiscuous architectural permutations might sprout like a glorious city of yore and that it could all be done to his bidding and profit is almost too much for him.

"I've got an option." Benivalle nods again, as though this was news not to be bruited. "The old guy who used to operate this vegetable stand"—his big mitt motions toward the tumbledown gray-plank produce shack—"his family owns it."

"MacDonald," I suddenly realize—and say.

"Okay," Benivalle says, like a cop. "You know him? He's dead."

"I used to buy tomatoes from him twenty-five years ago."

"I used to pick those freakin' tomatoes," Benivalle says matter-of-factly. "I worked for him. Like—"

"I probably bought tomatoes from you." I can't keep from grinning. Here is a human being from my certifiable past—not all that common if you're me—who may actually have laid his honest human eyes on my dead son, Ralph Bascombe.

"Yeah, maybe," Benivalle says.

"What happened to ole MacDonald?" I'm forgetting the option, the floodplain, inventory, footprint, usable floor space. Memory rockets to that other gilded time—red mums, orange pumpkins, fat dusty tomatoes, leathery gourds, sunlight streaming through the roof cracks in the warm, rich-aired produce stand. Ralph, age five or six, would march up to the counter and somebody—Tommy Benivalle, acned, furiously masturbating high schooler and reserve on the JV wrestling squad—would look gravely down, then slip my son a root beer rock candy on condition he tell no one, since Farmer MacDonald got a "pretty penny" for them. It became Ralph's first joke. Every penny a pretty penny.

"He passed." Meaning ole MacDonald. "Like I said. A few years ago." Tom Benivalle's not at ease sharing the past with me. He brushes a speck of phantom road grit off his oxford cloth shirtsleeve. On his breast pocket there's stitched a tiny colorful pheasant bursting into flight. He buys his shirts from the same catalog I buy mine—minus the pheasant.

Silence momentarily becalms us while Benivalle refinds the skein of business talk. He is not the bad guy I thought. I could mention my son. He could say he remembered him. "He's got a daughter up in Freylinghuysen," he says about the now dead owner. "I approached her about this. She was okay."

"You must've known her when you were kids."

Mike's still staring at the acreage in his mustard blazer, dreaming conquest dreams. A whole new *it* has bumped up onto his horizon. Lavallette no longer the final *it*. He and Mrs. Mahoney might see eye-to-eye again.

"Yeah, I sorta did," Benivalle says scratchily. "He worked at Bell Labs, the old man. My dad had a decorative-pottery place up in Frenchtown. They did some business." How do I know these natives? I should've been an FBI profiler. Sometimes no surprise can be a blessing. I, however, am not the business partner here. My job is to be the spiritual Geiger counter, and see to it Benivalle understands Mr. Mahoney has serious (non-Asian) backers who know a thing or two. I'm sure I've done that by now. Thoughts of my son go sparkling away.

"I'm going to take off," I say, turning toward Mike, who's still staring away, dazzled. "I've gotta see a man about a horse."

Benivalle blinks. "So, then, are you in the horse business?" It's his first spontaneous utterance to me—besides my name—and it causes him to ravel his brow, turn the corners of his mouth up in a non-smile, touch a finger to the stud in his earlobe and let his eyes examine me.

I smile back. "It's just an expression." Mike unexpectedly turns and looks to me as if I'd spoken his name.

"I get it," Benivalle says. He's ready for me to get going, for it to be just the two of them, so he can start making his spiel to Mike about having himself certified for all that government moolah so they can start moving Urdu speakers down from Gotham and Teaneck. He may think Mike's a Pakistani. My work here is done, and fast.

MIKE AND I begin our walk back across the gusty turn-out toward my Suburban. Sweet pungence of leaf-burn swims in the air from the linked back yards across Mullica Road, where a homeowner's daydreaming against his rake, garden hose at the ready, peering into the cool flames and curling smoke, indifferent to the good-neighbor ordinances he's breaching, woolgathering over how *things* should most properly *be*, and how they once *had been* when something he can't exactly remember was the rule of the day and he was young. It could all be put back into working order, he knows, if the Democrats could be kept from boosting the goddamned fucking election that he, because he was on a business trip to Dayton and had jury duty in Pennington the second he got home, somehow forgot to vote in. "Whatever It Takes" should be the battle hymn of the republic.

"So, I'll see you later," Mike says, nose in the breeze as we come to my parked vehicle. He's feeling tip-top about everything now, even though seeming eager is incautious.

"I'll be at the August," I say. Benivalle has already headed toward his Caddy. He has no inclination for good-byes with strangers. "Gladda meetcha," I shout to him in the stiff wind, but he's already mashing a little cell phone to his ear and can't hear me. "Yeah. I'm out here at the parcel," I hear him say. "It's all great."

"What do you think?" Mike says barely under his breath. His flat freckled nose has gone pale in the cold, his small pupils shining with hope for a thumbs-up. His spiffy business outfit—expensive shoes and blazer—makes him seem helpless. His lapel, I see, sports a tiny American flag in the buttonhole. A new addition.

"You just better be careful." My fingers are on the cold door handle.

Mike hands me the keys he's removed. "No choices are ever absolutely right," he says and frowns, trying to be confident.

"Plenty are absolutely crazy, though. This isn't Buddhism, it's business."

"Oh, yes! I know!" He consults the sky again. A front, maybe cold New Jersey rain, true harbinger of winter, is coming in now. I'm colder already, my hands frozen. My barracuda jacket is water-resistant, not waterproof. "Just don't let him talk you into signing anything." I'm climbing stiffly into the driver's side, where the seat's too far forward. "If you don't sign, they can't put you in prison."

Prison scares the crap out of him. Our bold, new-concept American lockups are the stuff of his nightmares, having seen too many documentaries on the Discovery Channel and knowing what happens on the inside to gentle souls like him.

"We'll talk about it tonight," I say out my window, which I'd like to close.

"You think belief's a luxury, I know." Breeze flaps his trouser legs. He's fidgeting with his gold pinkie ring without seeking my eye. Benivalle starts up his Coupe de Ville with a noisy screech of fan-belt slippage.

"I guess if you think it is, it is," I say, getting the seat resituated and not entirely sure what I mean by that.

"You talk like a Buddhist." He actually giggles, then narrows his little lightless eyes and hugs his blazered shoulders in the cold.

Anyone, of course, can talk *like* a Buddhist. You just turn every cornpone Will Rogers cliché on its ear and pretend it's Spinoza. It wouldn't be hard to be a Buddhist. What's hard is to be a realist. "Buddhism-schmuddhism," I say.

Mike enjoys coarse American talk for the same reason he enjoys random cursing—because it's meaningless. You can't insult the Buddha, only yourself for trying. "So, we can talk later?" He looks down at his big fake Rolex, as if time was what mattered now.

"We'll talk later, yep." My window's going up. He's retreating. Possibly the wind's chasing him, because he begins half-skipping, half-running/shuffling, everything but a cartwheel toward the waiting blue Cadillac. For a man of his size, race, age, religion and manner of fussy dress, he is a funny spectacle—though spirited, which can take you a far distance.

As I pull away, I take a departing look at the cornfield stretching down to Mullica Creek, its gentle fall and charming hardwood copse, soon to be overwhelmed by grumbling, chuffing, knife-bladed Komatsus and Kubotas, cluttered with corrugated culverts, rebar and pre-cut king posts, ready-mixers lined up to 206, every inch flattened and staked with little red flags prophesying megahouses waiting on the drawing boards. The neighbor across the road, watching his dreams go up in smoke, has his point: Someone should draw the line somewhere.

I say silent adieu to the ground my son trod and will no more. The old lay of the land. E-eye, E-eye, OOOOOOO.

CHAPTER 2

DRIVING THE scenic route back to Haddam—Preventorium
Road to the rock quarry (where certified mafiosi once dumped
their evidence), past the SPCA and the curvy maple-lined lane
along the mossy old Delaware Canal, past the estate where retired
priests snooze away days in tranquilized serenity and hopeful
non-reflection—I'm for an instant struck: What would real
scientists, decades on, say about us here on our own patch of
suburban real estate?

I knew a boy back at Michigan, Tom Laboutalliere, who dedicated his whole life to "reading" little birds-feet scratch marks
on ossified clods of ancient tan-colored mud and possibly turds.
From such evidence, he conjured what the ancient Garbonzians
were doing back in 1000 B.C. in *their* little square of earth. By
studying cubic tons of dirt—his field data—what he got his hands
on and sifted through screens were the Garbonzians' precious
laundry receipts. The little birds-feet tracks were actually their
writings, which made it unassailable, using infrared spectroscopy
and carbon dating, that a mighty lot of army uniforms had
needed repair and entrail despotting and caustic herbal soaks
between about 1006 and 1005. So that he concluded (everyone
was amazed) that a considerable amount of nonstop pulverizing,
disemboweling and tearing limb from limb had gone on during
that period, and—his great, tenurable discovery—that's why we
now think of those long-ago, far-distant folk as "warlike."

None of us should suppose that this type of years-on digging
won't winkle out our own naked truths. Because it will. Which
merits some consideration.

Most evidence, of course, will just be the stuff Mike and
I cruised past on Route 37 this morning, strewn along the road
shoulder, in the pine duff and dusty turn-outs. This civilization,
future thinkers will conclude, liked beer. They favored wood-
paper products as receptacles for semen and other bodily excre-
tions. They suffered hemorrhoids, occasional incontinence and

erectile dysfunctions not known to subsequent generations. They thought much about their bowel movements. Sex was an activity they isolated as much as possible from daily life. They disliked extraneous metal things. They were faltering in their resolve about permanence vis-à-vis possibility and change, as evidenced by their shelters being in good condition but frequently abandoned, with others seemingly meant to last only five years or less. I'm not certain what the signs about paint-ball wars will teach them, or, for that matter, Toms River itself, should it last another year. Fort Dix they'll understand perfectly.

But future delvers will also think—and Mike's and Tom Benivalle's plans lie in my brain like a piece of heavy driftwood—how much we all lived with, banked and thrived on, got made happy or sad by what was *already there*! And how little we ourselves *invented*! And by how little we *had* to invent, since you could get anything you wanted—from old records to young boys—just by giving a number and an expiration date to an electronic voice, then sitting back and waiting for the friendly brown truck. Our inventions, it'll be clear, were only to say yes or no, like flipping off a light switch or flipping it on. Future scholars might also conclude that if we ever did think of trying something different—living in the Allagash and eating only tubers; becoming a mystic, taking a vow of poverty and begging on the roadside in Taliganga; if we considered having six wives, never cutting our hair or bathing and holing up in an armed compound in Utah; in other words, if we ever gave a thought to worming our way outside the box to see what was out there— we must've realized that we risked desolation and the world looking at us with menace, knew we couldn't stand that for long, and so declined.

Possibly I tend toward this glum future perspective because, like millions of other journeying souls, I've lately received *the* call—from my Haddam urologist, possibly phoning from the golf course or his Beemer, casually commenting that my PSA "values" were "still higher than *we* like to see . . . so *we'd* better get you in for a closer looky-look." That can change your view, let me tell you. Or maybe it's because I've graduated to the spiritual concision of the Permanent Period, the time of life when very little you say comes in quotes, when few contrarian voices mutter doubts in your head, when the past seems more generic than specific, when life's a destination more than a journey and when who you feel yourself to be is pretty much how people will remember you once you've croaked—in other words, when personal integration (what Dr. Erikson talked about but secretly didn't believe in) is finally achieved.

Or possibly I take the view I do just because I've been a real estate agent for fifteen years, and can see that real estate's a profession both spawned by and grown cozy with our present and very odd state of human development. In other words, I'm implicated: You have a wish? Wait. I'll make it come true (or at least show you my inventory). If you're a Bengali ophthalmologist with your degree from Upstate and have no desire to return to Calcutta to "give back," and prefer instead to expand life, open doors, let the sun in—well, all you have to do is travel down Mullica Road, let your wishes be known to a big strapping guinea home builder and his smiling, nodding, truth-dispensing, dusky-skinned sidekick, and you and civilization will be on the same page in no time. They'll even name your street after your daughter—which those same scientists can later puzzle over.

Up to now I've thought this basic formula was a good thing. But lately I'm less sure I'm right—at least as right as I used to be. I can take the matter up with Mike in the car later, when home's in sight.

MIKE'S HANDOFF to Benivalle has taken less time than expected, and it's only noon when I merge onto westbound Brunswick Pike, the corner where once stood a big ShopRite when I lived nearby but which now contains a great silver and glass Lexus palace with wall-to-wall vehicles and a helipad X for buyers on the go, and across from it a giant Natur-Food pavilion where formerly stood a Magyar Bank. If I shake a leg and don't attract a speeding ticket, I can make the funeral home before they begin shooing mourners out to ready Ernie McAuliffe's casket for its last ride.

The Haddam cemetery—which I intend to avoid—lies directly behind where I once resided at 19 Hoving Road, and is the resting place of my aforementioned son Ralph, who died of Reye's at age nine and would be almost thirty now. He "rests" there behind the wrought-iron fence among the damp oaks and ginkgoes, alongside three signers of the Declaration, two innovators of manned flight and innumerable New Jersey governors. I don't go there anymore, as the saying has it. I've learned by trial and much error to accept that Ralph is not coming back to his mother and me. Though every time I venture near the cemetery, I dreamily imagine he still might—which I deem to be a not-good thought pattern, and to violate the Permanent Period's rule of the road about the past. Mike has told me the Dalai Lama contends that young people who die are our masters who teach us impermanence, and I've tried to think of things this way.

In truth, it's no longer even physically possible to cruise past my old Hoving Road house—a sweet, sagging, old Tudor half-timber on a well-treed lot, which I sold to the Theological Institute in the Eighties, and who then transformed it into an ecumenical victims' rights center. (Land-mine victims, children-soldier victims, African-circumcision victims, families of strangled cheerleaders, all became regular sights on the sidewalkless street.) However, due to fierce Nineties property-value wars, my former residence was demo'd the instant the Korean Fresh Lighters took over, and the ground sold for a fortune. Efforts were made to recycle the old pile using chain saws and flatbed trucks. Some ecumenicists wanted it hauled to Hightstown and rechartered as a hospice, whereas others wanted it moved to Washington's Crossing and turned into an organic restaurant. For a week, the neighborhood association, fearing the worst, stood a vigil and actually erected a human chain against the recycling people. But without notice, one night the Koreans dispatched a jumpsuited wrecking crew, trucked in dismantling equipment, trained two big klieg lights on the house, lighting up the neighborhood like an invasion from space. And by seven in the morning all four walls—within which I'd started a family, experienced joy, suffered great sadness, became lost to dreaminess, but through it all slept many nights as peaceful as a saint under the sheltering beeches and basswoods—were gone.

Legal remedies were sought—to enjoin something, punish someone. The neighborhood has many lawyers. But the Koreans instantly cashed in the lot for two million to a thoroughbred breeder from Kentucky with big GOP connections. In a year, he'd put up a lot-line to lot-line three-quarter-size replica of his white plantation-style mansion in Lexington, complete with fluted acacia-leaf columns, mature live oaks from Florida, an electric fence, mean guard dogs, a rebel flag on the flagpole and two Negro jockey statues painted his stable colors, green and black. "Not Furlong" is what he called the place, though the neighbors have found other names for it. All problems were deemed my fault for selling out originally back in '85. So mine is not a popular face around there now, though many of my old neighbors have also moved on.

BRUNSWICK PIKE glides me in through Rocky Ridge, back into Haddam Township, and becomes Seminary Street along the banks of the widened stream referred to by locals as Lake Bimble, for the German farmer who owned the river bank and, as a Tory in the Revolution, gave aid and comfort to Colonel Mawhood's troops, and who for his trouble got bound to a sack of ballast rocks and tossed in the stream—Quaker Creek—by General Washington's men, there to stay.

Since I lived here for twenty years, I know what to expect farther in on Seminary two days before Thanksgiving. A melee. People stocking up and leaving for Vermont and Maine, the cozy Thanksgiving states; others arriving for family at-homes, students back from Boulder and Reed, divorcées visiting children, children visiting divorcées—the customary midday automotive hector brought about by a town become a kind of love-it/hate-it paragon of suburban amplitude gone beyond self-congratulation to the point of entropy. (Greenwich minus the beach, times three.)

Plus, there's the further complication of the town fathers' decision to mount a Battle of Haddam re-enactment right in town. I read this in the Haddam *Packet*, which I still receive in Sea-Clift. Uniformed Redcoats and tattered Continentals in home-spun, carrying period musketry, eating homemade hardtack and wearing tricorn hats, jerkins and knee pants, their hair in pigtails, will be setting up drill fields, redoubts and headquarters all around the Boro, staging assaults and retreats, bivouacs and drumhead courts-martial, digging latrines and erecting tenting at the sites where these occurrences actually occurred back in 1780—though the current sites may now be Frenchy's Gulf, Benetton or Hulbert's Classic Shoes. This was done once before, for the bicentennial, and it's all happening again for the Millennium in an effort to rev up sidewalk appeal. Though some merchants—I heard this at the bank last week—are already sensing retail disaster, and have retained counsel and are computing lost revenue as damages. This includes the bank itself.

The other distraction making movement into the Square near-impossible is that the Historical Society, in a fit of Thanksgiving spirit and under the rubric of "Sharing Our Village Past," has converted the entire Square in front of the August Inn and the Post Office into a Pilgrim Village Interpretive Center. Two Am. Civ. professors from Trenton State with time on their hands have constructed a replica Pilgrim town with three windowless, dirt-floor Pilgrim houses, trucked-in period barnyard animals, and lots of authentic but unhandy Pilgrim implements, built a hand-adzed paled fence, laid in a subsistence garden and produced old-timey clothes and authentically inadequate footwear for the Pilgrims themselves. Inside the village they've installed a collection of young Pilgrims—a Negro Pilgrim, a Jewish female Pilgrim, a wheelchair-bound Pilgrim, a Japanese Pilgrim with a learning disability, plus two or three ordinary white kids—all of whom spend their days doing toilsome Pilgrim chores in drab, ill-fitting garments, chattering to themselves about rock videos while they hew logs, boil clothes, rip up sod, make soap in iron caldrons and spin more coarse cloth, but now and then pausing to step forth, just like soap-opera characters on Christmas Day, to deliver loud declarations about "the first hard days of 1620" and how it's impossible to imagine the character and dedication of the first people and how our American stock was cured by tough times, blab, blab, blab, blab—all this to whoever might be idle enough to stop on the way to the liquor store to listen. Every night the young Pilgrims disappear to a motel out on Route 1, fill their bellies with pizza and smoke dope till their heads explode, and who'd blame them?

Merchants on the Square—the Old Irishman's Kilt, Rizzuto's Spirits, Sherm's Tobacconist—have taken a more tolerant view of the Pilgrim shenanigans than they have of the battle re-enactors, who whoop and carry weapons, and stay out at the actual battlefield in Winnebagos and bring their own food and beer and never buy anything in town. The Pilgrims, on the other hand—which is probably how they were always viewed—

are seen as a kind of peculiar but potentially attractive business nuisance. It's hoped that passing citizens who pause to hear the overweight paraplegic girl give her canned speech about piss-poor medical facilities in seventeenth-century New Jersey, and how someone in her state of body wouldn't have lasted a week-end, will then be moved by an urge to buy a Donegal plaid vest or a box of toffees or Macanudos or half a case of Johnnie Walker Red.

There's even talk that a group representing the Lenape Band—New Jersey's own redskins, who believe *they* own Haddam and always have—is setting up to picket the Pilgrims on Thursday, wearing their own period outfits and carrying placards that say THANKS FOR NOTHING and THE TERRIBLE LIE OF THANKS-GIVING and stirring up a bad-for-business backlash. There's like-wise a rumor that a group of re-enactors will go AWOL, march to the Pilgrims' defense and re-enact a tidy massacre on the front steps of the Post Office. This is all probably skywriting by the boys at United Jersey and represents less truth than their wish that something out of the ordinary could happen so they can quit boring themselves to death approving mortgage after mortgage.

What it all comes down to, though, as with so many vital life issues and blood-boiling causes, is traffic and more traffic. An ambulance carrying our President and Pope John Paul couldn't make it the two blocks from the Recovery Room Bar to Caviar 'n Cashmere in less than three-quarters of an hour, by which time both these tarnished exemplars would be out on the street walking.

LONG MANORIAL lawns sweep down to the north side of Brunswick Pike, facing the lake, with heavy hemlock growth and rhododendron splurge giving the white, set-back, old-money mansions their modesty protection. In my years selling houses here, I sold three of these goliaths, two twice, once to a famous novelist. Still, I take my first chance to turn off, to avoid the town traffic, and pass along onto bosky, stable, compromise-with-dignity Gulick Road—winding streets, mature plantings, above-ground electric, architect-design "family rooms" retro-fitted onto older reasonable-sized Capes and ranches a year beyond their paint jobs. (I sold twenty of these.) Yukons and

Grand Cherokees sit in driveways. Older tree houses perch in many oaks and maples. New mullions have been added to old Seventies picture windows and underground sprinklers laid in. It's the suburban Sixties *grown out*, with many original owner-pioneers holding fast to the land and happy to be, their "new development" now become solidly *in-town*, with all the old rawness ironed out. It's now a "neighborhood," where your old Chesapeake, Tex, can take his nap in the street without being rumbled over by the bottled-water truck, where once-young families have become older but don't give a shit, and where fiscal year to fiscal year everybody's equity squeezes up as their political musings drift to the right (though it feels like the middle). It's the height of what's possible from modest beginnings, and as near to perfection as random settlement patterns and anxiety for permanence can hope for. It's where I'd buy in if I moved back—which I won't.

Though passing down these quiet, reserved streets—not splashy but good—I sometimes think I might've left for the Shore and Sea-Clift a bit too soon in 1992, since I missed the really big paydays (I still made a pot full). But by then I had an unusual son in my care, clinging precariously to his hold on Haddam High. (He actually graduated and left for college at Ball State—his odd choice.) I had a girlfriend, Sally Caldwell, who was giving me the old "now or never." I was forty-seven. And I was experiencing the early, uneasy symptoms—it pretty quickly got better—of the Permanent Period of life. I couldn't have told you what that was, only that after Paul left for Muncie, I began to feel a sort of clanking, mechanistic, solemn sameness about flogging these very houses, whereas earlier in my realty life I'd felt involved in, even morally committed to, getting people into the homes they (and the economy) wanted themselves to be in (at least for a while). Though what had always accompanied my long state of real estate boosterism was a sensation I've described in differing ways using differing tropes, but which all speak to the dulling complexity of the human organism. One such sensation was of constantly feeling *off-shore*, a low-level, slightly removed-from-events, wooing-wind agitation that doing for others, in the frank, plain-talk way I was able to as a house seller, generally assuaged but never completely stilled. *Experiencing the need for an extra beat* was another of my figures. This I'd felt since military school in Mississippi—as if life and its directives were never quite all they should be, and, in fact, should've meant more. Regular life always felt like an unfinished flamenco needing, either from me or a source outside me, a completing beat, after which tranquillity could reign. Women almost always did the trick pretty neatly—at least till the whole thing started up again.

There were other such expressions—some warriorlike, some sports-related, some hilarious, some fairly embarrassing. But they pointed to the same wearying instinct for *becoming*, of which realty is an obvious standard-bearer profession. I really did fantasize that if Clinton could just win the White House in '92, then a renaissance spirit would open like a new sun, whereby through a mysterious but ineluctable wisdom I would be named ambassador to France—or at least the Ivory Coast. That and a lot more didn't happen.

Only, neuron by neuron, over a period of months (this was nearing the middle of the doomed and clownish Bush presidency) I realized I was feeling different about things. I remember sitting at my desk at my former employer, the Haddam realty firm of Lauren-Schwindell, tracking down some computerized post-sale notes I'd made on a house on King George Road that had come back on the market six months later, sporting a 30 percent increase in asking, and overhearing a colleague three cubicles away saying, just loud enough for me to take an interest, "Oh, that was Mr. Bascombe. I'm sure he would never do or say that." I never found out what she was talking about or to whom. She normally didn't speak to me. But I went off to sleep that night thinking of those words—"Mr. Bascombe would never..."— and woke up the next morning thinking them some more. Because it occurred to me that even though my colleague (a former history professor who'd reached the end of her patience with the Compromise of 1850) could say what Mr. Bascombe would never do, say, drive, eat, wear, laugh about, marry or think was sad, Mr. Bascombe himself wasn't sure *he* could. She could've said damn near anything about me and I would've had to give the possibility some thought—which is why I'd never take a lie-detector test; not because I lie, but because I concede too much to be possible.

But very little about me, I realized—except what I'd *already* done, said, eaten, etc.—seemed written in stone, and all of that meant almost nothing about what I *might* do. I had my history, okay, but not really much of a regular character, at least not an inner essence I or anyone could use as a predictor. And something, I felt, needed to be done about that. I needed to go out and find myself a recognizable and persuasive semblance of a character. I mean, isn't that the most cherished pre-posthumous dream of all? The news of our premature demise catching everyone so unprepared that beautiful women have to leave fancy dinner parties to be alone for a while, their poor husbands looking around confused; grown men find they can't finish their after-lunch remarks at the Founders Club because they're so moved. Children wake up sobbing. Dogs howl, hounds begin to bark. All because something essential and ineffable has been erased, and the world knows it and can't be consoled.

But given how I was conducting life—staying offshore, waiting for the extra beat—I realized I could die and no one would remember me for anything. "Oh, that guy. Frank, uh. Yeah. Hmm . . ." That was me.

And not that I wanted to blaze my initials forever into history's oak. I just wanted that when I was no more, someone could say my name (my children? my ex-wife?) and someone else could then say, "Right. That Bascombe, he was always damn *blank*." Or "Ole Frank, he really liked to *blank*." Or, worst case, "Jesus Christ, that Bascombe, I'm glad to see the end of his sorry *blank*." These blanks would all be human traits I knew about and others did too, and that I got credit for, even if they weren't heroic or particularly essential.

Another way of saying this (and there're too many ways to say everything) is that some force in my life was bringing me hard up against what felt like my *self* (after a lengthy absence), presenting me, if I chose to accept it, with an imperative that all my choices in recent memory—volitions, discretions, extra beats, time spent offshore—hadn't presented me, though I might've said they had and argued you to the dirt about it. Here, for a man with no calculable character, was a hunger for *necessity*, for something solid, the thing "character" stands in for. This hunger could, of course, just as easily result from a recognition that you'd never done one damn substantial thing in your life, good or otherwise, and never would, and if you did, it wouldn't matter a mouse fart—a recognition that could leave you in the dol-drums' own doldrum, i.e., despair that knows it's despair.

Except, I'll tell you, this period—1990–92—was the most exhilarating of my life, the likes of which I'd felt once, possibly twice, but not more and was reconciled perhaps never to feel again, just glad to have had it when I did, but whose cause I couldn't really tell you.

What it portended—and this is the truest signature of the Permanent Period, which comes, by the way, when it comes and not at any signifying age, and not as a climacteric, not when you expect it, not when your ducks are in a row (as mine back in 1990 were not)—it portended an end to perpetual becoming, to thinking that life schemed wonderful changes for me, even if it didn't. It portended a blunt break with the past and provided a license to think of the past only indistinctly (who wouldn't pay plenty for that?). It portended that younger citizens might come up to me in wonderment and say, "How in the world do you live? How do you do it in this uncharted time of life?" It portended that I say to myself and mean it, even if I thought I said it every day and already really meant it: "This is how in the shit I *am*! My life is *this* way"—recognizing, as I did, what an embarrassment and a disaster it would be if, once you were dust, the world and yourself were in basic disagreement on this subject.

Following which I set about deciding how I should put the next five to ten years to better use than the last five—progress being the ancients' benchmark for character. I'd by then started to worry that Haddam might be *it* for me—just like Mike sweats it about Lavallette—which frankly scared the wits out of me. As a result, I immediately resigned my job at Lauren-Schwindell. I put my house on Cleveland Street on the rental market. I pro-posed marriage to Sally Caldwell, who couldn't have been more surprised, though she didn't say no (at least not till recently). I cashed in the Baby Bells I'd been adding to since the breakup. I made inquiries about possibilities for real estate at the Shore and was able to buy Realty-Wise from its owner, who was retiring to managed care. I made an unrejectable offer on a big tall-windowed redwood house facing the ocean in Sea-Cliff (the second-home boom hadn't arrived there yet). Sally sold her Stick Style beach house in East Mantoloking. And on June 1, 1992, with Clinton nearing the White House and the world seeming more possible than ever, I drove Sally to Atlantic City and in a comical ceremony in the Best Little Marriage Chapel in New Jersey, a pink, white, and blue Heidi chalet on Baltic Avenue, we tied the knot—acted on necessity, opted for the substantial in one simple act. We ended up saying good-bye to the day, my second wedding day and Sally's, too, and the first full day of the Permanent Period, eating fried clams and sipping Rusty Nails at a seaside fish joint, giggling and planning the extraordinary future we were going to enjoy.

Which we did. Until I came down with a case of cancer shortly after Sally's first husband came back from the dead, where he'd been in safekeeping for decades. Following which everything got all fucked up shit, as my daughter, Clarissa, used to say, and the Permanent Period was put to its sternest test by different necessities, though up to now it's proved durable.

MANGUM & GAYDEN Funeral Home, on one-block, oak-lined Willow Street, is a big yellow-and-brown-shingled Victorian, with a full-gingerbread porch above a bank of vociferous yews, with dense pachysandra encircling a large, appropriately-weeping front-yard willow and a thick St. Augustine carpet out to the sidewalk. For all the world, M&G looks like a big congenial welcoming-family abode where people live and play and are contented, instead of a funeral parlor where the inhabitants are dead as mallets and you feel a chill the instant you walk in the front door. What distinguishes it as a mortuarial establishment and not somebody's domicile is the discreet, dim-lit MANGUM & GAYDEN—PARKING IN REAR lawn sign, a side porte-cochère that wasn't in the original house design and two or three polished black Cadillacs around back with apparently nothing to do. A recent Haddam sign ordinance forbids any use of the word *funeral*, though Lloyd Mangum got his grandfathered. But nobody flying over at ten thousand feet would ever look down and say, "There's a funeral home," since it's nestled into a row of similar-vintage living-human residences that list for a fortune. Lloyd says his Haddam neighbors seem not to mind residing beside the newly dead, and proximity has never seemed to put the brakes on resale. Most new buyers must feel a funeral home is better than a house full of attention-deficit teens learning the snare drum. And Lloyd, who's a descendant of the original Mangum, tells me that mourners routinely stop by for a visitation with Aunt Gracie, then throw down a huge cash as-is offer for building and grounds before they're out the door. Lloyd and family, in fact, live upstairs.

I park a ways down Willow and walk up. The new weather announced in the skies over Mullica Road is quickly arriving. Metallic rain smell permeates the air, and clouds back over Pennsylvania have bruised up green and gray for a season-changing blow. In an hour it could be snowing—a sorry day for a funeral, though when's a good day?

Outside on the bottom front step, having a smoke, are Lloyd and another man known to me, both friends of the deceased and possibly the only other mourners. Ernie McAuliffe, to be honest, took his good sweet time departing this earth. Everybody who cared about him got to say they did three times over, then say it again. His wife, Deb, had long ago moved back to Indiana, and his only son, Bruno, a merchant mariner, came, said his brief strangled good-bye, then beat it. Ernie himself took charge of all funerary issues, including terminal care out at Delaware-Vue Acres in Titusville, and set out notarized instructions about who, what and when to do this, that and the other—no flowers, no grave-side folderol, no funeral, really, just boxed up and buried, the way we'd all probably like it. He even made arrangements with an unnamed care-giver to ease him out when it all got pointless.

I am, I realize, violating Ernie's wishes by being here. But his obit was in the *Packet* on Saturday, and I was coming over with Mike anyway. Why do we do things? For ourselves, mostly. Ernie, though, was a grand fellow, and I'm sorry he's no more. *Memento mori* in a sere season.

Ernie was, in fact, the best of fellows, someone anybody'd be happy to sit beside at a bar, a wounded Viet vet who still wore his dog tags but didn't let any of that bring him low or fill him with self-importance. He'd seen some ugly stuff and maybe did a bit of it himself. Though you wouldn't know it. He talked about his exploits, about that war and his fellow troopers and the politicians who ran it, the way you'd describe how things had gone when your high school football squad went 11–0 but lost the state championship to a scrappy but inferior team of small-fry opponents.

Ernie was brought up on a dairy farm near La Porte, Indiana, and went to a state school out there. When he left the Army minus his left leg, he went straight into the prosthetic-limb business as a supersalesman and ended up "opening" New Jersey to modern prosthetic techniques, then managing some big accounts and finally owning the whole damn company. Something about the savagery of war and all the squandered youth, he said to me, had made him feel prosthetics, rather than dairy herding, was his calling in this life, his way of leaving a mark.

Ernie, even with a space-age leg, was a great tall drink of water who walked up on the ball of his one good foot, which was barge material, wore his brown hair long and pomaded, with a prodigious side part that made him resemble a Forties Hollywood glamour boy. He also was said to possess the biggest dick anybody'd ever seen (he would sometimes show it around, though I never got to see it) and on certain occasions was given the nickname "Dillinger." He had a superlative sense of humor, could do all kinds of howling European accents and wacky loose-jointed walks and was never happier than when he was on the golf course or sitting with a towel draped over his unit, with his fake leg leaned against the wall, playing pinochle in the nineteenth hole at the Haddam Country Club. Deb was said to have gone back to Terre Haute for sexual reasons—probably so she could sleep with a normal man. Ernie, however, only spoke of her with resolute affection, as though to say, You can't know what goes on between a man and a woman unless you write the novel yourself. He never, for obvious reasons, lacked for female companionship.

Of my two fellow mourners on Mangum's front steps, the other is Bud Sloat, known behind his back as "Slippery Sloat." Both are in regulation black London Fogs, in tune to the weather. Lloyd is tall, bare-headed and solemn, though Bud's wearing a stupid Irish tweed knock-about hat and saddle oxfords that make him look sporting and only coincidentally in mourning.

Both Lloyd and Bud are members of the men's group that "stepped up" when Ernie found out he had lymphoma and started going down fast. They organized outings to the Pine

Barrens and Island Beach (close to where I live) and down to the
Tundra swan sanctuary on Delaware Bay, where they trekked the
beach (as long as Ernie was up to it), then sat around in a circle
on the sand or on the rocks and told stories about Ernie, sang
folk songs, discussed politics and literature, recited heroic poems,
said secularist prayers, told raunchy jokes and sometimes cried
like babies, all the while marveling at life's transience and at the
strange *beyond* that all of us will someday face. I went along once
in late October, before Ernie needed transfusions to keep himself
going. It was an autumn morning of pale water-color skies and
clear dense air—we were just down the beach from my house—
five of us late middle-agers in Bermudas and sweaters and tee-
shirts that said *Harrah's* and *Planned Parenthood*, plus ever-paler
one-legged "Whatcha" McAuliffe (his other nickname), looking green and limping along without much stamina or joie de
vivre. I thought it would just be a manly hike down the beach,
skimming sand dollars, letting the cold surf prickle our toes,
watching the terns and kestrels wheel and dip on the shore
breezes, and in that fashion we would re-certify life for those able
to live it.

Only at a certain point, the four others, including Lloyd and
Bud, circled round poor Ernie—stumping along on his space-
age prosthesis but still game in spite of being nearly dead—and
rapturously told him they all loved him and there was no one in
hell who was a bit like him, that life was here and now and needed
to be felt, that death was as natural as sneezing. Then to my shock,
like a band of natives toting a canoe, they actually picked Ernie
up and walked with him—peg leg and all—up on their shoulders
right into the goddamn ocean and, while cradling him in their
interlaced arms, totally immersed him while murmuring,
"Ernie, Ernie, Ernie" and chanting, "We're with you, my
brother," as if *they* had lymphoma, too, and in six weeks would
be dead as he'd be.

Once such bizarre activities get going, you can't stop them
without making everybody feel like an asshole. And maybe
calling a halt would've made Ernie feel lousier and even more
foolish for being the object of this nuttiness. One of the immersion team was an ex-Unitarian minister who'd studied anthro-
pology at Santa Cruz, and the whole horrible rigamarole was his
idea. He'd e-mailed instructions to everyone, only I don't have

e-mail (or I wouldn't have been within a hundred miles of the whole business). Ernie, however, because nobody had warned him, either, struggled to get the hell out of his captors' grip. He may have thought they were going to drown him to save him from a drearier fate. But the defrocked minister, whose name is Thor, started saying, "It's good, Ernie, let it happen, just let it happen."

Ernie's depleted blue eyes—his whites as yellow as cheap mustard—found me standing back on shore. For an instant, he gaped at me, his bony visage tricked and sad and too well loved. "What the fuck's this, Frank? What's going on?" He said this to me, but to everyone else, too. "What the fuck're you assholes doing to me?" It was at this point that they immersed him in the cold water, cradling him like a man already dead. He howled, "Ooooooowwoooo. Goddamn it's cold!"

"It's good, Ernie," Thor droned in his ear. "Just let it happen to you. Go down into it. It's *g-o-o-d*." Ernie's mouth turned down like a cartoon character's. His shoulders went limp, his head lolled, his dismayed gaze found the sky. Once they had him immersed, they touched his face, his chest, his head, his hands, his legs, I guess his ass.

"I'm dying of goddamn cancer," Ernie suddenly cried out, as if his dignity had suddenly been refound. "Cut this shit out!"

I didn't take part. Though there was a moment just as they lowered poor Ernie into the Atlantic's damp grasp (nobody stopped to think he might catch pneumonia) when he looked back at me again on the beach, his eyes helpless and resigned but also full of feeling, a moment when I realized they were doing for Ernie all the living can do, and that it was stranger that I was on the sideline and, worse yet, that Ernie knew it. You usually don't think about these things until it's too late. Even so, I'd never let anything like that happen to me, no matter how far gone I was or how beneficial it might be for somebody else.

"I MEAN, WHO let who down, for crap sake?" Bud Sloat says. "If you can't win your own goddamn home state, and the Dow's at ten forty-two, and your state's as dumb-ass as Tennessee, I'd quit. I'd just fuckin' quit."

Bud's not talking in the hushed tones appropriate to the dead-lying-inside-the-big-frosted-double-doors, but just jabbering on noisily about whatever pops into his head. The election. The economy. Bud's a trained attorney—Princeton and Harvard Law—but owns a lamp company in Haddam, Sloat's Decors, and has personally placed pricey one-of-a-kind designer lighting creations in every CEO's house in town and made a ton of money doing it. He's sixty, small, fattish and yellow-toothed, a dandruffy, burnt-faced little pirate who wears drugstore half glasses strung around his neck on a string. If he wasn't wearing his Irish knock-about hat, you could see his strawberry-blond toupé, which looks about as real on his cranium as a Rhode Island Red. Bud is a hard-core Haddam townie and would ordinarily be wearing regulation Haddam summer dress: khakis, nubble-weave blue blazer, white Izod or else a pink Brooks' button-down with a stained regimental tie, canvas belt, deck shoes and a little gold lapel pin bearing the enigmatic letters YCDBSOYA, which Bud wants everybody to ask him about. But the day's chill and solemnity have driven him back to baggy green cords, the dumbbell saddle oxfords and an orange wool turtleneck under his London Fog, so he looks like he's headed to a late-season Princeton game. He only lacks a pennant.

Bud's a blue-dog Democrat (i.e., a Republican) even though he's yammering, trying to act betrayed by fellow Harvard-bore Gore, as if he voted for him. Bud, though, absolutely voted for Bush, and if I wasn't here, he'd admit right now that he feels damn good about it—"Oh, yaas, made the practical business-man's choice." Most of my Haddam acquaintances are Repub-licans, including Lloyd, even if they started out on the other side years back. None of them wants to talk about that with me.

"How's old Mr. Prostate, Franklin?" Bud's worked up an unserious glum-mouth frown, as if everybody knows prostate cancer's a big rib tickler and we need to lighten up about it. My Mayo procedure came to light (regrettably) during our men's "sharing session" on the cold beach with Ernie in October, just before he got dunked in the ocean for his own good. We all agreed to tell a candid story, and that was the only one I had, not wanting to share the one about my wife hitting the road with her dead husband. I know Bud wants to ask me how it feels to walk down the street with hot BBs in your gearbox, but doesn't have the nerve. (For the most part it's unnoticeable—except, of course, you never don't know it.)

"I'm all locked and loaded, Bud." I stand beside them at the bottom of the steps and give Bud a mirthless line-mouth smile of no tolerance, which re-informs him I don't like him. Haddam used to be full of schmoes like Bud Sloat, yipping little Princetonians who never missed New Year's Eve at the Princeton Club, showed up for every P-rade, smoker, ball game and fund-raiser, and wore their orange-and-black porkpie hats and tiger pajamas to bed. These guys are all into genealogy and Civil War history, and like to sit around quoting Mark Twain and General Patton, and arguing that a first-rate education as prelude to a life in retail was exactly what old Witherspoon had in mind back in 17-what-ever. Bud's business card, in collegiate Old Gothic embossed with the Princeton crest and colors (I admit to admiring it), reads, *There's the Examined Life. And Then There's the Lamp Business.*

"Nothing's really happening inside now, Frank," Lloyd murmurs in his seasoned mourner's voice, cupping a smoke down by his coat pocket and letting a drag leak out his big nose. From where I stand, I can see right inside Lloyd's nostrils, where it's as dark as bituminous coal. Lloyd buried my son Ralph from out of this same house nineteen years ago, and we've always shared a sadness (something he's probably done with eight thousand people, many of whom he's also by now been called on to bury). Every time he sees me, Lloyd lays a great heavy mitt on my shoulder, lowers his bluish face near mine and in a Hollywood baritone says, "How're those kids, Frank?" As if Clarissa and Paul, my surviving children, had stayed eternally five and seven in the same way Ralph *is* eternally nine. Lloyd's as big, tall, sweet and bulky as Bud is fat, weasly and lewd—a great, potato-schnozzed, coat hanger-shouldered galoot who years ago played defensive end for the Scarlet Knights, has soulful mahogany eyes deep-set in bony blue-shaded sockets and always smells like a cigarette. It's as if Lloyd became an undertaker because one day he gazed in a mirror and noticed he looked like one. I'd be happy to be buried by Lloyd if I felt okay about being buried—which I don't. "We put Ernie in a viewing room for an hour, Frank, just in case, but we need to get him along now. You know. Not that he'd care." Lloyd nods professionally and looks down at his wide black shoe toes. A burning Old Spice cloud mingled with tobacco aroma issues from somewhere in the middle of Lloyd. I didn't intend to *view* Ernie, or even the box he's going out in.

From the side of the building, the headlights of a long black Ford Expedition glow out through the weather's gloom, ready to transfer Ernie to the boneyard, where a grave's probably already opened. Lloyd always uses SUVs for unattended interments. Without pageantry or a hushed ruffle, life's last performance becomes as matter-of-fact as returning books to the library.

"Do you know what the death woman said?" Bud Sloat's round pink face is tipped to the side, as though he's hearing music, his shrewd retailer's eyes hooded to convey self-importance.

"What woman? What's a death woman?" I say.

Lloyd exhales a disapproving grunt, shifts back in his under-taker brogans. Squeaky, squeaky.

"Well, you know, Ernie agreed to let this psychologist woman from someplace out in Oregon be present when he died. *Actually* died." Bud keeps his face cocked, as if he's telling an off-color joke. "She wanted to ask him things right up to the last second, okay? And then say his name for ten minutes to see if she could detect any efforts of Ernie wanting to come back to life." Bud frowns, then grins—his thin, purple and extremely un-kissable lips parted in distaste, indicating Ernie was indisputably not our sort (Old Nassau, etc.) and here's final proof. "Great idea, huh? Wouldn't you say?" Bud blinks, as if it's too astonishing for words.

"I guess I'd have to think about that," I say. Though not for long. This is news I don't need to hear. Though, of course, it's exactly what people who stand outside funeral homes while the body's inside cooling always yak about. Now it can be told: Who he fucked, aren't we glad we're smarter, where'd the money go, isn't it a credit to us he's in there and we're out here.

Bud wheezes a little laughlike noise down in his throat. "You need to hear what she said, though. This Professor Novadradski. Naturally it'd be a Ruskie."

I think a moment about Ernie mugging his "Rooshan" accent and pounding the table at the Manasquan Bar years and years behind us now, when Russian meant something. "*Nyet, nyet, nyet,*" he'd growled and shouted that night about some crazy thing, took off one of his loafers and pounded it like Khrushchev, sweated and drank vodka like a Cossack. We all laughed till we cried.

"What she said was—and I got this from Thor Blainer" (the defrocked Unitarian minister). "He said the male nurse out at Delaware-Vue came in and gave Ernie the big shot because he'd been having a pretty rough time there for a day or so. Just walked in and did the deed. And in about three minutes, Ernie quit breathing, without ever saying anything. Then this Russian woman—right down in his face—starts saying his name over and over. 'Er-nie, Er-nie. Vat're you tinking? How dus you feel? Dus you see some colors? Vich vunz? Are you colt? Dus you hear dis voice?' She said it, of course, in a soothing way, so she wouldn't scare him out of coming back if he wanted to."

Lloyd's heard enough and heads off around the side of the building to check on the Expedition, its headlights still shining into the mist. Some sound audible only to undertakers has reached his ears, alerting him that a new matter needs his expertise. He ambles away, hands down in his topcoat pockets, leaning forward like he's curious about something. Lloyd's heard these stories a jillion times: corpses suddenly sitting up on the draining table; fingers clutching out for a last touch before the fluid gurgles in; bodies inexplicably rearranged in the casket, as if the occupant had been capering about when the lights were out. The human species isn't supposed to go down willingly. Lloyd knows this better than Kierkegaard.

"Okay, Lawrence," I hear Lloyd say from around the side. "Let's get 'er going now."

A tall young black man dressed in a shiny black suit, white shirt and skinny tie, and bundled into a bulky green-and-silver Eagles parka with a screaming eagle over the left breast, emerges from the porte-cochère beside the building. He's flashing a big knowing grin, as if something supposed to be serious—but not really—has gone on inside. He stops and shares whatever it is with Lloyd, who's facing down, listening, but who then just shakes his head in small-scale amazement. I know this young man. He is Lawrence "Scooter" Lewis, surviving son of the deceased Everick Lewis, and nephew of the now also deceased Wardell, enterprising brothers who made buckets of dough in the early Nineties gentrifying beaten-up Negro housing in the Wallace Hill section of town and selling it to newcomer white Yuppies. I sold them two houses on Clio Street myself. Lawrence, I happen to know, went to Bucknell on a track scholarship but didn't last, then entered the Army Airborne and came home to find his niche in town. It's not an unusual narrative, even in Haddam. Scooter, who's younger-looking than his years, gives me a sweet smile and a small wave of unexpected recognition across the lawn, then turns and walks back toward his waiting Expedition before he's seen that I've waved back.

"Now hear me out, Frank." Bud's short upper lip begins to curl into a sneer. I'm not going to be glad to have heard this story, whatever it is. I hope Ernie has had the good grace in death to be still and not make a fool of himself. "The second this Ruskie gal quits saying 'Er-nie, Er-nie,' she puts her ear down close to him, where she can hear the slightest sound. And when the room's quiet, she hears—she swears—what sounds like a voice. But it's coming from Ernie's *stomach*!" Bud flashes another astonished smile, which wipes away his sneer. "I swear to God, Frank. *She* swears the voice was saying 'I'm here. I'm still here.' Out of his *goddamn* stomach." Bud looks exactly like the old-time actor Percy Helton, round, raspy-voiced, craven and mean, his fishy eyes saucered in mock horror that is actually gleeful. "Doesn't that beat the shit out of everything you ever heard?"

Bud, for some reason, opens his mouth as if a sound was meant to emerge, but none does, so that (having already looked in Lloyd's nose) I now have to see his short, thick, mealy, café au lait-colored tongue, broad across as Maryland, and, I'm sure, exuding vapors I don't want to get close to. Men. Sometimes the world is way too full of them. What I'd give this second for a woman's ministering smell and touch. Men can be the worst companions in the world. Dogs are better.

"She also said he was alive in a sexual sense. What do you think about that?" Bud blinks his sulfurous little peepers while fingering his half-glasses-on-a-string outside his black overcoat.

"Death's like turning off the TV, Bud. Sometimes a little light stays on in the middle. It's not worth wondering about. It's like where does the Internet live? Or can hermits have guests?"

"That's bullshit," Bud snarls.

"You probably hear more bullshit than I do, Bud." I smile another mirthless, unwelcoming smile.

Snow of the thin, stinging variety has begun to skitter before the burly November wind, turning the St. Augustine greener and crunchy. Sharp bits nick my ears, catch in my eyelids, sprinkle the jaunty-angled top of Bud's tweed hat. Contrary to expectation, I wish I was inside, standing vigil beside Ernie in his box, and not out here. I remember a night years past when a young, lean but no less an asshole Buddy Sloat—still practicing divorce law and before the unexamined life of lamps caught his fancy—started a row over, of all things, whether a deaf man who rapes a deaf woman deserves a deaf jury. Bud's view was he didn't. The other guy, an otolaryngologist named Pete McConnicky, a member of the Divorced Men's Club, thought the whole thing was a joke and kept looking around the bar for someone to agree with him and ease the pressure Bud felt about needing to be right about everything. Finally, McConnicky just smacked Bud in the mouth and left, which made everybody applaud. For a while, we all referred to Bud as "Slugger Sloat," and laughed behind his back. It'd be satisfying now to hit Bud in the mouth and send him back to the lamp store crying.

Bud, however, doesn't want to talk to me anymore. He watches the Black-Mariah Expedition creep out from the porte-cochère, wipers flapping crusts of new snow, big headlight globes cutting the flurry, gray exhaust thickening in the cold. Ernie McAuliffe's dark casket is in the windowed, curtained luggage-compartment, as lonely and uncelebrated as death itself—just the way Ernie wanted it, no matter how his belly ached to disagree. Scooter Lewis sits high in the driver's seat, shining face solemn in self-conscious caution. Lloyd watches from the grass beside the driveway. He probably has another of these occasions in half an hour. The funeral business is not so different from running a restaurant.

Unexpectedly, though, before Scooter can navigate the big Expedition out onto the street and turn up toward Constitution and the cemetery, a squad of Battle of Haddam re-enactors (Continentals) comes higgledy-piggledy, hot-footing it around the corner at the bottom end of Willow Street. These "patriots" are running, muskets in hand, heavy-gaited, their homespun socks ragged down to the ankles, shirttails flapping, beating a hasty retreat, or so it seems, from a smaller but crisply organized company of red-coated British Grenadiers hurrying around the same corner in a stiff little formation, their muskets at order arms, bayonets glinting, black regimental belts and boots, crimson tunics and high furry hats catching what muted light there is.

They present an impressive aspect. The Continentals have been whooping and shouting warnings and orders on the run. "Get to the cemetery and deploy." One's waving an arm. "Don't fire till you see the whites of your eyes." From the funeral home lawn, I see this man is an Asian and small and rounded in his homespuns, though his command voice has real authority.

The Redcoats, once onto the corner, very smartly form two lines of five, crosswise of the street, five kneeling, five standing behind. A tall, skeletal officer hurries up beside them and without any buildup barks an Englishy-sounding command, raises a bulky cutlass into the New Jersey air. The Grenadiers shoulder their weapons, cock their hammers, aim down their barrels and—right in the middle of Willow Street, in the cold misting snow, as it must've been back in 1780—cut loose up the street at the Americans, who're just in front of Mangum & Gayden's (in time to be shot) and blocking Scooter Lewis's path in his Expedition.

The English musketry produces a loud, unserious cracking sound and gives out a preposterous amount of white smoke from barrel and breech. The Continentals, swarming past the funeral home, turn as the volley goes off, and from various positions—kneeling, standing, crouching, lying on the yellow-striped asphalt—fire back with similar unserious cracks and smoke expenditures. And right away, two Brits go right over as stiff as duckpins. Three Continentals also get it—one who's taken cover behind the hearse's fender, with Ernie in the back. The Americans make a much more anguished spectacle out of dying than the English, who seem to know better how to expire. (It's a strange sight, I'll admit.) The remaining Grenadiers calmly begin to reload, using ramrods and flinting devices, while the Continentals—forefathers to guerrillas and terrorists the world over—just turn and begin hightailing it again, whooping and hoo-hawing up to Constitution, where they clamber around the corner and are gone. It hasn't taken two minutes to fight the Battle of Willow Street.

Lloyd Mangum, Bud Sloat and I, with Scooter behind the wheel of his hearse, have simply stood in the wet grass and borne silent witness. No humans have emerged from neighbor houses to inquire what's what. Musket smoke drifts sideways in the snowy, foggy Willow Street atmosphere and engulfs for an instant my Suburban, parked on the other side. The sound of the Continentals, shouting orders and yahooing, echoes through the yards and silent sycamores. Other muskets discharge streets away, other manly shouts are audible above the muffled sound of campaign snares and a bugle. It is almost stirring, though I'm not in the mood. Ernie, once a combatant himself, would've gotten a charge out of it. He'd have wondered, as I do, if any of the soldiers were girls.

The British—minus two—have now re-formed as a moving square and begun marching back around the corner onto Green Street. The three "dead" Continentals have recovered life and begun strolling back down Willow, muskets on their shoulders, barrel ends forward, looking to join up with their enemies, who're now waiting, dusting off their jodhpurs. A clattering blue New Jersey Waste truck lumbers around the corner. Two teenage black boys cling outside to the hold-on bars, making wagon-master noises to signal the stops. It's "pickup Tuesday." Oversized green plastic cans sit at the end of each driveway, beside red recycling tubs. Details I haven't noticed.

The black kids on the garbage truck say something sassy to the Continentals that makes the boys crack up and swing outward on their handgrips like amazing acrobats. Neither of them is fazed when one irregular points a musket at them and simulates a volley, though it makes the soldiers laugh as they disappear around the corner.

"You know what Ernie's putting on his gravestone?" Lloyd's come to stand beside me, Old Spice gunk a halo around him. He has a wheeze deep down in his chest, and the coarse black follicles around the helix of his left ear are the same as in his nose. Lloyd is a man not much made in America now, though once there were plenty: men without preconditions or sharp angles the world has to contend with, men who go to work, entertain important, unsensational duties, get home on time, mix a hefty brown drink after six, enjoy the company of the Mrs. till ten, catch the early news, then trudge off to bed and blissful sleep. I don't usually like being around men my age—since they always make me feel old—but Lloyd's the exception. I like him immensely, with his somber, pensive, throwback visage of times and shaving lotions of yore. He is good value—earnest, sympathetic, solid to the bone and not overcomplicated—just the way you'd hope your undertaker would be. Tom Benivalle, in his secret best sense of himself, is Lloyd, which is what I found likable about him. He's aware of who he pretends to be. Though Benivalle's the modern version, with angles and twitchy cellphone impatience that things might not turn out right. All of it in an Italian pasta box.

"What's that?" I say to Lloyd about Ernie's gravestone. Bud has wandered up the funeral home steps and is just entering the front door. Snow's falling harder now, though it won't last. My Philadelphia early-bird news channel didn't even mention snow when I woke at six.

"He's putting *He suffered fools cheerfully.*" Lloyd's pale blue lantern-jaw face rearranges itself from somber to happy.

I look at Lloyd again but, due to the difference in our heights, am forced—again—to look right up his hairy spelunkle of a left nostril. "That's great."

Scooter Lewis, in the Expedition, has let the New Jersey Waste truck rumble past and begins negotiating a respectful turn onto Willow. He has another serious game face on. No winks or smiles or eye rolls. The garbage truck boys stare back at the hearse mistrustfully.

"Ernie'd have liked having a battle in the middle of his funeral, don't you think, Frank? An un-funeral." Ernie liked to put *un* in front of words to make fun of them. Un-drunk. Un-vacation. Un-rich. "It was at a time when I was still un-rich." When he said it, we all said it. Un-fuck. Un-Jersey.

"I'm surprised everyone doesn't ask for a battle," I say. "Or at least a skirmish." I've never discussed "arrangements" with Lloyd, but perhaps I should, since I have a deadly disease.

"I wouldn't stay in business long if they did." Lloyd exhales a breath he seems to have been holding in for some time. Lloyd has seen Ernie in the last hour, dead as a posthole digger, but seems to be none the worse for it.

"What business would you be in, Lloyd, if you weren't in the dead-person business?"

"Oh, lord." He's watching the Expedition bearing our friend come to a stop at Constitution, red blinker flashing a left turn. Scooter, in the driver's seat, cranes his neck both directions, then eases out and silently disappears toward the cemetery. Lloyd is satisfied. "I've sure thought about it, Frank. Hazeltine"—Lloyd's well-upholstered wife, named for God only knows what tribe of abject Pennsylvania Kallikaks—"would like me to sell it out. To some chain. Quit livin' in a funeral home. Her family are all potato farmers in PA. They don't get this here. Kids're in Nevada."

One of Lloyd's three is my son Paul's age—twenty-seven—and, unlike my son, who has a career in the greeting-card industry, is a computer wizard who started his own mail-order business selling office furniture made from recycled organic food products and now owns six vintage Porsches and an airplane.

Lloyd frowns at the thought of Pennsylvania potatoes and retirement. "But I don't know."

"Is it the smell of the embalming fluid or the sob of the crowd, you think, Lloyd?" Lloyd doesn't answer, though he has a good sense of humor and I know is letting these words silently amuse him. It is his gift. There's no use having a somber day cloud everything.

"So what's the plan for Thanksgiving, Frank? The family? The works?" Lloyd's oblivious to what my "family" entails, except "those two kids." I've, after all, been gone eight years. Lloyd's likely picturing his own brood: Hazeltine, Hedrick, Lloyd, Jr., and Kitty—the funeral-directing Mangums of Haddam. "You're living where right now?" (As if I was a Bedouin.)

"Sea-Clift, Lloyd." I smile to let him know it's a positive change and he's asked me about it before. "Over on the Shore."

"Yep, I get it. That's nice. Real nice, over there."

We both turn to a storm door closing, a cough, a footfall. Bud's coming down the steps, walking a little gimpy, as if he's worried about slipping. The snow's sticking but no longer falling.

"Looks like you got some more business in there, Lloyd. The Van Tuyll girl. And who's that *old* party?" Bud resettles his dick under his London Fog, which is why he was walking bowlegged. He went in for a piss, which is what I'd like to do, but not in there.

"Harvey Effing's mother," Lloyd says reluctantly. "She was ninety-four."

"Oh my God," Bud says. He's been nosing around the other viewing rooms after his leak and without even taking off his Irish hat, having a whiff of different deaths. It's made him giddy. " 'Paging Mr. Effing. Call for Mr. Effing. Effing party of two.' We used to play that on Harvey up at the Princeton Club." Bud the clubman is pleased by this memory. He's done with the matter of noises from Ernie's innards and their possible cosmic significance. We're just three men out on the snowy front walk again, waiting for permission to disengage. To remain longer threatens divulgences, confidences, the connection of dots in no need of connecting. The job description for *mourner* is simply to stay on message.

I'm, however, hungry as a leopard and realize I'm standing with my mouth partway open in anticipation of food, just the way a leopard would. Having to piss a lot makes me not drink much, which makes me forget to eat. Though it's also because I have no more words I want to speak.

"How's the realty business, Frank?" Bud says insincerely.

"It's great, Bud. How's lamps?" I close my yap and try to smile.

"Couldn't be brighter. But let me ask you something, Frank." Bud pushes his little cold hands officiously down in his coat pockets and spaces his saddle oxfords wider apart and sways back like a racetrack tout.

The grassy ground is already turning bare again as the snow vanishes. It could easily begin to rain. I'm not sure I don't detect the pre-auditory rumble of thunder. "I hope it's simple, Bud." I'm not in the mood for complexity. Or candor. Or honesty. Or anything, including jokes.

"It's something I started asking people when I'm selling them a lamp, you know?" Bud beetles his brow in a look appropriate to philosophical inquiry.

I cast a wary eye Lloyd's way. He's looking at his brogans again, jeweled with dampness. I'm sure he's already taken this quiz.

"What've you learned in the realty business, Frank? In how many years now?"

"I don't remember."

"Pretty long, though. Twenty years?"

"No. Or yes. I don't remember."

Bud sniffs back through his little ruby-veined nose, then wags his shoulders like a boxer. "A while, though."

"I thought you liked the unexamined life, Bud."

"For selling lamps," Bud snaps. "I was at Princeton, Frank, with Poindexter and that crowd. Empirical all the way. I had a scholarship over to Oxford but went on and attended Harvard Law. It was the Sixties."

"I never believe people, Bud."

"Well, you can sure as shit believe that."

Bud's translucent eyelids snap like a crow's. He's misunderstood me. He thinks I've deprecated his academic accomplishment, about which I couldn't care less.

"That's my answer to your question, Bud. How could I not know you went to Princeton? You probably haven't told me more than four hundred times. I'm sure Harvey Effing's mother knows you went to Princeton. You probably reminded her when you were in there."

"Your answer is *what*?" Bud says.

"My answer is, I tend not to believe people."

"About what?"

Lloyd groans down in his tussive chest. All day, death, and now questions.

"About anything. It lets people act freely. I realized it one day. A guy told me he was driving back to his motel for his checkbook then coming right back to where we'd been looking at a condo over in Seaside Park. He was going to write me a check for twenty-five thousand on the spot. I knew he exactly intended to. And I was going to stand there and wait till he came back. But I realized, though, that I didn't believe a fucking thing he said. I just pretended to, to make him feel good. That's what I've learned. It's a big relief."

"Did the guy come back," Lloyd asks.

"He did, and I sold him the condo."

Bud's livery lips wrinkle in distaste meant to signify concern. "You've gotten deep since your prostate flare-up."

"My prostate didn't *flare up*, you asshole. It had cancer. I believe that, though. If you trust people unnecessarily, it incurs an obligation on everybody. Suspending judgment's a lot easier. Maybe you can do that with lamps."

"Makes sense," Lloyd says quietly. "I probably feel the same way." He lowers his big funereal brow at Bud as a warning.

"Whatever." Bud makes a display of looking around the empty yard, as if Harvey Effing's mother was calling him. The driveway's empty. Water's puddling from the melted snow. The postman, in his blue government sweater and blue twill pants, is just traversing the lawn from next door in some wiggly black galoshes he hasn't bothered to snap. He radiates a wide, welcoming postal-carrier got-something-for-you smile and hands Lloyd a stack of letters bound with a red rubber band.

"That's great," Lloyd grunts, and smiles but doesn't peek at his letters. Surely some are heart-warming thank-yous for all the above-and-beyond kindness by the M&G staff when Uncle Beppo was "taken," and for the extra time needed so a long-estranged brother could arrive from Quito, especially since Uncle B. wasn't discovered in his apartment until some time had passed. I wonder what Lloyd's answer was to the what-have-you-learned question.

"*Whatever*'s about it," I say to Bud, who's still gooning around the yard at nothing. I believe I detect a ghostly Parkinson's tremor in Bud's chin, something he may not know about him-self. His pudding chin is slightly oscillating, though it may be because I yelled at him and made him nervous. "I want you to understand, Bud. When I didn't believe the guy'd come back, it wasn't that I *dis*believed him. I just decline to make people have to bear extra responsibility for their own insecure intentions. Having to be believed is too big a burden. I thought you studied philosophy. It isn't so hard."

"Okay, that's fine." Bud smiles faintly and pats me softly on the front of my barracuda jacket, as if I was about to start throw-ing punches and needed calming.

"Fuck you, Bud."

"Yeah, yeah. Okay. That's great. Fuck me." Bud fattens his bunchy cheeks and smirks. The funeral contingent has now lost its funerary decorum. I'm, of course, largely to blame.

"Better get going." Lloyd's stuffing his mail into his overcoat pocket.

"Time to," Bud says. He's staring straight at Lloyd's chest, so as not to have to face me. "Hope you feel better, Frank."

"I feel great, Bud. I hope *you* feel better. You don't look so good."

"Chasing a cold," Bud says, and commences walking in his gimpy gait across the damp lawn, heading down Willow, back toward Seminary and the unreflective lamp business. It's why I hate men my age. We all emanate a sense of youth lost and tragedy-on-the-horizon. It's impossible not to feel sorry for our every little setback.

"Those kids coming to visit, are they?" Lloyd's happy to be upbeat.

"They sure are, Lloyd." We're watching Bud cross Willow, stamping grass and snow-melt off his oxfords, clutching his coat collar up around his neck. He doesn't look back, though he thinks we're talking about him. "You can't enter the same stream twice, can you, Frank?" Lloyd says.

I look squarely at Lloyd, as if by gazing on him I'll come to know what he means, since I don't have the vaguest idea, though I'm certain it has something to do with the life lessons we both know: takes all kinds; for every day, turn, turn, turn; life'd be dull if we were all the same. "Small blessings," I say solemnly.

"Thanks for showing up. We needed some bodies." This is not a pun to Lloyd. He is a born literalist and couldn't survive otherwise.

"It was a good thing," I lie, and think a thought about Ernie's epitaph and how smart a cookie he was to know what to say at the end. We should all be that smart, all heed the lesson.

SURPRISINGLY—though probably *not* that surprisingly—the inside of my Suburban when I climb in is gaseous with stinging, whanging anti-Permanent Period ethers that make me have to run the windows down to get a usable breath. Conceivably it's low blood sugar from being starved, which makes me clench my jaw. When you have cancer in your nether part, *plus* a bolus of radiant heavy metal—most of which has spent its payload by now, though it's my keepsake forever—your systems don't run on autopilot like they used to. Everything begs for suspicious notice —a headache, loose bowels, erectile virtuosity or its opposite, bloodshot eyes, extra fingernail growth. Dr. Psimos, my Mayo surgeon, explained all this. Though once my procedure was over, he said, nothing on a daily basis would be caused *per se* by my condition, unless I went prospecting for uranium, in which case my needle would point out the mother lode up my butt.

"It'll be in your mind, Frank, but that's about it," Psimos said, leaning back, self-satisfied in his doctor chair, like a forty-year-old lab-coated Walter Slezak. His tiny Mayo seventh-floor pale-green office walls were full of diplomas—Yale, the Sorbonne,

Heidelberg, Cornell, plus one designating him a graduate of the Suzuki Method of pianism. Those hirsute sausagey digits, capable of injecting hot needles into tender zones, also contained "The Flight of the Bumblebee" in their muscle memory.

It was our presurgical chat, the entire duration of which he sat teasing a bad backlash out of a tiny silver fly reel, using those same meaty fingers, assisted by a surgical clamp and some magnifying spectacles. Out his little window, the entire Mayo skyline—the bland tan hospital edifices, smokestacks, helipads, radar dishes, antennae, winking red beacons, everything but anti-aircraft batteries and ack-acks—projected the reassuring solidity of a health-care Pentagon to wayward pilgrim patients like me and the King of Jordan.

I didn't know what to say back. I hadn't had "a procedure" since once in the Marine Corps on my ailing pancreas, which got me out of Vietnam. I knew what was going to happen— the BBs, etc.—and figured the biopsy had already been worse. I wasn't scared till I found out I shouldn't be. "Most things that happen to me anymore happen in my mind," I said pathetically. My knees were shaking. I had on red madras Bermudas and a *Travel Is a Fool's Paradise* tee-shirt to try to look casual. I'm sure he knew what was happening.

It was a sunny, humid Minnesota Friday, last August. I'd watched the Olympic 4×100 relay that morning at the Travelodge. "Procedures," it seems, only take place on Mondays. But terrifying doctor chats are all slated for Fridays, to ensure that the maximum stomach-churning, molar-crunching jimjams will fill up your weekend.

"I'm just an ole surgeon around here, Frank." Psimos held his antique reel away from his jowly, mustachioed Walterish face and frowned at it through his magnifiers. "They don't pay me millions to think, just cut 'n paste stuff. I'll fix you up Monday so you're back firing. But I can't help what goes on in the brain department. That's over on West Eleven, across the street." He gave his heavy Greek brows a couple of insolent flicks.

"I'm looking forward to it," I said idiotically, my asshole as hard as a peach pit.

"I bet you are." He smiled. "I bet you really are."

And that was that.

*   *   *

ALL THIS woolly, stinging, air-sucking breathlessness inhabiting my Suburban is about nothing but death, of course—big-D *and* little-d. The Permanent Period is specifically commissioned to make you quit worrying about your own existence and how everything devolves on your *self* (most things aren't about "you" anyway, but about other people) and get you busy doin' and bein'—the Greek ideal. Psimos, I bet, practices it to perfection, on the links, at the streamside, in the operating theater, at the Suzuki and over lamb patties on the Weber. Surgeons are past masters at achieving connectedness with *the great other* by making themselves less visible *to* themselves. Mike Mahoney would love them.

Still, too much death can happen to you before you know it, and has to be staved off like a bad genie and stuffed back in its bottle.

I MOTOR SLOWLY past the trudging, bescroffled, pre-Parkinson-ian Bud Sloat, just crossing Willow in the mist, head down in his Irish topper and sad toupé, heading toward the back lot of the CVS and Seminary Street, where his lamporium sits next door to the Coldwell Banker. I have a thought to shove open the passenger door and haul him in out of the rain, put a better end to things between us. He's possibly as death-daunted as I am (even assholes get the willies). A moment of unfelt fellowship might be just the ticket to save us from a bad afternoon. But Bud's intent on missing the puddles and saving his saddle oxfords, his hands down in his topcoat pockets, and in any case he's the sort of jerk who thinks every unrecognized vehicle contains someone inferior and worthy of disdain. I couldn't stand the look on his face. In any case, I have nothing I could even lie about to make him feel better.

Though Bud's question about the real estate business has set off belated silent alarms, and I feel a sudden cringe up near my diaphragm, brought on by the thought that real estate *might be my niche* the way undertaking's Lloyd's and Bud's is lamps. A strangled voice within me croaks, Nooo, nooo-no-no, no. I should know that voice, since I've heard it before—and recently.

Tell a dream, lose a reader, the master said (I do my best to forget mine). But you can't un-know what you know, as attractive as that might be.

In two consecutive weeks now, I've twice dreamed that I wake up in the middle of my prostate procedure just as the BBs—which in the dream are actually hot—go rolling down a lighted slot into my butt, a slot that looks like a pinball-machine gutter that Psimos, dressed in tails, has moved into the OR. In another one, I'm shooting baskets in a smelly old wire-windowed gym and I simply can't miss—except the score on the big black-and-white scoreboard doesn't change from 0–0. In a third, I somehow know jujitsu and am boisterously throwing little brown men around in a room full of mattresses. In another, I keep walking into a CVS like the one on Seminary, asking the pharmacist for a refill of my placebos. And in still another, I wake up and realize I'm forty-five, and wonder how I managed to fritter so much of my life away. And there are others.

Life-lived-over-again dreams, these are—no question; and the little *no, no, no* anti-Permanent Period voice, an alarm bespeaking a sharp downturn in outlook, for which I have God's own plenty of excuses these days. When you start looking for reasons for why you feel bad, you need to stand back from the closet door.

However, one of the pure benefits of the Permanent Period—when you're as nose-down and invisible to yourself as an actualized unchangeable non-becomer, as snugged into life as a planning-board member—is that you realize you can't completely fuck everything up anymore, since so much of your life is on the books already. You've survived it. Cancer itself doesn't really make you fear the future and what might happen, it actually makes you (at least it's made me) not as worried as you were before you had it. It might make you concerned about lousing up an individual day or wasting an afternoon (like this one), but not your whole life. I try to impart this hopeful view to oldsters who wander down to the Shore in their blue Chrysler New Yorkers to "look at houses," but then get squirrelly about making a mistake, and end up scampering home to Ogdensburg and Lake Compounce, thinking that what I've told them is nothing but a sales pitch and I won't be around when the shit train pulls in and the house market bottoms out just as their adjustable mortgage starts to steeple (I certainly won't). But once I've explained that it's seashore property I'm showing them and God isn't making any more of it, and you can get your money out any day of the week, I just want to say: Hey! Look! Take the plunge. Live once. You're on the short end of this stick. He isn't making any more of *you*, either.

What I usually see, though, is nervous, smirking, irritable superiority (like Bud Sloat's) that's convinced there's something out there that *I* could never know about—or else I wouldn't be a know-nothing real estate agent—but that *they* goddamn well know all about. Most humankind doesn't want to give up thinking they can fuck up the whole works by taking the wrong step, by shoving the black checker over onto that wrong red square. It makes them feel powerful to believe they own something to be cautious about. These people make terrible clients and can waste weeks of your time. I've developed a radar for them. But in fairness to these reluctant home-seekers—their chins on their chests the way Bud's is today—and who're thinking more positively about having that aluminum siding installed instead of paying for a whole new place, or about buying that new pop-up camper or checking fares on Carnival Lines (however they can throw some money away, but not too much): There *are* legitimate downsides to the Permanent Period. Permanence can be scary. Even though it solves the problem of tiresome becoming, it can also erode optimism, render possibility small and remote, and make any of us feel that while we can't fuck up much of anything anymore, there really isn't much to fuck up because nothing matters a gnat's nuts; and that down deep inside we've finally become just an organism that for some reason can still make noise, but not much more than that.

This you need to save yourself from, or else the slide off the transom of life's pleasure boat becomes irresistible and probably a good idea.

CHAPTER 3

STOPPED AT the red light at Franklin and Pleasant Valley, my Suburban interior musty-damp and my feet warming with the defroster on high, the outside day has turned gloomy. Wind gusts against the hanging traffic light, making it yaw and twist and sway. Rain sheets the street. My car thermometer says the outside temp's dropped to thirty-six, and lights have prickled on inside houses. Haddamites are getting indoors, holding hats to heads. Pilgrims in the Square are packing it in. It's 1:00 p.m.

Something to eat and somewhere to piss are now high priorities, and I turn down Pleasant Valley toward Haddam Doctors Hospital, which has become my best-choice solo-luncheon venue since I moved away—in spite of its being the sad setting of my son's final hours so long ago. It's odd, I'll admit, to eat lunch in a hospital. But it's no stranger than paying your light bill at the Grand Union, or buying your new septic tank from the burial-vault dealer. Form needn't always follow function. Plus, it's not strange at all if you can get a decent meal in the process.

Decades ago, when I arrived in Haddam, you could grab a first-rate cheese steak in a little chrome and glass, plastic-booth diner lined with framed sports glossies and presided over by muttering old townies who wouldn't speak to you because you were an outsider. And there was still a below-street-level, red-walled Italian joint serving manicotti and fresh bluefish, where they'd let you read your paper, fill you up, then get you out for cheap. Cops ate there, as did seminary profs, ancient librarians and the storied old HHS baseball coach who'd had a cup of coffee with the Red Sox once, and who'd sneak over in his blue-and-white uniform for a double vodka and a smoke before afternoon practice.

I loved it here then. The town had the ambling, impersonal, middling pleasantness of an old commercial traveler in no real hurry to get anywhere. All of which has gone. Now either you're forced into mega-expensive "dining" or to standing in a line behind hostile moms in designer sweats pushing strollers into the Garden of Eatin' Health Depot and who're fidgeting over whether the Roman ceviche contains fish on the endangered list or if the coffee's from a country on the Global Oppression Hot 100. By the time you get your food, you're pretty much ready to start a fistfight—plus, you're not hungry anymore.

At Haddam Doctors, by contrast, strangers are always welcome, parking's easy in the visitors lot and it's cafeteria-style, so no waiting. There's no soul-less plastic ware. Everything's spotless, tables cleaned antibacterially in record time. The long apple-green dining hall has an attractive commissary busy-ness bespeaking serious people with serious things in mind. And the food's cooked and served by big, smiling, no-nonsense, pillowy black women in pink rayon dresses, who can make a meat loaf so it's better cold than hot, and who always slip a little ham bone into the limas so you get back to your car with a feeling you've just had a human, not an institutional, experience. The cooks' husbands all eat there—always the sure sign.

At lunch, you often share your table with some elderly gentleman with a wife in for tests, or a worried young couple whose child's there for back straightening, or just some ordinary citizen like me grabbing a plate lunch before hitting it again. Restrained but understanding smiles are all that's ever shared. ("We've all got our woes, why blab 'em?") Nobody opens up or vents (you might complain to some poor soul worse off than you). White-smocked M.D.'s and crisp-capped nurses sit together by the windows, chatting while patient families eye them hopefully, wondering if *he*'s the one and if they could interrupt for just one question about Grampa Basil's EKG. Only they don't. Stately decorum reigns. Occasionally, there's an outburst of strange laughter, followed by a few Turkish words from the blue-trousered floor orderlies that break through the tinkle and plink of eating and surviving. Otherwise, all is as you'd want it. (Oddly, there's no such positive ambience at Mayo—only an earth-tone, ergonomically-designed food court where patients stare wanly at other patients and pick at their green Jell-O.)

Plus, in Haddam Doctors, if anyone gets his Swiss steak down the wrong pipe or swallows an ice cube or suffers a grand mal, there's plenty of help—Heimlich masters, wall-mounted defibrillators and Thorazine injections in all the nurses' pockets. Beginning with when Ralph was a patient and his mother and I lived in the hospital days and nights, the most untoward thing I've witnessed was a streaker, a banker I knew who'd suffered reversals in the S&L crisis and ended up in the psycho ward, from which he made a brief but spectacular break (eventually, he got on at another bank).

However, when I wheel in toward Visitor Lot A, just after one, I see that something not at all regular's afoot at the hospital. The big, usually glassed-in front windows of the cafeteria—inside which the doctors and nurses usually sit—are at this moment being ply-boarded over, with yellow crime-scene tape stretched across. Several uniformed Haddam police and detectives wearing badges on cords around their necks are standing out in the sorry weather, writing notes on pads, taking pictures and generally reconnoitering the scene. Glass from the empty windows is strewn out on the damp grass, and tan wall bricks and aluminum splinters and cottony insulation have been spewed as far as the visitors lot. Police and fire department vehicles with flashers flashing are nosed at all angles around the doctors parking lot and the ER entrance, along with two panel trucks from network affiliates. A man and a woman with ATF stenciled on the backs of their windbreakers are conferring with a large man in a fireman's white hard hat and fireman's coat. Yellow-slickered police are carefully outlining bits of debris with spray paint, while others use surgical gloves and what look like forceps to tweeze evidence into plastic bags they drop into larger black garbage bags that other cops are holding.

Up the four stories of the hospital, faces are at all the windows, peering down. Two policemen in black commando outfits and holding automatic weapons stand at the lip of the roof like prison guards, watching the proceedings below.

What's happened here, I don't know. It can't be good. That I do know.

Suddenly, a *clack-clack* on my passenger-side window scares me out of my pants. A round, inquisitive woman's face, with a blue plastic-covered cop hat pulled down to her eyebrows, hangs outside the glass, staring in at me. An oversized black flashlight barrel shows above the window frame, its hard metal rim touching the glass, its beam shining over my head. The face's mouth moves, says something I can't make out, then a hand with pudgy fingers makes a little circular roll-'er-down motion, which I instantly perform from my side, letting in a gust of cold.

"Hi," the woman says from outside. She smiles so as not to seem officially menacing. "How're we doing, sir?" Her question intends that I need to be doing fine and be eager to say so. Rain mist has dampened her shiny black hat bill and made her cheeks shiny.

"I'm great," I say. "What's happened here?"

"Can you state your business here for me today, sir?" She blinks. She's a thick, pie-faced woman who looks forty but is probably twenty-five. Her teeth are small and white, and her lips thin and unhabituated to smiling except in official ways. She's undoubtedly been a law enforcement major somewhere and had plenty of practice looking in car windows, though her aspect isn't alarming, only definite. I'm not doing anything illegal—seeking lunch. Though also wanting pretty seriously to take a leak.

"I just came for lunch." I smile as if I'd divulged a secret.

The policewoman's smooth face doesn't alter, just processes info. "This is a hospital, sir." She glances up at Haddam Doctors four-story tan-brick façade as if to make sure she's right. On her yellow slicker a black name tag says *Bohmer* over a stamped-on black police badge. A microphone is Velcro'd to her left shoulder so she can talk and still hold a gun on you.

I know it's a hospital, ma'am, I'm tempted to say; my son died in it. Instead, I chirp, "I know it's a hospital, but the cafeteria's a super place for lunch."

Officer Bohmer's smile renounces a little of its definiteness and becomes amused and patronizing. She sees now that I'm one of *those* people, the ones who eat their lunch in the fucking hospital, who sit in libraries all day leafing through *Popular Mechanics*, World War II picture books and topless-native layouts in *National Geographic*s. The ones who don't fit. She's rousted my type. We're harmless when kept on a short leash.

"What happened inside there?" I ask again, and look toward the police goings-on, then back to Officer Bohmer, whose heifer eyes have fixed me again. Outside air is making my hands and cheeks cold. Her shoulder microphone crackles, but she doesn't attend to it.

"Tell me again, sir, what your business here is," she says in a buttoned-up way. She takes a peek through at the backseat, where I've got two Realty-Wise signs I'm taking to the office.

"I came for lunch. I've done it for years. The lunch is good. You should eat there."

"Where do you live, sir?" Staring at my signs.

"Sea-Clift. I used to live here, though."

Her eyes drift back to me. "You lived here in Haddam?"

"I sold real estate. I own my own company on the Shore. Realty-Wise."

"And how long have you lived over there?"

"Eight years. About."

"And you lived here before?"

"On Cleveland Street. And before that on Hoving Road."

"And could I just have a look at your driver's license?" Officer Bohmer is the picture of female resolve and patience. She glances up and over the hood of my Suburban, checking to see how quick her backup could arrive in case I produce a German Luger and not a billfold. "And your registration and proof of insurance."

I get about retrieving these documents—first from my wallet, then, under Officer Bohmer's interested eye, from the glove compartment, where a pistol would be if I had one.

She takes my documents in her pink digits, pinching the papers and getting them wet, looking up once to match my face to my picture. Then she hands them all back. More static crackles in her mike, a male voice says something that includes a number, and Officer Bohmer turns her chin to the little speaker and in a different, harder-edged voice snaps, "Negative on that. I'll maintain a twenty." The man's voice replies something unintelligible but also authoritative, and the transmission is over. "Thanks, that's great, Mr. Bascombe. Now I need you to turn 'er around and head on out again. Okay?"

"Can you tell me what happened over there?" I ask for the third time.

"Sir. A device detonated outside the cafeteria this morning."

A *device*. "What kind of device? Anybody hurt?" I say this to Officer Bohmer's raincoat belly.

"We're trying to find out what happened, sir."

In the blast area, I see police are huddling around something on the ground, and another uniformed officer is taking a photograph of it, the little digital camera held clumsily out in front of him.

Officer Bohmer's slick yellow raincoat front and imposing black flashlight barrel are all I can see from inside as she steps back from my window and with the flash makes a tiny sweeping movement to indicate what she'd like to see my car do. "Just turn 'er around right here," her police academy voice says again, "and take 'er right out the way you came."

A gas leak is what I'm thinking. Some pressurized container for hospital use only, that got too close to a pilot light. Yet something that requires the A T F?

My tires squeeze and scrape as I make the tight turn-around in the hospital drive—a Suburban doesn't change course easily. I take a look at the boarded cafeteria windows and the squads of police and firemen and hospital officials milling in the drizzle and the lights of their idling vehicles, the black-suited commandos standing roof guard just in case. The faces at the windows are all taking note of my car. "What's he doing?" "Read the license number." "Why are they letting him go?" "Who's to blame? Who's to blame? Who's to blame?"

Officer Bohmer is now gone from sight as I "take 'er right out." But another policeman in a yellow rain slicker and black cop's hat is up ahead, stopping cars as they turn in and dispatching them elsewhere.

"Any idea who did this?" I say to this new man as I idle past. He is an older officer I know, or once did, a big Polack with heavy brows, a pale, smooth face and mirthful eyes—Sgt. Klemak, a Gotham PD veteran, escaped to the suburbs. He once gave me an unjustified yellow-light summons that set me back seventy bucks, but wouldn't remember me now, which is just as well.

"We're doing our best out here, *sir*!" Sgt. Klemak shouts over the traffic and rain hiss. He seems to be having fun doing his job.

"Are you sure something exploded?" I'm speaking upward, rain needles pelting my nose and chin.

"You can go ahead and turn right, sir!" Officer Klemak says with a big smile.

"I hope you guys take care of yourselves."

"Oh, sure. Piece a cake. Just take 'er right around and have a splendid day. Get 'er home safely."

"That'd be nice," I say, then ease back out onto Pleasant Valley and put the hospital behind me.

I NOW HAVE a fierce need to piss. Plus, violent crime, instead of dousing my appetite, has inflamed it to queasiness. I drive straight out 206 to the remodeled Foremost Farms Mike and I passed earlier. I park in front, hustle in for my leak (which I now do more than seems humanly possible), then find the cold case, pick out a cellophane-sealed beef 'n bean burrito, radiate it in the microwave, draw a diet Pepsi, pay the Pakistani girl in the purple sari, then hustle back to my car and consume all in three minutes with paper napkins spread over my lap and jacket front. The burrito's been *hecho a mano* by the Borden Company down in Camden and is as hard as a cedar shingle, the interior as cold and pale as mucilage, and of course tastes wonderful. Although it's 180 degrees off my prostate-recovery, tumor-suppressing Mayo diet of 20 percent animal product, 80 percent whole grains, tofu and green tea, which only monks can survive on.

When I'm finished, I stuff my garbage in the can provided, then climb back in and turn on the local FM station, in case there's some news about the hospital incident. And indeed a metallic backyard-radio-station sound opens up—WHAD, the "Voice of Haddam," where I once recorded novels for the blind. *Static, static, static*—the rain's a problem. ". . . in Trenton have been dispatched . . ." *Static, static, static.* ". . . an average of ten threatening . . . a month . . . been . . . no name pending . . ." *Crackle, snap, poppety-pop.* ". . . all critical-care patients . . . mercy . . . a search is under way . . . Chief Carnevale stated. . . . credible . . ." *Static, static, static.* ". . . more on our regular . . ." *Ker-clunk* . . . "Strangers-in-the-night, dee-dah-dee-daaah-dah . . ."

Little help. But still. Hard to contemplate—a medium-anxiety, good-neighbor suburban care facility like Haddam Doctors, where the whole staff's from Hopkins and Harvard (no one tops in his class), all sporting eight handicaps, all divorced a time or two, kids at Choate and Hotchkiss, everyone as risk-averse as concert cellists (no one does serious surgery)—hard to contemplate *here* being the target of a "device." Unless somebody wanted his vasectomy reversed and couldn't, or somebody's tonsils grew back, or a set of twins got handed off to the wrong parents. Though these wrongs have tamer remedies than renting a U-Store-It, stockpiling chemicals and brewing up mayhem. You'd just sue, like the rest of humanity, and let the insurance companies take the hit. That's what they're there for.

WHEN I START up and defrost the windshield, it's suddenly 1:40. I'm due for my Sponsor visit on the affluent Haddam West Side at two.

Though as I wheel back out onto busy, rain-smacked 206 and head west, I recognize that while the willies I experienced after my funeral home visit certainly were due to a too-close brush with the Reaper (normal in all instances), they might also have been nothing more than the usual yellow caution flag, which signals that being marooned in your car on a dreary day in a cold town you once lived in, but don't now, can be chancy. Especially if the town is this one, and especially if you're in my state of repair. Activities may need to be curtailed.

I actually began experiencing adverse intimations about Haddam during my last years here, close to ten years ago (I always thought I loved it). And not that a realtor's view would ever be the standard one, since realtors both live life in a town yet also huckster that place's very spirit essence for whopper profits. We're always likely to be half-distracted from regular life—like a supreme court justice who resides in a place as anonymously as a postal employee but constantly processes everybody else's life in his teeming brain so he can know how to judge it. My life in Haddam always lacked the true resident's naïve, relief-seeking socked-in-ed-ness that makes everyday existence feel like a warm bath you relax into and never want to leave. Surveying property lines, memorizing setback restrictions, stepping off footprint limits and counting curb-cuts all work a stern warp into what might otherwise be limitless, shapeless, referenceless—and happily thoughtless—municipal life. Realtors share a basic industry with novelists, who make up importance from life-run-rampant just by choosing, changing and telling. Realtors make importance by selling, which is better-paying than the novelist's deal and probably not as hard to do well.

By 1991, the year before I left and the year my son Paul Bascombe graduated from HHS and headed off to Indiana to begin studies in Puppet Arts Management (he'd mastered ventri-loquism, did a hundred zany voices, told jokes and had already staged several bizarre but sophisticated puppet shows for his classmates), by then Haddam—a town where I'd felt genuine residence and that'd been the *mise-en-scène* for my life's most solemn adult experiences—had entered a new, strange and discordant phase in its town annals.

In the first place, real estate went nuts, and realtors even nuttier. Expectations left all breathable atmosphere behind. Over-pricing, under-bidding, sticker shock, good-faith negotia-tion, price reduction, high-end flux were all banished from the vocabulary. Topping-price wars, cutthroat bidding, forced com-pliance, broken lease and realty shenanigans took their place. The grimmest, barely habitable shotgun houses in the previously marginal Negro neighborhoods became prime, then untouch-able in an afternoon. Wallace Hill, where I sold my rental houses to Everick Lewis, was designated a Heritage Neighborhood, which guaranteed all the black folks had to leave because of taxes (many fled down south, though they'd been born in Haddam). Agents sold their own homes out from under their own families and moved spouses, dogs and kids to condos in Hightstown and Millstone. New college graduates passed up med and divinity school and buyers bought million-dollar houses from twenty-one-year-olds straight out of Princeton and Columbia with degrees in history and physics and who barely had their driver's licenses.

In '93, after I'd left, yearly price increases had hit 45 percent, there was no affordable housing anywhere and buyers were pay-ing full boat for tear-downs and recyclables and in some instances were burning houses to the ground. Some Haddam companies (not Lauren-Schwindell) required out-of-town clients to submit their AmEx number and authorize thousand-dollar debits just to be shown a house. Though by Christmas, there was nothing to show anyway, not even a vacant lot.

The end came personally for me at the convergence of three completely different (and unusual) events. One Saturday after-noon I was at my desk, typing an offer sheet on a property situated on the rear grounds of the former seminary director's residence, down the street from where I myself once lived on Hoving. The building was nothing but a rotting, ruined beaverboard shack that

had once been the Basque gardener's storage shed for toxic herbi-
cides, caustic drain openers, banned termite and Asian beetle
eradicators, and would've alerted the state's environmental
police except in Haddam, no inspection's required. As I filled out
the green blanks on my computer, occasionally staring longingly
out the front window at traffic-choked Seminary Street,
I began—because of the property I was selling and the preposterous price it was commanding—to muse that a malign force
seemed to be in full control of every bit of real property on the
seaboard, and possibly farther away. Possibly everywhere.

This force, I began to understand, was holding property hostage and away from the very people who wanted and often badly
needed it and, in any case, had a right to expect to own it. And
this force, I realized, was the economy. And the practical effect
of this force—on me, Frank Bascombe, age forty-five, of ordinary, unexalted and, up to then, realizable aspirations—was to
render everything too goddamn expensive. So much so that
selling even one more house in Haddam—and especially the
gardener's toxic hovel, on whose site was planned a big-
windowed, one-man live-in studio for a sculptor who mostly
lived in Gotham and was willing to pay 500K—was going to be
demoralizing as hell.

What I was thinking, of course, as cars edged thickly past the
Lauren-Schwindell window and passengers stared warily in at
me at my desk, knowing I was totaling figures that would give
them a heart attack—what I was thinking was real estate heresy.
I would get burned at the real estate stake by my agent colleagues
(especially the twenty-one-year-olds) if they knew about it.
What we were supposed to do if we had qualms—and surely
some did—was douse them. On the spot. Take a deep breath, go
wash your face, lease a new Z-car, buy a condo in Snowmass,
learn to fly your own Beech Bonanza, maybe take instruction in
violin making. But ship as much fresh money as possible to the
Caymans, then spend the rest of the time putting your feet up
on your desk and chortling about how work's for the other ranks.

Except everyone's entitled to some glimmering *sense of right*
in his (or her) own heart. And part of that sense of right—for
real estate agents anyway—involves not just what something
ought to cost (here we're always wrong) but what something *can*
cost in a world still usable by human beings. Every time I heard

myself pronounce the asking price of anything on the market in Haddam, I'd begun to feel first a sick, emptied-out, semi-nauseated feeling, and then an impulse to break into maniac laughter right in a client's startled face as he sat across my desk in his pressed jeans, Tony Lamas and fitted polo shirt. And that growing sense of spiritual clamor meant to me that right was being violated, and that my sense of usefulness at being what I'd been being was exhausted. It was a surprise, but it was also a big relief. It was like the experience of the sportsman who's shot ducks in the marsh all his life but one day, standing up to his ass in freezing water, with the sky silvered and dark specks on the horizon beginning to take avian shape, realizes he's killed enough ducks for one lifetime.

The second way I knew I'd reached the end of my rope in Haddam was simpler, though more garish and immediately life-diverting.

During the summer of 1991—when the daffy elder Bush was still ruffling his own duck feathers in the aftermath of Desert Storm—a home sale, on tiny Quarry Street, opposite St. Leo the Great Catholic Church, culminated in a SWAT-team extraction when the owner-occupant refused to vacate the house he'd signed papers and already closed on. The man ran right out of the lawyer's office, back across neighbors' front lawns to his erstwhile family home, where he took a position in an attic dormer window and, using a varmint rifle, held off Haddam police, two hostage-negotiators and a priest from St. Leo's for thirty-six hours before giving in, being led defiantly out the door in front of the same neighbors and the new owners, then riding off in chains to the state hospital in Trenton.

No one was hurt. But the reason for the behavior was the seller's discovery that his house had appreciated 18 percent between offer-acceptance and the lawyers' closing, which made the thought of all that lost money and the smirking ridicule from the neighbors, who were holding on for another season, just too much to bear. For weeks afterward, tension and threat hung over the town. Two new police officers were added. Threat sensitivity courses were made mandatory in our office, and a "conflict resolution half point" was added to closing costs when a bank approved super balloon notes to first-time buyers purchasing from sellers with greater than ten years' longevity.

Nothing, however, prepared anyone for the outlandish worst. A trucking magnate of Lebanese extraction made a full-price offer on a rambling, walled monstrosity far out on Quaker Road, owned by the reclusive grandson of a south Jersey frozen-potpie magnate, who'd turned up his nose at the family business to become a competitive stamp collector. The house was a great weed-clogged Second Empire mishmash with a rotted roof, sagging floor joists, scaling paint, disintegrating masonry and cellar dampness due to being in the floodplain. It wasn't even a candidate to be torn down, since regulations prohibited replacement. When I took the realtors' cavalcade tour, I couldn't find one timber or sill that wasn't corrupted by something. Everybody who showed it presented it as uninhabitable. The land, we felt, was a write-off to some rich tree-hugger conservationist who'd turn it into "wetlands" and make himself feel virtuous.

The trucking magnate, however, wanted to come in with a big improvement budget, rebuild everything up to code, restore the house to mint condition, plus add a lot of exotic fantasy landscaping and even let tame animals roam the grounds for the grandkids.

But when he submitted his full-price bid, saw it accepted, put three-quarters down as earnest money, the hermetic owner, Mr. Windbourne, decided to take the house off the market for a rethink, then a week later listed it again with a 20 percent increase in asking and had five new full-price offers by noon of the first day—two of which he accepted. The trucking guy, Mr. Habbibi, who was known in the Paterson area as a patient man who didn't mind using muscle when it was needed, naturally protested all this double-dealing, though none of it was illegal. He drove out to the Windbourne house in an agitated state but still in hopes of bettering the new offers and resuscitating his deal. Windbourne—wan, gaunt and blinking from long hours in the dark staring at stamps—came to the front door and said that the fantasy landscaping and tame animals sounded to him more suited to towns like Dallas or Birmingham, not Haddam. He laughed at Habbibi and closed the door in his face. Habbibi then drove to a marine supply in Sayreville (this is the strangest part, because Habbibi didn't own a boat), bought two marine flare pistols and two flares, drove back to Quaker Road, confronted Windbourne at his door and offered him the deal they'd already agreed to, plus

20 percent. When Windbourne again laughed at him, informed him this was America and that Habbibi had "loser's remorse," Habbibi went back out to his car, got his flare pistols, stood out in the yard of what he'd hoped would be his dream oasis, shouted Windbourne's name and shot him when he answered the door a third time. After which, Habbibi got back in his car, turned on the radio and waited for the police to show up.

Haddam house prices dropped 8 percent in one day (though that lasted less than a week). Habbibi was also trucked off to the loony bin. Windbourne's relatives drove up from Vineland and completed the sale to one of the other buyers. Realtors started carrying concealed weapons and hiring bodyguards, and the realty board passed an advisory to raise commissions from 6 to 7 percent.

At about this time, I was experiencing the first airy intimations of the Permanent Period filtering through my nostrils like a sweet bouquet of new life promised. Things had also gotten to a put-up-or-leave stage with Sally Caldwell. Selling houses in Haddam had evolved to a point at which I couldn't recognize my personal motives for even doing it. And on the waft of that bouquet and by the simple force of puzzlement, I decided it was time to get out of town.

But before I left (it took me to the sultry days of that election summer to get my affairs untangled), I noticed something about Haddam. It was similar to how the stolid but studious Schmeling saw *something* about the mute, indefatigable, but reachable Louis —in my case, something maybe only a realtor could see. The town felt different to me—as a place. A place where, after all, I'd dwelled, whose sundry homes and mansions I'd visited, wandered through, admired, marveled at and sold, whose inhabitants I'd stood long beside, listened to and observed with interest and sympathy, whose streets I'd driven, taxes paid, elections heeded, rules followed, whose story I'd told and burnished for nearly half my life. All these engraved acts of residence I'd dutifully committed, with staying-on as my theme. Only I didn't like it anymore.

THE DEVIL is in the details, of course, even the details of our affections. We'd, by then, earned a new area code—cold, unmemorable 908 supplanting likable time-softened old 609. New blue laws had been set up to keep pleasure in check. Traffic was deranging—spending thirty minutes to go less than a mile made everyone reappraise the entire concept of mobility and of how important it could ever be to get anywhere. Seminary Street had become the preferred home-office address for every species of organization whose mission was to help groups who didn't know they comprised a group become one: the black twins consortium; support entities for people who'd lost all their body hair; the families of victims of school-yard bullying; the Life After Kappa Kappa Gamma Association. Boro government had turned all-female and become mean as vipers. Regulations and ordinances spewed out of the council chamber, and litigation was on everyone's lips. A new sign ordinance forbade FOR SALE signs on lawns, since they sowed seeds of anxiety and a fear of impermanence in citizens not yet moving out—this was rescinded. Empty storefronts were outlawed *per se* so that owners forced to sell had to *seem* to stay in business. An ordinance even required that Halloween be "positive"—no more ghosts or Satans, no more flaming bags of feces left on porches. Instead, kids went out dressed as EMS drivers, priests and librarians.

Meanwhile, new human waves were coming, commuting *into* Haddam instead of *out to* Gotham and Philly. A small homeless population sprouted up. Dental appointments averaged thirteen months' advance booking. And residents I'd meet on the street, citizens I'd known for a generation and sold homes to, now refused to meet my eyes, just set their gaze at my hairline and kept trudging, as if we'd all become the quirky, invisible "older" town fixtures we'd encountered when we ouselves had arrived decades ago.

Haddam, in these devil's details, stopped being a quiet and happy suburb, stopped being subordinate to any other place and became a *place to itself*, only without having a fixed municipal substance. It became a town of others, for others. You could say it lacked a soul, which would explain why somebody thinks it needs an interpretive center and why it seems like a good idea to celebrate a village past. The present is here, but you can't feel its weight in your hand.

Back in the days when I got into the realty business, we used to laugh about homogeneity: buying it, selling it, promoting it, eating it for breakfast, lunch and dinner. It seemed good—in the

way that everyone in the state having the same color license plate
was good (though now that's different, too). And since the benefits of fitting in were manifest and densely woven through,
homogenizing seemed like a sort of inverse pioneering. But by
1992, even homogeneity had gotten homogenized. Something
had hardened in Haddam, so that having a decent house on a safe
street, with like-minded neighbors and can't-miss equity growth
—a home as a natural extension of what was wanted from life, a
sort of minor-league Manifest Destiny—all that now seemed to
piss people off, instead of making them ecstatic (which is how
I expected people to feel when I sold them a house: happy). The
redemptive theme in the civic drama had been lost. And realty
itself—stage manager to that drama—had stopped signaling our
faith in the future, our determination not to give in to dread,
our blitheness in the face of life's epochal slowdown.

In short, as I stood out on Cleveland Street watching green-
suited Bekins men tote my blanketed belongings up the ramp
under matching green-leaf, sun-shot oaks and chestnuts just
showing the pastel stains of autumn 1992, I felt Haddam had
entered its period of era-lessness. It had become the emperor's
new suburb, a place where maybe someone might set a bomb off
just to attract its attention. The mystics would say it had lost its
crucial sense of East. Though east, to the very edge, was the
direction I was then taking.

THE CIRCUMSTANCES of my Sponsor visit this afternoon—in
Haddam, of all places—are not entirely the standard ones.
Normally, my Sponsoring activity is centered on the seaside
communities up Barnegat Neck, where I know practically no
one and typically can swing by someone's house or office, or
maybe make a meeting in a mall or a sub shop, not use up a whole
afternoon and be back at my desk in an hour and change. But
yesterday, due to other volunteers wanting off for Thanksgiving,
I received a call wondering if I might be going to Haddam today,
and if so, could I make a Sponsor stop. I've kept my name on
the Haddam list since I'm regularly in and out of town, know
relatively few people anymore, and because—as I've said—
I know the town can leave people feeling dismal and friendless,
even though every civic nook, cranny and nail hole is charming,

well-rounded and defended, and as seemingly caring, congenial and immune to misery as a fairy-tale village in Switzerland.

Sally actually prompted my first Sponsor visits four years back. She'd grown depressed by her own work—a company that mini-bused terminally ill Jerseyites to see Broadway plays, provided dinner at Mama Leone's and a tee-shirt that said *Still Kickin' in NJ*, then bused them home. Constant company with the dying, staying upbeat all the time, sitting through *Fiddler on the Roof* and *Les Misérables*, then having to talk about it all for hours, finally proved a draw-down on her spirits after more than a decade. Plus, the dying complained ceaselessly about the service, the theater seats, the food, the acting, the weather, the suspension system on the bus—which caused employee turnover and inspired the ones who stayed to steal from the oldsters and treat them sarcastically, so that lawsuits seemed just around the corner.

In 1996, she sold the business and was at home in Sea-Clift for a summer with not enough to do. She read a story in the *Shore Plain Dealer*, our local weekly, that declared the average American to have 9.5 friends. Republicans, it said, typically had more than Democrats. This was easy to believe, since Republicans are genetically willing to trust the surface nature of *everything*, which is where most friendships thrive, whereas Democrats are forever getting mired in the meaning of every goddamn thing, suffering doubts, regretting their actions and growing angry, resentful and insistent, which is where friendships languish. The *Plain Dealer* said that though 9.5 might seem like plenty of friends, statistics lied, and that many functioning, genial, not terminally ill, incapacitated or drug-addicted people, in fact, had *no* friends. And quite a few of these friendless souls—which was the local hook— lived in Ocean County and were people you saw every day. This, the writer editorialized, was a helluva note in a bounteous state like ours, and represented, in his view, an "epidemic" of friendlessness (which sounded extreme to me).

Some people over in Ocean County Human Services, in Toms River, apparently read the *Plain Dealer* story and decided to take the problem of friendlessness into their own hands, and in no time at all got an 877 "Sponsor Line" authorized that would get a person visited by another tolerant and feeling human not of their acquaintance within twenty-four hours of a call. This Sponsor-visitor would be somebody who'd been certified not to be a pedophile, a fetishist, a voyeur or a recent divorcée, and also not simply someone as lonely as the caller. The cost of a visit would be zilch, though there was a charities list on a Web site someplace, and contributions were anonymous.

Sally got wind of the Sponsor Line and called to inquire that very afternoon—it was in September—and went over for a screening interview and, probably because of her work with the dying, got right onto the Sponsors list. The Human Services people had figured out a digitized elimination system to ensure that the same Sponsor wouldn't visit the same caller more than once, *ever*. Callers themselves were screened by psych grad students and a profile was worked up using a series of five innocuous questions that ferreted out lurkers, stalkers, weenie wavers, bondage aficionados, self-published poets, etc.

The idea worked well right from the start and, in fact, still works great. Sally started going on one but sometimes three Sponsor visits a week, as far away as Long Branch and as close in as Seaside Heights. The idea pretty quickly caught on in other counties, including Delaware County, where Haddam is. A cross-referenced list of people like me who operate in a wider than ordinary geographical compass was compiled. And after signing up, I made Sponsor visits as far away as Cape May and Burlington—where I do some bank appraisals—or, as here in Haddam today, when I just happen to be in the neighborhood and have some time to kill. I originally thought I might snag a listing or two, or even a sale, since people often need a friend to give them advice about selling their house, and will sometimes make a decision based on feeling momentarily euphoric. Though that's never happened, and in any case, it's against all the guidelines.

Nothing technical's required to be a Sponsor: a willingness to listen (which you need in liberal quantities as a realtor), a slice of common sense, an underdeveloped sense of irony, a liking for strangers and a capacity to be disengaged while staying sincerely focused on whatever question greets you when you walk in the door. There have been concerns that despite the grad student screening, innocent callers would be vulnerable if a bad-seed Sponsor made it through the net. But it's been generally felt that the gain is more important than the modest statistical risk—and like I said, so far, so good.

It turns out that the hardest thing to find in the modern world is sound, generalized, disinterested advice—of the kind that instructs you, say, not to get on the Tilt-A-Whirl at the county fair once you've seen the guys who're running it; or to always check to see that your spare's inflated before you start out overland in your '55 roadster from Barstow to Banning. You can always get plenty of highly specialized technical advice—about whether your tweeter is putting out the prescribed number of amps to get the best sound out of your vintage Jo Stafford monaurals, or whether this epoxy is right for mending the sea kayak you rammed into Porpoise Rock on your vacation to Maine. And you can always, of course, get very bad and wrong advice about most anything: "This extra virgin olive oil'll work as good as STP on that outboard of yours"; "Next time that asshole parks across your driveway, I'd go after him with a ball-peen hammer." Plus, nobody any longer wants to help you more than they minimally have to: "If you want shirts, go to the shirt department, this floor's all pants"; "We had those Molotov avocados last year, but I don't know how I'd go about reordering them"; "I'm going on my break now or I'd dig up that rest room key for you."

But plain, low-impact good counsel and assistance is at an all-time low.

I stress low-impact because the usual scope of Sponsor transactions is broad but rarely deep—just like a real friendship. "When you sharpen that hunting knife, do you run the stone *with* the cutting edge or *against* it?" For better or worse, I'm a man people are willing to tell the most remarkable things to—their earliest sexual encounters, their bankruptcy status, their previously unacknowledged criminal past. Though Sponsorees are not encouraged to spill their guts or say a lot of embarrassing crap they'll later regret and hate themselves (and you) for the minute you're gone. Most of my visits are, in fact, surprisingly brief—less than twenty minutes—with an hour being the limit. After an hour, the disinterested character of things can shift and problems sprout. Our guidelines specify every attempt be made to make visits as close to natural as can be, stressing informality, the spontaneous and the presumption that both parties need to be someplace else pretty soon anyway.

In my own case, my demeanor's never grim or solemn or clerical, or, for that matter, not even especially happy. I steer clear of the religious, of sexual topics, politics, financial observations and relationship lingo. (On these topics, even priests', shrinks' and money analysts' advice is rarely any good, since who has much in common with these people?) My Sponsor visits are more like a friendly stop-by from the bland State Farm guy, who you've run into at the tire store, asked over to the house to tweak your coverage, but who you then enlist to help get the lawn sprinkler to work. So far, my Sponsorees have done nothing to take extra advantage, and neither have I gone away once thinking a "really interesting" relationship has been unearthed. And yet if you impulsively blab to me that you stabbed your Aunt Carlotta down in Vicksburg back in 1951, or went AWOL from Camp Lejeune during Tet, or fathered a Bahamian baby who's now fighting for life and is in need of a kidney transplant for which you are the only match, you can expect me to go straight to the authorities.

With all these provisos and safety nets and firewalls, you might expect most callers to be elderly shut-ins or toxic cranks who've savaged all their friends and now need a new audience. Or else cancer victims who've gotten sick of their families (it happens) and just need somebody new to stare intensely into the face of. And some are. But mostly they're just average souls who need you to go out to their garage to see if their grandfather's hand-carved cherry partners' desk has been stolen by their nephew, the way it was foretold in a nightmare. Or who want you to write a dunning letter to the water department about the three-hour stoppage in June—while the main line was being repaired—demanding an adjustment in the next month's bill.

There are also prosperous, affluent, young-middle-aged, 24/7 type A's. These people are often the least at ease and typically want something completely banal and easy—to tell you a joke they think is hilarious but can't remember to tell anybody they know because they're too busy. Or women who want to yak about their kids for thirty minutes but can't because it's incorrect—in their set—to do that to their friends. Or men who ask me what color Escalade looks good against the exterior paint scheme of their new beach house in Brielle. But on three separate occasions—one woman and two men—the question I answered was (based on just two minutes' acquaintance) did I think she or he was an asshole. In each case, I said I definitely didn't think so.

I've begun to wonder, since then, if this isn't the underlying theme of most all my Sponsorees' questions (especially the rich ones), since it's the thing we all want to know, that causes most of our deflected worries and that we fear may be true but find impossible to get a frank opinion about from the world at large. Am I good? Am I bad? Or am I somewhere lost in the foggy middle?

I wouldn't ordinarily have thought that I'd get within two football fields of anything like Sponsoring, since I'm not a natural joiner, inquirer or divulger. Yet I know the difficulty of making new friends—which isn't that the world's not full of interesting, available new people. It's that the past gets so congested with lived life that anyone in their third quartile—which includes me—is already far enough along the road that making a friend like you could when you were twenty-five involves so much brain-rending and boring catching up that it simply isn't worth the effort. You see and hear people vainly doing it every day—yakkedy, yakkedy, yakkedy: "That reminds me of our family's trips to Pensacola in 1955." "That reminds me of what my first wife used to complain about." "That reminds me of my son getting smacked in the eye with a baseball." "That reminds me of a dog we had that got run over in front of the house." Yakkedy, yakkedy and more goddamn yakkedy, until the ground quakes beneath us all.

So—unless sex or sports is the topic, or it's your own children —when you meet someone who might be a legitimate friend candidate, the natural impulse is to start fading back to avoid all the yakkedy-yak, so that you fade and fade, until you can't see him or her anymore, and couldn't bear to anyway. With the result that attraction quickly becomes avoidance. In this way, the leading edge of your life—what you did this morning after breakfast, who called you on the phone and woke you up from your nap, what the roofing guy said about your ice-dam flashings—*that becomes all your life is*: whatever you're doing, saying, thinking, planning *right then*. Which leaves whatever you're recollecting, brooding about, whoever it is you've loved for years but still need to get your head screwed on straight about—in other words, the important things in life—all of *that's* left unattended and in need of expression.

The Permanent Period tries to reconcile these irreconcilables in your favor by making the congested, entangling past fade to beige, and the present brighten with its present-ness. This is the very deep water my daughter, Clarissa, is at present wading through and knows it: how to keep afloat in the populous hazardous mainstream (the yakkedy-yak and worse) without drowning; versus being pleasantly safe in your own little eddy. It's what my more affluent Sponsorees want to know when they make me listen to their unfunny jokes or crave to know if they're good people or not: Am I doing reasonably well under testing circumstances? (Thinking you're good can give you courage.) It also happens to be precisely the dilemma my son Paul has settled in his own favor in the embedded, miniaturized mainstream life of Kanzcity and Hallmark. He may be much smarter than I know.

Depth may be all that Sponsoring really lacks—with sincerity as its mainstay. Most people already feel in-deep-and-dense enough with life involvement, which may be their very problem: The voice is strangled by too much woolly experience ever to make it out and be heard. I know I've felt that way more in this fateful year than ever before, so that sometimes I think I could use a Sponsor visit myself. (This very fact may make me a natural Sponsor, since just like being a decent realtor, you have to at least harbor the suspicion that you have a lot in common with *everybody*, even if you don't want to be their friend.)

My other reason for getting involved in Sponsoring is that Sponsoring carries with it a rare optimism that says some things can actually work out and puts a premium on inching beyond your limits, while rendering Sponsorees less risk-averse on a regular daily basis and less like those oldsters in their blue New Yorkers who won't make a mistake for fear of bad results that're coming anyway.

And of course the final reason I'm a Sponsor is that I have cancer. Contrary to the TV ads showing cancer victims staring dolefully out though lacy-curtained windows at empty playgrounds, or sitting alone on the sidelines while the rest of the non-cancerous family stages a barbecue or a boating adventure on Lake Wapanooki or gets into clog dancing or Whiffle ball, cancer (little-d death, after all), in fact, makes you a lot more interested in other people's woes, with a view to helping with improvements. Getting out on the short end of the branch leaves you (has me, anyway) *more* interested in life—any life—not less.

Since it makes the life you're precariously living, and that may be headed for the precipice, feel fuller, dearer, more worthy of living—just the way you always hoped would happen when you thought you were well.

Other people, in fact—if you keep the numbers small—are not always hell.

The last thing I'll say, as I pull up in front at #24 Bondurant Court, residence of a certain Mrs. Purcell, where I'm soon to be inside Sponsoring a better outcome to things, is that even though other people are worth helping and life be fuller, etc., etc., Sponsoring has never actually produced a greater sense of connectedness in me, and probably not in others—the storied lashing-together-of-boats we're all supposed to crave and weep salty tears at night for the lack of. It could happen. But the truth is, I feel connected enough already. And Sponsoring is not about connectedness anyway. It's about being consoled by connection's opposite. A little connectedness, in fact, goes a long way, no matter what the professional lonelies of the world say. We might all do with a little less of it.

NUMBER 24, where lights are on inside, is built in the solid, monied, happy family-home-as-refuge style, houses Haddam boasts in fulsome supply, owing to its staunch Dutch-Quaker beginnings and to a brief nineteenth-century craving for ornamental English-German prettiness. Vernacular, this is sometimes called—neat, symmetrical, gray-stucco, red-doored Georgians with slate roofs, four shuttered front windows upstairs and down, a small but fancy wedding-cake entry, curved fanlight with formal sidelights, dentil trim and squared-off (expensive) privet hedges bolstering the front. Intimations of heterodoxy, but nothing truly eye-catching. Thirty-five hundred square feet, not counting the basement and four baths. A million-two, if you bought it this very afternoon—complete with the platinum BMW M3 sitting in the side drive—though with the risk that a surveilling neighbor will come along before you sign the papers and snake it away for a million-two-five so he can sell it to his former law partner's ex-wife.

Bondurant Court is actually a cul-de-sac off Rosedale Road. Three other residences, two of them certifiable Georgian stately homes, lurk deep within bosky, heavily treed lawns on which many original willows and elms remain. The third home-like structure is a pale-gray flat-roofed, windowless concrete oddity with a Roman-bath floor plan built by a Princeton architect for a twenty-five-year-old dot-com celebrity who no one speaks to for architectural reasons. Children aren't allowed to go there on Halloween or caroling at Christmas. Rumors are out that the owner's moved back to Malibu. I'm surprised not to see a Lauren-Schwindell sign out front, since one of my former colleagues sold him the lot.

Number 24—the great neighbor-houses' little sister—would be a great buy for a new divorcée with dough, or for a newly-wed lawyer couple or a discreet gay M.D. with a Gotham practice who needs a getaway. If I could've sold easy houses like this, instead of overpriced mop closets you couldn't fart in without the whole block smelling it, I might've stayed.

And like clockwork, as I stride up the flagstones toward the brass-knockered red door—two shiny brass carriage lamps turning on in unison—I experience the anti-Permanent Period williwaws lifting off of me and the exhilaration of whatever's about to open up here streaming into my limbs and veins like a physic. One could easily wonder, of course, about a Mr. Definitely Wrong being set to spring out from the other side of the heavy door—John Wayne Gacy in clown gear, waiting to eat me with sauerkraut. What would the termite guy or the Culligan Man do, faced as they are with the same imponderables on a daily basis? Just use the old noodle. Stay alert for the obviously weird, attend your senses, drink and eat nothing, identify exits. I've, in fact, never really feared anything worse than being bored to bits. Plus, if they're gonna, they're gonna—like the little town in Georgia the tornado ripped a hole through when everybody was at church on Sunday, believing such things didn't happen there.

Everything happens everywhere. Look at the fucking election.

Ding-dong. Ding-dong. Ding-dong.

A melodious belling. I turn and re-survey the cul-de-sac—wet, cold, bestilled, its other ponderous residences all bearing lawn signs: WARNING. THIS HOUSE IS PATROLLED. The big Georgians' many leaded windows glow through the trees with antique light, as though lit by torches. No humans or animals are in view. A police car or ambulance *wee-up, wee-ups* in the distance. Cold air hisses with the rain's departure. A crow calls from a spruce, then a second, but nothing's in sight.

Noises become audible within. A female throat is cleared, a chain lock slid down its track. The brass peephole darkens with an interior eye. A dead bolt's conclusively thrown. I rise a quarter inch onto my toes.

"Just a moment, pu-lease." A rilling, pleasant voice in which, do I detect, the undertones of Dixie? I hope not.

The heavy door opens back. A smiling woman stands in its space. This is the best part of Sponsoring—the relief of finally arriving to someone's rescue.

But I sense: Here is not a complete stranger. Though from out on the bristly welcome mat, the back of my head feeling a breeze flood past into the homey-feeling house, I can't instantly supply coordinates. My brow feels thick. My mouth is half-open, beginning to smile. I peer through the angled door opening at Mrs. Purcell.

It couldn't be a worse opening gambit, of course, for a Sponsor to stare simian-like at the Sponsoree, who may already be fearful the visitor will be a snorting crotch-clutcher escapee from a private hospital, who'll leave her trussed up in the maid's closet while he makes off with her underthings. The risk for doing Sponsor work in Haddam is always, of course, that I might know my Sponsoree: a face, a history, a colorful story that defeats disinterest and ruins everything. I should've been more prudent.

Except maybe not. Some days, I see whole crowds of people who look exactly like other people I know but who're, in fact, total strangers. It's my age and age's great infirmity: over-accumulation—the same reason I don't make friends anymore. Sally always said this was a grave sign, that I was spiritually afraid of the unknown—unlike herself, who left me for her dead husband. Though I thought—and still do—that it was actually a positive sign. By thinking I recognized strangers I, in fact, *didn't* recognize, I was actually reaching out to the unknown, making the world my familiar. No doubt this is why I've sold many, many houses that no one else wanted.

"Are you Mr. Fruank?" Dixie's definitely alight in the voice: bright, sweet and rising at the end to make everything a happy question; vowels that make *you* sound like *yew*, *handle* like *handull*. Central Virginia's my guess.

"Hi. Yeah. I'm Frank." I extend an affirming hand with a friendlier smile. I'm not a leering crotch-clutcher or a dampened-panty faddist. Sponsors omit last names—which is simpler when you leave.

"Well, Ah'm Marguerite Purcell, Mr. Fruank. Why don't you come in out of this *b-r-r-r* we're havin'." Marguerite Purcell, who's dressed in a two-piece suit that must be raw silk of the rarest French-rose hue, with matching Gucci flats, steps back in welcome—the most cordial-confident of graceful hostesses, clearly accustomed to all kinds, high to low, entering her private home on every imaginable occasion. Haddam has always absorbed a small population of dispirited, old-monied southerners who can't stand the South yet can only bear the company of one another in deracinated enclaves like Haddam, Newport and Northeast Harbor. You catch glimpses of their murmuring Town Cars swaying processionally out gated driveways, headed to the Homestead for golf-and-bridge weekends with other white-shoed W&L grads, or turning north to Naskeag to spend August with Grandma Ni-Ni on Eggemoggin Reach—all of them iron-kneed Republicans who want us out of the UN, nigras off the curbs and back in the fields, the Suez mined, and who think the country missed its chance by not choosing ole Strom back in '48. Hostesses like Marguerite Purcell never have problems money can't solve. So what am I doing here?

"Ahm just astonissshed by this weathuh." Marguerite's leading me through the parquet foyer into a living room "done" like no living room I've seen (and I've seen a few) and that the staid Quaker exterior gives no hint of. The two big front windows have been sheathed with shiny white lacquered paneling. The walls are also lacquered white. The green-vaulted ceiling firmament has tiny recessed pin lights shining every which way, making the room bright as an operating theater. The floors are bare wood and waxed to a fierce sheen. There are no plants. The only furnishings are two immense, hard-as-granite rectilinear love seats, covered in some sort of dyed-red animal skin, situated on a square of blue carpet, facing each other across a thick slab-of-glass coffee table that actually has fish swimming inside it (a dozen lurid, fat, motionless white goldfish), the whole *objet* supported by an enormous hunk of curved, polished chrome, which I recognize as the bumper off a '54 Buick. The air is odorless, as if the room had been chemically scrubbed to leave no evidence of prior human habitation. Nothing recalls a day when regular people sat in regular chairs and watched TV, read books, got into arguments or made love on an old braided rug while logs burned cheerily in a fireplace. The only animate sign is a white CO_2 detector mid-ceiling with its tiny blinking red beacon. Though on the wall above where a fireplace ought to be, there's a gilt-framed, essentially life-size oil portrait of an elderly, handsome, mustachioed, silver-haired, capitalist-looking gentleman in safari attire, a floppy white-hunter fedora and holding a Mannlicher .50 in front of a stuffed rhino head (the very skin used to make the couch). This fellow stares from the wall with piercing, dark robber-baron eyes, a cruel sensuous mouth, uplifted nose and bruising brow, but with a mysterious, corners-up smirk on his lips, as if once a great, diminishing joke has been told and he was the first one to get it.

"This wuss my husbund's favorite room," Marguerite says dreamily, still primly smiling. She establishes herself on the front edge of one of the red love seats, facing me across the aquarium table, squeezing together, then shifting to the side her shiny stockinged knees. She possesses thin, delicately veined ankles, one of which wears a nearly invisible gold chain flattened beneath the nylon. She is all Old Dominion comeliness, the last breathing female you'd think could stomach a room as weird as this. Obviously, she married it, but now that the Mister's retreated to his place on the wall, she doesn't know what in the fuck to do with it. This may be what she wants me to tell her. Anyone—but me—couldn't resist asking her a hundred juicy, prying, none-of-your-business questions. But, as with all Sponsor visits, I heed the presence of an invisible privacy screen between Sponsoree and self. That works out best for everybody.

From where I sit, Marguerite seems to have the lens softened all around her—a trick of the pin lights in the celestial green ceiling. She's maybe mid-Fifties but has a plush, young-appearing face she's applied a faint rouging to, a worry-free forehead, welcoming blue eyes, with an obviously sizable bustage under her rose suit jacket, and an amorous full-lipped mouth, through which her voice makes a soft whistling sound ("ssurely," "hussbund's"), as if her teeth were in the way. My guess is she's the hoped-for result of a high-end makeover—a length somebody might gladly go to for the chance of an enduring (and rich) second marriage. Her hair, however, is the standard bottle-brown southern *do* with a wide, pale, scalp-revealing middle part going halfway back, with the rest cemented into a flip that only elderly hairdressers in Richmond know how to properly mold. Southern socialites—my schoolmates' mothers at Gulf Pines Academy, who'd drive down from Montgomery and Lookout to speak briefly to their villainous sons through lowered windows of their Olds Ninety Eights—wore exactly this hair construction back in 1959. I actually find it sexy as hell, since it reminds me of my young and (I felt) clearly lust-driven fourth-grade teacher, Miss Hapthorn, back in Biloxi.

When she led me into the lifeless and over-heated living room, I noticed Marguerite stealing two spying looks my way as if I, too, might've reminded her of somebody and wasn't the only one searching time's vault.

And she's now examining me again. And not like the beguiling Virginia hostess who sparkles at the guest, hoping to find something she can adore so she can decide to change her mind about it later, but with the same submerged acknowledging I detected before. These magnolia blossoms, of course, can be scrotum-cracking, trust-fund bullies who secretly smoke Luckies, drink gin by the gallon, screw the golf pro and don't give an inch once money's on the table. Only they never act that way when you first make their acquaintance. I'm wondering if I sold her a house back in the mists.

Though all at once my heart, out ahead of my brain, exerts a boulderish, possibly audible *whump-whoomp-de-whomp*. I know Marguerite Purcell. Or I did.

The knees. The good ankles. The ghosty anklet. The bustage. The plump lips. The way the peepers fasten on me, slowly close, then stay closed too long, revealing an underlying authority making decisions for the composed face. (The lisp is new.) She may remember me, too. Except if I admit it, Sponsorship loses all purchase and I'll have to beat it, just when I got here.

Marguerite reopens her small pale blue eyes, looks self-consciously down, arranges her pretty hands on her rose skirt hem, flattens the fabric across her knee-tops, smiles again and recrosses her ankles. No one's spoken since we sat down. Maybe she's also having a day when everybody looks like somebody else and thinks nothing of this moment of faulty recognition. And maybe she's *not* the woman I "slept" with how many years back (sleep did eventually come), when her name was Betty Barksdale—"Dusty" to her friends—then the beleaguered, abandoned wife of Fincher Barksdale, change-jingling local M.D. and turd. He left her to join some foreign-doctors outfit in deepest Africa, where he reportedly went native, learned the local patois, took a fat African bride with tribal scarrings, began doctoring to the insurgents (the wrong insurgents) and ended up in a fetid, lightless, tin-sided back-country prison from which he eventually found his way to a public square in a regional market town, where he was roped to a metal no-parking post and hacked at for a while by boy soldiers hepped up on the amphetamines he'd been feeding them.

But even if Marguerite *is* the metamorphosed Dusty from '88, I may not be that easy to recollect. Most high jinks aren't worth remembering anyway. Behind her warm, self-conscious smile, she might be silently saying, What is it now? This guy? Frank ... um ... something? Something about when my first husband, something, I guess, didn't come back or some goddamn thing. Who cares?

I'd lobby for that. We don't have to revisit a tepid boinking we boozily committed upstairs in her green-shingled Victorian on Westerly Road that Fincher stuck her with. Though if it *is* her, I'd like (silently) to compliment the impressive metamorphosis to magnolia blossom, since the Dusty I knew was a smirky, blond, slightly hard-edged, cigarette-smoking former Goucher girl who made fun of her husband's blabbermouth east Memphis relatives and about what he'd think if he ever knew she was rogering the realtor. He never got to think anything.

Though the wellspring of transformation is almost always money. It works miracles. First Fincher's big life-insurance policies, then the lavishments of old Clyde Beatty Purcell all worked their changes. Ex-friends who knew her as sorrowing, needful Dusty could all go fuck themselves. (I'd like to know if I look as old as she does. Possibly yes. I've had cancer, I'm internally radiated, in recovery. It happens.)

Marguerite's warm society smile has faded to a querulous pert, designating confusion. I've become quiet and may have alarmed her. Her eyes elevate above my head to gaze toward the blocked-off front windows, as if she could see through them to the dying day. She wags her soft chin slowly, as though confirming something. "I don't want to talk about our politics, Mr. Frank, it's too depressin'." Politics is strictly verboten in Sponsoring anyway. Hard to think we could be on the same side. "In the *New Yawk Times* today, Mr. Bush said if Florida goes to the Dem-uh-crats, it could be ahrmed insurrection. Or worse. That rascal Clinton. It'ss shocking." She frowns with disdain, then she sniffs, her nose darting upward as if she'd just sniffed the whole disreputable business out of the air forever.

But with this gesture, the Marguerite-Dusty-Betty deal is sealed. In our night of brief abandon, after I'd shown her a gigantic Santa Barbara hacienda on Fackler Road (she wanted to squander all Fincher's money so he *couldn't* come home), we two wound up on bar stools at the Ramada on Route 1, with one thing following fumblingly the next. I had a well-motivated prohibition against casual client boinking, but it got lost in the shuffle.

As the night spirited on and the Manhattans kept arriving, Dusty, who'd begun referring to herself as "the Dream Weaver," gradually gave in to a strange schedule of abrupt smirks, fidgets, tics, brow-clenchings, lip-squeezings, cheek-puffings, teeth-barings and fearsome eye-rollings—as if life itself had ignited a swarm of nervous weirdness, attesting to the great strain of it all. It rendered our subsequent lovemaking a challenge and, as I remember it, unsuccessful, except for me, of course. Though the next morning when I was skulking out through the kitchen door (I thought before she could wake up), I encountered Dream Weaver Dusty, already at the sink in a faded red kimono, staring wanly out the window, hair askew and barefoot, but with an unaccountably graceful, empathetic welcome and a weak smile, wondering if I wanted an English muffin or maybe a poached egg before I disappeared. She was hollow-eyed and certainly didn't want me to stay (I didn't). But the night's stress-plus-booze-inspired tangle of tics, warps and winces had also vanished, leaving her exhausted but calm. Vanished, that is, except for one—the one I just saw, the tiny heavenward flickage of nose tip toward ceiling, punctuating a subject needing to be put to rest. Its effect on me now is to inspire not what you'd think, but even franker admiration for her reincarnation and the proficient adaptation to the times. How many of us, faced with a bad part to play, wouldn't like to slip offstage in act one, then reappear in act three as an entirely different personage? It's a wonder it doesn't happen more. My wife, Sally, did the exact opposite when, far along in the play, she went back to being the wife from act one who never got the ovation she deserved.

I look out the arched doorway to the parquet foyer and to closed doors leading farther into the house. Is anyone else in here with us? A loyal servant, a Cairn terrier, possibly old Purcell himself, hooked to tubes and breathing devices, up the back stairs, watching game shows.

"I don't want to talk about politics, either." I smile back like a kindly old GP with a pretty patient presenting with nonspecific symptoms that don't really bother her all that much. Possibly there are indistinct rumblings happening inside her brain—an English-muffin moment without a place in time.

"I have a strange question to ask you, Frank." Marguerite's delicate shoulders go square, her back straightens, fingers unlace and re-lace atop her shiny knees. Perfect posture, as always, ignites the low venereal flicker. You never know about these things.

"Strange questions are our stock-in-trade," I offer back genially.

"I don't suppose you're an expert in this." Eyelids down and holding. I nod, expressing competence. Marguerite has worked a little free of her plantation accent. She's more downtown *Balmur.* Her limpid blues rise again and seek the absent window behind me and blink in an inspiration-seeking way. "I have a very strange urge to confess something." Her eyes stay aloft.

I am as noncommittal as Dr. Freud. "I see."

The room's glistening white walls, firmamental ceiling and aquarium table holding motionless, creepily mottled goldfish all radiate in silent stillness. I hear a heat source *tick-tick-ticking.* One of the crows outside issues a softened caw. It's a *Playhouse 90* moment, one interminable soundless shot. How do you get a room to smell this way, I wonder. Why would you want it to?

Marguerite's slender left hand, on which there's a ring supporting an emerald as big as a Cheerios box, wanders to above her left breast, fingertips just touching a pin made of two tiny finely joined golden apples, then returns to her knee. "But

I really have nothing to confess. Nothing at all." Her gaze falls to me plaintively. It is the look of someone who's spent twenty-five years in customer service at the White Plains Saks, feels okay about it, but now realizes something more challenging might've been possible. It's disheartening to encounter this look in a woman you like. "It's a little unnerving," she says softly. "What do you think, Frank?" Her full lips push tantalizingly outward to signify candor.

"How long have you been feeling this way?" I am still all doctorish-Sponsorish concern.

"Oh. Sixss months."

"Did anything seem to cause it?"

Marguerite inhales a deep chest-swelling breath and lets it out. "No." Two blue eye blinks. "I keep thinking whatever it is will just come to me while I'm boiling a putatuh. Somebody'd abused me as a child, or my mother'd been a woman of mixed blood." Or you once fucked your realtor when you had a whole nuther identity. This trunk lid we won't open. "I certainly don't want something terrible to be true. If I've forgotten something terrible, I'm happy for it to stay that way."

"I can't blame you there." My eyes fasten on her for the benefit of verisimilitude.

"I call it a need to confess. But it's maybe something else."

"What else could you maybe call it?"

Marguerite suddenly sits up even more erectly, her softened features alert. "I haven't really thought about that."

"You might just have to make it up, then."

Her mouth now transforms into a mirthless almost-smile. I believe she may have quickly crossed her eyes and instantly uncrossed them—another of the Eighties-era tics. "I don't know, Frank. Maybe it's an urge to clear sssomething up."

My face, by practice, expresses nothing. Ann and I used to ask each other—when one of us would register a complaint the other couldn't properly address: "What's your neurosis allowing you to do that you couldn't do otherwise?" Mostly the answer was to complain and enjoy it. This might be the urge that Marguerite's experiencing. "Would you really like to know what to confess, no matter what?" I ask. "Or would you be happy to just quit feeling this way and never confess anything?"

"I guess the latter, Frank. Iss that horrible?"

"Maybe if you murdered somebody," I say. Put arsenic in their smoothie at the health club. "Did you murder anybody?" Fincher wouldn't count.

"No." She clasps her hands and looks distressed, as if she sort of wished she could say she *had* murdered somebody, make me believe it, then take it all back, leaving behind a zesty fragrance of doubt. "I don't think I have the right character for that," she says wondrously.

My bet, though, is she's never done anything wrong. Married a shit, been treated shabbily, forgettably rogered the realtor, but then reconstituted herself, married a better sod who left her well-off and didn't stick around for *forever*. It's not all that different from the story behind many doors I knock on, though it doesn't make much of a climax and I'm not usually a ghost presence. But—the guy with the sailboat that's driving him nuts; Bettina, the fractious Dutch housekeeper—there *is* the need to tell, which is its own virtue and complaint. That's why I'm here—it could be the modern dilemma. But like many modern dilemmas, it's susceptible to a cure.

"I'm not sure we have characters, Marguerite. Are you? I've thought a lot about it." I press my lips together to signal this is my judgment *in re* her problem. Any suspicion that I might *be* the problem is entirely nugatory.

"No." A quarter smile of recognition emerges onto her whole face. I wonder if I already said this to her sixteen years ago in some postcoital posturings. I hope not. "No, I'm not. I'm Episscopalian, Frank, but I'm not religious."

I give a wink of "me, neither" assurance. "We may think we have a character because it makes everything simpler."

"Yes."

"But what we do have for sure," I say supremely, "is memories, presents, futures, desires, hatreds, et cetera. And it's our job to govern those as much as we can. How we do that may be the only character we have, if you know what I mean."

"Yes." She is possibly stumped.

"*Your* job, I think, is to control your memory so it doesn't bother you. Since from what you say, it shouldn't bother you. Right? There isn't even a bad memory there."

"No." She clears her throat, lets her eyes drop. I may be veering near privileged subjects, where I don't want to veer, but the truth is the truth. "And how do I do that, Frank?" she says. "That's the problem, isn't it?"

"No. I don't think that's the problem at all." I'm beaming. I certainly *should* have been able to explain this decades back, in the kitchen, over our muffin. Isn't that where we want our casual couplings to lead us? To someone we can tell something to? Even if there isn't anything to tell. Maybe it's me who's reincarnated. "I don't think there *is* a problem," I say enthusiastically. "You just have to believe this feeling of wanting to confess something is a natural feeling. And probably a good omen for the future." My eyes roam up and catch the knowing gimlet eye of old Purcell, bearing down on me in his white-hunter outfit. I am your surrogate here, I think, not your adversary. It is the genius soul of Sponsoring.

"The future?" Marguerite clears her throat again, stagily. We've moved onto the bright future, where we belong.

"Sometimes we think that before we can go on with life we have to get the past all settled." I am as soulful as a St. Bernard. "But that's not true. We'd never get anyplace if it was."

"Probably not." She's nodding.

Then neither of us says anything. Silences are almost always affirming. I cast a wary eye down into the aquarium, glass as thick as a bank window and beveled smooth all around its rhomboid to guard against gashed shins, snagged hems, toddlers and pets poking their eyes out. My face is mirrored back in the Buick bumper—as rubbery as the Elephant Man. I see one of the huge, glaucal goldfish looking at me. How would one feed them? Probably there's a way. Possibly they're not real—

"Ah yew plannin' on a big Thanks-givin'?" I hear Marguerite say, Dixie, again, the music in her voice.

I smile stupidly across the table. When I first had my titanium BBs downloaded, I experienced all sorts of strange enervated zonings out and in, often at extremely unhandy moments— across the desk from a client who'd just signed an offer sheet obligating him to pay $75,000 if the deal fell through; or listening to a man tell me how the death of his wife made an instant sale a matter of highest priority. Then, ZAP, I'd be lost in a reverie about a Charlie Chan movie I saw, circa age ten, and whether it was Sidney Toler or Warner Oland in the title role. Again, Psimos says these "episodes" are not relatable to treatment. But I say baloney. I wouldn't have them if I didn't have what I *do have*. Either it was the BBs or the *thought* of BBs—a distinction that's not a difference.

"Do you have childrun?" I'm sure she's wondering what the hell's wrong with me.

"Yeah. Absolutely." I'm fuzzy-woozy. "They're coming. For Thanksgiving. Two of 'em." Sponsors aren't supposed to tell *our* stories. Expanded human contexts lead to random personal assessments. We're here to do a job, like the State Farm guy. Plus, now that we've gotten past it, I don't want to risk a needless *revisitus* of who was who, when *when* was when. It's not the key to Marguerite's mystery. There is no key. There is no mystery. We all live with that revelation.

I abruptly stand right up, straight as a sentry as if on command, but am woozy still. Satisfactory visit. Needs to be over. Done and done well. If I had a clipboard, it'd now be under my arm. If I had a hat, I'd be turning it by its brim.

"Are you leavin'?" Marguerite looks up at me, surprised, but automatically rises (a little stiffly) to let me know it's okay and not rude if I have to go. She looks hopefully across the strange aquarium table, then takes a hesitant turning step toward the foyer, her two feet going balky, as though they'd gone to sleep in their Guccis. "I 'magine you have other ssstops to make." (Do I walk like that?)

I'm eager to go, though still light-headed. Sponsor visits are more demanding than they seem and adieus can be unwieldy. People of both genders sometimes need to lavish hugs on you. I'm nervous Marguerite's going to spin round when we hit the parquet, take both my hands in her two warm ones, bull her way inside the invisible screen, peer into my bleary orbs, smile a smile of lost laughter and past regret and say something outrageous. Like: "We don't have to pretend anymore." Though we do! ". . . fate didn't intend us . . . it's true and it's sssad . . . but you've counseled me so well . . . couldn't you hold me for just a moment? . . ." I'll have a heart attack. You think you'll always be open to these impromptu clenches and whatever good mischief they lead to. But after a while you're not.

However, Marguerite says, "This election's made a mess out of everybody's Thanksssgiving, hasn't it, Fruank?" She turns to me in the entryway (I'm fearful) but is smiling ruefully, her veined hands folded at her rose pink waist like a schoolmarm. The little joined apples are glowing cheerfully. She clicks on the soft overhead globe, suffusing us in a deathly glow that guarantees, I trust, no smoochy-smoochy.

"I guess so." My eyes find the brass umbrella stand beside the door, as if one of the umbrellas is mine and I want it back. I must be going, yes, I must be going.

"You know, when I called to assk for a visit today—and I have these vissits quite often—I intended to ask for help in drafting a letter to President Clinton explaining all we have to be thankful for in this country. And then this other funny old business just popped up."

"Why'd you change your mind?" Why ask *that*! I've Sponsored so well up to now! I flinch and move my toes nearer the door. Cold breeze purrs beneath it, chilling my ankles and giving me a shiver. *Heat does not reach front foyer.* A prospective buyer wouldn't notice this till it's too late. I grasp the cold brass knob and twist-test it. Left, right.

"I'm really not sssure now." Marguerite's eyes cast down, as though the answer was on the floor.

I give the knob a quarter right twist, staring at the dark roots of Marguerite's hairline, up the regimental center part to nowhere. She looks up at me brazenly, eyes shining not with stayed tears but with resolve and optimism. "Do you think life's ssstrange, Frank?" At her waist, her fingers touch tips-to-tips. She's smiling a wonderful, positivistic Margaret Chase Smith smile.

"Depends on what you compare it to." If it's death, then no.

"Oh my." One eye narrows at me in tolerant ridicule. "That's really not a very good answser. Not for a ssmart boy like yew."

"You're right. Sorry."

"Let's just ssay it *isss* strange. That's the thought to ssay good-bye on, isn't it?"

"Okay." I give the ponderous door a ponderous tug. Cold damp instantly falls in on us like a tree.

"Thank you ssso much for coming." Marguerite cocks her pretty head like a sparrow, her nose flicking up. In no way does she mean "Thanks for coming back *finally.*" She extends a soft, bonily mature hand for me to grasp. I take it like a Japanese businessman, give her a firm double-hand up-down up-down, the kind I counsel Mike never to do, then turn loose quick. She looks in my eyes, then down to regard her empty hand, then smiles, shaking her head at life's weirdness. Women are stronger (and smarter) than men. Whoever doubted it? I attempt my manliest affirming smile, say *good* and *bye* between my lips and teeth, step out onto the bristly mat, into the frigid afternoon that looks like evening. Surprisingly, the red door closes hard behind me. I hear a lock go click, footsteps receding. Miraculously, and not a moment too soon, I'm history (again).

BACK IN the car, my heart—for reasons best known to Dr. DeBakey—*again* goes cavorting. *Whumpetty, whump-de-whumps* like a stallion in a stall when smoke's in the air. My scalp seizes. My skin prickles. Metallic ozone tang's in my mouth, as if something foreign had been in the car while I was inside. I sit and try to picture stillness, hold my cheek to the cold-fugged window glass, make myself simmer down so as not to lapse into "a state." Possibly I should put in my night guard.

Everyone's wondered: Will I *know* if I'm having a heart attack? The people who've had them—Hugh Wekkum, for one—say you can't *not* know. Only goofballs mistake it for acid reflux or over-excitement when you open the IRS letter. Unless, of course, you *want* to be in the dark—in which case everything's possible. EMS technicians testify—I read this in the Mayo newsletter I'm now sent whether I want it or not—that when they ask their patients, stretched out on sidewalks turning magenta, or doubled over in the expensive box seats at Shea, or being wheeled off a Northwest flight in Detroit, "What seems to be the trouble, sir?" the answer's usually "I think I'm having a fucking heart attack, you dickhead. What d'you think's wrong?" They're almost always right.

I am *not* having a heart attack, although having a Sea Biscuit heartbeat may mean something's not perfect, following on my partial fade-out inside Marguerite's. (The beef 'n bean burrito on an empty stomach is a suspect.) I take a peek through the hazy glass out at #24, cast in shapeless shadows. Lights downstairs are off, though the carriage lamps still burn. But Marguerite is now standing at an upstairs window, looking down at my car, wherein I'm trying to stop my galloping heart. I believe she's smiling.

Enigmatic. Knowing. I'm willing to bet she has no friends, lives isolated in the world of her inventions—helpfully underwritten by gobs of dough. I could go back inside and be her friend. We could speak of matters differently. But instead, I turn the key, set the wipers flopping, the defrost whooshing, the wheels to rolling—the bass *gur-murmur-murmur* of my Suburban's V-8 fortifying me just like the commercials promise. I am on my way to De Tocqueville and to Ann.

But. Let no man say here was not a successful Sponsoring—even if our present selves were under pressure from our past, which is what the past is good at. It's not so different from thinking you know people when you don't. Life *is* strange. What can we do about it? Which is why Sponsors are never concerned with underlying causes. My counsel was good counsel. Significant hurdles were cleared. One talked, one listened. Human character (or a lack thereof) was brought into play. A good future was projected. I'm actually now wondering if Marguerite could've been an older sister to Dusty and known nothing of me, only shared certain sibling nervous disorders. People, after all, have sisters. Whoever she was, she had legitimate issues I had a peculiarly good grasp on, and not just about reigniting the pilot light or reading the small print on the dehumidifier warranty. Something real (albeit invented) was bothering someone real (albeit invented). There are few enough chances to do the simple right thing anymore. A hundred years ago this week—in our grateful and unlitigious village past—this kind of good deed happened every day and all involved took it for granted. Looked at this way, Thanksgiving's not really a mess but more than anything else, commemorates a time we'll never see again.

I SHOULD SAY something about having cancer, since my health's on my mind now like a man being followed by an assassin. I'd like not to make a big to-do over it, since my view is that rather than *good* things coming to those who wait, *all* things—good, bad, indifferent—come to *all* of us if we simply hang around long enough. The poet wasn't wrong when he wrote, "Great nature has another thing to do to you and me . . . What falls away is always. And is near."

The telescoped version of the whole cancer rigamarole is that exactly four weeks after my wife, Sally Caldwell, announced she and her posthumous husband, Wally (a recent, honored guest in our house), were reconvening life on new footings and blah, blah, blah, blah, in earnest hope of gaining blah, blah, blah, blah, and better blah, blah, blah, blah, *I* happened to notice some dried brown blood driblets at about pecker height on my bed-sheets, and went straight off to Haddam Medical Arts out Harrison Road to find out what might be going on with what.

I was in robustest of health (so I thought) in spite of Sally's unhappy departure—which I assumed wouldn't last long. I did my sit-ups and stretches, took healthful treks down the Sea-Clift beach every other day. I didn't drink much. I kept my weight at 178—where it's been since my last year at Michigan. I didn't smoke, didn't take drugs, consumed fistfuls of daily vitamins, including saw palmetto and selenium, ate fish more than twice a week, conscientiously divided each calendar year into test results to test results. Nothing had come up amiss—colonoscopy, chest X ray, PSA, blood pressure, good cholesterol and bad, body mass, fat percentage, pulse rate, all moles declared harmless. Going for a checkup seemed purely a confirming experience: good-to-go another twelve, as though each visit was diagnostic, preventative and curative all at once. I'd never had a surgery. Illness was what others endured and newspapers wrote about.

"Probably nothing," Bernie Blumberg said, giving me a

wiseacre, pooch-mouthed Jewish butcher's wink, stripping his pale work gloves into a HAZARD can. "Prostatitis. Your gland feels a little smooshy. Slightly enlarged. Not unusual for your age. Nothing some good gherkina jerkina wouldn't clear up." He snorted, smacked his lips and dilated his nostrils as he washed his hands for the eightieth time that day (these guys earn their keep). "Your PSA's up because of the inflammation. I'll put you on some atomic-mycin and in four weeks do another PSA, after which you'll be free to resume front-line duties. How's that wife of yours?" Sally and I both went to Bernie. It's not unusual.

"She's in Mull with her dead husband," I said viciously. "We might be getting divorced." Though I didn't believe that.

"How 'bout that," Bernie said, and in an instant was gone— vanished out the door, or through the wall, or up the a/c vent or into thin air, his labcoat tails fluttering in a nonexistent breeze. "Well, look here now, how's that husband of yours?" I heard his voice sing out from somewhere, another examining room down a hall, while I cinched my belt, re-zipped, found my shoes and felt the odd queasiness up my butt. I heard his muffled laughter through cold walls. "Oh, he certainly should. Of course he should," he said. I couldn't hear the question.

Only in four weeks, my PSA showed another less-than-perfect 5.3, and Bernie said, "Well, let's give the pills another chance to work their magic." Bernie is a small, scrappy, squash-playing, wide-eyed, salt 'n pepper brush-cut Michigan Med grad from Wyandotte (which is why I go to him), an ex-Navy corpsman who practices a robust battlefield triage mentality that says only a sucking chest wound is worth getting jazzed up about. These guys aren't good when it comes to bedside etiquette and dispensing balming info. He's seen too much of life, and dreams of living in Bozeman and taking up decoy-carving. I, on the other hand, haven't seen enough yet.

"What happens if that doesn't work?" I said. Bernie was scanning the computerized pages of my blood work. We were in his little cubicle office. (Why don't these guys have nice offices? They're all rich.) His Michigan and Kenyon diplomas hung above his Navy discharge, next to a mahogany-framed display of his battle ribbons, including a Purple Heart. Outside on summer-steamy Harrison Road, jackhammers racketed away, making the office and the chair I occupied vibrate.

"Well"—not yet looking all the way over his glasses—"if that happens, I'll send you around the corner to my good friend Dr. Peplum over at Urology Partners, and he'll get you in for a sonogram and maybe a little biopsy."

"Do they do little ones?" My lower parts gripped their side walls. Biopsy!

"Yep. Uh-huh," Bernie said, nodding his head. "Nothin' to it. They put you to sleep."

"A biopsy. For cancer?" My heart was stilled. I was fully dressed, the office was freezing in spite of the warping New Jersey heat, and silent in spite of the outside bangety-bangety. Cobwebby green light sifted through the high windows, over which hung a green cotton curtain printed with faded Irish setter heads. Out in the hallway, I could hear happy female voices—nurses gossiping and giggling in hushed tones. One said, "Now that's Tony. You don't have to say any more." Another, "What a *rascal*." More giggling, their crepe soles gliding over scrubbed antiseptic tiles. This near-silent, for-all-the-world unremarkable moment, I knew, was the *fabled* moment. Things new and different and interesting possibly were afoot. Changes could ensue. Certain things taken for granted maybe couldn't be anymore.

I wasn't exactly afraid (nobody'd told me anything bad yet). I just wanted to take it in properly ahead of time so I'd know how to accommodate other possible surprises. If this shows a propensity to duck before I'm hit, to withhold commitment and not do *every goddamn thing* whole hog—then sue me. All boats, the saying goes, are looking for a place to sink. I was looking for a place to stay afloat. I must've known I had it. Women know "it's taken" two seconds after the guilty emission. Maybe you always know.

"I wouldn't get worked up over it yet." Bernie looked up distractedly, glancing across his metal desk, where my records lay.

My face was as open as a spring window to any news. I might as well have been a patient waiting to have a seed wart frozen off. "Okay, I won't," I said. And with that good advice in hand, I got up and left.

I WON'T BLUBBER ON: the freezing shock of *real* unwelcome news, the "interesting" sonogram, the sorry but somehow upbeat biopsy particulars, the perfidious prostate lingo—Gleason, Partin, oxidative damage, transrectal ultrasound, twelve-tissue sample (a lu-lu there), conscious sedation, watchful waiting, life-quality issues. There're bookstores full of this nasty business: *Prostate Cancer for Dummies*, *A Walking Tour Through Your Prostate* (in which the prostate has a happy face), treatment options, color diagrams, interactive prostate CD-ROMs, alternative routes for the proactive—all intended for the endlessly prostate-curious. Which I'm not. As though knowing a lot would keep you from getting it. It wouldn't—I already had it. Words can kill as well as save.

And yet. From the grim, unwanted and unexpected may arise the light-strewn and good. My daughter—tall, imperturbable, amused (by me) and nobody's patsy—re-arrived to my life.

Clarissa is twenty-five, a pretty, stroppy-limbed, long-muscled, slightly sorrowful-seeming girl with hooded gray eyes who'd remind you of a woman's basketball coach at a small college in the Middlewest. She has a square, inquisitive face (like her mother's), is pleasant around men without being much interested in them. She is sometimes profane, will mutter sarcastically under her breath, likes to read but doesn't finally say much (this, I'm sure, she got taught at Harvard). She wears strong contact lenses and frequently stares at you (me) chin down and for too long when you're talking, as if what you're saying doesn't make much sense, then silently shakes her head and turns away. She maintains a great abstract sympathy for the world but, in my mind, seems in constant training to be older, like children of divorce often are, and to have abandoned her girlishness too soon. She's said to have the ability to give memorable off-the-cuff wedding toasts and to remember old song lyrics, and can beat me at arm wrestling—especially now.

Though truth to tell, Clarissa was never a "great kid," like the bumper stickers say all kids have to be now. She was secretive, verbally ahead of herself—which made her obnoxious—sexually adventurous (with boys) and too good at school. The fault, of course, is her mother's and mine. She was loved silly by both of us, but our love was too finely diced and served, leaving her with a distrustful temper and pervasive uncertainties about her worth in the world. What can we do about these things after they're over?

Clarissa's and my relationship has been what anyone would expect, given divorce, given a brother she barely remembers but who died, given another brother she doesn't much trust or like, given a pompous stepfather she detested until he grew sick (then unexpectedly loved), given parents who seemed earnest but not ardent and given strong intelligence nurtured by years away at Miss Trustworthy's School in West Hartford. She and I together are fitful, loving, occasionally over-complicating, occasionally heated and rivalrous and often lonely around each other. "We're normal enough," Clarissa says, "if you back away a few feet"—this being her young person's faultless insight, wisdom not given to me.

I am, however, completely smitten by her. I do not believe she is permanently a lover of women, though I signed off on her orientation long ago and regret the dazzling Cookie's no longer around, since Cookie and I hit it off better than I do with most women. Clarissa's and my cohabitation during my convalescence has allowed her to think of me as a sympathetic, semi-complex-if-often-draining, not particularly paternal "older person" who happens to be her father, on whom she can hone her underused nurturing skills. And at the same time I've put into gear my underused fatherhood skills and tried to offer her what she needs—for now: shelter, a respite from love, a chance to exhale, have serious talks and set her shoulders straight before charging toward her future. It is her last chance to have a father experiencing his last chance to have the daughter he loves.

THREE WEEKS ago, the day after Halloween, Clarissa and I were taking my prescribed therapy walk together up the beach at Sea-Clift, me in my Bean's canvas nomad's pants and faded blue anorak (it was cold), Clarissa in a pair of somebody else's baggy khakis and an old pink Connemara sweater of mine. Dr. Psimos says these walks are tonic for the recovering prostate, good for soreness, good for swelling, and the sunlight's a proven cancer fighter. Walking around every day with cancer lurking definitely commits one's thoughts more to death. But the surprise, as I already said, is that you fear it *less*, not more. It's a privilege, of an admittedly peculiar kind, to get to think about death in an almost peaceful frame of mind. After all, you share your condition—a kind of modern American condition—with 200,000 other Americans, which is comforting. And this stage of life—well past the middle—seems in fact to be the ideal time to have cancer, since among its other selling points, the Permanent Period helps to cancel out even the most recent past and focuses you onto what else there might be to feel positive about. Not having cancer, of course, would still be better.

On our beach walk, Clarissa began declaiming lengthily about the presidential election (which hadn't happened yet). She detests Bush and adores our current shiftless President, wishes he could stay President forever and believes he exhibited "courage" in acting like a grinning, slavering hound, since, she said, his conduct "revealed his human-ness" (I was willing to take his human-ness on faith, along with mine, which we need not exhibit to people who don't want us to). It's clear she identifies him with me and would make unflattering high-horse excuses for me the way she makes them for him. These same-sex years of her life have left her not exactly a feminist, which she was in spades at Miss Trustworthy's, but strangely tolerant toward men—which we all hoped would be the good bounty of feminism, though so far have little to show for it. Looked at another way, I'm satisfied to have a daughter who has sympathy to excess, since she'll need it in a long life.

One of her current career thoughts for life after Sea-Clift and her life without Cookie, is to find employment with a liberal congressman, something Harvard graduates can apparently do the way the rest of us catch taxis. Only, she loathes Democrats for being prissy and isn't truly sure what party she fits in with. My secret fear is that she's pissed away her vote on sad-sack, know-it-all Nader, who's responsible for this smirking Texas frat boy stealing a march into the power vacuum.

When her declaimings were over, we walked along the damp sand without saying much. We've taken many of these jaunts and I like them for their freedom to seem everyday-normal and not just the discipline of disaster. Clarissa was carrying her black cross-trainers, letting her long toes grip the caked sand where the ocean had recently withdrawn. Tire tracks from the police patrols had dented the beach surface in curvy parallels stretching out of sight toward Seaside Park, where a smattering of autumn beach habitués were sailing bright Frisbees for Border Collies, building sand skyscrapers, flying box kites and model planes or just leisurely walking the strand in twos and threes in the breeze and glittering light. It was two o'clock, normally a characterless hour in the days after the time change. Evening rushes toward you, although I've come to like these days, when the Shore's masked with white disappearing winterish light yet nothing's nailed down by winter's sternness. I'm grateful to be alive to see it.

"What's it like to be fifty-six?" Clarissa said breezily, sandy shoes adangle, her strides long and slew-footed.

"I'm fifty-five. Ask me next April."

She adapted her steps to mine to stress a stricter precision for dates. I'm aware that she purposefully chooses subjects that are not just about her. She has always been a careful conversationalist and knows, in her Wodehousian manner, how to be a capital egg—though she's much on her own mind lately. "I'm wrong a lot more," I said. "That's one thing. I walk slower, though I don't much care. It probably makes you think I deal well with a challenging world. I don't. I just walk slower." She kept her stride with mine, which made me feel like an oldster. She's as tall as I am. "I don't worry very much about being wrong. Isn't that good?"

"What else?" she said, concertedly upbeat.

"Fifty-five doesn't really have all that much. It's kind of open. I like it." We have never discussed the Permanent Period. It would bore or embarrass her or force her to patronize me, which she doesn't want to do.

Clarissa crossed her arms, clutched her shoes, toes askew in a dancer's stride she used to practice when she was a teen. My own size tens, I noticed, were slightly pigeoned-in, in a way they never were when I was young. Was this another product of pro-state cancer? *Toes turn in. . . .*

"Who do you think's turned out better, me or Paul?" she said.

I had no answer for this. Though as with so many things people say to other people, you just dream up an answer—like I told Marguerite. "I don't really think about you and Paul turning out, *per se*," I said. I'm sure she didn't believe me. She's mightily concerned with the final results of things these days, which is what her furlough with me at the beach is all about in a personal-thematic sense: how to make her outcome not be bad, in the presence of mine seeming not so positive. A part of her measures herself against me, which I've told her is not advisable and encourages her to be even older than she can be.

Between my two offspring, she is the "interesting," gravely beautiful star with the gold-plated education, the rare gentle touch, the flash temper and plenty of wry self-ironies that make her irresistible, yet who seems strangely dislocated. Paul is the would-be-uxorious, unfriendly non-starter who pinballed through college but landed in the mainstream, sending nutty greeting-card messages into the world and feeling great about life. These things are never logical.

But when it comes to "turning out," nothing's clear. Clarissa's become distant and sometimes resentful with her mother since declaring herself to "be with" Cookie her sophomore year in college, and now seems caught in a stall, is melancholy about love and loss, and exhibits little interest in earning a living, pursuing prospects or making a new start—something I want her to do but am afraid to mention. Yet at the same time she's become an even more engaging, self-possessed, if occasionally impulsive, emerging adult, someone I couldn't exactly have predicted when she was a conventional, girlish twelve, living with her mother and stepfather in Connecticut, but am now happy to know. (I've loaned her Sally's beater LeBaron convertible as transportation, and since Halloween have put her to work with Mike making cold calls at Realty-Wise, which she halfway enjoys.)

Paul, on the other hand, has rigorously fitted himself in—at least in his own view. He's purchased a substantial two-story redbrick house (with his mother's and my help) in the Hyde Park district of K.C., drives a Saab, has gotten fat, endured early hair loss, raised a silly mustache-goatee, and—his mother's told me—asks every girl he meets to marry him (one may now have said yes).

But by striving hard to "turn out," Paul has rejected much, and for that reason replicated in early adulthood precisely who he was when he was a sly-and-moody, unreachable teenager, rather than doing what his sister did. And by finding a "home" institution that cultivates harmlessly eccentric fuzzballs like himself and lets them "thrive and create" while offering a good wage and benefits package, Paul has witnessed independence, success-in-his-chosen-environment and conceivably flat-out happiness. All things I apparently failed to provide him when he was a boy.

Paul now lives snugly in the very town where he finally, by a circuitous routing, graduated college—UMKC—(a certain kind of American male fantasy is to live within walking distance of your old dorm). He now attends three university film series a week, has all of Kurosawa and Capra committed to memory, admits to no particular political affinities, enrolls in extension courses at the U, sits on a citizen watchdog committee for crimes against animals and wears bizarre clothes to work (plaid Bermudas, dark nylon socks, black brogues, occasionally a beret—the greeting-card company couldn't care less). He has few friends (though three who're Negroes); he takes vacations to the Chiefs' training camp in Wisconsin, eats too much and listens to public radio *all day long*. He disdains wine tastings, book and dance clubs, opera, Chinese art, dating services and fly-tying groups, preferring ventriloquism workshops, jazz haunts downtown and hopeless snarfling after women, which he calls "moonlighting as a gynecologist." All he shares with his sister is a temper and a wish somehow to be older. In Paul's case, this means a life lived far from his parents—a fact that his mother finds to be a shame but to me seems bearable.

When I visited Paul in K.C. last spring—this was before my cancer happened and before Sally departed—we sat at a little bookshop/pastry/coffee place near his new house, which he wouldn't let me visit due to phantom construction work going on. (I never got inside, only drove past.) While we were sitting and both having a chestnut *éminence* and I was feeling okay about the visit (I'd stopped by on a trip to my old military school reunion), I imprudently asked how long he intended to "hold out here in the Midwest." Whereupon he viciously turned on me as if I'd suggested that dreaming up hilarious captions for drug-store card-rack cards wasn't a life's work with the same *gravitas* as discovering a vaccine for leukemia. Paul's right eye orbit isn't the exact shape as his left one, due to a baseball beaning injury years ago. His sclera is slightly but permanently blood-mottled, and the tender flesh encircling the damaged eye glows red when he gets angry. In this instant, his slate-gray right eye widened—significantly more than the left—as he glared, and his mustache-goatee, imperfect teeth and doofus get-up (madras Bermudas, thin brown socks, etc.) made him look ferocious.

"I've sure as fuck done what you haven't done," he snarled, catching me totally off guard. I thought I'd asked a newsy, innocent question. I tried to go on eating my *éminence*, but somehow it slid off its plate right down into my lap.

"What do you mean?" I grabbed a paper napkin out of the dispenser and clutched at the *éminence*, heavy in my lap.

"Accepted life, for one fucking thing." He'd become suffused in anger. I had no idea why. "I reflect society," he growled. "I understand myself as a comic figure. I'm fucking normal. You oughta try it." He actually bared his teeth and lowered his chin in a stare that made him look like Teddy Roosevelt. I felt I'd been misunderstood.

"What do you think *I* do?" I was leveraging the sagging pastry back up onto its lacy paper plate, having deposited a big black stain on my trousers. Outside the bookshop, a place called the Book Hog, shiny Buicks and Oldses full of Kansas City Republicans cruised by, all the occupants giving us and the bookstore looks of hard-eyed disapproval. I wished I was leagues away from there, from my son, who had somehow become an asshole.

"You're all about *development*." He snorted lustily, as if development meant something like sex slavery or incest. I knew he didn't mean real estate development. "You're stupid. It's a myth. You oughta get a life."

"I *do* believe in developments." I said, and geezered around to see who was moving away from us in the shop, sure some would be. Some were.

"If the key fits, wear it." Paul burned his merciless gap-toothed Teddy Roosevelt smile into me. His short, nail-gnawed fingers began twiddling. This conversation could never have happened between me and my father.

"What's your favorite barrier?" he said, fingers twiddling, twiddling.

"I don't know what you're talking about."

"The language barrier. What's your favorite process?" He smirked.

"I give up," I said, my crushed *éminence* pathetic and inedible back up on its greasy paper plate. Paul's eyes gleamed, especially the injured one. "I know you do. It's the process of elimination. That's how you do everything."

I was back in my rental car, needless to say, and headed to the airport in less than an hour. I will be a great age before I try my luck with a visit there again.

CLARISSA'S STATE of precarious maturation couldn't be more different. Since college, she's started a master's at Columbia Teachers, intending to do work with severely disabled teens (her brother's mental age), volunteered in a teen-moms shelter in Brooklyn, trained for the marathon, taken some acting lessons, campaigned for local liberals in Gotham and generally lived the rich, well-appointed girl-life with Cookie—who's a foreign-currency trader for Rector-Speed in the World Trade Center and owns a power co-op on Riverside Drive, looking out at New Jersey. All seemed in place for a good long run.

Only, during this Gotham time—four years plus since college—Clarissa has told me, her life seemed to grow more and more *undifferentiated*, "both vertically and horizontally." Everything, she noticed, began to seem a part of everything else, the world become very fluid and seamless and not too fast-paced, though all "really good." Except, she wasn't, she felt, "exactly facing all of life all the time," but was instead living "in linked worlds inside a big world." (People talk this way now.) There was school. There was her group of female friends. There was the shelter. There were the favorite little Provençal restaurants nobody else knew about. There was Cookie's many-porched Craftsman-style house on Pretty Marsh in Maine (Cookie, whose actual name is Cooper, comes from the deepest of unhappy New England pockets). There was Cookie, whom she adored (I could see why). There was Wilbur, Cookie's Weimaraner. There were the Manx cats. Plus some inevitable unattached men nobody took seriously. There were other "things," lots of them—all fine as long as you stayed in the little "boxed, linked" world you found yourself in on any given day. *Not* fine, if you felt you needed to live more "out in the all-of-it, in the big swim." Getting outside, moving around the boxes, or over them, or some goddamn thing like that, was, I guess, hard. Except being outside the boxes had begun to seem the only way it made sense to live,

the only "life strategy" by which the results would ever be clear
and mean anything. She had already begun thinking all this
before I got sick.

My coming down with cancer amounted to nothing less than
a great opportunity. She could take a break from her little boxed-
linked Gotham world, claim some "shore leave," dedicate herself
to me—a good cause that didn't require complete upheaval or
even a big commitment, but which made her feel virtuous and
me less bamboozled by death—while she lived at the beach
and did some power thinking about where things were headed.
"Pre-visioning," she calls this brand of self-involved thinking,
something apparently hard to do in a boxed-linked world where
you're having a helluva good time and anybody'd happily trade
you out of it, since one interesting box connects so fluidly to
another you hardly notice it's happening because you're so
happy—except you're not. It's a means of training your sights on
things (pre-visioning) that are really happening to you the instant
they happen, and observing where they might lead, instead of
missing all the connections. Possibly you had to go to Harvard
to understand this. I went to Michigan.

Clarissa seems to think I live completely in the very complex,
highly differentiated larger world she's interested in, and that
I "deal with things" very well all at once. She only believes this
because I have cancer and my wife left me both in the same year
and I apparently haven't gone crazy yet—which amazes her. Her
view is the view young people typically take of older citizens,
assuming they don't loathe us: That we've all seen a lot of stuff
and need to be intensely (if briefly) studied. Though surviving
difficulties isn't the same as surviving them well. I don't, in fact,
think I'm doing that so successfully, though the Permanent
Period is a help.

But there have been days during this rather pleasant, recupera-
tive autumn when I've looked at my daughter—in the kitchen,
on the beach, in the realty office on the phone—and realized
she's at that very moment pre-visioning me, wondering about
my life, reifying me, forecasting my eventualities as presenti-
ments of her own. Which I suppose is what parents are for. After
a while it may be *all* we're for. But there have also been gloomy
days when rain sheeted the flat Atlantic off New Jersey, turning
the ocean surface deep mottled green, and mist clogged the

beach so you couldn't see waves yet could view the horizon perfectly, and Clarissa and I were both in slack, sorry-sack spirits—
when I've thought she might fancifully envy me being "ill," for
the way illness focuses life and clarifies it, brings all down to one
good issue you can't quibble with. You could call it the one big
box, outside which there isn't another box.

Once, while we were watching the World Series on TV, she
suddenly asked if she might've had a twin sister who'd died at
birth. I told her no but reminded her she'd had an older brother
who died when she was little. And of course there was Paul.
It was just a self-importanc-ing question she already knew the
answer to. She was trying to make sure that what was true of
herself was what she knew about, and wanted to hear it from me
before it was too late. It's similar to what Marguerite asked in
our Sponsor visit. In a woman Clarissa's age, you could say it was
a respectable form of past-settlement, though again I'm not sure
a settled past makes any difference, no matter how old you get
to be.

And of course I know what Clarissa does not permit herself
to be fearful of, and is by training hard-wired to confront: *making
the big mistake.* Harvard teaches resilience and self-forgiveness and
to regret as little as possible. Yet what she *does* fear and can't say,
and why she's here with me and sometimes stares at me as if
I were a rare, endangered and suffering creature, is unbearable
pain. Something in Clarissa's life has softened her to great pain,
made her diffident and dodgy about it. She knows such fear's a
weakness, that pain's unavoidable, wants to get beyond fearing it
and out of those smooth boxes. But in some corner of her heart
she's still scared silly that pain will bring her down and leave
nothing behind. Who could blame her?

Is it from me, you might reasonably ask, that she's contracted
this instinct for crucial avoidance? Probably, given my history.

Looking after me, though, may be a good means to pre-vision
pain—mine, hers, hers about me—and make her ready, toughen
her up for the inevitable, the one that comes ready or not, and
that only your own death can save you from. It's true I love her
indefatigably and would help her with her "issues" if I could,
but probably I can't. Who am I to her? Only her father.

*   *   *

CLARISSA AND I reached our usual turn-around point on our beach walk—the paint-chipped, dented-roof Surfcaster Bar, built on stilts behind the beach berm and, due to the past summer's tourist fall-off, still open after Halloween. Is it the Millennium Malaise, the election, the stock market or everything altogether that's caused everybody in the country to want to wait and see? Knowing the answer to that would make you rich.

The shadowy, wide-windowed bar had its lights burning inside at a quarter to three. A few silhouetted Sea-Clift bibbers could be seen within. A forceful pepperoni and onion aroma drifted down to the beach, making me hungry.

Clarissa stood on one foot, putting her shoe on, a trick she performed with perfect balance, slipping it on behind her, mouth intent, lip bit, as if she was a splendid-spirited racehorse able to tend to herself.

We'd talked enough about how she and Paul had "turned out," about me, about what I thought about marriage now that my second one seemed in limbo. We'd talked about how we both felt estranged from world events on the nightly news. It bothered her that a story was important one week, then forgotten the next, how that had to mean something about disengagement, loss of vital anchorage, the republic becoming ungovernable and irrelevant. There wasn't much we disagreed on.

A colder midafternoon breeze plowed in off the ocean, elevating the kites and Frisbees to brighter heights. We were starting back. Clarissa put her arm on my shoulder and looked beyond me, up to the ghostly drinkers behind the Surfcaster's picture window. "Einstein said a man doesn't feel his own weight in free fall," she said, and looked away toward the pretty, clouded coastal heavens, then gave her head a shake as if to jog loose a less pretentious thought. "Does that go for women, do you think?"

I said, "Einstein wasn't that smart." I just felt good about the beach, the breeze, the scruffy little bar above us behind the dune, where men I'd sold houses to were spying down on Clarissa with admiration and desire for the great beauty I'd somehow scored. "He sounds serious but isn't. You're not in free fall anyway."

"I don't like binary ways of thinking. I know *you* don't."

"*And* and *but* always seem the same to me. I like it."

The long southerly coastline stretched toward my house and

now seemed entirely new, observed from a changed direction. Where we were walking was almost on the spot where the team of German sappers came ashore in 1943 with hopes of blowing up something emblematic but were captured by a single off-duty Sea-Clift policeman out for a night-time stroll with his dog, Perky. The sappers claimed to be escaping the Nazis but went to Leavenworth anyway and were sent home when the war was over. Local citizens of German descent wanted a plaque to commemorate those who resisted Hitler, but Jewish groups opposed and the initiative failed, as did an initiative for the policeman's statue. He was later murdered by shady elements who, it was said, got the right man.

From the south I breathed the pungent, sweet resinous scent from the National Shoreline Park, closed by then for the approaching winter. On the beach, discreetly back against the grassy berm, a family unit of Filipinos, one of our new sub-populations, was holding a picnic. These newcomers arrive in increasing numbers from elsewhere in the Garden State, take jobs as domestics, gardeners and driveway repairmen. One has opened a Chicago-style pizzeria beside my office. Another has a coin laundry. A third, a dirty-movie theater in Ortley Beach. Everyone likes them. Our VFW chapter officially "remembers" their brave support of our boys after the terrible march on Bataan. A Filipino flag flies on the 4th of July.

These beach lovers had established an illegal campfire and were laughing and toasting weenies, seated around on the cold sand, enjoying life. The men were small and compact and wore what looked like old golfer's shirts and new jeans and sported wavy, lacquered coifs. The women were small and substantial and peered across the sands at Clarissa and me with lowered, guilty eyes. *We're entitled*, their dark looks said, *we live here*. One man cheerfully waved his long fork at us, a blackened furter hanging from its prongs. A boom box played, though not loud, whatever Filipino music sounds like. We both gave a wave back and plodded toward home.

"As much as you think your life is just another life, it is, I guess," Clarissa said, her long legs carrying her ahead of me. A flat, nasal New England curtness had long ago entered her inflection, as if words were chosen for how she could say them more than for what they meant. She's young, and can still show it. She was now bored with me and was no doubt thinking about getting back to the house and on the phone to the new "friend" she'd tentatively invited for Thanksgiving but who didn't have a name yet—and still doesn't.

"Do you ever think that you were born in New Jersey and thanked your lucky stars, since you could've been born in south Mississippi like me and had to spend years getting it out of your system?" There was not much for us to talk about. I was vamping.

Something about the Filipinos had turned her disheartened. Possibly their small prospects had begun to seem like hers.

"I guess I don't think about that enough." She smiled at me, hands deep in her khaki pockets, her cross-trainers toeing through the tide-dry sand, eyes bent down. This was suddenly a female persona younger than she was and attractive to boys, who were now on the agenda. And then it vanished. "So, what're the big persuasive questions, Frank?" *Persuasive* was another favorite word, along with *vertical* and *horizontal*. It was serious-sounding and made her seem like a smart no-bullshitter. Not a kid. You're persuasive, you're not persuasive. She was trying to pre-vision me again.

"The *really big* ones. Let's see," I said. "Can I remember my shoes are in the shoe shop before thirty days go by and they get donated to the Goodwill? What's my PIN number? Which're the big scallops? Which Everly Brother's Don? Have I actually seen *Touch of Evil* or just dreamed I did? Like that." I turned my attention to an acute and perfect V of geese winging low a quarter mile offshore, headed, it seemed, in the wrong direction for the season. The eyesight's good, I thought, better than my daughter's, who didn't see them.

"Should I become like you, then?" Tall, handsome, unwieldy girl that she is, sharp-witted, loyal and as attentive to goodness as Diogenes, she almost seemed to want me to say, *Yep. And let me keep you forever; let nothing change any more than it has. Be me and be mine. I won't be me forever.*

"Nope, one of me's enough," is what I did say, and with a thud in the heart, watching the geese fade up the flyway until they were gone into a bracket of sun far out in the autumn haze.

"I don't think it'd be so bad to be you," she said. Outlandishly, then, she took my right hand in her left one and held it like she did when she was a schoolgirl and was briefly in love with me. "I think being you would be all right. I could be you and be happy. I could learn some things."

"It's too late for that," I said, but just barely.

"Too late for me, you mean." My hand in hers.

"No. I don't mean that," I said. Then I didn't say much more, and we walked home together.

WHAT CLARISSA *actually* did for me was take a firm grasp on the suddenly slack leash of my cancer-stunned life, which I'd begun to let slip almost the instant I got the unfavorable biopsy news.

You think you know what you'll do in a dire moment: pound blood out of your temples with your fists; scream monkey noises; buy a yellow Porsche with your Visa card and take a one-way drive down the Pan-American Highway. Or just climb into bed, not crawl out for weeks, sit in the dark with bottles of Tanqueray, watching ESPN.

What I did was transcribe onto a United Jersey notepad a shorthand version of what the doctor read off: my new diagnosis. "Pros Ca! Gleas 3, low aggr, confined to gland, treatment ops to disc, cure rate + with radical prostetec, call Thurs." This note I stuck on my electric pencil sharpener, then I drove up to Ortley Beach and showed a small sandy-floored, back-from-the-beach prefab to a couple who'd lost their son in Desert Storm and who'd lived under a cloud ever since, but one day snapped out of it and decided a house near the ocean was the best way to celebrate mourning's closure. The Trilbys, these staunch citizens were. They felt good about life on that day, whereas they'd been miserable for a decade. I knew they didn't want to go home empty-handed and had more to be happy about than I did to be morose. So, for a few hours I forgot all about my prostate, and before the hot August afternoon was concluded, I'd sold them the house for four twenty-five.

That night, I slept perfectly—though I did wake up twice with no thought that I had cancer, then remembered it. The next day, I called Clarissa in Gotham to leave a message for Cookie about some tech stocks she'd advised me to unload, and almost as an afterthought mentioned I might have to put up with "a little surgery" because the sawbones over at Urology

Partners seemed to think I had minor ... prostate cancer! My heart, exactly the way it did sitting out front of Marguerite's house, lurched *bangety-bang-bang* like a cat trapped in a garbage pail. My hands went sweaty on the desktop in my at-home office. I got light-headed, tight-brained, seemed unable to keep the receiver pressed to my ear, though of course it was mushed so close it hurt for a week.

"What kind of surgery?" Clarissa spoke with her competent, efficient cadence, like a veteran court clerk.

"Well, probably they just take it out. I—"

"Take it out! Why? Is it that bad? Do you have a second opinion?" I knew her dark eyebrows were colliding and her gold-flecked gray irises snapping with new importance. Her voice was more serious than I hoped mine sounded, which made me want to cry. (I didn't.)

I said, "I don't know." The receiver wobbled in my hand and pinched the helix of my ear.

"When're you seeing this doctor again?" She was terrifyingly businesslike. "This doctor" indicated she thought I'd gone to a cut-rate, drive-thru cancer clinic in Hackensack.

"Friday. I guess maybe Friday." It was Monday.

"I'll come down tonight. You've got insurance, I hope."

"It's not that urgent. Prostate cancer's not like bamboo. I'll survive tonight." I'd already looked at my Blue Cross papers, contemplated not surviving the night.

"Have you told Mom?"

I jabbingly imagined telling Ann—a "by the way" during one of our coffee rendezvous. She'd be not too interested, maybe change the subject: *Yeah, well that's too bad, ummm.* Divorced spouses—long divorced, like Ann and me—don't get over-interested in each other's ailments.

"Have you told Sally?" I sensed Clarissa to be writing things down: *Dad ... cancer ... serious.* She favored canary yellow Post-its.

"I don't have her number." A lie. I had a 44 emergency-only number but had never used it.

"Let's don't tell Paul yet, okay? He'll be strange." We didn't need to say he was already strange. "I can get a ride to Neptune with a girl in my theory class. You'll have to pick me up."

"I can drive to Neptune."

"I'll call when I leave."

"That's great." Great was not what I meant to say. Oh-no-oh-no-oh-no is what I meant to say—but naturally wouldn't. "What are we going to do?"

"Do some checking around."

I heard paper tearing on her end, then the other line go *click-click, click-click, click-click*. Someone else was needing her attention. "What about school?"

She paused. *Click-click.* "Do you want me not to come?"

I hadn't felt desperate, but all at once I felt as desperate as a condemned man. My way—the easy way—had seemed like the good way. Her way, the court clerk's way, was full of woe, after which nothing would be better. What do twenty-five-year-old girls know about prostate cancer? Do they teach you about it at Harvard? Can you Google up a cure? "No. I'm happy for you to come."

"Good."

"Thanks." My heart had gone back to, for my age, normal. "I'm actually relieved." I was smiling, as though she was standing right in front of me.

"Just don't forget to pick me up. Think Neptune."

"I can remember Neptune. Jack Nicholson's from Neptune. I've got cancer, but my brain still works."

CLARISSA MOVED herself in that night and in two days drove Sally's LeBaron to Gotham and brought back ten blue milk crates of clothes, books, a pair of in-line skates, a box of CDs, a Bose and a few framed pictures—Cookie and Wilbur and her, me and Cookie in front of a Moroccan restaurant I didn't remember, her brother Paul in younger days on her mother's husband's Hinckley in Deep River, a group of tall, laughing rowing-team girls from college. These she installed in the guest suite overlooking the beach. Cookie drove down on Thursday in her diamond-polished forest green Rover and stood around the living room smoking oval cigarettes, fidgeting and trying to act congenial. She knew something was happening to her, but wanted not to go to extremes.

When Cookie was leaving, I walked out to her car with her. She and Clarissa had stated their good-byes upstairs. Clarissa

hadn't come down. The story was that this was just until I got
back on my feet. Though I was on my feet.

As I've said, Cookie is teeth-gnashingly beautiful—small and
a tiny bit stout, but with a long, dense shock of black hair tinted
auburn, black eyes, arms and legs the color of walnuts, silky-
skinned, a round Levantine-looking face (in spite of her Down
East Yankee DNA), with curvaceous plum-color lips, a major
butt and thick eyebrows she didn't fuss over. Not your standard
lesbian, in my experience. Somewhere in the past, she'd incurred
a tiny, featherish swimming-pool scar at the left corner of her lip
that always attracted my attention like a beauty mark. She wore
a pinpoint diamond stud in her right ear, and had a discreet tattoo
of a heart with *Clarissa* inside on the back of her left hand. She
spoke in a hard-jaw, trading-floor voice trained to utter non-
negotiable words with ease. She's Log Cabin Republican if she's
an inch tall.

Cookie took my arm as we stood on the pea-gravel drive with
nothing to say. Terns cried in the August breeze, which had
brought the sound of the sea and an oceany paleness of light
around to the landward side of the house. A sweet minty aroma
inhabited her blue silk shirt and white linen trousers. I felt the
heft of her breast against my elbow. She was happy to give me
a little jolt. I was surely happy to have a little jolt, under the
circumstances. I was seeing the doctors again the next day.

"I feel pretty good, considering," Cookie said in her hard-as-
nails voice. "How do you feel, Mr. Bascombe?" She never called
me Frank.

I didn't want to ponder how I felt. "Fine," I said.

"Well, that's not bad, then. My girlfriend's taking a furlough.
You've got cancer. But we both feel okay." This was, of course,
the manner by which every man, woman, child and domestic
animal in Cookie's Maine family accounted for and assessed each
significant life's turning: dry, chrome-plated, chipper talk that
accepted the world was a pile of shit and always would be, but hey.

I wondered if Clarissa was at an upstairs window, watching us
having our brisk little talk.

"I'm hopeful," I said, with no conviction.

"I think I'll go have a swim at the River Club," she said.
"Then I think I'll get drunk. What're you going to do?" She
squeezed my arm to her side like I was her old uncle. We were

beside her Rover. Her name was worked into the driver's door, probably with rubies. My faded red Suburban sat humped beside the house like a cartoon jalopy. I admired the deep, complex tread of her Michelins—my way to sustain a moment with an arm wedged to her not inconsiderable breast. If Cookie'd made the slightest gesture of invitation, I'd have piled in the car with her, headed to the River Club and possibly never been heard from again. Lesbian or no lesbian. Girlfriend's father or no girl-friend's father. The world's full of stranger couples.

"I've got a good novel to read," I said, though I couldn't think of its author or its title or what it was about or why I'd said that, since it wasn't true. I was just thinking she was a stand-up girl, touching and unforgettable. I couldn't conceive why Clarissa would let her go. I'd have lived with her forever. At least I thought so that morning.

"Did you get rid of Pylon Semiconductor?"

"I'll do it tomorrow," I said, and nodded. Squeeze, squeeze, squeeze—my arm, arm, arm.

"Don't forget. Their quarterlies're out way below projected. There'll be a change at CFO. Better get busy."

"No. Yes." Wilbur, the mournful yellow-eyed Weimaraner, stood in the backseat, looking at me. Windows were left open for his benefit.

"You know I love Clarissa, don't you?" she said. I was learning to like her hacksaw delivery.

"I do." She was pulling away. This was all I was getting.

"Nothing good comes easy or simple. Right?"

"That's been my experience." I smiled at her. Can you love someone for three minutes?

"She just needs some context now. It's good for her to be here with you."

Context was another of their frictionless Harvard words. Like *persuasive*. It meant something different to my demographic group. To my quartile, context was the first thing you lost when the battle began. I didn't much like being a *context*—even if I was one.

"Where's *your* father," I asked. Her father was rich as a sheikh, I'd been told, had done things murky and effortless for the CIA sometime, somewhere. Cookie disapproved of him but was devoted. Another impossible parent in a long line.

Mention of the *pater* made her brain go spangly, and she smiled at me glamorously. "He's in Maine. He's a painter. He and my mom split."

"Are you *his* context?"

"Peter raises Airedales, builds sailboats and has a young Jewish girlfriend." (The venerable trifecta.) "So probably not." She shook her fragrant hair, then pressed a button on her key chain, snapping the Rover's locks to attention, taillights flashing *hello*. Wilbur wagged his nubby tail inside. "I hope you feel better," she said, climbing in. I saw the ghost outline of her thong through her white pants, the heart-breaking bight of her saddle-hard butt. She smiled back at me from the leather driver's capsule—I was gooning at her, of course—then let her gaze elevate to the house, as if a face *was* framed in a window, mouthing words she could take heart from: *Come back, come back.* She didn't know Clarissa very well.

"I'm hopeful, remember," I said, more to Wilbur than to her.

She fitted on her heavy black sunglasses, pulled her seat belt across and kicked off her sandals to grip the pedals of her rich-man's sporting vehicle meant for the Serengeti, not the Parkway. "Why does this feel so goddamned strange?" she said, and looked sorrowful, even behind her mirroring shades. "Isn't it strange? Does this feel strange to you?" Reflected in her Italian lenses I was a small faraway man, pale and frail and curved—insignificant in lurid-pink plaid Bermudas and a red tee-shirt that had *Realty-Wise* on it in white block letters. She switched on the ignition, shook out her hair.

"It's a little strange," I admitted.

"Thank you." She smiled, her elbows on the steering wheel. Frowning and smiling were not far apart in her repertoire and went with the voice. "Why is that?" Wilbur nuzzled her ear from the backseat. A plaid blanket had been installed—also for his benefit. She closed the door, laid her arm on the window ledge so I could see the heart with my daughter's name scored on her plump little dorsum.

"Uncharted territory." I smiled. A single limpid tear wobbled free from beneath her glasses' frame. "Ahhh." She might've noticed the tattoo.

"But it's all right. Uncharted territory can be good. Take it from me." I'd happily have adopted her if she wouldn't let me sleep with her at the River Club.

"Too bad you weren't my father."

Too bad you're not my wife, flashed in my mind. It would've been an inappropriate thing to say, even if true. She should've been with Clarissa, like I should've been with Sally. There were a hundred places I should've been in my life when I wasn't.

She must've thought it was a good thing to have said, though, because when I was silent, standing staring at her, what she said was, "Yep." She patted Wilbur's head on her shoulder, clamped the big Rover into gear—its muffling system tuned like a Brahms organ toccata—and began easing out my driveway. "Don't forget to sell your Pylon," she said out the window, wiping her tear with her thumb as she rolled over the gravel and onto Poincinet Road and disappeared.

WHAT CLARISSA did—while I drove off to the Realty-Wise office on Tuesday, indomitably showed two houses, performed an appraisal, scrounged a listing, attended a closing and generally acted as if I didn't have prostate cancer, just a touch of indigestion—was to attack "my situation" like a general whose sleeping forces have suffered a rear-guard sneak attack and who needs to reply with energetic force or face a long and uncertain campaign, whose outcome, due to attrition and insubordination and bad morale among the troops, is foregone to be failure.

Dressed in baggy gym shorts and a faded Beethoven tee-shirt, she brought her laptop to the breakfast room and set up on the glass-topped table that overlooks the ocean through floor-to-ceiling windows and simply ran down everything in creation that had to do with what I "had." She spent all week, till Friday, researching, clicking on this, printing that, chatting with cancer victims in Hawaii and Oslo, talking to friends whose fathers had been in my spot, waiting on hold for hot lines in Atlanta, Houston, Baltimore, Boston, Rochester, even Paris. She wanted, she said, to get as much into her "frame" as she could in these crucial early days so that a clear, confident and anxiety-allaying battle plan could be drafted and put in place, and all I (we) had to do was make the first step and the rest would take care of itself just the way we'd all like everything to—marriage, buying a used car, parenting, career choices, funeral arrangements, lawn care. I'd show up from the realty office in rambling but wafer-thin good spirits at 12:45, armed with a container of crab bisque or a Caesar salad or a bulldog grinder from Luchesi's on 98th Ave. We'd sit amidst her papers and beside her computer, drink bottled water, eat lunch and sort through what she'd learned since I'd escaped—on the run, you can believe it—five hours before.

I was far too young for "watchful waiting," she'd determined, whereby the patient enters a Kafkaesque bargain with fate that maybe the disease will progress slowly (or not progress), that normal life will fantastically reconvene, many years march triumphantly by, until another *whatever* picks you off like a sniper (hit by a tour bus; a gangrenous big toe) before the first one can finish you. It's great for seventy-five-year-olds in Boynton Beach, but not so hot for us fifty-fives, whose very vigor is the enemy within, and who disease tends to feast on like hyenas.

"You've got to do *something*," Clarissa said over her picked-at sausage and pepper muffaletta. She looked to me—her father in a faltering spirit—like a glamorous movie star playing the part of a fractious, normally remote but frightened movie daughter, performing just this once her daughterly duty for a dad who's not been around for decades but now finds himself in Dutch, and is played by a young Rudy Vallee in a rare serious role.

A second opinion was nondiscretionary—you just do it, she said, licking her fingertips. Though, she added (Beethoven glaring at me, leonine), that a nutritional history that's included "lots of dairy" and plenty of these rollicking sausage torpedoes was definitely one of many "contributing toxic elements," along with too little tofu, green tea, bulgur and flax. "The literature," she said matter-of-factly, stated that getting cancer at my age was a "function" (another of the banned words) of the unwholesome Western lifestyle and was "a kind of compass needle" for modern life and the raging Nineties tuned to the stock market, CNN, traffic congestion and too much testosterone in the national bloodstream. Blah, blah, blah, blah. Chinese, she said, never get prostate cancer until they come to the U.S., when they join the happy cavalcade. Mike, in fact, was now as much at risk as I was, having lived—and eaten—in New Jersey for more than a decade. He wouldn't believe a word of this, I told her, and would burst out yipping at the thought.

I looked wistfully out at the sparkling summer ocean, where yet another container ship was plying the horizon, possibly loaded with testosterone, seeming not to move at all, just sit. Then I imagined it filled with all the ordained foods I'd never eaten: yogurt, flaxseed, wheat berries, milk thistle—but unable to get to shore because of the American embargo. Come to port, come to port, I silently called. I'll be good now.

"Do you want to know how it all works?" Clarissa said like a brake mechanic.

"Not all that much."

"It's a chain reaction," she said. "Poorly differentiated cells, cells without good boundaries, run together in a kind of sprawl."

"Doesn't sound unfamiliar."

"I'm speaking metaphorically." She lowered her chin in her signature way to bespeak seriousness, gray eyes on me accusingly. "Your prostate is actually the size of a Tootsie Roll segment, and where *your* bad cells are, the biopsy says—down in the middle— is good." She sniffed. "Would you like to know exactly how an erection works? That's pretty amazing. Physically, it seems sort of implausible. In the books it's referred to as a 'vascular event.' Isn't that amusing?"

I stared across the table and did not know how to say "no more," other than to scream it, which wouldn't have sounded as grateful as I wanted to seem.

"It's interesting," she said, looking down at her papers as if she wanted to dig one out and show me. "You probably never had problems, did you, with your vascular events?"

"Not that often." I don't know why I picked that to say, except it was true. What we were talking about now was all strangely true.

"Did you know you can have an orgasm without an erection?"

"I don't want one of those."

"Women do it, sort of," she said, "not that you'd be interested. Men are all about hardness, and women are all about how things feel." *All about*: yet another item on the outlawed list. "Not too difficult to choose, really."

"This isn't funny to me," I said, utterly daunted.

"No, none of it is. It's just my homework. It's my lab report in my filial-responsibility class." Clarissa smiled at me indulgently, after which I went back to the office in a daze.

*   *   *

NEXT DAY, we met again over lunch and Clarissa, now dressed in a faded River Club polo and khaki trousers that made her look jaunty and businesslike, told me she basically had it all figured now. We could put a plan in force so that when I went back to Urology Partners in Haddam on Friday to review my treatment options, I'd be "holding all the cards."

Hopkins and Sloan Kettering were first-rate, but the real brain-trust treasure trove was Mayo in Rochester. This came from computer rankings, from a book she'd read overnight and from a Harvard friend whose father was at Hopkins but liked Mayo and could probably get us in in a jiffy.

The options, she felt, were pretty much straightforward. My Gleason score was relatively low, general health good, my tumor positioned such that radioactive iodine-seed implants, with a titanium BB delivery system, could be the "way to go" if the Mayo doctors agreed. Having "the whole thing yanked," she said (here her eyes fell to the toasted eggplant napoleon I'd bitten the bullet and brought back), was better in the philosophical sense that having no transmission is better than keeping an old beat-up one that might explode. But the side effects of "a radical" involved "lifestyle adjustments and a chance of impairment" (adult diapers, possibly a flat-line on my vascular events). The procedure itself was tolerable, though drastic, and in the end you might not live any longer, while "quality-of-life issues" could be "problematic."

"It's a trade-off," she said, and bit her lower lip. She looked across at me and seemed not to like this conversation. It was no longer a lab report, but words that shed shadowy light on another's future in, as it's said, real time. "Why not take the easier route if you can?" she said. "I would." As always, the best way out is not through.

"They put seeds in?" I said, baffled and contrary.

"They put seeds in," Clarissa said. She was reading from a sheet of paper she'd printed out. "Which are the size of sesame seeds, and you get anywhere up to ninety, under general anesthetic, using stainless-steel needles. Minimal trauma. You're asleep less than an hour and can go home or wherever you want to go the same day. They basically bombard the shit out of the tumor cells and leave the other tissue alone. The seeds stay in forever and become inert in about three months. Once they're in, there's some minor side effects. You might pee more for a while, and it might hurt some. You can't let babies sit in your lap, at first, and you have to try not to cough or sneeze real hard, because you can launch one of these seeds out through your penis—which I guess isn't cool. But you won't set off airport security, and the risk to pets is low. You won't infect anybody you *have sex*"—on the restricted list—"with. And you probably won't be incontinent or impotent. Most important"—she squinted at the paper as if her eyes were blurring, and scratched a finger into the thick hair above her forehead—"you won't be letting this take over the core of your manhood, and the chances are in ten years you'll be cancer-free." She looked up and turned her lips inward to form a line, as if this hadn't necessarily been so pleasant, but now she'd done it. "If you want me to," she said, picking up a scrap of eggplant and bringing it purposefully toward her mouth, "I'll go out to Mayo with you. We can have a father–daughter thing, with you having your radioactive seeds sown into your prostate."

"I don't think that's the job for the daughter," I said. I'd already decided to do whatever she said. Talking to your father about his dysfunctions and impairments wasn't a job for the daughter, either. But there we were. Who else would I want to help me? And who would?

"Okay," Clarissa said amiably. "I don't mind, though. I don't know what the daughter's job really is." She chewed her eggplant while staring at me, leaning on her knobby elbows. She looked like a teen eating a limp French fry. She quietly burped and looked surprised. "It'd be nice if the wife was around. That's a different screenplay, I guess. Marriage is a strange way to express love, isn't it? Maybe I won't try it."

I, at that instant, thought of "the wife," just like people do in movies but almost never in actual life. We usually think about absolutely nothing in these becalmed moments, or else about having our tires rotated or buying a new roll of stamps. Writers, though, like to juice these moments to get at you while you're vulnerable. What I actually *did* think of, however, was Sally— sitting down to this very glass-topped breakfast table last June, with the hot sun on the water and bathers standing in the surf, contemplating immersion. A tiny biplane had buzzed down the beachfront, pulling a fluttering sign that said NUDE REVIEW— NJ 35 METEDECONK. I had the *New York Times* flattened out to the sports page and was skimming a story about a Lakers win, before heading to the obits. It was the morning Sally told me she was leaving for Scotland with her long-presumed-dead former husband, Wally, who'd strangely visited us the week before. She loved me, she said, always would, but it seemed to her "important" (there are so many of these slippery words now) to finish "a thing" she'd started—her ossified marriage, which I'd thought was kaflooey. It seemed, she said, that I didn't "all that much need" her, and that "under the circumstances" (always treacherous) it was worse to be with someone who didn't need you than to let someone who maybe did be alone—i.e., Wally, a boy I'd actually gone to military school with but never knew before he showed up in my house. In other words (I supplied this part), she loved Wally more than me.

I sat there while Sally said some other things, wondering how in hell she could conclude I didn't need her, and what in hell "need" meant when another person's "need" was in question.

Then I cried. But she left anyway.

And that was that—right at the table where Clarissa said she'd go to Mayo with me to have my prostate radiated and (as the world says) "hopefully" my life saved.

"I understand the drive south of Red Wing along the Mississippi is gorgeous in the summer." Clarissa was standing, stacking my lunch plate onto hers.

"What's that?" My interior head, for many plausible reasons, felt restless—my grip on the moment, her offer, Sally's departure, the setting overlooking the Sea-Cliff beach, the idea of Red Wing, my newly defined physical condition and survival possibilities all scrabbling for attention.

"I was thinking about what I could do while you were in the hospital. I looked Minnesota up on the Web." She smiled the beautiful smile I knew would sink a thousand ships, but was now saving mine. "Minnesota's okay. In the summer anyway."

"I'm sorry, sweetheart. I wasn't paying attention." I smiled up at her.

"I don't blame you," Clarissa said, moving her long bones and having a stretch in the sunlight that fell in on us out of the August sky. Oddly enough, and for an instant, I felt glad about everything. "If I'd heard what you heard," she said, "I wouldn't pay much attention, either." And that was finally the way the whole matter was decided.

CHAPTER 5

THE DRIVE out to De Tocqueville minds the woodsy curves of King George Road away from Haddam *centre ville*, along the walled grounds of the Fresh Light Seminary, now (in the view of local alarmists) under the control of South Korean army factions. The tall, gaunt, flat-roofed old buildings the Presbyterians built loom beyond the darkening, oak-clustered Great Lawn like a New England insane asylum, though within, all souls are saved instead of lost. Single yellowed windows glow high up the building fronts. Fall classes are ended. Foreign students far from Singapore and Gabon, with no chance of travel home, are locked in their dorm rooms front-loading Scripture into their teeming brains, fine-tuning their homiletic techniques in front of the closet mirror, experiencing, no doubt, the first intimation that most believers aren't *real* believers and don't care what you say if you just take their minds off their woes. Some motivated seminarians, I see, have stretched a brash white-red-and-blue banner between two sentinel oaks, proclaiming BUSH IS GOD'S PRESIDENT AND CHARLTON HESTON IS MY HERO.

Traffic out King George has slackened to a trickle, as though a get-out-of-town-now whistle had sounded, whereas normally it's bumper-to-bumper down to Trenton, three to seven. But the nearing holiday and worsening weather have returned Haddam to its later-after-hours, nothing-happening somnolence, which all would love to legislate, with day workers, secretaries and substitute teachers broomed out back to their studio apartments and double-wides in Ewingville and Wilburtha.

Possibly it's a side effect of the Millennium (which doesn't seem to have other effects), or else it's my recent indisposed passage in life, but often these days I'm thunderstruck by the simplest, most commonplace events—or nonevents—as if the regular known world had suddenly illuminated itself with a likable freshness, rendering me pleased. Geniuses must experience this every day, with great inventions and discoveries the happy

results. ("Isn't it neat how birds fly. Too bad we can't...."
"If you just rounded off the sides of this granite block, you could
maybe move it a mite easier...." etc., etc.) My recent fresh realizations were on the order of being amazed that someone
thought to put a yellow light in between the green and the red
ones, or that everybody takes the road from Haddam to Trenton
for granted but nobody thinks what a stroke of brilliance it was
to build the first road. None of these has made me feel I could
invent anything myself, and I don't share my perceptions with
others, for fear of arousing suspicions that I've gone crazy due
to my treatment. And of course I don't have anybody to share
perceptions with anyway. (Clarissa would be bored to concrete.)
And to be truthful, my feeling of low-wattage wonder is usually
tinged with willowy sadness, since these alertings and sudden re-
recognitions carry with them the sensation of seeing all things
for the final time—which of course could be true, though I
hope not.

Not long ago, I was in my Realty-Wise office, at my desk
with my sock feet up, reading the National Realty Roundtable
Agents' Bulletin—a tedious article from their research department about *locked, float-down* mortgage rates being the wave of
the future—when my eye slipped down to a squib at the end that
said, "When asked what practical value there is in knowing if
neutrinos possess mass, Dr. Dieter von Reichstag of the Mains
Institute, Heidelberg, admitted he didn't have the foggiest idea,
but what really amazed him was that on a minor planet that circles
an average-size star (earth), a species has developed that can even
ask that question."

I'm sure this had some interesting connections to *locked, float-
downs* and to what amazing product enhancements they are in
the residential mortgage market (I didn't read to the end). But
the amazement Dr. von Reichstag admitted to is more or less
what I feel with frequency these days, albeit about less weighty
matters. Dr. von Reichstag may also feel the same sensation of
last-go-round somberness that I feel, since all new sensations
carry in their DNA intimations of their ending. Viewing the
new in this way almost certainly relates to having cancer, and
with being an older fast-fading star myself.

But driving out King George, on the road to meet my ex-
wife—a meeting I have trepidations about—I experience in this

late-day gloom another of my illuminations, one that interests me, even though it strikes me as tiresome. Simply stated: What an odd thing it is to *have* an ex-wife you have to have a *meeting* with! Millions, needless to say, do it day in and day out for legions of good reasons. Chinamen do it. Swahilis do it. Inuits do it. Anytime you see a man and woman sitting having coffee in a food court at the mall, or having a drink together in the Johnny Appleseed Bar, or walking side-by-side out of the Foremost Farms into a glaring summer sun holding Slurpees, and you instinctively force onto them your own understanding of what they could be up to (adulterers, lawyer–client, old high school chums), it's much more likely you're seeing an ex-wife and ex-husband engaged in contact that all the acrimony in the world, all the hostility, all the late payments, the betrayals, the loneliness and sleepless nights spent concocting cruel and crueler punishments still can't prevent or not make inevitable.

What *is* it about marriage that it won't just end? I've now had two go on the fritz, and I still don't get it. Sally Caldwell may be asking this question wherever she is with the shape-shifting Wally. I hope it's true.

But is this how life is supposed to be—loving someone, but knowing with certainty you'll never, never, never (because neither of you remotely wants it) have that person except in this sorry ersatz way that requires a "meeting" to discuss who the hell knows what? Clarissa doesn't agree and believes all things can be adjusted and made better, and that Ann and I can finally blubbety, blub, blub. But we can't. And, in fact, if we could, doing so would represent the very linked boxes Clarissa herself claims to hate. Only they'd be mine and Ann's boxes. A lot of life is just plain wrong. And the older I get, the more clearly and often wrong it seems. And all you can do about it—which is what Clarissa is trying to pre-vision—is just start getting used to it, start selecting amazement over bewilderment. This whole subject, you might say, is just another version of fear of dying. But my bet is 80 percent of divorced people feel this way— bewildered yet possibly also amazed by life—and go on feeling it until the heavy draperies close. The Permanent Period is, of course, the antidote.

The turn-off to De Tocqueville Academy is like the entrance to a storied baronial game preserve—a lichenous, arched stone gate carved with standing stags holding plaques with Latin mottoes on them. The gate alone would cause any parent driving little Seth or little Sabrina, in the backseat of the Lexus reading Li Po and Sartre three levels above their age group, to feel justly served and satisfied by life. "Seth's at De Tocqueville. It's rilly competitive, but worth every sou. His fifth-grade teacher's got a Ph.D. in philosophy from Uppsala and did his post-doc at the Sorbonne—"

Inside the gate, the road, murky in early-dark and drizzle, narrows and passes into first-growth hardwood, dense and primordial. Yellow speed moguls proliferate. Roadside signs let the uninitiated know what sort of place he or she's entering: We're Liberal! GORE FOR PRESIDENT placards just like out on Route 206 clutter the grassy verge as my headlights pass, while others demand that someone GET US OUT!, that PEACE IS WORTH VIOLENCE, that we all should STOP THE CARNAGE! I'm not sure which carnage they have in mind. There's one lonely Bush sign, which I'm sure has been put up to preserve the endowment, since no one here would vote for Bush any more than they'd vote for a chimp.

A pair of whitetails suddenly appears in my headlights, and I have to idle up close and beep-beep before they snort, flag their tails and saunter onto the road edge and begin nibbling grass, unfazed. De Tocqueville, back in the Twenties, was in fact a vaunted hunting woods for rich Gotham investment bigwigs (part of the carnage) and was then called Muirgris, which is embossed on the gate in Latin. Packard-loads of happy fat men in tweeds rumbled down on weekends, disported like pashas, drank like Frenchmen, consorted with ladies imported from Philly and occasionally stepped outside to blow the local fauna to smithereens, before packing up on Sundays and happily motoring home.

Muirgris is now De Tocqueville—and a bane of the old roisterers—a "sanctuary" overrun with deer, turkeys, skunks, possum, squirrels, raccoons, porcupines, some say a catamount and a bear or two, all of which enjoy refuge. Disgruntled Haddam home owners living outside the Muirgris boundaries have voiced complaints about predation issues (deer and bunnies eating their winged euonymus) and made dark threats about hiring professional hunter-trappers to "thin the herd" using controversial net-and-bolt devices, all of which has the gentle De Tocqueville staffers up in arms. There have been property-line confrontations, township-council shouting scenes, police called at late hours. Lawsuits have been filed as the animals have crowded inside, seeking protection, and new worries about Lyme disease, bird flu and rabies are now rumored. A relative of one of the original old sports, an interior design consultant from Gotham, gave a speech at commencement, saying his forebear would want Muirgris to stay up with the new century's values and be as "green" today as he was "bloody-minded" in his own time. So far, the issue is far from decided.

I wind a cautious way down to campus—speed bump to speed bump. The school's buildings are all sited around the old rogues' hunting lodge, a regal log and sandstone Adirondack-style dacha now converted into an "Admin Mansion," with earth-friendly faculty and classroom modules built down into the woods, as if prep school was a dreamy summer camp on Lake Memphrema-gog, instead of a hot petri dish where the future of the fortunate gets on track, while the less lucky schlump off to Colgate and Minnesota-Duluth. My son Paul didn't rate a sniff here ten years ago.

Ann's styleless brown Honda Accord sits alone in the shadowy, sodium-lit faculty lot, the rest of the De Tocqueville staff long gone for Turkey Day festivities. It's possible Ann wants to discuss the children today: Clarissa's revised gender agenda and lack of life direction; Paul's arrival tomorrow with a companion; how to apportion visiting hours, etc. She may, in fact, be afraid of Paul, as I slightly am, though he claims she's his "favorite parent." Having children can sometimes feel like a long, not very intense depression, since after a while neither party has much left to give the other (except love, which isn't always simple). You're each, after all, taken up with your own business—staying alive, in my case. And for reasons they have no control over, the children are always aware they're waiting for you to croak. Paul has expressed this very view as a "generic fact" of parent–child relations, point-blank to his mother, which is probably why she fears him. Clarissa's current gift-of-life to me is the rarest excep-tion, though one partly entered on by her—and why not—because it allows her to think of herself as equally rare and exceptional.

In any case, conversations with one's ex-wife always exist in a breed-unto-themselves/zero-gravity atmosphere that's attractive for its old familiarities, but finally less interesting than communication with an alien. Whenever I'm around Ann, no matter how civil or chatty or congenial we manage it, no matter what the advertised subject matter (it was worse when the kids were younger), her silent thoughts always turn to the old go-nowhere ifs and what-ifs, all the ways "certain people" (who else?) *should be*, but mysteriously are *not*. Try, try, try to be better. Award good-citizenship medals, wait patiently at bedsides, shell out my last dime for kids' therapy—still Ann can't ignore the one fatally blown circuit from long ago, the one that doused the lights and put karmic unity forever out of reach. The Permanent Period again stands me in good stead here by allowing me to take for granted exactly who I am—good, or awful—not who I should be, and along the way blurs the past to haze. But Ann is finally a lifelong essentialist and thinks there's a way all things *should* be, no matter how the land lies around her feet. Whereas I am a lifelong practitioner of choices and always see things as possibly different from how they look.

But even with these asymmetries being in continuous effect, I constantly carry around a sometimes heart-wrenching, hand-sweating fear that Ann will manage to die before I do (the odds there have clearly shifted to my favor). Each time I'm about to see her—the few times since she moved back to Haddam last year—I've sunk myself into a deep fret that she's about to release a truckload of bad news. A mysterious lesion, a "shadow," a changed mole, blood where you don't want blood, all requiring ominous tests, the clock ticking—all things I know about now. Following which, I won't know what the hell to do! If loving somebody you'll never really know again and only rarely see can be difficult—though I don't really mind it—think about having to *grieve* for that person long after any shared life is over, life that could've made grieving worthwhile. You think grief like that, grief once removed, can't be experienced? It can kill you dead as a mackerel. I, in fact, wouldn't last a minute and would head straight to the Raritan bridge at Perth Amboy and leave my car a derelict on the Parkway. Think about that the next time you see such a vehicle and wonder where the driver went.

*   *   *

DE TOCQUEVILLE Academy is a day school only. Even the Arab and Sri Lankan kids have well-heeled host families and good places to go—the Vineyard, the Eastern Shore—for holidays. A couple of dim fluorescent lights are left burning in the Admin Mansion, just like at the seminary, and down toward the classroom modules, past the postmodern ecumenical chapel, toward the glass-exterior athletic installation, a scattering of yellow lights prickles through the oaks and copper beeches as the day is ending. I'm confident I'm being observed on a bank of TV screens from some warm security bunker close by, the watchful crew standing around with coffee mugs, studying me, a "person of interest, doing what, we don't know," my name already jittering through the FBI computer at Quantico. *Am I wanted? Was I wanted? Should I be?* I'm surprised Ann can stand it here, that the practical-bone, non-joiner Michigan girl in her can put up with all this supervised, pseudo-communal, faux-humanistic, all-pull-together atmosphere that infests these private school faculties like mustard gas—everyone burnishing his eccentricities smooth so as to offend no one, yet remaining coiled like rattlers, ready to "become difficult" and "have problems" with colleagues whose eccentricities aren't burnished the same way. You think it's the psychotic parents and the hostile, under-medicated kids who drive you crazy. But no. It's always your colleagues—I know this from a year's teaching at a small New England college back in the day. It's the Marcis and the Jasons, the exotic *Ber*nards and the brawny Ludmillas, over for the Fulbright year from Latvia, who send you screaming off into the trees to join the endangered species hiding there. In-depth communication with smaller and smaller like-minded groups is the disease of the suburbs. And De Tocqueville's where it thrives.

Ann has given me directions to the indoor driving range where we're to meet. Footlights lead around the old plutocrats' hunting lodge, down a paved, winding trail under dripping trees, past brown-shingled, clerestoried class buildings, each with a low rustic sign out front: SCIENCE. MATH. SOCIAL STUDIES. FILM. LITERATURE. GENDER. Ahead, at a point farther into the woods—I see my breath in the cedar-scented air—I can make out a high lighted window. Below is a glass double door kept open just for me with a fat swatch of weather carpet. This I head for, my jaw tightening like a spring, my neck sweating, my hands fidgety. I don't feel at all vigorous, and vigorous is how I always want to feel when I present myself to Ann. I also don't feel at ease in my clothes. I've always been a dedicated solid-South, chinos, cotton shirt, cotton socks 'n loafers wearer—the same suiting I packed in my steamer trunk when I came up from Mississippi to Ann Arbor in '63, and that's done the job well enough through all life's permutations. It's not, in fact, unusual attire for Haddam, which again has its claque of similarly suited crypto-southerners—old remittance men who trace back to rich Virginia second sons of the nineteenth century and who arrived to seminary study bringing along their colored servants (which is why there was once a stable Negro population in the Wallace Hill section—now gentrified to smithereens). To this day, a seer-sucker suit, a zesty bow tie, white bucks and pastel hosiery are considered acceptable dress-up (post-Memorial Day) at all Haddam lawn parties.

Nowadays, though, and for no reason I understand, what I find myself wearing seems to matter less than it used to. Since August, I no longer look in mirrors or glance into storefront windows, for fear, I guess, I'll glimpse a worrisome shoulder slump that wasn't there before, or an unexplained limp, or my chin hung at a haggard angle on my neck stem. We're best on our guard against becoming the strange people we used to contrast ourselves favorably to: those who've lost the life force, lost the essential core vigor to keep up appearances, suffered the slippage you don't know has slipped until it's all over. I definitely don't want to find myself turning up at a closing wearing copper-colored Sansa-belts, a purple-and-green-striped Ban-Lon, huaraches with black socks and sporting a yawing, slack-jaw look of "whatever." Lost, in other words, and not remembering why or when.

In the present moment, it's my tan barracuda jacket I'm uneasy about. I bought it at a summer's-end sale from the New Hampshire catalog outfit I usually buy from, thinking it'd be nice to own something I'd never owned before—a wrong-headed impulse, since I now feel like some rube showing up to take flying lessons. Plus, there're the green-and-blue argyles and fake suede, Hush Puppy-like crepe-soled tie-ups I bought in Flint, Michigan, on a one-day trip in October. They were on sale in a shoe-store clearance where odd shoes in odd sizes were lined up on the sidewalk, and I felt like a fool not to find *something*, even if I never wore it. Which I now have. I don't know what Ann will think, having gotten used to seeing me the old way during years of divorced life. If I could, I'd ditch the jacket out here in the yew shrubs, except I'd freeze and catch cold—the BBs having done a job on my immune department. So, uneasiness or not, I'm consigned to present myself to Ann just as I am.

At the end of the winding asphalt path (it's only 4:00 p.m. but as good as dark), the Athletic Module is a state-of-the-art facility with lots of gigantic windows facing the woods, floating stairways and miles of corridors with exposed brightly-painted pipes and ductwork to give the impression the place had once been a power plant or a steel mill. It was designed by a Japanese architect from Australia, and according to the *Packet*, the Tocquies all refer to it as "Down Under," though the actual name is the Chip and Twinkle Halloran Athletic and Holistic Health Conference Center, since Chip and Twinkle paid for it.

Dim ceiling lights reflect off the long, echoing, buffed corridor floor when I step in where it's warm. Dank swimming pool water, sour towels, new athletic gear and sweat make the hot air stifling. I hear the consoling sound of a lone basketball being casually dribbled on a gym floor that's out of sight. No one's in the dark glassed-in events office. The turnstile is disengaged to let anyone pass. The indoor driving range is supposedly down the corridor, then right, then right again. I can't, though, resist a peek at the "Announcements" case by the events window. I regularly check all such notice boards in Sea-Clift—by the shopping carts at Angelico's, above the bait tank at Ocean-Gold Marina—standing arms folded, studying the cards for kittens lost, dinette sets to sell, collections of Ezio Pinza '78s, boats with trailers, boats without, descriptions of oldsters wandered off, the regular appeal for the young motorcycle victim in the ICU. Even Purple Hearts are for sale. You can eavesdrop on the spirit of a place from these messages, sense its inner shifts and seismic fidgets—important in my line of work, and more accurate than what the Chamber of Commerce will tell you. Real life writ small is here, etched with our wishes, losses and dismays. I occasionally pluck off a "For Sale by Owner" note and leave it on Mike's desk for follow-up—which usually comes to nothing. Though it might. I once saw the name of an old Sigma Chi brother on a notice board on Bourbon Street in New Orleans, where I'd gone to a realtors' meeting. Seems my onetime bro Rod Cabrero had been last seen there, and family members in Bad Axe were worried and wanted him to know he was loved— no residual bad feelings about the missing checks and stock options. Another time up in Rumson, right here in the Garden State, I saw a notice for a "large Airedale" found wandering the beach, wearing a tag that said "Angus," and instantly recognized it as the lost, lamented family treasure of the Bensfields on Merlot Court in Sea-Clift—a house I'd sold them less than a year before. I was able to effect the rescue and will get the listing again when they're ready to sell. Just like the home-for-sale snapshots we put in our office window, these message boards all say "there's a chance, there's hope," even if that chance and that hope are a thousand-to-one against.

Here, the "*Noticias del Escuela*" board is none too upbeat. "Have you been raped, fondled, harassed, or believe yourself to be, by a De Tocqueville faculty member, staff or security person? THERE'S HELP. Call [a phone number's supplied]." Another insists, "You don't have to be a minority to suffer a hate crime." (Another number offered.) A third simply says, "You can grieve." (No number is given, but a name, Megan, is in quotes.) There's also a schedule for blood testing (hepatitis C, AIDS, thyroid deficiency). A typed note is posted here from Ann about the Lady Linkster tryouts and team meeting. Another one says, "Fuck Bush," with the inflaming verb x-ed over. And one, in red, simply says, "Don't keep it to yourself, whatever it is. Culturally, we are all orphans." De Tocqueville seems not only funless but careworn and fatigued, where any time you're not studying, you'd better be worrying or dodging unwanted experiences. I'm glad Paul didn't get in, which isn't to say I'm thrilled with how things have gone.

Ann Dykstra is visible, alone and practicing, when I peer through the tiny door window into the blazing-lit inner sanctum of the indoor driving range (formerly a squash court). She doesn't know I'm here watching but is aware I *might* be, and so is going extra scrupulously through her ball placement, club-face address, feet alignment, shoulder set, weight distribution and outbound stare toward a nonexistent green. A white catch-net with golf balls scattered around has been established at the squash court's front wall, and behind it an enlarged color photograph of a distant links course on some coast of Scotland. All this is in preparation for her perfectly grooved, utterly fluid, head-down, knees-bent, murderous swing, the lethal metal-headed driver striking the nubbly ball so violently as to crush it into space dust. "This is how the fucker's done and always will be. No matter what asshole's watching or isn't"—is what I read this daunting display to say in so many words.

She doesn't glance toward the door, which I'm safe behind in the corridor darkness, but begins placing a second ball onto a pink rubber tee fixed into a carpet of artificial grass, and re-commences the fateful protocol of striking.

I don't want to go in. To enter will only ruin something that *is* and is perfect, by intruding a clamorous, troublesome, infuriating, chaotic *something else*. I'd forgotten, watching Ann through the peephole like a witness viewing a suspect, how much a perfect golf swing is an airtight defense against all bothersome "others." Once I knew that, long ago when I wrote sports: That for all athletes—and Ann's a good one—a perfect stroke protects against things getting over-complicated. I would actually slink away now if I could.

But just as I take an opportunistic look down the corridor with a thought to escape, Ann, I find, is staring at me—my partial, reluctant face obviously visible through the double-thick window. Her lips inside move in speech I can't hear. I again have an urge to run, become an optical illusion, down the hall, around a corner, be no more. But it's too late. Way too late for escape.

I push in the heavy, air-sucking door and Ann's words come into my ears. ". . . thought you were the security guy, Ramon," she says, and smiles cheerlessly at my presence. She has her driver in hand like a walking stick and goes back to addressing the new ball as if I *were* Ramon. "I don't like to be watched when I'm in here. And he watches me."

"You looked pretty solid." I'm guessing this is the appropriate compliment.

"How are you?" Ann calmly lays her club face to the ball's surface without touching it. I'm holding the heavy door open, barely inside. The brightly lit room smells like heated wood products.

"I'm great." I mean to act vigorous even if I'm not. Ann and I haven't seen each other in months. A chummy, hygienic phone chat would've been as good or better than this. The dense air is already thickening with ifs and what-ifs. "Nice place in here," I say, and look up and around. A black video camera's on a tripod to the left, a wooden team bench sits against the white squash court wall. The Scottish links course has been holographed right onto the plaster behind the catch-net. It could just as well be a chamber for a lethal injection.

"It's okay. They rigged this place up for me." Ann lightly taps her white ball off its tee, bends to retrieve it. She is turned out just as I've seen her all our life, married and apart—golf shorts (pink), white shoes (Reeboks with pink ankleless socks), a white polo with some kind of gold crest (De Tocqueville no doubt), white golf glove, and a pair of red sunglasses stuck in her hair like a country-club divorcée. She now exudes—unlike thirty years ago, when I couldn't get enough of her—a more muscular, broader-backed, stronger-armed, fuller-breasted, wider-hipped aura of athleticized sexlessness, which is still bluntly carnal but isn't helped by her blonded hair being cut in a tail-less ducktail a prison matron might wear, and her pale Dutch-heritage skin looking sweat-shiny and paper-thin. The fly of her shorts has inched down from the top button due to ungoverned belly force. I'm sorry to say there's nothing very appealing about her except that she's herself and I'm unexpectedly glad to see her. (Clenching has now made my third molar, left side, lower, begin to ache in a way that makes my jaw tighten. I should put in my night guard, which is in my pocket.)

Ann walks in a long, slightly up-on-toes gait over to the pine bench and leans her driver into a rack where other clubs stand. She sits on the pine and begins untying her golf shoes. I'm stationed in the doorway, feeling both reluctance and enthusiasm, longing and uxorious remorse. I don't know why I'm here. I wish I knew a hilarious golf joke but can only think of one that involves a priapic priest, a genie in a bottle and a punch line she wouldn't like.

"Somebody blew out the lunch room windows at the hospital," I say. Not a great conversation starter. Though why did no one at the funeral home mention it? News in Haddam must travel more slowly than ever. Everyone in his own space. Even Lloyd Mangum.

"Why?" Ann looks up from her shoelaces, bent over her thick, shiny knees. Pushing through her polo-shirt back is the wide, no-nonsense imprint of a brawny sports bra.

"I don't know. The election. People get pissed off. Doctors are all Republicans."

"How's real estate?"

"Always a good investment. They aren't making any more of it." I smile and round my eyes as a gesture of geniality.

Ann sets her Reeboks, toes out, under the bench atop the miserable green turf. She disapproves of my selling houses (Sally loved it, loved it that I think of real estate as related to Keatsian negative capability, with the outcome being not poetry but generalized social good with a profit motive). Ann fell in love with me when I was an aspiring (and failing) novelist, but since then has lived in Connecticut, grown rich and may have no use for negative capability. She may consider selling real estate to be like selling hubcaps on Route 1. She could be a Republican herself, though when I married her, she was a Soapy Williams Democrat.

I step all the way inside the warmed, dazzling, wood-scented room and let the door suck closed behind me. I don't know where to go or what to do. I need a golf club to hold. Though it's not so bad in here—unexpectedly satisfying, strangely intimate. We're at least alone for once.

"I have something I want to say to you, Frank." Ann leans back against the white wall, which has been recently repainted. She looks straight at me, her pale cheeks tightened and the downward tug at the corners of her mouth signifying importance of an ominous kind. Using my name always means "serious." I feel my hands and lips spontaneously (I hope invisibly) tremble. I do not need bad news now.

Ann wiggles her sock feet on the phony turf and looks down.

"Great"—my smile my only defense. Maybe it *is* great news. Maybe Ann's marrying Teddy Fuchs, the gentle-giant math teacher who everybody thought was a queer but was just shy and had to wait (till age sixty) for his camps-survivor mother to pass on. Or maybe Ann's decided to cash in Charley's annuity and live on the Costa del Sol. Or maybe she's figured out a meaningful new way to explain to me what an asshole I am. I'm all ears for any of that. Just nothing medical. I've had it with medical.

"Can I tell you a story?" She's still looking down at her pink socklets as if she drew assurance from them.

"Sure," I say. "I like stories. You know me." Her gray eyes dart up, warning against familiarity.

"I went into Van Tuyll's Cleaners the other day to check on a damage claim about a pair of pants they'd stained and hadn't paid me for. I was mad, and you can't really sue your dry cleaners over a pair of pants, but I thought of going in the shop and doing something disruptive to punish them. They really aren't very nice people."

Bring in some deer urine or maybe set a skunk loose behind the counter. I've thought of doing that. Just not a "device." I haven't moved an inch from where I've been under the too-warm lights.

"Anyway," Ann says. "When I got to the shop, down that little Grimes Street alley"—fine address for a dry cleaners—"a typed card was taped inside the door that said, 'We're closed due to the tragic death of our daughter Jenny Van Tuyll, who lost her life last Saturday in a traffic accident in Belle Fleur. She was eighteen. Our life will never be the same. The Van Tuyll family.' I actually had to sit down on the edge of the shop window to keep myself from fainting. It just overtook me. That poor Jenny Van Tuyll. I'd talked to her fifty times. She was as sweet as she could be. And that poor family. And there I was, mad about my goddamned Armani pants. It seemed so stupid." Ann squints at her feet, then raises her eyes to me.

Sad news. But not as bad as "I've got a fast-growing ence-phaloblasty and probably only about a month to keep breathing." "It's bad," I say gravely. Though I think: But you really can't feel worse about it just because of your Armani pants. They *are* a dry cleaners. You wouldn't even know about this if you weren't already mad at them.

Ann lowers her ocean-gray eyes, then lifts them to me signifi-cantly, and all the remembered shock and grief and impatience with me are absent from her gaze. An indoor driving range is an odd place to have this conversation. We have had a child to die, of course—in the very hospital where someone exploded a bomb today. Surely there's no need to talk about that now. For a while after Ralph's death, Ann and I met at the grave on his birthday. This being after our divorce. But eventually we just quit.

"Do you wonder, Frank, if when you feel something really forcefully—so forcefully you know it's true—do you ever wonder if how you feel is just how you feel that particular day and tomorrow it won't matter as much?"

"No doubt about it," I say. "It's a good thing. We need to question our strong feelings, though we still need to be available to feel them. It's like buyer's remorse. One day you think if you don't have a particular house, your whole life's ruined. Then the next day you can't imagine why the hell you ever considered it. Though plenty of times people see a house, fall in love with it, buy it, move in and never leave till they get taken out in a box." For some reason, I'm grinning. I wonder if the video camera that's pointed at me is operating, since something's making me uneasy, so that I'm racketing on like Norman Vincent Peale.

Ann has taken her red sunglasses out of her matron-athlete's hair and carefully folded them while I'm blabbering, as if whatever I'm saying must be endured.

"It's just hard to know," I say, and inch back against the door through which I spied Ann a while ago teaching a stern lesson to an innocent Titleist.

"I know I've told you this, Frank," she says, carefully laying her Ray-Bans on the pine seat beside her as a means of shutting me up about buyer's remorse. "But when Charley was so bad off, and you drove up those times to sit with him in Yale-New Haven, when his real friends got preoccupied elsewhere, that was a very, very excellent thing to have done. For him. And for me."

It only lasted six weeks; then off he went to heaven. Through his haze, Charley thought I was someone named Mert he'd known at St. Paul's. A few times he talked to me about his first wife and about important twelve-meter races he'd attended, and once or twice about his current wife's former husband, whom he said was "rather sweet at times" but "ineffectual." "A Big-Ten graduate," he said, smirking, though he was nutty as a coon. "You couldn't imagine her ever marrying that guy," he said dreamily. I told Charley the fellow probably had some good qualities, to which Charley, from his hospital bed, handsome face drained of animation and interest, said, "Oh, sure, sure. You're right. I'm too tough. Always have been." Then he said the whole thing over again, and in a few days he died.

Why would I do such a thing? Sit with my ex-wife's dying husband? Because it didn't bother me. That's why. I could imagine someone having to do it to me—a total stranger—and how nice it would be to have someone there you didn't have to "relate" to. I don't want to visit the subject again, however, and fold my arms across my chest and look down like a priest who's just heard an insensitive joke.

"It made me see something about you, Frank."

"Oh." Noncommittal. No question mark. I don't intend asking what it might be, because I don't care.

"It's something I think you would've said was always true about you."

"Maybe."

"I don't think I've always thought so. I might've when we were kids. But I quit about 1982." She picks up her white golf glove and folds it into a small package.

"Oh."

"You're a kind man," Ann says from the team bench.

I blink at her. "I *am* a kind man. I was a kind man in 1982."

"I didn't think so," she says stoically, "but maybe I was wrong."

I, of course, resent being declared something I've always been and should've been known to be by someone who supposedly loved me, but who wasn't smart or patient or interested enough to know it when it mattered and so divorced me, but now finds herself alone and it's Thanksgiving and I conveniently have cancer. If this is leading to some sort of apology, I'll accept, though not with gratitude. It could also still be a clear-the-decks declaration before announcing her engagement to oversized Fuchs. Our bond is nothing if not a strange one.

"You can't live life over again," Ann says penitently. She smiles up and across at me, as if telling me that I'm kind has gotten something oppressive off her chest. All dark clouds now are parting. For her anyway.

"Yeah. I know." A pearl of sweat has slid out of my hairline. It's hot as hell in here. What I'd like to do is leave.

"I didn't know if you really did know that." Ann nods, still smiling, her eyes sparkling.

"I understand conventional wisdom," I say. "I'm a salesman. Placebos work on me."

Ann's smile broadens, so that she looks absolutely merry. "Okay," she says.

"Okay," I say. "Okay what?" I glance at the tri-podded Sony, useful for showing Lady Linksters hitches in their backswings. "Is that goddamn thing turned on?"

Ann looks up at the black box and actually grins. Many years have elapsed since I've seen her so happy. "No. Would you like me to turn it on?"

"What's going on?" I'm feeling dazed in this fucking oven. It must be what a hot flash feels like. First you get hot; then you get mad.

"I have something to say." She is solemn again.

"You told me. I'm kind. What else? I accept your apology." Ungiven.

"I wanted to tell you that I love you." Both her hands are flat down beside her on the bench, as if she or the bench were exerting an upward force. Her gray eyes have trapped me with a look so intent I may never have seen it before. "You don't have to do anything about it." Two small tears wobble out of her eyes, although she's smiling like June Allyson. Sweat, tears, what next? Ann sniffles and wipes her nose with the side of her hand. "I don't know if it's again, or still. Or if it's something new. I don't guess it matters." She turns her head to the side and dabs at her eyes with the heel of her hand. She breathes in big, breathes out big. "I realized," she says mournfully, "it's why I came back to Haddam last year. I didn't really know it, but then I did. And I was actually prepared to do nothing about it. Ever. Maybe just be your friend in proximity. But then Sally left. And then you got sick."

"Why are you telling me this now?" My mouth's been ajar. These are not the words I want to say. But the words I want to say aren't available.

"Because I went to Van Tuyll's cleaners, and their pretty daughter was dead. And that seemed so unchangeable—dying just blotting things out. And I thought I'd invented ways to be toward you that let me pretend that being mad at you wasn't changeable, either—or whatever it is. But those ways can be blotted out, too. I guess there are degrees of unchangeableness. *Love*'s a terrible word. I'm sorry. You seem upset. I decided I'd just tell you. I'm sorry if you're upset." Ann hiccups, but catches her hiccup in her throat as a little burp, just like Clarissa. "Sorry," she says.

"Are you just telling me this because you're afraid I'm going to die, and you'll feel terrible?"

"I don't know. You don't have to do anything about it." She picks up her sunglasses and puts them back up in her hair. She reaches beneath the bench, produces a pair of brown penny loafers she puts on over her pink socks. She looks around where she's sitting for something she might be leaving, then stands in the blaring lights, facing me. "My coat's behind you." She's fast receding into the old protocols that she, for one moment, had gotten beyond and out into the open air, where she caught a good whiff and held it in her lungs. The poet promised, "What is perfect love? Not knowing it is not love, some kind of inter-change with wanting, there when all else is wanting, something by which we make do." I'm not making do well at all. Not achieving interchange. I am the thing that is wanting. After so long of wanting.

I turn clumsily, and there is Ann's jacket on a coat-rack I hadn't seen, a thin brown rayon-looking short topcoat with a shiny black lining—catastrophically expensive but made to look cheap. I take it off the old-fashioned coat tree and hand it over. Heavy keys swag inside a pocket. Its smell is the sweet powdery scent of womanly use.

"I'll let you walk me out to my car." She smiles, putting her brown coat on over her golfing uniform. She moves by, but I am not ready with a touch. She pulls open the air-sucking squash-court door. A breath of cool floods in from the corridor, where it'd seemed warm before. She turns, assesses the room, then reaches beyond me and snaps off the light, throwing us into com-plete, studdering darkness, closer together than we have been in donkey's years. My fingers begin to twitch. She moves past me into the shadowy hall. I almost touch the blousy back of her coat. I hear a boy's voice down the long hall. "You asshole," the voice says, then laughs—"hee, hee, hee, hee." A basketball again bounces echoingly on hardwood. *Splat, splat, splat.* A *kerchunk* of a gym door opening, then closing. A girl's voice—lighter, sweeter, happier—says, "You give love a bad name." And then our moment is, alas, lost.

*   *   *

IT'S ONLY 5:30, but already dead-end night-time in New Jersey. Nothing good's left of the day. Heading across the cold, peach-lit parking lot, Ann at first walks slowly, but then picks it up, going briskly along toward her Accord. The sulfur globes atop the curved aluminum stanchions light the damp asphalt but do not warm. All here seems deserted except for our two vehicles side-by-side, though of course we're still being watched. Nothing goes unobserved on this portion of the planet.

We have said nothing more, though we understand that saying nothing's the wrong choice. It is for me to declare something remarkable and remarkably important. To add to the sum of our available reality, be the ax for the frozen sea within us, yik, yik, yik, yik. Though I'm for the moment unable to fit my thoughts together plausibly or to know the message I need to get out. Ann and I are on a new and different footing, but I don't know what that footing might be. The Permanent Period and its indemnifying sureties are in scattered retreat out here in the post-rain De Tocqueville lot. They have sustained too many direct hits for one day and have lost some potency.

"I've lived here almost a whole year now." Ann walks resolutely beside me. "I can't say I love Haddam. Not anymore. It's odd."

"No," I say. "Me, either. Or, me, too."

"But . . ."

"But what?" We're back to our old intractable, defensible selves. Asking "What?" means nothing.

"But nothing." She fishes the clump of jingly keys out of her topcoat pocket and fingers through them beside her car. It was this way when we visited Ralph's grave on his birthday in the spring: a negotiated peace of little substance or duration, pleasing no one, not even a little. Then she says, "I suppose I should say one more thing." It's cold. Clouds are working against the moon's disk. I'm tempted to put a hand on her shoulder, ostensibly for warmth's sake. She is wearing golfing clothes, after all, in falling temps.

"Okay." I do not put a hand on her shoulder.

"All those things I said in there." She quietly, self-consciously clears her throat. I smell her hair, which still hints of the warm wood inside and something slightly acidic. "I meant all that. And what's more, I'd live with you again—where you live, if you wanted me to. Or not." She sighs a businesslike little sigh. No more tears. "You know, parents who've lost a child are more likely to die early. And people who live alone are, too. It's a toxic combination. For both of us, maybe."

"I already knew that." Everybody reads the same studies, takes the same newspapers, exhibits the same fears, conceives the same obsessive, impractical solutions. Our intelligence doesn't account for much that's new anymore. Only, I don't find that discouraging. It's like reading cancer statistics once you've been diagnosed—they become a source of misplaced encouragement, like reading last night's box scores. Misery may not love company. But discouragement definitely does. "Would-you-like-to-come-over-on-Thursday-and-have-Thanksgiving-with-me? I-mean-with-us-with-the-children?" With blinding swiftness these ill-conceived words leave my mouth, taking their rightful place among all the other ill-conceived things I've said in life and taking the place of something better I should've said but couldn't say because I was paralyzed by the thought of living with Ann and that she's now concluded I'm alone.

She clicks her car unlocked and swings the door out. Clean, new-car bouquet floods our cold atmosphere. The dimly lit cockpit begins pinging.

Ann turns her back to me as if to put something inside the car—though she's carrying nothing—then turns back, chin down, eyes trained on my chest, not my (shocked) face. "That's nice of you." She's smiling weakly, June Allyson-style again. *Ping, ping, ping.* It's other than the invitation she wanted and a poor substitute—but still. "I think I'd like that," she says, her smile become proprietary. A smile I haven't seen trained on me in a hundred years. *Ping, ping, ping.*

And just then, as when we are children sick at home with a fever in bed late at night, suddenly everything moves a great distance away from me and grows small. Softened voices speak from a padded tube. Ann, only two feet away, appears leagues away, her pinging Accord all but invisible behind her. The *pinging, ping, ping* comes as if from fresh uncovered stars high in the cold sky.

"That's great," her distant voice says.

Ann looks at my face and smiles. We are now not merely on different footings but on different planets, communicating like robots. "You'll have to give me directions, I guess."

"I will," I say robotically, cheeks and lips smiling a robot smile. "But not now. I'm cold."

"It *is* cold," she says, ignition key in hand. "When's Paul arriving?"

"Paul who?"

"Paul, our son." *Ping, ping.*

"Oh." Everything's smashing back into close quarters, the night hitting me on the nose. Real sound. Real invitation. Real disaster looming. "Tomorrow, I guess. He's en route." For some reason I say *route* to rhyme with *gout*, a way I never say it.

"Is that a new jacket," she asks. "I like it."

"Yeah. It is." I'm stumped.

She looks at me hard. "Do you feel all right, Frank?"

"I do," I say. "I'm just cold."

"There are a lot of things we haven't talked about."

"Yeah."

"But maybe we will." And instead of crossing the gulf of years to give my cold cheek a buss with cold lips, Ann gives me three pats on my barracuda jacket shoulder—pat, pat, pat—like a girl in a riding habit patting the shoulder of an old saddle nag she's just had a pleasant but not especially eventful ride on. "Paul's coming to my house for dinner tomorrow. I asked Clary, but she declined, of course." Same proprietary equitational smile and voice. Time for your rubdown and a nose bag. *Ping, ping, ping.* "I guess I'll see you for dinner Thursday."

"Okay."

"Call me. Tell me how to get there."

"Yes. I will. I'll call you." *Ping, ping.*

She looks at me as if to say, I know you might die right here and now, but we're going to pretend you won't and everything'll be fine, old fella. And it is in this manner we manage our good-bye.

AS IF SOMEONE, someone *else*, someone in a panic, someone like me but not me, was piloting my dark capsule, I am down the drizzly midnight De Tocqueville entrance lane like a NASCAR driver, my tires barely registering the speed moguls, skidding on each curve, sending deer, possum and catamount leaping into the sheltering woods, until I'm out past the signage, out the gate and *out*, back onto 27, headed into town. I of course have to piss.

And, no surprise, I am locked in a fury of regret, self-reproach and bafflement. Why, why, why, why, why did I *have* to ask? Why can't I be trusted *not* to ask? What hysteria chip in my personal hard drive impels me to self-evident disaster? Does anything teach us anything? Do seventeen years of perfectly acceptable divorced life, following clear-cut evidence of incompatibility, *not* dictate steering wide of Ann Dykstra, no matter how much I love her? *Does* cancer make you stupid as well as sick? If there was a Sponsor, a palmist, a shrink open late, dispensing mercy and wisdom to drop-ins, I'd beg, write a big check, dedicate quality hours. As stated, our intelligence doesn't account for much.

I wish, for the very first time, for a cell phone. I'd call Ann from the car and leave a cringing message: "Oh, I'm a terrible, terrible man. Mistake after mistake after mistake. You were always right about me. Just please don't come for Thanksgiving. We'd have an appalling time. I've booked you an A-list banquette at the Four Seasons, selected the right Dom Pérignon, arranged for Paul Newman and Kate Hepburn to be on your either side (where they'll definitely want to talk to you), ordered the baked Alaska in advance. Keep the limo, take a friend. . . . Just keep away on Thanksgiving. Even though you love me. Even if I'm dying. Even if you're lonely. Take my word for it."

If we'd only had our just-finished conversation on the phone —from home, without the tears, the sock feet, the lonely, converted, over-heated squash court—none of this would be happening. When I was at Mayo I met a hog farmer from Nebraska up on the urology floor, same as me, but who'd had a stroke and could barely speak to anyone. His happy, fat, grinning, scrubbed-face farm wife did the talking while he worked his eyebrows and nodded and smiled at me furiously but in total silence. Except on the phone, the wife told me, old Elmer'd yak and laugh and philosophize hours on end and never miss a beat or a connection, could even tell dirty jokes. Something's to be said for disembodied communication. Too much credit's given to the desultory *intime*. It's why the governor's never at the prison when the deed's being done.

I stop on the darkened roadside in front of a big, well-treed, hedge-banked, wide-lawned Norman Tudor that was actually moved to its present site twenty years ago from the Seminary grounds. There are few cars on this stretch of 27, so I can shuffle unnoticed up against the dark, dripping cedar hedge, in the damp leaf duff, and piss out the two cups I've accumulated since I can't remember when but which have suddenly begun to make me panicky. A diaper would be a fail-safe, but I'm holding the line there.

Then I'm back in the car and headed into Haddam, relieved, vaguely exhilarated, as only a blessed leak can bestow, though with my jaw screwed down even tighter, a faint flicker-rill in my lower abdomen more or less where I calculate my aggrieved prostate to be, my blood pressure for sure spiked, my life shortened by another thirty seconds—all this because I have now traitorously returned myself to the everyday, detail-shot, worry-misery-gnawing mind-set that I *hate*: how to un-invite the unwisely invited dinner guest who'll torpedo the otherwise-nice-enough family meal. This is what Clarissa experiences as linked boxes, the slippy-sliding world within worlds of every-one's *feelings* being on the line *all the time*, of perfect evenings with perfect overachiever dinner partners, the world of keeping calendars straight, of not forgetting to call back, always sending a note, the world of ducks-in-a-row, *i*'s dotted, *t*'s crossed and recrossed, of making sure the wrong person is *never* invited, or else everything's fucked up horrible and you're to blame and no one gets one ounce of closure. It's the world she's fled, the social Pleistocene tar pit that the Permanent Period is dedicated to saving you from by canceling unwanted self-consciousness, dim-ming fear-of-the-future in favor of the permanent, cutting edge of the present. By this measure, I shouldn't care if Ann comes to Thanksgiving dressed as Consuelo the Clown, squirts everybody with seltzer, honks her horn and sings arias till we're ready to strangle her. Because, in a little while it'll be over, no one will be any different and the day will end as it would've anyway: me half-asleep in front of the TV, watching the second game on Fox. It'd be a thousand times better—for my prostate, for my diastole and systole, for my life span, mandibular jaw muscles, embattled molars—for me just to rear back, har off a big guffaw, throw open the doors, push out the food, crack open my own big bottle of DP and turn ringmaster to the whole joyless tent-full.

Except that's not how I fucking well feel about it.

And how I *do* feel is not good. My Easter-egg-with-the-downsized-family-inside's been cracked. The usual Permanent Period protocols aren't restoring order. My brain's buzzing with unwanted *concerns* it wasn't buzzing with an hour ago.

When I first got my bad prostate news in August, and in the hours before Clarissa became my partisan-advocate, I stood out on the deck, stared at the crowded beach and silvered Atlantic and thought how just one day before this day I didn't know what I then knew. I tried to drift back to the bliss that didn't know enough to count itself bliss, have a moment of reprieve, stuff the genie back in. Several times I even said out loud to the warm wind and the aroma of sunblock and salt and seaweed, as transistors buzzed the top-40 countdown and no one noticed me watching from above—I'd say, "Well. At least nobody's told me I have cancer." But of course before fresh well-being could swell in my chest and return me inside with a precious moment captured, I was reduced to gulping, squeezing, straining tears and feeling worse than if I'd never kidded myself. Don't try this.

And what's zooming around my brain now is the certainty that Ann Dykstra knows next to nothing about me anymore—except what the kids tell her privately—nothing about Sally or about the particulars of my condition, and hasn't bothered to ask. That may be what she meant by "more to talk about," which puts it mildly. But for starters, I'm married and holding out hope I can stay that way. My medical condition is "subtly nuanced," though that may not mean much to her, since she buried one husband only two years ago. Women have things wrong with them just like men, and, as far as I can tell, don't act as bothered by it. Ann probably assumes I'm adrift and ought to be grateful for any life raft heaved my way. I'm not.

Plus, why would *she* be attracted to *me*? And now? I must be much paler from my ordeal. I'm definitely thinner. Am I stooped, too? (I said I never look.) Are my cheekbones knobby? My clothes grown roomy? I'm sure this is how old age and bad health dawn on you—gradually and unannounced. Just all at once people are trying to persuade against things you want to do and always have done: *Don't* climb that ladder. *Don't* drive after dark. *Don't* postpone buying that term life. The Permanent

Period, *again*, is set against this type of graduated obsolescence. But its strengths again seem in retreat.

Ann, of course, has also crudely played the "Ralph card" by referring to parents who lost children and the connecting path to early death—which is close to a cheap shot and offers no reason for us to get back together. I mean, if having my son die condemns me to an early exit, can that mean there are interesting new choices open that weren't before? Becoming a synchronized sky diver? Sailing alone around the world in a handmade boat? Learning Bantu and ministering to lepers? No. It's information that releases me to do nothing different and, in fact, almost challenges me to do nothing at all. It's like dull heredity, whereby you learn you have the gene that causes liver cancer, only you're too old for the transplant. Better not to know.

Though the truest, deep-background reason Ann is courting me (I know her as only an ex-husband can) is for a private whiff of the unknown, to provide the extra beat in her own life by associating it with a greater exigence than the Lady Linksters can offer: *me*, in other words, my life, my decline, my death and memory. Her daughter's on a similar search. If you think this kind of mischief is unthinkable, then think again. As I used to preach to my poor lost students at Berkshire College back in '83, when I wanted them to write something that wasn't about their roommate's acne or how it felt to be alone in the dorm after lights were out and the owls were hooting: If you can say it, it can happen.

CHAPTER 6

I MOTOR PAST the brick-and-glass-façaded village hall, lit up inside like a suburban Baptist church. Thick-chested policemen stand inside, talking casually while a poor soul—a thin, shirtless Negro—waits beside them in handcuffs. Does this bear on the Haddam Doctors Hospital "event" today? A known trouble-maker, one of the usual suspects in for a round of grilling? Since there are no TV cameras or uplink trucks out front, no flak jackets, no FBI windbreakers, no leg irons, my guess is not. Just someone who's had too much pre-holiday fun and now must pay the price.

Seminary Street, when I cruise in just past six, appears reduced to its village self. The streets crews have strung up red and green twinkly Christmas lights and plastic pine-needle bunting over the three intersections. (The "no neon" ordinance is a good thing.) A modest team of rain-geared believers is setting up a lighted crèche on the lawn at the First Prez, where in days gone by I occasionally snuck in for a restorative, chest-swelling sing. Two women and two men are kneeling in the wet grass, training and retraining misty floods and revolving colored lights into the manger's little interior, while others cart in ceramic wise men and ceramic animals and real hay bales to set the scene. All is to be up and going for the first holiday returnees.

Across the street—below the United Jersey Bank sign, its bleary news crawl streaming out-of-town events—a gaggle of local kids, all boys, stands slouched in the pissy weather, wearing baggy jeans cut off at the calves, long white athletic jerseys and combat boots. This is the Haddam gang element, children of single moms back-in-the-dating-scene, and dads working late, who arrive home too tired to wonder where young Thad or Chad or Eli might be, and head straight for the blue Sapphire in the freezer. These kids merely long for attention, possibly even a little tough-love discipline, and so are willing to provide it for each other, their mode of communication being bad posture, bad complexion, piercings, self-mortifications, smirky graffiti from Sartre, Kierkegaard and martyred Russian poets. In his day, Paul Bascombe was one of them. He once spray-painted "Next time you can't pretend there'll be anything else" on the wall of the high school gym, for which he was suspended, though he said he didn't know what it meant.

These idle kids—six of them, under the bright galloping news banner—are taunting the Presbyterian crèche assemblers, who occasionally look across Seminary and shake their heads sadly. Gamely, one ball-capped man comes out to the curb, where I stop at the light, and shouts something about lending a hand. The kids all smile. One shouts back, "Eat me," and the man— probably he's the preacher—fakes a laugh and goes back.

And yet, as it always could, the town works its meliorating blessing on me and my mood. There's nothing like a night-time suburban town at holiday season to anesthetize woe out of the feelable existence. I cruise down past the Square, where the Pilgrim Village Interpretive Center is now closed and padlocked against pranksters, the Pilgrims all hied off to their motel rooms, period animals stabled and safe in host back yards, the re-enactors disappeared into their Winnebagos, their uniforms drying, tomorrow's skirmishes vivid in their minds. At the I Scream Ice Cream, customers are crowded in under the lights, while others wait outside against the damp building, having a smoke. A thin queue has formed at the shadowy Garden Theater—a Lina Wertmüller offering I saw a hundred years ago, reprised for the holiday, the ship's-prow marquee proclaiming *Love and Anarchy*. It's the holiday. Not much is shaking.

My rendezvous with Mike at the August is not until 6:45. I have time to slide by my dentist's, on the chance he'll be in late doing a pre-holiday bridge repair and can make a quick adjustment to my night guard before I head out to Mayo next Tuesday. I turn around in the Lauren-Schwindell lot—my old realty firm. All's dark within, Real-Trons sleeping, desks clean, alarms armed, not open until Tuesday no matter who wants what. A big cheery orange banner in the window proclaims GOBBLE, GOBBLE, GOBBLE, which I understand means "Thanks."

I drive back up to Witherspoon, which goes direct to 206 and Calderon's office. The gang-posse hangs out under the bank sign, eyeing me pseudo-menacingly, though this time my notice is captured by the crawl, a miniature, bulb-lit Times Square above them, to which they're oblivious. *Quarterlysdown29.3 . . . ATTdown62% . . . Dowclose10.462 . . . HappyThanksgiving2000 . . . LLBeanChinamadeslippersrecalledduetodrawstringdefectabletochoke toddlerusers . . . PierreSalingertestifiesreLockerbiecrashsez "Iknowwho didit" . . . Airlineblanketsandheadrestssaidnotsanitized . . . Buffalo stymiedunder15"lakeeffectsnow . . . Horror storieswithFlaballots: "WhatinthenameofGodisgoingonhere?"workersez . . . NJenclave suffersmysteriousbombdetonlinktoelectionsuspec'd . . . Tropicaldepres Waynenotlikelytomakeland . . . BigpileupontheGarden State . . . HappyThanksgiving . . .*

These things are never easy to read.

I turn and pass down Witherspoon, the old part of Haddam, from when it was a real town—the old hardware, the old stale-but-good Greek place, the pole-less barbershop, the old Manusco photography gallery where everyone got his and her graduation portraits done until Manusco went to prison for lewdness. A new realtor's moved in here—Gold Standard Homes—beside the Banzai Sushi Den, where few customers are visible through the window. The tanning salon's in full swing for those heading to the islands. *Bombdeton . . . linktoelectionsuspec'd*— I "speak" these quasi-words in a mental voice that sounds portentous, though I don't think it could be true. Such a thought doesn't want to stay in mind and drifts away on the rainy evening's odd movie-street limbo, overtaken quickly by a thought that I can get my night guard fixed before heading home. I wonder, driving again along untrafficked Pleasant Valley Road past the cemetery fence, if I mentioned to Ann about the bomb, or if I told Marguerite during my Sponsor visit, or did she mention it to me, and did I go past Haddam Doctors before or after my funeral home stop? I can spend hours of a perfectly sleepable night wondering if I've kept such things straight, getting it all settled, then starting the process over, then wondering if I've contracted chemically induced Alzheimer's and pretty soon won't know much of anything.

Here again is the hospital, its upper stories lit up like a Radisson, its middle ones blacked out, its broken ground floor exterior turned incandescent by spotlights on metal scaffolds, shining alarmingly onto the distressed earth, turning the air pale metallic through the rain and dark. Humans—I see the FBI and ATF in blue rain jackets and white hard hats, and plenty of yellow-coated HPD—are in motion around the scene, so many hours after, their movement stylized and ominous. Yellow police tape cordons most of the grounds, and plenty of official vehicles, including an ambulance, a fire truck, more cruisers and two black panel trucks are parked helter-skelter inside the perimeter, as if something else is anticipated. No faces appear at the high hospital windows. The upper floors, the burn unit, the oncology ward, the ICU and maternity wings—the alpha and omega services—are in full swing, nobody with time for a crime scene outside. Officers, the same as earlier, their blue-flashing police cars parked up on the curb, wave me and the few other drivers on through. Red fusees sputter on the pavement.

Naturally, I'd love to shake loose some info, a name, a theory, a motive, a clue, but no one would spill any beans. "You'll know as soon as we know." "Everybody's doing their best out here." I stare up at the babyish rain-slick face of the young traffic cop, cold under his cop hat. He's rosy-cheeked, accustomed to smiling, but for the moment is as stern as a prosecutor. He peers inside my car with another practiced gaze. Anything suspicious here? Any tingle that says, "Maybe?" Any sign this could be Mr. Nutcase? A BUSH? WHY? sticker. A REALTOR sticker. Faded red Suburban with an Ocean County transfer station windshield sticker. *Haven't I seen you pass by here already today? Maybe you'd better pull over. . . .* I glide through, glancing in the rearview. He watches me as the red of my taillights fades into the dark, reads my license numbers, registers nothing, turns to the next car.

I turn onto Laurel Road, and immediately ahead is Calderon's office, on the back side of an older blond-brick Sixties dental plaza that fronts on 206 and where I've always used this rear entrance. As I cruise up Laurel, toward the little three-story cube down a flight of steps below a grassy embankment, I see two sets of lights are, in fact, glowing within. One suite, I know, is the *endo* guy, finishing off an after-hours root canal on some friend's impecunious sister. Another is the dental psychologist who works, evenings-only, on secretaries and dress-shop clerks who don't have the moolah for implants but still want to feel better about their smiles.

But no lights issue from Suite 308—Calderon's office. All's dark and buttoned up. Although up ahead, out at the curb as if awaiting a bus, is someone who actually looks like Calderon—topcoat, beret, a big-featured face distinguishable by black horn-rims and a black mustache I'm used to seeing sprouted behind his dental mask while he scrutinizes my bicuspids through a plastic AIDS shield. Here is my dentist—an odd vision to encounter after dark. Calderon's probably my age, the doted-on only son of Argentine renaissance scholar-diplomats who couldn't go home. He attended Dartmouth in the Sixties and settled in New Jersey after dental school. He's a tall, handsome, wry-mouthed, dyed-hair pussy hound, married to the fourth Mrs. Calderon, a young, tragically widowed, crimson-haired Haddam tax lawyer who makes poor Calderon dye his mustache, too, and work out like a decathlete at Abs-R-Us Spa in Kendall Park to keep him looking younger than she is. In his dental practice, Calderon affects bright tangerine clinical smocks, shows Gilbert Roland oldies on the patients' TV instead of tapes about what's wrong with your teeth and only hires blond knockout assistants who make the trip over worthwhile. He was briefly a member of our Divorced Men's Club in the Eighties and still is known to specialize in married female patients who require their cavities be filled at home. I'm always cheered up by my visits, since not only do I leave with shiny teeth, soft tissue checked, fillings tucked in tight and a feeling of well-being, but I'm also happy to pass an hour with another consenting adult who understands the lure of the Permanent Period but who hasn't had to dream it up the way I did. I, in fact, sometimes go right to sleep in the chair, with my mouth propped open and the drill whirring.

It makes me feel good now just to see Calderon waiting for who-knows-what out on the curb, though it's a long shot he'll take me back inside and knock off an adjustment.

I shoot down my driver's side window and angle over, satisfied if we only share a word. Calderon immediately smiles conspiratorially—with no idea who I am. Rain drizzle whooshes past on 206, thirty yards away.

"*Hola, Erno. ¿Dónde está el baño?*" I say this out my window—our usual palaver.

"*El Cid es famoso, ¿verdad?*" Ernesto beams a big scoundrel's smile, still not recognizing me, but putting his big veneers on display. His are white as pearls and made for him by a dental colleague at his wife's insistence. In his beret, he looks more like an old-timey film star than a philandering gum plumber. "Monet didn't have a dentist, I guess." This bears upon some lusty joke he told me the last time and has treated all his patients to for months. I don't remember it exactly, since I haven't been in since April. He doesn't know I've had/have cancer—which is a relief, since it makes me forget it. "What're you do-ing out here, *a-mi-go*, looking for houses to sell?"

Ernesto pretends to be more Latin than he is after thirty years. I've heard him on the phone with his denture lab in Bayonne. He could *be* from Bayonne. He does know who I am, though. Another small benison.

"I was hoping for a little after-hours dental attention." He'll think I'm kidding, but I'm not. Though having a night guard in my pocket feels ridiculous.

"No! *Hombre!* Don't tell me. Look at myself." He gaps back his topcoat to display a tuxedo with flaming red piping. His shoes are the shiny patent-leather species, and he's wearing a red bow tie and a red-and-green-striped cummerbund that does everything but blink and play music. Calderon's headed somewhere fancy, while I'm adrift on the back streets with a sore mandible. Who could expect a dentist to be late for a dinner party just because a patient's in need?

"So where's your big shindig?" I'm happy to get into the party spirit if I can't get my night guard fixed.

"Bet-sy went to see her old daddy in Chevy Chase. So . . . I am left alone once again *con* my thoughts. *¿Entiendes?* I'm going to New Jork to my club." Ernesto's donkey eyes brim with the promise of extramarital holiday high jinks. He's regaled me in the dentist's chair with winking accounts of his upper-Seventies "gentleman's club," where it's understood he'd be happy to take me and where I'd have the time of my life. Everything top-drawer. The best clientele—former Mets players, local news anchors, younger-set mafiosi. Black tie required, high-quality champagne on ice, the "ladies," naturally, all Barnard students with great personalities, making money for med-school tuition. I've pictured the "gentlemen" rumpus-ing round the plush-carpeted, damask-wallpapered rooms with their tuxedo pants off, in just their patent-leather pumps, dark socks and dinner jackets, comparing each other's equipment, of which it's my guess Ernesto probably has a prize specimen.

"Sounds like a blast," I say.

"Yeees. We have loads of fun. They send me down the leemo. Sometimes you should come with me." Ernesto nods to certify I wouldn't be sorry.

I have, just then, the recurrent aching memory of the long walk Clarissa and I took last August through the sun-warmed, healthy-elm-shaded streets of Rochester, a town noted for its prideful *there-ness* and for looking like a small Lutheran college town instead of medical ground zero. It was the Friday before my procedure on Monday, and we'd decided to walk ourselves to sweaty exhaustion, eat an early dinner at Applebee's and watch the Twins play the Tigers on TV at the Travelodge. We hiked out State Highway 14 to the eastern edge of town—on our feet where others were driving—beyond the winding streets of white-painted, well-tended, green-roof neighborhoods, past the Arab-donated Little League stadium and the federal medical facility and the Olmsted County truck-marshaling yard, beyond the newer rail-fenced ranch homes with snow machines, bass boats and fifth-wheelers For Sale on their lawns, past where a sand and gravel operation had cracked open the marly earth, and farther on to where dense-smelling alfalfa fields took up and a small, treed river bottom appeared, and the glaciated earth began to devolve and roll and slide greenly toward the Mississippi, fifty miles away. NO HUNTING signs were on all the fence posts. The summer landscape was as dry as a razor strop, the corn as high as an elephant's gazoo, the far, hot sky as one-color gray as a cataract. There was, of course, a lake.

On a little asphalt hillcrest beside where the highway ribboned off to the east, Clarissa and I stopped to take the view back to town—the great, many-buildinged Mayo colossus dominating the pleasant, forested townscape like a kremlin. Impressive. These buildings, I thought, could take good care of anybody.

Sweat had beaded on Clarissa's forehead, her tee-shirt sweated through. She passed a hand across her flushed cheek. A green truck with slatted sides rumbled past, kicking up hot breeze and sand grit, leaving behind a loud, sweetish aroma of pigs-to-market. "This is where America's decided to receive its bad news, I guess, isn't it?" She suddenly didn't like being out here. Everything was far too specific.

"It's not so terrible. I like it." I did. And do. "Given the alternatives."

"You would."

"Wait'll you're my age. You'll be happy there're places like this to receive you. Things look different."

"Maybe you should just move out here. Buy one of those nice, horrible houses with the green roofs and the green shutters and mullioned windows. Buy a Ski-Doo."

I'd already given that some thought. "I think I'd do fine out here," I said. We were both pretending I'd be dead on Monday, just to see how it felt.

"Great," she said, then turned dramatically on her heel to gaze down the highway eastward. We were traveling no farther that day. "You think you'd do fine anywhere."

"What's the matter with that? Is it a mark of something to be unhappy?"

"No," she said sourly. "You're very admirable. Sorry. I shouldn't pick on you. I don't know why I bother."

I started to say, Because I'm your father, I'm all that's left— but I didn't. I said, "I understand perfectly. You have my best interests at heart. It's fine." We started back walking to town and to the things town had in store for me.

ERNESTO STARES down at me off the curb the way he would if he was waiting for my mouth to numb up. It dawns on me he has no real idea who I am. I am real estate-related but possess no name, only a set of full-mouth X rays clamped to a cold white screen. Or maybe I'm the carpet-cleaning guy from Skillman. Or I own the Chico's on Route 1, a place I know he skulks off to with his Lebanese hygienist, Magda.

Up in my darkened rearview, I see what may be Ernesto's leemo, its pumpkin-tinted headlights rounding onto Laurel and commencing slowly toward us.

"What's up for Thanksgiving in *su casa*, Ernesto?" I have somehow become pointlessly cheery. Ernesto eyes the white stretch, then glances back at me warily, as if I might just be the wrong person to witness this. He flicks a secret hand signal to the driver, and in so doing makes himself look effeminate instead of *mal hombre machismo*. Maybe one of the nice-personality

Barnard girls with her gold-plated health report is waiting in the backseat, already popping the Veuve Clicquot.

"What's going on what?" he says, his horn-rims and beret getting misted, his smile not quite earnest.

"Thanksgiving," I say. "*¿Qué pasa a su casa?*" I'm deviling him, but I don't care, since he won't fix my night guard.

"Oh, we go to Atlantic City. Always. My wife likes to gamble at Caesars." He's departing now, inching crabwise toward the limo, which has halted a discreet distance down Laurel. In my side mirror I see the driver's door swing open. A tall chorus-girl-looking female in silver satin shorty-shorts, high heels and a white Pilgrim collar with a tall red Pilgrim hat just like on the Pennsylvania highway signs gets out and pulls open the rear door. "I have to go now." Ernesto looks back at me a little frantically, as if he might get left. "*Hasta la vista*," he adds idiotically.

"Hugo de Naranja to you, too."

"Okay. Yes. Thanks." In the mirror I see him hustle down the street, giving the chorus-girl driver a quick peck and scampering in the limo door. The Pilgrim chauffeur looks my way, smiles at me scoping her out, then climbs back in the driver's seat and slowly pulls around me and up Laurel Road.

It wouldn't be bad to be in there with ole Ernesto is what I think. Not so bad to have his agenda, his particular species of ducks lined up. Though my guess is, none of it would work out for me. Not now. Not in the state I'm currently in.

THE JOHNNY APPLESEED Bar, downstairs at the August Inn, where I'm meeting Mike Mahoney, is a fair replica of a Revolutionary War roadhouse tavern. Wide, worn pine floors, low ceilings, a burnished mahogany bar, plenty of antique copper lanterns and period "tack"—battle flags with snakes and mottoes, encrusted sabers, drumheads, homespun uniforms encased in glass, framed musket-balls, framed tricorn headgear—with (the *pièce de résistance*) a wall-sized spotlit mural in alarmingly vivid colors of a loony-looking J. Appleseed seated backward astride a gray mule, saucepan on head, a Klem Kadiddlehopper grin on his lascivious lips, mindlessly distributing apple seeds off the mule's bony south end. Which apparently was how the West was won. For years, Haddam bar-stool historians debated whether Norman Rockwell or Thomas Hart Benton had "executed" the Appleseed mural. Old-timers swore to have watched both of them do it at several different times, though this was disproved when Rockwell stayed at the inn in the Sixties and said not even Benton could paint anything that bad.

I'm always happy in here any time of day or night, its clubby, bogus, small-town imperviousness making me sense a safe haven. And tonight especially, following today, with only a smattering of holiday tipplers nursing quiet cocktails along the bar, plus an anonymous him 'n her tucked into a dark red leather banquette in the corner, conceivably doing the deed right there—not that anyone would care. A wall TV's on without sound, a miniature plastic Yule tree's set up on the bottle shelf, a strand of silver (flammable) bunting's swagged across the mirrored backbar. The old sack-a-bones bartender's watching the hockey game. It's the perfect place to end up on a going-nowhere Tuesday before Thanksgiving, when much of your personal news hasn't been so festive. It's one thing to marvel at what a bodacious planet we occupy, the way Dr. von Reichstag did, where humans ruminate about neutrinos. But it's beyond marveling that those humans can invent a concept as balming to the ailing spirit as the "cozy local watering hole," where you're always expected, no questions asked, where you can choose from a full list of life-restoring cocktails, stare silently at a silent TV, speak non sequiturs to a nonjudgmental bartender, listen (or not) to what's said around you—in other words, savor the "in but not all in," "out but not all out" zeitgeist mankind would package and sell like hoolahoops if it could and thus bring peace to a troubled planet.

After my sad divorce seventeen years ago, and before I was summoned to the bar of residential realty, I found myself on a stool here many a night, enjoying a *croque monsieur* from the upstairs kitchen, plus seventy or eighty highballs, sometimes with a "date" I could smooch up in the shadows, then later slithering (alone or à deux) up the steps out onto Hulfish Street and into a warm Jersey eventide with not a single clue about where my car might be. I frequently ended up lurching home to Hoving Road (avoiding busier streets, and cops), and diving straight into bed and towering sleep. I may have experienced my fullest sensation of belonging in Haddam on those nights, circa

1983. By which I mean, if you saw a fortyish gentleman stepping unsteadily out of a bar into a dark suburban evening, staring around mystified, looking hopefully to the heavens for guidance, then careening off down a silent, tree-bonneted street of nice houses where lights are lit and life athrum, one of which houses he enters, tramps upstairs and falls into bed with all his clothes on—wouldn't you think, Here's a man who belongs, a man with native roots and memory, his plow deep in the local earth? You would. What's belonging all about, what's its quiddity, if not that drunk men "belong" where you find them?

It's 6:25 and Mike is not yet in evidence. Hard to imagine what a diminutive Tibetan and a macaroni land developer could do *together* for an entire afternoon of rotten weather. How many plat maps, zoning ordinances, traffic projections, air-quality regulations, floodplain variances and EEOC regs can you pore over without needing sedation, and on the first day you ever laid eyes on each other?

From the elderly bartender, I order a Boodles, eighty proof, straight up, take a tentative lick off the martini-glass rim and feel exactly the way I want to feel: better—able to face the world as though it was my friend, to strike up conversations with total strangers, to see others' points of view, to think most everything will turn out all right. Even my jaw relaxes. My eyes attain good focus. The bothersome belly sensation that I probably erroneously associate with my prostate has ceased its flickering. For the first time since I woke at six in Sea-Clift and knew I could sleep another hour, I breathe a sigh of relief. A day has passed intact. It's nothing I take for granted.

My fellow patrons are all Haddam citizens I've seen before, may even have done business with, but who, because of my decade's absence, pretend never to have laid eyes on me. Ditto the bean-pole, white-shirted, green-plastic-bow-tied bartender, Lester, who's stood the bar here thirty years. He's a Haddam townie, a slope-shouldered, high-waisted Ichabod in his late sixties, a balding bachelor with acrid breath no woman would get near. He's given me the standard, noncommittal "What-chouhavin," even though years ago I listed his mother's brick duplex on Cleveland Street, next door to my own former house, where Ann now lives, presented him two full-price offers in a week, only to have him back out (which he had every right to do) and turn the place into a rental—a major financial misreading in 1989, which I pointed out to him, so that he never forgave me. Often it's the case that no matter how successful or pain-free a transaction turns out—and in Haddam there was never a bad one—once it's over, clients often begin to treat the residential agent like a person who's only half-real, someone they've maybe only dreamed about. When they pass you in a restaurant or mailing Christmas cards at the PO, they'll instantly turn furtive and evade your eyes, as if they'd seen you on a sexual-predators list, give a hasty, mumbled, noncommittal "Howzitgoin?" and are gone. And I might've made them a quick two mil or ended a bad run of vein-clogging hassles or saved them from pissing away all in a divorce or a Chapter 11. At some level—and in Haddam this level is routinely reached—people are embarrassed not to have sold their own houses themselves and resentful about paying the commission, since all it seems to involve is putting up a sign and waiting till the dump truck full of money stops out front. Which sometimes happens and sometimes doesn't. Looked at from this angle, we realtors are just the support group for the chronically risk-averse.

Lester's begun using the remote to click channels away from the hockey game, staring up turkey-necked, gob open at the Sanyo bracketed above the flavored schnapps. He's carrying on separate dialogues with the different regulars, desultory give-and-takes that go on night to night, year to year, never missing a beat, just picked up again using the all-purpose Jersey conjunction, *So*. "So, if you put in an invisible fence, doesn't the fuckin' dog get some kinda complex?" "So, if you ask me, you miss all the fuckin' nuance using sign language." "So, to me, see, flight attendants are just part of the plane's fuckin' equipment—like oxygen masks or armrests. Not that I wouldn't schtup one of them. Right?" Lester nibbles his lip as he flips past sumo wrestling, cliff divers in Acapulco, two people who've won a game-show contest and are hugging, then on past several channels with different people dressed in suits and nice dresses, sitting behind desks, talking earnestly into the camera, then past a black man in an ice-cream suit healing a fat black woman in a red choir robe by making her fall over backward on a big stage—more things than I can focus on in my relaxed, not-all-in, not-all-out state of mind.

Then all at once, the President, my president—big, white-haired, smiling, puffy-faced and guileless—*his* face and figure fill the color screen. President Clinton strolls casually, long-strided, across a green lawn, suppressing an embarrassed smile. He's in blue cords, a plain white shirt, a leather bomber jacket and Hush Puppies like mine. He's doing his best to look shy and undeserving, guilty of something, but nothing very important—stealing watermelons, driving without a learner's permit, taking a peek through a hole in the wall of the girls' locker room. He's got his Labrador, Buddy, on a leash and is talking and flirting with people off-camera. Behind him sits a big Navy copter with a white-hatted Marine at attention by the gangway. The President has just saluted him—incorrectly.

"Where's the fuckin' Mafia when you need them bastards?" Lester's growling up at the tube. He makes a pistol out of his thumb and index finger and assassinates the man I voted for with a soft pop of his lizard lips. "Ain't he havin' the time of his fuckin' life with this election bullshit. He loves it." Lester swivels around to his patrons, his mouth sour and mean. "Country on its fuckin' knees."

"Easier to give blow jobs," one of the regulars says, and thumbs his glass for a fill-up.

"And you'd know about that," Lester says, and grins evilly.

The couple in the back booth, who've been doing whatever away from everybody's notice, unexpectedly stands up, moving their banquette table noisily out of the way, as if they thought a fight was about to erupt or their sexual shenanigans required more leg room. All five of us, plus an older woman at the bar, have a gander at these two getting their coats on and shuffling out through the tables. Happily, I don't know them. The woman's young and thin and watery-blond and pretty in a sharp-featured way. He's a short-armed, gangsterish meat-pie with dark curly hair, stuffed into a three-piece suit. His trousers are unzipped and part of his shirttail's poked guiltily through the fly.

"What's your hurry there, folks?" Lester yaps, and leers as the couple heads for the red EXIT lozenge and up to the street.

The noisy drinker down the bar leans forward and smirks at me. "So whadda *you* think?" He is Bob Butts, owner (once) of Butts Floral on Spring Street, since replaced by the Virtual Profusion and going great guns. Bob is red-skinned, fattish and embittered. His mother, Lana, ran the shop after Bob's dad died in Korea. This was prehistoric Haddam, when it was a sleepy-eyed, undiscovered jewel. When Lana moved to Coral Gables and remarried, Bob took over the shop and ran it in the ground, gambling his brains out in Tropworld, which was new in Atlantic City. Bob's a first-rate dickhead.

The two men beyond him, I don't know, but are shady, small-time Haddam cheezers I've seen six hundred times—in Cox's News or in the now-departed Pietroinferno's. I have an idea they're involved with delivering the *Trenton Times* and possibly less obvious merchandise. The hatchet-faced, thin-haired woman, wearing a blowsy black dress suitable for a funeral, I've never seen, though she's apparently Bob's companion. It would be easy to say these four are members of a Haddam demimonde, but in fact they're only regular citizens holding out in defiance, rather than making the move to Bordentown or East Windsor.

"What do I think about what?" I lean forward and look straight at Bob Butts, raising my warming martini to my lips. President Clinton has disappeared off the screen. Though I wonder what he's doing in real time—having a stiff belt himself, possibly. His last two years haven't been much to brag about. Like Clarissa, I wish he was running again. He'd do better than these current two monkeys.

"All this election bullshit." Bob Butts cranes forward, then back, to get a better look at me. Lester's pouring him another 7&7. Bob's haggard lady friend gives me an unfocused, boozy stare, as if she knows all about me. The two *Trenton Times* guys muse at their shot glasses (root beer schnapps, my bet). "Some guy got blown up over at the hospital today. Bunch of pink confetti. This shit's gone too far. The Democrats are stealin' it." Bob's wet, bloodshot eyes clamp onto me, signaling he knows who I am now—a nigger-lovin', tax-and-spend, pro-healthcare, abortion-rights, gay-rights, consumer-rights, tree-hugging liberal (all true). Plus, I sold my house and left the door open to a bunch of shit Koreans, and probably even had something to do with him losing the flower shop (also true).

Bob Butts is wearing a disreputably dirty brown shawl-collar car coat made of a polymer-based material worn by Michigan frosh in the early Sixties but not since, and looks like hell warmed over. He has on chinos like mine and white Keds with no socks.

He's been in need of a shave for several days. His thin, lank hair is long and dirty and he could do with a bath. Obviously, Bob's experiencing a downward loop, having once been handsome, clever, gaunt to the point of febrile Laurence Harvey effemin-ance. Like Calderon, he cut a wide swath through the female population, who he used to woogle in his back room, right on the stem-strewn metal arranging table. That's maybe all you can hope for if you're a florist.

"I don't really see what the Democrats have to do with who-ever got blown up at the hospital," I say. I half-turn and take a casual, calculated look back at the Appleseed mural, brightly lit by a row of tiny silver spotlights attached to the low ceiling. By looking at goofball Johnny, I'm essentially addressing nut-case Bob. This is the message I want subliminally delivered. I also don't want Bob to think I give half a shit about anything he says, since I don't. I'm ready right now for Mike to show up. But then I can't resist adding, "And I don't see where the Democrats are stealing anything, unless getting more votes could be said to be a form of theft. Maybe *you* do. Maybe it's why you're not in the flower business anymore."

"Could be said." Bob Butts grins idiotically. "Could be said you're an asshole. That could be said."

"It's already been said," I say. I don't want to fan this disagree-ment beyond the boundary of impolite bar argument. I'm not sure what would wait out past that frontier at my age and state of health and with a big drink already under my belt. And yet the same irresistible urge makes me unable not to add, still facing the Appleseed mural, "It's actually been said by even bigger shit-heels than you are, Bob. So don't worry too much about surprising me." I shift around on my bar stool and entertain the rich thought of a second chilled Boodles. Only, I hear scuffling and wood being scraped. The hatchet-faced woman says, "Oh, Jesus Christ, Bob!" Then a bar stool like the one I'm sitting on hits the floor. And suddenly there's a fishy odor in my nostrils and mouth, and Bob Butts' small, rough hands go right around my neck, his whiskery chin jamming into my ear, his throat making a gurgling noise both mechanical, like a car with a bad starter, and also simian—*grrrrr*—into my ear canal—"*Grrrrr, grrrrr, grrrrr*"—so that I tip over off my bar stool, which tumbles sideways, and Bob and I go sprawling toward the pine floor.

I'm trying to grab a fistful of his reeking car coat and haul it in the direction I'm falling so he'll hit the floor first and me on top—which bluntly happens. Though the bar stool next to mine—heavy as an anvil—topples down onto me with a clunk in my rear rib cage that doesn't knock the breath out of me but hurts like shit and makes me expel a not-voluntary "oooof."

"Cocksucker, you cocksucker." Bob Butts is gurgling in my ear and stinking. "*Grrrr, errrr, grrrr.*" These are noises (I for some reason find myself *thinking*) Bob probably learned as a child, and that were funny once, but now come into play in a serious effort to murder me. Bob's grip isn't exactly around my windpipe, only my neck, but he's squeezing the crap out of me and digging his grimed fingernails into my skin. My flesh is stinging, but I don't feel shocked or in any jeopardy, except possibly from the fall.

No one else in the bar does anything to help. Not Lester, not the two *Trenton Times* palookas, not the witchy, balding woman in widow's weeds who's invoked Jesus Christ. They simply ignore Bob and me wrestling on the floor, as if a new bar customer, in for a Fuzzy Navel, might think it was great to see two middle-aged guys muggling around on the damp boards, trying to accomplish nobody's too sure what-in-the-fuck.

All of this begins to seem like an annoyance more than a fight, like having someone's pet monkey hanging on your neck, though we're down on the floor and the stool's on top of me and Bob's going "*Grrrr, errrr, grrrr*" and squeezing my neck, his breath and hair reeking like week-old haddock. Suddenly, I lose all my wind and have to buck the bar stool off my back to breathe, and in doing so I get my knee in between Bob's own squirming, jimmering knees and my right elbow into his sternum, just below where I could interrupt *his* windpipe. I lean on Bob's hard breast bone, stare down into his bulging, blood-splurged eyes, which register that this event may be almost over. "Bob," I half-shout at him. His eyes widen, he bares his long yellow teeth, refastens a fisted grip on my neck tendons and croaks, "Cocksucker." And with no further prelude, I go ahead and jackhammer my kneecap straight up into Bob's nuttal pouch pretty much as hard as I can— given my weakened state, given my lack of inclination and the fact that I've had a martini and had hoped the evening would turn out to be pleasant, since so much of the day hadn't.

Bob Butts erupts instantly in a bulbous-eyed, Gildersleevian

"*Oooomph,*" his cheek and lips exploding. His eyes squeeze melo-dramatically shut. He lets go of my neck and goes as flaccid as a lifesaving dummy. Instead of more "*Grrrr, errr, grrr,*" he groans a deep, agonizing and, I'll admit, satisfying "*Eeeeeuh-uh-oh.*"

"You fuckin' scrogged 'im, you cheap-ass son of a bitch," the hatchet-faced woman shouts from up on her bar stool above us, frowning down at Bob and me as if we were insects she'd been interested in. "Fight fair, fucker." She decides to toss her drink at me and does. The glass, which has gin in it, hits my shoulder, but most of its contents hit Bob, who's grimacing, with my elbow point—excruciatingly, I hope—nailed into his sternum.

"All right, all right, all right," Lester says behind the bar, as if he couldn't really give a shit what the hell's going on but is bored by it, his spoiled, impassive shoe-salesman's mug and his green plastic bow tie—relic of some desolate Saint Paddy's day—just visible to me beyond the bar rail.

"All right *what?*" I'm holding Bob at elbow point. "Are you going to keep this shit bucket from strangling me, or am I going to have to rough him up?" Bob makes another gratifying "*Eeeeeuh-uh-oh,*" whose exhalation is foul enough that I have to get away from him, my heart finally beginning to whump.

"Let 'im get up," Lester says, as though Bob was his prob-lem now.

Bob's blond accomplice hauls a big shiny-black purse off the floor beside her. "I'll get 'im home, the dipshit," she says. The two other bar-stool occupants look at me and Bob as if we were a show on TV. On the real TV, Bush's grinning, smirking, depthless face is visible, talking soundlessly, arms held away from his sides as if he was hiding tennis balls in his armpits. Other humans are visible around him, well-dressed, smooth-coifed, shiny-faced young men holding paper plates and eating bar-becue, laughing and being amused to death by whatever their candidate's saying.

Using the bar stool, I raise myself from where I've straddled Bob Butts, and feel instantly light-headed, weak-armed, heavy-legged, in peril of falling back over on top of Bob and expiring. I gawk at Lester, who's taking away my martini glass and scowl-ing at me while Bob's lady friend pulls him, wallowing, off the floor. She squats beside me, her scrawny knees bowed out, her skirt opened, so that I unmercifully see her thighs encased in black panty hose, and the bright white crotch patch of her undies. I avert my eyes to the floor, and see that my night guard has fallen out of my pocket in the tussle and been crunched in three pieces under the bar rail. It makes me feel helpless, then I scrape the pieces away with my heel. Gone.

Bob is up but bent at the waist, clutching his injured testicles. He's missing one of his Keds, and his ugly yellow toenails are gripping the floor. His hair's mussed, his fatty face blotched red and white, his eyes hollowed and mean and full of defeated despisal. He glares at me, though he's had enough. I'm sure he'd love to spit out one more vicious "Cocksucker," except he knows I'd kick his cogs again and enjoy doing it. In fact, I'd be glad to. We stand a moment loathing each other, all my parts—hands, thighs, shoulders, scratched neck, ankles, everything but my own nuts—aching as if I'd fallen out a window. Nothing occurs to me as worth saying. Bob Butts was better as a lowlife, floral failure and former back-room lady-killer than as a vanquished enemy, since enemy-hood confers on him a teaspoon of undeserved dignity. It was also better when this was a homey town and a bar I used to dream sweet dreams in. Both also gone. Kaput. On some human plain that doesn't exist anymore, now would be a perfect moment and place from which to start an unusual friendship of opposites. But all prospects for that are missing.

I turn to Lester, who I hate for no other reason than that I can, and because he takes responsibility for no part of life's tragedy. "What do I owe you?"

"Five," he snaps.

I have the bat-hide already in hand, my fingers scuffed and sticky from my busted knuckles. My knees are shimmying, though fortunately no one can see. I give a thought to collecting up my shattered night guard pieces, then forget it.

"Did you used to live here?" Lester says distastefully.

This, atop all else, does shock me. More than that, it disgusts me. Possibly I don't look exactly as I looked when I busted my ass to flog Lester's old mama's duplex in a can't-miss '89 seller's market—a sale that could've sprung Lester all the way to Sun City, and into a cute pastel cinder-block, red-awninged match box with a mountain view, plus plenty left over for an Airstream and a decent wardrobe in which to pitch sleazy woo to heat-baked widows. A better life. But I *am* the same, and fuck-face Lester needs to be reminded.

"Yeah, I lived here," I growl. "I sold your mother's house. Except you were too much of a mamma's-boy asshole to part with it. Guess you couldn't bear leaving your leprechaun tie."

Lester looks at me in an interested way, as if he'd muted me but my lips are still moving. He rests his cadaver hands on the glass rail, where there's a moist red rubber drying mat. Lester doesn't actually look much different from Johnny Appleseed, which may be why the August Inn people (a hospitality consortium based in Cleveland) keep him on. He still wears, I see, his big gold knuckle-buster Haddam HS ring. (My son refused his.) "Whatever," Lester says, then turns down the pasty corners of his mouth in disdain.

I'd like to utter something toxic enough to get through even Lester's soul-deep nullity. The least spark of anger might earn me the pleasure of kicking his ass, too. Only I don't know what to say. The two *Trenton Times* delivery goons are frowning at me with small, curious menace. Possibly I have morphed into something not so good in their view, someone different from who they thought I was. No longer the invisible, ignorable, pathetic drip, but a rude intruder threatening to take too much attention away from their interests and crap on their evening. They might have to "deal" with me just for convenience sake.

Bob Butts and his harridan lady friend are exiting the bar by way of the stairs up to Hulfish Street. "*Naaaa*, leave off, you asshole," I hear the old blondie growl.

"This fuckin' stinks," Bob growls back.

"*You* stink is what," she says, continuing with difficulty, one leaning on the other, up toward the cold outdoors, the heavy door going *click* shut behind them.

I stare a moment, transfixed by the bright apple-tinted Disneyish mural of clodhopper Johnny, straddling his plug bass-ackwards, saucepan on top, dribbling his seed across Ohio. These bars are probably a chain, the mural computer-generated. Another one just like this one may exist in Dayton.

I unexpectedly feel a gravity-less melancholy in the bar, in spite of victory over Bob Butts. In the ponderous quiet, with the Sanyo showing leather-fleshed Floridians at long tables, examining punch-card ballots as if they were chest X rays, Lester looks like a pallid old ex-contract killer considering a comeback. His two customers may be associates—silent down-staters handy with chain saws, butcher's utensils and Sakrete. It's still New Jersey here. These people call it home. It might be time to wait for Mike outside.

"Ain't you Bascombe somethin'?" One of the toughs frowns down the bar at me. It's the farther away one, seated next to the shot-glass rack, a round, barrel-chested, ham-armed smudge pot with a smaller than standard hat size. His face has a close-clipped beard, but his cranium is shaved shiny. He looks Russian and is therefore almost certainly Italian. He produces a short unfiltered cigarette (which Boro regulations profoundly forbid the smoking of), lights it with a little yellow Bic and exhales smoke in the direction of Lester, who's rummaging through the cash drawer. I would willingly forswear all knowledge of any Bascombe; be instead Parker B. Farnsworth, retired out of the Bureau—Organized Crime Division—but still on call for undercover duties where an operative needs to look like a real estate agent. However, I've blown my cover over Lester's mother's house. I feel endangered, but see no way free except to fake going insane and run up the stairs screaming.

So what I reluctantly say is, "Yeah." I expect the smudge pot to snort a cruel laugh and say something low and accusing—a widowed relative or orphan nephew I gave the mid-winter heave-ho to so I could peddle their house to some noisy Jews from Bedminster. I've never done that, but it doesn't stop people from thinking I have. Someone in my old realty firm for sure did it, which makes me a party.

"My kid went to school with your kid." The bald guy taps his smoke with his finger, inserts it in the left corner of his small mouth and blows more smoke out the front in little squirts. He lets his eyes wander away from me.

"My son Paul?" I am unexpectedly smiling.

"I don't know. Maybe. Yeah."

"And what was your son's name? I mean, what's his name?"

"Teddy." He is wearing a tight black nylon windbreaker open onto what looks like an aqua tee-shirt that exhibits his hard basketball-size belly. His clothes are skimpy for this weather, but it's part of his look.

"And where's *he* now?" Likely the Marines or a good trade school, or plying Lake Superior as an able seaman gaining grainy life experience on an ore boat before coming home to settle into life as a plumber. Possibilities are plentiful and good. He's probably *not* authoring wiseacre greeting cards and throwing shit fits because he feels underappreciated.

"He ain't." The big guy elevates his rounded chin to let cigarette smoke go past his eyes. His drinking buddy, a bony, curly-headed weight-lifter type with a giant flared nose and dusky skin—also wearing a nylon windbreaker—produces a Vicks inhaler, gives it a stiff snort and points his nose at the ceiling as if the experience was transporting.

I get a noseful clear over here. It makes the room suddenly wintry and momentarily happy again. "You mean he stayed home?"

"No, no, no," Teddy's father says, facing the backbar.

"So, where is he?" This is, of course, 100 percent none of my business, and I already detect the answer won't be good. Prison. Disappeared. Disavowed. The standard things that happen to your children.

"He ain't on the earth," the big guy says. "Now, I mean." He removes his cigarette and appraises its red tip.

No way I'm heading down *this* bad old road. Not after having had my own dead son flashed like a muleta by my wife I'm no longer married to. Since Ralph Bascombe's been absent from the planet, I haven't gone around yakking about it in bars with strangers.

I stand up straight in my now-soiled barracuda—sore kneed, neck burning, knuckles aching—and look expressionlessly at this short, cylindrical fireplug of a man who's suffered (I know exactly, or close enough) and has had to get used to it. Alone.

The big guy swivels to peer past his friend's face at me. His dark, flat eyes don't glow or burn or teem, but are imploring and not the eyes of an assassin, but of a pilgrim seeking small progress. "Where's *your* kid?" he says, cigarette backward in his fingers, French-style.

"He's in Kansas City."

"What's he do? He a lawyer? Accountant?"

"No," I say. "He's a kind of writer, I guess. I'm not really sure."

"Okay."

"What happened to your son?"

Why? Why can't I just do what I say I will? Is it so hard? Is it age? Illness? Bad character? Fear I'll miss something? What this man's about to say fairly fills the bar with dread, bounces off the period trappings, taps the drumheads, jingles the harnesses, swirls around Johnny Appleseed like a Halloween ghost.

"He took his own life," the palooka says without a blink.

"Do you know why?" I ask, full-in-now, with nothing to offer back, nothing to make a man feel better in this season when all seek it.

"Look at those fucks," Lester snarls. Candidate Gore and his undernourished running mate have commandeered the TV screen in their shirt sleeves, walled in behind stalks of microphones in front of an enormous oak tree, looking grave and silly at once. Gore, the stiff, is spieling on soundlessly, as if he's admonishing a seventh grader, his body doughy, perplexing, crying out to put on more weight and be old. "Haw!" Lester brays at them. "Whadda country. Jeez-o fuck." If I had a pistol I'd gladly shoot Lester with it.

"No. I don't." The big Trentonian bolts his drink and has a last drag on his smoke. He doesn't like this now, is sorry he started it. Just an idle question that led the old familiar wrong way. "What I owe you?" he says to Lester, who's still gawking at Gore and Lieberman gabbling like geese.

"A blow job," Lester says without looking around. "It's happy hour. Make me happy."

The skint-headed guy stubs his smoke in his shot glass, lays two bills on the bar but doesn't rise to the bait. I get another hot whiff of Vicks as the two men shift around to depart. Off the stool, the big guy's actually small and compact, and moves with a nice, comfortable, swivel-shouldered Fiorello La Guardia rolling gait, like a credible middleweight.

"Good talking to ya," he says. His taller, more threatening friend looks straight at me as he steps past, but then seems embarrassed and diverts his eyes.

"Remember what we talked about," Lester shouts as they head toward the stairs.

"You're already on the list," the bald guy's stairwell voice says as the metal door clanks open and their footfalls and muttering voices grow soft, leaving me alone with Lester.

Mike hasn't arrived. I stare at Lester's satchel-ass behind the bar as if it foretold a mystery. He glances around at me (I'm still queasy after my Bob Butts set-to). He has put on tortoiseshell-framed glasses and his practically chinless face is hostile, as if he's just before invoking his right to refuse to serve anyone. I could use the pisser. Once it was by the exit, but the old smoothed brass MEN plaque is gone and the wall's been bricked up. The gents must be upstairs in the inn.

"Who'dju waste your vote on?" Lester says. I transfer my stare from trousers seat to the plastic Christmas tree on the backbar. I'm unwilling to leave till Mike gets here.

"I voted for Gore." The sound of these four words makes me almost want to burst out laughing. Except I feel so shitty.

Lester bellies up to the bar in front of me. His frayed gray-white shirt bears tiny dark specks of tomato juice on its front. His black bartender trousers could use fumigating. He lays his big left hand, the one with the Haddam HS ring on it, palm-down on the eurathaned compass of the bar. The ring's *H* crest is bracketed by two tiny rearing stallions on either side, with the numeral 19 below one stallion, and 48 the other. I peer at Lester's fingers, which promise prophesy. He uses his other index finger to point toward his long left thumb. "Let me show you something," he says, sinister, matter-of-fact, staring down at his own fingers. "This is your Russian. This next one's your spic. This one's your African. This last one's your Arab or your sand nigger—whichever. You got your choice." Lester raises his eyes to me coldly, smiling as if he was passing a terrible sentence.

"My choice for what?"

"For what language you want to learn when you vote for fuckin' Gore. He's givin' the country away, like the other guy, except his dick got in his zipper." Lester, as he did earlier, nibbles his lip—but as though he might punch me. "You prob-ably respect my opinion, don't you? That's what you guys do. You respect everybody's fuckin' opinion. Except you can't respect *everybody's* opinion." Lester has made a brawler's fist out of his prophetic hand and leans on it to draw closer to me over the bar. Vile, minty fixative smell—something he's been told to use when he meets the public—has been adulterated by an acrid steam of hate. It would make me nauseated if I didn't think Lester was about to assault me.

"No," I say. "I don't respect your opinion." My voice, even to me, lacks determination. I stand back a step. "I don't respect your opinion at all."

"Oh. Okay." Lester smiles more broadly but keeps on staring hate at me. "I thought you thought everybody was just like everybody else, everybody equal. All of us peas in a fuckin' pod."

It *is* what I think, but I won't be able to explain that now. Precisely at this flash point—and surprisingly—Mike walks out of the stairwell and through the door of the Johnny Appleseed, looking like a happy little middle-manager, in his mustard blazer and Italian tassel-loafers, though he has the spontaneous good sense to halt under the red EXIT as if something was about to combust. It may.

"It *is* what I think," I say, and feel stupid. Lester's eye shifts contemptuously to Mike, who looks disheartened but is, of course, smiling. "And I think you're full of shit!" I say this too harshly and somehow begin to lose my balance on the tumbled-over bar stool I haven't had a chance to put back upright. I am falling yet again.

"Is the midget a friend of yours now?" Lester sneers, but his eyes stay nastily on Mike, object of all he holds loathsome, treacherous and wrong. The element. The thing to be extirpated.

I feel hands on my shoulder and lumbar region. I am now *not* falling (thank God). Mike has moved quickly forward and kept me mostly upright. "He *is* my friend," I say, and accidentally kick the bar stool against the brass foot rail with a loud clanging.

Lester just grimly watches the two of us teetering around the floor like marionettes. "Get out," he snarls, "and take your coolie with you." Lester is an old man, possibly seventy. But meanness and bile have made him feel good, able to take an honest pleasure in the world. Old Huxley was right: stranger than we *can* know.

"I will." I'm pushing against Mike with my left arm, urging him toward the exit. He has yet to make a noise. What a surprise all this must be. "And I'll never come in this shithole again," I say. "I used to like this place. You'd have been a lot better off if you'd sold your mother's house and moved to Arizona." Why I say these things—other than that they're true—I can't tell you. You rarely get the exit line you deserve.

"Blow it out your ass, you fag," Lester says. "I hope you get AIDS." He scowls, as if these weren't exactly the words he wanted to say, either. Though he's said them now and ruined his good mood. He turns sideways and looks back up at the TV as we meet the cold air awaiting us in the stairwell. A hockey game is on again, men skating in circles on white ice. The sound comes on, an organ playing a lively carnival air. Lester glances our way to make sure we're beating it, then turns the volume up louder for a little peace.

UP ON THE damp sidewalk bordering the Square, white HPD sawhorses have been established along the Pilgrim Interpretive Center's wattle fence so that during Pilgrim business hours pedestrians can stand and observe what Pilgrim life was once all about and hear Pilgrims deliver soliloquies. A youngish boy–girl couple in identical clear plastic jackets and rain pants stands peering over into the impoundment, shining a jumbo flashlight across the ghostly farm yard. The young husband's pointing things out to the young wife in a plummy English voice that knows everything about everything. They've let their white Shihtzu, in its little red sweater, go spiriting around inside the mucked-up yard, rooting the ground and pissing on things. "Ser-gei?" the husband says, using his most obliging voice. "Look at him, darling, he thinks this is all brilliant." "Isn't he funny? He's *so* funny," his young wife says. "Those hungry buggers would probably eat him," the young man observes. "Probab-lee," the wife says. "Come along, Ser-gei, it's 2000, old man, time to go home, time to go home."

Mike and I cross the shadowed Square to my car, parked in front of Rizutto's. Mike still has said nothing, acknowledging that I don't want to talk either. A Buddhist can nose out disharmony like a beagle scenting a bunny. I assume he's micromanaging his private force fields, better to interface with mine on the ride home.

All the Square's pricey shops are closed at seven o'clock except for the liquor store, where a welcoming yellow warmth shines out, and the Hindu proprietor, Mr. Adile, stands at his white-mullioned front window, hands to the glass, staring across at the August, where few guest rooms are lit. In steel indifference to the holiday retail frenzy elsewhere, nothing stays open late in Haddam except the liquor store. "Let 'em go to the mall if they need hemorrhoidal cream so bad." Shopkeepers trundle home to cocktails and shepherd's pie once the sun goes past the tree line (4:15 since October), leaving the streets with a bad-for-business five o'clock shadow.

Up on Seminary, where I cruised barely an hour ago, the news crawl at United Jersey flows crisply along. The stoplight has switched to blinking yellow. The Haddam gang element has skittered home to their science projects and math homework, greasing the ways for Dartmouth and Penn. The crèche is up and operating on the First Prez lawn—rotating three-color lights, red to green to yellow, brightening the ceramic wise men, who, I see, are dressed as up-to-date white men, wearing casual clothes you'd wear to the library, and not as Arabs in burnooses and beards. Work, I suspect, continues apace at the hospital—where someone got blottoed today. Ann Dykstra's home, musing on things. Marguerite's feeling better about what's not worth confessing. And Ernie McAuliffe's in the ground. Altogether, it's been an eventful though not fulfilling day to kick off a hopeful season. The Permanent Period needs to resurge, take charge, put today behind me, where it belongs.

In a moment that alarms me, I realize I haven't pissed and that I have to—so bad, my eyes water and my front teeth hurt. I should've gone upstairs in the Appleseed, though it would've meant beseeching Lester and letting him savor the spectacle of human suffering. "Hold it!" I say. Mike halts and looks startled, his little monk's face absorbing the streetlamp light. Good news? Bad news? More unvirtuous thoughts.

My car would make for good cover and has many times since the summer—on dark side streets and alleys, in garbage-y roadside turn-outs, behind 7-Elevens, Wawas, Food Giants and Holiday Inn, Jrs. But the Square's too exposed, and I have to step hurriedly into the darkened Colonial entryway of the Antiquarian Book Nook—ghostly shelving within, out-of-print, never-read Daphne du Mauriers and John O'Haras in vellum. Here I press in close to the molded white door flutings, unzip and unfurl, casting a pained look back up the side street toward the Pilgrim farm, hoping no one will notice. Mike is plainly shocked, and has turned away, pretending to scrutinize books in the Book Nook window. He knows I do this but has never witnessed it.

I let go (at the last survivable moment) with as much containment as I can manage, straight onto the bookshop door and down to its corners onto the pavement—vast, warm tidal relief engulfing me, all fear I might drain into my pants exchanged in an instant for full, florid confidence that all problems can really be addressed and solved, tomorrow's another day, I'm alive and vibrant, it's clear sailing from here on out. All purchased at the small cost of peeing in a doorway like a bum, in the town I used to call home and with the cringing knowledge that I could get arrested for doing it.

Mike coughs a loud stage cough, clears his throat in a way he never does. "Car coming, car coming," he says, soft-but-agitated. I hear girdering tires, a throaty V-8 murmur, the two-way crackle in the night, the familiar female voice directing, "Twenty-six. See the man at 248 Monroe. Possible 103-19. Two adults."

"Coming," Mike says in a stifled voice.

There's never very much and I've almost done it, though my unit's out and not easily crammed back in tight quarters. I crouch, knees-in to the door frame, piss circling my shoes. I cup my two hands, nose to the door glass the way Mr. Adile peered out from the liquor store window, and stare fiercely *in* with all my might—dick out, unattended and drafty. I'm hoping my posture and the unlikelihood that I'm actually doing what I'm doing will suppress all prowl-car attention, and that I won't be forced by someone shining a hot seal beam to turn around full-flag and set in motion all I'd set in motion, which would be more than I could put up with. Warm urine aroma wafts upward. My poor flesh has recoiled, my heart slowed by the cold pane against my forehead and hands. The Book Nook interior is silent, dark. My breathing shallows. I wait. Count seconds ... 5, 8, 11, 13, 16, 20. I hear, but don't see, the cruiser surge and speed up, feel the motor-thrill and the radio-crackle pulse into my hams. And then it's past. Mike, my Tibetan lookout, says, "They're gone. Okay. No worries." I tuck away, zip up quick, take a step back, feel cold on my sweated, battered neck, cheek and ears. I might be okay now. Might be okay. No worries. Clear sailing. All set.

*   *   *

MIKE SITS in motionless, ecclesiastical silence while I drive us home—Route 1 to 295 to NJ 33, skirt the Trenton mall tie-ups, then around to bee-line 195, to the Garden State toward Toms River. Cold rain has started again, then stopped, then started. The temperature's at 31, the road surface possibly coated with invisible ice. My suede shoes, I regret, smell hotly of urine.

Mike would've understood little of events at the Appleseed, only the last part, which seemed (mysteriously) concerned with him. And like any good Buddhist, he's decided the less made of negativity, the better. For all I know, he could be meditating. Anger is just attachment to the cycle of birth and death, while we live in thick darkness that teaches that all phenomena (such as myself) have inherent existence, and we must therefore distinguish between a rope and a snake or else be a dirty vase turned upside down and unable to gain knowledge. This was all in the book Mike left on my desk after my Mayo procedure. *The Road to the Open Heart*. Giving it to me represents his belief that I basically appreciate such malarkey, and that one of the reasons we get along so well and that he's become a fireball real estate agent is, again, that—due to my being "pretty spiritual" in a secular, pedestrian, all-American sort of way—we see many things the same. Namely, that few outcomes are completely satisfactory, it's better to make people happy—even if you have to lie—rather than to harm them and make them sad, and we should all be trying to make a contribution.

The Road to the Open Heart is a big, showy coffee-table slab chocked full of idealized, consciousness-expanding color photographs of Tibet and snowy mountains and temples and shiny-headed teenage monks in yellow-and-red outfits, plus plenty of informal snapshots of the Dalai Lama grinning like a happy politician while meeting world leaders and generally having the time of his life. Supposedly, the little man-god wrote the whole book himself, though Mike's admitted he probably didn't have time to "write" write it—one of the lies that make you feel better. Though it doesn't matter since the book is full of his most important teachings boiled down to bite-size paragraphs with easy-to-digest chapter headings even somebody with cancer could memorize, which was what the monks were doing: "The Path to Wisdom." "The Question We Should All Ask Ourselves." "The Sweet Taste of Bodhicitta." "The Middle

Way." Mike left a bookmark at page 157, where the diminutive holiness talks ominously about "death and clear light," followed by some more upbeat formulations about the "earth constituent, the water constituent, the fire constituent, and the wind constituent," followed by another photograph of the very view you've just been promised—if you're spiritual enough: an immaculate dawn sky in autumn. At this moment, the book's in a stack on my bedside table, and on one of these last balmy autumn days I intend to take it down to the ocean and send it off, since in my view the Lama's teachings all have the ring of the un-new, over-parsed and vaguely corporate about them—which, of course, is thought to be good, and a famous tenet of the Middle Way. What I needed, though, post-Mayo, was the New and Completely Unfamiliar Way. To me, the DL's wisdom also seemed only truly practicable if your intention was to become a monk and live in Tibet, where these things apparently come easy, whereas I just wanted to go on being a real estate agent on the Jersey Shore and figure out how to get around a case of prostate cancer.

Mike and I did talk about *The Road to the Open Heart* in the office one day while combing through some damage-deposit receipt forms to identify skippers—although our talk mainly concerned my son Ralph and was to the point that there are many mysteries and phenomena that can't be apprehended through sense or reason, and that Ralph might have a current existence as a mystery. It was then that he told me about young people who die young becoming masters who teach us about impermanence—which, as I said, I can buy, the Permanent Period not entirely withstanding.

Still, you can take the Middle Way only so far. Asserting yourself may indeed lead to angry disappointment—the DL's view—and anger only harms the angry and karma produces bad vibes in this life and worse ones in the next, where you could end up as a chicken or a professor in a small New England college. But the Middle Way can just as easily be the coward's way out. And based on what Mike probably heard back in the Johnny Appleseed, I'd feel better about him if he'd get in a lather about being called a coolie, insist we turn around, drive back to Haddam and kick some Lester ass, then head home laughing about it—instead of just sitting there in the reflected green dashboard glow composed as a little monkey under a Bodhi tree. East meets West.

I'm still feeling a little drunk, in addition to being roughed up, and may not be driving my best. My hands are cold and achy. My knees stiff. I'm gripping the wheel like a ship's helm in a gale. Twice I've caught myself broxing the be-jesus out of my unprotected molars. And twice when I took my eyes off the red taillight smear and the shoe-polish black highway, I found I was going ninety-five—which explains Mike's leaden silence. He's been scared shitless since Imlaystown, and is in a frozen fugue state, from which he's picturing the radiant black near-attainment as I send us skidding off into a cedar bog. I dial it back to seventy.

Today has gone not at all how I intended, although I've done nothing much more than what I planned—with the obvious exceptions of the hospital being detonated, having Ann ask me to marry her and getting into a moronic fight with Bob Butts. It's loony, of course, to think that by lowering expectations and keeping ambitions to a minimum we can ever avert the surprising and unwanted. Though the worst part, as I said, is that I've cluttered my immediate future with new-blooming dilemmas exactly like young people do when they're feckless and thirty-three and too inexperienced to know better. I wouldn't have admitted it, but I may still possess a remnant of the old feeling I had when *I* was thirty-three: that a tiny director with a megaphone, a beret and jodhpurs is suddenly going to announce "Cut!" and I'll get to play it all again—from right about where I crossed the bridge at Toms River this morning. This is the most pernicious of anti-Permanent Period denial and life sentimentalizing, which only lead you down the road to more florid self-deceptions, then dump you out harder than ever when the accounts come due, which they always do. It also suggests that I may not be up for controversy the way I used to be, and may have lapsed into personal default mode.

WE'RE NEARING the 195 junction with the Garden State, where millions (or at least hundreds of thousands) are now streaming south toward Atlantic City—not a bad choice for Turkey Day. It's the stretch of highway we detoured around this morning due to police activity. I shoot through the interchange as new lighted town signage slips past: Belmar, South Belmar, pie-in-the-sky Spring Lake, all sprawling inland from the ocean into the pine scrub and lowlands west of the Parkway. HUNGRY FOR CAPITAL. REGULAR BAPTIST CHURCH—MEET TRIUMPH AND DISASTER HEAD-ON. HOCKEY ALL NIGHT LONG. NJ IS HOSPITAL COUNTRY. Any right-thinking suburbanite would like to feel confident about these things.

I'm aware Mike's been cutting his eyes at me and frowning. He can possibly smell my soaked shoes. Mike occasionally broadcasts condescending, hanging-back watchfulness, which I take to mean I'm acting too American and not enough the velvet-handed secular-humanist-spiritualist I'm supposed to be. (This always pisses me off.) And perched on his seat in his fawn trousers, pink sweater, his ersatz Rolex and little Italian shoes with gold lounge-lizard socks, he's pissing me off again. I'm like chesty old Wallace Beery ready to rip up furniture in the bar-room and toss some drunks around like scarecrows.

"What the fuck?" I say, as menacing as I can manage. All around us are mostly tour buses, Windstars and church-group vans headed down to see Engelbert Humperdinck at Bellagio. Mike ignores me and peers ahead into the taillit traffic, little hands gripping the armrests like he's in a hurtling missile. "Are you going into the land-developing business and start throwing up trophy mansions for Pakistani proctologists and make yourself rich, or what? Aren't I supposed to hear the pitch and give you the benefit of my years of non-experience?" The aroma I've been sniffing since we left Haddam is not just urine but also, I think, garlic—not usual from Mike. Benivalle has given him the full gizmo—some gloomy *il forno* out on 514, where ziti, lasagne and cannoli hang off the trees like Christmas candy.

Mike turns a serious and judicious look my way, then returns to the taillight stream, as if he has to pay attention in case I don't.

"So? What?" I say, less Wallace Beery-ish, more mentorish Henry Fonda-like. The car in front of us is a wide red Mercedes 650 with louvered back windows and some kind of delta-wing radar antenna on the trunk. A big caduceus is bolted to the license plate holder and below it a bumper sticker says ALL LIFE IS POST-OP. GET BUSY LIVING IT. Back-lit human heads are visible inside, wagging and nodding and, I guess, living it.

"Not sure." Mike is barely audible, as if speaking only to himself.

"About what? Is Benivalle a cutie pie?" *Cutie pie* is our office lingo for shit-heel walk-ins who waste your time looking at twenty listings, then go behind your back and try to buy from the seller. *Cutie pie* sounds to us like mobster talk. We always say we're "putting out a contract" on some "cutie pie," then laugh about it. Most cutie pies come from far east Bergen County and never buy anything.

"No, he's not," Mike says morosely. "He's a good guy. He took me to his home. I met his wife and kids—in Sergeantsville. She fixed a big lunch for us." The ziti. "We drove out to his Christmas tree farm in Rosemont. I guess he owns three or four. That's just one business." Mike's laced his fingers, pinkie ring and all, and begun rotating his thumbs like a granny.

"What else does he do?" I'm only performing my agreed-to duty here.

"A mobile-home park that's got a driving range attached, and he owns four laundromats with Internet access with his brother Bobby over in Milford." Mike compresses his lips to a stern little line, all the while thumbs gyrating. These are rare signs of stress, the inner journey turning bumpy. Entrepreneurship clearly unsettles him.

"Why the hell does he need you to go into business with him? He's got a plate-full. Has he ever developed anything except Christmas trees and laundromats?"

"Not so far." Mike is brooding.

In Benivalle's behalf, he is, of course, the model of the go-it-alone, self-starter that's made New Jersey the world-class American small-potatoes profit leader it is. Before he's forty, he'll own a chain of Churchill's Chickens, a flush advertising business, hold an insurance license and be ready to go back to school and study for the ministry. Up from the roadside vegetable stand, he's exactly what this country's all about: works like a dray horse, tithes at St. Melchior's, has never personally killed anyone, stays in shape for the fire department, loves his wife and can't wait for the sun to come up so he can get crackin'.

Which doesn't mean Mike should risk his hairless little Tibetan ass in the housing business with the guy, back-loaded as that business is with cost over-runs, venal subcontractors slipping kickbacks to vendors, subpar re-bar work, off-the-books payouts to inspectors, insurers, surveyors, bankers, girlfriends, the EPA and shady guys from upstate—anybody who can get a dipper in your well and sink you into Chapter 11. Guys like Benivalle almost never know when to stay small, when a laundromat in the hand is worth two McMansions in the cornfield. This deal smells of ruin, and neither one of them needs a new ruin when 30-years are at 7.8, the Dow's at 10.4, and crude's iffy at 35.16.

"He's also got an eighteen-year-old who's mentally challenged," Mike says, and aims a reproving glower to indicate I'm, again, more American than he's comfortable with—though he's just as American as I am, only from farther east.

"So what? He's raking it in." A mind's picture of my son Paul Bascombe's angry face—not a bit challenged—predictably enters my thinking with predictable misgiving.

"His wife's not really well, either," he says. "She can't work because she has to drive little Carlo everywhere. They'll have to put him in a care facility next year. That's expensive." Mike, of course, has a seventeen- and a thirteen-year-old with his wife, now in the Amboys—little Tucker and little Andrea Mahoney. Plus, because he's a Buddhist, he's crippled by seeing the other guy's point of view about everything—a fatal weakness in business. I'm crippled by it, too, just not when it comes to giving advice.

"Yeah," I say, "but it's not *your* kid."

"No." Mike stops gyrating his digits and settles himself on the passenger's seat. He's thinking what I'm thinking. Who wouldn't?

We're suddenly five hundred yards from Exit 82 and Route 37. Our turn-off. I have no memory of the last 15.6 miles—earth traversed, traffic negotiated, crashes avoided. We're simply here, ready to get off. The red Mercedes with the caduceus dematerializes into the traffic speeding south—a Victorian manse on the beach at Cape May in its future, a high-roller suite at Bally's.

I slide us off to the right. And then instantly, even in the dark, the crumpled remains of a tour bus come into view. Undoubtedly it's the *bigpileuptheGardenState* that made the news crawl and stoppered the Parkway this morning when we tried to get on. The big Vista Cruiser's down over the corrugated metal barriers into the pine and hardwoods, flipped on its side like a wounded green-and-yellow pachyderm, left-side tires and undercarriage exposed to the night air, a gash opened in the graded berm, as if lightning had ripped through.

All passengers would be long gone now—medi-vac'd to local ERs or just limped away, dazed, into the timber. There's no sign of fire, though the big tinted vista windows have been popped out and the bus skin ripped open through the lettering that says PETER PAN TOURS (no doubt the Jaws of Life were used). Men in white jumpsuits are at this moment maneuvering a giant wrecker down the embankment from the Route 37 side, preparing to winch the bus upright and tow it away. No one who isn't getting off at Toms River would see anything, though an Ocean County deputy's at the ramp bottom, directing traffic with a red flare.

Neither Mike nor I speak as we slow and get directed by the deputy toward the left, in the direction of the bay bridge. Something about the accident requires a reining in on our conversation about Benivalle's family sorrows. Tragedies, like apples and oranges, don't compare.

Route 37 back through Toms River is changed from the Route 37 we traveled this morning. Road construction's shut down and the sky's low, mustard-colored and muffled, the long skein of traffic signals popping green, yellow, red through a salty seaside haze. Only it's not a bit less crowded—due to the Ocean County mall staying open 24/7, and all other stores, chains, carpet outlets, shoe boutiques, language schools, fancy frame shops, Saturn dealerships and computer stores the same. Traffic actually moves more slowly, as if everyone we passed this morning is still out here, wandering parking lot to parking lot, ready to buy if they just knew what, yet are finally wearing down, but have no impulse to go home. The old curving neon marquee at the Quality Court has had its WELCOME amended. No longer SUICIDE SURVIVORS, but JERSEY CLOGGERS and the BLIND GOLFERS' ASSOC are welcomed. The blind golfers have earned a CONGRATS, though they're unlikely to know about it.

My neck, arms, jaw and knuckles have gone on throbbing and burning where miscreant Bob Butts throttled me. Bob should be thinking life over in the Haddam lockup, awaiting my decision to bring charges. I've been able to let the unhappy prospect of Ann coming to Thanksgiving sink out of mind. But the slow-motion consumer daze on the Miracle Mile has revived it. It's the time of day in the time of year when things go wrong if they're going to.

In Ann's case, she simply didn't have any attractive Thanksgiving plans (not my fault), wished she did and exerted her will (strong-woman-getting-to-the-bottom-of-things) on *me*, in a depleted state. She's ignored Sally like temporary house help, played the sensitive dead-son card, the kind-man card, plus the L word, then stood back to watch how it all filters out. For years, I dreamed, shivered and thrilled at the idea of remarrying Ann. I pictured the whole event in Technicolor—though I could never (I wouldn't admit it) work the whole thing through to its fantastical end. There was always a *difficulty*—a door I couldn't find, words I got wrong—like in the dream in which you sing the national anthem at the World Series, except a lump of tar's for some reason stuck to your molars and your mouth won't open.

But this visit and all attached to it seem like the wrongest of wrong ideas even if I'm wrong as to motivation (I've had it with tonight). I don't even know Ann's politics anymore (Charley's I knew: Yale). I could also be impotent—though no trial runs have been attempted. She and the children have grinding life issues I don't want to share. And I have to piss too much to be perpetually amusing at dinner parties. Given Ann's power-point certainty about *everything*, I'd end up a will-less sheep at De Tocqueville faculty do's, a partial man who sees life from a couch in the corner. Plus, I have this sleeping-panther cancer that could roar back on me.

We all need to take charge of who we spend our last years, months, weeks, days, hours, minutes, seconds, final fidgeting eye-blinks with, who we see last and who sees us. Like the wise man said, What you think's going to happen to you after you die is what's going to happen. So you need to be thinking the right things in the run-up.

"They bundle up those Christmas trees so they look like torpedoes," Mike says out of the blue, taking his glasses off and rubbing them on his blazer cuff, blinking eyes attentively. We're passing the bonsai nursery, transformed now into a bulb-strung Christmas tree lot. "There's a big machine that does it. Then they're trucked out to vendors in Kansas. All Tommy's customers're in Kansas." He's thinking about commerce in general —if it's a good idea or if it could possibly be his punishment for cheating someone out of his wattle ten centuries back. Belief, in Mike's view, is not a luxury, but still needs to keep pace with known facts and established authority—in his case, the economy. It's the theory-versus-practice rub that all religions fail to smooth over.

We've passed beyond the mall-traffic chaos and are headed toward the bay bridge, along the strip of elderly clam shacks, red-lit gravel-lot taverns, Swedish massage parlors, boat-propeller repairs and boss&secretary tourist cabins from the Fifties, when it was a hoot to come to the Shore and didn't cost a year's pay. Out ahead spreads Barnegat Bay and across it the low sparse necklace lights of Sea-Clift, visible like a winter town on a benighted prairie seen from a jetliner. It's as beckoning as heaven. New Jersey's best-kept secret, where I'll soon be diving into bed.

Mike goes reaching under his pink sweater as if reaching for a package of smokes, his gaze cast over the dark frigid waters toward the bull-semen lab. And from his inside blazer pocket he produces, in fact, *a pack of smokes*! Marlboro menthols, in the distinctive green-and-white crushproof box—my parents' favorites and my own fag of choice during my military school days of experimentation eons ago. I could never hack it, though I perfected the French inhale, learned to finger a fleck off my tongue tip à la Richard Widmark and to hold one clenched between my teeth without smoke getting in my eyes.

But Mike? Mike doesn't smoke cigarooties! Buddhists don't smoke. Virtuous thinking can't possibly permit that. Does he know about his already-increased cancer susceptibility that comes with the oath of citizenship? To see him expertly strip open the pack like a fugitive is shocking. And revelatory—as if he'd started whistling "Stardust" out his butt.

I look over to be sure I'm not hallucinating, and for an instant veer into the other bridge lane and nearly wham us into a septic-service truck on its holiday way home. The truck's horn blares into the background, leaving me strangely excited.

"You mind if I smoke?" Mike looks preoccupied and vaguely ridiculous in his little dandy's threads. He even has his own matches.

"Not a bit." My surprise is really just the surprise of waking up to the moment in life I'm currently in: I'm in my car, driving over the Barnegat bridge with a forty-three-year-old Tibetan real estate salesman who's my employee and looking to me for advice about his business future and who's now smoking a cigarette! An act I've never known him to perform in eighteen months. We're a long way from Tibet out here. "I didn't know you were a Marlboro man."

He's already fired up, cracked the window and blown a good lung-full into the slipstream. "I smoked when I worked in Calcutta." He's referring to his telemarketer days of selling Iowa beef and electronic gadgets to New Jersey matrons from bullpens in the subcontinent. What a life is his. "I quit. Then I started again when I got separated." He takes another hungry suck. He already has it half-burned down, rich, stinging gray smoke hissing through the window crack. With one simple, indelible act he's no longer strictly a Tibetan, but has become the classic American little-guy, struggling under a wagonload of tough choices and plagued by uncertainties he has no experience with—in his case, about whether to become a sleazy land developer. It's our profoundest national conundrum: Are things getting better, or much worse? Poor devil. Welcome to the Republic.

"I was thinking when we were driving through Toms River." Mike actually plucks a fleck of tobacco off his tongue tip Dick Widmark-style. "All that mess back there, those people driving around aimlessly."

"They weren't aimless," I say. "They were looking for bargains." I'm still thinking about the septic truck that almost flattened us. Some guy heading home to Seaside Park, kids at the front windows, hearing the truck rumble in, happy wife, supper steaming on the table, brewsky already cracked, TV tuned to the Sixers.

"So much of life's made up of choosing things created by other people, people even less qualified than ourselves. Do you ever think about that, Frank?" He is graver than grave now, fag in mouth, its red tip a beacon as we reach the Sea-Clift end of the bridge. The illuminated NEW JERSEY'S BEST KEPT SECRET sign flashes past Mike's face and glasses. Once again, his snappy apparel and anchorman voice don't go together, as if someone else was talking for him. I'm about to be treated to some Buddhist ex cathedra homiletics in which I'm a hollow, echoing vessel needing filling with someone else's better intelligence—all because I'm patient and forbearing.

"We don't originate very much," Mike adds. "We just take what's already there."

"Yeah, I've thought about that." This very morning. Possibly he and I even talked about it and he's appropriated it and made it the Buddha's. I'm tempted to call him Lobsang. Or Dhargey—whichever one comes first—just to piss him off. "I'm fifty-five years old, Mike. I'm in the real estate business. I make a good living selling people houses they didn't *originate* and I didn't, either. So I've thought about a lot of these things over the years. Are you just a numbnuts?"

Lighted houses, wimmering up on the bay side as we circle off the bridge, are mostly ranches with remodeled camelbacks, and a few larger, modern, all-angles board-and-battens that solidify the tax base. I've sold a bunch of them and expect to sell more.

Mike further narrows his old-looking little eyes. This isn't what he expected to hear. Or what I expected to say.

"I mean, what about mindfulness being a glass of yak milk sitting on your head?" This is straight out of the Dalai Lama book, which I've read part of—mostly on the crapper. "I mean, you aren't acting very fucking mindful." I'm speeding again, off the bridge and onto Route 35, Ocean Avenue, the Sea-Clift main drag, also the main drag for Seaside Heights, Ortley Beach (with a different boulevard name), Lavallette, Normandy Beach, Mantoloking—concatenated seaside proliferance all the way to Asbury Park. Mike's Infiniti is parked at the office. I've so far given him little good advice about becoming a housing mogul. Possibly I have very little good advice to give. In any case, I'll be glad to have him out of the car.

Northbound Ocean Avenue is a wide, empty one-way separated from southbound Ocean Avenue by two city blocks of motels, surfer shops, bait shops, sea-glass jewelers, tattoo parlors, taffy stores (all closed for the season), plus a few genuine lighted-and-lived-in houses. In summer, our beach towns up 35 swell to twenty times their winter habitation. But at nine at night on November 21st, the mostly empty strip makes for an eerie, foggy Fifties-noir incognito I like. No holiday decorations are up. Few cars sit at curbs. The ocean, in frothy winter tumult, is glimpsable down the side streets and the air smells briny. Parking meters have been removed for the convenience of year-rounders. Two traditional tomato-pie stands are open but doing little biz. The

Mexicatessen is going and has customers. Farther on, the yellow LIQUOR sign and the ruby glow of the Wiggle Room (a summer titty bar that becomes just a bar in the winter) are signaling they're open for customers. A lone Sea-Clift town cop in his black-and-white Plymouth waits in the shadows beside the fire department in case some wild-ass boogies from East Orange show up to give us timid white people something to think about. A yellow Toms River Region school bus moves slowly ahead of us. We have now traveled as far east as the continent lasts. There's much to be said for reaching a genuine end mark in a world of indeterminacy and doubt. The feeling of arrival is hopeful, and I feel it even on a night when nothing much is going good.

Mike's clammed up since I scolded him about being mindful. We have yet to develop a fully operational language for conflict in the months he's been with me. And by being scolded, he's possibly been tossed back onto painful life lessons—the tele-marketers' bullpen with its cynical Bengali middle-management bullies; ancient, happy-little-brown-man stereotypes; muscular-McCain-war-hero imagery and plucky Horatio Algerish immi-grant models—all roles he's contemplated in his odyssey to here but that don't really cohere to make a rational world.

Though I don't mind if Mike's being pushed out of his comfort zone. He's like every other Republican: nervous about commitment; fearful of future regret; never saw a risk he wouldn't like somebody else to take. Benivalle may have done his dreams brusque disservice by putting his own little domestic Easter egg on display. Since what he's done is make Mike stop, think and worry—bad strategy if your customer's a Buddhist. Mike's now being forced to consider his own Big Fear—the blockade that has to be broken through sometime in life or you go no further. (I used to think mine was death. Then cancer taught me it wasn't.)

Mike now has to figure out if his big fear is the terror of going on ahead (into the mansioning business) or the terror of *not*; if he's ready to buy into the proposition most Americans buy into and that says "You do this shit until either you're rich or you're dead"; or if he's more devoted to his old conviction that dying a millionaire is dying like a wild animal, attachment leads to disappointment and pain, etc. In other words, is he really a Republican, or is this dilemma the greening of Mike? Flattening pretty cornfields for seven-figure mega-mansions isn't, after all, really *helping* people in the way that assisting them to find a modest home they want—and that's already there—helps them. Benivalle's idea, of course, is more the standard "we build it, they come," which Mike uncomfortably sniffed back in Toms River: If we build Saturns, they will want to drive them; if we build mini-crepe grills, they will want to eat mini-crepes; if we invent Thanksgiving, they will try to be thankful (or die in the process).

MY REALTY-WISE office sits tucked between a Chicago-Style Pizza that previously occupied my space, and the Sea-Clift Own-Make Candies, that's only open summers and whose owners live in Marathon. The pizza place is lighted inside. The tricolor flag still leans out from its window peg over the sidewalk (Italy is the official kingdom-in-exile on the Shore). Bennie, the Filipino owner, is alone inside, putting white dough mounds back in the cold box and closing down the oven until Saturday, when everybody will crave a slice of "Kitchen Sink." Some days, when the humidity's high, my office smells like rich puttanesca sauce. I can't tell if this inclines clients more, or less, to buy beach property, though when they aren't serious enough to get in the car and go have a look at something up their alley, I often later see them next door, staring out Bennie's front window, a slice on a piece of wax paper, happy as clams for having exercised self-control.

Mike's silver Infiniti, with a REALTORS ARE PEOPLE TOO sticker on the back bumper and a Barnegat Lighthouse license plate, sits in front of my white, summery-looking, cubed building, which announces REALTY-WISE in frank gold-block lettering on its front window like an old-time shirtsleeve lawyer's office. Home-for-sale snapshots are pinned to a corkboard that's visible inside the door. In general, my whole two-desk set-up is decidedly no-frills when compared to the Lauren-Schwindell architect's showplace on Seminary, which shouted Money! Money! Money! Nothing along this stretch of the Shore compares to Haddam, which is good, in my estimation. Here at this southern end of Barnegat Neck, life is experienced less pridefully, more like an undiscovered seacoast town in Maine, and no less pleasantly—except in summer, when crowds rumble and surge. When I came over with my broker's license in '92, seeking a place to set up shop, all my competitors gave me to understand that everyone was collegial down here, there was plenty of business (and money) to go around for someone who wanted not to work too hard but keep on his toes (handle summer rentals, own a few apartments, do the odd appraisal, share listings, back up a competitor if things got tight). I purchased old man Barber Featherstone's business when Barber opted for managed care near his daughter's in Teaneck, and everybody came by and said they were glad I was here—happy to have a realty veteran instead of a young cut-throat land shark. I took over Barber's basic colors —red and white (no motto or phony Ivy League crest)—substituted Realty-Wise for Featherstone's Beach Exclusives, and got to work. Anything fancier wouldn't have helped and eventually would've made everyone hate my guts and be happy to cut me off at the knees whenever they had the chance—and there are always chances. As a result, in eight years I've made a bundle, missed the stock market boom—and the correction—and hardly worked a lick.

The WE'RE OPEN sign's been left hanging inside the glass door since yesterday, and in the shadowy interior, where Mike and I sit at two secondhand metal desks I got at St. Vincent de Paul to make us not look like sharpsters but doers, the red pin light's blinking on the ceiling smoke alarm. Of course I have to piss again, though not frantically. Later in the day the urge is worse. Mornings and early afternoons, I often don't even notice. I can use the office facilities rather than wait for home (which could get tricky).

Mike is still aswarm with thoughts. He's stuffed another cigarette out the window and breathed a deep sigh of anti-Buddhist dismalness. His Marlboro and garlic, and my pissed-on shoes, have left my car smelling terrible.

There's no good reason to resume our conversation about mindfulness, glasses of yak milk, what we originate and what we don't. I have no investment in it and was only performing my role as devil's advocate. In my view, Mike is *made* for real estate the way some people are *made* to be veterinarians and others tree surgeons. He may have found his niche in life but hates to admit it for reasons I've already expressed. I would hate to lose him as my associate—no matter how unusual an associate he is. I might arrange to have a Sponsor visit him, some stranger who could tell him what I'd tell him.

Still, old Emerson says, power resides in shooting the gulf, in darting to an aim. The soul becomes. My soul, though, has become tired of this day.

"You're not under any big time constraint in all this, are you?" I say this to the steering wheel without looking at him. The interior instruments glow green. The heat's on, the car's at idle. "I'd be suspicious if there was some kind of rush. You know?"

"House prices went up forty percent last year. Money's cheap. That won't last very long." He is morose. "When Bush gets in, the minority program'll dry up. Clinton would keep it. So would Gore." He sighs again deeply. He dislikes Clinton for uncoupling China trade from human rights, but of course would fare better with the Democrats—like the rest of us.

"Does Benivalle like Bush?"

"He likes Nader. His father was a lefty." Mike absently pulls on his undersized earlobe. A gesture of resignation.

"Benivalle's green? I thought they were all cops. Or crooks."

"You can't generalize."

Though generalization's my stock-and-trade. And I like Benivalle less for getting in bed with the back-stabbing *Nadir*. "Isn't it odd that you like Bush, and he's killing off your minority whozzits. And you're thinking of going into business with a liberal."

"I don't *like* Bush. I voted for him." Mike impatiently unsnaps his seat belt. He has ventured valiantly forth as a brave citizen and come back an immigrant vanquished by uncertainty. Too bad. "I feel regret," he says solemnly.

"You haven't done anything bad," I say, and attempt a smile denoting confidence.

"It doesn't attach to doing." And he's suddenly smiling, himself, though I'm sure he's not happy.

"You just got out beyond your stated ideological limits," I say. "You can always come back. *Devil's advocate*'s just a figure of speech. My belief system hasn't defeated your belief system."

"No. I'm sure it hasn't." Mike frames his words as a verdict.

"There you go." Ours is a rare conversation for two men as different as we are to have in a car, though I wish it could be over so I could grab a piss.

"I understand you think this is not a good thing to do," he says.

"I don't want to keep you from anything but harm," I say. "You'll just have to understand what you understand."

BENNIE, THE pizzeria owner, has taken his Italian flag inside and is letting himself out his front door, locking up using a ring of keys as big as a bell clapper. He has his white apron draped over his arm for at-home laundering. He's a small, crinkly-haired, mustachioed man and looks more Greek than Filipino. He's wearing flip-flops, a red shirt and black Bermudas that reveal white ham-hock thighs. He glances at Mike and me, shadowy male presences in an idling Suburban, gives us a momentary stare, possibly puts us down for queers—though he should recognize me—then finishes his lock-up and walks away toward his white delivery van farther down the block.

Mike says he feels regret, but what he feels is lonely—though it's logical to confuse the two. He'll probably never feel true regret, which is outside his belief system. When he gets back to his empty house in Lavallette, he'll turn up the heat, call his pining wife in the Amboys, speak lovingly of reconciling, talk sweetly to his kids, meditate for an hour, connect some significant dots and pretty soon start to feel better about things. As an immigrant, he knows loneliness can be dealt with symptomatically. I could ask him over for Thanksgiving. But I've made a big-enough mess with Ann, and don't trust my instincts. Anything can be made worse.

In our silence, my mind strays to Paul again, already on his soldiering way over from the Midwest, his new "other" manning the map under the dim interior lights so there's no need to stop. (Why do so many things happen in cars? Are they the only interior life left?) I wonder where exactly they are at this moment. Possibly just passing Three Mile Island in his old, shimmying Saab? I already sense his commotional presence via consubstantive telemetry across the dwindling miles.

Mike's small, lined, smiling face waits outside my car door. Cold ocean fog swirls behind him, giving me a shudder. I've briefly zoned again. Oh my, oh me.

"Suffering, I think, doesn't happen without a cause." He nods consolingly in at me, as if I was the one in the pickle.

"I don't necessarily look at things that way," I say. "I think a lot of shit just happens to you. If I were you, I wouldn't think so much about causes. I'd think more about results. You know? It's my advice."

His smile vanishes. "They're always the same," he says.

"Whatever. You're a good real estate agent. I'd be sorry to lose you. This is the fastest-growing county in the East. Household income's up twenty-three percent. There's money to be made. Selling houses is pretty easy." I could also tell him there'd be virtually zero Buddhists in Haddam to be buddies with—just Republicans by the limo-full, who wouldn't associate with him, not even the Hindus, once they found out he's a developer. He'd end up feeling sad about life and moving away. Whereas here, he wouldn't. I don't say that, though, because I'm out of advice. "I'll be in in the morning," I say, all business. "Why don't you take the day and think about things. I'll steer the ship."

"Sure. Good. Okay." He goes reaching in his trousers for his keys. "Have a happy Thanksgiving." He puts the accent on the *giving*, not on the *thanks* as we longer-term Americans do.

"Okay." I sound and feel vapid.

"Do you explode fireworks?" His car lights flash on by themselves.

"Different holiday," I say. "This is just eating and football."

"I can't always keep things straight." He looks at me inside my cold cockpit and seems delighted. A minor holiday miscue lets him feel momentarily less American (in spite of his lapel-pin flag) and makes his other errors, failures and uncertainties feel more forgivable, just parts of those things that can't be helped. It's not a wrong way to feel—less responsible for everything. Mike closes the door, taps the glass with his pinkie ring and gives me a silly, grinning half bow with a thumbs-up, to which I involuntarily (and ridiculously) give him a half bow back, which delights him even more and into another thumbs-up but no bow. I am the hollow, echoing vessel between the two of us now. I have my patience and forbearance for my ride home, but as this long day of events comes to its close, I have little more to show.

PART 2

AT 3:00 A.M., I'm suddenly awake, which is not unusual these days. A late-night call to the toilet, or else something from the day ahead or the day past, abruptly breaking through the tent of sleep to invade my brain and set my heart to beating fast. Sleep's a gossamer thing for over-fifties, even women. Normally, I can breathe deep and slow, adjust my hearing to the hiss of the sea, project my mind into the oceany dark and am asleep without realizing I'm not awake. Though when that doesn't avail— and sometimes it doesn't—I seek repose by editing my list of prospective pallbearers, noting a crucial addition or deletion, depending on my mood, followed by a review of who I intend to leave what to when the day comes, then reviewing all the cars I've owned, restaurants I've eaten in and hotels I've slept in during my fifty-five years of ordinary life. And if none of these performs, I inventory all the acceptable ways of committing suicide (without scaring the shit out of myself—all cancer patients do this). And if nothing else works—sometimes that happens, too—I file through the names of every woman I ever made love to in my entire life (surprisingly more than I'd have thought), at which point sleep comes in half a minute, since I'm not really very interested, whereas with the others, I sort of am. Clarissa has told me that when sleep eludes her, she recites a South-Sea Fijian mantra, which goes: "The shark is not your demon, but the final resting place of your soul." This I'd find disturbing, so that if it ever did put me to sleep, it would give me a bad dream, which would then wake me up and I'd be stuck till morning.

My room now is cold and nearly lightless but for the red numerals on the clock, the ocean sighing toward daylight, still hours on. I've been dreaming I rescued a stranger from the sea outside my house and have been declared a hero (a sure sign of *needing* rescue). I awoke to hear the sound of my own name whispered in the night air.

"Frank-ee," I hear, "Frank-ee." My heart's racing like Daytona, my fingers and arms up to my shoulder webby and immobilized with slowed blood flow and dormancy. Normally, I maintain the recommended Dead Crusader position—flat on my back, feet together, wrists crossed on my chest as though a sword is in hand. But I'm surprisingly on my stomach and may possibly have been swimming in the sheets. My neck aches from my Bob Butts tussle. I've popped a sweat like an athlete on a jog. "Frank-ee." Then I hear boisterous laughing. "Haw, haw, haw." A door slamming. *Splat.*

When I arrived home last night from Haddam, a sports car, a shiny, pale blue, underslung Austin-Healey 1000, sat beside Sally's LeBaron convertible in the driveway, its motor warm (I checked). Green-numeral LIVE FREE OR DIE license plates. A red Gore sticker was half torn off its back bumper. Later, I climbed the stairs to my bedroom and heard Clarissa's radio, low and soft, tuned to the all-night jazz station in Philadelphia— Arthur Lyman playing "Jungle Flute" on a piano. A bottle lip clinked against a glass rim, a hushed man's (not a very young man's) voice was saying, humorously, "Not so bad. I wouldn't say. Not so bad." Silence opened as the two took in my footfalls and my door squeaking and a cough I felt required to cough, if only to say, Yes, things're fine. Fine, fine. Things're all fine. Then another tinkle-clink, Clarissa's languorous laugh, the word *father* casually spoken in a low but not too low voice, and then silence.

But now the door splat outside the house. My name whispered, then "Haw, haw, haw." Clearly, it's my neighbors.

Next door on Poincinet Road, eighteen feet from my south wall, my immediate neighbors are the Feensters, Nick and Drilla. I sold them their house in '97. Nick is a former Bridgeport firefighter who became a millionaire recycling old cathode-ray tubes, and then to his shock won the Connecticut lottery. Not the big one. But the big-enough one. He and Drilla had been weekenders in Sea-Clift, plus two set-aside weeks in August, consigning to me their pink, white-trimmed Florida-style bungalow on Bimini Street to rent for a fortune, May to October, which is our season. But when the big money rolled in, they sold the pink bungalow, Nick quit work, they pulled up stakes in Bridgeport and let me put them into #5 Poincinet Road—

a modern, white-painted, many-faceted, architect's dream/ nightmare with metal-banistered miradors, copper roof, decks for every station of the sun, lofty, mirrored triple-panes open on the sea, imported blue Spanish tile flooring (heated), intercoms and TVs in the water closets, in-wall vacuums and sound system, solar panels, a burglar system that rings in Langley, built-in pecky cypress everythings, even a vintage belted Excalibur that the prior owners, a gay banking couple with an adopted child who couldn't stand the damp, just threw in for the million eight, full-boat, as a housewarming present. (Nick sold it for a mint.)

The Feensters moved down, eager beavers, on New Year's Day, '98, ready to take up their fine new life. Only, their sojourn in Sea-Clift has turned out to be far from a happy one. I frankly believe if they'd stayed in Bridgeport, if Nick had stayed connected to the cathode-ray business, if Drilla had stayed working in the parts department at Housatonic Ford (where they loved her), if maybe they'd bought a transitional house in Noank and kept their rental here, practiced gradualism, not moved the whole gestalt in one swoop to Sea-Clift, where they didn't know anyone, had nothing to do, weren't adept at making new connections and, in fact, openly suspected everyone of hating them because of their ridiculous luck, then they might've been happier than a typical couple in the Witness Protection Program—which is how they seem.

Their Sea-Clift life seemed to go careening off the rails the instant they arrived. Our beach road, which contains only five houses, once contained twenty and stretched for a mile north along the beach, each large footprint facing the sea from behind a sandy, oat-grass hillock nature had placed in the ocean's way. We Poincinet home owners—three other residents, plus me (excluding the Feensters)—all understand that we hold our ground on the continent's fragile margin at nature's sufferance. Indeed, the reason there are now only five of us is that the previous fifteen "cottages"—grandiloquent old gabled and turreted Queen Annes, rococo Stick Styles, rounded Romanesque Revivals—were blown to shit and smithereens by Poseidon's wrath and are now gone without a trace. Hurricane Gloria, as recently as 1985, finished the last one. Beach erosion, shoreline scouring, tectonic shifts, global warming, ozone deterioration and normal w&t have rendered all us "survivors" nothing more than solemn, clear-headed custodians to the splendid, transitory essence of everything. The town fathers prudently codified this view by passing a no-exceptions-ever restriction against new construction down our road, grandfathering our newer, better-anchored residences, and requiring repairs and even normal upkeep be both non-expansive and subject to stern permit regulation. In other words, none of this, like none of us, is going to last here. We made our deal with the elements when we closed our deal with the bank.

Except the Feensters didn't, and don't, see things that way. They tried, their first summer, to change the road's name to Bridgeport Road, have it age-restricted and gated from the south end, where we all drive in. When that failed—at a tense planning-board meeting with me and other residents opposing—they tried to close access to the beach farther up, where the old cottages once sat in a regal row. Public use, they argued, deprived them of full enjoyment and drove values down (hilarious, since Adolf Eichmann could own a beach house down here and prices would still soar). This was all hooted down by the surfer community, the surf-casting community, the bait-shop owners and the metal-detector people. (We all again opposed.) Nick Feenster grew infuriated, hired a lawyer from Trenton to test the town's right to regulate, arguing on constitutional grounds. And when this failed, he stopped speaking to the neighbors and specifically to me and put up signs on his road frontage that said DON'T EVEN THINK OF TURNING AROUND IN THIS DRIVEWAY. KEEP OUT! WE TOW! BELIEVE IT! PRIVATE PROPERTY!!! BEACH CLOSED DUE TO DANGEROUS RIPTIDE. BEWARE OF PIT BULL! They also erected an expensive picket-topped wooden fence between their house and mine and installed motion-sensitive crime lights, both of which the town made them take down. Generally, the Feensters came to seem to us neighbors like the famous family that can't be made happy by great good luck. Not your worst-nightmare neighbor (a techno-reggae band or an evangelical Baptist church would be worse), but a bad real estate outcome, given that signs were positive at first. And especially for me was it a bad outcome, because while not wanting recipe swapping, drill-bit borrowing or cross-property-line chin-music razz-ma-tazz, I would still enjoy the occasional shared cocktail at sundown, a frank but cordial six-sentence exchange of political views as the paper's collected at dawn or a non-committal deck-to-deck wave as the sun turns the sea to sequined fires, filling the heart with the assurance that we're not experiencing life's wonders *entirely* solo.

Instead, zilch.

My misdelivered mail (Mayo bills and DMV documents) all gets tossed in the trash. Only scowls are offered. No apologies are extended when their car alarm whangs off at 2:00 p.m. and ruins my post-procedure nap. There's no heads-up when a roof tile blows loose and causes a behind-the-wall leak while I'm out in Rochester. Not even a "Howzitgoin?" on my return last August, when I wasn't feeling so hot. Twice, Nick actually set up a skeet thrower on his deck and shot clay pigeons that flew (I thought) dangerously close to my bedroom window. (I called the cops.)

At one point a year ago, I asked one of my competitors, in strict confidence, to make a cold call to the Feensters, representing a non-existent, high-roller, all-cash client, to find out if Nick might take the money and go the hell back to Bridgeport, where he belongs. The colleague—a nice, elderly ex-Carmelite nun who's hard to shock—said Nick stormed at her, "Did that asshole Bascombe put you up to this? Why don't you go fuck yourself," then bammed the phone down.

A couple of us up the road have discussed the mystery of what we think of as the "Toxic Feensters," standing out on sand-swept Poincinet on warm afternoons through the fall. My neighbors are a discredited presidential historian retired from Rutgers, who admitted fudging insignificant quotes in his book about Millard Fillmore and the Know-Nothing Party of 1856, but who sued and won enough to live out his years in style. (College lawyers are never any good.) There's also a strapping, bulgy-armed, khaki-suited petroleum engineer of about my age, from Oklahoma, Terry Farlow, a bachelor who works in Kazakhstan in "oil exploration," comes home every twenty-eight days, then returns to Aktumsyk, where he lives in an air-conditioned geodesic dome, eats three-star meals flown in from France and sees all the latest movies courtesy of our government. (I guarantee you're never neighbors with people like this in Haddam.) Our third neighbor is Mr. Oshi, a middle-aged Japanese banker I've actually never talked to, who works at Sumitomo in Gotham, departs every morning at three in a black limousine and never otherwise leaves his house once he's in it.

We're an unlikely mix of genetic materials, life modalities and history. Though all of us understand we've tumbled down onto this slice of New Jersey's pretty part like dice cast with eyes shut. Our sense of belonging and fitting in, of making a claim and settling down is at best ephemeral. Though being ephemeral gives us pleasure, relieves us of stodgy house-holder officialdom and renders us free to be our own most current selves. No one would be shocked, for instance, to see a big blue-and-white United Van Lines truck back down the road and for any or all of us to pack it in without explanation. We'd think briefly on life's transience, but then we'd be glad. Someone new and possibly different and possibly even interesting could be heading our way.

None of us can say we understand the unhappy Feensters. And as we've stood evenings out on the sandy road, we've stared uncomprehending down Poincinet at their showy white house marred by warning signs about towing and pit bulls and dangerous but fallacious riptides, their twin aqua-and-white '56 Corvettes in the driveway, where they can be admired by people the Feensters don't want to let drive past. Everything that's theirs is always locked up tight as a bank. Nick and Drilla go on beach power walks every day at three, rain, cold or whatever, yellow Walkmen clamped on their hard heads, contrasting Lycra outer garments catching the sun's glow, fists churning like boot-camp trainees, eyes fixed straight up the beach. Never a word, kind or otherwise, to anyone.

Arthur Glück, the defamed, stoop-shouldered ex-Rutgers prof, believes it's a Connecticut thing (he's a Wesleyan grad). Everyone up there, he says, is accustomed to bad community behavior (he cites Greenwich), plus the Feensters aren't educated. Terry Farlow, the big Irishman from Oklahoma, said his petroleum-industry experience taught him that conspicuous new wealth unaccompanied by any sense of personal accomplishment (salvaging cathode-ray tubes not qualifying as accomplishment) often unhinges even good people, wrecks their value system, leaves them miserable and turns them into assholes. The one thing it never seems to do, he said, is make them generous, compassionate and forgiving.

It seemed to me—and I feel implicated, since I sold them their house and made a fat 108K doing it—that the Feensters got rich, got restless and adventuresome (like anybody else), bought ocean-front but somehow got detached from their sense of useful longing, though they couldn't have described it. They only know they paid enough to expect to feel right, but for some reason don't feel right, and so get mad as hell when they can't bring all into line. A Sponsor visit, or a freshman course on Kierkegaard at a decent community college, would help.

With the clairvoyance of hindsight, it might also have worked that if the Feensters were dead set on Sea-Clift, they would've been smarter to stay away from ocean-front and put their new fecklessly gotten gains into something that would keep longing alive. Longing can be a sign of vigor, as well as heart-stopping stress. They might've done better down here by diversifying, maybe moving into their own Bimini Street bungalow, adding a second story or a greenhouse or an in-ground pool, then buying a bigger fixer-upper and fitting themselves into the Sea-Clift community by trading at the hardware store, subbing out their drywall needs to local tradesmen, applying for permits at the town clerk's, eating at the Hello Deli and gradually matriculating (instead of bulling in), the way people have from time's first knell. They could've invested their lottery winnings in boutique stocks or a miracle-cure IPO or a Broadway revival of *Streetcar* and felt they were in the thick of things. Later, they could've turned their cathode-ray-tube business into a non-profit to help young victims of something—whatever old cathode-ray tubes do that kills you—and made everyone love them instead of loathing them and wishing they'd go the hell away. In fact, if one or the other of them would get cancer, it would probably have a salubrious effect on their spirits. Though I don't want to wish that on them yet.

The bottom line is: Living the dream can be a lot more complicated than it seems, even for lottery winners, who we all watch shrewdly, waiting to see how they'll fuck it up, never give any loot away to AIDS hospices or battered children's shelters or the Red Cross, the good causes they'd have sworn on their Aunt Tillie's grave they'd bankroll the instant their number came up. This is, in fact, one reason I keep on selling houses—though I've had a snootful of it, don't need the money and occasionally encounter bad-apple clients like the Feensters: because it gives me something to feel a productive longing about at day's end, which is a way to register I'm still alive.

"FRANK-EE." A heavy pause. "Frank-ee." My name's being called from the chilled oceany night, beyond the windows I've left open to invigorate my sleep. There are no sounds from Clarissa's room, where she's entertaining Mr. Lucky Duck, and where they may even be asleep now—she in bed, he on the floor like a Labrador (there's so little you can do to make things come out right).

I climb stiffly out, blue-pajama-clad, and go to the window that gives down upon the sand and weedy strip of no-man's-land between me and the Feensters, the ground where the fence used to be. No light shines from the three window squares on the three stacked levels of white wall facing my house. We're bunched together too close in here despite the choker prices. Lots were platted by a local developer in cahoots with the planning board and who saw restrictions coming from years away and wanted to retire to Sicily.

Faint fog drifts from sea to land, but I can see a shadowy triangular portion of the Feensters' front yard, where the gay bankers planted animal topiary the Feensters have let go to hell in favor of aggressive signage. A grown-out boxwood rhino and part of a boxwood monkey are ghostly shapes in the mist. Seaward I can see the pallet of shadowed beach, with a crust of white surf disappearing into the sand. In the night sky, there's the icebox glow of Gotham and, in the middle distance, the white lights and rigging lines of a commercial fisher alone at its toils. In these times of lean catches, local captains occasionally dispose of private garbage on their overnight flounder trips. A fellow in Manasquan even advertises burials at sea (ashes only) beyond the three-mile limit, where permits aren't required. Many things seem thinkable that once weren't.

From between the houses, the Glücks' big tomcat, William Graymont, strolls toward the beach to scavenge what the shorebirds have left, or perhaps snare a plover for his midnight meal. When I tap the glass, he stops, looks around but not at me, flicks his tail, then continues his leisurely trek.

No one's said my name again, so I'm wondering if I dreamed

it. But all at once a light snaps on in the Feensters' third-floor bathroom, the Grecian marble ablution sanctum off the spacious master suite. Television volume blaring yesterday's news headlines goes on, then instantly goes silent. Drilla Feenster's head and naked torso pass the window, then pass again, her bottle-blond hair in a red plastic shower cap, heading for the gold-nozzled shower. Possibly it's their usual bathing and TV hour. I wouldn't know.

But then rounding the front outside corner of the house in pajamas, slippers, a black ski parka and a knit cap, Nick Feenster appears, talking animatedly into a cell phone. One hand holds the instrument to his ear like a conch shell, the other a retractable leash attached to Bimbo, their pug. A big man with a tiny dog could signal a complex and giving heart, if not straight-out homosexuality, but not in Nick's case. (Bimbo is the "pit bull" referred to on the sign.) Nick's gesturing with the hand holding Bimbo's leash, so that each time he gestures, Bimbo's yanked off his little front paws.

Nick's voice is loud but muffled. "Frankly, I don't get it," he seems to be saying, with gestures accompanying and Bimbo bouncing and looking up at him as if each jerk was a signal. "Frankly, I think you're making a *biiiig* mistake. A *biiiig* mistake. Frankly, this is getting way out of control."

Frankly. Frankly. Frank-ee. Frank-ee. There's so little that's truly inexplicable in the world. Why should it be such a difficult place to live?

The lighted bathroom square goes unexpectedly black—a purpose possibly interrupted. Nick, who's a husky, heavy-legged, former power lifter and has toted prostrated victims out of smoke-filled tenement stairwells, goes on talking in the cold, fog-misted yard (to whom, I don't even wonder). A yellow second-floor light square pops on. This in the cypress kitchen-cum-vu room—Mexican tile fireplace, facing Sonoran-style, silver-inlaid, hand-carved one-of-a-kind couches, Sub-Zero, commercial Viking, built-in Cuisinart and a Swiss wine cellar at cabinet level. Almost too fast, the first-floor window brightens. A sound, a seismic disturbance up through the earth's crust, permeating Nick's bedroom slippers—an intimation only misbehaving husbands can hear—causes Nick abruptly to snap his cell phone closed, frown a suspicious frown upwards (at me! He can't see me but senses surveillance). Then, in a strange, bumpy, big man's slightly balletic movement, reflecting the fact he's freezing his nuts off, Nick, with Bimbo struggling to keep up, beats it back around the house, past the topiary monkey and out of sight. Whatever he intends to say he's been up to outside—to Drilla, who's noted his absence and thought, *What the fuck?*— is just now larruping around in his brain like an electron.

I stare down into the sandy, weedy non-space Nick has vacated in guilty haste. Something's intensely satisfying about his absence, as if I'll never have to see him again. I think I hear, but probably don't hear, voices far away, buffered by interior walls, a door slammed hard. A shout. A breakage. The odd socketed pleasure of someone else's argument—not *your* night shot to hell, not *your* heart crashing in your chest, not *your* head exploding in anger and hot frustration, as when Sally left. Someone else's riot and bad luck. It's enough to send anyone off to bed happy and relieved, which is where, after a pit stop, I return.

UNTIL . . . MUSIC awakens me. *Dum-dee-dum-dee-dum, dum-dee-dum-dee-dum.*

My bedroom's lit through with steely wintry luminance. I'm shocked to have slept till now—7:45—with light banging in, the day underway and noise downstairs. Rich coffee and bacon-fat aromas mix with sea smells. I hear a voice particle. Clarissa. Hushed. "We have to be . . . He's still . . . not usually so . . ." Mutter, mutter. A clink of cup and saucer. Knife to plate. A kitchen chair scrapes. A car murmurs past on Poincinet Road. The sounds now of the ball getting rolling. I've clenched my teeth all night. Small wonder.

The music's from the Feensters'. Show tunes at high volume out the vu-room sliding door, past the owl decoy that keeps seagulls at bay. *My Fair Lady.* ". . . And *oooohhh*, the towering fee-ling, just to *kn-o-o-o-w* somehow you are *ne-ah*." The Feensters often sit out on their deck in their hot tub during winter, drink Irish coffee and read the *Post*, wearing ski parkas, all as a way of smelling the roses. This morning, though, music's needed to put some distance between now and last night, when Nick was "walking the dog" at 3:00 a.m.

I lie abed and stare bemused at the stack of books on my

bedside table, most read to page thirty, then abandoned, except for *The Road to the Open Heart*, which I've read a good deal of. Much of it's, of course, personally impractical, though you'd have to be a deranged serial killer not to agree with most of what it says. "On the one hand make concessions, on the other take the problem seriously." It's no wonder Mike does so well selling houses. Buddhism wrote the book on selling houses.

Recently I've also dipped into *The Fireside Book of Great Speeches*, a leftover from Paul's HHS Oratory Club. I've sought good quotable passages in case a moment arises for valedictory words this Thursday. The speeches, however, are all as boring as Quaker sermons, except for Pericles' funeral oration, and even *he's* a little heavy-handed and patented: "Great will be your glory if you do not lower the nature that is within you." When is that not ever true? Pericles and the Dalai Lama are naturals for each other. Convalescence is supposed to be a perfect time for reading, like a long stint in prison. But I assure you it isn't, since you have too much on your mind to concentrate.

The sky I can see from bed is monochrome, high and lighted from a sun deep within cottony depths—not a disk, but a spirit. It is a cold, stingy sky that makes a seamless plain with the sea— decidedly not a "realty sky" to make ocean-front seem worth the money. I'm scheduled for a showing at 10:15; but the sky's effect—I already know it—will not be to inspire and thrill, but to calm and console. For that reason I'm expecting little from my effort.

THE EXACT status of my marriage to Sally Caldwell requires, I believe, some amplification. It is still a marriage that's officially going on, yet by any accounting has become strange—in fact, the strangest I know, and within whose unusual circumstances I myself have acted very strangely.

Last April, I took a journey down memory lane to an old cadets' reunion at the brown-stucco, pantile-roof campus of my old military school—Gulf Pines on the Mississippi coast. "Lonesome Pines," we all called it. The campus and its shabby buildings, like apparently everything else in that world, had devolved over time to become an all-white Christian Identity school, which had itself, by defaulting on its debts, been sold to a corporate entity—the ancient palms, wooden goalposts, dusty parade grounds, dormitories and classroom installments soon to be cleared as a parking structure for a floating casino across Route 90.

During this visit, I happened to hear from Dudley Phelps, who's retired out of the laminated-door business up in Little Rock, that Wally Caldwell, once our Lonesome Pines classmate, but more significantly once my wife's husband, until he got himself shell-shocked in Vietnam and wandered off seemingly forever, causing Sally to have him declared dead (no easy trick without a body or other evidence of death's likelihood)—*this* Wally Caldwell was reported by people in the know to have appeared again. Alive. Upon the earth and—I was sure when I heard it—eager to stir up emotional dust none of us had seen the likes of.

Nobody knew much. We all stood around the breezy, hot parade ground in short-sleeve pastel shirts and chinos, talking committedly, chins tucked into our necks, the pale, wispy grass smelling of shrimp, ammonia and diesel, trying to unearth good concrete memories—the deaf-school team we played in football that hilariously beat the shit out of us—anything we could feel positive about and that could make adolescence seem to have been worthwhile, though agreeing darkly we were all of us pretty hard cases when we'd arrived. (Actually, I was not a hard case at all. My father had died, my mother'd remarried a man I pretty much liked and moved to Illinois, only I simply couldn't imagine going to high school with a bunch of Yankees—though, of course, I would someday become one of them and think it was great.)

The casino's big building-razing, turf-ripping machinery was already standing ranked along the highway like a small mean army. Work was due to commence the next morning, following this last muster on the plain. We had a keg of beer somebody'd brought. The Gulf was just as the Atlantic is in summer: brownish, sluggish, a dingy aqueous apron stretching to nowhere—though warm as bathwater instead of dick-shrinkingly cold. We all solemnly stood and drank the warm beer, ate weenies in stale buns and did our best not to feel dispirited and on-in-years (this was before my medical surprises). We chatted disapprovingly about how the Coast had changed, how the South had traded its tarnished soul for an even more debased graven image of gambling loot, how the current election would probably be won by the wrong dope. Surprisingly, many of my old classmates had gone to Nam like Wally and come back Democrats.

And then around 2:00 p.m., when the sun sat straight over our sweating heads like a dentist's lamp and we'd all begun to laugh about what a shithole this place had really been, how we didn't mind seeing it disappear, how we'd all cried ourselves to sleep in our metal bunks on so many breathless, mosquito-tortured nights on account of cruel loneliness and youth and deep hatred for the other cadets, we all, by no signal given, just began to stray away back toward our rental cars, or across the highway to the casino for some stolen fun, or back to motels or SUVs or the airport in New Orleans or Mobile, or just back—as if we could go back far enough to where it would all be forgotten and gone forever, the way it already should've been. Why were we there? By the end, none of us could've said.

How, though, do you contemplate such news as this possible Wally sighting? I had no personal memories of Cadet W. Caldwell, only pictures Sally kept (and kept hidden): on the beach with their kids in Saugatuck; a color snapshot showing a shirtless, dog-tagged Wally squinting into the summer sun like JFK, holding a copy of *Origin of Species* with a look of mock puzzlement on his young face; a few tuxedoed wedding photos from 1969, where Wally looked lumpy and wise and scared to death of what lay before him; a yearbook portrait from Illinois State, showing Walter "The Wall," class of '67, *plant biology*, and where he was deemed (sadly, I felt) to be "Trustworthy, a friend to all." "Solid where it counts" (which he wasn't). "Call me Mr. Wall."

These ancient, moistened relics did not, to me, a real husband make. Though once they had to Sally—a tall, blond, blue-eyed beauty with small breasts, thin fingers, smooth-legged, with her tiny limp from a tennis mishap—a college cheerleader who fell for the shy, heavy-legged, curiously gazing rich boy in her genetics class, and who smiled when she talked because so much made her happy, who didn't have problems about physical things and so introduced the trusting "Wall" to bed and to cheap motels out Highway 9, so captivating him that by spring break, "they were pregnant." And pregnant again and married by the time

Wally got called to the Army and joined the Marines instead, in 1969, and went off to a war.

From which, in a sense, he never returned. Though he tried for a couple of weeks in 1971, but then one day just walked off from their little apartment in the Chicago suburb of Hoffman Estates, never to return with a sound or a glimpse. Kids, wife, parents, a few friends. A future. Boop. Over.

This was the extent of my knowledge of Wally the uxorious. He was already legally "dead" when I came on the scene in '87 and tried to rent Sally some expandable office space in Manasquan. She'd identified me from a bogus reminiscence I wrote for the Gulf Pines "Pine Boughs" newsletter, though I had no actual memory of Wally and was merely on the Casualties Committee, responsible for "personal" anecdotes about classmates nobody remembered, but whose loved ones didn't want them seeming like complete ciphers or lost souls, even if they were.

The thought that mystery-man Walter B. Caldwell might still be alive was, as you can imagine, unwieldy personal cargo to be carrying home, Mississippi to New Jersey. There could probably be stranger turns of events. But if so, I'd like you to name one. And while you're at it, name one you'd find easy to keep as your little secret, something you'd rather not have spread around. No more details were available.

On arriving back to Sea-Clift (we're only talking about last April here!), I decided that rogue rumors were always shooting around like paper airplanes in everybody's life, and that this was likely just one more. Some old Lonesome Pines alum, deep in his cups and reeling through the red-light district of Amsterdam or Bangkok, suddenly spies a pathetic homeless man weaving on a street corner, a large, fleshy, unshaven "American-looking" clod, filthy in a tattered, greasy overcoat and duct-taped shoes, yet who has a particularly arresting, sweet smile animating tiny haunted eyes and who seems to stare back knowingly. After a pause, there's a second cadged look, then a long unformed thought about it afterward, followed by a decision to leave well enough alone (where well enough's always happiest). But then, in memory's narrow eye comes a fixifying certainty, an absolute recognition—a sighting. And ker-plunk: Wally *lives*! (and will be in your house eating dinner by next Tuesday).

In eight years of what I thought were much more than

satisfying-fulfilling marriage, not to mention almost thirty since Wally walked away and didn't come back, Sally had made positive adjustments to what might've driven most people bat-shit crazy with anger and not-knowing, and with anxiety over the anger and not-knowing. Therefore, to drop this little hand grenade of uncertainty into her life, I concluded, would actually be unfriendly (I'd decided by then it wasn't true, so it really wasn't a hand grenade in *my* life). But what was either of us supposed to do with the news, short of a full-bore "Have You Seen This Man?" campaign (I didn't *want* to see him), "aged" photos of Wally put up on Web sites, stapled to bulletin boards and splintery telephone poles beside aroma-therapy flyers and lost-cat posters, with appeals made to "Live at 5"?

After which he still wouldn't show up. Because—of course—he'd long ago climbed over a bridge rail or slipped off a boat transom or rock face in the remotest Arizona canyon and said good-bye to this world of woes. Someday, I fantasized, I would sit with Sally on a warm, sun-smacked porch by a lake in Manitoba—this being once our days had dwindled down to a precious few. I'd be pensive for a time, staring out at the water's onyx sheen, then quietly confide to her my long-ago gesture of devotion and love, which had been to shield her from faithlessly rumored sightings of Wally that I knew weren't a bit true (everyone embroiders fantasies to please themselves), and that would only have kept her from what rewarding life she and I could cobble together, knowing what we knew and feeling what we felt. In this fantasy, Sally for a while becomes agitated by my deception and presumption. She stands and walks up and back along the long knotty-pine porch, arms tightly folded, her mouth official and cross, her fingers twitching as the sun burns the surface of Lake Winnipegosis, canoes set forth for sunset journeys, kids' voices waft in from shadowy cottage porches deeper in the great woods. Finally, she sits back into her big green wicker rocker and says nothing for a long time, until the air's gone cooler than we'd like, and as that old lost life still clicks past her inner gaze. Eventually, her heart gives a worrisome flutter, she swallows down hard, feels the back of her hand going even colder (in this fantasy, we have become Canadians). She sighs a deep sigh, reaches chair-arm to chair-arm, finds my hand, knows again its warmth, and then without comment or query suggests we go inside for cocktails, an early dinner and to bed.

Case closed. RIP, Mr. Wall. My dream, instead of my nightmare, come true.

To which fickle fate says: Dream on, dream on, dream on.

Because sometime in early May—it was the balmy, sun-kissed week between Mother's Day and Buddha's birthday (observed with dignified calm and no fanfare by Mike) and not long after my own fifty-fifth (observed with wonderment by me)—Sally caught the United Shuttle out to Chicago to visit the former in-laws in Lake Forest. I'm always officially invited to these events, but have never gone, for obvious reasons—although this might've been the time. The occasion was the aged Caldwells' (Warner and Constance) sixtieth wedding anniversary. A party was planned at the formerly no-Jews-or-blacks-allowed Wik-O-Mek Country Club. Sally's two grim, grown but disenchanted children, Shelby and Chloë, were supposedly coming from northern Idaho. They'd long ago fallen out with their mom over having their dad declared a croaker—prematurely, they felt. You can only imagine how they loathe me. Both kids are neck-high in charismatic Mormon doings (likewise, whites only) out in Spirit Lake, where for all I know they practice cannibalism. They never send a Christmas card, though they plan to be in the "Where's mine?" line when the grandparents shuffle off. When I first met Sally, she was still making piteous efforts to include them in her new life in New Jersey—all of which they rebuffed like cruel suitors—until she was compelled to close the door on both of them, which thrilled me. Too much unredeemed loss can be fatal, which is one of the early glittering tenets of the Permanent Period, one I firmly believe in and was fast to tell her about. At some point—and its arrival may not be obvious, so you have to be on the lookout for it—you have to let life please you if it will, and consign the past to its midden (easier said than done, of course, as we all know).

When she drove her renter from O'Hare up to Lake Forest and up to the winding-drive, many-winged, moss-and-ivy-fronted fieldstone Caldwell manse that sits on a bluff of the lake, she entered the long, drafty, monarchical drawing room with her folding suitcase—she was considered a beloved family member and didn't need to knock. And there seated on the rolled and pleated, overstuffed Victorian leather settee, looking for all the world like the Caldwells' gardener asked in to review next season's perennial-planning strategies ("Did we do the jonquils right? Is there reason to keep the wistaria, since it's really not their climate?"), there was a man she'd never seen before but queerly felt she knew (it was the beady, piggy eyes). There was "The Wall." Wally Caldwell. Her husband. Back from oblivion, at home in Lake Forest.

In time, Sally told me all the useless details, which, once the trap was sprung, took on a routinized predictability—though not to her. One detail that stays in my mind to this steely-sky morning all these months later is Sally standing, suitcase in hand, in the long, lofty drawing room of her in-laws' castle, the must of age and plunder tangy in the motionless air, the leaded-window light shadowy but barred, the house silent behind her, the door just drifting closed by an unseen hand, the old fatigue of loss and heavy familiarity permeating her bones again, and then seeing this lumpy, bearded, balding gardener type, and beaming out a big welcome smile at him and saying, "Hi. I'm Sally." To which he—this not-at-all, no-way-in-hell Wally, with a frown of inner accusing and insecurity, and in a vaguely Scottish accent—says, "I'm Wally. Remember me? I'm not entirely dead."

It is proof that I love Sally that when I replay this moment in my brain, as I have many times, I always wince, so close do I feel to her—what? Shock? Shocked by her shock. Celestially reluctant to have happen next what happened next. The only thing worse would've been if *I'd* been there, although a murderous thrashing could've turned the tables in my favor, instead of how they did turn.

I don't know what went on that weekend. Pensive, hands-behind-the-back walks along the palliative Lake Michigan beach. Angry recrimination sessions out of earshot of the old folks (her kids, blessedly, didn't show). Moaning-crying jags, shouting, nights spent sweating, heart-battering, fists balled in fury, frustration, denial and crass inability to take all in, to believe, to stare truth in the beezer. (Think how *you'd* feel!) And no doubt then the rueful, poisoned thoughts of *why*? And why *now*? Why not just last on to the end on Mull? (The craggy, wind-swept isle off Scotland's coast where Wally'd moled away for decades.) Mull life over till nothing's left of it, soldier the remaining yards alone instead of fucking everything up for everybody—again. TV's much better at these kinds of stories, since the imponderableness of it all conveniently is swept away when the commercials for drain openers, stool softeners and talking potato chips pop on, and all's electronically "forgotten," during which time the aggrieved principals can make adjustments to life's weird wreckage, get ready to come back and sort things out for the better, so that after many tears are shed, fists clenched, hearts broken but declared mendable, everyone's again declared "All set," as they say in New Jersey. All set? Ha! I say. Ha-ha, ha! Ha, ha-ha-ha! All set, my ass.

Sally flew home on Monday, having said nothing of johnny-jump-up Wally during our weekend phone calls. I drove to Newark to get her, and on the ride back could tell she was plainly altered—by something—but said nothing. It is a well-learned lesson of second marriages never to insist on what you absolutely don't have to insist on, since your feelings are probably about nothing but yourself and your own pitiable needs and are not appropriately sympathetic to the needs of the insistee in question. Second marriages, especially good ones like ours seemed, could fill three door-stop-size reference books with black-letter do's and don'ts. And you'd have to be studious if you hoped to get past Volume One.

I, of course, assumed Sally's strange state had to do with her kids, the little devil Christians out in Idaho—that one of them was in detox, or jail, or was a fugitive or self-medicating or in the nut house, or the other was planning a lawsuit to attach my assets now that therapy had unearthed some pretty horrendous buried episodes of abuse in which I was somehow involved and that explained everything about why his life had gone to shit-in-a-bucket, but not before some hefty blame could be spread around. My fear, of course, is every second husband's fear: that somebody from out of the blue, somebody you won't like and who has no sense of anything but his or her own entitlement to suffering—in other words, children—will move in and ruin your life. Sally and I had agreed this would not be our fate, that her two and my two needed to think about life being "based" elsewhere. Our life was ours and only ours. Their room was the guest room. Of course all that's changed now.

When we reached #7 Poincinet Road, the sky was already

resolving upon sunset. The western heavens were their bright-est-possible faultless blue. Pre-Memorial Day beach enthusiasts were packing up books and blankets and transistors and sun reflectors, and heading off for a cocktail or a shrimp plate at the Surfcaster or a snuggle at the Conquistador Suites as the air cooled and softened ahead of night's fall.

I put on my favorite Ben Webster, made a pair of Salty Dogs, thought about a drive later on up to Ortley for a grilled bluefish at Neptune's Daily Catch Bistro and conceivably a snuggle of our own to the accompaniment of nature's sift and sigh and the muttered voices of the striper fishermen who haunt our beach after the tide's turn.

And then she simply told me, just as I was walking into the living room, ready for a full debriefing.

Something there is in humans that wants to make sure you're doing something busying at the exact instant of hearing unwel-come news—as though, if your hands are full, you'll just rumble right on through the whole thing, unfazed. "Wally? Alive? Really? Here, try a sip of this, see if I put in too much Donald Duck. Happy to add more Gilbey's. Well, ole Wall—whadda ya know? How'd The Wall seem? Don't you just love how Ben gets that breathy tremolo into 'Georgia on My Mind.' Hoagy'd love it. Give Wally my best. How was it to be dead?"

I should say straight out: Never tell anyone you know how she or he feels unless you happen to be, just at that second, stabbing yourself with the very same knife in the very same place in the very same heart she or he is stabbing. Because if you're not, then you don't know how anybody feels. I can barely tell you how *I* felt when Sally said, "Frank, when I got to Lake Forest, Wally was there." (Use of my name, "Frank," as always, a harbinger of things unpopular. I should change my name to Al.)

I know for a fact that I said nothing when I heard these words. I managed to put my Salty Dog down on the glass coffee-table top and lower myself onto the brown suede couch beside her, to put both my hands on top of my knees and gaze out at the darkening Atlantic, where the ghostly figures of the high-booted fishermen faced the surf and, far out to sea, the sky still showed a brilliant reflected sliver of azure. Sally sat as I did and may have felt as I did—*surprised.*

Sometimes simple words are the best, and better than violent

images of the world cracking open; or about how much everything's like a sitcom and what a pity William Bendix isn't still
around to play Wally—or me; or better than the ethical-culture
response, that catastrophe's "a good thing for everybody," since
it dramatizes life's great mystery and reveals how much all is
artifice—connected boxes, world-within-worlds—the trap
Clarissa's trying to break free of. How we express our response
to things is just made-up stuff anyway—unless we tip over dead
—and is meant to make the listener think he's getting his
money's worth, while feeling relief that none of this shit is
happening to him personally. *Surprised* is good enough. When
I heard Wally Caldwell, age fifty-five, missing for thirty years,
during which time many things had happened and substantial
adjustments were made about the nature of existence on earth—
when I heard Wally was alive in Lake Forest and had spent the
weekend doing God knows what with my wife, I was surprised.

Sally knew I might be surprised (and again, I *was* surprised),
and she wanted to make this news *not* cause the world to crack
open, for me to go hysterical, etc. She'd had three days with Wally
already. She had gotten over the shock of an older, bearded, avuncular and strange Wally hiding out in his parents' house like some
scary older brother with a terrible wound, whom you only see
fleetingly behind shadowy chintz curtains in an upstairs dormer
window, but who may be heard at night to moan. Her attitude
was—and I liked it, since it was typical of her get-up-and-fix-
things attitude—that while, yes, Wally's reappearance *had* caused
some tricky issues to pop up, needing to be resolved, and that
while she understood how "this whole business" maybe put me
in an awkward position (vis-à-vis, say, the past, the present and
the future), this was still a "human situation," that no one was a
culprit (of course not), no one had bad will (except me) and we
would all address this as a threesome, so that as little damage as
possible would be done to as few a number of innocent souls and
lives (I might've known who the left-unprotected innocent soul
would turn out to be, but I didn't).

Wally's story, she told me, sitting on the suede couch that faced
out to the darkened springtime Atlantic, as our Salty Dogs turned
watery and dark descended, was "one of those stories" fashioned
by war and trauma, sadness, fear and resentment, and by the
chaotic urge to escape all the other causes, aided by (what else?)

"some kind of schizoid detachment" that induced amnesia, so that for years Wally wouldn't remember big portions of his prior life, although certain portions were crystal clear.

Wally, it seems, couldn't put everything all together, though he admitted he hadn't just gone out to pick up the *Trib* thirty years ago, bumped his head getting into his Beetle and suffered a curtain to close. It had to have been—this, he no doubt admitted on one of their cozy Lake Michigan beach tête-à-têtes—that "something unconscious was working on him," some failure to face the world he confronted as a Viet vet with a (minor) head wound, and a family, and a future as a horticulturist looming, the whole undifferentiated world just flooding in on him like a dam bursting, with cows and trees and cars and church steeples swirling away in the gully-wash, and him in with it. (There are good strategies for coping with this, of course, but you have to want to.)

Cutting (blessedly) to the chase, Wally's trauma, fear, resentment and elective amnesia had carried him as far away from the Chicago suburbs, from wife and two kids, as Glasgow, in Scotland, where for a time he became "caught up" in "the subculture" that lived communally, practiced good feeling for everything, experimented with cannabis and other mind-rousing drugs, fucked like bunny rabbits, made jewelry by hand and sold it on damp streets, practiced subsistence farming techniques, made their own clothes and set their communal sights on spiritual-but-not-mainstream-religious revelation. In other words, the Manson Family, led by Ozzie and Harriet.

Eventually, Wally said, the "petrol" had run out of the communal subculture, and with a satellite woman—a professor of English, naturally—he had migrated up to the wilds of Scotland, first to the Isle of Skye, then to Harris, then to Muck, and finally to Mull, where he found employment in the Scottish Blackface industry (sheep) and finally—more to his talents and likings—as a gardener on the laird's estate and, as time went on, as head gardener and arborist (the laird was wild for planting spruce trees), and eventually as the estate manager for the entire shitaree. A complete existence was there, Wally said, a long way from Lake Forest "and that whole life" (again meaning wife and kids), from the Cubs, the Wrigley Building, the Sears Tower, the river dyed green—*again*, the whole deluging, undifferentiated crash-in of modern existence American-style, whose sudsy, brown tree-trunk-littered surface most of us somehow manage to keep our heads above so we can see our duty and do it. I'm not impartial in these matters. Why should I be?

In due time, the lady friend—"a completely good and decent woman"—got tired of life on Mull as a crofter's companion and returned to her job and husband—likewise a professor, in Ohio. A couple of local lassies moved in and, in time, out again. Wally got used to living semi-officially in the manager's stone cottage, scrubbing the loo, restocking the fridge with haggis, smoking fish, burning peat, reading *The Herald*, listening to Radio 4, snapping on the telly, sipping his cuppa, keeping his Wellies dry and his Barbour waxed during the long Mull winters. This was the wee life, the one he was suited for and entitled to and where he expected his days to end amongst the cold stones and rills and crags and moors and cairns and gorse and windblown cedars of his own dull nature—here in his half-chosen, half-fated, half-fucked-up-and-escaped-to destination resort from life gone kaflooey.

Enter then the Internet—in the form of the old laird's young son, Morgil, who'd taken the reins of the property (having been to college at Florida State) and who'd begun to suspect that this lumpy American in the manager's accommodation was probably other than he'd declared himself, was possibly an old draft dodger or a fugitive from some abysmal crime in his own country, from which he'd exiled himself, some guy who dressed up in clown suits and ate little boys for lunch. The standard idea of America, viewed from abroad.

What young Morgil found when he checked—and who'd be shocked?—was a "Wally Caldwell" Web site the old Lake Forest parents had erected as a long last hope, or whatever inspires Web sites (I don't maintain one at Realty-Wise, though Mike does, www.RealtyTibet.com, which is how Tommy Benivalle found him). No outstanding warrants, Interpol alerts or Scotland Yard red flags were attached to the site, only several sequentially aged photos of Wally (one actually in a Barbour) that looked exactly like the Wally out planting spruce sprigs and pruning other ones like a character out of D. H. Lawrence. "Please contact the Caldwell Family if you know this man, or see him, or hear of him. Amnesia may be involved. He's not dangerous. His family misses him greatly and we are now in our eighties. Not much time is left."

Young Morgil didn't feel it would be right to send a blind message out of the blue—that a cove of Wally Caldwell's general description was working right on old Cullonden, on the Isle of Mull, under the name of Wally Caldwell. It'd be better, he gauged, to tell Wally, even at the risk of its being sensitive news that might wake him up from a long dream of life and dash him into a world he had no tolerance for, send him screaming and gibbering off onto the heath, his frail vessel cracked, so that all his ancient parents would have to show for their Web site was a pale, broken, silent man in green pajamas, who seemed sometimes to smile and recognize you but mostly just sat and stared at Lake Michigan.

Morgil tacked a note to Wally's door the next morning—a color printout of the Caldwell home page—the computerized middle-aged face side-by-side with a yearbook photo from Illinois State ("Call me Mr. Wall"). No mention was made of Sally, Shelby and Chloë, or that he'd been declared *expired*. The only words it contained were his parents' tender entreaties: "Come home, Wally, wherever you are, *if* you are. We're not mad at you. We're still here in Lake Forest, Mom and Dad. We can't last forever."

And so he did. Wally crossed the sea to home and the welcome arms of his mom and dad. A changed bloke, but nonetheless their moody, slow-thinking son, all things suddenly glittering and promise-laden, whereas before all had been a closed door, a blank wall, an empty night where no one calls your name. I know plenty about this.

Which was the strange tableau my unsuspecting wife walked in upon, carrying her suitcase and lost memories, expecting only a "drinks evening" with the in-laws, followed by some whitefish au gratin, then early to bed between cold, stiff sheets and the next day making nice with elderly strangers at the Wik-O-Mek, trying patiently, pleasantly to re-explain to them exactly who she was (a former daughter-in-law?). But instead, she found Wally, bearded, older, fattish, balded, gray-toothed, though still innocent and vague the way she'd once liked, only dressed like a Scottish gamekeeper with an idiotic accent.

She was surprised. We were both surprised.

When she'd told me this whole preposterous story, it'd long gone dark in the house. Chill had filtered indoors off the surface of the moonlit sea. She sat perfectly still, peering out at the high tide, the fishermen vanished to home, a red phosphorescence seeding the water's swell. I left and came back with a sweater I'd bought years before in France, when I'd been in love in a haywire way (my then-beloved is now a thoracic surgeon at Brigham and Women's), though my love story, then, had an all-round satisfactory end that left life open for new investigations and not obstructed by problematical, profoundly worrisome insolubles.

Sally put on the sweater Catherine Flaherty had settled into on cold French spring nights facing the Channel. She hugged her arms the way Catherine had, burying her cold chin into the crusted, musty-smelling nap, giving herself time to think a clear thought, since Wally was in Lake Forest and I was here. All the safety netting of *our* little life was still up to catch her, and she could—as it seemed to me she should—just forget the whole commotion, writing it all off as a dream that would go away if you let it. My heart went out to her, I'll admit. But I also understood there could be no tweezing and tracing of slender filaments back through the knot to make loose ends become continuous and smooth. They weren't loose ends. These were what I called *my life*. And even though they were short, blunt and more frayed than what I'd rather, they were still what I had. If I'd known what awaited me, I might've phoned up some boys in Bergen County who owed me a favor and had 'em fly out and perform a penitential errand on Wally's noggin.

There are many different kinds of people on the planet—people who never let you forget a mistake, people who're happy to. People who almost drown as children and never swim again, and people who jump right back in and paddle off like ducks. There are people who marry the same woman over and over, while others have no scheme in their amours (I'm this man. It's not so bad). And there are definitely people who, when faced with misfeasance of a large and historical nature, even one that needn't cloud the present and forbid the future, just can't rest until the misfeasance is put right, redressed, battered to dust with study and attention so they can feel just fine about things and go forward with a clear heart—whatever that might be. (The opposite of this is what the Permanent Period teaches us: If you can't truly forget something, you can at least ignore it and try to make your dinner plans on time.)

In Sally's behalf, she was dazed. She'd gone to Illinois and seen a ghost. Everything in life suddenly felt like a cold higgle-piggle. It's the kind of shock that makes you realize that life only happens to you and to you alone, and that any concept of togetherness, intimacy, union, abiding this and abiding that is a hoot and a holler into darkness. My idea, of course, would've been to wait a week or two, go about my business selling houses, book a Carnival Cruise vacation to St. Kitts, then in a while nose back in to see how the land lay and the citizenry had re-deployed. My guess was that with time to reflect, Wally would've disappeared quietly back to Mull, to his spruce and cairns and anonymity. We could exchange Christmas cards and get on with life to its foreshortened ending. After all, how likely are any of us ever to change—given that we're all in control of most things?

Again, of course, I was wrong. Wrong, wrongety, wrong, wrong, wrong.

At the conclusion of Sally's long recitation of the lost-Wally saga, a chronicle I wasn't that riveted by, since I didn't think it could foretell any good for me (I was right), she announced she needed to take a nap. Events had pretty well wrung her out. She knew I was not exactly a grinning cheerleader to these matters, that I was possibly as "mixed-up" as she was (not true), and she needed just to lie in the dark alone for a while and let things— her word—"settle." She smiled at me, went around the room turning on lamps, suffusing the dark space she was then abandoning me to with a bronze funeral-parlor light. She came around to me where I'd stood up in front of the couch, and kissed me on my cheek (oh Lord) in a pall-bearerish, buck-up-bud sort of way, then ceremoniously mounted the stairs, not to *our room*, not to the marriage bower, the conjugal refuge of sweet intimacies and blissful nod, but to the *guest room*!—where my daughter now sleeps and also "sleeps" with new Mr. Right Who Drives A Fucking Healey.

I might've gone crazy right then. I should've let her mount the stairs (I heard the guest room floorboards squeezing), waited for her to get her shoes shucked and herself plopped wearily onto the cold counterpane, then roared upstairs, proclaiming and defaming, vilifying and contumelating, snatching knobs off doors, kicking table legs to splinters, cracking mirrors with my voice—laying down the law as I saw it and as it should be and as it served and protected. Let everybody on Poincinet Road and up the seaboard and all the ships at sea know that I'd sniffed out what was being served and wasn't having it and neither was anybody else inside my walls. One party left alone to his heartless devices, in his own heartless living room, while another heartless party skulks away to dreamland to revise fate and providence, ought to produce some ornate effects. No fucking way, José. This shit doesn't wash. My way or the highway. Irish (or Scots) need not apply. Members only. Don't even think of parking here.

But I didn't. And why I didn't was: I felt secure. Even though I could feel something approaching, like those elephants who feel the stealthy footfalls of those Pygmy spear toters far across savannas and flooded rivers. I felt at liberty to take an interest, to put on the white labcoat of objective investigator, be Sally's partner with a magnifying glass, curious to find out what these old bones, relics and potsherds of lost love had to tell. These are the very moments, of course, when large decisions get decided. Great literature routinely skips them in favor of seismic shifts, hysterical laughter and worlds cracking open, and in that way does us all a grave disservice.

What I did while Sally slept in the guest room was make myself a fresh Salty Dog, open a can of cocktail peanuts and eat half of them, since bluefish at Neptune's Daily Catch had become a dead letter. I switched off the lights, sat a while in the leather director's chair, hunkered forward over my knees in the chilly living room and watched phosphorescent water lap the moonlit alabaster beach till way past high tide. Then I went upstairs to my home office and read the *Asbury Press*—stories about Elián González being pre-enrolled at Yale, a plan to make postmodern sculpture out of Y2K preventative gear and place it on the statehouse lawn in Trenton, a CIA warning about a planned attack on our shores by Iran, and a lawsuit over a Circuit City in Bradley Beach being turned down by the local planning board—with the headline reading HOW'S THE DOWNTICK AFFECTING HOLIDAY SHOPPING?

I rechecked my rental inventory (Memorial Day was three weeks away). I took note that the NJ Real Estate *Cold Call* reported four million of our citizens were working, while only 4.1 percent of our population was not—the longest economic boom in our history (now giving hissing sounds around the edges). Finally, I went back down, turned on the TV, watched the Nets lose to the Pistons and went to sleep on the couch in my clothes.

This isn't to suggest that Wally's re-emergence hadn't caught my notice and didn't burn my ass and cause me to think that discomforting, messy, troublesome readjustments wouldn't need to take place, and soon. Readjustments requiring Wally being declared un-dead, requiring divorcing, estate re-planning and updated survivorship provisos, all while recriminations cut the air like steak knives, and all lasting a long time and raking everybody's patience, politeness and complex sense of themselves over the hot coals like spare ribs. That was going to happen. I may also have felt vulnerable to the accusation of marital johnny-come-lately-ism. Though I'd have never met Sally Caldwell, never married her (I might still have romanced her), had it not been that Wally was gone—we all thought—for good.

What I, in fact, felt was: on my guard—but safe. The way you'd feel if crime statistics spiked in your neighborhood but you'd just rescued a two-hundred-pound Rottweiler from the shelter, who saw you as his only friend, whereas the wide world was his enemy.

Sally's and my marriage seemed as contingency-proof as we could construct it, using the human materials we're all equipped with. The other thing about second marriages—unlike first ones, which require only hot impulse and drag-strip hormones—is that they need good reasons to exist, reasons you're smart to pore over and get straight well beforehand. Sally and I both conducted independent self-inquiries back when I was still in Haddam, and each made a clear decision that marriage—to each other—promised more than anything else we could think of that would probably make us both happy, and that neither of us harbored a single misgiving that wasn't appropriate to life anyway (illnesses—we'd share; death—we'd expect; depression—we'd treat), and that any more time spent in deciding was time we could spend having the time of our lives. Which as far as I'm concerned—and in fact I know that Sally felt the same—we did.

Which is to say we practiced the sweet legerdemain of adulthood shared. We formally renounced our unmarried personalities. We generalized the past in behalf of a sleek second-act mentality that stressed the leading edge of life to be all life was. We acknowledged that strong feelings were superior to original happiness, and promised never to ask the other if she or he really, really, really loved him or her, in the faith that affinity was love, and we had affinity. We stressed nuance and advocated that however we seemed was how we were. We declared we were good in bed, and that lack of intimacy was usually self-imposed. We kept our kids at a wary but (at least in my case) positive distance. We de-emphasized becoming in behalf of being. We permanently renounced melancholy and nostalgia. We performed intentionally pointless acts like flying to Moline or Flint and back the same day because we were "archaeologists." We ate Thanksgiving and Xmas dinners at named rest stops on the Turnpike. We considered buying a pet refuge in Nyack, a B&B in New Hampshire.

In other words, we put in practice what the great novelist said about marriage (though he never quite had the genome for it himself). "If I should ever marry," he wrote, "I should pretend to think just a little better of life than I do." In Sally's case and mine, we thought a *lot* better of life than we ever imagined we could. In the simplest terms, we really, really loved each other and didn't do a lot of looking right or left—which, of course, is the first principle of the Permanent Period.

Because today is November 22nd and not last May, and I have cancer and Sally is this morning far away on the Isle of Mull, I am able to telescope events to make our decade-long happy union seem all a matter of clammy reasons and practicalities, as though a life lived with another was just a matter of twin isolation booths in an old Fifties quiz show; and also to make everything that happened seem inevitable and to have come about because Sally was unhappy with me and with us. But not one ounce of that would be true, as gloomy as events became, and as given as I am to self-pity and to doubting I was *ever* more than semi-adequate in bed, and that by selling houses I never lived up to my potential (I might've been a lawyer).

No, no, no, no and no again.

We *were* happy. There was enough complex warp and woof

in life to make a sweater as big as the fucking ocean. We lived. Together.

"But she couldn't have been *so* happy if she left, could she?" said the little pointy-nose, squirrel-tooth, bubble-coifed grief counselor I sadly visited up in Long Branch just because I happened to drive by and saw her shingle one early June afternoon. She was used to advising the tearful, bewildered, abandoned wives of Fort Dix combat noncoms who'd married Thai bar girls and never come home. She wanted to offer easy solutions that led to feelings of self-affirmation and quick divorces. Sugar. Dr. Sugar. She was divorced herself.

But that's not true, I told her. People don't always leave because they're unhappy, like they do in shitty romance novels written by lonely New England housewives or in supermarket tabloids or on TV. You could say it's my fatal flaw to believe this, and to believe that Wally's return to life, and Sally leaving with him, wasn't the craziest, worst goddamn thing in the fucking world and didn't spell the end of love forever. Yet that's what I believed and still do. Sally could decide *later* that she'd been unhappy. But since she left, the two polite postcards I've received have made no mention of divorce or of not loving me, and that's what I'm choosing to understand.

WHEN SALLY came down later that night and found me asleep on the couch beside the can of Planters with the TV playing *The Third Man* (the scene where Joseph Cotten gets bitten by the parrot), she wasn't unhappy with me—though she certainly wasn't happy. I understood she'd just come unexpectedly face-to-face with *big contingency*—the thing we'd schemed against and almost beaten, and probably the only contingency that could've risen to eye level and stared us down: the re-enlivening of Wally. And she didn't know what to do about it—though I did.

All marriages—all everythings—tote around contingencies whether we acknowledge them or don't. In all things good and giddy, there's always one measly eventuality no one's thought about, or hasn't thought about in so long it almost doesn't exist. Only it does. Which is the one potentially fatal chink in the body armor of intimacy, to the unconditional this 'n that, to the sacred vows, the pledging of troths, to the forever *anythings*. And that is: There's a back door *somewhere* to every deal, and there a draft can enter. All promises to be in love and "true to you forever" are premised on the iron contingency (unlikely or otherwise) that says, Unless, of course, I fall in love "forever" with someone else. This is true even if we don't like it, which means it isn't cynical to think, but also means that someone else—someone we love and who we'd rather have *not* know it—is as likely to know it as we are. Which acknowledgment may finally be as close to absolute intimacy as any of us can stand. Anything closer to the absolute than this is either death or as good as death. And death's where I draw the line. Realtors, of course, know all this better than anyone, since there's a silent Wally Caldwell in every deal, right down to the act of sale (which is like death) and sometimes even beyond it. In every agreement to buy or sell, there's also the proviso, acknowledged or not, that says "unless, of course, I don't want to anymore," or "that is, unless I change my mind," or "assuming my yoga instructor doesn't advise against it." Again, the hallowed concept of character was invented to seal off these contingencies. But in this wan Millennial election year, are we really going to say that this concept is worth a nickel or a nacho? Or, for that matter, ever was?

SALLY STOOD at the darkened thermal glass window that gave upon the lightless Atlantic. She'd slept in her clothes, too, and was barefoot and had a green L.L. Bean blanket around her shoulders in addition to the French sweater. I'd opened the door to the deck, and inside was fifty degrees. She'd turned off *The Third Man*. I came awake studying her inky back without realizing it was her inky back, or that it was even her— wondering if I was hallucinating or was it an optical trick of waking in darkness, or had a stranger or a ghost (I actually thought of my son Ralph) entered my house for shelter and hadn't noticed me snoozing. I realized it was Sally only when I thought of Wally and of the despondency his renewed life might promise me.

"Do you feel a little better?" I wanted to let her know I was here still among the living and we'd been having a conversation earlier that I considered to be still going on.

"No." Hers was a mournful, husky, elderly-seeming voice.

She pinched her Bean's blanket around her shoulders and coughed. "I feel terrible. But I feel exhilarated, too. My stomach's got butterflies and knots at the same time. Isn't that peculiar?"

"No, I wouldn't say that was necessarily so peculiar." I was trying my white investigator's labcoat on for size.

"A part of me wants to feel like my life's a total ruin and a fuck-up, that there's a right way to do things and I've made a disaster out of it. That's how it feels." She wasn't facing me. I didn't really feel like I was talking to *her*. But if not to her, then to who?

"That's not true," I said. I could understand, of course, why she might feel that way. "You didn't do anything wrong. You just flew to Chicago."

"There's no sense to spool everything back to sources, but I might've been a better wife to Wally."

"You're a good wife. You're a good wife to *me*." And then I didn't say this, but thought it: And fuck Wally. He's an asshole. I'll gladly have him big-K killed and his body Hoffa'd out for birdseed. "What do you feel exhilarated about?" I said instead. Mr. Empathy.

"I'm not sure." She flashed a look around, her blond hair catching light from somewhere, her face appearing tired and marked with shadowy lines from too-sound sleep and the fatigue of travel.

"Well," I said, "exhilaration doesn't hurt anything. Maybe you were glad to see him. You always wondered where he went." I put a single cocktail peanut into my dry mouth and crunched it down. She turned back to the cold window, which was probably making her cold. "What's he going to do now," I said, "have himself re-incarnated, or whatever you do?"

"It's pretty simple."

"I'll keep that in mind. What about the being-married-to-you part? Does he get to do that again? Or do I get you as salvage?"

"You get me as salvage." She turned and walked slowly toward me where I sat staring up at her, slightly dazzled, as if she *was* the ghost I'd mistook her for. Her little limp was pronounced because she was beat. She sat on the couch and leaned into me so I could smell the sweated, unwashed dankness of her hair. She put her hand limply on my knee and sighed as if she'd been holding her breath and didn't realize it till now. Her coarse blanket prickled through my shirt. "He'd like to meet you," she said. "Or maybe I want him to meet you."

"Absolutely," I said, and could identify a privileged sarcasm. "We'll invite some people over. Maybe I'll interest him in a summer rental."

"That's not really necessary, is it?"

"Yes. I'm in command of my necessaries. You be in command of yours."

"Don't be bad to me about this. It flabbergasts me as much as it does you."

"That isn't true. I'm not exhilarated. Why are *you* exhilarated? I answered that *for* you, but I don't like my answer."

"*Mmmmmm*. I think it's just so strange, and so familiar. I'm not mad at him anymore. I was for years. I was when I first saw him. It was like meeting the President or some famous person. I know him so well and then there he is and of course I don't know him. There was something exciting about that." She looked at me, put her hands atop each other on my cold knee and smiled a sweet, tired, imploring, mercy-hoping smile. It would've been wonderful if we hadn't been talking about her ex-dead husband and the disaster he was casting our way, but instead about how good something was, how welcome, how much we missed something we both loved and now here it was.

"I don't feel that way," I said. I was on solid ground not feeling what she felt. It occurred to me that how she felt toward Wally was a version of being married to him, which was a version of the truth I mentioned before and couldn't argue with. But I didn't have to like it.

"You're right," she said patiently.

And then we didn't speak for a little while, just sat breathing in the cold air, each of us fancifully, forcefully seeking a context into which our separate views—of Wally, and disaster—could join forces and fashion an acceptable and unified response. I was further from the middle of events and had some perspective, so that the heavier burden fell on me. I'd already started suiting up in the raiments of patient understander. Oh woe. Oh why?

"Something has to happen," Sally said with unwanted certainty. "Something had to happen when Wally left. Something has to happen now that he's back. *Nothing* can't happen. That's my feeling."

"Who says?"

"Me," she said sadly. "I do."

"*What* has to happen?"

"I have to spend some time with him." Sally spoke reluctantly. "You'd want to do the same thing, Frank." She wrinkled her chin and slightly puffed her compressed lips. She often took on this look when she was sitting at her desk composing a letter.

"No, I wouldn't. I'd buy him a first-class ticket to anyplace he wanted to go in Micronesia and never think about him again. Where're you planning to spend time with him? The Catskills? The Lower Atlas? Am I supposed to be there, too, so I can get closer to *my* needs? I'm close enough to them now. I'm sitting beside you. I'm married to you."

"You *are* married to me." She actually gasped then and sobbed, then gasped again and squeezed my hand harder than anybody'd ever squeezed it, and shook her head from side to side, so tears dashed onto my cheek. It was as if we were both crying. Though why I would've been crying, I don't know, since I should've been howling again, shouting, waving my bloody fists in the air as the earth split open. Inasmuch as, with her certainty dawning like a new alien sun, split it did, where it stays split to this day.

I'LL MAKE the rest short, though it's not sweet.

I buttoned the buttons on my moral investigator's labcoat and got busy with the program. Sally said she'd be willing to invite Wally down to Sea-Cliff—either to a rental she would arrange for him (using who as agent?), or to our house, where he could put up in one of the two guest rooms for the short time he'd be here. The oddest things can be made to seem plausible by insisting they are. Remember Huxley on Einstein. Remember the Trojan Horse. Or else, Sally said, she and he could "go away somewhere" (the Rif, the Pampas, the Silk Road to Cathay). They wouldn't be "together," of course, more like brother and sister having a *wander*, during which crucial period they'd perform what few in their situation (how many are in that situation?) could hope to perform: a putting to rest, an airing, a re-examination of old love allowed to wither and die, saying the unsayable, feeling the unpermitted, reconciling paths not taken and those taken. Cleanse and heal, come back stronger. Come back to me. Yes, there might be some crying, some shouting, some laughter, some hugging, some crisp slappings across the face. But it would be "within a context," and in "real time," or some such nonsense, and all those decades would be drained of their sour water, rolled up and put away like a late-autumn garden hose, never to leave the garage again. In other words, it *was* a "good thing" (if not for everybody)—life's mystery dramatized, all is artifice, connected boxes, etc., etc., etc.

Interesting. I thought it was all pretty interesting. A true experiment in knowing another person—me knowing her, *not* her knowing Wally, who I didn't give a shit about. A revealing frame to put on Sally's life and into which I could see, since this was between Sally and me—which I still think is true. Can you always tell a snake from a garden hose?

The Silk Road strategy didn't appeal to me, for obvious reasons. I suggested (these things *do* happen) that we invite The Wall down for a week (or less). He could bivouac upstairs, set out all his toilet articles in the guest's bath. We could meet the way I used to meet Ann's previous, now dead, architect husband, Charley O'Dell—with stiffened civility, frozen-smile, hands-in-pockets mildness that only now and then sprang into psychotic dislike, with biting words that wounded and the threat of physical violence.

I could do better. I had nothing to fear from an *ex*-dead man. I'd tin his ears about the real estate business, let him experience Mike Mahoney, talk over the election, the Cubs, the polar ice cap, the Middle East. Though mostly I'd just stay the hell away from him, fish the Hendrickson hatch at the Red Man Club, spend a day with Clarissa and Cookie in Gotham, test-drive new Lexuses, sell a house or two—whatever it took, while the two of them did what they needed to do to get that moldy old hose put away on the garage nail of the past tense.

On the twenty-ninth of May, Wally "the Weasel," as he was known in military school, my wife's quasi-husband, father of her two maniac children, Viet vet, combat casualty, free-lance amnesiac, cut-and-run artist *par excellence*, heir to a sizable North Shore fortune, meek arborist, unmourned former dead man and big-time agent of misrule—my enemy—*this* Wally Caldwell entered my peaceful house on the Jersey Shore to work his particular dark magic on us all.

Clarissa and Cookie came down for the arrival to give moral

support. Clarissa, who was still wearing a tiny diamond nostril stud (since jettisoned), felt it was an "interesting" experiment in the extended-family concept, but basically nonsensical, that something was "wrong" with Sally and that I needed to keep my "boundaries" clear and that they (being Harvard lesbians) knew all about boundaries—or something to that effect.

Sally became convulsively nervous, oversensitive and irritable as the hour of Wally's arrival neared (I affected calm to show I didn't care). She snapped at Clarissa, snapped at me, had to be talked to by Cookie. She smoked several cigarettes (the first time in twenty years), drank a double martini at ten o'clock in the morning, changed her clothes three times, then stood out on the deck, sporting stiff white sailcloth trousers, new French espadrilles, a blue-and-white middy blouse and extremely dark sunglasses. All was a calculated livery betokening casual, welcoming resolution and sunny invulnerability, depicting a life so happy, invested, entitled, entrenched, comprehended, spiritual and history-laden that Wally would take a quick peek at the whole polished array—house, beach, lesbian kids, damnable husband, unreachable lemony ex-wife, then hop back in his cab and start the long journey back to Mull.

I will concede that the real Wally, the portly, thin-lipped, timidly smiling, gray-toothed, small-eyed, suitcase-carrying, thick-fingered bullock who struggled out of the Newark Yellow Cab, didn't seem a vast challenge to my or anyone's sense of permanence. I had perfect no-recollection of him from forty years ago and felt strangely, warmly (wrongly) welcoming toward him, the way you'd feel about a big, soft-hearted PFC in a Fifties war movie, who you know is going to be picked off by a Kraut sniper in the first thirty minutes. Wally had on his green worn-smooth corduroys—though it was already summery and he was sweltering—a faded, earthy-smelling purple cardy over a green-and-ginger rugger shirt, under which his hod-carrier belly tussled for freedom. He wore heavy gray woolen socks, no hat and the previously mentioned smelly but not mud-spackled Barbour from his days nerdling about the gorse and rank topsoil of his adopted island paradise.

He brought with him a bottle of twenty-year-old Glen Matoon and a box of Cohiba *Robustos*—for me. I still have the cigars at the office and occasionally consider smoking one as a joke, though it'd probably explode. He also brought—for Sally—a strange assortment of Scottish cooking herbs he'd obviously gotten for his parents at the Glasgow airport plus a tin of short-cakes for "the house." He was at least six feet two, newly beard-less and nearly bald, weighed a fair seventeen stone and spoke English in a halting, swallowing, slightly high-pitched semi-brogue with a vocabulary straight out of the Seventies U.S. He said Chicago Land, as in "We left Chicago Land at the crack of dawn." And he said "super," as in "We had some super tickets to Wrigley." And he said "z's," as in "I copped some righteous z's on the plane." And he said "GB," as in "I banged down a GB" (a gut bomb) "before we left Chicago Land, and it tasted super."

He was, this once-dead Wally, not the strangest concoction of *Homo sapiens* genetic material ever presented to me (Mike Mahoney has retired that jersey number), but he was certainly the most complexly pathetic and ill-starred—a strangely wide-eyed, positive-outlook type, ill at ease and conspicuous in his lumpy flesh, but also strangely serene and on occasion pompous and ribald, like the down-state SAE he was back when life was simpler. How he made it in Mull is a mystery.

Needless to say, I loathed him (warm feelings aside), couldn't comprehend how anybody who could love me could ever have loved Wally, and wanted him out of the house the second he was in it. We shook hands limply, in the manner of a cold prisoner exchange on the Potsdam bridge. I stared. He averted his small eyes, so I couldn't feel good about being insincerely nice to him and show Sally this was worthy of my patience—which I know she hoped.

I spoke tersely, idiotically. "Welcome to Sea-Clift, and to our home," which I didn't mean. He said something about "whole layout's . . . super," and that he was "chuffed" to be here. Clarissa instantly took me by the crook of my elbow and led me out to the road in front of the house, where we stood without speaking for a while in the thick spring breeze that stirred the vivid shore-line vegetation toward Asbury Park and points north. Dust from the town front-loader far up the beach, its yellow lights flashing, indicated civic efforts to relocate mounds of sand that had drifted over the promenade during the winter. We were making ready for Memorial Day.

Arthur Glück's dog, Poot, part Beagle, part Spitz, that looks like a dog from ancient Egypt and scavenges everyone's house (except the Feensters'), waited in the middle of Poincinet Road, staring at Clarissa and me as though it was clear even to him that something very wrong was underway, since events had driven all the humans out to the road in the morning, where it was his turf, his time, and where he knew how things worked.

Clarissa let go of my arm and just sat down in the middle of the sandy roadway—her gesture for separating us two from Sally and Wally, who'd already by fits and starts disappeared inside the house, though the door was left open. No one would've been driving down the road. Still, her gesture was a stagy, unplanned one I appreciated, even though it made me nervous and I wished she'd get up. Cookie, wise girl, had decided on a walk up the beach. I should have gone with her.

"You're a *way* too tolerant dude," Clarissa said casually, keeping her seat in the road, leaning back on one elbow and shielding her eyes from the noon-time sun. I felt even more awkward because of where she was and what she wasn't feeling. "Which isn't to say Mr. Wally isn't pretty much a *Wind in the Willows* kind of character in need of a good ass-kicking. It's pretty zen of you. In the girl community, this wouldn't stand up." Clarissa's nose stud sparkled in the brassy light, and made me touch my nose, as though I had one in mine. She was wearing tissue-thin Italian sandals that exhibited her long tanned feet and ankles, and a pair of cream-colored Italian harem pants with a matching tank top that showed her shoulders. She was like a mirage, languorous but animated.

"I'm not zen at all." Mike's hooded-eye, scrunched face appeared in my mind like one of the Pep Boys. He knew nothing of this day's events, but definitely would've approved of what I was doing.

"Don't you feel strange? It's pretty strange to have old Wally down here for a visit." Clarissa wrinkled her nose and squinted up at me as if I was the rarest of vanishing species.

"I had a good picture in my mind of how this would all happen," I said. "But now that he's here, I can't remember it." I looked at the house, my house, felt stupid being out in my road. "I think that's very human, though, to expect something and then have the expected event supplant the expectation. That's interesting."

"Yep," Clarissa said.

What I didn't say was even odder. That while I felt officially pissed off and deeply offended, I was not feeling that this fiasco was a real fiasco, or that my life was fucked up, or that any of the important things I hoped to do before I was sixty were going to be impossible to do. In other words, I felt tumult, but I also felt calm, and that I'd probably feel different again in another thirty minutes—which is why I don't pay fullest attention to how I feel at any given moment. If I'd told this to Clarissa, she would've thought I was suffering from stress-induced aphasia, or maybe having a stroke. Maybe I was. But what I knew was that you're stuck with yourself most of the time. Best make the most of it.

Clarissa struggled onto her feet like a kid at school after recess. She dusted off the seat of her pants and gave her hair a shake. It would've been a perfect day for a flight to Flint. Maybe by cocktail hour all would be settled, Wally packed off in another yellow taxi and happy to be, life resumable back at the Salty Dog stage, where I'd departed it a few days before.

"Is Sally a second child?" We were still standing in the middle of the road, as though expecting something. I was taking pleasure in the flashing yellow light of the town's front-loader, a half mile up the beach.

"She had a brother who died."

"I'm trying to be sympathetic to her. Second children have a hard time getting what they need. I'm a second child."

"You're a third child. You had a brother who died when you were little." Clarissa has scant memory of her dead brother and no patience with trying to feel what she doesn't really feel. Me, I feel like I'm Ralph's earthly ombudsman and facilitator to the living. It is my secret self. I give (mostly) silent witness.

"That's right." She was briefly pensive then, in deference to "my loss," which was her loss but different. "If Mom came back from the dead, would you invite her over for a visit?"

"Your mother's not dead," I said irritably. "She's living in Haddam."

"Divorce is kind of like death, though, isn't it? Three moves equal a death. A divorce equals probably three-quarters of a death."

"In some ways. It never ends." And how would this day rate, I wondered. Six-sixteenths of a death? About the same for Sally.

And who cared about The Wall? Morbid dimness had always complicated his life, landing him over and over in strange situations, and not knowing what to do about it.

"I'm just trying to distract you," Clarissa said. "And humor you." She rehooked her arm through mine and bumped me with her girl-athlete's shoulder. She smelled of shampoo and clean sweat. The way you'd want your daughter to smell. "Maybe you should keep a diary."

"I'll commit suicide before I keep a fucking diary. Diaries are for weaklings and old queer professors. Which I'm not."

"Okay," she said. She was never sensitive to insensitive language. We were starting to stroll up Poincinet Road, past the fronts of my neighbors' houses—all similarly handsome board-and-batten edifices with green hydrangeas ready to sprout their showy blooms. Ahead, where our newer settlement stopped and where the old mansions had been blown away, there was open, sparsely populated beach and grass and sea. I could see a tiny ant in the hazy distance. It was Cookie. Poot, the Egyptian dog, had found her and was trotting along.

"I thought life isn't supposed to be like this when you love someone and they love you," I said to Clarissa, more speculative than I felt. "That intelligence won't get you very far. That's your father's perspective."

"I knew that." She kicked road sand with her rubied toenail. Already things with her and Cookie were wearing through. I couldn't have known, but she could. "What do you think's gonna happen?"

"With Sally and Wally?" I gave myself a moment to wonder, letting sea breeze make my ears feel wiggly, my view of the beach grown purposefully wide and generous. Such views are supposedly good for the optic muscle, and the soul. Something seemed to be riding on what I said, as if I was the cause of whatever happened to us all. "I can guess," I said breezily, "but I tend to guess bad outcomes. Most horses don't win races. Most dogs finally bite you." I smiled. I felt foolish in the situation I was in.

"Let's hear it anyway," Clarissa said. "It's good to pre-vision things."

"Well. I think Wally'll stay around a few days. I'll forget exactly why I don't like him. We'll talk a lot about real estate and spruce trees. We'll be like conventioneers in town from Iowa.

Men always do that. Sally'll get sick of us. But then by accident, I'll walk into a room where they are, and they'll immediately shut up some highly personal conversation. Maybe I'll catch them kissing and order Wally out of the house. After which, Sally'll be miserable and tell me she has to go live with him."

Cookie was waving to us from out on the beach, waving a stick that Poot expected her to throw. I waved back.

Clarissa shook her head, scratched into her thick hair and looked at me with annoyance, her pretty mouth-corners fattened in disapproval. "Do you really believe that?"

"It's what anybody'd think. It's what Ann Landers would tell you—if she isn't dead."

"You're crazy-hazy," she said and punched me too hard on the shoulder, as if a slug in the arm would cure me. "You don't know women very well, which isn't news, I guess."

Cookie's clear, happy voice was already talking over the distance, telling something she'd seen out in the ocean—a shark's fin, a dolphin's tail, a whale's geyser—something the dog had gone after, trusting his Egyptian ancestry against impossible odds. "I don't believe it," Cookie said gaily. "You guys. You should've seen it. I wish you could've seen."

I wouldn't have been wrong about Sally, even not knowing women very well, and never having said I did. I'd always been happy to know and like them one at a time. But about some things, even men can't be wrong.

WALLY WAS in my house in Sea-Clift for five uncomfortable days. I tried to go about my diurnal duties, spending time early-to-late in the office where I had summer renters arriving, plumbers and carpenters and cleaning crews and yard-maintenance personnel to dispatch and lightly supervise. I sold a house on the bay side of Sea-Clift, took a bid on but failed to sell another. Mike sold two rental houses. He and I drove to Bay Head to inspect an old rococo movie house, the Rivoli Shore—where Houdini had made himself disappear in 1910. Maybe we wanted to buy it, find somebody to run it, go into limited partnership with a local Amvets group, using state preservation money and turn it into a World War II museum. We passed.

Normally, I'd have been home for lunch, but in grudging

deference to what was going on in my house, I ate glutinous woodsman's casserole one day, Welsh rarebit another, ham and green beans a third at the Commodore's table at the Yacht Club, where I'm a non-boating member. Two times, I ate at Neptune's Daily Catch, where I had the calzone, flirted with the waitress, then spent the afternoon at my desk, burping and thinking philosophically about acid reflux and how it eats potholes in your throat. I explained to Mike that Sally was having an "old relative" to visit, though another time I said an "old friend," which he noticed, so he knew something was weird.

Each evening I went home, tired and ready for a renewing cocktail, supper and an early-to-bed. Wally was most times in the living room reading *Newsweek*, or on the deck with my binoculars, or in the kitchen loading up a dagwood or outside having a disapproving look at the arborvitae and hydrangeas or staring out at the shorebirds. Sally was almost never in sight when Wally was, leaving the impression that whatever they were carrying on between them during the day and my absence—hugging, face slapping, laughing that ended in tears—was all pretty trying, and I wouldn't like seeing her face then, and in any case she needed to recover from it.

Toward Wally—who'd taken to wearing gray leisure-attire leather shorts that exposed his pasty bulldog calves above thick black ankle brogues and another rugby shirt, this time with *Mackays* printed on front—toward Wally, I dealt entirely in "So, okay, howzit goin'?" "Did you get to do some walking?" "Are they feeding you enough in here?" "Thought of going for a swim?" And to me, Wally—large, sour earth-smelling, full-cheeked, with a tired, timid smile I disliked—toward me, Wally dealt in "Yep." "Super." "Oh yeah, hiked up to the burger palace." "Great spread here, looverly, looverly."

I certainly didn't know what the hell any of us were doing—though who would? If you'd told me the two of them never so much as spoke, or went for polka lessons, or read the *I Ching* together, or shot heroin, I'd have had to believe it. Was it, I wondered, that everything was just too awkward, too revealing, too anxious-making, too upsetting, too embarrassing, too intimidating, too intrusive or just too private to exhibit in front of me—the husband, the patient householder, the rate-payer, the sandwich-bread buyer? And also now a stranger?

Sally made dinner for us all three on night two. A favorite—lamb chops, Cajun tomatoes and creamed pearl onions. This was not the worst dinner I ever attended, although conceivably it was the worst in my own house. Sally was nervous and too smiley, her limp worsening notably. She cooked the lamb chops too long, which made her mad at me. Wally said his was "astounding" and ate like a horse. I had three stout martinis and observed the dinner was "perfect, if not astounding." And, as I'd predicted, I forgot more or less who Wally was, let myself act like he was one or the other of Sally's cousins, talked at length about the history of Sea-Clift, how it had been founded in the Twenties by upstart Philadelphia real estate profiteers as a summer resort for middle-middle citizens from the City of Brotherly Love, how its basic populace and value system—Italians with moderate Democratic leanings—hadn't changed since the early days, except in the Nineties, when well-heeled Gothamites with Republican preferences who couldn't afford Bridgehampton or Spring Lake started buying up land from the first settler's ancestors, who pretty quick wised up and started holding on to things. "Okay. Sure, sure," Wally said, mouth full of whatever, though he also said "thas brillian" a few times when nothing was brilliant, which made me hate him worse and made Sally get up and go to bed without saying good night.

In bed each night with Sally returned—though asleep when her head hit the pillow—I lay awake and listened to Wally's human noises across in "his" room. He played the radio—not loud—tuned to an all-news station that occasionally made him chuckle. He took long, forceful pisses into his toilet to let off the lager he drank at dinner. He produced a cannonade of burps, followed by a word of demure apology to no one: "Oh, goodness, who let that go?" He walked around heavily in his sock feet, yawned in a high-pitched keening sound that only a man used to living alone ever makes. He did some sort of brief grunting calisthenics, presumably on the floor, then plopped into bed and set up an amazing lion's den of snarfling-snoring that forced me to flatten my head between pillows, so that I woke up in the morning with my eyes smarting, my neck sore and both hands numb as death.

During the five days of Wally's visit, I twice asked Sally how things were going. The first time—this was two seconds before she fell into sleep, leaving me in bed listening to stertorous Wally—she said, "Fine. I'm glad I'm doing this. You're magnificent to put up with it. I'm sorry I'm cranky. . . ." *Zzzzzzz.* Magnificent. She had never before referred to me as magnificent, even in my best early days.

The other time I asked, we were seated across the circular glass-topped breakfast table. Wally was still upstairs sawing logs. I was heading off to the Realty-Wise office. It was day three. We hadn't said much about anything in the daylight. To freshen the air, I said, "You're not going to leave me for Wally, are you?" I gave her a big smirking grin and stood up, napkin in hand. To which she answered, looking up, plainly dismayed, "I don't think so." Then she stared out at the ocean, on which a white boat full of day-fishermen sat anchored a quarter mile offshore, their short poles bristling off one side, their boat tipped, all happy anglers, hearts set on a flounder or a shark. They were probably Japanese. Something she noticed when she saw them may have offered solace.

But "I don't think so"? No grateful smile, no wink, no rum mouth pulled to signal no worries, no way, no dice. "I don't think so" was not an answer Ann Landers would've considered insignificant. "Dear Franky in the Garden State, I'd lock up the silverware if I were you, boy-o. You've got a rough intruder in your midst. You need to do some night-time sentry duty on your marriage bed. Condition red, Fred."

WALLY GAVE no evidence of thinking himself a rough intruder or a devious conniver after my happiness. In spite of his strange splintered, half North-Shore-fatty, half earnest-blinking-Scots-gardener persona (a veteran stage actor playing Falstaff with an Alabama accent), Wally did his seeming best to spend his days in a manner that did least harm. He always smiled when he saw me. He occasionally wanted to talk about beach erosion. He advised me to put more aluminum sulfate on my hydrangeas to make the color last. Otherwise he stayed out of sight much of the time. And I now believe, though no one's told me, that Sally had actually forced him to come: to suffer penance, to show him that abandonment had worked out well for her, to embarrass the shit out of him, to confuse him, to make him miss her miserably and make me seem his superior—plus darker reasons I assume are involved in everything most of us do and that there's no use thinking about.

But what else was she supposed to do? How else to address past and loss? Was there an approved mechanism for redressing such an affront besides blunt instinct? What other kind of synergy reconciles a loss so great—and so weird? It's true I might've approached it differently. But sometimes you just have to wing it.

Which explains my own odd conduct, my fatal empathy (I guess), and even Wally's attempts to be stolidly, unpretentiously present, subjecting himself to whatever penitent paces Sally put him through in the daylight, essaying to be cordial, taking interest in the flora and fauna and in me at cocktail hour, eating and drinking his scuppers over, burping and snorting like a draft horse in his room at night, then making an effort to get his sleep in anticipation of the next day's trials.

He and I never talked about "the absence" (which Sally said was his name for being gone for nearly thirty years) or anything related to their kids, his parents, his other life and lives (though of course he and Sally might've). We never talked about when he might be leaving or how he was experiencing life in my house. Never talked about the future—his or Sally's or mine. We never talked about the presidential election, since that had a root system that could lead to sensitive subjects—morality, dubious ethics, uncertain outcomes and also plainly bad outcomes. I wanted to keep it clear that he was never for one instant welcome in my house, and that I pervasively did not like him. I don't know what he thought or how he truly felt, only how he *was* in his conduct, which wasn't that bad and, in fact, evidenced a small, unformed nobility, although heavy-bellied and gooberish. I did my best. And maybe he did his. I picked up some interesting tips about soil salinity and its effect on the flowering properties of seashore flora, learned some naturopathic strategies for combating the Asian Long-Horned Beetle. Wally heard my theories for combating sticker shock and enhancing curb appeal, got some insider dope about the second-home market and how it's always wedded to Wall Street. There was a moment when I even thought I *did* remember him from eons ago. But that moment vanished when I thought of him together with Sally on the beach while I was alone eating tough, frozen woodsman's casserole at the Yacht Club. In the truest sense, we didn't get anywhere with each other because we didn't want to. Men generally are better at this kind of edgy, pointless armistice than women. It's genetic and relates to our hoary history of mortal combat, and to knowing that most of life doesn't usually rise to that level of gravity but still is important. I'm not sure it's to our credit.

WALLY EVENTUALLY departed on the morning of day five. Sally said he was going, and I made it my business to get the hell out of the house at daybreak and ended up snoozing at my desk until Mike arrived at eight and acted worried about me. I hung around the office the rest of the morning, catching cold calls, running credit checks on new rental clients and talking to Clarissa in Gotham. She'd called every day and tried to liven things up by referring to Wally as "Dildo" and "Wal-Fart" and "Mr. Wall Socket," and saying he reminded her of her brother (which is both true and not true) and that maybe the two of them could be friends because they're "both so fucking weird."

Then I drove home, where Sally kissed me and hugged me when I walked in the door, as if I'd been away on a long journey. She looked pale and drained—not like somebody who'd been crying, but like somebody who might've been on a roadside when two speeding cars or two train engines or two jet airplanes collided in front of her. She said she was sorry about the whole week, knew it had taken a toll on all of us, but probably mostly me (which wasn't true), that Wally would never again come into the house, even though he'd asked her to thank me for letting him "visit," and even though having him here, as awful as it was, had served some "very positive purposes" that would never have gotten served any other way. She said she loved me and that she wanted to make love right then, in the living room on the suede couch, where this had all started. But because the meter reader knocked at the front door and Poot started barking at him out in the road, we moved—naked as two Bushmen—up to the bedroom.

Next day I assumed—believed—matters would begin shifting back toward normal. I wanted us to drive over to the Red Man

Club for an outing of fishing, fiddlehead hunting and a trek along the Pequest to seek out Sampson's Warbler pairs that nest in our woods and nowhere else in New Jersey. I intended to put in an order for a new Lexus at Sea Girt Imports—a surprise for Sally's birthday in three weeks. I'd already made a trip up there to consult color charts and take a test drive.

Sally, though, seemed still pale and drained on Saturday, so that I canceled the Red Man Club and (thank goodness) didn't get around to the Lexus.

She stayed in bed all day, as if she herself had been on a long and arduous journey. Though the journey that had left her depleted had left me exhilarated and abuzz, my head full of plans and vivid imaginings, the way somebody'd feel who'd gotten happy news from the lab, a shadow on an X ray that proved to be nothing, bone marrow that "took." While she rested, I drove myself over to the movies at the Ocean County Mall and saw *Charlie's Angels*, then bought lobsters on the way home and cooked them for dinner—though Sally barely rallied to work on hers, while I demolished mine.

She went to bed early again—after I asked if maybe she should call Blumberg on Monday and schedule a work-up. Maybe she was anemic. She said she would, then went to sleep at nine and slept twelve hours, emerging downstairs into the kitchen Sunday morning, weak-eyed, sallow and sunk-shouldered—where I was sitting, eating a pink grapefruit and reading about the Lakers in the *Times*—to tell me she was leaving me to live with Wally in Mull, and that she'd decided it was worse to let someone you love be alone forever than to be with someone (me!) who didn't need her all that much, even though she knew I loved her and she loved me. This is when she said things about the "circum-stances" and about importance. But to this day, I don't under-stand the calculus, though it has a lot in common with other things people do.

She was wearing an old-fashioned lilac sateen peignoir set with pink ribbonry stitched around the jacket collar. She was thin-armed, bare-legged, her skin wan and blotchy from sleep, her eyes colorless in their glacial blue. She was barefoot, a sign of primal resolution. She blinked at me as if sending me a message in Morse code: Good-bye, good-bye, good-bye.

Oh, I protested. May it not be said I failed of ardor at that crucial moment (the past, critics have attested, seems settled and melancholy, but I was boisterous in that present). I was, by turns, disbelieving, shocked, angry, tricked-feeling, humiliated, gullible and stupid. I became analytical, accusatory, revisionist, self-justifying, self-abnegating and inventive of better scenarios than being abandoned. Patiently (I wasn't truly patient; I wanted to slit Wally open like a lumpy feed sack) and lovingly (which I surely was), I testified that I needed her the way hydrogen needs oxygen—she should know that, had known it for years. If *she* needed time—with Wally, in Mull—I could understand. I lied that I found it all "interesting," although I admitted it didn't make me happy—which wasn't a lie. She should go there and do that. Hang out. Plant little trees in little holes. Go native. Act married. Talk, slap, hug, giggle, groan, cry.

But come home!

I'd tear down conventional boundaries if we could just keep an understanding alive. Did I say beg? I begged. I already said I cried (something Clarissa chided me for). To which Sally said, shoulders slack, eyes lowered, slender hands clasped on the table top, her little finger lightly touching the covered Quimper butter dish she at one time had felt great affection for, and that I subsequently winged across the room and to death by smithereens, "I think I have to make this permanent, sweetheart. Even if I regret it and later come crying to you, and you're with some other woman, and won't talk to me, and my life is lost. I have to."

Strange grasp on "permanent," I thought, though my eyes burbled with tears. "It's not like we're dealing with hard kernels of truth here," I said pitiably. "This is all pretty discretionary, if you ask me."

"No," she said, which is when she took her wedding ring off and laid it on the glass pane of the table top, causing a hard little *tap* I'll never, ever, forget, even if she comes back.

"This is so terrible," I said in full cry. I wanted to howl like a dog.

"I know."

"Do you love Wally more than you love me?"

She shook her head in a way that made her face appear famished and exhausted, though she couldn't look at me, just at the ring she'd a moment before relinquished. "I don't know that I love him at all."

"Then what the fuck!" I shouted. "Can you just *do* this?"

"I don't think I can't do it," Sally—my wife—said. And essentially that was that. Double negative makes a positive. She was gone by cocktail hour, which I observed alone.

SOMEWHERE ONCE I read that harsh words are all alike. You can make them up and be right. The same is true of explanations. I never caught them smooching. Probably they didn't smooch. Neither did they stop mid-sentence in an intimate moment just when I strode through a door (I never strode through any without whistling a happy tune first). Sally and I never visited a counselor to hash out problems, or ever endured any serious arguments. There wasn't time before she left. Apart from when I first knew Sally, Wally had never been a feature of our daily converse. Everybody has their casualties; we get used to them like old photographs we glance at but keep in a trunk. To understand it all in the way we understand other things, I would have to make an explanation up. The facts, as I knew them, didn't say enough.

For the first week after Sally left, I cried (for myself) and brooded (about myself) as one would cry and brood upon realizing that marriage to oneself probably hadn't been so great; that I maybe wasn't *so* good in bed—or anywhere—or wasn't good at intimacy or sharing or listening. My *completelys*, my *I love yous*, my *my darlings*, my *forevers* weighed less than standard issue, and I wasn't such an interesting husband, in spite of believing I was a very good and interesting husband. Sally, possibly, was unhappy when I thought she was ecstatic. Any person—especially a realtor—would wonder about these post-no-sale issues just as a means of determining what new homework he was now required to do.

What I decided was that I may never have seemed to Sally to be "all in," but that "all in" is what I goddamn was. Always. No matter how I felt or described my feelings. Anything more "all in" than me was just a fantasy of the perfidious sort manufactured by the American Psychiatrists Association, that Sisyphus of trade groups, to keep the customers coming back.

Bullshit, in other words.

I *was* intimate. I *was* as amorous and passionate as the traffic would bear. I *was* interesting. I *was* kind. I *was* generous. I *was* forbearing. I *was* funny (since that's so goddamned important). I shared whatever could stand to be shared (and not everything can). Women both hate and love weakness in men, and I'd had positive feedback to think I was weak in the right ways and not in the wrong. Of course, I wasn't perfect at any of these human skills, having never thought I *had* to be. In the fine print on the boilerplate second-marriage license, it should read: "Signatories consent neither has to be perfect." I did fine as a husband. Fine.

Which didn't mean Sally had to be big-H happy or do anything except what she wanted to do. We're only talking about explanations here, and whether anything's my fault. It was. And it wasn't.

My personal view is that Sally got caught unawares in the great, deep and confusing eddy of contingency, which has other contingency streams running into it, some visible, some too deep-coursing below the surface to know about. One stream was: That just as I was enjoying the rich benefits of the Permanent Period—no fear of future, life not ruinable, the past generalized to a pleasant pinkish blur—*she* began, in spite of what she might've said, to fear permanence, to fear no longer *becoming*, to dread a life that couldn't be trashed and squandered. Put simply, she wasn't prepared to be like me—a natural state that marriage ought to accommodate and make survivable, as one partner lives the Permanent Period like a communicant lives in a state of grace, while the other does whatever the hell she wants.

Only along galumphs Wally, turf-stained, resolutely unhandsome, vaguely clueless from his years in the grave (i.e., Scotland). And suddenly one of the prime selling points of second marriage—minimalization of the past—becomes not such a selling point. First marriages have too much past clanking along behind; but second ones may have too little, and so lack ballast.

Heavy-footed, un-nuanced, burping, yerping Wally may have reminded Sally there was a past that couldn't be generalized, and that she had unfinished business in the last century and couldn't reason it away in the jolly manner that I'd reasoned myself into a late-in-life marriage and lived happily by its easy-does-it house rules. (Millennium angst, if it's anything, is fear of the past, not the future.) In fact, with Wally both behind and also suddenly lumped in front, it's good odds Sally never experienced the

Permanent Period, and so had no choice but to hand me her wedding ring like I was a layaway clerk at Zales and push herself out of the eddy of our life and take the current wherever it flowed.

Though I'll admit that even on this day, the eve of Turkey Day, I'm no longer so blue about Sally's absence, as once I was. I don't feature myself living alone forever, just as I wouldn't concede to staying a realtor forever and mostly tend to think of life itself as a made-up thing composed of today, maybe tomorrow and probably not the next day, with as little of the past added in as possible. I feel, in fact, a goodly tincture of regret for Sally. Because, even though I believe her sojourn on Mull will not last so long, by re-choosing Wally she has embraced the impossible, inaccessible past, and by doing so has risked or even exhausted an extremely useful longing—possibly her most important one, the one she's made good use of these years to fuel her present, where I have found a place. This is why the dead should stay dead and why in time the land lies smooth all around them.

THIS MORNING, I've scheduled the 10:15 showing at my listing at 61 Surf Road, and following that, at 12:30, a weeks-planned meet-up in Asbury Park with Wade Arcenault, my friend from years back, to attend a hotel implosion—the hotel in question being the elegant old Queen Regent Arms, remnant of the stately elephants from the Twenties, surrendering at last to the forces of progress (a high-end condo development). Wade and I have been to two other implosions this fall, in Ventnor and Camden, and each of us finds them enjoyable, although for different reasons. Wade, I think, just likes big explosions and the controlled devastation that follows. In his young life, he was an engineer, and watching things blow up is his way of coping with being now in his eighties, and of fortifying his belief that the past crumbles and that staring loss in the face is the main requirement for living out our allotment (this is as spiritual as engineers get). On the other hand, I'm gratified by the idea of an orderly succession manifesting our universal need to remain adaptable through time, a lesson for which cancer is the teacher, though my reason may not finally be any different from Wade's. In any case, going along with Wade injects an interesting and unusual centerpiece activity into the course of my day, one that gives it shape and content but won't wear me out, since at the end I'll have Paul to contend with. (Business itself, of course, is the very best at offering solid, life-structuring agendas, and business days are always better than wan weekends, and are hands-down better than gaping, ghostly holidays that Americans all claim to love—but I don't, since these days can turn long, dread-prone and worse.)

This morning, however, has already turned at least semi-eventful. Up and dressed by 8:30, I spent a useful half hour in my home office going over listing sheets for the Surf Road property, followed by a browse through the *Asbury Press*, surveying the "By Owner" offerings, estate auctions, "New Arrivals" and "Deaths," all of which can be fruitful, if sometimes disheartening. The *Press* reported on the Peter Pan tour-bus accident Mike and I saw yesterday—three lives "eclipsed," all Chinese-American females on an Atlantic City gaming holiday from their restaurant jobs on Canal Street, Gotham. Others were injured but lived.

The *Press* also reported that the presumptive (and devious) Vice-President-in-waiting for the Republicans has suffered a mild heart trembler, and farther down the page that the device that exploded at Haddam Doctors took the life of a security guard named Natherial Lewis, forty-eight—which startled me. Natherial is/was the uncle of young Scooter Lewis, who chauffeured Ernie McAuliffe to his resting ground yesterday, and so must have known nothing of his own loss at the time, although today he's thinking on death with new realities installed. I knew Natherial when he himself was a young man. Several times when I was at Lauren-Schwindell, I employed him to retrieve wayward FOR SALE signs after Halloween pranksters had swiped them from front yards and set them up in front of area churches or their divorced parents' condos. Nate always thought it was funny. I'll phone in flowers through Lloyd Mangum, who'll be overseeing. New Jersey is a small place, finally.

When I looked up from my paper, though, and out the window—my home office gives onto the front, and down Poincinet Road toward the state park where Route 35 ends and a few old seasonal businesses are in sight (a chowder house, the Sinker Swim Doughnut)—I couldn't stop remembering something Clarissa was talking about on our after-Halloween beach walk: That she felt strangely insulated from contemporary goings on. Which, as I've said before, is also true for me. I watch CNN every night, but never afterward think much about anything I see—even the election, as stupid as it is. I've come to loathe most sports, which I used to love—a loss I attribute to having seen the same things over and over again too many times. Only death-row stories and sumo wrestling (narrated in Japanese) can keep me at the TV longer than ten minutes. My bedside table, as I've said, has novels and biographies I've read thirty pages into but can't tell you much about. A couple of weeks ago, I decided I'd write a letter to President Clinton—the opposite of Marguerite's letter—detailing the sorry state of national affairs (much of it his fault), suggesting he'd be wise to nationalize the Guard and protect the future of the Republic with regard to the "rogue state of Florida." But I didn't finish it and put it in a drawer, since it seemed to me the work of a crank that would've earned me a visit from the FBI.

But what I wondered, at my desk with a copy of the *Asbury Press*, gazing out my window, was—it was a kind of minor revelation: Am I not just feeling what plenty of other humans feel all the time but don't pay any attention to? People with no worrisome follow-up tests next Wednesday, civically alert citizens, members of PA/Cs, schmoes who haven't lost their spouses to a memory of love lost? And if so, do I even have any excuse to feel insulated? At the end of this reverie, I took out my half-written letter to the President and threw it in the trash and promised myself to write a better one, posing more constructive questions I can work on in the meantime—all in an effort to seem less like a nutter and a complainer, and to do whatever the hell we're all supposed to do to display we're responsible and doing our best to make life better.

I HAD SEVERAL calls waiting before setting off for Surf Road. One from the Eat No Evil people in Mantoloking, wanting to know if gluten-free, no-salt bread in the organic turkey stuffing would be desired, or if the standard organic Saskatchewan spelt was okay. And could they come at 1:45 instead of 2:00? Another was from Wade, a nervous-nelly call to be sure we're meeting at the Fuddruckers at Exit 102 on the Parkway at 12:30, and to say that he was bringing his own sandwich which he can eat while the Queen Regent comes down (this needed no answer). Another, which I also didn't answer, was from Mike, apologizing for engaging in the "non-virtuous action of senseless speech" last night—which he certainly did—and accusing himself of covetousness, which I take as a sign that he's maybe saying no to the Montmorency spaghetti and that I can keep him as a trusted employee and house-selling house-a-fire.

The fourth call, however, was from Ann, and strummed an ominous minor bass chord in my chest as it bespoke fresh assumptions I don't share but may have seemed to share at the end of a long and wearisome day.

"It's easier to leave this as a message than to say it to you,

Frank." My name again. Years ago, when we were married, Ann used to call me "Tootsie," which embarrassed me in front of people, and then for a while she called me "Satch"—for private personal reasons—this being before "shit-heel" finally won the day. "I didn't really think ahead much about what I said tonight. I just blurted it. But it still seems right to me. You acted completely stunned. I'm sure I scared you, which I'm sorry about. I certainly don't have to come to Thanksgiving dinner. You were just sweet to ask. You were very good tonight, by the way, the best I can remember you—to me, anyway." Cancer obviously agrees with me. "Charley knew what a good man you were, and said so, though probably not to you." Definitely not. "He always thought I'd have been happier married to you than to him. But you can't recalculate, I guess. We act on so many things we don't know very much about, don't you think? It's no wonder we're all a little fucked up—as they say in Grosse Pointe. Anyway, the idea of underlying causes to things has started to oppress me. I didn't tell you, did I, that I considered attending the seminary after Charley died. It was probably why I came back here. Then I decided religion was just about underlying causes, things that are hidden and have to be treated like secrets all the time. And I—" *Click.* Time was up.

I sat at my desk, deciding if I wanted to hear the rest, which waited in message five. Humans generally get out the gist of what they need to say right at the beginning, then spend forever qualifying, contradicting, burnishing or taking important things back. You rarely miss anything by cutting most people off after two sentences. Ann's spiel about how much we all don't know about everything we do is linked thematically to Mike Mahoney's fourth-grade perception on the Barnegat bridge last night that we all live in houses we didn't choose and that choose us because they were built to somebody else's specifications, which we're happy to adopt, and that that says something about the price of baloney. Each has the specific gravity of a rice-paper airplane tossed from the top of the Empire State Building that soars prettily before it's lost to oblivion. Another example of non-virtuous speech. Maybe Ann's now dabbling in Eastern religions, since her old-line Reform Lutheranism stopped packing a wallop.

Except. Our ex-wives always harbor secrets about us that

make them irresistible. Until, of course, we remember who we are and what we did and why we're not married anymore.

Message five. "Okay, sweetie, I'll get this over with. Sorry for the long message. I've had a glass of New Zealand sauvignon blanc." Long messages ask for but don't allow answers, which is why they're inexcusable. "I just want to say that I can't get over the long transit we all make in our lives. The strangest thing we'll ever know is just life itself, isn't it?" No. "Not science or technology or mysticism or religion. I'm not looking for underlying causes anymore. I want things to be evident now. When I saw you tonight, at first it was like being in a jet airplane and looking out the window and seeing another jet airplane. You see it, but you really can't appreciate the distance it is from you, except it's really far. But by the end, you'd gotten much closer. For the first time in a very long time you were good, like I said in my last message, or maybe I said it at school. Any-hoo, I just thought of one last thing, then I'm going to bed. Do you remember once when you took the little kids to see a baseball game? In Philadelphia, I guess. Charley and I were somewhere on his boat, and you had them down there. And some player, I guess, hit a ball that came right at you. Of course you remember all this, sweetheart. And Paul said you just reached up with one hand and caught it. He said everybody around you stood up and applauded you, and your hand swelled up huge. But he said you were so happy. You smiled and smiled, he said. And I thought when he told me: That's the man I thought I married. Not because you could catch an old ball, but because that's all I thought it took to make you happy. I realized that when I married you I thought I could make you happy just like that. I really did think that. Things made you happy then. I think you gave that ball to Paul. I have it somewhere. So okay. Life's an odd transit. I already said that. It'll be nice to see Paul tomorrow—at least I hope it will. Good night." *Click.*

"It's also true . . ." I said these words right into the receiver, with no one on the other end, my fingers touching my Realtor of the Year crystal paperweight from my early selling days in Haddam. It was holding down some unopened mail beside the phone. ". . . It's also true"—and here I quit speaking to no one—"that we conjure up underlying causes and effects based on what we want the underlying causes to be. And *that's* how we get things *all fucked up.*" But in any case, Ann would've done better marrying me *precisely* because I could catch a line drive with my bare hand, and then letting that handsome, manly, uncomplicated facility be the theme of life—one I might've lived up to—rather than thinking she could ever make me *happy*! The kind of happy I was that day at the Vet when "Hawk" Dawson actually doffed his red "C" cap to me, and everyone cheered and I practically convulsed into tears—you can't patent that. It was one shining moment of glory that was instantly gone. Whereas life, real life, is different and can't even be appraised as simply "happy," but only in terms of "Yes, I'll take it all, thanks," or "No, I believe I won't." Happy, as my poor father used to say, is a lot of hooey. Happy is a circus clown, a sitcom, a greeting card. Life, though, life's about something sterner. But also something better. A lot better. Believe me.

THERE WAS a sixth call. From my son Paul Bascombe, on the road, telling me he and "Jill" wouldn't make it in tonight—last night, now—due to "hitting the edge of some lake-effect snow" that "has Buffalo paralyzed clear down into western PA." They were "hoping to push on past Valley Forge." Weighty pauses were left between phrases—"has Buffalo paralyzed," "lake-effect snow," "western PA"—to denote how hysterical these all are, requiring extra time for savoring. The two of them, he said, "almost picked up a flop in Hershey." I've invited them to stay here, but Paul doesn't like my house and I'm happy for them not to. I have a sense, of course, that Paul has surprises for us. Something's in his flat, no-affect, Kanzcity-middlewestern, put-on phone voice that I don't like, since he seems to strive too hard to become that strange overconfident, businessy mainstreamer with a mainstreamer's sealed-off certainty riven right into the lingo. I haven't given up on the notion of things generally "working out," or with either of my children "fitting in," but I'd also be pleased if they both thought these things had happened. I halfway expected Paul to say he'd "rest in the City of Brotherly Love," but he couldn't have suppressed a shout of hilarity, which would've ruined it.

Nine years ago, when he was an unusual and uninspired senior at Haddam HS—it was during the two years when Ann's husband, Charley, had his first cruel brush with colon cancer and Ann simply couldn't deal with Paul *and* Clarissa—Paul lived with me in the very house on Cleveland Street where he'd lived as a little boy, the house I bought from Ann when she moved away from Haddam and married Charley, and of course the very house she lives in this morning. It was the time when Ann—for some good reasons—thought Paul might have Asperger's and was forcing me, at great expense, to drive him down to Hopkins to be neurologically evaluated. He *was* evaluated and *didn't* have Asperger's or anything else. The Hopkins doctor said Paul was "unsystematically oppositional" by nature and probably would be all his life, that there was nothing wrong with that, nor anything I could do or should want to, since plenty of interesting, self-directed, even famous people were also that. He named Winston Churchill, Bing Crosby, Gertrude Stein and Thomas Carlyle, which seemed a grouping that didn't bode well. Though it was amusing to think of all four of them writing greeting cards out in K.C.

The day from that relatively halcyon time which I remember most feelingly was a sunny Saturday morning in spring. Forsythias and azaleas were out in Haddam. I had been outside bundling the wet leaves I'd missed the fall before. Paul had few friends and stayed home on weekends, working on ventriloquism and learning to make his dummy—Otto—talk, roll his bulging eyes, mug, agitate his acrylic eyebrows over something Paul, his straight man, said needed to be made a fool of for. When I came in the living room from the yard, Paul was seated on the old hard-seated Windsor chair he practiced on. He looked dreadful, as he usually looked—baggy jeans, torn sweatshirt, long ratty hair dyed blue. Otto was perched on his knee, Paul's left hand buried in his complicated innards. Otto's unalterably startled, perpetually apple-cheeked oaken face was turned so that he and Paul were staring out the window at my neighbor Skip McPherson's Dodge Alero, which McPherson was washing in front of his house across the street.

I was always trying to say things to Paul that were friendly and provoking and that made it seem I was an engaged father who knew things about his son that only the two of us *could* know— which maybe I was. These were sometimes dummy jokes: "Feeling a little wooden today?" "Not as chipper as usual?" "Time to branch out." It was one reliable strategy I'd found that offered us at least a chance at rudimentary communication. There weren't many others.

Otto's idiot head swiveled around to peer at me when I came through the front door, though Paul maintained an intense, focused stare out at Skip McPherson. Otto's get-up was a blue-and-white-plaid hacking jacket, a yellow foulard, floppy brown trousers, and a frizz of bright yellow "hair," on top of which teetered a green derby hat. He looked like a drunk bet-placer at a second-rate dog track. Paul had bought him at a going-out-of-business magic shop in Gotham.

"I've decided what I want to be," Paul said, staring away purposefully. Otto regarded Paul, batted his eyebrows up and down, then looked back at me. "The invisible man. You know? He unwinds his bandages and he's gone. That'd be great." Paul often said distressing things just to be, in fact, oppositional and usually didn't really know or care what they meant or portended.

"Sounds pretty permanent." I sat on the edge of the over-stuffed chair I usually read my paper in at night. Otto stared at me, as if listening. "You're only seventeen. Somebody might say you just got here." Otto spun his head round full circle and blinked his bright-blue bulbous eyes, as if I'd said something outrageous.

"I can act through Otto," Paul said. "It'll be perfect. Ventriloquism makes the best sense if the ventriloquist's invisible. You know?" He kept his stare fixed out at Skip, who was working over his hubcaps.

"Okay," I said. Somebody might've interpreted this as a silent "cry for help," an early warning sign of depression, some anti-social eruption in the offing. But I didn't. Adolescent jabber designed to drive me crazy, is what I thought. Paul has put this instinct to work in the greeting-card industry. "Sounds great," I said.

"It's great and it's also true." He turned and frowned at me.

"True. Okay. True."

"Greet 'n true," Otto said in a scratchy falsetto that sounded like Paul, though I couldn't see his whispering lips or his suppressed pleasure. "Greet 'n true, greet 'n true, greet 'n true."

That's all I remember about this—though I didn't think about it at the time in 1991. But it's probably not something a father could forget and might even experience guilt about, which I may have done for a while, but stopped. I also remember because it reminds me of Paul in the most vivid of ways, of what he was like as a boy, and makes me think, as only a parent would, of the progress that lurks unbeknownst in even our apparent failures. By his own controlling hand, Paul may now be said to have gotten what he wanted, willed invisibility, and may already be far down the road to happiness.

CLARISSA'S BEAU, the New Hampshire Healey 1000 guy, I'm grievously forced to meet as I make my hurried trip through the kitchen, wanting to catch a bite and beat it. I intentionally stayed in my office, hoping the lovebirds would get bored waiting for Clarissa's "Dad" and head out for a beach ramble or a cold Healey ride for a shiatsu massage up in Mantoloking. I could meet him later. But when I head through, my Surf Road listing papers in hand, aiming for a fast cup of coffee and a sinker, I find Clarissa. And Thom. (As in "Hi, Frank, this is my friend Thom"—I'm guessing the spelling—"who I woogled the bee-jesus out of all night long in your guest room, whether you approve or don't." This last part she doesn't say.)

The two of them are arranged languidly, side-by-side, yet somehow theatrically *intent* at the glass-topped breakfast table, precisely where Sally gave me my bad news last May. Clarissa's wearing a pair of man's red-and-green-plaid boxer shorts and a frayed blue Brooks Brothers pajama shirt—mine. Her short hair's mussed, her cheeks pale, her contacts are out, and she has her long-toed bare feet across the space of chairs in Thom's lap and is studying an Orvis catalog. (All evidence of a "committed relationship" with another female *gone*. Poof. Things happen too fast for me—which, I guess, is a given.)

Thom's frowning hard over an open copy of what looks like *Foreign Affairs* (thick, creamy, deckled pages, etc.) and looks up to smile weakly as my fatherly identity is expressed (in my own kitchen). I mean to proffer only the most carefully crafted, disinterested and hermetically banal sentiments and damn few of them, for fear I'll say extremely wrong things, after which terrible words from my daughter's razor tongue will lacerate my head and heart.

Only, Thom's *old*—at least *forty-six*! And even bumbling through my kitchen like a renter and barely daring a look or to meet his dark eyes—my listing papers being my something to hold on to—I know this character's rap sheet. And it has DANGER stamped on it in big red block letters. Clarissa has carefully mentioned nothing about him in the last days, only that he "teaches" equestrian therapy to Down's syndrome kids at a "pretty famous holistic center" over in Manchester, where she volunteers a day a week when she isn't working in my office. She's intended him to attract absolutely no vetting commentary from me. Apparently the "whole thing"—the connected boxes versus the complex, well-differentiated big swim I was unarguably in—was still pretty precarious, and she didn't need other people's (mine, her mother's) views making her difficult life harder to navigate. This is all re-conveyed to me now in my kitchen with one look of post-coital lassitude and menace.

Thom, however—Thom is no mystery. Thom is known to me and to all men—fathers, especially—and loathed.

Tall, rangy, long-muscled, large-eyed, smooth-olive-skinned Amherst or Wesleyan grad—read Sanskrit, history of science and genocide studies, swam or rowed till books got in the way; born "abroad" of mixed parentage (Jewish-Navajo, French, Berber—whatever gives you charcoal gray eyes, silky black hair on the back of your hands and forearms); deep honeyed voice that seems made of expensive felt; intensely "serious" yet surprisingly funny, also touchingly awkward at the most unexpected moments (not during intercourse); plays a medieval stringed instrument, of which there are only ten in existence; has mastered *Go*, was once married to a Chilean woman and has a teenage child in Montreal he's deeply committed to but rarely sees. Worked in Ghana for the Friends Service, taught in experimental schools (not Montessori), built his own ketch and sailed it to Brittany, wears one-of-a-kind Persian sandals, a copper anklet, black silk singlets suggesting a full-body tan, sage-colored desert shorts revealing a shark bite on his inner thigh from who-knows-what ocean, and always smells like a fine wood-working shop. He's only at the Equestrian Center now because of an "awakening" on the Going to the Sun Highway, which indicated he had yet to fully deliver on his "promise." And since he'd grown up with horses in North Florida or Buenos Aires or Vienna, and since his little sister had

Down's, maybe there was still time to "make good" if he could just find the right place: Manchester, New Jersey.

And oh, yes, along the course, he also wanted to make good on some men's daughters and wives. On Clarissa. My Clarissa. My prize. My lifesaver. My un-innocent innocent. She was number 1001.

If I had a pistol instead of a handful of house-for-sale sheets, I'd shoot Thom right in the chest in the midst of their cheery bagel 'n cream cheese, eggs 'n bacon ambience, let him slump onto his *Foreign Affairs* and drag him out to the beach for the gulls. (Since I've had cancer, I've compiled an impressive list of people to "take with me" when things get governmentally irreversible—as they soon will. If I survive the hail of bullets, I'll happily spend my last days in a federal lockup with books to read, three squares, and limited TV in the senior block. You can imagine who I'll be seeking out. Thom is my new entry.)

". . . This is my dad, Frank Bascombe," Clarissa mutters, head down over her Orvis catalog. She casually retracts her shoe-less foot out of Thom's lap, gives her big toe a good scratching, then absently, lightly fingers the tiny red whelp where her diamond nose stud used to be. Breakfast dishes are disposed in front of them—bagel crescents, melted butter globs, a bowl of cereal bits afloat on a gray skim of milk product.

I proffer a hand insincerely across Clarissa. "Hi there," I say. Big smile.

"Thom van Ronk, sir." Thom looks up suddenly from *Foreign Affairs*, now smiling intensely. He shakes my hand without standing. Van Ronk. Not a Berber, but a treacherous Walloon. Clarissa could've been smarter than this.

"What's shakin' in *Foreign Affairs*, Thom?" I say. "Brits still won't go for the Euro? Ruskies struggling with a market economy? The odd massacre needing interpreting?" I smile so he knows I hate him. Every person he's ever known hates him—except my daughter, who doesn't like *my* tone of voice and glares up from her page of Gore-Tex trekking mocs to burn a dead-eyed frown into me promising complex punishments later. They'd be worth it.

"Your son, aka my brother, paid us a visit already this morning," Clarissa says, nestling her heel back comfy into Thom's penile package, while he re-finds his place in his important reading material. They seem to have known each other for a year. Possibly they're already on the brink of the kind of familiarity that leads to boredom—like a ball bearing seeking the ocean bottom. I hope so. Though neither of my wives ever stuck her heel into my package while fingering up breakfast crumbs. At Harvard, there's probably a course for this in the mental-health extension program: Morning-After Etiquette: Do's, Don'ts, Better Nots. "He seemed—surprise, surprise—extremely weird." She casts a bored look out at the beach to where the Shore Police are grilling some local teens freed from school for the holiday. "He's not as weird, though, as his girlfriend. Miss Jill." She frowns at the boys, four in all, with shaved heads, butt-crack jeans, long Jets and Redskins jerseys. Two enormous, hulking, hatless policemen in shorts are making the boys form a line and turn their pockets out alongside the black-and-white Isuzu 4 × 4. All of them are laughing.

Clarissa, I understand to be musing over the fact that mere mention of her brother makes her revert to teen vocabulary ten years out-of-date, when Paul was "weird beyond pathetic, entirely out of it, deeply disgusting and queer," etc. She's sophisticated enough not to care, only to notice. She and her strange brother maintain an ingrown, not overtly unfriendly détente she doesn't talk about. Paul admires and is deeply in love with her for being glamorous and a (former) lesbian and for stealing a march on transgressive behavior, which had always been his speciality. (I'm sure he was pleased to meet Thom.) Clarissa recognizes his right to be an insignificant little midwestern putz-burger, card writer and Chiefs fan, someone she'd never have one thing to do with if he wasn't her brother. It's possible they're in contact about their mother and me by e-mail, though I'm not sure when they last saw each other in the flesh, or if Clarissa could even be nice to him in person. Parents are supposed to know these things. I just don't.

Though there's also an old, murky shadow over their brother–sister bond. When Paul was seventeen and Clarissa fifteen, Paul in a fit of confusion apparently "suggested"—I'm not sure how—that he and Clarissa engage in a "see-what-it's-like" roll in the hay, which pretty much KO'd further sibling rapport. It's always possible he was joking. However, three years ago—he told his mother this—Paul was summoned to Maine by Clarissa and

Cookie, given a ticket to Bangor, brought down to Pretty Marsh by bus, then forced to sleep in a cold cabin and endure an inquisition for misfeasances he wouldn't go into detail about (reportedly "the usual brother–sister crap"), though clearly for trying to make Clarissa do woo-woo with him when she was underage and his sister. Paul said the two women were savage. They said he should be ashamed of himself, should seek counseling, was probably gay, wasn't manly, had self-esteem issues, was likely an addicted onanist and premature ejaculator—the usual things sisters think about brothers. He told Ann he finally just gave in (without specifically admitting to what) when they said none of it was his fault, but was actually Ann's and mine, and that they felt sorry for him. Then they each gave him a hug that he said made him feel crazy. They ended the afternoon with Paul showing them some of his sidesplitting "Smart Aleck" cards—the Hallmark line he writes for out in K.C.—and throwing his voice into the bedroom, and laughing themselves silly before sitting down to a big lobster dinner. He went home the next day.

"What's wrong with Jill?" I say.

"Way-ell." Clarissa casts an eyebrows-raised look of appraisal up at me. She can't see well without her contacts.

Thom suddenly snaps to, grins, showing huge incisors, blinks his eyes and says, "What? Sorry. I wasn't listening."

"Did he tell you she only has one hand? I mean she's perfectly okay. They probably love each other. But yeah. It's fine, of course. It's not a problem."

"One hand?" I say.

"The left one." Clarissa bites the corner of her mouth. "I mean she's right-handed, so to speak."

"Where'd it go?" I have both of mine. Everybody I know has both of theirs. I of course know people suffer such things—all the time. It shouldn't be a shock that Paul romances a girl with only one arm. But it is. (Never wonder what else can happen next. Much can.)

"We didn't get into it." Clarissa shakes her head, her foot still tucked away in plain sight into Thom's man department. "I guess they met on-line. But she actually works where he works, whatever that's called. The card company." (She knows what it's called.)

I say, "Maybe she works in the sympathy-card department."

Clarissa smiles an unfriendly smile and gives me one of her long looks that means everything I say is wrong. "A lot of people who write sympathy cards have disabilities themselves. She did tell us that—apropos of nothing. They didn't stick around that long. I think he wants to surprise you." She prisses her lips and goes back to her Orvis catalog.

Clarissa, who's my only earthly ally, if provoked in front of Thom, will jump to Paul's and one-arm Jill's defense for anything inappropriate in my body language, facial expression, much less my word-of-mouth. Never mind that she thinks it's all the strangest of strange. Paul may have hired an actor to bring home just to drive us all crazy. It's in his realm. Otto in a skirt.

"They said they were going to 'pick up a motel room.'" Clarissa's very businessy-sarcastic now because she wants to be—but I can't be. "They're going to Ann's for dinner." (First names only here.) I don't want to tell her I've invited Ann for Thanksgiving and hear from her what an insanely bad idea it is. "Surprises all around. She'll flip." Clarissa executes a perfectly glorious smile that says, I wish I could be there.

Words, I find, are not in full abundance. "Okay," I say.

"*We're* going to Atlantic City, by the way." She extends a hand over onto velvety Thom's singleted shoulder and rolls her eyes upward (in mockery). Thom seems confused—that so much could go on in one family in so short a period of time without any of it being about him. "We'll be back in the morning." More woogling, this time at Trump's. "I'm going to try my luck at roulette." She pats Thom's tawny, muscular thigh right where the shark took its nip or where he rappelled down the face of Mount whatever. Maybe they'll see the Calderons at the free high-roller buffet.

"Then I think I'll just go off and try to sell a house." I grin insincerely.

"Okay now, is that what you do?" Thom blinks at me. The widely separated corners of his mouth flicker with a smile that may be amused or may be amazed but is not interested.

"Pretty much."

"Great. Do you do commercial or just houses?" His smile's tending toward being amused. I'm sure his father did commercial in Rio and printed his own currency.

"Mostly residential," I say. "I can always use a mid-career

salesman, if you're interested. I have a Tibetan monk working for me right now who's maybe going to leave. You'd have to take the state test, and I get half of everything. I'd put you on salary for six months. You'd probably do great."

Amazement. His teeth are truly enormous and white and unafflicted by worry. He likes flashing them as proof of invulnerability.

"I've got my hands pretty full at the Down's center," he says, smiling self-beknightedly.

"Do those little devils really stay on a horse without being wired on?"

"You bet they do," Thom says.

"Does riding horses cure Down's syndrome?"

"There isn't any *cure*." Clarissa smacks shut her Orvis catalog and retracts her heels from Thom's scrotal zone. It's time to go. This is her house, too, she wants me to understand—though it isn't. It's mine. "You know it doesn't cure Down's syndrome, you cluck." She starts gathering dishes and ferrying them noisily to the sink. "You should come over and volunteer, Frank. They'll let you ride a pony if you want to. No wires." Her back is to me. Thom's gazing at me wondrously, as if to say, Yep, you're getting a good scolding now, I'm sorry it has to happen, but it does.

"Great," I say jovially, and give Thom a chummy grin that says we men are always in the line of female fire. I pop the spindled listing sheets in my palm—three times for emphasis. "You kids have yourselves some fun pissing Thom's money away."

"Yeah, we will," Clarissa says from the sink. "We'll think of you. Paul has a time capsule with him. I almost forgot. He wants us to put something in it and bury it someplace." She's smirking as she rinses cups and doesn't turn around. Though this occasions a troubled look from Thom, as if Paul's a sad soul who's made all our lives one endless hell on earth.

"That'll be great," I say.

Clarissa says, "What're you going to put in it?"

"I'll have to think. Maybe I'll put in my Michigan diploma, with a listing sheet. 'Once there was a time when people lived in things called houses—or in their parents' houses.' You can put your old—"

"I'll think about me," Clarissa says. She knows what I was about to suggest. Her nose stud.

I consider confessing that I've invited her mother for Thanksgiving—just to discourage Thom from coming. But I'm late and don't have time for an argument. "Don't forget you're the acting lady of the house tomorrow. I'm depending on you to be a gracious hostess."

"Who's the husband?"

"I hope you sell a house," Thom says. "Is that what you want to do? My dad was in real estate. He sold big office buildings. He—" I'm on my way to the front door and miss the rest.

CHAPTER 9

UP AGAIN, old heart. Everything good is on the highway. In this instance, New Jersey Route 35, the wide mercantile pike up Barnegat Neck, whose distinct little beach municipalities—Sea-Clift, Seaside Park, Seaside Heights, Ortley Beach—pass my window, indistinguishable. For practical-legal reasons, each boro has its separate tax collector, deeds registry, zoning board, police, fire, etc., and local patriots defend the separate characters as if Bay Head was Norway and Lavallette was France. Though I, a relative newcomer (eight years), experience these beach townlettes as one long, good place-by-an-ocean and sell houses gainfully in each. And particularly on this cold, clearing morning when it's reassuring as a Fifties memory all up the Shore, I thank my lucky stars for landing me where they did.

Christmas decorations are going up in the morning sunshine. The streets crew is stringing red-and-green plastic bunting to the intersection wires, and swagging the firemen's memorial at Boro Hall. Candy-cane soldiers have appeared on the median strip, and a crèche with bearded, more authentic burnoose-clad Semites is now up on the lawn of Our Lady of Effectual Mercy. No revolving lights are in place. A banner announcing a Cadillac raffle and a Las Vegas Night stands on the lawn by the announcements case offering CONFESSIONS ANYTIME.

In Frederick Schruer's *History of Garden State Development: A Portrait in Contrasts, Conflicts and Chaos* (Rutgers, 1984), Sea-Clift is favorably referred to as the "Classic New Jersey Shore Townlette." Which means that owing to the beach and the crowds, we're not a true suburb, though there're plenty of pastel split-levels on streets named Poseidon, Oceania and Pelagic. Neither are we exactly a fishing village, though flounder fishermen and day charters leave from the bayside wharf. We're also not exactly a resort town, since most of the year tourists are gone and the steel Fun Pier's ancient and the rides closed for being life-threatening. There's not even that much to do in summer except float along in the crowds, hang out in the motel or on the beach, eat, drink, rent a boogie board or stare off.

There *is* a mix, which has encouraged a positivist small-businessman spirit that's good for real estate. The 2,263 year-rounders (many are south Italians with enormous families) run things, own most of the businesses, staff the traffic court, police and fire—which makes Sea-Clift more like Secaucus than the ritzier enclaves north of us. Our town fathers long ago understood that xenophobia, while natural to the species, will get you broke quick in a beach town, and so have fostered a not so much "*Mia casa é tua casa*" spirit as a more level-headed "Your vacation is my financial viability" expedience, which draws eight jillion tourists to our summer streets, plus a stream of new semi-affluent buy-ins from Perth Amboy and Metuchen, all of it spiced with Filipinos, Somalians and hard-working Hondurans (who come for the schools) to brew up a tranquil towny heterogeneity that looks modern on paper without feeling much different from the way things have always felt.

For me, transacting the business of getting people situated under roofs and into bearable mortgages and out again, Sea-Clift couldn't be a better place—real estate being one of our few year-round business incubators. People are happy to see my face, know that I'm thriving and will be there when the time comes, but still don't have to have me to dinner. In that way, I'm a lot like a funeral home.

VERY LITTLE's abuzz and about today in spite of Thanksgiving being tomorrow. A few home owners down the residential streets are employed in pre-holiday cleanup, getting on ladders, opening the crawl space for termite checks, putting up storms, spooling hoses, closing off spigots, winterizing the furnace. In a town where everybody comes in the summer, now's when many year-rounders take their three-day trips—to Niagara and the Vietnam Memorial—since the town's theirs and empty and can be abandoned without a worry. Which doesn't make *now* a bad selling season, since niche buyers come down when the throngs are gone, armed with intent and real money to spend.

Of course, now's when any prudent newcomer—a software kingpin with new development dollars—would notice all that we *don't* offer: any buildings of historical significance (there are no large buildings at all); no birthplaces of famous inventors, astronauts or crooners. No Olmsted parks. No fall foliage season, no sister city in Italy or even Germany. No bookstores except one dirty one. Mark Twain, Helen Keller or Edmund Wilson never said or did anything memorable here. There's no Martin Luther King Boulevard, no stations on the Underground Railroad (or any railroad) and no golden era anyone can recollect. This must be true for plenty of towns.

There is, however, little teen life, so car thefts and break-ins are rare. You can smoke in our restaurants (when they're open). The Gulf Stream moderates our climate. Our drinking water's vaguely salty, but you get used to it. We were never a temperance town, so you can always find a cocktail. College Board scores match the state average. Two Miss Teenage New Jerseys ('41 and '75) hail from here. We stage an interesting Frank Sinatra impersonator contest in the spring. Our town boundary abuts a state park. Cable's good. And for better or worse, the hermit crab is our official town crustacean—though there's disagreement over how large the proposed statue should be. You could also say that for a town founded by enterprising Main Line land speculators on the bedrock principles of buy low/sell high, we've exceeded our municipal mission with relatively few downsides. Since we're bounded by ocean and bay, there're few places where planning problems could ever arise. Water is our de facto open space plus a good population stabilizer. For a time, I sat on the Dollars For Doers Strike Council, but we never did much besides lower parking fines, pass a good-neighbor ordinance so tourists could reach the beach via private property, and give the Fun Pier a rehabilitation abatement the owners never used. Our development committee extended feelers to a culinary arts academy seeking growing room—though we didn't have any. There was a citizen's initiative for a new all-cement promenade, but it failed, and for establishing a dinosaur park, though we hadn't had any dinosaurs and couldn't legally claim one. Still, as old-timey, low-ceiling and down-market as Sea-Clift is, most people who live here like it that way, like it that we're not a destination resort but are faithful to our original charter as a place an ordinary wage earner comes for three days, then beats it home again—a town with just a life, not a lifestyle.

*   *   *

I MAKE A stop by my office to pick up the Surf Road keys. Inside, it's shadowy and dank, my and Mike's desktops empty of important documents. Mike's computer (I don't own one) beams out his smiling picture of himself and the Dalai Lama, which coldly illuminates his Gipper portrait and his prayer flags on the wall. The office has a stinging balsam scent (mingled with a pizza odor through the wall) from the one time Mike burned incense in the john—which I put a stop to. The house keys, with white tags, are on the key rack. I have a quick piss in our bare-bones bathroom. Though when I come out, I see through the window that a car's stopped out front by my Suburban, a tan Lincoln Town Car with garish gold trim and New York plates. Since it's too early for a Chicago-style pizza, these are doubtless showcase shoppers eyeballing the house snapshots in the window. They'll be scared off when they see me, sensing I might drag them in and bore them to death. But not today. I frown out at the car—I can't see who's inside, but no one climbs out—then I go back in the bathroom, close the door, stand and wait thirty seconds. And when I come out, as if by magic the space is empty, the Lincoln gone, the morning, or what's left of it, returned to my uses.

THE CLIENT for my Surf Road showing is a welding contractor down from Parsippany, Mr. Clare Suddruth, with whom I've already done critical real estate spadework the past three weeks, which means I've driven him around Sea-Clift, Ortley Beach, Seaside Heights, etc., on what I think of as a lay-of-the-land tour, during which the client gets to see everything for sale in his price range, endures no pressure from me, begins to think of me as his friend, since I'm spending all this time with nothing promised, comes after a while to gab about his life—his failures, treacheries, joys—lets me stand him some lunches, senses we're cut out of the same rough fustian and share many core values (the economy, Vietnam, the need to buy American though the Japs build a better product, the Millennium non-event and how much we'd hate to be young now). We probably *don't* agree about the current election hijacking, but probably *do* see eye-to-eye about what constitutes a good house and how most buyers are better off setting aside their original price targets in favor of stretching their pocketbooks, getting beyond the next dollar threshold—

where the houses you *really* want are as plentiful as hoe handles—
and doing a little temporary belt-tightening while the economy's
ebb and flow keeps your boat on course and steaming ahead.

If this seems like bait-and-switch hucksterism, or just old-
fashioned grinning, bamboozling faithlessness, let me assure you
it's not. All any client ever has to say is, "All right, Bascombe,
how you see this really isn't how I see it. I want to stay *inside*, not
outside, my price window, exactly like I said when I sat down
at your desk." If that's your story, I'm ready to sell you what
you want—if I have it. All the rest—the considered, heartfelt
exchange of views, the finding of common ground, the beginning of true (if ephemeral) comradeship based on time spent
inside a stuffy automobile—all *that* I'd do with the Terminix guy.
A person has only to know his mind about things, which isn't as
usual as it seems. I view my role as residential agent as having a
lay therapist's fiduciary responsibility (not so different from being
a Sponsor). And that responsibility is to leave the client better
than I found him—or her. Many citizens set out to buy a house
because of an indistinct yearning, for which an actual house was
never the right solution to begin with and may only be a quick
(and expensive) fix that briefly anchors and stabilizes them, never
touches their deeper need, but puts them in the poorhouse anyway. Most client contacts never even eventuate in a sale and, like
most human exposures, end in one encounter. Which isn't to
say that the road *toward* a house sale is a road without benefit or
issue. A couple of the best friends I've made in the real estate
business are people I never sold a house to and who, by the end
of our time together, I didn't *want* to sell a house to (though I still
would've). It is another, if unheralded, version of the perfect real
estate experience: Everyone does his part, but no house changes
hands. If there weren't, now and then, such positive outside-the-
envelope transactions, I'd be the first to say the business wouldn't
be worth the time of day.

I SWING OFF Ocean Avenue at the closed-for-the-season
Custom Condom Shoppe ("We build 'em to your specs") and
motor down toward the beach along the narrow gravel lane of
facing, identical white and pastel summer "chalets," of which
there must be twenty in this row, with ten identical parallel lanes

stacked neighborhood-like to the north and south, each named for a New Jersey shorebird—Sandpiper, Common Tern, Plover (I'm driving down Cormorant Court). Here is where most of our weekly renters—Memorial Day to Columbus Day—spend their happy family vacations, cheek-to-cheek with hundreds of other souls opting for the same little vernal joys. At several of these (all empty now), more pre-winter fix-up is humming along—hip roofs being patched, swollen screen doors planed, brick foundation piers regrouted after years of salt air. Three of these chalet developments lie in the Boro of Sea-Clift, where I own ten units and, with Mike's help, manage thirty more. These summer chalets and their more primitive ancestors have been an attractive, affordable feature of beach life on south Barnegat Neck since the Thirties. Five-hundred-square-foot interiors, two tiny bedrooms, a simple bath, beaverboard walls, a Pullman kitchen, no yard, grass, shrubbery, no a/c or TV, electric wall heaters and stove, yard-sale decor, no parking except in front, no privacy from the next chalet ten feet away, crude plumbing, tinted, iron-rich water, occasional gas and sulfur fumes from an unspecified source—and you can't drive vacationers away. A certain precinct in the American soul will put up with anything—other people's screaming kids, exotic smells, unsavory neighbors, unsocialized pets, high rents (I get $750 a week), car traffic, foot traffic, unsound construction, yard seepage—just to *be* and be able to brag to the in-laws back in Parma that they were "a three-minute walk to the beach." Which every unit is.

Of course, another civic point of view—the Dollars For Doers Strike Council—would love to see every chalet bulldozed and the three ten-acre parcels turned into an outlet mall or a parking structure. But complicated, restrictive covenants unique to Sea-Clift require every chalet owner to agree before the whole acreage can be transferred. And many owners are among our oldest Sea-Clift pioneers, who came as children and never forgot the fun they had and couldn't wait to own a chalet, or six, themselves and start making their retirement nut off the renters—the people they had once been. Most of the people I manage for are absentees, the sons and daughters of those pioneers, and now live in Connecticut and Michigan and would pawn their MBA's before they'd sign away "Dad's cottage." (None of them, of course, would spend two minutes inside any of these sad little shanties themselves, which is when I get in the picture, and am happy to be.)

These days, I do my best to upgrade the ten chalets I own, plus all the ones I can talk my owners into sprucing up. Occasionally I let a struggling writer in need of quiet space to finish his *Moby-Dick*, or some poor frail in retirement from love, stay through the winter in return for indoor repairs (these guests never stay long due to the very seclusion they think they want). Looked at differently, these chalets would be a perfect place for a homicide.

Three Honduran fix-up crews (all legal, all my employees) are at work as I drive down Cormorant Court. From the roof of #11, one of these men (José, Pepe, Esteban—I'm not sure which), suited up in knee pads and roped to a standpipe, replacing shingles, rises to his feet on the steep green asphalt roof-pitch and into the clean, cold November sky, leans crazily against his restraint line and performs a sweeping hats-off Walter Raleigh-type bow right out into space, a big *amigo* grin on his wispy-mustachioed face. I give back an embarrassed wave, since I'm not comfortable being *Don Francisco* to my employees. The other workers break into laughing and jeering calls that he (or I) is a *puta* and beneath contempt.

CLARE SUDDRUTH is already out front of the fancy beach house he thinks he might like to buy. Surf Road is a sandy lane starting at the ocean end of Cormorant Court and running south a quarter-mile. If it were extended, which it never will be due to the same shoreline ordinances that infuriate the Feensters, it would run into and become Poincinet Road a mile farther on.

Clare stands hands-in-pockets in the brisk autumn breeze. He's dressed in a short zippered khaki work jacket and khaki trousers that announce his station as a working stiff who's made good in a rough-and-tumble world. The house Clare's interested in is—in design and residential spirit—not so different from my own and was built during the blue-sky development era of the late Seventies, before laws got serious and curtailed construction, driving prices into deep space. In my personal view, 61 Surf Road is not the house a man like Clare should think of, so of course he *is* thinking of it—a lesson we realtors ignore at our peril. Number 61 is a mostly-vertical, isosceles-angled, many-windowed, many sky-lighted, grayed redwood post-and-beam, with older solar panels and inside an open plan of not two, not three, but six separate "living levels," representing the architect's concern for interior diversity and cheap spatial mystery. More than it's right for Clare, it's perfect for a young sitcom writer with discretionary scratch and who wants to work from home. Asking's a million nine.

How the house "shows," and what the client sees from the curb—if there was a curb—are only two mute, segmented, retractable brown garage doors facing the road, two skimpy windows on the "back," and an unlocatable front door, through which you go right up to a "great room" where the good life commences. I don't much like the place since it broadcasts bland domiciliary arrogance, typical of the period. The house either has no front because no one's welcome; or else because everything important faces the sea and it's not your house anyway, why should you be interested?

Clare's a tall, bony, loose-kneed sixty-five-year-old, a bristle-haired Gyrine Viet vet with a thin, tanned jawline, creased Clint Eastwood features and the seductive voice of a late-night jazz DJ. In my view, he'd be more at home in a built-out Greek revival or a rambling California split-level. "Thornton Wilders," we call these in our trade, and we don't have any down here. Spring Lake and Brielle are your tickets for that dream.

But Clare's recent life's saga—I've heard all about it—has led him down new paths in search of new objectives. In that way, he is much like me.

Clare's standing beside my Realty-Wise sign—red block letters on a white field plus the phone number, no www, no virtual tours, no talking houses, just reliable people leading other people toward a feeling of finality and ultimate rightness. Clare turns and faces the house as I drive up, as if to allow that he's been waiting but time doesn't mean much to him. He's driven down in one of his company's silver panel trucks, which sits in the driveway, ONLY CONNECT WELDING painted in flowing blue script. His schoolteacher wife dreamed it up, Clare told me. "Something out of a book." Though Clare's no mutton-fisted underachiever who married up. He won a Silver Star with a gallantry garnish in Nam, came out a major and did the EE route at Stevens Tech. He and Estelle bought a house and had two quick kids in the Seventies, while Clare was on the upward track with Raytheon. But then out of the blue, he decided the laddered life was a rat-race and took over his dad's welding business in Troy Hills and changed its name to something he and Estelle liked. Clare's what we call a "senior boomer," someone who's done the course creditably, set aside substantial savings, gotten his kids set up at a safe distance, experienced appreciation in the dollar value of his family home (mortgage retired), and now wants a nicer life before he gets too decrepit to take out the garbage. What these clients generally decide to buy varies from a free-standing condo (we have few in Sea-Clift), to a weekend home near the water (these we have aplenty), to a "houseboat on the Seine"—aka something you park at a marina. Or else they choose a real honest-to-God house like this one Clare's staring up at: Turn the key, dial up the Jacuzzi. The owners, the Doolittles—currently in Boca Grande—detected the tech-market slowdown in September, were ready to shift assets into municipals and conceivably gold and are just waiting to back their money out. So far, no takers.

The other characteristic on Clare's buyer's profile is that three years ago—by his own candid recounting (as usual)—he fell in love with somebody who wasn't exactly his wife, but was, in fact, a fresh hire at the welding company—someone named Bitsy or Betsy or Bootsy. Not surprisingly, big domestic disruptions followed. The kids chose sides. Several loyal employees quit in disgust when "things" came out in the open. Welding damn near ceased. Clare and Estelle acted civilly ("She was the easy part"). A sad divorce ensued. A marriage to the younger Bitsy, Betsy, Bootsy hastily followed—a new life that never felt right from the instant they got to St. Lucia. A semi-turbulent year passed. A young wife grew restive—"Just like the goddamn *Eagles* song," Clare said. Betsy/Bitsy cut off all her hair, threw her nice new clothes away, decided to go back to school, figured out she wanted to become an archaeologist and study Meso-American something or other. Somehow she'd discovered she was brilliant, got herself admitted to the University of Chicago and left New Jersey with the intention of morphing her and Clare's spring–fall union into something rare, adaptable, unusual and modern—that he could pay for.

Only, at the end of year one, Estelle learned she had multiple sclerosis (she'd moved to Port Jervis to her sister's), news that galvanized Clare into seeing the fog lift, regaining his senses, divorcing his young student wife. ("A big check gets written, but who cares?") He moved Estelle back down to Parsippany and began devoting every resource and minute to her and her happiness, stunned that he'd never fully realized how lucky he was just to know someone like her. And with time now precious, there was none of it he cared to dick around with. (As heartening and *sui generis* as Clare's story sounds, in the real estate profession it's not that unusual.)

Which is when Sea-Clift came into play, since Estelle had vacationed here as a child and always adored it and hoped. . . . Nothing now was too good for her. Plus, in Clare's estimation our little townlette was probably a place the two of them would die in before the world fucked it up. (He may be wrong.) I've driven him past thirty houses in three weeks. Many seemed "interesting and possible." Most didn't. Number 61 was the only one that halfway caught his fancy, since the inside was already fitted with a nursing home's worth of shiny disabled apparatus, including—despite all the levels—a mahogany side-stair elevator for the coming dark days of disambulation. Clare told me that if he likes it when he sees it, he'll buy it as is and give it to Estelle—who's currently holding her own, with intermittent symptoms—as a one-year re-wedding/Thanksgiving present. It makes a pretty story.

"DRY AS MY Uncle Chester's bones out here, Frank," Clare says in his parched but sonorous voice, extending me a leathery hand. Clare has the odd habit of giving me his left hand to shake. Something about severed tendons from a "helo" crash causing acute pain, etc., etc. I always feel awkward about which hand to extend, but it's over fast. Though he has a vise grip even with his "off" hand, which fires up my own Bob Butts injuries from last night.

Clare produces his steady, eyes-creased smile that projects impersonal pleasure, then crosses his arms and turns to look again at 61 Surf Road. I'm about to say—but don't—that the worst droughts are the ones where we occasionally get a little rain, like yesterday, so that nobody really takes the whole drought idea seriously, then you end up ignoring the aquifer until disaster looms. But Clare's thinking about this house, which is a good sign. The color listing brochure I'm holding is ready to be proffered before we go in.

Down Surf Road (like my road, there are only five houses), a bearded young man in yellow rubber coveralls is scrubbing the sides of a white fiberglass fishing boat that's up on a trailer, using an extended aluminum hose brush—a blue BUSH-CHENEY sign stuck up in his weedy little yard. From back up Cormorant Court I hear the sharp *shree-scree* of a saber saw whanging through board filaments, followed by the satisfying bops of hammers hitting nails in rapid succession. My unexpected *jefe* presence has set my Hondurans into motion. Though it's only a game. Soon they'll be climbing down for their pre-lunch marijuana break, after which the day will go quickly.

The cold seaside air out here has a fishy and piney sniff to it, which feels hopeful in spite of the unpredictable November sky. My Thanksgiving worries have now scattered like seabirds. A squad of pigeons wheels above, as far beyond a jet contrail— high, high, high—heads out to sea toward Europe. I am rightly placed here, doing the thing I apparently do best—grounded, my duties conferring a pleasant, self-actualizing invisibility—the self as perfect *instrument*.

"Frank, tell me what this house'll bring in a summer?" Clare's mind is clicking merits–demerits.

I assume he's talking about rent and not a quick flip. "Three thousand a week. Maybe more."

He furrows his brow, puts a hand to his chin and rests it there— the standard gesture of contemplation, familiar to General MacArthur and Jack Benny. It is both grave and comical. Clearly it is Clare's practiced look of public seriousness. My instant guess is we'll never see inside #61. When clients are motivated, they don't stand out in the road talking about the house as if it'd be a good idea to tear it down. When clients are motivated, they can't wait to get in the door and start liking everything. I'm, of course, often wrong.

"Boy, oh boy." Clare shakes his head over modernity. "Three G's."

"Pays your taxes and then some," I say, breeze waffling my listing brochure and stiffening my digits.

"So who all's moving down to Sea-Clift now, Frank?" More standing, more staring. This is not a new question.

"Pretty much it's a mix, Clare," I say. "People driven out of the Hamptons. And there's some straight-out investment beginning. Our floor hasn't risen as fast as the rest of the Shore. No big springboard sales yet. Topping wars haven't gotten this far down. It's still a one-dimensional market. That'll change, even with rates starting to creep. A really good eight-hundred-thousand-dollar house is already hard to find." I take a glance at my sheet, as if all this crucial data's printed there and he should read it. I'm guessing coded chalk talk will appeal to Clare-the-small-businessman, make him think I'm not trying very hard to sell him the Doolittles' house, but am just his reliable resource for relevant factual info to make the world seem less a sinking miasma. Which isn't wrong.

"I guess they're not making any more ocean-front, are they?"

"If they could, they would." In fact, I know people who'd love to try: interests who'd like to "reclaim" Barnegat Bay and turn it into a Miracle Mile or a racino. "Fifty percent of us already live within fifty miles of the ocean, Clare. Ocean County's the St. Petersburg of the East."

"How's *your* business, Frank?" We're side-by-side—me a half step behind—staring at silent multi-this, multi-that #61.

"Good, Clare. It's good. Real estate's always good by the ocean. Inventory's my problem. If I had a house like this every day, I'd be richer than I am."

Clare at this instant lets go a small, barely audible (but audible) fart, the sound of a strangled birdcall from offstage. It startles me, and I can't help staring at its apparent point of departure, the seat of Clare's khakis, as if blue smoke might appear. It's the ex-Marine in Clare that makes such nonchalant emissions unremarkable (to him), while letting others know how intransigent a man he is and would be—in a love affair, in a business deal, in a divorce or a war. Possibly my reference to being rich forced an involuntary disparaging gesture from his insides.

"Tell me this now, Frank." Clare's stuffed both hands in his khaki side pockets. He's wearing brown-and-beige tu-tone suede leisure sneakers of the sort you buy at shoe outlets or off the sale rack at big-box stores and that look comfortable as all get out, though I'd never buy a pair, because they're what *doozies* wear (our old term from Lonesome Pines), or else men who don't care if they look like doozies. The Clint Eastwood look has a bit of doozie in it. Old Clint might wear a pair himself, so uncaring would he be of the world's opinion. "What kind of climate have we got, I mean for buying a house?"

I hear my workers up Cormorant Court begin laughing and their hammering come to a halt. "¡Hom-bre!" I hear a falsetto voice shout. "Qué flaco y feo." One needn't wonder. Something involving somebody's "chilé."

"I'd say that's a mixed picture, too, Clare." He already knows everything I know, because I've told him, but he wants me to think he takes what we're doing seriously—which means to me this is a waste of my time, which I in fact do take seriously. Clare came into the picture saying he was ready to buy a house sight unseen, maximize the quality-of-life remaining for his dear-stricken-betrayed-but-timeless love Estelle. Only, like most humans, when it gets down to the cold nut cutting, it's do-re-mi his heart breaks over.

"Money's cheap down here, Clare," I say, "and the mortgage people have got some interesting product enhancements to shift weight toward the back end—for a price, of course. Like I said, our inventory's down, which tends to firm up values. Most sales go for asking. You read the technology sector's ready to cycle down. Rates'll probably squirt up after Christmas. You'd hate to buy at the top with no short-term resale potential, but you can't take your cue from the wind, I guess. We saw a forty percent price increase in two years. I don't tell clients to go with their hearts, Clare. I don't know much about hearts."

Clare gazes at me, brown eyes squinted near-to-closing. I've probably said too much and strayed over into sensitive territory by referring to the heart. This sleepy-eyed look is a recognition and a warning. Though I've found that in business, a quick veer into the soft tissue of the personal can confuse things in a good way. Clare, after all, has given me a giant earful—probably he does everyone. He's just suddenly gotten leery about forging an unwanted connection with me. But ditto. I like Clare, but I want him to spend his money and feel good about giving part of it to me.

"Can I show you something, Frank?" Clare peers down at his doozie tu-tones as if they were doing his thinking for him.

"Absolutely."

"It won't take a minute." He's already moving—in a bit of a slinking, pelvis-forward gait—along the driveway toward the back of the Doolittles', between it and the next-door neighbor's, a dull two-story A-frame that's boarded for the winter and has a dead look: basement windows blocked with pink Styrofoam, plants covered with miniature wooden A-frames of their own, the basement door masked with plyboard screwed into the foundation. Winter gales are expected.

"I took a walk around here while I was waiting," Clare's saying as he walks, but in a more intimate voice, as if he doesn't want the wrong people hearing this. I'm following, my listing materials stuffed in my windbreaker pocket. The Doolittles' house, I can see, is in need of upkeep. The side basement door is weathered and grayed, the veneer shredded at the bottom. A scimitar of glass has dropped out of a basement window and shattered on the concrete footing. Something metal is whapping in the wind above the soffits—a loose TV cable or a gutter strap—though I can't see anything. I wonder if the solar panels even work. The house could do with a new owner and some knowledgeable attention. The Doolittles, who're plastic surgeons in joint practice, have been spending their discretionary income elsewhere. Though they may soon have less of it.

Clare leads around to the "front" of the house, between the windowed concrete basement wall and the ten-foot sand dune that's covered with dry, sparse-sprouted sea rocket from the summer. The dune—which is natural and therefore inviolable—is what keeps the house from having a full ocean view from the living room, and probably what's retarded its sale since September. I've put into the brochure that "imagination" (money) could be dedicated to the living room level (moving it to the third floor) and "open up spectacular vistas."

"Okay, look at this down here." Clare, almost whispering, bends over, hands on his knees to designate what he means me to see. "See that?" His voice has grown grave.

I move in beside him, kneel by his knee on the gravelly foundation border and stare right where he's pointing at an outward-curving section of pale gray concrete that's visible beneath the sill and the footing. It is one of the deep-driven piers to which the well-named Doolittles' house is anchored and made fast so that at times of climatological stress the whole schmeer isn't washed or blown or seismically destabilized and propelled straight out to sea like an ark.

"See that?" Clare says, breathing out a captured breath. He gets down on both knees beside me like a scientist and brings his face right to the concrete pillar as if he means to smell it, then puts his index finger to the curved surface.

"What is it?" I say. I see nothing, though I'm assuming there *is* something and it can't be good.

"These piers are poured far away from here, Frank," Clare says as if in confidence. "Sometimes Canada. Sometimes upstate. The Binghamton area." He employs his finger to scratch at the transparent lacquer painted on the pier's exterior. "If you pour your forms too early in the spring, or if you pour them when the humidity's extremely high … well, you know what happens." Clare's creased face turns to me—we're very close here—and smiles a closed-mouth gotcha smile.

"What?"

"They crack. They crack right away," Clare says darkly. He has a pale sliver of pinkish scar right along the border of his Brillo-pad hairline. A vicious war wound, possibly, or else something discretionary from his second marriage. "If your manufacturer isn't too scrupulous he doesn't notice," Clare says. "And if he's unscrupulous he notices but then has this silicone sealer painted on and sells it to you anyway. And if your home builder or your G C isn't paying attention, or if he's been paid not to pay attention or if his foreman happens to be of a certain nationality, then these piers get installed without anybody saying anything. And when the work gets inspected, this kind of defect—and it *is* a serious defect and oughta show up—it might be possible for it not to get noticed, if you get my drift. Then your house gets built, and it stands up real well for about fifteen years. But because it's on the ocean, salt and moisture go to work on it. And suddenly—though it isn't sudden, of course—Hurricane Frank blows up, a high tide comes in, the force of the water turns savage and Bob's your uncle." Clare turns his gaze back to the pier, where we're crouched like cavemen behind the musty quick-lime-smelling Doolittle house, which is built, I see, on much worse than shifting sand. It's built on shitty pilings. "These piers, Frank. I mean"—Clare pinches his nose with distaste and home-owner pity, pressing his lips together—"I can see cracks here, and this is just the four to five inches showing. These people have real problems, unless you know a sucker who'll buy it sight unseen or get an inspector who needs a seeing-eye dog."

Clare's breath in these close quarters is milky stale-coffee breath and makes me realize I'm freezing and wishing I was two hundred miles from here.

"It's a problem. Okay." I stare at the innocent-looking little curve of gray pier surface, seeing nothing amiss. The thought that Clare's full of shit and that this is a softening-up ploy for a low-ball offer naturally occurs to me, as does the idea that since I can't see the crack, I don't have to bear the guilty knowledge that adheres to it. A thin file of stalwart ants is scuttering around the dusty foundation, taking in the air before the long subterranean winter.

"A problem. *Definitely*," Clare says solemnly. "I was raised in a tract home, Frank. I've seen bad workmanship all my life." He and I are straggling to our feet. I hear youthful boy-and-girl voices from the beach, beyond the dune bunker.

"What can you do about a problem like that, Clare?" I dust off my knees, stuffing the listing sheet farther down in my pocket, since it won't be needed. I experienced a brief stab of panic when Clare revealed the cracked pier, as if this house is mine and I'm who's in deep shit. Only now, a little airy-headed from bending down, then standing up too fast, I feel pure exhilaration and a thrumming sense of well-being that this is not my house, that my builder was a board-certified UVa architect, not some shade-tree spec builder (like Tommy Benivalle, Mike's best friend) with a clipboard and some plan-book blueprints, and who's in cahoots with the cement trade, the Teamsters, the building inspectors and city hall. Your typical developer, Jersey to Oregon. "I'm fine." These murmured words for some reason escape my lips. "I'm just fine."

"Okay, there's things you can do," Clare's saying. "They're not cheap." He's looking closely at me, into my eyes, his fingers pinching up a welt of nylon on my windbreaker sleeve. "You all right, old boy?"

I hear this. I also hear again the sound of youthful boy–girl voices beyond the dune. They emerge from a single source, which is the cold wind. "You look a little green, my friend,"

Clare's friendly voice says. I'm experiencing another episode. Conceivably it's only a deferred result of my floor struggle with Bob Butts last night. Yet for a man who hates to hope, my state of health is not as reliable as I'd hoped.

"Stood up too fast," I say, my cheeks cold and rubbery, scalp crawly, my fingers tingling.

"Chemicals," Clare says. "No telling what the hell they spray back here. The same thing's in sarin gas is in d-Con, I hear."

"I guess." I'm fuzzy, just keeping myself upright.

"Let's grab some O$_2$," Clare says, and with his bony left fist begins hauling me roughly up the dune, my shoes sinking in sand, my balance a bit pitched forward, my neck breaking a sweat. "Maybe you got vertigo," Clare says as he guys me up toward the top, his long legs doing the work for my two. "Men our age get that. It goes away."

"How old are you?" I say, being dragged.

"Sixty-seven."

"I'm fifty-five." I feel ninety-five.

"Good grief."

"What's the matter?" Sand's in my shoes and feels cool. His doozie loafers must be loaded, too.

"I must look a lot younger than I am."

"I was thinking you did," I say.

"Who knows how old anybody is, Frank?" We're now at the top. Lavender flat-surfaced ocean stretches beyond the wide high-tide beach. A smudge of gray-brown crud hangs at the horizon. Breeze seems to stream straight through my ears and gives me a shiver. For late November, I'm again dressed way too lightly. (I believed I'd be inside.) "I look at twenty-five-year-olds and somebody tells me they're fifteen," Clare natters on. "I look at thirty-five-year-olds who look fifty. I give up."

"Me, too." I'm already feeling a bit replenished, my heart quivering from our quick ascent.

Thirty yards out onto the beach and taking no notice of our appearance—legionnaires topping a rise—a group of teens, eight or nine of them, is occupied by a spirited volleyball game, the white orb rising slowly into the sky, one side shouting, "Mine!" "Set, seeeet-it!" "Bridget-Bridget! *Yours!*" The boys are tall, swimmer-lanky and blond; the girls semi-beautiful, tanned, rugged, strong-thighed. All are in shorts, sweaters, sweatshirts and are barefoot. These are the local kids, gone away to Choate and Milton, who've left home behind as lowly townie-ville but are back now, dazzlingly, with their old friends—the privileged few, enjoying the holidays as Yale and Dartmouth early-admissions dates grow near. Too bad my kids aren't that age instead of "grown." Possibly I could do my part better now. Though possibly not.

"You back in working order?" Clare pretends to be observing the volleyballers, who go on paying us no attention. We are the invisibles—like their parents.

"Thanks," I say. "Sorry."

"Vertigo," Clare says again, and gives his long over-large ear a stiff grinding with the heel of his hand. Clare clearly likes the prospect from up here. It's the view one would get from a "reimagined" floor three of the big-but-compromised Doolittle house behind us. Maybe his mind will change. Maybe cracked piers aren't so troublesome. Things change with perspective.

"You're from California, you don't count," a girl volleyballer says breezily into the breeze.

"*I* count," a boy answers. "I absolutely count. *Ro*-tate, *ro*-tate."

"Could you entertain a quasi-philosophical question, Frank?" Clare's now squatted atop the dune and has scooped up a handful of sand, as though assaying it, sampling its texture.

"Well—"

"Pertains to real estate. Don't worry. It's not about my sex life. Or yours. That's not philosophical, is it? That's Greek tragedy."

"Not always." I am on the alert for some heart-to-heart I lack the stomach for.

Clare half closes his creased submariner's eye at the brown horizon murk then spits down into the sand he's just released. "Do you imagine, Frank, that anything could happen in this country to make *normal* just not be possible?" He continues facing away, facing east, as if addressing an analyst seated behind him. "*I* actually tend to think nothing of that nature can really happen. Too many checks and balances. We've all of us manufactured reality so well, we're so solid in our views, that nothing can really change. You know? Drop a bomb, we bounce back. What hurts us makes us stronger. D'you believe that?" Clare lowers his strong chin, then cranks his skeptical gaze up at me, wanting an answer in kind. His kind. His kind of stagy seriousness. *Semper Fi*, Hué 'n Tet, the never-say-die Khe Sanh firebase of '67 seriousness. All the things I missed in my rather easy youth.

"I don't, Clare."

"No. Course not. Me, either," he says. "But I *want* to believe it. And *that's* what scares the shit right out of me. And don't think they're not sitting over there in those other countries that hate us licking their chops at what they see us doing over here, fucking around trying to decide which of these dopes to make President. You think these people here"—a toss of the Clare Suddruth head toward crumbling 61 Surf Road—"have foundation problems? *We've* got foundation problems. It's not that we can't see the woods for the trees, we can't see the woods *or* the fuckin' trees." Clare expels through his schnoz a breath heavy and poignant, something a Clydesdale might do.

"What does it have to do with real estate?"

"It's where I enter the picture, Frank," Clare says. "The circuit my mind runs on. I want to make Estelle's last years happy. I think a house on the ocean's the right thing. Then I start thinking about New Jersey being a prime target for some nut with a dirty bomb or whatever. And, of course, I know death's a pretty simple business. I've seen it. I don't fear it. And I know Estelle's gonna probably see it before I do. So I go on looking at these houses as if a catastrophe—or death—*can't* really happen, right up until, like now, I recognize it *can*. And it shocks me. Really. Makes me feel paralyzed."

"What is it that shocks you, Clare? You know everything there is to be afraid of. You seem way ahead of the game to me."

Clare shakes his head in self-wonder. "I'm sitting up in bed, Frank—honest to God—up in Parsippany. Estelle's asleep beside me. And what I go cold thinking about is: If something happens—you know, a bomb—can I ever sell my fucking house? And if I buy a new one, *then* what? Will property values even mean anything anymore? Where the hell are we then? Are we supposed to escape to some other place? Death's a snap compared to that."

"I never thought about that, Clare." As a philosophical question, of course, it's a lot like "Why the solar system?" And it's just about as practical-minded. You couldn't put a contingency clause in a buy–sell agreement that says "Sale contingent on there being no disaster rendering all real estate worthless as tits on a rain barrel."

"I guess *you* wouldn't think about it. Why would you?" Clare says.

"You said it was pretty philosophical."

"I know perfectly well it all has to do with 'Stelle being sick and my other relationship ending. Plus my age. I'm just afraid of the circumstances of life going to hell. Boom-boom-boom." Clare's staring out to sea, above the heads of the lithe, untroubled young volleyballers—a grizzled old Magellan who doesn't like what he's discovered. Boom-boom-boom.

Clare's problem isn't really a philosophical problem. It just makes him feel better to think so. His problem with circumstances is itself circumstantial. He's suffered normal human setbacks, committed perfidies, taken some shots. He just doesn't want to fuck up in those ways again and is afraid he can't recognize them when they're staring him in the face. It's standard—a form of buyer's remorse experienced prior to the sale. If Clare would just take the plunge (always the realtor's warmest wish for mankind), banish fear, think that instead of having suffered error and loss, he's *survived* them (but won't survive them indefinitely), that today could be the first day of his new life, then he'd be fine. In other words, accept the Permanent Period as your personal savior and act not as though you're going to die tomorrow but—much scarier—as though you might *live*.

How, though, to explain this without arousing suspicion that I'm just a smarmy, eel-slippery, promise-'em-anything sharpster, hyperventilating to unload a dump that's already crumbling from the ground upward?

You can't. *I* can't. As muddled as I feel out here, I know the Doolittles' house has serious probs, may be heading toward teardown in a year or two, and I would never sell this house to Clare and will, in fact, now have to be the bearer of somber financial news to the Doolittles in Boca. All's I can do is just show Clare more houses, till he either buys one or wanders off into the landscape. (I wonder if Clare's a blue state or a red state. Just as in Sponsoring, politics is a threshold you don't cross in my business, though most people who look at beach houses seem to be Republicans.)

Somewhere, out of the spheres, I hear what sounds like the

Marine Corps Hymn played on a xylophone. *Dum-dee-dum-dum-dum-dum-dum-dee-dum, dum-dum-dum-dum-dum-dum-dum.* It's surprisingly loud, even on the dune top in the breeze. The volleyball kids stop rotating, their heads turn toward us as if they've registered something weird, something from home or further back in the racial fog.

Clare goes fumbling under his jacket for a little black hand-tooled holster looped to his belt like a snub-nose. It's his cell phone, raising a sudden call to arms and valor—unmistakable as *his* ring and *only* his, in any airport, supermarket deli section or DMV line.

"Sud-druth." Clare speaks in an unexpected command voice—urgent message from the higher-ups to the troops in the thick of it down here. His snapped answer is aimed into an impossibly tiny (and idiotic) red Nokia exactly like every one of the prep school girls has in her Hilfiger beach bag. "Right," Clare snaps, jabbing a thumb in his other ear like a Thirties crooner and lowering his chin in strict, regimental attention. He steps away a few yards along the dune, where we are trespassers. Every single particle of his bearing announces: All right. *This* is important. "Yep, yep, yep," he says.

For me, though, it's a welcome, freeing moment, unlike most cell-phone interruptions, when the bystander feels like a condemned man, trussed and harnessed, eyes clenched, waiting for the trap to drop. The worst thing about others blabbing on their cell phones—and the chief reason I don't own one—is the despairing recognition that everybody's doing, thinking, saying pretty much the same things you are, and none of it's too interesting.

This freed moment, however, strands me out of context and releases me to the good sensations we all wish were awaiting us "behind" every moment: That—despite my moment of syncope, my failed house-showing, my crumbling Thanksgiving plans, my condition, my underlying condition, my overarching condition—there is still a broad fertile plain where we can see across to a white farmhouse with willows and a pond the sky traffics over, where the sun is in its soft morning quadrant and there is peace upon the land. I suddenly can feel this. Even the prep school kids seem excellent, promising, doing what they should. I wish Clare could feel it. Since with just a glimpse—

permitted by a kindly, impersonal life force—many things sit right down into their proper, proportionate places. "It's enough," I hear myself breathing to myself. "It's really enough."

"Yep, yep, yep." Clare's internalizing whatever's to be internalized. Get those fresh troopers up where they can see the back side of that hill and start raining hellfire down on the sorry bastards. And don't be back to me till that whole area's secured and you can give me a full report, complete with casualties. Theirs *and* ours. Got that? Yep, yep. "I'll get home around one, sweetheart. We'll have some lunch." It is a homelier communiqué than imagined.

Clare punches off his Nokia and returns it to its holster without turning around. He's facing north, up the shore toward Asbury Park, miles off, and where I'll soon be going. His posture of standing away gives him the aura of a man composing himself.

"Everything copacetic?" I smile, in case he should turn around and unexpectedly face me. A friendly visage is always welcome.

"Yes, sure." Clare does turn, *does* see my welcoming mug— a mug that says, We aren't looking at a house anymore; we're just men out here together, taking the air. The volleyballers have formed a caucus beside their net and are laughing. I hear one of *their* cell phones ringing—a gleeful little rilling that exults, *Yes, yes, yes!* "My wife, Estelle—well, you know her name." Clare glances toward the calm sea and its white filigree of sudsy surf, over which gulls are skimming for tiny fleeing mackerel. "When I'm gone for very long, it's like she thinks I'm not coming back." He dusts his big hands, cleaning off some residue of his call. "Of course, I did go away and didn't come back. You can't blame her."

"Sounds like it's all different now."

"Oh yeah." Clare runs his two clean hands back through his salt 'n pepper hair. He is a handsome man—even if part doozie, part fearful shrinker from the world's woe and clatter. We have things in common, though I'm not as handsome. "What were we gassing about?" His call has erased all. A positive sign. "I was bending your ear about some goddamn thing." He smiles, abashed but happy not to remember. A glimpse of my wide plain with the house, sun, pond and willows may, in fact, have been briefly his.

"We were talking about foundations, Clare."

"I thought we were talking about fears and commitments." He casts a wistful eye back at #61's troubled exterior—its weathered soffits, its gutter straps (defects I hadn't noticed). I say nothing. "Well," Clare says, "same difference."

"Okay."

"Somebody else'll want this place." He offers a relieved grin. Another bullet dodged.

"Somebody definitely will," I say. "You can bet on it. Not many things you can bet on, but on that, you can."

"Good deal," Clare says.

We find other things to talk about—he is a Giants fan, has season tickets—as I walk him back down and out to his Only Connect truck. He's happy to be heading home empty-handed, happy to be going where someone loves him and not where somebody's studying archaeology. I'm satisfied with him and with my part in it all. He is a good man. The Doolittles, I'm sure, after a day of raging, then brooding, then grudging resolution, could easily decide to come down on their asking. Houses like theirs change hands every four to six years and are built for turn-over. Not many people feel they were born to live in a house forever. I'll sell it by Christmas, or Mike will. Possibly to Clare. They truly aren't making any more of it here at the beach. And in fact, if the Republicans steal the show, they'll soon be trucking it away.

ON MY WAY back out Cormorant Court, Clare blinks his lights, and I pull over in front of a chalet where my red-and-white realty-wise sign stands out front. The Hondurans lounge on the little front steps, eating their lunches brought from home.

Clare idles alongside, his window already down so we can confer vehicle-to-vehicle in the cold air. Possibly he wants to set matters straight about my BUSH? WHY? bumper sticker, which I'm sure he doesn't approve of. I should probably peel it off now.

"What's the story with these?" he half shouts through his window (his passenger seat's been removed for insurance reasons). He's now wearing a pair of Foster Grants that make him look more like General MacArthur. He's talking about the chalet being spiffed up.

"Same old," I say. "I sell. You buy."

Clare's tough Marine Corps mouth, used to doing the talking, all the ordering, assumes a wrinkled, compromised expression of deliberate tolerance. He knows the opportunity to be taken seriously even by me is almost over. He gets most things—it's one of his virtues. But I'm as happy to sell him one of these as I am the Doolittles'. I've shown many a client a house they didn't want, then sold them a chalet as a consolation prize. Although blending business (potential rental income) with sentimental impulses (buying a house for the dying wife) can be troublesome for buyers. Internal messages can become seriously mixed, and bad results in the form of lost revenues ensue.

"What's the damage?" Clare says from the financial safety of his work truck.

"A buck seventy-five." Add twenty-five for wasting my time this morning, and since he's obviously got the scratch. "Walking distance to the beach."

"Rent 'em year-round?" Clare's smiling. He knows what a schmendrick he is.

"Make your nut in the summer. Seven-fifty a week last year. I take fifteen percent, get my crew in for upkeep. Capital improvement's yours. You probably clear seven per summer, before taxes and insurance. You really need to own three or four to make it happy." And you have to keep your heart out of your pocketbook. And this last summer wasn't that great. And Estelle won't like it. Clare's probably not ready for all this.

"That's assuming some miserable asshole doesn't sue you," he says out of the echo chamber of his truck. He may have heard me say something I didn't say. But he's refound his authority and begun frowning not at me but out his windshield toward NJ 35 at the end of Cormorant Court.

"There's always that." I smile a zany smile of *who cares*.

"Fuckin' ambulance chasers." Clare's two divorces could conceivably have left a bad taste in his mouth for the legal profession. He shakes his head at some unavenged bad memory. We've all been there. It's nothing to share the day before Thanksgiving. I try to think of a good lawyer joke, but there aren't any. "I see you voted for Gore. The patsy." He's acknowledging my BUSH? WHY? sticker.

"I did."

He stares stonily ahead at nothing. "I couldn't vote for Bush.

I voted for his old man. Now we're in the soup. Wouldn't you say?"

"I think we are."

"God help us," Clare says, and looks puzzled for the first time.

"I doubt if he will, Clare," I say. "Are you staging a big Thanksgiving?" I'm ready to part company. But I want to celebrate Clare-the-redeemed-Republican with a warm holiday wish.

"Yeah. Kids. Estelle's sister. My mom. The clan."

It's nice to know Clare has a mom who comes for holidays. "That's great."

"You?" Clare shifts into gear, his truck bumping forward.

"Yep. The whole clan. We try to connect." I smile.

"Okay." Clare nods. He hasn't heard me right. He idles away up toward 35 and the long road back to Parsippany.

SINCE THERE'S no direct-est route to Parkway Exit 102N, where Wade's already fuming at Fuddruckers, I take the scenic drive up 35, across the Metedeconk and the Manasquan to Point Pleasant, switch to NJ 34 through more interlocking towns, townships, townlettes—one rich, one not, one getting there, one hardly making its millage. I love this post-showing interlude in the car, especially after my syncope on the dune. It's the *moment d'or* which the Shore facilitates perfectly, offering exposure to the commercial-ethnic-residential zeitgeist of a complex republic, yet shelter from most of the ways the republic gives me the willies. "Culture comfort," I call this brand of specialized well-being. And along with its sister solace, "cultural literacy"— knowing by inner gyroscope where the next McDonald's or Borders, or the next old-fashioned Italian shoe repair or tuxedo rental or lobster dock is going to show up on the horizon—these together I consider a cornerstone of the small life lived accept-ably. I count it a good day when I can keep *all* things that give me the willies out of my thinking, and in their places substitute vistas I can appreciate, even unwittingly. Which is why I take the scenic route now, and why when I get restless I fly out to Moline or Flint or Fort Wayne for just a few hours' visit—since there I can experience the new and the complex, coupled with the entirely benign and knowable.

Cancer, naturally, exerts extra stresses on life (if you don't instantly die). We all cringe with cancer *scares*: the mole that doesn't look right; the lump below our glutes where we can't monitor it, the positive chest X ray (why does *positive* always mean fatal?) resulting in CAT scans, blood profiles, records reviews from twenty years back, all of which scare the shit out of us, make us silent but wretched as we await the results, entertaining thoughts of apricot treatments in Guadalajara and inquiries about euthanasia for nonresidents in Holland (I did all these). And then it's nothing—a harmless fatty accumulation, a histoplasmosis scar from childhood—innocent abnormalities (there *are* such things). And you're off the hook—though you're not unfazed. You've been on a journey and it's not been a happy one. Even without a genuine humming tumor deep in your prostate, just this much is enough to kill you. The coroner's certificate could specify for any of us: "Death came to Mr. X or Ms. Y due to acute heebie-jeebies."

But then when the sorry news *does* come, you're perfectly calm. You've used up all your panic back when it *didn't* count. So what good is calm? "Well, I'm thinking we'd better do a little biopsy and see what we're dealing with...." "Well, Mr. Bascombe, have a seat here. I've got some things I need to talk to you about...." Be calm now? Calm's just another face of wretched.

And then what follows *that* is the whole dull clouding over of *all* good feeling, *all* that normally elevates days, moods, reveries, pretty vistas, *all* the minor uplifts known to be comforting.... Crash-bang! *Meaningless!* Not *real* reality anymore, since something bad had *always* been there, right? The days before my bad news, when I had cancer but didn't know I had it and felt pretty damn good—all of those days are not worth sneezing at. *Good* was a lie, inasmuch as my whole grasp on life required that nothing terrible happen to me, *ever*—which is nuts. It did.

So the on-going challenge becomes: How, post-op, to maintain a supportable existence that resembles actual life, instead of walking the windy, trash-strewn streets in a smudged sandwich board that shouts IMPAIRED! FEEL SORRY FOR ME! BUT DON'T BOTHER TAKING ME SERIOUSLY AS A WHOLE PERSON, BECAUSE (UNLIKE YOU) I WON'T BE AROUND FOREVER!

I wish I could tell you I had a formula for changing the character of big into small. Mike has suggested meditation and a trip to Tibet. (It may come to that.) Clarissa's been a help—though I'm ready for her life to re-commence. Selling houses is clearly useful for making me feel invisible (even better than "connected"). And Sally's absence has not been a total tragedy, since misery doesn't really want company, only cessation. Suffice it to say that I mostly do fine. I overlook more than I used to, and many things have just quit bothering me on their own. Which leads me to think that my "state" must not be such a thoroughly bad or altered one.

And I'll also admit that in the highly discretionary lives most of us lead, there *is* sweet satisfaction to this being *it*, and to not having *it* be always out there to dread: the whacker coronary; both feet amputated after paraskiing down K2 on your birthday; total macular degeneration, so you need a dog to help you find the can. This longing for satisfaction, I believe, is in the hearts of those strange Korea vets who admit to wartime atrocities they never committed and never would've; and may be the same for poor friendless Marguerite, back in Haddam, wondering what she has to confess. There *is* a desire to face some music, even if it's a tune played only in your head—a desire for the real, the permanent, for a break in the clouds that tells you, This is how you are and will always be. Great nature has another thing to do to you and me, so take the lively air, the poet said. And I do. I take the lively air whenever I can, as now. Though it's that *other thing* great nature promises that I rely on, the thing that quickens the step and the breath and so must not be thought of as the enemy.

I HATCH A thought as I cross the Manasquan bridge and near the 34 cut-off: to stop at the Manasquan Bar for a beer and a piss in its nautical, red-lit cozy confines. Years ago, with a cohort of fellow divorcés, I would drive over from Haddam once a month, just to get out of town, seeking night-time companionship and large infusions of gin and scotch that always sent us back into the dark to Hightstown, Mercerville and home with a better grasp on our griefs and sorrows. A quick re-savoring of those old days—the rosy perpetual indoor bar light and beery bouquets—would, I'm sure, extend the good feeling I've concocted. But a piss is what I really need and a beer is not, since a beer would just require another piss sooner than I now consider normal (hourly). Plus, any venture into the swampy vapors of time lost—no matter how good I'd feel—could prove precarious, and make me late for Wade.

Instead then, I take 34 straight inland, north through suburban Wall Township, which is not truly municipal or even towny, but dense and un-centered, a linear boilerplate of old strip development, skeins of traffic lights and jug-handles with signage indicating Russians, Farsi speakers, Ethiopians and Koreans live nearby and do business. A cellular tower camouflaged to look like a Douglas fir looms up at an uncertain distance above roofs and fourth-growth woodlots. The Manasquan River winds past somewhere off to the left. But little is discernible or of interest. It is actually hard to tell what the natural landscape looks like here.

I pull in for my long piss at a Hess station across the avenue from Wall Township Engine Company No. 69, where a Thanksgiving CPR clinic's in progress on the station-house apron. Burly firefighters in black-and-yellow regalia are demonstrating modern resuscitative techniques on plastic mannequins and on citizens craving resuscitating firsthand. Cheerleaders from the Upper Squankum Middle School are running a five-dollar car wash at the curb. Inside the station house, so the sign-on-wheels says, selected items from the Hoboken Museum's traveling Frank Sinatra collection are on display, along with a DNR exhibit entitled "What to Do When Wild Animals Come to Call." A handful of citizens mills around on the asphalt—tall and skinny Ethiopians, with a few smaller Arabs in non-Arab sweaters— all having a perusal of the pumper rig and the hook 'n ladder, stealing nervous glances at the female dummy the firemen are working on and taking leaning peeks in at the Old Blue Eyes display. It is all a good civic pull-together, even if Thanksgiving's a quaint mystery to most of them and business is poor hereabouts. Rich soil is here for municipal virtues, though the philosopher would never have planted them in Wall Township.

AT GARDEN State Exit 102N, it's half past noon, a cold November sun shining high. The Queen Regent implosion is scheduled for one, and since I haven't answered Wade's calls, he's likely to be fidgety and cross. In my view, oldsters with virtually zilch to do should squander their hours like sailors on shore leave, but instead end up hawking the clock and making everybody miserable, while us working clods would like to throw our watches in the ocean (I don't own one).

When I pull up, Wade is seated on the curb under the yellow awning of the Fuddruckers, which appears to be out of business, along with the empty Sixties-era mall just behind it, whose long, vacant parking lot awaits reassignment. Wade starts theatrically tapping the face of his big silver and turquoise wristwatch and scowling when I wheel in beside his ancient tan Olds. I should've been here yesterday, or at least two hours ago, and now I've jeopardized his day.

"Did you get lost in Metedeconk?" he says, struggling up onto his tiny feet, getting his balance on the blue disabled sign. Metedeconk represents an insider joke I know nothing about.

"I did," I say through my window. "They all asked about you." I stay put behind the wheel. The warmer inland air carries a seam of dry cold as traffic swishes noisily on the Parkway.

"I know who asked about me, all right." He's shuffling— bow-legged, stiff-hipped, arms slightly held out like an outrigger. Wade says he's seventy-four, but is actually over eighty. And though he's dressed in youthful sporting attire—baggy pink jackass pants with a semaphore pattern, sockless white patent-leather slip-ons and a bright yellow V neck—he looks decrepit and shabby, as if he'd slept in this outfit for a week. "We're going in my vehicle," he growls, eyes fixed on the pavement in front of him as if its surface was tricking around.

"Not today," I say, cheerfully.

Wade is a menacing driver. He regularly runs stop signs, drives thirty-five on the Turnpike, barges through intersections, leans on his horn, has his turn signal constantly on, shouts religious and gender epithets at other drivers, and, because he's considerably shrunken, can barely see over his dashboard. He shouldn't be allowed near the driver's seat. Though when I've counseled him, during our monthly lunch at Bump's, that it's time to hang up his duster and ride, his blue eyes snap, his teeth clack, his foot and knee tremor starts whapping the table leg. "So are you volunteering to drive me? Good. I'll let you drive me—and wait for me everyplace I go until I'm ready to go home. Sounds perfect. Do you think I *like* to drive?" He has his point. Though I often think that death will come to me not naturally, but by being backed over by some stiff-necked old lunatic like Wade in front of the Marshalls in Toms River.

I sit my seat, shaking my head, which is certain to piss him off.

Wade pauses between our two vehicles and glowers at me. "Mine's all rigged up." Meaning his car seat's shoved up, his hemorrhoid donut's strapped to the extra cushion, the radio's tuned to a hillbilly station he likes in Long Branch, and the beaded back supporter that helps his arthritis is bungeed to the driver's side. For years, Wade worked as a toll taker at Exit 9 on the Turnpike and believes repetitive stress plus exhaust fumes degraded his skeleton and compromised his immune system, resulting in shrunkenness and unexplained night pains. I've explained to him he's just old.

"I've got a wife and children to think about, Wade." I'm waiting for him to get in.

"Hah! The missing wife. That's a good one." Wade knows all about my marital hiatus, as well as my prostate issues and most of the rest of my story, which he takes no interest in unless he can make a joke out of it (his own prostate is a memory). Due, I believe, to an occasional mini-stroke, Wade also sometimes confuses me with his son, Cade, a New Jersey State Trooper in

Pohatcong, Troop W. And at other times, for reasons I don't understand, he calls me "Ned." This kind of impairment could pass for useful disinterest, I've thought. So that if Wade wasn't occasionally ga-ga and didn't yak your ear off, I'd get him certified to Sponsor fellow seniors out at the Grove, the staged senior community where he lives in Bamber Lake, where they hold weekly wine tastings, senior art openings and jigsaw puzzle contests, and boast gold-standard tertiary care, in-house cardiac catheterization, their own level-one trauma center, with six class-A hospitals a twenty-minute ambulance ride away, but where Wade says the oldsters are always looking for something extra.

Wade has given in to riding in my car and has crawled into his Olds to retrieve his brown-bag lunch and his video cam so he can eat while the Queen Regent falls in on herself and also get the whole thing on tape for public exhibit. At the Grove, he says, he's an A-list dinner guest and much sought after by the ladies as a raconteur.

"We're all better off to get over our pain," Wade says in a muffled voice inside his passenger's door. He's referring to my absent wife. He's on his hands and knees, fishing for something on the floorboard and making Frankenstein noises, his pink-pants ass in the air. I would help, but it's part of our compact that he never needs help. I stare glumly in at his inflatable hemorrhoid donut.

"I think you're a walking advertisement for a long life," I say, though he can't hear me. I could just as easily say, I'd like to string you up by your ankles and put a stopwatch on how long it takes your head to explode, and it would mean the same. Wade's not a proficient listener, which he credits to having had a full life and a reduced need to take anything in anymore.

"On the other hand." He's grunting, backing out, hauling his sack lunch and his Panasonic. "I'd kill myself if I wasn't afraid of the fucking pain." He stands up on the Fuddruckers' asphalt, facing inside his car as if I was there instead of behind him. He's become an odd-looking creature, after being pretty normal-looking when I first knew him. While his hands and arms and neck are dry and leathery as an alligator, his small head is round and pinkish-orange, as if he'd been boiled. He's fashioned his white hair into a Caesarian back-to-front comb-down that makes a bang, which—depending on barbershop visits—can be a simple-sad oldster fringe or else a Beatle-length mop that makes him appear seventy, which is how he more or less looks now. Add to this that when he takes off his glasses, his blue left eye wanders off cockeyed, that he wears a big globby hearing device in each ear, is an inexpert face shaver, plus always gets too close to you when he talks (spritzing you with Listerine spit), and you have a not always attractive human package.

When I first knew Wade, sixteen years ago, he lived in the suburb of Barnegat Pines, with his now-deceased second wife, Lynette, and son, Cade. I was then lost in hapless but powerful love for his daughter, Vicki—an oncology nurse and major handful of daunting physical attainments. It was three years after my son died, and one after my divorce from Ann, a time when my existence seemed in jeopardy of fading into a pointless background of the onward rush of life. Wade was then a level-eyed, crew-cut engineer and truth seeker. He'd seen confusion in life, had looked the future in the eye and gotten down to being a solid citizen/provider who understood his limits, maintained codes and was glad to welcome me as a unique, slightly "older" son-in-law candidate. My present take on Wade comes mostly from those long-ago days. I didn't see him at all for sixteen years and only refound him four months back when Cade presented me with a speeding ticket on my way back late from the Red Man Club and I noticed the ARCENAULT on his brass name plate. Blah, blah, blah, blah, blah . . . I ended up calling Wade because as he wrote out the summons, Cade—thick-browed, fat-eared, wearing a black flak jacket and a flat-top—said that "Dad" had become "like a pretty sad case" and "maybe wouldn't last a lot longer" and that they (Cade and Mrs. Cade) had "pretty much our own lives up in Pohatcong, kids and whatever," and didn't make it down to visit the old man as often as they should. "Things like that are too bad in a way," he observed. And, oh, by the way, that'll be ninety clams, plus costs, plus two points, have a nice day and keep 'er under fifty-five.

I ended up rendezvous-ing with Wade at Bump's and reaffiliating. And in a short while, I managed to reconcile Wade *years back*—frontier Nebraskan with a trim physique and a Texas Aggie engineering degree, with Wade *today*—orange-skinned, obstreperous bang-wearer and sour-smelling, weirdly dressed crank; and, by the force of my will, to make a whole person out of the evidence. Aging requires reconciliations, and nobody said getting old would be pretty or the alternative better.

What Wade and I actually do for each other in the present tense, and that makes putting up with each other worth the aggravation, is a fair question. But when he's in his right head—which is most of the time—Wade's as sharp as a Mensa member, still sees the world purely as it is and for this reason is not a bad older friend for me, just as I'm not a bad younger companion to keep him on his toes. We share, after all, a piece of each other's past, even if it's not a past we visit. We also like each other, as only truly consenting adults can.

ASBURY PARK, which we pass through and where I've done some bank work, has unhappily devolved over the years into a poverty pocket amidst the pricey, linked Shore communities, Deal to Allenhurst, Avon to Bay Head. Those monied towns all needed reliable servant reserves a bus ride away, and Asbury was ceded to the task. Hopeful Negroes from Bergen County and Crown Heights, Somalis and Sudanese fresh off the plane, plus a shop-keeper class of Iranis for whom Harlem was too tough, now populate the streets we drive down. Occasionally, a shady Linden Lane or a well-tended Walnut Court survives, with its elderly owner-occupant tending his patch while values sink to nothing and the element pinches in. But most of the streets are showing it—windows out, mansions boarded, grass gone weedy, side-walks crumbling, informal automotive work conducted curb-side, while black men wait on corners, kids ply the pavements on Big Wheels, and large African-looking ladies in bright scarves lean on porch rails, watching the world slide by. Asbury Park could be Memphis or Birmingham, and nothing or no one would seem out of place.

"One in five non-English speakers, right?" Wade's watching out his window, fingering his diabetic's Medi-Ident bracelet and looking abstracted. He's infected the interior of my car with his sour, citrusy elder-smell—mostly from his yellow sweater—that mingles with Mike's stale Marlboro residue from last night, making me have to crack open my window. He shoots me a fiery glance when I don't answer his non-English-speaker non-question, pink tongue working his dentures (his "falsies") as if he's warming up for verbal combat. Wade is of a generally conservative belief-base but wouldn't vote for dumb-ass Bush if the world was ablaze and Bush had the bucket. He grew up poor, lucked into A&M, worked two decades in the oil patch in Odessa and views Republicans as trustees for keeping government on the sidelines, out of his boudoir, the classroom and the Lord's house (where he's not a frequenter). Isolation's the way to go, keep the debt below zero, inflation nonexistent, blubbety-blubbety. Any kind of sanctimony's for scoundrels—hence the hatred of Bush. Smiling Rocky was Wade's hero, though he's voted Democrat since Watergate. "Housing's leveled off. D'you read that?" he says, just to make noise.

"Not where I live," I say.

"Oh, well of course," Wade says. "Being what you are, you'd know that. That's the kind of stuff you're the expert in. The rest of us have to read about it in the papers."

AT STRAIGHT-UP one o'clock, the day's turned warmer than in Sea-Clift. A pavement of gray clouds has streaked open up here to reveal febrile blue out over the ocean we're approaching. The day no longer feels like the day before Thanksgiving, but a late-arriving Indian summer afternoon or a morning in late March when spring's come in like a lamb. A perfect day for an implosion.

The Queen Regent sits opposite the boardwalk and the crumbling Art Deco convention hall—home to luckless club fights and poorly attended lite-rock record hops. Noisy gulls soar above and around the Queen's battlements, where she stands alone on a plain against the sky, as if the old buff-colored hospital-looking pile of bricks was occupying space no longer hers. Though even from a distance she's hardly an edifice to rate a big send-off: Nine stories, all plain (and gutted), with two U-shaped empty-windowed wings and a pint-size crenellated tower like a supermarket cake. A previously-canopied but now trashy glassed-in veranda faces the boardwalk and the Atlantic, and a wooden water tower with a giant TV antenna attached bumps above the roofline. Once it was a place where felt-hatted drummers could take their girlfriends on the cheap. Families with too many kids could go and pretend it was nice. Young honeymooners came. Young suicides. Oldster couples lived out their days within sound of the sea and took their meals in the dim coffered dining room. Standing alone, the Queen Regent looks like one of those condemned men from a hundred revolutions who the camera catches standing in an empty field beside an open grave, looking placid, resigned, distracted—awaiting fate like a bus—when suddenly volleys from off-stage soundlessly pelt and spatter them, so they're changed in an instant from present to past.

All around the Queen Regent is a dry, treeless urban-renewal savanna stretching back to the leafless tree line of Asbury. Where we're currently driving were once sweller, taller hotels with glitzier names, stylish seafood joints with hot jazz clubs in the basement, and farther down the now-missing blocks, tourist courts and shingled flop-houses for the barkers and rum-dums who ran the Tilt-A-Whirl on the pier or waltzed trays in the convention hall, which itself looks like it could fall in with a rising tide and a breeze. Today it is all a PROGRESS ZONE! a sign says, WITH LUXURY CONDO COMMUNITY COMING!

Wade has his silver Panasonic up and trained tight on the Queen Regent through the wide windshield glass. His is the awkward kind you peer *down* into like a reverse periscope, and operating it through his bifocals makes him crank his mouth open moronically and his old lips go slack. He seems to believe the Queen is about to go down any instant.

"Drive us around to the front, Franky. What're we doin' over here?" He flashes me a savage gaping grimace. The V of Wade's yellow velour sweater, under which is only bare skin, shows his chicken chest with sparse white pinfeathers sprouting. I've seen Wade naked once, in his "flat" in Bamber Lake, when I arrived early for dinner. I haven't gone back.

A tall cyclone fence, however, has been stretched around the Queen Regent, razor wire on top to discourage souvenir seekers and preservationist saboteurs who're always around looking to monkey-wrench a decent implosion. We the public can't go where Wade wants us to, or, in fact, get within three football fields of the site, since Asbury Park police and a cadre of blue-tunicked State Troopers have rigged a traffic diversion using cones and Jersey barriers and are forcing us off onto (another) Ocean Avenue and away from the hotel entirely. We can both see where a crowd of implosion spectators has been marshaled into a temporary grandstand the imploding company, the Martello Brothers—FIREWORKS, DETONATING, RAZING FOR PASSAIC AND CENTRAL JERSEY—has put up behind another cyclone fence at the remote south end of the Progress Zone, across from another big sign that says THIS STREET ADOPTED BY ASBURY PK CUB PACK 31. Some land—I'm thinking, as we follow Ocean Avenue toward the Temporary Parking—is better off with a few good condos.

"You can't see a fucking thing from over here." Wade's twisted in his seat, straining to see back to the Queen Regent, his throat constricted, his voice raised a quarter octave while he forces his Panasonic up to his bifocals in case the whole shebang goes down while I'm parking. "It might as well be the White Sands Proving Ground out here. What're they afraid of, the god-damn peckerwoods?" Wade never cursed when I first knew him and was wooing his daughter like Romeo.

"I'm sure insurance stipulates—"

"Don't get me going on those shitheads," he says. "When Lynette died, I didn't get a cryin' nickel." Lynette was Wade's wife number two, a tiny Texas termagant and Catholic crackpot who left him to enter a Maryknoll residence in Bucks County, where she became a Christian analyst auditing the troubled life stories of others like herself, until she had an embolism, assigned her benefits to the nuns and croaked. I've heard quite a bit about all that since the summer, and I consider it one of the fringe benefits of not marrying Wade's daughter, Vicki, that I missed having Lynette as my mother-in-law. Wade doesn't always perfectly remember I was ever in love with Vicki, or why he and I know each other. Vicki, however—he told me—has now changed her name to Ricki and lives a widow's life in Reno, where she works as an ER nurse and never ventures back to New Jersey. God works in sundry ways.

I've driven us around to the temporary parking remuda behind the Martello Brothers' bleachers. Back here are two trucked-in Throne Room portable toilets—always good to find—and several land yachts and fifth-wheel camper rigs, indicating that other implosion enthusiasts have spent the night to get the best seats. I've barely stopped and Wade is already quick out and stumping around toward the side of the bleachers, Panasonic in one hand, greasy sandwich bag in the other, not wanting to miss anything, since we're five minutes late.

The whole setup's like an athletic event, a Friday pigskin tilt between Belvedere and Hackettstown in the brittle late-autumn sunshine—only this tilt's between man's hold on permanence and the Reaper (most contests come down to that). The crowd around the front of the bleachers is exerting a continuous anticipatory hum as I approach. A raucous male voice shouts, "Not yet, not yet. Please, not yet!" An African-looking woman in a flowered daishiki has set up a makeshift table-stand, selling *I Went Down with the Queen* and *The Queen Regent Had My Child* tee-shirts. A large black man has secured the "Chicago Jew Dog" concession and is cooking franks on a black fifty-gallon drum. I'm famished and buy one of these in a paper napkin. Bush and Gore placards are leaned against the fence in case anyone wants to recant his vote. The Salvation Army has a tripod and kettle off to the side, with a tall blue-suited matron clanging a big bell and smiling. There are lots of Asbury Park cops. Everything is here but someone singing karaoke.

When I get near the edge of the grandstand (Wade has disappeared), I can see that the crowd's being addressed by a small stout man in a yellow jumpsuit and gold hard hat, who's talking through a yellow electric bullhorn. He's in the middle of declaring that thousands of man-hours, four million sticks of dynamite, nine zillion feet of wire, brain-scrambling computer circuitry, the services of two Rutgers Ph.D.'s, plus the generous cooperation of the Monmouth County Board of Supervisors and the Asbury Park city council, plus the cops, have made *here* be the safest place to be in New Jersey, which makes the crowd snicker. This man I recognize as "Big Frank" Martello of the fabled brothers. Big Frank is a homegrown Jersey product who, after mastering percussive skills blowing up VC caves in the Sixties, came home to Passaic, turned away from the family's business of loan-sharking and knee-restructuring, took a marketing degree at Drew and went into the legit business of blowing things to smithereens for profit (the fireworks came along later). Being the oldest, Frank sent his six siblings to college (one is a dentist in Middlebush), and little by little absorbed the ones who were inclined into the business, which was in fact, booming. There they thrived and became a famed family phenomenon the world over—a sort of black-powder Wallendas—capable of astounding destructive dexterities, pinpoint precision and smokeless, dustless, barely noticeable obliterations in which buildings safely vanished, sites were cleaned and the craters filled so that the concrete trucks could be all lined up for work the following day.

I'm acquainted with Big Frank "the legend" because his brother Nunzio, the dentist, made inquiries about a snug-away for one of his girlfriends in Seaside Heights. While we cruised the streets, one thing led to another and the family saga got unspooled. Nunzio finally bought a lanai apartment for his honey down in Ship Bottom, and I'm sure is happy there.

Big Frank's riling up the crowd—about two hundred of us— to a modest pitch, cracking dumb New Jersey Turnpike and Turkey Day jokes, taking off his yellow hard hat and dipping his dome to show us how few hairs his dangerous job has left him, then strutting around arms-crossed in front of the bleachers, like Mussolini. The crowd includes plenty of young parents with their kids in crash helmets, off for school holidays, plus a good number of older couples representing the land yachts and fifth-wheelers, who conceivably honeymooned in the Queen Regent, skating nights on the hardwood floors of the convention hall way back when. There's also, of course, the inevitable collection of singleton strangees like Wade and me, who just like a good explosion and don't need to talk about it. All are seated in rows, knees together, sunglasses and headgear in place, staring more or less raptly at a red plunger box Big Frank has stationed on a red milk crate in front of the temporary fence on which is attached a sign inscribed with his well-known motto, WE TAKE IT DOWN.

From where I'm standing to the side of the bleachers, eating my Jew Dog, I can see the red plunger is ominously *up*. Though no wires are connected. The whole plunger business, I suspect, is a fake, the critical signal likely to be beamed in from Martello Command Central in Passaic, using computer modeling, high-tolerance telemetry, fiber optics, GPS, etc. Nobody there will hear or see a thing but what's on a screen.

I cast up into the bleachers, half-wolfed hot dog in hand, seeking Wade's orange face, and find it instantly, sunk in the crowd at the top row. He's glowering down at me for not being up where he is, with a good view across the Progress Zone to the far away Queen Regent. Wade makes an awkward, spasmic hand gesture for me to get my ass up there. It's a movement a person having a heart attack would make, and people on either side of him give him a fishy eye and inch away. ("Some smelly old nut sat beside us at the implosion. You can't go anywhere—")

But I'm in no mood for climbing over strangers to achieve closer bodily contact with Wade—plus, I have my dog, and am as happy here as I'm likely to get today. The sun at the crowd's edge feels good, the air rinsed clean like a state fair on the first afternoon before the rides are up. No matter that we're in a no-man's-land in a dispirited seaside town, waiting to watch an abandoned building get turned to rubble—the second explosion I've been close to in two days.

I wave enigmatically up to Wade, raise my hot dog bun, point to my wrist as if it had a watch on it that said zero hour. Wade mouths back grudging words no one can hear. Then I turn my attention back to Big Frank, who's standing beside his red plunger box while a skinny white kid with technical know-how, wearing a plain white jumpsuit, screws wires to terminals on top, looking questioningly up at Big Frank as if he doesn't think any of this is going quite right. In the distance, through the fence and across the three football fields, I can make out small human figures moving hastily inside the Queen Regent's secure perimeter toward what must be the exit gates. Many more blue-and-white Asbury PD cruisers are now apparent, all with their blue flashers going. Yellow traffic lights I also hadn't noticed are blinking along the emptied streets. A police helicopter, an orange-striped Coast Guard chopper and a "News at Noon" trafficopter are hovering just off the boardwalk in anticipation of a big bang soon to come. The Salvation Army bell is clanging, and for the first time I hear hearty, sing-song human voices chanting from somewhere "Save the cream, save the cream," which, of course, is "Save the Queen, save the Queen." The chanters are nicely dressed (but unavailing) landmark loonies who've been forced into a spot outside some white police sawhorses, where they can make their voices heard but be ignored.

Big Frank, through his electric megaphone, which makes his strong New Jersey basso seem to come out of a cardboard box, is spieling about how the "seismic effects" of what we're about to witness will be detectable in China, yet the charges have been so ingeniously calculated by his family that the Queen Regent will fall straight down in exactly eighteen seconds, every loving brick coming to rest in arithmetically predetermined spots. "Nat-ur-al-ly" there'll be some dust (none of it asbestos), but not even as much, he's saying, as a stolen garbage truck would kick up in Newark—this is also due to climatological gauging, humidity indexing, plus fiber optics, lasers, etc. The sound will be surprisingly modest, "so you might want to hire us to renovate your mother-in-law's house in Trenton, hawr, hawr, hawr." A Coast Guard cutter is stationed just off the boardwalk ("In case one of my brothers gets blown out there"). Scuba divers are in the water. Fish and geese migration patterns won't be disrupted, nor will air quality or land values in Asbury Park—a murmur of general amusement. Likewise hospital services. "All efforts, in other words," he concludes, "have been expended to make the demolition nuttin' more than a fart in a paint bucket."

Big Frank stumps heavily off his central master of ceremonies spot to confer, head-down, with the skinny technician kid, plus two other swart-haired parties in red jumpsuits, who look like they might be filling station employees, though for all I know are the Rutgers Ph.D.'s. One of these red-suits hands Big Frank a set of old-fashioned calipered earphones with a mouthpiece attached. Big Frank, hard hat in hand, holds one phone to his ear, seems to listen intently to something—a voice?—coming through, then begins barking orders back, his meathead's big mouth cut into a downward swoop of anger, his head nodding.

Conceivably something's amiss, something that might postpone the big mushroom cloud and send us all cruising back down the streets of Asbury Park seeking substitute excitements. A hush of waiting has fallen over the hurly-burly, and a low hum of individual voices and single laughters and beer-can pops arises. A rich fishy smell drifts in off the sea—contributor, no doubt, to the Queen Regent's run of bad luck, since it comes from discharge practices long banned, though the pollutants are still in the soil and the atmosphere. From some undetermined place, there's a high-pitched mechanized *whee-wheeing* in the air, like the ghost of an empty ferris wheel at the boardwalk Fun Zone, where millions idled and thrilled and smooched away summer evenings without a care for what came before or

next. To me, there's good to be found in these random sensations. I've made it my business at this odd time of life, when
the future seems interesting but not necessarily "fun," to permit
no time to be a dead time, since you wouldn't want to forget
at a later, direr moment what that earlier, possibly better, day
or hour or era was "like"; how the afternoon felt when the
implosion got canceled, what specific life got lived as you
awaited the Queen Regent's decline to rubble. You definitely
would want to know that, to have that on your mind's record
instead of say, like poor Ernie, hearing the thanatologist droning, "Frankee, Frankee? Can you hear me? Can you hear any-
ting? Is you all de vay dead?"

Then . . . *boom, boom, boom, boom. Boomety-boom. Boom, boom.
Boomety-boomety!* The Queen Regent is going. Right now. I'm
happy I didn't duck out to the Throne Room.

Innocent puffs of gray-white smoke, small but specific and
unquestionably consequential, go *poof-poof-poof* all up and down
the Queen's nine-story height, as if someone, some authority
inside, was letting air out of old pillows, sweeping her clean,
putting her in top form for the big reopening. Birds—the gulls
I'd seen before, diving, swooping and wheeling—are suddenly
flying away. No one warned them.

Our entire crowd—many are standing—exhales or gasps or
sighs a spoon-moon-Juning "ahhhh" as if this is the thing now,
finally, what we've come for, what nothing else can ever get
better than.

Big Frank's staring, startled, right along with us, his big baldy
head still calipered, his mouth gapped open, though he quickly
closes it hard as an anvil, nostrils flaring. The two swarthy red-
suited assistants have backed away as if he might start wind-
milling punches. The skinny kid who'd wired the plunger box
is blabbing into Big Frank's sizable ear, though Big Frank's
staring out at the building being consumed in smoke, the plunger
still stagily *up* at his feet.

Boom. Boom. Boomety-boom. Again, puffs of now grayer smoke
squirt out all around the Queen Regent's foundation skirting,
and another big one at the top, from the crenellated crown. And
now commences a set of larger sounds. These things never go
off with one bang, but more like a percussive chess game—the
pawns first, then the bishops, then the knights. Whatever's left

stands and fights but can't do either. At least that's how it happened down in Ventnor.

Now another series of *boom-booms*, bigger towering ones erupt from the Queen Regent's core. The old dowager has yet to shudder, lean or sway. Possibly she won't go down at all and the crowd will be the winner. Some yokel up in the stands laughs and yaps, "She ain't fallin'. They fucked this all up." Spectators have begun smiling, looking side to side. Wade, I can see, is getting all on tape. The Grove ladies will love him even more if the Queen survives. Big Frank's now glaring. I can read his lips, and they say, Fuck you. It'll fuckin' fall, you pieces of shit.

Just then, as the Queen Regent is holding firm and the copters are darting in closer from over the water, and some of the Asbury cops with flashers are moving along Ocean Avenue in front of the convention hall, and our crowd has started clapping, whooping and even stomping on the risers (Big Frank looks disgusted in his caliper headgear, and no doubt's begun calculating who's gonna catch shit)—just then, as the demolition turns to un-demolition—a scrawny, dark-skinned black kid of approximately twelve, wearing a hooded black sweatshirt, baggy dungarees down over big silver basketball sneakers and carrying a plastic Grand Union bag containing a visible half gallon of milk, a kid who's been standing beside me, letting his milk carton bap against my leg for five minutes as if I wasn't there, *this* kid suddenly makes a springing, headlong dash from beside me, out across the front of the crowd, and with one insolent stomp of his silver foot whams down the red plunger of the phony detonator box, then goes whirling back past me around the end of the grandstand, darting and dodging through the standees toward the parking lot, where he disappears around a big Pace Arrow and is gone. "Motherfuckin' *boool*shit" is all I'm certain he says in departure, though he may have said something more.

And now the Queen Regent is headed down. Maybe the plunger did it. Black smoke gushes from what must be the hotel's deepest subterranean underpinnings, her staunchest supports (this will be what the Chinese seismographers detect). Her longitude lines, rows of square windows in previously perfect vertical alignment, all go wrinkled, as if the whole idea of the building had sustained, then sought to shrug off a profound insult, a killer wind off the ocean. And then rather simply, all the way down she comes, more like a brick curtain being lowered than like a proud old building being killed. Eighteen seconds is about it.

A clean vista briefly comes open behind the former Queen—toward Allenhurst and Deal—leafless trees, a few flecks of white house sidings, a glint of a car bumper. Then that is gone and a great fluff of cluttered gray smoke and dust whooshes upward and outward. We spectators are treated to a long, many-sectioned, more muffled than sharp progression of rumblings and crumblings and earth-delving noises that for a long moment strike us all silent (it must be the same at a public hanging or a head lopping).

Someone, another male, with a Maryland Tidewater accent, shouts, "*Awww*-raaiight. Yoooooo-hoo." (Who are the people who do this?) Then someone else shouts, "Aww-right," and people begin clapping in the tentative way people clap in movies. Big Frank, who's stood glaring across the empty Progress Zone, turns to the crowd with a smirk that combines disdain with derision. Someone yells, "Go get 'em, Frank!" And for an instant, I think he's shouting encouragement to me. But it's to the other Frank, who just waves a sausage hand dismissively—know-nothings, jerkimos, putzes—and with his two red-suited lieutenants, stalks away around the far side of the bleachers and out of sight. One could hope, forever.

WADE'S GONE pensive as we walk back across the grass lot to my Suburban, a mood that's infected other spectators retreating to their campers and SUVs and vintage Volvos. Most conduct intimate hushed-voice exchanges. A few laugh quietly. Some brand of impersonal closure has been sought and gained at no one's expense. It's been a good outing. All seem to respect it.

Wade, however, is struggling some with his motor skills. How he climbed the bleachers, I don't know, though he seems a man at peace. He's told me that after Lynette retreated to the Bucks County nunnery and he'd retired from the Turnpike, he decided to put his Aggie engineering degree to use for the public's benefit. This involved trying out some invention ideas he'd logged in a secret file cabinet down in his Barnegat Pines basement (plenty of time to dream things up in the tollbooth). These were good ideas he'd never had time for while raising a family, moving up to New Jersey from the Dallas area and working a regular shift at Exit 9 for fifteen-plus years. His ideas were the usual Gyro Gearloose brainstorms: a lobster trap that floated to the surface when a lobster was inside; a device to desalinate seawater one glassful at a time—an obvious hit, he felt, with lifeboat manufacturers; a universal license plate that would save millions and make crime detection a cinch. If he could dream it up, it could work, was his reasoning. And there were plenty of millionaires to prove him right. You just had to choose one good idea, then concentrate resources and energies there. Wade chose as his idea the manufacture of mobile homes no tornado could sweep away in a path of destruction. It would revolution-ize lower-middle-class life, Florida to Kansas, he felt certain. He took half his lump-payment Turnpike pension and sank it in a prototype and some expensive wind-tunnel testings at a private lab in Michigan. Naturally, none of it worked. The coefficients to wind resistance proved 100 percent relatable to mass, he said. To make a mobile home not blow away—and he knew this outcome was a possibility—you had to make it really heavy, which made it not a mobile home but just a house you wouldn't think to put up on wheels and move to Weeki Wachee. And apart from not working, his prototype was also far too expensive for the average mobile-home resident who works at the NAPA store.

Wade lost his money. His patent application was turned down. He damn near lost his house. And it was at that point, twelve or so years ago (he told me this), that he began taking an interest in demolitions and in the terminus-tending aspects of things found in everyday life. It's hard to argue with him, and I don't. Though selling real estate, I don't need to say, is dedicated to the very opposite proposition.

A small plane pulls a banner across the blue-streaked Nov-ember sky above us, heading north into the no-fly zone now abandoned by the Coast Guard and the "News at Noon" copters. BLACK FRIDAY AT FOSDICKS? the trailing sign says. No one in the departing crowd pays it any attention. Up ahead, a black man is helping the Salvation Army woman lift her red kettle into a white panel truck. Several landmark protestors are trailing their signs behind them as they seek their vehicles, satis-fied they've again done their best. No one's much talking about the Queen Regent, now a rock pile awaiting bulldozers and fresh plans. Many seem to be chatting about tomorrow's turkey and the advent of guests.

"What do you hope for, Franky?" Wade has taken a grip of my left bicep and given me his Panasonic, which is surprisingly light. He's eaten his sandwiches and left the sack behind. My Suburban's at the far end of the parked cars. Wade intends, I know, to leap-frog on to weightier matters. The reminder of his own end, concurrent with the Queen Regent's demise, fastens him down even more firmly to the here and now.

"I'm not a great hoper, Wade, I guess." We're not walking fast. Others pass us. "I just go in for generic hopes. That good comes to me, that I do little harm and die in my sleep."

"That's a lot to hope for." His grip is pinching the shit out of me right through my windbreaker. Then he unaccountably loosens up. Vehicles are starting around us, back-up lights and taillights snapping on. "I'm not alive from the waist down any-more. How 'bout you?" Wade isn't looking at me, but staring toward what's ahead—my Suburban, which has an altered look about it.

"I'm shipshape, Wade. Fire in the hole." I'm reliant on Dr. Psimos's assessment, and on how things seem most mornings. You could say I have high hopes for life below the waist.

"I've plateaued," Wade says irritably. "Left it all in the last century." He's frowning, as if he, too, has spied something wrong up ahead of us. The Millennium clearly has different resonances for different age brackets.

"Maybe enough's enough, Wade. You know?"

"So other people tell me."

What Wade and I have seen altered about my car is that the driver's-side backseat window's been smashed and glass particles scattered on the sparse grass. Below the door, on top of the glittering glass, is a flesh-colored Grand Union plastic bag with the milk carton inside. Though when I pick it up, it's as heavy as a brick, and on closer notice I discover that the Sealtest carton inside—a pink-toned photograph of a missing teen on the label —actually contains a brick. The carton's mission hasn't been what it seemed when I felt it bumping my leg, its little brigand owner awaiting his chance at mischief. Did he sense I was a Suburban owner? Was I under surveillance from the beginning?

This is why I never hope: Hoping is not a practical mechanism for events that actually happen.

"Little pissmires nailed you," Wade snarls, taking in the damage, completely clear-brained, bifocals flashing at the chance to be permissibly pissed off, instantly intuiting the whole criminal scenario. "Too bad Cade's not here," he says, "though they probably didn't leave any prints." He hasn't seen the actual culprit, only the virtual one (the real one's spitting image). "Shouldn't of stuck that stupid sticker on your bumper." He scowls, walking around behind my car, assessing things like a cop, his little bandy-legged self full-up with race bile, which makes me angrier than the busted window—and fingers me as a typical liberal. "They probably hate fat-ass Gore worse than they hate shit-for-brains," he says. (His only name for Bush.) Wade's mouth wrinkles into a twisted, unhumorous smile of seen-it-all pleasure. "What'd they get? Did you leave your billfold in there?"

"No." I touch my lumpy back pocket, then peer inside the mostly glassless window hole, trying not to touch a sharp edge. Glass kernels carpet the backseat and floor. Sunlight on the roof has turned it hot and boggy inside. The deed can't be more than five minutes old. I stand up and look longingly around, as if I could rerun things, set a guiding, weighted hand onto little Shaquille's or little Jamal's sun-warmed head, walk with him over to the boardwalk for a funnel cake and some unangrified, nonjudgmental, free-form man-to-man about where one goes wrong in these matters. Possibly he's a member of Cub Pack 31 and is at work on his larceny merit badge.

Nothing's present in the backseat but a torn-out *Asbury Park Press* real estate page, a couple of red-and-white bent-legged Realty-Wise signs and the pink Post-it with Mike's directions to Mullica Road. That seems long ago. Though yesterday wasn't better than today. If anything, it was worse. I haven't been in a fistfight today or had my neck twisted (yet). I haven't been vilified, haven't gotten in deep with my ex-wife, haven't gone to a funeral. It may not be the right moment to count my blessings, but I do.

An enormous Invector RV as big as a team bus, with Indian arrow markings on its side, comes rumbling past us, its owner-operator a tiny balding figure with sunglasses inside the slide-back captain's window. He frowns down at me with empathy and stops. He's a "Good Sam" and has the smiling, stupid mouthy-guy-with-the-halo decal on one of his back windows. These birds are always Nazis. The captain's sweet-faced wife's behind him in the copilot's space, craning past to see down to me and my lower-case woes. I know she feels empathy for me, too. But being peered down at, shattered glass around my feet, my car busted and an orange-skinned old loony as my teammate, makes me feel a wind-whistling loss far beyond empathy's reach.

"Vehicle crime's up twenty percent due to the Internet," the Invector captain says from behind his sunglasses, surveying the scene from above. He's weasly, with a puny little mustache that he may have just started. His wife's saying something I can't hear. Another man and woman, their lifelong friends, plus the square head of a Great Dane, appear in the back living-quarters window. All stare at me gravely, the dog included.

"What'd he say?" Wade says from behind my car.

I can't repeat it. A saving force in the universe forbids me. Something tells me these travelers are from central Florida, possibly the Lakeland area, which makes me hate them. I shrug and look back at my window hole. I'm still holding Wade's Panasonic, as if I was taping everything.

"No use callin' the cops," the land-yacht driver says, down from his little window. His wife nods. Their passengers have pulled the café curtains farther apart and are rubber-necking me and Wade and my broken vehicle. Both are holding tall-boys of Schlitz. I am another feature of the interesting New Jersey landscape, a textbook case of worsening crime statistics. Eighty percent of murders are committed by people who know their victims, which means many murders are probably not as senseless as they seem.

"I guess," I say, and fake a grateful smile upward.

"Oh yeah!" From somewhere, a hidey-hole the police wouldn't find—in a safe box, a glove compartment, under the sun visor—the land-yacht guy produces a nickel-plated revolver as big as Wade's video cam, from whose barrel end he coolly blows invisible smoke like an old-west gunfighter who is also a good samaritan. "They don't fuck with me," he smirks. His wife gives him a halfhearted whap on the shoulder for language reasons. Their friends in the back laugh soundlessly. I'm sure they're all Church of Christers.

"That oughta do it," I say.

"That already *has* done it," he says. "I'm ex-peace officer." He lowers his big Ruger, S&W, Colt, whatever, smiles a goofy sinister smile, then revs his Invector into new life, issuing an order over his shoulder to his passengers, who disappear from the window. He sets some kind of blue ball-cap with U.S. Navy braiding onto his skint head. "Buckle up. We're casting off," a man's voice says inside. The captain's wife mouths something to me as her window of opportunity closes, but I can't hear for the motor noise. "Okay," I say. "Thanks." But it's the wrong thing to say as they sway away over the dry grass toward new marvels awaiting them.

COLD PRE-THANKSGIVING winds whistle through my broken back window, stiffening my neck and making me feel like I'm catching something, even though I had a flu shot and am probably not. The advance weather of tropical depression Wayne is moving up the seaboard, and the once-nice sky has quilted into dense cotton batting, the cold sun that warmed us in the bleachers now retired. It's November. Nothing more nor less.

The Queen Regent's big finish has contributed little to Wade and me, only a bleak and barren humility, suggesting closure's easier to wish for than locate. Driving back out Lake Avenue toward the Fuddruckers—through a precinct of crumbling mansions, a Dominican "hair station," the Cobra motorcycle club and the Nubian Nudee Revue, all bordering a pretty green lake with low Parisian bridges crossing to a more prosperous town to the south (Ocean Grove)—I spy my little culprit window smasher, tootling along down the crumbling sidewalk in his big silver shoes and hooded sweatshirt, under the heavy hand of the Chicago Jew-Dog purveyor, a giant coffee-black Negro with woolly hair and big inner-tube biceps. Wade's mooning out the window, sees these citizens and makes a satisfied grunt of approval, as if to say, See, now. More of this kind of parental oversight will get you less of that other stuff . . . pass on the vital gnosis of the civilization . . . a sense of what's right . . . intact units, yadda, yadda, yadda. Better than a perp walk into social services in plastic bracelets, I'll concede, and drive us on.

Wade is exhausted. His rucked hands, in the skinny lap of his jackass pants, have begun just noticeably to tremble, and his old white-fringed head won't exactly be still and is ducked, anticipating sleep—which he complains he does little of. He smells possibly more sour, and one of his scuffed patent-leather slip-ons taps the floor mat softly. Old people, no matter what anyone says, do not make the best company when spirits flag. They tend to sink toward private thoughts or embarrassed, uncomprehending silence, from whose depths they don't give much of a shit about anybody else's private thoughts—all the "great experience" they carry become essentially useless. Not that I blame him. Seeing an implosion has given him the peek into oblivion he wanted. It simply hasn't changed anything.

I remember, years ago, after my father died and my mother and I were living in a sandy, ant-infested asbestos-sided house near Keesler, my mother one morning backed our big green Mercury right over my little black-and-white kitten, Mittens. Apparently nothing caught her notice, because she continued out onto the street and drove away to her job. It was not the best time in her life. But Mittens made a terrible squawling scream I heard inside the house. And when I raced out in a panic of knowledge and cold helplessness, there was the sad, mangled little cat, not long for the planet, flopping and wriggling, making awful strangling noises out of his crushed little gullet and turning me crazed, since my mother was gone and no one was there to help.

Next door, on our neighbor's front porch, was the neighbor lady's—Mrs. Mockbee's—antique old daddy, a dapper turkey-necked fossil who told my mother he'd fought in the Civil War but of course hadn't. Still, he called himself Major Mockbee and sat long days on his daughter's concrete porch in a straw boater, red bow tie, suspenders, spats and seersucker suit, chewing, spitting and talking to himself while Keesler Saber jets flew over.

He alone was there when Mittens got flattened by my mother's Merc. The only adult. And it was to him I fled, my mind a fevered chaos, across the driveway in the sweltering Mississippi morning, across the damp St. Augustine and up the three steps onto the porch. The poor little cat had already grown quiet, breathing his troubled last. But I pushed his smushed limp body straight into Major Mockbee's field of vision—he knew me, we'd spoken before. And I said, tears squirting, my heart pounding, my limbs aching with fear (I shouted, really), "My mother ran over my cat. I don't know what to do!"

To which Major Mockbee, after spitting a glob over the porch rail into the camellias, clearing his acrid old throat and putting on a pair of wire spectacles to have a better look, said, "I believe you've got yourself a Persian. It looks like a Persian. I'd say something's wrong with it, though. It looks sick."

Unfair, I know. But truth is truth. I sometimes think of old people as being *like* pets. You love them, amuse yourself *with* them, tease and humor them, feed them and make them happy, then take solace that you're probably going to live longer than they will.

Back in the Barnegat Pines days of '84—when Wade took life more as it tumbled, projected a seamless, amiable surface, kept his garage neat, his tools stowed, his oil changed, tires rotated, went to church most Sundays, watched the Giants not the Jets, prayed for both the Democrats *and* the Republicans, favored a humane, Vatican II approach to the world's woes, inasmuch as we live amid surfaces, etc.—back then I just assumed he, like the rest of us (prospective son-in-laws think such things), would wake up one morning at four, feel queasy, a little light-headed, achy from that leaf raking he'd done the evening before and decide not to get up quite yet. Then he'd put his head back to the pillow for an extra snooze and somewhere around six and without a whimper, he'd soundlessly buy the farm. "He usually didn't sleep that late, but I thought, well, he's been under a strain at work, so I just let him—" Gone. Cold as a pike.

Only, age plays by strange rules. Wade's now survived happiness to discover decrepitude. To be alive at eighty-four, he's had to become someone entirely other than the smooth-jawed ex-Nebraska engineer who was cheered to see the sun rise, cheered to see it set. He's had to *adapt* (Paul would say "develop")—to shrink around his bones like a Chinaman, grow stringy, volatile, as self-interested as a pawnbroker, unable to see his fellowmen except as blunt instruments of his demon designs. Apart from merely liking him, and liking to match Wade-remembered to Wade-present tense, I'm also interested for personal reasons in observing if any demonstrable good's to be had from getting as old as Methuselah, other than that the organism keeps functioning like a refrigerator. We assume persistence to be a net gain, but it still needs to be proved.

"Why don't you come down to my place for dinner?" Wade says gruffly out of the blue, more energetic than I expected.

"Thanks, but I've got some duties." Not true. We're re-crossing 35, the route I'll take home. Some commercial establishment—I don't know where, but cultural literacy tells me it's there—will be eager to fix my back window, if only in a temporary way until after the holiday. Busted Back Windows R-Us.

"What the hell duties have *you* got?" Wade cuts his jagged eyes at me, working his tongue tip along his lower lip. He gives one bulky beige hearing device a jab with his thumb. "You don't have a new girlfriend, do you?"

"I have a wife. I have *two* wives. At least I—"

"Hah!" Wade makes a strangled noise that could be a cough or a last gasp of life. "You know the penalty for bigamy? Two wives! I had two. I'm single now. Never had so much fun." Wade's forgotten we're acquainted. He'll be calling me Ned next. Ned might be better than Frank now, since Frank's not feeling so enthusiastic.

Evenings down at the Grove are not for everybody. Dinner's at 6:00 and over by 6:25. Then the inmates (the ones that can) scuttle out to the common room for rapt-silence CNN viewing and alarming postprandial personal odors. Meals are color-coded—something brown, something red, something that once was green, with tapioca or syrupy no-sugar fruit to follow. If I went with Wade, we'd arrive early, have to wait in his two-room "en suite," full of his bric-a-brac, his bathroom full of medicines, his framed Turnpike battle insignias and vestigial home furnishings from Barnegat Pines. We'd watch a *Jeopardy* rerun, then get in an argument, like we did the one time I was a guest and unexpectedly saw him naked. It's no wonder Cade and family stay up in Pohatcong and don't much look in. What can you do? Things are what they are. If we hang on too long, we reach the back side of the Permanent Period, where life doesn't grow different, there's just more of it until the lights go dim.

"I've got a surprise for you." Wade's white slip-on's still tapping the floor mat, but his hand-trembling and neck-ducking have ceased. I've turned up the heater due to the back window draft. Suburbans have world-beating comfort systems, which is a reason to own one.

Wade claims he indulges in unbridled semi-sexual liaisons with several of the grannies at the Grove—in spite of being dead below the belt line. He charms them with his implosion videos and spicy narratives about things he's seen in the backseats of stretch limos passing through his tollbooth. During my one visit, he had a tiny powdery-cheeked, pink-haired lawyer's widow in her seventies as his squeeze. They smirked and winked, and Wade made lewd innuendos about night-time feats he was still capable of after two vodka gimlets and a Viagra chaser.

"I'd love to, but I've got a house-full back home," I say, easing into the Fuddruckers' lot across from the streaming Parkway. Wade's Olds sits nosed under the faded yellow awning. A blue-and-white Asbury Park PD cruiser with a Bush sticker is parked across the lot, its hatless occupant observing traffic through the intersection. Technically, I have *no one* waiting at home. Paul and the unusual Jill have checked into the Beachcomber and are dining at Ann's. Clarissa's off on her heterosex escapade with honey-voiced Thom. My house is ringingly empty on Thanksgiving eve. How does that happen?

"But how 'bout I mention there's somebody back at my place who'd love to lay eyes on you?" Wade's damp mouth wallops shut, suppressing a smile. He's up to mischief, stroking his Caesarish comb-down like an old Arab. One of his wrinkle-cheeked old squeezes no doubt has a freshly widowed sister from the Wildwoods who's a "young sixty-eight" and on the hunt.

"I need to get this window fixed, Wade."

"It's what?" Wade looks affronted. His tongue darts in and out like a viper's.

"My window." I motion backward with my thumb. "It's trying to rain."

"You're cracked! You need a new connection, mister. There's something hollow under you, you know that?" Wade's suddenly talking way too loud and vehement for our close quarters. He's been sneaking up on this with his questions about hoping and my sexual problems and barbs about my absent wife.

We're stopped alongside his Olds. I check in the rearview to see if the cop's surveilling us, which of course he is. Possibly the empty Fuddruckers' lot is a rendezvous point in the white-slave market.

Wade's eyes fix on me accusingly, making me feel accused. "I don't think that's true, Wade."

"You're a goddamn house peddler. You hang around with strangers all the time. You're gonna be poopin' in a bag one of these days—if you live long enough. Which you may not." His old mouth does something between a terrible grin and a furious frown. It's close to the look my son Paul turned on me last spring in K.C. Only Wade's upper falsie set sinks a millimeter, so he has to clack it back up with his lowers. I'm happy Wade's still in touch with who I am.

"Well." I glance again at the Asbury cop.

"Well what?" Wade dips his head like a goose, snorts, then suddenly stares down at his big watchband as if he was on a tight schedule.

Cold air is still drawing in on my neck. "It may not seem like it, Wade," I say softly, "but I'm connected enough. Real estate's a good connecter."

"Bullshit. It's putting stitches in a dead man's arm." He blinks, ducks, saws his wrist—the one with his Medi-Ident—across his red nose, then grabs his Panasonic off the seat. "You're an asshole."

"I just told you how I feel about things, Wade. I wasn't trying to piss you off. My belief is we all have an empty spot underneath us. It doesn't hurt anything." I tap my foot on the brake. This needs to end now.

"You're in a dangerous spot, Franky." Wade pops open his big door. "However old you are. Fifty-what?"

"Two." Which feels better than fifty-five. I gently bite down on a welt of my left cheek—a bad sign. I'm not going to the Grove with Wade and make woo-woo with some retired reference librarian from Brigantine. I'd end up driving home to Sea-Clift with black vanquishment filling my car like cyanide.

"Fifty-two doesn't mean *anything!*" Wade croaks. "You're *between* everything good when you're fifty-two. You need to get hooked up or you're screwed. I married Lynette when I was fifty-two. Saved my ass."

Wade of course has told me *never* to get married again, and

Lynette, after all, left him for the Lord. Plus, I believe I'm still married. "You were lucky."

"I was *smart*. I wasn't lucky." Wade levers one trembling sock-less white-shoed foot out and down onto the pavement, then the other, then cautiously scoots his scrawny ass off the seat, holding the door handle for support, emitting a tiny effortful grunt.

"I guess we might as well think our life's the way it is 'cause that's how we want it, Wade."

"Haw!" He's studying down at his feet as if to be sure they know their assignments. "That's in your brain."

"That's where a lot of stuff goes on."

"Think, think, thinky, think. In *your* life it does. Not mine." Wade gives my car door a fearsome, dismissive bang shut.

I power down the passenger window so he's not shut out. "Don't think I don't appreciate your thinking about me." Think, think, thinky, think.

"I'll tell my daughter you gotta think about gettin' your window fixed instead of seein' her." Wade's mouth wrinkles up bitterly as he starts his staggering departure.

Daughter?

"Which daughter?" I say through the window.

"Which daughter?" Wade's red-rimmed eyes glare in at me, as if I knew we'd been talking about his daughter this whole time, and why was I being such a stupe? Stupe, stupe, stupey, stupe. "I only have one, you nunce. Your girlfriend. You farted around with her till you ran her off right in my front yard. You're a nunce, you know that? You like being a nunce. You get to do a lot of good thinking that way." Wade starts struggling toward the front of my car, heading toward his Olds, his Panasonic bumping my fender panels he's holding onto for balance. I can only see the upper half of him, but he's not looking at me, as if I'd stopped existing in here.

But. Daughter!

For these weeks, traveling to the odd implosion here, another there, a cup of chowder or a piece of icebox pie in a Greek diner, I've all but expunged from my thoughts the truth that Wade is father to Vicki (now Ricki), my long-gone dream of a lifetime from when I, as a divorced man, wrote for a glossy New York sports magazine, horsed around with women, suffered dreami-ness both night and day and had yet to list my first house. I rashly, wrongly loved nurse Arcenault with my whole heart and libido, was ready to tie the knot, move to Lake Havasu and live in an Airstream off savings (I had none). Only she lacked the necessary whatever (love for me) and sent me packing. So Wade's wrong about who heave-ho'd who. Vicki shortly afterward married a handsome, clean-cut Braniff pilot, moved to Reno, became a trauma nurse at St. Crimonies, eventually was widowed when Darryl Lee crashed his spotter plane in Kuwait under the command of Bush #1.

I haven't seen, spoken to or thought much about Vicki/Ricki, who I guarantee was a yeasty package, since '84, and wouldn't recognize her if she shot out of Fuddruckers on a pair of roller skates. Although *daughter* sets loose deep space-clearing stirrings. Not that I want to see her any more than I want to see the reference librarian from Brigantine. But the thought of Vicki/Ricki—once a bounteous, boisterous, fine-thighed and raven-haired dreamboat—sets my ribs atremble, I'm not ashamed to say it. On the other hand, driving to the Grove on the night before Thanksgiving for a surprise face-to-face, followed by an unwieldy *intime* in some ennui-drenched south Jersey "steak place," at the conclusion of which she and I disappear in opposite directions into the teeming night, is far from anything I want to happen to me. Even though I have nothing else to do: early to bed amid sea breezes after maybe getting my window fixed.

"Maybe Ricki and I can have lunch once the holiday's over," I say insincerely out the window to where Wade has navigated around the front of my car. I don't want him to feel condescended to on the topic of his marriageable daughter. I have some experience there.

"What?" he snaps. He's putting his video cam down on the passenger's side seat as if it was his honored guest.

"Tell Ricki I said howdy."

"Yeah, I'll do that."

"When am I likely to see you again? When's our next blow-up?" Wade has forgotten I've invited him for Thanksgiving, an offer I now silently retract in self-defense.

"I dunno." He's begun crawling into his car from the wrong side.

"Wade, are you okay in there?" My smile dwindles to a half smile of concern.

"How do I look?" His baggy ass and the scuffed soles of his slip-ons face me out of his open car door.

I could get the Asbury cop to come confiscate Wade's car keys if I thought he'd lost his marbles and presented a threat to the public. Except I'd have to drive him home. "You got your keys?" I sing out hopefully.

"Kiss my ass." He's struggling down onto his donut, his feet to the floor, back to his cushion. I hear him breathe sternly. "Goddamn piece of shit."

"What's happening in there, Wade? You need some help?"

Wade burns a scowl back at me, then looks at his instruments. "Goddamn door's busted. Some idiot woman backed into me at CVS. Now get your silly ass out and close my door. You nunce." He's got his little biscuit hands fastened to the wheel at ten and two, like Mike Mahoney. His keys dangle from the ignition, where they've been the whole time. He gets her cranked as I get out into the cold. It's sizing up to rain more. Yesterday's weather is hanging over the seaboard like a bad memory. Plus there's tropical disturbance Wayne.

"I wanted you to get to see Vicki," Wade says. "She wants to see you." He can't remember her new name and won't look at me, only out at the Fuddruckers' chained and locked front door. He's resigned more than mad and, like all good fathers, ineptly keeping vigil for his offspring's improvement. "We'll have lunch" is not what he wants to hear. Wade wants me in the steak place with his honey bunch, ordering our third martini, with love—belated, grateful, willing, candid, budding and, above all, permanent—saturating the dark, rich airs like gardenias. It's his last try to set things right before his hour's called.

Though based on history, there's nothing I can do. The last thing Vicki Arcenault ever said to me sixteen years ago, from her bachelorette apartment in Pheasant Run on the Hightstown Pike, by phone to my former, since-demolished family home in Haddam, was, "Woo, boy-hidee, you like to of fooled me." She talked in a wide, east Dallas, barrel-racer lingo, just right for barrooms, bronco-buster sex and no bullshit but hers. I loved it.

"How did I fool you, sweetheart? I love you so much," I said. It was spring. The copper beech was in abundance. The wistaria and lilacs in bloom. The dreamy time of love's labors lost.

" 'Sweetheart'?" she pooh–poohed. "Love *me*? Opposites cain't love. Opposites just attract. And we're done through with that. Least I am. But I almost took a tumble. I'll give you that." I remember her wonderful tongue-cluck, like a jockey signaling giddy-up.

"I still want you to marry me," I said. And I dearly did—would've in a minute and been happy. Although it would've been the lamp business more than the realty business, the unexamined life more than the life steeped in reflection and contingency. Win–win.

"Yeah, but first we'd get married"—I knew she was beaming her big Miss Cotton Bowl smile—"and then we'd have to get divorced. And I need somebody who'll get me all the way to death. And that id'n you."

Death. Even then!

"I'll give a call in the next couple days, Wade." I'm leaning into his open door, radiating bad faith. "Maybe Ricki'll have time to grab lunch. It'd be good to catch up." The prospect makes my brain swell.

Wade carefully uncouples his spectacles from his crusted ears and gives his old eyes a good knuckle-kneading that's probably painful. He turns toward me, sockets hollowed, pale and knobby, his left pupil orbited out to left field. Age is not gentle or amusing.

"I can't talk you into it?" he says, insulted.

"I guess not, Wade." I smile the way you would into the upside-down mirror of an iron-lung patient. "I'll call. We'll stage a lunch."

"You're not vital anymore. You know that?" He sniffs as if my words carried a bad odor, then looks disgusted and shakes his head. His Olds is idling. The Asbury cop, his gray exhaust visible in falling temps, eases out into traffic and slowly motors away. The wind has a bite that stings my butt. Across the access road, the Parkway groans with the *hum-bum-bum* sounds of pre-Thanksgiving hurry-up.

"I'm working on vital," I say. "It's on my short list." I try a smile.

"Hunh," Wade grumps. He doesn't know what I'm talking about. "You're a nunce. I already said that."

"Could be true." I'm holding his car door open.

"Remember the three boats, Franky?" The three boats parable is Wade's favorite. He's told me the three boats story six times in support of six different points of reference—most recently the presidential race and the American people's blindness to the obvious.

"I do, Wade. I only get three boats."

"What?" He can't hear me. "You only get three, and you already had two." He gives me a mean threat-look across the seat, where his silver Panasonic lies full of new implosion footage. "This is your last one." My first pair of boats, I take it, symbolizes my two marriages, though they could also reference my prostate condition.

"Okay, I'll give it some serious thought. Maybe it'll make me more vital. I hope so."

"How long has it been for you?" Wade drops the Olds into gear, causing a sinister metal-on-metal *ker-klunk*.

"How long's what been? There's been a lot of 'it's' this year. Hard to keep 'em straight."

"Since you were with anybody?" His scraggly old brows dart up lewdly.

"Since I was *with* anybody?" Wade's lips tremble with a hint of below-the-belt seaminess. "What do you mean?" I'm still holding open the passenger door, but I must be squeezing it, because my thumb's gotten numb. What's the matter with the world all of a sudden?

"Ah, forget it. The hell with you." He's scowling up into his rearview. Conversation over. He's ready to make a move.

"I don't want to think about the implications of what you're saying, Wade." Why does this sound so pompous and stupid?

"Yeah, yeah," Wade growls. "Think, think, thinky, think. Where do you think you're gonna end up?"

"Go fuck yourself. Okay?" I stand back and give his car door a powerful slam closed. I can just hear him say, "Yeah, maybe I will."

Wade's begun backing up, using his mirror in the tried-and-true manner of the old and joint-frozen. I have to step lively since he hauls on the wheel like a stevedore, swerves and nearly swipes my foot. I can see his mouth working, in furious converse with the face in the rearview.

"Be careful, Wade," I call out. He's glued to his mirror and can't see the fat red postpole holding aloft the gold sunburst Fud-druckers' WORLD'S GREATEST HAMBURGERS sign, plus a smaller white one that says EAT HEALTHY! TRY AN OSTRICH BURGER!

The old Eighty Eight crunches straight into the postpole with a hollow metallic *bung* noise, the whole vehicle caroming back and jangling to a stop, giving Wade a jolt inside. He glowers up at the mirror, half-cocks his head around as three black letters off the Ostrich Burger sign spiral down—the *O*, the *N* and the *H*—and clatter onto his rusted-through vinyl roof.

Wade's twisted around, facing back, able now to see the pipe he's smacked. Without looking, he sends the Olds lurching forward in "D," burns rubber, then stabs the brakes and stops again, the motor racing to indicate he's somehow gotten into "N."

"Wade!" I shout. "Hold it. Hold it." I'm coming to give assistance, in spite of Wade being the shameless procurer for his own daughter. I'll have to take charge of him now, transport him home in *my* vehicle, meet Vicki/Ricki, go to dinner, etc., etc., none of which I want to do. Too bad the Asbury cop's left already. He could arrest Wade, call the EMS and Ricki could claim him in the Monmouth County ER, where she'd know all the procedures.

Wade's mouth's still working vigorously. He fires a look of betrayal out at me, seeing I'm coming to help him. I'm to blame for all of this. If I'd gone down to the Grove and made everybody happy, none of this horseshit would be happening. I don't know what made me think I could befriend the father of a former love interest who spurned me. These conjunctions aren't meant to happen except among the primitive Yanomami. Not in New Jersey.

Wade's staring down at his dashboard. Rust and road crap have dislodged from the Olds' chassis, though nothing seems broken or hanging. One of the Ostrich Burger letters has slid off his roof and lodged under the passenger-side wiper blade. It is an *H*. The sign now reads EAT EALTHY.

I step out in front of Wade's car and raise my hand like an Indian. I see he's furious. He could easily run me over. You read about these deaths in the paper every day. Wade grimaces at me through the windshield. His engine suddenly kicks up a mighty *whaaaa*, and I start backpedaling, my hand still up in the original peace sign, and almost stumble back on my ass as he socks it into

"D" again and the Olds springs ahead with a screech, headed toward the EXIT and the traffic-clogged business street leading to the Parkway. I'm all out of the way but can feel the Olds' side panel whip past me. It's as if I'm not here, not even a holiday statistic. Wade's fighting the wheel to get himself into the EXIT side of the curb-cut. His shoulder dips left, his hands still at ten and two. *Brack, brack, brack.* The old Eighty Eight judders, bucks, then judders again—probably the parking brake's on—heading across the empty lot into the ENTRANCE side, not the EXIT. "Wade!" I shout again, and start walking toward his car, its brake lights glowing, exhaust shooting out. I'll help him. I'll drive him. The Olds dips stopped, then noses out toward the traffic that's backed up at the red light. Though the red immediately goes to green, and the cars commence smoothly forward. Wade's head is oscillating back and forth, hawking a place in the line, his mouth still going. I'm moving toward him. I haven't helped him. I'm very aware of that, but I will—for all the difference it'll make. A young woman in a blue Horizon full of kids smiles at Wade, waves a hand, motions his beater out into the flow. And in just that number of precious seconds and before I can get there to give help, Wade smoothly becomes traffic, his taillights blending into the flux of the street and on under the Parkway overpass. And gone.

CHAPTER 12

EYES PEELED, I cruise busy 35 South—Bradley Beach, Neptune, Belmar. I'm expecting a storefront to be open at 3:30 on Thanksgiving eve, with glass on the menu. These places thrive on every street corner in America, though they vanish when you want one. Cultural literacy's never perfect.

Wintry effluvium has turned my vehicle into an icebox, and I've cranked the heat up on my feet, my belly already sensing a mixed signal from my hot dog. The three boats parable is, in fact, a useful moral directive, and though Wade would sneer at me, in my own view I've heeded it by giving a wide berth to the Grove and Vicki/Ricki, or whatever her name is. Of course, my more natural habit would be to consider most all things as mutable, and to resist obstinance in human affairs, an attitude which has helped me to think more positively about Sally's return and not to be flattened like roadkill by her abandoning me (I think of myself as a variablist). The realty profession itself thrives on the perpetual expectation of changes for the better, and is permanently resistant to the concept of either the rock or the hard place. Ann, however, once pointed out to me that a variablist can be a frog who sits in a pan of water, looking all around and feeling pretty good about things, while the heat's gradually turned up, until cozy, happy pond life becomes frog soup.

In the three boats story, a man is floating alone in an ocean without a life jacket when a boat passes by. "Get in. I'll save you," the boatman says. "Oh, no, it's fine," the floating man answers, "I'm putting my faith in the Lord." In time, two more boats come along, and to each rescuer the man—usually me, in Wade's telling—says, "No, no, I'm putting my faith in the Lord." Eventually, and it isn't very long in coming, the man drowns. Yet when he stands up to meet his Maker at the fated spot where some rejoice but many more cower, his Maker looks sternly down and says, "You're a fool. You're assigned to hell forever. Go there now." To which the drowned man says, "But your honor, I put my faith in you. You promised to save me." "Save you!?" fearsome God shouts from misty marmoreal heights (and this is the moment the old liver-lipped procurer of his own daughter likes most, when his scaly eyelids blink down hard and his tongue darts like a grinning Beelzebub). "Save you? *Save you?*" God thunders. "I sent you three boats!" And off goes Frank forever.

The last time Wade told this story—in reference to who the American people should've chosen but probably didn't in this doomed election now awaiting God's wrath—God supposedly said, "Three *fucking* boats! I already sent you three *fucking* boats, you morons. Now go to hell." God, Wade believes, sees most things as they are and has no trouble telling it.

But the point's plain. Drowning men save themselves, no matter how it looks from the shore and even though it's not always easy to assess your own situation. Vicki/Ricki's my last boat, Wade believes. Though in my view (and what could she look like after sixteen years), she's only a ghost ship out of the mists. To drive to the Grove and reconnect with that old life would be treacherous even for a variablist—as asinine as Sally heading off to Mull or Ann wanting to forge a new union with me. In the modern idiom, that boat won't float. And I'm resolved to stay here even in the deep water, waiting for the next one, even if it's the boat to you-know-where.

THE FIRST glass place I see—Glass, Glass, & More Glass—is closed, closed, & more closed. The second, Want a Pane in the Glass? in the 35 U-Need-It Strip Mall, has its metal grate chained to the sidewalk and everything dark within. The third, in Manasquan—forthrightly called Glass?—appears open, though when I walk inside the dingy, echoing, oily-lit front showroom with its big sheets of plate glass leaned against the walls, there's not a soul in evidence. I step through a door to a long, cold, shadowy room with empty wide-topped tables where glass could be cut. But no one's around—no sounds of skilled labor in progress, or the after-work noises of back-room pre-holiday whiskey cheer. Which suddenly turns me spooky, as if a storage bin of cooling corpses awaits beyond the next door, a pre-holiday revenge-hit by elements from north of here.

"Hello," I timidly call out—but only once—then, quick as a flash, beat it back to my freezing car.

It has somehow become four o'clock. Daylight's sunk out of the invisible east. Sunset's at a daunting 4:36. Brash wind and slashing rain sheets have begun whacking my windshield and beading moisture on the backseat. Headlights are now in use. It's drive-time, the race home, the time no one but the doomed want to be on our nation's roadways—including me, with nobody waiting at the doorway, no plans to make the hours resemble the true joy of living.

A drink's what I require. I usually hold the line till six, a discipline well known to weary corporate accountants, single-handed sailors and hard-luck novelists in need of cheering. But six is a state of mind, and my state of mind says it's six, which even out front of the spooky Glass? confers a jollying self-confirming certainty that positive elections can still be mine—not just refusals to drive Wade to the Grove or to romance the unspecified Ricki. I can have a drink. *Some* good things, warm sensations, await me.

I'm once again only a stone's short throw from the old Manasquan Bar, below the river bridge, where I took the 34 cut-off earlier. There I can certainly have a drink (and a piss) in familiar, congenial surroundings. Save an Hour, Save an Evening—the late-occurring motto for the day.

The Manasquan, which I head straight toward, would ordinarily—as I said before—be off-limits to me due to its anchorage in the past and prone-ness to fumy nostalgias. In the middle Eighties, it had its scheduled and amiable purpose. After a night's chartered fishing excursion on the *Mantoloking Belle*, the Manasquan was the Divorced Men's special venue for demonstrating residual rudimentary social, communicative and empathy skills (we actually weren't very good at any of these things and not good at fishing, either), and we all fled to it the instant we stepped off our boat—our legs rubbery, arms weak from manning our rods, thirsts worked up. The charter captain's mustachioed brother-in-law owned the place—an extended family of crafty Greeks. And it sat where it sat—hard by the dock—to make sure the Mouzakis family got all our money before sending us home happier but wiser. Which, as if by magic, is what happened—until it didn't, at which point and by no agreed-upon signal, we all quit going and consigned it to the past and oblivion, where we wished our old marriages would go.

Though I sense I have nothing to fear now from the Manasquan, for reason of its prosaic, standard-dockside, snug-away character—the red BAR sign on its shingled roof, muted rose-blue accent lights, tar-ry nautical smells, plenty of cork buoys and shellacked swordfish husks on the walls alongside decades of dusty fishermen photos. It will be as it was years back: detoxified and inoculated by inauthenticity, with no negative juju powers to give me the creeps about not throwing my life over to become a second mate on a halibut hauler off the Grand Banks, and instead being a realtor—or a State Farm agent in Hightstown, or a garden supply owner-operator in Haddam, or a podiatrist in Rocky Hill—all those things we were back in '83. Of course, I anticipated the same at the Johnny Appleseed last night, with sorry results.

I take the Manasquan jug-handle and loop down around to the small embarcadero fronting the River Marina, where banners are still up from the annual striper derby in September, an antique fair and last summer's Big Sea Day on the beach. All is familiar—the Mouzakis Paramount Show Boat Dock and the lowly Manasquan itself, red BAR warmly glowing through the early-evening rain.

Although names have changed. The Paramount Dock is now Uncle Ben's Excursions. The old *Belle*, with a fresh pink paint job, is dimly visible at the dock's end, bearing the name *Pink Lady*. The shingled, barn-roofed Manasquan, once in neon above the portholed entry, has become Old Squatters, with a plain black-letter sign hung to the door itself.

And by a good stroke, across the puddled lot from the dock and bar, there's now, outside the old Quonset shed where nautical gear was once stored for the charter business, a shingle that says BOAT, CARS, TRAILER REPAIRS. NO JOB TOO ABSURD. Lights are on in the garage and the tiny office. I swing around, stop in front and walk up to ask about a back-window repair.

Inside, a small black-haired man in need of a shave is seated behind the counter, close to a gas space heater, listening to a Greek radio station playing twiny bouzouki music while he eats an enormous sandwich. A long-legged, peroxided, pimpled kid with tattoos on his arms, possibly the son, sits in a tipped-back dinette chair across the tiny overheated office, bent over a foxed copy of *The Great Gatsby*—the old green-gray-and-white Scribner Library edition I read in "American Existentialism and Beyond" in Ann Arbor in 1964. For decades, I reread it every year, exactly the way we're all supposed to, then got sick of its lapidary certainties disguised as spoiled innocence—something I don't believe in—and gave my last copy to the Toms River Shriners' Xmas Benefit. Garage mechanics, of course, play a pivotal role in Fitzgerald's denouement, transacted scarcely a hundred miles from here as the gull flies. It is this boy, I'm certain, who's authored the sign outside, and he I address about my window.

His eyes raise above his book top and he smiles a perfectly receptive smile, though the older attendant never looks at me. He may only wait on other Greeks.

"Okay," the boy says before I can explain the whole situation and how little I'll be satisfied with. "I'll do it. Duct tape okay?" He looks back with interest to his page. He's near the end, where Meyer Wolfsheim says, "When a man gets killed I never like to get mixed up in it in any way. I keep out." Sound advice.

"Great," I say. "I'll head over to the Manasquan and try the cocktails." I offer a nod of trust that promises a big tip.

"Leave me them keys." He's wearing a blue mechanic's shirt with a white patch that says *Chris* in red cursives. Likely he's a Monmouth College student on Thanksgiving break, the first of his immigrant family to blub, blub, blub. I'm tempted to poll his views about Jay Gatz. Victim? Ill-starred innocent? Gray-tinged antihero? Or all three at once, vividly registering Fitzgerald's glum assessment of our century's plight—now blessedly at an end. The "boats against the current, borne back ceaselessly into the past" imagery is at odds with the three boats imagery of the old Nick Carraway doppelganger, Wade. It's possible of course that as a modern student, Chris doesn't subscribe to the author concept *per se*. I, however, still do.

Keys handed off, I head across the drizzly gravel lot to the Old Squatters né Manasquan, heartened that the time-honored shade-tree way of doing business "While-U-Wait" is still a tradition in this part of our state—among immigrants anyway—and hasn't caved in to the franchise volume-purchasing-power mentality that only knows "that's on back order" or "the manufacturer stopped making those"—the millennial free-enterprise canon in which the customer's a bit-part player to the larger drama of gross accumulation (what the Republicans want for us, though the liars say they don't).

Dense, good bar smell meets me when I step inside, surprising for being the exact aroma I remember—stale beer, cigarette smoke, boat tar, urinal soap, popcorn, wax for the leather banquettes, and floor-sweep granules—a positive, good-prospects smell, though probably best appreciated by men my age.

The dark-cornered, barny old room looks the same as when Ernie McAuliffe pounded his fists on the table and racketed on about Ruskies—the long-raftered ceiling, the long bar down the right side, back-lit with fuzzed red and blue low-lights and ranked rows of every kind of cheap hooch you'd dream of, all reflected in a smoky mirror on which the management has taped a smiling cartoon turkey with a cartoon Pilgrim pointing a musket at it. Two patrons sit at a table at the booth-lined rear wall. There's a tiny square linoleum dance floor, where no one ever danced in my day, and hung above it a mirror-faceted disco ball useful when things are jumping, which I don't remember ever being the case. Once the Manasquan served a decent broasted-chicken basket and a popcorn-shrimp platter. But no one's eating, and no food smell's in the atmosphere. The swinging chrome doors to the kitchen are barred and padlocked.

I am, though, happy to arrive, and to take a stool at the near end of the bar, with a view toward the other patrons—two women drinking and talking to the bartender.

AS I LEFT Asbury Park, with Wade careering off toward what destiny I don't know, and an empty nest awaiting me and the weather swarming into my car, I tried—just as I did the day I returned from Mayo last August, radiating anti-cancer contamination like Morse code—to imagine what a really good day might be. And in each instance I thought of the same thing (this strategy, as childlike as it seems, ought not be scoffed at).

Two years ago, Sally and I set off on one of our cut-rate one-day flying adventures—this time to Moline—with the intention of taking an historic boat trip down the Mississippi, visiting some interesting Algonquian earthworks, seeing a Civil War ironclad that had been hauled out of the muck and given its own museum, and maybe stopping off at the Golden Nugget casino, which the same Algonquians had built to recoup their dignity. We planned to finish the day with an early dinner in the rotating tenth-floor River Room of the Holiday Inn-Moline, then get back on the plane in time to be home by 3 a.m.

But when we got to the departure dock of the romantic old paddle-wheeler, the S.S. *Chief Illini*, a storm began dumping every manner of precip on us—snow, rain, sleet, hail, arriving by turns with a coarse wind at their backs. We'd bought our tickets off the Internet ahead of time, but neither Sally nor I wanted any part of a river cruise, wanted only to head back up the old cobbled streets of the historic district in search of a nice place to have lunch and to hatch a new plan for the hours that remained—possibly a leisurely trip through the John Deere Museum, since we had time to kill. I went aboard and told the boat captain, who was also the concessionaire and proprietor of the cruise business and owner of the *Chief Illini*, that we were sacrificing our tickets due to weather skittishness but wanted him to know (since he seemed personable and accommodating) that we'd be back another time and buy more tickets. To which the captain, a big happy-faced galoot dressed in his river pilot's blue serge uniform with gold epaulettes and a captain's cap, said, "Look here, you folks, we don't want anybody not to have a good time in Moline. I know this weather's the pits and all. I'll just return your money, and don't you sweat it. We're not in the business here in River City to take anybody's dough without rendering a first-class service. In fact, since you've come all this way"—he didn't know we'd flown from Newark but recognized we probably weren't locals—"maybe you'll be my guest at the Miss Moline diner my sister runs, where she makes authentic Belgian waffles with farm-fresh eggs and homemade sticky buns. How 'bout I just give her a call and say you're on your way up there? And here're some tickets to the John Deere Museum, the best one you'll find from here to South Dakota."

We didn't end up eating at the Miss Moline. But we did take in the museum, which was well-curated, with interesting displays about glaciation, wind erosion and soil content that explained why in that part of America you could grow anything you wanted pretty much anytime—forget about the growing season.

When I think about it now, here in the Manasquan—or the Old Squatters—with my window being fixed while I take my ease in these familiar detoxified surrounds, I can almost believe I made it up, so perfect a day did it produce for Sally and me, and so enduring has it been as illustration of how things can work out better than you thought—like now—even when all points of the spiritual weather vane forecast dark skies.

"OKAY, I COULD aks you again, but it ain't good to wake up de dead." A small mouse-faced woman with a silver flat-top and two good-sized ears full of tiny regimented gold loops stacked lobe to helix, faces me across the empty bar surface. A look of wry, not hostile, amusement sits on her lips, though her lips also have a permanent wrinkle to their contours, as if harsh words had once passed through but things had gotten better now.

I don't know what she's been saying, but assume it's to do with my drink preference. I've decided on the time-honored high-ball, the all-around drinker's drink, to commemorate the old divorced men, many of whom have now died. It's perfect for me in my state. "I'd like a tall bourbon and soda on ice, please."

"Dat ain't what I sed. But whatever."

I smile pointlessly. "Sorry."

"'I aksed wuz you sure you wuz meetin' your friends in de right place here." The bartender casts a look around down the bar toward her customers, two large older women elbowed in over birdbath-size cocktails, covertly eyeing me but clearly amused.

"I think so." Her accent is pure swamp-water coon-ass, straight from St. Boudreau Parish, far beyond the Atchafalaya. She's trying to be nice, making me know as gently as possible that the atmospheric old Manasquan has become a watering hole for late-middle-passage dykes and possibly I might be happier elsewhere, but I don't have to leave if I don't want to.

Except I couldn't be happier than to be here amidst these fellow refugees. The nautical motif's intact. The framed greasy-glass heroic fish photos still cover the walls with coded significance. The light's murky, the smells are congenial, the world's held at bay, as in the storied Manasquan days. Probably the drinks are just as good. I couldn't care less whose orientation's bending its big elbow beside mine. In fact, I feel a strong Darwinian right-ness about what was once a hard-nuts old men's hidey-hole transitioning into a safe house for tolerant, wry, full-figured, thick-armed goddesses in deep mufti (one's wearing a Yankees cap, another a pair of bulgy housepainter's dungarees over a Vassar sweatshirt). My own daughter used to be one of their number, I could tell them—but possibly won't.

"I used to come in here when Evangelis owned it," I say grate-fully, referring to old Ben Mouzakis's sister's husband.

"Fo' my time, dahlin'," the bartender croons, organizing my highball. I see she has a vivid green tattoo on her skinny neck, inches below her ear. Gothic letters spell out TERMITE, which I guess could be her name, though I'm not about to call her that.

"How's ole Ben doing?"

"He's okay. He in the whale-watch bidnus anymore." My drink set down in front of me, Termite (I'm only calling her that privately) begins giving a sink full of dirty glasses the three-tub, suds-rinse-rinse treatment, her little hands nimble as a card sharp's. "Dat ole charter boat bidnus played out. He got into burials-at-sea for a while. Den dat crapped. Annend dis whale thing jumped up."

"Sounds great." I take a first restorative sip. Termite has poured me a double dose of Old Woodweevil, meaning it's happy hour. Soon the bar will be filling up with big women fresh from jobs as stevedores, hod carriers and diesel mechanics—happy warriors happy to have a place of their own. I wonder if Clarissa has a tattoo someplace I don't know about, and if so, what does it say? Not Dad, we're sure of that.

The two shadowy women from the rear booth, one in a floral print muumuu her belly doesn't fit into too well, the other in a bulky red turtleneck, stand up and walk arms around each other to the antique jukebox. One puts in a quarter and cues up Ole Perry singing "I'll Be Home for Christmas," then they begin slowly to dance to the sweet-sad melody underneath the un-moving disco globe.

"She'd fuck a bullet wound, *that* skanky bitch," I hear one of the two full-figured gals at the bar—the one in the Yankees cap—saying to Termite, who's back down where they are, conniving about one of their friends.

"Well, guess what?" Termite is brazenly smirking, rising up onto her toes on the duckboards better to get into the faces of the two women patrons. "Ah ain't no fuckin' bullet wound. I heeerd dat. You know what ahm sayin'?" She shoots a sudden feral look my way, then lowers her voice to a big stage whisper. "Ahmo be dat bitch's worst nightmare." Termite, I see, wears an enormous Jim Bowie sheath knife on her oversized silver-studded black bruiser-belt that's drawn up so tight she must have trouble breathing. She herself is entirely in black—jeans, boots, tee-shirt, eyeshadow—everything but her silver flat-top, ear decor and TERMITE tattoo. I imagine she's already been a lot of people's nightmare, though she's been completely welcoming to me and could bring me another highball and I wouldn't mind it. My car window's not fixed yet, and the roof's drumming with sheets of merciless rain I'm happy to be out of.

Termite sees me angling for her eye and leaves the disputers and saunters down to me, still carrying most of her fuck-you attitude with her. She's skinny-bowlegged in her jeans, with excessive space between her taut little spavined thighs, so that she swaggers like the long-departed Charley Starkweather, no small-change nightmare himself.

"How *you* doin'? You still thirsty?" She rests her little hands on the bar rail and tap-taps an oversized silver thumb ring against the wood. "You suck dat one down like you needed it."

"It was good," I say. "I'll have another one just like it." I have to take my piss now. My eye wanders to where the gents used to be.

"Oh yeah, dey good." Termite's filling my glass where it sits, using the old ice, lots of whiskey and a quick squirt from the soda gun. "It's over in dat corner," she says, seeing where I'm looking without looking there. "Light's burnt out. It don't get the use it used to."

"Great." I slide off my stool and test my walking stability, which is solid.

Termite flashes a nasty smile down at her two friends as I go, and in the same stagy voice says, "It might be a ole alligator in dere, so you better be careful."

"Or worse," one of the girls cracks back, and snorts.

"Okay," I say. "Will do."

Inside the GENTLEMEN door, nothing's forbidding. The

ceiling bulb actually works, though the grimy porcelain fixtures are decrepit Fifties-era Kohler, the hand-dryer fan's hanging on a screw, and the woolly old window vent whose outside cover bangs in the wind lets cold mist in onto the layer of brown that gunks up everything. Still, the pissing facility's perfectly usable. No alligators.

Plenty of messages have been left on the wall for future users to ponder, all illustrated with neatly-penciled, magic-markered or rudely carved depictions of the engorged male equipment, plus a variety of women with miraculous breasts, several demonstrating uncanny coupling postures. Appeals are made for the "Able-bodied Semen," the "Lonely Hards Club" and "Fearless Fast-Dick Dick-tective Agency." One, to the side of the urinal, has the nostalgic old 609 area code, with a request for "Discreet Callers Only." Several messages propose reckless sexual chicanery with members of the Mouzakis family, including Grandma Mouzak and the Mouzakis pet sheep, Mouzy, who's shown scaling a fence. The only items of unusual note as I complete a long, knee-weakening piss—other than the BUSH-GORE BOTH SUCK, lipsticked onto the scaly old mirror—is a chartreuse cell phone, a little Nokia that's been tossed in the urinal as a gesture, I suppose, of dissatisfaction with its service. And beside it on the rubber grate is a half-eaten lunch-meat sandwich on white bread. It feels odd to piss on a sandwich and simultaneously into the ear hole of the miniature green telephone. But I'm past having a choice. My time in unlikely men's rooms has tripled since my Mayo insertions, and I tend not to be as finicky as I once was.

When I re-take my place at the bar, feeling immensely better, my fresh highball's waiting along with a new twin. Ms. Termite has stayed at my end and wants to be friendly, which makes me even happier to be here.

"So whadda you do? You some kinda salesman?" She hauls a soft pack of Camels out of her jeans, retrieves one with pinched lips and lights it with a silver Zippo as big as a Frigidaire. *Click-crack-tink-snap.* She exhales a gray smoke trickle out the corner of her mouth, skewing her lips like a convict. "Mind if I smoke? Ain't spose to, but fuck it."

"You bet," I say, grateful for the forbidden aroma in my nostrils. When Mike fired up last night, I realized you don't smell it as much as you used to. I'm tempted to bum one, though I haven't smoked since military school and would probably suffocate. "I *am* a salesman," I answer. "I sell houses."

"Where at? Florida? One-a dem?"

"Right down in Sea-Clift. A ways south of here. Not far, really."

"Oh yeah? Well ain't dat sump'n." Eyes squinted, her smoke in the corner of her mouth, Termite goes searching under the bar and produces a copy of the *Shore Home Buyer's Guide*. The East Jersey Real Estate Board publishes this guide, and if Mike Mahoney's done his homework, there's a boxed Realty-Wise ad in the south Barnegat section showing 61 Surf Road, which the storm outside—vanguard of tropical depression Wayne—may now be washing out to sea.

"I been lookin'," Termite says.

"What kind of place you lookin' for?" I drop my *g*'s as a gesture of camaraderie. Termite would be a challenging client, though possibly I could let Mike do the honors. He'd think it was great—and it would be.

"Oh. You know." She plucks a fleck of tobacco off her tongue tip and in doing so gives me a glimpse of a silver stud punched through her tongue skin like a piece of horse tack. I want it to be still so I can get a better look, but in an instant it's flickered and gone. "Just sump'n grand, overlookin' de ocean and dat don't cost nothin'. Maybe sump'n somebody died in, like what used to be about the Corvette dat girl died in in Laplace and dey couldn't get the smell out, so they had to junk it. I could live with it. You got sump'n like dat? Where was it you live?"

"Sea-Clift."

"Okay." She sucks a molar and rolls her punctured tongue around her cheek at the concept of a town by that name. "Course, I got my momma. She in the wheelchair since I don't know when."

"That's nice," I say. "I mean it's nice she can live with you. It's not nice she's in a wheelchair. That's not nice."

"Yeah. Diabetes amputated her leg off." Termite frowns as if this was, for her, personally painful.

"I see."

The two big ladies down the bar are re-animating their conversation at higher decibels. "Every time I get on a fuckin' plane, I think, This sumbitch is gonna blow up. Makes me sleep better if I just accept it." The couple from the back booth are still dancing, though Perry has long ago finished his Christmas song.

"Look. Lemme aks you somethin'." Termite hikes her booted foot onto the lip of the rinse sink and holds her smoke like a pencil between her thumb and index finger. In spite of her tough-as-rivets, knife-wielding personal demeanor—little biceps veined and sculpted, brown eyes slightly, skeptically bulged, ringed fingers raw and probably callused from pumping iron—she is not the least bit masculine. In fact, she's as feminine as Ava Gardner—just not in the same way as Ava Gardner. Her waist, with her big silver and black belt pulled tight, is as tiny as a dragonfly's. And her breasts, possibly encased in something metal under her black muscle shirt, are sizable breasts no man would sniff at. I'd like to know what her mother calls her at home. Susan or Sandra or Amanda-Jean. Though she'd pop you in the kisser if you breathed it. "Where you come from originally?"

"I'm pure cracker," I say. "Mississippi."

"I heeerd dat," Termite sneers. A lineage check means we're aiming toward subject matter her customers down the bar wouldn't tolerate, something, in her experience, only another southerner could possibly comprehend: exactly why your colored races are constitutionally unsuited to work a forty-hour week; the consequences of their possessing statistically proven smaller brains; why they can't swim or leave white women alone. It's too bad there can't be something good to come from being a southerner. However, I'm getting happily drunk on my second highball and these are subjects easily skirted.

"Okay. See. I read this." Termite inches in close to the bar, drops her voice. "Your brain don't have no manager, see. Not really. It's just like a plant. It go dis way, den it go dat way. Dey ain't no *self* ever runnin' it. It just like adapts. We all just like accidents dat we got minds at all." Her little rodent's face grows solemn with the dark implications of this news. I know something about this matter from my bathroom study of the Mayo newsletter, where such matters are regularly reported on. The mind *is* a metaphor. Consciousness *is* cellular adaptation, intelligence *is* as fortuitous as pick-up sticks. All true. I only hope Termite's not vectoring us toward adumbrations about The Lord and His Overall Design. If she is, I'll run right out into the storm. "You know what ahm sayin'?" She's whispering in a secret-keeping voice the other bar patrons aren't supposed to hear. "You know what ahm sayin'?" she says again.

"I do."

"Millennium! What fuckin' Millennium?" The big boisterous girls are getting drunker, too, and have decided they've got the place to themselves, which they nearly do. No one's come in since I did. "I musta been in the crapper when that happened!"

Termite gives them a disgusted look and begins spindling the *Shore Home Buyer's Guide* into a tight tube, scrolling it smaller and smaller into itself until it looks solid. "So, see," she says, still confidentially. "Like I'm fifty-one"—I'd have said forty—"and I try to like test ma mind sometimes. Okay?" I smile as if I know, and simultaneously try to know. "I try to think of a specific thing. I try to remember somethin'. To see if I *can*. Like—and it's usually a name—de name of dem flowers with red berries on 'em we useta always have at Christmas. Or maybe something'll come up when ahm talking, and I wanta say, 'Oh, yeah, that's like . . .' Den I can't think of it. You know? They's just a hole there where what I want to say ought to be. It ain't never nuttin important, like what's Jack Daniel's or how you make a whiskey sour. It's like ahm sayin', '. . . and den we all drove over to Freehold.' But den I can't say Freehold. Dat ain't the best example. 'Cause I can say Freehold, whatever. But if I give you a good example, den I won't think of it. I can't even think of a good example. You know what I'm talkin' about with dis thing?"

Termite takes a long consternated drag on her Camel, then douses it in the rinse sink and tosses the butt into a black plastic garbage can behind the bar, blowing smoke straight down without lowering her head.

"I've had that happen to me plenty of times," I say. Who hasn't? This is the kind of pseudo-problem that would easily succumb to a Sponsor call. And as always, my solution would be: Forget the hell about it. Think about something better—a new apartment with a wheelchair ramp and maybe a Jenn-Air and lots of phone jacks. Your mind's not the fucking Yellow Pages. You've got no business asking it to perform tasks it's not interested in just so you can show off. To me, it's a worse signal that anybody would ever worry about these things than that he/

she can't remember every little bit of nibshit minutiae you can dream up but that maybe doesn't even exist.

"Pyracantha?"

"Say what?" Termite blinks at me.

"That Christmas flower with the red berries."

"Dere it is, okay. But dat ain't all. 'Cause the real baddest thing is that when I can't get what you just said into my mind, den I worry about dat, and den dat like opens the floodgates for stuff you wouldn't believe."

"What stuff?"

"Stuff I don't wanna talk about." Termite guardedly eyes the two large-bodies down the bar again, as if they might be snickering at her. They are, in fact, pulled in close together, whispering, but holding hands like married bears.

"But I mean, true stuff?" I'm wondering but not wondering very hard.

"Yeah, true stuff. Stuff I don't like to think about. Okay?"

"You bet." I take a subject-changing sip of my—now—third happy-hour highball. I may have had enough. I don't have the stamina I used to. I'm also on the brink of a discussion that threatens to tumble into seriousness—the last thing I want. I'd rather talk about beach erosion or golf or the Eagles' season or the election, since I'm sure these girls have to be Democrats.

"You think ahm losing my mind?" Termite asks accusingly.

"Absolutely not. I *don't* think that. Like I said. I've had that happen to me. Your mind's just got a lot in it." Tattoo and piercing decisions, who's a good knife sharpener, her invalid mom.

"'Cause Mamma thinks mebbe I'm losing it. Ya know what ahm sayin'? And sometimes *I* think I am, too. When I want de name of some got-damn red flower, or whatever dat woman's name is who's the Astronaut—whatever—then I can't think of it." Her lips curl in a smile of disgust with herself—a look she's used to.

And then, in by-the-book bartender protocol, she turns and walks away, resuming something with the lovebirds who've been smooch-dancing to Perry. I hear her say, ". . . they just treat Thanksgiving like it really meant somethin'. What I want to know is, what *is* it?"

"Me, too," one of the slow dancers speaks, with an echo that registers sadly in the bar.

Termite's left me the spindled *Home Buyer's Guide.* I intend to show her my ad and leave my card. Sometimes a new vista, a new house number, a new place of employ, a new set of streets to navigate and master are all you need to simplify life and take a new lease out on it. Real estate might seem to be all about moving and picking up stakes and disruption and three-moves-equals-a-death, but it's really about arriving and destinations, and all the prospects that await you or might await you in some place you never thought about. I had a drunk old prof at Michigan who taught us that all of America's literature, Cotton Mather to Steinbeck—this was the same class where I read *The Great Gatsby*—was forged by one positivist principle: to leave, and then to arrive in a better state.

I take this opportunity to climb off my stool and walk to the porthole door and have a check across the lot to find out if my car window's ready. It isn't. Chris, the Fitzgerald scholar, has pulled it into the fluorescent-lit garage bay and is moving around the murky shop interior, seeming to be in search of the right materials for the job. The other man, small and raffish and unshaven, stands at the office door, looking up at the rain-torn skies as if into a cloud of sorry thoughts. Edward Hopper in New Jersey.

I reclaim my bar stool and remind myself to grab another piss or be faced with again relieving myself in the rain, behind some darkened Pathmark, where I've already been caught more than once by security patrols, resulting in a lot of unwieldy explanation. In each instance, however, the officers were moonlighting middle-age cops and completely sympathized.

Termite's staying down with the girls at the end of the bar. No one else has shown up for happy hour (weather and the holiday are always negatives). I leaf through the *Buyer's Guide,* perusing the broker-associate faces in their winning, confidence-pledging smiley cameos. The glam Debs, Lindas and Margies with their golden silky hair, big earrings, plenty of lens gauze to disguise what they really look like, and the men all blow-dried Woodys and mustachioed Maxes in hunky poses—blue jeans, open-collar plaids, tasteful silver accessories and gold throat jewelry. Most of what's for sale are "houses," our term of art for cookie-cutter ranches and undersized split-levels—nothing different from our basic inventory in Sea-Clift. Every few pages, there's a grandiose one-of-a-kind "palatial beach estate" that doesn't list the price but everyone knows is seizure-inducing.

My 61 Surf Road listing is back on page ninety-six, a boiler-plate box with the Doolittles' house in washed-out color, a shot captured by Mike using our old Polaroid. It strikes me again, even knowing what I now know, that it's as good as there is at this location, at this time, at this price. There are nicer listings in Brielle, but at twice the ticket. Monday morning, I'll call Boca and discuss options regarding foundation issues and amending the disclosure statement. "Foundation needs attention" is natur-ally a death knell in a saturated market unless the buyer sees the whole thing as a tear-down. My bet is the Doolittles jerk the listing and hand it to a competitor who knows nothing about the foundation. I'm not sure I'd blame them.

"Hey! You!" the big Yanks-cap mama bear down the bar (she's shit-faced) is addressing me. I smile as if I'm eager to be spoken to. "You wouldn't happen to be named Armand, would you? And you wouldn't happen to be from Neptune, I guess?"

"Or Ur-a-nus." Her can't-bust-'em friend bursts out a guffaw.

"Nope. Afraid not." Smiling back winningly. "Sea-Clift."

"Told ya," the overall woman gloats.

"Big deal. Well then, do you wanna dance? I promise I'm a woman."

"He doesn't give a shit," her companion stage-whispers, lean-ing in front of her to grin down at me. "Look at him." More laughing.

"That's really nice. But no thanks," I say. "I'm taking off pretty soon."

"Who isn't?" she growls. "Tough luck for you. I'm a good dancer."

"On her feet and yours, too," her friend mocks.

"You two should dance," I say.

"There you go," the second woman agrees.

"*Where* I go?" the first woman grumbles, and they immedi-ately forget about me.

It is a fine and fortunate feeling to be beached here—stranger and welcomed onlooker. I could've easily gotten mired into nowhere-no-time, with only the night's dark cave in front of me.

But I'm not. I'm found, though I'm not sure anyone but me would see it like that.

Still, my day has accomplished much of what I wanted when I set forth—which is full immersion in events. Three occurrences have been of a positive nature: a good if unproductive house showing, a successful implosion and a salubrious interlude here. Versus only two and a half of a low-quality: a not-good kitchen encounter with my daughter and her beau; my car busted into; Wade blowing a gasket and ending up—where? (Home, I hope.)

Any of the latter events would be enough to set a man driving to North Dakota, ending up at a stranger's farmhouse east of Minot, pleading amnesia and letting himself be sheltered for the day—Turkey Day—before regaining his senses and heading home. Suffice it to say, then, that when you see a man bending an elbow, head down, shoulders hunched before a dark brown drink, chatting elliptically, *sotto voce* with the barkeep, looking tired-eyed, boozy, but apparently happy, you should think that what's being transacted is the self giving the self a much-needed reprieve. The brain may not have a true manager, but it's got a boss. And it's you.

Several pairs of fresh patrons have rumbled in out of the rain, which turns the bar more festive. All the ladies—a couple being 200-plus-pounders—are in some species of loose-fitting work clothes with durable footwear, as if they were members of the pipe fitters' union. Some have donned amusing headgear (a pink beret, a zebra-striped hard hat, a backwards Caterpillar cap), and they're all in cracking good spirits, know everyone else's name and are joking and ribbing one another just like a bunch of men—though these women are younger than men would be, and more amiable and tolerant, and would undoubtedly make better friends.

They each give me a surreptitious appraising eye upon entering and share a quick naughty remark, as if I was actually a woman. One or two of them smile at me in a haughty way that means, we're happy you're here, we're on our best behavior, so you better be on yours (which I intend to be). Termite, they all treat like a beloved little sister, but a scandalous little sister with a vicious mouth any parent would have trouble with. She stalks the duckboards with their drink orders, calling everyone "gents" and "goyls" and "douchebags," occasionally wisecracking something down to me that I'm not supposed to answer. She drifts my way, eyes snapping, offers me something known as an "Irish Napalm" that the "goyls" all like, and that's served on fire. "They'll all be wanting 'em in a minute," she says in a tough, loud voice over the enlarged noise, "after which all shit'll break loose in here. Anyway, an-y-way." She's forgotten about having talked to me twenty minutes ago about being afraid she's going crazy.

"De thing I want to know," she says, leaning in again, tiny eyes slitted, as if this is definitely not for general consumption, her right hand resting on her bowie knife handle, "is—when did everything get to be about bidnus? You know what ahm sayin'? Bidnus this, bidnus that."

One thing I hadn't noticed, now that Termite's moved in close to me again, is that she's wearing silvery orthodontic appliances on her lower incisors, in addition to her silver tongue rivet—which makes her look even stranger.

"The business of business is business," I say with a frank expression to suggest I know what that means.

"Okay." She nods, then glances over her shoulder at her bar full of business, as if the new raucousness in here gives us some privacy we hadn't had. "You a good listener. Did ma old husband, Reynard, hear one thing I ever said, ah mighta been stayed married to dat knucklehead. You know what ahm sayin'? But no way. Uh-uh. Wudn' no listenin' involved. Just him talkin' and me jump'n round like a old hop-frog."

"That's too bad. Some men aren't good listeners, I guess."

"Oh yeah." She sucks a tooth and looks down. "You a good-lookin' man, too. You got you a good young hotsy down-ere where you livin' at Sea-what's-it-called?" Termite suddenly smiles at me both directly and sweetly, a smile that features her lower line of silver braces, and tentatively advances a thought that a better, stronger bond might form between us, with other things possibly permissible.

"I do," I cheerfully lie. I'm picturing my daughter with poly-ethnic Thom, who I hope never to see again.

Termite's sweet smile turns instantly professional-impersonal. "Yeah. Well. Das good. Yep," she says crisply. "Happy hour almost over wid. You need anything?"

"I'm already happy," I say, wanting to sound affirming about all her life's prospects but one.

"Dere you go," she says, and turns straight away again and saunters down the duckboards, proclaiming, "Now ya'll fatsos try to control ya'll selves."

"Fuck you and that goat you rode in on, you skinny little bitch," one of the women shouts in merry mirth, and they all convulse full-throated.

I BROWSE BACK through the curled pages of the *Buyer's Guide*, wanting to give mechanic Chris another ten minutes. These publications can actually be the most helpful and news-packed that any citizen could hope for when entering a community or region where he knows no one and might grow dispirited and feel tempted just to head home to Waukegan. In the interest of plain and simple commerce, but for the price of nothing, the *Guide* provides a well-researched list of "essential services," crisis numbers, "Best Bet" Italian, Filipino and Thai cuisines, walk-in wellness clinics, an e-mail address for a mortgage-consultant clearing house, emergency dental care and pet health hot-line numbers, oxygen tank delivery, bump shops and bail bondsmen. And, of course, bi-weekly training classes in the real estate profession. There's even a list of local numbers for Monmouth and Ocean County Sponsors Anonymous. Plus, many small-business opportunities are advertised, situations where you can walk in and take over like I did. I always find one or two new summer rental properties every year by leafing through these pages on slow Saturday afternoons in January—often chalets I could buy myself if they're in presentable shape, or manage for a good fee if they're not. I also read through these crowded pages just to acquire (by osmosis) some sense of how we're all basically doing, what we need to be wary of, look forward to or look back on with pride or relief. These spiritual sign-pointers are revealed to me in old fire stations, rectories or Chrysler agencies that are for sale, or once-thriving businesses in turnaround, or the number of old homes versus new ones on the sale block, or the addresses and plat maps of new constructions, the ethnicity (gauged by the names) of who's selling what, who's doing the cooking or who's going out of business. And finally, of course, what costs what, versus what used to cost what. There's in fact a listing in the middle Green Pages of every property sold in Monmouth and Ocean counties and how much was paid and by whom—sure signs of the time. Little of this will be anything I make a note about or mention to Mike in our Monday strategy breakfasts at the Earl of Sandwich. It's just the soft susurrus, the hick and tick of the engine that warms us when it's cold, soothes us when it's beastly, and that we all hear and feel on our arms, necks and faces like atmosphere, whether we know it or whether we never do.

On page sixty-four, however, amidst all that's familiar, a new *Guide* feature attracts my eye, part of a double-truck layout for the Mengelt Agency in Vanhiseville. Mengelt offerings are generally small, characterless scrub lots in old interior suburbs on their way to extinction, exactly like the ones Mike and I rode past on our trip to Haddam. The Mengelt motto, in hopeful serifs, is, "We find your home. You find the happiness." There's the usual row of tiny page-bottom snapshots showing the mostly unsmiling, mostly female Mengelt agents—a new batch of Carols, Jennifers and a Blanche—contributing to the impression that the institution of marriage may be losing some traction in Vanhiseville.

But in a larger framed box, under the title "Profiles in Real Estate Courage," is a sharp color photo of "Associate of the Month" Fred Frantal, smiling and cherub-cheeked, a sausage of a fellow with a round weak chin, crinkly hair, a fuzzy mustache and two happy, saucerish eyes. Fred's wearing a red-and-green lumberjack shirt that hints of a decent-size personal sculpture below the frame. And under his picture there's printed a lengthy story apparently pertaining to Fred, which the Mengelt associates want the world to know about. I'd probably be smart to plaster Mike's squinting, beaming mug onto our ad, with a boiled-down account of his improbable but inspirational life's journey from Tibet to the Jersey Shore. It would attract the curious, which is often where commerce begins.

"'Frog' Frantal," the Mengelt story goes, "is not just our *Associate of the Month* but our *Associate of the Millennium*. A two-year Vanhiseville resident and graduate associate from Middlesex Community College, Fred got gold-plated lucky when he married Carla Boykin back in '82 and moved to Holmeson to be an EMS technician for the H'son Rescue Unit, where he saved many lives and made a big impression on many others. Fred and Carla raised two great kids, Chick and Bev, and have always trained Rottweilers. The Frantals moved to Vanhiseville in 1998, when Fred retired from the FD, having earned his real estate license at night. He joined the Mengelt family last year and made an instant impact here, too, on our residential sales, due to his EMS contacts and generally positive outlook (he loves cold calls). Fred's a Navy vet, a brown belt in tae kwon do, an avid surfcaster and snowmobiler, a Regular Baptist Church member and these days is in demand as a motivational speaker on youth and grieving issues. Sadly, last winter tragedy struck the Frantals, when their son Chick, 20, was killed by a drunken snowmobiler in eastern PA. We all mourned Fred and Carla's loss. But with support of friends, loved ones and the Mengelt crew, Fred's back and ready to list your house and sell you another one. Frog has topped our leaders board eight of the last ten months, and deserves the distinction of *Associate of the Millennium*. He believes that whatever doesn't kill you makes you stronger, and that you meet triumph and disaster and make friends with both. If either of these describes your current real estate situation, give Fred a call at (732) 555–2202, or e-mail him at frog@mengelt.com. Happy Thanksgiving from all of us!"

Voices in the bar. Laughter. The tinkle-clinkle of glasses. Shuffle of booted feet, squeezing bar-stool leather, heavy coats rustling, exhale of heavy breaths. Outside, there's the hiss of wind, the spatter splat of rain on the metal roof. A sigh of a door closing. These sounds of mutuality and arrival recede down a hallway, yet grow more distinct, as though I viewed the livening bar on a screen, with the sound track elsewhere.

Down the bar, little silver-haired Termite frowns toward me, narrows her eyes suspiciously, then turns back to the bar full of women, all laughing at something. Someone says, pretty loud, "So it turns out, see, that China's *really fucking BIG.*" "Whoa," someone else says.

I am, I now perceive, immobilized on my stool, though in no danger of toppling off. I don't feel drunk, though I could be. My head isn't swimming. My extremities aren't dulled or immobilized. I'd recognize all the money denominations in my pocket if I had to, could pay my tab and walk right out into the stormy parking lot and take command of my vehicle (which must be fixed by now). Yet I'm heavy-armed and moored to the bar rail, my heels stuck to the brass footrest. My empty highball glass seems small and distant—once again, as when I was a feverish kid and the contents of my room got pleasantly distant, and the sound of my mother's footsteps in another room were all I experienced of ambient sound.

I've said it before. I do not credit the epiphanic, the seeing-through that reveals all, triggered by a mastering detail. These are lies of the liberal arts to distract us from the more precious here and now. Life's moments truly come at us heedless, not at the bidding of a gilded fragrance. The Permanent Period is specifically commissioned to combat these indulgences into the pseudo-significant. We're all separate agents, each underlain by an infinite remoteness; and to the extent we're not and require to be *significant*, we're not so interesting.

And yet. In this strange, changed state I for this moment find myself, and for reasons both trivial and circumstantial (the bar, the booze, the day, even Fred Frantal), my son Ralph Bascombe, age twenty-nine (or for accuracy's sake, age nine), comes seeking audience in my brain.

And I am then truly immobilized. And with what? Fear? Love? Regret? Shame? Lethargy? Bewilderment? Heartsickness? Whimsy? Wonder? You never know for sure, no matter what the great novels tell you.

It may go without saying, but when you have a child die— as I did nineteen years ago—you carry him with you forever and ever after. Of course you should. And not that I "talk" to him (though some might) or obsess endlessly (as his brother, Paul, did for years until it made him loony), or that I expect Ralph to turn up at my door, like Wally, with a wondrous story of return or of long, shadowy passageways with luminous light awaiting, from which he bolted at the last second (I've fantasized that could happen, though it was just a way to stay interested as years went by). For me, left back, there's been no dead-zone sensation of life suspended, hollowed, wind-raddled, no sense of not leading my *real* life but only some consolation-prize life nobody would want—I'm sure that can happen, too.

Though what *has* developed is that my life's become alloyed with loss. Ralph, and then Ralph being dead, long ago became embedded in all my doings and behaviors. And not like a disease you carry that never gets better, but more the way being left-handed is ever your companion, or that you don't like parsnips and never eat them, or that once there was a girl you loved for the very first time and you can't help thinking of her—non-specifically—every single day. And while this may seem profane or untrue to say, the life it's made has been and goes on being a much more than merely livable life. It's made a good life, this loss, one I don't at all regret. (The Frantals couldn't be expected to believe this, but maybe can in time.)

Of course, Ralph's death was why Ann and I couldn't stay married another day seventeen years back. We were always thinking the same things, occupying and dividing up the same tiny piece of salted turf, couldn't surprise and please each other the way marrieds need to. Death became all we had in common, a common jail. And who wanted that till our own deaths did us part? There would be a forever, we knew, and we had to live on into it, divided and joined by death. And not that it was harder on us than it was on Ralph, who died, after all, and not willingly. But it was hard enough.

Out of the rosy bar-light distance, as though emerging from a long passageway, so long she'll never reach me in my state—I'm drunk, okay—is Termite, thumbs provocatively in her black denim pockets, inquisitive grin on her mousy mouth, eyes shining, fixed on me. We are like lovers who've become friends late in life: She knows my hilarious eccentricities and failures and only takes me half seriously. I love her to bits but no longer feel the old giddy-up. We could spend hours now just talking.

"You know all what I was yakkin' about back den? I'm probably gon' forget about it tomorrow. It ain't permanent—goin' crazy. You know whut ahm sayin'?" She sweeps away my empty highball glass, drops it *plunk* into the sudsy sink. "Do you say *drought* or *drouth*?" She stares across at me, though her face has turned suspicious in a hurry, as though I'd offered her a counterfeit tenner. She takes a step back, cocks her flat-topped head, her mouth curls cruelly the way I knew it could. "Whut's wrong witch you?"

Unexpectedly, my eyes flood with tears, my hot cheeks taking the runoff. I've known about them for the better part of a minute but have been stuck here, unable to blink or wipe my nose with my sleeve or to think about a trip to the gents or about seeking a breath of rescue in the out-of-doors. I don't know what to say about *drought* or *drouth*. *Dry* comes into my mind, as does *I'm in a terrible state*. Though like a lot of terrible states, it doesn't feel so bad.

"I-I—" My old stammer, not heard from in years but always lurking were I to laugh inconsiderately at another stammerer—which I never do—now revisits my glottus. "I-I-I don't know." I want to smile but don't quite make it.

Termite's hard little ferret's eyes fix on me. She performs one of her flash glances back down the bar, as if my predicament needs to be kept under wraps. "Wadn't nuthin *I* said," she announces, but not loud.

"N-n-n-o." My hands clutch the *Buyer's Guide* and give it another fierce re-spindling. *N* is a hard one for stutterers. My chest empties as if somebody has just stamped on it. Then it heaves a big sigh-sounding noise, which I manage not to let out as a groan, though stifling it hurts like hell. I have to get out of here now. I could die here.

"You piss drunk is all," Termite snarls. This is not old-lovers-become-friends. This is, "I've seen the likes of you all my life, been married to it, fucked it, wallowed in it, but I'm well out of it as you see me now." That's what this is.

"Ahhh, yeah." This time an actual groan issues forth. Then more tears. Then a shudder. What's going on? What's going on? What's going on?

"Jew drive here?"

"Yeah." I reach my nose with my jacket sleeve and saw back and forth.

"You drive off and git in a wreck and kill some kid, you ain't sayin' you been in here. You got dat? I'm spose to take dem keys"—She regards me with revulsion, right hand on her silver bowie knife hilt. How can things change so fast? I haven't done anything—"but I don't wanna touch you." She snorts back a stiff breath, as if I smell bad.

I am climbing off my bar stool, feeling light-headed but terribly heavy, like a sandbag puppet.

"Y'hearin' what ahm sayin'?" Her eyes narrow to a threat. Termite might be her real name.

"Okay. Sure." From my pocket I produce a piece of U.S. paper currency along with my Realty-Wise card. It could be a million-dollar bill. These I place on the bar. "Thanks," I say, my mouth chromy. My hands are cold, my feet thick.

Termite doesn't regard my pay-up. I've become her problem now, something else to lose sleep over. Will there be repercussions? Her job in jeopardy? Jail time? One more thing not to be thankful for.

But I'm already away, heading for the door, my gait surprisingly steady, as if the way out was downhill. I am, in fact, not drunk. Though what I am is a different matter.

RAIN NEEDLES sting my cheeks, nose, brow, chin, neck when I make it out into the dark parking lot—painful but alerting. It was burning up in there, though I was frozen. Again, I may be catching something.

Cars with cadaverous colored headlights pass over the Route 35 bridge, motoring home to relatives, a quiet night before the holiday tangle, a long weekend of parades, floating balloon animals, football and extra plate-fulls. I have no idea what time it is. Since Spring Ahead gave way to Fall Back, I've been uncertain. It could be six or nine or two a.m. Though I'm clear-headed. My heart's beating at a good pace. I even give a sudden optimistic thought to Ann and Paul (and Jill) in Haddam, enjoying each other's company, reacclimating, forging new bonds. I don't feel panicky (though that could be a sure sign of panic). It is merely odd to be here now—the opposite of where the evening seemed to be heading, though, again, I had no plans.

But bad luck, bad luck heaped on bad luck! The Quonset across the lot looms dark and silent, from all appearances closed up forever, the big metal door rolled down, the office—I can see from here—wearing a fat bulletproof padlock that catches a glint off the sulfur lights from the boatyard next door. Cut-out turkeys and Pilgrims in happy holiday symbiosis are taped to the window there, too. NO JOB TOO ABSURD.

I am incensed—and breathless. If I could just get out of here, I'd gladly hunt down the faithless Chris asleep somewhere, and strangle him in front of his father, uncle, whatever, then smoke a cigarette before attacking the old man with a pair of needle-nose pliers. Except I spy a rear bumper's shine, a BUSH? WHY? sticker and a pale-blue-and-cream AWK 486, *Garden State* plate—mine. My Suburban's parked in the oily shadows between the Quonset and a pile of tire discards. *Left out*, where I'm supposed to find it. I'll send young Chris a whopper check that'll pay his way through Monmouth and pave the path to dental school. If he'd hung around, I'd have bought him a shore dinner and told him about the things in life he needs to beware of— starting with lesbian bars and the false bonhomie of treacherous little coon-ass bartenders.

I hustle through the remnant mist, avoiding the lakes and flooded tire tracks. Most of the women in Squatters seem to have arrived in pickups with chrome toolboxes or else junker Roadmasters with rusted rocker panels. Despite the shadows, Chris, I can see, has performed a creditable repair, including sweeping out the broken glass. My window's masked by multiple layers of gray duct tape backed by a slat of jigsawed plywood fitted to the hole. I could drive it this way for weeks and be fine.

The driver door's unlocked and the interior I crawl into stiff and cold and dank. My eyes are still flooding with unavailing tears. But I am eager to get going.

Only where are the keys? The ones with the fake Indian arrowhead and miniature beaded warrior-shield fob made by the retarded son of Louis the Dry Cleaner and for sale on a card for three dollars (and you'd better buy one or your shirts come back with their buttons crunched). I handed them to Chris just before the "boats against the current, borne back ceaselessly" part. He had them, or the car wouldn't be here and fixed. I saw it half-in the lighted garage bay when I checked—how long ago? Twenty minutes. How can a place of business go dark and its employees vamoose like ghosts all in twenty minutes? Why wouldn't he just skip across and give me the high sign, a hand signal, a raised eyebrow, two monosyllables—"Yer done." Cultural literacy should make this kind of masculine transaction a no-brainer— even in Greece. But not in Manasquan.

I go rifling through all the places keys can hide. The visor. The side map pocket. The glove box—full of extra chalet keys. The ashtray. Under the rubber floor mat. In the fucking cup holder. Tears are flowing, my fingers clammy, stinging when I scrape them on every sharp or rough surface. I've given my extra set to Clarissa in case I fall over dead and there're complications with the authorities about getting my valuables sacked up and returned in a timely fashion. These things happen. How mindless would it have been to have Assif Chevrolet-GMC requisition twenty extras to distribute in every corner of my existence. I swear that on Monday, when I take my window hole for proper fixing (assuming I make it to then), I'll issue the order no matter the cost, even though computer chips aren't cheap. I consider getting out in the cold and crawling underneath, probing my bunged fingers under the gritty bumpers, into the wheel wells, inside the grille face. Though I'd only soak myself and compromise my flu-shot immunity. In any case, I know the sons of bitches aren't there. They're hanging "safely" on a fucking nail in the office, attached to a paper tag that says "Older dude. Red Sub keys. Payment due," meaning the little Greek cocksuckers didn't trust me to pay the twenty-five bucks the moment the sun comes up tomorrow; were happier to let me do whatever in hell a human being does in asshole Manasquan outside a dyke bar, the night before Thanksgiving, when you're too crocked to call the police. While-U-Wait, my ass.

I pound my fists on the steering wheel until they ache and it's ready to crack. "Why, why, why?" These actual words come with an all-new freshet of frustrated tears. Why did I do what's so ill-advised? Why did I risk the Manasquan, knowing what might lurk here? Why did I, a nunce, trust a Greek? One who reads Fitzgerald? Faithless Chris, himself a callow young Nick. Why, oh why did I rashly count my blessings and leave myself at risk? *Thanksgiving?* Thanksgiving's bullshit.

I should've driven down to the Grove with Wade, hied off with a mid-forties-body-style Ricki, downed the martinis, eaten the hanger steak, skived away in the night, right to the blind golfers Quality Court to test the lead left in the ole pencil. What higher ground am I occupying? For what greater purpose am I preserved? Do I have anything to accomplish before I'm sixty that makes an unserious boinking a bad idea when it never was before? Am I preserving clarity? Am I too good, too intent, too loyal, too cautious, too free to grab a little woogle when it's offered and otherwise in short supply?

Tears and more tears come fairly flooding. Rage, frustration, sorrow, remorse, fatigue, self-reproach—a whole new list. Name it, I've suddenly got it. I gawk around through the fogged windows at the Squatters' lot. A low-rider Chevette idles through and noses into the handicapped space. Two women in big coats climb out, one on crutches, and move slowly through the doors, which when open cast a blue-red blur into the night, where I'm trapped, wanting, needing someone to help me. No one inside would even remember me, though probably plenty possess automotive skills.

It's another moment for cell-phone service. A chance to use the Triple-A I never bought. The ideal dilemma for an in-car computerized hot-line-to-Detroit for dispatched emergency assistance—though my Suburban's a '96. Too old. Of course, there aren't pay phones anymore.

And for God's sake and beyond all: What *else* is happening to me out here? I'm not about to *die* (I don't think). "Bascombe was discovered deceased in his car outside a Manasquan bump shop, across from an alternative night spot on Thanksgiving morning. No further details are available." No, no, no. Except this feeling I'm having *reminds* me of death and presents itself as pain right where my heart ought to be; only nothing's spazzing down my arm, no light-headed, gasping or blue-faced constriction. It's as if I'd done death *already.* Though I'd give anything, promise any promise, admit anything just to not feel this way, to see instead a hopeful, trusting Sponsoree materialize out of the misty night, seeking good counsel for his or her issues and shifting the focus away from mine. Since mine seem to be not that I'm dying, but that I just have to *be* here in some fearsome way— and me the last person on earth to truckle with stagy ideas of *be*-ness. *Be*-ness means business to me. (What is it about being trapped in your cold vehicle with no help coming and the promise of the night spent curled up like a snake in the luggage compartment that gives rise to the somberest of thoughts: the finality of one's *self,* in defeat of all distractions put in the way? Possibly it's cloying Thanksgiving *it*self—the recapitulative, Puritan and thus most treacherous of holidays—that clears away the ordinary pluses and leaves only the big minuses to be totaled.)

Of course, anyone could tell, even me, that it's the Frantals' sad family mini-saga that's whop-sided me into painful, tearful grieving (if you've lost a child, other people's child-loss stories magnetize around you like iron filings). And what else would you call my symptoms but grieving? Inasmuch as tucked away in the *Home Buyer's Guide,* where I'd least expect it, is the juggernaut of *acceptance*—grief's running mate. *Their* acceptance—of life's bounty and its loss—which the world can honor, in the Frantals' case, by plunking down some earnest money on a cunning Cape on Crab Apple Court.

But what the hell more do *I* need to accept that I haven't already, and confessed as the core of my *be*-ness? That I have cancer and my days are numbered in smaller denominations than most everyone else's? (Check.) That my wife's left me and probably won't come back? (Check.) That my fathering and husbanding skills have been unexemplary and at best only serviceable? (Check.) That I've chosen a life smaller than my "talents" because a smaller life made me happier? (Check, check, double check.)

More tears are falling. I could laugh through them if I didn't have a potentially self-erasing pain in my chest. What is it I'm supposed to accept? That I'm an asshole? (I confess.) That I have no heart? (I don't confess.) But what would be the hardest thing to say and mean it? What would be the hardest for others? The Frantals? For Sally? For Mike Mahoney? For Ann? For anybody I know? All good souls to God?

And of course the answer's plain, unless we're actors or bad-check artists or spies, when it's still probably plain but more tolerable: that your life is founded on a lie, and you know what the lie is and won't admit it, maybe can't. Yes, yes, yes, yes.

Deep in my heart space a breaking is. And as in our private moments of sexual longing, when the touch we want is far away, a groan comes out of me. "Oh-uhhh." The sour tidal whoosh the dead man exhales. "Oh-uhhh. Oh-uhhh." So long have I *not* accepted, by practicing the quaintness of acceptance by. . . . "Oh-uhhh. Oh-uhhh." Breath-loss clenches my belly into a rope knot, clenching, clenching in. "Oh, oh, ohhhhhpp." Yes, yes and yes. No more no's. No more no's. No more no's.

A SINGLE RAIN spatter strikes the hood of my cold vehicle. I'm roused and gaunt, mouth open. Ears stinging. Fists balled. My feet ache. My neck's stiff. My interior parts feel wounded, as if I'd been sealed in a barrel, tupped off a cliff, then rolled and rolled and rolled, bracing myself inside until stopped, upon a dark terrain I can't see but only dream of.

"What now?" These are spoken words I manage. In the rear-view, through the fogged back glass, there's still the red smear of BAR across the lot. Two cars are left—the low-rider and a big Ram club cab. It feels late. Traffic on the 35 bridge has thinned to a trickle. "What now?" I offer again to the fates. I breathe a testing breath (no heart pain), then a deeper, colder one I fill my chest with and hold for my inner parts to register back. My temples go bump-bump-bump-bump behind my eyes, which feel tight. It's better to close them, hands in my lap, cold knees together, elbows in, cranium on the headrest, chest expanded with held-in air. Dampness sits in the cockpit. I breathe out my deep inhale. And though it's said (by ninnies) that we can never experience the exact moment of sleep's arrival, still—and in a speed that amazes me—I do. "So it turns out, see, that China's *really fucking BIG*" are the words I'm thinking, and they are like velvet with their comfort.

TAP, TAP, TAP. *Tap, tap, tap.* A pale moon's face, young, mostly nose and chin and eyebrows, hangs outside my window glass—apprehensive, puzzled, a slight uncertain smile of wonder.

Is he dead? Is it too late?

At first it doesn't scare me. And then, when I realize how deep in sleep I've been, I'm startled. My eyes blink and blink again. My heart goes from imperceptible to perceptible. Robbed, blud-geoned, dragged, heels in the muck, to the cold Manasquan and schlumped onto the tide like a rolled-up rug. I shrink from the glass to escape. I utter a small frightened sound. "Aaaaaaaaaa."

The moon's mouth is moving. Its muffled voice says, "I went to a club over in . . ." *Static, static, static* . . . "I seen your vehicle from the bridge . . . like . . ." *Static, static.*

I gawk through the glass, unable to fix on the face. My cheeks are cobwebby, my mouth bitter and dry. I'm frozen in my jacket and thin pants, but I'm willing to go back to sleep and be murdered that way.

". . . So, are you, like, okay?" the pimpled young moon mouth says.

"Yep," I say, not knowing who to.

But criminals don't wonder if you're okay. Or they shouldn't.

The muffled voice outside says, "Did you find your keys?" An agreeable grin says, You're a poor dope, aren't you? You don't know a goddamn thing. You'll always have to be helped. I push at the window button. Nothing happens. I struggle at the ignition, where there's no key inserted. Things fall into place.

Chris speaks something else, something I can't make out. I push open the heavy-weight door right into his chest and forehead as I hear him say ". . . under the mat."

I stare up. He is no longer in his blue mechanic's shirt that shows off his tattoos, but in a Jersey long-coat of inexpensive green vinyl manufacture, which makes him look like a seedy punk and is meant to. He's cold, too, his hands stuffed in his shallow pockets. He's rocking foot to foot. His nose is running, his forehead reddened, his hair a yellow tangle. But he is in positive spirits, possibly a little wine-drunk or stoned.

Cold air smacks my cheeks. "What time is it?"

Chris breathes out a congested nasal snurf. "Prolly. I don't know. Midnight." He looks over to Squatters. The BAR sign's dark, but visible. No cars sit outside. Route 35's a ghost highway, the bridge empty and palely lit. A garbage truck with a cop car leading it, blue flasher turning, moves slowly south toward Point Pleasant. "I seen your rig still here. I go, 'Uh-oh, what the fuck is this?'" Chris shudders, tucks his chin into his lapel and breathes inside for warmth.

"I looked under the goddamn mat," I say. I'm feeling extremely rough, as if I'd been manhandled for the second night in a row. I'm grinding my molars and must look deranged.

"That mat out front of the office," Chris says, fidgety, chin down, pointing around toward the front door at a mat that's invisible from my car. "We leave 'em there. That way, the car looks like it's just sitting."

"How the hell am I supposed to know that?"

"I don't know," says Chris. "It's how everybody does it. How'd you get in?"

"It was unlocked." I am slightly dazed.

"Oh. Man. I messed that up. I shoulda locked it. Lemme get them keys."

Chris doesn't act like a struggling American Existentialist scholarship boy at Monmouth, but a sweet, knuckleheaded grease monkey weighing a stint in trade school or the Navy. He is who he ought to be. It is a lesson I could apply to my son Paul if I chose to, and should.

Chris hustles back with my arrowhead fob, but grinning. "Didn't you get cold in 'ere?" He swabs his nose, sucks back, hocks one on the gravel. He is someone's son, capable of a good deed performed without undue gravity. He has saved me tonight, after nearly killing me. I now see he has SATAN inked into the flesh of his left metacarpals and JESUS worked into the right ones. Both inexpertly done. Chris is on a quest, his soul in the balance.

"Yeah, but it was fine," I say. "I went to sleep. How much for the window?" I straighten my left leg, where I'm sitting half out the door, so I can reach my billfold. I'm tempted to ask who's winning his soul. Old number 666 rarely has a chance anymore except in politics.

"Thirty," he says. "But you can mail it to him. It's all shut up. I gotta get home. Tomorrow's a holiday. My wife'll kill me."

Wife! Chris has one of those *already*? Possibly he's older than he looks. Possibly he's not even Greek. Possibly he's a father himself. Why do we think we know anything?

"Me, too." A marital lie to make me feel better. "Thanks." I effect a sore-necked look back at the duct-taped window, seemingly as impregnable as a bank.

"No problem," Chris says. His skin-pink Camaro with a bright green replacement passenger door sits idling behind us, headlights shining, interior light on, its door standing open. "You'd be surprised how many of them babies I fix a month." He grins again, a boyish grin, his teeth straight, strong and white. He's leaving, rescue complete, heading home to his Maria or his Silvie, who won't be mad, and will thrill to his return (after modest resistance).

"How old are you?" It seems the essential question to ask of the young.

"Thirty-one." A surprise. "How 'bout you?"

"Fifty-five."

"That ain't so old." His breath is thin smoke. His vinyl coat affords little warmth. "My dad's, like, fifty-six. He does these tough-guy competitions for his age group, up at the convention hall in Asbury. He's on his fourth wife. Nobody fucks with him."

"I bet not."

"Bet they don't fuck with you," Chris says to be generous.

"Not anymore they don't."

"There you go." He breathes down into his lapel again. "That's all you gotta worry about."

"Happy Thanksgiving," I say. "Early." We are beating on, Chris and me, against the current.

"Oh yeah." He looks embarrassed. "Happy Thanksgiving to you, too."

CONCEIVABLY IT'S TWO. I've avoided clocks on my drive home, likewise during the passage through my empty house. Knowledge of the hour, especially if it's later than I think, will guarantee me no sleep, promising that tomorrow's celebration of munificence and bounty will degrade into demoralized fatigue before the food arrives.

Clarissa's bedroom window's been left open, and I crank it closed, intentionally noticing nothing. I listen to none of my day's messages. I've shown one house to one serious client on the day before Thanksgiving, a day when most toilers in my business are headed off to convivial tables elsewhere. For that reason I'm ahead of the game—which is generally my tack: With few obligations, turn freedom into enterprise. Thoreau said a writer was a man with nothing to do who finds something to do. He would've made the realty Platinum Circle. His heirs would own Maine.

But passing by my darkened home office a second time, I'm unable to resist my messages. After all, Clarissa herself might've called with a plea that I shoot down and collect her at the elephant gate at the Taj Mahal. In my unwieldy state of acceptance, I concede that something once unpromising could show improvement.

Clare Suddruth has, not surprisingly, called at six—a crucial interval, and at the vulnerable cocktail hour. He says he definitely wants to "re-view" the Doolittle house on Friday, if possible. "At least let's get through the damn front door this time." He's bringing "the boss." "At my age, Frank, there's no use worrying about the long run in anything." He says this as if I hadn't spoon-fed him those very words. Estelle, the MS survivor, has been counseling with Clare about matters eschatological. I'm just relieved not to have to call the Drs. Doolittle with unhappy news that would cost me the listing. Though Clare's the type to come in with a low-ball offer, consume weeks with back-and-forth and then get pissed off and walk away. My best strategy is to say I'm tied up until next week (when I'll be at Mayo) and hope he gets desperate.

Call #2 is from Ann Dykstra, more cut-and-dried-businessy than last night's sauvignon blanc ramble about what a good man I am, what a long transit life is, me snagging the Hawk's liner at the Vet in '87. "Frank, I think we need to talk about tomorrow. I'm thinking maybe I shouldn't come. Paul and Jill just left, which was very strange. Did you know she only has one hand? Some awful accident. Maybe I'm just saving myself." What's wrong with that? "Anyway, maybe I'm getting ahead of myself on several fronts. I sort of sense you may feel the same. Call me before you go to bed. I'll be up."

Too late.

Call #3 listens to my Realty-Wise recording, waits, breathes, then says "Shit" in a man's voice I don't recognize and hangs up. This is normal.

Call #4 is from the Haddam Boro Police—putting me on the alert. A Detective Marinara. The room where he's speaking is crowded with voices and phones ringing and paper rattling. "Mr. Bascombe, I wonder if I could talk to you. We're investigating an incident at Haddam Doctors on eleven twenty-one. Your name came up in a couple of different contexts." A tired sigh. "Nothing to be alarmed about, Mr. Bascombe. We're just establishing some investigative parameters here. My number's (908) 555-1352. That's Detective Mar-i-nar-a, like the sauce. I'll be working late. Thanks for your help." *Click.*

What investigatory parameters? Though I know. The boys at Boro Hall are hard at it, connecting dots, leveling the playing field. My license number was mentally logged by Officer Bohmer. Dot one. My years-old connection with the grievously unlucky Natherial (who couldn't have been the target) has been cross-referenced from his list of life acquaintances. Dot two. Possibly my passing association with Tommy Benivalle (who's conceivably under indictment somewhere) has hit pay dirt via the FBI computer. Dot three. My fistfight with Bob Butts at the August has disclosed an unstable, potentially dangerous personality. Dot four. Who of us could stand inspection and not come out looking like we did it—or at least feeling that way? I am again a person of interest and my best bet is to call and admit everything.

Call #5 is, also predictably, from Mike, at ten, and sounds as if he may have been into the sauce (he's a Grand Marnier man). Mike hopes that I've enjoyed an excellent day with my family around me (I haven't); he also notes that Buddha permits individuals to make decisions without giving offense because "the nature of existence is permanent, which can include temporarily taking up a quest to free oneself from the cycle of time." There's more, but I don't intend to hear it at what is probably two-something. He'll be naming streets in Lotus Estates by Monday. His arc is shorter than most.

I'm relieved there's no call-out-of-the-weirdness from Paul, and half-relieved/half not that there's nothing from Wade. Nothing's from Clarissa. And I'll be honest and admit, in the new spirit of millennial necessity, that not a night begins and ends without a thought that Sally Caldwell might call me. I've played such a call through my brain cells a hundred times and taken pleasure in each and every one. I don't know where she is. Mull or not Mull. She could be in Dar es Salaam, and I'd welcome a call gratefully. A lot of things seem one way but are another. And how a thing *seems* is often just the game we play to save ourselves from great, panicking pain. The true truth is, I wish Sally would come home to me, that we could be we again, and Wally could wear a tartan, hybridize many trees and be satisfied with his hermit's lot— which he chose and, for all I know, may long for, given the kind of lumpy-mumpy bloke he was in this house. Possibly I will call her on Thanksgiving, use the emergency-only number. Nothing has qualified as an emergency—but may.

The sea and air outside my window are of a single petroleum density, with no hint of the tide stage. One socketed nautical light drifts southward at an incalculable distance. I've always attributed such lights to commercial craft, dragging for flounder, or a captaincy like the *Mantoloking Belle*, commandeered by divorced men or suicide survivors or blind golfers out on the waves for a respite before resuming brow-furrowing daylight roles. Though I know now, and am struck, that these can be missions of another character—grieving families scattering loved ones' ashes, tossing wreaths upon the ocean's mantle, popping a cork in remembrance. Giving rather than taking.

When our sweet young son Ralph breathed his last troubled breath in the now-bomb-shattered Haddam Doctors, in time-dimmed '81 (Reagan was President, the Dodgers won the Pennant), Ann and I, in one of our last free-wheeling marital strategizings—we were deranged—sought to plot an "adventurous but appropriate" surrender of our witty, excitable, tender-hearted boy to time's embrace. A journey to Nepal, a visit to the Lake District, a bush-pilot adventure to the Talkeetnas—destinations he'd never seen but would've relished (not without irony) as his last residence. But I was squeamish and still am about cremation. Something's more terrifying than death itself about the awful, greedy flames, the sheer canceling. Whereas death seems a regular thing, a familiar, in no need of fiery dramatizing, orderly to the point of stateliness, just as Mike says. I couldn't cremate my son! Only to have him come back in powdered form, in a handy box, with a terrifying new name I'd never forget in four hundred years: *Cremains!* I've scattered the ashes of two Red Man Clubmen, and these residues turn out not to be powdered nearly *enough*, but are ridden through with bits of bone—odorless gray grit—like the cinders we Sigma Chi pledges used to shovel onto the front walk of the chapter house in Ann Arbor.

Ann felt exactly the same. We had two other children to think about; Paul was seven, Clarissa five. Plus, there was no way to transport a whole embalmed body on an around-the-world victory lap. It would've cost a fortune.

For a few brief hours, we actually thought about, and twice talked of donating Ralph's physical leavings to science, or of possibly going the organ donor route. Though we pretty quickly realized we could never bear the particulars or face the documents or stand to have strangers thank us for our "gift," and would never forgive ourselves once the deeds were done.

So finally, with Lloyd Mangum's help, we simply and solemnly buried Ralph in a secular ceremony in the "new part" of the cemetery directly behind our house on Hoving Road, where he rests now near the founder of Tulane University, east of the world's greatest expert on Dutch elm disease, a stone's throw away from the inventor of the two-level driving range and, as of yesterday, in sight of Watcha McAuliffe. Interment at sea—a shrouded bundle sluiced off the aft end of a sport-fishing craft with a fighting seat and a flying deck, performed under cover of darkness and far enough out so the Coast Guard wouldn't come snooping—wasn't an option we knew about. But it's on my list for when my own time arrives and final thoughts are in the ballpark.

But. Acceptance, again. What have I now accepted that visits me in my stale bedroom, where I'm warm and dank beneath the covers, my stack of unread books beside me, and at an unknown but indecent hour? What is it that rocked me like an ague, turned me loose like a flimsy ribbon on a zephyr? All these years and modes of accommodation, of coping, of living with, of negotiating the world in order to fit into it—my post-divorce dreaminess, the long period of existence in the early middle passage, the states of acceptable longing, of being a variablist, even the Permanent Period itself—these now seem *not* to be forms of acceptance the way I thought, but forms of fearful nonacceptance, the laughing/grimacing masks of denial turned to the fact that, like the luckless snowmobiler Chick Frantal, my son, too, would never *be* again in this life we all come to know too well.

It's *this* late-arriving acknowledgment that's unearthed me like a boulder tumbled down a mountain. *That* was my lie, my big fear, the great pain I couldn't fathom even the thought of surviving, and so didn't fathom it; fathomed instead life as a series of lives, variations on a theme that sheltered me. The lie being: It's not Ralph's death that's woven into everything like a secret key, it's his *not death*, the *not* permanence—the extra beat awaited, the mutability of every fact, the grinning, eyebrows-raised chance that something's waiting even if it's not. These were my sly ruses and slick tricks, my surface intrigues and wire-pulls, all played *against* permanence, not *to* it.

Hard to think, though, that the Frantals alone could've sprung me this far loose with their sad acceptance *qua* sales pitch. Chances are, with the year I've had, I was headed there anyway, preparing to meet my Maker. When I asked what it was I had to do before I was sixty, maybe it's just to accept my whole life and my whole self in it—to have that chance before it's too late: to try again to achieve what athletes achieve when their minds are clear, their parts in concert, when they're "feeling it," when the ball's as big as the moon and they hit it a mile because that's all they can do. When nothing else is left. The Next Level.

A cooling tear exits my eye crease where I'm turned on the

pillow to face the inky sea. The single-lighted ship is nearly past the window's frame. Possibly they do more than one cremains box per night if no mourners are along. This could be what the funeral business means when it says "We're trustworthy." No tricks. No shameless practices. No doubling up. No tossing Grandma Beulah in the dumpster behind Eckerd's. We do what we say we'll do whether you're along or not. A rarity.

Somewhere below the ocean's hiss I hear Bimbo's doggy voice, musical within the Feensters' walls, yap-yap-yap, yap-yap-yap. Then a muffled man's voice—Nick—not decipherable, then silence. I detect the murmur of the Sumitomo banker's limo as it motors down Poincinet Road past my house for his early morning pickup, hear two car doors close, then the murmured passage back. No Thanksgiving for the Nikkei.

My last tear, after this many, and many more not shed, is a tear of relief. Acceptable life frees you to embrace the next thing. Though who's to say it all wouldn't have worked fine anyway—those familiar old rejections and denials performing their venerable tasks. Years ago, I knew that mourning could be long. But *this* long? Easy to argue some things might be better left alone, since permanence, real permanence, not the soft blandishments of the period I invented, can be scary as shit, since it rids you of your old, safe context. With whom, for instance, am I supposed to "share" that I've accepted Ralph's death? What's it supposed to *mean*? How will it register and signify? Will it be hard to survive? Can I still sell a house? Will I want to? And how would it have been different if I'd accepted everything right from the first, like the CEO of GE or General Schwarzkopf would've? Would I be living in Tokyo now? Would I have died of acceptance? Or be in Haddam still? God only knows. Maybe all would've been about the same; maybe acceptance is over-rated —though the shrinks all tell you different, which just means they don't know. After all, we each carry around with us plenty of "things" that're unsatisfactory, "things" we're wanting to undo or ignore so other "things" can be happier, so the heart can open wider. Ask Marguerite Purcell. As I said, acceptance is goddamned scary. I feel its very fearsomeness here in my bed, in my empty house with the storm past and Thanksgiving waiting with the dawn in the east. Be careful what you accept, is my warning—to me. I will if I can.

Out in the dark, I hear a motorcycle, nazzing, gunning, high-pitched, somewhere out on Ocean Avenue, though it fades. Then I think I hear another car, a smaller foreign one with narrow-gauge tires and a cheap muffler, slowing at my driveway. For a moment, I think it's Clarissa, home now, with Thom in the Healey, or alone in a rented Daewoo—safe. I'll hear the front door softly open and softly click closed. But that's not it. It's only the *Asbury Press*. I hear music from the carrier's AM as his window lowers and the folded paper whaps the gravel. Then the window closes and the song fades—"Gotta take that sentimental journey, sen-ti-men-tal jour-ur-ney home." I hear it down the street and down into my sleep. And then I hear nothing more.

PART 3

CHAPTER 13

BRRRP–BRRRRP! Brrrp-brrrrp! Brrrp-brrrrp! Brrrp-brrrrp!

My Swiss telephone, stylish, metal, minuscule (a present from Clarissa on my return to the land of the living), sings its distressing Swiss wake-up song: "Bad news, bad news for you (and it ain't in Switzerland, either)."

I clutch for the receiver, so flat and sleek I can't find it. My room's full of morning light and cottony, humid, warmer air. What hour is it? I knock over my pile of books, detonating a loud and heavy clatter.

"Bascombe," I say, breathless, into the tiny voice slit. This is never how I answer the phone. But my heart's pounding with expectancy and a hint of dread. It's Thanksgiving morning. Do I know where my daughter is?

"Okay, it's Mike." This is not how he talks, either. My answer-voice has startled him. He says nothing, as if someone's holding a loaded gun on him.

"What time is it?" I say. I'm confused from too deep sleep, where I believe I was having a pleasant dream about eating.

"Eight forty-five. Did you hear my message last night?"

"No." Half true. I didn't listen past the Buddhist flounces and flourishes.

"Okay—" He's about to tell me it's been one heckuva hard decision, but the world's a changing place and, even for Buddhists, is entirely created by our aspirations and actions, and suffering doesn't happen without a cause and effort is the precondition of positive actions—the very reason I didn't listen last night. I'm in bed, fully clothed, with my shoes still on, the counterpane wrapped around me like a tortilla. "Could you drive over to 118 Timbuktu at eleven and meet me?"

"What the hell for?"

"I sold it." Mike's accentless voice is fruity with exuberance. "Cash deal."

"One eighteen Timbuktu's *already* sold." I'm about to be

aggravated. Acceptance is right away posing a challenge. I'm relieved, of course, it's not Clarissa telling me she and lizard Thom are married, that I somehow missed all the big clues yesterday. "It's up on trucks," I say. "I'm moving it over to 629 Whitman." Our Little Manila section, which has begun gentrifying at an encouraging rate. He knows all this.

"My people want the house right now, as is." It's as though the whole idea tickles him silly and has elevated his voice half an octave. "They want to take over the moving and put it on a lot on Terpsichore that I'm ready to sell them."

"Why can't this wait till Monday?" I'm about to doze off, though I have to piss (the third time since 2 a.m.). Outside my open window, up in the scrubbed azure firmament, white terns tilt and noiselessly wheel. The air around my covers feels soft and cushiony-springlike, though it's late November. Laughter filters up from the beach—laughter that's familiar.

"You hold the deed on that, Frank." Mike uses my name only at moments of all else failing. Usually, he calls me nothing at all, as if my name was an impersonal pronoun. "They have to buy it direct from you. And they're ready right now. I thought you might just drive over."

He, of course, is right. I sold 118 Timbuktu in September to a couple from Lebanon (Morris County), the Stevicks, who planned to demolish it first thing next spring and bring in a new manufactured dwelling from Indiana that had a lifetime guarantee and all the best built-ins. I stepped back in and offered to take the house in lieu of commission, since it's a perfectly good building. They agreed and I've been arranging to move it to a lot I own on Whitman, where it'll fit in and bring a good price because the inventory's low over there. At 1,300 sq. ft., it'll be bigger than most of its Whitman Street neighbors and be exactly the kind of small American ranch any Filipino who used to be a judge in Luzon, but who over here finds himself running a lawn-care business, would see as a dream come true. Arriba House Recyclers (Bolivians) from Keansburg have been doing the work on a time-permits basis, and throwing me a break. I'm looking at a good profit slice by the time the whole deal's over. Except, if I sell it off the truck like a consignment of hot Sonys, get a good price (less Mike's 2 percent), dispense with the rigamarole of moving a house up Route 35, getting a foundation dug and poured and utilities run, paying for all the permits and line-clearance fees, I'd need to have my head examined not to do Mike's deal on the spot. It's true that as deeded owner, only I can convey it if we're conveying this morning. (We call deals like this WACs, for "write a check.") Only I'm not certain I have the heart for real estate on Thanksgiving morning, even if all I have to do is say yes, sign a bill of sale and shake a stranger's hand. The Next Level and universal acceptance may be closing the shutters on the realtor in me.

I haven't spoken for several moments, and may have gone to sleep on the phone. I hear laughing again, laughing that's definitely known to me but unplaceable. Then a voice talking loudly, then more laughter.

"Can we do it?" Mike's voice is forceful, anxious, fervent—odd for a Tibetan who'd rather cut a fart in public than seem agitated. Possibly I've discouraged him. What about Tommy Benivalle?

"Will I come where?"

"To Timbuktu." A pause. "One eighteen. Eleven o'clock."

"Oh," I say, pushing my head—still sore from Bob Butts' wrenching it—deep into the yielding pillow, letting air exit my lungs slowly, then breathing in body odor in my winding-sheet, loving being where I am, but where I cannot stay much longer. "Sure," I say. "Sure, sure."

"Terrific!" Mike says. "That's terrific." He says "terrific" in his old Calcutta telemarketer style, as when a housewife in Pennsauken tumbled to a set of plastic-wicker outdoor chairs and a secret bond was forged because she thought he was white: "Terrific. That's terrific. I know you're going to enjoy that, ma'am. Expect delivery in six to ten weeks."

THE LAUGHING voice, the laughing man I see when I stand to the window for the day's first gaze at the beach, the sky, the waves is my son Paul, hard at work with a shovel, digging a hole the size of a small grave in the rain-caked sand between the beach and the ocean-facing foundation wall of my house, where some rhododendrons were planted by Sally but never thrived. The hole must be for his time capsule, which Clarissa told me about but which doesn't seem present now. What would a time capsule look like? How deep would you need to bury one for it to "work"? What haywire impulse would make anyone think this is a proper idea for Thanksgiving? And why do I not know the answer to these questions?

Paul is not alone. He's spiritedly shoveling while talking animatedly from three feet down in his hole to the tiny Sumitomo banker, Mr. Oshi, who's surprisingly back from work and standing motionless beside Paul's hole, dressed in a dark business suit as shovel-fulls of sand fly past onto a widening pile. Paul's hair looks thinner than when I saw him last spring, and he's heavier and is wearing what look like cargo shorts and a tee-shirt that shows his belly. He has the same goatee that connects to his mustache and surrounds his mouth like a golf hole. Though his haircut, I can see, is new—a style that I believe is called the "mullet," and that many New Jersey young adults wear, and also professional hockey players, but that on Paul looks like a Prince Galahad. Mr. Oshi appears to be listening as Paul yaks away from his hole, haw-hawing and occasionally gesturing out toward the ocean with his shovel (from my utility room, no doubt), nodding theatrically, then going on digging. Mr. Oshi may also be trying to speak, but Paul has him trapped—which is his usual conversational strategy. Two dachshunds are rocketing around off the leash through the dune grass (where they're forbidden) and out onto the beach, then back round the house and the hole and out of sight. These must be Mr. Oshi's wiener dogs, since he's holding in each hand what looks like a sandwich bag of dog crap that I'm sure he'd like to get rid of. Such is the private nature of neighborly life on Poincinet Road, that I've never seen these dogs before.

As the first thing one sees on Thanksgiving morning, it's an unexpected sight—my son and Mr. Oshi in converse. Though I'm sure it's what the higher-ups in Sumitomo hope for when they dispatch a Mr. Oshi to the Shore: chance encounters with the natives, cultural incumbency taking root, exchange of ground-level demographic and financial data, gradual acceptance of *differences*, leading quickly to social invisibility. Then *bingo!* The buggers own the beach, the ocean, your house, your memories, and your kids are on a boat to Kyoto for immersion language training.

Still, it's saving that I've seen Paul before he sees me, since I'd begun—terrible to admit this—to dread our moment of meeting following last spring's miscommunication. I've pictured myself standing in the middle of some indistinct room (my living room); I'm smiling, waiting—like a prisoner who hears the footfalls of the warden, the priest and the last-mile crew thudding the con-crete floor—anticipating my son to come down a flight of stairs, open a closed door, emerge from a bathroom, fly unzipped, and me just being there, grinningly *in loco parentis*, unable to utter intelligible sounds, all possible good embargoed, nothing prom-ising ahead. No wonder fathers and sons is the subject of enig-matic and ponderous literatures. What the hell's it all about? Why even go near each other if we're going to feel such aversion? Only the imagination has a prayer here, since all logic fails.

What I desire, of course, is that the freshening spirit of accept-ance render today free of significant pretexts, contexts, sub-texts—texts of any kind; be just a day when I'm not the theme, the constant, not expected to make things better, having now, with an optimistic outlook, put holiday events into motion. (I'm by nature a better guest than a host anyway.) But isn't that how we all want Thanksgiving to be? Perfectly generic—the state of mind we enjoy best. In contrast to Xmas, New Year's, Easter, Independence Day and even Halloween—the fraught, load-bearing holidays? We all project ourselves, just the way I do, as regular humans capable of experiencing a regular human holiday with selected others. And so we should. It was what I intended: Acceptance—a spirit to be thankful for.

Only easier said than done.

The beach beyond the grassy furze—where my son's digging away and lecturing poor captive Mr. Oshi—is nonetheless a good beach for a holiday morning. After last night's drought-ending rain, the air has softened and become salt-fragrant and lush, trop-ical depression Wayne having missed its chance with us. Light is moist and sun-shot. A tide is changing, so that fishermen, their bait pails left back on the sand, have edged out into the tame surf to cast their mackerel chunks almost to where a pair of wet-suited kayakers is plying a course up the coast. Tire tracks dent the beach where the Shore Police have passed. A few straggler tourists have returned with the good weather to stroll, throw Frisbees, shout gaily, let their kids collect seashells above the waves' extent. Mr. Oshi's dachshunds skirmish about like water sprites. Surely here in the late-autumnal tableau one can feel the holiday's sweetness, the chance that normal things can happen to normal folk, that the sun will tour the sky and all find easy rest at day's end, full of gratitude on gratitude's holy day.

Though my son's vocalizing and excavating make me know that for normal things to happen to normal folk, some selected normal folk in a frame of mind of acceptance, prudence and gratitude need to get kick-started and off the dime. Since the day is full, and it is here.

I'VE AWAKENED to several new certainties, which make themselves known, as certainties often do, when I'm in the shower—the first pertaining to the day's clothing commitments. As I've already said, I prefer mostly standard-issue "clothes." Medium-weight chinos I buy from a New Hampshire mail-order firm where they keep my size, cuffing preferences, inseam—even which side I "dress" on—stored in a computer. I generally wear canvas or rawhide belts, tabbed to the season; white or pale oxford-cloth shirts, or knitted pullovers in a variety of shades—both long sleeve and short—along with deck shoes, penny loafers or bluchers all from the same catalog, where they showcase everything on unmemorably attractive human mannequins, pictured beside roaring fireplaces, out training their Labradors or on the banks of rilling trout streams. I hardly have to say that such clothing identifies me as the southern-raised frat boy I am (or was), since it's a style ideal for warm spring days, perched on the balcony at Sigma Chi, cracking wise at passing Chi O's, books to bosoms, headed to class. These preferences work very well in the house-selling business, where what I wear (like what I drive) is intended to make as little statement as possible, letting me portray myself to clients as the non-risk-taking everyman with a voice of reason, who only wants the best for all, same as they want for themselves. Which happens to be true.

However, for today I've decided to switch away from regular clothes, based on the first perceived certainty: that something different is needed. My new attire is *not* to dress up like a Pilgrim, ready to deliver an oration like the kids over in the Haddam Interpretive Center. I merely mean to wear blue relaxed-fit 501s—I had them already, just never thought to put them on—

white Nikes from a brief try at tennis two years back, a yellow polo and a blue Michigan sweatshirt with a maize block-M, which the alumni association sent me for becoming a lifetime member (there was other stuff—a substandard-size football, a Wolverine bed toy, a leather-bound volume of robust imbibing songs—all of which I threw in the trash). I'm dressing this way strictly for Paul's benefit, since it will conceivably present me as less obviously myself—less a "father," with less a shared and problematic history, even less a real estate agent, which I know he thinks is an unfunny joke (a greeting-card writer being a giant step up). Dressing like an orthodontist from Bay City down for the Wisconsin game will also portray me as a willing figure of fun and slightly stupid in a self-mortifying way Paul generally appreciates, permitting us both (I hope) to make wry, get-the-ball-rolling jokes at my expense.

My father always wore the same significant blue gabardine suit, with a button-hole poppy in his wide lapel, for Thanksgiving dinner, while my mother always wore a pretty one-piece flowered rayon dress—pink azaleas or purple zinnias—with sling-back heels and blazing stockings I hated to touch. Their attire lives in my mind as the good touchstone for what Thanksgiving symbolized of material and spiritual life—steadiness. I had a blue Fauntleroy outfit given to me by Iowa grandparents, although I hated every minute I had it on and couldn't wait to wad it in the back corner of my closet in our house in Biloxi. But my parents didn't experience the same challenges with me that I face with Paul—resentment, zany oppositional behavior, too-abundant access to language, eccentric every-day appearance—jeopardy, in other words. Plus, at the Next Level, all things count more and can be ruined. So you could say that I'm building a firewall, allowing myself to become an accepting new citizen of the new century, walling myself off from being an asshole by dressing exactly like one in hopes everybody will get my well-intended message.

The second batch of certainties I've awakened clear-headed about and mean to put into motion even before heading to Timbuktu are: (1) call Ann to make sure she doesn't show up today (there is acceptance here, but it's of rejectionist character); (2) call the Haddam PD to be certain Detective Marinara understands I'm not a hospital bomber, but a citizen ready to help in any way

I can; (3) send the thirty dollars plus a tip to the car repair, though I lack the address, so will have to deliver it in person; (4) call Clarissa's cell phone to find out her arrival time to start hostessing Thanksgiving—and to make certain she's not married; (5) call Wade in Bamber Lake; (6) put in an overseas call to Sally to inform her that after careful thought I officially accept the logic that it's worse to let a person you love be alone forever when you don't have to—and I'm that person.

Actually, I *have* done some homework on this last topic and now believe that "Sally–Wally"—I think of them in the same spirit as "priced to sell," "just needs love," "move in today"—makes about as much sense as wanting your dead son to come back to life, or wanting to marry your long-divorced former wife, and has the same success potential: Zero. And therefore *something* different and *better* has to goddamn happen *now*—and will—just like when Wally showed up at my doorstep as empty-headed as a rutabaga, and *something* had to happen then. And did.

I definitely, however, am not going to tell Sally I have, or did or still do have a touch of cancer, since that could be viewed as a cheap late-inning win strategy—and might even be—and therefore prove unsuccessful. One of the hidden downsides of being a cancer victim/survivor is that telling people you've got it rarely comes out how you want it to, and often makes you feel sorry for the people you tell—just because they have to hear it—and spoils a day both of you would like to stay a happy day. It's why most people clam up about having it—not because it scares them shitless. That only happens the first instant the doctor tells you and doesn't really last that long, or didn't in my case. But mostly you don't tell people you've got cancer because you don't want the aggravation—the same reason you don't do most things.

FROM MY desk upstairs, where I go to make my calls, I detect unfamiliar noises downstairs. It's too bad the prior owners never carried out their retrofitting plans for a maid's quarters/back staircase, so I could see what's what down there now. Paul, I believe, is still outside digging and lecturing Mr. Oshi, since his voice is still audible, laughing and yorking like a used-car salesman. This noise downstairs, then—morning TV noise, plates rattling, strangely heavy footfalls, a feminine cough—can only be Jill, the one-handed girl (which I'll believe when I see).

Call one I decide to make to the Haddam PD. Detective Marinara won't be there anyway and I can just leave my cooperative citizen's message. Only he *is* there, picks up on the first half ring with the standard indifferent-aggressive TV cop greeting, full of dislike and spiritual exhaustion. "*Mar*-i-nara. Hate Crimes."

"Hi, it's Frank Bascombe over in Sea-Clift, Mr. Marinara. I'm sorry, I didn't get your call till late." I must be lying and am instantly nervous.

"Okay. Mr. Bascombe? Let me see." Pages shuffling. *Clickety-click, click-click.* My name's on a list, my number traced automatically. "Okay. Okay." *Clickety-click-clickety.* I imagine the youthful bland face of a small-college dean of students. "Looks like—" A heavy sigh. Words come slowly. "We got a match. On your VIN at the crime scene yesterday. This is about the explosion here in Haddam, at Doctors Hospital. You might've read about it."

"I was *there*!" I blurt this. Producing instant galactic silence on the line. Detective Marinara may be flagging to other cops at other desks, silently mouthing, "I got the guy. I'll keep him on the line. Get the Sea-Clift police to pick him up. The fuck."

"Okay," he says. More silence. He is trained to be as emotionless as a museum guard. *These people always call. They can't stand not to be noticed. Actually, they want to be caught, can't bear freedom; you just have to not get in their way. They'll put the noose around their own necks.* I'm sure he's right.

More *clickety-clicking.*

"I mean, I was there because I came over to eat lunch at the hospital." I'm fidgety, self-resentful, breathless. Paul's voice is still audible through the bedroom window, in through my office door. Distant children's voices are behind his. Out of the empty blue empyrean, I hear the calliope sounds of a Good Humor truck patrolling the beach, appealing to the hold-out holiday visitors, people not talking to the police on Thanksgiving Day about bloody murder.

"I see." *Click, click, click.*

"I used to live in Haddam," I say. *Clickety-click.* "I sold houses there for seven years. For Lauren-Schwindell. I actually knew

Natherial. Mr. Lewis. I mean, I knew him fifteen years ago. I haven't seen him in blows. I'm sorry he's deceased." Am I not supposed to know it was Natherial, and that he's dead? I read it in the newspaper.

Silence. Then, "Okay."

I hear more kitchen noises downstairs. Something made of glass or china has shattered on the floor, something a girl with only one hand might easily do. The TV volume jumps up, a man's voice shouts, "Ter-*rif*-ic! And what part of Southern California do you hail from, Belinda?" Then it's squelched to a mumble. "You say you knew Mr. Lewis?" Detective Marinara speaks in a monotone, very cop-like. He's typing what I'm saying. My worries are his interests.

"I did. Fifteen years ago."

"And, uh, under what circumstances were those?"

"I hired him to go find For Sale signs that had gotten stolen from properties we had listed. He was real good at it, too."

"He was real good at it?" More typing.

"Yeah. But I haven't seen him since." *Which is no reason to kill him* is what I'd like to imply. My innocence seems bland and inevitable, a burden to us both. The HPD apparently hasn't yet linked me to the August Inn dust-up with Bob Butts. I must seem exactly the harmless, civic-minded cancer victim I am. Of course this is the plodding police work—the investigative parameters, the mountain of papers, the maze of empty hunches, dismal dead ends and brain-suffocating phone conversations— that will relentlessly lead to the killer or killers, like the key to Pharaoh's tomb. But for a moment, on Thanksgiving morning, it has led to Sea-Clift and to me.

"And you live where?" Detective Marinara says. Possibly he yawns.

"Number seven Poincinet Road. Sea-Clift. On the Shore." I smile, with no one to see me.

"My sister lives up in Barnegat Acres," he says. "It's on the bay."

"A stone's throw. It's nice over there." Though it isn't so nice. The water has a sulfurous bite and a cheesy smell. Quirky bay breezes hold acrid fog too close to shore. And it's not far from the shut-down nuke facility in Silverton, which depresses house sales to flat-line.

"So." More typing, a squeak of Detective M's metal chair, then an amiable sniff of the constabulary nose. "Would you be willing, Mr. Bascombe, to drive over tomorrow and take part in an identification protocol?"

"What's that? Mine or somebody else's?"

"Just a lineup, Mr. Bascombe. It's not very likely we'll even do it. But we're trying to enlist some community cooperation here, do some eliminating. We've got witnesses we need to double-check. It'd be a help to us if you'd agree. Mr. Lewis has a son in the department here." (A cousin to young Lawrence, the hearse driver.)

"Okay. You bet." If I don't agree, my name goes into another pile, and the next person I'm interviewed by won't be yakking about his sister Babs in Barnegat Acres but will be one of the neatnik, black-belt karate guys with Arctic blue eyes in an FBI windbreaker. It lances into my brain that I haven't called Clare Suddruth back yet but am supposed to show him 61 Surf Road tomorrow. Then I remember I intend not to be available.

"Okay, then, that's all set," Detective Marinara says, more clicking. "Will. Participate. In. IDP. And . . . that's great."

"I'm happy to. Well. I'm—"

"Yep," Marinara says. "Ya still in the realty business over there?"

"Sure am. Realty-Wise. You want to buy a house on the ocean? I'll sell you one."

"Oh yeah, I just gotta get these citizens over here to quit killing each other, then I'll be over with you."

"That's a tall order but a noble quest, Detective."

"It's changed, Mr. Bascombe. It's a big difference than when you lived over here."

Just as I thought! He knows all about me. My life's displayed on his green screen. My mother's maiden name, my freshman GPA, my blood pressure, my tire pressure, my Visa balance and sexual preference. Probably he can see when I'm scheduled to die.

"People get rich, they get upset a lot easier. They keep me hoppin', I'll tell you that. Homicide rate's inchin' up in Delaware County. You don't hear about it. But I hear about it."

"Is your family together for Thanksgiving?"

"Oh, well. I'm workin', ain't I? Let's don't go down that road. You just have a good one."

"It's always complex."

"Whew. You got that right. Thanks for your cooperation, Mr. Bascombe. We'll be contacting you about tomorrow." And *click*, Marinara's gone, sucked into a computer dot just as I hear my son outside shout out, "He who smelt it, dealt it. That's all I know." It's hard to know what he's talking about, but my guess is the election.

"I CALLED LAST night," Ann Dykstra-Bascombe-Dykstra-O'Dell-Dykstra says before I can say it's me. I've called her cell. Where is she? In an underwear boutique at the Quaker Bridge Mall? On the 18th at HCC? In the can? You have no control over where your personal private voice is being heard, what audience it's being piped into, who's lying about who's where. It's an intrusion but isn't quite. I was ordering two cubic yards of pea gravel at the Garden Emporium in Toms River last week, and the customer beside me at the register was blabbing away, "Listen, sweetheart, I've never been so in love with anybody in my whole fucking life. So just say yes, okay? Tell that imbecile to go fuck himself. We can be on Air Mexico to Puerto Vallarta at ten o'clock tonight—"

"We need to talk about some things, Frank," Ann says in a disciplined voice. "Did you just elect to *not* call me last night?"

"This *is* calling you. I wasn't home last night. I was busy." Sleeping in my car. I've now showered and shaved and positioned myself, in my plaid terry-cloth robe and fleece mukluks, in as steadfast a sitting position as possible at my desk, coccyx flush to the chair back, feet flat to the floor, knees apart but nervous, breath regulated. It is the posture for hearing disappointing biopsy reports, offer turn-downs and "Someone's been badly injured" calls. It's also the posture for *delivering* bad news.

Yet I'm already on the defensive. My toes curl in my mukluks; my sphincter reefs in. And I'm the *delivering* party: Don't come here today. Or ever. My heart thumps as if I'd sprinted up a fire escape to get here. Ann has perfected the skill of making me feel this way. It's her golfer's inner meritoriousness. I'm forever the hunch-shouldered, grinning census taker at the door; she, the one living the genuine life. I have my questionnaire and my stubby pencil but will never know what reality—the one behind her, within the complex rooms—is all about. Hers is the voice of reasoned experience, sturdy values, good instincts and correct outlook (no matter how conventional); I am outside the threshold, the regretted one in need of sobering lessons. It's why she could turn away from me seventeen years ago and never (until now) look back. Because she was right, right, right. It's amazing I don't hate her guts.

"I think Gore should concede, don't you?"

"No."

"Well. He should. He's a sap. The market'll go crazy if he wins." Sap. The all-around Michigan term of disparagement. Her father characterized me as a sap when Ann and I were dating. "Where'd you find that sap?" Its sound twists a tighter knot in my gut. No one ever gets called a sap without feeling he probably is one.

"He may be a sap, but the other guy's unmentionably stupid." I can't actually mention the other guy's name.

"What did John Stuart Mill say?"

"I don't know. He didn't say it was better to have a stupid President."

"Better to have a happy, unmentionable pig than a something, something something."

"That's not what he said." And it's not what I want to talk about. Mill would've supported Gore and the whole ticket and feel betrayed just like I do.

"Have you talked to Paul?" She is progressing down a checklist.

"No. He's out on the beach right now, digging a grave for his time capsule. I haven't talked to Jill, either."

"Well, she's interesting. She's different." I hear Paul laugh again, then shout, "G'day, mate." Possibly Mr. Oshi has freed himself.

"Listen," I say. "About today. I mean this afternoon."

Dense silence. Different from the galactic dead space Detective Marinara receded into. This silence of Ann's is the silence known only to divorced people—the silence of making familiar but unwelcome adjustments to evidence of continued bad character, of second-tier betrayals, unreasonable requests, late excuses, heart stabbings that must be withstood but are better defeated in advance. It's what communication becomes between the insufficiently loved. "I'm not coming," Ann says, seemingly without emotion. It's the same voice she'd use to cancel a hair appointment. "I think we are who we are, Frank."

"Yeah. I sure am."

"Since Charley died, I've had this feeling of something about to happen. I was waiting for something. Moving down from Connecticut seemed to be getting close to it. But I don't think I thought it was you." I am entombed in the silence she was just entombed in. Now comes revised testimony (including Charley's) of my foul, corrupt and unacceptable nature. I wonder if she's pacing her living room like an executive or sitting on a bench with her clubs, awaiting her tee time, while she dispenses with me again. "But then you got sick."

"I wasn't sick. Not *sick* sick. I had prostate cancer. Have. That's not sick." It's just fatal. SBD. I'm still the census taker, weakened by illness but still in need of reproval and some lessons.

"I know," Ann says officiously. I hear her footsteps on a hard floor surface. "Anyway, I didn't *really* think it was you."

"I get it." A stack of mail's on my desktop under my Realtor of the Year paperweight. It's unopened since Tuesday—a measure of my distraction, since I'm usually eager to read the mail, even if it's steak-knife catalogs or a pre-approved platinum-club membership. I don't think I'm going to be allowed to say what I want to say, which is all right. "What do you think it was? Or who?" I'm staring at the cover of the AARP magazine—a full-color (staged) photograph showing a silver-haired gent lying on a city street looking dead, but being worked on by heavy-suited firemen in fireman hats, equipped with oxygen cylinders, defibrillator paddles, with intubation paraphernalia standing at the ready. A silver-haired old lady in an electric blue pantsuit looks on, horrified. The headline reads RISK. WILL THERE BE TIME?

"Gee, I don't know," Ann says. "It's strange."

"Maybe you missed Charley. Didn't you meet him at Haddam CC? Maybe you thought you'd find him again." No use mentioning her thoughts of the seminary.

"You didn't like Charley. I understand that. But *I* did. You were jealous of him. But he was a fine man."—In death, and when he thought my name was Mert. "He was the love of my life. You don't like hearing that. You're not a very good judge of people." Whip. Crack. *Pow!* But I'm ready for it. The slow-rhythm meticulousness of Ann's rhetorical style is always an indicator that I'm coming in for a direct hit. All bad roads lead to Frank. We have, of course, never talked about Sally—my wife —in the entire eight years I've been married to her. Now might be the optimum moment to set me straight about that misstep, since it's led me where it's led me: to this conversation. I'm not surprised to learn that I don't win the "love of my life" gold medal. Except in rogue bands of lower primates, you don't abandon the love of your life. Death has to intervene.

Out my front window, beyond the low hedgement of arbor-vitae, I spy Mr. Oshi moving in quickened, mechanized Japanese banker steps along Poincinet Road, hustling back to his own house to bolt the door. His business suit still looks neat, though he's holding one Dachshund under his arm like a newspaper and he still has both plastic bags of dog shit. His other wiener's prancing at his feet. Mr. Oshi takes a quick, haunted look toward my front door, as if something might rush out at him, then hastens his steps on to home.

I have not spoken into the receiver since Ann fingered me as a bad judge of human flesh, in preparation for apprising me that my marriage to Sally was a lot of foolishness that led to no good, whereas hers to architect Charley was the stuff myth and legend are made of.

"I have something I want to say to you," Ann says, then sighs heavily through her nose. I believe she's stopped pacing. "It's about what I said when you were at De Tocqueville on Tuesday."

"What part?"

"About wanting to live with you again. And then when I left a message that night."

"Okay."

"I'm sorry. I don't think I really meant all that."

"That's okay." An unexpected wrench in my heart, with no pain associated.

"I think I just wanted to come to a moment, after all these years, when I could say that to you."

"Okay." Three okays in a row. The gold standard of genuine acceptance.

"But I think I just wanted to say it for my own purposes. Not because I really needed to. Or need to."

"I understand. I'm married anyway."

"I know," Ann says. Once again, it's good there're telephones for conversations like this. None of us could stand it face-to-face. Hats off to Alexander Graham Bell—great American—who foresaw how human we are and how much protection we need from others. "I'm sorry if this is confusing."

"It's not. I guessed if I wasn't a good choice once, I'm probably not now, either." For every different person, love means something different.

"Well, I don't know," she says disapprovingly but not sadly. A last disapproval of me as I genially disapprove of myself.

It's tempting to wonder if a new goodly swain's now in her picture, with a more attractive lunch invitation. That's usually what these recitations mean but don't get around to admitting. Teddy Fuchs, maybe. Or a friendly, widowed Mr. Patch Pockets, a gray-maned De Tocqueville Colonial history teacher, someone "youthful" (doesn't need Viagra), coaches lacrosse and feels simpatico with her golfing interests. Amherst grad, Tufts M.A., a summer retreat in Watch Hill and whose grown kids are less enigmatic than our two. It would be a good end to things. They can be "life companions" and never marry except when one of them gets brain cancer, and then only as encouragement for life's final lap. I approve.

"Is that all right?" Ann says, self-consciously sorrowful.

"It *is* all right." I could let her know I'd already figured out that getting divorced after Ralph died just deprived the two of us of the chance to get properly divorced later on, and for simpler reasons: that we weren't really made for each other, didn't even love each other all that much, that the only lasting thing we did love about each other was that we each had a child who died (forgetting the two who didn't die), which admittedly is a strange love and, in any case, wasn't enough. Better, though, just to let her believe she's the one who knows mystical truths, even if she doesn't really know them, just feels them all these years later. Ann may be many good and admirable things, but a mystic is not one of them.

In the stack of unopened letter-mail, beneath the Mayo newsletter, a Thank You from the DNC, circulars for a 5-K race and the Pow-R-Brush Holiday promotion in Toms River, I spy a square blue onionskin envelope—not the self-contained kind

I always open wrong because it can't be opened right, and end up tearing and reading in three damaged pieces, but a fuller, sturdier one—on whose pale tissue-y surface is writing I recognize, the writer's firm hand flowing with small peaked majuscules and even smaller perfectly formed, peaked and leaning minuscules: Frank Bascombe, 7 Poincinet Road, Sea-Clift, New Jersey 08753. USA.

"We just have to be who we are, Frank," Ann is saying for the second time.

"You bet." I separate the letter from its cohort and stare at it.

"You sound strange, sweetheart. Is this upsetting you? Are you crying?"

"No." I almost miss the "sweetheart." But how did I miss this letter—of all letters? "I'm not crying, I don't think."

"Well. I haven't told you Irma's ready to die. Poor old sweetie. She spent her life believing my father should've moved out with her from Detroit to Mission Viejo thirty years ago, which of course he never would've, because he was tired of her. She has Alzheimer's. She thinks he's arriving next week, which is nice for her. I wish she and the children could've been closer. They're like you are about personal connections."

"Really?" The salmon-colored stamp bears a stern-looking profile of the Queen of England in regnal alabaster, framed in fluted molding. It's the most exciting stamp I've ever seen.

"They're mostly okay without them, of course. At least not strong ones anyway." Cookie never counted to her.

"I understand."

"I'm sorry if all this is distressing you. I made a mistake and I regret it."

"Well—" Fingering the letter's heft upon my fingertips, I raise it to my nostrils and breathe in, hoping for a telltale scent of its far-off sender. Though it bears only a starchy stationery odor and the unsweet aroma of stamp glue. I hold it to the window light—there's no return address—and turn it front to back, bring it instinctively to my nose again, touch my tongue tip to its sealed flap, put its smooth blue finish to my chin, then my cheek and hold it there while Ann continues blabbing at me.

"Paul said last night Clary has a new beau."

"I—" Thom. The multicultural cipher.

"Has Paul told you yet that he wants to leave K.C. and come work in the realty office with you? He's—"

Whip. Crack. *Pow!* Again. I am *not* ready. My swelling heart as much as founders. I don't hear the next thing she says, though my mind offers up "You know a heart's not judged by how much you love, but by how much you're loved by others." I don't know why.

But. The *mullet*? My son? A promising second career after greeting cards? Chauffeuring clients around Sea-Clift? Holding court in the office? Farming listings? Catching cold calls? Wandering through other people's precious houses, stressing the distance to the beach, the age of the roof, the lot-line dimensions, the diverse mix here in New Jersey's Best Kept Secret? He could bring Otto out and sing a chorus of "Shine on, Harvest Moon," like he used to do when he lived with me. "Realty-Wise. This is Paul. Our motto is, He Who Smelt It, Dealt It."

"I haven't heard about that," I say. Whip-sawed.

"Well, you will. I assumed you'd asked him, since your surgery last summer and all of that. We talked a bit about that. I'm surprised you two hadn't—"

"I didn't have surgery. I had a procedure. They're different." I was going to tell him about my condition. And I didn't ask him to "join the firm," *because I'm not crazy.* I realize what an ideal job writing greeting cards is for my son.

"Women know about things like procedures, Frank."

"Good for women. I'm not a woman yet."

"I know you're angry. I'm sorry again. I used to wonder if you ever *got* angry. You never seemed to. I always understood why you didn't make it in the Marines."

"I *was* sick in the Marines. I had pancreatitis. You didn't even know me then. I almost died."

"We don't have to be angry at each other, do we? You may not realize it, but you don't want to go any further with this, either."

"I realize it." Sally's blue letter is pinched between my thumb and forefinger as though it might float upward and I need to cling to it for my life's sake. "That's what I called to say. You just beat me to it."

"Oh," Ann says. Ann my wife. Ann my not wife. Ann my never-to-be. The things you'll never do don't get decided at the end of life, but somewhere in the long gray middle, where you can't see the dim light at either end. The Permanent Period tries to protect us from hazardous moments like this, makes pseudo-acceptance only a matter of a passing moment. A whim. Nothing that'll last too long. Which is why the Permanent Period doesn't work. Acceptance means that things, both good and sour, have to be accounted for. Relations, as the great man said, end nowhere.

"I encouraged Paul to come work with you. I think that would be good."

I'm stunned silent by this preposterous prospect. Anger? If I spoke, I would possibly start cursing in an alien tongue. This is the stress Dr. Psimos advised me to avoid. The kind that burns out my soldier isotopes like they were Christmas lights and sends PSA numbers out of the ballpark. I'd like to say something apparently polite and platitudinous yet also shrewdly scathing. But for the moment, I can't speak. It is entirely possible I *do* hate Ann's guts. Odd to know that so late along. Life *is* a long transit when you measure how long it takes you to learn to hate your ex-wife.

"Maybe we just don't need to say anything else, Frank."

Mump-mump, mump. Mump. Silence.

I hear her chair squeak, her footsteps sounding against hard-wood flooring. I picture Ann walking to the window of 116 Cleveland, a house where I once abided and before that where she abided, following our divorce, when our children were children. She is once again its proprietor, fee simple absolute. The big eighty-year-old tupelo out front is now spectral but lordly in its leaflessness, its rugged bark softened by the damp balmy air of false spring. I've stood at that window, my breathing shallowed, my feet heavy, my hands cold and hardened. I've calculated my fate on the slates of the neighbors' roofs, their mirroring windowpanes, roof copings and short jaunty front walks. This can be both consoling (You're here, you're not dead), and unconsoling (You're here, you're not dead. Why not?). The past just may not be the best place to cast your glance when words fail.

Mump-mump.

My silence speaks volumes. I hear it. My voice is trapped within.

Mumpety-mump. Mump. Mump.

"Well," I hear Ann say. More steps across the hardwood. Fatigue shadows her voice. "I don't know," I hear her say. Then *ping-ping*. I hear a truck in the street, outside her window—in Haddam (this I can picture)—backing up. Miles from where I stand. *Ping! Ping! Ping! If you can't see me, I can't see you.* I wait, breathe, say nothing. "Well," Ann says again. Then I believe she puts the phone down, for the line goes empty and our call in that way ends.

MY DARLING FRANK,

I would like to write you something truly from my heart that would reveal me, good and bad, and make you feel better about things. But I'm not sure I am capable. I'm not sure I know my truest feelings, even though I have some. I don't have any idea what you could be thinking. I guess I have Thanksgiving envy, since I've been thinking about you, and about that nice Lake Laconic we went to before. I bet you're doing something really interesting and good for T'giving. I hope you're not alone. I bet you're not, you rascal. Maybe you've connected with some snappy realtor type and are headed somewhere out of town (I hope not to Moline). What I'm feeling now, true feelings or not, is that everything in my life is just all about me, and I can't find a way to change the pronouns. I'm aware of myself, without being very self-aware. My kids would agree—if they spoke to me, which they don't. But does that make any sense? (Possibly I won't send this letter.) I think I should apologize for all that happened last June—and May. I <u>am</u> sorry for the difficulty it caused you. It's probably hard to understand that someone can love you and feel great about everything, and then leave with her ex. I always thought people decided they were unhappy first, and <u>then</u> left. But maybe things in life are just fine and then you do some crazy thing, and decide later if you were. Unhappy, that is. What's that the evidence of? But I can't really be sorry for doing it, so why apologize only for half? This sounds like something you would say maybe about selling a house to somebody, some house you didn't approve of, except you knew the people needed a home. If I'm right (about you), you'll think this is funny and not very interesting—something a person from south-central Ohio would do. You <u>are</u> like that.

When I left with Wally last June, I just wasn't feeling enough. I couldn't take others in. You, for instance—hardly at all. It was so shocking to experience Wally. I made him come, by the way. He didn't want to and was pretty embarrassed, you might've noticed. I think I just left on an idea—to go back and experience something I never got to experience before. (That word's coming up a lot.) I've never even been stupid enough to think anyone can do that. You really ought to leave some things where they lay, whether you got to feel them or not. I think that now. I don't think I'm sounding breezy here, do you? I don't want to. I'm not breezy at all. Coming to the end of the millennium year, I wonder if I've been affected by it at all? Or if all this tumult and upset is the effect of it. Has it affected you yet? It hadn't last spring, I don't think. We're both "only children." Maybe I just fear death. Maybe I feared that you and I weren't going anywhere and never realized it before. I am not very reflective. You know that. Or at least I wasn't before. I ask questions but don't always answer them or think about the answers.

I don't want to go into too much detail here. I know I went away with Wally for my own reasons, probably selfish. And by August, I knew I wouldn't stay much longer. He was a strange man. I loved him once, but I think I may have driven him crazy at least twice. Because the whole thing thirty years ago was that he was just very unhappy living with me, and couldn't tell me. So he left. It's so simple. I can't say what we both knew back then. Probably very little. We did try to enlist the children's sympathies this time. But they are both crazy as bats and treated us as though we were lunatics and wouldn't talk to us and receded into their nutty beliefs, even though we said to them, "But we're your parents." "Who says?" they said. I guess I think they're lost to me.

I would've left then (late August), but I got concerned about Wally. He began eating very little and lost a lot of weight. He would sit in the bathtub until the water was freezing (we lived in his cottage, which was okay, if small). I would see him standing out in his little row of apple trees he loved, just talking and talking, to no one—though I guess it was to me. I would catch him looking strangely at me. And then he began going for swims in the ocean. He was a very large white figure out there, even with his lost weight. I think, as I said, I drove him crazy. Poor man.

I don't want to tell all the rest of it. Sooner or later you'll find out. The best way out may not be through, though. Whoever said that?

But I am not in Mull anymore. (Isn't that a funny name? Mull.) I am in a place called Maidenhead, which is funny, too, and is in J.O.E. (Jolly Old England). Talk about wanting to go back in time! I've come all the way back to Maidenhead. From Mull to Maidenhead. That's a hoot. It is just a suburb here, not very nice or very different than any other one. I am doing temporary work in a sweet little arts centre (their spelling), where they need my skills for organizing older citizens' happiness. It is like Sponsoring, although old English people are easier than our old people by a lot. England is not a bad place to be alone (I was here twice before). People are nice. Everyone gives solid evidence of feeling alone a lot, but seems to think that's natural, so that they don't get terribly, terribly invested in it. Unlike America where it's just one mad fascination after another one, but no one's any more invested—or so it seems to me. I did not vote, by the way, and now things are in this terrible twist with Bush. Can you believe it? Can that numskull actually win? Or steal it? I guess he can. I'm sure you voted, of course, and I'm sure I know who you voted for.

How are your kids? Are you and Paul still feuding? Is Clarissa still being a big lesbian? (I bet not.) Who else do you see? Are you selling a lot of houses? I bet you are. (You can tell I'm fishing.) I am fifty-four this year, which of course you know. And I am not a grandparent, which is very odd, even though my children dislike me so much— for what, I don't know exactly. I am thinking of going to a retreat in Wales—something Druidic—since I feel I'm heading someplace but don't feel too confident about it. Though I am pretty comfortable in my skin. Being fifty-four (almost) is also odd. It kind of doesn't have an era, and I know you believe in all human ages having a spiritual era. This one I don't know. I think everybody needs a definition of spirituality, Frank (you have one, I believe). You wouldn't want to go on a quiz show, would you, and be asked your definition of spirituality and not know one. (Apropos this retreat.) June doesn't seem that far back to me. Does it to you? I can't say that how things are now is how I thought they would end up. Though maybe I did.

But I do want to say something to you (a good sign, maybe). I want to tell you one reason why I'm sure I love you. There are people we can be around, and we take them for granted sometimes, and who make us feel generous and kind and even smarter and more clever than we probably are—and successful in our own terms <u>and</u> the world's. They are the ideal people, sweetheart. And that's who you are for me. I'm sure I'm not that way for you, which bothers me, because I think I'm kind of a roadblock for you now. No one else is like that for me, and I don't know why you are that way, but you are. So just in case you were wondering.

(The reason I'm writing this is to see how it comes out. If it seems okay, then you're reading it "now.") Finally (thank God, huh?), I don't know if I want to be married to you anymore. But I don't know if I want a divorce, or if I can't live without you. Is there a precise word for that human state? Maybe you can make something up. Maybe New Jersey is it. Though here in Maidenhead (what a name!), where for some reason tourists come, I hear Americans saying they're from all over. Iowa and Oregon and Florida. And I think—that doesn't matter anymore. Maybe it would be good to move away from New Jersey. Maybe all we need is a change. Like the hippies used to say when there were so many of them, and they were begging quarters back in the Loop in Chicago: "Change is good." I thought that was a riot. At least we don't have cancer, Frank. So maybe we have some choices to make together still. I also want you to know—and this is important—that you were not boring in bed, if you ever worried about that. I'll call you on Thanksgiving, which is not a holiday in Maidenhead so I can probably use the trunk line at the arts centre. Love with a kiss. Sally (your lost wife).

I'M SHOCKED. Humbled. Emptied. Amazed. Provoked. Delighted. Thrilled to be all. If man be a golden impossibility, his life's line a hair's breadth across, what is woman? A golden possibility? Her life's line a lifeline thrown to save me from drowning.

I'm ready to wire greenbacks—except it's Thanksgiving. Mr. Oshi could be of service, though he's probably huddled in his house. I'll send solicitors out to Maidenhead in a black saloon car to spirit Sally down to Heathrow, provide a change of clothes, get her into the VIP lounge at BA and right into a first-class seat—on the Concorde, except it crashed. I'll be waiting at Newark Terminal 3 with a dinner-plate smile, all slates cleaned, agendas changed for the future, bygones trooping off to being bygones. Cancer's a dot we'll connect in due time. Since she doesn't know I have/had it, it's almost as if I don't/didn't—so powerful is her belief, so unreal is cancer to begin with.

Except there's no call-back number here. No 44 + bippety, bippety, bippety, bip. When I come back from Timbuktu, I'll coax the Maidenhead Arts Centre number out of *inquiries*, where they're always helpful (our *information* won't give you the time of day). Or else I'll declare an emergency.

I go to the window again in my terry-cloth robe, my heart pumping, a zizzy bee-sting quiver down my arms and legs, my bare feet cold on the floor planks. "Is this really happening?" I say to the window and the beach beyond, in a voice someone could hear in the room with me. Is this happening? Is there a celestial balance to *things*? A yin/yang? Do people come back once they've gone away to Mull? Life is full of surprises, a wise man said, and would not be worth having if it were not. My choice then, since I have a choice, is to believe they do come back.

Out upon the dun Atlantic, a Coast Guard buoy tender sits bestilled on the water's roll, its orange sash promoting bright, far-flung hope—the same it gives to all sailors adrift and imperiled. I train my powerful U-boat-quality binoculars, given to me by Sally, on its decks, its steepled conning bridge, its single gray gunnery box, its spinning radar dish, the heavy red nun already winched aboard. Fast-moving miniature sailors are in evidence. A davit's employed, a dory's lowering off the landward side. Sailors are there, too. No doubt this is a drill, a dry run to pass the time on Thanksgiving, when all would be elsewhere if only our shores were safe. I pan across the swells (how do they ever find anything?), but there is nothing visibly afloat. I put the lens bottles to the window glass and lean into the ferrules, as if finding a foreign object was essential to a need of mine. Only nothing's foreign. A second red buoy, whose bell I sometimes hear in the fog or when the wind blows in, rocks in the slow swell, its red profile low, its clapping now inaudible. I, of course, can't find what they're after. And maybe it's nothing, a coordinate on a chart, a signal down deep they must track to be accomplished sailors. Nothing more.

I sweep down the beach and find the surfcasters—close-up— in their neoprenes and watch caps, their backs to the shore, up to their nuts in frigid, languid ocean, their shoulders intent and hunched, their long poles working. A blue Frisbee floats through my circled view. A white retriever ascends to snare it. I find the Sea-Clift Shore Police's white Isuzu trolling back along its own tracks, the uniformed driver, as I am, glassing the water's surface. For a shark fin. A body (these things happen when you live by the sea). A periscope. Icarus just entering the sea, wings molten, eyes astonished, feet spraddling down.

And then I see my son Paul again, wading out of the surf in his soaked cargo shorts, his pasty belly slack for age twenty-seven. He is shoeless, shirtless, his skull—visible through his mullet— rounder than I remember, his beard-stached mouth distorted in a smile, hands dangling, palms turned back like a percy man, his feet splayed and awkward as when he was a kid. He does not look the way you'd like your son to look. Plus, he must be frozen.

I track down to the hole he's dug beyond the hydrangeas, and it's there, "finished," coffin-shaped, not large, ready for its casket to be borne down. My shovel stands in the sandpile to the side.

When I find Paul again, he's seen me glassing him like a sub-captain and has fixed his gaze back on me, his red-lipped smile distorted, his feet caked with sand, pale legs wide apart like a pirate's. He flags his bare arm like one of those drowners out of reach—lips moving, words of some sentiment, something possibly that any father would like to hear but I can't at this distance. Paul cocks his fists up in a Charlie Atlas muscle man's pose, jumps sideways and bears down stupidly and shows his soft abs and lats. The young Frisbee spinners, the elderly walkers in bright sweats, the metal-detector cornballs, a late-arriving fisherman just wading into the sea—all these see my son and smile an indulgent smile. I wave back. It's not bad to wave at this remove as our first contact. On an impulse, I put down my binocs and give my own Charlie Atlas double-bicep flexer, still in my tartan robe. And then Paul does his again. And we are fixed this way for a moment. Why couldn't we just stop here, not go on to what's next—be two tough boys who've fought a draw, stayed unvanquished, each to leave the field a victor? Fat Chance.

IN FRONT of my closet mirror, I get into my 501s, my Nikes and my block-M sweatshirt with the yellow polo underneath. I am Mr. Casual Back to Campus, booster dude and figure of whole-some ridicule. I have called Clarissa and left a message: "Come home." I have called Wade and left a message: "Where are you?" Clearly, I'm fated to wait for Sally's call, at least until I'm back from Timbuktu and can make calls of my own. I have another full-out yearning for a cell phone, which would render me avail-able (at all times) to hear her voice, answer a summons and go directly to Maidenhead if necessary—though she would need to know *my* number. I'd gladly forget Thanksgiving (like any other American). Most of my guests have been decommissioned any-way. I'd take the organic turkey, the tofu stuffing, the spelt, the whatever else, straight down to Our Lady of Effectual Mercy, where the K of C ministers to Sea-Clift's neediest and thank-fulest. Or else I'd put it in Paul's time capsule and bury it for later generations to puzzle over.

I am, however, exhilarated, and take a last scrutinizing look at myself. I look the way I want to—dopey but defended—the gen-ial Tri-cities orthodontist. Though as usual, exhilaration doesn't feel as good as I want it to—as it used to—since all sensation, good or bad, now passes through the damping circuitry of the cancer patient, victim or survivor. The tiramisu never tastes as sweet. The new paint job doesn't shine as bright. Miss America's glossy life-to-come wears a shadow of lurking despair, her smile a smile of struggling on in a dark forest. That's what we survivors get as our good luck. Though think about the other poor bas-tards, the ones who get the real black spot—not just my gray one—and who're flying home to Omaha this morning, urged to put their affairs in order.

I've, however, learned to let exhilaration be exhilaration, even if it only lasts a minute, and to fight the shadows like a boxer. Staring at the mirror, I give myself a slap, then the other side, then again, and once more, until my cheeks sting and are rosy, and a smile appears on my reflection's face. I blink. I sniff. I throw two quick lefts at my block-M but hold back on the convincer right. I'm ready to step into the arena and meet the day. Once again, it's Thanksgiving.

"I'M TAKING this bad-boy outside to see how it fits," Paul's saying energetically. I've come down munching a piece of bacon, following voices to the daylight basement, chilly mausoleum of old Haddam furniture—my cracked hatch-cover table, my nubbly red hide-a-bed, my worn-through purple Persian rug, several non-working brass lamps bundled in the corner and a framed map of Block Island, where Ann and I once sailed when we were kids and thought we loved each other. I've thought of opening things up down here as a rumpus room.

I'm already smiling as I come to the bottom of the stairs, very conscious of my booster-club get-up, though Paul is just exiting the sliding glass door to the beach, toting his time capsule, which is a chrome bomb-shaped cylinder as long as two toasters. A tall young blond woman he's been talking to is in the middle of the room and she looks at me. She's beside the defunct old rabbit-eared DuMont that was my mother's and that I've kept as a memento, and she unexpectedly smiles back widely to broadcast her surprise and enthusiasm—for me, for Paul, for the overall good direction things are taking down here. This is Jill, dressed—I don't know why I'd expect any different—in bright red coveralls with a white long-john shirt underneath and some kind of green wooden clog footwear that makes her look six foot seven, when she may only be six three. Her long yellow hair hangs straight past her shoulders and is parted in the middle Rhine maiden-style, exposing a wide Teutonic forehead. Her generous mouth is unquestionably libidinous, though her sparkling dark eyes are welcoming—to me, in my own basement. A great relief. And as advertised, at the bottom of her left sleeve is the alarming hand absence, though there's good evidence of a wrist. Here, I realize, is the girl who may become mother of my grandchildren, mourner when my obsequies are read out, will tell vivid rambling tales of my exploits once I'm gone. It'd be good to get off on the right foot with her. Though in a day's time, I've met two of my children's chosen ones. What's gone wrong?

"Hi, I'm Frank," I say. "You must be Jill."

"Listen, Frank," Paul's saying, just leaving through the door. "You wanna come out and attend the trial internment?" He may mean *interment*, but possibly not—though he's talking too loudly for indoors. He pauses, grinning from behind his smudged specs (we're all grinning down here), his capsule clasped to his wet tee-shirt, which bears an Indian-warrior profile in full eagle-feather war bonnet—the Kansas City Chief. Paul's still barefoot, still has his gold stud in his left ear. He looks like the guy who delivers the *Asbury Press* before dawn out of his backseat-less '71 Cutlass and, I suspect, lives in his car.

"You bet I want to." I make a step forward. "Let's do it." But he's already out the sliding door, heading toward his site. My positive response hasn't registered. I look to Jill and shake my head. "We don't communicate perfectly all the time."

"He'd really like you to approve of him," Jill says in a slightly nasal midwestern voice. Though startlingly and with an even bigger, eager-er smile, she strides across the linoleum and with her right hand extended gives mine a painful squeeze, the kind lady shot-putters give each other outside the ring. Her smile makes me look straight at her nose, which is noble and makes her wide eyes want to draw in, in concentration, toward the middle. One central incisor has shouldered a half-millimeter over onto its partner, but not to a bad effect. In someone less impos-ing, this could be a signal to exercise caution (turbulent brooding over life's helpless imperfections, etc.), but in Junoesque Jill, it is clearly trifling, possibly a giggle, in contrast to her injury and to how monstrously beautiful she otherwise is. I like her completely and wish I wasn't wearing this preposterous get-up. She looks admiringly out the glass door at Paul, who's already down inside his hole, bent over, apparently testing the dimensions of things. "He's really a big fan of yours," she says.

"I'm a big fan of his," I say. Jill exudes a faint lilac sweetness, though the air's gone musty as a ship's hold down here. Jill lets her friendly dark eyes roam all around the low-ceilinged basement and sniffs. She smells it, too. I amiably swallow my last bit of bacon—left in plain sight (by who?) on a paper towel in the kitchen. I want to say something forward-thinking about my son, but being up close to his sweet-smelling, pulchritudinous squeeze is far from what I thought would be happening, and I'm not exactly sure what's appropriate to say. Physical closeness to an abject (and smaller) stranger, however, doesn't seem to faze her one bit. Clarissa's the same—relaxed, defensible boundaries —something my age group didn't understand. I could ask Jill how she likes New Jersey so far or how everything went with Ann last night (though I don't want to mention Ann's name), or what's a bounteous beauty like her doing with an oddment like my son. But what I do say, for some reason, is, "What happened to your hand?"

Which doesn't faze her one bit more. She looks down at the vacant sleeve end, then raises it to eye level. She is still very close to me. A pink stump becomes visible, starting (or ending) where her carpal bone would be, the flesh finely stitched to make a smooth flap. Jill's happy demeanor seems undiminished by a hand being conspicuously not there. "If everybody would just *ask* like that," she says happily, "my life'd be easier." We both look straight at the stump like surgeons. "I was in the Army, in Texas," she says, "training for land mine work. And I guess I got the worst-possible grade. I shouldn't have been doing it, as big as I am. It's better if you're small." She moves the appendage around in a tight little orbit to exhibit its general worthiness and I suppose to permit me to touch it, which I don't think I'll do. I've never knowingly been this close to or conversant with an amputee. Doctors get used to these things. But no one much gets anything cut off in normal real estate goings-on. Without meaning to, I inch back and give her what I hope is an affirming nod. "So when I got to Hallmark," she goes on chattily, "they thought, Well, here's a natural for the sympathy-card depart-ment." I knew it. "Which I was, but not because of my hand, but because I'm really sympathetic." She rolls her eyes and shakes her head as though getting rid of that ole hand was the best-possible luck.

"So, is that where you two met, then?" I say. Out the corner of my eye, I uncomfortably spy Paul crawling back out of his hole, dusting off his knees, looking as if he'd just invented fluid mechanics. His silver capsule lies in the beach grass. He begins speaking toward the hole as if someone, a member of his crew, was still down there doing last-minute deepening and manicuring.

"We really met on the Internet," Jill says, "though I'd already seen him at a film series and knew he'd be interesting. Which he is." She stows her stump in her red coveralls pocket and warmly regards my son, who's still outside talking away. I should go out there. Though my instinct is to stay where I am and chat up the big blondie, even if the big blondie belongs to my son and only has one hand. "We were really shocked when we finally met face-to-face at a bookstore"—conceivably the place where I got into hot water last spring—"and realized we were both writers at Hallmark." In a bikini, Jill probably looks like young Anita Ekberg (minus a hand). It's difficult to envision Paul, who's a lumpy five ten, raree-ing around with her in his little Charlotte Street billet. Though no doubt he does. "Odd couple's redundant is what we think," Jill says. I've begun to think about what Paul, in his rage last spring, told me about his job—that it was the same as what Dostoyevsky or Hemingway or Proust or Edna St. Vincent Millay did: supplied useful words to ordinary people who don't have enough of them. I, of course, thought he was nuts.

But suddenly, here is something crucial. I could spend the next six weeks locked in a room with these two, learn how Jill felt about boot camp, learn the mascot's name of her girls' basketball team, where she was the center, learn how she found her star-crossed way to K.C., how she came to write Ross Perot's name in on her presidential ballot; and possibly at the same time get to know Paul's closely guarded ideas about matrimony (coming as he does from a broken home), get his overview about parity in the NFL, hear his long-term thoughts for leaving Hallmark and joining Realty-Wise—things most fathers hear. But I still wouldn't know much more that's important about them as a couple than I do after these five perfectly good minutes. It's electrifying to think Jill's a lusty young Anita Ekberg, and interesting to know that Paul is interesting. But they are what they seem—which is enough to be. I don't want to change them. I'm willing and ready to jump right to the climax, confer fatherly blessings on their union (if that's what this is) before Paul makes it back inside. If they make each other happy for two seconds, then they can probably last decades—longer than I've lasted. I bless you—I say these words silently in anticipation of leaving. I bless you. I bless you. *Sum quod eris, fui quod sis.*

"Did you really go to Michigan?" Jill steps back and takes a look at my block-M, a studious cleft formed between her dark eyebrows. She leans forward and gives me the sensation of being loomed over. Obviously, she doesn't see my outfit as comical.

"Did I what?"

"My dad went to U of M," she says.

"Did he? Great."

"I'm from Cheboygan." She holds up her right hand to exhibit how much the state of Michigan—lower peninsula only—resembles a hand. With her stunted left arm, she taps the hand at about where the town of Cheboygan lies, near the top. "Right there on Lake Huron," she says, making Huron sound like *Hyurn*. I knew a boy from Cheboygan back in the icy mists. Harold "Doodlebug" Bermeister, defense-man on our pledge hockey team, who longed to return to Cheboygan with his B.S. and buy a Chevy franchise. Doodlebug got blown to cinders in Vietnam the year he graduated and never saw Cheboygan again. No way this Jill is Doodlebug's daughter. She's twice as tall as he was. But if she *is* a wandering Bermeister and life's a long journey leading to my son, it doesn't need any explaining. I accept. Though you could work up a good greeting card out of the whole improbability, something on the order of "Happy Birthday, son of my third marriage to my foster sister of Native American descent."

"I never really got up there," I say in re Cheboygan.

"It's where they have the snowmobile hall of fame," she says earnestly.

Paul's letting himself back in through the sliding glass door, his capsule wedged under his arm pigskin-style, wiping his bare feet on the rug and still talking away as if we'd all been outside doing things together. With his smudged glasses, mullet, his beard-stache and general unkempt belly-swell under his Chiefs shirt, Paul looks oddly elderly and therefore ageless—less like the *Asbury Press* guy and more like one of the beach loonies who occasionally walk into your house, sit down at your dinner table and start babbling about Jesus running for president, so you have to call the police to come haul them away. These people never harm anything, but it's hard to see them (or Paul) as mainstream.

"So. You got it all set?" I say and give him one of our sly-shrewd chivvying looks, meant to draw attention to my Bay City orthodontist outfit. Such greeting is our oldest workable code: common phrasings invested with secret double, sometimes quadruple "meanings" that are by definition hilarious—but only to us. As a troubled boy of tender years, Paul was forever antici-pating, keeping steps ahead, as if the left-behind brother of a dead boy had to be two boys, doubly, even triply aware of everything, could not just be a single yearning heart. Other priorities tended to get overlooked, and our code became our only way to con-verse, to keep love fitfully in sight and the world beneath us. In adulthood, of course, this fades, leaving just a vapor of lost never would-bes.

"Sherwood B. Nice," Paul says—not really an answer—though he elevates his chin in a victorious way, possibly having to do with Jill. In the corner of his right eye, a small dent retains an apple redness from the terrible beaning at age fifteen, which he claims not to remember. I've never been sure how well he sees, though the doctors back then said he'd have vitreous swimmers, shortened depth perception, and in later life could face problems. Elevating his chin to see out the bottom of his eyes is compensa-tory. None of this, naturally, is ever discussed. "So. Aaaallll at once," Paul immediately starts in, bringing his time capsule over to the hatch-cover table. It is his patented Tricky Dick voice. "Just out of nowhere, out of the clear blue." He hoods his eyes and extends his schnoz like Nixon. "I realized. That what I really needed to do, you understand, was to help others. It was just *that* simple." He gives his jowly face a solemn pseudo-Nixon head shake. "I hope you all can understand what I'm getting at here." This may be his reaction to my get-up. I'm satisfied, though as always to me he is a borderless uncertainty. I don't even feel like his father—more like his uncle or his former parole officer. It's good if Jill, queen of Cheboygan, can try to admire, understand and please him, and he her. I bless you. I don't know what we're supposed to do now. "How's your mom?"

"She's not coming over today," Paul says. He's monkeying with his time capsule while I'm standing here. It has a little silver side door that slides open to permit installation of sacred artifacts.

Where do you get one of these things? Is there a Web site? Why are we even down here where I never come? "She said you had cancer. How's that going?" He frowns at me, then down again, as though this was another encoded joke of ours.

"Oh, it's great," I say. "I have a prostate full of radioactive BBs I didn't have when I saw you last."

"Cooo-ul. Do they hurt?"

"It—"

"My stepfather had that," Jill says, the cleft reappearing between her wide-set eyes. A show of sympathy.

"How'd *he* do?"

"He died. But not from that."

"I see. Well, this is all pretty new to me." I say this as if we were talking about changing car-repair affiliations. I smile and look around my shadowy basement. In addition to the Block Island map, there's a large hanging framed reproduction left by the prior owners, depicting the *Lord Barnegat*, famed two-masted whaling schooner that plied the ocean right outside in the 1870s and is currently in a museum in Navesink. I should toss out all this shit and turn the space into a screening room for resale to TV people. "I don't see life as a perfect mold broken," I say uncomfortably when neither of them says anything more about my having cancer. Possibly Jill and I share this point of view. What else has Ann blabbed to them?

The cancer topic has struck them both mute, the way it does most people, and I feel suddenly stupid standing here dressed like a nitwit, as if none of us has anything to say to the other on any subject but my "illness." Aren't they in the greeting-card business? Though probably we're all three waiting for one of us to do something unforgivable so we can convulse into a throat-slashing argument and Paul can grab Jill and clear out back to K.C. I think again of him whonking away with this bounteous, one-handed Michigan armful and I admit I'm happy for him.

"The caterers'll be here at one-forty-five," I say to have something to say so I can leave. "Did your sister say when she might be back?"

Mention of Clarissa instantly inscribes a displeased/pleased smile on Paul's beard-encircled lips. His sister is, of course, his eternal subject, though she has always treated him like a dangerous mutant, which he relishes. By taking possession of the most-unsettling-life-course trophy, she has further put him off his game. Jill could be his attempt to wrest back the trophy.

"So did you meet Gandhi's grandson?" Paul smirks while he goes on fiddling with his time capsule, though he's nervous, his eyes snapping at Jill, who regards him encouragingly. His mouth breaks into a derisive grin. "He's into fucking equitation therapy. Whatever that is. He's probably writing a semi-autobiographical novel, too." Paul combs one hand back through his mullet and frowns with what I'm supposed to know is dismayed belief. "I like asked him, 'What's the most misunderstood airline?' And he goes, 'I don't know. Royal Air Maroc?' I go, 'Fucking bullshit. It's Northwest. It flies to the Twin Cities of Minneapolis and Saint Paul. No contest.'" Paul's lip curls in its right corner. Something's setting him off.

"Maybe he didn't understand what you were getting at," I say to be fatherly. "I'm guessing she's not too serious about him anyway."

"Oh, what a *giant* relief *that* is." Paul's odd round face assumes an expression of profoundest disdain.

"I thought he seemed pretty interesting," Jill says—her first semi-familial utterance and the first uncoded words anybody's spoken since Paul came back inside. Although, of course, she's wrong.

"He's a butthole. Case closed," Paul snarls. "'Are you all right? Are *you* all right?' He's like a fucking nurse. He's one of those dipshits who's always asking people if they're all right. 'Are you all right? How 'bout you? Are *you* all right, too? Do you want a fucking foot massage? How 'bout a back rub? Or a blow job? Maybe a high colonic?'" In this frame of mind, as a junior at Haddam High, Paul used to get so angry at his teachers, he'd beat his temples with his palms—the universal SOS for teen troubles ahead. It's hard to imagine him selling residential real estate.

"I think you should let this go, okee, honey?" Jill says and smiles at him.

Paul glowers at Jill, then at me, as if he's just exited a trance—blinking, then smiling. "Issat it?" he says. "You done? That be all? You want cheese on that?" It's possible he might bark, which is also something he did as a teen.

Someplace, from some sound source I can't locate, as if it came out of the drywall, I hear music. Orchestral. Ravel's *Bolero*—the military snares and the twiny oboes, played at high volume. No doubt it's the Feensters. What more perfect Thanksgiving air? Possibly they're in the hot tub, staging a musicale for the beach visitors and, of course, to aggravate the shit out of me. At Easter, they played "The March of the Siamese Children" all day long. Last 4th of July, it was "Lisbon Antigua" by Pérez Prado, until the Sea-Clift Police (summoned by me) paid them a courtesy call, which started a row. It's conceivable that in the cathode-ray tube business, Nick got too close to some bad-actor chemicals that are just now being registered in his behavior. To ask them to turn it down would invite a fistfight, which I don't feel like. Though I'm happy to call the police again. Then, just as suddenly, *Bolero* stops and I hear voices raised next door and a door slam.

"Look here, you two." I'm tempted to say *lovebirds*, but don't. "I've got some bees wax of my own to take care of before the food gets here. I want you to treat the place like you own it."

"Okay. That's great." Jill puts her arms behind her and nods enthusiastically.

"No, but wait!" Paul says, and suddenly abandoning his time capsule, he essentially rushes me across the basement. I manage to take one unwieldy backward-sideways step, since he seems maybe to want to go right by me and head up the stairs—to where, I haven't the foggiest. But instead, he lurches straight into me, thudding me in the chest, expunging my breath and clamping his terrible grip on me. "I haven't given you a hug yet, *Dad*," he howls, his whiskery jaw broxed against my shaved face, his belly to my belly. He's got me grappled around my shoulders, his bare knee, for some reason, wedging between mine the way a high school gorilla would body-press his high school honey. My shocked eyes have popped open wider, so that I see right down into his humid manly ear canal and across the red bumpy landscape of his awful mullet. "Oh, I've been *so* bad," he wails in deepest, crassest sarcasm, clutching me, his head grinding my chest. I want to flee or yell or start punching. "Oh, *Christ*, I've just been so terrible." He's taken me prisoner—though I mean to get away. I'm backed into the narrow stairwell and manage to anchor one Nike against the bottom riser. Except with Paul grasping and rooting at me, I miss my balance and start listing backward, with him still attached, his glasses frame gouging my cheek. "Ooooh, ooooh," he boo-hoos in mock contrition. We're both going over now, except I catch a grip, hand-rasping and painful, on the banister pole, which stops us, saving me from knocking the crap out of myself—snapping a vertebra, breaking my leg, finishing the job Bob Butts started. What's wrong with life?

"What the fuck, you idiot," I say, clung to the sloping banister like a gunshot victim. "Are you losing your fucking mind?"

"Bonding." Paul expels a not-wholesome breath into the front of my block-M sweatshirt. "We're bonding."

"Sweetie?" Jill's beseeching voice. At the angle I'm suspended, and from behind the top of Paul's head, Jill's wide, disconcerted face comes into view, looking troubled, as she's trying to gain a one-handed grip on Paul's back to pry him off me before I lose my own hand-hold and brain myself on the riser edge. "Sweetie, let your dad up now. He's gonna hurt himself."

"It's *so* important," Paul murples.

"I know. But—" Jill begins raising him like a child.

"Get off me." I'm struggling, trying to shout but breathless. "Jesus Christ." What I'd like to do is wham a fist right in his ear, knock him into a stupor, only I can't turn loose of the banister without falling. But I would if I could.

"Come on, Sweetie." Jill has both her milky arms—hand and handless—about Paul's sides. My nose is against her shoulder—the sweet smell of lilacs possibly associated with her Ekberg bosoms. Though it's still an awful moment.

And then I'm loose and able to pull myself up. Paul is six inches in front of me, his bleared right orb glowing behind his spectacles, his mouth gaping, heaving for air, his gray pupils fixed on me.

"What's wrong with you?" I let myself sit down onto the third stair leading up to the kitchen. I'm still breathless. Jill still has a wrestler's grip around the middle of Paul's red Chiefs shirt. He looks dazed, surprised but pleased. He may feel things couldn't have turned out better.

"Are you one of those people who shies away from physical intimacy with loved ones?" He's now speaking in a deep AM dee-jay voice, dead-eyed.

"Why are you such an asshole, is what I want to know."

"It's easier," he snaps.

"Than what, for Christ's sake? Than to act like a human being?"

Paul's round face inches closer. Jill's still got him. His body smells metallic—from his time capsule—his breathing stertorous as a smoker's (which I hope he isn't). "Than being like you." He shouts this. He is furious. At me.

Except I haven't done anything. Meant no harm or injury—other than to love him, which might be enough. This is all loss. "What's so terrible about me? I'm just your old man. It's Thanksgiving Day. I have cancer. I love you. Why is that so bad?"

"Because you hold everything fucking *down*," Paul shouts, and he accidentally spits in my face, catching my eyelid. "You smother it."

"Oh bullshit." I'm shouting back now. "I don't smother *enough*. How the hell would you know? What have you ever restrained?" I almost blurt out that someone ought to smother *him*, though that would send the wrong message. I begin hoisting my aching self off the stair, using the banister. "I've got things to do now. Okay?" My hand burns, my knees are quaky, my heart's doing a little periwinkle in its cavity. Outside the sliding glass door, where the light's diaphanous, the late-morning beach—what I can see of it—stretches pristine, sprigged up with airy yellow beach grass and dry stems. I wipe my son's cool saliva off my eyelid and address Jill, who's peering at me as if I might expire like her stepfather in Cheboygan. I wonder if I'd get used to her having only one hand. Yes.

I try to smile at her over my son's shoulder, as if he wasn't there anymore. "Maybe you two just oughta take a long walk down the beach."

"Okee," Jill says—good, staunch Michigan beauty who sees her job.

"You need to take the hostility quiz." Paul's eyes dance behind their specs. "It was on a napkin in a diner down in Valley Forge."

"Maybe I'll do that later." I am defeated.

" 'How many times a week do you give the finger? Do you ever wake up with your fists clenched?' Let's see—" He's forgotten how I smother things and make his difficult life unlivable. I'm sure he meant it when he said it. His mind is cavorting now, his way of letting the past go glimmering. " 'Do you think people are talking about you all the time? Do you think a lot about revenge?' I forget the rest." He stares expectantly, blinking, as if he needs re-acclimating—to me, to being here, to his niche in the world. There is nothing wrong with my son. It's us. *We're* not normal. No wonder life seems better in Kansas City.

I have nothing available to say to him. He has placed himself outside my language base, to the side of my smothering fatherly syntax and diction, complimentary closes, humorous restrictive clauses and subordinating conjunctions. We have our cocked-up coded lingo—winks, brow-archings, sly-boots double, triple, quadruple entendres that work for us—but that's all. And now they're gone, lost to silence and anger, into the hole that is our "relationship." I bless you. I bless you. I bless you. In spite of all.

CHAPTER 14

HURRIEDLY NOW, or I'll have nothing to show for the day. It's past 10:30. I head up Ocean Ave, my duct-taped window holding fast. I check the news-only station from Long Branch for something on the Haddam hospital explosion that might keep me out of the lineup tomorrow. But there's only holiday traffic updates, a brewing controversy over the new 34-cent stamp, last night's Flyers' stats and Cheney doing swell in the Georgetown Hospital.

I'm certain I've missed Mike's house prospects, though I may not now be in the best realty fettle—after my "conflict" with my son—and am just as likely to scare clients away. Plus, I'm missing my call from Sally and, at the very least, depriving myself of an easeful morning in bed following last night's ordeal. I'd like to settle my blood pressure and stopper the seep of oily stress into my bloodstream before I show up in the phlebotomy line at Mayo on Wednesday. Even in stolid Lutheran Rochester, where sheikhs, pashas and South American genocidists go for tune-ups, and where they've seen everything, I still want to make as good a biomedical impression as possible, as if I was selling myself as a patient. If Paul's right that I hold everything down, my wish would be that I could hold down more.

Sea-Clift, viewed out my Suburban window on late Thanksgiving morning, is as emptied, wide-streeted and spring-y as Easter Sunday—despite the Yuletide trimmings. No cars are parked along the boulevard shopfronts. Wreathed traffic lights are flashing yellow. The regular speed trap—a black-and-white Plymouth Fury "hidden" behind the fire station load lugger—is in position and manned (we locals know) by a rubber blow-up cop named "Officer Meadows" for a since-deceased chief fired for sleeping on the job. My Realty-Wise office at 1606 looks unpromising as I pass it. Only the crime-barred Hello Deli and Tackle Shop is lighted inside and doing business—three cars angled in, another Salvation Army red-kettle tender out front chatting with a pair of joggers in running gear. The Coastal Evacuation signs leading to the bay bridge and points inland appear to have been heeded, leaving the rest of us to fend for ourselves.

A beach town in off-season doldrum may seem to have blissfully reclaimed its truest self, breathing out the long-awaited sigh of winter. But in Sea-Clift, a nervous what-comes-next uneasiness prickles down the necks of our town fathers due to last summer's business slowdown. Growth, smart or maybe even stupid, is the perceived problem here; how to grow an entrepreneurial culture where our hands-on family-based service commitment could survive till doomsday (because of the beach), but will never go all the way to gangbusters without a tech sector, a labor-luring signature industry, a process-driven mentality or a center of gravity to see to it we get rich as shit off beaucoup private dollars. In other words, we're just a place, much like another.

I, of course, moved here for these very reasons: because I admired Sea-Clift's *face* to the interested stranger—seasonal, insular, commuter-less, stable, aspirant within limits. There was no space to grow *out* to, so my business model pointed to in-fill and retrench, not so different from Haddam, but on a more human scale. My house-moving plan on Timbuktu is the perfect case in point. You could teach it over at Wharton. To me, commerce with no likelihood of significant growth or sky-rocketing appreciation seems like a precious bounty, and the opposite of my years in Haddam, when *gasping increase* was the sacred article of faith no one dared mention for fear of the truth breeding doubt like an odorless gas that suffocates everybody.

Mine, of course, is not the view of the Dollars For Doers Strike Council, who sit Monday mornings in the fire station bullpen and who've seen the figures and are charged to "transition" Sea-Clift into the "next phase," from under-used asset to vitality pocket and full-service lifestyle provider using grassroots support. This, even though we all like it fine here. Permanence has once again been perceived as death.

This fall, after the summer down-tick—fewer visitors, fewer smoothies and tomato pies, fewer boogie-board and chalet rentals (I credit the election and the tech-stock slide)—new plans went on the table for revitalizations. The Council floated a town naming-rights initiative to infuse capital ("BFI, New Jersey" was seriously suggested, but met with a cold shoulder from citizens). A proposal came up to abandon the "seasonal concept" and make Sea-Clift officially "year-round," only no one seemed to know how to do that, though all were for it until they figured out they'd have to work harder. There was support for dismantling a light-house in Maine and setting it on the beach, but regulations forbid new construction. The Sons of Italy offered to expand the Frank Sinatra contest to include a permanent "New Jersey Folk Tradi-tions" exhibit to go on the Coastal Heritage Trail (no one's taken this seriously). The most ambitious idea—which *will* take place, though not in my lifetime—is to reclaim acres of Barnegat Bay itself for revenue-friendly use: a human tissue-generator lab or possibly just a golf course. But no one's identified partnering capital or imagined how to buy off wetlands interests. Though one day I'm sure a man will rollerblade from where the Yacht Club used to be across to the condom plant in Toms River with-out noticing that once a great bay was here. The only new idea that seems to be genuinely percolating is an Internet rental-booking software package (Weneedabreak.com) that's worked in towns farther north, and that Mike's all for. In all these visionings, however, my attitude's the same: Quit fretting, keep the current inventory in good working order, rely on your Fifties-style beach life and let population growth do its job the way it always has. What's the hurry? We've already built it here, so we can be sure in time they'll come. This is why I'm not on the Dollars For Doers anymore.

JUST AHEAD, at the left turn onto Timbuktu Street, I see the scheduled Turkey Day 5-K Sea-Clift-to-Ortley-and-back road race nearing its start time in front of Our Lady of Effectual Mercy R C church. A crowd—a hundred or so singleted body types—mingles on the cold grassy median right where I have to turn. The runners—string-thin men and identical females in weightless shorts, expensive-as-hell running shoes, numbered Turkey Day racing bibs and plastic water bottles—are dedi-catedly goading themselves into road race mentality, stretching and twisting, prancing and bending and ignoring one another, hands on hips, heads down, occasionally erupting into violent bursts of in-place jogging to fire their muscles into exertion mode. They are, I have to say, a handsome, healthy, sinewy, finely-limbed bunch of sociopathic greyhounds. Most are in middle years, all obviously scared silly of serenity and death, a fixation that makes them emaciate themselves, punish their bones and brains (many of the women quit menstruating or having the slightest interest in sex) and cut themselves off from friend, foe and family—everyone except their "running friends"—in order to pad out along the dark early-morning streets of America, demonstrating sentience. My time in the USMC, three decades back, and in spite of what Ann says about my suitability, made me promise myself that if I got out alive, I'd never hasten a step as long as I lived, unless real life or real death was chasing me. I pretty much haven't.

On the margins of the crowd are the usual wheelchair athletes —chesty, vaguely insane-looking, leather-gloved men and women strapped into aerodynamic chairs with big cambered wheels and abbreviated bodies like their owners. There are also spry oldsters—stiff, bent-over and balding octogenarians of both genders, ready to run the race with extinction. And set apart from these are the true runners, a cadre of regal, tar-black, starved-looking, genuine Africans—women and men both, a few actually barefoot—chatting and smiling calmly (two talk on cell phones) in anticipation of tearing all the neurotic white racers brand new Turkey Day assholes. For all the runners, it's hopeful, I know; but to me it's a dispiriting spectacle to witness on a morning when so much less should be strived for under a wide, pale-clouded and slightly pinkish sky. I feel the same way when I go in a hardware store to have a new tenant's key cut and smell the cardboard and corrugated-metal and feed-store aromas of all the dervish endeavors a human can be busily up to if he's worth a shit: recaulking that shower groin with space-age epoxies, insulating the weather-side spigot that always freezes, re-hanging the bathroom door that opens the wrong way and clutters the nice view down the hall that reveals a slice of ocean when the trees aren't in leaf. It gives me the grims to think of what we humans do that no one's life depends on, and always drives me right out the door into the street with my jagged new key and my head spinning. It's no different from Mike's idea of putting up magnum-size "homes" on two-acre lots with expectations of luring hard-charging young radiologists and probate lawyers who'd really be just as happy to go on living where they live and who need six thousand square feet like they need a bone in their nose. Neither am I sure that the second-home market, where I ply my skills, is immune from the same complaint.

Sea-Clift police are of course a presence, a pair of thick-necks in helmets and jodhpurs on giant white-and-black Kawasakis, waiting to be escorts. A green EMS meat wagon sits beyond the crowd at the curb, its attendants sharing a smoke and a smirk. The priest from Our Lady of Effectual Mercy, Father Ray, wearing his dress-down everyday white surplice, has mounted a metal stepladder at the curb and is using a bullhorn and an aspergill to bless the race and runners: May you not fall down and bust your ass; may you not tear your Achilles or blow out an ACL; may you not have an aneurysm in your aorta with no one to give you last rites; may you have a living will that leaves all to the RC Church; now run for your lives in the name of the Father, the Son, etc., etc., etc.

I need to make my turn here, cross the median cut and the white markings the race organizers have painted on the pavement. All the milling soon-to-be-racers give me and my Suburban the cloudy eye, as if I might be about to plow into them, cut a bloody swath right through. What's this Suburban all about, their hard looks say. Do you *need* a boat that big? There oughta be a special tax on those. What's with the window and the fucking tape? Is this guy local?

I'm grinning involuntarily as I make the turn, my head ducking, nodding unqualified 5-K approval along with my guilty admission that I'm not one of them, not brave enough, will have to try harder. I mustn't accidentally hit the horn, punch the accelerator, veer an inch off course, or risk setting them to yelling and contesting and reviewing their civil rights. But seeing them congregated and intent, so pre-preoccupied, so vulnerably clad and unprotected, so much one thing, makes me feel just how much I'm a realtor (in the bad sense); even more so now than in my last Haddam days, when I felt coldly extraneous and already irremediably what I was—a house flogger, cruising the periphery of all the real goings-on: the shoe-repair errands, the good-results doctor and dental visits, the 5-K races, the trips to the altar to kneel and accept the holy body and blood of kee-rist on a kee-rutch. I felt something akin to this somber sensation when I didn't give Bud Sloat a ride in Haddam on Tuesday.

But I'm sorry to be here feeling it now. Though it is but another in the young day's cavalcade of good-for-my-soul, Next Level acceptances for which I'll be thankful: I am this thing, seller of used and cast-off houses, and I am not other. It's shocking to note how close we play to unwelcome realizations, and yet how our ongoing ignorance makes so much of life possible. However, gone in a gulp are all the roles I might still inhabit but won't, all the new learning curves I'd be good at, all the women who might adore me, the phone calls bearing welcome news and foretelling unimagined happiness, my chance to be an FBI agent, ambassador to France, a case worker in Mozambique—the one they all look up to. The Permanent Period permitted all that, and the price was small enough—self-extinguishment, becoming an instrument, blah, blah, blah. And now it's different. The Next Level means me to say yes to myself just when it feels weirdest. Is this what it means to be mainstreamed like my son?

"I'm one of you," I want to say to these joggers out my window like a crowd in a jogger republic undergoing a coup. "The race is ahead of me, too. I'm not just this. I'm that. And that. And that. There's more to me than meets your gimlet eye." But it isn't so.

A bare coffee-colored arm flags out of the milling crowd, with a squat body attached and a face I know above the three blue stars 'n bars of the Honduran flag worn as a singlet. This is Esteban, from the Cormorant Court roofing crew, waving happily to me, *el jefe*, his gold restorations flashing in the hidden sun's glint. He's socked into the runner crowd, way more a part of things than I feel. My thumb juts to tap the horn, but I catch myself in time and wave instead. Though it's then I have to press across the opposing lane of Ocean Ave and onto Timbuktu. The electric carillon in Our Lady commences its pre-race clamor, startling the shit out of me. The runner crowd shifts as one toward the starting line and up goes the gun (Father Ray is the shooter). I carry through with my turn, extra careful, since the motorcycle cops are eyeing me. But in an instant, I'm across and anonymous again as the gun goes off and the beast crowd swells with a sigh, and then all of it's behind me.

*   *   *

MIKE MAHONEY—bony, businesslike, crisply turned-out realty go-getter—is the first human I see down Timbuktu. He's out in the street beside his Infiniti with its REALTORS ARE PEOPLE TOO sticker and Barnegat Lighthouse license tag, waving, a happy grin on his round flat face, as though I'd gotten lost and just happened down the right street by dumb luck. He's wearing his amber aviators and clutching a bouquet of white listing sheets. Twenty yards beyond him is a beige Lincoln Town Car, the exact model Newark Airport limo drivers drive. Outside the Lincoln waits a small, ovoid mustachioed personage in what looks like, through my windshield, a belted linen-looking suit that matches the Town Car's paint job, into which the man almost perfectly blends. This is the client Mike has somehow convinced to hang around. I'm a half hour late—for reasons of my difficult son—but frankly don't much care.

Timbuktu Street is a three-block residential, connecting Ocean Avenue to Barnegat Bay out ahead. The closed-for-the-season Yacht Club is at the end to the left, and across the gray water the low populous sprawl of Toms River is two-plus miles away. The bay bridge itself is visible, though at 11:30 on Thanksgiving morning, it is not much in use.

Houses on Timbuktu (Marrakesh Street is one street south, Bimini one street north) are all in the moderate bracket. The bay side is naturally cheaper than the ocean side, but prices go up close to the water, no matter what water it is. Most of these are frank plain-fronted ranches, some with camelbacks added, some with new wood-grained metal siding, all hip-roofed, three-window, door-in-the-middle, pastel frame constructions on small lots. Most were put up en masse, ten streets at a time, after Hurricane Cindy flattened all the aging cypress and fir bungalows the first Sea-Clift settlers built from Sears kits in the Twenties. A few of those '59-vintage owners are still around, though most houses have changed hands ten times and are owned by year-rounders who're retired or commute to the mainland, or who keep their houses as rentals or a summer bolt-hole for the extended family. Several are owned and kept in mint condition by Gotham and Philadelphia policemen and firefighters who store their big trailered Lunds and refurbished Lymans, shrink-wrapped in blue plastic, on their pink-and-green crushed-marble "lawns." These small streets, with their clean-façade, well-barbered, moderately-priced dwellings (250–300 bills) are, in fact, the social backbone of Sea-Clift, and even though most newcomers are Republicans, it's they who oppose the Dollars For Doers schemes to grow out the economy like a mushroom.

It's also these same home owners who're made rueful by the sight of a neighbor house being torn off its foundation and trucked away, leaving behind scarred ground that once was a compatible vista, to be replaced by some frightening new construction. The worst is always assumed. And even though the identical houses along these identical, all but tree-less streets are simplicity and modesty's essence, and finally no great shakes, that's exactly how the owners want it, and know for certain a new house of unforeseeable design will rob their street of its *known* character and kick the crap out of values they're looking to cash in on. I've already received concerned calls from the Timbuktu Neighbors Coalition, advancing the idea that I "donate"(!) the emptied lot at 118 for a passive park. Though even if I wanted to (which I don't), no one in the Coalition would keep it up or pay the liability premiums, since many Coalition-owners are absentees and quite a few are elderly, on fixed whatevers. Eventually, the "park" would turn into a weedy eyesore everyone'd blame me for. Prices would then fall, and everyone would've forgotten that an attractive new house could've been there and made everything rosy. Better—as I told the Coalition lady—to sell the lot to some citizen who can afford it, then let the community do what communities do best: suppress diversity, discourage individuality, punish exuberance and find suitable language to make it seem good for everyone and what America's all about. Placards (like election placards) still stand in some yards, shouting SAVE TIMBUKTU FROM EVIL DEVELOPERS!!! Though the house at 118 is already up on steel girders and in a week will be history.

Mike's heading toward my driver's window as I pull to the curb. He's smiling and glancing back, nodding assurances to his client and generally brimming with house-selling certainty.

"I got tied up," I say out the window, and look annoyed.

"It's better, it's better," Mike says in a whisper, then has another glance at the Town Car clients. He looks like a dashboard doll, since he's wearing a strange knee-length black knitted sweater with a mink-looking collar, a Black Watch plaid sports-car cap, green cords and green suede loafers with argyle socks. It would seem to be his Scottish ensemble. "It's good to make them wait." He has drawn close to my face, so that I'm almost nose-into the fur trim on his sweater. The breeze on the bay side of Barnegat Neck is stouter than I expected. Inland weather is bringing change. We'll have a proper blustery Thanksgiving cold snap before the day's done. I bend forward against my steering wheel and give a look through the windshield up at pleasant, leaf-green #118, hiked up on dull red girders that have several impressive-looking hydraulic jacks under them, so the entire house, sill and all, has been elevated five feet off its brick founda-tion, exposing light and air and affording a view to the back yard. Two sets of heavy-duty tires and axles await use in what was once the front yard, in preparation for actually moving the house—which, like its neighbors, is unornamented, aluminum-sided, with brighter, newer green roof shingles mixed with old. The Arriba house movers have put their enigmatic sign up in the yard: EL GATO DUERME MIENTRAS QUE TRABAJAMOS.

This is the first time I've seen 118 up on its sleds, and I frankly can't blame the neighbors for feeling "violated," which is what the Coalition lady said before she started to cry and told me I was a gangster. It's not a very good thing to do to a street's sense of integrity—prices or no prices—to start switching houses like Monopoly pieces. I'm actually sorry I've done it now. It would've been better if the new owners had torn 118 down as planned and put their new house up in its dust. Orderly resi-dential succession would have been satisfied, although possibly nobody would've been any happier. All the more reason to let Mike sell it to his clients right off the sleds and shift the focus to them—who at least plan to live in it, albeit someplace else.

"I've been telling them inventory's down a third and demand's kicking up." Mike's whispered breath is warm and once again has tobacco on it. He practices all kinds of breath-purifying tech-niques, as if that's the thing buyers look for first. His Infiniti has a Dalai Lama-approved incense air-freshener strung to the rear-view, and his car seats are always strewn with Clorets and Dentyne papers. But today's efforts are so far unavailing.

I stare curiously out at Mike's shiny round face—a face of high, faraway mountain crags, clouded pinnacles and thinnest airs, all forsaken for the chance to sell houses in the Garden State. And just for that instant, I cannot for the life of me think of his name—even though I just thought it. I'd like to say his name, frame a question in a confidential manner that lets him know I'm behind his deal 110 percent, and why doesn't he just take my thumbs-up from right here in the car. I'll wave a cheery welcome aboard to the fat little Hindu (or Mohammedan or Buddhist or Jainist or whatever he is), then motor off to be home when Sally calls and Clarissa returns with tales. Possibly Jill will have given Paul a sedative and we can all watch the Patriots pregame on Fox before the food's festive arrival.

Only, my mind has problematically swallowed up this bright-eyed little brown man's name, even though I can tell you every-thing *else* there is to know about him. Gone from me like a leaf in the wind.

"Uhmmm," I say. Of course I don't need to know his name to carry on a conversation with him. Though not knowing it has had the added defect of sweeping clean the conversational path from in front of me, like the police sweeping pedestrians from in front of the 5-K to Ortley and back. I remember all *that* perfectly! What the hell's going on? Am I having a stroke? Or just bored to nullity by one more house going on the sale block? This may be how you know you've reached the finish line in real estate. I even remember *that*.

I smile out at this strangely dressed, burbling little man, hoping to neutralize alarm from my face. Though why should there be any? Whatever we're about to do—I assume sell a house—doesn't seem to require me. I peer out toward the small pear-shaped man in his wrong-season suit, beside his Lincoln, which wears what looks like blue-and-white Empire State plates and also, I see now, a blue BUSH sticker on its left bumper. He has his short fat-man's arms folded and is staring thoughtfully at 118 up on its girders, as if this is a marvelous project he's now in charge of but needs to study for a while. The Town Car appears packed with shadowy human cargo—three distinct heads in back, plus a dog staring through the back window, its tongue out in a happy-dog laugh.

I look back at this diminutive unnamed man at my window. It's possible I don't look normal. "So," I say, "are we all set, then?" I smile exuberantly, suddenly invigorated with what I'm here for and ready to do it—press the flesh, seal the deal, say howdy and make the outsider feel wanted—things I'm good at. "I'm ready to meet the pigeon," I say for some reason, which seems to distress and sink the grin on ———'s round mug. Bill, Bert, Baxter, Boris, Bently . . . I'll come to it.

"Mr. Bagosh, Frank," ——— says, *sotto voce* through my window. Frank. Me.

——— smiles in at me faintly. His thumb is, I can see, twisting his pinkie ring. Thank goodness he doesn't know I can't say his fucking name. He'd think I'm demented. Which I'm not. This kind of thing happens. Possibly vertigo again.

"How is it again?" I say.

"Bagosh," Carl, Carey, Chris, Court, Curt, Coop says, pushing his listing papers into his silly sweater's side pocket, then pulling down on his sports-car cap to look more official. He doesn't want me involved in this now. Something doesn't feel right. He sees his deal evaporating. But I'm doing it, if only because I don't know how to leave. He casts a guarded look at my block-M sweatshirt. Then behind his aviators, his eyes drift down to my jeans, as if I might not be wearing pants at all.

"Bagosh it *is*." I start out of the car, surprisingly feeling damn good about selling a house on Thanksgiving. Cash deal to sweeten the pot—if I remember right. I actually love this kind of shirt-sleeve, write-a-check, hand-it-over deal. Real estate used to have plenty of them. Nowadays, parties are walled off from exposure, require exit strategies, escape hatches in case a sparrow flies against a screen on the third Tuesday and this is thought to be a bad omen. America is a country lost in its own escrow.

I don't know why I can't say Ed, Ewell, Ernie, Egbert, Escalante, Emerson, Everett's name, but I can't. He's Tibetan. He's my associate. I've known him for a year and a half. He and his wife are estranged, with genius-level kids. He's a Libertarian but a social moderate. A Buddhist. A tiger in our trade, a clothes-horse, a happy little business warrior. I just can't come up with his handle, even out on chilly Timbuktu, with a mind-clearing whistle-breeze gusting off the bay. Maybe I should ask to borrow his business card to make a note.

Mr. Bagosh is heading toward us with a big pleased grin on his plump lips. He has a toddling-sideways motoring gait you sometimes see experienced waiters use. What I couldn't see from the car is that he's wearing walking shorts with his belted Raj jacket, plus rattan loafers and socks of the thinnest white silk up to his knees. We are in Rangoon (when it was still Burma). I'm just out of the cockpit of my Flying Fortress, ready for a gin-rickey, a good soak, a new linen suit of my own and some social introductions. This man—Bagosh—coming across the lobby is just the fellow to make it all happen (in addition to being a spy for our side).

"Bagosh," this good man says into the Barnegat breezes, far from Rangoon, here now on Timbuktu. He must've thought it'd be warm here.

"Bascombe," I say in the same robust spirit.

"Yes. Wonderful." We clasp hands. He gives me his two-hander, which is okay this time. "Mr. Mahoney has told me superior things about you."

Bingo! But *Mahoney*? I wouldn't have guessed it. I extend to Mr. Mahoney an affirming business associate's smile. Mike. All is normal again. We at least know who we are.

"I love your house!" Mr. Bagosh nearly shouts with pleasure. In his toddling way, he half-turns and regards 118 up on its severe machinery, as if it was a piece of rare sculpture he was connoisseur to. "I want to buy it right now. Just as we see it here. Up on its big boats. Whatever they are." He leans back and beams, as if saying "its big boats" afforded him inexpressible pleasure.

"Well, that's what we're here for." I nod at Mr. Mahoney at my side. He's re-examining his listing sheets and looking more confident. I have the rich, ineradicable fetor of English Leather burning in my nostrils and also, I believe, on my hand. It's no doubt Mr. Bagosh's signature scent since his school days in Rajpur or some such outpost.

"We're down from the Buffalo area, Mr. Bascombe," Mr. Bagosh says pridefully. "I own an awards and trophies business, and my business has been good this year." He has twinkling black eyes, and his fine white hair has been choreographed into a swirling comb-down from the far reaches that complements a little goatee, which is not so different from my son Paul's beard-stache, only presentable. On anyone but an Indian—if that's what he is—this configuration would make him look like a masseur. The three of us, me in my block-M and Nikes, Mike in his Scotch get-up, Bagosh in his tropical lounging-wear, are probably the strangest things anyone on Timbuktu—a street of cops, firemen, Kinko's managers and plumbers—has yet witnessed, and might make them all less sorry to see the house head down the road.

"I'm not sure what that is," meaning the "awards business," though I have an idea.

"Oh, well," Mr. Bagosh says expansively in a plummy accent. "If you become a salesman of the year in New Jersey. And you receive a wonderful awahd for this honor. We supply this awahd—in the Buffalo area. In Erie, as well. We're a chain of six. So." His mouse-brown face virtually glows. Possibly he's five eight and sixty, and obviously happy to see the complex world in terms of bestowing awards on inhabitants and to make a ton of money doing it. "We say ours is a rewarding business. But it has been very profitable." This is his standard joke and makes him lower his eyes to stifle a look of pleasure.

"That's great." I pass an eye over his Town Car, which has all gold accessories—gold door handles, gold side mirrors, gold and silver hubcaps and gold window frames. Even the famed Lincoln hood ornament is gold-encrusted. It is the car I saw at the office yesterday. In the passenger's seat, a swarthy Madonna-faced woman with dense black hair and a pastel scarf covering part of her head is talking non-stop into a cell phone and paying no attention to what we're doing. In the back I count possibly three sub-teen faces (there could be more). A large-eyed girl peers at me through the tinted window. The others—two slender boys with vulpine expressions—are fidgeting with handheld video gizmos as though they don't know they're in a car in New Jersey. The dog is not to be seen.

But *ecce homo*—Bagosh. Family number two is my guess. The cellphone Madonna looks not much older than Clarissa and is probably a mail-order delivery from the old country, where she may have been unmarriageable in ways Buffalo residents couldn't care less about. A young widow.

"I guess a lot more people are getting awards now," I say.

"Oh my, yes. It's very good today. Very positive. When my father started in the business in 1961, everyone said, 'Oh, Sura, my God. This doesn't make sense. There's no possible way for you. You're mad as a hatter.' But he was smart, you know? When

I finished at Eastman and came into the firm, he had two stores. And now I have six. Two more next year, maybe." Mr. Bagosh links his manicured fingers across the belted front of his Raj cabana jacket and rests them on his prosperous little belly—one pinkie wears a raucous diamond Mike is probably envious of. He's a better candidate for one of the mansionettes Mike's planning in Montmorency County than for 118. Though he may already have one of those in Buffalo, and maybe in Cozumel. In any case, the first commandment of residential sales is never to question the buyer's motives. Leave that for the lawyers and the bankruptcy referees, who get paid to do it.

"Is there anything I can tell you about the house?" I have to say something to merit being here. I look down at my Nike toes and actually give the asphalt a tiny Gary Cooperish nudge.

"Oh no, my goodness," Mr. Bagosh exults. His teeth are straight and white and uniform—top of the line, in dental terms. "Your Mike here has done his job splendidly. I could use twenty of him."

Stood off to the side so the two of us can talk, Mike, I see, is unsmiling. Being commodified in front of me is distasteful to him and will make skinning money off this gentleman less than a hardship. I'm certain he's reciting his Ahimsa, since he's begun gazing up into the sky as if a passing pelican was his soul dispersing to bliss. When reason ends, anger begins. Mike's little flat face, I think, looks weary.

"Have you even been *in* the house?" I say for no particular reason.

"No, no. But I really don't—"

"Let's just have a look," I say. "You don't want any surprises once it's yours."

"Well—" Bagosh shoots a dubious look at Mike and then over to the Lincoln, where his girlfriend, wife, daughter, grand-daughter is still yakking on the phone. A hurry-the-hell-up frown wrinkles her features, as if she's wanting lunch and to be rid of the kids. I see the dog now, a black Standard Poodle seated beside her in the driver's seat, staring out toward Barnegat Bay, a block and a half away, where a late-staying pair of Tundra swans browses on the weedy shore. In his doggy mind, they are his future. "It's conceivably not safe, I think," Bagosh says, his smile gone measly. In fact, both the house and the red girdering have

PELIGRO! NO ENTRADA! painted on in big, crude, no-nonsense letters. Except I know the Bolivians crawl these houses like lemurs and the whole rigamarole's solid as a bank.

"*I'm* gonna have a look," I say. "I think you should, too. It's just good business." I'm only doing this to put chain-store, second-family Bagosh through some hands-on experience he won't enjoy—this, because he gloated over Mike's subaltern status (and voted for Bush). Though it's Mike's fault for thinking he can sell a house to an Indian and not feel cheated. Last year, he sold a condo to a Chinese family and accepted an invitation to dinner once they moved in. I asked him how it had gone, and he answered that the little man-god no longer opposes Chinese sovereignty and that Buddhists bear exile well.

Mike projects a beetled expression and definitely does not support a trip inside the house or hauling his customer up with me. He's worried what the place looks like—huge cracks in the ceilings, floor joists compromised by wet rot—the cold vastness of all that's unknown but not good and therefore *peligro*. Only a nitwit would expose a client to the unexpected when cash is smiling at you. Despite being a Buddhist—full of human compassion for all that lives, and who views real estate as a means of helping others—when it comes to clinching deals, Mike sees clients as rolls of cash that happen to be able to talk. He is no more bothered by Bagosh's undervaluing his essence than if Bagosh fell down and barked like a dog. To Mike—eyes blinking, hands thrust into his absurd sweater pockets—Bagosh is "Mr. Equity Takeover." "Mr. Increased Disposable Income." It wouldn't matter if he was a Navajo. I've never felt exactly that way in fifteen years of selling houses. But I'm not an immigrant, either.

Bagosh, against his will and judgment, but shamed, has begun clambering up onto the girder behind me, bumping the back of my Nikes with his noggin and making me breathe in big burning whiffs of his English Leather. He's taking deep grunting breaths as he ascends, and because he's a shrimp, has to struggle up on his bare knees to reach the red girder surface.

Once onto the flat I-beam, however, it's easy to step along past the front window, holding to the siding panels, and to walk straight to the front door opening that gives entry to the house. Bagosh keeps crowding me on the girder, breathing unevenly, a couple of times saying, "Yes, yes, all right, this is fine now," and smiling wretchedly when I look back at him. We're only eight feet off the ground here and wouldn't do any damage if we did a belly flop.

But there's a nice new view to take in from here, one I'm happy to have and that makes the whole climb-up worthwhile, no matter what we discover inside. Getting a new view—even of Timbuktu Street—is never a waste of time. From here the community is briefly re-visioned: Mike Mahoney down in the street, looking skeptically up at us; our three cars; Bagosh's little closeted brood, all now watching us—the wife at the window, smiling a smile of disapproval. The view stresses the good uniformity of the houses, with their little crushed-marble front yards of differing hues (grassy green, a pink, two or more oceany blues). Few have real trees, only miniature Scotch pines and skimpy oak saplings. None have political placards (meaning the Republicans have won), though several still have their SAVE TIMBUKTU FROM EVIL DEVELOPERS!!! protests. Some yards have boats stored and others feature white statuary of Ole Neptune leaning on his trident—purchasable off the back of trucks on Route 35. No house has nothing, though the effect is to re-enforce sameness: three windows (some with decorative crime bars), center door, no garage, fifty-by-a-hundred-foot lots the original way the (not yet evil) developer designed it. A housing concept which permits no one ever to feel he was *meant* to be here, and so is happy to be, and happier yet to pack up and go when the spirit moves him or her—unlike Haddam, which operates on the Forever Concept but is really no different.

Up the street toward Ocean Avenue, where the 5-K racers have disappeared and the carillon tower at the RC chapel is just visible, some owners are out busying. A man and his son are erecting an Xmas tree in a front yard, where the MIA flag flies on its pole below the Italian tricolor. A man and wife team is painting their front door red and green for Yuletide. Across at 117, in the skimpy back yard, a wrestling ring's been put up and two shirtless teens are throwing each other around, springing off the ropes, taking goofy falls, throwing mock punches, knee lifts and flying mares, laughing and growling and moaning in fun. Number 117, I see, is for sale with my competitor Domus Isle Realty and looks fixed up and spruced for purchase. To the west, the bay stretches out toward the scrim of Toms River far beyond the white Yacht Club mooring markers set in rows. A few late-season sailors are out on the water, seizing the holiday and the land breeze for a last go.

"Ahhhh, yes, now. This is very fine now, isn't it?" Bagosh is close to my shoulder, taking the view, and has actually fastened ahold of my arm. This may be as far above ground as he's been without walls around him. His English Leather is happily beginning to dissipate in the breeze. His womanish knees have smudges from clambering onto the girder. We're outside the vacant front doorway, at a level where the sill comes to my waist. Mike, at street level, is frowning at the bay. He is envisioning better events than these.

"We have to go inside still," I say. "You have to inspect your house." This is purely punitive. I've, of course, already been in the house when it was attached to the ground and I was selling it to the Morris County Stevicks following the departure of the previous owners, the Hausmanns. Though climbing up and in constitutes a pint-size good adventure I didn't expect and is much more rewarding than fighting with my son.

"I'll certainly inspect it when these moving chaps finish," Bagosh says, and widens his onyx eyes in a gesture of objection that seems to agree.

"You'll own it by then," I say, and start pulling myself over the metal sill strip that's half-worked out of its screw holes and a good place to get a nasty cut.

"Yes. Well—" Bagosh casts a fevered frown down at his luxury barge, clearly wishing to be driving it away. He coughs, then laughs a little squealy laugh as I reach down from the doorway and haul him up into the house that will soon be his.

But if it's good to see the familiar world from a sudden new elevation, it may not be to see inside a house on girders, detached from the sacred ground that makes it what it is—a place of safety and assurance. This is what Mike was trying to make me understand by saying nothing.

Down on the street, temps must be low forties, but inside here it's ten degrees colder, and still and dank as a coal scuttle and echoey and eerily lit. It's different from what I thought—without being sure what I thought. The soggy-floored living room–dining room combo (you enter directly—no foyer, no nothing) is tiny but cavernous. The stained pink walls, old green shag and picture-frame ghosts make it feel not like a room but a shell waiting for a tornado to sweep it into the past. Leaking gas and backed-up toilets stiffen the cold internal air. If I was Bagosh, I'd get in my Town Car and not stop till I saw the lights of snowy Buffalo. Good sense is its own reward. I may be losing my touch.

"O-kay! Well. Yes, yes yes. This is fine," Bagosh says jauntily. We're both too big for the cramped, emptied living room, our footfalls loud as thunder.

I walk through the kitchen door to a tiny room of brown-and-gold curling synthetic tiles, where there's no stove, no refrigerator, no dishwasher. All have been ripped out, leaving only their unpainted footprints, the rusted green sink and all the metal cabinets standing open and uncleaned inside. There's a strong cold scent in here of Pine-Sol, but nothing looks like it's been scrubbed in two hundred years. Police enter rooms like this every day and find cadavers liquefying into the linoleum. It didn't look like this when I showed it to the Stevicks.

Bagosh is heading down the murky hall that separates the two small bedrooms and ends in the bath—the classic American starter-home design. "Okay, this is fine," I hear him say. I'm sure he's frozen in his shorts. The Hausmanns lived in these rooms twenty years, raised two kids; Chet Hausmann worked for Ocean County Parks and Lou-Lou was an LPN in Forked River. Life worked fine. They were normal-size people, with normal-size longings. They bought, they saved, they accrued, they envied, they thrived and enjoyed life right through the Clinton adminis-tration. The kids left for other lives (though Chet "the Jet" Jr.'s currently in rehab #2). They grew restless for Dade County, where Lou-Lou's parents live. Things seemed to be changing here—though they weren't. So they left. Nothing out of the ordinary, except it's hard to see how it could've happened inside these four walls, or, if it did, how things could look like this four months later. Empty houses go downhill fast. I should have been more vigilant.

I have a look out the kitchen window into the ditched-up and vacant back yard, and the square, fenced back yards of Bimini Street. Several houses there are closed and boarded for the season, though some have dogs chained up and clothes on the line. Up on Ocean Avenue, the noon carillon at Our Lady has begun chiming "O come, all ye faithful, joyful and triumph-ant—" Then the wail of a farther-off siren signals the hour. Sirens are rare in Sea-Clift in the off-season, though routine in summer.

"O-kay!" I hear Bagosh say conclusively. It's time to leave. I've said not a word since forcing us to come in here.

And then there's a loud, violent, scrabbling, struggling com-motion down the hall, where Bagosh is carrying out his un-willing presale inspection. "Oh my Gawd," I hear him shout in a horrified voice. Then *bangety, bangety, bang-bang*. The sound of a man falling. I'm moving, without bidding myself to move, across the mud-caked floor of the back family room, with its water-clouded picture window overlooking the wrecked back yard. It's less than twenty feet to the hallway entrance and another twelve down the passage. It's possible Bagosh has come upon the overdosed Chet, Jr., is all I can think. Then "Ahh-hhh," I hear poor Bagosh shout again. "My Gawd, oh my Gawd." I still can't see him, though unexpectedly I'm faced with *me*, reflected in the mirror on the dark bathroom medicine chest at the end of the hallway. I look terrified.

"What's wrong? Are you all right?" I call out. Though why would he be all right and be howling?

Then out from the right bedroom, where I take it Bagosh is and has hit the floor, a good-size bushy-tailed red fox comes shooting into the hallway. "Ahhh," Bagosh is wailing, "my-Gawd, my-Gawd." The fox stops, paws splayed, and fixes its eyes on me, hugely blocking the path of escape. Its eyes are dark bullets aimed at my forehead. Though it doesn't pause long, but turns and re-enters the room where Bagosh is, provoking another death wail (possibly he's being ripped into now and will have to undergo painful rabies shots). Immediately, the fox comes rocketing back out the bedroom door, claws scrabbling powerfully to gain purchase. For an instant, its spectral, riotous eyes consider the other tiny bedroom—the kids' room. But without another moment's indecision, the fox fires off straight toward me, so that I stagger back and to the left and pitch through the arched doorway into the living room and right off my feet onto the filthy green shag, where I land just as the fox explodes after me through the door, claws out and scrabbling right across my block-M chest, so that I catch a gulp of its feral rank asshole as it springs off, straight across to the metal threshold and out into the clean cold air of Timbuktu, where, for all I know, Mike may believe the fox is me, translated by this house of spirits into my next incarnation on earth. Frank Fox.

CHAPTER 15

WHEN THE Bagoshes' taillamps have made the turn up onto Ocean Avenue and disappeared ceremoniously into the post noon-time, holiday-emptied streets, Mike and I have ourselves a side-by-side amble down to the bay shore, malodorous and sudsed from last night's storm.

Sally will have called by now. Paul will have answered and could possibly have blurted things I don't want her to know (my illness, for one). Though Clarissa will be home, and the two of them can have a sister–brother parsing talk about my "condition," my upcoming Mayo trip, etc., etc. Possibly Clarissa could also talk to Sally, fill in some gaps, welcome her back on my behalf, no recriminations required. As is often the case, one view is that life is as fucked up as ground chuck and not worth fooling with. But there's another view available to most of us even without becoming a Buddhist: that with an adjustment or two (Sally moving home to me, for instance), life could perhaps be fine again. No need for a miracle cancer cure. No need for Ann Dykstra to vaporize off the earth. No need for Clarissa to marry a former-NFL-great-become-pediatric-oncologist. No need for Paul to dedicate himself to scaling corporate Hallmark (new wardrobe concepts, a computerized prosthesis for his sugar pie). I can't say if this view is the soul of acceptance. But in all important ways, it is the Next Level for me and I am in it and still taking breath regularly.

Mike and I trek stonily down toward the bay's ragged edge. He, it seems, has a proposition for me. The not-good outcome of the Bagosh deal, he believes, only underscores the wisdom and importance of his plan, as well as the "time being right" for me. There's a bravura opportunity for "everybody," should I take him seriously, which I do. I'm always more at home with chance and transition than with the steady course, since the steady course leads quickly, I've found, to the rim of the earth.

The Bagoshes, not surprisingly, couldn't get away from us fast enough. Bagosh emerged uninjured from his ordeal—a small tear in his linens, a scuffed wrist (no chance of a bite), his hair disfigured. But the sight of the fleeing fox incited the big poodle, Crackers, to a primordial in-car carnivore rage, so that the kids got deep scratches, broke their computer games and eventually had to pile out on the street, letting Crackers give pursuit out of sight. (He came back on his own.) Mrs. Bagosh, if that's who the Madonna-faced woman was, didn't leave the front seat, never lowered her window, did nothing more than say nothing to anyone, including her husband, a silence lasting up to Ocean Avenue, I suspected, but no longer.

Bagosh himself couldn't have been nicer to me or to Mike. Mike couldn't have been nicer. And neither could I, since I was responsible for everything. Bagosh said he would "definitely" buy the house on Monday. He and his family, however, had Thanksgiving reservations in Cape May that night, planned to travel up to Bivalve to see the snow geese wintering ground, then on to Greenwich, Hancocks Bridge and around to the Walt Whitman house in Camden before driving home weary but happy on Sunday, back to Buffalo, where there's now ten feet of snow. He'd be calling. The story made him happy to tell. And even though Mike knew Bagosh had at that moment a choker wad of greenbacks in his shorts pocket and could've counted out big bills while I executed a quit-claim deed on my Suburban hood, he seemed jolly about money he would never see. He actually took off his sports-car cap, revealed his bristly dome, rubbed his scalp and joked with Bagosh about what a dog's breakfast the Bills were making of the regular season, but that with luck a new O.J. would come along in the draft—a possibility that made them both laugh like Polacks. They are both Americans and acted like nothing else.

When the Bagoshes were all loaded in and maneuvering the big Lincoln around on Timbuktu, Mike stood beside me, hands thrust in his sweater pockets. "Wrong views result in a lack of protection, with no place to take refuge," he announced solemnly. I took this to mean I'd fucked up, but it didn't matter, because he had more significant things in mind.

"I loused this up," I said. "I apologize."

"It's good to *almost* sell a house," he said, already upbeat. The Bagosh children were waving at us from inside their warm, plush car (unquestionably at the command of their father). The little girl—wispy, sloe-eyed, with a decorative red dot on her forehead—held up Crackers' paw so he could wave, too. Mike and I both waved and smiled our good-byes to dog, money and all as the Lincoln, its left taillight blinking at the intersection, rumbled out of sight forever.

"I'd rather have their money than their friendship," I said. I noticed that I'd ripped my 501s somewhere in the house. My second fall of the day, third in two days. A general slippage. "Did he say what he thought he wanted the house for?"

"He didn't know," Mike said. "The idea just appealed to him. It's why I didn't want him to go inside." He looked at me to say I should've known that, then smiled a thin, indicting smile meant not to be condescending.

"I'm an essentialist in things," I said. "I believe humans buy houses to live in them, or so other people will."

Mike didn't attempt a reply, just looked up at the frosted clouds quickly forming. I cast a speculative eye up at the unsold green house, raised and allowing the glimpse of fenced back yards on Bimini Street. Possibly Thanksgiving wasn't really a great day to sell a house. On a day to summon one's blessings and try to believe in them, it might be common sense not to risk what you're sure you have.

LAST NIGHT's storm has widened the bay's perimeter and shoved water up onto Bay Drive, where it exudes swampy-sweet odors of challenged septics. Yellow fluff rides in the weeds where the black-billed swans have foraged. This part of the bay shore has remained undeveloped due to Seventies-era open-space ordinances mandating jungle gyms, slides and merry-go-rounds for younger, child-bearing families in the neighborhood. These apparatuses are here but now disused and grown dilapidated on the skimpy beach. A billboard announcing WE CAN DO IT IF WE TRY has been erected on the bay's sandy-muddy shore. I'm not sure what this message means. Possibly save the bay. Or possibly that condos, apartments and shops will soon be here where there's now a pleasant vista across the water, and that the families with kids will have to do their own math or else take a flying fuck at a rolling doughnut.

The two swans have moved off among the Yacht Club buoys. Bits of white Styrofoam, yellow burger wrappers and a faded red beach ball have washed in among the weeds with last night's blow. A gentleman is working alone on his black-hulled thirty-footer, readying it for winter storage. His white-helmeted kid plays with a cat on the dock plankings. Thanksgiving now and here feels evasive, the day at pains to seem festive. It's cold and damp. The usual band of bad air along the far, cluttered Toms River horizon has been washed away in the night. I have noted in our walk down that I am not keen to walk as fast as Mike, whose little green loafers step out lively as he talks in his businessy voice. I'm hoping not to forget his name in mid-announcement of his developer plans. I want to be upbeat and comradely—even if I don't feel that way. We can, after all, always set aside our real feelings—which usually don't amount to a hill of beans anyway, and may not even be genuine—and let ourselves be spontaneous and bounteous with fast-flowing vigor, just as when we're at our certifiable best. This is the part of acceptance I welcome, since it has down-the-line consolations.

On our walk down, Mike has said matter-of-factly that the last two nights have been a "great sufferance" to him, that he dislikes dilemmas (the middle way should preclude them), hates causing me "uncertainty," is uncomfortable with ambition (though he's been practicing it for a coon's age), but has had to concede these "pressures" are a part of modern life (here in America, apparently not in Tibet) and there's no escaping them (unless of course you can get stinking rich, after which you have no real problems). I was curious if he was fingering a pack of Marlboros in his sweater pocket and would've preferred to be puffing away Dick Widmark-style as he spieled all this out to me.

I've begun to enjoy the lake-like bay, the clanking halyards of the remaining Yacht Club boats, the rain-cleared vista across to the populous mainland, even the distant sight of the newer homes down the shore, from the go-go Nineties. There's nothing wrong with development if the right people do the developing. At the gritty water's edge, with the wind huskier, I can see that the WE CAN DO IT billboard has a tiny Domus Isle Realty logo at its bottom corner, an artist's conception of a distant desert atoll with a lone red palm silhouetted. Unfortunately, though maybe only in my view, the desert-island motif calls to mind

Eniwetok, not some South Sea snug-away where you'd like to buy or build your dream house, but in any case has nothing at all to do with Sea-Clift, New Jersey. I've met the owners, two former sports-TV execs from Gotham, a husband and wife team, and by most accounts, they're perfectly nice and probably honest.

Farther down Bay Drive, where it approaches the first of the newer Nineties homes, a two-person survey crew has set up—a man with a tall zebra stake and a girl bent over a svelte-looking digital transit on a tripod. Something's already afoot, out ahead of public approval and opinion. These two are working where a sign designates CABLE CROSSING. I can make out the tiny red digitalized numerals in the transit box, glowing at me each time the young surveyor girl stands up to take a sight line.

There's absolutely no reason to drag out Mike's epic new-vistas announcement and spend all day out here where it's cold and gusty. I'm ready to get on board, whatever it is. I regret our last collaboration hasn't been a money-maker. Averages of showings-to-sales run 12 percent, and we came close on an un-promising day. I want to get home in case Sally hasn't called. But because Mike's a Buddhist, he can only proceed the way he wants to proceed and not the way anybody else does, which means he often has to be humored.

In my rising spirit, I take a cold seat on the low barn-red kids' merry-go-round and give it a rounding push with my toe, so that Mike has to come where I am to speak his piece.

"So're we gonna jump into the McMansion business with our new pecorino *cumpari*?" I say, and give another spin around. The wrecked old contraption squalls with a metal-on-metal *skweeeee-er* that unfortunately nullifies my spirited opening. I'm succeeding in feeling munificent, but can't be sure how long it'll last.

"Tom's a real good guy," Mike says gravely.

I can't hear that well as the merry-go-round takes my gaze past the surveyors, across the bay, past the Nineties housing, then back to Mike, who's stationed himself legs apart, arms folded like an umpire. His brow's furrowed and he looks frustrated that I won't be still.

"Yep, yep, yep," I say. "He seemed pretty solid—for a bozo developer." Benivalle, however, also once knew my precious son Ralph—whose death I have now accepted—and thus occupies a special place in my heart's history book. But I don't want to piss Mike off after I've queered the Bagosh deal like an amateur, so I stop the merry-go-round in front of him and offer up a general smile of business forgiveness for quitting on me when I'm not feeling my best.

"I think now's the right time to make a change," Mike says, seeming to widen his eyes to indicate resolution, his pupils large behind his glasses. "I think it's time to get serious about real estate, Frank. Bush is going to win Florida, I'm sure. We'll see a turn-around by fiscal '01." I don't know why Mike has to sear his little self-important gaze into my brain just to tell me what he's going to do.

"You could be right." I try to look serious back. I'd like to take another spin on the old go-round, but my ass is frozen on the boards and what I need to do is stand up. Only then I'd tower over Mike and ruin his little valedictory. I just want him to get on with it. I've got places to go, telephone calls to answer, children to be driven crazy by.

"People need to stay the course, Frank," he says. "If it isn't broken, don't break it, you know. Stick with old-fashioned competence. Thanksgiving's a good time for this." Mike un-corks a giant happy-Asian smile, as if I'd just said something I haven't said. He's, of course, kidnapping Thanksgiving for his own selfish commercial lusts, the same as Filene's. "I've got a new person in my life," Mike says.

"A new what?" I suspected it.

"A new lady friend." He rises fractionally on the soles of his shoes. "You'll like her."

"What about your wife?" And your two kids at their laptops? Don't they get to make the transition, too? What about the soulful, clear-sighted immigrant life that delivered you to me? And old-fashioned competence not breaking what isn't broken? "I thought you two were reconciling."

"No." Mike tries to look tragic, but not too. He doesn't want to go where what he's said gets all blurred up with what he means. A true Republican.

But it's okay with me. I don't want to go there either.

"Love-based attachments," Mike says indistinctly enough that I don't hear the next thing he says—lost in the breeze—some-thing about Sheela and the kids in the Amboys, the discarded part of his history the business biographers will gloss over in the cover stories once he and Benivalle break through to developer's paradise: "Little Big Man: Tiny Tibetan Talks Turkey to Tantalize Trenders, Trenton to Tenafly." But who could a new squeeze be—suitable for a fortysomething Himalayan in the lower echelons of the realty trade? And in New Jersey? An arranged union, like Bagosh, with a Filipina daughter grown too long in the tooth for her own kind? A monied Paraguayan military widow seeking a young "protégé"? A Tibetan teen flown in like a pizza, on a pledge he'll care for her always? I wonder what the Dalai Lama says in *The Road to the Open Heart* about monogamy. Probably not much, given his own curriculum vitae.

"So, is that all the news that's fit to tell?" From my cold merry-go-round, I can address Mike at eye-level. His plaid cap has drifted down an inch and off to the side, so he looks once again like a pint-size mobster.

"No. I want to buy you out." His now invisible eyes go grim as death. Then again his mouth cracks a big smile, as if what he's just said was absolutely hilarious. Which it isn't.

My own mouth opens to speak, but no words are ready.

"I've tamed myself," Mike says, jubilant. A lone passing duck quacks one quack high in the misty sky, as if all the creatures agree, yes, he's tamed himself.

"From what?" I manage. "I didn't know you needed taming. I thought you were rounding up your courage."

"They're the same." He, as usual, gets instantly giddy at talk like this—word riddles. "There's some unhappiness never to be as rich as J. Paul Getty." Another of Mike's earthly deities. "Filthy rich," he adds buoyantly. "But I can make money, too. Helping people this way can make money."

He means helping them out of their cash. There's a reason these people don't get cancer in their countries. And there's a reason we do. We make things too complicated.

"I believe you want to think about this proposal," he says. His tough little hands are clasped priest-like. He likes being the presenter of a proposal. *Believe, want, think*—these are words used in new ways.

"I don't want to sell you my business," I say. "I like my business. You go develop McMansions for proctologists."

"Yes," he says, meaning no. "But if I make a good business proposal and pay you a lot of money, you can transfer ownership, and everything will stay the same."

"Everything's already the same. It ain't broke. Due to old-fashioned competence. Mine."

"I knew you'd say this," Mike says happily. For the first time since I've known him, he's talking like the departed Mr. Bagosh, with whom he shares, after all, a stronger regional bond than he shares with me. "I think we should agree, though. I've thought about this a great deal. It'll give you time to travel."

Travel is code for my compromised health status, which Mike is officially sensitive to, and means in Mike's enlightened view— Buddhist crappolio—that I "need" to ready myself for the final conjugation by taking a voyage on the *Queen Mary* or the *Love Boat*. He's "helping" me, in other words, by helping me out of business. "I've got time to travel," I say. "Why don't we not talk about this anymore. Okay?" I attempt a faint smile that feels unwelcome to my cold cheeks. Munificence is gone. I don't like being strong-armed or felt sorry for.

"Yes! Okay!" Mike exults. "This is just what I thought. I'm satisfied." It's all about him, his confidence level, his satisfaction. I'm as good as out of work, a cat in need of herding.

"Me, too. Good. But I'm not going to sell you Realty-Wise." I give my sore knees a try at prizing me up off the butt-froze planks. I hold onto the curved hang-on bar that wants to glide away and spill me over. Mike semi-casually secures a light grip on my sweatshirt sleeve. But I'm up and feel fine. The bay breeze cools my neck. My eyes feel like they've both just freshly opened all the way. Down Bay Drive, the boy–girl surveyors are walking side-by-side toward a yellow pickup parked farther along the curve, where houses are. One holds the collapsed tripod, the other the striped pole.

"So, you're not going into business with what's his name?" I say gruffly.

Mike dusts his little hands together as if dirt was on them. He's pretending we didn't have the conversation we just had, and that he feels good about something else. It's possible he'll never bring this subject up again. Intention is the same as action to these guys. "No," he says, pseudo-sadly.

"That's probably smart. I didn't want to say that before."

"I think so." He gives his little Black Watch cap a straightening as we begin walking back to the cars.

Mike is pleased by my rebuff of his unfriendly takeover try. He knows I know it's nothing more than what I did with old man Barber Featherstone and how the world always works. Plus, he's smart. He knows he's succumbed to the little leap into the normal limbo of life. That he's facing down the big fear of "Is this it?" by agreeing "Yes, this *is*." He also knows I might sell him Realty-Wise after all, possibly even very soon, and that he can then start video-taping virtual tours, building Web-based rental connections, adding a new Arabic-speaking female associate, change the company name to Own It . . . TODAY!.com, subscribe to recondite business studies from Michigan State and concentrate more on lifestyle purchasing than essentialist residential clientele. In two to twelve years, when he'll be my age now, he'll be farting through silk. One hardly knows how or when or by what subtle mechanics the old values give way to new. It just happens.

"TOMMY BENIVALLE taught me some invaluable—" Mike's maundering on as we trudge at my slower pace back up Timbuktu. Ahead, his new-values silver Infiniti and my broke-window, old-values, essentialist Suburban sit end to end in front of 118, perched sturdily up on its girders. "Only a fool—" Mike rattles on. I'm not interested. I was his mentor and am now his adversary—which probably mean the same thing, too. I admire him but don't particularly like him today, or the fresh legions he commands. How much life do I have to accept? Does it all come in one day?

"So, are you putting on a big holiday feed bag with your new squeeze?" I say this just to be rude. We stand mid-street, looking exactly like what we are—a pair of realtors. Mike's eyes move toward my Suburban. The duct-taped back window may be a worrisome sign that he needs to hurry up with his business proposal, get the deal nailed down before the mental-health boys show up. There *was* the puzzling scene at the August on Tuesday. I could be discovered tomorrow sitting silently in the office, "just thinking." He could be forced to negotiate with Paul.

"She's got her big place up in Spring Lake. The kids come.

They're Jewish. It's a big scene." Mike nods a sage "not my kind of thing" nod. He's gone back to talking like a Jerseyite.

But I knew it! A dowager, a late-model divorcée like Marguerite. She's adopted "little Mike-a-la," who's giving her "investment counsel" over and above his unspecified services of a consensual nature. The kids, Jake, a Columbia professor, Ben, a fabric artist on Vinalhaven, and one daughter, Rachel, who lives alone in Montecito and can't seem to get started. They all keep the zany parent on a frugal budget so she can't ruin their retirements with her funny enthusiasms. Mike's "interesting," a minority, resembles the Dalai Lama—plus, who cares, if he makes "Gram" happy and keeps her away from ballroom dancing. At least he's not a Mexican.

"Do they let you carve the turkey and serve?" I don't try to suppress a smirk, which he hates but won't show. He knows what he's up to and doesn't care if I know. It's business, not a love-based attachment.

"I'll just drop by late," he says, and frowns, not at me, but at how he'll pass the night. He is, as we all are, taking his solaces as they come. "I have the business proposal already written up." He produces a white Realty-Wise business envelope from his sweater pocket, rolled up with the listing sheets for 118. This he proffers like a summons, bowing slightly. I'm not sure Tibetans even bow. It may be something he picked up. Though I, the defendant, accept it and bow back (which I can't seem to prevent myself from doing) before folding it and stuffing it in my Levi's back pocket like junk mail.

"I'll read this someday. Not today."

"That's splendid." He is elated again. It pleases him to conduct business in the street, in the elements, far from the ancestral cradle. To Mike, this is a sign of progress: the old lessons from the life left behind still viable here in New Jersey.

"Am I going to see you again?" My hand's on my cold door handle. "I don't know what you're doing. I thought you were moving your base of operations over to Mullica Road. You're a mystery wrapped in a small enigma."

"Oh, no." His smile—all intersecting angles—radiates behind his specs. He's risen onto his little toes again, Horatio Alger-style. "I work for you. Until you work for me. Everything's the same. I love you. I keep you in my prayers."

I'm fearful he may hug, kiss, high-five or double-hander me. Two male hugs in one morning is a lot. Men don't have to do that all the time, even though it doesn't mean we're not sensitive. I open the car door and stiffly get myself inside before the inescapable happens. I shut the door and lock it. Mike's left standing out on Timbuktu in his black sweater with its fake-fur collar and his little Black Watch cap. He's speaking something. I can hear the buzz of his voice, but not the sense, through the window. I don't care what he's saying. It's not about me. I get the motor started and begin to mouth words he'll "understand" through the window glass. "Abba-dabba, dabba-dabba, dabba-dabba-dabba, dabba-dabba," I say, then smile, wave, bow in my car seat. He says something back and looks triumphant. He gives me the thumbs-up sign and nods his head proudly. "Abba dabba, dabba, dabba-dabba," I say back and smile. He nods his head again, then steps back, effects a small wave, laughs heartily. And that is it. I'm off.

CHAPTER 16

A DUAL SENSATION—pleasure and enthusiasm—unexpectedly skirls through my middle by the time I reach Ocean Avenue; and alloyed with it is another bracing sensation, from my arms down to my fists, of complete readiness to "take hold." I actually envision these words—*take hold*—in watery letters like an old eight-ball fortune. And there's also, simultaneously, a seemingly opposite feeling of *release*—from something. Sometimes we know complex pressures are building and roiling, and can finger exactly what they're about—a gloomy doctor visit, a big court case before a mean-spirited judge, an IRS audit we wish to God wasn't happening. And other times, we have to plumb the depths, like seeking a warm seam in a cold pond. Only, this time it's easy. Full, pleasurable release and bold, invigorating authority both exude from the sudden, simple prospect of handing over the Realty-Wise reins to Mike Mahoney.

At first blush, of course, it's a heresy. Except, life on the Next Level is only what you invent. And as Mike pointed out two days ago (and I scoffed at), residential real estate's all about what somebody invented. I could sign the papers right now and be on top of the world. Even if it's the worst idea in the world and leaves me rudderless, with yawning angst-filled days during which I never get out of my pj's, it still feels like the right invention now. And now is where I am. (This feels, of course, like a Permanent Period resurrection. But if it is, I don't care.)

There's no sign of returning 5-K runners here at the corner, or much mid-day traffic, not even post-race street litter—only the starting line, whitewashed across the north-bound side of the avenue. A black man—the docent at Our Lady—is just now carting Father Ray's aluminum blessing ladder across the lawn to an arched side doorway. He leans the ladder against the stucco exterior, steps in the door, closes it behind him and does not come out again.

My instinct now is to turn right and get myself home—a

better second act with my son, the hoped-for return of my daughter, the crucial call from Sally. The resumption of the day's best, if unlikely, hopes for itself.

Only another powerful urging directs me not to turn right, but to cross the median and go left, and north, up the peninsula toward Ortley Beach. I know what I'm up to here. I'm empowered by the dual sense of release and take hold, which don't come often and almost never together, and so must be heeded as if ordained by God.

There are—I admit this at risk to myself, though all men know it's true and all women know men think it—there *are* ideal women in the world. Sally said it about me in her letter—which means the same is true for how women calculate men. In my view, there's at least one ideal person for all of us, and probably several. For men, these are the women who make you feel especially smart, that you're uniquely handsome in a way you yourself always believed you were, who bring out the best in you and, by some generosity or need in themselves, cause *you* to feel generous, clever, intuitive as hell about all sorts of things and successful in the world exactly the way you'd like to be. Pity the man who marries such a woman, since she'll eventually drive him crazy with undeserved approval and excessive, unwanted validations. Not that I'd know, having married two "challenger" types, who may have loved me but never looked upon me with less than a seasoned eye, and whose basic watchwords to friend and foe alike were, "Well, let's just see about that. I'm not so sure." In any case, they both left me flat as a flounder—though Sally may be coming back at this moment.

These ideal women can actually *make* you be smarter than you are, but are finally only suitable for fleeting escapades, for profound and long-running flirtations never acted on, for unexpected driving trips to Boston or after-hours cocktails at shadowy red-booth steak houses like the one Wade Arcenault tried to lure me to yesterday with his Texas-bred, ball-crusher, definitely *not* ideal daughter, Vicki/Ricki, who anybody'd be smart to steer wide of, but who I once unaccountably wanted to marry. These women are also meant for sweetly intended, affectionate one-nighters (two at the max), after which you both manage to stay friends, conduct yourselves even better than before, possibly even "enjoy" each other a time or two every six months or six years, but never consider getting serious about, since everybody knows that serious ruins everything. Marguerite might've qualified, but wasn't truly ideal.

Perfect for *affairs* is what these women are. They almost always know it (even if they're married). They realize that given the kind of man they find attractive—usually ruminant loners with minimal but quite specific needs—to strive for anything more lasting would mean they'd soon be miserable and hoping to get things over with fast, and so are happy for the escapade and the cocktails and the rib-eye and the one-nighter where everything works out friendly, and then pretty quick to get back in their own beds again, which is where they (and many others) are happiest.

"Enlightened" thought by headshrinkers with their own rich broth of problems has twisted these normal human pleasures and delights into shabby, shameful perversions and boundary violations needing to be drummed out of the species because someone's always seen as the loser-victim and someone's definition of wholesome and nurturing doesn't always get validated. But we all know that's wrong, whether we have the spirit to admit it or don't. Women are usually full participants in everything they do (including heading off to Mull), and I'm ready to say that when it comes to wholesome, nurturing and long-lasting, a frank, good-hearted roll in the alfalfa, or something close to it, with an enthusiastic and willing female is about as nurturing and wholesome as I can imagine. And if it doesn't last a lifetime, what (pray tell me) does, except marriages where both parties are screaming inside to let light in but can't figure out how to.

The old release-and-take-hold has worked its quickening magic on me and routed me north toward Neptune's Daily Catch Bistro and (I hope) to Bernice Podmanicsky, who may be my savior for the day just when a savior's needed. Sally's call offers some things, but pointedly not others. And she herself authorized a female companion for the day. I'd be a fool to pass on the opportunity, should there be one.

Bernice Podmanicsky, who's one of the wait-staff at Neptune's, is my candidate for the aforementioned ideal woman. A lanky, full-lipped, wide-smiling brunette with big feet, a hint of dark facial hair, but oddly delicate hands with shiny pink nails, a proportionate bosom, solid posterior and runway-model ankles (always my weakness once the butt's accounted for), Bernice would be considered pretty by some standards, though not by all: mouth too big (fine with me); hair taking root a sixteenth of an inch too far down the forehead (ditto); augmented eyebrows (neutral); libidinous chin dimple when she smiles, which is often; fortyish age bracket (I prefer women with adult experience). Altogether, hard not to like. I've known Bernice three years, ever since her long-standing love relationship in Burlington, Vermont, blew a tire and she came down to live in Normandy Beach with her sister Myrna, who's a Mary Kay franchisee. Waitressing was what she'd always done since college at Stevens Point, where she took art (waitressing leaves time for drawing). She is a reader of serious novels and even abstruse philosophical texts, owing to her father, who was a high school guidance counselor in Fond du Lac, and her mother, who's in her seventies and a serious painter in the style of Georgia O'Keeffe.

I actually like Bernice immensely, though there hasn't been any but the most casual contact between us over the course of the three years. When Sally was my regular dinner companion, Bernice was gregarious and jokey and impudently friendly to both of us. "Oh, you two again. Somebody's gonna get the wrong idea about you. . . . And I guess you'll have the bluefish rare." But when Sally left, and I was often alone at a window table with a gin drink, Bernice was more candid and curious and personal and (on occasion) clearly flirtatious—which I was happy about. But mostly she was interested and corroborative and even spontaneously complimentary. "I think it's odd but completely understandable that a man with your background—writing short stories and writing sports and a good education—would be happy selling houses in New Jersey. That just makes sense to me." Or "I like it, Frank, that you always order bluefish and pretty much dress the same way every time you come in here. It means you're sure about the little things, so you can leave yourself open for the big ones." She smiled so as to show her provocative dimple.

I told her about my Sponsoring activities and she said I seemed, to her experience, unusually kind and sensitive to others' needs. Once she even said, "I bet you've got a big lineup at your door, handsome, now that you're single again." (I've heard her call other men "handsome" and could care less.) I decided *not* to tell her about the titanium BBs situation, for fear she'd feel sorry for me—I couldn't see a use for pathos—but also because talking about the BBs can convince me I've lost the wherewithal even if I still have the wherefore.

Several times, I've stayed late at the Bistro, feeling better about myself and also about Bernice. Sometimes her shift would end and she'd come out from the kitchen in a pea jacket over her pink waitress dress and walk over and say, "So, Franklin"—not my name—"happy trails to you." But then she'd sit and we'd talk, during which occasions I'd become the funniest, cleverest, the wisest, the most instructive, the most complex, enigmatic and strangely attractive of all men, but also the best, most attentive listener-back that anybody on earth had ever heard of. I'd quote Emerson and Rochefoucauld and Eliot and Einstein, remember incisive, insightful but obscure historical facts that perfectly fitted into our discussions but that I never remembered talking about to anyone else, all the while dredging up show-tune lyrics and Bud & Lou gags and statistics about everything from housing starts in Bergen County to how many salmon pass through the fish ladder up at Bellows Falls in a typical twenty-four-hour period during the spring run. I became, in other words, an ideal man, a man I myself was crazy about and in love with and any-body else would be, too. All because—though I never specifically said so to her—Bernice was herself an ideal woman. Not ideal *per se*, but ideal *per diem*, the only place ideal really makes much difference. I realize as I say all this that my "Bernice experience" and my current willingness to rekindle it represents another small skirmish into the Permanent Period and away from the strict confines of the Next Level. Sometimes, though, you have to seek help where you know you can find it.

On late after-shift evenings, I sometimes would walk outside the Bistro with Bernice onto the warm beach-town sidewalk, when the air was cooling and things were buzzing last summer and, later on, after my procedure, and when most visitors had gone home in September. We'd stand at the curb or walk, not holding hands or anything like that, down to the beach and talk about global warming or Americans' inexplicable prejudice against the French or President Clinton's sadly missed opportu-nities and the losses that won't ever be recovered. I always had, when I was with Bernice, unusual takes on things, historical perspectives I didn't even know I possessed, bits of memorized speeches and testimony I'd heard on Public Radio that somehow came back to me in detail and that made me seem as savvy as a diplomat and wise as an oracle, with total recall and flawless sense of context, all of it with a winning ability to make fun of myself, not be stuffy or world-weary, but then at a moment's notice to be completely ready to change the subject to something she was interested in, or something else I knew more about than anybody in the world.

In all of this rather ordinary time together, Bernice had persistently positive things to say about me: that I was young for my age (without knowing my age, which I guessed she guessed was forty-five), that I led an interesting life now and had a damn good one in front of me, that I was "strangely intense" and intuitive and probably was a handful, but not really a type-A personality, which she knew she didn't like.

I said about her all the good things that I thought: that she was "a major looker," that her independent "Fighting Bob" La Follette instincts were precisely what this country needed, that I'd love to see her "work" and had a hunch it would wow me and I'd be drawn to it, implying but not actually saying that *she* wowed me and I was drawn to her (which was sort of true).

Once, Bernice asked me if I'd like to take a drive and smoke some reefer (I declined). And once she said she'd finished a "big nude" just that day and would be interested to know what a guy with my heightened sensibilities and intuition would think about it, since it was "pretty abstract" (I assumed it was a self-portrait and burned to see it). But I declined that, too. I understood that how we felt, standing out on the curb or at the edge of the beach, where the street came to an end and the twinkling shank of the warm evening opened out like a pathway of stars to where the old ferris wheel turned like a bracelet of jewels down at the Sea-Clift Fun Pier—I understood that how we felt was good and might conceivably get better if we had a Sambuca or two and a couple of bong hits at her place and took a look at her big nude. But then pretty quickly who we really were would assert itself, and it wouldn't feel good for long and we'd end up looking back at our moment on the curb, before anything happened, with slightly painful nostalgia—the way emigrants are said to feel when they leave home, thrilled to set sail for the new land, where life promises riches but where hardships await, and in the end old concerns are only transported to a new venue, where they (we) go back to worrying the same as before. When you're young, like my daughter, Clarissa, and maybe even my son, you don't think like that. You think that all it takes is to get free of one box and into a bigger one out in the mainstream. Change the water in your bowl and you become a different fish. But that's not so. No siree, Bob, not a bit. It's also true that because of the fiery BBs in my prostate, and despite early-morning and even occasionally late-night erectile events giving positive testimony, I wasn't sure of my performance ratings under new pressures and definitely didn't want to face another failure when so few things seemed to be going my way.

Now, though, I believe is the time—if ever one was ordained —for Bernice and me to lash our tiny boats together, at least for the day, and set sail a ways toward sunset. Nothing permanent, nothing that even needs to last past dark, nothing specifically venereal or proto-conjugal (unless that just happens), but still an occasion, an eleventh-hour turn toward the unexpected—the very thing that can happen in life to let us know we're human, and that could even prove I'm the handful Bernice always knew I'd be and perhaps still am. All this, of course, if it seems like a good idea to her.

Neptune's Daily Catch Bistro, I already know from our local Shore weekly, is serving its twenty-dollar turkey 'n trimmings buffet to all Ortley Beach seniors, eleven to two. Bernice— because she casually told me—is without companionship today and only working to give herself something to do, then heading home with a jug of Chablis to "watch the Vikes and Dallas at 4:05," before turning in early. My guess is if I cruise in right at one, almost now, and tell her I'm taking her away for a holiday feast, she'll beg off with the boss, leave her apron on the door-knob, see the whole idea as a complete blast that I've had planned for weeks, feel secretly flattered and relieved and sure she's had me pegged right and that I'm fuller of surprises than she ima-gined and that all her appreciation of me these years wasn't wrong or wasted. In other words, she'll recognize that I recog-nize *her* as the ideal woman, and that even if she's home in time for the nightly news, she'll have gotten more than she bargained for—which is all that usually counts with humans.

And as an added inducement, bringing Bernice Podmanicsky for Thanksgiving dinner will drive my kids crazy. Worse than if I'd brought home a Finnish midget from the circus, a six-foot-eight fag comb-out assistant from Kurl Up 'n Dye in Laval-lette, or a truckload of talking parrots that sing Christmas carols *a cappella*. It'll drive them—Paul especially—into paralyzed, abashed and scalding, renunciating silence, which is what I may now require of my Thanksgiving festivity. Loathing will run at warp speed. Sinister "What's happened to *him*?" grimaces will radar between siblings who already don't like each other. Your kids may be the hapless victims of divorce and spend their lives "working out" their "issues" on everybody in sight, but they damn straight don't want you to have any issues, or for *their* boats to get rocked while they're doing their sanctified "work." They want instead for you to provide them a stable environment for their miseries (they might as well *be* adopted). Except my view is that if kids are happy to present us aging parents with their own improbabilities, why not return the favor? A diverse table of Paul, Jill, Clarissa, Thom, Bernice and myself seems more or less perfect. As is often the case, given time, "things" come into better focus.

And yet. Best case? It could bring out the unforeseeable best in everybody and cause Thanksgiving to blossom into the extended-family, come-one-come-all good fellowship the Pilgrims might (for a millisecond) have thought they were ringing in by inviting the baffled, mostly starved Indians to their table. Paul's time capsule could turn out to be the rallying projectile he may—or may not—want it to be. Clarissa could send Thom away two-thirds through the bulgur course, and we could all laugh like chimps at what a sorry sack he was. Bernice could do her full repertoire of America's Dairyland imitations. We might even ask the Feensters in and watch them combust. I could be made happy by any or all or none of these, and the day could end no worse than it began. Though I'd still like Bernice Podmanic-sky with me, just as my personal *friend* against the difficulties that are likely waiting. She would think it was all—whatever it was—a riot or a trip or awesome, and be agreeable when we excused ourselves from the table to take a sunset stroll on the beach, where we could both make ourselves feel ideal all over again, after which I could take her home for the second half of the

Vikes' game—which I might stay for. I'd tell Sally all about it later and be certain she wouldn't care.

CENTRAL BOULEVARD enters Ortley Beach from Seaside Heights without fanfare—both being Route 35—the same no-skyline weather-beaten townscape of closed sub shops, blue Slurpee stands, tropical fish outlets and metal-detector rentals, where I'm thinking the 5-K runners must have now come and gone, since I see none of them. In the election three weeks ago—the life-threatening part of which is still unsettled in the Florida court—Ortley Beach gave its own voters their chance to ratify a non-binding "opinion" by the Boro attorney that the town could secede from New Jersey and join a new entity called "South Jersey." But like our naming-rights initiative, this was hooted down by Republicans as being fiscal suicide, not to mention civically odd and bad for business. Sea-Clift—nearer the end of Barnegat Neck, and farther south—would've ended up marooned in "Old Jersey," tolls could've been exacted just for the privilege of leaving town, while Ortley would have had a different governor and a state bird. Municipal conflict would've erupted, had cooler heads not prevailed. Though even now I see a few inflaming SECESSION OR DIE stickers still plastered on stop signs and a few juice-shop windows. It's always been a strange place here, though you can't tell by looking.

What I see as I approach the Neptune's Daily Catch doesn't make my heart hopeful. No cars are parked in front. The blue neon fish sign is turned off. As I pull to the curb, inside appears empty. Grainy daylight falls in through the big windows, turning the interior dishwater gray. Chairs are upside down on tabletops. Next door, the Women of Substance second-hand shop is closed. The Parallel Universe video arcade is open three doors down, but only a thin bald man's standing in the door alone, reading a magazine. Four men in khaki clothing and heavy corduroy jackets wait at the corner under the Garden State Parkway sign, smoking cigarettes and drinking coffee from the Wawa across Central. Mexicans, these are. Illegals—unlike my Hondurans—hoping to be picked up for a job across the bridge, unaware today's a holiday. They eye me and laugh as if I'm the cops and they're invisible.

The thought, however, that I may be wrong and Bernice is inside at a back table having an Irish coffee alone, awaiting opening time, makes me get out and peer through the plate-glass window. Arnie Sikma, the owner, is an old Reed College SDSer who's evolved into a community-activist, small-business booster, and has stuck various groups' advertising stickers on his front window beside the door. ORTLEY, AN UNUSUAL NAME FOR THE USUAL PLACE. WE ROOT FOR THE PHILLIES. SUPPORT OUR TROOPS (from Gulf War days). PROTECT RAPTORS, NOT RAPISTS. THIS, TOO, SHALL PASS—JERSEY SHORE NEPHRO-LOGY CLINIC. PEOPLE HAVE TO DIE . . . SOMEWHERE (a hospice in Point Pleasant).

But no Bernice when I peer in between my cupped hands. Or anyone. Arnie's left the Christmas Muzak on outside—"Good King Wenceslas" sung by a choir. "Yon-der pea-sant, who is he, where and what his dwel-ling—" No one out in the cold hears it but me and the Mexicans.

Though a hand-written note scotch-taped to the door announces that, "We will be closed Thanksgiving Day due to a loss in our family. God Bless You All. The Mgt."—naturally a sign that alarms me. Since does it mean *family* family (Arnie's of Dutch extraction in Hudson, New York, up-river—a distant relation of the original patroons)? Or does it mean extended family? The Neptune's Daily Catch Bistro "family" of trusted employees. Does it mean Bernice, heretofore scheduled to work the buffet? Though wouldn't it mention her name—like the Van Tuyll daughter Ann told me about two nights ago? "Our trusted and beloved Miss B—"

A hot sizzling sensation spreads up my cold neck, then spreads down again. How can I find out? I once called *information* to learn if Bernice was listed, in case I someday decided to call her and needed to be made to feel like my best self in return for a movie ticket to the Toms River Multiplex and a late dinner at Bump's. I found out she possessed a phone but didn't choose to list its number. Waitresses rarely do. I couldn't very well tell the oper-ator, "Yeah, but she thinks I'm great. It's fine. I won't give the number to anybody or do anything weird." Those innocent days are behind us now.

Gusty ocean air with a strong grease smell in it pushes a white Styrofoam container along the sidewalk—the kind of container you'd carry your unfinished fried calamari home in. One of the khaki-suited Mexicans gives the container a soccer kick out into the boulevard, which inspires another, smaller Mexican to address the box with a complex series of side kicks and heel kicks that finally send it flying in the air. His associates all laugh and sing out "Ronal*dito*," which amuses the kicker, who sashays back up onto the curb and makes them all howl.

A skinny, elderly bald man in red running shorts and a blue singlet with a 5-K card on his chest—#174—glides past us up Central on bulky in-lines, arm swings propelling him like a speed skater, one hand tucked behind, his old eagle's face as serene as the breeze. He is heading home. The Mexicans all eye him with amusement.

I gaze up to the woolen sky and think of good-soul Bernice, her sweet breath, full smiling lips, dainty ankles, dense virile hair not everyone would go for and that possibly I didn't go for or else I'd know her phone number. Where is she today? Safe? Sound? Not so good? How would I find out? Call Arnie Sikma at home the minute I arrive. Ask for her number as a special favor. High up and to the north, a pale blue and optimistic fissure has opened in the undercloud. Two jet con-trails, one southerly, one headed east and out to sea, have crossed there, leaving a giant and, for an instant, perfect X at 39,000 feet above where I am, in Ortley, outside a good fish place, contemplating the life of a friend. X marks my spot (and every place else that can see it). "Begin here. This is where I left it. This is where the gold is. This is—" what?

Only the most dry-mouthed Cartesian wouldn't see this as a patent signal, a communiqué from the spheres, an important box on an important form with my name on top—X'd in or X'd out, counted present or absent. You'd just need to know what the fucker means, wouldn't you? There may have been others. Two swans on the bay shore. A quick red fox in the bedroom. A letter. A call. Three boats. All can be signage. I'd thought Ralph's finality, my acceptance and succession to the Next Level and general fittedness to meet my Maker were my story, what the audience would know once my curtain closed—my, so-to-speak, character. "He made peace with things, finally, old Frank." "He was kind of a shit-bird, but he got it sorted out pretty good just before—" "He actually seemed clear-sighted, damn near saint-like toward the end there—" This happens when you have cancer, though it's not a fun happening.

Except now there's *more*? Just when you think you've been admitted to the boy-king's burial chamber and can breathe the rich, ancient captured air with somber satisfaction, you find out it's just another anteroom? That there's more that bears watching, more signs requiring interpretation, that what you thought was all, isn't? That this isn't *it*? That there's no *it*, only *is*. Hard to know if this is heartening or disheartening news to a man who, as my son says, believes in development.

The cloud fissure has now closed primly, and what was a sign—like a rainbow—is no more. Somehow I know that Bernice Podmanicsky is not the family member lost. She'd laugh to know I even worried about her. "Oh, handsome"—she'd beam at me—"I didn't know you cared. You're just such an unusual man, aren't ya? A real handful. Some lucky girl—" It's odd how our fears, the ones we didn't know we had, alter our sight line and make us see things that never were.

The Mexicans are all looking at me as if I've been carrying on a boisterous conversation with myself. Possibly it's my block-M. I should take it off and give it to them. Their faces are serious, their small grabby hands jammed in their tattered jacket pockets. Their expectancy of work is being clouded over by my suspicious starings into the Bistro and the firmament. They are religious men and on the lookout for signs of their own, one of which I may have become. Possibly I'm "touched" and am about to be drawn up into heaven by a lustrous beam of light and they (in the good version) will find true vocations at last: to tell the thing they saw and of its wonders. Is that not the final wish of all of us on earth? To testify of our witness to wonders?

But as an assurance, since I cannot ascend to heaven in front of them today, I'd still like to speak something typically First World and welcoming, put them off their guard. We are together, after all. Simple me. Simple them.

Only when I turn their way, a welcome grin gladdening my cheeks, my eyes crinkling up happy, my mind concocting a formulation in their mother tongue—"*Hola. ¿Cómo están? ¿Pasandan un buen día?*"—they stiffen, set their narrow shoulders and lock their knees inside their khakis, their faces organized to say they want *nada* of me, seek no assurance, offer none. So that all I can do is freeze my grin like a crazy man caught in his craziness. They look away at the empty boulevard to search for the truck that isn't coming. For all five of us, together and apart, the moment for signs goes past.

HEADED HOME now, fully contextualized, vacant of useful longing. Bernice could've conferred a sporty insularity, made me feel my own weight less. Even un-ideal women can do this. But help's not available, which is a legitimate mode of acceptance. It just doesn't feel good.

Traffic lights are working again, candy-cane ornaments weakly lit. Commerce is flickering to life as I drive out of Seaside Park and re-enter Sea-Clift. LIQUOR has illuminated its big yellow letters at noon, and cars are flocking. The drive-thru ATM at South Shore Savings is doing a smart business, as is the adult books, Guppies to Puppies and the bottle redemption center—the former Ford dealership. The Wiggle Room has opened up, and a hefty blue New Jersey Waste snail-back is swaying into its back alley. There are even tourists outside the mini-golf/batting cage, their nonchalant gestures betraying seasonal uncertainty, their gazes skyward. The green EMS wagon rests back in its Fire Department bay, the same crew as earlier out front under the waving American flag, sharing a smoke and a joke with the two jodhpured motorcycle cops who guarded the race. The Tru-Value is holding its "Last Chance Y-2K Special" on plastic containers and gas masks. THE FUTURE WAS A BOMB, their hand-lettered sign says.

Many of the 5-K runners are here straggling home along the sidewalks and down the residential side streets, their race run, their faces relaxed, limbs loosened by honest non-cutthroat competition, their water bottles empty, their gazes turned toward what's next in the way of healthy, wholesome Thanksgiving partaking. (There's no sign of the Africans.) I still wouldn't want to be any of them. Though one scrawny red-shoed runner waves at my car as I pass—I have no idea who—someone I sold a house to or busted my ass trying, but left a good impression of the kinda guy I am. I give a honk but head on.

When I cruise past my Realty-Wise office, Mike's Infiniti sits by itself in front. The pizza place is lighted and going, though no one seems to want a pizza for Thanksgiving. Doubtless, Mike's at his desk tweaking his business plan, re-conferring with his new friend, the money bags. He may be trying the Bagosh family on his cell before they hit the Parkway after lunch. I lack the usual gusto to go have a look-see at what he's up to—which makes business itself seem far away and its hand-over a sounder idea. How, though, will I feel to "have sold" real estate and sell it no more? The romance of it could fade once the past tense takes over. Different from, "Well, yeah, I usta fly 16's up in that Bacca Valley. Pretty hairy up there." Or, "Our whole lab shared credit on the malaria cure." The only way to keep the glamour lights on in the real-estate commitment is to keep doing it. Do it till you drop dead, so you never have to look back and see the shadows. Most of the old-timers know that, which is why so many go feet first. This won't please Mike, but fuck Mike. It's my business, not his.

Ahead, beyond the old shuttered Dad 'n Lad, where the Boro of Sea-Clift originally ended because the topsoil ran out and the primeval white sand beach took up, the old Ocean Vista Cemetery, where Sea-Clift's citizens were buried back in the Twenties, lies shabbily ignored and gone to weeds. The Boro officially maintains it, keeps up its New Orleans-style wrought iron fence and little arched filigree gate that opens pleasantly down a slender *allée* three-quarters of a city block toward the sea, where the ocean vista's long been blocked by grandfathered frame residences that have gone to seed themselves but can't be replaced. No one is currently at rest in Ocean Vista, not even gravestones remain. The ground—alongside the Dad 'n Lad—looks like nothing but a small-size shard of excess urban landscape awaiting assignment by developers who'll tear down the whole block of elderly structures and put up a Red Roof Inn or a UPS store—the same as happened on a grand scale in Atlantic City.

The particular reason our only town cemetery no longer has residents is that the great-great-grandchildren of Sea-Clift's first Negro pioneer, a freed slave known only as "Jonah," somehow discovered him interred plumb in the middle of the otherwise-white cemetery, and began agitating at the state level for a monument solemnizing his life and toilsome times as a "black trailblazer" back when being a trailblazer wasn't cool. Jonah's progeny turned out to be noisy, well-heeled Philadelphia and

D.C. plutocrat lawyers and M.D.'s, who wanted to have their ancestor memorialized as another stop on the Coastal Heritage Trail, with an interactive display about his life and the lives of folk like him who valiantly diversified the Shore—a story that was possibly not going to be all that flattering to his white contemporaries.

Whereupon all hell broke loose. The town elders, who'd always known about Jonah's resting place and felt fine about him sharing it with their ancestors, did not, however, want him "stealing" the cemetery and posthumously militating for importance he apparently hadn't claimed in life. Jonah had his rightful place, it was felt, among other Sea-Clifters, and that was enough. The grandchildren, however, sniffing prejudice, commenced court proceedings and EEOC actions to have the Boro Council sued in federal court. Everything got instantly blown out of proportion, at which point an opportunistic burial-vault company with European Alliance affiliations in Brick Township offered free of charge to dig up and re-inter anybody whose family wanted its loved one to enjoy better facilities in a new and treeless memory park they had land for out Highway 88. Everyone—there were only fifteen families— said sure. The town issued permits. All the graves—except Jonah's—were lovingly opened, their sacred contents hearsed away, until in a month's time poor old Jonah had the cemetery all to his lonesome. Whereupon, the litigious Philadelphians decided Jonah and his significance had been municipally disrespected and so applied for a permit themselves and moved him to Cherry Hill, where people apparently know better how to treat a hero.

The town is still proprietor of the cemetery and awaits the happy day when the Red Roof site-evaluation crew shows up seeking a variance and a deconsecration order. For a time—two winters ago—I proposed buying the ground myself and turning it into a vernal park as a gesture of civic giving, while retaining development rights should the moment ever come. I even considered not deconsecrating it and having myself buried there— a kingdom of one. This was, of course, before my prostate issues. I'd always pondered—without a smidge of trepidation—where I'd "end up," since once you wander far from your own soil, you never know where your final resting place might be. Which is why many people don't stray off their porch or far from familiar sights and sounds. Because if you're from Hog Dooky, Alabama, you don't want to wind up dead and anonymously buried in Metuchen, New Jersey. In my case, I thought it would've saved my children the trouble of knowing what in the hell to do with "me," and just deciding to entrust my remains to some broken-down old Cap'n Mouzakis who'd "return" me to the sea from whence as a frog I came. You could say it's a general problem, however—uncertainty over where and how you want to be eternally stowed. Either it represents your last clinging to life, or else it's the final muddled equivocation about the life you've actually lived.

Not surprisingly, insider development interests on the Dollars For Doers Council saw disguised dreams of empire behind my petition and declined my cash offer for the cemetery. The "civic giving" part put them on their guard. Which was and is fine with me. Money not spent is money saved, in my economy. Though it has left as an open subject the awkward issue of my ending-up formalities. I have a will which leaves the house and Realty-Wise to Sally and all remaining assets to the kids—not much, though they'll get plenty from their mom, including a membership in the Huron Mountain Club. But that picture's different since Sally left for Mull, and could shift again, since she could come back and Mike now wants the business. I'd even thought the three of us nuclear-family components might sit around a con-genial breakfast table during the coming days and talk these sensitive matters into commonsense resolution. But that was prior to re-exposure to Paul (and Jill), and hearing of his secret dreams to be my business partner. And before Clarissa hied off to Atlantic City, leaving me with the uneasy sensation she'll return changed. In other words, events have left life and my grasp on the future in as fucked-up a shape as I can imagine them. Life alters when you get sick, no matter what I told Ann. Don't let any of these Sunny Jims tell you different.

WHAT I DON'T expect to find in my driveway is activity. But activity is what I find. Next door at the Feensters', as well. Thanksgiving, in my playbook, is an indoor event acted out between kitchen and table, table and TV, TV and couch (and later bed). Outdoor activity, particularly driveway activity, fore-shadows problems and events unwanted: genies exiting bottles, dikes bursting, de-stability at the top—anti-Thanksgiving grem-lins sending celebrants scattering for their cars. The outcome I didn't want.

The Feensters appear unimplicated. Nick has set up shop in his driveway and is giving his twin '56 vintage Vettes the careful hand-waxing they deserve and frequently get (cold-weather bonding issues, what the hell). Drilla, in a skirt and sweater, is seated on the front step, hugging her knees and petting Bimbo in her lap as if now was July. Nick is, as usual, luridly turned out in one of his metallic Lycra bodysuits—electric blue, showing off his muscles and plenty of bulgy dick—the same outfit the neigh-borhood is used to seeing during his and Drilla's stern-miened beach constitutionals, when they each listen to separate Walk-men. Though because it's wintry, Nick has added some kind of space-age silver-aluminum anorak you'd buy in catalogs only lottery winners from Bridgeport get sent for free. Seen through his derelict topiary, he is a strange metallic sight on Thanksgiving. Though if Nick wasn't such an asshole, there'd be something touching about the two of them, since clearly they don't know what to do with themselves today, and could easily end up gloomy and alone at the Ruby Tuesday's in Belmar. Likewise, if Nick weren't such an asshole, I'd walk over and ask them to come join our family sociality, since there's too much food anyway. Possibly next year. I give him a noncommittal wave as I pass and turn in my own drive. Nick repays it with a black stare of what looks like disgust, though Drilla, clutching the dog, waves back smally and smiles in the invisible sunshine—her smile indicating that if a man like Nick is your husband, nothing's easy in life.

However, it's my own driveway that's cause for concern. If I'd noticed in time, I might've driven back to the office, listened to Mike's business proposal, sold the whole shitaree, then come home a half hour later in a changed frame of mind.

Paul and his lofty Jill are out on the pea-gravel drive in holiday attire and absorbed in an arms-folded, head-nodding confab with a man I don't know but whose chocolate brown Crown Vic sits on the road by the arborvitae and Paul's ramshackle gray Saab. Possibly this is a client prospect who's tracked me down, holiday or no, in hopes I'll have the key to the beach house he's noticed in the *Buyer's Guide* and can't wait to see. Paul may be dry-running his new agent's persona, gassing about time capsules, greeting-card pros and cons, the Chiefs' chances for the Super Bowl and how special it is being a New Jersey native.

Only this guy's no realty walk-up, nor is his car a usual car. His body language lacks the tense but casual hands-in-pockets, feet-apart posture of protective customer indecision. This man is dapper and small, with both hands free at his sides like a cop, with thick blunt-cut Neapolitan hair, a long brown leather jacket over a brown wool polo and heavy black brogues with telltale crepe soles. He looks like a cop because he is a cop. Plenty of ordinary Americans living ordinary citizen lives dress exactly this way, but nobody looks this way dressed this way but cops. It's no wonder crime's on the uptick. They've given away the element of surprise to the element—to the window bashers, hospital bombers and sign stealers of the world.

But why is a cop in my driveway? Why is his brown cop car with MUNICIPAL license plates conspicuously parked in front of my house on Thanksgiving, dragging my family outside when law-abiding citizens should be inside stuffing their faces and arguing?

Clarissa. A heart flutter, a new burning up my back. He is an emissary of doleful news. Like in *The Fighting Sullivans*, when the grief squad marches up the steps. Her re-entry to conventionality has already come to ruin. Not thinkable.

All three turn as I climb out, leaving Mike's business plan on the seat, my gait hitched again and slowed. I'm smiling—but only out of habit. The Feensters—I couldn't hear it from my car— have their boom box at its usual high decibels, apparently to aid in waxing. "Lisbon Antigua" again—their way of getting their Thanksgiving message out: Fuck you.

"Hi," I say. "What's the trouble here, Officer?" I intend this to be funny, but it isn't. There can't be bad news.

"This is Detective Marinara, Frank," Paul says in the most normal of imaginable voices, tuned to the exquisite pleasure of saying "Detective Marinara." I can smell cops. Though this, thanks to the signs above, will not be about Clarissa, but me.

Paul and Jill—she's looking at me sorrowfully, as though I'm Paul's crippled parent—have transubstantiated themselves since our basement get-together. Jill has severely pulled much of her long, dense yellow hair "back," but left skimpy fringe bangs, plus a thick, concupiscent braid that swags down behind her like a rope. From her travel wardrobe, she's chosen a green flare-bottomed pantsuit with some sort of shiny golden underhue and a pair of clunky black shoes that show off the length of her feet and that, as an ensemble, renders her basically gender-neutral. She's also attached a flesh-tinted holiday hand prosthesis, barely detectable as not the real thing, though not flexible like a hand you'd want. Paul, from somewhere, has found a strange suit—a too-large summer-weight blue-gray-and-pink plaid with landing-strip lapels, gutter-deep cuffs and English vents—a style popular ten years before he was born and that everyone joked about even then. With his mullet, his uncouth beard-stache and ear stud, his suit makes him look like a burlesque comedian. He looks as if he could break out a ukelele and start crooning in an Al Jolson voice. Just seeing him makes me long for sweet and affirming Bernice. She could set things right in a heartbeat, though I don't really know her.

"I'm impressed with your place here, Mr. Bascombe." Detective Marinara scans around and grins at the way some people can live, but not him: ocean-front contemporary, lots of glass and light, high ceilings—the works. He's a small, handsome, feline-looking man with long, spidery fingers, dark worried eyes and a small shapely nose. He could've been a sixth-man guard in Division III, maybe for Muhlenberg, who only heeded the call to police work because of his "soshe" degree and a desire to stay close to his folks in Dutch Neck. These guys make detective in a hurry and aren't adept at cracking skulls.

"I'd be happy to sell it to you," I say, and try to look happy. "I'll move out today." I'm not comfortable standing in front of my house with a cop, as if I'm soon to be leaving in handcuffs. Though it could happen to any of us.

"I was down at my sister's," Detective Marinara says. "I told you she lives in Barnegat Acres." His interested eyes survey around professionally. They pass my busted duct-taped window, Sally's LeBaron, pass the Feensters, my son, Jill. "They do the whole Italian spread," he says. "You need to take a breather though. So I wandered down here. Your son happened to be outside."

"We asked Detective Marinara to have Thanksgiving with

us," Paul says with barely suppressible glee at the discomfort this will cause me (it does). His fingers, I can see, are working. When he was a boy, he "counted" with his fingers—cars on the highway, birds on wires, individual seconds during our lengthy disciplinary discussions, breaths during his therapy sessions at Yale and Hopkins. He eventually quit. But now he's counting again in his weird suit, his warty fingers jittering, jittering. Something's wound him up again—a cop, of course. Jill is aware and smiles at him supportively. They are an even stranger pair all dressed up.

"That'd be great," I say. "We've got plenty of free-range organic turkey."

"Oh, no. I'm all set there. Thanks." Marinara continues panning around. This is not a social visit. He pauses to give a lengthy disapproving stare at Nick Feenster, buffing his Vettes in his Lycra space suit, Pérez Prado banging up into the atmosphere, where a whoosh of blackbirds goes over in an undulant cloud. "That's a plate-full over there, I guess."

"It is," I admit. Though the old sympathy again filters up for the poor all-wrong Feensters, who, I'm sure, suffer great needless misery and loneliness here in New Jersey with their Bridgeport social skills. My heart goes out to them, which is better than hoping they'll die.

Nick has seen Detective Marinara and me observing him across the property line. He stands up from buffing, his Lycra further stressing his smushed genitals, and gives us back a malignant "Yeah? What?" stare, framed by topiary. He doesn't know Marinara's the heat. His lips move, but "Lisbon Antigua" blots out his voice. He jerks his head around to fire words off to Drilla—to crank up the volume, probably. She says something back, possibly "don't be such an asshole," and he waves his buffing pad at us in disgust and resumes rubbing. Drilla looks wistfully out toward where Poincinet curves to meet 35. She'd be a better neighbor married to someone else.

"I could flash my gold on that clown, tune him down a notch." Marinara shoots his sweater cuffs out of his jacket sleeves. An encounter would feel good to him about now. Conflict, I'm sure, calms him. He's a divorcé, under forty. He's full of fires.

"He'll quit," I say. "He has to listen to it, too."

Marinara shakes his head at how the world acts. "Whatever." It is the policeman's *weltanschauung.*

Exactly then, as if on cue, the music stops and airy silence opens. Drilla—Bimbo under one arm—stands and walks inside, carrying the boom box. Nick, his voice softened to indecipherability, speaks something appeasing to her. But she goes inside and closes the front door, leaving him alone with his buffing implements. It's the way I knew it would happen.

I am thinking for this instant, and longingly, about Sally, whose call I've now missed. And about Clarissa. It's 1:30 already. She should be home. The Eat No Evil people will be here soon. All this brings with itself a sinking sensation. I don't feel thankful for anything. What I'd like to do is get in bed with my book of Great Speeches, read the Gettysburg Address out loud to no one and invite Jill and Paul to go find dinner at a Holiday Inn.

The mixed rich fragrance of salt breeze, Detective Marinara's professional-grade leather coat and no doubt his well-oiled weapon tucked on his hip, all now enter my nostrils and make me realize once again that this is not a social call. Nothing can make a day go flat like a police presence.

Paul and Jill stand silent, side-by-side in their holiday get-ups. They say nothing, intend nothing. They are as I am—in the thrall of the day and the law's arrival.

"This is not a social call, I don't think."

"Not entirely." Detective Marinara adjusts his cop's brogues in the driveway gravel. His precise, intent features have rendered him an appealing though slightly sorrowing customer—like a young Bobby Kennedy, without the big teeth. I have the keenest feeling, against all reason, that he could arrest me. He's sensed "something" in my carriage, in my house's too rich *affect* (the redwood, the copper weather vane), my car, my strange children, my white Nikes, something that makes him wonder if I'm not at least complicitous *somewhere.* Surely not in setting a bomb at Haddam Doctors and heedlessly taking the life of Natherial Lewis, but in *something* that still requires looking at. And maybe he's exactly right. Who can say with certainty that he/she did or didn't do anything? Why should I be exempted? Lord knows, I'm guilty (of something). I should go quietly. I don't say these words, but I think them. This may be what Marguerite Purcell experienced, though I'll never know.

What I do say apprehensively is, "What gives, then?" The corners of Paul's mouth and also his bad eye twitch toward me. "What gives, then?" is gangster talk he naturally relishes.

"Just standard cop work, Mr. Bascombe." Marinara produces a square packet of QUIT SMOKING, NOW gum from his jacket pocket, unsheathes a piece, sticks it in his mouth and thoughtlessly pockets the wrapper. Possibly he wears a nicotine "patch" below his BORN TO RUN tattoo. "We're pretty sure we got this thing tied up. We know who did it. But we just like to throw all our answers out the window and open it up and look one last time. You were on our list. You were there, you knew the victim. Not that we suspect you." He is chewing mildly. "You know?"

"I tell people the same thing when they buy a house." I do not feel less guilty.

"I'm sure." Detective Marinara, chewing, looks appraisingly up at my house again, taking in its modern vertical lines, its flashings, copings, soffit vents, its board-and-batten plausibility, its road-facing modesty and affinity for the sea. My house may be an attractive mystery he feels excluded from, which silences him and makes him feel out of place now that he's decided murderers don't live here. Belonging is no more his metier than mine.

"Must be okay to wake up here every day," he says. Paul and Jill have no clue what we're talking about—my car window, an outstanding warrant, an ax murder. Children always hear things when they don't expect it.

"It's just nice to wake up at all," I say, to be self-deprecating about living well.

"You got that right," Marinara says. "I wake up dreading all the things I have to do, and every one of them's completely do-able. What's that about? I oughta be grateful, maybe." He gazes up Poincinet Road, along the line of my neighbors' large house fronts to where only empty beach stretches far out of sight. A few seaside walkers animate the vista but don't really change its mood of exclusivity. The air is grainy and neutral-toned with moisture. You can see a long way. On the horizon, where the land meets the sea, small shore-side bumps identify the Ferris wheel Bernice and I admired on our evenings together months ago. I wonder again where and how my daughter is, whether I've missed Sally's call. Important events seem to be escaping me.

"Detective Marinara was considerate enough to give me his business card to put in the time capsule." Paul speaks these words abruptly and, as always, too loud, like someone introducing quiz-show contestants. Jill inches in closer, as if he might lift off like a bottle rocket. She touches her prosthesis to his hand for reassurance. "I gave him one of my Smart Aleck cards." Paul, my son, mulleted, goateed, softish and strange-suited, again could be any age at this moment—eleven, sixteen, twenty-six, thirty-five, sixty-one.

"Okay, yeah. Okay." Marinara jabs a hand (his wristwatch is on a gold chain bracelet) into his leather jacket pocket, where his QUIT SMOKING packet went, and fishes out a square card, which he looks at without smiling, then hands to me. I have, of course, seen Paul's work before. My impolitic response to it was the flash point in last spring's fulminant visit. I have to be cautious now. The card Marinara hands me seems to be a photograph, a black and white, showing a great sea of Asians—Koreans, Chinese, I don't know which—women and men all dressed in white Western wedding garb, fluffy dresses and regulation tuxes, all beaming together up into an elevated camera's eye. There must be no fewer than twenty thousand of them, since they fill the picture so you can't see the edge or make out where the photograph's taken—the Gobi Desert, a soccer stadium, Tiananmen Square. But it's definitely the happiest day of their lives, since they seem about to be married or to have just gotten that way in one big bunch. Paul's sidesplitting caption below, in red block letters, says "GUESS WHAT????" And when opened, the card, in bigger red Chinese-looking English letters, shouts "WE'RE PREGNANT!!!"

Paul is staring machine-gun holes into me. I can feel it. The card I stupidly didn't respond to properly last spring featured a chrome-breasted, horse-faced blonde in a Fifties one-piece bathing suit and stiletto heels, grinning lasciviously while lining up a bunch of white mice dressed in tiny racing silks along a tiny starting stripe. It was clearly a *still* from an old porn movie devoted to all the interesting things one can do with rodents. The tall blonde had dollar bills sprouting out her cleavage and her grin contained a look of knowing lewdness that unquestionably implicated the mice. Paul's caption (sad and heart-wrenching for his father) was "Put Your Money Where Your Mouse Is."

I didn't think it was very funny but should've faked it, given the fury I unleashed.

But this time, I'm ready—though the cold driveway setting isn't ideal. I've slowly creased my lips to form two thick mouth-corners of insider irony. I narrow my eyes, turn and regard Paul with a special Chill Wills satchel-faced mawp he'll identify as my instant triple-entendre tumbling to all tie-ins, hilarious special nuances and resonances only the truly demented and ingeniously witty could appreciate and that no one should even be able to think of, much less write, without having gone to Harvard and edited the *Lampoon*. Except *he* has and can, even though he's in love with a big disabled person, is twenty pounds too pudgy and has mainstreamed himself damn near to flat-line out in K.C. You can hang too much importance on a smile of fatherly approval. But I'm not risking it.

"Okay, okay, okay," I say in dismissal that means approval. Standard words of approval would be much riskier. I do my creased-mouth Chill Wills mawp again for purposes of Paul's re-assessment and so we can travel on a while longer functioning as father and son. Parenthood, once commenced, finds its opportunities where it can. "Okay. That's funny," I say.

"I'm willing to admit"—Paul is officiously brimming with pleasure, while smoothing his beard-stache around his mouth like a seamy librarian—"that they rejected that one as too sensitive, ethnically. It was one of my favorites, though."

I'm tempted to comment that it pushes the envelope, but don't want to encourage him. His plaid joker's jacket is probably stuffed with other riotous rejects. "Grape Vines Think Alike." "The Elephant of Surprise." "The Margarine of Error." "Preston de Service"—all our old yuks and sweet guyings from his lost childhood now destined for the time capsule, since Hallmark can't use them. Too sensitive.

And then for the second time in ten minutes we are struck dumb out here, all four of us—me, Marinara, Paul and Jill—aware of something of small consequence that doesn't have a name, as though a new sound was in the air and each thinks the others can't hear it.

Loogah-loogah-loogah, blat-blat-blat-a-blat—a sound from down Poincinet Road. Terry Farlow, my neighbor, the Kazakhstan engineer, has fired up his big Fat Boy Harley in the echo chamber

of his garage. We all four turn, as if in fear, as the big CIA Oklahoman rolls magisterially out onto his driveway launching pad,
black-suited, black-helmeted as an evil knight, an identically
dressed Harley babe on the bitch seat, regal and helmeted as a
black queen. *Loogah, loogah, loogah.* He pauses, turns, activates
the automatic garage-door closer, gives his babe a pat to the knee,
settles back, gears down, tweaks the engine—*blat-a-blat-BLAT-
blat-blat-blat*—then eases off, boots up, out and down Poincinet,
idling past the neighbors' houses and mine with nary a nod
(though we're all four watching with gaunt admiration). He
slowly rounds the corner past the Feensters'—Nick ignores
him—accelerates throatily out onto 35, and begins throttling up,
catches a more commanding gear, then rumbles on up the highway toward his Thanksgiving plans, whatever they might offer.

To my shock, I can't suppress the aching suspicion that the
helmeted, steel-thighed honey, high on the passenger perch,
gloved hands clutching Terry's lats, knees pincering his buns,
inner-thigh hot place pressed thrillingly to his coccyx, was
Bernice Podmanicsky, my almost-savior from the day's woolly
woes, and who I was just thinking might still be reachable.
Wouldn't she know I'd sooner or later be calling? The Harley,
already a memory up Route 35, stays audible a good long time,
passing through its gears until it attains its last.

I've handed back Detective Marinara's "We're Pregnant"
card. He studies it a moment, as though he'd never really looked
before, then effects a mirthless, comprehending smile at all the
grinning brides and beaming grooms. This is not what Paul had
in mind: vague amusement. I'm close enough to smell Marinara's
QUIT SMOKING gum, his breath, cigarette-warm and medicine-
sweet. He dyes his hair its shiny shade of too-black black, and
down in his bristly chest hair, tufted out of his brown polo, he
wears a gold chain—finer than his watchband—with a gold heart
and tiny gold cross strung together. My original guess was Dutch
Neck, but now I think Marinara hails from the once all-Italian
President streets of Haddam—Jefferson, Madison, Monroe,
Cleveland, etc.—a neighborhood where I once resided, where
Ann resides today and where once Paul and Clarissa were sweet
children.

"Maybe you want to come in and try that organic turkey,"
I say. "And some organic dressing and mock pumpkin pie with

plain yogurt for whipped cream." Paul and Jill grin warm encouragement for this idea, as if Detective Marinara was a homeless man we'd discovered to have been a first violinist with the London Symphony and can nurse back to health by adopting him into our lives and paying for his rehab.

"Yeah. No," Marinara says—proper Jersey syntax for refusal. He cranes his fine-featured head all around and winces, as if his neck's stiff. "I gotta get back to my sister's to get in on the fighting. This is just, you know—" He smiles a professional, closed-mouth smile and plunges both hands in his brown jacket pockets, giving Paul's "We're Pregnant" card a good crunching. "You'll still come over and do our show-and-tell for us, will you?" He now reminds me of a young Bob Cousy in his Celtic heyday, all purpose and scrap, maximizing his God-givens but strangely sad behind his regular-Joe features.

"Absolutely. Just tell me when. I'm always happy to come to Haddam." (Not at all true.)

"Like I said. We think we got him. But you never know."

"No, you don't." I'm not asking who's the culprit, in case I sold him a house or he was once a fellow member in the Divorced Men's Club.

"You go to Michigan?" Marinara side-eyes my maize-and-blue block-M as if it was worthy of esteem.

"I did."

He sniffs and looks around as Nick Feenster's entering his house, carrying his buffing supplies clutched to his electric blue chest. At the door, he turns and gives us all a look of warning, as if we were gossiping about him, then regards his twin Corvettes the same way. It's cold as steel out here. I'm ready to get inside.

"I wanted to go there," Marinara says, wagging his shoulders an inch back and forth with the thought of Michigan.

"What stopped you?"

"I was a Freehold kid, you know?" Wrong again. "I got all intoxicated with the band and the neat football helmets and the fight song. Saturday afternoons, leaves turning. All that. I thought, Man, I could go to Michigan, I'd be, you know. All set forever."

"But you didn't go?"

"Naaaa." Marinara's bottom lip laps over the top one and presses in. It is a face of resignation, which no doubt strengthens his aptitude for police work. "I was the wrong color. Scuse my French."

"I see," I say. I'm of course the wrong color, too.

"I did my course over at Rutgers-Camden. Prolly was better, given, you know. Everything. It isn't so bad."

"Seems great to me." I shiver through my thighs and knees from the accumulating cold. It's just as well, I think, that Detective Marinara has his family to go back to. Police, by definition, make incongruous guests and he could turn unwieldy with a glass of merlot, once he got talking. Though he doesn't seem to want to leave, and I don't want to abandon him out here.

"Okay. So. Good to meet you. I'll be in touch tomorrow." He smiles, proffers a hand to me, a hand as soft as calfskin and delicate—not large enough to palm a basketball. I have yet to hear his first name. Possibly it's Vincent. He extends his smile to Paul and Jill, but not a hand. "Thanks for the card," he says, and seems pleased. Detective Marinara is, in fact, a regular Joe, could've been my little brother in Sigma Chi, done well in management or marketing, settled in Owosso, become a Michi-ganian. He might never have given the first thought to carrying a shield or a gun. It's often the case that I don't know whether I like fate or hate it.

"Great to meet you," I say. "Have a happy Thanksgiving."

"Yeah. That'd be different." He shrugs, his smile become sun-less but mirthful. Then he's on his way, back to his cruiser, his radio (hidden somewhere on his person) crackling unexpectedly with cop voices. He doesn't look back at us.

CHAPTER 17

INSIDE, BEHIND the coffered front door of the steam bath that's become my residence, in the candle-lit dining room that's too small and boxy and windowless (a design flaw fatal to resale), arrayed on the Danish table accoutred with bone china, English cutlery, Belgian crystal, Irish napkins as wide as Rhode Island, two opened bottles of Old Vine Healdsburg merlot, all courtesy of Eat No Evil, who've arrived early and paved every available table inch with pricey ethical food, including an actual, enormous, glistening turkey, is: Thanksgiving, broadcasting its message through the house with a lacquered richness that instantly makes my throat constrict, my cheeks thicken, my saliva go ropy and my belly turn bilgy. It's exactly the way I ordered it. But just for the moment, I can't go in the room where it is. No doubt my condition's asserting itself through the belly and up the gorge.

"Isn't it great?" Jill's ahead, beaming, peeking in at the flickering festive room, not wanting to enter before I do, eyes wide back to Paul and me like a daughter-in-law, her prosthesis tucked behind her.

"Yeah," I say, though the whole spread looks like a wax feast in a furniture store showroom. If you put a knife to the turkey or a spoon to the yellow squash or a fork to the blamelessly white spuds, it would all be as hard as a transistor radio. And at the last second before entering, I swerve right, and into the kitchen, where there are windows, big ones, and a door out, giving air, which is what I need before I chuck up. "Yeah, it is," I say as I push open the sliding door and struggle onto the deck for the ocean's chill that'll save a big mess (I'm also dying to grab a leak). You can say yours is a "nontraditional" Thanksgiving when you have cancer and the sight of food makes you sick and you nearly piss your pants and the police check in and your wife's split to England—which isn't counting your kids. From out here, Drilla Feenster's in view, deck to deck, alone in her hot tub—naked, it would seem—listening to "The March of the Siamese Children" (clearly her favorite) on the boom box, drinking some kind of milky white drink from a tall glass and staring out past the owl decoy to the sea. Bimbo sits on the hot tub ledge beside her, staring in the same direction. I must be invisible to her.

"Who turned the fucking heat up to bake?" I say back through the open doorway into the kiln of a kitchen, where Jill and Paul have stopped, looking concerned by the fact that I am (I can feel it) pale as a sheet. "Where's Clarissa?"

The beach and ocean are oily-smelling, the sand stained lifeless brown and packed by the tide. Long yellow seaweed garlands are strewn from the turbulence at sea (these are what stink). Two hundred yards out, a black-suited surfer sits his board, prow-up, on the barely rising sheen of ocean. Nothing's happening. Paul's time-capsule hole and pile of sand are the only things of note close by.

"There's a kind of story involved in that," Paul says from the kitchen, through the door out to the deck. A small bird-like female is visible behind the stove island in the kitchen, holding a dish towel, insubstantial through the mirroring glass. She's got up in a floppy white chef's toque and a square-front tunic that engulfs her.

"Who's that?" I say. The sight of this tiny woman makes me unexpectedly agitated—and also enervated. I'm sure this is the way the dying man feels as his final breaths hurry away and word goes through the house: "It's time, it's time, he's going, better come now." The room fills with faces he can't recognize, all the fucking air he'd hoped to salvage is quickly sucked up. It's the feeling of responsibility colluding with pointlessness, and it isn't good.

"That's Gretchen," Paul says. I feel like I've entered a house not my own and encountered circus performers—the one-handed mountain woman, the midget chef, the wise-cracking pitchman in the horse-blanket suit. Everything's gone queer. It wasn't supposed to.

"What's *she* here for?" I'm now burning to piss. Were it not daylight and Drilla not in her hot tub in full view, I'd lariat out right here, the way I do all the time behind Kmart.

"She's part of the food," Paul says, and looks uncomfortably at Jill, who's beside him. "She's nice. She's from Cassville. She and Jill both do yoga."

"Where's your sister?" I snap. "Did Sally call me?"

"She did," Paul says. "I told her that you were doing fine, that your prostate stuff was a lot better and probably in remission, and that you and I had—"

"Did you say that to her?" My lips stiffen to a grimace. This was *my* news. My story to spin, to bill me as more than a penile has-been. Guilt, shame, regret will now cloud all Sally's intentions toward me. Love will never have its second chance. She'll be on a plane to Bhutan by sundown. I'll become a pitiful thing in her horoscope ("Better watch your p's and q's on this one, hon"). I could strangle my son and never think of him again.

"I just thought she prolly knew about it." Paul elevates his chin semi-defiantly, thumbs over his belt cow-puncher-style. This is his new take-charge posture—somewhat compromised by his suit. Tiny Gretchen stares out at me apprehensively, as if I was being talked off a high ledge. She doesn't know who I am. Introductions were neglected. "She said she'd be here tomorrow. She seemed a little distressed, I guess."

I, of course, was too busy *not* selling a cracker box on wheels to awards-store Bagosh and hunting for—and not finding—Bernice Podmanicsky. At the Next Level, the old standards vanish. You don't know where your interests lie or how to contact them. "Where's your sister. Did she call?"

"Okay." Paul casts a fugitive look around the kitchen. Jill is nowhere in sight now. Probably she's snuffing the dining room candles so the smoke alarm doesn't go off.

"Okay? Okay what?" Paul stands his ground, separated by the open sliding doorway, his brow heavy, his damaged eye twitching but focused. What's wrong here? What's the story? *Is* she hurt, after all? Maimed? Dead? And everyone's too embarrassed to tell me? Me, me, me, me. Why does so much have to be about me? That's the part of life that makes you want to end it.

"She, like, called right after you left and talked to Jill and said she'd be late because there were some issues with dumb-fuck whatever. Thom."

"Tell me what issues." Atlantic City's eighty miles south. I can be there in a twinkling (and be glad to go).

"She didn't say. Then half an hour later she called back and asked to talk to you, and you were gone, I guess."

"Yeah. So? What'd she say? What's this about?"

"I didn't know then. She asked for Mom's cell and I gave it to her." Paul isn't used to being the bearer of important news that doesn't seek its source from his everlasting strangeness. For that reason, he's reverted to talking like a halting seventeen-year-old.

"Is that it?" It. It. It. And why am I hearing about *it* on the deck and not twenty minutes ago instead of "We're Pregnant"? My fists ball up hard as cue balls. I've gratefully lost the urge to piss, though I might've pissed and not noticed. That's happened. Little Gretchen's still staring at me, dish towel in hand, as if I'm an intruder wandered in off the beach. "Is that *it*? Is there anything *else* to the fucking story? About *your sister*?"

"Okay." Paul blinks hard, as if he's recognized I might do something he might not like. I may look frightening. But what I am is scared—that my son is about to calmly mention, "Well, like, um, I guess Clarissa got decapitated. It was pretty weird." Or "Um . . . some guys wearing hoods sort of kidnaped her. One guy, I guess, saw her get shot. We aren't too sure—" Or "She was, I guess, trying to fly off the thirty-first floor. But she didn't really get too far. Except like down." This is how real news is imparted now. Like reading ingredients off the fucking oatmeal box.

"Would *that* 'okay' be the same 'okay' as the first 'okay' that meant *not* okay?" I say. I'm staring a hole in him. "What the fuck's the matter with you, Paul? What's happened to your sister?"

"She's in Absecon." His gray eyes behind his lenses roll almost out of sight in their sockets, as if under slightly different circumstances this information could be hilarious. Paul sways back on his heels and drops his hands to his sides.

"Why?" My heart's going thumpa-thumpa.

"She and Thom got into some kind of fight. I don't know. Clary took his keys and went and got his car"—the Healey—"and started driving back up here. But then shit-for-brains called the police and said it was stolen. And the police in Absecon, I guess, tried to pull her over. And she panicked and drove into one of those lighted merge-lane arrows on a trailer at Exit Forty, and knocked it into a highway guy and broke his leg." Paul runs his left hand back through his mullet, and for an instant closes his eyes, then opens them as if I might be gone, suddenly, blessedly.

"How do you know this?" My chest is twittering.

"Mom told me." His hands slip nervously down into his baggy plaid suit-pants pockets.

"Is she in Absecon, too?" Where the fuck *is* Absecon?

"I guess. Yeah."

"Is your sister hurt?" Thumpa-thumpa-thump, thump.

"No, but she's in jail."

"She's in *jail*?"

"Well. Yeah. She hit that guy." Paul's gray eyes fix on me as though to render me immobile. They blink. He coughs a tiny unwarranted cough and begins to say something else, his hands in his pockets.

But I'm already moving. "Well, Jesus Christ—"

I shoulder past him into the kitchen, past Gretchen and go for the stairs, skinning off my block-M, already contemplating how I will portray myself as a good, solid, not-insane-but-still-distressed father to all of ranked Absecon officialdom justifiably angry about one of their own being mowed down by my daughter. Ann, I absolutely know, will bring a lawyer. It's in her DNA. My job will be simply to get there—down there, over there, wherever.

STANDING SHIRTLESS in my closet, I immediately understand that regulation realtor clothing's what's called for—attire that causes the wearer to look positive-but-not-over-confident, plausible, capable but mostly bland on first notice; suitable for meeting a client from Clifton, or the FBI. In the real estate business, an agent's first impression is as an attitude, not a living being. And for that, I'm well provided. Chinos (again), pale blue oxford button-down, brown shell cordovans, nondescript gray socks, brown belt, navy cotton V neck. My uniform.

From inside my closet, I can hear the high-pitched nazzing, ratcheting, gunning, insect-engine noise of a dirt bike out on the beach. Local ball-cap hooligans, younger siblings of the prep school kids from yesterday, freed up—due to relaxed holiday police staffing—to go rip shit over our fragile shore fauna and pristine house-protecting dunes. If I weren't on a dire mission, I'd call the cops or go put a stop to things myself. Possibly they'll drive into Paul's time-capsule bunker.

As I tie my shoes, I meditate darkly (and again) upon the very

model of young manhood I once had in mind for my daughter—
not to *marry* necessarily, or run away with, but to seek out as a
good starter boyfriend. There was just such a staunch fellow
when she was at Miss Trustworthy's. A small, wiry, bespectacled,
slate blue-eyed, blinking Edgar-of-Choate, who went on to read
diplomatic history at Williams and Oxford but chose the family
maritime law practice on Cape Ann, who coxed the heavy-
weight eight, could do thousands of knuckle push-ups, had an
intense, scratchy, yearning voice, dressed more or less like me,
and who I liked and encouraged (and who Clarissa humored
and also liked), even though we all knew she was destined for a
sage older man (who also remarkably resembled me), a fact that
young Edgar didn't seem to mind the hopelessness of, since a
chassis like Clarissa Bascombe was way beyond the planet Pluto
in terms of his life's hopes. All seemed safe and ideal. Clarissa
would begin adult life believing men were strange, harmless
beings who couldn't always be taken completely for granted,
needed to be addressed seriously (now and then), but ultimately
were hers for the taking—low-hanging fruit for a girl who'd
seen some things. Edgar is now a hang 'em high prosecutor out
in Essex County in Mass.—and a Republican, natch. I hardly
have to say that a perilously bogus over-oiled character like van
Ronk-the-equestrian is not the safe finish line for which good,
solid Edgar was ever the starting gate. Beware when you have
children that your heart not be broken.

Outside, the bracking, whining dirt-bike racket hasn't stopped, has, in fact, seemed to migrate down through the space
between my and the Feensters' houses (where I observed Nick
having his secret phone rendezvous two nights ago). The ruckus
carries out to the front, where the vandals, I'm sure, are whipping
out toward 35 before the police can trap them. "The March of
the Siamese Children" is still blaring off the Feensters' deck. As
I finally take my long, jaw-clenching piss, I'm able to think that
Absecon and whatever yet transpires there may offer the only
relief and achievement the holiday will deliver to me. Although,
did I not hear my son say that Sally would arrive? Tomorrow?
A good sign.

Jill, large and green-suited, Paul, fidgety and zoot-suited,
loiter in the front foyer, waiting on me like scolded servants. Jill's
hands are clasped behind her, schoolmarm-style—a habit. Both

are grave but seem confident there's nothing they can do. Our decommissioned and paralytically expensive Thanksgiving feast lies cooling, inedible and uncelebrated on the dining room table. The Men's Ministry at Our Lady can come for it in a panel truck—and throw it in the ocean if they want to. Minuscule white-suited Gretchen is nowhere in sight. She may have been smart enough to leave.

My furniture, when I stop to put on my barracuda jacket, all seems bland and too familiar, but also strange and unpossessed— the couches, tables, chairs, bookcases, rugs, pictures, lamps—not mine. More like the decor of a Hampton Inn in Paducah. How does this happen? Does this mean my time here is nearing its end?

"I'm heading to Absecon, okay?" I have seen an Absecon exit on the Garden State but never gotten off.

"I'm going with you," Paul announces commandingly.

"No way. You almost fucked this all up." It's still a furnace in here. Sweat sprouts in my hairline. My jacket—slightly grimed from my Bob Butts one-rounder—is the finishing touch of persuasive but distressed fatherdom.

"That's really not fair." Paul blinks behind his glasses. I didn't notice before, but Otto, Paul's dummy—his stupid blue eyes popped open, lurid orange hair, hacking jacket, fingerless wooden mitts, black patent-leather pumps with white socks, plus his green derby all making him appear perfectly at home in my house—is seated at the table-full of food like a stunned guest. Thanksgiving is all his now.

"I can't explain it to you right now, Paul. But I will. I love you." I'm moving out the front door. Outside, the dirt-bike noise is intense, as if whoever it is, is running a gymkhana around my or the Feensters' front yard. Nick will be out if he isn't already, primed to deal cruelly, etc., etc. It could be a chance for us to act in concert, only I have to leave. My daughter's in jail.

"I think you need me with you. I think—" Paul's saying.

"We'll talk about it later."

Then abruptly all is silenced outside—*no-noise* as palpable as noise.

And I feel just as suddenly a sensation of *beforeness*, which I've of course felt on many, many days since my cancer was unearthed, the sensation of when there was no cancer, and oh, how good that was—*before*—what a rare gift, only I was careless and didn't notice and have kicked myself ever since for missing it.

But I feel that same *beforeness* now. Though nothing's happened that a *before* should be expected. Unless I've missed something—more than usual. The Next Level wouldn't seem to be in the business of letting us miss important moments. Still, why does *now*—this moment, standing in my own house—feel like *before*?

"What's going on out there?" Paul says in a superior-sounding voice. His gray eyes bat at me. These words come from some old movie he's seen and I have, too. Only he means them now, looks stern and suspicious, moves toward the doorknob, intent on turning it—to get to the bottom of, shed some light on, put paid to. . . .

"No! Don't do that, Paul," I say. We all three look to one another—wondrous looks, different looks, because we are all different, yet are joined in our *beforeness*. It's quiet outside now—we all say this with our silence. But it's just the usual. The holiday calm. The peace of the harvest. The good soft exhale along this stretch of nice beach, the last sigh and surrender the season is famous for.

"Let me look," I say, and go forward. "I'm leaving anyway."

Paul's brow furrows. Even in his horse-blanket suit, he is imploring. He heard what I said. "I'm going with you," he says.

It's hard to say no. But I manage. "No."

I grasp the warm knob, give it a turn and pull open my front door.

And, just as it's supposed to, everything changes. *Before* is everlastingly gone. There is only everlastingly *after*.

At first, I see nothing strange from my doorway, into which a cold gasp floods by my damp hairline. Only my hemispheric driveway. The high seaboard sky. My Suburban, its window duct-taped. Paul's junker Saab behind the arborvitae. Sally's LeBaron. Sandy Poincinet Road, empty and mistily serene toward the beach. And to the left, the Feensters' yard with its sad topiary (the monkey, the giraffe, the hippo all neglected). Nick's aqua Corvettes, enviably buffed, the upbraiding signs—DON'T EVEN THINK OF TURNING AROUND. BEWARE OF PIT BULL. DANGEROUS RIPTIDES. Nothing out of the ordinary. William

Graymont, who's caught something—possibly a bird—stands under the monkey, calmly staring down at his kill.

I begin walking toward my vehicle. Paul and Jill stand in the doorway behind me.

Where's the clamorous, peace-destroying dirt bike, I wonder. Can it have simply vanished? I open the driver's door, thoughts of Absecon re-encroaching with unhappy imagery—Clarissa in a room wearing beltless jailhouse garb; a two-way mirror with smirking men in suits behind it; an Oriental detective—a female—with small clean hands and a chignon; loathsome Thom at a desk, filling out forms. Then Clarissa remote from every-thing and everyone, forever. I test the gray duct tape across my broken window with an estimating poke—it gives but holds. Then Sally re-enters—on a Virgin flight from Maidenhead. How am I to re-establish myself as a vigorous, hearty, restless, randy Sea Biscuit, who's also ready to forgive, forget, bygones staying bygones? I give Paul and Jill a fraught frown back where they stand in the doorway, followed by a bogus Teddy Roosevelt thumbs-up like Mike's. A flight of geese, audible but invisible, passes over—honk-honk-honk-honk-honk in the misted air. I raise my eyes to them. "What the hell happened to your win-dow?" Paul in his silly suit says, starting heavily out the door.

"Nothing," I say. "It's fine. It'll be fine."

"I should go with you." He's crossing the driveway, for some reason putting his hands on his hips like a majorette.

And that is when all hell breaks loose at the Feensters'.

From inside their big white modernistic residential edifice—the teak front door, I can see, is left open—comes the blaring, grinding, reckless start-up whang of a dirt bike. Possibly it's sound effects, something Nick's ordered from an 800 number on late-night TV, delivered in time for the holidays. *The Sounds of Super-X.* Give those neighbors something to be thankful for—when it's turned off.

Paul and I stare in wonder—me across my Suburban hood, he mid-driveway. Inside the Feensters', the dirt-bike racket winds up scaldingly, very authentic if it's a recording—*raaa-raaa-raaa-raaa-raaaaaaaaaaaa-er-raaaaaaa.* I hear, but am not sure I hear, Drilla Feenster in a shrill operatic voice say, "No, no, no, no, no. You *will* not—" Her voice gets husky, insisting "no" to be the only acceptable thing about something. And then, through the

Feensters' open front door, wheeled up and rared back on its thick, black, cleated, high-fendered rear tire, a monstrous, gaudy, electric-purple Yamaha Z-71 "Turf Torturer" screams straight out onto the front drive, where the Corvettes are and the cat was. Astride the bike, captaining it, is a small-featured miniature white kid wearing green-and-black blotch camo, paratrooper boots, a black battle beret and a webbed belt full of what look to me like big copper-jacketed live rounds. (There is no way to make this seem normal.) The instant the bike touches front wheel down in the Feensters' driveway, the kid snaps the handlebars into a gravel-gashing, throttle-up one-eighty that spins him around to face the house, at the same time giving the Yamaha more *raaaa-raaaa-raaaa-rer-raaaas*—popping the clutch out, in, out, spewing gravel against the Corvettes and looking neither left (at Paul and me, astonished across the yards) nor right, but back into the house, his face concentrated, luminous.

It's not possible to know what's happening here, only that it is happening and its consequences may not be good. I look at Paul, who looks at me. He seems perplexed. He is a visitor here. Jill steps out into the driveway to view things better. Gretchen has come to the door still in her chef's hat and carrying a large metal kitchen spoon.

"Go back inside." I say this loudly to Jill over the bike whine. The kid rider now takes note of me, fastens his eyes on me (he could be fourteen), then looks intently back through the Feensters' open door, where someone he's communicating with must be. He's wearing an earpiece in the ear I can see, and his lips are moving. The kid rider points over to me and wags his gloved finger for emphasis. "You go back inside, too," I say to Paul and turn to go in myself—just for the moment, lock the door, wait this one out. These sorts of things usually pass if you let 'em.

Then I hear Drilla inside saying over again, "No-no-no-no-no-no." And then very sharply, possibly from the Great Room—where there are Jerusalem marble countertops, copper fixtures, mortised bamboo floors, no expense spared top to bottom—there come two short metallic *brrrrp-brrrrp!* noises. And Drilla stops saying "No-no-no-no."

"Oh, *man*," Paul says mid-driveway.

Almost in the same instant as the *brrrrp-brrrrp* sounds, Nick Feenster appears, marching out the door, bulky and muscular in his electric-blue Lycra get-up—no anorak. He is barefoot, being led like a prisoner by another undersized white kid, the match of the first one, camo'd, booted, beret'd and web-belted, but who is holding pressed to Nick's jawbone an oddly shaped, black boxy contraption with a stubby barrel that looks like a kid's gun and is—unless someone else is still in the Feensters' house—what I just heard go *brrrrp-brrrrp*. Nick's eyes cut over to me across the yards through his topiary as he's being shoved ahead. His walking style is bumpy, a bulky man's gait. His jowly face is stony, full of hatred, as if he'd like to get his hands on the parties responsible, just have five minutes alone with one or all of them.

I have no idea what this is that's happening in the yard. I look at Paul, who's motionless, hands riding his hips in his plaid suit, staring across the yard as I've been. He is transfixed. Jill is a few steps behind and motionless, her generous mouth opened but silent, hands (real and inauthentic) clasped at her waist. Little Gretchen has disappeared from the doorway.

"Go inside. Call somebody," I say—to Paul, to Jill, to both of them. "Call 911. This is something. This isn't good."

And as if her switch has been thrown, Jill turns and walks directly back inside the front door without a word.

"You go inside, I said," I say to Paul. I have to have them inside, so I can know what to do. But Paul doesn't budge.

Nick Feenster, when I look again, is exactly where he was in his driveway. But the kid from the fiery purple Yamaha is just getting in the driver's seat of one of the Corvettes—becoming instantly invisible behind the wheel. The big bike has been allowed to fall on its side in the gravel but is running. The other boy's still holding the black machine pistol under Nick's chin. They're stealing his cars. That's all this is. This is about stealing cars. They get the keys and then they shoot him. He knows this.

The Corvette rumbles to life. Its headlights flick on, then off, its fiberglass body trembling. Then the kid is quick out of it, hurries around, jumps in the other Corvette. He has both sets of keys. The second aqua-and-white Corvette cranks and shimmies and vibrates. Smoke puffs out of its dual pipes. The kid revs and revs the big mill, just like he did the Yamaha, but then drops it in reverse, sends it springing backward, spewing gravel underneath, then (I can see him looking down at the gear shifter) he yanks it down into first, rips a buffeting, wheel-tearing power left in the gravel and, in a clamor of smoke and engine racket and muffler blare, gurgle and clatter, spins out of the Feensters' driveway, bouncing out onto Poincinet Road and straight away toward Route 35.

"They're going to shoot Nick," I say—I suppose—to Paul, who hasn't gone inside the way I told him to. The boy with the machine pistol is talking to Nick, and Nick, at the point of the stubby barrel, is talking to the boy, his lips moving stiffly, as if they were discussing something difficult. I hear a siren not so far away. A silent alarm has gone off. The police will have stopped the first boy already, and none of this will go much further. I begin walking toward Nick and the boy, who're still talking. I lack a plan. I'm merely impelled to walk across the driveway and the tiny bit of scratchy lawn separating our two houses to do something productive. You're not supposed to think thoughts in these moments, only to see things distinctly for the telling later: the remaining vibrating aqua-and-white Corvette; the topiary monkey and the hippo; the cottony sky; Nick's house; the kid with the machine pistol; Nick, muscular and stern-jawed in his blue Lycras and big bare feet. Though I do think of the boy, this lethal boy with his gun, threatening Nick. But as if he was a mouse. A tiny mouse. A creature I can corner and trap and hold in my two hands and feel the insubstantial weight of and keep captured until he's calm. They're still talking, this boy and Nick. Behind me, I hear Paul say, "Frank." Then I say, "Could I just.... Could I just ... get a little involved here in this?" And then the boy shoots Nick, shoots him straight up under the jaw. One *brrrrp!* I am beside the measly topiary giraffe and say, "Oh, gee." And almost as an afterthought, more a choice of activities he didn't know he'd have to make, the boy shoots me. In the chest. And that, of course, is the truest beginning to the next level of life.

CHAPTER 18

I WONDER AT what Ms. McCurdy saw as she fell. What were her last recorded visual inputs before she closed her amazed eyes upon this toilsome, maybe not entirely bad life forever? Did she get to see the crack-brained Clevinger squeeze the final round into his melon? Did she see her astonished nursing students get the education of their lives? Did she see, for one last eye flutter, the sands of Paloma Playa or glimpse an oil derrick out at sea? A bather? A man standing in a tepid surf, looking back at her curiously, waving good-bye? I have the hope of a man who never hopes.

You're told about the long, shimmering corridor with the spooky light at the end and the New Age music piped in (from where?). Or of the chapter-by-chapter performance review of your muddled life, scrolling past like microfiche while you pause at death's stony door for some needed extra suffering. Or of the foggy, gilded, curving steps leading to the busy bearded old man at the white marmoreal desk with the book, who scolds you about the boats he's already sent, then sends you below.

Maybe for some it happens.

But what I tried very, very hard to do, there on Nick Feenster's lawn, was keep my eyes open, stay alert, maintain visual contact with as much as possible, keep the dots connected. Shooting three living humans apparently does not make a big impression on a fourteen-year-old, because even before I let myself kneel on the lawn and take notice of the two holes in my barracuda jacket high up in my left pectoral region, then look up at the boy with an odd sensation of gratitude, he'd already climbed into Nick's Corvette and put it into clunking gear, after which he wheeled around in the driveway and roared off, narrowly missing Nick and geysering gravel in my whitening face, turning onto Route 35, where possibly the Sea-Clift police were already waiting to catch him as he headed onto the Toms River bridge.

My son Paul appeared at once to aid me where I lay on the

lawn, as did Jill. Oddly enough, Paul kept asking me—I was awake for all of this—if I felt I was going to be all right, was I going to be all right, was I going to be all right. I said I didn't know, that being shot in the chest was often pretty serious. And then Detective Marinara arrived—I may have dreamed this—having decided to celebrate Thanksgiving with us after all. He said—I may have dreamed this, too—that he knew quite a lot about bullet wounds to the chest, and mine might be all right. He called an ambulance from the radio in his jacket pocket.

And it came. I was lying on the cold ground, breathing shallow but religiously regular breaths, staring up glass-eyes into the misty sky, where I again could hear the geese winging through the smoky air, even see their spectral bodies, wings set, barely agitating. A stocky red-haired man with a red beard and a purple birthmark on his lower lip arrived and looked down at me. He had a hypodermic syringe in his mouth and a pink-tubed stethoscope around his rucked neck. "So, how's it going there, Frank?" he said. "You gonna die?" He had one of the clotted Shore accents and grinned at me as if my dying was the furthest thing from his mind. "You ain't gonna gork off on us, are you? Right here on your own lawn, in front of God and everybody. And on Thanksgiving? Are you, huh? That wouldn't be too cool, big ole boy. Ruin everybody's day. Specially mine." He was giving it to me in the arm. The ground was very cold and hard. I wondered if the bullets (I didn't know how many, then) had entered my chest and gone out the other side. I wanted to ask that and to explain that it wasn't my lawn. But I must've lost consciousness, because I don't even remember the needle being taken out, only that I hadn't been called "big ole boy" in a long time. Not since my father called me that on our golfing days on the sun-baked Keesler course, when he would smack the living shit out of the ball, then look down at me, with my little junior clubs, and say, "Can you hit it that far, big ole boy? Let's see if you can, big ole boy. Give her a mighty ride." It's worth saying that it doesn't hurt *that* much to be shot in the chest. It was something I always wondered about as far back as my Marine Corps days, when people talked a lot about it. There's the hit and then it's hot and hurts some, then it's numb. You definitely hear it. *Brrrrp!* You instantly feel strange, surprised (I was already cold, but I felt much colder) and then you—I, anyway—just kneel down to try to get some rest, and there's the feeling then that everything's going on without you. Which it pretty much is.

Of course—anyone would expect the rest to happen—I wake up in the Sea-Clift EMS truck, strapped to a yellow Stryker stretcher, shirtless and jacketless, covered with a thin pink blanket, my feet toward the back door. It is just like all the movies portray it—a fish-eye view, a jouncing, swerving ride under an elevated railroad in the Bronx, siren *whoop-whooping*, diesel motor growling, lights flashing. The fluorescent light inside is lime green, barely sufficient for decent patient care. The turns and roaring motorized dips make me roll against my nylon belt restraints. There's the smell of rubbing alcohol and other disinfectants and aluminum. And I believe I've died and this is what death is—not the "distinguished thing," but a swervy, bumpy ride with a lot of blinking lights all around you that never ends, a constant state of being in between departure and arrival, though that might be just for some. I'm bandaged and strung up to a collapsing clear plastic drip bag, and wearing a mask to aid my breathing. I can see the scruffy, heavy-set, red-bearded guy in a white shirt with his stethoscope, sitting beside me, talking to someone else in the compartment who I can't see, talking in the calmest of voices, as if they're on break from the produce department at Kroger's and taking their time about clocking back in. They talk about the 5-K race and some guy they thought had "stroked out" but, it turns out, hadn't. And some woman with a prosthetic leg whom they admired but couldn't see having decent sex with. And about how no one would catch them out running in the street on Thanksgiving when they could be home watching the Sixers, and then something about the police saying the boys who'd shot me and Nick (and possibly Drilla) being Russians: "Go figure." I am gripping. My hand can touch something cold and tubular, and I would like very much to sit up and see out the little louvered side windows to find out where we are. The clock on the wall here says it's 2:33. But when I stir toward rising, the red-bearded EMS guy with the purple birthmark says, "Well, our friend's come alive, looks like," and puts a big freckled hand heavily on my good shoulder so that I can see he's wearing a milky blue plastic glove. I'm aware that I say from under my mask, "It's all right, I don't have AIDS." And that he says, "Sure, we know. Nobody does. These gloves are just my fashion statement." And I may say, "I do have cancer, though." And he may say, "In-te-*rest*-ing. Four inches lower and this would be a more leisurely trip." Then I relax and stare at the dim, rocking, metallic-gray ceiling as the boxy crate roars on.

The ceiling has a color snapshot of a thinner version of the red-haired paramedic in an Army desert uniform, kneeling, smiling down at me from a faraway land, and above his head a thought-balloon says "Oxygen In Use. Ha-ha-ha-ha-ha." I may dream then that we're passing onto the long bridge to Toms River, across Barnegat Bay, and that these two men are talking and talking and talking about the election and what a joke it is: "suspended agitation," "diddling while home burns," how no one has loyalty to our sacred institutions anymore, which is a national disgrace, since institutions and professions have always carried us along. In their view, it is a nature–nurture issue, and they agree that nurture is, while not everything, still very impor-tant (which I don't feel so sure about). And then I think someone, I'm not sure who, is flossing his teeth and smiling at me at the same time.

And at this point it becomes clear to me (how does one know such things?) that I'm not going to die from merely being shot in the chest by some little miscreant mouse who needs to spend some concentrated time alone thinking about things, particularly about his effect on others. Now, today, may be an end—time will tell what of—but it is not *the* end the way Ernie McAuliffe's and Natheriel Lewis's ends were unarguably *the* end for those good and passionate souls. And Nick, too, who can't have sur-vived his wounds. To know such a thing so clearly is a true mystery, but one does, which puts an interesting spin on the rest of life and how people pretend to live it, as well as on medical care and on religion and on business and the pharmaceutical industry, real estate—most everything, when you get right down to it.

I could, of course, die in the hospital. Thousands do, victims of lawless pathogens that make their home there, felled by an otherwise-non-fatal wound; or I could suffer my titanium BBs to turn traitor to my tissues and become my worst enemy. These things are statistically possible and happen. Listen to *Live at Five* or read the *Asbury Press*. Nature doesn't like to be observed, but can be.

Whoop-whoop, whoop-whoop! Blaaaant, blaaaant! Vroom, vroom.
"That's right, that's it. Just sit there. You mother*fucker*! I gotta
dead guy in he-ah, or soon will. Ya silly son of a bitch."

It's good to know they actually care—that it's not like driving
a beer truck or delivering uniforms to Mr. Goodwrench. What
is their average time in traffic, one wonders.

BANG! BANG! Bangety-ruuuump-crack. We've hit something now. "That's right, asshole. That's why I got this cow-
catcher on this baby, for assholes like you!" *Vroom, vroom, vroom-
vroom.* We're off again. It can't be far now.

When I'm turned loose from this current challenge, I am
going to sit down and write another letter to the President,
which will be a response to his yearly Thanksgiving proclama-
tion—generally full of platitudes and horseshit, and no better
than poems written for ceremonial occasions by the Poet
Laureate. This will be the first such letter I've actually sent, and
though I know he will not have long to read it and gets letters
from lots of people who feel they need to get their views aired,
still, by some chance, he *might* read it and pass along its basic
points to his successor, whoever that is (though of course I
know—we all do). It will not be a letter about the need for more
gun control or the need for supporting the family unit so four-
teen-year-olds don't steal cars, own machine pistols and shoot
people, or about ending pregnancies, or the need to shore up
our borders and tighten immigration laws, or the institution of
English as a national language (which I support), but will simply
say that I am a citizen of New Jersey, in middle age, with wives
and children to my credit, a non-drug user, a non-jogger, without cell-phone service or caller ID, a vertically integrated non-
Christian who has sponsored the hopes and contexts and dreams
of others with no wish for credit or personal gain or transcendence, a citizen with a niche, who has his own context, who does
not fear permanence and is not in despair, who is in fact a realtor
and a pilgrim as much as any. (I will not mention cancer survivor,
in case I'm finally not one.) I'll write that these demographics
confer on me not one shred of wisdom but still a strong personal
sense of having both less to lose and curiously more at stake. I will
say to the President that it's one thing for me, Frank Bascombe, to
give up the Forever Concept and take on myself the responsibilities of the Next Level—that life can't be escaped and must

be faced entire. But it's quite another thing for him to, or his successor. For them, in fact, it is very unwise and even dangerous. Indeed, it seems to me that these very positions, positions of public trust they've worked hard to get, require that insofar as they have our interests at heart, they must graduate to the Next Level but never give up the Forever Concept. I have lately, in fact, been seeing some troubling signs, so that I will say there is an important difference worth considering between the life span of an individual and the life span of a whole republic, and that. . . .

"Absecon," I hear someone say. "That's Ab-*see*-con." That's not how I've been pronouncing it, but I will forever. Surely we're not going to a hospital there. "When I was a kid, in Absee-con—" It's the big red-headed Army medic, blabbing on in his south Jersey brogue. "My old man useta go to Atlantic City. They still had real bums over there then. Not these current fucks. This was the Seventies, before all this new horseshit. He'd go get one a these bums and bring him home for Thanksgiving. You know? Clean him up. Give him some clothes. Useta look for bums about his own size. My mom useta hate it. I'll tell ya. We'd—"

We are slowing up. The siren's gone silent. The two men inside with me are moving, legs partly bent, stooping. A two-way radio crackles and sputters from someone's belt beside my face. The clock says it's 3:04. "Could be you'll want some backup," a woman's metallic voice says from a place where it sounds like the wind's blowing. "Oh boy. Ooooohh boy. Oh man," the woman's faraway voice says. "This is somethin'. I promised you fireworks." Sputter and fuzz. And we are, because I can feel it, backing up and turning at once. I strain against my webbed restraints to see something. My hands are cold. I feel my upper chest to be cold, too, and numb. A randy taste has dislodged from somewhere in my mouth. My chest actually hurts now, I have to admit. I'm not breathing all that well even with oxygen in use, though I'm glad to have it. "Delivery for occupant," I hear a man's voice say. "He had a big heart, my old man." The medic is speaking again, "For all the good it did 'im." The red-bearded face is peering down into mine out of the minty fluorescence. "How ya doin', big ole boy? You holdin' up?" the red mouth with the birthmark says. His blue eyes fix on me suspiciously. I wonder what my own eyes say back. "How'd you like your ambulance ride? Just like TV, wasn't it?"

"Life's interesting," I say from under my mask.

"*Oh* yeah."

Suddenly, there's lots of outside light and a burst of cold air. The door, which I can see, has opened, and my stretcher is moving. The face of a bright-eyed, smiling young nurse, a black woman in a long white labcoat, and corn-rows with gold beads intertwined and tortoiseshell glasses, is staring into my face. She's saying, "Mr. Bascombe? Mr. Bascombe? Can you tell me how you feel?"

I say, "Yes. I don't feel like a big ole boy, that's one thing."

"Well then, why don't you tell me how you are," she says. "I'd like to know."

"Okay," I say. And as we move along, that is what I begin to do—with all my best concentration, I begin to try to tell her how I am.

THANKSGIVING

VIOLENCE, THAT IMPOSTER, foreshortens our expectancies, our logics, our next days, our afternoons, our sweet evenings, our whole story.

At 23,000 feet, the land lies north and east to the purple horizon. Terminal moraine, which in summer nurtures alfalfa fields, golf courses, sod farms, stands of yellow corn, is now masked and frozen white, fading into dusk. Wintry hills pass below, some with frail red Christmas lights aglitter on tiny porches, then a gleaming silver-blue river and the tower trail of our great midwestern power grid. It is all likable to me. Minnesota.

My fellow passengers on Northwest Flight 1724 (world's most misunderstood airline), all thirty of us, are Mayo bound. O'Hare straight up to Rochester. The blond, heavy-boned, duck-tailed flight attendant—a big Swede—knows who her passengers are. She acts jokey-light-hearted if you're just flying up for a colonoscopy—"the routine lube job"—but is chin-set, hard-mouth serious if your concerns are more of an "impactful," exploratory nature. As usual, I fall into the mid-range of patient-passenger profiles—those who're undergoing successful treatment and on our way to Rochester to hear encouraging news. At 23,000 feet, no one is the least bit reluctant to discuss personal medical problems with whoever fate has seated next to them. Above the engines' hum, you hear earnest, droning heartland voices dilating on what an aneurysm *actually* is, what it feels like to undergo an endoscopy or a heart catheterization ("The initial incision in your leg's the goddamn worst part") or a vertebra fusion ("They go in through the front, but of course you don't feel it, you're asleep"). Others, less care-laden, discuss how "the Cities" have changed—for the better, for the worse—in the years they've been coming up here; where's the best muskie fishing to be found (Lake Glorvigen); whether it was King Hussein or Saddam Hussein who was a Mayo patient once upon a time (AIDS and "the syph" are rumored); and what a good newspaper *USA*

Today has turned out to be, "especially the sports." Many tote thick manila envelopes containing crucial evidentiary X rays from elsewhere. BRAIN, SPINE, NECK, KNEE are stamped in red. I have only myself—and Sally Caldwell—plus a prostate full of played-out BBs destined to be with me forever. And I have my thoughts for a sunny prognosis and a good start to year two of the young Millennium, which includes a new direction in the Presidency—one it's hard to see how we'll survive—though the enfeebled new man's little worse than his clownish former opponent, both being smirking cornpones unfit to govern a ladies' flower show, much less our frail, unruly union.

Sally, beside me on the aisle of our regional Saab 340 turbo-prop, is reading a book encased in one of the crocheted book cozies women years ago employed to sneak *Peyton Place* or *Bonjour Tristesse* into the beauty parlor (my mother did it with *Lady Chatterley's Lover*), books requiring privacy for full enjoyment. Sally's reading a thick paperback called *Tantrism and Your Prostate*, by a Dr. White. She's assured me there're strategies woven into his recommendations that are part of our (my) natural maturing process and pretty much common sense anyway, and will clear out a lot of underbrush and open up some new paths we'll both soon be breathless to enter. The sex part is still a source of concern—for me but not, apparently, for Sally—since we've yet to fully reconvene since she returned from Blighty and I cleared customs at Ocean County Hospital from my successful gunshot surgery, which left amazingly small scars and wasn't nearly as bad as you'd imagine (pretty much the way it happens on *Gunsmoke* or *Bonanza*). I *did* wake up on the operating table, though the Pakistani surgeon, Dr. Iqbal, just started laughing at my shocked, popped-opened peepers and said, "Oh, well, my goodness, look who can't stand to miss anything." They put me out again in two seconds, and I have no memory of pain or fear, only of Dr. Iqbal laughing. The two .32 slugs are at home on my bedside table, where I have in the past two weeks studied them for signs of significance and found none. Sally believes there's nothing to worry about on the sexual front and that she knows everything'll kick into gear once I regain full strength and get some good news in Rochester.

Sally's hand, her right hand, grazes mine when we encounter turbulence and go buffeting along over the oceany chop, while our fellow passengers—all regional flying veterans and all fatal-ists—start laughing and making *woo-hoo*-ing noises. Someone, a woman with a nasal Michigan voice, says, "Up-see-daisee. Ain't this fun now?" None of us would mind that much if our ship went down or was hijacked to Cuba or just landed someplace other than our destination—some fresh territory where new and unexpected adventures could blossom, back-burnering our inevitables till later.

Since she's been back from her own *Wanderjahr*, Sally has seemed unaccountably happy and hasn't wanted to sit down for a full and frank debriefing, which is understandable and can wait forever if need be. I was in the hospital some of the time, anyway, and since then there's been plenty to do—police visits and sit-down interviews with prosecutors, an actual lineup at the Ocean County Court House, where I identified the perpetrators, all this along with Clarissa's difficulties in Absecon. (The pint-size accomplices were twins *and* Russians, boyfriends of the faithless Gretchen. It turns out there's a story there. I, however, am not going to tell it.)

Paul and Jill, it should be said, proved to be much better than average ground support in all our difficulties, although they've now driven back to K.C. to celebrate the Yule season "as a couple." Paul and I were never precisely able to get onto the precise same page because I was in the hospital, but we now seem at least imprecisely to be reading the same book, and since I was shot, he has seemed not as furious as he was before, which may be as good as these things get. I don't know to this moment if he and Jill are married or even intend to be. When I asked him, he only smoothed his beard-stache and smiled a crafty, uxorious smile, so that my working belief has become that it doesn't matter as long as they're "happy." And also, of course, I could be wrong. He did, as an afterthought, tell me Jill's last name—which is Stockslager and not Bermeister—and I'll admit the news made me relieved. But again, as to Sally's and my true reconciliation (in both the historical and marital senses), it will come in time, or never will, if there's a differ-ence. In her letter, she said she didn't know if there was a word that describes the natural human state for how we exist toward each other. And if that's so, it's fine with me. *Ideal* probably wouldn't be the right word; sympathy and necessity might be important components. Though truthfully, love seems to cover the ground best of all.

When she arrived the day after Thanksgiving, Sally carried with her a wooden box containing Wally's cremains. (I was zonked in the Ocean County ICU and she didn't actually bring the box up there.) Wally, it seems, had just been a man who no matter how hard he tried could never find full satisfaction with life, but who actually came as close to happiness as he ever would by living alone, or as good as alone, as a bemused and trusted arborist on a remittance man's estate (there are words for these people, but they don't explain enough well enough). His nearly happy existence all went directly tits-up when Sally forcibly re-inserted herself into his life for reasons that were her own and were never intended to last forever—though poor Wally didn't know that. After a few weeks together on Mull, Wally grew as grave as a monk, then gradually morose, apparently feared his paradise on earth would now not be sustainable, but could not (as he couldn't from the start) explain to Sally that marriage was just a bad idea for a man of his solitary habits. She said she would've welcomed hearing that, had tried lovingly to make him discuss it and put some fresh words in place, but hadn't succeeded and saw she was spoiling his life and was already planning to leave. But with no place else to run away to, and not realizing he could just stay in Mull, and thus in a fit of despair and incommunicable fearfulness and sorrow, Wally took a swim with a granite paving stone tied to his ankle and set his terrible fears and unsuitedness for earth adrift with the outward tide. She said when he was found he had a big smile on his round and innocent face.

Sally has admitted—seated at the same glass-topped breakfast table overlooking the ocean where she'd told me she was leaving and gave me her wedding ring only a short, eventful six months ago—that she simply never made Wally happy enough, though she loved him, and it was too bad they couldn't have gotten a divorce like Ann and I did and freed each other from the past. In time, I will find words to explain to her that none of this is as simple as she thinks, and in doing so possibly help explain herself *to* herself, and let her and Wally off some hooks—one of which is grief—hooks they couldn't get off on their own. It's my solemn second-husbandly duty to do such things. In these small ways, there's been appreciable progress made in life in just the twelve days since I got out of Ocean County. We both feel time is precious, for obvious reasons, and don't want to waste any of it with too much brow beetling.

In any case, I rescheduled my Mayo post-procedure checkup, which will be tomorrow at nine with blunt-fingered Dr. Psimos. And since Chicago was, in a sense, on the way, Sally asked me to go with her to Lake Forest to present a solid-front *fait accompli* when she delivered Wally's ashes to the aged parents. It is an unimpartably bad experience to have your son die *once* in a lifetime, as my son Ralph did. And even though I have officially accepted it, I will never truly get over it if I live to be a hundred—which I won't. But it is unimpartably worse and in no small measure strange to have your son die *twice*. And even though I knew nothing to say to his parents and didn't really want to go, I felt that to meet someone who knew Wally as an adult, as I did in a way, and who knew his odd circumstances and could vouch for them, and who was at the same time a total stranger they'd never see again, might prove consoling. Not so different from a Sponsor visit, when you settle it all out.

The elderly Caldwells were rosy-cheeked, white-haired, small and trim Americans, who welcomed Sally and me into their great fieldstone manse that backs up on the lake and is probably worth eight million and will one day be turned into a research institute run by Northwestern to study (and interpret) whatever syndrome Wally suffered from that made everybody's life a monkey house. I couldn't help thinking it could also be turned into four luxury condos, since it had superb grounds, mature plantings and drop-dead views all the way to Saugatuck. A big conical blue spruce was already up and elaborately lighted in the long drawing room with the stone fireplace, where Sally (I guessed) first re-encountered Wally last May. The Caldwells were soon to be off to a *do* at the Wik-O-Mek that evening and wanted us to come along and stay over, since there would be dancing. I'd have died before doing anything like that and, in fact, managed to work into the conversation that unfortunately I'd recently been shot in the chest (which seemed not to surprise them all that much) and had trouble sleeping, which isn't true, and Sally said we were really just stopping by on our way up to Mayo for my checkup and needed to get going—as if we were driving all the way. They both acted cheerful as could be, fixed us each an old-fashioned, talked dishearteningly about the election (Warner described all their neighbors as decent Chuck Percy Republicans) and how they felt the economy was headed for recession, witness the tech sector and capital-spending cuts. Constance took grateful but unceremonious possession of Wally's ashes—a small box upholstered in black velvet. They both guardedly mentioned Sally's two children in a way that made me sure they sent them regular whopper checks. Then they talked about what an exotic life Wally had chosen to live—"Strange and in some ways exciting," Constance said. We all sat around the huge but cozy spruce-and-apple-wood-scented room and drank our cocktails and thought about Wally as if he was both with us and as if he had never lived, but definitely not as though he'd sharked my wife away from me—even if unwillingly. At some point all four of us started to get not-surprisingly antsy and probably fearful of our words beginning to take on meanings we might regret. Sally and Constance excused themselves, in a southern way, to go upstairs together with the cremains box. Warner took me out the French doors to the low-walled patio, which was snowy and already iced in. He wanted me to see the lake, frozen and blue, and also where he'd put up his fancy covered and heated one-man practice tee he could use all winter. He wondered if I played golf—as though he was sizing me up as a son-in-law. I said no, but that my former wife was a golf coach and played for the Lady Wolverines in the Sixties. With a pixyish grin—he looked nothing like Wally, which leads to speculation—he said he'd played for the purple and white when he came back from the Marianas. We had nothing else to say after that, and he walked me around the outside of the big rambling house through the gleaming crust of snow to where the ladies were just then exiting the front door (it was their standard way to hustle you out). And in no more than three minutes, after we'd all uncomfortably hugged one another and said we'd definitely visit somewhere, someday on the planet, Sally and I headed out the drive, out of Lake Forest, back toward the Edens and toward O'Hare.

But since there was still plenty of light left and I had my old orienteering feel for streets and cardinal points—realtors all think we have this, but can be calamitously wrong—I said I wanted to drive past my mother's last address in Skokie, where she'd lived while I was in college, with Jake Ornstein, her good husband, and where she'd died in 1965. We got off at Dempster Avenue and drove east to where I thought it would intersect, via a tricky set of small-street maneuverings, with Skokie Boulevard. Everything felt familiar to me, equipped as I was with the sense of near-belonging I'd had from thirty-five years ago, when I used to ride over from Ann Arbor on the old New York Central and be picked up at the LaSalle Street Station by my mother. But when I got to where I thought Skokie Boulevard should've been (possibly my old-fashioned was working on me), there was a big but past-its-prime shopping mall, with an Office Depot and a poorly patronized Sears as its anchors and a lot of vacant store spaces in between. I realized then that somewhere toward the back of the employee-parking section of the Sears was where my mother and Jake's house had been—a blue-roofed, single-dormer, center-stoop, quasi-Colonial Cape where my mother had lived out her last days, and where I'd gone to see her before being officially rendered an orphan at age nineteen.

"Do you know where your mom's buried?" Sally was driving our renter Impala and wasn't in a hurry, since her duties toward Wally and herself were now forever discharged. She'd happily have driven around all day.

I said, "It's one of those places where you just see miles of granite headstones and freeways go by on three sides. I could probably find it from the air. She's buried beside Jake."

"We can look for it," she said, widening her eyes like a challenge. "I think it'd be nice if you went there once before you died. Not that you're in jeopardy of dying. At least you better not be. I have plans for you." That was our sexual code in prior days. "I've got plans for *you*, buster." An eyebrow cocked. I'd certainly like those plans to see good results again soon.

"I hope you do," I said. We were again headed back toward the Edens and the route to the airport. "It's enough that I tried to find it. She'd think that was good. It's one of the ways life's like horseshoes."

"There're more than you know, you know." She smiled broadly at me, her eyes shiny in a way I hadn't seen them shine in a while. This also clearly meant something amorous and made me happy, though also apprehensive that something close to amorous was all I was expected to manage. We got to the airport with two hours to spare.

I will say that in the days since Sally's return, some of which time I was in the hospital in Toms River, before I walked out as a convalescing man, holey-chested as a minor-league saint, she has treated me—as I feared she might—with kid gloves, almost as if in some karmic way she believes she caused what happened to me. I probably have not objected enough, though Mike Mahoney says karma doesn't work like that. Still, Sally often seems to be "attending" to me, and sometimes addresses me in an over-animated third-person manner—spirited attendant to fractious attendee: "So what does Frank have on his mind today?" "So is Frank going to clamber out of bed today?" I've heard this is what people do in therapy sessions when straight talk hits the wall. "Frank believes, or at least is willing to specu-late, that Sally is overcompensating for prior behavior that requires no compensation, and Frank is wishing it would stop." I actually said this to her. And for a day she turned silent and evasive, even a little testy. But by the second day, she was cheerful again, though still more solicitous than makes me happy.

I'm actually ready to believe that what any marriage might need is a good whacking abandonment or betrayal to test its tensile strength (most of them survive that and worse). In any case, I'm pretty well over being angry and feel an exhilarated sense of necessity just to be alive still and have her back. Mar-riage, in fact, does not even feel much like marriage anymore, even though Sally has asked for her wedding ring back (but has yet to put it on). Possibly it never really felt like marriage, and that in spite of two efforts I don't know what marriage is. Maybe it's not our natural human state, which is why Paul only smiled when I asked him about it.

But in these days since being shot in the chest, as this Millen-nial plague year ends and the confounding election's finally resigned to, what I've begun to feel is a growing sense of enlight-enment, even though I have plenty of pain from my bullet holes. Enlightenment often gets lost in intimate life with another per-son: the positive conviction, for instance, that the person *you are now* would make precisely the same choices you're living with and that your life is actually the way you want it. That enlight-ened understanding can get lost. Life with Sally returned to

Sea-Clift feels, in fact, less like a choice I made long ago, and more like the feeling of meeting someone you instantaneously like while on a walking trip along the Great Wall, and who seems sort of familiar and who by the end of the day you decide to share your pup tent with.

Not that I'm totally in the clear. If I intend to be healed and be a full participant more than an attendee, I believe I will have to become more interesting *per se*. Although being shot with a machine pistol by a fourteen-year-old assassin and living to tell about it gives me a good, unconventional story that most people probably won't have. I may also need to become more intuitive, which I would've said I was anyway, until cancer got in the picture. And possibly I could stand an improved sense of spirituality—which Sally seems to have come home with, and Mike Mahoney sells like popsicles. "Faith is the evidence of things unseen" always seemed a reasonably reliable spiritual credo to have, and evoked me to myself in a secular sense—though you could also say it gave rise to problems. Or: "In an age of disbelief ... it is for the poet to supply the satisfactions of belief in his measure and his style"—except of course I am not a poet, though I've read plenty of them and find their books easy to finish. But in the most purely personal-spiritual vein—since I took two slugs four inches above my own—the best motivational question in the spirituality catechism, and one seeking an answer worth remembering, may *not* be "Am I good?" (which is what my rich Sponsorees often want to know and base life on), but "Do I have a heart at all?" Do I see good as even a possibility? The Dalai Lama in *The Road to the Open Heart* argues I definitely do. And I can say I think I do, too. But anymore— as they say back down in New Jersey—anymore than that is more spiritual than I can get.

How any of this jibes with acceptance and the Next Level, I'm not sure. Self-improvement as a concept already smacks of the Permanent Period, of life you *can* live over again, which is a thought I've put behind me now but may be harder to outlive than it seems. Truly, at a certain point around the course, can you do much to change your chances? Isn't it really more a matter of readying? Of life as prelude?

*   *   *

IN A PURELY itemized way, then, these things are now of record at the end.

I've always liked the joke about the doctor coming into the examining room, holding a clipboard, wearing his stethoscope and mirrored visor, and saying, "I've got good news and bad news. The bad news is you have cancer and you'll be dead in a week. The good news is I fucked my nurse last night."

My good news is I have cancer, but I sleep better than ever since being shot and nearly offed. The Ocean County Hospital doctors said this is not unusual. Death can take on a more contextualized importance relative to our nearness to it. And truthfully, I do not fear death even as much as I used to, which wasn't much, although these things can get hidden. I did not, for example, get on the plane today and feel as I once felt—that I recognized the flight attendant from other flights (they never recognize me) and that therefore my odds of averting disaster were shortened. Neither today did I feel the urge I've felt for years—even on my happy, worry-erasing trips to Moline and Flint—to repeat my traveler's mantra upon taking my seat: "An airplane is forty tons of aluminum culvert, pressure-packed with highly volatile and unstable accelerants, entering a sky chock-full of other similar contraptions, piloted by guys with C averages from Purdue and carrying God only knows what other carnage-producing incendiary materials, so it's stupid not to think it will seek its rightful home on earth at the first opportunity. Therefore today must be a good day to die." I used to take strength from those words, spoken silently as I watched my luggage ride the conveyor and the baggage handlers secretly stealing glances up at my face in the window and mouthing words I couldn't lip-read but that seemed to be directed to me, smirking and laughing while they sent on board whatever fearsome cargo the other people were carrying (these baggage people rarely fly themselves).

For item number two, my strange syncopes have quit occurring since I was wounded. Why, I can't say, but it may be that I meditate now without really realizing it.

On other fronts, the mystery of Natherial Lewis's death was brought to a sad but sure solution—one that seems unrelated to a hate crime. A simpler matter than guessed was at its heart, as is often true in these cases. A man of the Muslim faith desired to "send a message" to a medical doctor of the same persuasion who, this first man believed, lived too much in the world of infidels and needed reminding. The medical doctor, of course, had already left to spend Thanksgiving in Vieques on the day the reminder was delivered—which must have proved to the bomb maker he was right. Only Natherial was there in the cafeteria, in the early a.m., listening to his transistor radio, looking out the window, watching dawn come up on the hospital grounds, waiting to go home and to bed—which he never did. No one was supposed to be hurt, the guilty man said. It was just a message.

Meanwhile our long drought is officially declared ended in New Jersey on the strength of tropical depression Wayne, which never became a hurricane but brought a change for all. Some people associate the dry season's ending with the election being settled and a hoped-for upturn in the economy. But these people are Republicans who'll do fine no matter who's elected. They are the ones who sell you water in a desert.

On a less optimistic note, Wade Arcenault has, unhappily, died. Of a stroke. A general system failure. "Eighty-four," as Paul Harvey would say, on the Sunday after Thanksgiving. No surprise to him and probably not disappointing, either, if he knew anything about it. I did not go to the funeral because I was in the hospital and didn't hear until later. Though I wouldn't have gone. Wade and I were not the kind of friends who need to attend each other's funerals. In any case, his daughter, Ricki, and his thick-necked policeman son, Cade, were there to send him on to glory. Ricki called me in the hospital and sounded much the same as when I last saw her sixteen years ago, her voice a bit deepened and made less confident by time. I pictured her with a mall haircut, an extra thirty pounds strapped to her once-wonderful hips and a look of non-acceptance camouflaged behind a big Texas smile. "Deddy liked you s'much, Frank. Like me, I guess—hint, hint. It made a big difference to him havin' you be his big buddy. Life's peculiar, idn't it?" "It is," I said, staring apprehensively out my hospital window down onto Hooper Avenue choked with Christmas shoppers and misted with tiny snowflakes. I hoped she wasn't calling from downstairs or out in her car, and wasn't about to come check me out, being a nurse and all. But she didn't. She was always a smarter cookie than I was a cookie. She told me that she'd discovered the Church of Scientology and was a better person for that, though at her

age she doubted anybody would ever love her for what she was—
which I said was dead wrong (I couldn't remember what her
exact age was). Our conversation did not range far after that.
I think she would've liked to see me, and some parts of me
would've liked to see her. But we were not moved enough to do
that, and in a while we said good-bye and she was gone forever.

On the nearer-to-home front, Clarissa Bascombe's scrape
with local law in Absecon was indeed serious, but ended not
nearly as badly as it might've. Her mother *did* bring down a
lawyer from Haddam, a big, blond, handsome Nordic-looking
palooka with eyes on both sides of his head—who I'd seen a
hundred times and never paid any attention to, and who, I
believe, is Ann's new goodly swain—not the patch-pockets
history teacher I previously imagined. She told me this lawyer,
Otis—I don't know if that's his last name or his first—had "good
connections," which meant either the mob or the statehouse,
whatever the difference might be. But by six p.m. Thanksgiving
Day, this Otis had Clarissa sprung from the Absecon lockup and
had made allegations that the police applied reckless and undue
force by running her off the road and into the blinking lane-
change arrow and on into the NJDOT employee, whose foot
was only sprained and may have been sprained a week before.
Otis also claimed Clarissa had possibly been the victim of date
rape, or at the very least of a pretty scary dating experience that
amounted to assault, leaving her traumatized—as good as innocent. She was actually fleeing for her safety, he said, when she
made contact with the Absecon police. Thom may pay the
freight for this or he may not, since he naturally turns out to have
a past no one knew about but, also naturally, has mouthpieces of
his own. It's enough that Clarissa was unharmed and will eventually look less like a fool than she felt at the time. When she arrived
at the hospital late on Thanksgiving night, when I'd been in
surgery and was just waking up, feeling surprisingly not so bad
but out of my head, she stood close by my bed, gave me her
serious stare, put her two hands on my wrist below where they
had me strung up to fluids and infusions and heartbeat monitors,
then smiled gamely and said in what I remember as an extremely
softened, chastened, worn-out, had-it-with-life voice, "I guess
I've become number one in number two." This was our joke of
possibly longest standing and refers to a sign we once saw on a

septic-service truck on the back roads of Connecticut, when she was just a girly girl and I was an insufficient father trying to find sufficiency. There were, or seemed to be, others in the room with her—Ann, possibly Paul, possibly Jill, possibly Detective Marinara. I may have dreamed this. Along the top of the green wall, where it corniced with the white ceiling, was a frieze bearing important phrases that the hospital authorities wanted us patients to see as soon as we opened our eyes (if we did). What I read said, "When patients feel better about their comfort level they heal faster and their length of stay is shortened."

I looked at my sweet daughter, into her fatigue-lined, handsome face, at her thick honeyed hair, strong jaw, her mouth turned down at the corners when her smile was gone. I could see then, and for the first time, what she would look like when she was much older—the opposite of what a father usually sees. Fathers usually think they see the child in the adult's face. But Clarissa would look, I thought, just like her mother. Not like me, which was acceptable along with the rest. I thought as I lay there, how few jokes we'd shared and how rarely I had seen her laugh since she'd become a grown-up. And while you could say the fault for that belonged to her mother and me, that fault in truth was mostly mine.

I said something then, in my daze. I believe I said, "I should've spent more time with you when you were young."

She said, "That's not true, Frank. I didn't want to spend more time with you then. Now's better." That's all I remember from those early hours in the hospital and from my daughter, who's now back "camping out" with Cookie in Gotham, which pleases me, since she may have decided that "the big swim," the "out in the all of it" were just mirages to keep her from accepting who she is, and that the smooth, gliding life of linked boxes may not be the avoidance of pain but just a way of accepting what you can't really change. It's possible she's come to feel fortunate.

THE PASSENGERS across the aisle from Sally have turned out to be Kansas Citians, a jolly, rotund couple named the Palfreymans. Burt Palfreyman is hairless as a cue ball, from chemo, and as blind as Milton from retinal cancer, but full of vim and vigor about a whole new round at "the clinic." He's had many others and tells

Sally his hair's getting tired of growing in and has just decided to stay gone. They don't say what's ailing Burt this time, though Natalie mentions something about "the whole lymph system," which can't be good. Sally remarks that my son lives in Kansas City, too, and works for Hallmark, news that turns them reverent, provoking approving nods, though Burt's nod is more toward the seat-back in front of him. "First-class outfit," Burt says soberly, and Natalie, who's pleasingly rounded, with frizzed salmon-colored hair and puffy cheeks gone venous with worry and long life, stares over at me, around Sally, as if I might not know what a first-class outfit Hallmark really is and that that's a serious lapse of info, needing correction. I smile back as if I cannot speak but can nod. "It's all family-owned," she says. "And they do absolutely everything for Kanzcity." Burt grins at nothing. He's wearing a blue velour lounging outfit with purple piping down the legs and looks as comfortable as a blind man can look in an airplane. "They're right up there with UPS," Burt says (which he calls "ups"), "or any of those big outfits when it comes to employee benefits, compassionate leave, that kind of thing. Oh yeah. You bet." He might've worked for them in the Braille card department.

Sally touches my left hand as if to say, Don't let these nice souls give you the blues. We'll be landing soon.

Natalie goes on to say that Burt has just retired after thirty-five years working for a company that makes laundry starch—another solid family-owned outfit in K.C.—which made a place for him in the accounting department once his eyes got to be a problem. They have kids "out west," which Sally admits she does, too, allowing Natalie to know we're second-timers. Natalie says the two of them are thinking of going ahead and moving up to Rochester after selling their family home in Olathe. "At least get a condo," she says, since they're up and back so much now. They like Burt's cancer doctor, who's had them to dinner once, and feel they could fit well into the Rochester community, which is not so different from K.C. "A good deal less crime." They'll just need to get used to the winter, which seems a fun idea to her. They've made some "relator" appointments to see some places in between Burt's tests. "Health's the last frontier, isn't it?" Natalie hoods her eyes and looks straight to me, as if this is a fact men need to be aware of. I smile back a smile of false approval, though my mind runs to the idea of a barium enema self-administered on a cold bathroom floor, which is what I always think of when I envision my "health"— either something not good or else something that was good but will soon be no more. A permanent past tense. A *lost* frontier, not just the last one. *Health*'s a word I never use.

Getting on to the end, then.

Paul, as I said, along with Jill, has returned to K.C. and to the sweet feasible life of greeting cards and giving words to feelings others lack their own words for. On the day I left the hospital, we buried Paul's time capsule behind the house in a quiet ceremony that was very much like burying a dog or a goldfish. Paul put in some of his riotous rejects, Jill put in a lock of her yellow hair for purposes of DNA, later on. Detective Marinara (whose name turns out to be Lou) put in a broken pair of handcuffs Paul had wangled out of him, in addition to his police business card. Sally put in a smooth granite pebble off the beach at Mull and another off our beach in Sea-Clift. Clarissa, with Cookie present, put in the mahogany gearshift knob off Thom's Healey. Mike put in his signed Gipper photo and a green prayer flag. Ann did not attend, although she was invited and may now have made some positive strides with her daughter. I, as a joke, put in one of the spent titanium BBs (packaged in a plastic baggie), which I apparently "passed" on the operating table in Toms River, no doubt when I woke up in mid-surgery and everyone had a good laugh at my expense. Paul was pleased, made a couple of corny wisecracks about the Millennium, and then we covered the little missile up with sand. (I'm sure in the next big blow it'll be unearthed and washed away and turn up in Africa or Scotland, which will work out just as well.) For whatever Paul may have said to Ann or Ann to him about wanting to break into the real estate industry, this never came up between us—a relief, since his style of everyday mainstream life would never adapt well to the need to coax and coddle and be confessor, therapist, business adviser and risk assessor to the variety of citizen pilgrims who cross my threshold most days. He would like them, do his level best for them, but ultimately think everything they said was a riot and wouldn't understand the heart from which their words drew strength—much as he doesn't understand mine. He is a different kind of good man from most. And though I love him and expect him to live long and thrive, I don't truly understand him much, cannot do much for him except be happy he's where he is and with his love, and that he will know increase in his days. Perhaps over time, if I have time, I will even come to know them better than I do.

As to Mike and the sale of Realty-Wise, I have elected to take a Tibetan partner. In the time that I was laid up, he not only sold the Timbuktu house-on-wheels to a wholly different Indian client—they apparently come in droves when they come—but also sold 61 Shore Road, cracked piers and all, plus four chalets, to Clare Suddruth, who showed up Friday morning after Thanksgiving with Estelle, having called the emergency number when I didn't answer, and was so eager to get his money out of his pocket and into somebody else's that Mike feared he might be "losing an inner struggle" (experiencing a psychotic detachment) and possibly wasn't responsible for his acts. A call to the bank settled that. Mike also turned down a listing on the Feensters' beach house when he was approached by poor dead Drilla's sister, and discreetly passed the business along to Sea-Vu Associates. Nick, it turns out, had many more enemies than the two Russian kids, and had not been as fastidious in his personal affairs as would've been needed to keep him above ground.

At first, Mike didn't see how partnership would suit his ambitions or his arrangements with his Spring Lake dowager. But I convinced him that in the long run, which might not be such a long run, all will be his to buy out. I said I was not ready for *éminence grise* status or to retire to an island, and that in the coming housing climate with a big shiny bubble around it, he'd be smarter to be half-in instead of all the way, to retain some liquidity, keep a diverse portfolio and his options open for the deal you can't see coming until it's suddenly there. He has his children to think about, I reminded him, and a soon-to-be former wife he may someday feel differently about. We're not having a new shingle made or opening a bigger office, though we've subscribed to the Michigan State *Newsletter* and to "Weneedabreak.com." On his business card it will soon say "Mike Mahoney, Co-Broker," and he is thinking of enrolling in an executive boot camp in the Poconos, which I approve of. On the scale of human events and on the great ladder that's ever upward-tending, this has left him satisfied. At least for now.

*　　*　　*

WINDS BUFFET US. Our flying culvert makes a sudden shimmy-ing *eee-nyaw-eee* noise, and a tiny red seat belt emblem illumi-nates above me. The big brassy stewardess, whose name tag says Birgit, stands up like a friendly stalag matron and begins talking into a telephone receiver turned upside down, working her dark mannish eyebrows at the comedy of knowing none of us can understand anything she says. Though we're all veterans of this life. We know where we're descending to. No one's surprised or applauding. "Here goes nuttin'," someone says behind me and guffaws. Sally Caldwell, sweet wife of my middle season, squeezes my hand, smiles a falsely gay smile, rolls her eyes dream-ily and leans to give me a "be brave" kiss on my oddly cold cheek.

Below us I see the whited landscape stamped out in squares despite the early snow and failing light. It is nearly four. We pass, lowering, lowering over farms and farmettes and farm-equipment corrals, single stores with gas pumps along the ribbon of Route 14, where Clarissa and I walked and talked and sweated last August. Settlement's thickening and widening to include vacant baseball diamonds, a Guard armory with starred tanks and trucks out back (in case the fuckers make it this far inland, and they might), the Applebee's, the red blinking tower of an old AM transmitter morphed now into all new radiography—cell phone, cable, radar, NORAD, government surveillance. I don't yet see the great Mayo citadel with its own antennas and helipads, ICBM launchers and surface-to-air missiles to shoot down marauding microbes, but it's there. It's what we've come for. I press my cheek to the cold window, try to see the airport out ahead, establish the world on a more human scale. But I see only another jet, tiny and at an incalculable distance, its own red beacons winking, vectored for some different landing.

It is, of course, only on the human scale, with the great world laid flat about you, that the Next Level of life offers its rewards and good considerations. And then only if you let it. A working sense of spirituality can certainly help. But a practical acceptance of what's what, in real time and down-to-earth, is as good as spiritual if you can finagle it. I thought for a time that practical acceptance, the final, certifying "event" and extra beat for me had been my breathless "yes, yes," to my son Ralph Bascombe's death, and that I would never again have to wonder if how I feel now would be how I'd feel later on. I felt sure it would be. *Here* was necessity.

But get shot in the heart and live, and you'll learn some things about necessity—and quick. Lying in my ultramodern hospital bed in Toms River, looped to this machine and that fluid, with winter's woolen days coming on, I determined to be buried in powdered form somewhere at sea off Point Pleasant (it seemed simplest), and set about the solemn details that only a cold hospital room in New Jersey can make seem congenial: compiled my list of pallbearers, jotted down some basic obituary thoughts, concluded how I wanted my assignables assigned, to whom and with what provisos; who to take the business (Mike. Who else?). Happily, there wasn't so much. For a day or two afterward, I lay there and it all made me glad, and I thought I'd feel glad that way forever. Only by day three, I'd started to feel differently about everything—saw that what I'd decided was a mistake, probably a vanity—I'm not sure why. But right then and there, in that motorized bed with a hospital priest shanghaied from his every-day death duties and not at all sure if what he was doing was right, I fired all my pallbearers, forgot about a sea-burial, tore my organ-donor card in half and executed a document provided in the "welcome kit" by the hospital ethicist, consigning all my mortal leavings to science—the option I and Ann had failed for lack of courage to choose for our first son years ago. The medical kids, I felt, would treat me with all the dignity and compassion I'm due and no doubt with a measure of irreverence and amuse-ment, which seemed right and a better way to turn a small event —my death and life—into a slightly less small one, while keeping things simple and still making a contribution. Not a contribution you can see from a satellite, like Mount St. Helens or the Great Wall, but one that puts its money where its mouth is.

On the day I got home from the hospital, the weather turned ice-cream nice, and the low noon sun made the Atlantic purple and flat, then suddenly glow as the tide withdrew. And once again I was lured out, my pants legs rolled and in an old green sweatshirt, barefoot, to where the soaked and glistening sand seized my soft feet bottoms and the frothing water raced to close around my ankles like a grasp. And I thought to myself, standing there: *Here* is necessity. *Here* is the extra beat—to live, to live, to live it out.

We are going down fast now. Sally clutches my fingers hard, smiles an encouragement. The big engines hum. Our craft dips, shudders hard, and I feel myself afloat as the white earth rises to meet us—square buildings, moving cars, bundled figures of the other humans coming into clear focus as we descend. Some are watching, gaping up. Some are waving. Some turn their backs to us. Some do not notice us as we touch the ground. A bump, a roar, a heavy thrust forward into life again, and we resume our human scale upon the land.

ACKNOWLEDGMENTS

Independence Day:

I wish to thank the Lyndhurst Foundation and the Echoing Green Foundation for their generous support while I wrote this book. I wish also to express great gratitude to my friends Angela and Rea Hederman, Pam and Carl Navarre, Amanda Urban and, again, Gary Fisketjon . – RF

The Lay of the Land:

An unusual and embarrassing number of people made significant contributions to the writing of this book, none as illuminating, as consequential and as sweetly given as those made by Kristina Ford. My dear friends Gary Fisketjon, Amanda Urban, Gill Coleridge and Gabrielle Brooks have again given me the benefit of their judgment and encouragement, which have been indispensable. I wish also to thank Liz Van Hoose, Jennifer Smith, Amy Loyd, Field Maloney and Richard Brody for their kindness in extending the range of my notice. I'm grateful to Alexandra Pringle and Nigel Newton, to Olivier Cohen, to Elisabeth Ruge and Arnulf Conradi, to Claus Clausen, Jorge Herralde and to Inge and Carlo Feltrinelli for their trust in me. I'm also indebted to Katherine Hourigan, to Lydia Buechler, Carol Edwards and Margaret Halton for their generosity. I wish to thank Helen Schwartz for her essential writing on New Jersey houses, Deborah Treisman for her editorial counsel, Rachel Bolton for her trust, Tom Campbell for his saving advice and Debra Allen for her friendship for this work and for me. It is also true that I would not have written this book had I not met Mike Featherston, and would not have felt I could write it had I not met Dennis Iannaccone and Paul Principe, the kings of the New Jersey Shore. Finally, I wish to express my lifetime's gratitude and affection to Christopher and to Koukla MacLehose, for expanding the horizon I see, and for their enduring friendship. – RF

This book is set in BEMBO which was cut
by the punch-cutter Francesco Griffo
for the Venetian printer-publisher
Aldus Manutius in early 1495
and first used in a pamphlet
by a young scholar
named Pietro
Bembo.